Created By: Bill Webb
Developer and Project Manager: Mark Greenberg
Associate Developer: Greg Vaughan
Authors: Casey W. Christofferson, Matthew J. Finch, Mark Greenberg, Tom Knauss, Patrick Lawinger, Rhiannon Louve, Vicki Potter, Anthony Pryor, Ken Spencer, Greg Vaughan, Bill Webb, and Thom Wilson
Producer: Zach Glazar
Editors: Jeff Harkness, Vicki Potter, and Mark Greenberg
Art Director: Casey W. Christofferson
Layout and Book Design: Charles A. Wright
Cover Art: Colin Chan
Interior Art: Colin Chan, Santa Norvaisite, Michael Syrigos, Adrian Landeros, and Artem Shukaev; with Brian LeBlanc, Eric Lofgren, Jeremy McHugh, and Tyler Walpole
Cartography: Robert Altbauer
Special Thanks: To all of the authors, editors, artists, cartographers, and playtesters over the years who contributed to the products set in the Lost Lands and helped bring this world to life!
Dedication: To our amazing fans and backers, who supported our products and enabled us to finally publish this massive and long-awaited compendium of the Lost Lands!

And a Special Dedication to:

Richard, Eric, Kurt, Victor, Scott, Mike, and Dean – my original party from the 1970s
Clark, John, Dale, JP, and Ian – the intrepid super-party from the college years
Louis, Jen, Ed, Michelle, Terrace, and Brian – after all, the gods say the dwarf should open it!
Jillian, John, Claudia, Rocco, Maggie, and Cash – my genius kid group that makes me wake up and plan early
Gary and Bob – I look forward to rolling dice with you again in the future (but not yet)

FROG GOD GAMES IS:

Bill Webb, Matthew J. Finch, Zach Glazar, Charles A. Wright, Edwin Nagy, Mike Badalato

ADVENTURES WORTH WINNING

FROG GOD GAMES
ISBN: 978-1-62283-822-6

TABLE OF CONTENTS

Welcome to the World of the Lost Lands! 3

Introduction 4

Chapter I: Overview of the Lost Lands 5

Chapter II: Peoples of the Lost Lands 12

Chapter III: A Brief History of the Lost Lands 27

Chapter IV: Religions of the Lost Lands 39

Chapter V: Gazetteer of the Lost Lands 40

Western Akados 40

The Green Warden Forest and the Free Coast 77

Southwest Akados 102

The Haunted Steppes 119

The Lands of Reme 138

South-Central Akados 156

Southeastern Akados 208

Eastern Akados & The Stoneheart Mountains 263

Northeastern Akados 315

The Northlands 334

Northern Libynos 355

Eastern Libynos 379

Central Libynos 405

Southern Libynos 442

Appendix I: The Lost Lands Timeline 466

Appendix II: Pantheons & Gods of the Lost Lands 487

Welcome to the World of the Lost Lands!

After more than 40 years and much collaboration with dozens (hundreds!) of people in the industry, from conventions, and in my home games, my campaign world is finally seeing press. The roots of this effort go back to 1977, when gaming was still wild and free.

Everything then was DIY and free form. We had no supplements and had to use books as the basis for what we created. We were inspired by Tolkien, Howard, Lovecraft and others (and in my case, several Sci-Fi authors as well). The only campaign setting that was (even partially) fleshed out was the Empire of the Petal Throne, at a towering $25 price tag ($108 in today's dollars). Later came Judges Guild and the Wilderlands, and eventually Greyhawk, Forgotten Realms, and other worlds that inspired thousands of gamers.

What you have in your hands now is my version of a game world . . . vast and full of adventure. The only changes from the original map (which hangs above my dining room table) are that all the intellectual property violation references have been changed to prevent lawsuits! My limited brain capacity has been supplemented by some of the great RPG authors of our time—Greg Vaughan, Matt Finch, Vicki Potter, Pat Lawinger, Anthony Pryor, Rhiannon Louve, Tom Knauss, Mark Greenberg, Ken Spencer, Casey Christofferson, and Thom Wilson, and many, many others that have helped me create material over the last 19 years.

A special shout out to Mark Greenberg, who after retiring as a corporate attorney, decided to come on board as a project manager for this beast. Let's hope that he sticks around after this!

All in all, the whole team worked very hard to create this book. I believe that no other world setting has ever been created for use in the game that incorporates this level of detail in a complete package. The word count is astonishing (even more than Slumbering Tsar or the Blight), and cross references have been worked in to provide reference to our existing body of work.

You will find within these pages not only the standard canon from our prior works, but expanded histories and links detailing everything from the fall of Tsar to the creation of the Wizard's Wall. Much of the world has been derived from actual play, and the parts that are not from a game were certainly created with the intention of being used for such.

So, practice your weightlifting and enjoy reading this encyclopedia (cyclopean?) monster of a book. I hope that you will have as much fun playing in my game world as I have had creating it.

Bill Webb
11/21/19

Introduction
The Lost Lands

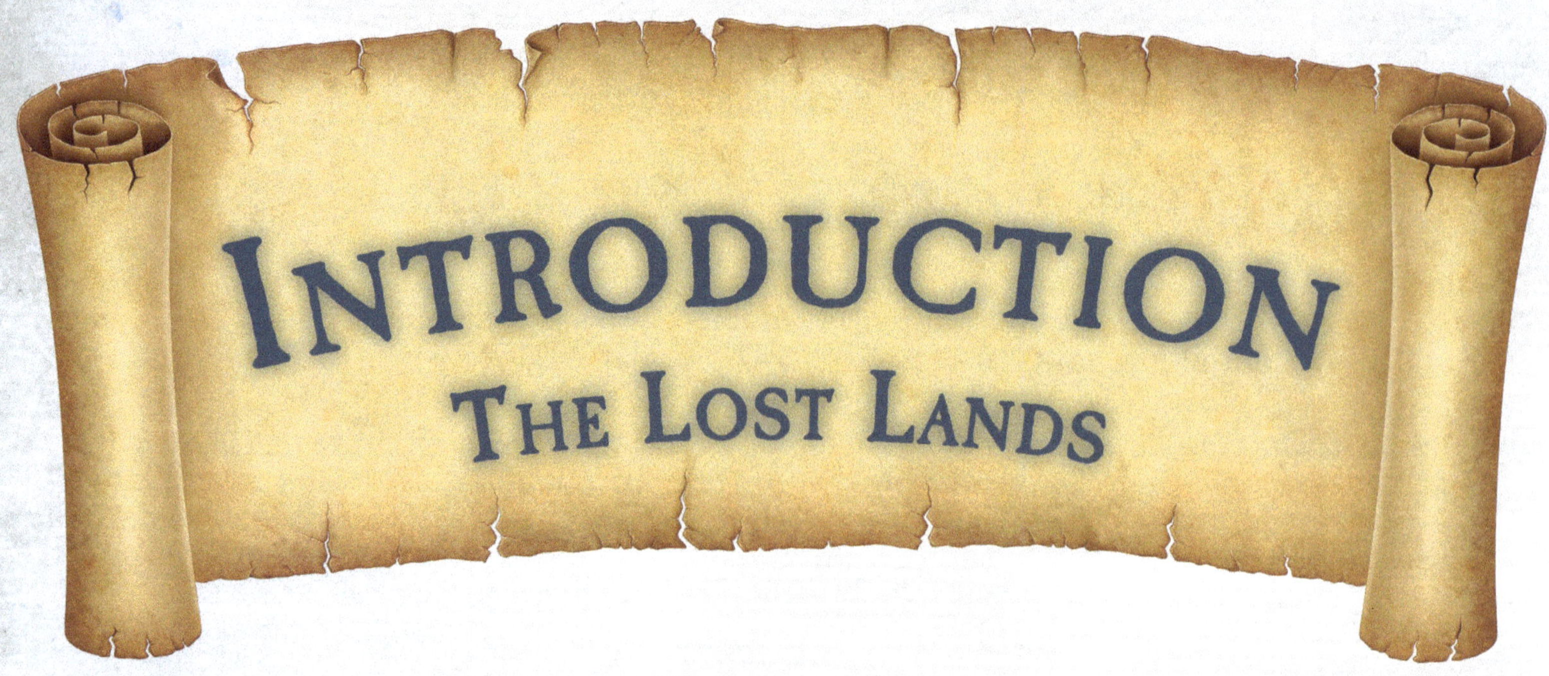

The Lost Lands …

… the campaign world of **Necromancer Games** and **Frog God Games** for almost 20 years …

… home to locations now legendary in the annals of roleplaying, from the depths of the massive dungeons of Rappan Athuk, to the city of Bard's Gate, the Desolation of Tsar, the Blight, the demon-tainted Sundered Lands, the chaotic tumult of the Borderland Provinces, and the fabled Northlands.

Between these covers is the definitive guide to the world of the Lost Lands. Herein you will find a description of the lands and seas and the skies above, the people who populate the world, an overview of its history, a summary of its religions, and an enormous gazetteer with thousands of entries covering nations, cities, temples, ruins, mountain ranges, waterways, and other geographical features.

For the first time, in a single volume, are detailed descriptions of the continents of Akados — where most of the previously published adventures have been located — and far Libynos, including kingdoms and locations that have been only hinted at before. Here can be found the locations of your favorite adventures, all set into the historical and physical context of the entire world, alongside new lands that have never before been revealed.

Welcome to the Lost Lands. A lifetime of adventures awaits!

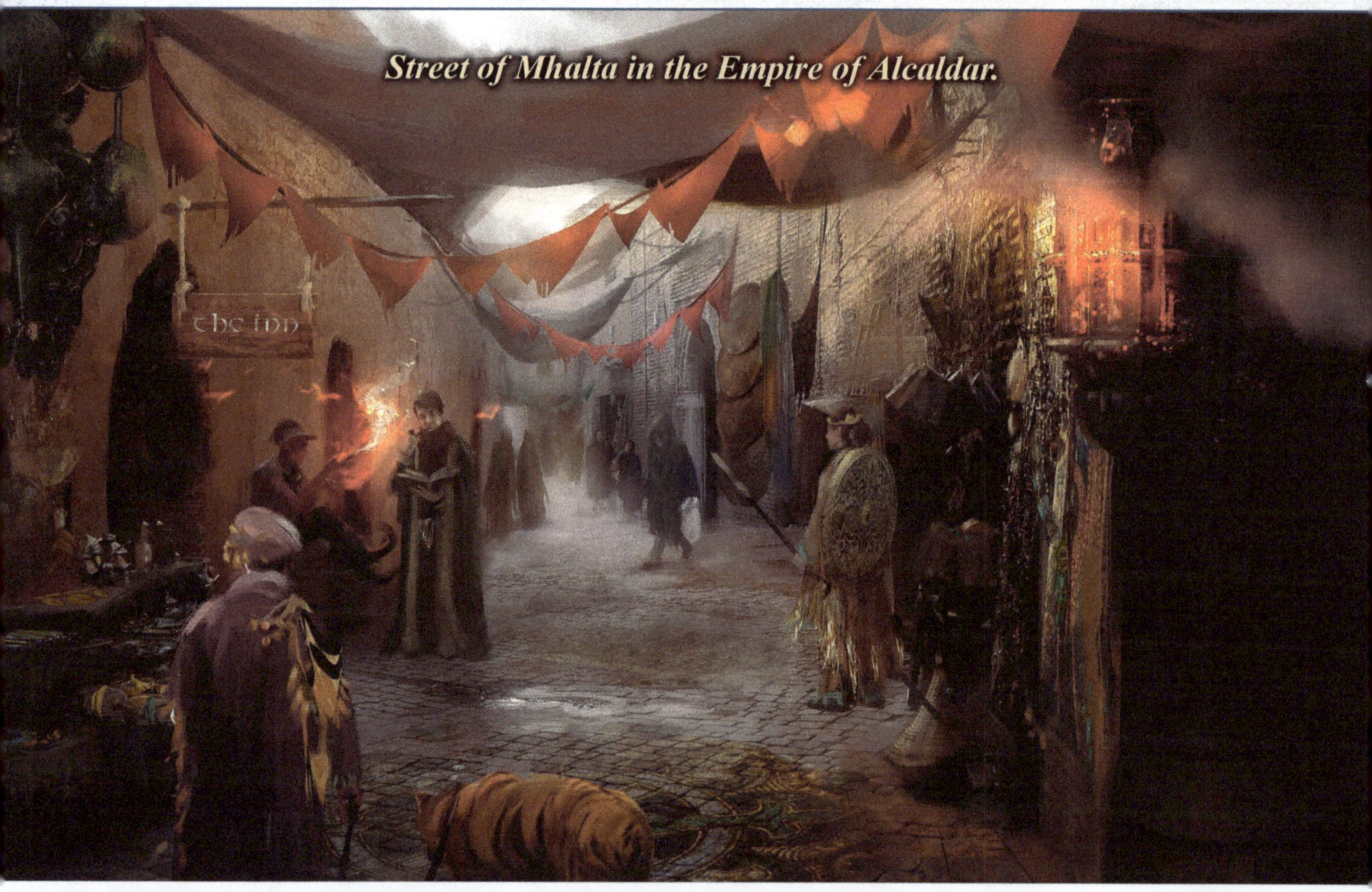

Street of Mhalta in the Empire of Alcaldar.

CHAPTER I
OVERVIEW OF THE LOST LANDS

The world of the Lost Lands has been known by many names over many thousands of years. To the ancient Phoromyceaens, it was Erce the Mother. In the desert lands of Khemit, it was called Geb, while to the people of Far Jaati, it was Kala. The ancient Hyperboreans called the world Boros, the same name they gave to the continent from which they came, and the name that was most used for the world during the millennia of their empire. To the Heldring, the world is called Eorth, while to the Northlanders it is Midgard. But today, the most common name for the world is Lloegyr, or the Lost Lands, the name it was given by the Daanites after their leader Daan overthrew the undead imperatrix of Hyperborea (and was himself slain), bringing to an end the Hyperborean era.

The world of the Lost Lands is large. The globe's circumference is approximately 50,400 miles, nearly twice that of our Earth.

The known world includes two populated continents, Akados in the west and Libynos in the east. To the north, under a deep sheet of ice, is the lost continent of Boros, from which the ancient Hyperboreans once came and to which they returned when they withdrew almost a thousand years ago. Whether they live there still, and in fact whether anyone at all can be found in that frozen land, remains the subject of speculation. To the south are islands scattered over thousands of miles of open ocean, sometimes called the islands of Arkanos, which legend says are all that remains of a mighty southern continent, now almost entirely sunken beneath the waves.

Those southern seas are known as Mother Oceanus and reach unknown distances to the east, south, and west. Great lines of impenetrable storms known as the Tempest Meridians lie far to the east of Libynos and far to the west of Akados, barring the way to whatever might be in the seas beyond. The Great Ocean Ûthaf is to the north of Akados and Libynos. And between those two continents is the Sinnar Ocean.

The world circles a sun that is slightly more orange than Earth's. Two moons — Narrah, the Pale Sister, and smaller Sybil, the Dark Sister — appear in the night sky alongside several wandering stars and uncountable other stars.

And in dimensions beyond are other planes of existence, homes of gods and demons.

Such are the bounds of the Lost Lands.

LANDS AND SEAS OF THE LOST LANDS

THE LANDS

There are three continents in the known Lost Lands: Akados in the west; Libynos in the east; and lost Boros in the north, now buried beneath hundreds of feet of glacial ice.

AKADOS

Akados is the largest of the known continents of the Lost Lands. Through its center runs the greatest of the world's mountain ranges, the Stonehearts, from the icebound far north to the heart of the continent in the south. In the southwest, the Crescent Sea divides the western lands of the Green Realm and the Xha'en Hegemony from the former lands of the Hyperborean Empire of the Foerdewaith. And in the far northeast is the Irkainian Peninsula, which reaches out to the shores of Libynos, separated only by the narrow Mulstabhin Passage and Krivcycek Island.

The climates within Akados are vast. In the northwest are the trackless plains of the Haunted Steppes; to the north, the forests and icy rivers of the Northlands and the taiga and tundra beyond; in the northeast, the Vast and Irkainian Deserts; and in the southwest, the mighty forests of the Green Realm.

Akados was the first land conquered by the Hyperboreans when they marched forth from their homeland in Boros to the north. As a result, many of the human kingdoms and realms of Akados can trace their origins to provinces of that empire and look back to the Hyperborean era as a golden age of peace and prosperity. Only the far western portion of the continent, beyond the Crescent Sea — where can be found the Green Realm of the wild elves, the Xha'en Hegemony, Gtsang Prefecture, and Anaros Island — never felt the rule of the imperators.

Akados is also home to the largest groups of non-humans in the world, including the wild elves of the Green Realm, the high elves of the forests of eastern Akados, and the clans of the mountain dwarves in the Stonehearts and other mountain ranges of the continent.

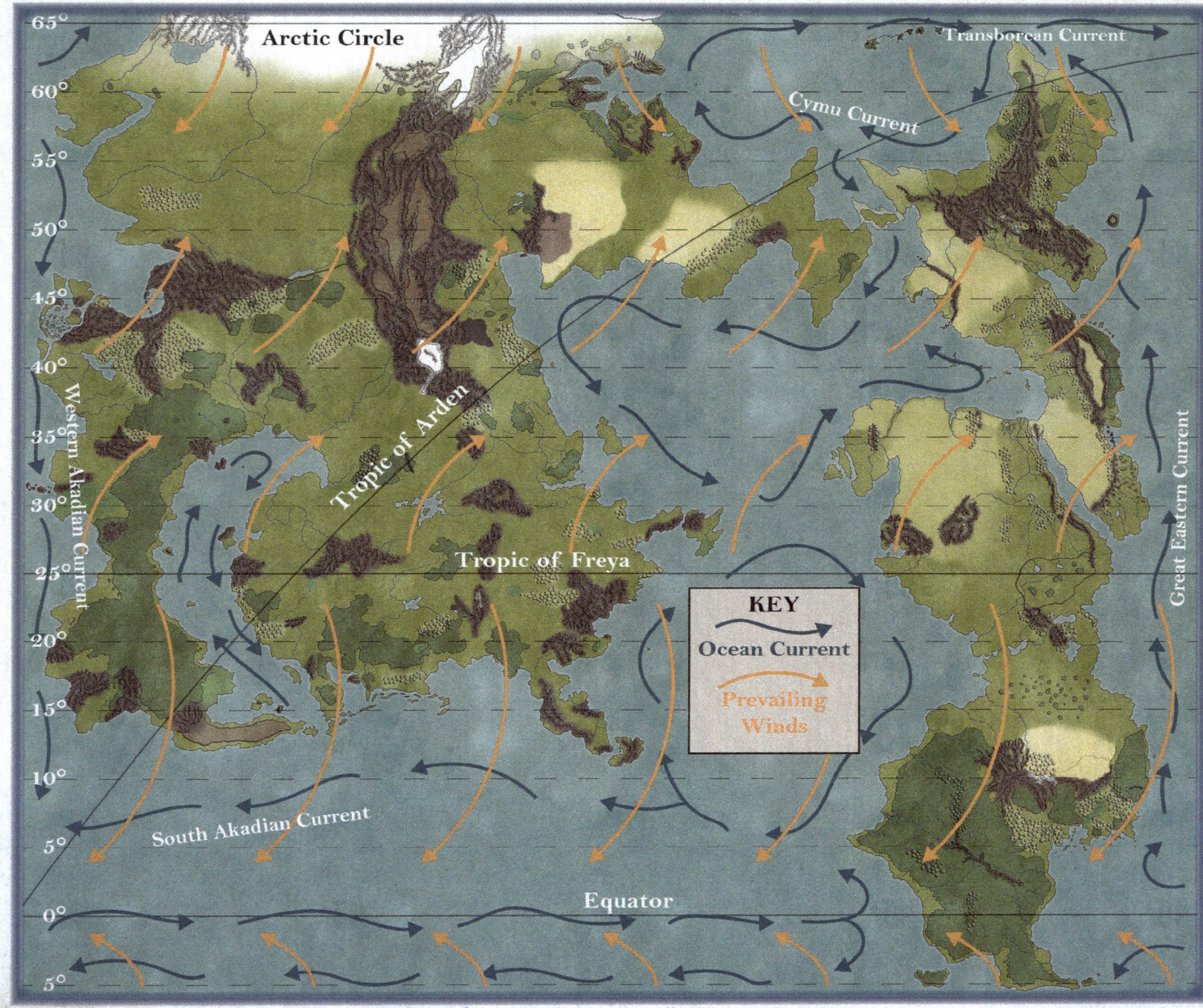

Arctic Circle
Transborean Current
Cymu Current
Western Akadian Current
South Akadian Current
Tropic of Arden
Tropic of Freya
Equator
Great Eastern Current
KEY
Ocean Current
Prevailing Winds
65°
60°
55°
50°
45°
40°
35°
30°
25°
20°
15°
10°
5°
0°
5°

Libynos

The continent of Libynos is much longer north to south than it is wide east to west. The Sea of Baal, a huge arm of the Sinnar Ocean, nearly cuts the continent in two, dividing north Libynos from central and southern Libynos. The Zakros and Scythirian Mountains dominate the northern part of the continent, separating the lands of the ancient western city-states from the equally old Jaati in the north and the Jungle of Malagro along the eastern coast. In southern Libynos, a series of lakes called the Channel Lakes runs through the middle of the continent, and beyond that to the south are the peaks known as the Hollow Spire Mountains.

Much of northern and central Libynos is dominated by deserts. The great Maighib Desert runs the entire breadth of the continent from Khartous and the shores of the Sinnar Ocean in the west to Numeda and the Boiling Sea in the east. Farther north is the Desert of Oreb, in the midst of the Scythirian Mountains, and northwest of that is the Ashurian Desert. Even southern Libynos boasts a desert, the Kanderi south of the Channel Lakes.

Although the Hyperboreans colonized many lands on Libynos, far less of that continent bears the traces of those conquerors than does Akados. When the polemarchs of the imperium first arrived on the western continent, they found humans living in sparse, nomadic tribes, severely pressed by the elves of the interior forests. With such a fragmented existing culture, the nations that developed on Akados took on a decidedly Hyperborean flavor as they adopted the traditions and religion of their conquerors.

Libynos, on the other hand, hosted civilizations that were ancient even when the first Hyperboreans arrived on their shores. Many cities of Istaflumina, Jaati, and Khemit, and the Antioch City-States, predated the Hyperborean arrival. Other folk of Libynos never truly fell under the sway of the conquerors. When confronted by the Ashurian Desert in the north and the jungles of the south, the Hyperboreans usually chose to settle only on the margins, at coastal locations or slightly inland near large rivers where they could trade with those in the interior without needing to mobilize sufficient forces to conquer and hold such inhospitable lands. As a result, when the Hyperboreans left, most of the peoples of Libynos returned to their former ways. The one exception, however, being Alcaldar, a Hyperborean colony that survived the end of the empire.

Beyond Libynos to the northeast are said to be the legendary Oestryn Islands, the last land before reaching the Tempest Meridians in the east.

Lost Boros

Little is known today of Boros. From this continent came the Hyperboreans when they marched south to Akados. And to Boros did they return when they withdrew following the end of their empire. Once said to be a temperate land, it has been covered with glaciers of ice since the poles of the world shifted in 2491 I.R. The relationship between the Shadowlands of northern Akados, beyond the Haunted Steppes, and Boros is unknown. Though the sea ice makes a demarcation between land and water uncertain, it is believed that parts of what is known as the Far North, beyond the Northlands, are in fact on the continent of Boros. More exploration will be necessary to determine the truth of this proposition.

In any event, the ancient and original homeland of the Hyperboreans — and the remains of their civilization — are today somewhere on Boros, now buried under hundreds of feet or more of ice.

The Oceans

There are three great seas of the known Lost Lands: Mother Oceanus, Great Ocean Ûthaf, and the Sinnar Ocean.

Mother Oceanus

Mother Oceanus, also sometimes called Great Oceanus or just Oceanus, is the largest ocean in the world. Her northern boundary is easy to define — the southern coast of Akados, the Sinnar Ocean, and southern Libynos. But if there are eastern, western, or southern limits, none can say.

As far as is known, no large landmasses lie in Mother Oceanus. Very old legends tell of a great continent once far to the south, known as Notos, that sank ages ago in a terrible cataclysm. If such tales are true, little of these lands remains today other than scattered groups of islands, which some cartographers refer to collectively as the Arkanos Islands.

On one such island, located across more than 2,000 miles of open ocean from the southern shores of Akados, is the infamous Razor Coast, which is visited by ships from Castorhage, the Kingdom of Oceanus, and Alcaldar. Even farther south, according to tales told in wharf-side bars, are more islands — some covered with jungle, others by desert — that are populated by folk unknown in the northern lands. To the east, between the Razor Sea and the coast of Libynos, lie the Aizanes Islands that are home to a tribal people known as the Tulita. And nearby are the island homes of the so-called Pirate Confederacy.

Also said to be in Mother Oceanus, somewhere southwest of Akados, is the fabled Island of Ra, where the equator meets the Tropic of Arden. And at the extremes of Mother Oceanus, far to the west of Akados and far to the east of Libynos, are the Tempest Meridians: walls of fearsome, raging storms that no known ships have yet to penetrate. Various kingdoms of locathah, merfolk, nereid, tritons, sea elves, and sahuagin can be found in the waters of Mother Oceanus, and in the deeps, monsters of terror and darkness.

Beyond the few known islands, untold thousands of miles of great, rolling waves and often brutal storms challenge any who might decide to sail beyond the sea lanes marked on mariners' maps.

Along the southern shore of Akados, the South Akadian Current flows from east to west. Ships sailing from the Sinnar to the Mouth of Akados and the Crescent Sea take advantage of this current, as well as the prevailing winds here south of the continent, which bear from the northeast. The return trip east, however, tends to be much slower, with ships having to combat the current and the wind. A northern equatorial countercurrent some 500 to 750 miles south of the South Akadian Current flows east all the way to the shores of Libynos. Some captains seek out this current, but its distance from Akados, and the dangers of the deep waters and the fickle storms of Mother Oceanus, mean only the bravest or most desperate choose such routes.

Other than by way of brief references, the lands and seas of Mother Oceanus, including the Isle of Ra, the Razor Coast, and the Aizanes Islands, are outside the scope of this volume.

Great Ocean Ûthaf

Great Ocean Ûthaf is the ocean of the northern hemisphere, including the Far North, and surrounds Boros and touches both the eastern shores of Libynos and the western shores of Akados. It is said that nothing larger than a modest island rises above the waves in all of Great Ocean Ûthaf, and that before the creation of the Tempest Meridians, one could sail all the way around the world without seeing a sign of land (a task said to have been accomplished by ancient Jaati of northeastern Libynos, who legends say sailed east until they landed at Gtsang some 15,000 years ago). Whether anything in fact can be found beyond the barriers of the Tempest Meridians remains little more than idle speculation and the subject of fevered stories told by aged sailors.

Along the western coast of Akados, the Western Akadian Current flows north to south and brings chill waters, clouds, and rain to the Thousand Rocks, Gtsang, and the Xha'en Hegemony. This current continues south until it joins with the South Akadian Current of Mother Oceanus, and then turns to the unknown west.

To the east of Libynos, the warm waters of the Great Eastern Current flow from the equator, following the shores of the continent north until it reaches the northernmost point of Libynos. There, the current, still holding the warmth of its equatorial origins, turns west to flow along the northern shore of Irkainia toward the mouth of the North Sea. This stretch of the current is known as the Cymu Current, after a group of volcanic islands through which it passes on its way west. Near the mouth of the North Sea, the great river of water turns clockwise and heads north and east, becoming the Transborean Current. From here, as the current passes the Seal Coast and other shores of the Far North, the waters take on icemelt and icebergs calving from the glaciers of Boros and becomes an oceanic river of cold water that runs east. At a point far to the east of Libynos, the current meets the Tropic of Arden somewhere in the vicinity of the Oestryn Islands. Here, the power of the Tropic enters the ocean waters, and the current again warms as it continues on its way east into the unknown reaches where the Tempest Meridians waits.

Sinnar Ocean

The Sinnar Ocean separates Akados on the west from Libynos to the east. It is divided roughly in half into northern and southern sections, where Ramthion Island of Akados reaches out toward the east and the islands of Caddesh some 1,000 miles distant.

In the northern Sinnar Ocean, the current flows counterclockwise, bringing ships from Endhome, Eastgate, and Port Clar to the Sea of Baal. In the southern Sinnar, the current flows clockwise, favorable for those ships of Akados seeking port in Alcaldar, the Channel Lakes, or the Southern Paramountcies of Libynos.

Though the Sinnar is much smaller than either Mother Oceanus or Great Ocean Ûthaf and is regularly crossed by seaborne traffic, sailors and captains know well not to take this ocean lightly. Mighty storms

are common, both in the north where they originate beyond Irkaina in the icy north and in the south where they rush in from the open seas of Mother Oceanus. Vessels here are known to vanish without a trace, and sometimes reappear, undamaged and intact but without a crew. Various creatures of the depths live beneath the surface of the Sinnar and sometimes threaten those who sail its waves. Somewhere in the southern reaches is said to be a great city of the sahuagin.

Beyond the Bounds of the World

The astrologers of Hyperborea knew well that Lloegyr is a planet circling a yellow-orange star. Orbiting in turn about this world are two moons, Narrah the Pale Sister and Sybil the Dark Sister. In addition, at least three "wandering stars" in the sky were recognized as other planets, also in orbit around the sun. Some have speculated that those other celestial bodies may be home to their own unique inhabitants, and possibly entire civilizations.

Yet all of what we can see is not all that the universe holds. There are other planes of existence, far dimensions that can only be reached by powerful magic or long-lost gates. Such planes or other realms include Alfheim, Niðavellir and Svartalfheim (believed to be separate locations within the same plane of existence), from whence came the elves, the dwarves and the drow, respectively; the Upper Planes, including the Seven Heavens, Elysium, Arcadia, and Asgard; the Lower Planes, such as Abyss, Tarterus, Hades, Gehenna, and the Nine Hells; and the Ginnungagap, also called the Yawning Void, which touches and intrudes upon those infernal domains, but also occupies the nothingness that lies beyond their bounds.

Weather and Climate of the Lost Lands

Similar to the Earth, the climate of Lloegyr is heavily influenced by the axial tilt of the planet, which is approximately 25 degrees relative to its orbital plane with the sun.

As a result, the northernmost latitude at which the sun can appear to be directly overhead, on the summer solstice, is at 25 degrees north. This latitude is also known as the Tropic of Freya. On Akados, it runs through the Worntooth Peaks, the southern extent of the Blackrock Mountains, the southern fiefdoms of the Kingdom of Foere, and Old Burgundia to the east. Similarly, the southernmost latitude at which the sun can be directly overhead, on the winter solstice, is at 25 degrees south, known as the Tropic of Mithras. This latitude is well south of the southern shores of both Akados and Libynos, though some say it is near the location of the Razor Coast.

The equator lies approximately 1,700 miles south of Akados, and crosses Libynos in the region of the Southern Paramountcies.

The arctic circle on Lloegyr is at approximately 65 degrees north; at this latitude and farther north, the midnight sun (when in the summer the sun never appears to set) is visible at least one day of the year. Above this latitude are the Shadowlands north of the Haunted Plain, the northernmost reaches of the Stonehearts, the Far North and, somewhere, the continent of lost Boros.

Another factor unique to Lloegyr also has a substantial effect on the climate of Akados and Libynos. When the god Arden sacrificed himself to banish invading hordes of the frog demon Tsathogga in −182 I.R., the very fabric of the world was rent, creating what is now known as the Tropic of Arden. Unlike the other tropics which parallel the equator, the Tropic of Arden lies at an oblique angle to the equator, which it crosses in Mother Oceanus at a point southwest of Akados (where legend says can be found the Isle of Ra). From there, the Tropic reaches the coast of Akados near the Cinderhame Mountains, and then crosses, in turn, the southernmost reaches of the Green Realm, the Crescent Sea, the Kingdom of the Vast, the Plains of Eaux and the northern domains of Foere, the southern Stonehearts and the Dragon Hills. From there, the Tropic passes over the Gulf of Akados, and then through Irkaina and the northernmost regions of Libynos.

More than just a geographic designation, the Tropic of Arden in fact constitutes a powerful atmospheric effect that refracts the sun's light in ways that change the climate of areas a thousand miles or more to either side of the Tropic. Part of the effect seems to redirect solar energy from lands in the Tropic's influence in the southwest toward the northeast. As a result of this effect, the southern regions of Akados are much more temperate and less tropical than would be expected of such southerly latitudes; and in fact, the Helcynngae Peninsula, not far from the equator, has the cool climate one would normally only see in a region much farther north. On the other hand, the area around Freegate on the coast of the Gulf of Akados is known for its remarkably subtropical clime.

Passing over the northern Gulf of Akados and Irkaina, the Tropic of Arden heats and desiccates the air, giving rise to both the Vast and Irkainian Deserts, while also creating an odd coriolis effect that brings moisture off the northern Sinnar to the Buntesveldt and Pelshtaria. In Libynos, the Tropic causes the Ashurian Desert and the Maighib Desert to be hot and dry though they are in northern and middle latitudes, respectively, while across the Jungteran Mountains it brings warmth and moisture to the lands of Jaati and the northeast coast of the continent.

Prior to the shift of the world's poles in 2491 I.R., the angle between the equator and the Tropic of Arden was substantially less, mitigating the effect the Tropic had on weather and climate. Since the pole shift, however, the angle increased substantially, which has resulted in a concomitant increase in the effect the Tropic has, particularly the regions farther north.

Skies of the Lost Lands

The world of Lloegyr circles a yellow-orange sun known by the Foerdewaith as Rana. Among the Ashurians, it is called Tascheter; to the Hyperboreans, Solanus; and Mitra among the Jaata.

The night sky is dominated by the two moons that orbit the world: Narrah, also known as Luna, the Pale Sister, and Sybil, the Dark Sister. Narrah is larger and bright, showing a crater-scarred face much like Earth's moon. Legends in some parts of the world, such as in the Yolbiac Vale, claim that denizens of Narrah invaded the Lost Lands in the distant past. The goddess Narrah is associated with this moon. Sybil is smaller and dim, appearing an almost bluish-black when full in the night sky. Evil portents attend this moon, which is associated with the goddess Cybele. Times when both moons are full in the sky are of particular importance to a number of faiths.

Wheeling over the night skies of Lloegyr are a multitude of stars. Among the best known are Oliarus, the Pole Star (known to the Daanites

Zodiacal Constellations

Name	Meaning	Aspects
Calade	Hawk of Fate	Associated with Arden in Hyperborean and pre-Hyperborean times, now associated with the Tropic of Arden
Draconis	The Dragon	On certain (un)holy days, the planet Xharos/Erebos is the dragon's eye
Irminsul	Pillar of the Gods	The star Irminsul is at its peak
Nodens	God of the Sea	
Skiðblaðnir	Ship of the Gods	Also known as Sektet, Ra's Solar Barge
The Host	The Army	Appears as a hazy expanse of starlight
The Ninefold Lamp		An important constellation to the old gods (Daanite/Ancient Ones)
The Sickle		Called the Wheel by the followers of Jamboor
The Sphinx	The King of Boros	Associated with the Great Sphinx of Khemit; symbol of the Imperial Mercantile League
The Springald	The Crossbow	Also known as the Hammer or Donar's Hammer, appears to be striking toward Yales/Jörmungandr
The Tesseract		Shaped like a square of four stars within a larger square of four stars
The White Wolf		
Yales	The Devil	Also known as Jörmungandr the World Serpent among the Northlanders and Apep the Eater of Souls in Khemit

as Sidhe, the Star of the Otherworld); Solaris, the Lightstar, which was the pole star before the world's poles shifted in 2491 I.R.; Aether, Star of the Upper Air; the Blót Star, or the Star of Sacrifice; Irminsul, the Pillar of the Gods; and Eärendel, the star of the morning.

In the astrology of the Hyperboreans, which has been passed down to many of the cultures of Akados and Libynos, the stars combine to form various constellations. Two such are known as Freya and Mithras. Thirteen other constellations, which proceed one after another in a great circle about the sky, form the zodiac, which defines the 13 lunar months of the year. The zodiacal constellations are presented on the previous page.

In addition, certain other "wandering stars" travel among the fixed stars in the night sky in patterns that the wise can come to understand. Among these are Mulvais the Red Star, Cyril the Blue Chariot, and Xharos the Black Star (also known as Erebos, the Dark Star, and the Lower Air). The astrologers of ancient Hyperborea believed these to actually be other planets circling the sun in far-distant orbits, just as does Boros. The Hyperboreans also believed that other planets existed in addition to these three, but that they are so far away that they remain unseen by mortal eyes. Some have speculated that those other celestial bodies could be home to their own unique inhabitants and possibly entire civilizations.

TIME AND CALENDARS OF THE LOST LANDS

When the Hyperboreans came south out of Boros to invade the lands of Akados and Libynos, they brought with them a calendar that to this day remains the basis for the calendars of most cultures around the world.

In the Hyperborean calendar, a week consists of seven days. A fortnight is a period of two weeks with a festival day in between, and so consists of 15 days. Two consecutive fortnights make a month of 30 days. There are 12 months in each year, which also includes a High Holy Day on each solstice and each equinox. As a result, a year consists of 364 days, which is very close to the length of an actual solar year. Approximately every 250 years, the churches join in a conclave at which they agree to add a number of additional days to the year — usually as additional holy days at the solstices — to ensure that the seasons continue to occur at the correct times each year.

Unlike the civil and religious calendar, astrologers follow a 13-month calendar that is lunar and reflects the passage of the moons through the zodiacal constellations.

In 2768 I.R., Overking Magnusson of Foere imposed the common calendar that is now in use throughout most of Akados in honor of his completion of the imperial capital of Courghais. It shows evidence not just of its origin in Hyperborean astrology, but also reflects the impact of other peoples on the Foerdewaith, including the years of Heldring occupation following the departure of the Hyperboreans. The latter influence is particularly notable in the names for the months (many of which end in "mond," a derivative of the Heldring word for month) and in the names of the days of the week (all of which end in "dag," a derivative of the Heldring word for day).

Common Name	Hyperborean Name	Earth Equivalent
Oeros	Firstmonth	January
Foeros	Secondmonth	February
Freyrmond	Thirdmonth	March
Eostre	Fourthmonth	April
Tiwemond	Fifthmonth	May
Daan	Sixthmonth	June
Haymond	Seventhmonth	July
Hummidos	Eighthmonth	August
Mithrond	Ninthmonth	September
Blótmond	Tenthmonth	October
Winterfyll	Eleventhmonth	November
Yule	Twelfthmonth	December

The High Holy Days of each year are the two solstices and the two equinoxes. In southern Akados, the exact dates of the solstices and equinoxes are determined by the Order of Corollaries at the Reliquary of Jamboor in the Rampart Mountains. Such dates are not considered part of the month in which they fall.

DAYS OF THE WEEK

Solsdag	For Solanus, the Goddess of the Sun
Ardsdag	For Arden, the God of Life (formerly Anumesday)
Djinsdag	For Da-Jin the God of Death
Mootsdag	The Day of the Market
Manesdag	The Day of Souls
Sistersdag	For Narrah and Sybil, the Goddesses of the Moons
Thingsdag	The Day of the Government (for the Heldring assembly)

Not all peoples of the Lost Lands use this calendar. Castorhage adopted a slightly modified version of it. On Akados, the Xha'en Hegemony, Gtsang Prefecture, and Anaros Island have separate and unique calendars. Most of the major cultures on Libynos also have their own calendars, though many in large cities are aware of the Foere system, particularly merchants and sailors who have need of a way to coordinate oceanic shipments.

In the calendar of Foere, dates are still tracked by the Hyperborean Imperial Record (I.R.), for which year 1 is the year in which the Battle of Hummaemidon occurred. Those outside the historical dominion of the Hyperboreans and Foerdewaith, or where the depth of their influence

MAJOR CALENDARS OF THE LOST LANDS

Calendar	Abbreviation	Year 1	Event	Principally Used By
Erylle Cycle	E.C.	–6484 I.R.	First Elven Exodus	Elves
Xha'en Calendar	XC	–1302 I.R.	Founding of city of Xha'ahan	Xha'en Hegemony, Gtsang Prefecture, Anaros Island
Imperial Record	I.R.	1 I.R.	Battle of Hummaemidon	Former Hyperborean and Foere domains
Blessed Year	B.Y.	482 I.R.	Year Mah-Barek arrived in Ashurian Desert	Caliphate and worshippers of Mah-Barek
Huun Chronicle	H.C.	2496 I.R.	Founding of Huun nation	Huun
New Khemit Reckoning	N.K.R.	2632 I.R.	Release of Khemit from Hyperborean hegemony	Khemit and traders in Sea of Baal

was limited, usually use a different, local calendar. Such others include the Erylle Cycle among the elves, the Reckoning of Kings in Khemit, the Xha'en Calendar, the Blessed Year calendar in the Ammuyad Caliphate, and the Huun Chronicle. In some regions, multiple calendars may in fact be in use; in Khemit, for example, many dates are given by the applicable year of a given dynasty.

TECHNOLOGY IN THE LOST LANDS

The information blocks for many entries in Chapter V contain a line called "Technology Level." This item indicates the level of technological achievement generally found throughout the land in question. Exceptional individuals or groups may have access to a higher technology level or live at a lower level, but for a given area this should give a general guideline of the types of weapons, armor, and equipment found there. These levels can vary even between neighboring nations as one may be more insular and cut off from outside contact and ideas while another may be open to a great deal of trade that brings in new innovations from outside.

It should be noted that the technology levels presented herein are not meant to represent real-world advancements in technology. There is, perhaps, a loose correlation in some of it, but it is instead intended to represent the developments of technology in the world of the Lost Lands.

The technology levels used in Chapter V are as follows:

STONE AGE

Materials: clay vessels, furs, hides, horn, stone tools and weapons, some copper, wood
Armor: hide armor
Weapons: dagger, javelin, shortbow, spear
Warfare: ambush, raiding bands, single combat
Settlements: rock shelters, semi-permanent camps
Social Organization: tribes/bands
Transportation: paddled craft, trained animals
General: animal domestication, fire, horticulture, log rollers

BRONZE AGE

Materials: bronze tools and weapons, crude glass items, linen, papyrus, wool
Armor: breastplate, leather armor, padded armor
Weapons: composite shortbow, short sword
Warfare: organized armies, city walls (large city-states only)
Settlements: capitals, cities, towns
Social Organization: city-states
Transportation: chariot, oars, sails, side rudder, wheel
General: agriculture, corbelled arch, hand loom, lever, oil lamp, plow, potter's wheel, pulley, sundial

IRON AGE

Materials: cotton textiles, iron and steel tools and weapons, parchment
Armor: ring mail, scale mail, studded leather
Weapons: longbow, longsword
Warfare: cataphracts, catapults, hill forts
Social Organization: nations/empires
General: arch, dome, locks, loom, screw, water wheel

DARK AGES

Materials: cold iron, felt, porcelain, silk, silvered weapons
Armor: chain shirt, chainmail
Warfare: fortified towns (wooden stockades)
General: horn window panes, hourglass, masterwork items

HIGH MIDDLE AGES

Materials: adamantine, mithral
Armor: half-plate armor
Weapons: composite longbow, greatsword, lance
Warfare: castles, cavalry
Social Organization: guilds
Transportation: stern rudder, stirrup
General: Gothic arch, lantern, spinning wheel, waterclock, windmill

MEDIEVAL

Materials: paper
Armor: full plate, tower shield
Weapons: bastard sword, crossbow, rapier, warbow
Warfare: trebuchet
Transportation: astrolabe, compass
General: buttons, crude glass window panes, mechanical clock, mirror, power loom

RENAISSANCE

Materials: finely-ground glass
Transportation: caravels, coach lines
General: fine glass windows, glass lenses, printing press

In certain published works by **Frog God Games** set in the Lost Lands, such as *The Blight* and *Razor Coast*, available technology includes such things as gunpowder, cannons, and ironclad warships. Given that much of the Lost Lands are at levels where such advances do not exist (Medieval, High Middle Ages, and even Dark Ages being common), the possession of such superior technology by other realms poses issues of consistency. Would not those with access to steam power and cannons rule the waves? Wouldn't heavy armor such as plate cease to be in use in a world where handguns are available? This problem is even noted in the introduction to the Swords & Wizardry version of *Razor Coast*, which suggests that the Razor Coast be separated from areas of a traditional fantasy campaign by a planar barrier, a physical barrier, enormous distances, or barriers in space or time.

For players and Gamemasters who prefer a fantasy setting without advanced technology, we have written this volume to exclude references to gunpowder, cannons, handguns, steam power, and ironclads. For those purposes, it is assumed that Castorhage does not have access to such technology. As the Razor Coast does not work well in a pre-17th century setting, that region is not covered by this volume, though some references are included in various places. A GM preferring a lower technology setting will have to modify *The Blight* accordingly if that text is used, as well as determine how to include the contents of *Razor Coast*, or whether to design such region afresh.

Those who prefer a higher level of technology, or those not concerned with having divergent technology levels, are free to include that technology and incorporate *The Blight* and *Razor Coast* as published.

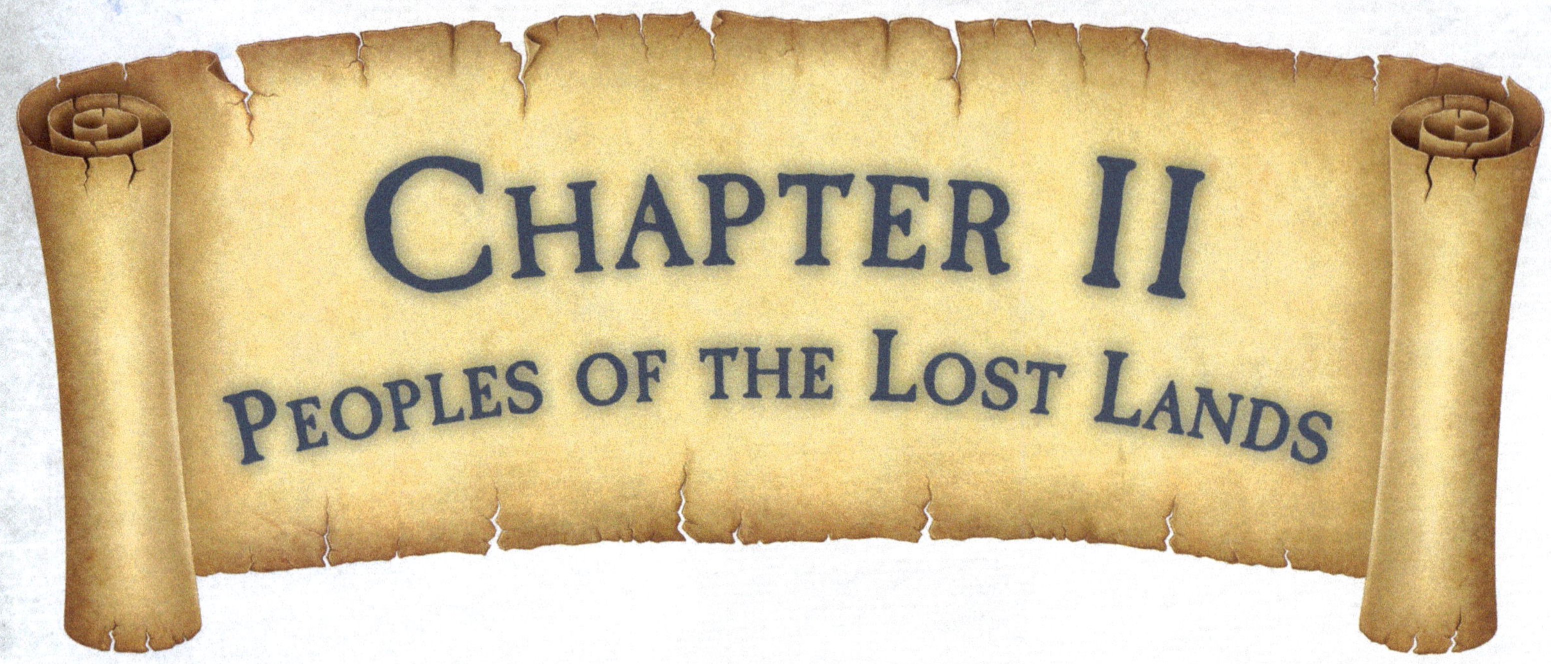

The origin of humans in the Lost Lands is shrouded in the mystery of ancient eons. Evidence of Neolithic groups of humans dates back at least as far as the so-called Age of Man, perhaps 100,000 years ago. A few scholars have, based on very sparse evidence, suggested that some humans may have in fact lived in far earlier times, though such views are controversial to say the least.

A vast diversity of people now populates the Lost Lands. In most regions of the world today, the local folk either view their region as an ancestral homeland or based on legends and myths can tie themselves to a group that migrated to their present location at some time in the past. Many groups show clear evidence of being the result of the intermingling of two or more earlier populations that, for a period of time, found themselves living in close proximity to one another.

While the humans of the Lost Lands vary substantially in appearance from one group to another, in many ways their differences in culture and tradition outweigh differences in physical characteristics. The summary in this chapter attempts to set forth some of the more notable distinctions, but it should be noted that any description of a group of people by definition must speak in generalities, and variations and exceptions in even the smallest populations certainly exists. In addition, this is not intended to be a comprehensive identification of all human and non-human folk in the world, omitting some that either are not numerous or have had a very limited impact on others in the Lost Lands, as well as others that are perhaps yet to be revealed.

A substantial majority of the non-human races, such as elves, dwarves, gnomes, and halflings, in the Lost Lands settled on Akados. The Green Realm of southwestern Akados is the homeland for the largest population of wild elves in the world, while high elves can be found principally in the central and eastern parts of the continent. Nearly all of the dwarven clans who came to the world from Niðavellir made their eventual homes in the great mountain chains of Akados, and most particularly in the Stonehearts; though hill dwarves are spread more widely around the world and even have a sizable population in Shamash Kush in eastern Libynos. But as a general rule, fewer of the non-human races will be seen in Libynos than in Akados.

HUMAN FOLK OF AKADOS

ANARI

The Thousand Rocks and Anaros Island are home to the Anari, a hardy and skilled people known for their martial expertise and artisanship. According to their legends, the Anari once lived on the continent to the east and fled to their current island homelands to escape a terrible war and an army of demons led by evil gods and powerful sorcerers. The Anari themselves date their arrival on the islands to 1313 XC (or 11 I.R.), which has led some scholars to speculate that the Hundaei may have been the proximate cause of the Anari's flight.

The Anari appear to be related to the Xha'en people, though they tend to be a bit shorter on the average than their continental cousins. Much like the Xha'en, Anari typically have dark hair, usually brown or black though red hair is not uncommon, and tawny skin tones. Their eyes tend to be black, brown, or dark green.

Culturally, Anari are part of a feudal society where duty to a lord is considered a paramount virtue. However, nobles are expected to share hardship with their people. In times of crisis, food, water, shelter, and other necessities are shared among all Anari regardless of their social status. Monastic study and skill at arms are also highly prized by the Anari, whose monks and warriors are among the finest in the world.

The Anari speak their own language, also known as Anari, and use a syllabic alphabetic writing system derived from that in use in Xha'en.

BERRINI

The folk known as the Berrini live between Irkaina and the Northlands, primarily in Brounthia, including Hesten and Monrovia. Their name is derived from Lake Berring, which is near the center of their homeland. Among themselves, they sometimes refer to their people as the Hibor.

In fact, the Berrini are largely descended from ancient Hyperboreans who settled the region thousands of years ago. When the Great Darkness fell upon the Gulf of Akados in 1491 I.R. following the destruction of Tsar, the people of this region lost almost all contact with the rest of the Hyperborean Empire. Although the Great Darkness lasted only three years, the creation of the Burning Waste ensured that they remained mostly isolated from their kin through the eventual end of the empire.

Though intermarriage with the local plains tribes has undoubtedly occurred, the physical characteristics of the Berrini are certainly quite distinct from any

of their neighbors. They tend to be lean and pale-skinned, with sharp facial features and dark hair, though some families have very fair, often straw-gold hair. Eye colors are almost uniformly light, from blues to greens to even pale golds. Those who have studied the Berrini note similarities between them and the people of Freegate who also claim Hyperborean heritage.

The Berrini speak a language they also call Hibor, a heavily modified dialect of High Boros. Most Berrini also speak Common.

CASTORHAGERS

Scholars debate whether the folk of Castorhage (known as Castorhagers in polite society and "Blighters" everywhere else) should be considered a unique ethnicity. Most of the people of the city-state are derived from various groups found throughout central Akados, and in that regard are similar to those who are labeled Foerdewaith. That being said, Castorhagi society has existed on Insula Lymossus for more than 3,500 years, and the culture and outlook of the people have clearly been heavily influenced by the city in which they live.

This is most clearly the case with respect to the people known as the "Blighted" who make up perhaps a third of the human population of the city. They bear the mark of living in the Blight in body and soul, and show an unusual degree of physical affinity for their position or occupation, as if the city has crept into them and become a part of their very being. Though the Blighted are ordinary on the streets of the city-state, outsiders find something just a bit off about them, as if they carry with them a bit of the ill-regarded city.

Castorhagers are divided into several different castes, the most common of which are the Lowfolk. They speak Common (or a slightly modified version thereof).

CORALITE

The Coralites, once known as the Yalts, occupied the lands now known as the Domain of Hawkmoon in southeastern Akados until 2496 I.R., when they sailed *en masse* to a coral reef in the Sinnar Ocean where they founded the city of Coralis.

A peaceful folk, Coralites stand four to five feet tall and have a bulky build. Their skin is a deep, rich chocolate color, and their hair is long, dark, and streaked with red or blonde. Both men and women wear garments of diaphanous silk in bright, vibrant colors. The Coralites are known for their art, learning, and music. They have evolved to facilitate underwater exploration around their reef and are able to dive to 1,000 feet without suffering negative effects.

Coralites speak their own unique language.

DAANITES

The native residents of the island of Ynys Cymragh (known as Insula Extremis to the Hyperboreans), Daanites tend to be well-muscled if a bit shorter than the average, with ruddy or freckled skin, and hair ranging from brown to red. Their eyes likewise range from brown to blues and greens. They are rare sights outside of their island, though some trade widely, as far as Castorhage.

The folk of Ynys Cymragh took the name Daanite in honor of their high king Daan, who perished after slaying the undead imperatrix of Hyperborea at Tircople in 2584 I.R. Most people of Akados hold the Daanites in varying degrees of reverence for their sacrifice in ending that dark queen's rule.

The Daanites speak their own language, known as Ogham, though most speak Common as well. The formal name of the world, Lloegyr, is derived from Ogham, and literally means "Lost Lands" in that tongue. While most use the term to refer to the entire world, when Daanites use it they mean the world other than their home island of Ynys Cymragh.

ERSKAELOSI

The Erskaelosi were, in origin, a nomadic group of people who wandered the Irkainian Peninsula from the lands of the Buntesveldt to what is now the Principality of Pelshtaria. At the time of the Great Darkness, many of them fled west and south, but found little welcome and less opportunity in their travels until they finally reached the Kingdom of Burgundia on the Sinnar Coast. There they constructed the city of Tyr as a new homeland.

After the fall of Burgundia in 3354 I.R., many displaced Erskaelosi began to wander once again. The wide-open places of the Unclaimed Lands of the northern Borderland Provinces and the Plains of Mayfurrow north to the Dragon Hills proved to be sparsely settled and offered a degree of freedom from persecution not experienced since the height of Burgundia. Mayfurrow has since become a more settled realm with only a few small bands of Erskaelosi wandering about, always careful to avoid agitating the villages and steadings of the plains. But to the north many large bands of Erskaelosi still run free.

While the Erskaelosi get along well with Plainsmen and the Riverfolk, they tend to be looked at suspiciously by city folk, who often see them not so much as neighbors but rather as a potential threat. For their part, the bluff and boisterous Erskaelosi have no qualms about reinforcing these stereotypes as an excuse to drink hard and play hard.

Erskaelosi tend to be tall and stocky, with weather-beaten — often freckled — skin, and brown or black hair worn long and loose by men and women alike. Their eyes range from dark browns to bright greens. They are usually garbed in rough skins and are prone to tribal symbols tattooed or branded upon their face, arms, and chest.

The people who now live in the Buntesveldt and, to a lesser degree, Pelshtaria, share a heritage with the Erskaelosi, but centuries of intermarriage with Hyperboreans, other tribes, and Ashurians from the Caliphate led these peoples to deviate substantially in culture and appearance.

FOERDEWAITH

The Foerdewaith are by far the most commonly found ethnicity in the eastern half of Akados. These humans descend from the many indigenous tribes that dwelt in the lands conquered by Hyperborean thousands of years ago. During the years of Hyperborean rule, they largely assimilated into an amalgamated people, though regional differences certainly existed. After being left behind when the Hyperboreans withdrew from Akados, these folk eventually became part of the hegemony of Foere started by Macobert, the first Foerdewaith overking. Although the Foerdewaith were identified as a single people during the height of the Foerdewaith monarchy, this was true only as an ethnicity and a broadly shared cultural heritage from the Hyperboreans and the later rule of the overkings. Most Foerdewaith throughout Akados identify themselves as members of smaller regions. The term Foerdewaith is now commonly used to refer to the inhabitants of the Kingdom of Foere and those (mainly the nobility) who can trace ancestries leading back to the kingdom. These "Foerdewaith of Foere" consider the bloodline to be a sign of superiority.

The Foerdewaith of western Akados tend to have fair skin and aquiline features, with darker hair colors and eyes of gray, blue, or violet. Those of eastern Akados tend to broad features; brown, light brown, or blond hair; tan to light-brown skin; and brown, black, green, or hazel eyes. The Foerdewaith of southern Akados have lighter skin tones with brown to blond to red hair, and deep brown to light hazel eyes.

Almost all Foerdewaith speak Common, though some eastern Foerdewaith traditionalists still speak Gasquen.

GAELEEN

A people unique to the Gaelon Valley, these riverfolk ply the waters of the mighty Gaelon, fishing with line and hook and nets in large family groups from light, flat-bottomed skiffs. They sell their catch at the great trade-road bridges, in the markets of wealthy Endhome, or among the innumerable villages that line the shores up and down the river and its countless tributaries.

The Gaeleen deny any relation to the peoples of the Kingdoms of Foere and instead claim to have been born of the river itself and use their tendency to be skilled swimmers as alleged "proof" of the fact. Scholars scoff at this and surmise that the Gaeleen may be a remnant of a much-earlier people called the Phoromyceaens who once inhabited the region of Endhome and the Duskmoon Hills before disappearing from the historical record long ago. The Gaeleen are a smaller folk than the typical Foerdewaith, with skin tones that easily hold a tan from working on the waters under the sun all day long. Their hair ranges from dirty blonds to dark browns, with darker shades frequently being sun-bleached to a much lighter hue due to their chosen vocation, and eyes tending toward greens and blues. The Gaeleen are great storytellers and renowned singers, who often claim to "sing the fish into their nets" as they ply the waters of the Gaelon.

Gaeleen speak the singsong Gaeling tongue, but most know Common as well.

GIANT-BLOODED

The Northlanders hate giants, especially in regions plagued by hordes of these monsters, such as Estenfird or Vastavikland. Yet sometimes a union between a giant and a Northlander occurs, and the result is the giant-blooded. Occasionally, a giant-blooded child is born to two Northlanders, for it is said that the taint of giant blood corrupts for a dozen generations. However the unfortunate thing is conceived, it is usually killed at birth, for most Northlanders will not accept the shame of such an abomination. Still, some are allowed to live and find a place in Northlander society (or, sometimes, among giants), though always at the fringes and never with full acceptance.

Giant-blooded are huge, often well over eight feet tall, hairy, brutish in body and mind, and prone to tempers and passions beyond that of normal men. Their hair is coarse, as are their features, and cleft lips, missing or extra digits, enlarged foreheads, and other unsightly things are common. They are also not terribly bright as the giant blood seems to dim the intelligence of the human to produce individuals who have trouble with even the most mundane of tasks. Giant-blooded are not patient and often give in to impulses and desires, often of a fell nature.

GTSANG

According to their legends, the modern-day Gtsang are the descendants of a group of Jaata who colonized the lands north of the Tsendakar Mountains 150 centuries ago. Whatever the truth of this may be, over 15 millennia the Gtsang have adapted to their homeland, evolving both physically and culturally. They tend to be short (though taller than modern-day Jaata), with skin of various shades of light brown, dark eyes (usually black or dark gray), and fine, black hair. Many Gtsang boast arm or facial tattoos that become increasingly elaborate the higher one is in Gtsang society.

Though the Gtsang are friendly and outgoing, they are also somewhat isolationistic, the result of long years spent in a small and well-protected land far away from outside influence. They are superb craftsfolk, artisans, and performers, and their works of philosophy, magic, and faith are among the wisest and most scholarly in all of Akados. They speak their own language, which bears enough resemblance to Meeruwhan to support their origin story.

HELDRING

The fair-skinned Heldring have lived on the Helcynngae Peninsula for as far back as histories reach. After the fall of Hyperborea, their longships full of vicious raiders landed on the coasts of Akados and swept all before them as they established colonies along large stretches of the Sinnar Coast. Many current-day residents of these regions still bear the distinct characteristics of the Heldring in their ancestry. Eventually, the armies of the overking of Foere drove the Heldring from continental Akados back to their peninsula, where they live to this day. One key result of the Foere conquest, however, was the conversion of the Heldring from the worship of Hel to the faiths of Thyr and Muir.

The Heldring tend to be a tall, broad-shouldered people, many with fair hair and, among the men, prone to thick beards. They speak their own tongue of Helvaenic, though many also speak Common.

JAUNDOOL

According to rumor, the Jaundool are an isolated tribe of folk who lived within Yolbiac Vale long before the coming of the Hyperboreans, and who live there still. The appearance of the Jaundool remains subject to conjecture and uncertainty, and some scholars question whether they were in fact actually human. Some speculate that the Jaundool interbred with Hyperborean settlers following the conquests of Oerson, and that some who still live in the area may, unbeknownst to them, in fact have Jaundool blood in their veins.

KAF

The Kaf are uncommon in Akados, being unique to only one place on the continent: the Kildren Peninsula and nearby Sand Hills where they roam, hunt, and conduct some trade with coastal cogs or the occasional merchants that they approach on the Soldier's Road. No other known enclaves of the Kaf exist in the rest of Akados or Libynos. They speak a language called Ruiki and are the only known speakers of that language.

Their principal settlement is Kaf Village, but smaller farms and villages are scattered across the peninsula. Scholars who know of them tend to think they may be related to the K'Haln located north beyond the river Xircos, but no firm connection to the horse people has been established. Records also don't show how or when the Kaf came to dwell on Kildren Point.

The Kaf are fierce horse warriors that fight with lance, shortbow, and saber. They wear armor of layered leather and onion-domed helmets that have a fringe of fur. They tend to have pale skin with straight black hair and black eyes, and the men are prone to beards and moustaches. Most Kaf have high, angular cheekbones that give them a fierce predatory look and a reputation for a sour disposition. They dress in colorful pants and vests with felt jackets. They are known to be cheerful and boastful at feast but hard and taciturn at other times.

KOUI

The Koui are the original inhabitants of the Bream Islands of western Akados and appear to be related to the Senge tribesfolk of the mainland. They live in slate-roofed stone huts in villages of 10 to 50 souls and maintain small fishing boats or coracles. The Koui follow a simple subsistence economy and survive on fish, abalone, and seaweed. Generally left to their own devices by the Xha'en, the Koui have lived in this fashion for thousands of years, with most of their villages clustered around the southern ends of the three Bream Islands.

Like the Senge, Koui tend to be short and lean, with hair of light or chestnut brown and honey or golden skin tones. With their life outdoors on windswept islands, most Koui have weather-beaten skin by the time they reach adulthood. Both men and women usually keep their hair long, though they wear it tied in the back in tight braids.

NORTHLANDERS

The most populous cultural and racial group in the Northlands are, unsurprisingly, the Northlanders themselves. Most Northlanders are of above-average height and weight for a human, though they do not exceed human norms for size. In skin, eye, and hair color they tend toward the lighter shades, though dark brown hair and eyes, as well as black, are not uncommon. Northlanders are also well known for being clean and for regularly bathing. These hardy folk see no problem with diving into a winter-chilled stream provided they can quickly exit and get back into the warmth of a hall.

Men and women wear their hair long and in braids, though women's hair tends to be longer. Men and women engaged in more-active pursuits, wear trousers, a long tunic, and shoes of wood or leather. Women's clothing tends toward dresses, aprons, and smocks, and both genders wear several layers, especially in winter, as well as cloaks and hats. Although women occasionally wear men's clothing, men rarely are seen in women's clothing.

NÛKLANDERS

Beginning at Nieuburg in Estenfird and reaching north to the Endless Glacier that marks the edge of the world lays Nûkland. The Nûklanders are a different race than the human Northlanders, a race that foreigners would describe as elven. The average Nûklander is short, slender of build, and dark of skin and hair. They have long faces with small, broad noses, pointed ears, and eyes possessing slightly folded lids. Nûklanders have a second inner eyelid that is transparent and seems to serve to protect the eye from the sun and cold, but also gives them the look of perpetually staring, as they rarely blink. Despite their slight build, Nûklanders do not suffer from the great cold of their icy homeland; indeed, they tend not to feel the cold at all due to their innate resistance derived from their inherently magical nature.

While the Northlanders consider the Nûklanders to be natives of the area, they are in fact rather recent settlers, having been led to their current homeland nearly 3,000 years ago by a god the Nûk have since abandoned.

OCEANDERS

Though not an ethnicity in its own right, in recent years it has become more common for citizens of Pontos Island to be considered a distinct group. In truth, they are simply another of the vast number of peoples melded together into the amalgamation of folk known as the Foerdewaith, but their success in remaining a rival empire for the last 300 years has caused their claims of racial distinction to gain some traction.

Oceanders look much like other Foerdewaith, with perhaps their skin slightly more sun-darkened by years spent at sea and eyes a bit more creased from squinting against the glare off the waves. They tend toward shorter hair and fewer beards than their land-bound cousins, though this is by no means universal among them.

PLAINSMEN

The term Plainsman is used in eastern Akados, and particularly in Bard's Gate, to refer to the nomadic folk of the plains of Reme. These are the folk of the Loreclans, ancient inhabitants of the Rhemish plains, who are known there (and described below) as Rhemans.

RAMITHI

Before the coming of the Hyperboreans, a number of human clans lived on Ramthion Island. These piratical people were known for raiding shipping as far north as Legions Bay and as far south and west as the Mouth of Akados. Though the Hyperboreans colonized the island, the local clans remained frustratingly independent and chafed under the attempts of the imperators to bring them to heel, though they were eventually driven to the swampy peninsula known as the Sea Dagger. When Curgantium was destroyed and the Plains of Suilley and the Matagost Forest were set aflame, the Hyperboreans withdrew, while groups of refugees fled across the Dardanal Straight to Ramthion Island, where the local clans welcomed them.

The refugees settled in the lowlands of the rest of the island, and for a while there was peace.

Unfortunately, Ramthion's respite did not last long, for soon the bloodthirsty Heldring invaded, and the islanders traded one oppressor for another. Together, the old Ramithi clans and the newly settled refugees resisted the Heldring invaders and eventually succeeded in driving them off the island.

Through their collective efforts, the refugee settlers and the old Ramithi clans intermarried with each other and came to identify themselves as one people. Today, all of the native inhabitants of the island identify themselves as being directly descended from the Ramithi clans, though probably only around 20 percent have any more than a fictional blood tie. The Ramithi have tawny skin and dark hair. They are usually shaven with elaborate moustaches and sideburns. Their heritage is that of a sea people, but they have had to become warlike over the generations due to repeated invasions of their home island.

The Ramithi exclusively speak Gasquen and refuse to speak Common with its Helvaenic influences.

RHEMAN

The Rhemans are the original inhabitants of the plains of Reme. A nomadic, horse-riding folk, they are distantly related to the Hundaei of old and their descendants, the Shattered Folk of the Haunted Steppes. Since time immemorial, they have been divided into groups of extended and interconnected families known as Loreclans.

Many Rhemans continue their nomadic traditions today and live on the endless plains of Reme. The largest of the nomadic Loreclans include the Grass Sailors, the Quick Knives, the Stone Faces, the Thunder Riders, the Stone Walkers, and the Beast Takers. However, the close relationship between Reme and Foere over thousands of years has, without doubt, changed the character of Reme. Today, roughly a third of the humans in the grand duchy have some degree of Foerdewaith ancestry, although these are clustered mostly in cities, towns, and other substantial settlements. Adoption of Foerdewaith culture is more widespread in Reme than actual Foerdewaith ancestry, for the cultural impact of Reme's alliance of convenience with Foere extended into the Loreclans of the plains as well as the cities. The common tongue is used as a trade language to overcome Loreclannic dialects of Kirkut, jewelry is heavily influenced by Foerdewaith craftsmanship, and — perhaps oddly, perhaps not — plays and music from Foere are performed enthusiastically by amateur troupes even deep in the plains by purely nomadic Loreclans.

The connection between the Rhemish Loreclans and the Shattered Folk is not just one of ancestry, however. Every 50 years, families among the Shattered Folk beyond the Crynnomar Gap are permitted to petition for a right to settle in the Rhemish plains, and a lottery is held to determine who may immigrate. Those permitted to settle usually join existing Loreclans in the plains of Reme, though occasionally they may form new clans with a direct grant of range lands to be held thereafter.

Much like their kin among the Shattered Folk, Rhemans have skin tones that range from a burnt sienna to mahogany and have almost universally straight, black hair — usually worn long — that tends to gray early, though hair of a deep red is occasionally seen. They tend to have long limbs and lean muscle. Beards and excessive body hair are rare, while their eyes are almost always black or deep brown. Among the nomadic groups, tattoos are fairly common, though not as frequently seen as among the Erskaelosi.

RIVERFOLK (ARKAJI)

The Riverfolk have fished the waters and hunted the banks of the Stoneheart River for centuries, though their origin before entering the record of Bard's Gate around 3036 I.R. during the year of the Hard Cold remains a mystery. Before then, they were virtually unknown in the city and only sporadically commented on in the city's annals as boatfolk who plied the Stoneheart under the forest eaves. The Riverfolk speak their own language of Kra, and some speak intelligible Common as well.

Known among their own folk as the Arkaji, the Riverfolk live primarily within the Stoneheart Forest, in the eastern stretches of the central swamp, in particular. Their talent for handling shallow-draft watercraft in the swamps and upon the river is peerless. As a result, a large number of the Riverfolk can be found in Bard's Gate or upon the river waters in service to the city at any given time, and even into the lower Stoneheart Mountains and as far down the Great Amrin River as Eastgate. However, the Riverfolk avoid leaving the confines of the riverbanks for the open sea, but none has ever said what it is they fear.

The Riverfolk have pale pinkish skin tones prone to sunburn and freckling, eyes ranging from deep blue to pale, nearly colorless, and bristly and curly hair and beards (or thick sideburns at least) ranging in color from auburn to black with many going stone gray at an early age. They claim to be descended from the Arcadians of the ancient mountain kingdom of Arcady and take their name for themselves as a corruption of that long-lost people, but their language of Kra bears no resemblance to the Khemitian that was spoken by the folk of Aka Bakar's kingdom. Some few scholars speculate that they may indeed be a last offshoot of some Hyperborean strain, and indeed their language does contain many parallels with old High Boros. Despite some superficial similarities, they do not appear to be in any way related to the Gaeleen of the Borderland Provinces.

SEAGESTRELANDERS

Southwest of the Northlands lies the Seagestreland, a forested band that stretches between the shores of the North Sea and the vast plains of the Sea of Grass. This forest, and the plains beyond, is home to hundreds of warring tribes known collectively as the Seagestrelanders. These tribes are human, but of a different origin than the Northlanders. They speak several different languages and possess a very different culture (in fact, several different cultures).

It is difficult to describe the average Seagestrelander, as there is truly no such thing. The vast majority are smaller in frame and stature than the towering Northlanders, tend toward equally pale complexions, but have darker hair and eyes. They are human, and number few mixed-races among themselves, having no half-elves or half-orcs, and rarely produce a giant- or troll-blooded child.

In general, Seagestrelanders pursue three main lifestyles: farming, fishing, and herding, with cattle, horse, and sheep being the most common livestock. Along the forested coast, the former two go hand in hand, and most tribes practice both in roughly equal measure. Along the Dnipir River, farming is the most popular occupation of the tribes, while out on the Sea of Grass it is herding that dominates. Hunting and trading, as well as raiding, heavily supplement all three.

SENGE

The Senge are the original inhabitants of the Plains of Xha, or at least were living there when the ancestors of the Xha'en people arrived thousands of years ago. Those two peoples clashed in ancient times, until the Senge were finally defeated in the year –1302 I.R. (0 XC). Following their defeat, the Senge were largely driven to the plains east of the Sengejia Hills. Then in –187 I.R. (1115 XC), the city of Xha'ahan completed the Lujhiran Dam, which flooded the plains the Senge lived in and created Lake Pantai. As a result, they were forced even farther into the hills where they dwell to this day in small villages along the Upper Pantai River.

The Senge are not particularly aggressive, though they keep to themselves and avoid contact with the Xha'en to the extent possible. Given their proximity to the city of Aphapor, however, they have developed some trade with that city, which agreed to provide a portion of their produce to the tribes to pacify them after the dam was completed. In their lands, however, strangers are treated with suspicion and generally shunned. Senge villages are overseen by clan hetmen and supported by shamans who have been known to cast powerful druidic spells in defense of their territory. Senge trade handicrafts, furs, and produce for metal tools, clothing, and livestock.

The Senge appear to be related to the Koui, the natives of the Bream Islands. They tend to be short and lean, with brown hair of varying shades, and honey or golden skin tones. Though they can grow beards, most Senge men choose to be cleanshaven, with some shaving their heads as well.

SHATTERED FOLK

The Shattered Folk are the remnant of the once-mighty empire of the Hundaei. Destroyed in their civil war of two millennia earlier and hunted by the vicious humanoids of the Haunted Steppes, the Shattered Folk now exist as scattered tribes that roam the vast steppes as nomads and herders. There are hundreds of tribes ranging in size from a few dozen members to thousands, and some are friendly with each other, though many more either war upon those they meet or simply flee. These tribes are generally ruled by a chief, sometimes through a hereditary lineage but equally often through egalitarian selection, depending on the individual tribe.

There is a still a strong culture of horse warriors among the tribes that runs back through their blood to the mighty hordes of the Hundaei, but they are now small and localized and lack the unity that once made them a powerful nation. When brought to battle, they prove to be brave and skilled horse warriors — after all, survival in the Haunted Steppes is no mean thing, and they have had generations to hone their skills in this hostile environment. Most Shattered Folk avoid contact with outsiders. However, the two largest confederations, the Elitan-i-pan of the western plains near the coast and the Campacha in the south, recently began trading with merchants from Castorhage, Gtsang, Reme, and Foere, and some have even experimented with permanent settlements and agriculture.

Every 50 years, a number of families of Shattered Folk are chosen by lottery to move south of the Wizard's Wall to the plains of Reme. The majority of those choosing to relocate come from the Campacha.

The Shattered Folk tend to be long-limbed and leanly muscled, with dark eyes (black being most common) and skin ranging from deep golden tones to chestnut brown.

TROLL-BLOODED

Troll-blooded are found almost exclusively in the Northlands, but even there, they are rare in the extreme. Interactions between humans and trolls are rarely anything other than killing and eating, and thus almost never produce troll-blooded offspring. Still, it does happen, and like giant-blooded, troll blood corrupts for generations, meaning that two humans can produce a troll-blooded child. The fruits of these unions are even more cursed than the giant-blooded, for if there is anything the Northlanders hate more than giants, it's trolls.

Troll-blooded who are not slain at birth must face the hatred of their neighbors and an all-consuming drive to eat. They are always hungry, and due to their nature and digestive systems, they need to consume far more meat than anything else. This makes keeping a troll-blooded fed throughout the long winters a daunting task. Settlements that host troll-blooded over the winter often find that by spring they have a dearth of rats, cats, and dogs, assuming that the livestock haven't already been pillaged.

Troll-blooded are feral, savage, creatures, at least in appearance if not in behavior. They are tall, but not much taller than most men, and have a hunched posture. Their skin is greasy and tends toward a greenish tint, their hair is straight and black, and their eyes range from red to blue. Like their troll relatives, the troll-blooded have long limbs and short torsos; in fact, their hands easily reach to their knees when standing. These hands grow long talon-like nails that can rend steel. It is the face that is the most troll-like, having a long, narrow nose, high cheekbones, and a mouth filled with sharp teeth. Despite these inhuman features, most troll-blooded retain some signs of their human heritage, usually in their facial expressions or as a glint of intelligence in their eyes.

UPLANDERS

The Uplanders are an honorable and proud folk living primarily in the upper portions of the mountain valley of the River Eamon in the Stoneheart Mountains. They tend to divide themselves along clan lines, with the Angus of Dun Eamon being the primary chieftain of the premier clan. Though they often exhibit a tendency to believe themselves superior to those who do not hail from their homeland, Uplanders are known to be hardworking and have a reputation for honestly and fair dealing that, on occasion, may exceed the truth of the situation.

They are of average height, with lighter skin tones tending toward freckles, and hair ranging from browns to auburn to shocking shades of red. Eyes range from brown or hazel to gray to blue or green. While most Uplanders remain in the Eamon valley, others have taken to trading, and enclaves of these folk can be found as far as Castorhage.

Uplanders speak Common.

VANIGOTHS

The Vanigoths are a large but widely dispersed nation of human barbarians predominantly found in the Wilderland Hills and the plains between the Lorremach Highhills and the Forlorn Mountains. They are most likely mixed descendants of Heldring invaders and the pre-Hyperborean tribes of the Plains of Sull.

It is extremely rare for the disparate Vanigoth tribes to unite under a leader, although they have their own king in the fortress of Aen Vani deep in the Wilderland Hills. The Vanigoths take battle-trophies from their victims, usually the head and some other trophy, often a hand or finger.

The Vanigoths speak their own language of Vanigothic derived from a mixture of Old Sulli and Helvaenic, although most of them can communicate in a rudimentary Common.

XHA'EN

The Xha'en are an ancient people who have inhabited the western lands of Akados for thousands of years. Originally living in small nomadic groups, they spread over an enormous range from the Tsendakar Mountains in the north to the Utterends in the south, and between the Caerulean Ocean in the west to the forests of the Green Realm in the east. Over many centuries, they moved from a hunter-gatherer culture to a more settled agrarian lifestyle, particularly in the rich farmlands of the Plains of Xha, where villages grew into towns, and towns grew into cities, eventually becoming some of the largest in all Akados. Their expansion brought the Xha'en into conflict with the other people of the plains, the Senge, but by –1302 I.R. (0 XC), those others were defeated and driven to the east near the Sengejia Hills.

Today, most Xha'en live in the Xha'en Hegemony, an empire of city-states and territories, all of which owe allegiance to the emperor in the city of Xha'ahan. After millennia of uninterrupted development, the Xha'en are highly advanced in the fields of art, science, magic, architecture, and military development, and have developed an elaborate hierarchical culture. While old tribal traditions still hold sway in villages and in the countryside, most city-dwelling Xha'en are sophisticated and well-educated and hold to the pursuit of learning and worshipping the gods of the Imperial Pantheon.

Xha'en society is bound up in a complex web of laws, traditions, and bureaucracy, and people of all levels are expected to know the rules under which they must live. On the other hand, there is also a long tradition of revering those who overcome unjust limitations imposed by the culture, and many of the heroes of Xha'en legend are notorious for their iconoclastic and subversive ways — though always within certain acceptable bounds.

For nearly the entire history of their people, the Xha'en have lived almost exclusively within the bounds of the hegemony, isolated from most of the other great cultures of Akados. Only in recent years have outsiders come to do more than visit, most particularly when Castorhage established colonies on the Bream Islands starting in 3210 I.R. In turn, some Xha'en have now begun to travel outside their lands, and a sizable mercantile enclave now exists in Castorhage itself.

Given their wide distribution and centuries of development, the Xha'en vary significantly in appearance. Northern Xha'en tend to be taller, while those from the southern cities are somewhat shorter, with broader, stronger builds. Complexion ranges from tawny in the north to rich bronze in the south. Mountain-dwelling Xha'en tend toward a rich ochre tone. Nearly all Xha'en have black hair, though red and brown are sometimes seen. Facial hair is rare, while eyes are generally dark — black, brown, and rarely a very deep green.

Human Folk of Libynos

Alcaldrich

The Alcaldrich are the natives of the Empire of Alcaldar in central Libynos. In origin, Alcaldar was a Hyperborean colony, one of the few in central or southern Libynos that extended into the interior of the continent. As a result, when the Hyperborean Empire fell, Alcaldar survived, maintaining many of the traditions of the empire, though assimilating with the indigenous Libynosi of the region. Today, the Alcaldrich have themselves colonized other lands, conquering the old kingdoms in the Channel Lakes region and settling in places such as the island of Estallia and along the coast of the Yingozi Woodlands. Ships from Alcaldar can be found in most ports of the Lost Lands, even as far as the Razor Coast.

Most Alcaldrich have skin tones ranging from light olive to tan to leather-brown, with hazel or brown eyes, though some have green or even blue. Hair color ranges from dark blond in the upper class through a range of browns all the way to black, and, very rarely, red. Their heights tend to be average, though members of the noble classes tend to be taller, with skin the color of old ivory.

They speak their own tongue of Alcaldrich, which is descended from High Boros.

Antiochians

The folk of the Antioch City-States are known as Antiochians. Mainly descended from Ashurian stock, some people also have Hyperborean heritage from the years of empire. They share a common language, though each city-state tends to have a separate dialect that is an amalgam of Old Boros and Semuric.

Most Antiochians have light tan or pale olive skin, however, instead of the darker complexions typical of Ashurians. Eye colors tend toward brown and hazel, though some, particularly those with lighter skin tones, may have green or deep blue eyes. Hair color is typically brown or auburn. Among the Antiochians, skin color is not considered important, though lighter tones tend to brand one as "city folk" in most rural areas. They tend to be taller than average but with slender builds.

Though most Antiochans are in their city-states, they can be found in many trading cities throughout Libynos, and even in major ports on Akados.

Ashurians

Ashurian is a general label applied to many peoples of northern and western Libynos, all of whom can broadly trace their ancestry back to the ancient Assurian Empire. Though there is great diversity in their appearance, most Ashurians are of a darker complexion, with common skin tones often resembling light brown leather or the light brown of dried tobacco leaves. Their hair color can range from black to dark brown, occasionally to reddish brown. Eye colors are typically brown or black, though some hazel is not uncommon. Slender builds are typical, but almost every body type can be seen somewhere among the Ashurian populations.

Today, Ashurians can be found throughout much of northern and central Libynos and even in northeastern Akados. Those who still dwell in or near the Ashurian Desert are likely closest in appearance to their original forebears in the Assurian Empire. Elsewhere, intermarriage with other groups has led to the wide variation now seen in their populations. Today, Ashurians make up large majorities of the Ammuyad Caliphate, Pelshtaria, other parts of eastern Irkaina, Khartous, and islands in the Sea of Baal; many Ashurians are also present in the Antioch City-States and the desert countries of Guurzan and Caddesh.

Other than in the Antioch City-States, the countries where Ashurians are a majority all speak Semuric, a language based on the speech of the ancient Assurians.

Baalathites

The Baalathites are the people of Baalthaaz and Ifthaaz in northern Libynos, as well as the original inhabitants of what is now the Khemitian Governate of Tahmakht. They are seldom found outside the lands surrounding the Sea of Baal.

Baalathites tend to have dark olive skin, with prominent noses and very dark brown or black hair, though lighter brown hair is not unheard of. Their eyes are usually brown, dark green or black, and very rarely, hazel or dark blue. Natives of Ifthaaz have an average range of heights and body types, while those of Baalthaaz tend to be taller and more muscular. Baalathites speak their own tongue, which appears unrelated to either Khemitian or Semuric.

Bhanakhirans

The Bhanakhirans are natives of southern Libynos, in the forests, jungles, and coastal regions west of the Hollow Spire Mountains. They primarily live in cities along the coast and in towns and villages within the interior, usually near rivers. Tribes in the Yingozi Woodlands and the northern part of the Mengamuk Forest often have some Bhanakhiran ancestors, and so may have similar features. Other than merchants and traders, few Bhanakhirans leave their homeland.

Most Bhanakhirans have golden-brown skin the color of amber, with straight, dark hair that ranges mostly from dark brown to black. Their eyes are primarily brown or black. On occasion, reddish-brown hair and deep green eyes are seen, which may be evidence of some Hyperborean

ancestry. They tend to be shorter than average, though taller than the people of Jaati. Plumpness is considered a mark of wealth and status among these folk.

They speak a language known as Bhanikhat, largely a unique tongue of the region, though there is clear evidence of Hyperborean influence from the years of that empire's colonial period in southern Libynos. As a result, anyone who has studied High Boros should be able to understand simple phrases and words in Bhanikhat.

EQUATORIANS

These folk are the people of Sensibar, Tulyamin, and villages in the southern part of the Seething Jungle in south Libynos. They are seldom seen anywhere outside of their homelands or the major cities of the Reaping Coast.

Most Equatorians have skin the color of ebony or onyx, with black or brown eyes, and tend to be tall. They have black hair that curls very tightly, which some wear in tight braids, often elaborately done, while others keep their hair cut quite short or even shaven. Traditionally, Equatorians dress in bright earthy colors or jewel tones and adorn themselves lavishly with gold and silver or strings of shells or beads.

Sensibrites and some tribes in the Seething Jungle place great importance on being addressed by appropriate titles and expect people to show them the respect due their positions. Those in Tulyamin tend to be much more casual about such matters.

Equatorians speak the Zenzin language.

HUUN

The Huun are the people of the Huun Imperium, with their homeland in the Desert of Oreb, a high, isolated desert plateau in eastern Libynos. They claim descent from the ancient Hundaei clans of the Great Steppes of Akados, making them the inheritors of an ancient legacy of enmity to Hyperborea. Their physical similarities to others who trace their origin to the Hundaei, as well as the parallels between their language and Kirkut, support such claims, though how they traversed the distances between the Great Steppes and western Libynos remains a mystery to Akadian scholars.

For over 250 years, the Huun Imperium and the Foerdewaith of Akados fought four crusades for dominion over the Sacred Table and the city of Tircople in eastern Libynos. Three years ago, an army of Huun recently appeared at the very verge of the Lyre Valley and held Bard's Gate captive within its siege line for more than a year before disappearing just as swiftly in retreat before the approaching forces of the overking of Foere. The Huun remain some of the most feared warriors in all of the Lost Lands.

Most who encounter Huun outside the high desert meet only armored warriors in battle. Very few (typically limited to merchants or traders from Ifthaaz or the Malagro) can claim any other relationship with the folk of the Imperium, and they do not discuss such things.

Huun skin-tones tend toward the dark red-brown color of mahogany to walnut brown, while their eyes are usually black, but may also be gray or brown. Their hair tends to be black and straight; men and women usually wear their hair long, though hairstyles tend to be simple and many warriors keep their hair short. The tallest Huun are barely above average height, and most are shorter than average. They tend to be slender, but muscular.

The Huun language is different from any other in Libynos, having the most similarity to the Kirkut of the ancient Hundaei, though there is clear evidence of influence from most local tongues, such as Semuric. Their warriors are also known to employ a silent Huun Hand Speech for use in battle and when stealth is an imperative.

ISTAFLUMINAN

The Istafluminans are the natives of the fertile river plains and rolling hills bounded by the deep Ashurian Desert on the west and the high Zakros Mountains on the east. Their cities are some of the oldest in the world, many of which were founded at the very dawn of human civilization. Today, their merchants can be found throughout much of northern and central Libynos, from the Ammuyad Caliphate to Khemit. The Adenians have even established colonies in Jaati and on Tyrnos Island.

To an outsider, Istafluminans would easily be classified as Ashurians, though they consider themselves of separate ethnicities. Istafluminans have somewhat darker skin than most Ashurians, with black or brown eyes and almost uniformly black hair. Both women and men elaborately style their hair, though some cut it short or even shave their heads. Men often have well-kept beards, often styled, though some do choose to be cleanshaven. The people of the Zakros Mountains — the Adenians, Hurardu, and Kymmurean tribes — are somewhat taller than average, with slightly lighter skin.

Istafluminans speak Hakhaddic, which as a spoken language seems to have some similarities to Semuric, though the written forms are very different.

JAATA

The Jaata are native to the lands of far northeastern Libynos. Despite its location at a high northern latitude, Jaati is kept warm by the waters of the Great Eastern Current, along with the odd effects of the Tropic of Arden. Most Jaata live in coastal cities or villages that line the many rivers of the region, while much of the interior is sparsely populated.

Among the shortest of humankind, the Jaata also tend to be slender, though they still can be quite strong, which often surprises those not familiar with their people. They have skin color that ranges from the golden-brown of sandalwood to deep browns of rosewood or walnut, with eyes that are almost always black, and black hair that is usually fine and straight. Women usually grow their hair long and braid or wrap it, while men seldom grow hair past their shoulders but cultivate their beards carefully. Usually fine-featured and graceful, the Jaata are considered by many outsiders to be the handsomest people in the world.

Jaata often wear clothes of colorful silk, along with jewelry of gold and silver. Such jewelry is a symbol of status but also a way to carry one's wealth, so most people wear some all the time and even more on special occasions.

The Jaata trade widely and form enclaves in many large cities. One of the largest is in Shabbis, and a large population even lives as far as Castorhage in Akados. They speak Meeruwhan. The Jaata are believed to be distantly related to the Gtsang of western Akados, who are said to have migrated from Jaati thousands of years ago.

KALDILOORAN

These folk are native to the westernmost extent of southern Libynos on the coast of the Sinnar Ocean and live in the fertile, if narrow, coastal plain and dense interior rainforest. Named after a chieftain who united them from many related tribes, all Kaldiloorans are considered to be part of the family of the prince, with chieftains being "cousins" who are in charge of smaller houses under the great house of the prince. As infants, they are given facial tattoos that designate their house, so it is possible to recognize where a Kaldilooran was born if one understands the patterns. Needless to say, anyone without facial tattoos is immediately revealed as an outsider.

Kaldiloorans tend to be of average height or taller, with skin tones the warm browns of cardamom or cloves, or a few shades darker. Their hair is usually dark brown, thick and curly, worn less than shoulder length or bound in a thick tail. Their eyes are also usually dark brown, though both black hair and black eyes are not uncommon.

Kaldiloorans typically dress in cotton or linen, often in natural colors, or (especially in cities) wear silk in muted colors. Clothing is not considered a status symbol among these people, and outside cities is sometimes very simple indeed. Kaldiloorans traders can be found around the southern coasts of Libynos and have been known to sail south and west to the Aizanes Islands and (rarely) as far as the Razor Coast.

A number of the folk who live in the region but outside Kaldiloora appear to be closely related to the Kaldiloorans. The River People of the Delta, for example, seem to be quite closely related, though they have more variations in appearance, some of which has been attributed to the presence of fey blood. And the inhabitants of the Mengamuk Forest also look much like Kaldiloorans, though they tend to be a little shorter on average. The residents of Kaldiloora and the Mengamuk Forest speak a language known as Gonidal.

KHEMITITES

Khemitites are the people of the Triple Kingdom of Libynos, a land of living gods and ancient civilizations. They are quite rare outside their own kingdom and the lands they have conquered, though the benefits of trade have seen Khemitites sail to far ports, and sometimes settle small merchant enclaves. Even a city as far as Bard's Gate in Akados has a permanent (if small) population of Khemitites, largely due to the presence of the Temple of Bast there and the special relationship it has enjoyed in the city since the time of the Shabbisian plagues.

Khemitites generally distance themselves from those they see as foreign barbarians — barbarians who were able to conquer their lands in centuries past, but barbarians nonetheless. Even when living in foreign lands, they are rarely seen in public, preferring to remain sequestered in their fortified compounds and manses surrounded by soldiers of their own land and priests of their own religions.

Though a distinct group, modern Khemitites can claim descent from many different peoples, including Hyperboreans and Nubarans, and accordingly they can exhibit a wide range of characteristics. Nevertheless, most Khemitites have darker skin that is often the color of nutmeg or teak wood. Most have brown eyes, but black, green, gray, and hazel are not uncommon. Their hair is usually black or dark brown, though lighter-skinned Khemitites may have medium-brown hair. They are usually short, though some families are known to be of average or greater height.

Many Khemitites, particularly those of the noble and merchant classes, prefer to wear diaphanous tunics and gowns, skillfully crafted adornments of gold and jewels, and have kohl-limned eyes.

Khemitites speak Khemitian, which is used in many ports throughout Libynos, and some of their scholars are even able to read the hieroglyphic language of Ancient Kemitian.

LAGISH

The Lagish folk live in the Grasslands of Wahm and the Yingozi Woodlands and are the natives of the Channel Lakes region. At one point, those who lived near the Channel Lakes developed a semi-agricultural society centered around a number of settlements, which collectively was known as the Kingdom of Ka'dufaar. When the Alcaldrich conquered the region some 275 years ago, they put all of those settlements to the torch (one of which was rebuilt and became the city of Caduvar). Today, the Lagish are almost exclusively a nomadic, tribal people. Though they continue to tell stories of the glory of their former kingdom, they seem to have grudgingly accepted their new lives, trading with their former Alcaldrich enemies and even adopting their language. Two of the larger Lagish tribes are the Moglai and the Mwandu.

Mostly of average height, those of unmixed heritage have rich brown skin tones, with hair and eyes of deep brown to black, and occasionally dark green eyes. However, many of the Lagish have some amount of Alcaldrich or Bhanakhiran heritage, and so show some characteristics typical of those groups.

Lagish living in the woodland areas have largely retained the use of their original tongue, while many of the tribes near Alcaldar or the Channel Lakes adopted Alcaldrich as their primary language. Lagish are seldom found anywhere other than their native homelands and the margins of neighboring countries.

LITTORIC

The indigenous folk of the jungles along the eastern coast of Libynos, including the Mguru of the Malagro and the tribes of Ambicuaria, are members of a group known as the Littoric. They tend to have the same rosewood or walnut brown complexions as the Jaati, black eyes, and coarse, black hair, often grown long enough to braid in charms and totems. Shorter than the average, they are still taller than the typical Jaati.

Littoric folk are typically xenophobic, do not take kindly to strangers wandering in their lands, and similarly are almost never seen anywhere other than their jungle homeland.

MAIGHIB DESERTFOLK

The historical range of the Desertfolk includes almost all of the Maighib, which nearly crosses the entire breadth of Libynos. They are the deep desert tribes of Khartous, Guurzan, Khemit, and Qesh, as well as the people of Numeda. While most Desertfolk still live nomadic lives, about one-third of the general population of Guurzan and many in Caddesh are descended from the Desertfolk.

Their skin tones are mostly rich bronze in color, darker than a typical Ashurian, with eyes that are usually dark brown or black. Their hair is black or very dark brown. Men tend to grow beards easily from the teen years. They are typically slightly taller than Ashurians or Khemitites, Numedans being the tallest of the group. Though there are many differences between the different tribes that make up the Desertfolk, they all tend to wear loose-fitting, comfortable clothing suited to a nomadic desert life.

The Desertfolk originally spoke a group of related languages, with enough diversity that distant tribes would not be able to understand one another. Many, particularly those far from cities, continue to speak dialects of these varied tongues. Other Desertfolk have, to one extent or another, adopted, or at least have some passing familiarity with, Semuric or Khemitian.

Except for trading in the towns of Guurzan, Khartous, or Khemit, most Desertfolk seldom wander far from their ancient nomadic lands. Numedans travel a bit more widely, but even they are rarely seen outside the areas of the Sea of Baal or the Ruby Sea, unless they have been hired as mercenaries.

MEROWEN

The Merowen are a widely-dispersed ethnic group that includes the people of Axuum, Aethiope, Imya, Kazania, Meroë, Qesh, and the former country of Nubara. They usually have skin with the dark reddish-brown to brown-black colors of peppercorns, and black hair with tight curls. Their eyes are usually dark brown, though they may be black or (rarely) dark green. Most Merowen tend to be taller than average.

Though styles differ widely among the various cultures that include the Merowen folk, women in general often wear their hair loose or in a scarf or multiple braids, while men usually keep their hair short or even shave their heads. Many men choose to be cleanshaven, and if beards are worn, they tend to be kept short and thin.

Deferring to the dominant culture in the region, most Merowen speak Khemitian, though Kazania managed to retain its own language.

Merowen travelers can be found as far as large cities in northern Khemit, while their traders typically venture along the Ruby Sea, south to the Channel Lakes and the northern Reaping Coast, and east to the Boiling Sea.

REAPING COAST

The folk of the Reaping Coast are an agglomeration of many different ethnicities. Those found here may claim ancestry from Hyperborean-era colonists, Lagish tribesfolk, Equitorans, and travelers from as far as Foere and Castorhage. As a result, there is no typical resident of these lands.

RIVER PEOPLE

These people are the natives of the land between the Lenggor River and the Ular River and their various tributaries in southwestern Libynos, including the area near the Sinnar Coast known as the Delta. Other than those who choose to live in the Delta and trade with outsiders, they tend to be reclusive and stay deep in the forests and jungles of the interior.

As a general rule, the River People look much like their Kaldilooran neighbors to the south, but have more variation in height, hair color, eye color, and skin tones. Some of this is attributed to the possible presence of fey blood among the River People. In addition, the beliefs, traditions, and religion of the River People are entirely different from any of those who live elsewhere in southern Libynos.

In the interior, the River People speak their own strange language, which appears to be unrelated to any other known tongue. In the Delta, they use a trade tongue (called Delta Speech) that consists of a debased version of their own language combined with Hyperborean and various terms borrowed from Bhanakhirin and Gonidal (the language of the Kaldiloorans).

OTHER HUMAN GROUPS

GHAZAKS

The Ghazaks are nomadic bands of Semuric-speaking peoples who wander the island-realm of Mulstabha between Akados and Libynos. These small family and clan groups of tall, pale-skinned, white-haired humans are as phenotypically different from the Mulstabhins as could be imagined, yet they alone are able to move unhindered through Mulstabhin territory with impunity. Most folk think it is because there are so few of them and that they represent no threat or great burden to the city-state, while others claim it was because they inhabited the island long before the Mulstabhins. Still others whisper that it was the ghazaks who first taught the secrets of Mulstabhin astrology to the ephemerides. Whatever the reason, the ghazaks are few in number and are rarely seen in their wanderings upon the island.

MULSTABHINS

The Mulstabhins are the folk of Krivcycek Island in the Mulstabhin Passage between the continents of Akados and Libynos. The island is also sometimes referred to as Mulstabha, which, somewhat confusingly, is also the term for their leader. They are the people of the Land of the Bull from the Sea, so named for their founder, a Libynosi minotaur and pirate who founded the citadel of Jem Karteis. They share Krivcycek Island with local tribes of peoples known as the Ghazaks.

The folk of Mulstabha make almost all other foreign visitors seem mundane and approachable. Their habit of holding themselves aloof from the local residents makes the Khemitites look warm by comparison, and their rigid system of castes make the Jaata system seem flexible. The fact that they keep to themselves and share almost nothing of themselves or their home with anyone makes them seem only more exotic and powerful. They are tall and lean, with skin the color of mahogany, and wiry black hair with blue or brown eyes. Descended from a mixture of ancient sea peoples and Libynosi, they are unlike any other known people in the world in appearance or culture.

Mulstabhins speak Semuric.

Hyperboreans

Scholars the world over, from Castorhage to Pharos, consider the Hyperborean race as a distinct lineage to be extinct. The last remnant of that ancient people disappeared from Tircople 900 years ago, and from Akados a century before that. Though many records of those times exist, oddly enough a description of a typical Hyperborean does not, and accordingly what they looked like remains a subject of intense scholarly debate.

There are some folk within the Lost Lands who claim direct or near descent from the Hyperboreans, such as the citizens of Freegate in Akados and the Berrini between the lands of Irkaina and the Northlands. There are good historical reasons to accept their assertions, though the fact that Berrini and Freegaters look little like one another may make it difficult to accept the truth of both simultaneously. Of course, centuries of intermarriage with locals has undoubtedly affected both peoples and led to necessary divergence of their characteristics.

Wanderers

The term Wanderer refers to a mix of different peoples and even races — humans of many and mixed lineages, half-orcs, even some halflings and other assorted odds and ends, all of whom are exiles from their own lands, who have come together as a group and have truly created their own society. They are mainly recognized in the vicinity of Bard's Gate on Akados, where they live nomadic lives in small groups that wander across the wide expanses of the plains to the east and west of that city and the valley between. Given this, they are not truly an ethnic group, at least not yet, though some scholars suggest that they could become one in time.

The Non-Human Races

Dwarven Folk

The first dwarves arrived in the Lost Lands just under 15,000 years ago from their homeland of Niðavellir, part of the same plane of existence as the elven Alfheim and the drow Svartalfheim. They were in the midst of a war with the drow when they discovered the secrets of the gates to Boros originally created by the elven god Wayland the Smith. The dwarves opened multiple new gates between the worlds, and soon the conflict between the two races spilled through. The dwarves soon found themselves embroiled in the Gods' War and allied with the gods of good against the gods of evil (with whom the drow joined).

Over the ensuing centuries, the dwarves spread throughout many lands of Boros (or, as they still call it, Midgard). The planar gates were eventually all destroyed or forgotten, until the dwarves lost contact with their homeland.

Yet in their new world, the dwarves began to acclimate to their new homes and divided into distinct groups based on where they settled. Those who came to live amid the peaks of Akados became the mountain dwarves; those who settled in the hills became hill dwarves. The Ankhurans of far western Akados are certainly dwarves, though their origin seems unconnected to any of their cousins throughout the world. There are also the sand dwarves of Libynos, the gray dwarves (also known as duergar), and the deep dwarves of the Under Realms, as well as certain more recently-recognized groups such as the street dwarves of Bard's Gate.

All dwarves, however, are known for their stolid resilience, stubbornness, and sheer tenacity in the face of trial and hardship. As they say, better to chip at a granite boulder than to try to change the mind of a dwarf.

Hill Dwarves

The most common type of dwarf seen outside the deep mountains are hill dwarves. These ruddy-skinned, stocky folk have beards and/or sideburns that tend to be thick and in hues of dirty blond to dark brown. They are mainly miners and craftsmen and can be found throughout the world, from the Xha'en Hegemony to Reme to the Plains of Mayfurrow, and eastward to the hills of Irkaina and Shamash Kush in Libynos. They get along quite well with humans and can tolerate elves, having not been a party to either the battle at Lake Crimmormere or the Great Betrayal at Hummaemidon. They tend to avoid their mountain dwarf cousins, however, as the two groups have little love for each other.

Mountain Dwarves

Mountain dwarves tend to stay within their mountain dwellings, though some do travel for trade or adventure to cities not far from their people. They tend to be taller than hill dwarves, with pale skin, black or gray hair, and full, thick beards.

It is said that the mountain dwarves were originally all part of a single clan whose greatest king was Karam Ezun the Wyrmkiller. Since those ancient days, however, the mountain dwarves have divided into nine Great Mountain Clans. These are Clan Craenog of the central Stoneheart Mountains; Clan Ironskull of the Blackrock Mountains; Clan Targ, now a scattered folk, originally from the Forlorn Mountains; Clan Koth, also scattered, from somewhere in the Stoneheart Mountains; Clan Krazzadak, who lost their home in the Shengotha Plateau when ice covered it, who live yet in the Stonehearts and their capital of Abad Durahai; Clan Flammeaxte of the Deepfells; Clan Bulghoi of the Kal'Iugus Mountains; and Clans Duhnbeyl and Tusov, whose locations are uncertain.

Mountain dwarves generally do not have good relations with any other folk, even their hill dwarf cousins. However, the Silverhelm Clan of the northern Lyre Valley in the Stoneheart foothills, a part of the Great Mountain Clan Krazzadak, is an anomaly in that they are on good terms with the humans of Bard's Gate.

Ankhuran Dwarves

Found only in their homeland in the Tsendakar Mountains of far western Akados, Ankhuran dwarves are a quiet, almost taciturn group, who usually wear elaborate tunics, shirts, and trousers embroidered with mandalas and geometric patterns. Unlike many other dwarves, they favor bright colors such as reds and yellows, sometimes garishly contrasting with darker blues or greens.

Ankhuran dwarves tend to wear their hair long and often woven into multiple braids. Embroidered, soft conical hats with the top pulled forward are common headgear, as are skullcaps and headbands. The Ankhurans do not make quite such a fuss about beards as other dwarves, and male Ankhurans often go unshaven or wear short beards that are sometimes shaved into elaborate patterns. Ankhuran women favor face paints or tattoos, also in traditional geometric patterns that are often quite beautiful and extensive. Males usually do not decorate their faces, save for ear- and lip-rings.

Elven Folk

Much like the dwarves of Boros, the elves came from another plane of existence, from their homeland known as Alfheim. They arrived in several waves via planar gates created by the god Wayland the Smith beginning some 17,000 years ago. Initially, few were permitted to pass the gates, most of whom were among the most noble of the elves, ancestors of today's grey elves of the Emerald Mountains. Over the next several millennia, other groups of elves managed to cross in small numbers and largely settled in remote locations. Only in –6484 I.R., at the same time the Three Gods banished Orcus to the far plane of void known as the Ginnungagap, did a large wave of elves come to Boros during what is known as the First Exodus.

The arrivals from the First Exodus settled mainly in the Great Akadonian Forest that then stretched across almost all of southern Akados. These were the ancestors of today's wild elves (those who refused to follow Valenthlis and withdrew west to the Green Realm) and high elves (who followed Valenthlis, fought aside the Hyperboreans at Hummaemidon, and live today in eastern Akados largely in friendship with the human realms).

High Elves

Most elves encountered in eastern Akados or in human cities elsewhere are high elves, most initially hailing from the Forest Kingdoms to the east of Bard's Gate or from the Harwood Forest. Many high elves are subjects or vassals of the elven kingdom of Parnuble and revere the beloved queen of that realm and gladly rise to defend her honor. Most high elves have honey-blond hair, though some have black hair, and blue, green, or sapphire eyes.

Though preferring forests, many high elves encountered outside their homelands are widely traveled and cosmopolitan, and are on friendly terms with humans, as well as gnomes and halflings. They are reasonably tolerant of hill dwarves, but dislike mountain dwarves. They find wood elves to be fascinating throwbacks, view the wild elves as arrogant and insular, and generally hold grey elves in legendary awe. They hate drow on general principle.

Wild Elves

Though likely the most numerous of the elven kindreds in the world, the wild elves are almost never seen outside their forests in the Green Realm and Green Warder Nations. They are the descendants of those elves who refused to make peace with the humans of Akados and chose to retreat to the west to avoid civil war with their high elf kin. These are also the elves that suffered the wars with the humanoid tribes of the Haunted Steppes at the Crynnomar Gap and who erected the Green Warder monoliths to prevent future human incursions into their lands.

Most wild elves have flowing black hair, eyes of black, browns, or grays, and rich woody-brown skin, though some may have silver or honey-blond hair, and golden or amber eyes.

Wild elves are coolly indifferent toward their high elven kin (whom they view as having betrayed elvenkind by making peace with humans) and half-elves (whom they view with a mixture of pity and disgust). While wild elves would likely feel kinship with wood elves, they would also consider them crude and barbaric. They think little of gnomes and halflings, and view all humans and dwarves with outright hostility. If possible, drow are killed on sight.

Wood Elves

The wood elves are the seemingly feral remnant of the elves that neither followed the ways of Valenthlis nor chose to depart eastern Akados during the Second Exodus. They usually live in small, isolated enclaves scattered in woodlands throughout central and eastern Akados. While they may be less overtly hostile to humans than their wild elf cousins of the Green Realm to the west, these sylvan folk are nonetheless more prone to isolationism and insular defense of their territories than the high elves. Usually, conflict is the result where human settlements encroach on wood elf lands. The one exception seems to be around Bard's Gate, where the wood elves of the region hold the queen of Parnuble in high regard and respect the peaceful relationship she has engendered with the local humans. As a result, the occasional wood elf can even be seen walking the streets of Bard's Gate.

Wood elves tend to be shorter than high elves, slightly stockier, with darker earth-tone skin, and hair of dark brown or muted auburn, and eyes of black, brown or, occasionally, leaf green. Unlike their kinfolk, some wood elves are able to grow beards.

Compared with their high elf kin, wood elves tend to have somewhat cruder technology but are more in touch with nature and druidic magic. In point of fact, they usually have a haughty disdain for most high elves and look down on half-elves as half-breeds. They get along with gnomes, have a neutral to slightly-hostile attitude toward humans and halflings, and actively dislike half-orcs and dwarves. Like their other cousins, they hate drow. Being quite an insular folk, the wood elves have little knowledge of wild elves or grey elves and would be both fascinated by and cautious of such folk.

Grey Elves

The grey elves, mysterious and fey, are the legendary monarchs of the elven race, sequestered in the Emerald Mountains deep in the Green Realm. It is to these kings and queens that the wild elven high lords swear fealty. They are an inherently magical race and are renowned for the depths of their knowledge and wisdom. To their other elven kin, they are known as the Hidden Ones or the Shining Ones.

Grey elves tend to a much paler cast than other elves, with hair ranging in color from white to silver, sometimes with a tint of bluish-gray. Their eyes are bright blue, silver, completely colorless, or amber. They stand taller than all other elves and are as at home upon the waves as on land.

Grey elves are friendly though aloof with wild elves, whom they see as their rightful subjects. High elves and wood elves are likewise seen as subjects, though gone astray and without proper guidance. They think little of half-elves as a debased offshoot and consider them more akin to humans than elves. They tolerate humans, gnomes, and halflings and are generally unfriendly with dwarves, though they reserve a special respect for those dwarves directly related to the dwarven high kings of old, for theirs is a shared history. Grey elves find drow to be fascinating and seek to learn all they can of their subterranean kin. A grey elf is extraordinarily unlikely to be encountered anywhere outside the Emerald Mountains.

Dark Elves (Drow)

The drow are the descendants of the natives of Svartalfheim who warred with the dwarves of Niðavellir and came over to Akados through the gates the dwarves built, eventually siding with the evil gods in the Gods' War. They have lived in the depths of the Under Realm ever since, in their own cities such as Thoth Kathalis underneath the Mons Terminus mountains, and in one city on the surface, Vilik Strad on the Talanos Peninsula of far southwestern Akados. Hating most other races and being hated in return, few drow are ever seen outside their own realms. The one exception might be the grey elves of the Emerald Mountains, where a mutual curiosity seems to hold.

Half-Elves

Many half-elves trace their ancestry to the aftermath of the Hyperborean wars, though many others are the offspring of more recent interbreeding between humans and elves (usually high elves). As a general matter, half-elves are accepted by most human realms on Akados, particularly where they are more common; in some locales where they are rare, they may be seen as a bit of an oddity, though they still would not elicit hostility. As evidence of their acceptance, particularly in eastern Akados, many leaders of human cities are and have been half-elves.

Half-elves and high elves are usually on quite friendly terms. Ironically, it is among their other cousins that half-elves are most likely to meet animosity. Typically, wild elves and wood elves would view half-elves as half-breeds, while grey elves would think of them as little more than humans. Only in some of the eastern lands of Akados would wood elves be willing to accept half-elves as companions or friends.

GNOMES

The vast majority of gnomes in the Lost Lands live on Akados and can be found in many locations and cities throughout the continent. Some also live in Libynos, mainly in the region of the Hollow Spire Mountains in the south of the continent.

Rock gnomes are the common gnomes of the Lost Lands, and the ones most typically encountered in cities or other settled areas. They are found more frequently in the central and western portions of Akados but live as far east as the city of Bard's Gate. Rock gnomes generally settle in small villages in hilly regions, and mostly try to stay out of the affairs of other folks. They are known for raising fruit trees, herbs, and bees; gnomish wines and honey are well-regarded and can fetch good sums in trade.

Their deep gnome cousins, the svirfneblin, are almost never seen outside their mountain homes. Their city of Alesardin in the Stoneheart Mountains is regularly in conflict with the nearby dwarven clans. Also in the Stonehearts, on the Ice Plateau, are the ice gnomes, or barbegazi, who are shunned by all of their cousins.

HALFLINGS

The presence of halflings is virtually ubiquitous throughout the whole of Akados, particularly in the lands that at one time or another were under the dominion of the Kingdom of Foere. Their original homeland may be in the area of the Dale and the Low Country, in the western part of the Principality of Olduvar, though there is some support for their origin in the Old Tors in the holdings of the overking of Foere.

Most halflings live rustic lives, often in the countryside, where they plant gardens, grow grains, and raise sheep and other smaller livestock. Some, however, have found their way to major towns or cities, and in some cases have reached heights of substantial influence and wealth, becoming successful merchants, guildmasters, or business owners. Some few have even found a degree of notoriety as adventurers or rogues, a status that secretly pleases many of the otherwise quiet halfling folk.

LANGUAGES OF THE LOST LANDS

Hundreds if not thousands of languages are spoken in the Lost Lands. At one point in time, most of the human population of the world lived in small, relatively isolated tribes or clans, each of which developed its own tongue (or divergent dialects of regional languages). Over thousands of years, each of these different languages diverged, merged, and influenced each other, in a complex tapestry that can, even to experts, be bewildering.

That being said, certain languages have had outsized influence on the modes of speech in the world. A number of current languages either are descended from or were heavily influenced by the High Boros spoken by the Hyperborean Empire. Even though now separated by thousands of miles, many folk who claim Hundaei ancestry speak a language clearly descended from Kirkut, including the Shattered Folk, the Rheman Loreclans, the tribes of the Sea of Grass, and even the Huun of Libynos. And throughout Libynos, the Semuric tongue of the ancient Assurian Empire has spread far and wide to form the basis for scores of languages now in use throughout that continent.

Set forth below is a table of many of the major languages of the Lost Lands, followed by a brief consideration of a few of the more widespread or influential tongues.

COMMON LANGUAGES OF THE LOST LANDS

Language	Original Speakers	Used Today By
Anari	Anari	Anari
Common	Varied	Many throughout Akados
Erskin	Erskaelosi	Erskaelosi
Gasquen	Foere tribes	Foere nobility, Ramithi
Helvaenic	Heldring	Heldring
High Boros	Hyperboreans	None
Khemitian	Khemit	Khemit, traders in Libynos
Kirkut	Hundaei (varied dialects)	Rhemans, Shattered Folk, tribes of Sea of Grass, Huun
Kra	Arkaji	Arkaji (Riverfolk)
Meeruwhan	Jaata	Jaata, merchants in northern Libynos
Nørsk	Northlanders	Northlanders, others in the Northlands
Ogham	Folk of Ynys Cymragh	Daanites
Semuric	Assurian Empire	Many throughout Libynos
Xha'en	Plains of Xha tribes	Xha'en, many in western Akados

WESTERLING (COMMON)

The common language of most of Akados, Westerling (as it is known outside of Akados) or Common (as it is usually known locally) is the language spread throughout the continent by the Kingdom of Foere. It began as something of a pidgin tongue that took words and construction from the Gasquen of Foere and High Boros as well as other Akadian tribal languages, and introduced a strong influence of Helvaenic from the era of the Heldring conquests. Over time, Common became a full language, and, once it was adopted for the purposes of trade, diplomacy, and soldiering, the most effective at permitting communication by a wide variety of peoples. Today, the vast majority of people in the parts of Akados once dominated by the Foerdewaith speak Common as the regular language, and most merchants and traders on the continent (even those from Libynos) use it in the ordinary course.

GASQUEN

Gasquen was the language of the original tribe of Foere from whom Macobert descended. Unique in its linguistic etymology, its scope of use was originally limited to central Akados around the Star Sea. With the spread of the Foerdewaith empire, Gasquen was picked up in many places to identify with the new overking. But even Macobert himself realized that Gasquen was inadequate to communicate within his growing empire and set about establishing the Westerling military tongue as a vernacular to be used commonly among all his disparate peoples. Gasquen is now found only in isolated areas or noble courts that wish to strongly identify with Old Foere. In the Sundered Kingdoms, the Ramithi, who hate the Heldring influence on the Common tongue, speak Gasquen almost exclusively as a means of emphasizing their cultural identity in the face of generations of invasion of their island.

HELVAENIC

Helvaenic is the language of the Helcynngae Peninsula and is the only tongue that most Heldring use when in their homeland. Wherever populations with strong Heldring ties exist (which today includes the parts of eastern Akados they at one time conquered), Helvaenic is likely to be spoken as a household language if not in daily dealings. From a wholly different etymological family then High Boros, some of that ancient language has nevertheless found its way into Helvaenic after millennia of (often hostile) contact between the two cultures. Of any existing languages, Helvaenic is most similar to the Nørsk language spoken in the Northlands, though that language appears to be a simpler, more linguistically pure version.

HIGH BOROS

The stilted and archaic language of ancient Hyperborea and the little-known land of its origin in Boros on the World Roof provides the common roots of or contributes to almost all human languages in Akados and Libynos today, and bits and pieces have found their way into non-human languages such as Elven as well. However, despite this universal relation that the language has to so many others, it is an all-but-dead language itself, more likely to be found in old tomes and dusty archives than on the lips of living speakers. Only two locations in Akados continue to use a version of High Boros: the anachronistic city of Freegate and the Berrini living between Irkaina and the Northlands. Even in those cases, most know and use Common with visitors or while abroad.

KHEMITIAN

One of the oldest human languages in the world, Khemitian is the spoken language of the ancient kingdom of Khemit in Libynos and the second-most commonly spoken language in Libynos next to Semuric. Its written form is heavily influenced by High Boros from when the Hyperborean Empire stretched across Akados and to the far coast of Libynos as well. Its older written form, the hieroglyphic language of Ancient Kemitian (sometimes rendered as Ancient Khemitian), however, is very different and bears no relation to High Boros.

KIRKUT

Kirkut is an entire language family rather than a single language, with distinctive dialects spread across much of the world. It is derived from the Hundish language of the ancient Hundaei Empire, and so forms the basis of the current tongues of those claiming descent from those tribal clans: from the Shattered Folk of the Haunted Steppes to the Rheman Loreclans, the Ulnat of the Far North, the tribes of the Sea of Grass, and the Huun of Libynos. The long years and far distances that have separated these people, however, mean that the languages they in fact speak are now widely varying dialects that are so different that the speaker of one may be almost entirely unable to understand the language of another.

SEMURIC

Semuric originated in the Assurian Plains, considered by many scholars to be the cradle of humanity on Lloegyr. Khemitian makes claim to being the older language simply because Khemit emerged first as a single kingdom, and its language has changed less over the ensuing millennia. If Semuric has been subject to more change, it is because it has spread much farther across the continent of Libynos. Semuric is principally spoken in the lands of the Ashurians of north, central, and western Libynos and extends west most of the way across the Isthmus of Irkaina but is the true lingua franca of Libynos, and many Libynosi know it as at least a second language.

The following history, brief as it is, includes far more information than even the most respected scholar of the Lost Lands could ever know. Most educated people will be aware of the basic history of their kingdom, and maybe a close neighboring kingdom or two, going back perhaps two or three centuries. Certain legends or stories of ancient times may be common knowledge, if particularly important to the local community. Residents likely also know some history of their city, if they live in one. And almost everyone has heard stories of the ancient Hyperboreans and, where relevant, the Foerdewaith. But that is likely to be the extent of the historical knowledge of even a literate and well-read individual. That, and the creation myths and legends of their own religion.

Scholars in major cities know more, of course, but even there, most only have expertise in a specific area or topic. No one has the breadth of knowledge set forth below, and it should be parceled out accordingly.

More details about the history of specific regions, nations, and cities may be found in the applicable entries in the Gazetteer in Chapter V. Other details and specific dates are included in the timeline in Appendix I at the end of this volume.

CREATION OF THE WORLD AND THE AGE OF GODS

The beginning of the world is shrouded in myth and mystery. Many religions and cultures have their own creation stories, most of which are entirely inconsistent with each other. As of yet, scholars have not been able to piece together a single origin on which they can agree.

That being said, most scholars subscribe to the view that the world is incredibly ancient. Evidence has been found that suggests that the continents were at one point connected in one supercontinent, sometimes referred to as Hyperboros, which eventually split into the known continents of Akados, Boros, and Libynos. Given the speed at which the landmasses appear to move, some of the wise in Courghais, Reme, Bard's Gate, and Castorhage postulate an age of the world of billions of years.

Most scholars have also come to a consensus that the world's creation resulted from the actions (whether intentional or not) of one or two primordial elemental forces. Not necessarily gods in the strict sense, these fundamental powers have been given various names by those cultures that refer to them, including Erce, Boros (from whence came the name of both the northern continent and the world), Ymir, and Behemoth. Some of these forces may be native to our plane of existence, while others may have come from the upper or lower planes.

According to the oldest and darkest legends, there came a time, long after the world formed but eons ago yet, that chaotic beings of enormous power arrived on the world from beyond the stars. In many ways neither gods nor demons, they have come to be referred to as the Great Old Ones. Some of their names have also come down to us, including Hastur, the Unspeakable One; Cybele, the Great Mother, the Black Goat of the Woods; and Tsathogga, the Demon Frog God, the Devouring Maw, who is also said to be a demon lord. The Great Old Ones and their unhuman servitor races populated the world and are believed to have bred beasts for labor and food.

Eventually, the Great Old Ones warred among themselves during a period called the Primordial Wars. None now knows which one of them ended up ascendant. It is thought that Tsathogga was not victorious, but that he and his tsathar servitor race survived the Primordial Wars by retreating into desolate swamps and caverns, though they lost much of their power elsewhere in the world.

The end of the Age of Gods is traditionally marked by an event known as the Judgment of Xtu. According to the legends that speak of this time, a fiery object from the skies crashed into eastern Libynos and annihilated a portion of the eastern side of the continent and devastated the populations of the Great Old Ones' nonhuman servitor races and the great beasts inhabiting the world. Where the object struck, hundreds of thousands of square miles of land were effectively vaporized. The seas rushed into the massive crater and created the Boiling Sea, which exists today as a part of Mother Oceanus along the east coast of Central Libynos near Imya and the Jungle of Malagro.

AGE OF DRAGONS

The next age of the world is typically known as the Age of Dragons. With the Great Old Ones rendered powerless, dead, or imprisoned, elemental and primal dragons arrived on Boros, likely from the Inner Planes, and defeated the remnants of the prior nonhuman races and took the land for themselves.

Very little is known of this era. It is believed that the division between chromatic and metallic dragonkind originated during this time and led to a conflict known as the Dragon Wars. Both great lizards as well as serpent-folk were either brought to the world or bred by the great dragons as food or to fight battles for them. And toward the end of this era, giants are said to have arrived from Jotunheim to fight the dragons for dominion over the world.

There is no agreement as to why this era ended, though it appears that the dragons and giants battled among themselves until they were all driven to the corners of the world. Into the vacuum came new powers,

Elves ambush a Hyperborean patrol in the forests of southeastern Akados.

the first beings known as gods. And toward the end of this age, humans arrived on Boros. As to the origins of humans, the diversity of stories and legends are impossibly inconsistent. Some say that humans were already here, in hiding, and that the gods found them and brought them out of the darkness. Other religions claim one god or another created humans. Whatever the case, humans began to spread across the continents of the world.

Age of Man

Evidence of Neolithic human groups can be found throughout all of the continents of the Lost Lands. When and how they first arose, and whether or in what way they might have been related, is uncertain. It has been noted that one symbol, roughly looking like a cube within a cube (an object known as a tesseract), can be found in cave art and other petroglyphs in many locations separated by thousands of miles.

These early people must have come into contact with the serpent-folk and giants who had been around for, at that point, perhaps hundreds of thousands of years, evidenced by certain obscure legends that come down to us from that time.

During this period, the earliest human proto-civilizations arose. Evidence of agriculture and the beginnings of communities from this time can be found in the regions that would become Khemit, Istaflumina, and Jaati on Libynos, and in the future lands of the Xha'en in western Akados. Based on relics dating from this period, the larger communities appear to have been theocracies, with some evidence of brutal traditions and the enforcement of loyalty through blood. From their weaponry and armor and burials evincing terrible injuries, it is clear that, even in these earliest years, there was conflict among the nascent human realms. In one consistency across thousands of miles, the religious image of the tesseract is widely recognized as a symbol of life and the natural order.

Most scholars assume that the people of the northern continent of Boros, the ancestors of the Hyperboreans, had their origin during this time as well, although no evidence or records have yet been found that could confirm this hypothesis. In addition, there are legends concerning a southern continent, now lost, which was called Notos, on which civilization also arose.

Age of Strife

The first human city-states were founded during the era known as the Age of Strife, which began roughly 18,000 years ago. Cities such as Erethu, Gessh, and Ur on Libynos grew large, built surrounding walls, and conquered the neighboring countryside. Around the same time, the explorer Koshag of Ur sailed the Sinnar Ocean and established the City-State of Xantollan on Pontos Island, the earliest city on Akados. And about 15,700 years ago, colonists from the northeastern coast of Libynos (the location of the modern Jaati) found their way to the west coast of

Akados (legend says by crossing Mother Oceanus the long way), where they founded Gtsang.

During this period, the worship of many gods spread throughout the human realms, along with the understanding that the deities belonged to various groups, or pantheons. Many of the gods first to be worshipped were benign, of light and agriculture, of land, sea, and air. But not all. Some stories suggest the malign influence of older, non-human races in the introduction of the worship of various evil deities. However it occurred, certain human realms adopted the ways of beneficent deities, while others devoted themselves to gods of darkness. Soon, strife between these city-states and kingdoms of Libynos erupted into war.

The legends of the elves and dwarves indicate that those races first arrived on Boros over the course of this age. Some 17,000 years ago, the elven god Wayland the Smith unlocked the secret to passing between the elven homeland of Alfheim and the world of Boros, and some among the elves, or Alfar, crossed through. For many years, the way was kept a closely guarded secret; the earliest visitors were limited to the noblest of the elves, whose descendants are said to be the grey elves of the Emerald Mountains of Akados. Over time, some other Alfar passed between the worlds, but only in small numbers, and settled in remote locations, and for reasons yet to be determined.

Some two millennia after Wayland first discovered the secret of the planar gates, the dwarves of Niðavellir (which, depending on who you ask, is either a region of Alfheim, or is closely connected to it) came into conflict with the elves of a realm called Svartalfheim, who in time became the drow, or dark elves. During the course of this war, the dwarves discovered the secrets of the gates of Wayland the Smith and proceeded to construct gates of their own. Unlike the Alfar gates made by Wayland that broached wild areas of Boros little populated by sentient folk, and through which only small numbers of Alfar were permitted to pass, the dwarves opened multiple gates into the deep places of Boros, and in no time the conflict between the dwarves and dark elves spilled through unchecked.

The world they found was one already at war, scarred by the clash of great powers. The strife between the followers of the gods of good and the gods of evil had spread to the Outer Planes, into a conflict known as the Gods' War. The drow soon joined with the evil gods in the Gods' War, while the dwarves and Alfar allied with the deities of good. Eventually, at great cost, the last general of the forces of darkness was overthrown, and the god Thyr ended the Gods' War, and with it the Age of Strife.

Oddly, the dwarves of Ankhura, in the Tsendakar Mountains of northwestern Akados, are said to have already been in their mountain fastnesses when Gtsang was founded. If that is true, the dwarves of this realm would have arrived independently of, and substantially earlier than, their fellows who used the dwarven gates created at the time of the Gods' War. The dwarves of Ankhura do not provide any insight as to when or how they may have come to their homes in the Tsendakars, simply maintaining that they always lived in those mountains.

AGE OF KINGS

Though elves and dwarves now lived on Boros, the Age of Kings was in many ways the first great age of humanity. This period, starting around 12,000 years ago, saw the rise of the Phoromyceaen civilization. Not a single empire, the Phoromyceaens spread from an unknown point of origin to found independent city-states across much of the world, all of which, for some as yet undiscovered reason, were built underground. Though a solidly Bronze Age culture (and outside their cities, essentially Neolithic), they were magically advanced, with sorcerer-kings or priest-kings ruling most of their cities. Some of those ancient rulers are said to have survived the fall of their civilization and become lichs, enduring to this day in the hidden depths of the world.

Among the cities founded by the Phoromyceaens were Barakus, beneath the Duskmoon Hills of the Sinnar Coast of Akados, which was abandoned in –6627 I.R.; Lyemmos, on the island of the Crescent Sea now known as Insula Lymossus, which was swallowed by a massive sinkhole in –6484 I.R.; Nestril, the ruins of which are said to be hidden under the eaves of the Forest of Parna, also in eastern Akados; and Tharistra, on the plains west of the Gulf of Akados, possibly in the vicinity of Stoneheart Valley.

In addition, it is believed that during these years a great empire arose on the legendary continent of Notos in the seas south of Akados. Nothing but myths and tales survive of this power, if indeed it ever existed. Before the end of this age, the myths say that Notos was destroyed in a cataclysm and sank beneath the seas, leaving only a scattering of islands above the waves that today are known as the Islands of Arkanos.

In this age, a mighty god walked among the people of Akados. He was Arvonliet, an angelic being of almost painful splendor known as the Prince of Beauty and also as the Bringer of Light for his radiant presence. He brought great achievement, artifice, and indulgence to his followers, and if he also introduced jealousy, spiteful competition, and vice, for long years no one was the wiser. For Arvonliet was not only the self-proclaimed Prince of Beauty but also the Prince of Hate. It is said that Arvonliet either destroyed or corrupted all the Phoromyceaen cities and brought an end to that civilization throughout the world.

To ensure his dominion over the lands of Boros, Arvonliet began construction of a permanent gate to his home plane of the Abyss. At last, the gods of good realized the peril the world was in. Together, the three sibling gods Thyr, Muir, and Kel overthrew Arvonliet, driving him from Boros and casting him into the outer plane Ginnungagap. To ensure he would not return, the gods created a mystical ward known as the Keltine Barrier, over which they raised a mighty range of peaks, the Stoneheart Mountains. Ever after, Arvonliet would no longer be either beautiful or light, and became known as Orcus.

Whether a coincidence or otherwise, at almost the same time as the defeat of Arvonliet, some event in the realm of Alfheim led to a large migration of elves from their homeland to Boros. Known as the First Exodus of the Elves, the cause for the sudden influx of population is unknown, except perhaps to the grey elves of the Emerald Mountains, who do not speak of such things. The vast majority of the arrivals fled to the southern reaches of Akados, into deep forests that extended almost from the western edge of the continent to the shores of the Sinnar Ocean in the east. There they founded new elven realms far from the humans of Akados.

Thus ended the Age of Kings in –6484 I.R.

AGE OF SILENCE

With the Phoromyceaen city-states in ruin, a new dark age settled on Akados. The embryonic Xha'en folk of western Akados and the people of Gtsang, in their mountain fastness, survived relatively unscathed. Similarly, the nascent Libynosi societies that were to become Khemit, Istaflumina, and Jaati were largely unaffected by the events so far from their homes. But for the rest of Akados, the people effectively returned to a Neolithic existence, living in scattered tribes and eking out a meager existence.

Evidence for one proto-culture of this dark age, known as the Andøvan or Ancient Ones, can be found in eastern Akados and the Northlands. They were a mixture of hunters, growers, and breeders of horses, and their magic was in the strength of the natural world and its creatures. They were clad in hides and wielded weapons of wood and stone, though it is said some knew the secret of making bronze. Shamans called upon the spirits of the land and the middle air. They communed with many different types of spirits, and some of them were what would now be called demons, such as Pazuzu, King of the Demons of the Wind. The legend of Aracor of Fair Island (now called Ramthion Island), and the arrival of the Obelisks of Chaos on the Plains of Sull, come to us from this time (see *Cults of the Sundered Kingdoms*). The Ancient Ones also populated much of the Northlands, where they flourished for a time but eventually fell before an onslaught of giants, trolls, and troll-kin. They vanished by the time the ancestors of today's Northmen arrived, leaving behind only barrow mounds, earthen hill forts, and enigmatic rings of standing stones upon the heights. Those ancients are still held in a mixture of awe and fear by modern Northlanders, their barrow fields still haunted by the specters of their civilization that walk the night-darkened hills and forests (see *The Northlands Saga Complete*).

As the years of the Age of Silence passed, the human realms on Akados and Libynos gradually became more complex and urbanized.

In Istaflumina in northern Libynos, the cities of Gessh in the Kingdom of Hakhad, and Erethu, Irrech, and Ur in the Kingdom of Zumaru became centers of civilization during this time, with their king-priests commanding the loyalty of tens of thousands. In –1518 I.R., the Lower Kingdom and Middle Kingdom of Khemit merged to become the Conjoined Double Kingdom, beginning the First Dynasty under the Pharaoh Narmar.

On Akados, the city-state of Xha'ahan (a derivative of the word Xha'en, the name the folk of the region have given to themselves for thousands of years) was founded soon after the final defeat of the Senge in –1302 I.R., designated as Year 0 in the official Xha'en calendar (XC). And in –722 I.R., the first Yaltic Dynasty of Hawkmoon on eastern Akados was founded.

In the late seventh century prior to the Imperial Record, however, a shadowy group called the Cult of Aurikas arose in southern Libynos. Akruel Rathamon, the high priest of this cult, consolidated political power and brought various tribal folk under Aurikas' banner. By –613 I.R., the cult and its disciples were committing unnamable atrocities in the god's name in the lands along the Reaping Sea. It was soon discovered that Aurikas was, in fact, the ancient demon-god Orcus, seeking vengeance for his prior defeat. And again, the gods responded. Shah Rasalt, a Khemitian priest of Arden, raised an army in the name of his god to bring war to the burgeoning empire of Akruel Rathamon. Over 25 years, the forces contested in what became known as the War of Divine Discord. At last, in –579 I.R., Shah Rasalt used the *scepter of faiths* to defeat (but unfortunately not destroy) the vampire death-priest Akruel Rathamon as he marched across Libynos along the coast of the Reaping Sea. Shah Rasalt and his army then turned and marched hundreds of miles into the Seething Jungle to destroy the death-priest's remaining forces at the jungle temple of Al-Sifon. With the task complete (or so he thought), Shah Rasalt returned to his desert temple to die an old man.

But the forces of evil were not done with Boros yet. In –182 I.R., the frog demon Tsathogga unleashed a horde of demons in Irkaina in far northeastern Akados. The god Arden again intervened, this time sacrificing himself to entrap the horde and stop the invasion. In the cataclysm of the god's sacrifice, the very fabric of the world was rent, and the odd atmospheric effect of the Tropic of Arden was created, permanently changing the climate of lands ranging from the far south of Akados to the northern extent of Libynos and beyond.

As these events were unfolding, a new civilization appeared on the continent of Boros, also called the World Roof, far to the north. In those days, prior to the polar shift, much of that continent was not ice-covered, and in fact was reasonably temperate. There, the Borean Empire, the first Empire of Hyperborea, arose, adopting and consolidating a new pantheon of gods that would soon sweep much of the world. For in –109 I.R. they sent an army to Akados and changed history forever.

THE HYPERBOREAN AGE

The remainder of the history of the Lost Lands set forth below is principally a high-level summary of the events relating to the Hyperborean Empire and its successors. We focus on Hyperborea because of the profound impact that empire had on nearly the entire continent of Akados, as well as much of Libynos, over thousands of years. Details of the history of other regions, and specific areas within the empire, can be found in the related entries in Chapter V. In addition, other details and dates may be found in the timeline contained in Appendix I at the end of this volume.

THE MARCH OF OERSON (–109 I.R. TO –91 I.R.)

The recorded history of the Lost Lands begins in –109 I.R., more than 3,600 years ago, when a phalanx of ancient Hyperborea led by the Polemarch Oerson descended from the continent of Boros through what are now the Northlands and into the fertile heart of Akados.

At that time, the Hundaei roamed across the Great Steppes in their numberless hordes, and the majority of southern Akados was covered in a great primeval forest claimed by kingdoms of wild elves who fiercely guarded their boundaries, confining the Neolithic human clans to scattered enclaves across the continent. The legion led by Oerson marched along the eastern slopes of the Stoneheart Mountains and began making inroads into the great forest. The elves were unprepared for a concentrated assault by a professional army, and it was almost a year before they were able to gather in sufficient numbers to drive the tree-cutting Hyperboreans out of their woodland home. In the meantime, elven settlements had been raided and burned, leaving many elves dead. With the aid of the new reinforcements, the elves pushed Oerson's legion back to the edges of the forest and set an armed vigil along this expansive front.

Reluctant to dare the ambushes and traps of the wild elves again, but not content to admit defeat, Polemarch Oerson spent 10 years expanding his conquests along the edge of the Great Akadonian Forest, initiating skirmishes with elven watchers and conquering the scattered human tribes that he ran across. These tribal warriors — no matter how fierce — were no match for the discipline and effectiveness of the Hyperborean phalanx and its heavily armored pikemen. Stone and copper weapons broke against bronze breastplates and hoplon shields, and bronze-headed sarissa pikes and javelins easily tore through hide armor and furs. Those tribes that Oerson did not destroy were assimilated into his legion, their ferocity harnessed and redirected. After organizing these woods-wise warriors and teaching them to work together, Oerson released them beneath the boughs of the forest eaves to hunt their hated elven adversaries.

The elves had long fought off incursions by the human tribes and were adept at ambushing them and picking apart their war-bands through traps and sniping. Those tactics still took a heavy toll on the human tribal warriors, but now the invaders attacked in great numbers, organized and guided to support each other and envelop the elven defenders. Even as thousands of humans fell victim to the long arrows of the elves, so too did many elves fall, quickly depleting their normal reserves of guardians. And while this occurred, Polemarch Oerson continued his circumnavigation of the forest and the absorption of human tribes, swelling the ranks of his army with auxiliary levies.

In the face of this unprecedented threat upon their realm, the elven high lords called for aid from throughout the elven nations of Akados. The guardians of the forest eaves were augmented by the archers and soldiers of the forest's deep interior kingdoms — even from so far as the fabled elven cities of Elenis Tuath and Solis Alunaris — and a great elven host gathered in numbers never before seen in Akados. But even the stealth of the elves could not keep this host a secret, and Oerson's legion caught wind of its approach. Thus began the Perilous March, a year-long retreat by the legion northward, retracing the route it had taken along the forest's edge, all the while being harassed and pursued by the elven host. Though far enough from the forest's edge that the elves could not risk leaving the protection of the sheltering trees to make a full assault, the Hyperboreans were subjected to what seemed a never-ending series of surprise attacks and ambushes that continually whittled away at their forces and took an increasing toll on their morale.

Eventually, the elven host forced the legion into a lightly wooded vale upon the northern slopes of the Stoneheart Valley near Lake Crimmormere. Exhausted and low on supplies, the Hyperboreans found themselves trapped in the valley and took up a defensive position in their tortoise-like chelone formations with shields above and before. The elves, sensing a final victory against the despised humans, advanced into the valley against the outnumbered defenders.

But as the elven spearmen and archers advanced, they discovered that Oerson had not been idle the last 10 years: He had struck an alliance with the mountain dwarves of the Stoneheart clans. Dwarves now emerged from hidden caves along the valley's upper slopes to send landslides of carefully prepared boulders and scree down into the elves' flanks. Hidden pits opened beneath the rear ranks of the elves to swallow many of their archers and most of their small cavalry force. From these holes streamed columns of doughty dwarven warriors. Then as the elves found themselves crippled on their flanks and enveloped from behind, the heavy phalanx of the legion advanced from its defensive posture.

The slaughter was terrifying, and legend holds that seven generations of the flower of elven civilization was destroyed that day, leaving only the very old and the very young alive within the forest. When darkness finally came that evening and the few surviving elven warriors were able to escape back into the trees, there was no doubt that Polemarch Oerson had made the Hyperboreans conquerors and the new masters of Akados.

The Rise of Hyperborea (–90 I.R. to –1 I.R.)

The polemarch pressed his advantage and pushed into the interior of the forest along with his dwarven allies, the surviving elven tribes retreating before him. His great sweep went uncontested and managed to reach all the way to the neck of the Helcynngae Peninsula. Here his advance was checked by the barbarian tribes that had heard of his approach and amassed their own war-bands to face the invaders. The mountain dwarves marching with Oerson were of little help, as they were more interested in plundering abandoned elven enclaves than facing a new host of human adversaries. Leaving a defensive screen of rival tribesmen across the neck of the peninsula, Oerson turned his legion back and instead pressed through the southern foothills of the Stoneheart Mountains until he reached the coast of the Crescent Sea. Once there, he sent half of his legion back to retrace the route he had marched over the last two decades to bring reinforcements from Hyperborea while the other half remained with him to build the new Hyperborean city of Remenos.

With news of the success of Oerson's legion reaching the land of Boros, additional legions began moving south to reinforce the garrisons left along the way by Oerson and further expand the acquisitions of the conquering Hyperboreans. The savage tribes of the Heldring on the Helcynngae Peninsula remained unbeaten, and a string of forts was eventually built across its neck, connected by a wall called the Helwall. A series of roads were cut through the vast forest of Akados, and settlements and forts were built all along its length to prevent any further incursions by vengeful elven tribes. The mountain dwarves, having sated their lust for elven treasure and mayhem, returned to their own mountain fastnesses and maintained a distant diplomacy with the new human settlements. By the time of Oerson's death at the ripe age of 131, as many as a half million Hyperborean immigrants had settled in Akados, and a fragile peace had descended across their holdings.

In –17 I.R., during the time of Oerson's grandchildren, Oesson and Oeric, the monarchs of distant Boros doubled their demand for tribute from the Hyperborean colonies in Akados and sent episcopi — inspectors general with authority to rule alongside the colonial governors to ensure a full tallying of tribute owed — to the hundreds of Hyperborean garrisons and settlements. By then, the Hyperborean immigrants and their assimilated tribes constituted a population of millions and had built their own burgeoning war machine of 20 legions, each with as many as 30,000 men. For a time, the colonies grudgingly acquiesced to the new demands, but each year the demands grew greater. After six years of rising tributes and imperious tax collectors, the colonies erupted in a popular uprising. The polemarchs of the legions and military governors of the many garrisons and towns appointed Oesson and Oeric as co-regents. The episcopi were lynched in the streets and their heads sent as tribute back to Boros instead. Oesson and Oeric moved from the prosperous port of Remenos to the more central settlement of Curgantium and there raised the Tower of Oerson, a citadel to serve as the heart of their new Hyperborean kingdom and a bastion of defense for the realm.

War was now inevitable. Though it took over a decade, Boros raised 27 legions and marched them south to bring the colonies back into submission. On the plains east of the Stoneheart Mountains in the area called Hummaemidon, the Boros legions were met by the Hyperborean legions led by Polemarch Asenna. With his mountain dwarf allies, Asenna managed to trap half of the Boros legion against the flank of the mountains and cut the other half off from reinforcing them. But Crassin and Odontius, Boros' polemarchs, had their own surprise ready for Asenna. They had sailed a fleet of triremes around the Irkainian Peninsula far to the east through the treacherous Mulstabhin Passage and then west across the northern Sinnar Ocean to the Gulf of Akados. With this fleet, Telamon, Boros' navarch, brought the legions of Odontius and landed them behind the Hyperboreans' positions to catch Asenna's legions between the two armies.

Seeing the new legions approaching from the rear, the dwarven army turned from the field and formed a wedge and attempted to retreat to the foothills south of their position where hidden cave entrances would allow them to withdraw back into their cavern realms. The legions of Odontius proved too many, however, and the dwarves found themselves surrounded. Asenna, meanwhile, abandoned by his dwarven allies and pressed from both ahead and behind by the enveloping legions of the two polemarchs, created his own defensive position and led his men in their death paean to Mithras.

However, the battle did not end as anticipated, for suddenly the exposed flank of Odontius' phalanx came under a withering hail of arrows fired from the rolling hills to their south. As the Borean legionnaires turned to lock shields against this new threat, the dwarven wedge they had pinned down renewed the fury of its assault and sought to break through and escape to the hills. Seeing the developments to the south, Asenna split his own legions, leaving half to hold those of Crassin in place and the other half to exploit the weakness caused by the dwarves as they managed to divide the now-disorganized legions of Odontius. Crassin watched helplessly as the legions of Odontius, now assaulted by arrows from the hills, the dwarven wedge, and half of Assena's legions, were cut to pieces. He was unable to reinforce Odontius, but the split of Asenna's forces allowed his own legions to make an orderly withdrawal back north. Of the 27 legions that marched forth from Boros, only eight escaped to the north.

Asenna himself was killed in the battle, but his strategos survived to see the source of their salvation: A horde of elven archers descended from the hills as the last of Odontius' legionnaires fell. Now the elves turned their bows and spears upon the approaching dwarves who howled their battle cries in return and charged into the fray. However, the mountain folk were already badly depleted by the battle with the Boreans, and the elves were still fresh, having spent only arrows in the fight and not yet blood. The three strategos that commanded the southern half of the Hyperborean legions then made a fateful decision. In what it known as the Great Betrayal among the dwarven clans of the Stoneheart Mountains and the Reconciliation by the elves of eastern Akados, the Hyperborean phalanx charged into the rear flank of the retreating dwarves. The carnage was awful and casualties high as the stubborn dwarves fought on to the very last. But in the end, the exhausted human phalangites looked warily across the piled bloody carcasses of the dwarves at the equally exhausted elven spearmen and were astonished by what they saw: Many among the elven warriors were taller and less fair than their elven brethren. Nearly half of the elven force was composed of half-elves.

Truce was called, and the Hyperborean strategos met with the elven and half-elven high lords that commanded the elven force. They learned that while the battles of three generations earlier had seriously depleted the population of the slow-to-reproduce elves, atrocities committed by the Hyperborean and tribal raiders had resulted in an entire generation of half-elf bastards, and in numbers much greater than the usual elven birth rate. These half-elven children were a shock to the insular wild elves. In many of the surviving communities, they were known as the "war-dead" and were considered abominations to be abandoned to die of exposure. But in many of the diminished communities, the numbers of the half-elves and their quick maturation was the only means of survival through the following decades. Finally, a schism had broken out between the wild elf high lords who condemned the new race of half-breeds and the high lords whose communities benefited from their presence and held no grudge against them for the circumstances of their birth.

Around −27 I.R., a charismatic half-elf by the name of Valenthlis came of age and began demanding the rights and dignity of the half-elves be honored. Anger against 60 years of oppression broke out and resulted in violence among the shadows of the deep forest. Queen Vaissilune herself was slain and buried in a cavern deep beneath the eastern Akadonian Coast.

Unwilling to see even more elves slaughtered at the hands of their kin, those who opposed Valenthlis withdrew to the far west to the realms of Elenis Tuath and Solis Alunaris beyond the Crescent Sea. This became known as the Second Exodus of the Elves, and those who went west named themselves the wild elves, as they refused to accept accommodation with those of part-human birth. Those who allied with Valenthlis now took a new name for themselves — the high elves — as they believed their willingness to join with their fellows was the moral path.

In the 90 years since the massacre at Lake Crimmormere, the Hyperboreans and the high elves of eastern Akados had stayed far away from the domains of the other. When word of the march of the Boros legions had made its way into the forest's interior reaches, the lords of the high elves gathered. Some argued that they should remain within the protective eaves of the forest and take no sides in the coming conflict. Others, with Valenthlis most prominent, feared that the newcomers would, in their numbers, seek to further encroach on the forests to seek out new lands. They believed that intervening on behalf of the Hyperboreans would be to their benefit and might help forge an alliance with the humans. While siding with their former enemies was anathema to some, others noted that more than four human generations had passed, and the actual perpetrators of atrocities against the elves were now long dead.

In the end, the lords of the high elves of eastern Akados resolved to come to the assistance of the nascent Hyperborean realm. When they saw the retreat of the Stoneheart dwarves who had ambushed their kin at Lake Crimmormere, long-pent-up fury erupted, and the elves rushed to the attack. The pragmatic decision of the Hyperborean strategos to betray their erstwhile dwarven allies and side with the elves cemented a lasting peace between the Hyperboreans and the high elves of eastern Akados. It also created a simmering grudge between the humans and the Stoneheart dwarves that lasted for thousands of years.

The final, oft-overlooked, result of the Battle of Hummaemidon was that the trireme fleet anchored on the nearby coast did not receive word of the disaster of the Boros legions and remained unconcerned, assuming victory to have been assured. Instead, they were caught off guard as elves and tribal warriors suddenly streamed aboard their anchored vessels in the night and captured more than 150 ships. Thus was born the great Hyperborean navy, which until that time had been greatly underdeveloped with only a few local curraghs and merchant galleys to its name. Now the waters along the eastern and southern coasts of Akados could be tamed, and the Mouth of Akados come under the full control of the Hyperboreans. The port of Remenos rose to great prominence and prosperity, and the great sea citadel of Castorhage was constructed on Insula Lymossus to control the Crescent Sea.

FORMATION OF EMPIRE (1 I.R. TO 12 I.R.)

With the great victory at Hummaemidon and the capture of the Boros fleet, the kingdom of the Hyperboreans began a new wave of expansion. The legions were still largely intact after the battle and found themselves swelling in number with the addition of thousands of half-elf volunteers who wished to make their fortunes in the armies of their fathers. Oesson remained on the throne in the city of Curgantium, while Oeric led these legions afield in the expansion of the nascent empire.

The Hyperborean legions first turned east to the Isthmus of Irkaina, where they faced the Irkainian tribes, which, though fierce, were no match for the disciplined legions augmented by elven archers and tribal cavalry. Crossing the Mulstabhin Passage, they entered Libynos proper and marched through the Ashurian desert, then south to the cities in the plains and hill country between the northern shore of the Sea of Baal and the Scythirian Mountains to the north. One city after another around the eastern shores of the Sea of Baal fell to the legions until they reached the Triple-Kingdom of Khemit. Even that nation, ancient and powerful, fell before Oeric's armies, their soldiers assimilated into the forces of the empire.

Shortly after the conquest of Khemit, Oeric received a vision that he claimed came from the goddess Muir. He saw a pristine tableland vale encircled by a ring of mountains. He was told that he must build a city on this Sacred Table that would become the greatest in the world and that would serve as a bastion of the goddess's virtuous faith. Oeric marched north through Numeda and the throne-lands of Ift and Baal to the eaves of the Scythirian Mountains where he found a pass east through the peaks. Leading his legion on, he came at last to the table of his vision. In this place, Oeric founded the city of Tircople. He abdicated his right to the throne of Hyperborea and took on the humble robes of a penitent, becoming known as the Pontifex of the Three and establishing a monastery to Muir in the newly built city of Tircople.

While Oeric conquered the lands of northern and middle Libynos, the triremes of the Hyperborean navy explored the southern reaches of the continent and established colonies at the mouths of major rivers. Inland, the deep forests and jungles proved an insurmountable barrier for the thinly stretched empire, so at the rivers' mouths they stayed, using local tribes to bring back treasures from the interior.

With the abdication of his brother, Oesson took the golden regent circlet sent back to Curgantium by Oeric and had it and his own melted together and reforged into a royal crown. He then took up sole residence in the Tower of Oerson and had himself crowned as imperator of the Hyperborean Empire. This momentous and unifying action was taken not a moment too soon, for shortly thereafter came attacks by bands of vicious horsemen issuing from passes through the Stoneheart Mountains. The Hundaei hordes had arrived.

INVASION OF THE HUNDAEI (13 I.R. TO 686 I.R.)

Riders of the Great Steppes, the Hundaei noticed the arrival of the Hyperborean legions a century earlier but paid scant attention to them, occupied as they were with their own internal clan warfare. However, a Great Khan had arisen as first among the many khans of the Hundaei, and for the first time the entire population of the Hundaei horse warriors gathered into one great Invincible Horde. With the aid of the mountain dwarves seeking revenge on the Hyperboreans, the horse warriors took secret paths through the Stoneheart Mountains and found themselves within the fat and poorly defended heartland of the new Hyperborean Empire.

Though the Hyperborean legions were battle tested and peerless in warfare, the Hundaei came at their settlements from a direction that was thought to be safely sealed by the ramparts of the Stoneheart Mountains while most of the legions were deployed halfway across two continents from Occibolos to Tircople. The Hundaei quickly stormed through the towns they encountered, burning them out and putting their inhabitants to the sword. They even successfully besieged several walled cities and left them in ruins. Their incursion made it as far as the regional capital at Apothasalos, where the horse-riders were finally stopped by two legions led by the polemarch Gnassus. When additional legions approached, the Hundaei were forced to withdraw, eventually back to the mountain passes, where the Hyperboreans could not pursue without entering the territory of their dwarven enemies.

Great Khan Jaganga had successfully raided deep into Hyperborea and taken much plunder, but he had made no gains of territory. Over the next five centuries, Hundaei hordes would make lightning raids deep into Hyperborea to burn and plunder, while the Hyperborean legions would in turn seek out safe passes over the mountains to create temporary beachheads on the Great Steppes beyond. The horse warriors could never defeat the legions in a stand-up fight, and the legions could never force the Hundaei riders to engage in such a fight. Neither side made great gains against the other, and both suffered terrible losses at the others' hands. But no upper hand could ever be gained, and the war stretched on seemingly without end.

Despite the threat of the Hundaei to the west, Hyperborea flourished. The line of imperators descended from Oesson were intermittently wise or warlike or foolish, but the prosperity and military might of the empire was such that even the poor rulers did not cause any precipitous declines. The great woodlands of eastern Akados were slowly deforested, giving way to rich pasture and farmlands to feed the burgeoning empire, and tribute poured in from its far-flung corners. The folk of the Ashurian desert, and the coastal lands, the throne-lands of Ift and Baal, Numeda, and Khemit were absorbed into the empire, while colonies along the coast of southern Libynos thrived, though the tribes of the deserts and jungles continued to make war among themselves, sometimes requiring the empire to intervene. Sea trade flourished as well, bringing goods and travelers from all over the empire. Remenos became the greatest port city of the empire, and all overland trade in the heart of the empire passed through Curgantium.

The empire did find a western bound, however, just beyond Remenos. Northward were the Hundaei, and to the west were the wild elves of the Green Realm. With so much other land to conquer, the cost of exploration farther west seemed to far outweigh any benefits, so few if any gave those regions further thought. As a result, the western shores of Akados and the city-states of Xha'ahan, Jhohir, and Rojhah, as well as Gtsang, remained beyond the ken of the Hyperboreans.

One beneficiary of the growing sea trade was the island of Insula Extremis across a narrow strait at the far end of the Helcynngae Peninsula. Its denizens were not related to the warlike Heldring of the peninsula, who were largely contained there by the Helwall. When the triremes of the Hyperboreans came to their island, the folk of Insula Extremis accepted the offer to join the empire and embraced the new civilization, in time forsaking the old ways of the Ancient Ones from whom they were descended.

By the time six centuries had passed, the Hyperboreans had gained the upper hand in their conflict with the Hundaei. They had made peace with tribes of Irkainian hill dwarves and from them learned the secrets of ironworking and steel. With these improvements in weaponry, they were able to push back the less-numerous mountain dwarves until they took refuge in their deep halls under the mountains and rarely, if ever, emerged. With control of the mountain passes, the Hyperboreans were able to put multiple legions into the Great Steppes. Armed with steel pikes and swords and improved iron scutum shields and cuirasses, those legions took a terrible toll on any Hundaei that they were able to bring to battle.

The pressure of the Hyperborean legions during the reign of Great Khan Ogedane eventually forced some clans of the Hundaei to expand into the northwestern corner of the Great Steppes at the foot of the Nam-i-Budhani, the Lost Mountains — territory long taboo to the horse clans of the Hundaei — and to settle in and around the shores of dark Lake Hali. These clans were ostracized by their fellows for daring to settle along the forbidden shores. What transpired with these clans is unknown, but within a year, clan war erupted among the Hundaei of the northwestern steppes and eventually expanded to consume the entire nation.

The civil war grew so vicious that by the time word reached the Hyperborean frontier on the far side of the Great Steppes, more than half the population of the Hundaei had already been slain. Within two years of the war's start, the Hundaei had ceased to exist as an organized people. Hyperborean scouts found the Great Steppes in places to be littered with the skulls of the once-great nation, now reduced to a few roving bands that fled from all contact.

Pax Hyperborea (687 I.R. to 2490 I.R.)

With the Hundaei threat finally eradicated, nothing stood in the way of the empire and its continued growth and prosperity. To commemorate this time of Hyperborean transcendence, a new city was established in the Piedmont Highlands to serve as a crown jewel in the midst of the long Boros Road where the Hundaei no longer threatened. The city was called Tsen and was built upon ground sacred to the ancient faith of Arden. It grew in knowledge, wealth, and sophistication to become known as the City of Wonders and rival even the imperial capital at Curgantium.

With the Hundaei horde shattered and dispersed, humanoid tribes of orcs, gnolls, goblinoids, and even giants increased in number and power on the Great Steppes. Unable to cross the Stoneheart Mountain passes (where the mountain dwarves barred the way), the humanoid tribes looked south to the Crynnomar Gap and soon were making war against the wild elves in the forests south of the gap and north of the lands of Remenos.

The wild elves of the Green Realm held this forested land as a bulwark against the hated humans, from which they would launch raid into the lands of Remenos from time to time to ensure their borders were respected. They resisted the arrival of the humanoid bands, fearing that they would turn west and attempt to raid farther into elven lands. A call went out to all the elves of the Green Realm, even as far as Solis Alunaris, for warriors to gather and defend the gap between the Stoneheart Mountains and the Deepfells. Barely recovered from their costly wars against the humans in past generations, the tribes and kingdoms of wild elves sent their warriors and, in their pride, refused to call upon their high elf kin to the east for assistance. The Crynnomar Gap was to be their line of defense.

The watchful Hyperboreans of Remenos noticed when the marauding elves of their northern marches began to disappear. Tentative expeditions were sent forth to scout out the land, and all returned with tales of abandoned settlements and signs of a hasty withdrawal. The military governor (or harmost) of Remenos saw an opportunity to log the pristine woodlands in that region and expand the domain under his control. By the time the elven war-bands returned south from the Crynnomar Gap after 13 years of exhausting battle in which the humanoids were finally driven back into the steppes, they found that the Remenos frontier had expanded deep into their forests, and an entire legion was firmly entrenched in the heart of their old lands south of the gap. Lacking the will to fight anew, they withdrew westward around the northern shore of the Crescent Sea, deeper into the woods of the Green Realm, where erected a new line of defense. Monoliths imbued with ancient magics, now known as the Green Warders, were set from the Impossible Peaks to the north all the way south to the Hellgate Peaks to bar the passage of any humans across this new frontier. The Green Realm was forever closed to the presence of humans.

After 800 years of glory, the might of Tsen ended in a single night. For several decades, the folk of Tsen had been fighting a war of attrition with tribes of humanoids and inhuman marauders that seemed to spring from the ground of the surrounding hills and nearby plains. Finally, Tsen mobilized its army and marched forth to draw the marauders into open battle where they could be decisively defeated. On that fateful morning, some survivors outside the city reported seeing a white feathered serpent rising from the gulf far to the south and flying through the sky toward Tsen. Whatever the meaning of that portent, the city ceased to exist in a single act of cataclysmic devastation the likes of which had never been seen before upon the face of the world. Hyperborea's crown jewel was no more and has remained an uninhabitable wasteland ever after.

Whether connected to the fall of Tsen or mere coincidence, over the next three years a dense, dark haze settled over the Gulf of Akados in the northern Sinnar Ocean. During these years, which came to be known as the Great Darkness, the sun's light was diffuse and weak during the day, and at night the stars were entirely invisible, only a faint lightening of the sky revealing the location of Narrah, the great moon. Crops failed and, without stars visible to guide ships, shipping routes to the ports of the gulf as far south as Freeport were abandoned. Tens of thousands perished from starvation, and refugees fled to regions far from the gulf, where the light of the sun and stars still shone. After three years, however, the haze finally dissipated, and slowly people returned to the lands about the gulf, and shipping lanes reopened.

Not long after the fall of Tsen, a new kingdom arose on the Feirgotha Plateau of the Stoneheart Mountains. The Khemitite wizard Aka Bakar, who had been apprenticed to the archmage Alycthron the Dragon Lord, founded this kingdom after fleeing the court of the prince of Pharos and somehow absconding with a third of that city-state's legion. With his own magics and the force of his loyal Khemitite soldiers, Aka Bakar carved the Kingdom of Arcady in the midst of the dwarven clanholds of the Stonehearts and held it for nearly a century against dwarven assaults. Yet Arcady did fall, in a short war of slaughter and desolation, but only as a result of a massive surprise invasion by the combined hobgoblin armies of the Deepfells to the west and the Stonehearts and the apparent sudden madness of Aka Bakar himself. The archmages Alycthron and Margon ended the devastation and defeated Aka Bakar, after which they disappeared into the heart of Libynos on some mysterious errand and were not seen again for centuries.

THE FALL OF THE EMPIRE (2491 I.R. TO 2515 I.R.)

As the Hyperborean Empire approached its 25th century, signs of decline were becoming readily apparent. An apathy had settled over its capital and provinces, and corruption was rampant in government. Fewer lands seemed open for conquest and plunder. The legions were reduced in number from 46 at the empire's height to 12 as funds to finance these juggernauts of men and materiel became harder to find.

Then in 2491 I.R., something of unknown origin but enormous power occurred, and the world wobbled on its axis. Both lands and seas were stricken by a season of unearthly storms and tidal waves. Far out in the oceans, east of Libynos and west of Akados, great lines of impenetrable, eternal storms arose, now known as the Tempest Meridians. What might be beyond the storms none could say, though diviners named something in the midst of the storms the Goitre. Whatever may be the case, no longer could one sail the long way around the world.

Over a period of three weeks known as the Troubled Span, the poles of the world shifted. The north pole, which had previously been in the Great Ocean Ûthaf beyond the Lost Mountains at the edge of the Great Steppes, moved to a point directly upon the continent of Boros. This brought about a sudden and radical change of climate, and a thick sheet of ice began to form over that land, which proceeded to creep down into what was now the Far North.

As the weather shifted and ice began to cover the roof of the world, the auguries in the Tower of Oerson were poor. When the high wizards and priests of the empire gathered to reverse the drastic change to the climate of their world, the results were cataclysmic. They spent five years researching and preparing a ritual to return the world to its proper alignment so that the stars would once again follow their old paths across the sky. When all was in readiness, Imperator Obraskius oversaw the inauguration of the monthlong ritual himself. But some powers, perhaps, are simply too great to be harnessed by mortal man, and the attempt by the haughty Hyperboreans was just such an instance. At the climactic moment of the ritual, when the world was to set itself aright upon its celestial foundation once more, the pent-up magic was released in an uncontrollable wave of destruction. The Tower of Oerson was thrown down, and fires consumed Curgantium. The flames spread to the plains around the city, and soon raging wildfires marched across the heartland of the empire, burning all in their path. The fires raged across the plains and forests of eastern Akados for three years. By the time they had at last burned themselves out, a quarter of the empire's population died due to either the immediate destruction or the resulting famine that followed in the next few years.

Rather than try to survive in the midst of such desolation, the surviving Hyperborean elite chose to relocate east and make their new capital at Tircople. They left behind their many subject tribes to fend for themselves in the wasted lands and removed their garrisons that had for so long kept the peace in Akados.

THE LEGION OF KING DAAN (2516 I.R. TO 2584 I.R.)

The first of the tribes to arise in the wake of the Hyperborean withdrawal was the Heldring of the Helcynngae Peninsula. They surged across the Helwall and began their own age of conquest, though the burned-out and desolate lands they found in the old hinterlands of Hyperborea quickly checked their advance once they had captured the Sinnar Coast. At that point, they turned their sights upon Insula Extremis across the narrow channel at the end of their peninsula. Without the Hyperborean triremes and galleys to protect the island, the Heldring began building longboats, which they landed on its shores to seek land and plunder.

The warriors of Insula Extremis at first held off these incursions, but soon the chieftains among the island's clans began to war among themselves. Taking advantage of the internal conflict, the Heldring seized a small kingdom when a chieftain hired them as mercenaries in a battle with his rivals. Using this foothold, the Heldring slowly increased their lands on the island until Daan, the son of a local chieftain who had served in the Hyperborean legions and a minor Hyperborean noblewoman, returned to Insula Extremis. Daan himself was a hipparchos cavalry officer in the legions and served for long years in the Irkainian Peninsula. When the Hyperboreans withdrew from Irkaina following the destruction of Curgantium, Daan, together with his father's auxiliary phalangites and his own horsemen native to Insula Extremis, were abandoned and left to find their own way home.

The journey across eastern Akados took the small force three years until they finally reached a friendly port that would transport them and all of their mounts to Insula Extremis. When Daan and his army arrived on the island, they found the situation dire, with the Heldring kingdoms expanding. Daan had learned much from fighting the Irkainians and had developed his own hipparchia of heavy cataphracts that combined the heavy armor of the phalanx with the mobility of the cavalry. This force of armored, lance-wielding horsemen was unlike anything the Heldring had ever encountered, and in his first engagement Daan routed and utterly destroyed a much-larger force of Heldring shield-warriors.

Shortly after this engagement, the folk of the island named Daan as the polemarch of Insula Extremis and placed the salvation of the island in the hands of Daan and his cataphracts. For 10 long years, they battled the Heldring and bested them in every engagement, until finally in one great pitched battle near the Spring of Agedium, Daan's cataphracts and the combined armies of the island's petty kingdoms broke the power of the Heldring on the island and drove them back to the sea.

However, Daan knew that it was only a matter of time before the Heldring ships began to arrive in force again. Throughout the duration of the war against the Heldring, Daan had repeatedly written to the Hyperboreans at Tircople, invoking the name of his father and his mother's family to beg for help from the legions. No answer was ever received until finally, shortly before the Battle of Agedium, a reply was received from Imperatrix Trystecce of Tircople advising that if the islanders would send their kings as representatives, she would hear their pleas for aid and consider what help Tircople could send. So even as the warriors of Insula Extremis girded for the great campaign that would end at Agedium, the petty kings of the island and their advisors and heirs took ship from their port at Dunkelding to beseech the court of the imperatrix.

Daan was victorious at Agedium and anxiously awaited word from Tircople as the months passed, but none came. Eventually, the seers and druids of the island were employed to find some clue as to the fate of the kings in Tircople. To their horror, the divinations revealed that the emissaries of Insula Extremis had been imprisoned at Tircople by the court of the apparently mad imperatrix. Realizing the Hyperboreans had abandoned and betrayed them, Daan saw no choice but to march on Tircople itself to overthrow this corrupt monarch and rescue the kings of Insula Extremis.

Daan spent five years building his army. He took ship across the strait with what forces he had and began recruiting among the disenfranchised former subjects of Hyperborea. His first stop was among the burghs and halls of the Heldring, who though beaten and incapable of fielding a new army themselves, still retained many restless and leaderless warriors lusting for battle and plunder. Many embraced the offer of their erstwhile enemy and joined his growing army, many even training upon the great warhorses to become cataphracts. And as his army grew, Daan headed north through the devastated heartlands of Akados where thousands of dissolute folk flocked to his banner at the promise of glory and justice.

Daan's army continued to grow, and it encountered its first Hyperborean legion as it crossed the Isthmus of Irkaina. But though the legion was well equipped and well led by its strategos and had nearly the numbers as accompanied Daan in his own army, it was not experienced in dealing with the thundering charge of a formation of cataphracts. While Daan's archers and peltasts forced the legionnaires to huddle within their chelones, the lance-wielding horsemen burst upon their formation and overran them in droves. The battle was short, and the badly-injured strategos had only enough time to formally yield his forces to Daan before succumbing to his own wounds.

Daan spent three years consolidating his forces and pushing toward Tircople. During that time, he smashed three more Hyperborean legions, including one composed of the charioteers of Khemit, and his own legion swelled its ranks with recruits from among the former imperial provinces he crossed and deserters from the Hyperborean legions. Finally, with his host numbering well over 50,000, he crossed the Scythirian Mountains and came to Tircople. He watched as the final legion deployed outside the city's walls fled in full retreat toward the Sea of Tyre. And there the legion of Daan stopped and waited. One messenger was sent to the gates to demand the return of the kings of Insula Extremis and their retinues, but no other action was taken, and no other words were exchanged. Daan had brought the Hyperborean Empire to its knees and awaited its capitulation.

On the third night, the release of a catapult sounded, and a large bundle flew over the walls of Tircople and landed before the lines of Daan's legion. An inspection showed it to be a huge tarp holding the severed heads of all the hostages taken by the imperatrix. The catapult was likewise the signal to attack, as suddenly the ground around the city erupted and hordes of undead abominations poured forth to attack the besiegers. The Hyperboreans, once the greatest rulers and the light of civilization in the world, had turned to dark rites and darker allegiances to save themselves. The legion of Daan was decimated but not destroyed by the sudden attack, and even as Daan deployed his heavy cataphracts

and phalanx to deal with the undead hordes, he ordered his auxiliary troops to advance upon the walls of Tircople with ladders and ropes while siege engines pounded away at its gates and towers.

The battle for Tircople was long and vicious, and after four days the gates were breached, and the legion of Daan poured into the city streets. They did not loot or burn, but only attacked defenders who threatened them as they made their way to the Imperial Palace. Daan rode at the head of his cataphracts and was the first to reach the palace and smash through the ranks of more undead that barred the way. Daan fought through the horde and reached the throne room to face Imperatrix Trystecce, where he and his companions discovered to their horror that the imperatrix herself was an undead lich of surpassing power. Daan's cataphracts were not only superb heavy cavalry but were also heroes and warriors of renown and now faced off against the horror that was the queen of Hyperborea. Though many of his company died that day, Daan himself gave the final blow to the lich-queen and ended her reign over Tircople and Hyperborea. Her phylactery bore a vicious trap, however, and when Daan destroyed it, it exploded. As the smoke cleared, the corpse of the lich-queen was dust, and Daan the Polemarch of Insula Extremis lay dead of a hundred cursed wounds.

Honoring Daan's final orders, the legion left Tircople unsacked. The legionnaires returned to their own lands or sought out new opportunities, while the surviving 50 horsemen of Daan's cataphracts carried their lord's body back to Insula Extremis. He was interred in a crypt in a hidden location somewhere on the island and pronounced the high king for all time. Then the second sons and cousins of the executed kings renounced the imperial name of the island and restored its ancient name, Ynys Cymragh, and declared their tribes henceforth as the united tribe of the Daanites. They rechristened the channel to the Helcynngae Peninsula as the Straits of Daan and swore an oath that no man would cross it and live until their high king had returned and ruled over the island once again. The rest of the world they simply called Lloegyr, the Lost Lands — the name by which the world came to be known among the common folk, who thenceforth grew up on tales of Daan and his legendary cataphracts.

THE KINGS OF FOERE (2585 I.R. TO 2842 I.R.)

Following the death of the imperatrix, anarchy reigned over Akados for years as the disparate peoples of the former empire struggled with the absence of Hyperborean rulership. On Libynos, the end of empire took a little longer, but after only a few decades, the new imperator and the surviving legions vanished in the north. The tribes of Irkaina spoke of the Hyperboreans crossing the isthmus toward their ancestral home of Boros, with columns of warriors and refugees marching silently northward into the cold wastes. The Hyperboreans had departed for their homeland, abandoning Akados and Libynos without a word of explanation.

In the void left by the absence of the Hyperboreans in Akados, wars raged between petty kings seeking to obtain and hold lands, wealth, and warriors. One such kingdom in central Akados was Foere. Their king, a half-elf named Macobert, had been a chiliarch (battalion commander) of the Hyperborean legion that faced the Cataphracts of Daan in battle decades earlier. Upon his return to Foere, he quickly overthrew the petty king and installed the military tradition from his time in the legion. Breeding his own war mounts, he created his own heavy cavalry from among the lords of Foere, much like the old Hyperborean hippeis class. Trained in cavalry tactics and the use of combined arms, they became the single-most deadly fighting force since the Cataphracts of Daan.

These Knights of Macobert served as the anchor for his army and allowed him to defeat and unite all of the petty kingdoms around until soon one Kingdom of Foere ruled in central Akados. In his 260th year, King Macobert marched his vast host, led by his thousands of knights, in a long pilgrimage across Irkaina to distant Tircople. There he reclaimed the city, cleared the High Altar of Muir, and had himself crowned Macobert I, Overking of the Hyperborean Monarchy of the Foerdewaith.

The City of Courghais, Imperial Capital of Foere.

Subsequent overkings consolidated the Foerdewaith hegemony over Akados and maintained their control of Tircople as a distant client kingdom. Even the mighty Heldring of the Helcynngae Peninsula were defeated in battle and brought under the banner of Foere.

The first real troubles to threaten the Hyperborean Monarchy occurred after Foerdewaith explorers and settlers migrated through the Crynnomar Gap into the Great Steppes. By now, the Hundaei Khanate was a distant memory, and only scattered bands of riders known as the Shattered Folk continued to dwell upon the expansive plains. Foerdewaith settlers found little to fear from these small groups, and soon small settlements and colonies of Foere began to spring up on the fringes of the steppes.

THE COLONIZATION (2843 I.R. TO 2957 I.R.)

In 2843 I.R., Queen Beraia, wife of Overking Paulus, gave birth to twin sons, Kennet and Cale. None knew which was the elder, since the queen died in childbirth and the royal physiker, having been drunk at the time, was summarily executed on orders of the overking. As the twins grew, the empire was wracked by fears of civil war when Paulus should die. But when Paulus did pass, the twins revealed a wisdom beyond their years. Kennet was crowned the sole overking of the Hyperborean monarchy. Cale, meanwhile, abdicated his claim to the throne, and in return received sole control of the rich port of Reme (formerly known as Remenos) as well as all the nearby marches that controlled access to the Crynnomar Gap.

With the full support and resources of Courghais at his disposal, Cale began the Great Colonization, a mass migration of settlers into the fertile and largely unoccupied grasslands of the Great Steppes. Within 70 years, a string of settlements sprang up along the base of the surrounding mountains and in an unbroken chain across the steppes to the western coast more than a thousand miles away. Then the colonists reached the shores of Lake Hali in the far northwest. There they found better organized and aggressive tribes of humanoids, which suddenly descended in hordes onto the Great Steppes. The widely scattered settlements were ill-prepared, and many were sacked and burned before the Foerdewaith were even aware of the threat. With additional military assistance from Courghais, the colonists fortified their steadings and slowly pushed back the humanoid marauders until a tense stalemate settled in.

The stalemate did not last long. Less than two decades later, the floodgates opened once again in a horde that poured forth from the Lost Mountains in numbers not seen since the great elven defense of the Crynnomar Gap, and this time accompanied by creatures of Shadow, the sceadugenga, or shadow-walkers. The horde descended in a tide that rolled south, burning and destroying settlements as it went. Finally, at a battlefield now known as Cale's Doom, the legion of Cale and the remaining colonial irregulars met the humanoids and shadow walkers. The legion fell where it stood, with tens of thousands dead. Grand Duke Cale himself was among the missing.

Refugees from the settlements poured into Reme, and the army of the Foerdewaith prepared to march north to try to stop the oncoming horde. In this time of Reme's greatest need, the powerful archmages Margon and Alycthron reappeared, having vanished from the knowledge of men more than 10 centuries before. At the Crynnomar Gap, where the gathering legions of Foere stared across a field at seemingly endless numbers of humanoids, the wizards called upon ancient and forgotten magics. The ground before the legions broke and tilted steeply backward to create a slope where only a flat plain had stood before. The hordes beyond the break watched as the tilted ground rose in a massive escarpment of earth and stone before them, rising hundreds of feet and stretching all the way from the flanks of the Stoneheart Mountains, across the Crynnomar Gap, to the flanks of the Deepfells more than 500 miles distant. With such an unscalable height — thereafter known as the Wizard's Wall — blocking their path into the human lands, the humanoid hordes were turned back.

Sorrowful even in victory at the loss of the colonies and anyone trapped below on the plains beyond the Wizard's Wall, the soldiers of Foerdewaith turned their backs upon the House of Cale and began the long march home. Garrisons were left along the length of the broken escarpment to ensure no attempts were made to scale the wall and sneak into the human lands beyond, but never again, swore the folk of Foere, would they cross the Crynnomar Gap and enter what became known as the Haunted Steppe beyond.

THE GREAT CRUSADES (2958 I.R. TO 3207 I.R.)

Ever since its founding by Oeric of Hyperborea, Tircople had stood as a bastion of the Hyperborean gods on the continent of Libynos. It was primarily dedicated, however, to the goddess Muir, whose High Altar was established in the city as the center of her worship in the world. Outside the city in the surrounding mountains was a secret shrine to her said to have been blessed by the goddess herself, making the site even more holy in the eyes of the faithful. Oeric, having abdicated the throne of the Hyperborean Empire to his brother, was anointed as the Pontifex of the Three, a triumvirate of ancient Hyperborean deities of whom only Thyr and Muir were remembered — the identity of the third deity having been lost somewhere in the distant past. Pontifex Oeric thus established a long line of high priests who cared for the weighty spiritual matters of the empire from their holy city while the political matters of the empire were administered from Curgantium. This arrangement persisted throughout the life of the empire with a heavily traveled pilgrim's road maintained between the heartlands of the empire in Akados and distant Tircople.

In the waning days of the empire, however, the imperator moved the capital from ruined Curgantium and relocated it to Tircople where the High Altar of Muir came to double as the Imperial Palace. Also at this time, the office of pontifex became absorbed by the imperators who took the mantle of political and spiritual leader of the empire on themselves when Imperator Garsune "discovered" Pontifex Maximilian murdered at the beginning of the Twelve Nights of Blood in 2509 I.R. Garsune's reign was short-lived, however, as he mysteriously fell from the topmost spire of his palace and was succeeded by his wife, the ageless Imperatrix Trystecce. It was the hero Daan who discovered that she was actually a foul lich and destroyed her, bringing about the end of the lines of both imperators and pontifices.

In 2744 I.R., when Macobert marched on Tircople, he replaced the line of the imperators by having himself crowned Overking of the Hyperborean Monarchy of the Foerdewaith, and lots were cast to choose a new Pontifex of the Three between the high priests of Thyr and Muir who had traveled with Macobert. Gesselrod, a priest of Thyr, was chosen as pontifex, and the high priest of Muir, Sagrilaer, chose to stay in Tircople and re-consecrate the High Altar of Muir. Seeing the state into which the city of Tircople and its many holy sites had fallen, Sagrilaer proposed to create an order of knights dedicated to Muir. With the pontifex's blessing, he established the Holy Order of Justicars which, drawing upon the traditions of both the Knights of Macobert and the Cataphracts of Daan, would be defenders throughout the world of justice and the virtues of paladinhood. Sagrilaer placed the order under the command of a high lord who would be the military defender of Tircople, and second only to the pontifex in power within the churches of Thyr and Muir.

As the first high lord, Sagrilaer grew the order from a dozen worthy knights to an entire battalion of mounted heavy horsemen ready to bring the sword of truth wherever it was needed throughout the Kingdom of Foere. As the number of Justicars grew, Sagrilaer appointed a grandmaster to oversee the order in its duties abroad, while the office of the high lord focused on the defense of Tircople. Eventually, only a company of Justicars remained in Tircople, while the rest rode far and wide to discharge their holy duties and bring justice to the downtrodden.

The Hyperboreans and, later, Foerdewaith were not the only peoples to focus their attention upon Tircople and its Sacred Table in the Scythirian Mountains, however. A Libynosi ruler, who styled himself the king of kings and claimed his folk were descended from the ancient Hundaei race, received a vision granted by the death god Nergal that said the Sacred Table was sacred to his faith because it bore the entrance to the Underworld hidden within its cliffs. King of Kings Ossimandius declared the Foerdewaith anathema and led his people, called the Huun, in a holy war against them. The Huun swept over the mountains and slaughtered the inhabitants of Tircople and the valley basin. Almost the entire body of Justicars on the Sacred Table fell in the onslaught, alongside both the pontifex and the first high lord.

In Courghais, Overking Granicus learned of this attack and called upon the people of Foere to liberate the Sacred Table in what he named the Great Crusade. Armies were raised from across Foere by Justicars throughout the lands. With potentially hostile inhabitants in Irkaina and northwestern Libynos, an overland march was deemed too long and costly. Instead, a great flotilla was raised and sailed east through the Canal of the Pharaohs in Khemit, and thence to the Wasted Desert that lay west of the Sea of Tyre on the eastern coast of Libynos. The crusader army landed and attacked the lightly defended eastern approach without remorse. The unprepared Huun were driven before them, and Tircople and the Sacred Table were recaptured.

Fortresses were erected at strategic points in the Scythirian Mountains and along the coasts. To create a powerful presence capable of repelling future invasions, a series of Crusader States were established along a section of the eastern shore of Libynos west of the Sea of Tyre and on a group of islands offshore, which became known as the Crusader Coast.

Ten years later, the Huun struck back and recaptured the Sacred Table along with some of the Crusader States, and besieged Tircople. Yurid, the new overking, called for a second Great Crusade to relieve the besieged holy city. The crusader armies joined with the armies of the surviving Crusader States, and once again the Huun were driven from the Sacred Table and the siege of Tircople lifted.

A century passed, and the Crusader States prospered. The Order of Justicars grew under the half-elf Elanir, the second high lord, though now it kept its forces marshaled primarily in and around the Crusader States to guard against further incursions by the Huun, who still lived in the mountains to the south around the Desert of Oreb. But in time, the vigil of the Justicars grew lax and the Crusader States sank into peaceful forgetfulness, while the long-lived King of Kings Ossimandius (or another Huun leader who claimed to be the same person) consolidated power. The Huun struck again, the coastal Crusader States fell, the Sacred Table was overrun, and Tircople was sacked. The inhabitants of all were put to the sword. Only the island Crusader States survived, and all they could do was watch in horror as their brethren cities ashore were fired to light up the entire coast at night in a ghastly spectacle.

Overking Oervid called for a Third Great Crusade, which gathered once again from all across Foere and took ship for the Crusader Coast. But this time the Huun were ready for them and waited at the shore for the ships to land. It was said that the immortal king of kings and his high priests called upon their dark gods, and a great monsoon sprang up as the flotilla neared the coast and smashed the fleet. Survivors unlucky enough to be washed ashore along the coast were hunted by the gathered Huun spearmen and executed before being cast back into the sea. The Third Great Crusade ended in failure before it even stepped foot on Libynos.

The Huun held Tircople and the Sacred Table for 30 years, fighting off occasional raids from the island Crusader States, before a Fourth Great Crusade could be gathered. This one was led by Overking Oessum VIII himself, a pious and devoted warrior of Muir. The flotilla landed safely on the island of Cyproean and remained there for eight years as Oessum slowly gathered more crusaders to his banner. A third high lord, Ethelgart of Berrocburh, was named while this army gathered, and new Justicars were inducted into the order from among the crusaders. Finally, the crusader army made plans to embark for the coast where the forces of the Huun waited in numbers unequaled by any prior Huun army. It is said that Ossimandius himself led the army from his great war chariot pulled by elephants culled from the forests of Far Jaati. The crusaders disembarked and marched across the Wasted Desert toward the west where the escarpment rises to the Sacred Table. Reaching the escarpment, they began their climb up the Crusaders' Road, at the top of which the Huun army awaited, expecting to destroy the Foere as they tried to reach the plateau. But as the first of the crusaders approached the top, a ripple of confusion ran through the Huun forces from the rear.

During the years of preparation on Cyproean, Oessum had not been idle. His messengers had flown back and forth between the chieftains of the hill dwarf clans of Shamash Kush. He had convinced these chieftains of the dangers posed by the proximity of the Huun to their homeland, and the clans had marched secretly over the Scythirian Mountains and now tore into the rear positions of the Huun on the Sacred Table. Portions of the Huun army turned to meet this new threat, robbing the front lines of the ability to prevent the crusaders from advancing onto the Table. Soon, the Huun found themselves trapped between the two armies on a pair of small mounts on the eastern edge of the Sacred Table called the Sickles. The battle was fierce and the outnumbered crusaders hard pressed, but the morale of the Huun was already broken and, after much costly battle in which the majority of the Justicars were slain in suicidal charges upon Ossimandius' bodyguards, the crusaders carried the day. The king of kings abandoned his famed war chariot on the field and was last seen fleeing south toward Oreb with the survivors of his personal bodyguard, while the main body of his force was smashed to ribbons.

The Sacred Table and Crusader States were secure, and Tircople was once again in the hands of the Foerdewaith. High Lord Ethelgart called for a new pontifex to be ordained. Unfortunately, Overking Oessum VIII was killed in the battle and died without an heir. Distracted by the political struggles to agree on a new overking, the leaders of Foere left Tircople to its own devices, and no pontifex was ordained. Finally, the aged Graeltor, Oessum's uncle who had administered Foere in Oessum's absence, was crowned overking in Courghais.

THE AGE OF BREAKING (3208 I.R. TO PRESENT)

The reign of Graeltor was not long. Shortly after his coronation, a delegation of religious leaders in Courghais approached him about the threat rising in the wastes north of Bard's Gate where the temple-city of Orcus known as Tsar was threatening trade between Foere and the Isthmus. Though the temple-city had been there for many years, Graeltor declared his own Great Crusade to destroy the city, which he dubbed the Army of Light. The siege of Tsar lasted for over a year and claimed tens of thousands on both sides.

Then in distant Libynos, swarms of invading Mguru tribesmen emerged from the Malagro Jungle and overran Tircople and the Sacred Table, reducing it to a burning waste. News of this atrocity shocked the Army of Light and shook its morale. Yet shortly thereafter, the forces of Tsar suddenly retreated from the field and led the vengeful Army of Light on a long chase down the Gulf of Akados coast. The army of Tsar was driven into the Forest of Hope, and the Army of Light followed. Both disappeared under the forest canopy, and no sign of either has been seen since.

The shock of the loss of so much of the realm's nobility and greatest warriors shook Foere to its core. Uprisings started to occur across the kingdom, with few knights or noblemen to put them down. Three years later, the broken Graeltor died in his bed, passing the crown to his largely unknown and untested grandson Oedwin. Shortly thereafter, Ramthion Island declared its independence from Foere, beginning what is known as the Foerdewaith Wars of Succession. Two years after that, the Grand Admiral of Pontus Tinigal withdrew from Foere and declared himself Emperor of the Oceans Blue, and established the Kingdom of Oceanus on Pontos Island. Efforts by the Foerdewaith to recover these lost provinces failed, and in short order other Foere lands followed suit, including Burgundy, Suilley, the Vast, North Heath and, in a devastating blow, Reme.

During the three centuries since, the power of Foere has continued to decline, and many areas on its periphery have fallen increasingly into chaos and disorder. Where once the legions of empire kept the peace, now bandits and monsters roam, and good folk bar their doors and keep fires burning through the perilous night.

Just three years ago in 3514 I.R., an event occurred that shook the kingdoms of Akados as a Huun army of the apparently immortal King of Kings Ossimandius appeared on the northern border of the Desolation of Tsar, past the ruins of Oxibbul. Never before had a Huun army set foot on the shores of Akados. It advanced southward until it reached the Lyre Valley, where it found its way blocked by Bard's Gate and so laid siege to the city. King Ovar the Magnificent, the overking of Courghais, hastily called for a new Great Crusade against the age-old enemy and rallied the nobles and men-at-arms of Foere and its former provinces to the defense of Bard's Gate. But first he unleashed a fleet of ships against the sambuks of Ossimandius' navy in the Gulf of Akados. A combined Foerdewaith and Heldring armada delivered a crushing defeat to the Huun ships and forced them into a retreat back up to the coasts of the Sea of Spices.

With their supply lines disrupted by the loss of its naval support, the besieging Huun forces withdrew from the walls of Bard's Gate and retreated back across the Desolation with the crusader army in pursuit. The last reports from the front were of the crusading army pursuing the Huun into the wastes of the Irkainian Desert to draw them into battle, but nothing further has been heard for two years. With no word from the king of Foere nor any of the lesser rulers who marched with him, the Lost Lands are once again on the verge of turmoil as the rule of law is stretched by the absence of so many lords and men-at-arms. And rumors that King Ovar has returned to his Throne Tower of the citadel Caene, arriving alone at night astride his trained black dragon, has only further sparked talk of rebellion and betrayal. The Lost Lands are in need of heroes now more than ever.

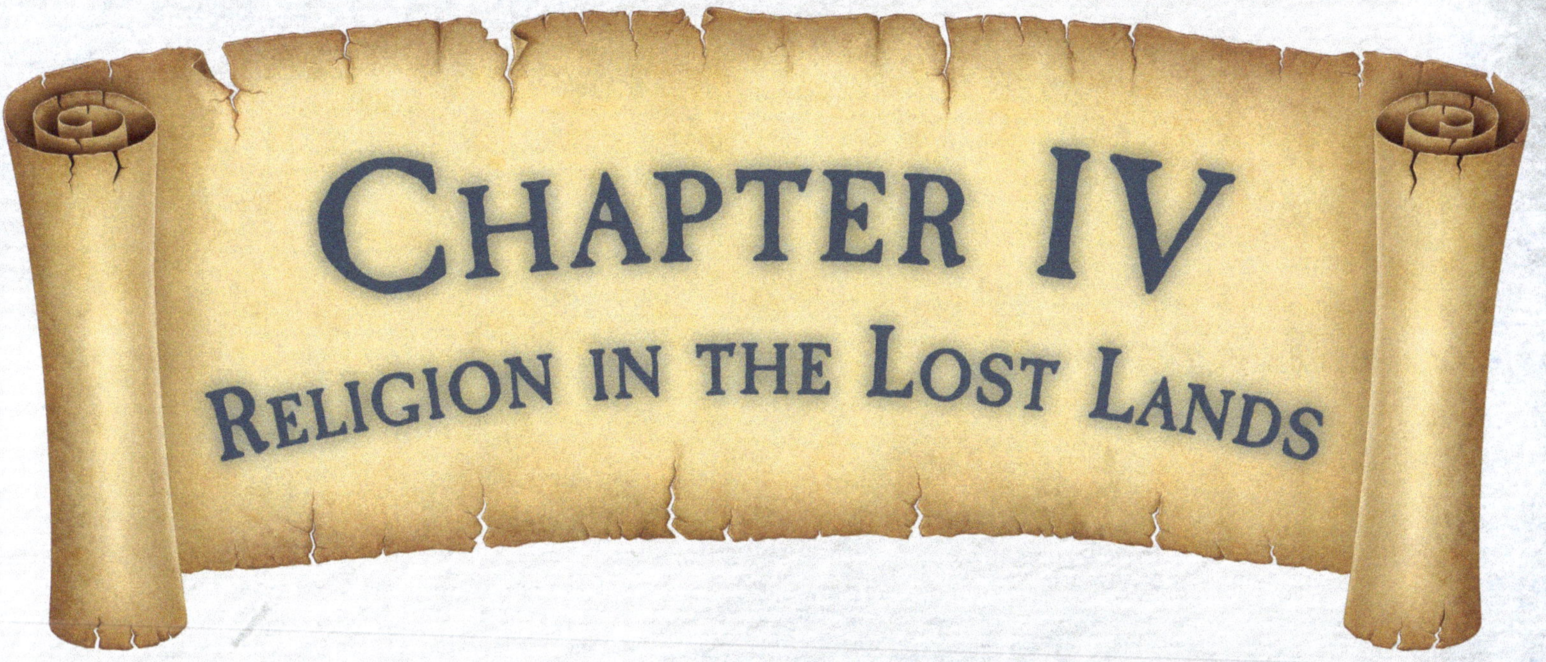

CHAPTER IV
RELIGION IN THE LOST LANDS

The exact number of deities worshipped in the Lost Lands is undoubtedly unknowable. Some gods are ancient in origin, and today may be nearly or entirely forgotten. Some new gods may be venerated by only a small number of people in one location, while others may be prayed to by many people in many different places and even under different names.

Most of the folk of the Lost Lands worship an interconnected group of deities, divided into what are known as pantheons. Whether the gods consider such divisions relevant is unknown. Certainly, some gods have been adopted by several groups of disparate peoples, and accordingly are included in more than one pantheon, suggesting that these categories may be more a human construction than anything else. That being said, deities certainly do share bonds with one another, some friendly and some antagonistic, so in some sense affiliations do represent reality.

A full discourse on the gods of the Lost Lands is beyond the scope of this volume and is expected to be addressed in a future publication. In the meantime, it can be noted that the most important pantheons today include the Foerdewaith (which represents an intermingling of the ancient Hyperborean gods and those of the tribes of central Akados, principally Foere); the Xha'en Imperial Pantheon; the gods of the Heldring and the Northlands; the Annunaki pantheon; the gods of Khemit; the deities of nature and the earth; and the various pantheons of the non-human races (such as the elves, dwarves, and gnomes).

One religious symbol that has acquired nearly universal significance is the tesseract, usually shown as a square within a square or, in three dimensions, a cube within a cube. Variations of this symbol can be found as early as the Neolithic folk predating the first human settlements on Akados. To this day, it remains an important icon of Thyr and Muir, and the great cathedral of the Foerdewaith pantheon in Courghais is known as the Cathedral of the Tesseract. The reason for its widespread relevance remains a subject of controversy among scholars.

Appendix II at the end of this volume provides a table of the major deities of the most important pantheons, with essential information concerning their areas of influence.

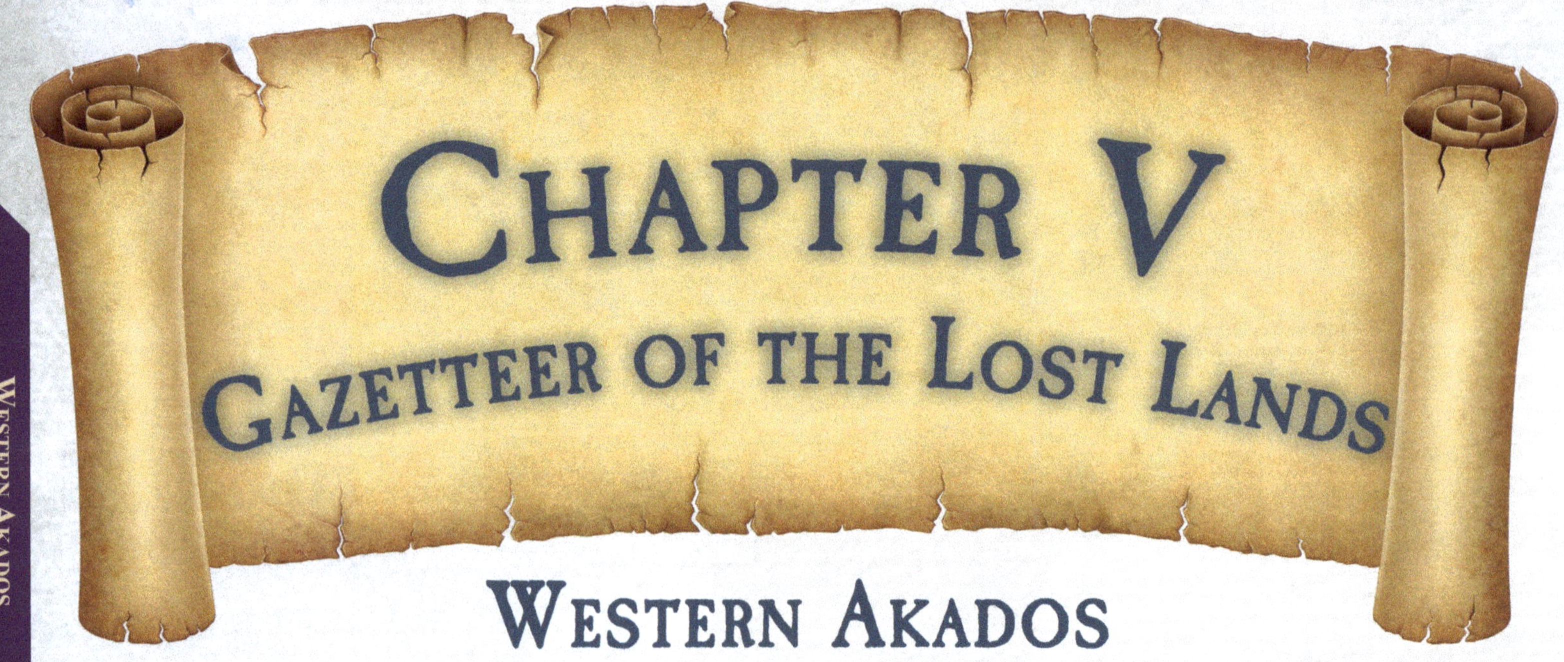

Chapter V
Gazetteer of the Lost Lands

Western Akados

Political Subdivisions of Western Akados

Xha'en Hegemony (sometimes, Xi'en)

(SHAH-en)

Capital: Xha'ahan
Notable Settlements: Thanalos, Djir, Rojhah, Tsadar, Jhohir
Ruler: Emperor Sajrac su Kar Rachar
Government: hereditary monarchy (empire; local government varies by tradition)
Population: 17,700,000 (16,180,000 Xha'en, 500,000 Senge, 400,000 halfling, 200,000 hill dwarf, 150,000 mountain dwarf, 100,000 tabaxi, 75,000 half-elf, 75,000 tengu, 20,000 wild elf)
Monstrous: barghest, bat swarms, bugbears, centaurs, cockatrice, crabs (giant), dryads, eagles, eagles (giant), elephants, ettercaps, ettins, fomorians, fire giants, hill giants, stone giants, gnolls, goblins, griffons, hags, hobgoblins, hyenas, hyenas (dire), kobolds, leopards, lions, lions (dire), lycanthropes (weretiger), lycanthropes (wereboar), lycanthropes (wererat), lycanthropes (werewolf), manticores, megafauna (arsinoitherium, glyptodon, megaloceros, megatherium), merfolk (coastal regions), minotaurs, mummies, nagas, ogres, oni, perytons, phoenix, rakshasa, rats, rats (dire), sahuagin (coastal regions), satyrs, sea serpents (coastal regions), sphinx, tengu, tigers, tigers (dire), treants, troglodytes, trolls, vampires, yeti, worgs
Languages: Xaon, Guivoc (The Utterends)
Religion: the Imperial Pantheon, numerous tribal pantheons, ancestral spirits, and animism
Resources: cloth, copper, fishing, foodstuffs, gems, gold, glass, grain, iron, livestock (cattle, goats, horses), manufactured goods, opium, pottery, silver, timber
Currency: Xha'en
Technology Level: Renaissance (Xha'ahan city), Medieval (large cities), High Middle Ages (smaller cities), Dark Ages (towns, villages and countryside)

The mighty Xha'en Hegemony (sometimes written Xi'en by those of other nations) is a union of several powerful city-states united under the hereditary rulership of an emperor or empress based in the ancient city of Xha'ahan. Secure behind the imposing slopes of the Impossible Peaks and the near-impenetrable depths of the Great Akadonian Forest, the Hegemony has grown and prospered over millennia into a powerful and sophisticated state that is only now developing full contact with the outside world.

The Hegemony's borders range from the semi-autonomous Gtsang Prefecture in the north, along the edge of the Great Akadonian Forest to the east and the wild regions of the Utterends in the south. To the west lies the Caerulean Ocean (known as the Nether Sea to the folk of Castorhage) — dark, vast and mysterious.

Many outsiders are entirely unfamiliar with the Hegemony, and first-time visitors are likely to be astonished that such a great state has evolved in isolation. While many portions of the Hegemony still live following the ancient ways, Xha'en city-states contain numerous wonders of art, architecture, and science that equal or exceed those of kingdoms such as Foere and Oceanus.

Outside visitors to the Hegemony are rare, and locals tend toward suspicion (in the countryside) and curiosity (in cities). Ever-present Imperial officials are quite interested in the affairs of visitors, and often insist upon official passes and fees. Foreigners will find themselves watched closely and sometimes even followed. This is not to say that the Xha'en are openly hostile, but a healthy level of caution prevails in most of their interactions with foreigners.

History and People

The ancient Xha'en people have occupied western lands for thousands of years, and in that time many kingdoms and empires have risen and fallen. Today's Xha'en are believed to be descended from the primeval nomadic folk of western Akados, the original progenitors of such races as the Hundaei and the clans of Reme. Originally hunter-gatherers, the Xha'en settled in the fertile Plains of Xha, where they adopted a more agrarian culture and built permanent settlements while farming and herding livestock.

For many millennia, the population of the Xha region remained relatively low, but as they prospered and their numbers grew, the Xha'en came into conflict with the Senge, the area's other inhabitants. After generations of sporadic warfare and migration, the Senge were slowly forced from their traditional lands and into the hill country to the east. They still exist today, but as a minority in the greater Xha'en Hegemony.

The Hegemony as such did not exist for several millennia to come, as various city-states and small nations rose, fought, and fell. This era, known as the Thousand Kingdoms, is one of the most popular in Xha'en art, literature, and theater. Those days are said to have witnessed acts of great heroism and fell villainy, as well as mighty sorceries, the blackest of necromancy, and the forging of legendary artifacts.

Western Akados
Farthest Point
Neer
Greater Bream
Lesser Bream
The Thousand Rocks
Kuseve Gulf
Mt. Shir
Shir Meadows
Mt. Yojunar
Bream Straits
Ctsang Prefecture
Duam
The Deepfells
Devil's Finger
Namia Forest
Ashen Hills
Anaros Isle
Ui'aharti
Ochotan
Least Bream
Ilthanic Fortress
Dwarven Kingdom of Ankhura
Odanishana temple
Kamatkhan
Kraken's Teeth
The Sinking Place
Eisenwood
Jhadarah
She Fench Sea (aka Urni Hosoeta)
Iron Octogon
Tsendakan Mountains
Harrowfar
The Front
Quy Island
Quy Tar
Lujhiran Dam
Xhanhan Aphapor
Alo River
Kabanila R.
Sengetia Hills
Serpentai River
Batto River
The Impossible Peaks
Endless Hills
Westwood
Acfler River
Tanner's Green
Tower of Jhedophar
Windreft
Jhohin
Rojhah
Lake Pantai
Tsadar
Xha'en Hegemony
South Pantai R.
Plains of Xha
Taode River
Shawa River
Serpent's Coil
Duchy of West
Sea Kingdom of Caerulea
Qalen Delta
River Road
Qalen R.
Aban Rha
Thanaloa
The River
Eloikan River
Circle of the Wild
Green Wanderer
Forest's Bones
Onthenkan River
Hollow Mountain
Naelec
Sessamon
Cealos
Lacamon
Djin
Earos Hills
Monkey's Laughter
Anasandin
Green Warden
Caerulean Ocean
Cholama
Ejindor
Ghon Complex
Odarnadan Mountains
Inoni River
Family of Thorn
The Kingdom of Wolves
Forest
Tranith
Soohr-Ahmaad
Hearthfire Pass
The Cauldron
Tahngari
Perilous Kaf
Chafa Temple
Shandaren
The Otterends
Tchor-i-kahn
Quiris Meadow
Elenis Tuath
Sentinels of the Trees
Limariel
Fringe
Median
Free Coast
Queensribbon River
Saefier River
Timb
Mudspit Peninsula
Kanuba Mountains
Il
Poolar
Im

Legend
● Town or Village
◉ City
✪ Capital or Free City
✸ Imperial Capital
■ Fortress or Citadel
⁚⁚ Ruins
▲ Place of Interest
〜 Road
⌇ Trail or Unused Road
⋯ Mountain Pass
✕ Battlefield

The greater history of the Xha'en Hegemony, spanning as it does over three millennia, is a long and complex story. Brief histories can only touch on its high points, as a full study of the Hegemony would take several lifetimes. The city-state of Xha'ahan (a derivative of the word Xha'en, the name the folk here have given to themselves for thousands of years) was founded soon after the final defeat of the Senge in –1302 I.R., now designated as Year 0 in the official Xha'en calendar (XC). As years lengthened into centuries, Xha'ahan grew larger and more influential, dominating the neighboring cities of Tsadar and Aphapor.

Xha'ahan's explorers reached out across the region and made contact with many other entities, including the efreeti of Soohr-Ahmaad. The Xha'ahan quickly realized that the efreeti were extremely powerful and some called for a campaign of conquest, but these foolish voices were quickly silenced by those who knew that such an act could lead only to disaster. Instead, complex treaties were signed with the efreeti, the contents of which remain a mystery to this day. Some scholars point to the efreetis' mystical powers and legendary wish-granting abilities and note the continued success of the Xha'ahan, suggesting that there may be some connection. For their part, Xha'en officially recognizes Soohr-Ahmaad but have very little to do with the strange state and its equally strange inhabitants.

With or without efreeti aid, Xha'ahan cemented its dominance in 1115 XC (–187 I.R.) with the construction of the engineering marvel called the Lujhiran Dam, named for the Xha'ahan queen Lujhira sa Bhor Ahra. Intended to prevent the annual flooding of the Alu and Pantai rivers and thus free up vast stretches of the Plains of Xha for settlement, the great project resulted in the creation of the vast body of water now called Lake Pantai, and just coincidentally the submergence of Agretor, one of Xha'ahan's chief rival cities. Xha'ahan's allied cities Tsadar and Aphapor now sit on the edge of a great body of water, which allows direct access between the city-states by boat. With the loss of the Pantai lowlands, greater emphasis was placed on the Xha farmlands freed up by the dam's construction. Great aqueducts and canals were constructed to replace the yearly floods while also providing a controlled source of irrigation to the plains.

The dominance of Xha'ahan was challenged in 1447 XC (145 I.R.) when the cities of Jhohir and Rojhah formed a confederacy, sharing a single legislative group of nobles and a military commander. As Jhohir was the dominant party, this state came to be known as the Jhohir Confederacy, and it lasted nearly 400 years before falling to internal discord and external defeat. In 1834 XC (532 I.R.), a mighty flotilla of vessels filled with Jhohir and Rojhah warriors set sail, intent on the conquest of the Thousand Rocks and the great Anaros Island beyond. The Anari, long thought to be uncultured barbarians, took umbrage at this act and fought back, battling the invaders for each rock. Bad weather descended on the Sheltered Sea as well, with the wind battering ships, waves sinking dozens of vessels, and the chill cold spreading across the land to slow and sicken the mainland warriors. When at last the invaders had had enough, they returned home, greatly weakened and diminished. At this point, a ferocious squabble between the two states broke out over who bore responsibility for the disaster, and by the end of 1837 XC (535 I.R.) the once-proud confederacy lay in tatters, with each of its partners now going its own way.

The Xha'en Hegemony as it is known today was founded in 2700 XC (1398 I.R.) when Lord Vaelos su Dis Ahra, of the clan Ahra (Kingfisher), declared the three allied cities — Xha'ahan, Tsadar, and Aphapor — to be a single union. Already ancient, Xha'ahan became the center of a new and growing empire. In 2845 XC (1543 I.R.), the city of Rojhah fell after a long siege. A puppet ruler was installed by the ruling Ahra clan, and the following year the port city of Jhohir accepted the inevitable and agreed to peacefully join the Hegemony, followed in 2848 XC (1546 I.R.) by Aban Rha and Thanalos.

The luck of the gods was with the new state, for just a few years later in 2856 XC (1554 I.R.), a massive tidal wave swamped the region's west coast and devastated the city of Tianos, one of the last holdouts against the Hegemony. A massive series of offshore earthquakes triggered this disaster and also spread destruction across the undersea Kingdom of Caerulea, but no one among the Xha'en was aware of this until several years later when raids by the desperate sea-kingdom began to pick off merchant shipping. By the time Caerulean forces began to attack coastal regions of Quy Island and the Xha shore, the Xha'en realized that they were facing a new and until-now unknown threat.

The coastal cities, still reeling from the aftereffects of the great tidal wave, attempted to band together to face their attackers, but the Caeruleans were cunning, and with the ocean as their secret, utterly unseen highway, could strike anywhere. Forces from across the Hegemony were called up to man coastal garrisons. Mounted troops and messengers were posted at regular intervals to quickly respond and spread the word of raids as they occurred. In response, the Caeruleans began to raid in greater numbers and brought substantial forces ashore and struck several locations simultaneously. False raids intended to draw off defenders were common, and soon the entire coast and Quy Island beyond was aflame with a war between civilizations. Hostilities lasted until 2878 XC (1576 I.R.), when the two peoples, exhausted from conflict, finally settled a treaty that ended the raids.

The seemingly inevitable march of the Ahra clan to total dominance halted abruptly in 2883 XC (1581 I.R.) when assassins felled the Emperor Gyris su Ard Ahra and his family. In a brilliant coup, the independent Ophronya (Peacock) clan seized power and declared their home city of Djir to be the new seat of the Hegemony.

The Ophronya Dynasty's end came after a long, slow decline and ended with a descent into madness on the part of the so-called Boy Emperor Ziris su Dos Ophronya, who took the throne at age 11 in 3062 XC (1760 I.R.). Prone to fits of rage and irrational behavior, the young ruler was hopelessly mad by his 20th birthday. A council of nobles met in secret and decided to depose the emperor with the help of several allies in the royal guard. In early 3083 XC (1781 I.R.), a mysterious fire in the imperial palace claimed the life of the emperor. Immediately, stories circulated that Ziris immolated himself while commanding the fire to stop burning. Thoroughly discredited, the Ophronya dynasty ended.

The leader of the rebellious nobles, Sarilla sa Dan Huris of clan Huris, proclaimed herself empress and thus began the rule of what many believe to be the greatest of all Xha'en dynasties. Under the Huris Dynasty, art, music, and science prospered with noble sponsorship. Cities grew, and huge public works were constructed. The dynasty reached its height under Emperor Takar su Pan Huris when the Hegemony's capital moved back to the city of Xha'ahan in 3223 XC (1921 I.R.). This move led to a revolt by southern nobles who saw their power slipping away. For a time, the rebels met with success until 3230 XC (1928 I.R.), when Takar su Pan's forces emerged victorious from the epic Battle of Taode River. Over the next five years, the Hegemony reconquered the rebel cities one by one, and the surviving rebels fled to the Utterends where, to hear the Xha'en tell it, they were forced to survive as bandits.

With the Hegemony reunited, the Huris clan returned to their program of civil works by building roads, fortresses, toll stations, port facilities, and similar improvements. Great works of art and music were displayed in the capital and elsewhere. Engineering, astronomy, biology, and medicine all advanced as well. Temples trained clerics and warriors in the healing and martial arts, and colleges of magic were founded to expand and codify the science of the arcane.

But this order and advancement came at a price. A rigid caste system grew up under the Huris, with peasants at the bottom and nobles at the top. Taxes were often penurious, and those who could not pay found their property confiscated and their families forced into indentured servitude. Thus, a class of virtual slave labor arose, a system that persisted for centuries. So while one may marvel at the great buildings, monuments, roads, and other works created during the Huris dynasty, they were accomplished on the backs of slaves and at the cost of countless lives.

Legal rigidity increased under the Huris as well. Laws were established by a council of scholars under the emperor's guidance. While these laws were intended to be rational and relatively benign, they were enforced with ruthless efficiency by the official constabulary, even if they proved to be misguided or unintentionally cruel. To enforce the law, the Huris' rulers decreed the creation of a class of traveling judges — specially-trained warriors, many with some knowledge of magic — who wandered the Hegemony to hear cases and deliver their judgements on the spot. These warrior judges became the Huris' most feared servants, and legends are told of their adventures to this day.

The authoritarian Huris faced many challenges during their years in power. Most prominent was the so-called Ghost Plague that began in 3414 XC (2112 I.R.). First in small villages, then in larger settlements, and finally in the streets of major cities, the spirits of the dead began to wander, moaning and begging for food and to be reunited with their loved ones. In time, the spirits grew hostile and attacked those who could not help them, driving out entire towns. It fell to the warrior judges, Imperial priests, and others skilled in dealing with the undead to clear abandoned towns and buildings of their unwanted inhabitants. The plague continued for two years and ended as quickly as it began. Though theories abound as to the plague's origins, no one today knows for certain why it happened.

Like the previous dynasties, the Huris eventually fell into decline and vanished, but their end was more dramatic than most. Aging Emperor Amaran su Bha Huris had always feared death, and despite his advisors' assurances that he would ascend to heaven and take his place alongside the other great rulers, he began to seek out a way to cheat mortality. His experiments took him down a very dark road, and when he began to hold court wearing fanciful masks, even his closest advisors began to suspect that something was very wrong with the emperor.

In 3697 XC (2395 I.R.), 20 years after his experiments began, Emperor Amaran's advisors demanded that he abdicate in favor of a council of regency. In reply, Amaran revealed what many had long suspected, that he was an undead horror, and that his royal guard had been replaced by undying resurrected corpses. All would bow before him, Amaran declared, and serve the new unending Immortal Dynasty. For long years the Hegemony suffered under the undead emperor's yoke. Amaran's necromantic minions spread across the land, occupying villages and cities, and carried off innocent citizens to be transformed into undead or to feed their master's ever more horrific experiments. Even execution or death from torture did not end the suffering of Amaran's victims, for many of them rose again as undead servitors, or as the dreaded Immortal Guard, Amaran's elite warriors. As the emperor's atrocities grew and the people suffered, an uprising was all but inevitable. Once more, civil war raged across the Hegemony, and this time the nation fought for its very survival.

By 3777 XC (2475 I.R.), the rebels gained the upper hand and laid siege to Amaran's palace. For his part, the lich-emperor crafted a powerful ritual that he believed would raise all the dead in the Hegemony as his servants. Amaran's mad scheme was to transform the Xha'en state into a land of the undead that would never die and be forever subject to his whim. Only drastic action could stop the mad lich, and it fell to a band of heroes — a misfit band that included an Anari Uarsinsi warrior, a stern imperial soldier, a battle-priest, a sorceress, a warrior judge and even an outlaw rogue — to scour the land for the lost Ahra dynasty artifacts that could destroy him. In the end the adventurers, known today as the "Heroic Seven" succeeded, facing down the emperor just as his terrible ritual began. In the battle that followed, most of the heroes perished, but the undead emperor was destroyed forever, along with all the wonders of the imperial palace. The Immortal Dynasty was over.

In the aftermath, the nation rebuilt under the relatively benign Tilgi (Ibis) Dynasty. The reign of the Tilgi was marked by its very mundanity as the nation prospered and the more rigid and cruel of the old dynasty's laws were relaxed. The Tilgi died out peacefully, as was their nature, to be replaced with the more aggressive and militaristic Rachar Dynasty in 4258 XC (2956 I.R.).

The Tilgi Dynasty was not without its momentous events, however. The Xha'en had always been aware of a greater world beyond their borders, and certain ambitious families such as the Y'lshon of Quy Island sought to increase their personal fortunes and influence by seeking trade with distant nations, especially the city-state of Castorhage, whose penal colonies were known to occupy the eastern shore beyond the Great Akadonian Forest. In 3809 XC (2507 I.R.), the Y'lshon received imperial permission to send vessels south around the Talanos Peninsula and into the Crescent Sea. After several unsuccessful ventures, the trading junk *Bounteous Harvest* made the journey and reached Castorhage, offering Hegemony silk, artwork, and foodstuffs in exchange for Castorhagi gold, livestock, and manufactured goods. The journey was long and arduous, but the *Harvest* caused a sensation when it returned in 3811 XC (2509 I.R.). A trickle of trade commenced, with individual ships braving the journey to ferry goods back and forth while bringing both nations news and information about the other. It was not until 3888 XC (2586 I.R.) that the twin Castorhagi regents King Alar and Queen Elspeth finally sealed a permanent trade agreement with the Hegemony that triggered an even greater flow of trade and also a steady stream of immigrants from the Hegemony to Castorhage where the Xha'en quickly became one of the largest minority groups in the city-state. A door to the outside world had finally opened, but it would be some time before that opening widened to more than a crack.

It was another disaster, this time on land, that finally established real relations between Xha'en and the Caerulean sea kingdom. Beginning in 3826 XC (2524 I.R.), a sea-borne plague spread by tainted fish consumed the Hegemony — first in coastal cities, then farther east. The plague was quick, debilitating, and deadly without treatment or healing magic. The sickness even proved resistant to magical cures, for those treated by clerics often fell ill again immediately. When folk started to sicken in the capital city of Xha'ahan, Emperor Alnand su Var Tilgi summoned his advisors to deal with the situation.

Some advisors believed the Caeruleans themselves spread the plague to weaken or exterminate the Xha'en in preparation for a renewal of hostilities. Others advised caution and a measured, diplomatic approach to the problem. The emperor sided with those who counseled caution, much to the anger of the war faction. Diplomats were dispatched to the undersea kingdom while a renegade faction of nobles and officers plotted an attack on Caerulea.

Even as the diplomats were on their way, a flotilla of Xha'en vessels set sail with elite warriors equipped with water-breathing magic. A heavy, costly strike against the sea kingdom would surely trigger a strong response, thus forcing the emperor into war, a situation that the conspirators considered vital before the plague killed or incapacitated too many Xha'en.

Fortunately for the Caeruleans and the peace of the region, the legendary Warrior Judge Samadar foiled the plot after learning of it from a drunken nobleman and immediately moving to stop it. In a fierce showdown, the conspirators were arrested, and their orders were countermanded just in time to allow the diplomatic mission to proceed.

As it transpired, the Caeruleans were aware of the plague and provided a cure. Distributed throughout the Hegemony, the merfolk's potion stopped the sickness in its tracks and vastly improved relations between the two nations.

Today, under Emperor Sajrac su Kar Rachar, the Hegemony stands at a crossroads as the outside world begins to intrude. An intelligent and forward-thinking monarch, Sajrac su Kar has chosen a path of cautious engagement by sending diplomatic expeditions to Foere and several other western nations while expanding trade with Castorhage. Though the arrival of Castorhagi colonists on the Bream Islands in 4512 XC (3210 I.R.) sent shockwaves through the Hegemony, Sajrac su Kar sees the presence of the Castorhagi naval yards and citadels on the Breams as an opportunity to actually engage with outsiders and has also expanded his contacts there. Unfortunately for him, an unscrupulous Castorhagi governor may have plans of his own, for the foreign military presence has been steadily growing over the past few years.

The Hegemony's population is largely human, and many of the indigenous peoples have been absorbed into the Xha'en culture. A few exceptions exist, such as the Senge, the descendants of the region's original inhabitants. Today, most Senge dwell in the Sengejia Hills and live in small villages along the Upper Pantai River. The Senge were already declining by the time Lake Pantai flooded their original homeland after the construction of Lujhiran Dam. Retreat to the hills proved costly, and many Senge perished. Today, they exist semi-autonomously, keeping to themselves and avoiding contact with the Xha'en.

The Senge are not particularly aggressive, though strangers are treated with suspicion and generally shunned. Senge villages are overseen by clan hetmen and supported by shamans who are known to cast powerful druidic spells in defense of their territory. Senge trade handicrafts, furs, and produce for metal tools, clothing, and livestock.

The native Bream islanders who live in small villages along the shoreline resemble the Senge and are believed to be close relatives who chose to settle on the islands rather than the plains at some distant point in the past.

Non-humans occupy an unusual place in the Hegemony, for many clans of halflings and dwarves occupied regions conquered by the Xha'en, and the hostile Eloitan elves occupy the depths of the eastern forest. A small population of half-elves exists in the Hegemony but they are generally shunned by human and elven societies.

Most halfling communities were agrarian and could do little to stem the tide of Xha'en migration. The Xha'en often displaced these villages and killed or enslaved their people, or transported them to less-favorable regions. Today, small communities of halflings persist, especially in the southern portions of the Plains of Xha.

Dwarven settlements dot the Sengejia Hills or are dug deep beneath the Tsendakar and Odarnadar Mountains. For the most part, the Xha'en left these groups in peace, and today they remain fairly isolated, keeping to themselves and sometimes trading with the Xha'en.

In the south, particularly the Utterends, the situation is far more chaotic, with humans and non-humans existing side-by-side and sometimes coming into conflict. Officially, the Hegemony includes the Utterends and nearby territories on its official maps and in the emperor's decrees, but in reality, only a portion of the region comes under Hegemonic control.

RELIGION

During their early agrarian days, the Xha'en worshipped a variety of ancestral and nature spirits, propitiating them in annual rituals. These spirits were highly localized and varied across the region. Most did not adhere to a single pantheon, and it was commonly believed that all of the local entities coexisted, with each group being in charge of its chosen territory. No general concept of afterlife existed beyond a general belief in reincarnation.

The founding of the Hegemony changed all this. The ancestral spirits of the Ahra clan were elevated to the status of true gods, and their worship became mandatory. Priests were sent throughout the Hegemony to establish temples and to see to it that the locals worshipped in the approved manner. Local pantheons were allowed to continue, as displacing them might cause widespread disruption and unrest, but all citizens of the new Hegemony were required to worship the Imperial Pantheon as well.

Like the Hegemony itself, the Imperial Pantheon is rigidly structured, with the great god Ara at its head. Ara is an androgynous deity who gave birth to all the races of humanity and also the other gods. The remainder of the pantheon consists of six gods — Dakhan (war and justice), Gorni (mountains), Jatan (sun and moon), Noradu (nature), Oba (oceans), and Zakur (planting) — and an equal number of goddesses — Banra (the underworld), Estia (the sky), Lainu (lakes and rivers), Meita (the harvest), Quana (love and mercy), and Yainda (childbirth). Zakur and Meita are both agricultural deities and divide duties between the planting season (Zakur) and the fall harvest (Meita).

TRADE AND COMMERCE

Wealthy and largely self-sufficient, the Hegemony engages in extensive internal trade, with goods transported within its own frontiers. Livestock, produce, textiles, and timber flow from the northern regions south, while raw materials such as silver and iron come from the mines of the Odarnadar

Mountains and gemstones are mined amid the treacherous volcanic peaks of the Cauldron. The waters of the Caerulean Ocean are rich with the bounty of the sea, providing all varieties of food to the Hegemony from the fishing villages that dot the eastern shore. Off the coast, the shipwrights and mariners of Quy Island provide ships and crews for the Hegemony.

Foreign trade exists, though today the Hegemony has official trade agreements with only the city-state of Castorhage and its colonies on the Bream Islands. Hegemony goods are exchanged for gold or manufactured goods, and Xha'en immigrants continue to travel to the city-state, growing in importance and bringing their cultural traditions (including less-savory aspects of Xha'en society such as the Triad criminal gangs) to the eastern lands.

The Hegemony also maintains trade relations with the Anari of the Thousand Rocks. Fish, ceramics, and copper ore are imported from the islands in exchange for grains, cattle, tools, and smelted copper. While a few emperors over the centuries considered conquering the islands, the beneficial economics of the status quo always prevailed.

The mountainous Gtsang Prefecture is an odd exception to Xha'en dominance and maintains its effective independence due to its inaccessibility while at the same time paying lip service to the Hegemony with small tribute payments. The economic benefits of this relationship outweigh the expense and inconvenience of outright conquest, as the mines of the Tsendakar Mountains are the Hegemony's only reliable source of tin, and it is generally known that the Gtsang are easily able to destroy their mines in the event of invasion. While the Hegemony could reopen these mines if destroyed, it would be an incredibly expensive undertaking. The Tsendakar mines are also the biggest source of gold in the Hegemony, making the region even more valuable.

The growth of the Tycho Free States has opened another avenue of trade, but the elves of Eloitan and the Green Warder States have so far prevented the establishment of overland trade. Contact with the Free States must be by ship only, but the voyage south then north into the Crescent Sea is difficult and expensive.

With the ascension of the relatively enlightened Emperor Sajrac su Kar, the Hegemony seems poised to end its long isolation. Diplomatic and trade delegations make perilous journeys to distant lands such as Foere, Oceanus, and elsewhere, and goods from the Hegemony now flow to eastern kingdoms other than the Xha'en's old trading partners, the Castorhagi.

Loyalties and Diplomacy

Separated from the rest of the world by imposing mountain ranges and tangled forest, the Hegemony has existed in something of a bubble for much of its history. While relations with the Thousand Rocks, Gtsang Prefecture, and the sea Kingdom of Caerulea have long been established, these are neighboring states that cannot be ignored. For many long years, the only truly foreign power that the Hegemony traded with was the City-State of Castorhage.

Emperor Sajrac su Kar's advisors have told him that the world is changing, and that the old ways are fading, which will require new paths of thought and action. To this end, he has begun to reach out to other states of Akados, sending diplomatic missions to Foere, Bard's Gate, and elsewhere. The Castorhagi have been trading partners for a long time, but the volume of trade was always strictly controlled — this too may be changing as a growing number of Xha'en emigrants make their home in Castorhage, taking with them many cultural and social practices and institutions. The appearance of Castorhagi colonists on the Bream Islands three centuries ago created yet another crack in the Hegemony's walls of isolation, and now the emperor hopes to further expand his nation's outside contacts, using the Breams as one route to the greater world and its riches.

A handful of Xha'en merchants also made their way through the northern reaches of the Great Akadonian Forest, risking attack by hostile wood elves and dangerous creatures, to trade with the young Tycho Free States, and more eastern goods have begun to appear within Xha'en borders. These steps toward opening up Xha'en to the outside world are thus far relatively tentative but may grow in time.

Government

While the Xha'en's state is officially called a Hegemony, it is ruled by a hereditary monarchy based in the city of Xha'ahan (excluding the period in which the capital was officially moved to the city of Djir). Its great city-states — Jhohir, Aphapor, Tsadar, Rojhah, Thanalos, and others — in turn exercise authority over surrounding territories, making them de facto provinces in a larger empire.

The Hegemony's history is divided into dynasties, beginning with the founding House of Ahra (the Kingfisher). Four other dynasties — the Ophronya (Peacock), Huris (Ostrich), Tilgi (Ibis) and the present-day Rachar (Heron) — rose and fell, either peacefully or violently, and the succession continued uninterrupted for four and a half millennia.

Over the centuries, the occupant of the Imperial Throne has ranged from a powerless figurehead to an absolute monarch, with stops at

Crime in the Hegemony

As a highly lawful state, the Xha'en Hegemony abhors crime and harshly punishes even the most minor and mundane of offenses. All the same, the Hegemony is a human state, and like all humans, the Xha'en themselves are imperfect and vulnerable to corruption. Despite the best efforts of local magistrates, warrior judges, and the Silent Demons (the emperor's secret police), crime exists and flourishes in many places in the Hegemony.

While there are extensive petty crimes and many local crime bosses, particularly in slums and poorer villages, the two major axes of illegal activities are the Crimson Mask and the Triads, two groups that take quite different approaches to lawlessness. The Crimson Mask is a very old organization, run primarily by the Vilgyr clan of Djir. While this identification suggests that rooting out the Crimson Mask would be an easy task — after all, with supreme authority, why can't the emperor simply arrest every member of the Vilgyr family? — in reality, the Vilgyr themselves are quite adept at hiding in plain sight, often with a complex and sophisticated network of secret identities, legitimate business, and safehouses. The Crimson Mask has often been compared to a hydra, for when one head is killed, two more seem to take its place at new and even better hidden locations. The Crimson Mask also commands a secret network of assassins who are said to be able to kill anyone if their price is met (the price for the emperor is, naturally, so high that almost no one can afford to pay, though the Mask's assassins insist that they would be equal to the task should they ever be called upon).

The Triad gangs, on the other hand, are a far more diffuse and harder to identify group. These are independent entities organized according to very old traditions that may date to before the founding of Xha'ahan city itself. The name "triad" is based upon the gangs' use of triangular symbology, as well as the philosophy that their practices require a combination of three forces — heaven, earth, and spirit. Five major Triads — and numerous smaller ones — are believed to exist in Xha'en. Triads are involved in almost every criminal enterprise within the Hegemony and beyond, including smuggling, murder, theft, the sale of narcotics, prostitution, and slavery. Branches of the Triads have made their way beyond the Hegemony and are especially active among the Xha'en immigrants in the city of Castorhage.

XHA'EN DYNASTIES

Xha'en Calendar	Dynasty
1115–2883	Ahra
2883–3063	Ophronya
3063–3702	Huris
3703–4258	Tilgi
4258–Present	Rachar

almost every level in between. Today, the power of the emperor appears to be on the increase, with the vital and intelligent Sajrac su Kar reclaiming some of the throne's old authority. Already he has undercut the privileges of nobles in other provinces and insists that they pay taxes and visit Xha'ahan at least once every two years to report on conditions in their homelands. He has placed much of the army under his and his advisors' direct control, and dispatched diplomatic missions far abroad, triggering a growing flow of trade from the east.

How well the emperor's reforms will succeed remains to be seen. Many nobles chafe at his new taxes and decrees, and a significant number of priests of the Imperial Pantheon express conservative views and call for a return to older, more isolationist policies. A small but powerful group of nobles has banded together to form a secret society known as the White Serpent, but so far their plots against the emperor have been foiled with the aid of the warrior judges and the Silent Demons.

MILITARY

Traditionally, the Hegemony's military is made up of several armies, each maintained and commanded by its city-state of origin. Also by tradition, the army of Xha'ahan is required to be the largest and most powerful. As the Hegemony has few enemies, these armies have dwindled somewhat over the generations, and today serve mostly to safeguard the country against bandits, put down local uprisings, and patrol the border. Nevertheless, some ancient traditions continue, and the Hegemony military still contains skilled and even legendary warriors.

While armies differ in appearance and composition from one city-state to the next, all use similar military technologies and tactics. The bulk of the army is infantry, divided between unarmored skirmishers equipped with shortbows, medium infantry in leather armor (often derived from the tanned hides of elephants and rhinoceros as well as horses and cows) armed with well-engineered crossbows, and heavy infantry in chain mail or plate, usually armed with large two-handed weapons such as glaives, mauls, and halberds. Weapons and armor bear design motifs and details that are unique to their cities of origin.

Most mounted troops ride horses. The horse-archers of Thanalos are considered the finest in the realm and carry on the traditions of excellent horsemanship developed by their distant ancestors. The knights of Xha'ahan wear heavy scaled armor and fight with great lances and swords, while the lancers of Aban Rha are lightly-armored, mobile, and deadly as both scouts and shock cavalry.

Several unusual units exist within the Hegemony's military, though most of their greatest exploits took place in the distant past. The Tiger-Riders of Xha'ahan are probably the best known of these elite groups. An all-female unit of armored warriors, mounted on tigers bred for both size and ferocity and armed with lances, swords and bows, the Tiger-Riders are credited with winning numerous battles for the Hegemony's leading city-state. Their numbers have dwindled over time, and where once over a thousand served at the personal command of the emperor, only a single regiment of 300 remains.

The city-state of Djir was long able to resist the dominance of Xha'ahan through the excellence and professionalism of its army, which included its legendary aerial cavalry, mounted on griffons from the Odarnadar Mountains. Like the Tiger-Riders, the Griffon Knights are

today a shadow of their former selves, consisting of a single squadron of six, maintained almost entirely due to tradition.

Despite the suppression of halflings throughout the Hegemony, the city-state of Rojhah maintains better relations with its halfling population and has for many generations maintained several regiments of halfling skirmishers equipped with bows, slings, and darts. These halflings are employed as scouts and rangers and often participate in successful campaigns on behalf of the Hegemony. Other non-humans occasionally serve with the Hegemony military, usually as contractors or mercenaries — dwarven engineers and half-elf scouts are most commonly employed in this fashion.

Arcane and divine magic have played important roles in the Hegemony military, even more than in the eastern kingdoms. An entire coterie of battle-wizards serves the emperor and can be called up on extremely short notice. It was this command of magic and its application to warfare that helped Xha'ahan dominate the region's other city-states, and the emperor continues to maintain a large number of these battle-wizards. In the past, each regiment of the Hegemony's united army contained one or more war-priests who commanded both offensive and healing magic, though this tradition is currently in decline along with other military practices.

The Xha'en maintain only a small standing navy, as few major threats come from the sea. Emperors in need of ships can press civilian vessels into service or commission the construction of ships intended for short-term, fairly limited purposes such as amphibious invasion or the suppression of piracy. The need for either function passed long ago, and today the Hegemony remains a largely non-naval power. The vessels of Ankhura and Castorhage patrol the outer waters but are restricted from approaching the Xha'en coastline too closely.

Overall, the Hegemony military remains strong and is easily the equal of any nation that might present a threat, but generations of relative peace have sapped much of Xha'en's more militaristic tendencies, and today the army has been largely relegated to civil duties and the suppression of minor threats to the nation. Emperor Sajrac su Kar has undertaken a program of modernization, sending diplomats to study foreign militaries, reorganizing old and inefficient units, and putting the armies of the Hegemony's various member-cities under his own direct command. Needless to say, this irritates many of the cities' nobles, especially members of the radical White Serpent Society.

MAJOR THREATS

The Xha'en Hegemony is one of the most stable of known nations. Safe behind nearly-impassible mountains and forests, the Hegemony has few real outside enemies, and those within its borders lack the power to do more than inconvenience the emperor.

The nearest states with any power are the relatively new Tycho Free States located on the eastern side of the near-impenetrable Great Akadonian Forest. Engaged mostly in a struggle for growth and survival, these states have little interest in antagonizing their larger neighbor to the west and welcome the handful of Xha'en merchants who make the difficult journey through the forest to trade.

The Utterends in the south are the least-settled portion of the Hegemony and are home to independent groups of humans and non-humans. Relations with these groups vary, from friendly trade agreements to outright hostility, with human bandits, humanoid raiders, and angry warlords attacking Xha'en settlements and merchants. The Xha'en military responds to these provocations, but the sheer inaccessibility of much of the region limits their effectiveness.

The most significant threats to the Hegemony come from inside its own borders. A new emperor has taken the throne, hoping to awaken a sleepy nation and set it back on the road to greatness. To this end, Sajrac su Kar has rattled many cages — taking greater control of the state military, dismissing advisors and bureaucrats from old families, improving local administration, sacking corrupt governors, and making tentative moves toward ending the Hegemony's isolation from the rest of the world.

While these moves have met with some approval, especially from younger and more progressive Xha'en, they have been frowned upon by an increasingly alarmed establishment. Established noble houses, the rulers of various city-states, military officers, and doctrinaire priests of the Imperial Pantheon have all expressed dissatisfaction and, in some cases, outright defiance of the new emperor's edicts.

A few nobles banded together into a secret society known as the White Serpent and intend to depose or kill the emperor. So far, the emperor has survived two attempts on his life by masked assassins, and has dispatched his secret police, the Silent Demons, to find out who is behind the conspiracy and bring them to justice.

The Hegemony has maintained trade relations with Castorhage for centuries and has come to warily accept the presence of Castorhagi colonists on the Bream Islands. However, the expansion of both nations' influence may lead to conflict. Some believe that the Breams' governor, Lord Duke Taneth, is building up naval and land forces with the intention of invading Quy Island, thus expanding his nation's holdings and potentially provoking war with the Hegemony. This outcome, sure to be disastrous for all involved, is one that all save Taneth and his allies seem determined to avoid.

WILDERNESS AND ADVENTURES

Although it remains one of the largest and most powerful states in Akados, the Xha'en Hegemony is not well-known outside its frontiers, and opportunities abound for those who wish to travel there, as well as those who were born and bred in the region. Surrounded by a changing world, the Hegemony will soon be experiencing seismic changes in its culture and society, surely creating many chances for adventure and good fortune.

The central regions of the Hegemony — the lands around Lake Pantai and the fertile Plains of Xha — have been settled for millennia. Other regions, such as the wild Sengejia Hills, the rugged Tsendakar Mountains, and wilderness in the Utterends remain lightly populated, minimally settled, and largely unexplored.

The depths of the northern Akadonian Forest — and particularly the wild elven realm of Eloitan — present a significant barrier between the Hegemony and the growing Tycho Free States to the east. These former penal colonies have vital economies and may prove important in the new trade routes springing up along the Crescent Sea and linking the Free Coast to the great city of Castorhage and other ports. The forest is indeed an imposing barrier, thick with ancient trees, tangled undergrowth, treacherous ravines, and deep, swift rivers. The presence of hostile local wildlife is only the beginning of the challenges facing those who would venture into the forest. The Eloitan elves, xenophobic and hostile to all but their own kind, lie in wait for unwary travelers.

All of these factors make crossing the forest a near-suicidal proposition, yet eager merchants and explorers on both sides continue to make inroads, venturing into the forest and — rarely — actually making it out alive. Rumors of treasure — lost elven gold, hollow hills that contain the wonders of the ancient reptilian civilization that once flourished here, and the remains of the old Castorhagi fortresses — continue to draw adventurers despite a depressingly high fatality rate.

Many other adventuring opportunities present themselves, even in the relatively cosmopolitan regions of the Hegemony. The Crimson Mask and the Triads control most of the Hegemony's crime, and also maintain an extensive smuggling and assassination network — both enterprises that adventurers may encounter or be drawn into. The nobles of the city of Djir maintain a private hunting preserve in the nearby Earos Hills, where they seek out the region's exotic megafauna, and these expeditions always require assistance from professional trackers, hunters, and explorers. Diplomatic and trade parties regularly visit the Sea Kingdom of Caerulea and the dwarves of Ankhura, and those parties often require aid from warriors, mages, healers, and the like.

XHA'AHAN, CITY OF (CAPITAL)

Ruler: Emperor Sajrac su Kar Rachar
Government: hereditary monarchy
Population: 1,000,000 (mostly Xha'en, small numbers of halflings and dwarves)
Technology Level: Renaissance

The grand city and capital of the Hegemony, Xha'ahan has occupied its current site for nearly three and a quarter millennia. Starting life as a small river town in what was subsequently declared to be Year 0 XC, Xha'ahan grew steadily in population and influence, particularly after the construction of the Lujhiran Dam in 1115 XC (−187 I.R.). During this period, the Xha'en engaged in a series of public works and improvements, demolishing old neighborhoods and rebuilding along carefully planned lines. The resulting city consisted of three distinct sections, each enclosed by graceful crenelated walls: the Imperial Palace that rises majestically from the precise center of Xha'ahan; the Inner City, home to nobles, temples, government offices, and bureaucrats; and the Outer City where most of Xha'ahan's residents live, along with much of the merchant class. Paved streets and canals crisscrossing the Outer and Inner Cities allow a relatively free flow of traffic, and both the Inner and Outer walls are accessible through massive gates, two per side, for a total of eight on each wall.

Over generations, Xha'ahan's population has spilled out beyond the Outer Wall to form vast labyrinthine slums where crime and violence flourish. Also beyond the Outer Wall lies the Xha'ahan army's main encampment, where the bulk of the city's military, including the legendary Tiger-Riders, are permanently stationed.

While it is not the most ancient city in the region (the mystical settlement of Duam in the Gtsang Prefecture takes that honor), Xha'ahan retains a palpable sense of history. Structures from the earliest periods of Xha'ahan history stand side-by-side with modern apartments, shops, and government buildings. Cobbled streets rise above broad canals crossed at regular intervals by picturesque bridges. Boats of every description make their way across the city by water, while the streets are crowded with foot traffic, wagons, and dray beasts.

The Inner City is graced with public parks, the estates of the wealthy, statuary, gilded temples, and stern government buildings. Prominent features include the Azure Tower, a decorative structure built early in the city's history that provides a panoramic view of the surrounding countryside, and the Great Observatory of Xha, another tower surmounted by a water-powered clock and an elaborate array of telescopes, astrolabes, armillary spheres, and other astronomical devices. Here, scholars and priests chart the heavens and make note of significant celestial events.

The Imperial Palace towers over the rest of the city. Its walls were first laid down during the great rebuilding of 1115 XC (−187 I.R.) and have been added to over centuries. Dark red and decorated with yellow-gold protective icons, the palace is considered to be the sole domain of rulers and their households. This tradition has waxed and waned over the years, and today the Emperor Sajrac su Kar has opened up the palace and allows visits from priests, government officials, and even a handful of foreign dignitaries, including representatives of the High Burgess of Bard's Gate and an official diplomatic delegation from the eastern nation of Foere.

ABAN RHA, CITY OF

Ruler: Princess Iriku sa Dri
Government: hereditary monarchy
Population: 185,000 (180,000 Xha'en, 5,000 halflings)
Technology Level: Medieval

Located in the heart of the fertile Plains of Xha, Aban Rha is the breadbasket of the Xha'en Hegemony, surrounded by vast fields of grain and seemingly-endless orchards of fruit trees. Its walls, parks, and public buildings are all decorated with colorful agricultural symbols, lucky signs, and motifs suggesting fertility and rich harvests.

Agricultural goods from Aban Rha are shipped throughout the Hegemony — north to Rojhah, east along the wide Taode River and the River Road, and down to Thanalos and the southern provinces beyond. During harvest season, caravans enter and leave the city around the clock.

As a result, Aban Rha is a prosperous city with little severe poverty. While the peasants are still poor, they are generally better off in terms of food and shelter than Xha'en elsewhere in the Hegemony.

Rich Aban Rha citizens, on the other hand, are the wealthiest in the land, with the exception of the emperor himself. Vast sprawling estates surround the city, and countless luxurious mansions fill the city proper. Gilded barges ply the river alongside lumbering merchant vessels, lavishly decorated with decadent accommodations and small armies of servants. Elaborate processions leave the city in good weather to travel the countryside, setting up extensive encampments where the wealthy can "enjoy the wonders of nature." Lavish parades, festivals, and mock-battles are held on holidays and at the whim of the rich.

The inhabitants of other cities, especially the grim militarists of Tsadar and the old wealth of Djir, frown upon the excesses of Aban Rha, though it's known that outsiders often travel here to partake of its pleasures and wonders. Aban Rha nobles are generally considered to be somewhat boorish, vulgar types who flaunt their wealth in pointlessly ostentatious ways. For their part, the Aban Rha don't seem terribly concerned, for no matter how judgmental the rest of the world may be, Aban Rha gold is always accepted everywhere.

APHAPOR, CITY OF

Ruler: Prince Ydirac su Qol and Princess Amaya sa Qol
Government: hereditary monarchy
Population: 210,000 (177,500 Xha'en, 15,000 Senge, 9,000 halflings, 8,000 hill dwarves, 500 other)
Technology Level: High Middle Ages

Located along the shores of Lake Pantai and just south of the Sengejia Hills, Aphapor has a reputation as an open and tolerant city, where the wary Senge tribesmen can come to trade and treat with the Xha'en, and where goods from the wilds and exotic lands to the east can be obtained.

Aphapor grew up amid the chaos of the Thousand Kingdoms period, cementing its role as a crossroads and trading city with its central location amid several other growing city-states. Though it was never as populous or powerful as Xha'ahan or Tsadar, Aphapor nevertheless became an important member of the alliance that led to the formation of the Hegemony, transforming its trade and mercantile contacts into a diplomatic network, and sending its ambassadors to the cities of the Plains of Xha ready to negotiate, threaten, or cajole those reluctant to join the new nation.

Aphapor's loyalty to the Hegemony was tested somewhat when the Lujhiran Dam flooded the old Pantai Lowlands where the city maintained extensive agricultural interests, reducing Aphapor's access to neighboring territories. Official protests — couched in respectful but ominous terms — were sent to Xha'ahan, for the once-prosperous city began to suffer from its isolation, with food shortages and population pressures growing.

Fortunately for all, the issue was resolved peacefully, with Xha'ahan contributing to the construction of extensive lakeside shipping facilities, signing lucrative agreements with the Aphapor government, and assisting in the clearing of new lands for farming. A second diplomatic tightrope act was needed to pacify the Senge, who resented the city's expansion into their lands — the Senge had been forced out of their ancestral territories already, and now despite their overall pacifistic nature, they were reluctant to be squeezed out again.

This dilemma was also solved through diplomacy, with the city ceding arable territory to the Senge, offering them exclusive employment, and distributing a portion of their farms' produce directly to the tribes free of charge. This last practice continues today and is accepted by Aphapor farmers as the "Senge Tax." After several decades of tension, Aphapor's relations with its neighbors began to improve.

Aphapor today is a picturesque city, its white walls rising above the waters of Lake Pantai, and surrounded by a network of roads, small villages, farms, and Senge encampments. The city's reasonably good relations with the Senge has led to a bit of a cultural renaissance within Aphapor. Senge artwork, folklore, and music are all studied and archived here, along with histories of ancient cultures and nations that occupied Xha'en lands in the distant past. The Hegemony's tentative contact with eastern states such as Castorhage, Reme, and Foere is followed

with great interest, and generally supported. A trickle of goods from the Tycho Free States and elsewhere has found its way into Aphapor, where they are studied and consumed with great enthusiasm. The city's rulers, Prince Ydirac su Qol and Princess Amaya sa Qol, have on occasion dressed their official guards in the styles of other nations, and have officially sponsored work to translate works of eastern literature and drama into the Xaon tongue.

DJIR, CITY OF

Ruler: Great Prince Nalas su Tan Djir
Government: hereditary monarchy
Population: 500,000 (451,950 Xha'en, 23,000 mountain dwarves, 15,000 halflings, 9,000 hill dwarves, 1,000 half-elves, 50 wild elves)
Technology Level: Medieval

Djir is generally acknowledged to be the second most-influential city in the Hegemony and was even the Hegemony's capital for a time. Its status was eventually revoked and primacy returned to the mighty Xha'ahan, but Djir emerged unharmed. Its ruler, once dubbed "emperor," is today given the slightly less grand but still impressive title of "great prince."

Surrounded by a tall hexagonal wall, Djir is built in a different style than its rival, with tall red stone buttressed towers, squat square homes with spacious central courtyards, public plazas, and great aviaries where many exotic breeds of bright-feathered birds can be seen. The city's phoenix-sigil symbolizes its fascination with winged creatures, as does its legendary griffon cavalry, once the pride of Djir's military but now reduced in the long peace to a single squadron of six individuals based at the city's central edifice, known as the Phoenix Palace.

Like Xha'ahan, Djir's population has expanded beyond its graceful city walls, but adequate planning and public funding largely prevents the creation of slums or other ugly sprawls. Districts beyond the wall are administered with the same level of bureaucratic efficiency as the rest of the city, and feature the same broad streets, attractive buildings, and public spaces.

Despite its beauty and tranquility, all is not well within Djir, for it is known that the Crimson Mask criminal syndicate controls much of what goes on there, with many nobles and officials in its pay. Though the city of Djir presents a pristine and spotless image to the world, the Crimson Mask represents a rot at its heart.

EJINDOR, PREFECTURE OF

Capital: Ejindor (population 85,000)
Ruler: Governor Jerain sa Kha
Government: vassal of Xha'en
Population: 500,000 (336,500 Xha'en, 65,000 halfling, 40,000 tengu, 18,500 tabaxi, 17,000 half-elf, 12,000 hill dwarf, 11,000 other)
Resources: cloth, dyes, fishing, foodstuffs, grain, trade hub
Currency: Xha'en, mixed
Technology Level: Medieval

The prefecture of Ejindor consists primarily of the trade city of Ejindor and surrounding farms. Though on its official maps the Xha'en Hegemony extends much farther south and east than the prefecture of Ejindor, in practical terms, Ejindor functions as a border town between the Hegemony and the wilder lands beyond it. As such, the population of the city and the surrounding countryside tends to include more than the average of Xha'en's various minority peoples, particularly tengu, tabaxi, halflings, and half-elves. In addition, the average monthly population of foreigners visiting the city of Ejindor is nearly 10 times that of other typical cities in the Hegemony.

For these reasons, as well as the prefecture's proximity to the controversial Ghon Complex boarding school, laws in Ejindor are strict, curfews early, taxes high, and the military ever-present. Despite these potential drawbacks, however, Ejindor has a reputation for treating visitors well and all residents fairly. Governor Jerain sa Kha is largely beloved by her citizens, known for her wise and measured interpretations of even the strictest laws, and her just sentencing when punishment is necessary.

RELIGION

Though Governor Jerain sa Kha personally observes only Imperial Pantheon religious practices and holidays, all religions willing to play well with their neighbors are welcome in Ejindor and are permitted to make public their festivals. The summer solstice festival is especially multicultural and considered by seasoned travelers to be a must-see event in the region.

TRADE AND COMMERCE

Trade and commerce are the primary reasons for Ejindor's existence. Without them, the city would be neither so large, nor so diverse, nor so economically relevant to southern Xha'en. It boasts several great public markets, the largest of which is the river market, where one can buy fish and seafood of all kinds, as well as foreign goods brought to Ejindor up the Jhoni River. This is also where locals come to sell any goods found to be in high demand among river merchants and captains.

The farmers' market on the east side of the city is where farmers bring in the fruits of their fields and sell delightful local confections, and where visitors from surrounding regions bring livestock for sale. Finally, to the south of the city stands the smaller, covered, year-round market hall where the finest of local crafts and creations are sold alongside the works of famous Xha'en tradespeople and exotic foreign riches from all over the world. The indoor market is the most heavily guarded (and taxed), but it cannot be argued that its offerings are a wonder to behold, even in the dead of winter (when it tends to be dominated by goods crafted from materials gathered in the Cauldron to the south of the prefecture).

LOYALTIES AND DIPLOMACY

Ejindor is a loyal vassal-prefecture of the Xha'en Hegemony but it often finds itself in a delicate place politically as it is so far away from the center of Xha'en's politics and has such a large and constant influx of foreign contact. To avoid arousing suspicions of sedition, Ejindor puts on twice the show of imperial loyalty that other Xha'en cities might do. Governor Jerain sa Kha manages this balance with grace and dignity, but not without a certain degree of discord between herself and Grand Teacher of the Ghon Complex, the other most powerful appointed leader in the region.

Indeed, though even Governor Jerain sa Kha only knows or suspects less than half of the "education" techniques being used to influence the Ghon Complex children, rumor has it that a small rebel organization has sprung up in Ejindor with the intention of staging a prison break and freeing the Ghon Complex children. If Governor Jerain sa Kha knows of any such thing, it would appear she has chosen to turn a blind eye, which could potentially bring terrible ramifications down on Ejindor if the situation were presented to the emperor in the wrong way.

GOVERNMENT

Governor Jerain sa Kha has authority to run Ejindor as she sees fit, though the commander of the local military garrison reports to military superiors elsewhere in the Hegemony rather than to the governor. Governor Jerain sa Kha and Commander Mornys su Rin work well together, however, so this division of authority does not interfere with the smooth functioning of the prefecture. Governor Jerain sa Kha serves as primary lawmaker (after the emperor, of course) and judge and makes all non-military appointments, prioritizing skill and integrity above connections or flattery. Military appointments are the province of Commander Mornys su Rin, who also oversees the military in their regular service as the watch and police.

MILITARY

Unless Ejindor is actively threatened by war, defense of the town is left to the larger-than-average resident garrison of professional soldiers. These troops enforce the curfew, guard the town's imperial taxes until they can be shipped north, and otherwise function as police. Their unit includes two wizards and two clerics, none of whom is particularly high in rank or skill.

MAJOR THREATS

The Jhoni Falls to the north do much to defend Ejindor from river-borne threats, and the town maintains good (or at least civil) relations with all its neighbors. The threat of retaliation from the might of Xha'en is enough to make any force think twice about attacking the city. As such, the greatest threats to Ejindor tend either to be economic, such as the tengu bandits that disrupt shipping in the Jhoni Canyon, or come from individual monsters, such as the salamanders that have been known to follow the Jhoni River downstream from the Cauldron in summer.

Of course, one looming threat is the eventual loss of Governor Jerain sa Kha. Under Governor Jerain sa Kha's rule, the markets thrive and, despite the high imperial taxes, the citizens mostly prosper. The only problem is that Jerain sa Kha is 87 years old. She is improbably hale for her age as well as sharp of faculties, but even the healthiest of humans — even with unlimited access to magical healing — must ever more often play dice with death the older they get. Jerain sa Kha is aware that one day soon her luck will run out, and mortality will win the round. She is doing her best to prepare her people for her passing, but the future of Ejindor remains uncertain.

The Ejindor prefecture is an appointed rather than inherited position. Jerain sa Kha has begun to float suggestions for her successor to representatives of the court at Xha'ahan, but so far none has been all that favorably received. For now, Jerain sa Kha remains alive and well, and Ejindor is a happy and diverse city, strict laws notwithstanding. Only time will tell what the emperor will decide in appointing the next prefect.

GHON COMPLEX

(GOAN, one syllable)

Ruler: Grand Teacher Almalandra sa Pol

Government: Xha'en imperial appointment

Population: 412 (354 Xha'en, 20 Senge, 15 halfling, 10 tengu, 6 hill dwarf, 5 half-elf, 1 mountain dwarf, 1 tabaxi)

Technology Level: Medieval with some Renaissance tools

The Ghon Complex, named for its founder Ghon su Pol (grandfather of the current Grand Teacher), is a prison-like boarding school in the southwestern Xha'en Hegemony. Whenever a dissident, rebel, traitor, or other political criminal is convicted in the Xha'en Hegemony, presuming said criminal is sufficiently high-profile, high-status, or wealthy, that criminal's children, young siblings, and sometimes even nieces or nephews are sent to the Ghon Complex for education, training, and propaganda.

The outside of the complex appears to be a sprawling military fortress, nigh-impenetrable and crawling with guards. Inside, other than the solitary confinement chambers in the basement, the Ghon Complex is open and cheery, well-appointed, and full of gardens, practice yards, and other deceptively inviting facilities. It boasts one of the largest (and most painstakingly curated) libraries in all of Xha'en.

HISTORY AND PEOPLE

Founded in 4763 XC (3461 I.R.) as part of a "compassionate" consolidation of the new Rachar dynasty's power, the Ghon Complex was formed with the idea that the young children of dissidents and traitors need not necessarily be executed to prevent them from following in their parents' footsteps (as was sometimes done during older dynasties) or expensively imprisoned for life (as was done during much of the Tilgi dynasty). Instead, it was suggested that young children of political criminals could be placed in a special school to teach them to grow up as useful and honorable citizens, potentially able to cleanse their family names of all rebellious taint. Thus, the Ghon Complex was born.

While the education that the Ghon Complex children receive is relatively high caliber — offering many noble skills such as reading, calligraphy, gardening, classical dance, and music, and even science, magic, tactics, swordplay, and other martial arts for those deemed sufficiently loyal — it is nevertheless a highly manipulative program designed to destroy independent thinking and to obscure all the faults and flaws of the Hegemony.

The history taught at the Ghon Complex is particularly fictionalized, making all the rulers out to have been glorious, honorable, and wise, with the sole exception of the lich-emperor, who is portrayed as a usurper. All dissidents, rebels, traitors, and similar are portrayed as cruel villains, including the children's own relatives. While treatment is usually strict but humane, children showing even the slightest signs of "following in traitorous footsteps" are harshly punished, with methods ranging from extra chores, to missed meals, to public canings, to solitary confinement.

RELIGION

Religious practice in the Ghon Complex is highly ritualized and entirely compulsory for all residents. Other practices may be tolerated in private, so long as the practitioner is believed to revere the Imperial Pantheon above all else, and the specific practices in question have not been deemed seditious.

LOYALTIES AND DIPLOMACY

Though the Ghon Complex is dogmatically loyal to the emperor and the Hegemony, it is not universally beloved by the Xha'en people. For the most part, the activities of the Ghon Complex are kept secret, and it is advertised only as a special school for children chosen by the emperor. It is not entirely certain even the extent to which the emperor has been accurately informed of the Ghon Complex's methodology.

For those who know the truth, the Ghon Complex is controversial, and it does have powerful enemies within the empire. Because of its purpose of "inspiring loyalty to the emperor," however, openly opposing the complex can be somewhat tricky, politically speaking. As such, a subtle political dance goes on continuously behind the scenes within the imperial court, wherein enemies of the complex try to have it shut down, while those sympathetic to its methods and purpose defend it and keep it funded.

GOVERNMENT

Unusually militaristic in organization for a school, the Ghon Complex is ultimately under the absolute dictatorship of Grand Teacher Almalandra sa Pol. A serious and oddly compassionate-seeming woman, Almalandra is adamant that her school is beneficial to society and kind to the children. If nothing else, she does not speak inaccurately when she says that older policies toward the children of political criminals were crueler still, and that many lands still practice worse atrocities. However misguided and disturbing, the Ghon Complex is at least intended to reform and teach rather than to merely torment or control.

MILITARY

The Ghon Complex is always heavily guarded by imperial troops under Almalandra sa Pol's command. While the Ghon Complex teachers are included in the population statistics, the military presence is not, especially since its complement may be doubled or tripled if any particularly politically volatile children are in residence. Assigned companies are rotated out regularly to avoid soldiers learning too much about the specific children in residence or why they are there.

JHOHIR, CITY OF

Ruler: Prince Aranis su Tan Darondan
Government: hereditary monarchy
Population: 325,000 (247,000 Xha'en, 35,000 halflings, 30,000 mountain dwarves, 11,000 hill dwarves, 1,000 Senge, 100 half-elves, 900 others)
Technology Level: Medieval

Located along a broad strait sheltered by the Island of Quy, Jhohir is the Xha'en Hegemony's leading port city and hosts ship traffic from all along the western Xha'en coast. Extensive docking, repair, and warehousing facilities are maintained by the Darondan clan, who have been masters of this city-state for several millennia.

In the past, Jhohir was a powerbroker in the struggles for dominance in the Xha'en region. Shipping and mercantile contracts from the Darondan were used to favor one city-state over another, and Jhohir mercenaries fought for any city that could pay their price. Strict neutrality kept the city relatively safe, but the rise of Xha'ahan and the eventual formation of the Hegemony significantly reduced Jhohir's influence and forced the Darondan to focus more on their shipping and trade functions.

Though the Darondan clan, in theory, rules the city and its members or their close associates hold all major offices, the true power in the city is the local chapter of the Triads, which controls a secret network of criminals, killers, and smugglers. Triad operatives hold obscure but significant positions throughout Jhohir, and nothing comes into or goes out of the city without the express permission of the Triad leader, a mysterious boss whose true identity is not known, though some claim that she masquerades as a humble beggar or cart seller. Under her guidance, Jhohir has become one of (if not the) major centers of Triad strength in the Hegemony, and so far, few suspect the full extent of its influence.

Otherwise, Jhohir is what one might expect in an ancient city that is crossroads to an empire — noisy, dirty, crowded, with a huge gulf between the walled and guarded mansions of the wealthy and the rude hovels of the poor, which continue to spread around the city like a dark stain. Folk of every description can be found here, from arrogant Xha'en nobles (the Darondan are the most arrogant of the lot, aware as they are of their family's past greatness, and how far they have fallen since the glory days) to humble Gtsang monks, Anari merchants and their guards, exotic southerners including the occasional cat- or ravenfolk, and even a handful of Senge tribesfolk who have made the long journey here to obtain food and clothing for their people in exchange for handmade goods or service to wealthy patrons.

ROJHAH, CITY OF

Ruler: Prince Inodaren su Ber
Government: hereditary monarchy
Population: 420,000 (325,350 Xha'en, 85,000 halflings, 9,000 hill dwarves, 250 Senge, 100 half-elves, 300 others)
Technology Level: Medieval

Rojhah is one of the oldest cities in the Hegemony, and for a time threatened to eclipse Xha'ahan as the region's dominant state. Seeing the futility of a long, drawn-out military or economic conflict with their rivals, the folk of Xha'ahan chose the diplomatic route and formed alliances and trade relationships with Rojhah that eventually led to the formation of the Hegemony. The union proved prosperous to both sides, and now Rojhah is a wealthy, cosmopolitan settlement in the middle of the fertile Plains of Xha.

Though halflings often fare poorly in competition with humans in the Hegemony, Rojhah and its environs represent a better life for many small folk. Halfling farms dot the countryside, a thriving halfling quarter boasts shops, merchants, inns, and restaurants, and several regiments of halfling bowmen and slingers can be found in Rojhah's army.

Rojhah is not an especially attractive city, with ancient weathered walls and vast, dingy stands of undistinguished buildings and streets that are often choked with commerce and filthy with the passage of countless thousands. Even the grand palaces of the wealthy and the stern government structures are strangely mundane. All the same, Rojhah is a vital city with an ancient and vibrant culture — music, opera, sculpture, and ceramics are all considered the finest in Xha'en lands, drawing visitors and patrons from all across the vast lands of the Hegemony. The Rojhah Opera House has been the scene of many classic performances and the premieres of numerous shows that went on to become enduring classics.

THANALOS, CITY OF

Ruler: Prince Yonnis su Ang
Government: hereditary monarchy
Population: 580,000 (505,500 Xha'en, 40,000 halflings, 17,000 hill dwarves, 8,000 tabaxi, 4,500 tengu, 3,000 half-elves, 1,600 Senge, 400 others)
Technology Level: Medieval

Located at the southern end of the great River Road to Tsadar, Thanalos is the southernmost great city on the Plains of Xha and as such is the leading transportation hub of the Xha'en Hegemony. So important is access to and from this city that its great walls were disassembled long ago, leaving the city to sprawl unchecked across the flatlands around it.

A striking combination of modernity and the rustic frontier, Thanalos stands at a crossroads between the urbane north and the wild south. The old city — that portion of Thanalos that lies within the old, now-demolished walls — boasts many magnificent structures that date back to before the founding of the Hegemony, carefully maintained and repaired by the city's leaders. A near-religious respect for the past is common among Thanalos' nobility, for many have ancestries that can be traced back thousands of years. This backward-looking attitude stands somewhat at odds with the rest of the city, which is inhabited by thousands of new arrivals, many from such distant lands as the Utterends. Here, buildings are built overnight, shops and stalls crowd the chaotic streets, trade caravans are constantly coming and going, and the population rises and falls unexpectedly. The focus is on the future, on expansion and on new ways of living, doing business, and making money. As the stodgy nobles remain in their ancient buildings dreaming of the past, the city's new inhabitants have created a vital and chaotic society where almost anything can be bought and sold, crime runs rampant and fortunes can be made and lost in the course of a single day.

Tsadar, City of

Ruler: Princess-General Hilelia sa Fahn Tsadar
Government: hereditary monarchy
Population: 375,000 (354,600 Xha'en, 15,000 halflings, 3,000 hill dwarves, 1,200 Senge, 1,000 half-elves, 200 others)
Technology Level: Medieval

Before the birth of the Xha'en Hegemony, numerous city-states competed for dominance, and with its elite footmen and fearsome scythed chariots, Tsadar was among the leading powers. Ultimately worn down by the growing influence of Xha'ahan, Tsadar eventually joined in alliance with its former enemy and was rewarded with a leading role when the great Hegemony was finally born.

Tsadar remains a stern military state. Though its warriors are not the most numerous in the Hegemony army, they are acknowledged to be the finest. The armories and smithies of Tsadar produce high quality weapons and armor, though long years of relative peace have made their martial prowess less significant to the Hegemony as a whole.

The city itself is perfectly square, with thick, battlemented walls that slant inward to shrug off siege missiles, and heavy gates crafted from iron and steel. Like other Xha'en cities, Tsadar cannot contain the entirety of its population, but the outlying communities are carefully planned and laid out, with grids of paved streets and farmlands of near geometric perfection.

The creation of Lake Pantai when Xha'ahan erected the Lujhiran Dam changed the city's geography somewhat. The main walls sit atop a bluff above the new artificial lake, with switchbacks leading down to the water where docks and warehouses have been constructed to accommodate lake traffic.

The Utterends

Capital: Shan'daren
Notable Settlements: Chafa Temple, Quiris Meadow, Tchur-i-kahn, Tahngari
Ruler: none (High Duke chosen in times of war; Lord Dragon consulted for conflict resolution)
Government: nomadic bands.
Population: 120,000 (39,000 Xha'en, 34,000 tengu, 27,000 tabaxi, 13,500 lizardfolk, 6,000 wild elf, 500 other)
Monstrous: stirges, spire monkeys, giant silverfish, chike, serpent creepers, boobries, tombotu, blaze boas, hanu-nagas, malkeens, bloodsoaker vines, vile drakes, wood elementals (any region); giant flying piranha, bloodworms, gray dragons (coastal regions only)
Languages: Guivoc, Elven, Xha'en, Tengu, Tabaxi, Common, Draconic
Religion: ancestral spirits, animism, tribal pantheons
Resources: rare magical herbs, rare poisons, rare intoxicants, tabaxi steel
Currency: gold, silver, steel, and iron ingots; barter; Xha'en
Technology Level: Iron Age

A proud and ancient mélange of nomadic people dwell in a vast and deadly swamp once considered in Xha'en legend to be the location of the utter ends of the earth. This is the nation most commonly referred to as the Utterends (or variously Gyuubou, Guivo, or Gibo in different local tongues). To outsiders, the Utterends often seem like a hellhole: sweaty, primitive, and perilous, but that is only the barest surface of this deep and complex land.

It is true that the creatures of the Utterends, both magical and mundane, are often deadly and terrible, many venomous or bloodthirsty, and some even possessed of a vile and cruel intelligence. The Utterends are not an easy place to make one's abode. Nevertheless, these terrifying swamps have become a haven and a refuge to many who call it home.

An isolated pocket of improbable weather, the Utterends are heated by winds blowing down from the Cauldron to the north, hotspring runoff from several springs on the mountains' southern half, and by underwater springs and volcanoes off the coast, a continuation of the Cauldron range. This combination creates a unique climate in all the world, with bizarre wildlife and weather seemingly wholly divorced from the seasons around them.

Never cold and always damp, the Utterends has a "dry" season in what surrounding regions call late winter and most of spring, and a monsoon season that ramps up in late spring and doesn't typically wind down until "winter" solstice. This pattern (and the heat) makes the Utterends' main agricultural cycle quite short, with a planting celebration for the new year and harvest before summer solstice. A second harvest cycle takes place during the wetter months for plants that prefer to be partially submerged.

Many rare and valuable plants grow well in the humid Utterends, though all attempts at agriculture here come with a plethora of other challenges. It is perhaps due to the sheer diversity of hardships in the Utterends' region that so many disparate peoples have been able to come together to form a cohesive society based upon mutual cooperation, support, and boundless hospitality.

History and People

As far as the historical record can show, tabaxi were the original natives of the Utterends. Locked in constant war with the brutal chike, the desperately beleaguered tabaxi began a millennium-spanning tradition (unlike no other known tabaxi community in the world) of welcoming any and all fellow humanoids willing to fight alongside them in their struggle for survival. The earliest remains of this culture show that it was bloody and warlike, nearly as cruel as that of the chike themselves, and that the first group to join the tabaxi were the lizardfolk, who immigrated north and west from the Akadonian Forest. Humanoid cats and lizards shared the land in close alliance and learned to prosper together.

The next group to join the Utterends mix were tengu, who moved south from the Xha'en region in response to human expansion. The tengu, too, formed a friendly alliance with the others and brought with them new types of military tactics and a partial tempering of bloodthirsty patterns. Records of this era are sparse, but the bas-relief sculptures all over the Chafa (or Tcha-i-F'ha) Temple walls indicate repeated attempts to make peace with the chike during the next several centuries and to bring them into the multi-species fold. But such efforts were met always by rejection, misdirection, or betrayal. No chike records of the era have been found.

Local legend says that 5,000 years passed this way, though elven scholars believe this number to be wild hyperbole.

The next group to join the growing Utterends culture came nearly 1,600 years ago, in and around Xha'en Calendar year 3230 (1928 I.R.). These were an influx of Xha'en rebels defeated in their attempt to oust the powerful Huris dynasty and driven into the Utterends to escape Imperial retaliation for their treason. This influx marked the beginning of the Guivoc language, as well as a more streamlined integration of the three humanoid peoples with their new human immigrants. What had formerly been a trade pidgin of Tabaxi, Draconic, and Tengu was joined by Xha'en and recorded using Xha'en characters on scrolls for the first time. Several multi-species communities sprang up during this period, and the pidgin evolved into a full-vocabulary creole. The Guivoc creole has since become the dominant language of the region, though all four of the languages it is derived from are still spoken in places, and most inhabitants speak at least three local languages.

Though no one knows precisely how it happened, the next major event in Utterends' history was the Dragon Plagues in XC 3678–83 (2376–81 I.R.). During this period, a wave of hideous, magic-resistant poxes swept through the Utterends, annihilating the majority of the region's reptilian humanoids and dragon-related creatures. Ordinary reptiles and non-dragon magical beasts were unaffected, but all other dragonids and humanoid reptilians were felled by the thousands. These species-spanning poxes are believed to be the work of Xha'en Emperor Amaran su Bha (later revealed to be a lich), perhaps as an unintended side-effect of experiments regarding undead dragons. Wherever the plagues came from, their death toll was high, and they departed as mysteriously as they arrived.

When the plagues finally passed, many species were extinct in the Utterends, including kobolds, black dragons, hydras, and countless others. The lizardfolk population dwindled into the hundreds, though by a cruel twist of fate, the ever-hostile chike population recovered from the plagues within three generations, due largely to differences in chike versus lizardfolk reproduction. Most dragonids common in the region today are species that arrived to carve a niche for themselves in only the last few centuries, and chikes and lizardfolk remain the only reptilian humanoids in the Utterends.

Following this regional tragedy, the culture of the Utterends was badly shaken, as some lizardfolk found themselves no longer able to relate to their less-bereaved neighbors. Inter-community disagreements became heated, and a band of lizardfolk leaders set out to consult a solitary gold dragon believed to have survived the plague. This dragon had indeed survived, albeit scarred and blinded beyond the ability of any magic to cure (as was typical for the consequences of this particular wave of plagues). Despite his own suffering and grief at all he had lost, he advised the Guivoc lizardfolk, and ultimately all of the Guivoc peoples, to take this regional trauma as an opportunity to grow closer as a people and to improve their way of life.

This era saw local improvements in many aspects of life for the Guivoc people. Once again peace was sought with the chike. The blind gold dragon, Mikan (referred to almost exclusively in history texts as the Lord Dragon, though he has never held any official status in the Guivoc legal code), went personally to serve as mediator between chike and Guivoc communities. The chike insulted the Guivoc delegation, poisoned them, and attacked while they were ill. Mikan defended the helpless Guivoren and, recognizing the poison used, brewed an antidote in time to save most of them, but his interference was claimed by the chike to prove he was never a neutral mediator, and retroactively adopted as the justification for the attack.

Subsequent scholars have postulated that — like true dragons and some extraplanar beings — some inherent aspect of chike physiology makes it impossible for them to behave in any way other than overt hostility. They certainly tend toward brutality amongst themselves — not just toward the Guivoren — but it is yet unknown whether such hypotheses are fair to the chike. Regardless, no subsequent attempts at reconciliation have succeeded either, in more than 1,000 years.

Guivoc culture, however, made a meteoric rise after the Dragon Plagues ceased. Soon, the lich-emperor Amaran su Bha, still enthroned in Xha'ahan, noticed their economic and military power. With Xha'en having long claimed the Utterends as imperial territory, the undead emperor began to extort exorbitant taxes from the Guivoc people. The people of the Utterends rejected his demands and defiantly declared their nation of Guivo to be officially independent of Xha'en. They spent the rest of the lich-emperor's reign effectively cut off from the outside world, with undead forces boxing them in by land and sea, and the elves of the Green Warden Forest unwilling in that period to have any dealings with a "human-loving" nation, or with a nation they saw as being probably full of spies for the lich king.

The deadly Cauldron Mountains became the only route into or out of the Utterends, and since it only led right back to lich-oppressed Xha'en, this perilous passage offered less in the way of aid for the Utterends than it did a string of Xha'en refugees to Guivo fleeing their undead overlord. Within the Utterends, the chike chose to side with the lich king for reasons of their own, and the Utterends spent decades fighting for its life.

Through it all, the Guivoc people remained steadfast in their commitment to the Lord Dragon's compassionate wisdom, and Utterends' histories record that the Utterends provided succor and supplies at one point during those benighted times to the band of heroes who ultimately recovered the Ahra artifacts that were used to depose the lich.

Once Xha'en was saved and the Tilgi dynasty begun, the Utterends were again ignored by an empire busy licking its wounds. But as both nations recovered from that terrible time, later emperors remembered that the Utterends' declared independence was never legally acknowledged by the Hegemony, and that Xha'en still claimed the marshy territory as its own. Armed "tax collection" forces were turned away at the Utterends' borders, by violence if necessary, but always as compassionately as possible. Diplomats sent to Xha'en seeking official recognition of Guivoc statehood were variously ignored or even imprisoned for insurrection.

To this day, Xha'en claims the Utterends as part of the Hegemony, acknowledges none of Guivoc history, and insists that the Guivoren are "bandits," savages eking out a squalid living in the fetid swamps the emperor cannot be bothered to "clean up." The swamps themselves, as well as the geography around the Utterends, have protected the Guivoren from true invasion or occupation by Xha'en forces. Xha'en can and periodically does cut off the Utterends from contact or trade with any but the Cauldron and the Green Warden Forest, and this has significantly stifled the Utterends' economic growth. But what Xha'en can't do is field forces that can survive the perilous Utterends' swamps and marshes well enough to defeat Guivoc natives on their home territory. No leader since the lich-emperor has been foolish enough to try.

Influenced by the Lord Dragon (now a Great Wyrm) and by their money-averse elven neighbors, the Guivoc people have chosen to accept this state of affairs with Xha'en peacefully. The chike remain a more pressing problem since they too are warriors native to the swamp and not so easily defeated by compassionate means. Though generally considered to be of near-animal intelligence and barely able to use simple tools, the chike are wily and tough, and they reproduce as quickly as the food supply allows (unlike the lizardfolk, whose former numbers have still never recovered from the Dragon Plagues).

The Guivoc have largely found means to defend themselves from chike raids, and they stay out of chike territory whenever possible. Other language-capable creatures in the Utterends, such as the tombotu and malkeens, have allied themselves with Guivoc culture even when they have elected not to join it. The chike prey upon these creatures as well, and on anything else they find within their grasp, though they are known occasionally to ally themselves for brief periods with hanu-nagas or a gray dragon on the coast. Guivoc culture interacts with these elements of the Utterends wilderness only if necessary, in self-defense.

The rest of the time, the Guivoren pursue peaceful occupations such as fine art, education, poetry, and music. They trade with the Green Realm and the Cauldron, and have established a discreet trade relationship with Ejindor, one wherein so long as they never mention where they are from, the Ejindor officials never accuse them of being "Utterends' bandits." As simply "traveling merchants" therefore, they are able to participate in the Ejindor markets and bring home books, tools, and new technologies from all over the world for their libraries and schools.

Some have remarked that the Guivoren have grown so peace-loving and intellectual that were it not for the ever-present chike threat forcing them to keep their swords sharp, they would lose all interest in the art of war and be easily subsumed by Xha'en. Whether or not that is the case, what has indeed become true is that those who know the people of the Utterends well have come to see them as a haven for refugees from oppression. Xha'en discontents of many species have continued to find a home there over the centuries, so long as they are willing to abide by Guivoc laws. Even occasional Green Warden elves, sick of the anti-human bigotry and isolationism of their homeland, have found the humidity and stirges to be worth the advantages of the warm community that the Guivoc culture can offer.

The Lord Dragon, for his part, is alive and well, and spends most of his time wandering the Utterends, disguised in whatever humanoid form takes his fancy, hiding his blindness with magic and draconic abilities as best he can (since few types of blindness are not magically curable, and the condition would otherwise give him away). Scarred old Mikan does not rule the Utterends and does not wish to and avoids making "Lord Dragon" appearances whenever possible. But he always appears when he is needed. It is believed that he is not yet 2,000 years old, and that as a gold dragon (a particularly long-lived species), he may last two millennia yet or more. Some have speculated that without his influence, the perilous Utterends would quickly descend to their former bloodthirsty ways. But for now he lives, and Guivoc is a just and compassionate place.

Religion

Religion in the Utterends tends to be celebratory and closely tied to the natural world. Most people mix and match all the common religions of the region together in personalized, private worship, and public ceremonies tend to be vaguely worded so as to appeal to as many types of belief as possible.

The most important religious site in the Utterends is the ancient stone temple at Chafa (or Tcha-i-F'ha in Tabaxi). The Chafa Temple is carved in intricate and lovely bas-relief with the ancient history and legends of the early Utterends' peoples. The temple is dedicated to all Utterends' ancestors, and it is where the histories, both local and foreign, are kept, guarded from tampering and humidity alike by a dedicated clergy of scholar-priests.

The Chafa Temple is also a place for communities to mourn departed loved ones or to pray to direct ancestors. When a nomadic band arrives at Chafa each year, a large community funeral is held (in addition to the smaller, personalized funeral that takes place just after a death). This group grief ritual focuses on gratitude for everything the departed offered to the community while alive, and on convincing the departed that it is safe for them to leave their loved ones behind and move on to the next life, by demonstrating — through feasting, dance, gifts, and kind words — just how well the communities care for one another and how loved and appreciated the bereaved are by the living people around them.

Trade and Commerce

In addition to rare plants that can be more easily cultivated in the Utterends' strange climate, and to the unique and often poignant works of art produced by the Guivoc people, the Utterends are most particularly known for tabaxi steel. Tabaxi are understood to be gifted with weapons, intuitively able to understand them. The tabaxi of the Utterends have honed and perfected this talent, such that Guivoc tabaxi weaponsmiths are known to be some of the best in the world.

Any maker-marked weapons produced in the Utterends are considered to be masterwork, as even non-tabaxi smiths must meet exacting traditional standards to ply their trade in the region, but something about tabaxi senses gives them a particular edge in the weaponsmithing process, and thus far only tabaxi smiths have ever passed the grueling examinations required by the Utterends' smiths guilds for the right to incorporate the elite "four claws" mark into their maker stamps.

Four-claws smiths are able to use the smells, sounds, and feel of every moment in the ritualized and time-consuming traditional Utterends' steel-making process to pull the natural magic of the land into their craft. As a result, any weapon, tool, or armor with a significant steel component made by a four-claw smith is inherently magical, even if the smith is not a spellcaster. Some four-claws smiths have more ability

than others, and four-claw caster-smiths can do more still, but any four-claw Utterends' smith produces exclusively magical steel goods.

The Guivoc culture being what it is, even the most pacifist smiths are still usually willing to craft weapons in some circumstances. The Guivoren know that even the compassionate are sometimes forced to defend themselves and their homes. However, many Guivoc smiths will not craft weapons for people they do not know or trust. Others exact a vow to never use their weapons for unnecessary harm, accepting customer responses with varying degrees of naivete (or shallow ritualism). Few smiths craft weapons for resale to strangers, but tools or defensive items (such as amulets, bracers, bucklers, helms, etc.) are often pre-crafted and sold to merchants or sent to market in Ejindor.

Large steel items such as tower shields or full plate armor usually require that a buyer bring the required iron as part of payment in advance and be willing to wait long enough for the iron to be processed into steel before the item can be crafted. This is because the Utterends are in fact a terrible place to find iron. Mining is extremely difficult in the wet marshes, and all the old above-ground sources have been long-since exhausted. Thus, for all the excellence of Guivoc steelmaking, the vast majority of their raw iron must now be imported from outside. For this reason, quality raw iron can be worth as much as copper in the Utterends, and steel ingots of four-claw smith quality are worth as much as gold. Precious metals are otherwise worth comparable amounts to their values in other places and are often used in sculpture.

Loyalties and Diplomacy

Despite Xha'en's claims to the contrary, the Utterends maintain their independence and do not offer fealty to any other nation. Isolated as they are, the Utterends are also largely lacking in allies, as the elves are too insular and few of the intelligent creatures living in the Cauldron Mountains share a worldview compatible with Guivoc philosophies. In many ways, the ever-brutal chike have an easier time forming (brief, treacherous) alliances than do the Guivoc given their location. This is one of many reasons why it is so often believed that the Utterends will only maintain their open-hearted attitudes for as long as the Lord Dragon yet lives. Without his influence and protection, it seems likely that the Guivoc people would experience a great deal more pressure to conform to prevailing attitudes around them.

Government

Guivoc government is as minimal and localized as possible, and no one person is ever permitted to hold a great deal of power over others. Small nomadic communities (usually no more than 300 people) choose their own leaders however they wish, often by consensus. Professional guilds are larger, some spanning the entire Utterends, but these never have a single leader, and are instead often governed by large councils.

A typical way for guild councilmembers to be chosen is that they must be nominated (without volunteering) by three guild members in good standing who are not already on the council. Should nominated individuals choose to accept nomination, their credentials are presented to the council, along with all other nominees. The council then votes among the nominees, using a ritual voting process wherein choices are ranked by preference so that the nominee with the broadest appeal to the largest number of voters is selected. Decisions of the council are made through a similar process and are usually quite slow. Councilmembers typically serve five-year terms, with a limit of no two terms in a row and an unlimited possibility of re-selection after any five-year period not spent on the council.

Crime is usually handled by community leaders, or, if applicable, by the relevant guild. Unless the crime is violent, punishment is meted out in hours of some form of service to the community, with certain privileges revoked until service hours are completed. Violent crime leads to imprisonment and rehabilitation efforts the first time, longer imprisonment and more intensive rehabilitation efforts the second time, and the third time to permanent exile from the Utterends, enforced where possible by *geas* or other magic. Suspected criminals may always appeal their sentences to the Guild of Justice, which handles disputes between communities and studies international law, among other things. Further appeals go to the Chafa Temple, where priests of knowledge use magic to determine the lies or truth of all parties involved. The final tier of appeal is finding the Lord Dragon and convincing him to hear the case, which is far easier said than done.

The Lord Dragon's interference is more likely when the Guild of Justice finds itself unable to mediate a major internal dispute, as old Mikan dislikes internal conflict in his chosen homeland and will, if he has to, go out of his way to help everyone get along. The Guild of Justice was founded primarily with the intent of making sure the citizens of Guivo try the Lord Dragon's patience as rarely as possible.

MILITARY

Most adult Guivoc have some combat training due to the perilous nature of the Utterends' swamps. Typically, communities organize their members into small militias to defend their own people. In addition, citizens may volunteer (or be selected by lots if volunteers are insufficient, though this is rare and unenforced) to spend up to a year at a time serving as guards for various facilities such as the Chafa Temple or the great smithies. A year spent as a guardian is a common cultural practice for Guivoren and is a highly respected occupation, especially for young adults. It is a rare able-bodied Guivoren who has the luxury to "get soft" and cease daily battle drills or turns taken on watch for the community.

For national defense, there is the Guild of Protectors. Those who choose to dedicate their professional lives to the safety of Guivo may join this guild, which organizes regular patrols of the wilderness and borders throughout the Guivoc regions of the Utterends.

The various Guivoc military units are the only places within Guivoc culture where individuals may hold a great deal of authority over other individuals in a strict hierarchy. However, even here many rules are in place to prevent corruption or power-hoarding, and military rank is often determined by election or consensus, and relatively easy to strip from officers. A centralized command is authorized with unilateral decision-making abilities only when a threat to the Utterends is deemed to be of emergency status. During such a time period, a high duke (usually an experienced veteran with a reputation for tactical and logistical skill) is empowered to command all Utterends' warriors for a clearly pre-determined, finite period of time. When the threat or duration passes, the Utterends' military returns to its more typical localized state.

MAJOR THREATS

The Utterends themselves are extremely threatening, packed with monsters and things that can poison a person. This alone is enough of a threat to keep the Utterends eternally on its toes. Another threat would be the way the Xha'en Hegemony is sometimes able to harshly curtail travel and trade between the Utterends and the outside world. If this were ever to take place during a major crop failure, thousands of people could find the insular Green Warden elves the only thing standing between themselves and starvation — a chilling prospect indeed.

Should the Utterends' chike population ever be convinced to organize and rally behind a single, clever leader, the Guivoc nation would be hard-pressed to defend its many tiny, mobile communities. Fortunately, the chike have thus far always been fragmented and — albeit wily — predictable in tactics, in much the way clever pack hunters can be. Their passing alliances with evil beings in the past have yet to extend all the way to obedience or loyalty.

Finally, one thing that would shake the Guivoc nation to its foundations would be the death of the Lord Dragon, for any reason. This is perhaps another reason why he prefers to make himself so hard to find.

WILDERNESS AND ADVENTURES

Due to the harsh environment and high prevalence of monsters, the Utterends' population is unusually small for so otherwise healthy a community. Even humans seem to breed more slowly here, with mothers rarely producing a child more often than once every four to five years, for reasons only partially understood. Because of this, nearly all of the Utterends is wilderness, the only exceptions being the nation's few permanent structures, and wherever a group of nomads is currently camped.

In general, the traditional nomadic routes are safer than other parts of the region, both because no population of monsters can gain a deep foothold there, and because the Guild of Protectors keeps the traditional routes better-patrolled than other parts of the Utterends. The most dangerous areas of the Utterends are the northwest and the coast.

The northwest region of the Utterends sees a larger influx of monsters wandering down from the Cauldron into the swamps and is also the area of highest chike concentration. In addition, the Mudspit Peninsula is partially submerged for half of each year, such that all the peninsula's water is brackish and foul, and travelers unable to drink saltwater (as the Utterends' species of chike are able to do) must pack enough water along to make the hundred-plus-mile trek across it.

The Utterends' coast is bathwater warm for much of the year, but in addition to being muddy and stirge-infested, it is also quite popular among young gray dragons, for reasons unknown (especially since gray dragons typically prefer coastal hills and mountains to mud and muck). It is commonly believed that the Lord Dragon comes to shoo such interlopers away on a semi-regular basis, but no one knows why they keep coming back. Some believe there must be a large gray dragon population in the Cauldron, or even some heretofore undiscovered island off the coast that is covered in gray dragons. Whatever the cause, the Utterends' coastline has a recurring baby dragon problem. Thus far, few juveniles or young adult dragons have been spotted (and none older), but even the little ones are dangerous.

SHAN'DAREN, CITY OF

Ruler: none
Government: guild council
Population: 1,500 year-round (varies seasonally) (500 Xha'en,
   425 tengu, 340 tabaxi, 150 lizardfolk, 75 wild elf, 10 other)
Technology Level: Iron Age

Shan'daren is a treetop city, modeled after a northern wild elven basic structural design but with an entirely Guivoc aesthetic. Certain practical aspects are different from elven cities as well in order to adapt the design to the peculiarities of old growth cypress trees, to increase air flow on hot days, and to slow damage to the building materials from humidity, among other things. All open spaces are draped with fine-woven mosquito netting for a surprisingly decadent overall appearance in the way that the lovingly-crafted and practical netting resembles chiffon or other luxury fabrics.

Shan'daren was constructed during the reign of the Xha'en lich-emperor in order to address a need for a secure and centralized command base for Guivoc resistance operations. In times of war, it is just that; but in times of peace, the many and various national guild councils instead use it as a headquarters in order to aid in the smooth running of the guilds. The high command tree fort, whenever there is no high duke to occupy it, is used instead by council members assigned by their guilds as guild ambassadors who are tasked with coordinating governance efforts between different guilds.

While the Guild of Protectors does organize volunteer guards to keep Shan'daren safe from monsters, no other service positions are permitted in Shan'daren. Councilmembers must make time and work together to keep the place clean, do other necessary chores, and cook their own meals. Exceptions to the ban on service positions can be situationally lifted for councilmembers who are ill or disabled, but the social pressure is strong to do as much as one can for oneself, save on Healers Guild orders. Food in Shan'daren must be purchased from a guild's budget, and life in Shan'daren, in general, is mildly ascetic with a work-focused atmosphere.

Nomadic communities alter their routes to pass through Shan'daren any time they feel the need to consult with one of the guild councils.

CHAFA TEMPLE

Ruler: none
Government: priesthood
Population: 400 year-round (varies seasonally) (135 Xha'en,
   120 tabaxi, 110 tengu, 25 lizardfolk, 5 wild elf, 5 other)
Technology Level: Iron Age

Originally called by its Tabaxi name, Tcha-i-F'ha — after an ancient local folk hero who is said to have stolen a whole series of useful crafts and tools from the gods, one at a time — the Chafa Temple is probably the most beautiful structure in all the Utterends. Nearly 100 feet tall and more than 300 feet per side, this stepped pyramid spirals upward from the more solid earth of the north-central Utterends. Its top is capped with a graceful stone dome and spire above a ritual space dedicated to all ancestors and their knowledge. The path up to this shrine moves in a long, squared spiral from the ground, and every wall of the pathway is lined with ancient bas-reliefs depicting the history and legends of those who built the temple long ago. Built before the influx of humans to the Utterends, the bas-reliefs notably depict mostly tabaxi and lizardfolk, with a few tengu at the lower levels where the most recent sculptures were placed.

While a few other ruins from that era dot the Utterends, only Chafa Temple was built of an imported stone from the Odarnadar Mountains located hundreds of miles to the north. This stone has withstood the test of time in a way that the other temples of the era have not, and it is a source of great pride for the Guivoc people. As nomads, they have made few permanent structures over the centuries, and the Chafa Temple is precious to them.

The only year-round inhabitants of Chafa are the priests of knowledge, but all nomadic groups stop here once a year just before monsoon season to consult with the priests, exchange community books at the temple library (a more recent but still beautiful stone outbuilding surrounded by the clergy's modest dwellings), and to celebrate the ancestors in a huge, multi-community festival.

Quiris Meadow

Ruler: none
Government: none
Population: 1,200 year-round (varies seasonally) (450 Xha'en, 385 tabaxi, 315 tengu, lizardfolk, 35 wild elf, 15 other)
Technology Level: Iron Age

Located in the eastern Utterends, Quiris Meadow is a vast stretch of the best farmlands in the region. As the Guivoc culture has grown, so have its agricultural requirements, yet the practicality of the Guivoc nomadic lifestyle is inarguable in a region where most structures quickly rot and crumble, and stable ground is so scarce for half the year. The Quiris Meadow has become Guivo's compromise in order to maximize food production.

Nomadic communities arrive near the end of the rainy season at the "meadow," which is farmed in the natural-looking elven style rather than human-style single-crop rows, such that it really does look like a giant meadow. Here, they take what they need from the reserve stores in great storehouses and silos at the edge of the swampish lands, leave any dried or preserved spare goods they acquired in their wanderings (nothing of high monetary value), and go to work planting the fields for the year. Each community has a traditional plot to care for, but all harvested goods are stored together, and distribution is managed in several ways, though the task primarily is organized by the Farmers Guild which assigns some members to stay with the meadow year-round.

Once planting is accomplished, a community chooses a need-proportional number of volunteers to remain behind and tend the fields through the growing season. The communities depart by their various dry-season routes for more old-fashioned gathering of wild plants, fishing and trapping, and other pursuits. Then, near the end of the dry season, groups make their way back to the meadow for harvest time and help bring in the crops, celebrate together, and participate in another exchange of spare goods.

A new (or the same) group of volunteers is chosen to stay behind and spends the rainy season preserving and guarding perishable goods, and if a community's supplies run low during the rainy season, couriers can be sent back to the meadow for more. The Utterends are extremely fertile throughout the region, so in most years there is a fair amount of excess, and the Farmers Guild keeps the whole thing organized to generate as little waste as possible. The Guild of Protectors focuses a great deal of its efforts on defending the Quiris Meadow.

Tahngari, City of

Ruler: none
Government: council of elders
Population: 5,000 year-round (varies seasonally) (1,600 Xha'en, 1,450 tengu, 1,050 tabaxi, 560 lizardfolk, 250 wild elf, 90 other)
Technology Level: Iron Age

Tahngari is a stone city built into a series of cliffs along the southeastern edge of the Cauldron Mountains, well north and east of chike territory and near the entrance to Hearthfire Pass. The city was founded by the first tengu immigrants to arrive in the Utterends region, and a few parts of it remain to this day inaccessible by people unable to fly. Most of the city, however, has been built to cater to all Guivoc species, and Tahngari has become a fixture of Guivoc culture.

Tahngari is where the volunteer guardians of Hearthfire Pass make their base of operations, and it also contains an extensive healing community, including a small natural hotspring in the foothills below. Though it is not part of the annual migration path of any of the nomadic Guivoc communities, the sick and injured often make their way to Tahngari for healing, mostly during the dry season when travel is safer, so even in Tahngari, the population does seasonally fluctuate.

In addition to those ill and injured who only visit long enough to be healed, Tahngari is home to a community of the elderly who have begun to find a nomadic lifestyle difficult. Not all of the Utterends' elderly come here to retire. Some join the Priests of Knowledge or are called to serve so often in various guild councils that travel away from Shan'daren is rarely a concern. Others, mostly craftspeople, find room to settle in Tchur-i-kahn, and other still are willing and able to continue traveling with their home communities until the day they die. Nevertheless, Tahngari has the highest population of elderly Guivoren per capita, and is therefore considered a repository of wisdom.

Local Tahngari legend claims that the Lord Dragon visits the Tahngari hotsprings when he feels the need to engage in intelligent conversation.

Tchur-i-kahn, City of

Ruler: none
Government: Guild of Smiths
Population: 2,000 year-round (varies seasonally) (775 tabaxi, 520 Xha'en, 360 tengu, 265 lizardfolk, 70 wild elf, 10 other)
Technology Level: Dark Ages/Medieval

Tchur-i-kahn is a city of smithies. Built atop the point of highest elevation in all the Utterends (a jumble of low, rocky hills), Tchur-i-kahn is at least as ancient in its foundations as the Chafa Temple. This is where the Tabaxi first learned to smelt and forge, and some of the oldest stone forges are still preserved, used today for gold and silver works (since they cannot be made hot enough for smithing iron and steel).

Over time, Tchur-i-kahn has grown in size, technology, and importance, and has come to be another major annual stop for the Guivoc nomadic communities. While the rocky hills remain high and dry all year round, able to support a modest monsoon-season population, the ground around the hills is all marsh during the rains, unsuitable for large camps of people. In the dry season, however, the areas around the Tchur-i-kahn hills are hospitable and rich with life. Communities therefore come here to camp for a time on their way back to Quiris Meadow for the harvest season and have turned Tchur-i-kahn into a grand annual market taking place usually at a midpoint between Spring Equinox and Summer Solstice, in line with the Utterends' unusual harvest cycle.

This tradition has, in the eyes of some, given the Guild of Smiths (who largely run the city) an inflated share of national power, and the Guild of Smiths' council has thus become one of the hardest guild councils to join and one of the easiest to be expelled from. While this may have prevented corruption on the council, it has unfortunately promoted a certain degree of disorganization, and market time in Tchur-i-kahn is usually a jumbled chaos.

A smaller festival takes place in Tchur-i-kahn each year during monsoon season and is attended by only a few volunteer representatives of each community every year. This is the birthday celebration of the Lord Dragon. It is said that the Lord Dragon claimed his birthday was just after Fall Equinox in order to prevent the Guivoc people from making a fuss over him every year, but they still do — it's just a smaller fuss than it might otherwise have been.

In a large gathering hall, each nomadic community that sent representatives presents a work of art from its own band that is dedicated to the Lord Dragon. These are judged by all attendees and prizes are awarded to the communities of the winners in various categories such as poetry, performance art, sculpture, etc. All entries (or transcripts thereof) are displayed in the gathering hall until market season the following year to make sure the Lord Dragon has a chance to see them, but it is said that he makes his way in secret to the ceremony every year without fail to hear performances and poems in person. For this reason, attendees are always on their best behavior since they all know that any other attendee might be the Lord Dragon in disguise.

It is unknown whether the Lord Dragon actually appears at his birthday celebration each year, but some say he once promised someone that he would, and he is known to always keep his promises if at all possible.

GTSANG PREFECTURE

(G'tsahng)
Capital: Duam
Ruler: Svaame-Anahbi Ojun Ahujawahl
Government: theocracy
Population: 325,000 (305,000 Jaata, 20,000 Xha'en)
Monstrous: basilisks, bat swarms, eagles (giant), frost giants, hill giants, griffons, harpies, hippogriffs, ogres, manticores, perytons, rakshasas (rumored), trolls, wyverns, yeti
Languages: Meeruwhan, Xaon
Religion: Mithraldism, Path of the Circle
Resources: copper, grain, silver, tin
Currency: Xha'en currency
Technology Level: Medieval

The name Gtsang Prefecture is a bit misleading, for this autonomous state is a part of the Xha'en Hegemony in name only. Independently ruled for more than 15,000 years, the city of Duam and its surrounding lands are among the oldest continually-occupied realms in Akados. Its rulers pay a token tribute of 100 gold coins to Xha'ahan each year, and generally go about their business unmolested, sometimes providing sorcerous, scientific, or martial aid to the Hegemony.

The Prefecture is separated from the Hegemony by the treacherous Tsendakar Mountains and are accessible only along a narrow and perilous path grandly known as the Heavenly Road (named for its nearness to the heavens rather than its heavenly qualities). A small ribbon of trade and travel stretches along the road, and traffic between the Prefecture and the Hegemony is infrequent but growing in significance. The Tsendakar Range harbors the legendary Udanishanti Temple, where both Xha'en and Gtsang students come to learn the way of the sword.

The people of Gtsang are not Xha'en — rather they are the descendants of Jaata colonists who first traveled here approximately 15,700 years ago. A small number of Xha'en live in the Prefecture, with most making a living as miners, shopkeepers, and subsistence farmers. Rumors persist that a handful of rakshasas also live here, carefully concealing their true identities with illusion and secretly running the Prefecture from the shadows.

HISTORY AND PEOPLE

Settled over 15 millennia in the past, the city-state of Duam is the second-oldest human settlement in Akados, surpassed only by Tros Zoas, built on the foundations of ancient Xantollan on Pontos Island in the Sinnar Sea. According to their most ancient tales, colonists from the land that is now Far Jaati on the distant continent of Libynos made the perilous voyage across the Great Ocean Ûthaf in relatively primitive ships, eventually landing in the Gtsang region 15,700 years ago. How

they made such a long and difficult journey (or whether this is nothing more than a myth) is not known for certain, but the Gtsang themselves believe that they succeeded only with the blessings of Mithras Himself.

The hilly lands of Gtsang seemed perfect for the colonists — a fertile realm protected by the towering Tsendakar Mountains to the south and adjacent to rich fishing waters. The main city of Duam was founded soon after landfall, and within a few generations the tiny colony began to grow.

The folk who settled Gtsang appear to have initially been a highly religious magiocracy founded on the principals of Mithraldism (see below) that emphasized spiritual learning combined with the absolute authority of the jaaduga, or mage-king. These early mage-kings were trained in the ways of Mithras by the priestly caste of Anahbi — many Jaaduga were themselves priests. In this fashion, a highly lawful and good society was founded in the new land.

For centuries, Gtsang remained hidden from the outside world and shunned contact with the ancestors of the Senge tribes who even then inhabited the lands south of the Tsendakar Range. These early years proved challenging for the new colony, for although it was blessed with cool summers and mild springs, the region proved treacherous in fall and winter as fierce storms swept down from the north and seasonal rains set rivers to flood. The hills and mountains contained other hazards, and for the first few generations the Gtsang were forced to deal with raids or outright invasion by fierce creatures such as yetis and frost giants. A warrior class emerged over these years as Mithraldic monks began to train in esoteric martial arts, and metalsmiths began to craft weapons intended solely for the defense of the nation.

The colonists found other friends in the region as well, for the Ankhura dwarves had inhabited the Tsendakar Range for generations. Though they were themselves an insular people, the dwarves made tentative contact with the humans and offered trade and possible diplomatic relations. A wary friendship began as Ankhuran smiths trained the Gtsang in the secrets of ironworking and the forging of steel, and the Gtsang provided a small amount of their precious crops in exchange.

For three millennia, the realm tottered on the edge of subsistence. But ever so slowly, Gtsang began to prosper through the sheer determination of its people and the strength of its community. It was nearly 12,000 years ago, well before the founding of the Xha'en Hegemony, that the Gtsang community faced its first true crisis.

Any society is bound to change over three millennia — those that do not are doomed to waste away and perish. The Gtsang were no different in this, moving away from the society of their founding colonists and evolving to live in a new and very different environment. The power of the mage-kings grew as the Anahbi began to lose influence. Originally, the Anahbi themselves selected the mage-king's council, but as time passed, the mage-kings increasingly selected their own advisors, eventually shunning the priest class altogether. With the wise advice of the Anahbi gone, the Jaaduga grew more independent and began to seek council on spiritual planes, calling up ghosts, extraplanar entities, and even demons. In this fashion, the mage-kings began to move toward chaos and madness.

The end of the Jaaduga came when the Mage-King Lakhsa made a fearful bargain with the ogre mage Amnu-Paket, promising the monster any worldly reward in exchange for absolute wisdom. The bargain was predictably fixed — Lakhsha was driven mad by the knowledge he gained and Amnu-Paket demanded rulership of Gtsang as his price. Ascending the throne, he became known as the Red King.

At first, the ogre mage's rule proved a mixed blessing to Gtsang, for though he was a thoroughly evil being, Amnu-Paket realized that the power and security of his new domain depended on the health and welfare of "his" people. Utterly ruthless with his enemies, and demanding absolute obedience from his subjects, Amnu-Paket nevertheless led Gtsang, for a time, to unparalleled prosperity. Crops were plentiful, animals grew fat and productive, and peace (of a sort) ruled the land. Well-fed and content, the folk of Gtsang were willing to overlook their supernatural monarch's wicked tendencies and rationalize away conduct that they had, until recently, believed to be abhorrent.

Amnu-Paket shunned the former capital city of Duam and instead decreed the construction of a vast palace crafted from a single colossal emerald to be built upon the sheer walls of Mount Batekun, the tallest peak in the Tsendakar Range. This great structure, the Tu Chai Palace, served as the Red King's home for the next five centuries as his grip on the land grew tighter.

Despite his initial attention to the welfare of the Gtsang, Amnu-Paket over time came to see humans as weak and inefficient. He began to hatch plans to replace the humans of Gtsang with evil creatures who would be more obedient and work harder in his name. Humans would survive, of course, but only as slaves to his dynasty. Dreams of empire and conquest began to grow in his inhuman mind, and both the offshore islands and the plains south of the Tsendakar seemed ripe for absorption, along with legions of human slaves.

In all this time, the Anahbi priest caste had not been idle. As the Red King's influence spread, the priests traveled the land, seeing to the needs of the people and forming alliances with the old warrior castes, disaffected sorcerers, and the martial monks of the few remaining monasteries. The dwarves of Ankhura, long distressed by the Red King's presence, agreed to send both warriors and weapons.

Amnu-Paket's intentions soon became clear to even the most loyal of his citizens. He had raised an army of hobgoblins and summoned several powerful rakshasa to serve as generals and advisors. It was only a matter of time before the humans of Gtsang were wholly supplanted in favor of more loyal (and coincidentally evil) creatures, and after five centuries the people of the land were ready to rebel. The priests had their own army, and now as the Red King's wicked schemes were about to bear fruit, they struck.

War came to a land that had been at peace for three and a half millennia. Bands of martial warriors and elite fighters armed with dwarven steel weapons struck at hobgoblin commanders, depriving Amnu-Paket's army of leadership, while secretly-trained peasants and those Gtsang who still followed the old warriors' way took on the bulk of the Red King's forces. Surprised by the sudden uprising, Amnu-Paket's army retreated into the mountains, falling back on his fastness at the Tu Chai Palace.

The siege of the Red King's palace lasted nearly three years and cost countless lives. In the end, unable to break Amnu-Paket's defenses, the Anahbi and their arcane allies, including Ankhuran keepers of ancient and dangerous knowledge, risked a fearsome spell that, if unsuccessful, might curse the entire realm. Fortunately for them, the ritual was a success and cast a terrible curse on Amnu-Paket that burned him to ashes while transforming the once-fearsome Tu Chai Palace into a normal-sized emerald. Amnu-Paket's ashes were placed in a small golden receptacle and (supposedly) safely stored in the magically shrunken palace. For many more generations, both the emerald and the ashes contained within were held safe in Duam, but were eventually lost, finding their way, it is said, into the hands of the Cult of Orcus and the lost city of Tsar. (See *The Slumbering Tsar Saga* by **Frog God Games**.)

With the fall of the Red King, the priests of Mithras sought to establish a new system of government that would avoid the mistakes of the past. Now Gtsang was overseen by the Svaame-Anahbi, or priest-lord, who was in turn overseen by a new council of Anahbi, whose approval was needed for all major decisions, who selected their own members, and who could not be replaced or disempowered. Once more, strict adherence to and training in the principles of Mithraldism was required of anyone who wished to participate in government, and the realm returned to its rigid but good-aligned nature.

Little changed in the realm for several more millennia, until at last the founding of the Xha'en Hegemony awakened Gtsang and brought it into direct contact with the outside world. Protected by the mountains and sea, and accessible overland only along the narrow and winding Heavenly Road, Gtsang had escaped notice for many ages, but as the Xha'en grew in power and the Hegemony spread its influence, the priest-lord and his advisors knew something had to be done.

War with the Hegemony was unthinkable — though the Xha'en would surely lose thousands attempting to force their way along the Heavenly Road, Gtsang was vulnerable to attack from the sea, and any conflict between the two states would be disastrous for both.

And so, in 2945 XC (1643 I.R.), the Priest-Lord Amaa, with the support of his council, agreed to join the Hegemony, at that time led by the ascendant Ophronya Dynasty, with its capital in the city of Djir. The Ophronya were also aware of the difficulties involved in conquering the tiny state, and readily agreed to generous terms. The Gtsang were to continue to be self-governed and the priest-lord would have authority over the region. A small tribute of 100 gold pieces would be paid yearly, and the Gtsang would give the Hegemony favored status when negotiating trade and other agreements.

It was at this time that Gtsang's other great institution was formed. Martial artists and warriors from the Prefecture, the Hegemony, and the Thousand Rocks formed the Udanishanti Temple (a compound Gtsang/Anari word that roughly translates to "service to heaven") deep in the mountains where they would train legendary fighters who would help defend the entire region, incorporating martial traditions from all three nations. The temple remains to this day, well-hidden in the mountains and accessible only to those individuals who are truly dedicated to the art of the sword. The temple is the only location outside of the island of Anaros where a warrior can be trained in the ways of the Uarsinsi, the noble sword fighters of the Anari. Those trained in the temple serve all across western lands, for no student is turned away due to nationality, gender, or religion. Even a tiny handful of easterners from Castorhage, Bard's Gate, Vast, Reme, and elsewhere are known to have received training there.

The entire region was thrown into confusion in 4523 XC (3221 I.R.) when settlers from the city-state of Castorhage settled on the island of Greater Bream and founded the outpost of Farthest Point. The Castorhagi had always been distant and relatively unknown to the Gtsang, though it was known that the Xha'en Hegemony traded with them. Now, as the new outpost grew and a Castorhagi trade delegation arrived in Duam, the Gtsang were forced to accept that these outsiders had established a foothold in the region and were unlikely to leave. To almost everyone's surprise — not least the Gtsang themselves — the Anahbi agreed to trade with the Castorhagi, and goods began to flow between the Prefecture and the new colonies. Actual sea travel between Gtsang and the Breams began as well, with a few small, crude docking facilities being established in Gtsang fishing villages.

Today, the Anahbi still govern a peaceful and pastoral realm, though now the outside world is fully aware of the Prefecture's existence. Its inaccessibility helps protect Gtsang, but more foreigners have appeared within its borders, including a small but growing number of Xha'en settlers and Castorhagi traders. Though the state is outwardly peaceful and tranquil, some disturbing rumors continue to be told, the most persistent of which is that the descendants of Amnu-Paket's rakshasas still exist, living as humans and keeping their true heritage a secret while plotting to return to power. The teachings of Mithras still guide the Gtsang, however, and despite their continuing allegiance to the Xha'en Hegemony, the region remains autonomous and largely free. How long before Gtsang's isolation and independence are challenged in a changing world is anyone's guess, however.

RELIGION

The original settlers in the region of Gtsang were members of the Mithraldic sect — devout followers of Mithras (also referred to as Mitros or Mithros). Believing that divine knowledge can be transferred from Mithras to his worshippers through a class of priestly teachers known as Anahbi, the Mithraldi favor intellect and spirituality over the supposed pleasures and temptations of the material world.

Mithraldism is an extremely old branch of the Mithraic faith and represents perhaps its most ancient and original version. While essentially a monotheistic faith, Mithraldism nevertheless venerates Mithras as a god of the sun served by three elemental entities that most incorrectly identify as "angels" or "demigods" — Miotes, the spirit who led humanity to learning and civilization; Myskes, the deliverer who rescued humans from the darkness of ignorance and superstition; and Neh, the messenger who delivers wisdom directly from the divine spirit of Mithras.

This complex faith requires considerable study and has many legends and sacred texts, though it lacks the various mystery cult aspects that are practiced by other peoples. Mithraldic priesthood demands years of patient study, and Anahbi are all highly learned in history, science, and philosophy. While officially sworn to non-violence, Mithraldic priests are allowed to use their martial skills to defend the innocent and protect the faith from its enemies.

Several monastic orders also exist, with monks who are devoted to separating themselves from worldly pleasures and beliefs, focusing on spiritual perfection and the contemplation of what is usually called the White Light of Mithras. Mithraldic monks share some elements with the warrior-monks of Xha'en, often wandering the land and tending to the sick and the poor. Many tales are told of simple monks who outwit demons, warlords, and monsters while using only their spiritual enlightenment and weaponless martial arts.

While the faith of Mithras continues to hold sway in Gtsang, several contending schools of faith also exist, with the ascetic Path of the Circle being the most prominent. Developed in Gtsang, then spread to the steppelands by the monk Bledja Ulgar and expanded upon by successive philosophers, this system is as much philosophy as faith, teaching as it does that an individual's perception shapes reality. The so-called "gods" were originally thought of as simply beings who have attained an imperfect state of enlightenment called Falsana that grants limited immortality and the ability to perceive multiple realities simultaneously. Over the centuries, the path's initial atheistic theology evolved (in part due to pragmatic concerns) to the point that the gods are revered but as enlightened teachers rather than deities. While this philosophy/religion is today confined mostly to the steppelands north of the Hegemony, it has also grown and flourished in the Prefecture, with several small monasteries established to teach new followers.

TRADE AND COMMERCE

Though the region is largely self-sufficient, the Gtsang Prefecture maintains some trade relations with the Ankhuran dwarves and exchanges local produce and cattle for fish with the Thousand Rocks. Trade with the Xha'en has grown slowly since Gtsang's union with the Hegemony, with caravans making their way along the treacherous Heavenly Road along with a trickle of Xha'en settlers who have established farms and small communities within the Prefecture.

When the cunning Castorhagi established their colonies on the Bream Islands 300 years ago, they immediately began to cement their position in hopes of heading off any Hegemony interference. A trade delegation to the Prefecture yielded results with surprising swiftness, and goods began to flow between the two regions, a situation that continues today.

LOYALTIES AND DIPLOMACY

The Gtsang people's primary loyalty is to their nation and to the teachings of Mithras, but they are pragmatic enough to know that they are now part of a larger state in the form of the Xha'en Hegemony. While in most cases diplomatic duties have been taken up by the officials of the Hegemony, the Gtsang maintain good relations with the Ankhuran dwarves and the Thousand Islanders. Relations with the Bream Island colonies are a bit trickier, as the presence of the Castorhagi is a bit of a tender subject with the Xha'en and other locals. While full diplomatic relations with Castorhage have not been established, a small but robust flow of trade continues between Gtsang and the Breams.

Along with their token tribute of 100 gold pieces a year, the Gtsang are also obligated to offer favorable trade agreements with the Hegemony, and also send martial artists and spellcasters to help the Xha'en. Warriors and monks trained at the Udanishanti Temple serve throughout the region, acting as soldiers, military advisors, and even diplomats for the Gtsang, the Hegemony, and the Thousand Rocks. In general, the Prefecture's agreements with the Xha'en have been beneficial to both states, and remain in place, even after long centuries.

GOVERNMENT

Upon its founding, Gtsang was governed by the principles of Mithras and led by a benevolent Jaaduga, or mage-king, trained and advised by the Anahbi priests. Though successful for many years, the system eventually fell into decline, with the power of the priests reduced systematically over

three millennia until at last the Mage-King Lakhsa ceded power to the ogre mage Amnu-Paket. After the wicked Red King was overthrown and destroyed by an army of Anahbi-led rebels, a new system was created by the victorious priests. Now, a Svaame-Anahbi or Priest-Lord ruled the land with assistance from Mithraldic clerics and Gtsang arcanists.

This theocratic system weathered many challenges over the subsequent millennia and endures today with few changes. This is largely due to the Gtsang's lawful nature, and with the government's flexibility — new Svaame-Anahbi are selected by the priests and wizards of the advisory council and rule with their consent. Incompetent or incapacitated Priest-Lords may be removed and replaced, and if no suitable candidates are found, the council can rule as a group.

MILITARY

Gtsang has no standing military, but in times of crisis can call up a large number of warrior-priests and monks, trained peasant infantry, and mages. These groups can be further reinforced by Anari Uarsinsi warriors from the Thousand Rocks and armored dwarf soldiers from Ankhura who have maintained a close relationship to the Gtsang. Fortunately, the Gtsang have not faced any external threat in millennia, and today can also rely upon the Xha'en Hegemony for defense.

WILDERNESS AND ADVENTURES

Most of Gtsang Prefecture north of Tsendakar Range is cultivated, hilly land, settled continuously for millennia. From the lower slopes of the Tsendakars rises the pale marble wonder that is the ancient city of Duam, a labyrinth of streets and buildings of unbelievable age, full to overflowing with the collected wisdom of centuries. Only a handful of outsiders has ever visited Duam or the Prefecture beyond it, and those that do come for knowledge and enlightenment.

The wild mountains hold the greatest dangers, as they are still home to some of Gtsang's most ancient enemies — wild yeti and tribes of frost giants. Legend holds that some of the Red King's fierce hobgoblin warriors survived their master's destruction and live on in the jagged crags of the Tsendakars.

KAMATKHAN

Hidden deep in the Tsendakar Mountains, this narrow valley supports a tiny village and monastery where over six centuries ago the aged Gtsang monk Qataz developed a philosophy that rejected the gods and proclaimed the individual as the ultimate arbiter of reality and spiritual enlightenment. These teachings he shared with the monk Bledja Ulgar to create what is today known as the Path of the Circle. This faith/philosophy is still practiced in the Gtsang Prefecture but made the most significant inroads in the Haunted Steppes and its environs, where Bledja journeyed to spread his new way of thought and faith. The Path that is practiced today differs somewhat from Qataz and Bledja's original vision, in that the gods continue to be revered, though not as supreme beings, and respect for existing institutions is encouraged (a pragmatic political concession that has allowed the Path its continued existence).

DUAM, CITY OF

Ruler: Svaame-Anahbi Ojun Ahujawahl
Government: theocracy
Population: 85,000 (75,500 Jaati, 9,500 Xha'en)
Technology Level: Medieval

This city at the center of the isolated Gtsang Prefecture is the second-oldest settlement in all of Akados. Founded by Mithradic colonists reportedly from the land now known as Far Jaati, Duam began life as a rude huddle of huts surrounded by a rough palisade, but soon the hospitable nature of Gtsang brought peace and prosperity to the colonists. Within a few generations, what had been a primitive village was the spiritual center of a thriving new nation.

Duam sits on a low hill surrounded by well-tended farmlands and Mithradic shrines crafted of pale stone. The city is unwalled and arranged in the form of a six-pointed star bounded by whitewashed roads. Each point of the star is dedicated to different functions — three are residential, two mercantile, and one public — with each filled with shines, temples, and parks. The religious and administrative center is in the hexagonal center of the city and sports large and elaborate temples, some of which have stood here for millennia. In the center is the tower of Mithros, where the Svaame-Anahbii or Priest-Lord and an advisory council of Anahbii (priests) and Bedhka (mages) apply a light but firm hand to the nation's governance. Few suffer in Duam and the city does not experience the crowding, crime, and poverty found in other Xha'en cities.

ANKHURA

(An-koo-ra)
Capital: Iron Octagon
Notable Settlements: Ithanic Fortress
Ruler: Grand Matron Ninsar Hamura
Government: hereditary monarchy
Population: 1,150,000 (mountain dwarf)
Humanoid: mountain dwarf (many)
Monstrous: bat (dire), bat swarms, cave fishers, giant centipedes, doppelgangers, goblins, gray ooze, ogres, piercers, purple worms, ratfolk, ropers, shoggoths, skeletons, giant spiders, stirges, trolls, violet fungi, wights
Languages: Ankhuran
Religion: Masakhan
Resources: copper, gemstones, gold, iron, mithral, silver, tin
Currency: Ankhuran
Technology Level: Medieval/Renaissance

The ancient Ankhuran civilization existed before the arrival of humans to the lands now known as the Gtsang Prefecture, and continues to exist today, deeply entrenched among the grim slopes of the western Tsendakar Mountains, with the mighty Ithanic Fortress as its imposing face to the outside world.

Though they are physically similar to the dwarves elsewhere in the world, the Ankhurans are quite distinct culturally, leading some to suggest that they may be the direct descendants of the original dwarves, living in relative isolation, unchanged while the rest of the dwarven peoples evolved to new lands and climates. The Ankhurans themselves are notoriously tight-lipped about their history and hold the secrets of their subterranean realm close to their chests.

HISTORY AND PEOPLE

The earliest history of the Ankhurans is shrouded in the impenetrable mists of time. They present a dilemma to historians, as their civilization was well established and thriving when humans arrived in the region more than 15,000 years ago, before the legendary appearance of the dwarves in eastern Akados. This suggests that either the Gtsang histories are incorrect or the Ankhuran dwarves predate their eastern relatives.

The Ankhurans themselves are no help as they simply claim that "we have always been here" and let it go at that. As the prehistory of the Ankhurans remains a sealed puzzle box, the only option left to scholars is to study the dwarves' history since their first contact with humans.

The dwarves were quick to make contact as soon as they were aware of the newcomers' presence, dispatching envoys into the hill country and establishing diplomatic relations with Gtsang. Representatives were taken to the Ankhuran realm where they witnessed the wonders of a truly ancient land that lay largely hidden in the mountains with only the impressive Ithanic Fortress visible to outsiders.

A stern but goodhearted people, the Ankhurans watched the Gtsang develop as decades stretched into centuries, then into millennia, and engaged in low-level trade and occasional cultural exchange. When the wise but cruel Red King Amnu-Paket rose to power as a result of corruption and evil in the heart of Gtsang's rulers, the Ankhurans were alarmed. Safe for the moment in their mountain fastness, the dwarves knew that it was only a matter of time before the greedy Red King came for them. Though confident of their ability to defend themselves, the Ankhurans knew that any conflict would devastate the region and cost countless lives. So they began a quiet but determined campaign to undermine Amnu-Paket and aid those in Gtsang who resisted.

When the uprising finally came, Gtsang warriors and priests alongside Ankhuran soldiers assailed Amnu-Paket's forces and drove his minions from power and pursued them into the mountains and laid siege to the seemingly-impenetrable Tu Chai Palace.

There, the Ankhurans shared some of their most ancient secrets and allowed the Anahbi priests — Gtsang spellcasters who had thrown their lot against the Red King — to cast a powerful ritual that destroyed Amnu-Paket and freed the nation from his tyranny. Grateful to the dwarves for their help, the Gtsang priests swore that the knowledge they had been given would never be used for evil purposes, though rumors persist that the powerful Ankhuran rituals were transcribed and saved in a great book that remains well-guarded in the city of Duam.

Fortunately for the dwarves and everyone else, the priests kept their promise, and harmony reigned in relations between the two nations. When the Xha'en Hegemony was founded in 2700 XC (1398 I.R.), the Ankhurans were once more concerned with the growing power of the humans and immediately dispatched emissaries to secure their independence and lay the groundwork for peaceful relations. The Xha'en had little interest in conquering an underground realm full of dwarves and so readily agreed. Today, Ankhuran armor, weapons, arts, and crafts can be found throughout the Hegemony, commissioned directly from dwarven artisans.

RELIGION

As with most everything else, the dwarves are relatively tight-lipped about their religion. It is known that they are monotheistic and revere a single creator god named Masakhan, and their reverence for the heroes of the past suggests that they believe that especially accomplished dwarves join their creator as divine beings devoted to law and good. This is an earned status — those who do not achieve greatness in their lifetime are reincarnated and given another opportunity, while those who are evil and unredeemable are snuffed out and cease to exist, thus making certain that only the truly good can return. Priests provide guidance to worshippers regarding proper conduct, behavior, and the right path to true goodness.

TRADE AND COMMERCE

The Ankhurans are not an especially isolationist nation, nor are they overly friendly with outsiders. They retain a typically dwarven skill in trade and craftsmanship, however, and have maintained mercantile relationships with the region's humans since their arrival some 15,000 years ago. More recently, the Castorhagi of Bream approached the dwarves, opening up some commerce and further cementing the status of the Bream colonies as a permanent fixture in the region.

There is little that the humans harvest or manufacture that the dwarves need, so trade is mostly in terms of gold, silver, and exotic items that tickle the Ankhurans' stern fancy. Fabrics, works of art, unusual foods such as citrus fruit, and poultry are all traded for Ankhuran crafts, tools, weapons, armor, and mechanical devices. Trade usually takes place in human lands, or at the Ithanic Fortress, which is normally accessible to humans by sea.

LOYALTIES AND DIPLOMACY

Steadfast and independent, the Ankhurans nevertheless value peace and friendly relations with their human neighbors. Dwarven emissaries visit and even dwell among the humans of Anaros, Xha'en, and Gtsang, while human diplomats are allowed into some of the less-sensitive regions of the Ankhuran kingdom. The Castorhagi have been treated with a little more reserve, though diplomatic missions have been exchanged between Ankhura and Bream in recent years, which the humans hope will lead to full diplomatic relations.

The dwarves are also willing to send their veteran warriors to aid their neighbors should any outside force threaten the general peace, though it usually has to threaten Ankhura itself to trigger such a response. The most prominent such incident was when the dwarves aided the Gtsang in their war against the Red King Amnu-Paket.

Besides their tentative contacts with Castorhage, the Ankhurans do not maintain relations with any nation outside the Xha'en region. In fact, most outsiders are completely unaware of the kingdom's existence, a fact which is fine with the Ankhurans.

GOVERNMENT

The dwarves' government is hierarchal and family-structured, with a grand matron or patron (or sometimes both in the case of married monarchs) at its head, and lesser matrons and patrons below. In general, a given matron or patron has authority over all those of lesser rank, though it is considered polite and proper to couch all "commands" in the form of requests. These requests are almost always carried out however, though subordinates always have the opportunity to question them or request clarification. Rarely must a high-ranking matron or patron demand obedience, nor are they ever outright refused. Controversial orders are sometimes discussed (occasionally at length) and may be modified by consensus. Though this system seems odd to outsiders, the Ankhurans have been practicing it for millennia and it seems to work well for them.

Other officials bear far less grandiose titles than their human equivalents — overseer being the rough equivalent of "duke" and manager more or less equivalent to "baron." Investitures such as "knight" and "lord" don't exist in the Ankhurans' largely egalitarian society, though great heroes who perish in battle are enshrined as (for the lack of a better term) "saints" and are believed to directly serve Masakhan in the afterlife.

MILITARY

Though they are loath to admit it, the Ankhurans are in reality a military state, with much of their society devoted to defending the kingdom and holding off terrible threats from deep below.

While their armor and weapons are every bit as strong, durable, and often as magical as those of other dwarven nations, the Ankhurans favor steel imbued with bronze coloration and classically designed muscled or decorated breastplates and conical helms. Unlike dwarves elsewhere in Akados, the dwarves of Ankhura prefer swords over axes, usually with heavy, curved blades such as falchions, khopesh, or yataghans. Ankhuran shields are square and semi-cylindrical, allowing Ankhuran warriors to deploy with locked shields to block corridors and ward off missile fire. Ranged weapons include powerful shortbows and elaborate, intricately-designed crossbows with many different innovations such as self-loading mechanisms, accurate sights, and security latches that prevent their unauthorized use.

A small Ankhuran navy is based out of the port facilities below the Ithanic Fortress. These vessels patrol the waters of the Bream Straits (wary of incidents with the Castorhagi navy, which is also present there), the Kuseye Gulf, and the Thousand Rocks. While at top speed, Ankuran ships can challenge the fastest-oared or sailing vessels afloat, they seldom venture farther afield. In past years, the Ankhuran warships helped fight pirates and smugglers, but recently they have acted more as a mobile search-and-rescue force to aid vessels in distress or to help out in cases of natural disaster.

The Ankhuran warrior class is a distinct group, usually living separately from others and intermarrying within its own ranks. Children are allowed to choose their own path, but almost invariably continue in their parents' martial lifestyles. Warriors engage in ritual scarification, even males who normally leave their faces unadorned.

The highest rank in the Ankhuran military is Primary, equivalent to a general or field marshal, naturally followed by the Secondary (colonel or major) and Tertiary (captain). Below this are various grades of officers, each identified by command or responsibility. The Ankhuran equivalent to sergeant or non-commissioned officer is Master.

While the Ankhurans do not have the same berserker traditions as some dwarves and humans, they do consider death in service to the nation as the highest of honors. Barracks areas throughout Ankhura are decorated with shrines, statues, and images of past warriors who fell in battles unknown to anyone outside the subterranean realm. In some cases, these heroes gave their lives in conflicts that might have ended in regional, or even global catastrophe, against unspeakable horrors from the deep levels, and lie unknown to any but their fellow Ankhurans.

MAJOR THREATS

Almost nothing aboveground threatens the Ankhuran Kingdom, and the imposing edifice of the Ithanic Fortress is a tangible symbol of the dwarves' strength and ability to defend themselves. The Ankhurans are also quite capable of responding to dangers on the surface, as they did when they sent warriors to aid in the Gtsang's battles against Amnu-Paket. The truest and most alarming threats to Ankhura, and to the world beyond, lie in the deep spaces far below, and almost no one on the surface is aware of them.

The tunnels and warrens beneath the Tsendakar Mountains and elsewhere in Xha'en are home to subterranean races — derro, goblins ratfolk, and others — that struggle ceaselessly against both each other and the Ankhurans. The dwarves are able to defend themselves handily against these foes, and most battles involve fending off raids or punitive attacks into enemy territory. There are tales of periodic derro invasions, goblin migrations, and explosions of ratfolk population that lead to large-scale conflicts, but these are rare.

Known only to very few, the Ankhurans' most ancient and dangerous foes lurk in the labyrinthine tunnels that lie beneath the kingdom's lowest levels. No one knows who dug these tunnels; perhaps they have always been there. The Ankhurans will not even acknowledge that they exist, but a handful of inquisitive visitors and illicit explorers from the surface world — those who survived with their bodies and sanity intact at any rate — have described them.

The tunnels are said to twist and turn in strange ways that induce sickness, mental instability, and even physical pain. They appear to exist in more than three dimensions, looping back on themselves or delivering confused travelers to entirely different locations, hopelessly lost and on the verge of madness. A few observers have spoken quietly of disturbing carvings and runes that run all along the tunnels — runes that alarmingly resemble the characters of the Ankhuran phonetic alphabet.

The tunnels are the least of the deep horrors, for a few hushed rumors have filtered down from the tight-lipped Ankhurans that suggest the tunnels are inhabited by entities every bit as alien and disturbing. These horrors seem to originate someplace deeper yet, where even the Ankhurans refuse to go, and periodically surge up from the depths to assail the dwarves' kingdom in ferocious attempts to break out onto the surface.

When this happens, the Ankhurans go to war with absolute society-wide dedication. Every Ankhuran fights when the horrors come. Entrances to the surface are sealed, diplomats withdrawn, tradeposts closed, and visitors are unceremoniously escorted out. No one knows exactly how the Ankhurans face the horrors — that these wars take place at all is little more than whispered rumor. But the dwarves' fatalistic determination suggests that that this is an ancient and extremely important conflict. Claims exist that the Ankhurans possess some very old magic, rituals, artifacts, and devices that are essential in their battles against the horrors of the deeps, and that one such ritual was used to defeat the Red King Amnu-Paket. Again, the Ankhurans say little to nothing about such matters, but those who know the dwarves well are assured that the horrors, and the measures to which the Ankhurans go to keep them contained, are all too real.

WILDERNESS AND ADVENTURES

The Ankhuran kingdom is located beneath the inhospitable and largely impassable Tsendakar Mountains. Entrances to the kingdom are hidden throughout the region, though generally only the Ankhuran dwarves themselves can locate and operate them. The Ithanic Fortress is accessible from above, but the landward route is over a narrow and treacherous mountain trail that many have tragically failed to traverse.

Access from the sea is much easier, as the fortress has extensive port facilities far below its peak.

Travelers in the mountains may find themselves lost, starving, injured, and attacked by hostile denizens such as goblins, frost giants, and yetis, in which case the Ankhuran dwarves may appear from hidden entrances to aid the unfortunates. Such contact probably leads adventurers into the kingdom itself, at least those portions where outsiders are allowed. Trusted outsiders may sometimes be recruited to help the dwarves fight off attacks by goblins or ratfolk, but the struggle against the deep horrors is usually reserved for the Ankhurans alone. Being allowed into the dwarves' confidence sufficiently to know the truth about the horrors may be the basis of an especially involved series of adventures.

Delving into the mysteries of the dwarves' origins and their connection to the depths below may also be possible, though doing so without the Ankhurans' consent quickly earns their enmity. As a rule, Ankhurans do not murder, but those who learn too much may find themselves imprisoned or have their memories obscured through arcane means, possibly leading to even greater complications. Only the most trusted and reliable of outsiders can be taken into the dwarves' confidence, and then only if absolute secrecy is sworn.

Tales among the Xha'en say that Ankhuran treasures and artifacts may lie hidden or forgotten in the mountains as well. It is known that the dwarves hold the secret of powerful magical rituals, and some old stories suggest that they crafted especially dangerous artifacts to battle unspecified enemies in the distant past. These secrets and artifacts, along with fabulous treasure, may be hidden in the craggy Tsendakar peaks. No one has thus far ever discovered such treasures, but this has not stopped greedy explorers from venturing to the region, often failing so catastrophically as to require rescue from the Ankhruans, the very folk that they intended to rob.

THE IRON OCTAGON (CAPITAL)

Ruler: Grand Matron Ninsar Hamura
Government: hereditary monarchy
Population: 95,000 (Ankhuran dwarf)
Technology Level: Medieval/Renaissance

The Ankhuran seat of government is a central citadel called the Iron Octagon, a heavily-fortified location under the peak of Mount Babokha. Here, the Grand Matron Ninsar Hamura oversees the domain, protected by elite Ankhuran veterans. Various lesser matrons and patrons travel to the Octagon regularly, and the entire fortress is a constant beehive of activities. Outsiders are rarely allowed into the Octagon, as the place is full of sensitive information about the inner workings of the kingdom and — more alarmingly — about the horrors that dwell far below.

ITHANIC FORTRESS

Ruler: Matron Nakhala Hosh
Government: military fortress
Population: 105,000 (99,000 Ankhuran dwarf, 3,000 Jaati, 2,500 Xha'en, 500 other)
Technology Level: Medieval/Renaissance

The dwarves of Ankhura, the subterranean kingdom that occupies the western portion of the Tsendakar Mountains, are an insular but good-aligned lot. Their main connection to the outside world is through the gray stone Ithanic Fortress, an artificial massif that dominates the coastline along the southern Bream Straits. A casual viewer might see the fortress as just another grim gray mountain, but closer observation reveals that the entire crag is carved with Ankhuran runes, and its peak is crafted in the shape of an Ankhuran dwarf warrior with a conical helm.

The fortress is accessible by land over a long and circuitous trail that connects to the Heavenly Road in the east, and by sea through sturdy stone docks that lead to enclosed ship pens, connected via a series of stairs, elevators, and lifts to the fortress nearly 10,000 feet above. Here, visitors and merchants can interact with the dwarves, who, despite their insularity, are friendly and hospitable. The dwarves also maintain a small but efficient fleet of warships that can be called into action in the event of piracy, disasters, or raids by hostile sea creatures.

A number of Ankhuran officials oversee the fortress's operation. The Matron Nakhala Hosh is the current senior manager, and she runs the place with singular efficiency. Unusually for an Ankhuran dwarf, she has spent several years among the humans in the Xha'en Hegemony and understands their strange ways better than most. Her top military officer, Primary Fehna Khe, is a veteran of many underground battles and has a rare understanding of the horrors that dwell deep below. The fortress itself has fought off several major attacks by goblins and continues to be a stronghold of Ankhuran influence in the mountains and along the Bream Straits.

THE WESTERN ISLES
THE BREAM ISLANDS

(Breem)
Capital: Farthest Point
Notable Settlements: Neer
Ruler: Governor Lord Duke Taneth
Government: Colonial governorship
Population: 50,000 (35,000 Castorhagi, 14,000 Koui, 1,000 Xha'en)
Monstrous: none
Languages: Common
Religion: Castorhagi, Xha'en Imperial Pantheon, animism (Koui)
Resources: fishing, ironwork, manufactured goods, shipbuilding, shipbuilding supplies
Currency: Castorhagi currency
Technology Level: Renaissance

Wild and sparsely populated, the Bream Islands were long the domain of the Koui — simple fisherfolk who lived on the coastline, scratching out a meager living from the sea. All that changed in 4512 XC (3210 I.R.) when King Worrn II of Castorhage issued a decree calling for the exploration of the Nether Sea (as the Caerulean Ocean was called) and colonization of the Bream Islands. This act caused an unexpected crisis in the Xha'en Hegemony and ended with a foreign presence directly on the Xha'en's doorstep. Cautious relations continue to this day, though the Xha'en's new emperor is using the Castorhagi presence as a possible route to full contact and open trade with the outside world.

HISTORY AND PEOPLE

The Breams' original inhabitants, known as the Koui, appear to be related to the Senge tribesfolk of the mainland. They live in slate-roofed stone huts in villages of 10–50 and maintain small fishing boats or coracles. The Koui follow a simple subsistence economy, surviving on fish, abalone, and seaweed. Generally left to their own devices by the Xha'en, the Koui have lived in this fashion for thousands of years, with most of their villages clustered around the southern ends of the three Bream Islands.

The city-state of Castorhage was the Hegemony's only truly foreign trading partner, having established official mercantile relations in 3888 XC (2586 I.R.). However, it was not until 4512 XC (3210 I.R.) that King Worrn II of Castorhage decided that the city needed overseas colonies, and commanded that settlers be dispatched westward. The near-empty northern reaches of the Bream Islands presented the colonists with a risky but very real opportunity, with the hope that Castorhage's previous relationship with the Hegemony would lessen hostility and help avoid open conflict.

The Castorhagi exploration vessel *Brave* made landfall in the Breams in 4515 XC (3213 I.R.) and found the islands suitable for colonization. A Castorhagi fleet arrived in the early summer of 4523 XC (3221 I.R.) and quickly established an outpost that was dubbed Farthest Point. Within weeks, several crude stone structures and a palisade had been built, and when unsuspecting Xha'en fishermen discovered it late in the fall, the outpost was well established and defended by well-armed Castorhagi soldiers. Farthest Point's governor, Duke Lord Kestrel, had not been idle either, having dispatched a trade delegation to the Gtsang Prefecture and persuaded the notoriously isolationist inhabitants to open a small trading post.

Winter storms set in by the time news reached Empress Ilesa sa Yn Rachar and further investigation of the newcomers would have to wait until the following spring. As soon as the weather was favorable, an official delegation, accompanied by a strong force of Xha'en soldiery, sailed to the Breams to report on and, if necessary, destroy the foreign colonists.

The Castorhagi were decadent and ancient to be sure, but they were anything but stupid. The arrival of the Xha'en was inevitable, and Duke Lord Kestrel was as prepared for the event as anyone could be under the circumstances. He greeted the Xha'en delegation with deference, flattery, and declarations of friendship, reminding the Xha'en of their two nations' long friendship, and presented gifts and offered tribute to the Hegemony in exchange for the colony's independence.

Despite the Hegemony's significant power and influence, the Xha'en delegation was somewhat taken aback at Castorhage's diplomatic assault, and despite some misgivings, relayed Kestrel's offer back to Empress Ilesa. Unsurprisingly, her court was thrown into confusion by these events, with some demanding open war with the "invaders" and others counseling a peaceful resolution and pointing to the centuries-long trade relationship between the two powers. Fortunately for all, Ilesa sided with the peace faction and agreed to let the colony stay, so long as yearly tribute was paid. The Castorhagi were allowed to build a second outpost on Greater Bream, but further expansion was limited, and any approach to the Xha'en mainland was strictly forbidden.

For their part, the Castorhagi stuck scrupulously to the letter of this agreement and established the outpost of Neer, then greatly expanding facilities on Farthest Point until it was a fully-functioning fortress, a major shipyard, and important waypoint for Castorhagi traffic north toward the city's new colonies along the Elitani coast. Both settlements proved vital when they supplied and supported Castorhage's fleet in the defeat of the Sea-Throng of the Sinking Place in 4773 XC (3471 I.R.) and as a refuge for damaged Castorhagi vessels after their disastrous defeat on the Kraken's Teeth in 4793 XC (3491 I.R.).

The two Bream settlements have continued to grow in recent years as trade along the Caerulean coast grows and ships move in larger numbers from Castorhage and the Free States to the new Elitani colonies. The Breams may well prove still more important as the Xha'en Hegemony and its new emperor move to end centuries of isolation, for now the Xha'en have established a permanent diplomatic mission there, and more Xha'en immigrants have begun traveling to live and work in the teeming districts of Castorhage.

The islands are growing more cosmopolitan by the day, with traders of several nations and ancestries arriving to help with mercantile endeavors. Elves, dwarves, halflings, and others are now seen among the crowds of Castorhagi traders, sailors, soldiers, and officials.

Religion

As in Castorhage proper, actual "religion" is something of a misnomer, for dozens of faiths compete for prominence. The settlements of Neer and Farthest Point boast places of worship for several of Castorhage's true gods, including Baphomet, Mithras, and Mother Grace, but the most popular true gods are probably Mammon, a god of ruthless commerce and prosperity, and Sister Shadows, who is especially popular with shipwrights and some mariners.

The Koui, who still practice their subsistence economy along the Breams' southern coastlines, generally follow the Xha'en pantheon, with a scattering of animistic local spirits, household gods, and entities of the sea that must be propitiated to bring rich hauls of fish.

Trade and Commerce

As the Bream colonies were founded for trade and support of trade, it's not surprising that they are today centers of exchange for the region, and vitally important to Castorhage's growing colonial empire. Regular trade with the insular Gtsang was established early, with finished goods and foodstuffs sent to the Prefecture in exchange for raw ore, fabrics,

and artwork. Trade was similarly established with the Thousand Rocks, and many Bream warriors bear weapons of Anari steel, and Bream nobles wear garments of Anari silk.

Full and official trade relations with the Hegemony had existed since well before the colony's establishment, though the quantities of actual trade were relatively small. This situation is changing as the Emperor Sajrac su Kar has begun to negotiate and expand his contacts with the outside world.

Farthest Point's naval facilities are increasingly vital as well, and now Hegemony vessels — fishing ships and even naval craft — have begun to make port there, seeking assistance from the skilled Castorhagi shipwrights.

Loyalties and Diplomacy

The Breams occupy a somewhat delicate position: an outpost of the growing influence of Castorhage next door to the ancient power of the Xha'en Hegemony. Officially, Neer and Farthest Point are colony cities, and the Hegemony claims the remainder of the Breams, though there has never been a significant Xha'en presence there. The two outposts have expanded over the years to the very limits allowed by treaty, and now that a friendlier and far more outgoing monarch sits upon the Xha'en throne, Queen Alice's diplomats have begun to make polite but insistent requests to expand Castorhagi influence to the entirety of all three isles.

The Breams' value as naval facilities for vessels traveling to and from the Castorhagi colonies in the north has also increased the influence of the islands' governor and made the office a highly desirable one. The current governor, Lord Duke Taneth, is also an influential nobleman who hopes one day to ascend to the rank of Justice and is willing to move heaven and earth to do so. Such is his ambition that he has managed to double the naval resources assigned to Farthest Point and station several elite regiments of Castorhagi troops at Neer under the pretense of providing security for merchant and colonial traffic bound for Elitani lands to the north. Hushed rumors suggest that Taneth's goals are far more elaborate, and that he intends to provoke a diplomatic incident with the Hegemony over maritime routes near Quy Island. In the ensuing conflict, Taneth hopes to use his crack Castorhagi troops and warships to sweep aside Hegemony defenders and add Quy to Castorhage's empire. While the long-term consequences of such an ill-advised strategy should be obvious to even the dullest observer, the soaring heights of Taneth's ambitions may not allow him to see disaster in the offing.

The Castorhagi are aware of the existence of the Kingdom of Caerulea, but so far have made no effort to approach the state or establish diplomatic relations. Castorhagi vessels travel unmolested in the region, and captains are usually careful about what they throw overboard for fear of offending the merfolk. A growing number of officials have called for direct contact with Caerulea, but so far Governor Taneth has refused.

Government

The greater colony of Bream is under the overall command of an appointed governor, usually of ducal rank. Each of the two citadels is in turn commanded by a military officer, both subordinate to the governor in civil matters. As noted, the position of governor has gained significant influence as the Breams grow more important to Castorhage, and Lord Duke Taneth is an especially notable example of the ambitious Castorhagi nobleman hoping to increase his personal power. The two garrison commanders, Lord General Aldus and Lady General Gentari, are both skilled professionals who have few ambitions beyond military service — a situation that Taneth himself arranged when he saw to their assignments.

Military

Farthest Point is currently the most important Castorhagi outpost in the far west, equipped as it is with extensive shipbuilding and repair facilities. Supplies are shipped from the Forest Coast and elsewhere to keep the shipyards working at peak effectiveness, and thanks to Governor Taneth's influence, a full squadron of warships, including the *Strategos*, are currently assigned to provide protection for the port and for vessels bound to and from the northern colonies.

Taneth has made certain that only the best and most competent Castorhagi soldiers and sailors are assigned to the Breams. Soldiers, knights, and engineers all have excellent arms and armor, and some are entirely equipped with weapons of Anari steel. Unbeknownst to the Xha'en, the Castorhagi have also equipped the fortresses with defensive weapons such as anti-ship ballistae and fire-throwing war engines; these are kept hidden should hostilities with the Hegemony ever break out.

While Castorhagi numbers are markedly inferior to the seemingly-endless manpower commanded by the Xha'en, their position on the Breams would allow them to hold out for a significant period, and their powerful warships outclass the Hegemony navy in almost every category. On the other hand, choking the Breams off from supplies would be relatively simple, and any relief from Castorhage would take months or even years to arrive. War between the two states would clearly be a long, drawn-out affair likely to sap both societies and economies, so cooler heads on both sides believe it should be avoided. Unfortunately, rumor has it that Governor Taneth himself is willing to risk confrontation simply to advance his own political fortunes.

Major Threats

The Breams currently face no overt threats save for the harsh environment of the Caerulean Ocean and the sheer distance to the city of Castorhage. Potential enemies surround the Breams, of course, which has necessitated an elaborate diplomatic balancing act. Tribute is sent to the Hegemony every year, while trade is maintained with Gtsang, the Thousand Rocks, and the dwarves of Ankhura.

The greatest potential threat to the Breams, of course, is the Xha'en Hegemony, and the Castorhagi have remained here at the Xha'en's indulgence for three centuries. Even if meddlers such as Governor Taneth don't succeed in triggering a disastrous conflict between Castorhage and the Hegemony, there remains a distinct possibility that a war faction or other group hostile to the colony might rise in influence or, worse yet, replace the emperor entirely.

Wilderness and Adventures

The Breams are for the most part rocky, windswept wilderness, with settlements only on their coastlines. There are a few exceptions, such as the great mountains of Shir and Kor on Lesser Bream. The islanders tell tales of the hero Nandase, whose bones are said to lie at the summit of Mount Kor. Pilgrims can supposedly receive blessings and good luck when they pray at this site, but the route up the mountain is deadly, plagued by fierce griffins, giant eagles, and, in some stories, vengeful spirits. One of the few green and pleasant regions in the Breams are the forests and meadows at the base of Mount Shir, which the islanders say are inhabited by nature spirits who are kind to those who treat the land well and vengeful to those who mistreat it. A small sect of druids dwells here in caves and tends the land.

A few legends speak of ogres, trolls, giants, and various species of ogre magi that live in the island's rugged interior, occasionally preying upon the unfortunate fisherfolk of the southern coast. Whether these stories are true or not has never been determined.

Shir Meadows

Though the vast bulk of the Breams are windswept rock, with some patches of twisted trees, scrub, and lichen, the valley between Mount Kor and Mount Shir is an odd (and some would say arcane) exception. Here, dense pine forest surrounds a series of alpine meadows, full of wildlife and rich, rugged beauty. A clan of good fey are said to dwell here apart from the rest of the world and protected by a small sect of human Koui druids. These druids defend the area against intruders and keep the area healthy, while dwelling in the caves that are found among the crags of Mount Shir. The Koui themselves hold the meadows sacred and come here only in solemn religious pilgrimages in the late spring. Once there, they leave offerings to the fey and the druids, engage in quiet prayer and enjoy the beauty before returning home. The Castorhagi are interested in the meadows but are wise enough not to violate them for fear of offending the Koui and possibly triggering an incident with the Anari or the Xha'en.

Farthest Point, Colony Town of

Ruler: Lord Duke Taneth (governor), Lady General Gentari (military commander)
Government: colony
Population: 14,000 (almost all Castorhagi, handful of Xha'en and Koui)
Technology Level: Renaissance

Established three centuries ago by an expedition from the city-state of Castorhage, Farthest Point was the first foothold by a foreign power in the Xha'en region and caused considerable consternation among the imperial court. The outpost survived through skillful diplomacy and good fortune, and today is a significant location for the Castorhagi, with extensive shipyards, barracks, sturdy walls, and port facilities. Trade delegations from the Hegemony, the Thousand Rocks, and the normally-insular Gtsang Prefecture are also here helping to establish a mercantile connection that the emperor and the Castorhagi hope keeps the peace and fosters ties between the disparate nations.

Farthest Point has grown in size and prominence over the years, as Castorhage's colonies in the Elitani lands to the north expand. Supply vessels, merchant ships, and ships of the Royal Castorhage Navy make port here. A small fleet of Castorhagi warships has been permanently assigned here at the insistence of the colony's governor, Lord Duke Taneth. Though he maintains this is entirely for defensive purposes, it is widely thought that he intends to create a diplomatic incident with the Hegemony as a pretext for invading Quy Island and wants to use his newly-reinforced fleet to do it.

Neer, Colony Town of

Ruler: Lord Duke Taneth (governor), Lord General Aldus (military commander)
Government: colony
Population: 7,000 (almost all Castorhagi, handful of Xha'en and Koui)
Technology Level: Renaissance

Established in 4576 XC (3274 I.R.) on Lesser Bream island, this outpost added more protection and influence to the established Castorhagi presence elsewhere in the Breams. Today it consists of a single-walled citadel surrounded by a small settlement with attached ship repair and boatbuilding facilities. Governor Taneth also increased the outpost's garrison from 1,000 to nearly 5,000, forcing the construction of new barracks, armories, and storehouses. Some question Taneth's motives for this increase, and some go so far as to suggest that this is an invasion force to be used against the Hegemony to increase Taneth's status and influence in Castorhage.

Neer has begun to service overflow traffic from the nearby facilities at Farthest Point. The Xha'en continue to keep a wary surveillance of the outpost, though as with Farthest Point, they sometimes take advantage of ship repair services here.

Anaros Island and the Thousand Rocks

Capital: Ui'aharti
Notable Settlements: Ochotari
Ruler: Eldest Saharwa Terq
Government: feudalism
Population: 1,200,000 (almost all Anari, with a small number of scattered Xha'en, Jaati, Koui)
Monstrous: ankhegs, giant boars, giant elk, goblins, green hags, insect swarms, ogres, oni, owl bears, perytons, giant spiders, stirges, wolves, wolves (dire)
Languages: Anari, Xaon
Religion: Ni Araha and Yisya Thun
Resources: alchemical reagents, cloth, copper, fishing, gems (pearls), glass, ironwork, linen, pottery, shipbuilding
Currency: Anari
Technology Level: Medieval

The Thousand Rocks is a single domain under the spiritual (if not political) leadership of an individual with the title of Eldest who dwells in an inaccessible temple high on Mount Yu'unar. A brave and stoic people, the Anari are known throughout the Xha'en Hegemony as skilled warriors who have developed a vibrant culture and society almost through will alone, transforming a resource-starved land into a strong nation with rich traditions.

HISTORY AND PEOPLE

The Anari are related to the Xha'en people. Physically, they are quite similar, though the Anari are somewhat shorter on average and red hair is not uncommon. Though the story of how they got to Anaros and the Thousand Rocks is shrouded in legend, it is believed that they came seeking refuge from a pressing nomadic tribe, possibly the Hundaei — the Anari themselves date landfall from 1313 XC (about 11 I.R.). Most stories say that these Anari were refugees from a terrible war far to the east and that they arrived on the islands after fleeing from an army of demons led by evil gods and powerful sorcerers.

The leader of these refugees — once more, according to legend — was the demigoddess Ni Araha, a deity of justice and mercy who had taken a mortal husband, the warrior-king Yisya Thun. Ni Araha and Yisya Thun would lead their people as they colonized Anaros and spread across the Thousand Rocks, and their children — all imbued with various semi-divine powers — would found all the important institutions that govern Anari society. The office of the Eldest, the various noble houses, the traditions of the Uarsinsi warriors, the collective society that shares its resources in times of trouble, the ascetic houses of monks where martial arts and divine magic are taught — all of these are said to have originated with Ni Araha and Yisya Thun's children, whose descendants are believed to still dwell among the Anari today.

The Anari survived on the rocks for nearly a half-millennium, only barely acknowledged by the powerful Xha'ahan city-states to the east. Some trade and travel took place, but for the most part Anaros and the Thousand Rocks were left to their own devices. All that changed in 1834 XC (532 I.R.) when the forces of the Jhohir Confederacy made landfall in the rocks, intending to sweep over the Anari and greatly expand their burgeoning empire.

The Anari, well-schooled in the ways of the warrior and aware of the threat that the confederacy represented, fought back with hit-and-run tactics, sapping the enemy's manpower and supplies even as they retreated island by island. On occasion, the Anari called up the mightiest of their warriors, known as the Uarsinsi, and made a stand, inflicting further losses on the confederacy until at last, plagued by shortages, sickness, and terrible storms that smashed their vessels to kindling, the invaders gave up and returned home, greatly weakened and reduced in number. The defeat proved a death-blow to the confederacy, and within three years, the state utterly collapsed, its two member-cities now independent and hostile toward one another.

The Anari continued to enjoy their independence, and their defeat of the confederacy lent them an almost-mystical reputation. When the Xha'en Hegemony finally subdued the former members of the Jhohir Confederacy and forged a single state in 2700 XC (1398 I.R.), diplomats were immediately dispatched, and treaties signed, guaranteeing independence to the Anari. A new era of cooperation followed as the Anari helped found the Udanishanti Temple in the Tsendakar Mountains and actually sent Uarsinsi warriors to aid in training and supervising Hegemony military formations.

In 3250 XC (1948 I.R.), the Anari faced a new threat: an invasion from the sea. Strange scaled creatures emerged from the surf along Anaros Island's western shore, attacking villages and dragging victims into the sea. These were not the merfolk of Caerulea — far from it. A great surge in the population of sahuagin had driven the sea devils to attack the land for food, and after initial shock and confusion, the Anari fought back, going so far as to seek help from the Caerulean Kingdom, whose rulers eventually lent aid and helped defeat the invasion from the sea. The inhabitants of western Anaros Island still speak of this terrible struggle and remain on guard against another such attack.

Today, Anaros Island and the Thousand Rocks persist as an independent state and neighbor of one of the most powerful empires in the world. A stream of trade flows between the Rocks and Xha'en Hegemony and to the Bream Islands to the north. The swordsmiths, Uarsinsi warriors, and monks of Anari maintain their fearsome and near-legendary reputation, while from the heights of Mount Yu'unar, the Eldest oversees a nation that needs little real oversight.

RELIGION

The islands' native faith arrived with the refugees — as legend tells it, they were accompanied by the demigoddess Ni Araha and her husband, the mortal hero Yisya Thun. Ni Araha was the last survivor of her pantheon, which had been slaughtered and thrown down by an alliance of demons and evil gods. Over generations, new aspects of the faith emerged, and when Yisya Thun died, he and Araha ascended to the heavens, leaving their children and children's children to watch over the people of the Thousand Rocks.

With her fellow gods dead, Ni Araha urged the Anari to adopt a new faith that revered the divine spark that dwelled in all living things and natural objects. This faith is somewhat druidic in nature and many Anari priests and monks have access to druid spells. The only true "gods" that the Anari revere are Ni Araha and Yisya Thun, who watch over the lives of their followers but rarely intervene.

TRADE AND COMMERCE

For many centuries, the Anari managed on their own, growing their own food and crafting their own clothing, utensils, and vessels, then sharing equally during times of need. A small amount of trade existed between the Thousand Rocks and the Xha'en states, but this situation changed abruptly after the Anari's defeat of the Jhohir Confederacy. With their reputation as indomitable warriors firmly established, the other Xha'en cities agreed to leave the islands in peace, and when the Xha'en Hegemony was created, diplomatic relations were immediately established.

Since then, trade between the Thousand Islands, the Hegemony, and the Bream Islands has flourished. Anari weapons, ceramics, and fabrics are exchanged for foodstuffs, livestock, timber, and other vital materials in a mutually beneficial arrangement that helps to cement peace and good relations between the various nations.

The Anari themselves have a surprisingly flexible economy that combines a fairly robust trade and barter system with a collective process that takes effect in times of difficulty. Poor crops, bad weather, natural disasters … these events cause misery throughout the islands, and when they do occur, it is considered incumbent upon those with more to share with those who have less. Once the crisis passes, society returns to its normal practices, with commerce going back to its usual pace.

LOYALTIES AND DIPLOMACY

The Thousand Rocks is not officially allied to any state but it maintains peaceful relations with the Castorhagi of the Bream Islands and the Xha'en Hegemony. This is not to say that the Anari are unwilling to aid their neighbors in time of crisis — far from it. Anari weapons equip many Xha'en warriors, and Anari Uarsinsi warriors help train fighters in the Udanishanti Temple high in the Tsendakar Mountains. The Anari are friendly toward the folk of the Gtsang Prefecture and the dwarves of Ankhura as well.

GOVERNMENT

The Anari practice a rather unusual form of government, with the nation under the spiritual leadership of the Eldest, who dwells in an isolated temple high on Mount Yu'unar (or Mount Harthnow as the Castorhagi call it). Those with news or requests must usually come personally before the Eldest, which can be accomplished only by negotiating the perilous route to the temple up sheer mountain slopes above sickening heights. The Eldest also commands a group of flying messengers who ride great snowy owls, but such measures are employed only in times of emergency or when speed is of the essence.

The rationale behind this unusual system is that only those with truly significant issues will approach the Eldest. Other matters are dealt with by local governors who are appointed either by the Eldest or by a local council of nobles. These individuals are generally expected to consider the welfare of their communities and see to it that no one goes hungry or is otherwise neglected. They must also maintain bands of Uarsinsi warriors and other military forces sufficient to defend their districts in times of crisis. Governors who fail in these duties may find themselves removed from office, investigated, or even arrested.

The method of selecting a new Eldest is unknown to those outside of the Anari. Some statements by locals seem to suggest that the Eldest is in fact either immortal or fantastically long-lived, which seems absurd.

MILITARY

As there has not been a major military crisis in the Thousand Rocks for many, many years, it would not be surprising if the military were to be in decline, as it is in the Xha'en Hegemony. This is not the case, however, and the long-standing tradition of martial excellence among the Anari is as strong today as it was a millennium ago.

The islands' regular defenders are a skilled class of professional swordsmen who also serve to keep the peace, enforce governors' decrees, track down criminals, and aid in civil projects. The sense of duty that is instilled in each warrior means that even these seemingly menial tasks are considered to be honorable chores and are done without complaint. Among these are those trained in the highest of martial arts, the noble warriors known as the Uarsinsi.

In times of crisis, local militias are raised with able-bodied civilians armed, armored, and trained by their governors. For the most part, these times of crisis consist of natural disasters such as floods, tidal waves, and earthquakes, so as with the warriors, the army of the Anari exists primarily for civil purposes. Should the region come under attack however, the Anari army is fully capable of defending the islands against invasion.

MAJOR THREATS

As of today, no major outside powers threaten the Thousand Rocks. The Anari's reputation as invincible warriors has served them well and held the Xha'en Hegemony at bay for generations and kept the Castorhagi of the Bream Islands from investigating the region too closely. Sahuagin raids occasionally threaten Anaros Island from the seaward side, but local garrisons are assigned to deal specifically with such attacks, and they try to respond quickly.

WILDERNESS AND ADVENTURES

The Thousand Rocks that dot the Sheltered Sea are well named. Some are simply single bare spurs of rock projecting above the waves, sometimes supporting a single small dwelling. Others are larger, with villages and even a small amount of arable land. Among the rocks, the real wilderness lies underwater, where pearl divers seek riches and various sunken wrecks contain valuable cargo. The wildlife of the area can be hostile and includes sharks and octopi of enormous size as well as whales and other larger species that are dangerous simply due to their size.

Much of Anaros Island remains rugged, unsettled wilderness, and it is known that wild animals and hostile creatures such as ogres, goblins, and hags make their home there. Many stories are told about the island prior to human settlement, and some of these involve incidents during the Age of Dragons. One epic cycle claims that Anaros Island was once connected to the mainland, and that battles between two great alliances of dragons shattered the land and created the Sheltered Sea and the scattered islands of the Thousand Rocks. Remnants of the battle are believed to be found throughout the region, and one legend even suggests that the grand palace of an ancient gold dragon is somehow hidden on Anaros Island itself. There, it is said, the great being slumbers amid untold riches.

ANAYINONOS FORGE

Popular legend holds that Anari weapons are supernaturally sharp and imbued with amazing qualities, able to cut through almost any other material, and in the hands of a skilled Uarsinsi warrior, all but invincible. This legend is carefully encouraged and maintained by Anari swordsmiths, who have made mountains of gold from the Hegemony and others willing to pay for the weapons. In reality, the islands' iron is of such poor quality that it must be worked with quantities of charcoal over a very long period to be made suitable for weapon production. While the resulting steel is indeed of high quality, it is not magical, nor is it especially superior to many other forms of steel. Nevertheless, the Anari swordsmith's art requires surpassing skill and talent, for the blades produced are both beautiful and functional. Several elite Hegemony units are equipped with Anari weapons, and the sword of an Uarsinsi warrior must be of the most flawless manufacture.

Anayinonos Forge is probably the most famous swordsmithy in Anari and is located near the great city of Ui'aharti. Here, master sword-makers have practiced their trade for centuries, producing amazing weapons of all kinds. Each year, the Eldest himself requests the manufacture of a new sword, which is delivered to Aliyashinsah Temple via owl-rider and placed in a specially-designed display hall. None of the Eldest's swords has ever been used in battle.

UI'AHARTI, CITY OF (CAPITAL)

(wee-a-HAR-tee)
Ruler: Great Elder Domah Kald
Government: oligarchy
Population: 120,000 (almost all Anari)
Technology Level: Medieval

Located in a bay in the middle of the eastern coast of Anaros Island, Ui'aharti is the largest and most important city of the Anari. While the nation is generally overseen by the Eldest from the Warrior's Temple on Mount Yu'unar, Ui'aharti is the nation's cultural and economic center. Several colleges of excellent repute found in the city educate the youth of the nobility alongside some number from the countryside and even a few from outside Anaros Island in arts, philosophy, and magic. Some 15 schools of martial arts are in the city, and each provides instruction in a different master's style of swordplay or unarmed combat. Many nobles and merchants who oversee the more practical day-to-day Anari matters live here in aesthetic splendor, and their estates are marvels of art and architecture.

The collective nature of Anari society holds sway here as well, and even powerful nobles are expected to share their wealth with the less fortunate. Each day, poorer Anari visit these estates to meet with chamberlains and other officials to receive grants of money or food as needed. More generous nobles tend to wield more influence, while stingy families may find themselves ostracized and cut off from contact with the Eldest.

OCHOTARI, CITY OF

Ruler: City Elder Lashinsa Nudu
Government: oligarchy
Population: 75,000 (almost all Anari)
Technology Level: Medieval

Situated in the center of the Sheltered Sea, amid the jumbled chaos of the Thousand Rocks, Ochotari is more town than city. The steep slopes of Ososar Island rise sharply behind it, sculpted into steps of terraced farms, where rice and other crops are cultivated. Ochotari itself clings to a semicircular bay, usually crowded with tiny, one- and two-crew fishing vessels.

Besides it being the largest settlement in the Thousand Rocks, Ochotari is most remarkable for its rich oyster beds, and the high-quality pearls that they produce. An entire society of pearl divers exists here to harvest oysters for food and pearls. Although they are assisted by their own squad of spellcasters who provide *water breathing* and other useful spells, a pearl diver's life is a hazardous one, for the bay also harbors a number of dangerous species such as tiger seals — an especially aggressive species of carnivorous pinniped — and cove sharks, a large and particularly toothy breed that has developed a taste for humans. These, as well as currents, submerged rocks, entanglements, and related hazards make the pearl divers among the most celebrated and admired folk in the Thousand Rocks, and the Eldest has even recognized them as vital members of society and directed that the craft of pearl diving never be allowed to decline or die out.

ALIYASHINSAH, TEMPLE OF

Ruler: Eldest Saharwa Terq
Government: Oligarchy
Population: 800 (almost all Anari)
Technology Level: Medieval

Known as the Warrior's Temple, Aliyashinsah is the spiritual heart of Anari culture, and home to the nation's leader, the Eldest. Located on the highest peak of Mount Yu'unar on Anaros Island, Aliyashinsah is a wonder of aesthetics and construction, standing serenely with a commanding view of the nearby Bream Islands, the scattered Thousand Rocks, and the vastness of the Caerulean Ocean beyond. Most days, however, the mountain is shrouded in clouds, closing it into its own world, and shutting it off utterly from the world beyond. Snow lies thick on the ground for much of the year.

The location of the temple was a willful and conscious one — making the Eldest Saharwa Terq all but inaccessible ensures that only the most important matters are brought before him, and the isolation allows the ruler to pay mind to truly deep and spiritual issues. The Eldest spends most of his days in quiet contemplation, addressing matters of governance and society only as absolutely needed. The needs of the Eldest and maintenance on the temple are carried out by a staff of priests, monks, and white-armored Uarsinsi warriors who swear lifetime oaths of personal service.

The Eldest and his advisors are aware that the temple's isolation might prove a liability in an emergency, so Aliyashinsah is also home to a squadron of aerial messengers known as the White Wings who ride giant snowy owls and bring and dispatch important news, visitors, and supplies. The White Wings are legendary throughout Anaros Island and the Thousand Rocks and are the subject of many tales of their bravery, loyalty, and steadfastness.

QUY ISLAND

Quy Island is the only offshore holding of the Xha'en Hegemony, located a few miles off of the western coast of the continent and home to several thousand Xha'en, mainly farmers and fishers. The city of Jhadarah sits on the island's north coast, and is home to the wealthy Y'lshon family, whose vessels first undertook the long journey to Castorhage to establish the first connection between the Hegemony and the outside world.

QUY TAR, FORTRESS OF

Ruler: Governor I'iris sa Ad Dharas
Government: military
Population: 3,000 (almost all Xha'en)
Technology Level: Medieval

This fortress guards the island of Quy, off the Xha'en coast. Here, a garrison of about 1,000 warriors and a dozen Xha'en warships is permanently stationed, though over the years the need for such a large group has been questioned. The emperor has maintained the garrison however, partially out of tradition, and partially out of wariness of the Castorhagi colonies on the Bream Islands to the north. While so far the Castorhagi have given no reason to suspect their intentions, the current schemes of Governor Lord Duke Taneth have roused some suspicion in the Hegemony, with a few of the emperor's advisors suggesting that he may be preparing for war.

JHADARAH, CITY OF

Ruler: Lord Teskec su Ric Y'lshon
Government: oligarchy
Population: 11,000 (almost all Xha'en)
Technology Level: Medieval

The largest settlement on Quy Island, Jhadarah is the domain of the Y'lshon family, wealthy merchants who have lived here for millennia. Shipbuilding and fishing facilities nearby drive the city's economy, while the Y'lshon's merchant fleet is based out of the city's sheltered bay. The city's ancient seaward walls stand weathered and overgrown with vines and shrub trees and retain a few traces of their original carvings and battlements.

The city's most prominent feature is the oldest continuously operating temple to the god Jatan in the Xha'en Hegemony. Located on the heights above the weathered buildings of Jhadarah's noble quarter, the temple is staffed by a group of six ancient priests and a number of younger monks who carry out the place's day-to-day running. Its true age isn't certain, but it is known to have been old when the city of Xha'ahan was founded more than 4,000 years ago. The common belief is that High Priest Arku is immortal, for he has held the post for as long as anyone alive today can remember. Arku is a wizened, ancient creature, almost blind and capable of communicating only in a faint whisper, but it is said that he can see the past and future with perfect clarity and will impart wisdom to those he considers worthy. He refuses to reveal future events however, for he claims that the gods themselves might be overthrown if anyone were to know what he knows. Exactly what this means no one knows, but a steady stream of pilgrims comes from all across the Hegemony to visit the temple. Few are deemed worthy to even enter the temple, let alone commune with the Ancient One, but those who do are said to return changed forever, with a light of true wisdom burning in their eyes.

SOOHR-AHMAAD

(SHYOOR-uh-MAHD, r slightly rolled)
Ruler: Suzerain Tahmani Kohr
Government: constitutional monarchy
Population: 3,000 (?) (efreeti)
Monstrous: none (in city limits)
Languages: Auran, Ignan, Infernal, Common
Religion: unknown
Resources: unknown, though residents do seem wealthy
Currency: mixed, primarily Xha'en
Technology Level: unknown, but at least High Middle Ages

This small, well-fortified town of efreeti is highly secretive and does not allow visitors within its gates. Outside their great, steel-spiked, stone town wall, a sumptuous "trade hall" — finely furnished and strewn with velvet and silk — has been built where visitors are invited to sell wares or services. The resident efreeti spend a great deal of money there, and never sell anything. In a magically scry-proof and soundproof backroom off the trade hall, efreeti leaders hold secret council with their hired scouts and spies, never inviting even these trusted servants inside the town proper.

Those who have had glimpses inside the gate or over the walls report a town that might support 2,000 to 4,000 efreeti. No other species have been noted, not even as servants. The homes inside seem to be of fine quality and very defensible. The streets are clean. No one who has seen more than that has shared what they have learned — assuming any lived to tell the tale.

HISTORY AND PEOPLE

Little is known of the residents of Soohr-Ahmaad. What locals have pieced together over the centuries may or may not be accurate, but it is commonly believed that the Soohr-Ahmaadin efreeti are descendants of a group banished from the City of Brass long ago. A thousand conflicting rumors argue as to why.

Whatever the reason for their banishment (assuming even that part of the tale is accurate), the Soohr-Ahmaadin efreeti behave toward their neighbors with a legalistically cruel sense of "fairness." All the intelligent communities and monsters in the Cauldron mountain range and its immediate surroundings, including the Xha'en Hegemony itself, have made extensive and complex agreements with the Cauldron efreeti (though the Xha'en Hegemony would never publicly admit to such a thing).

The primary way in which the Soohr-Ahmaadin efreeti interact with surrounding communities is in the hiring of scouts and spies to keep track of the world around them. Through the questions their employers ask, these hirelings are able to discern a little of their employers' motivations. According to some, even after many centuries away from the City of Brass, the Soohr-Ahmaadin efreeti remain paranoid that the Grand Sultan will yet send forces to destroy them. Similarly, they are fearful of meddling from the Hellsgate Peaks devils, whom they suspect of coveting their territory. For these reasons, the Soohr-Ahmaadin efreeti are always in search of news of devils or other efreeti. According to rumor, they are sometimes willing to pay in wishes, if adventurers will make secret expeditions into the Hellsgate Peaks (hundreds of miles away from the Cauldron range) to acquire military intelligence about the devils and their hidden city. Thus far, no such expedition has been known to succeed.

The Soohr-Ahmaadin efreeti never speak of why they were banished, why the Grand Sultan might still hold a grudge, why the devils might be plotting against them, or why they are so insular that they don't even keep slaves in their community as most efreeti do (at least, none that any outsiders have seen). They also seem to be bottomlessly wealthy and able to defend their community from incursion despite engaging in only one-sided commerce, no conquest, and not even any known mining activities.

It is commonly suspected that the efreeti guard some magnificent stolen artifact, one which provides their great wealth without them needing to lift a finger, and for the continued secrecy of which they might gladly die. In perfect accordance with their own laws and with their agreements with surrounding communities, the Soohr-Ahmaadin efreeti capture and execute all who attempt to solve the mysteries of their ongoing residence in the Cauldron mountain range.

Trade and Commerce

Soohr-Ahmaadin coin is mixed, but almost always current and local, with Xha'en being the most common. No one knows where or how they get it, or what skills, crafts, or trades the town possesses. The efreeti purchase almost anything of fine crafting from those who come to trade with them, even tools and weapons that no one ever sees them use. They do sometimes wear the jewelry or clothing they purchase, and traders have also observed them eat and drink.

The products in highest demand at the Soohr-Ahmaad trade hall are fine incense, high quality Xha'en rice wine or tea blends, and luxuriously preserved sweets. Ordinary food staples are sometimes purchased, but never in the quantities required to feed the entire community. Other than the spies and scouts, the efreeti show no interest in hiring services unless they can be performed on the spot. Musicians are sometimes paid to play in the trade hall, for example, and those who service weapons or repair clothing get customers now and again, among others.

There is talk of expanding the trade hall to allow privacy for a massage parlor or brothel, but traders say there is always such talk, and the project never begins. Perhaps the leadership of Soohr-Ahmaad does not want its citizenry to become quite so relaxed around outsiders.

In any event, however they acquire their coin, the Soohr-Ahmaadin efreeti offer a major boon to the business of all traders in their region, which makes them quite popular with their neighbors, despite their cruel and inflexible policy toward trespassers.

Loyalties and Diplomacy

As far as anyone knows, Soohr-Ahmaad is entirely independent, a miniature city-state. It has no official acknowledgement as such and seeks none, but extremely detailed arrangements exist between itself and all neighboring military powers — including the powerful Xha'en Hegemony — making it illegal for anyone to attack them, take possession of their land, or enforce external laws of any kind within their town walls.

Government

The Soohr-Ahmaadin efreeti make no secret that their suzerain was elected for life by the people, and that while her authority is generally accepted in all matters, her power can occasionally be held in check by a community council. Who sits on the council and why or for how long has not been shared with outsiders.

Military

Though the majority of the Soohr-Ahmaadin efreeti are never seen with weapons in the trade hall, the locals insist that every force that has ever assaulted Soohr-Ahmaad has failed. Many, traders report, have made the attempt, from human bandits to Cauldron fire giants to various monsters, often in search of whatever bottomless wealth store the efreeti possess. Whenever such a thing occurs, the traders who rely upon Soohr-Ahmaad's business for their livelihoods watch the proceedings intently from a safe distance. They report skilled defense of the walls by powerful warriors and impressive mages, the greatest of which is believed to be Suzerain Tahmani herself.

The Soohr-Ahmaadin forces always use the minimal force necessary to utterly destroy their enemies. They never attack, but if anyone attacks them, they show no mercy whatsoever. They do not allow fleeing attackers to escape, if at all possible, and they take no prisoners. They also never make sorties outside their walls, and when sieges have been attempted, they have simply waited for the threat to give up and go away (often encouraged by pressures from surrounding communities, who miss the profits of the trade hall). It would appear that wherever the efreeti get their money, they also have access to unlimited food stores.

It is not known what percentage of the Soohr-Ahmaad population participates in its defense when it is threatened.

Major Threats

According to the scouts and spies that serve the Soohr-Ahmaadin efreeti, the only things they fear are devils and other efreeti. If they do guard some precious artifact that grants their endless prosperity, one would assume that stealing or destroying said artifact would harm Soohr-Ahmaad greatly. However, Soohr-Ahmaad residents seem to feel confident that their secrets of secure abundance are safe from their Cauldron, Xha'en, and any other plane-local neighbors.

Wilderness and Adventures

While no one enters Soohr-Ahmaad besides its efreeti residents, the wilderness between Soohr-Ahmaad and its neighbors can be difficult to traverse at times. Wealthy merchants who sell their wares at the Soohr-Ahmaad trade hall rarely make the trek in person. Instead, they hire hardy and/or local agents to do their buying and selling and often send along a few guards to defend their merchandise on the road.

At the bottom of the road leading up to Soohr-Ahmaad, on the Xha'en side, a local adept sells potions of fire resistance at inflated prices, warning always of salamanders, rasts, mephits, or the occasional thoqqua on the trail. It is not inaccurate that some creatures normally native to the elemental plane of fire do make the volcanic Cauldron their home. Occasionally, there are bandits, some of whom might have a fire giant among them. It is true as well that with all the geysers and hotsprings in the area, much of the road is often shrouded in mist or steam, which allows for easy ambush at times.

Traders who make the trek regularly know that the road to Soohr-Ahmaad and its trade hall is usually clear, but you never go unarmed, you stay on the trail, and you always bring healing and fire resistance from somewhere with reasonable prices. If possible, it is recommended to travel quietly and to avoid advertising one's wealth.

SEA KINGDOM OF CAERULEA

(Kay-roo-lee-ah)

Capital: Sessamon (pop. 750,000)

Notable Settlements: Cealos (pop. 100,000), Cholama (pop. 100,000), Lacamon (pop. 250,000), Naelaec (pop. 350,000)

Ruler: King Avilon II

Government: monarchy

Population: 3,000,000 (2,000,000 merfolk, 750,000 aquatic elves, 250,000 tritons)

Humanoid: merfolk (many), aquatic elves (many), tritons (many)

Monstrous: aboleths, bunyips, giant crabs, dolphins, dragon turtles, sea drakes, giant eels, grindylows, sea hags, hippocampi, jellyfish swarm, giant jellyfish, kelpies, killer whales, krakens, locathah, merfolk, merrow, manta rays, reefclaws, sahuagin, scyllas, sea serpents, giant sharks, sharks (dire), skum, stingrays, giant octopus, giant seahorse, giant squid, tritons, water orms, whales, great white whales

Languages: Aquan

Religion: Eashe the Sea Mother

Resources: fishing, gems, sea plants, sculptures, jewelry

Currency: Caerulean

Technology Level: Medieval

The Caerulean Ocean lies to the west of the Xha'en Hegemony, a vast, dark body of water, largely unexplored, that has never been crossed in living memory. Beneath these forbidding waters lies a realm of wonder and surprising beauty, the undersea realm known as Caerulea. Ruled for thousands of years by a single royal family of merfolk, Caerulea has existed separately, following its own history and fighting its own cataclysmic wars, well hidden from the prying eyes of surface peoples. Only when the realm collided violently with the growing power of the Xha'en Hegemony did the region become known to outsiders.

As much empire as kingdom, Caerulea is divided among three distinct major groups as well as several smaller ones. The upper depths are inhabited by the sea elves, who live in dwellings of coral, magically altered into homes and utilitarian structures. These elves serve as the military class and, more recently, as a diplomatic corps, capable of surviving for long periods on the surface where they can meet and negotiate with the humans of Xha'en and other lands. Along the deeper waters of the coastal shelf, the ruling class of merfolk hold sway, while the extended slope between the edge of the Akadonian shelf and the fearsome abyss farther out to sea is the realm of the nomadic tritons who pay fealty to the royal family and serve as frontier scouts, hunters, and explorers.

HISTORY AND PEOPLE

Like other peoples, the folk of Caerulea have their own creation myths. Caerulean priests and teachers speak of a great oceanic god who created the merfolk to be its chosen servitors, seeing to the health and well-being of the sea and tending to its creatures. The tritons were granted the deeper waters as their home, but commanded to serve the merfolk, and the aquatic elves are said to have migrated from afar, having taken to the sea to avoid disaster on land. Arriving in Caerulean waters, the elves offered their services as warriors and hunters, and the merfolk welcomed them freely. For countless years, the merfolk claim, this situation endured, and they lived at peace, divided into many different kingdoms, all existing in harmony.

Caerulea's written history extends back to the Age of Kings, over 100 centuries ago, when it was only one of a dozen or so aquatic states, though it had been ruled by a single family for countless generations. The renegade mer-sorceress Awalea, who deeply resented the royal family's vast power and influence, took several followers into the undersea wilderness where they became leaders of an alliance of renegade merfolk, tritons and evil sea creatures including sahuagin,

aquatic demons, and grindylow in an attempt to overthrow Queen Caelass. Other kingdoms were drawn into the conflict, with some backing the rebels and some the royal family.

As the great Phoromycean civilization arose on land, as the foundations of the city of Barakus were laid, and as the Jaati city of Duam grew, a vast and terrible conflict raged unseen beneath the waves, invisible even to the folk of Gtsang, who sat literally on the doorstep of the Caerulean realm. A few mariners reported strange events at sea — unexpected storms, weird mid-ocean waves, and lights flashing in the depths — but for the most part, Awalea's War was fought in isolation, well away from the surface.

The conflict raged for decades. Communities were uprooted, coral fortresses shattered, and monstrous creatures used by both sides. Krakens, giant whales, devil rays, and horrors from the deepest depths fought and ravaged the realm. At long last, the rebels were defeated, and their surviving armies scattered. Of the evil sorceress Awalea, no sign was ever found, and to this day she lives on as an evil legend, often blamed for any misfortunes suffered by the kingdom or its inhabitants.

At the end of this long and painful conflict, Queen Caelass, long grown weary of war and killing, abdicated in favor of her son, Caelon. The new king, young and inexperienced, struggled to heal a kingdom devastated by war, and was soon in thrall to several scheming advisors, chief among them Count Isachla. This unscrupulous individual and a cabal of corrupt sea-priests and power-hungry nobles sought to become the power behind the throne, manipulating King Caelon and persuading him to expand the kingdom to first encompass those rival kingdoms that did not support Queen Caelass, and then the others. Through aggressive diplomacy and warfare where it was needed, Caerulea soon had absorbed all the other states, reducing them to mere principalities. The tritons and sea elves were also repressed, and some were reduced to virtual slavery.

As Caelon matured, he also grew stronger-willed, finally declaring his independence from Isachla's circle of "advisors." He relaxed many harsh laws and restored rights to the sea elves and tritons and gave the conquered kingdoms greater autonomy. When the duplicitous count hatched a conspiracy against the obstreperous monarch, Caelon responded harshly by arresting the conspirators and executing their leaders.

So it remained until well after the Xha'en arrived in their homeland and drove out the Senge tribes and the city of Xha'ahan grew to prominence. The Xha'en Hegemony prospered for over a century, unaware of the undersea kingdom's existence. But this was soon to change. In 2856 XC (1554 I.R.), a massive undersea earthquake ripped through the kingdom and unleashed several submerged volcanoes. The tremors shattered numerous Caerulean cities while the boiling lava, hot mud, and ash that surged up from below fouled the waters, killing millions of fish and poisoning thousands of merfolk.

Shortages and deprivation followed, along with unrest throughout the kingdom as the common folk felt the pinch of hunger. King Chalaine and his advisors were in a dilemma, lacking the population and material to expand significantly beyond their own frontiers. The deeper oceans and open sea were vast but had few resources to help the struggling kingdom. Only on the surface, where human ships plied the waves and humans raised crops and herds, could the kingdom obtain the food and materials that it needed.

Raids on the surface began with a few carefully-planned attacks, designed to appear as if ships were wrecked or lost in bad weather. It was not until the Caeruleans began to openly take ships and raid coastal areas that the Xha'en realized the full extent of the danger.

The Caeruleans held the upper hand in the early stages of the struggle as their sea-elf warriors were able to survive for long periods on land, striking anywhere and vanishing before the Xha'en could respond. Triton infiltrators could sneak into harbors, sinking and burning vessels and escaping with impunity, and merfolk magic was able to harness the sea itself against the humans. But slowly the humans reinforced their local garrisons and added extensive mounted and flying troops to counter the enemy's mobility. Ankhuran warships were deployed to escort merchant and fishing vessels, and Xha'en spellcasters were trained in spells designed specifically to repel aquatic foes. Water-breathing spells allowed the Xha'en to take the war to the Caeruleans as well.

The struggle eventually ground to a stalemate, as neither side could gain a clear advantage. Caerulean attacks on land and Xha'en assaults against the undersea kingdom were costly but could not hold territory, and both sides had secure central provinces to provide supplies, manpower, and other resources. Finally in 2878 XC (1576 I.R.), after nearly two decades of open warfare, the two sides exchanged emissaries and began to negotiate a peace settlement. The effects of the quake and volcanoes had largely subsided by this time, cities had been rebuilt, and schools of fish had returned in even greater numbers than before, so the causes of the conflict had largely abated. A treaty was signed, and both powers agreed that they could largely ignore each other.

Peace was maintained for almost a millennium before another crisis arose in the form of a sea-borne plague that devastated the Xha'en Hegemony. Though many of Emperor Alnand su Var Tilgi's advisors blamed the Caeruleans and called for a renewal of hostilities, cooler heads prevailed after a traitorous plot to attack the merfolk and trigger a war was uncovered and stopped. Xha'en diplomats made contact with the Caerulean Queen Iulea, who agreed to help the humans treat the plague. War was averted, and the two nations at last cemented the peace.

The Caeruleans noted with interest and no small amount of alarm the coming of the Castorhagi and the settlement of the Bream Islands. A new surface power was rising, and the sea-folk felt it best to avoid direct contact. When their ancient enemies in the Sinking Land began to attack sea traffic to and from the Breams however, the royal family decided to do something. Unknown to the Castorhagi, Caerulean warriors struggled against the Sea-Throng, and actually aided in the humans' great victory of 4773 XC (3471 I.R.), when the Castorhagi fleet defeated the enemy at the Battle of Quandary Deep. Once the fight was over, the Caeruleans returned to their policy of avoidance, assuming that the Castorhagi would approach the sea-kingdom when it was ready.

Good, or at least neutral, relations with the Xha'en have continued to this day. For the most part, the Hegemony and the undersea kingdom keep to themselves, occasionally coming into conflict over fishing grounds, and occasionally cooperating to face down a mutual threat.

The situation beneath the waves is a bit less settled, as the Caerulean Kingdom has its own neighbors and enemies, as described below. The royal family maintains its rule unchallenged, despite grumbling from nobles and occasional internal squabbles. The tritons of the lower depths continue to practice their nomadic ways, fishing and patrolling the kingdom's frontiers and occasionally venturing into the deeper waters below. In the shallower waters, the sea elves have begun to build structures, some reaching above the waves, and have been known to guide vessels through treacherous waters or rescue victims of shipwrecks. Caerulean warriors continue to patrol the Sinking Land and have on several occasions held back new incursions, while keeping their activities secret from the Castorhagi.

Those who visit this wondrous realm are almost always changed by the experience, for the sheer wild, alien beauty of the kingdom is a sight to behold. Vast castles of gleaming stone and magically-transformed living coral fill deep canyons, covered in bright sea plants, with schools of rainbow-hued fish darting in and out of waving kelp forests. Inside these buildings, light is provided by clouds of bioluminescent fish and small organisms, and the king's royal throne room is illuminated by large and terrifying angler fish, whose great light-emitting organs have been enhanced to provide light almost as bright as on the surface. Legions of sea-elf warriors swim in elaborate three-dimensional formations, sometimes riding great seahorses, lungfish, or eels. Merfolk sorcerers command the secret magics of the sea. Vast temples to the ocean gods rise gracefully from the sea floor, glimmering in dozens of shades of blue and green. Many a surface visitor has come to love this realm, and many are reluctant to leave.

Religion

The Caeruleans worship a pantheon of deities under the supreme guidance of Eashe the Sea Mother, who is thought to be related to the Mother goddess worshipped by the Talorani. A group of demigods governs various aspects of the sea subordinate to the Sea Mother. Among these demigods are Taela, goddess of plenty, Tymannum, god of war and battle, Cehenasla, goddess of healing and mercy, and Udamata, god of arts and architecture. All are of good alignment — the Caeruleans do not have anything like an evil pantheon, for they believe that evil beings cannot be gods. Dark entities of divine-level power are all considered demons, while practitioners of evil magic such as the hated and feared sea-witch Awalea live on in legends and popular tales.

Trade and Commerce

Before the war with the Xha'en, the Caeruleans were content with producing their own resources and trading with neighboring oceanic states and nomadic tribes. Once the war was over and better relations established with the surface folk, a small amount of trade began, with the Caeruleans exchanging fish and other foodstuffs for artwork, gemstones, and various goods magically or otherwise treated against the ravages of seawater.

Loyalties and Diplomacy

While the kingdom does not maintain full diplomatic relations with the Xha'en Hegemony (few on either side would like to spend much time in the other's realms after all), the outright hostility of the past has evolved into mutual respect and a live-and-let-live attitude on both sides. Conflicts are kept to a minimum, and those that do arise are settled diplomatically, often with the exchange of emissaries — Xha'en spellcasters venture below with the assistance of water-breathing magic, and sea elf diplomats journey to the surface. Neither Caerulea nor Xha'en has the resources or the stomach for another full-scale conflict.

Undersea, the situation is somewhat more complex, as the kingdom is actually a patchwork of smaller principalities, each with its own rulers, and other states and powers exist beneath the ocean, unknown (and largely unknowable) to the surface world. Caerulea is known to maintain diplomatic ties to a number of other states, some of which are populated by merfolk, and others that are home to different undersea creatures. The vast Caerulean Ocean also harbors numerous creatures of vast age and intelligence, including aboleth, evil kraken, ancient giant cetaceans, and in the depths, beings of a nature that is almost entirely alien to those who dwell on the surface. The Caeruleans are aware of these creatures as well, and alternately maintain friendly contact or keep them under wary surveillance.

Government

The sea kingdom's borders are ill-defined, even by its rulers, as the sea is a constantly changing environment. In all, about a dozen smaller principalities are united under the royal family, each with its own prince or princess. Each of the principalities is governed similarly to the larger state, with elders and nobles advising each monarch.

The royal house of Laesaela has ruled since the kingdom's founding, though it has been challenged more than once, most prominently when the sorceress Awalea raised an army of evil sea creatures and demons to overthrow her rightful queen. For the most part, however, the royal family tries to maintain the peace, allowing principalities to go their own way and govern as they see fit, so long as they do not unduly oppress, overtax, or aggravate the common people.

The sea elves of the upper ocean are a stern and noble lot, unshakably loyal to their merfolk monarchs. These folk make up the elite branches of the Caerulean military, as they are able to fight equally well on land and at sea. Their relatively small numbers and inability to sustain long supply lines limits their activities against the surface, but they are a powerful group nonetheless.

Down the continental slope, the tritons live in clan-based groups that travel from place to place with little in the way of permanent settlements. Each clan swears allegiance to the royal family, and are obligated to send scouts, warriors, or workers if called upon. For the most part, the tritons see this as an annoying but necessary duty, for they are aware of the dangers that might rise up from the abyss and know that they need the protection of the merfolk and the sea elves.

Military

The Caerulean military is a sight to behold, with aquatic forces of all kinds combining into a single body to face down the kingdom's enemies. Legions of aquatic elven infantry make up the bulk of the merfolk's forces. Clad in seashell armor, each is armed with a pair of wicked spears and a crossbow. Cavalry is mounted on large swimming mounts, with giant sea horses and hippocampi for the light riders, and sharks or orca for the heavier forces. Merfolk aquamancers and priests of Tymannum supplement battle formations with arcane or healing magic.

Tactics are adapted to the merfolk's undersea kingdom. Formations are three-dimensional, with height, width, and depth rather than the simple lines and squares of land warfare. Brave but inexperienced Xha'en warriors venturing into the depths on punitive missions learned this to their misfortune.

The merfolk also use war engines, particularly giant spear throwers intended to impale larger foes or damage enemy fortifications. There are vast fortresses in the sea crafted from living coral, stone, and other materials, stronger for being surrounded by the dampening effects of water. They are also roofed over, for once more the three-dimensional nature of oceanic warfare requires changes from land-based battles.

Assaults on land require significant changes in tactics and approach. Surface warfare falls primarily to the aquatic elves, who can survive out of water for extended periods. Merfolk lack legs and have only limited abilities on the surface, so usually only officers and spellcasters participate, their abilities modified by magic amulets that extend their endurance out of water. Weapons are enhanced with magic and poisons from various deadly sea creatures, so wounds from Caerulean spears, harpoon guns, and ballistae are especially dire.

Land forces are also aided by specially-bred and magically-enhanced giant armored lungfish capable of carrying up to two riders or small war engines such as catapults or ballistae. These creatures are slow and ponderous but highly resistant to damage and all but implacable, advancing determinedly, stopping only if actually killed or dismembered.

In the past, especially against powerful foes, Caerulean druids, priests, and other spellcasters could summon or control the largest creatures of the deep, including titanic whales, colossal sea turtles, pods of orca, and giant sharks. A few intelligent creatures such as sea dragons and kraken have been persuaded to aid the merfolk in battle as well. As noted, many battles involving these titans take place far from the sight of surface dwellers who have no clue of the massive forces struggling beneath the waves.

Major Threats

Though the most prominent conflict in the eyes of humans was the great war between the Xha'en Hegemony and Caerulea, to the merfolk, humans are only one of many potential threats to their kingdom. Elsewhere in the sea are kingdoms of sahuagin, tritons, and even rumored settlements of aquatic elves, as well as tribes of scrag, grindylow, and other intelligent sea creatures unknown to humans. Nomadic merfolk and tritons wander the ocean as well, swimming from place to place following schools of fish and warm weather.

While the kingdom maintains relations with many of these groups, particularly merfolk and creatures of good alignment, conflict with the others is a regular event, as sahuagin raid outlying settlements and grindylows hunt merfolk for food. Large-scale warfare is rare, but can occur, as it did when an alliance of sahuagin swept into the kingdom 200 years ago and overwhelmed Caerulean garrisons and enslaved entire communities. The ensuing struggle was difficult and at last the enemy was driven from Caerulean territory, but the cost was high.

The Caeruleans view the monstrous inhabitants of the Sinking Land with special horror and have fought a long war against them for centuries. Beginning in 4572 XC (3270 I.R.) when Castorhagi vessels were attacked by the monsters of the Sea-Throng, the Caeruleans struck back, engaging the throng in an underwater war that was hidden from the surface folk. The great Castorhagi victory at Quandary Deep in 4773 XC (3471 I.R.) took place with secret assistance from Caerulean warriors, and to this day Caerulean patrols help keep the Sea-Throng from returning.

The Caeruleans do not talk about their war with the Sinking Land, nor have they ever revealed who the true masters of the Sea-Throng are. The Caeruleans' fear of the Sea-Throng may be well-founded, for those few scholars who are aware of the conflict and the sea-folks' participation believe the Sinking Land's rulers to be the terrible aboleth — utterly alien entities that lurk in the deepest trenches and enslave other races, twisting and transforming them into hideous slaves. The Caeruleans themselves do not even acknowledge that the aboleth exist, but their continued vigilance regarding the Sinking Land suggests that they know far more than they are willing to admit.

Other threats to the kingdom are equally dire, including demons and other hostile extradimensional entities summoned by the kingdom's enemies, or spontaneously drawn to the region by surges of ancient chaos magic. Undead are also a rare but alarming event, and the deep depths of the oceanic trenches that lie beyond Akados' continental shelf harbor stranger things still. Rumors suggest that tribes of twisted merrow — horribly changed merfolk transformed into evil monstrosities — dwell in the unplumbed depths, and that the Caerulean Kingdom is always on its guard against their return. In Caerulean legend and folklore, the sea-witch Awalea still lives on, her life extended by unnatural magics, gathering merrow and other horrors to her cause and plotting vengeance against the royal family.

Wilderness and Adventures

The sea is a vast and unexplored wilderness, and other things even more hostile than sahuagin lurk in the depths. Surface folk who venture to the kingdom face significant challenges, above and beyond the need to survive underwater. Moving and thinking in three dimensions proves difficult for surface-dwellers, and disorientation is a common issue. Also, the sea has no roads or signs that are recognizable by outsiders. Landmarks and permanent features can be used to navigate underwater, but smart travelers will engage a local guide — merfolk or tritons being the most frequently employed for this task.

Many of the region's inhabitants are creatures of downright infernal nature such as the giant devil rays of the open sea — malicious, intelligent and skilled in druidic magic, they are an especially grave threat to those merfolk who travel any distance from the kingdom. Punitive or rescue missions against the devil rays often take place after encounters with these evil creatures.

Many parts of the ocean are imbued with negative energy, a result of extremely ancient events that transpired eons ago as gods and demons contended for dominance over a young world. This magic has persisted, with a variety of woeful results. Planar gateways sometimes open unexpectedly and draw hostile entities into the ocean. Unexpected bursts of necromantic energy may yield undead horrors, from the dead of the sea or from the remains of drowned mariners. Mutative chaos energy may transform mundane sea creatures into horrific monsters.

Diplomatic missions to the undersea kingdom are not common, but take place when important matters such as trade, warfare, or natural disaster are to be discussed. These expeditions are difficult and usually undertaken only by the most experienced officials. They also require guards and escorts, jobs that are ideal for veteran adventurers. These expeditions invariably involve encounters with hostile sea life and possibly enemies of the Caerulean Kingdom, and usually involve rich rewards to the survivors.

Freelance adventurers have been known to venture into Caerulean territory in order to explore sunken treasure wrecks or to delve into abandoned structures built by the merfolk and others. As with the escort missions, such ventures are quite perilous but can yield significant rewards. The Caeruleans themselves, though a generally good-hearted folk, may take a dim view of surface-dwellers sneaking into their realm to steal.

The Abyss

The Akadonian continental shelf extends about 50 miles off the coastline of the Xha'en Hegemony. It is there that the Kingdom of Caerulea flourishes and most of their settlements exist. Other undersea kingdoms and groups prefer these relatively shallow waters as well due to their tolerable temperatures and teeming sea life. Beyond the shelf lies the somewhat deeper and colder Akadonian Plateau that extends for another 100 miles before giving way to the steep continental slope. The Caeruleans maintain some settlements and fortresses on the plateau, and nomadic nereids, merfolk, devil rays, and related species travel here frequently. It is the black, cold open waters beyond the continental slope that fill the Caeruleans with dread.

Several deep trenches extend from the continental slope, but none is deeper than that directly opposite the Xha'en coastline and the sea kingdom's frontier. This deep, known only as the "Abyss," is known to harbor forces that terrify the Caeruleans and (should they ever become known) the surface world as well. Here, in absolute darkness, protected by miles of cold, deadly water, dwell the aboleths — creatures that may have existed from the dawn of time, possibly even before the coming of the gods. Though these monstrous tentacled beings are rarely seen, their appearance inevitably heralds horror and disaster, as they or their twisted minions emerge from the Abyss to take prisoners or ravage the upper reaches of the sea for their own alien, incomprehensible purposes. It is known, though rarely spoken of openly, that the Caeruleans have fought several disastrous wars with the horrors, though details are scarce. The merfolk do not like to speak of these creatures and their ways, possibly because some of their own number were taken and enslaved in wars, then sent back to plague the merfolk.

The extent of the Abyss is not known for certain. A few especially brave tritons have ventured into its upper reaches and reported the presence of other creatures almost as disturbing as the aboleth. No one is certain whether these others are in league with the aboleth, but stories suggest the presence of grindylows, aquatic undead, sea demons, and even dark, twisted merrow who lurk in the deep, plotting vengeance against those who exiled them. These last are often associated with the legendary sea-witch Awalea, though most "sensible" merfolk believe she is nothing more than a myth designed to frighten naughty youngsters into obedience. However, a few claim to know better …

Geographic Features and Points of Interest in Western Akados

Alu River

Like the Pantai, the Alu River was once an untamed waterway that flooded regularly and washed away homes, farms, and whole villages. In 1115 XC (−187 I.R.), the Xha'en erected the great Lujhiran Dam and flooded the lowlands upstream and permanently tamed the Alu and the Pantai rivers. Today, the Alu is far more sedate, flowing sluggishly through the foothills of the Tsendakar Mountains before emptying into the ocean at the city-state of Jhohir. Nowhere near as filthy as the crowded South Pantai River, the Alu acts as a highway for the towns along its banks. Graceful stands of trees grow along its banks in many places, including the picturesque northern Xha'en willow, an especially large and attractive species.

Anaros Island

The Anari who inhabit this forested, stormy island are renowned throughout the Hegemony as tough, skilled warriors with a deeply stoic martial philosophy. Anaros Island itself serves as the leading member of a confederacy of small communities and states scattered throughout the Thousand Rocks. The Eldest, the region's spiritual leader, dwells in the distant temple Aliyashinsah located at the peak of Mount Yu'unar.

Anaros Island seems the ideal place to breed a nation of warriors. Cold, with rocky shores and thick pine forests, the island is unprotected from the storms that roar in from the west, but also provides shelter to the smaller islands of the Thousand Rocks. Its minimal resources and arable land force its people to live in a stratified, yet also surprisingly egalitarian, society where all are cared for and hardships are shared. It cannot be said that no one goes hungry on Anaros Island, but if some go hungry, all go hungry, including even the most influential nobles. A popular proverb asserts that "The branch may break, but the tree stands strong."

Bakko River

The Bakko originates in the high slopes of the Impossible Peaks before meandering through the Sengejia Hills and joining the larger Taode River southeast of Tsadar. Several villages of Senge tribesmen are located along its length.

Bream, Greater

Rocky, windswept, and covered in scrub pine and brush, Greater Bream is not an especially hospitable place. Named for its northernmost location among the Breams rather than its size or importance, Greater Bream was always sparsely inhabited by the Koui fisherfolk, relatives of the Senge tribesfolk of the Xha'en Hegemony. These folk live on the island to this day, in small hamlets clustered along the southern coast, sheltered from the ferocious storms that batter the seaward side of the island. The northern portion of the island is dominated by relative newcomers, however — colonists from the city of Castorhage built the outpost of Farthest Point which, along with the newer citadel of Neer, services the growing traffic of Castorhagi and other vessels bound for the Elitani colonies in the north.

So prominent are the Castorhagi works there that today even ships from the Xha'en Hegemony put in for repairs and refitting, activities which the emperor hopes improves relations with the Castorhagi and eventually leads to full diplomatic ties.

The interior of the island is mostly scrubland dotted here and there with stands of wind-stunted trees and a few real forests. Wildlife consists mostly of smaller predators such as wild dogs, felines, and raptors that prey upon mice, rabbits, and snakes. The island harbors no truly dangerous natural creatures, though the gangsters of the Triads are believed to control some villages and maintain safehouses here for their assassins and criminals on the run.

Bream, Least

This southernmost of the three Breams also has the smallest population, owing to its relatively inhospitable terrain and climate. A few Koui villages scrape out a living from the sea along the island's western shore, but the remainder of the place is windswept and rocky, with almost no arable land and few plants beyond lichen, scrub, and wind-warped pines.

Bream, Lesser

Contrary to its diminutive name, Lesser Bream is actually the largest of the three Bream Islands. Similar in climate and terrain to its neighboring islands (see Greater Bream entry), Lesser Bream occupies the middle portion of the three and is similarly home to independent villages of fisherfolk. Larger and somewhat more fertile, Lesser Bream also contains a few Koui farming communities that produce grains, tubers and berries. These farms are mostly located in Lesser Bream's eastern coastal regions, as the southern end of the island grows progressively rugged, finally rising to the twin peaks of Mounts Kor and Shir, with the Shir Meadows in the vale between.

Bream Straits

This narrow waterway lies between the Bream Islands and the Xha'en mainland.

Caerulean Ocean

This vast and seemingly endless body of water stretches west from the coast of the Xha'en Hegemony. Known to the Castorhagi as the Nether Sea, it has proved far larger than explorers anticipated, and its full extent remains unknown. Great oceanic kingdoms such as the merfolk's realm of Caerulea thrive unseen beneath the ocean's waters, and its depths hide many things that are best left unseen.

The Cauldron

Named for its many geysers and hot springs, the Cauldron, much like the Hellsgate Peaks to the north of the Free Coast, is a cluster of highly volcanic mountains located in the southern Xha'en region. Though not part of the same mountain range as the Hellsgate Peaks, dwarven scholar-druids have claimed the Cauldron sits along the same great crack beneath the surface of the world, and that this great underground crack, which they call a "fault line," also causes the regular earthquakes that rumble beneath the ground in the southern region of the Hegemony. A more popular theory is that an ancient deity of fire was defeated and slain in the region, and that her angry ghost gives rise to all the local volcanoes. Earthquakes, it is said, are simply her attempts to raise new volcanoes, while geysers and hot springs are thought to be young volcanoes, not yet fully developed. If the right rituals to appease her rage were ever to be found, so it is claimed, all the seismic and volcanic activity in the area would cease forever.

In any event, the terrain and populations of the Cauldron are similar to the Hellsgate Peaks in that many fire- and heat-loving people and monsters choose to make the small mountain range their home. The Cauldron is somewhat more easily traversed by nonmagical means than the Hellsgate Peaks, however, as the geysers are far more active than the volcanoes, and said volcanoes are in turn more easily predicted and understood in their activity than those of Hellsgate. Thus, some of the wider passes through the Cauldron range are generally reliable if a party is well-prepared and able to defend themselves.

Also unlike the Hellsgate Peaks, the Cauldron is known for neither devils nor red dragons but instead for a close-knit community of efreeti in the secretive and difficult-to-access village of Soohr-Ahmaad.

Earos Hills

Nestled between the forbidding Eloitan region of the Green Warden Forest and the peaks of the Odarnadar Mountains, the arid Earos Hills are sparsely populated and wild. Grassy or forested hills are interspersed with rift valleys inhabited by megafauna such as mammoths, daeodon, giant sloths, paraceratherium, glyptodon, giant otters, saber-toothed cats, and others. Much of the region has been left in its natural state by the nobles of the city of Djir who use the Earos as a sort of a private hunting preserve. In the spring and summer, elaborate caravans venture out of Djir, guided by professional hunters who lead their wealthy employers on long, luxurious hunts to seek the rare and exotic species that flourish here. While outsiders are not strictly forbidden to venture into the Earos Hills, they may find themselves actively discouraged from exploring by nobles and their hired bullies. The nobles of Djir generally consider the hills to be theirs and theirs alone and have little tolerance of visitors.

There are good reasons to risk the nobles' ire however. Mighty mammoths have roamed this region for aeons, and tales are told of fabulous "graveyards" where ancient mammoth skeletons can be excavated, along with a fortune in ivory. Other stories, actively discouraged by the Djir nobles, suggest that remnants of the region's oldest intelligent inhabitants, an advanced race of reptilian humanoids who ruled during the Age of Dragons, may be found here in small numbers protecting powerful magical artifacts that they no longer understand.

Heavenly Road

Winding perilously through the treacherous peaks of the Tsendakar Range, this grandly-named narrow passage is the only land route between Gtsang Prefecture and the Xha'en Hegemony. The very difficulty of this road is what assured Gtsang's independence for so long, and this protection continues to this day, allowing the folk of Gtsang to gain the benefits of Hegemony membership without the onerous taxes and regulations levied against folk in the remainder of the Xha'en state.

Though it is narrow, winding, and slow to navigate, the road is surprisingly safe if it is treated with sufficient care and respect.

Monks and Uarsinsi warriors from the Udanishanti Temple regularly patrol the path to make sure that travelers are safe and that no "undesirables" are allowed to enter the Gtsang Prefecture. Unfortunately, this definition also includes rootless adventurers and wanderers, so those venturing to Gtsang seeking their fortune had best have travel papers, or at least a convincing story, at the ready.

Udanishanti patrols also try to keep the path clear of hostile creatures, but the mountains harbor a number of dangerous species and this can prove difficult. Unwary travelers may encounter giants, griffons, yetis, or goblins. Dealing with these creatures often falls to the dwarves of Ankhura who also call the mountains home and maintain the Ithanic Fortress in the western region of the mountains. The dwarves generally leave security along the road to the patrols but have been known to intervene and rescue lost or threatened travelers.

The Impossible Peaks

Tall, cold, and forbidding, these mountains are well-named. Along with the Green Warders of the Akadonian Forest, the Impossibles form the eastern frontier of the Xha'en region, separating it from its nearest neighbor, the Grand Duchy of Reme. While some stories circulate about secret passes and a handful of explorers claim to have crossed them, there are no confirmed tales of the Impossibles ever being traversed. While they are neither as extensive as the Stonehearts nor as tall as the Deepfells, the Impossible Peaks may be the most rugged mountain range in Akados, full of sheer rock faces, deep rifts and ravines, treacherous icefalls and snow deep enough to bury a city. Constantly wreathed in clouds and storms, very little is known of the mountains' true geography or whether their highest peaks harbor anything besides quick death for travelers.

As with the Tsendakar Mountains, however, there are clearly subterranean passages beneath the Impossibles, for reports of marauding ratfolk, goblins, and worse circulate through the foothills to the east and west. The Senge tribes of the Sengejia Hills speak of mysterious raiders who descend from the mountains under the cover of night to steal crops, cattle, and even children, while stories of goblin attack have come from as far away as Harrowfar and Tanner's Green. While some of these raiders may be hill-dwellers, there is little evidence to support this, suggesting that the mysterious attackers come from the Impossible Peaks, where it is theorized that they dwell in underground cavern complexes.

The lower slopes of the Impossible Peaks, where the craggy mountains fade into rugged hills, are also inhabited by various hardy wildlife species such as mountain goats, sheep, and snow leopards. In the past, tribes of hill and frost giants have made their homes there as well, but there have been no reliable sightings of giants in generations, leading many to suggest that they are extinct in the region.

Jhoni River

From a source on the north side of the Cauldron mountain range, the Jhoni River runs primarily northward to the Caerulean Ocean. Though the southern portion of the Jhoni is hot and smells unpleasantly of sulfur due to the high volcanic activity near its source, many small tributaries flow into it along its route and dilute it into a relatively normal river by the time it reaches the bustling Ejindor river docks.

Not far north of Ejindor, the Jhoni plummets down the tall and rocky Jhoni Falls, into a sheltered grotto where many river vessels typically stand at anchor. The rest of the Jhoni's journey northward is through a narrow canyon, such that its mouth pours forth between two sheer cliff faces, which explains why no coastal city has sprung up beside it. Instead, ships small enough to make the somewhat narrow voyage sail up to the Jhoni Falls where an ingenious winch and pulley system hauls smaller landing craft up the side of the falls and allows them to paddle the rest of the way to Ejindor for the region's major commerce.

In weather and river flow, the Jhoni is a safe and predictable passage during all seasons but the winter floods, though experienced captains know to bring appropriate guards and equipment for dealing with the

Tengu bandits that unpredictably attack some Jhoni Canyon vessels, and whose lair has yet to be found.

The Jhoni is always an unusually warm river due to its Cauldron source, and both fishing and river sports are quite popular in Ejindor, even in colder months. The river is barely lukewarm by that point in its journey, but it never freezes, nor does it experience flooding due to any sort of spring thaw. It floods when it rains, rarely to any inconvenient degree for Ejindor residents, and the waters recede when the rain stops. Only in the Jhoni Canyon is this a danger, as the narrow canyon walls funnel the floodwaters into dangerous rapids. A good river captain knows to watch the weather in the vicinity and allow the river time to subside after any flood-worthy rainstorm.

KAHARIS RIVER

This short river flows swiftly from the slopes of the Tsendakar Mountains, joining the Alu River between the cities of Xha'ahan and Jhohir. A famous willow that hangs over the river near the town of Xe'qun is said to be haunted by the spirit of a woman who drowned herself in the river over a faithless lover. If visitors rest at the foot of this willow and tell their own sad tales of lost love, it is believed that the ghost will speak to them and tell them strange secrets.

THE KRAKEN'S TEETH

These imposing rocks are the upper peaks of the mountains that once surrounded the flooded lowlands now known as the Sinking Place. They and the other peaks that lie just beneath the surface form a deadly barrier capable of tearing out the hulls of passing ships and keeping the creatures of the Sinking Place secure from attack from the surface.

KUSEVE GULF

No expedition has ever successfully found the bottom of the suboceanic rift that lies at the junction of the Bream and Anaros islands. Many superstitions surround this ill-omened stretch of water, and ship captains refuse to cross it at night or during full moons. Even the deep-diving tritons of the Caerulean kingdom avoid the region. Some legends claim that a titanic beast slumbers there, or that the trench is so deep that it reaches to another plane full of fell water demons that sometimes emerge to trouble the surface-dwellers and unfortunate mariners.

LAKE PANTAI

Thousands of years ago, this vast artificial lake was called the Pantai Lowlands, and was home to Senge tribesmen. Later, the Xha'en Agretor clan settled here and founded a vast and powerful city-state along the Pantai River that rivaled the growing influence of Xha'ahan. The cunning Xha'en ended Agretor's ascendancy by damming the Pantai, flooding the lowlands and transforming the region into what was redubbed Lake Pantai. Now, the cities of Xha'ahan, Aphapor, and Tsadar rise from the shores of the lake, with regular water travel between them. In addition to submerging the troublesome city-state, the dam also wrought untold havoc on the local environment and caused droughts across the Plains of Xha and required the construction of a vast canal and aqueduct network to bring water to Xha'en farms. These difficult days are long past, and the battered ecosystem has readjusted to the new reality — the Xha'en themselves even take fish from the lake, and the tamed South Pantai River is a major travel route through the central provinces of the Hegemony.

As an entirely artificial construction, the lake is free of many natural hazards of the region, and its economic importance has grown over the centuries. There is one major exception to the lake's relative placidity however, for the death of Agretor has never fully vanished from Xha'en memory. Many tragic tales have been told of the last days of the Agretor, and of the Senge tribesfolk displaced by the Pantai's flooding — despite the Hegemony's official focus on the glories of the dam's construction and its significance as a symbol of Xha'en superiority. Some tales claim that the city still exists in the depths of Lake Pantai, inhabited by the

shades of its old inhabitants who still relive their lives as their resentment and rage at the Xha'en festers and grows. Stories of phantoms, shades, mysterious mists, and even cannibalistic undead rising from the waters of Lake Pantai are told in hushed whispers, and invariably silenced by government bureaucrats. Yet the tales persist, and one day they may actually prove true.

LUJHIRAN DAM

This marvel of engineering was built in 1115 XC (−187 I.R.) when many of Akados' inhabitants still lived in highly primitive conditions. Raised on the Alu River and intended to prevent the annual flooding of the Pantai, the dam succeeded almost too well, flooding the Pantai Lowlands and depriving the plains of water, necessitating the construction of canals, channels, and aqueducts to bring water back to the Plains of Xha in a more controlled fashion. It also utterly tamed the Alu and the Pantai rivers, transforming them into far more placid (and in the case of the South Pantai River, far filthier) waterways. The dam itself was crafted of fitted stones laid individually along the Alu's riverbed and in from its banks between the Pantai Lowlands and the flat floodplains north of Xha'ahan City. Some claim that high sorcery and elaborate rituals were also used in the construction, for the dam remains intact and functional three and a half millennia later. To be sure, the dam has been renovated and repaired over the years; at one point during the Huris Dynasty, a second, stronger dam was built, essentially adding a second wall to the first, but the structure's longevity nevertheless supports the notion that arcane or supernatural forces were used in its erection. In addition to its flood control functions, the dam also drives great grinding stones that produce flour and meal for the Hegemony.

MOUNT KAPE

The highest point of Least Bream Island is a prominent, snow-clad landmark for mariners, and is said to contain an ancient temple to prehistoric, possibly pre-human, gods, but the region is wild and inaccessible, so no one has yet been able to verify these rumors.

MOUNT KOR

One of the two prime peaks located on the southern end of Lesser Bream Island, Mount Kor rises 6,000 feet beside its slightly taller sibling, Mount Shir. The bones of the hero Nandase supposedly lie at the summit, and those who venture here are said to receive his blessing.

MOUNT SHIR

Rising to 6,500 feet, Mount Shir is the taller of the two mountains located on the southern tip of Lesser Bream. Its lower slopes are forested, and foothills contain several lush alpine meadows, in sharp contrast to the island's harsh, windswept terrain. A small sect of Koui druids tends to these natural areas and dwell in the caves found among the crags of Mount Shir.

MOUNT YU'UNAR

Located at the very northern tip of Anaros Island, this mountain is known as Mount Yu'unar in the Anari language, meaning White Peak. On Castorhagi maps it is labeled Mount Harthnow, after the captain of the Castorhagi vessel *Brave,* who mapped the peak in 4516 XC (3214 I.R.). It soars nearly 8,000 feet above the cold, crashing waves of the Bream Straits. At its peak stands Aliyashinsah, the Warrior's Temple and spiritual heart of the Anari people, where the Eldest dwells in isolation, contemplating the world that stretches out below him. Access to the temple is by a number of risky climbing routes and winding paths above yawning depths, and many who seek audience with the Eldest never reach their goal.

ODARNADAR MOUNTAINS

According to Ankhuran stone-scholars, the Odarnadar Mountains came to be as part of the same ancient geologic events that led to both the Cauldron to the southwest and the Impossible Peaks to the northeast, though the Odarnadars are neither like those other ranges. The Odarnadar Mountains are neither steep and cold nor riddled with volcanoes; instead they are lush and green save for the tops of the tallest peaks, with broad, sloping sides covered in deep, ancient forests.

The soil here is not good for planting or grazing, and even a gentle mountain makes for a harsher way of life than the plains and hills below, so the majority of the Odarnadar Mountains remain untouched by civilization. Exceptions include the deep-cut farming and grazing terraces in the lower northern slopes near the foot of the range, as well as the various iron and gem mines higher up on the same side. There is also a well-maintained, broad pass through the middle of the range, running roughly north-south, which is loosely guarded by Xha'en troops from late spring to early fall, for uses both mercantile and military.

Outside these exceptions, the Odarnadar Mountains are a place of pristine nature as far as the eye can see. However, this is not to say that they are harmless to travelers. Aside from the one guarded pass, the majority of the mountain range is home to all manner of perilous wildlife, including at least one large pack of dire wolves, many other dire animals, megafauna from the Earos Hills, and any number of forest- and mountain-dwelling magical creatures.

It has been said that the Odarnadar Mountains are guarded by some powerful being that protects them from being despoiled beyond certain encroachments. According to rumor, this entity might be an ancient mountain god, a gold or green dragon, a kirin, or an immortal druid. Animistic shrines dot the side of the road along the guarded pass through the mountains, and while the druids who maintain them say they are devoted only to the land itself, the travelers who stop beside them to pray or to leave offerings of coin, food, and pretty stones will tell you they are praying to almost every conceivable entity for safe passage through its territory.

And, indeed, the road itself is usually as safe as any wilderness travel can be expected to be. Those who step off the road outside the marked camping areas, however, are indeed known at times to disappear or to be found slain by wild beasts. Whether this is simply because they have left the safety of the guarded road or because they transgressed against the unspoken rules of whatever entity may or may not claim the Odarnadar Mountains as its territory is perhaps a matter best left to personal interpretation, as those who know the truth, if any, aren't talking.

PANTAI RIVER

The broad Pantai River is central to the history and civilization of the Xha'en region. Originally flowing unrestricted from high in the Impossible Peaks, the Pantai brought water to the rich and fertile Plains of Xha, allowing the development of agriculture and permanent settlements by the region's original inhabitants, the Senge tribesfolk. This fertility came with problems however, for the Pantai periodically flooded the region, washing away towns and farms. It was the Xha'en who ended this ancient cycle by erecting the mighty Lujhiran Dam on the Alu River to the north, permanently flooding the Pantai Lowlands and freeing the plains from the threat of flooding. Today, the northern portion of the Pantai River remains, bringing fresh water from the mountains to the artificial Lake Pantai, from which the river's lower portion, the South Pantai River, now flows, into the teeming settlements and farms of the Plains of Xha.

PERILOUS KAF

Once, long ago, there lived a mad wizard who chose to name her rambling, asymmetrical, gravity-defying tower "the Kaf." Many have speculated that this word had some meaning in some extraplanar language that the wizard spoke, or that it relates somehow to the Kaf

people of the Kildren Peninsula, but if so, the significance was lost upon the wizard's death. Also lost upon her death was the structural integrity of her improbably constructed fortress, and before her elven allies had even finished lighting her pyre, her tower crumbled to ruins, destroying most of her centuries of acquired knowledge and treasure — or so it was thought.

Decades later, a group of treasure hunters passed through the region and poured over the jumbled stone ruins, in case the elves had missed anything of value. During the process, one of their number stumbled through a broken stone trapdoor into what was, at first, believed to be a simple basement. Excited by their discovery, the treasure hunters descended into the passage below, where they stayed for several days. Only two ever made it out alive, both badly injured, but one of them managed to bring out with her a golden statue enchanted to temporarily increase the intelligence of those touching it.

Sale of the statue made the two treasure hunters wealthy for life, and both retired from adventuring. They documented what they had experienced on a series of beautifully illuminated scrolls titled "The Perilous Kaf: A Labyrinth of Terror." The scrolls described wealth and treasures but also knowledge beyond all imagining squirreled away in seemingly random pockets throughout an incomprehensible system of tunnels and honeycombing passages, all enchanted to magically shift and change shape from time to time.

These passages were guarded by traps both mechanical and magical, all enchanted to mend themselves if broken. In addition, various corridors housed guardians in the form of golems, animated objects, and other magical constructs, or were enchanted to summon living monsters to attack in accordance with unpredictable predetermined criteria.

"The Perilous Kaf cannot, in our opinion, be safely explored by mere mortals," the scrolls conclude. "We were the best of our profession with the best equipment, and we believe we saw less than half of the wizard's mad underground maze. Indeed, we believe that even she could no longer access most of her creation, unless some mystical key to her puzzle was lost in her tower's rubble. We cannot recommend that anyone ever attempt such an expedition again."

Despite such dire warnings, however, the scrolls do include a detailed map to the portions of the Kaf that the treasure hunters were able to explore, with extensive survival advice for those who would follow in their footsteps. Many have done so, and few have survived to tell the tale. Fewer still have had any better success than the first expedition, and none has managed to map the full Kaf.

The last known location of the scrolls of the Kaf is the treasury of the Xha'en emperor. By imperial decree, the Kaf itself has been sealed with a great iron gate. Too many have lost their lives in its depths to no purpose, and the empire fears what dangerous artifacts might be brought to the surface should an expedition ever succeed. It is said, however, that copies of the scrolls can be found here and there among the wealthier members of Xha'en's criminal underworld. Some such copies are fakes or otherwise inaccurate, but it is said that at least one copy is a perfect replica of the original (or even that it IS the original, and the emperor has an excellent forgery).

Any explorers with a chance of survival would have no difficulty bypassing the emperor's iron gate and lock, so the Kaf is still explored from time to time. What no one has found yet is whether the original treasure hunters were correct that some additional key is needed to solve the maze. The wizard's elven allies did recover some treasures from the fallen tower. Could this hypothetical key be among them? And if so, who has it now? Perhaps the scrolls' authors are correct that the mysteries of the Perilous Kaf will never be solved, but … perhaps not?

QALEN DELTA

The great Qalen River terminates on the Xha'en coast northwest of the city of Thanalos, along the southern edge of the Plains of Xha. Agriculturally rich and densely populated, the Qalen Delta is the source of a significant portion of the Xha'en Hegemony's grains, alfalfa, rice, and fruit.

Qalen River

Since the mighty Pantai was split in two and tamed by the construction of Lujhiran Dam, the Quan has taken its place as the longest continuous river in the Xha'en Hegemony, flowing along the southern edge of the Plains of Xha. Broad and old, the Quan follows a serpentine path, with various bends and oxbows throughout.

Quy Island

This large, forested island lies a few miles off the west coast of Akados. It is home to several thousand Xha'en who make their living farming and fishing. It has one substantial settlement, the city of Jhadarah on the island's northern coast.

The island's interior is largely wild and unsettled, and is home to deer, black bears, foxes, and similar woodland creatures. While the eastern coast of Quy is relatively placid, the northern and western coasts are windy, rugged places periodically lashed by storms and high waves. A few communities cling to the rocks here, braving the high seas for their rich haul of ocean fish. Legends of the seas abound here, for just a few miles beyond the island, the Akadonian continental shelf drops abruptly, plunging to immeasurable depths, said to contain both wonders and horrors. Every few years, tales surface of great monsters ascending from the deep to ravage Quy fishing fleets before returning to the abyss.

Quy Strait

A broad and deep strait, this stretch of ocean lies between Quy Island and the Xha'en Hegemony, and is a popular route owing to its relative calm and easily navigated waters.

River Road

This broad road stretches between Tsadar and Thanalos. Fully paved and well maintained, it is vital to trade and transport through the central regions of the Xha'en Hegemony. Warriors from both cities regularly patrol its length, and it is normally crowded with traffic each way.

Sengejia Hills

The rugged, nearly trackless foothills of the Impossible Peaks are home to the Senge clans, the last descendants of the region's original inhabitants who fled here in the face of Xha'en aggression. While the Senge are not a hostile or warlike people, they remain insular and distrustful of outsiders, which is not entirely unreasonable given their tragic history. The hills are a rough place, and the Senge scratch out a bare living through subsistence farming, herding, and occasional trade with the Xha'en. The hills themselves are covered in hardy grasses and occasional stands of white oak and smoke trees. The broad Pantai River is the largest waterway in the region and dotted with many small Senge settlements. Most other rivers are small, and many are seasonal. Wildlife is similarly hardy, with a few large predators such as dire wolves and hyenas, smaller predators such as foxes and coyotes, and herd animals such as deer, vicuna, and an especially fleet species of antelope called the kuailu. The region is also home to hill giant and gnoll tribes and is sometimes ravaged by ratfolk from the caverns beneath the Impossible Peaks. The Senge themselves fear to stray too far from home at night, as stories of lycanthropes and roaming ghosts and revenants are common.

Shawa River

A short, fast-flowing river, the Shawa is a major tributary of the larger Qalen River.

The Sheltered Sea (aka Umi Hosoeta)

This body of water located between Anaros Island and the Xha'en mainland contains the bulk of the Thousand Rocks, which range in size from tiny outcroppings to larger islands capable of supporting houses and small communities. Legend holds that the rocks were once part of a single landmass that connected Anaros Island to the mainland, but that they were shattered and flooded during a battle between rival dragons during the Age of Dragons.

Sho River

The Sho takes a circuitous route from the Odarnadar Mountains, through the Earos Hills and the Green Warden Forest before joining the Qalen River along the southern edge of the Plains of Xha. It is little traveled and there are no settlements on its banks, owing to its proximity to the elven domains.

The Sinking Place

This mysterious region is said by the Gtsang to have once been above water, but over centuries was slowly and deliberately drawn beneath the waves, probably by the hostile forces that rule the place. Today, only the upper peaks of the mountains that once surrounded the Sinking Place remain above the surface, forming a potent barrier against large-scale incursion.

The region is known to harbor many hostile sea-creatures, many of which attack passing vessels with clear malevolence — sea serpents, kraken, aquatic demons, and other lesser-known species have been sighted here. Not only do these creatures represent a real danger to shipping, but they appear to be controlled by some sort of greater intelligence.

In 4572 XC (3270 I.R.), a Castorhage trade fleet set out from Lesser Bream, only to be attacked by sea creatures on their return from Elitan-i-pan. While the event was a tragedy of catastrophic proportions, it proved to be only the beginning of the Breams' troubles in the region. Over the next three years, attacks grew in number and intensity, and in 4575 XC (3273 I.R.), Castorhage Admiral Milo Skanter led a fleet of 12 ships into the area to hunt down and destroy the monsters. The expedition ended in disaster as an overwhelming horde of sea monsters emerged from the Sinking Place, with only a single ship escaping. It was not until 4773 XC (3471 I.R.) that the Sea-Throng was finally brought to bay at the Battle of Quandary Deep. Though the throng was defeated and wiped out or put to flight, the Sinking Place remains firmly under their control, and outside ships visit the region at their own peril.

No one on the surface knows who truly rules the Sinking Place. The sea-folk of Caerulea are said to have extensive knowledge, but in typical fashion are quite reluctant to share information with surface-dwellers.

South Pantai River

Beyond the placid surface of Lake Pantai, the vast body of water created by the damming of the Alu River, the once-wild Pantai River, now flows peacefully into the Plains of Xha where it is diverted into canals and channels to aid in irrigation. Now broad, slow, and fully tamed, the South Pantai serves as a highway of sorts, with extensive boat and ferry traffic up and down its length. Its pacification has had consequences of course, for it is now full of silt and only the most robust fish species survive — mostly carp and some large catfish. Waste from the city of Rojhah also fouls the water, and by the time it reaches the sea far to the west, the South Pantai is dark, muddy and largely lifeless.

Taode River

The graceful Taode originates in the Impossible Peaks and winds lackadaisically across the Plains of Xha. It is broader and less prone to flood than the old Pantai River, and before the coming of the Xha'en was settled by the Senge, who traveled on and fished in its waters. It remains important to the region today, though the Xha'en have diverted much of its flow into canals for the irritation of Xha farms and settlements.

The Thousand Rocks

Anaros Island forms a long, narrow wall that protects this rocky archipelago from the worst of the storms from the Caerulean Ocean, allowing its inhabitants to wrest a living from the sea and their islands' rocky soil. Most inhabitants of the Thousand Rocks are Anari, though some Xha'en have migrated here to try their luck. Most fail, leaving the isles to their original inhabitants.

There may well be a thousand or more rocks in the Sheltered Sea, especially if one counts the uninhabitable spurs of rock that rise from the waves all across the region. Larger rocks, marginally more hospitable, harbor the region's humans, who live in small villages or hamlets, fishing or farming during the few pleasant months of the spring and summer. Some of these hamlets are tiny, with only a dozen or so inhabitants, and a few harbor solitary dwellings where individual families live in utter isolation. Lone hermits also live here in huts that cling to the coldest and loneliest of rocks.

Like the Anari of the main island, Thousand Rock folk are a stoic and self-reliant lot, dedicated to a life of labor and deprivation, assured of nothing save reincarnation to still more toil. A few seek spiritual enlightenment as monks or take the path of the warrior, but most remain here for their entire lives, rarely seeing anything beyond their home islands.

Tsendakar Mountains

Rising majestically along the northern coast of the Xha'en Hegemony, the Tsendakar range provides further security and is yet another major factor in the ancient nation's isolation and continued tranquility. Impassable save for a single route known as the Heavenly Road, the mountains are largely wilderness, unexplored and deadly to outsiders. Yeti and frost giants lurk among icy peaks, snow griffons and ice drakes prey on the unwary, and treacherous crevasses, all but bottomless, crisscross the range, sometimes hidden beneath debris or drifts. The Tsendakar are rich with folklore and history, for the fearsome Tu Chai Palace of the tyrannical Red King was located here. The legendary Udanishanti Temple, where anyone who makes the difficult journey can train in the ways of the Uarsinsi, is located along a side trail of the Heavenly Road. And there are legends of lost gods, forgotten heroes, and ancient treasures to be found throughout the range.

Beneath the Tsendakars lies the Kingdom of Ankhura, a dwarven nation like no other. Hidden passages to Ankhura are in many locations, but most are so well concealed that only Ankhuran dwarves can find them. Lost travelers are sometimes rescued by the dwarves, though they are reluctant to share their secrets. The undermountain passages also contain hostile creatures — goblins, ratfolk, and others. The Ankhurans are stingy with their secrets, but stories are also quietly told that the dwarves have knowledge of deeper and more terrifying things in the lightless depths beneath their lowest chambers.

Udanishanti Temple

Standing at the top of a long and winding staircase that rises from the Heavenly Road in the treacherous Tsendakar Mountains, the Udanishanti Temple has stood here for centuries, a monument to martial excellence and spiritual perfection. Built on five levels, each progressively higher up the mountain than the previous one, the temple is a wonder of aesthetic construction, incorporating dragon symbology throughout.

Founded by the Anari of the Thousand Rocks soon after the founding of the Xha'en Hegemony, the temple's doors are open to any who can reach them, though the training regimen within has proven far too challenging for the vast majority of students. Here, principles of martial combat based upon the Anari warrior model are taught, along with other unarmed martial arts, as well as calligraphy, poetry, dance, archery, and meditation. Under the guidance of Headmaster Omronris, the temple has trained warriors from Anaros Island, Gtsang, the Hegemony, and the Utterends, as well as a handful of outsiders from as far away as Castorhage who have made the perilous journey here. Not all students need to be human, either — a good number of elves and dwarves have come to learn the ways of the blade at the temple. It is even said that some kenku and tabaxi from the far south have attended the school, and that they bore the master's teachings back to their own people.

Xha, Plains of

This vast and fertile plain has been continuously settled and cultivated for millennia. The plains were originally inhabited by the Senge, peaceful agrarians and herders who were unable to stem the tide of Xha'en migration. Within a few generations of their arrival, the Xha'en had forced the Senge into the hill country to the east and entirely taken over the Plains of Xha. The construction of the Lujhiran Dam prevented the annual flooding that swamped the region, while permanently flooding the Pantai Lowlands. While this allowed for more permanent settlements in the Xha region, it also deprived the area of irrigation and forced the Xha'en to build canals and aqueducts to provide water to local farmers. Today, the area is thickly populated with numerous farms and villages, roads, inns, government buildings, barracks, and similar signs of civilization. As the heavily-settled center of a great nation, the Plains of Xha is possibly one of the safest regions in all Akados.

THE GREEN WARDEN FOREST AND THE FREE COAST

POLITICAL SUBDIVISIONS OF THE GREEN WARDEN FOREST AND FREE COAST

THE GREEN WARDEN NATIONS

Capital: none

Notable Settlements: Anasanalin (61,000), Elenis Tuath (200-600, seasonal), Family of Thorns (47,000) Forest's Bones (38,000), The Kingdom of Wolves (59,000), Lintariel (52,000), Monkey's Laughter (53,000) Sentinels of the Trees (60,000), Serpent's Coil (42,000)

Ruler: none currently (a high monarch is chosen in times of war with outsiders)

Government: hereditary monarchy (Anasanalin, Lintariel), semi-democratic republic (Forest's Bones, Sentinels of the Trees), semi-democratic monarchy (The Kingdom of Wolves), nomadic bands (Monkey's Laughter), martial meritocracy (Family of Thorns), nomadic bands/monarchy mix (Serpent's Coil), theocracy (Elenis Tuath)

Population: 413,000 (wild elves 411,000, other humanoid 2,000)

Monstrous: dire or giant animals native to the region (including but not limited to local breeds of monkeys, apes, pandas, red pandas, wolves, foxes, many snakes, birds, and occasional tigers), plant-type creatures native to the region (any, but especially treants, shambling mounds), awakened plants/trees, awakened animals, satyrs, pixies, centaurs, lycanthropes (various) dryads, unicorns, nymphs, other fey, owlbears, various undead (Forest's Bones region, Great Road ruins environs), wyverns, pseudodragons, other temperate forest creatures native to the region

Languages: Elven, Sylvan, Druidic, some Common

Religion: Animism, Arialee, local deities

Resources: magical resources, spices, timber (responsibly harvested in careful moderation), rare woods, dyes, spirits, cloth, pottery, foodstuffs

Currency: barter and gift, mixed

Technology Level: usually High Middle Ages

The Green Warden Nations are a collective of fragmented wild elven peoples loosely allied in their guardianship of the Green Warden Forest. They are peoples dedicated as well to preserving as much as they can of all that they, and all elves, have lost. They prize tales of the past — both the glorious past from before the humans came, and the terrible past of wars and horrors and loss.

Each of the Green Warden Nations is different from the others. The people are all similar: stately elves with flowing black hair, eyes of black, browns, or grays, and rich woody-brown skin. Culturally, however, these elves are more diverse than the humans who encounter them often assume. They are a nation because they have decided to ally as one, but they are proud of their differences, and they honor the divergent ways in which each nation keeps its history alive.

One thing Green Warden elves do share is that humans never see their settlements. Ever. Each nation handles this resolution differently, but for the last several generations, the elves of the Green Warden Forest never allow any human eyes to set sight on their homes. They also do not draw maps of their nation and navigate instead by their deeply-instilled knowledge of the forest itself, by a system of coded signs and symbols hidden among the trees, and — in a pinch — magic.

HISTORY AND PEOPLE

Long, long ago, the forest was vast and stretched across the continent. When humans began to cut and burn the trees, the elven people scattered, fought, hid, or made peace as best they could. The wild elves retreated to the far southwest to protect the remains of the Great Akadonian Forest from human invasion. There, in a mighty and terrible ritual that took a full year to cast, the wild elves raised the Green Warder monoliths in 725 I.R., a magic to keep all enemies of the forest from being able to enter it … from the north.

Strategically, it was a well-chosen position for the spell, and for more than 1,500 years it kept the elven peoples isolated from most of the rest of the world. The early Xha'en peoples to the west did come to encroach upon the western edge of the forest, but there was much wilderness between them and the remains of the elves' homeland. Even to this day, the Xha'en have never mounted a serious incursion against the Green Warden Forest. To the east, however, what had seemed a harmless stretch of coastline was "discovered" by Castorhage, and in 2301 I.R. they set up penal colonies alongside the eastern forest.

After 1,500 years, not even the elves had living memory of the conflicts that first raised the Green Warders. After a few diplomatic overtures from Castorhagi Queen Malice, the elves began to feel that perhaps the days of enmity with humans had passed. Indeed, her outreach was so generous, and their economy so quickly improved by Castorhagi trade, the wild elves and fey gifted her with the Courtyard of Oak — a living courtyard — that was carefully nurtured and tended on its journey across the sea to her court in Castorhage.

Such friendship was not to last, however. Queen Malice's great grandson, Lertis Tevoy, decided (for reasons no one ever fully understood) to break every treaty Castorhage and the Green Realm had ever made. He began an incursion into the forest to build a road. The elves attempted to dissuade the Castorhagi humans from following their king's bizarre order, but they could not be convinced, and no diplomatic plea to King Lertis was ever acknowledged. When all else failed — in 2349 I.R. after the 37th tree was slain to make room for the road — the elves, fey, and awakened plants and animals of the northern Green Realm went to war with their human neighbors.

King Lertis Tevoy responded by doubling down on his devotion to his incomprehensible road, committing thousands of troops and driving the road all the way into the forest, almost to the edge of the Green Realm's former summer capital, Elenis Tuath. The history of Elenis Tuath is told elsewhere, but when the humans arrived, it had been evacuated save for a few monks whom the invaders slaughtered.

At that point, the elves, who had previously sought to limit the conflict, ceased efforts at self-restraint and escalated to new and far bloodier tactics. Within a week of the attack on Elenis Tuath in 2369 I.R., Fort Tevoy was sacked and its garrison destroyed. It was another four years before the Forest Coast War finally ended, but by then it had cost Castorhage millions in gold and nearly 80,000 lives. Losses did not approach such a scale on the elven side, even when including felled trees as casualties. Having had to mortgage the Castorhagi crown jewels to pay the war debts, King Lertis Tevoy was betrayed by his own half-brother Terrance Acquiri, who, with the support of the city's nobles, was named king (and nicknamed King Acquire). In short order the new king, seeking a final end to the conflict, made a wary peace with the wild elves.

This new state of affairs was far from friendship, however, and in 2383 I.R. the Green Realm lost all contact with the elves and fey in Castorhage who tended the still-living Courtyard of Oak. To this day, no clear explanation for their disappearance has been given, and relations with Castorhage have never improved.

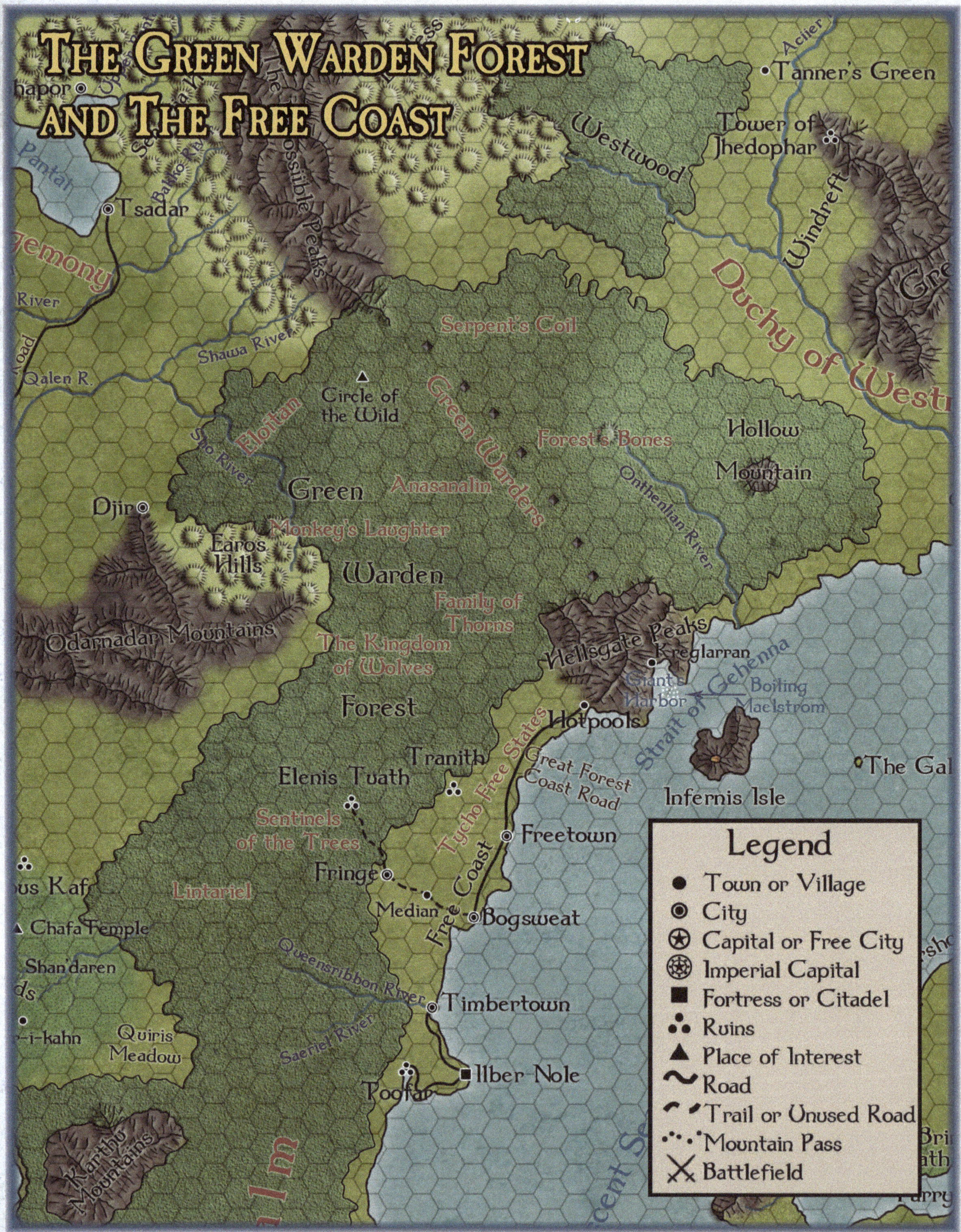

The Green Warden Forest and the Free Coast
Tanner's Green
Acier
Tower of Jhedophar
Windreft
Duchy of West...
Gre...
Westwood
hapor
Pantah
Tsadar
gemony
River
Road
Qalen R.
Serpent's Coil
Green Wardens
Shawa River
Elontan
Circle of the Wild
Forest's Bones
Hollow Mountain
Sho River
Onthenlian River
Green Warden
Anasanalin
Djir
Monkey's Laughter
Earos Hills
Warden
Family of Thorns
Hellsgate Peaks
Kreglarran
Odarnadar Mountains
The Kingdom of Wolves
Giant Harbor
Strait of Gehenna
Boiling Maelstrom
Forest
Hotpools
Infernis Isle
The Gal...
Tranith
Great Forest Coast Road
Elenis Tuath
Tycho Free States
Sentinels of the Trees
Freetown
us Kafr
Lintariel
Free Coast
Fringe
Median
Bogsweat
Chafa Temple
Shan'daren
ds
Queensribbon River
Timbertown
-i-kahn
Quiris Meadow
Saeriet River
...sho...
Bri... ...ath
...arry
Roofar
Ilber Nole
Karthu Mountains
lm
...cent Se...

Legend
● Town or Village
◉ City
✪ Capital or Free City
✸ Imperial Capital
■ Fortress or Citadel
⁘ Ruins
▲ Place of Interest
〜 Road
⌒ Trail or Unused Road
⋯ Mountain Pass
✕ Battlefield

A wild elven ritual at a Green Warder Monolith.

The humans remaining in the Castorhagi Forest Coast colonies saw less and less contact and support from their rulers and grew ever warier of the threat of their elven neighbors as the years went by. In addition to the dangers from the close-by forest, the isolated human colonies found themselves beset by pirates on the seas and other difficulties. On the elven side, they largely ignored the human settlements, with the exception of Fringe, a town on the forest's edge that had long since driven out all Castorhagi loyalists and begun independent operation. With that group alone, the nearby wild elves (specifically, the Sentinels of the Trees) were willing to trade.

Other parts of the forest remained extremely anti-human, on all sides, to the point that when petitioned by Xha'en refugees and even by Utterends' tengu and tabaxi to aid the Xha'en empire in deposing Amaran su Bha, the lich-emperor, the wild elves of the Green Realm turned them away and simply shut their borders against the undead threat, waiting for it to go away and barely noticing when it did.

With time, the Forest Coast War fell out of living elven memory, and eventually out of living memory for even most of the fey and awakened trees. Ignoring the now-militarily-irrelevant, coast-dwelling humans became habit, as did mercilessly slaying them if they harmed a tree without permission or refused to leave the forest when told. Instead of their human neighbors, the elves began to turn on one another.

Sometime during this period, elves loyal to the Matriarch of Anasanalin, one of the Green Realm's oldest family lines, found the Green Warder monolith known as Tyriem broken and thrown down, his songs silenced. Though many elves and fey heard or felt a great crash that night as the top of the stone fell to earth, and a few believed they'd seen flickers of eldritch light in that direction, no direct witnesses have ever come forward, nor have any theories been advanced as to how such a thing could have been accomplished.

After that, the forest began to change. In the corner that Tyriem had guarded, just near the southernmost foothills of the Impossible Peaks, incursions of monsters began to make their way into the forest to challenge the local elves. Some communities were able to hold a line of defense, but others were caught up in the influx of horror and forced to fight for their lives.

At the same time, the northern Green Realm elves, especially those along the Forest Coast and those nearest to the Impossible Peaks, began to have fierce disagreements with the southern Green Realm and the court at Solis Alunaris. The northern elves had begun to feel that they were being used by the southern elves, to enable their complacency in the face of the ever-expanding human world. To have a Green Warder so mysteriously slain was terrifying to the northern wild elves, who felt that at any moment the other six might follow and allow rampaging hordes of humans to instantly descend on them.

The final straw came when hostilities broke out between the wild elves living north and east of Tyriem and those living south and west of the felled Warder. While their elven neighbors, including the Anasanalin family, attempted to mediate the conflict, the court of the Green Realm dismissed the issue as one might the squabbling of young siblings. Seeking a neutral mediator, the northern elves looked to the Gardener of Elenis Tuath for wisdom, and she was able to broker a grumbling peace. Seeing that they had handled their problem by themselves without any aid from their southern rulers, a movement arose in the north to choose their own leadership and formally secede from the Green Realm.

It took 100 years, but in the end, the current Green Warden Nations were established. Nine nations, with Lintariel as the southernmost and Elenis Tuath enshrined as a tiny, neutral nation unto itself, were acknowledged and empowered to oversee their own territories as they saw fit, and conventions were established to provide for action in concert when necessary for their mutual interest and defense. When all was agreed, talks with the southern Green Realm began, and were concluded surprisingly quickly and peacefully due to a multitude of factors, including the coincidence of the talks with certain events taking place in the south at the time.

The entire Green Realm north of the Ilber Peninsula became known as the Green Warden Nations. However, before the matter was settled, diplomacy broke down between Eloitan, the elves in the heart of the growing corruption around the felled Warder stone, and all of their neighbors. In the end, the elves of Eloitan chose not to finalize their agreement with the other eight nations and have governed themselves in isolation ever since.

The remaining eight nations in the Green Wardens coalition are: Serpent's Coil in the far north, just above Tyriem's fallen monolith; Forest's Bones to their east, still north of the line of Green Warders and including Hollow Mountain as well as most of the "unquiet" realms where the forest's fallen defenders sometimes continue their stewardship even after death; Anasanalin, stretching through the forest south of the Warders, save for the parts considered Eloitan territory; Monkey's Laughter, Eloitan's neighbors to the south and west; the Kingdom of Wolves in roughly the center and center-west of the Green Warden Nations; the Family of Thorns near the Hellsgate Peaks and the northern Forest Coast; Sentinels of the Trees along the rest of the Forest Coast border and all but surrounding Elenis Tuath; and Lintariel for the western half of the southernmost portion of the Green Warden Nations' territory.

While this new arrangement of nations healed relations with the southern Green Realm such that trade and diplomacy increased dramatically and a formal alliance was forged within a generation, internal matters for the Green Warden Nations were less simple. Each nation had long celebrated its own diverse culture (a major reason for their secession in the first place), but now that they were largely self-governed, they found that their differences with one another, particularly in ideology, only increased.

The Eloitan elves have never been coaxed into the coalition despite several attempts, and they accuse the Green Warden Nations of using them as a bulwark in the same way that the south was said to have used the north. Serpent's Coil elves accuse those of the Eloitan of colluding with the monsters that plague their region, and Serpent's Coil rumor suggests that it was Eloitan elves who were responsible for the felling of Tyriem. There are also some who believe that, whether they felled the monolith or not, the Eloitan have been subtly affected by its fall and have themselves wandered down the path of corruption. Anasanalin and Monkey's Laughter have had better relations with their Eloitan neighbors, occasionally even providing assistance to the ever-challenged community, but Monkey's Laughter in turn has developed an antagonistic relationship with the Kingdom of Wolves, whom they accuse of arrogance and treating them like a vassal state. The Kingdom of Wolves, in turn, accuses Monkey's Laughter of refusing to deal with the thieves and raiders from their territory who have assaulted Wolf villages.

Anasanalin and the Sentinels of the Trees both protest against Family of Thorns' xenophobic policies toward outsiders, while the Thornsibs accuse the Anasanalions of living too far from any human populations to know what they are talking about, and the Sentinels of having gone soft or even betrayed the forest. The Sentinels, Lintarions, and Wolfsibs — all of whom share borders with independent Elenis Tuath — constantly accuse one another of attempting to gain undue influence over the Gardener of Elenis Tuath … and so on.

When nearly 900 years had passed since the last of Castorhage's direct crimes against the Forest Coast Nation, the remains of the Forest Coast colonies, along with a few new settlements, officially declared their independence from Castorhage and united to form the Tycho Free States. Now the fragmented nations of elves and humans share a long border along which they have complicated and varied relationships.

Thus far, the Sentinels of the Trees have in fact been quite friendly with Fringe (which they have come to consider to be almost a vassal state) and, to a lesser extent, with the leader of Freetown, and have maintained decent, wary relations with greedy Timbertown. Trust is thin, however, and even the Sentinels of the Trees are rarely friendly with humans. Some of the fey in the Green Warden still remember human betrayal, and the elves do listen to their tales. The Family of Thorns will have nothing to do with the Tycho Free States and seems only to grow more hostile toward them as the humans gain in wealth and population. If Fringe were to petition the Sentinels to defend the Free States against the Family of Thorns, some postulate that hostility might erupt between the two Green Warden Nations.

Indeed, internally, the Nations have continued to deal with strife in many areas, and it has come to the point that — while neither nation has sought to leave the Green Warden coalition — Monkey's Laughter and the Kingdom of Wolves are almost constantly at odds with one another. Hostilities are rarely bloody, and the casualty count has yet to exceed a dozen, even after decades, but every time their other neighbors help the Wolfsibs and Apesibs to establish a truce, one or the other side breaks it again in a vindictive raid over some past slight or other. It is suspected that Serpent's Coil may be engaged in a similar long-term conflict with Eloitan, but if so, neither they nor the Eloitan elves speak of it to the rest of the Nations. Though most elves in the region are willing to aid the Eloitan should it be needed, there is still widespread suspicion of the realm and a possible darkness festering in its heart.

While most within and without the forest believe the elves would unite as one if presented with a sufficiently threatening common enemy, some fear that such a unity could not be maintained for long. If an enemy were patient enough, the Nations would likely fragment, with none having the military might necessary to defend the forest from incursion — especially not if any more of the Green Warders fall.

Religion

Reverence for Arialee is the dominant religion in Anasanalin and Lintariel, and tied for dominance in Sentinels of the Trees and Elenis Tuath. It is the second most popular religion in the Kingdom of Wolves and Forest's Bones, and it is common in every Green Warden Nation. Of the eight nations, it is least common in Serpent's Coil.

Animism is the dominant religion in Family of Thorns, the Kingdom of Wolves, and Monkey's Laughter. It is tied for dominance in Elenis Tuath and Sentinels of the Trees, and is the second most common religion in Serpent's Coil, Anasanalin, and Lintariel. Even where its popularity is lowest, in Forest's Bones, it is still practiced in a majority of households as a secondary addition to other religious practices. Nearly all families in the Green Warden Nations practice animism to some degree, blending it seamlessly with their other beliefs, if any.

In Serpent's Coil, the dominant worship is of a lesser-known local deity called the Tree of the World, whose roots feed on death and whose fruit gives life, and whose servant is a great serpent. Interpretations of this deity have sprung up throughout the Nations, with two wildly different versions popular as a fad among younger elves in Anasanalin and Family of Thorns. It is believed that the dangerous cult growing in the Hollow Mountain region of Forest's Bones' territory may be a disturbing offshoot of Tree of the World worship, since mention has been heard among cultists of a "Tree That Sees," but the Hollow Mountain cult version is very different from the others, if so.

In Forest's Bones, the dominant religion is ancestor-worship, with strong animistic overtones. Ancestor reverence is common throughout the Green Warden Nations, but only in Forest's Bones, Anasanalin, and Sentinels of the Forest does it commonly take on a true prayer or devotion element. In Anasanalin and Sentinels of the Trees, ancestor-worship is a common element included in some types of animism, but in Forest's Bones it takes precedence over the animistic aspects of the belief systems, and many outside Forest's Bones find the Boneguards' obsession with the dead to be morbid.

Trade and Commerce

The Green Warden Nations do most of their trading with one another and with the Green Realm to the south. Exceptions include the close trade relationship between Sentinels of the Trees and the town of Fringe in the Tycho Free States, as well as the arrangement some Sentinel elves have made with Captain Akadearg of Freeport to sell sustainably- and responsibly-harvested lumber. Family of Thorns' elves participate in trade with the intelligent magical creatures of the Hellsgate Peaks and have been accused of selling human prisoners as slaves to Hellsgate Peaks' devils. Lintariel elves have limited trade with Xha'en and more extensive trade relations with the Utterends' nomads. Any other external trade relationships have not been made public by the Green Warden elves engaging in them.

All eight of the Green Warden nations are nutritionally self-sustaining, and capitalism, money, and materialism in general tend to be culturally despised, particularly in Monkey's Laughter, such that trade is not a prized value in any of the Green Warden Nations, and all would question not just the utility but even the wisdom of deliberately seeking economic growth. The Green Warden Nations concentrate instead on magical education as their primary source of influence. All spellcasting classes are more common and respected in the Green Warden Nations than is typical of the world around them, with druidry being a quite typical life-path and sorcerers being revered as blessed children.

Magical power is infinitely more desired than wealth throughout the Green Warden, as is knowledge.

Loyalties and Diplomacy

The closest ally of the Green Warden Nations is the Green Realm to the south. The Green Warden Nations keep no other official allies and are extremely standoffish when other nations attempt to initiate diplomatic relations. The notion of a Tycho Free States embassy has been rejected multiple times. Xha'en has been permitted regular ambassadorial visits to the outer edge of Lintariel territory, and a Green Warden ambassador has visited each of the last three Xha'en emperors once to ensure ongoing peace with Xha'en, but even with that illustrious empire no permanent embassy is maintained. The Green Warden elves prefer to keep to themselves and be left alone.

Government

Outside times of war or great necessity, the Green Warden Nations are governed by a council of the leaders of the eight Nations. When any of the leaders cannot be present, a representative is sent to the council instead. If a vote results in a tie, one of the eight leaders is randomly selected, and that leader may cast a second vote.

On a few rare occasions, the eight leaders choose to empower the Gardener of Elenis Tuath as a wise and neutral figure to make economic and diplomatic decisions for the nation as a whole, but only for a brief and pre-determined period. The Gardener of Elenis Tuath has, in the past, been sent as an ambassador to Xha'en as well. In times of war, the eight leaders would in theory select one from among themselves to serve as High Monarch (or High King) until the end of the war, though no military conflicts have been considered sufficiently serious for such a unification since the Green Warden Nation was formed.

Below the highest leaders, each Nation is governed differently. Anasanalin is a semi-hereditary monarchy, its leader known by a genderless elven term (tala) commonly translated as duke or duchess. Positions of authority under the tala are either appointed by the tala or hereditary, depending on the position. A council of 13 elders — elected for life by all language-capable Anasanalin citizens over age 300, regardless of species — appoints each new tala, who must come from the same historic family among the Anasanalin. The council is also empowered to depose a tala under certain circumstances and approves the partners with whom the tala is permitted to officially breed.

The council uses this authority to seek to enhance the wisdom, even-temper, intelligence, confidence, health, and magical ability of those who may become tala in the future, with secondary concerns being battle prowess and beauty. Though tala may marry whomever they wish, heirs produced by matches outside the council-selected pool must pass a grueling qualification process to be considered worthy. Inbreeding is carefully avoided, and the partner pool often includes commoners or even elves from other Green Warden Nations. Most tala have been wizards (including the current duchess), but sorcerers are selected whenever an available heir meets the elders' criteria for good leadership and shows sorcerous talent.

In the Family of Thorns, the Council of Elders system is similar to Anasanalin's, but the Thornsib elders preside over the choice of a warlord rather than a tala. The warlord is selected by ritual tournament every 10 years, with no term limits. The council may call a special tournament before a term is up if a warlord is found to be weak or treasonous. All other positions of authority are either appointed by the warlord, appointed by the council, or determined by tournament. Magic is permitted and encouraged in the ritual tournaments, and most warlords have had some magical ability in addition to physical prowess. The current warlord is a druid.

Forest's Bones is ruled directly by an elected Council of Elders that selects a military leader only in times of conflict, to be removed as soon as there is peace. Other authority positions are appointed by the council, through means as diverse as tournaments, other contests, popular vote, divination, or simply a vote by the council itself.

The Kingdom of Wolves is one of the few Nations to call its leader king or queen. The Kingdom contains 11 noble families, which it has come to style the "Great Packs." Each citizen swears fealty to the hereditary leader of a Pack of its choice (with a ritualized process for transferring loyalty from one Pack to another, save in times of war). The matriarchs and patriarchs of all of the Great Packs make up the Royal Council, which shares power with the king or queen though a highly ritualized legal system. The Royal Council selects a new monarch when the previous one dies and also has a say in which of a councilor's heirs succeed to the council when a Pack matriarch or patriarch dies. Councilors representing larger packs get more votes than smaller packs. A breeding system similar to that of Anasanalin attempts to ensure that the matriarchs and patriarchs on the council and the monarchs are all sound of mind and temperament.

Like Anasanalin, Lintariel is ruled by a tala (duke or duchess). This leader is always the head of the ancient Lintariel family, though the heir must be acclaimed by the majority of all elder citizens of Lintariel (over 300 years) to be considered capable of inheritance. If biological heirs are not found suitable, the tala must officially adopt someone the elders will acclaim. The Lintariel tala must always have at least one such acceptable heir, and usually a preapproved line of succession is maintained at least five people down in case of disaster. All other governing positions within Lintariel are appointed by the tala, who has absolute authority and can be deposed only by three respected priests of Arialee who can provide evidence of divine decree, or theoretically by the Gardener of Elenis Tuath if all seven other Nations chose to empower such interference (which would not be undertaken lightly).

Monkey's Laughter consists of many small nomadic clans, each of which is governed by clan elders and an elected chieftain. Any independent group of 20 or more citizens of the Nation (including fey, some monsters, and awakened plants and animals) may appoint a chieftain. Many of the chieftains gather every 10 winters to vote on a national representative to sit on the Green Warden Leaders' Council. But many chieftains do not bother, and the national representative rarely speaks for even half of the Monkey's Laughter clans. Clans whose chieftains do not acknowledge the representative often refuse to abide by decisions of that representative. The current representative, Nynarinel the Sharp, is unusually beloved by the Monkey's Laughter populace and has curried and maintained the support of all of the largest and many of the smaller clans' leaders. Even she, however, cannot be said to "govern" the Monkey's Laughter nation. In truth, hardly anyone in Monkey's Laughter has real authority.

Sentinels of the Trees is governed by a Council of Healers. Anyone able to demonstrate healing ability (magical or otherwise, of animals and humanoids, plants, or even of hearts) is granted "healing citizen" status and may vote on the selection of members to the 19-member Council of Healers. The Council of Healers appoints all other major positions, including a permanent duke to command the military and a high minister to sit on the Green Warden Leaders' Council. Whenever a member of the Council of Healers dies, the election process to select a new one is long and chaotic, as locally-appointed officials attempt to determine who is and isn't a "healing citizen."

Serpent's Coil, like Monkey's Laughter, has little central governance and consists of self-governing nomadic clans. However, the Serpent's Coil clans have a more structured legal system and methodology for electing a representative, called the King or Queen of Serpents. The Monarch of Serpents is beholden to the clan chieftains and easily deposed, but technically holds absolute authority, especially in military matters, so long as the majority of chieftains continue to choose to obey.

MILITARY

Though it varies somewhat from Nation to Nation, for the most part, the Green Warden professional military consists entirely of troops other nations would consider special forces or shock troops. Rangers are common, as are other stealth-based classes, with various forest specialization. Spellcasters are unusually common in the Green Warden, and a Green Warden army would never lack sufficient healers, mages, or supporting casters. The Green Warden wild elves take military tactics using magic for granted, so common is spellcasting among their peoples.

In times of war, all able-bodied adults may be urged to volunteer as additional support to the professional forces, but even these less-trained troops are likelier than average soldiers to know a few spells, own a minor magical item, have non-humanoid allies, or be frighteningly stealthy. In addition, with some local variation for specific species, the Green Warden military is adept at coordinating battle efforts with various animal, plant, and monster units.

If the military of the Green Warden has a weakness (other than being relatively small in number), it is that the differently-organized and -motivated units of the various Nations are likely to have trouble coordinating, should they ever need to fight together as one.

MAJOR THREATS

Despite the constant (and typically anti-human) shield-rattling of many Green Warden citizens, in practical terms, the Green Warden faces few military threats from outside their borders. The forest is defended by too much magic and too many monsters to make invasion cost-effective, especially in territory so well-suited to guerrilla tactics, and the wild elves do not appear to guard great wealth (at least, not of any varieties that seem easy to steal). All in all, the Green Warden's neighbors are generally content to leave them alone.

The far greater threats come from less overt sources. In Forest's Bones, disappearances around Hollow Mountain are increasing. It is still unknown why the northernmost Green Warder fell, and in Monkey's Laughter and Serpent's Coil, foul monsters from Eloitan are an omnipresent hazard. Family of Thorns faces similar difficulty from monsters from the Hellsgate Peaks. In many parts of the Nations, especially in disputed lands between them (as none of the Nations are well demarcated, maps being a cultural taboo), infighting and intrigues among the wild elves themselves threaten to poison the Green Warden as a whole.

In addition, as the Tycho Free States grow in population and economic relevance, radical elements in Sentinels of the Trees and especially Family of Thorns grow ever more eager to provoke conflict with the humans. At this time, the Green Warden would almost certainly triumph in such a conflict. However, the Free States have friends in Reme, Castorhage, and even Foere. If the wild elves were seen by the outside world to have become a threat to humankind, a multi-nation retaliation for violence against the Free States might prove devastating for the Green Warden peoples. In this sense, one of the greatest potential threats to the Green Warden is its own radical fringe.

WILDERNESS AND ADVENTURES

With rare exceptions, all of the Green Warden Forest might as well be wilderness to outsiders. Some communities use magic or misdirection to mask their villages from prying eyes, while others hide their homes in trees or caves, or simply post sentries to see to it that no outsiders ever approach their settlements uninvited. Many are nomadic, keeping no permanent dwellings, and these pack up and move if their camps are observed. However the goal is accomplished, it is taboo to allow outsiders — especially humans — to lay eyes on a permanent Green Warden settlement. For this reason, the only Green Warden region that traveling adventurers are likely to see is wilderness. Indeed, even Green Warden agriculture is never farmed in traditional rows. Rather, it is gardened in so harmonious a way as to be indistinguishable from natural forest to all but the most perceptive and plant-savvy observers.

The least "wild" Nation in the Green Warden is Anasanalin, and some of the treetop villages in that region (including the Anasanalin tala's tree-mansion) are not considered to be sufficiently hidden by members of other Nations. Since Anasanalin is surrounded on all sides by other Nations, however, it is unlikely that intruders would penetrate deeply enough to encounter its settlements in the first place. Additionally, to all non-locals, the forest floor beneath a treetop village should be considered wilderness for the purpose of many sorts of threats. For example, it is not uncommon for Green Warden villages to be guarded by tigers, apes, dire animals, or even treants or unicorns.

ELENIS TUATH

(EL-ih-nis TOO-ahth)
Ruler: Gardener Findolel
Government: theocracy
Population: 200-600 wild elves (including seasonal pilgrims)
Technology Level: mixed (High Middle Ages, but residents prefer Iron Age technology)

This small, self-governing spiritual community, built in the ruins of an ancient elven city, is of great import to the surrounding Green Warden Nations and often serves as a place of mediation for disputes. The order's elected leader, known as the Gardener, has also now and again been sought for judgment on important crimes or invested with very high temporary authority by the various dukes and monarchs of the surrounding fragmented Green Warden peoples.

This is done because Elenis Tuath is seen as owing allegiance only to the forest as a whole, and as being above mundane political squabbles. This perception in turn makes control of Elenis Tuath a potentially very powerful position, despite all appearances. As a consequence, the residents of Elenis Tuath never accept any form of money for any reason: They seek to avoid undue influence or even the appearance of undue influence over the Gardener from anyone, from anywhere.

The remains of the old city, and especially its fair temple, are a marvel of structural and magical engineering, full of sweeping arches, lace-like flying buttresses, and gloriously intricate (though now shattered) glass-paned windows. Though much of the ruins are indistinguishable from natural rocks, or buried in ivy, it is impressive how much remains upright — of the temple especially — despite the damage taken over the centuries.

The crowning glory of the temple (and indeed of the whole city) is the great statue of Arialee, which is carved into a nearby hillside and seamlessly appears to be emerging from the earth. Though somewhat stylized in the manner of its era, this classic example of the reclining Arialee — great with child in a local variation of her "Spring" iconography — remains one of the world's greatest works of art.

HISTORY AND PEOPLE

Once the summer capital of the Court of the Green Realm, Elenis Tuath (a name meaning, very roughly, Oneness with Nature) was mostly abandoned long before humans came to the region. The architecture and materials were constructed using technology that the elves had lost ages ago, and as the capital fell slowly into disrepair, the court found it more and more a painful reminder of former glory.

As Elenis Tuath's population thinned ever further and the court became less likely to visit each summer, the former grand community shrank until little remained but its greatest and most beautiful structure, even lovelier than the court's summer palace: a proud, ancient temple to the fey goddess of nature, Arialee. Today, even that great temple is now a crumbling ruin, a bitter reminder to the elves of the Green Warden Forest of their culture's decline.

By the time diplomatic relations broke down between the Green Warden elves and the Castorhagi settlers on the coast, and the Great Road crawled ever deeper into the heart of the forest, the Green Realm's old summer capital was already mostly empty, and even the worship of the goddess Arialee had dwindled at that time among the northern wild elves. As Elenis Tuath had become entirely indefensible, the Green Realm leaders chose to evacuate the few remaining residents rather than fight to defend a place that caused them only pain.

The temple, by then, was sparsely tended by only a few monks, all of whom lacked the necessary ability to keep the statue from being covered in foliage without harming the plants, which their religion at the time forbade outside strictly nutritional needs. Thus, the statue was overgrown and largely forgotten. Nevertheless, the monks refused to evacuate and chose to stay with the temple as emissaries of peace.

Due to a freak misunderstanding and poor leadership among the Castorhagi forces, the near-abandoned temple was not only unable to serve as a peaceful embassy, it was outright sacked. The forest around it was cruelly burned, and the resident monks were slaughtered. When other elves came to investigate the forest fire, besides the charred evidence of this terrible crime, they found the newly uncovered statue of Arialee marred by the flames to forever appear as if tears streaked her face as she gazed out over the now-ruined temple and city.

The monks' remains were laid reverently to rest, and the statue became a potent symbol of elven pride and grief forever after. Once the elves retook that part of the forest, it didn't take long for a new order of priests, druids, and monks to spring up — an eclectic group of different local orders united by a dedication to preserving the natural forest and what remains of elven culture.

This new and revitalized Order of Remembrance still tends to the statue, once again training the foliage to enhance it rather than ever obscure or damage it, and many Green Warden elves make pilgrimages each spring to give offerings at the simple stone shrines now built at the ever-weeping Arialee's feet. The ruined temple, however, is left untouched, as a monument to grief and loss. The resident faithful make their homes in deliberately temporary little huts among the nearby city ruins. They rebuild the huts each fall to serve as winter shelter and burn them in controlled summer bonfires as a ritual of the eternal sorrow of impermanence.

RELIGION

Nature is the key unifying element of the religions observed by the Order of Remembrance. Animism holds the most sway among the residents, and the current Gardener is primarily an animist himself. Worship of Arialee is almost as prevalent as direct communion with the land, and many members of the order preach that the two outlooks are simply different ways of looking at the same thing. Other nature and healing deities are occasionally revered by individuals within the order.

The Order of Remembrance is profoundly anti-materialistic. In addition to the preservation of nature and the forest, the order values honesty, hard work, accountability, and knowledge of history.

LOYALTIES AND DIPLOMACY

Owing fealty to only the land itself, the Order of Remembrance remains carefully neutral among all the various Green Warden Nations. During times of war, one of the Nations' leaders is selected as a temporary High King; in matters of diplomacy or peaceful trade, the Green Warden Nations' leaders have been known to transfer much of their authority to the Gardener at Elenis Tuath and empower this holy individual to make major decisions and sign documents on behalf of the entire Green Warden realm. During such periods, it could be said that all the nations of the Green Warden owe their fealty to Elenis Tuath, but the Order of Remembrance deliberately gives itself no means to capitalize on such a circumstance.

The current Gardener, Findolel, has never been granted such authority. He gives no sign of coveting power of any kind.

GOVERNMENT

The Order of Remembrance is highly organized, with the Gardener at the head supported by the elders, who are in turn supported by the watchers. Elders are all members of the order at least 250 years of age, so long as they have ever been watchers. The Gardener (always an elder) is elected to 20-year terms by the elders, with no term limits. Watchers are members of the order who have been fully vested for at least 20 years. The structure beyond that is quite complicated, with each elder or watcher having authority over different aspects of daily life and pilgrim-management in Elenis Tuath.

Within the bounds of the Elenis Tuath ruins, the Gardener's word is absolute law, enforced by the elders and watchers. The Gardener can be removed from office early if found to be guilty of deliberately (or through criminal negligence) harming the forest. Detailed scriptural history itemizes what sorts of events could be or have in the past been deemed to harm the forest.

MILITARY

Elenis Tuath has no military as such, and bearing arms is not permissible anywhere within the limits of the old city. However, the order does boast many clerics, druids, monks, and any number of sympathetic local monsters, animals, and magical creatures. When the person telling you to leave your weapons at the gate is petting a six-foot tiger at the time, the presence of a military is often considered to be unnecessary.

MAJOR THREATS

While Elenis Tuath is sometimes considered to be "dangerously" close to the human-dominated territory of the Tycho Free States, it is unlikely to be threatened by humans or other foreigners any time soon. The Green Warden Forest is very well defended. A much greater threat to the region is posed by the rest of the Green Warden Nations surrounding them. Should any of the surrounding dukes and monarchs see a chance to exert inappropriate influence over Elenis Tuath in any way, it could have disastrous effects on the stability of the entire region.

Gardener Findolel has held his position for 30 years and is widely respected. Thus far, he seems to be adept as a mediator and diplomat and also entirely incorruptible. His mild demeanor and grandfatherly smile, however, have made it difficult for some to take him seriously. Such people worry that his appearance of "softness" already undermines the unity of the Green Warden Nations, though many others find his even temper and objectivity to make him the worthiest Gardener that has been seen in centuries. Only time will tell if his leadership will ever be of more than passing import to the loosely allied nations around him.

WILDERNESS AND ADVENTURES

The Order of Remembrance is located on the south side of the ruins of the city, clustered in little huts and a small natural grotto between the remains of the Temple of Arialee and Arialee's weeping statue. Even in spring, when the order sees its highest influx of visiting pilgrims, the elven population of Elenis Tuath rarely spills out over the former temple grounds. The rest of the city, though watched over and lightly gardened by the order, belongs to the plants, animals, fey, and other creatures. It is a quite dangerous place to explore without a local or druid guide.

Dangerous, yes, but fascinating. Most of the ruins have been examined thoroughly by the order over the centuries, but plenty of nooks and crannies could have been overlooked that contain the gods only know what ancient elven mysteries, not to mention the potential for harmful or corrupted creatures taking up residence in some crumbling structure or other without the order having noticed.

Finally, on the southeast edge of the ruined city, one can find the crumbling and overgrown remains of the Castorhagi Great Road project. This stretch of the Great Road is famously haunted. Undead found there are always incorporeal and rarely more than sad or disturbing apparitions with no power to affect the living, but now and again something might trigger a change in one of the restless dead, from mere messenger of sorrow to active instrument of vengeance, especially if a human were to return to Elenis Tuath.

ELOITAN, ELVEN TRIBE OF

(Eh-loy-i-tan)
Ruler: none
Government: tribal hierarchy
Population: 125,000 (est.) (wild elves)
Monstrous: ankheg, assassin vines, bears, bears (dire), bugbears, chimerae, faerie dragons, green dragons, dryads, ettin, ettercaps, goblins, hags, leopards, lycanthropes (wereboar), lycanthropes (werewolves), nymphs, giant owls, ogres, owlbears, pseudodragons, panthers, satyr, skeletons, snakes (poisonous), giant snakes, giant spiders, sprites, stirges, treants, trolls, unicorns, giant wasps, will-o'-wisps, wolves, wolves (dire), zombies

Languages: elvish
Religion: Arialee/druidism
Resources: gems, magical resources, timber
Currency: barter
Technology Level: Bronze/Iron Age

The name Eloitan is a corruption of a very old elvish term originally meaning "Verdant Heart." The wild elves who dwell in this region, on the very eastern frontier of the Xha'en Hegemony, are among the most insular and dangerous in Akados, shunning even relations with the neighboring Green Warden Nations and the elves of the Green Realm. Many of their fellow elves feel that there is a darkness here that gnaws at the hearts of the Eloitan folk and affects the land itself, transforming it into a hostile, perilous place, as if the entire region is a single living organism that is inimical to all life save its own.

HISTORY AND PEOPLE

The Third Exodus of the Elves saw the westward retreat of elvenkind in the face of advancing human civilization, falling back into the remnants of the ancient Akadonian forests west of the Crescent Sea, leaving the Green Warders behind to guard against incursion. The elves who settled in the north-western portions of the forest bordering on the Plains of Xhas dubbed their region the Eloitan.

Originally known as the River Singers, they had been great artisans — singers, musicians, players, balladeers, bards — but after this third forced exodus, they were hardened, embracing a fanatical self-reliance and separatism from the rest of the world. Though initially there was tentative contact between them and the Xha'en to the west, this ended quickly as the humans, ever seeking new lands and resources, began to move into the forest, felling trees and building roads and settlements. The elves of the Eloitan quickly struck back, raiding Xha'en settlements along the forest's edge and killing lone foresters and hunters. The Xha'en responded, sending punitive expeditions into the forest in a low-level conflict that lasted for decades.

The last chance for trust between Xha'en and Eloitan was lost. The forest elves would tolerate no further incursions and broke off all contact with the humans. These were elven forests, and elven forests they would remain — only the utter extermination of the Eloitan folk would change that. The wild elves would die rather than take even a single step backward.

The Eloitan's insularity extended even to the other elves of the Green Realm. At first, the shared sense of hardship and heritage bound the forest elves together, but the Eloitan, stern and unyielding in their dedication to the old ways, began to drift away. When the elves of the northern forests split off from the Court at Solis Alunaris and became the Green Warden Nations, Eloitan ultimately refused to join and went their own way. Formal cordiality devolved into cold indifference and in some cases outright hostility, for Eloitan warriors sometimes clashed with Green Warden elves, especially those of the Serpent's Coil, whose territories adjoined the Eloitan.

At the same time, Green Warden elves began to sense a change in the Eloitan region. Some elves believe that the destruction of the Green Warder monolith Tyriem may have marked the beginning of the Eloitan's descent, bringing a shadow to the entire forest region. Since that day, the Green Warden elves say, Eloitan has been slowly but steadily transforming into a dark and dangerous place. Natural creatures have grown larger and more aggressive. Hostile humanoids such as goblins and gnolls wander these woods, and even more fearsome creatures like ettin, ettercaps, giant spiders, and other arachnids have seen their populations increase. Violence in the once-peaceful region has grown and sometimes spread to affect adjoining regions of the Xha'en Hegemony.

With this has come greater conflict between Eloitan and the Green Warden Nations, particularly the Serpent's Coil — itself one of the more fearsome wild elf nations. Open conflicts between the two have grown more frequent in recent years, sufficient to concern even the other elven nations, with some leaders sounding the alarm and openly considering whether something needs to be done.

Most humans, especially those of the Xha'en Hegemony, consider the Eloitan elves to be primitive savages with little regard for life or civilization. On the contrary, of course, like the nearby Green Warden Nations, the Eloitan are anything but primitive, though they have willfully embraced a far simpler and less technological existence than the humans.

Eloitan elves usually live in temporary or semi-permanent camps throughout the region, moving as the seasons dictate and the welfare of the tribe demands. They are an unmaterialistic people, preferring to hunt with flint- or obsidian-tipped weapons (or, rarely, artifacts left over from before the Exodus), and wearing clothing derived from animal hides and natural fibers. Fur cloaks are worn in the cold winter months, while simple loincloths or less are favored during the heat of summer. Body decorations in the form of pigments, tattoos, or scarification are common, with each tribe having its own unique motifs and practices.

Long-lived, the elves have few children and the birth of a child is cause for great celebration by a tribe and its neighbors. Youngsters mature much more slowly than humans and are carefully taught the ways of their tribes. Normally, children are considered adults at age 20, when they most closely resemble humans of ages 12 to 14. These new adults are expected to immediately take on adult responsibilities such as hunting, fishing, farming, and training for battle with the other tribal warriors.

The scarcity of children, as well as some very old societal practices, has encouraged the development of group marriage among the Eloitan, a situation in which several individuals of varying gender live in a loose group, caring for each other and, if necessary, raising children collectively. A child usually refers to all males in his group as "father" and all women as "mother," as specific parentage is often not known for certain.

RELIGION

The wild elves retain some elements of their people's ancient faiths, but other deities have arisen more in keeping with their current status as keepers of the forest and defenders of nature. The fey goddess Arialee is most commonly worshipped and thought to be the primary deity among a host of nature spirits and elementals who make up the rest of the Eloitan elves' pantheon. The mysterious nature god known as the Green Father is also worshipped, but usually by the druids alone, who carry out his rituals in secret, and receive messages from the great deity delivered by intelligent white ravens.

Various demigods and spirits, often associated with very specific local regions, all serve under Arialee, who is considered to be kind and benevolent, but must still be respected and appeased. The wild elves truly believe that every plant, animal, and natural object possesses its own spirit, and that some even contain the spirits of their own ancestors who can be summoned through ritual and called upon for wisdom. An Eloitan legend speaks of an entire tribe of wild elves that sought refuge in the plants and animals of its region to escape persecution, and that may someday return.

Priestly duties are carried out by a shaman class that practices druidic magic and cares for the natural life of the forest. These druids usually dwell apart from the tribes but can be approached for advice or called upon for divine assistance. These druids are among the most fanatical of the region's defenders, and often use their magic mercilessly against trespassers and innocent travelers alike.

TRADE AND COMMERCE

Trade is an entirely internal matter for the Eloitan elves, as, with very few exceptions, outsiders are forbidden. Most tribes subsist on hunting and gathering and maintain a fairly non-material culture, living in skin tents, hunting with bow and spear, fishing with net or bow, sometimes engaging in a small amount of cultivation, or keeping small herds of goats. Trade usually takes place in spring and summer as tribes trade excess food, tools, weapons, clothing, and animals among themselves. From time to time, goods from Xha'en or the Tycho states may be available for trade, the result of successful raids on unfortunate communities or travelers.

LOYALTIES AND DIPLOMACY

The elves of Eloitan are loyal to no one save each other — not even the elves of the Green Warden Nations. Folklore and history have shown that non-elves are untrustworthy and should be either driven out of elven lands or slain without mercy if they refuse. Humans are usually attacked if encountered, which forces them to rely on stealthy passage through the treacherous depths of this ancient forest. Other elves are allowed to enter the region but are often followed and treated with suspicion.

Prisoners are rarely taken, though in recent years disturbing reports have emerged and suggest that some Eloitan communities have taken to capturing enemies and putting them to torment before finally killing them. The truth of these rumors is not yet known, but they are disturbing and consistent with the suggestion that the Eloitan's character has grown even darker over the centuries.

The Eloitan do not maintain formal relations with the Green Warden Nations, though from time to time they accept aid or in especially dire circumstances, offer it themselves. For the most part, however, the Eloitan consider the Green Warden elves to have strayed from the paths of ancient wisdom and authority, and shun contact. In some cases, the Eloitan come into open conflict with their fellow elves, especially the Serpent's Coil. The two groups clash over control of various sacred sites such as the Circle of the Wild and the site of Tyriem's warder.

GOVERNMENT

The elves of Eloitan have nothing resembling a central government, instead consisting of small tribes ranging from 20 to 200 members scattered across the region. Though once their forebears followed a single monarch, the move back toward a "purer" and less technologically-advanced society also encouraged reversion to earlier cultural practices. Most of their communities are overseen by a chief — usually an older, accomplished warrior, hunter, or druid. These chiefs can be of any gender and are selected by the other elders of the tribe upon their predecessor's death or disability.

Chiefs are assisted by councils of elders, usually the oldest of the tribe. These groups are also of mixed genders, and though their advice does not have to be followed, it is considered very unwise to ignore them. Councils are able to remove incompetent chiefs from power and accordingly reduce their status though this occurs only rarely.

Some Green Warden elves who have visited the Eloitan region report that in some communities, the priestly class has grown in influence, sometimes dictating decisions to chiefs and elders. When taken with the rumors of tortured prisoners and violence growing in the heart of the Eloitan region, these reports are even more alarming.

MILITARY

All adult elves, including those who have just reached adulthood, are expected to fight and defend the tribe. About half to two-thirds of each tribe is capable of fighting at any time.

Eloitan warrior bands are highly effective at skirmish and hit-and-run, attacking the enemy without warning before vanishing among the trees. Tribal warriors fight unarmored with spears, longbows, clubs, and flint knives. Some tribes employ hide or turtle-shell shields, and others use less-familiar weapons such as atl-atl and stone-bladed clubs. A few weapons that date back to before the Exodus exist, and these are carefully guarded by tribes and revered as sacred objects.

Warbands are often accompanied by druids who use their magic to enhance warriors and confuse the enemy. Many druids also command creatures of the wild — animal companions as well as ordinary creatures under druidic influence — that can attack the enemy from unexpected quarters, perform reconnaissance, or carry messages.

MAJOR THREATS

Although the Eloitan once considered the humans of the Xha'en Hegemony to be their greatest threat, a growing sense among the Eloitan is that all peoples beyond their borders are dangerous, including other elven nations. Icily polite relations with the Green Warden elves continue, and the Eloitan accept and offer aid in times of trouble, but it seems that the isolated realm is growing ever more estranged from their fellow elves. Some among the Green Warden Nations, in fact, fear that skirmishes between Eloitan and the Serpent's Coil elves may erupt into open warfare over sacred sites.

Though the Xha'en see the forest as a vast untapped source of timber and other resources, their past incursions into the area have ended badly, and at this point most Xha'en keep their distance.

The forest's other denizens have been growing more aggressive in recent years. Significant numbers of goblins, gnolls, giants, and fey of every sort and alignment plague the Eloitan, often requiring several tribes to combine forces to face the challenge. Of these, the goblins are the most persistent. Their warriors are almost as cunning and dangerous as those of the Eloitan themselves and their evil spellcasters specialize in summoning or compelling some of the forest's more dangerous inhabitants — giant spiders, cave bears, dire wolves, serpents, carnivorous worms, birds of prey, and the like — to serve them and attack the elves. Battles with the goblins sometimes go on for days, with each side sneaking through the woods, attacking, retreating, and counterattacking over and over until both are exhausted and forced to withdraw. The goblins rarely attack to seize or hold territory — they are most interested in theft and mayhem.

The fey are a different matter, for the elves of old maintained a special relationship with the creatures of faerie. In the past, the elves and good-aligned fey kept to themselves, occasionally joining forces to battle mutual foes such as evil fey and undead. The wild elves' relations with the good fey have been strained, however, as the Eloitan grow more suspicious of outsiders. Conflicts between the elves and the good fey are usually inconclusive, and typically end with either the fey or the elves moving away from the source of the conflict.

War with the evil fey are far more serious affairs, for they are as hateful toward the elves as the elves themselves are to humans and dwarves. Evil fey consider the elves — and their good cousins as well — to be interlopers who have no right to live in the region, and frequently engage in bloody raids, lay traps, and kidnap unfortunate elves and subject them to fearsome torments. Elven children are an especially popular target for the dark fey, and these are sometimes replaced with wicked changelings. For the most part, the evil fey and the elves avoid each other, for struggles are invariably costly and end tragically for both sides.

Alarmingly, some of the stories of tortured prisoners and powerful priests are accompanied with evidence that a few Eloitan communities have made peace with the evil fey and might even be cooperating with their former enemies.

WILDERNESS AND ADVENTURES

The woods of the Eloitan are notoriously wild and dangerous. Even without the hazards presented by the wild elves, the forest, which is full of natural hazards such as pits, ravines, and thickets, is a fearsome place. Even the mundane creatures of the woods — bears, wolves, panthers, boars, etc. — are especially fierce and cunning, and larger species such as cave bears, giant boars, and dire variants of ordinary creatures are quite common and extremely aggressive. It is as if the wildlife of the forest burns with the same fury toward outsiders as the wild elves.

Monsters are even worse, with tribes of gnolls, goblins, ettercap, and ettins. Giant spiders, scorpions, and insects often lair in trees or underground, making even the shortest of journeys in the forest extremely hazardous, and as previously noted, fey — both good and evil — defend their territory fiercely.

Reasons exist to venture into Eloitan, though not everyone agrees that they are good reasons. Certainly, the lure of a permanent trade route between the ancient Xha'en Hegemony and the young and growing Tycho states is a potent motivation, with potential riches awaiting anyone who establishes such a connection. Eloitan is only the first step of such a journey, but the elf tribes are determined to make that step a costly one.

TYCHO FREE STATES
(ALSO SPELLED TAICHO)

(TYE-cho)

Capital: none

Notable Settlements: Bogsweat, Freetown, Fringe, Hotpools, Ilber Nole, Median, Timbertown

Ruler: Chief Magistrate Kemma Philben

Government: confederation of independent city-states

Population: 450,000 (196,000 Tycho ethnicities, 80,000 halfling, 65,000 Foerdewaith, 50,000 half-elf, 30,000 mixed or other ethnicity human, 15,000 hill dwarf, 4,000 Xha'en, 3,500 half-orc, 2,500 high elf, 2,000 lizardfolk, 1,000 tengu, 500 mountain dwarf, 500 other)

Monstrous: dire or giant animals native to the region (including but not limited to local breeds of monkeys, apes, pandas, red pandas, wolves, foxes, many snakes, birds, and occasional tigers) (all wilderness areas), awakened plants/trees, awakened animals, satyrs, pixies, centaurs, other fey, plant-type creatures native to the region (any, but especially treants, shambling mounds), lycanthropes (various, usually non-evil) dryads, unicorns, nymphs, owlbears, wyverns, pseudodragons, other temperate forest creatures native to the region (forest edge regions); worgs, harpies, occasional manticores or chimerae (remote, non-forested areas); stirges, will-o-wisps, chuuls (marshes, especially near Bogsweat); fire giants, red dragons, salamanders, or other fire-elemental-related beings (far northern Tycho, near the Hellsgate Peaks); giant or dire sea life, nixies, or the rare sea hag (coastal waters)

Languages: Common, Elven, sometimes others

Religion: varies regionally

Resources: timber, medicinal herbs, fishing, rare herbs and spices, naval mercenaries, salt, shipbuilding and repair, shipbuilding supplies, quarry stone, trade with elves, sea transport, pearls, grain, foodstuffs, furs, hotsprings

Currency: mixed

Technology Level: Medieval (most cities), Dark Ages (remote areas)

Located on the Free Coast between the Hellsgate Peaks and the southern end of the Ilber Peninsula, the Green Warden Forest, and the Crescent Sea, the Tycho Free States are officially just over 275 years old, one of the youngest nations in the region. Parts of the Free States' history goes back thousands of years, however, long enough for individual states in the confederacy to have developed vastly different cultures from one another, despite a common origin.

The name "Free Coast" was originally coined shortly after the official withdrawal of Castorhage from the region in order to distinguish between the Tycho Forest Coast (formerly the Forest Coast Work Colonies) and the rest of the Forest Coast to the south. Initially, it was rarely used by local inhabitants (who were more likely to say "North Coast") and was more a conceit of mapmakers and politicians.

In recent generations, however, as the descendants of the Tycho Free States' founding citizens grow further removed from their origin as a penal colony, the "Free" Coast has become known for its high rate of indentured servitude among the populace. This irony has led to the long-standing map-marked title for the area finally coming into general use among the Tycho Free States' indentured poor and neighboring peoples.

Indentured service in the Tycho Free States is normally imposed as a result of the failure to pay debts or as a punishment for certain crimes. Although permanent slavery is technically illegal, the economy of the region increasingly relies on an ever-growing class of indentured servants, and many local laws make it difficult for those finding themselves in this status to escape their bonds. In addition, a small illegal slave trade can be found running a nomadic operation up and down the

Free Coast. With the exception of the renowned privateer Evangeliana Akadearg, the Tycho Free States' leaders have yet to fully acknowledge, much less address, this elusive new danger in Free Coast waters.

With impassibly rocky coastlines in some areas and easily defensible, well-hidden natural harbors in others, the Free Coast is exceedingly difficult to police. This in itself explains much of the military history and survival of the Tycho Free States, and now encourages a growing tradition of illicit activities in the region. The most dangerous region of the Free Coast is in the north, where ash and steam from the Strait of Gehenna are frequently blown south to obscure northern Free Coast waters and harbors. It is believed that slavers may have a secret base in this region, and that some may in fact be in league with devils from the Hellsgate Peaks.

Outsiders tend to know the Free States by several different, often conflicting reputations. It is a land of liberty and populist values. It is a land of indenture and oppression. It is a land of piracy and anarchy. It is a land of heroes and naval might. It is the human nation with the single best trade relationship with the Green Warden Forest. It has an antagonistic relationship with its elven neighbors and may at any point provoke a war with them. It is a land of overcrowded little cities and ancient, beautiful roads. It is a land of trackless and treacherous wilderness. It is a land of extravagant wealth and a land of humble simplicity. All of these statements are true and not true, depending on where one looks.

History and People

Starting in 2301 I.R., Castorhage established a string of penal colonies on the northern Forest Coast to work convicts and harvest the plentiful trees of the Green Realm. Eventually, King Lertis Tevoy of Castorhage provoked armed conflict with the wild elves of the nearby forest when he tried to build a great road piercing the heart of the Green Realm. The war was ruinous for Castorhage and resulted in the near-total destruction of the Forest Coast Work Colonies. By 2373 I.R., the great road project was abandoned, and Ilber Nole was left as the only remaining fortification on the Forest Coast. By the following year, King Lertis was overthrown by his half-brother and sold into slavery to pay for the debts he incurred in the war.

After peace was restored with the elves, Castorhage continued to send convicts and other undesirables to the Forest Coast. The island nation had less luck maintaining control over its colonies, as other outcasts and those seeking political freedom also began to relocate there. By 2854 I.R., the settlements of the Forest Coast ceased payment of taxes to Castorhage, and despite various threats, Castorhage in effect lost control of its colonies there. Attempts by Castorhage to reassert dominion were thwarted by the Grand Duchy of Reme, which preferred independent cities along this critical line of Crescent Sea shortline. In the 3230s, a group of Reme-influenced philosophers and revolutionaries founded Timbertown on principles they believed at the time would lead to a natural meritocracy. They set about freeing the oppressed populace of Pearlhaven. Finally, in 3240 I.R., Castorhage lost the Short War with Reme, and agreed to permanently absolve all claims to the Forest Coast. The next year, in 3241 I.R., the Tycho Free States were founded.

Timbertown, Pearlhaven (which returned to its former penal colony name of Bogsweat), and Fringe became the first three States on the Free Coast, and leaders from these three vastly different regions collaborated on and eventually signed the Tycho Free States Accords. These leaders, however, knew more about grand ideals than they did about actual governance, so the accords have proven over the intervening years to be a minimal legal system at best, and barely more than a loose alliance at worst. Few other nations have taken the Free States seriously as a unified entity, and it remains common practice to deal with each local leader as a wholly independent entity. Some see the entire Free Coast as vassal states either to the elves of the Green Warden Forest or to Reme.

However, in the last 20 years much has changed in the Free States. Timbertown's economy has leapt astronomically, and Bogsweat has been nearly keeping pace. At the same time, a vigilante privateer by the name of Evangeliana Akadearg took it upon herself to hunt down and attack slaver ships all over the Crescent Sea to bring the freed slaves home with her to a small harbor on the northern Free Coast. Eventually, this harbor became a town, and — as its reputation spread for harboring all "refugees from injustice" with no questions asked — the town became a city, and soon Freetown was large enough to sign the Free States Accords in 3502 I.R. "Captain" Akadearg's flotilla of loyal ships instantly doubled the Free States' navy, vastly increasing the nation's military pull with surrounding entities.

More changes followed swiftly on Freetown's heels. While the chaotic young city continued to grow far too fast for its own infrastructure or minimal legal system, the infamous pirate haven of Ilber Nole, on the Free States' southern edge, decided suddenly to clean up and start behaving like a real community. The people of the Free States were understandably skeptical of this change of heart, but when the Ilber Nole pirate flotilla came to the Tycho navy's aid in its next conflict, Ilber Nole's head of state, Andre Turotimis, was also invited to sign the Free States Accords in 3511 I.R., further increasing the nation's naval might.

In the nearly seven years since the number of Tycho Free States officially increased to five, the rest of the world began taking more notice of the sometimes quite backward confederacy. Indeed, the Free States seemed to be taking themselves more seriously as well. In 3513 I.R., at the most recent Free States Conference of Leaders, more new laws and ordinances were drawn up than ever before in the nation's history, and the five cities' chosen representatives elected a new and energetic chief magistrate who has proven herself devoted to unifying and regulating her nation.

Chief Magistrate Kemma Philben is the first Tycho chief magistrate born of the local Tycho ethnicity. The Tycho people are a mix of the prisoners, slaves, outcasts, and dreamers who have been coming, voluntarily or involuntarily, to the Free States region for more than 1,000 years. While more recent human arrivals to the Free Coast may evidence their forbears' ethnic identities, those whose ancestors have been living in the region for centuries have together formed a blended people, impossible to lump in with any of the other ethnicities around them.

Taking their name (as does the nation itself) from a corruption of an elven term meaning "marshy coast" (a name only accurate in the Bogsweat region of the Tycho Free States, but due to misunderstanding considered in local legend to be the elven name for the Free Coast), the Tycho people have a darker complexion than is typical for humans native to the Crescent Sea region, reflective of the disproportionately multicultural nature of the Castorhagi labor colonies (and some say more of the dark-skinned local elven blood than the elves would ever admit, though the hardy Tycho build is hardly elfin).

Tycho folk are typically shorter than those of Foerdewaith ethnic background, generally broader of build, with higher and wider cheekbones. Despite their darker skin for the region, it is not wholly uncommon for Tycho individuals to have red hair and gray or green eyes, though black or dark brown hair and brown eyes are far more common. In other respects, they tend to resemble other Crescent Sea human populations, which is to be expected, considering that the Tycho mix had a healthy helping from Castorhage's and surrounding regions' poor as well.

Because the Tycho people are descended from the poor and oppressed of the Free Coast region, they have not typically been in good position to profit from the Free States' burgeoning economy. Indeed, they are not even the largest human ethnic group on the Free Coast (that being more recent immigrants of various strains of Foerdewaith stock from across the Crescent Sea). Nevertheless, in Kemma Philben they finally have their first Tycho chief magistrate, and she is thus far proving well-suited to the position.

Of course, humans make up less than two-thirds of the Free States' humanoid citizens, and with the exception of half-elven Evangeliana Akadearg, and occasional half-elven leadership in Fringe, no non-human has ever yet held high office in the Tycho Free States. Halflings, the nation's largest humanoid minority, make up almost 18% of the population but hold very little political power.

Most of the Free States' halflings arrived as indentured servants. Halfling immigrants were courted (and misled, and badly oppressed) by the Castorhagi because it was believed that smaller workers would be easier to control. Now, centuries later, the Free Coast has become these halflings' home, and they would like to be treated as equals with their human neighbors, without regard to physical stature.

Similar stories can be told for many humanoid or ethnic minority populations in the Free States, all of whom would like to enjoy what the Tycho humans currently, finally have: a chief magistrate who resembles their own people.

TRADE AND COMMERCE

Though for the most part Free States' trade and commerce are best discussed in the context of each individual state, all of which deal in different trades, one interesting aspect of Tycho commerce is how much of it is internal. The Free Coast region is sufficiently diverse in trade goods and in food production that if the Free States trade among themselves, the nation requires few imports in providing for its populace. The more closely-knit and reliant upon one another the Tycho Free States become, the more economic power the nation is able to wield as a whole.

That being said, coastal Timbertown, complete with its timber industry-supported shipbuilding and ship-repair docks, has become the natural place for the majority of Crescent Sea foreign trade with the Free States. Timbertown merchants are becoming ever more inventive in finding ways to make more money on every sale than do the producers of the goods in question, even if said goods were produced in other Tycho Free States. This gouging has led to heated policy disagreements between the various states' leaders and a growing fear among other Tychoans that Timbertown leaders are out to wrest control of the entire nation for themselves.

LOYALTIES AND DIPLOMACY

Each state in the Tycho nation largely maintains its own independent diplomatic relationships. This is especially true in regard to the Green Warden elves who have markedly different policies toward Timbertown than toward Fringe, for example, and would prefer to have nothing to do with the rest of the Tycho nation. However, there are diplomatic relationships that the Tycho Free States engage in as a whole, such as the uncomfortable peace with North Heath for several years now, following an unsuccessful naval assault by the larger nation (or by rogue elements within it, if North Heath diplomats are to be believed).

The most important of the Tycho Free States' diplomatic relationships, however, is that with Reme. Without Reme, the Tycho Free States would never have been able to break free of Castorhagi control. Over the centuries, Reme repeatedly found it to be desirable to frustrate Castorhagi interests in the Forest Coast, and Reme was the first nation to officially acknowledge the legitimacy of Tycho's independence and the Tycho Free States Accords.

As a consequence, the Free States have carefully maintained good relations with this ally and benefactor, and even Timbertown offers Reme merchants particularly favorable trade arrangements.

GOVERNMENT

The Tycho Free States government is difficult to define. The accords contain certain pacts and regulations intended to maintain a close military and economic alliance between confederacy members, and are otherwise largely permissive. A population must exceed a defined threshold and have a legally-defined leader to qualify for membership, as well as being willing to unify with the other members and abide by the decisions of the Leaders' Council and any rulings of the chief magistrate that member states are required to follow. A qualifying population is considered a member state only if a two-thirds majority of the member states' current leaders choose to affirm membership and invite a signature on the magically-preserved Tycho Free States Accords document.

For the most part, the chief magistrate has little authority within the claimed territory of the member states and is tasked instead with the administration of Tycho territory that isn't claimed by member states. To accomplish this, each state sends one representative per thousand citizens in its average annual population (states determine for themselves how representatives are selected) to an annual summer conference in

Median, a town built for this purpose along the old Great Road between Fringe and Bogsweat. These representatives provide authority and direction to the chief magistrate in any mutual international matters and in governing unincorporated territory within the Free Coast region. Every four years, the leaders of each of the states meet at Median in a Leaders' Council, and every other Leaders' Council they meet to elect a chief magistrate for a term of eight years.

The Free Coast has been well settled for over 1,000 years, but outside the larger settlements, the unincorporated territories are sparsely inhabited, usually requiring little attention from the chief magistrate. Current projects on the mind of the chief magistrate, other than international diplomacy, include the organization of attempts to clean up and repair all that remains of the Castorhagi Great Road (outside the forest, of course) in order to improve transport and make it easier for outlying farms to bring their produce and livestock to markets or ports.

MILITARY

The military of the Tycho Free States is almost entirely naval. On the sea, the Free States are as well-defended as could be expected for their population, if not better. On land, however, the Free States have little that constitutes an army. Military activities on land tend to provoke harsh protests from the far more powerful Green Warden elves, leaving the Free States in the uncomfortable position of needing to rely on geography and the wild elves' mercy to protect them from overland invasion.

That said, there are enough monsters threatening the edges and wilderness areas of the Tycho Free States that a total lack of military would be disastrous. As such, the Free States do keep a small professional defense force to deal with threats to the countryside's security in unincorporated territory. These defenders are well trained, often rangers, but in sheer numbers an entirely inadequate force if any army were to invade the Free States by land.

MAJOR THREATS

The Tycho Free States face threats on all sides. To the east, however respected their navy (and allies) may be, they are nevertheless outnumbered and outclassed by other navies in the Crescent Sea, and hardly unassailable were they to be seriously attacked. To the south, even assuming that Andre Turotimis' reformation is sincere, Ilber Nole has a long tradition of piratical occupation, and might slip back into threatening habits if anything were to happen to the current charismatic leader. Without Turotimis and his flotilla providing defense, the increasingly wealthy Free States ports would only seem more enticing to those in search of plunder.

To the west, the Tycho region is, as always, threatened by the magically superior elves and their powerful forest-dwelling allies, and to the north, no one really knows how great a threat the Hellsgate Peaks' devils might be to the Free Coast, or what may be the source of the mysterious disappearances in Hotpools.

Finally, the Tycho Free States are threatened from within, both by the growing power of the greedy in nearly every state, and by the increasing division between the various states' political and economic philosophies. At any point, some believe, the Tycho Free States could fragment into civil conflict, either one state against another or an uprising of the oppressed against oppressors.

WILDERNESS AND ADVENTURES

Other than the edges of the wood to the west and the occasional wandering monster in the marshes or remote areas, the most dangerous and mysterious region of the Tycho Free States is undoubtedly Hotpools, with its history of unexplained disappearances, and its possible connection to the devils of the Hellsgate Peaks.

MEDIAN, VILLAGE OF

Founded sometime after the beginning of the Tycho Free States' confederacy, Median is a village that exists for the purpose of governmental decision-making, mediation of disputes, and national infrastructure management. It is normally a tiny little town in the middle of an otherwise featureless stretch of road, save for the annual midsummer conventions of Free States' governmental representatives, the larger convention every four years for the Leaders' Councils and the election every eight years of a chief magistrate. During these times, the population balloons into the thousands, with the states' representatives, leaders' entourages, and many citizens who come to make appeals, have disputes settled, and sell goods to everyone else in attendance.

Some have attempted to call Median the Free States' capital, but legally speaking, the Tycho Free States do not have a capital, as the central government exists to serve and coordinate the state governments, rather than to rule over them. Median is officially, therefore, a neutral meeting point, no more.

Bogsweat, City of

Ruler: Headman Valor Forswythe
Government: council
Population: 9,900 (4,100 Tycho ethnicities, 2,900 halfling, 2,000 Foerdewaith, 600 half-elf, 280 other or mixed ethnicity human, 20 other)
Languages: Common
Religion: local interpretations of Brine, Father Canker, Mother Grace, and Sister Shadows, combined with animism and the Loa
Resources: fishing, grain, herbs, medicinal herbs, magical herbs, pearls
Currency: mixed
Technology Level: mostly High Middle Ages

Bogsweat is a humble collection of closely-packed villages in the middle of a giant brackish marsh on the Free Coast. Incorporated together, the villages make up just barely a large enough community to have been one of the founding members of the Tycho Free States, third to sign the Tycho Free States Accords.

History and People

The oldest surviving Castorhagi town on the Free Coast, Bogsweat was among the original penal work colonies commissioned by Queen Malice in 2301 I.R. Though too small to appear on most maps, several little streams come together to form a swampy wetlands and estuary just to the west of Bogsweat's humble brick huts and storehouses. Bogsweat was unique among the labor camps in that its location was chosen for peak food production, and prisoners sent to Bogsweat worked to produce exports for sale to line Castorhagi pockets and also to feed the rest of the Forest Coast Work Colonies.

For this reason, even after King Lertis began his ill-advised Great Road project and pulled all other laborers out of their "colonies" and put them to work on the road, Bogsweat was the only such town to remain continuously populated, hard at work with fishing, farming of staples, and cultivating herbs both medicinal and magical. Positioned as they were, largely inaccessible to the north and west due to miles of marsh and swamp, and with their backs to the (at the time) Castorhagi-dominated sea, Bogsweat was touched by the war only in that it now had to provide for thousands of soldiers and sailors as well as its fellow labor colonies.

After the Great Road was abandoned, King Acquire lost interest in the Forest Coast colonies and gave governorship of Bogsweat to an irritating courtier who'd done him an important favor. The courtier, one Lord Governor Merris, excitedly departed for his new position, convinced he could make himself fabulously wealthy there. Merris ordered a disastrous foray into major export crops like cotton and tobacco despite the region's inappropriately moist soil for either plant. The more money he lost on the venture, the more convinced he became that "next year" the harvest would bathe him in gold.

During this time, the Bogsweat population swelled to the maximum that could be supported by the region, with most inhabitants still being indentured laborers (either punitively or through self-indenture to pay off debts). Only the presence of this pool of poorly-treated, near-slave labor enabled Merris to turn anything like a profit from his ridiculous orders to his subjects. Merris did die modestly wealthy, but the culture of Bogsweat was forever altered by his practices.

Every governor after him continued the reliance on large populations of ill-treated indentured labor, but these chose their projects more wisely, including not only high-yield crops such as a nutritious rice brought back from trade with Xha'en, but also dangerous fishing practices and oyster beds. Bogsweat's name was changed to Pearlhaven, a place for the wealthy to make themselves wealthier by working the indentured poor (not uncommonly) to death.

This state of affairs continued quietly, despite all the upheaval in Castorhage, until Pearlhaven was sacked by pirates in 2797 I.R., while Castorhage lay stricken with plague. In addition to all the pearls waiting at the docks to be shipped to jewelers all over the world, the pirates also stole all of the governor's vast wealth, his excessively-stocked armory, and his seal of office. The pirates used this loot (and a fair amount of trickery) to sack Ilber Nole as well, Castorhage's last remaining fortification on the Forest Coast. With the plague in full force, all communication between the Forest Coast and Castorhage ceased.

The pirates decided to seize Pearlhaven for themselves. The Castorhage-appointed governor was deposed and replaced by a tyrannical pirate captain as the small settlement's so-called "king." Unfortunately, so much was destroyed in the sacking of the town that Pearlhaven's wealth was slow to recover, made worse by previous overfishing and mismanagement. In an ironic turn of events, the grandson of the original pirate king was forced to re-pledge fealty to Castorhage to maintain his control of the town and accepted a change in title back to governor. Although Castorhage was happy to accept the payment of taxes and to provide extremely modest naval support in return, the interest of the Castorhagi rulers in the Forest Coast was in decline, and a reduced-productivity Pearlhaven was largely ignored.

The next generations of governors (now an inherited position) departed from a model of indentured servitude in favor of outright enslavement of large portions of the populace, a change that did not sit well with Pearlhaven's more liberty-minded neighbors. In 3236 I.R., Pearlhaven was once again sacked, this time by revolutionaries bent on freeing the Forest Coast from "all bondage." Despite the good intentions of their liberators, the newly freed slaves were left largely to fend for themselves and pick up the pieces of the destroyed community and decide on a means of self-government.

When the Forest Coast colonies officially declared independence from Castorhage in 3241 I.R., the first elected headwoman of Pearlhaven — chosen for the position largely because she had received an education before the misfortunes that made her a slave — signed the independence declaration and Free States Accords as Alice, Headwoman of Bogsweat.

Her decision was controversial at first, but Alice argued that Pearlhaven was a name born of injustice and suffering, and the community should not want to invite such a thing ever again. Rather than advertising themselves as pearls to be stolen or bought and sold, the residents would be better served by a humble name that would keep outsiders away. The residents put the name to a vote and narrowly chose to follow Alice's advice of returning the region's name to Bogsweat.

Though Bogsweat is adjacent to no actual bogs, most of the region is marshy, muddy, and damp, uncomfortably humid in the summers, and prone to mosquitoes. Without the pearl association, few would want to live there who weren't born there. Nevertheless, Bogsweat's rice paddies, cultivation of rare herbs, fishing hauls, and oyster beds have made the town prosperous enough that its name isn't always enough to deter a perceptive outsider from seeking their fortune here, legally or illegally.

Religion

Bogsweat religion is humble, quiet, insular, and a bit odd, much like the region itself. It combines animistic and tribal beliefs and practices from all over the world (beliefs which Bogsweat inherited from its multicultural work-camp and slave ancestors) with local re-interpretations of a few Castorhagi deities and other spirit beings. Believers top all this off with local quirks and superstitions. Technically, all religions are welcome in Bogsweat, but locals do look askance at any who won't participate in the regional festivals.

TRADE AND COMMERCE

Bogsweat has much of value to trade, and in recent years made arrangements with Freetown shipping vessels to distribute its goods more effectively, leading to a surge of economic growth not entirely welcome in the insular little region.

Bogsweat still produces fine pearls, though this is less advertised to outsiders than it was during the Pearlhaven era. In addition, Bogsweat produces many tons annually of spare rice for sale, and the Bogsweat herb fields are the true backbone of the region's economy. Dried herbs from Bogsweat are ubiquitous in apothecary shops and magical supply markets throughout the Crescent Sea and beyond.

The Free Coast now offers a great deal of competition in the fishing industry, so Bogsweat concentrates more on its own specialties, fishing more for sustenance than commerce. That said, Bogsweat folk are adept at preserving fish and roe, and some other fishing communities bring their excess to Bogsweat for smoking, salting, or pickling.

LOYALTIES AND DIPLOMACY

A full member of the Tycho Free States, Bogsweat is standoffishly friendly with its fellow states. Protected now by Freetown and the rest of the Tycho navy, most residents of Bogsweat prefer to keep their heads down and ignore the outside world. That said, Headman Valor is known among the rest of the Tycho government as an excellent diplomat and deal-maker. His political capabilities are more appreciated at the meetings of the Free States' heads than they are at home.

GOVERNMENT

Bogsweat adult citizens of good standing vote for the headperson and for a "people's judge" whose job it is to curb the powers of the government whenever necessary. The headperson appoints a council of nine elders from any "respectable townspeople of grandparenting age or older," and this council makes most of the region's decisions.

Despite the populist ideals underlying this system, the last several headpeople have continually appointed the wealthiest landowners to the council of elders, and the members of the town's watch seem to all be relatives of said landowners and of late far more concerned with the protection of their landowning relatives than with defending and policing the general populace. The last several people's judges have either been toothless, been bought by the elders, or died early.

Laws in Bogsweat are, therefore, wandering steadily back toward a feudalistic model, and indentured servitude has once more become a commonplace and accepted moneymaking practice.

MILITARY

Other than the bullying watch, Bogsweat has almost no military whatsoever. Individual landowners hire their own mercenary security forces, and the region as a whole relies on the rest of the Tycho Free States for protection. When additional forces are needed, the town must usually hire outsiders.

MAJOR THREATS

It is not impossible that Bogsweat could once again be targeted by pirates, though the Tycho navy has protected them thus far. Other threats include a regular stirge problem, and the occasional will-o'-wisp or chuul. The latter two threats are often more than Bogsweat can handle alone and have led to the hiring of mercenaries on all previously recorded occasions.

In addition, due to recent shifts in Bogsweat's government, greedy resource management has again become the rule, and Bogsweat's poor grow hungrier. Rumor even claims that some Bogsweat landowners are illegally importing slave labor and magically *geasing* the slaves not to speak of the crimes committed against them.

Rumor also whispers of dangerous magical experiments being performed on plants and sea life in irresponsible attempts to increase yield and profits and to allow better fishing competition with surrounding communities. If this is the case, it cannot be long before the perennially benighted community of Bogsweat faces the worst fallout of rampant greed that it has ever seen.

WILDERNESS AND ADVENTURES

The marshes surrounding Bogsweat are mostly long-tamed and monster-free, with the exception of an unusually high stirge population that keeps coming back no matter what the locals do. However, the Bogsweat marshes do attract the occasional dangerous invader. Will-o'-wisps and chuuls are encountered a few times a decade, and legend tells of a couple of black dragons in the distant past, one of which was probably actually a hydra, depending on the version of the tale that one hears.

FREETOWN, CITY OF

Ruler: Captain Evangeliana Akadearg
Government: crude democracy
Population: 16,000 (3,300 Foerdewaith, 2,500 Xha'en, 2,400 half-elf, 2,200 human mixed ethnicity, 1,400 halfling, 1,000 Tycho ethnicities, 1,000 half-orc, 800 high elf, 600 other human, 400 dwarf, 400 other)
Languages: Common, Xha'en, Elven
Religion: eclectic, informal, celebratory
Resources: fishing, sea transport and hauling, naval might
Currency: mixed
Technology Level: Medieval

Freetown is the largest city in the Tycho Free States that was not built before the Free States gained independence. Its architecture, such as it is, is all recent construction, mostly of wood. Few regulations and near-nonexistent oversight have led to streets that are entirely unnavigable, as well as dangerously ramshackle structures, often built of reclaimed materials from shipwrecks or other decommissioned vessels.

For all its flaws, however, Freetown is largely beloved by its residents. Populated by a multicultural, multi-species hodgepodge of freed slaves, refugees, outlaws, and various other fugitives, in addition to a few local fishing folk, Freetown is a city of wild opportunity for many who have never had opportunities before.

HISTORY AND PEOPLE

Young for its ever-burgeoning size, Freetown was founded by Evangeliana Akadearg, a vigilante (some say pirate) sea captain with a predilection for attacking slave ships and freeing all the slaves. When said slaves had nowhere else to go, she at first offered them jobs on her crew, but such a life did not appeal to every freed slave. Eventually, in answer to the growing need, Akadearg offered to help them build a new town, and once it was built, she was overwhelmingly elected its leader.

Since then, it has grown far too quickly for its own good, with not just more freed slaves but all manner of refugees, fugitives, and anyone with nowhere else to go.

RELIGION

Religion in Freetown is as chaotic and freeform as everything else in the city. People are tolerant of one another's faiths because they have to be. Everyone is surrounded by people completely different from themselves. Already, the town is becoming a stewpot of synchronistic "heresies," with new and mix-and-match religions and holidays springing up all over the place. If there is any theme or overall "feel" to Freetown religion, it is "festive." Freetowners love an excuse to celebrate.

TRADE AND COMMERCE

Freetown's primary food source is fishing, and many community members are fishers. However, most of Freetown's money and other goods come from longer seafaring voyages, and many citizens spend much of the year away from town. Freetown ships hire themselves out in transportation of goods and passengers, or to serve as mercenary military vessels. Ships directly loyal to Captain Akadearg largely support themselves by stealing from slavers or the more murderous sort of pirates, with occasional careful forays into the more political sorts of privateering.

LOYALTIES AND DIPLOMACY

Freetown was granted permission to incorporate by the Tycho Free States, and when its population grew large enough for it to be considered a city-state by Tycho legal definitions, Captain Akadearg was invited to sign the Free States Accords, which she did. Now a full "state" in the Tycho Free States, Freetown owes loyalty and alliance to its fellows, and to all of the Free States' other allies.

GOVERNMENT

A master of shipboard swordplay, high seas tactical maneuvering, and inspired leadership, Captain Akadearg (who insists that her title is "captain" no matter her elected position in the town or how many ships she commands) might as well technically be a reigning monarch. Freetown laws are poorly defined, giving their elected leader a great deal of power. Thus far, the good captain has made little use of her legal authority, in either just or unjust ways, making Freetown barely shy of an amiable anarchy.

Interestingly, Captain Akadearg is also a savvy businesswoman and has made a mint by dealing with the elves to buy and sell naturally fallen lumber from the Green Warden Forest, such that she is also well known in Timbertown to the south. Unfortunately, however, the good captain's many talents do not extend to urban planning, which makes her a strange leader for Freetown, to say the least.

Captain Akadearg's leadership abilities are sufficient to keep crime remarkably low (especially considering the high Freetown population of former convicts) and economic growth on a steady rise. Only time will tell how long such a balance can be maintained.

MILITARY

Though their army is small, Freetown is hardly undefended. Captain Akadearg has long commanded a fair handful of battle-ready ships full of loyal veteran sailors, and she is now officially the head of the Freetown Navy. This small and ragtag-looking flotilla is well-trained and well-utilized, such that they are considered a major player on the waters of the western Crescent Sea, a scourge to all slavers in the region.

Besides Akadearg's loyal navy, other battle-ready ships do make port at Freetown. Though these usually hire themselves out as mercenary vessels, such as to escort wealth-filled merchant ships, most have a standing agreement with Freetown to sail with the navy in times of war.

MAJOR THREATS

Freetown is well defended by sea and largely surrounded by allies on land. Like any community in the half-wild Tycho Free States, Freetown must occasionally contend with monsters wandering into town or threatening crops or livestock in outlying farms, but the primary threats to Freetown come from within.

The town's poor building choices, in particular, hang over it like an axe waiting to fall. One visiting druid described the place as not just a fire hazard but as a mass pyre that simply has yet to be lit. The overworked and inexperienced elected city council organized fire evacuation routes and water brigades, and the city is fortunately built so close to the sea that much of it is either on stilts above the waves or literally floating on pier-like structures in the water, such that a good bucket brigade would be able to put out small fires quickly in most of the city. A large fire is another story, however.

Then again, the risk to the town from storms and flooding (or, in places, sinking due to leakage) is at least as considerable as the risk of fire, and for that Freetown has yet to organize any countermeasures beyond Captain Akadearg paying a few wizards and druids out of pocket to protect the city during storm season.

FRINGE, CITY OF

Ruler: Governor Kimmerlyn Syrris
Government: republic
Population: 13,000 (5,100 Tycho ethnicities, 3,900 half-elves, 2,500 halflings, 800 Foerdewaith, 500 high elves, 150 other human ethnicities, 50 other)
Languages: Common, Elven, some Sylvan
Religion: Arialee, Animism
Resources: forest marble quarry, trade with the Green Warden
Currency: mixed, barter, Green Realm
Technology Level: primarily Medieval

Fringe has the distinction (if half-elves are counted as human, as per wild-elven reckoning) of being the sole human-majority community in regular trade with the Green Warden Nations. Though Fringe is a founding state of the Tycho Free States, and a Fringe leader was first to sign the Free States Accords, Fringe is considered by some (especially within the Green Warden Nations) to be very nearly an elven vassal state.

Other than friendship with notoriously unfriendly elves, Fringe is known primarily for a type of marble unique to the Green Warden region. Shot with veins and patches of an improbably gemlike dark green, forest marble is prized the world over, perhaps all the more so because of Fringe's careful quarrying practices, which incidentally also ensure that the global supply of forest marble remains rare and precious.

HISTORY AND PEOPLE

Fringe began as a Castorhagi penal colony, beside an outcropping of a stone discovered to be a beautiful green-variegated marble, dubbed forest marble. Originally named "Stonecut," the town's popular nickname became "Fringe" within a few years of its construction, because it was the farthest inland of all the labor towns and because it was built just under the fringes of what the early residents cheerfully called the "Malice Forest" after Queen Malice of Castorhage, who commissioned the colonies.

The quarry at Fringe was known up and down the Forest Coast as the worst of the labor camps, with dangerous practices and conditions, as well as the most back-breaking labor. Due to the rare beauty and practical utility of forest marble, however, Fringe was also the largest money-producer for Castorhage of all the original penal colonies. When the first wild elf raid on the town occurred, Queen Malice was quick to make peace with these wary neighbors by offering generous trade agreements and other concessions to keep them happy.

For this reason, mining and agricultural practices in Fringe have always been careful and clean, with no major incursions into the forest and very little damage to any of the surrounding wilderness, other than the rock of the quarry itself. These concessions made friendship between Fringe and the wild elves easier than it could otherwise have been. With the understanding that the forced laborers at the quarry were criminals serving their sentences, the elves simply remarked that humans must produce a great many terrible criminals for so many to deserve such treatment.

All could have continued like this indefinitely, if not for King Lertis Tevoy's mad insistence on building a road deep into the forest, not only destroying large swaths of the wilderness but flagrantly disrespecting wild elven territory. The Forest Coast War followed, sometimes referred to as the Mortgage War, because King Lertis was forced to mortgage the Castorhagi crown jewels in order to pay his debts after the extremely costly venture was finally abandoned.

During the war, a fortress was built at Fringe in order to defend the quarry. Several battles were fought there, but the governor of Fringe at that time, one Lady Governor Avarice, was a skilled leader and excellent tactician. She held the defenses at Fringe with minimal casualties on either side and brutally punished any of her soldiers who behaved with dishonor or unnecessary cruelty toward the elven enemy. Due to her longstanding familiarity with the local elven leaders and their appreciation for Fringe's respect of the forest, Fringe was granted similarly honorable treatment in return.

It was not long before Governor Avarice lost all respect for her sovereign. Nicknamed for her devotion to the acquisition of wealth, she found King Lertis' poor financial decision-making an embarrassment. Citing strictly financial reasons, she began to engage in fewer hostilities with the enemy. Careful never to overtly disobey her monarch, Avarice's subtle subversion was secretly looked upon with sympathy and approval by several of the king's financial advisors, as well as some of the nobility.

Governor Avarice disappeared from Fringe in 2371 I.R. Upon investigation, it was discovered that all of the quarry's pre-cut supply of marble, as well as all the governor's own riches from her mansion, were also missing — a process that would have taken months to accomplish without alerting anyone to the activity. Mere weeks after her disappearance, the vice-governor assumed the post of governor and declared Fringe independent of Castorhage and sued for peace with the elves. Upon observing that Fringe was turning away all Castorhagi soldiers and work parties, the elves accepted the proposed treaty and ceased all hostilities with Fringe.

Six years later, three years after the war had ended, Lady Avarice reappeared in Castorhage without explanation for her absence. She was welcomed back into the town, and eventually died a rich woman. Sixty years after Governor Avarice's death, secret communications came to light between herself and Terrance Aquiri, later known as King Acquire. It turned out that in exchange for a full pardon for desertion and a guarantee of no scandal, Governor Avarice agreed to arrange and broker the deal to sell King Lertis into slavery, revealing for the first time that King Acquire knew far ahead of time that his half-brother would mortgage the crown jewels to pay his debts.

In the meantime, Governor Petram, a philosopher and populist at heart, began to improve conditions in Fringe, starting by forgiving the financial debts of all Fringe's debt-based indentured workers and halving the remaining sentences of the rest. He also decreased daily required work hours and improved quarry safety. Finally, he revealed a project he had been working on in his spare time for the past 15 years: a proposed legal system for an experimental republic.

The Fringe republic model allows the vote only to resident, tax-paying landowners, but since most of the city was at that time a penal colony, Governor Petram allowed a one-time election in which all residents were allowed to participate, and the proposed republic was overwhelmingly adopted, affirming Petram as governor.

RELIGION

Though worship of Arialee, alongside a forest-centric animism, dominates Fringe's spiritual life, Fringe's religious practices are unique, including an annual spring flower-sculpture of Arialee that is allowed to dry over subsequent months and is burned in a giant bonfire every harvest season, as well as a late winter three-day chanting vigil (taken in shifts) to wake the plants and call them up from the earth.

The most incomprehensible religious practice in Fringe, from the perspective of most outsiders, is the dawn gratitude service. Every day at dawn (or just before, if farm duties require it), anyone who intends to work that day is expected to rise and engage in ritualized poses and chanting for two turns of the glass, at least. Residents say that in addition to the spiritual benefits of spending the morning in gratitude for nature itself, this daily practice gets the blood flowing, offers healthy stretching, and opens up the lungs, which results in better energy during the day, less soreness, and fewer labor-related injuries.

Unfortunately, it also alienates anyone with a less dawn-oriented internal clock, including many mostly-nocturnal humanoids. Individuals who regularly fail to participate in "dawn gratitudes" are often viewed with vague suspicion by the locals and possible enemies of the forest (even if they are Green Warden wild elves).

On the more popular side of things, Fringe religion is quite sexually permissive and tolerant of intoxicants and celebration of all varieties. For some outsiders, this permissiveness presents a confusing dichotomy, given the Fringe predilection for strict discipline, hard work, and rising early to pray.

TRADE AND COMMERCE

Fringe has always supported itself primarily through the quarrying and sale of forest marble, but it must be noted that Fringe's ability to trade with the Green Warden is also a major source of its economic stability. Fringe sells marble, spends the money it gains on goods and luxuries it knows will appeal to even the anti-materialistic Green Warden elves, trades those to the elves for elf-made magical items, rare herbs and woods, elf-brewed spirits, and other items Fringe merchants can turn around and sell for a high price to other humans. Since Fringe has exhausted its original forest marble quarry and may not find another in its territory when the second runs out, trade with the elves is an important economic backup strategy for Fringe residents.

LOYALTIES AND DIPLOMACY

Fringe participates actively in Tycho Free States' lawmaking and governance and maintains healthy relationships (and plenty of disagreements) with its fellow Free States. Despite the Green Warden perception of Fringe as a near vassal state, Fringe relies more heavily on its fellow Free States for its economic stability and political security. Few Free States' citizens see Fringe as disloyal, and many are cognizant of the important influx of rare and magical goods that Fringe's trade with the wild elves provides.

The good relationship between Fringe and its wild elf neighbors is carefully maintained, in part through a continuing commitment to preserving the wilderness around them. Due to this longstanding tradition of cultural exchange, the population of Fringe includes a much higher than average percentage of half-elves, and even a few resident elves.

As Fringe becomes known as a place that accepts half-elves with little prejudice, half-elf immigrants from other parts of the world sometimes come here seeking acceptance. Not all of them find it, as Fringe has very specific, traditional ideas of how people ought to live, and the residents tend to dislike change intensely. Fringe-born half-elves, however, usually speak well of their home.

GOVERNMENT

Fringe has, surprisingly, remained a republic for the last 1,200 years. Hardly any of Petram's original proposal remains in the legal code (save where it is profoundly modified by amendments, clarifications, and exceptions), but all land-owning and tax-paying residents may vote on nearly every decision the government makes, including all government appointments of any authority, and Fringe is one of the few of Tycho's tiny city-states to have legally classified indenture as a form of slavery and forbidden it. Governors are now elected to five-year terms, with no term limits, and Governor Kimmerlyn Sirris, in her fourth term, is largely beloved.

MILITARY

Ever since Fringe's first defection from Castorhage during the Mortgage War, Fringe has not maintained a professional military. Instead, all able-bodied adults take one shift per week in the town watch, which is organized and directed by a handful of full-time watch constables and sergeants, most of whom are rangers by training. These watch professionals are an entirely peacekeeping force and resort to violence only in self-defense or defense of Fringe citizens. The citizen watch is trained to avoid violence at all costs, unless specifically directed otherwise by a constable or sergeant.

Some believe that this lack of military, especially for a community so close to a famously hostile border, is not only foolish but an invitation to be attacked. In practice, Fringians have found that a wholly peaceful, harmless appearance is perhaps the only consistent way to disarm the wary Green Warden wild elves and maintain their precious trade relationship. Of course, if Fringe were bordered by the Family of Thorns Nation of the Green Warden confederacy instead of Sentinels of the Trees, this attitude of deliberate defenselessness might indeed provoke wanton hostility from radical elements. Fringe's military strategies are catered to the culture of the elves it encounters most consistently.

MAJOR THREATS

Even aside from the potential threat of radical anti-human elements within the Green Warden Nations, not all is wonderful in Fringe. Foreigners can face standoffishness or outright prejudice from native Fringians, and Fringe also faces an ever more concerning gap between the wealth of the shrinking number of landowners and that of the growing number of citizens denied the vote for not owning property. Unrest is on the rise, and none can yet predict what will become of the difficulties. Strangely, a growing number of Fringe citizens seem to believe that doing away with their republic and returning to a feudalistic dictatorship would somehow solve their problems of power inequality.

More troublingly still, some Fringe citizens have begun to complain of headaches, dizziness, inexplicable loss of time or memory, and extreme mood swings. Some blame a supposed curse on the new marble quarry, opened only a few years ago, after the centuries-old original quarry was finally exhausted. Others believe they have seen one or more mysterious figures lurking in the dark around the town and suspect direct magical interference. Governor Syrris has sent for experts on stone, on magic, and on medicine to come consult on the ailments, but thus far no clear conclusions have been drawn.

Wilderness and Adventures

Fringe is close enough to the Green Warden Forest that its quarry, outlying farms, and even — on rare occasions — its westernmost streets can be visited by various interesting "wildlife," including dangerous dire animals and plant creatures. Since these creatures are accepted as neighbors by the wild elves (many of whom can speak with them, after all), it would be considered in poor taste to harm them in defense of the city. When Fringe's watch encounters a creature it cannot safely handle alone, the beast may do considerable damage before help sufficiently powerful to subdue and relocate the creature without harming it can arrive.

In addition, it would be greatly useful to Fringe residents if anyone were to discover the source of the strange illness sweeping the city and how to cure it. Is this a plot by elven radicals? Human radicals attempting to provoke a war? Is it really a curse on the new quarry? Or the accidental side effect of someone's magical research? Whatever the cause, the citizens of Fringe would like to know the truth.

Ilber Nole, City of

(ILL-bur NOLL)

Ruler: Free Corsair Andre Turotimis, Commodore
Government: semi-democratic monarchy
Population: 9,600 (5,300 various human ethnicities, 1,300 half-elf, 1,200 half-orc, 600 high elf, 500 lizardfolk, 400 tengu, 300 other)
Languages: Common
Religion: many, none dominant or official
Resources: naval might, mercenary sailors, defensibility
Currency: mixed
Technology Level: Medieval/Renaissance

Ilber Nole is a small city-state sprung up around the only Castorhagi fort on the Free Coast to survive the war with the elves and conflicts with pirates. It has recently joined the Tycho Free States. However, most outside Ilber Nole still believe it to be a den of pirates.

The fort itself is known to be impenetrable and full of ingeniously designed traps. It is said that a single well-supplied soldier could hold off an army or navy for days, and that four soldiers sleeping in shifts could hold it until they died of old age. Well-supplied is the key to that claim, however, as Ilber Nole is easy to cut off from resupply by land or by sea and contains no internal source of fresh water. Any army with enough magic to create food and water from nothing for all its troops probably also has enemies with wizards who can blast right through the cliff itself from a nice, safe distance.

History and People

Ilber Nole began as the largest of the Castorhagi fortifications on the Forest Coast, and it was also the first constructed, commissioned by Queen Malice to oversee her penal colonies and defend against sea raiders. Built partway into a natural cliff face out on the point of the Ilber Peninsula, the Ilber Nole (Nole being an archaic term for "defensible location" in a strategy game apparently popular with Ilber Nole's first commanding officer) is one of the most easily defended locations in Akados.

To date, it has never been breached (at least, not while defended). Indeed, during the Mortgage War, Ilber Nole was utterly ignored by the wild elves, who saw its location to be of no tactical advantage to them. Its position is most useful against naval assaults, which was a concern of neither the elves nor the Castorhagers on the Forest Coast. Thus, it survived the conflict untouched.

Ilber Nole was used to good tactical advantage by Castorhage against Crescent Sea raiders and pirates on numerous occasions and is thought to have served as a deterrent and tactical inconvenience to Reme forces over the centuries. Then, in 2797 I.R., a group of pirates disguised themselves as Castorhagi naval officers and forged a document turning control of the fort over to themselves, using the stolen seal of the governor of Pearlhaven (Bogsweat). Intent more on plunder than on gaining a permanent base of operations, the pirates, once inside the fort, proceeded to sack it rather than capturing it and sent the fort's tiny garrison away unarmed and in their underwear. The pirates celebrated wildly for a few days on the fort's supply stores and then moved on.

Between the garrison's shame at having been tricked and the total lack of contact with Castorhage (which was suffering from plague at the time and was later blocked from re-establishing contact by Reme's machinations), none of those Castorhagi soldiers ever returned to Ilber Nole, and the place remained abandoned for some time.

Eventually, its availability was discovered by a wandering beggar who then set himself up as a miniature king in the region. King Bo died without issue, but not before he and his associates managed to damage the fort's entrance (and failed to repair any of the damage done by the celebrating pirates). Between the two, the fort's defensibility lay marred for generations, and for a time it changed hands regularly, with no one bandit ever keeping hold of it long enough to enact the repairs that would restore its impregnability. After the place was emptied twice in five years by two separate cholera outbreaks — both too deadly to even leave time for a healer to arrive — Ilber Nole gained a reputation for being cursed and stood mostly uninhabited for another cluster of decades.

In 3145 I.R., a pirate named Rosvo suddenly declared himself the tyrant of Ilber, and it was discovered that he'd managed to secretly repair the Ilber Nole fortress's defenses and also improve them.

When asked about the curse, Rosvo replied that when he'd taken the place, it was so filthy inside that he could only suspect that the cholera outbreaks were due to poor hygiene and nothing mystical whatsoever. Rosvo also improved the indoor plumbing, replacing what had been little more than a grated chute into the sea, flushed by bucket, to an elaborate pump system allowing for running water and even hot baths. Unfortunately, he was unable to add a freshwater well, so all the water in the facility is brackish, and the pumps require regular maintenance to avoid clogging or degradation from the salt.

Rosvo was killed in a ship-to-ship battle somewhere east of Tandril Island, but his daughter, Rosita, inherited the fort from him and turned away from piracy. She instead made a name for herself as a tinker and further improved Ilber Nole's defenses with complex clockwork traps, alarms, concealed passages, and a retractable system for transporting people and goods up and down the cliffs to anchored ships below.

Rosita's descendants held the place for about 200 years and used it for a variety of purposes and ultimately established healthy trade relations and a great deal of respect with surrounding communities. A town grew up around the fort, complete with outlying farms, and the so-called Ilber Tyranny became a surprisingly prosperous little city-state — until a naïve, young Rosvo the Second married an alluring older woman who turned out to be another pirate captain. Young Rosvo was kept captive for many years in his own fortress, while his wife made a bloody fortune and eventually attempted to conquer the other Tycho Free States.

This ended poorly for her, and rather quickly, as she was killed in the very second battle of her campaign and her forces broke and scattered. Unfortunately for Rosvo the Younger, however, one of her subordinates, calling herself Lady Stiletto, took this opportunity to murder him and set herself up as tyrant instead in 3359 I.R. Stiletto began what is still commonly considered to be the current era of Ilber Nole as a dangerous pirate nation and threat to the entire Crescent Sea.

Succession of the Ilber Tyranny thereafter passed repeatedly by murder and betrayal, with not a single tyrant either inheriting the position or being elected by the populace. The city-state surrounding the fortress has suffered greatly, at times because it is not nearly so defensible as the fortress and at other times due to cruel and irresponsible leadership. In 3458 I.R., Tyrant Hen was discovered to be engaged in the slave trade in defiance of Tycho Free State law. An unsuccessful attempt was made by the Free States to oust him from his fortress, and then a blockade was set up to starve him out — with the unfortunate side effect that any slaves who were unable to escape and surrender to the blockade, as other town refugees had done, instead starved to death before Hen could be defeated.

When Tyrant Hen publicly demonstrated his willingness to eat his slaves before surrendering, his third in command murdered him and his lieutenant and ran up a flag of truce. Making a deal with the Tycho forces, this subordinate of Tyrant Hen became the next tyrant, in line with what had become Ilber Nole tradition.

Subsequent tyrants have been relatively decent leaders to the fortress's little surrounding city-state, even building an outer wall to protect the citizens, but the threat of piracy posed by the fortress to surrounding communities has not abated. The north side of the Ilber Peninsula is relatively sheltered from typical Crescent Sea weather patterns, and a permanent pirate dock and pirate-loyal fishing village have sprung up there over the years under the protective watch of Ilber Nole. The town and dock can be safely assaulted by land and have indeed been destroyed three times (most recently in 3492 I.R.), but since Ilber Nole itself remains unassailable, the pirate port is always rebuilt.

The current tyrant, Andre Turotimis, poses something of an enigma to the world around him. He hates to be called tyrant and instead claims his title to be "Free Corsair" or at most "commodore." He has not explained his past to even his closest lieutenants and allies, though he communicates and behaves as if well-educated in many subjects and has the look of a man who has traveled and seen much. He speaks an unknown number of languages, and his own slight accent is definitely foreign but difficult to place. His skin is notably dark for the region, even among the ethnically diverse pirate population, and his black hair is especially curly, but he has told no one his origins. Lieutenants and lovers have revealed that his back is scarred as if by the lash, and his wrists and ankles as if by shackles. He tries not to let strangers notice either and grows silent and brooding if asked about them.

He claims, and his lieutenants support him on this, that he won the leadership of Ilber Nole in a game of chance. Since he took control of the fortress and the surrounding city-state, Turotimis has been hailed as the wisest and most benevolent ruler since Tyrant Rosita. Romantic poetry extols him as having the dignity, courtesy, and poise of a prince, and his handsome face and figure are said to break hearts wherever he goes.

Returning to the Rosvo family tradition, Andre Turotimis has made diplomatic contact with all his neighbors, and is engaged in fair and lawful trade with them. Furthermore, in 3511 I.R., in gratitude for his heroic defense of the Free Coast from a brief naval conflict with North Heath, Commodore Turotimis received controversial but official recognition from the Tycho Free States' leaders as a genuine head of the Ilber Nole state and has signed the Free States Accords as a member.

As far as anyone has been able to prove, neither Andre Turotimis nor his exceedingly loyal immediate subordinates have broken any Tycho laws since he signed the accords, but he has been repeatedly accused of continuing his career of piracy whenever he leaves Free Coast waters. It is also claimed that he maintains membership in a highly unsavory pirate confederacy to the south, and many suspect him of merely playing nice and using his charm and good looks to lull the Tycho Free States into complacency.

Commodore Turotimis and Captain Akadearg of Freetown had an extremely public maritime policy argument at the last meeting of the leaders of the Free States, just four years ago, and it was clear from their words that the two had known one another a long time. Though Captain Akadearg is considerably older, none would deny her blade-sharp beauty. Ever since her dramatic disagreement with Turotimis, it has been widely assumed that the two are lovers. Some say Turotimis is reforming himself and his crew for her sake, while others assume that only she can stop whatever nefarious plot he has in mind, and that he has therefore chosen to seduce her, to slow her wits in his regard. No proof of any such association exists, and neither entertains questions about the other.

TRADE AND COMMERCE

Ilber Nole produces just enough food to feed itself, and few other goods. All of the city's wealth comes from its "naval activities" (both legitimate and illegal).

GOVERNMENT

Andre Turotimis owns the Ilber Nole itself and would thus be difficult to oust from power should he choose to resist. However, like many pirate captains, he was elected to his position by his crew, and the captains of the other vessels in his flotilla elected him as their commodore with (presumably) the endorsement of their own crews. Albeit running unopposed, Turotimis also asked for and was given the popular acclaim of the common folk of the Ilber Nole city as their leader, making him technically sort of democratically elected.

That said, and regardless of his humility in refusing to style himself a king (or tyrant) as previous Ilber Nole rulers have done, Andre Turotimis is effectively an absolute monarch, with no laws in place to gainsay his whims. Thus far, his rule is very much in line with maritime tradition: highly disciplined where practicality demands it, and totally libertine in all other respects.

MILITARY

Ilber Nole is home to what is effectively a truly excessive professional military for a community its size. Many of the pirates turned Free States' sailors are veteran combatants, and despite a certain piratical wildness to the Ilber Nole "navy," the ships are disciplined once at sea. Turotimis is a fair naval tactician and not above listening to his advisors. Since shouldering the defense of the Free Coast alongside the rest of the Tycho navy, Turotimis has been undefeated on the water.

MAJOR THREATS

Threats to Ilber Nole depend on where its loyalties actually lie. If Andre Turotimis is what he seems, then upcoming threats might stem from his mysterious past or his former piratical allies. If he is, as many suspect, playing some kind of con on the Tycho Free States, then most seem to place their hopes in Captain Akadearg of Freetown to bring him to justice.

Either way, Ilber Nole is extremely well defended. Andre Turotimis and his subordinates and subjects have more to fear from espionage and betrayal than from any kind of direct assault.

TIMBERTOWN, CITY OF

Ruler: rotating Timber Council chair
Government: plutocratic oligarchy touted as a meritocracy
Population: 9,000 to 22,000, seasonal (typical peak population: 14,000 Foerdewaith, 3,300 Tycho ethnicities, 1,600 other human ethnicities, 1,000 halfling, 900 half-elf, 800 hill dwarf, 300 half-orc, 100 other)
Languages: Common, Elven (used primarily for official business with elves)
Religion: varied
Resources: timber, salt, fishing, foodstuffs, furs, shipbuilding, shipbuilding supplies
Currency: mixed
Technology Level: Medieval

Founded just in time to be large enough to participate in writing the Tycho Free States Accords, Timbertown was built atop the ruins of a long-abandoned Castorhagi labor colony called Treefall. As can be discerned from the thematic similarity between the old and current name, the town is ideally located for the transportation, curing, and export of timber. Poised at the very well-behaved mouth of the Queensribbon River, Timbertown is where all the lumber felled farther up the Queensribbon is hauled ashore, prepared for sale and sea voyage, and then hoisted aboard merchant ships for distribution.

There are three main sections to the Timbertown city-state. East Town sits right near the sea and is primarily dedicated to fishing, crabbing, ship-building, and sea salt refinement. West Town sits on the river a little farther inland and is primarily dedicated to the timber industry. North Town, above and between the two, is more like a kind of trading post for farmers, hunters, trappers, and other rural or wilderness professions.

All three of Timbertown's populations fluctuate wildly with the seasons, with variations from industry to industry. West Town is all but deserted in spring and early summer, as loggers trek upriver to fell trees and send them back down lashed together in large rafts. North Town, by contrast, sees a steady influx of seasonal residents beginning in late-spring, reaching its peak population for the year at the fall harvest festival and dropping off sharply again for winter.

East Town's population is the most stable, with the majority of residents living in the city year-round. However, because of the seasonal influx of people during the late summer and early fall in both West and North towns, many Crescent Sea independent merchant ships put to port in Timbertown for several months of each year, stopping for repairs and allowing their sailors to work seasonally as additional fishers because there would otherwise never be enough food in town to satisfy the hardworking and hungry loggers who produce no food of their own. Some of these ships overwinter in the large natural harbor south of Timbertown, adding yet another quirk to the Timbertown population flux.

Religion

Another Free States town with a large indentured population, Timbertown's chief article of faith is that those who work hard and work smart will always do well. Thus, you can tell who the hardest, smartest workers are by who has the most money.

Many gods are worshipped, and any religions common anywhere around the Crescent Sea can be found here, but in permanent Timbertown residents there is almost always this "cosmic fairness" overlay to any worship: the people doing well are the best people, and the people doing poorly must deserve it somehow.

Trade and Commerce

Trade and commerce are everything to Timbertown, with the highest profits coming in, on average, from the timber for which the town is named. The second most lucrative profession in Timbertown is sea salt refinement. Timber-uns have been known to claim their salt tastes the best in all the world and is the secret to the excellence of Bogsweat's salted fish.

Loyalties and Diplomacy

Of all the "states" in the Tycho Free States, Timbertown has the most delicate balancing act to play with their elven neighbors in the Green Warden Forest. Timbertown values place profits above all else, but the elves couldn't care less about money, and are concerned only for the wellbeing of the forest and its living things. The elves are also typically believed by Timber-uns to all be archdruids and human-haters.

Timbertown is bitter about the military superiority that requires them to follow elven rules about land-use along the edge of the forest, and now and again a greedy or desperate Timbertowner crosses a line with regards to elf-imposed regulations. So far, the Timbertown government has always managed to respond to such infractions in a manner that keeps the elves placated, but many believe that relations between Timbertown and the Green Warden Nations are a powder keg waiting to blow, and this in turn shakes the foundations of the ever-wary peace between the Free States and the Nations.

Within the Free States, Captain Evangeliana Akadearg of Freetown, to the north, owns and operates a highly successful lumber business through Timbertown. Wealthy and successful enough to sit on the Timber Council every year, she is the elected leader of another town and does not maintain a residence in Timbertown, thus barring her from council membership. Nevertheless, being wealthy, she embodies the ideals of success foundational to the Timbertown faith … and she is highly and vocally critical of the Timbertown system and works constantly to teach ideals of freedom and justice whenever she passes through the region.

It is broadly understood that if Timbertown's poor and indentured were ever to rise up against their oppressors, Captain Akadearg would be there to support them with her Freetown "navy." In the meantime, she is suspected of regularly harboring fugitives from Timbertown "justice" and spiriting them away northward to her own city-state.

Government

The leaders of Timbertown are always the 19 wealthiest business owners in the city. Each fall, after harvest season, all registered taxpayers in the city are encouraged to gather together, where they elect a team of auditors who spend the winter reviewing the finances of those who might be among the town's wealthiest people. At Winter Solstice, the top 19 become the year's Timber Council and elect a new chair from amongst themselves every season.

The make-up of this council rarely shifts much from year to year. Timbertown laws overwhelmingly favor the wealthiest, most-established business-owners over the poor and over the smaller business-owners. Order in Timbertown is maintained almost entirely by employers who punish the crimes of their employees in whatever way they see fit (with docking of pay being a common punishment). Independent workers who commit crimes are either punitively indentured for a specified period or driven from town, as is anyone convicted of the crime of unemployment.

Employers who commit crimes are generally fined. If the fine is more than they can pay, their assets are seized as a punitive tax, and they and their families are indentured to pay the debt. Their employees are given one month (or three months in winter) to find new work before being convicted of willful unemployment. The Timber Council's job, other than its own prosperity, is to mediate disputes between business owners. In general, they tend to find in favor of the wealthier party, save when political or business machinations would for some reason make it more advantageous to find in favor of the smaller business.

The majority of Timbertown residents seem to stubbornly believe that this is the way things should be, and that if they are smart enough and work hard enough, they too will one day be rich enough to sit on the Timber Council and tell other people what to do.

Military

Timbertown keeps a small, largely-mercenary militia and navy to defend its wealth from thieves and pirates. Any larger force, however, tends to be taken as hostile posturing by the elves, who would prefer there be no armed forces anywhere in the Free States, especially in Timbertown.

Major Threats

Timbertown faces three potential major threats. Always in the forefront of the Timbertown lumber-barons' minds are the elves. While in reality, the elves are only likely to become a threat if the town's agreements with them are broken, their proximity, power, and alien thinking make the threat seem larger in Timbertowner minds.

A more constant threat is that of coastal piracy. While matters have improved since the Ilber Nole community signed the accords to join the Free States, relations between Timbertown and Ilber Nole are wary, and many Timber-uns believe that the Ilber Nole pirates only bide their time, waiting to attack. Should relations between Timbertown and Captain Akadearg of Freetown ever sour, Timbertown could find itself insufficiently defended by sea, easy prey for reavers.

Finally, Timbertown's policies toward its own people threaten the city-state from the inside. If unrest ever rises high enough for the common folk to question whether the rich really are better than they are after all, a civil uprising is likely.

Wilderness and Adventures

Timbertown itself is very orderly. Monster invasions are bad for business. However, in the tree farms upriver, many strange and dangerous creatures are known to wander from the natural forest to the artificial one, causing problems for loggers on a semi-regular basis. Most of these creatures are natural or magical animals, unaligned and incapable of speech, while a few are mischievous fey or other dangerous creatures simply out for a stroll.

In general, these creatures are on perfectly good terms with the Green Warden elves — or are even Green Warden citizens — and must therefore be handled with exaggerated care in order to avoid a diplomatic incident. On other occasions, wicked fey or similar beings have been known to attempt to use the Timbertown tree farms as a means of sneaking into the Green Warden Forest. Such a tactic has never been known to succeed, but it can certainly cause trouble for Timbertowners in the process.

Settlements of the Hellsgate Peaks

The Hellsgate Peaks are volcanically active, and home to, among others, red dragons, salamanders, elementals of fire and, according to rumor, perhaps the largest population of devils in permanent residence on the Material Plane. Yet it boasts two settlements of note. On the shore of Giant's Harbor, a steam-hidden, eddying harbor within the Strait of

Gehenna, sits the fire giant village of Kreglarran. And just to the south of the mountains in a sheltered harbor is Hotpools, a destination for those seeking the healing waters of the pools or guidance into the mountains.

KREGLARRAN, FIRE GIANT VILLAGE OF

Ruler: Chief Aemtian Flaemroch
Government: hereditary chiefdom
Population: 280 fire giants
Monstrous: fire giants, red dragons, salamanders, devils, and other fire-elemental-related beings
Languages: Kreglarran Giant, standard Giant, Common, Draconic, Infernal
Religion: various giant deities
Resources: fishing, shells, pearls
Currency: mixed
Technology Level: Medieval

This fishing village is one of the most unusual in the world. Situated on the shore of Giant's Harbor, sandwiched between the perilous Strait of Gehenna to the south and the violently volcanic Hellsgate Peaks to the north (and west, and east), Kreglarran is home to an isolated population of fire giants. Content to fish and bathe in the hot and plentiful waters of their harbor (or the occasional nearby lava flow), Kreglarran fire giants are fiercely territorial warriors — because to be anything else would be suicide in the monster-infested, devil-beleaguered Hellsgate Peaks — but they are only warlike when they have to be. The rest of the time, Kreglarran fire giants are fair and honest in trade, and generally friendly, if wary of outsiders (any of whom could be devils in disguise or greedy treasure hunters looking to ravage their harbor for petty wealth schemes).

In the Kreglarran giants' local dialect (related to Giant, but incomprehensible to outsiders), Kreglarran means "pleasant home," which is exactly what the hot, humid, steam-clouded little harbor is to them. Interesting fish, starfish, and exceedingly useful sea plants are harvested in quantities sufficient to allow for profitable trade with surrounding communities, and the eternally scorching, volcanically-altered weather is very much to fire giant taste. Fortunately for visitors or those seeking to trade with the giants, most villagers who participate in trade with outsiders speak at least one of the other local languages, such as standard Giant, Westerling (Common), Draconic, or Infernal.

Though the trading of ruby mussel shells and the harvesting of lava pearls could win them vast wealth in the outside world, the Kreglarran fire giants prefer to keep such treasures to themselves. Lava pearls are harvested on only the rarest and most sacred of ritual occasions, such as the death of the village elder, or the selection of a new village warlord. Ruby mussel shell is also considered sacred and rarely allowed to leave the village, but the shells are collected all along the beach of Giant's Harbor and are used in much of Kreglarran's art and ritual.

On rare occasions, a trusted friend of the community is granted a ruby mussel shell as a gift. Only slightly less rarely, a greedy community member might be persuaded to smuggle out a few shells, with the right incentives, but these usually are second-rate shell fragments of lesser luster and brilliance than those prized within the village. Kreglarran fire giants are not friendly to those who seek to steal their precious shells or pearls.

HOTPOOLS, VILLAGE OF

Ruler: Mayor Alvindor Mesk
Government: elected mayor and council of wealthy citizens
Population: 280 (175 Tycho ethnicities, 40 mixed or other ethnicity human, 20 halfling, 15 Foerdewaith, 15 mountain dwarf, 10 half-elf, 5 half-orc)
Monstrous: fire giants, red dragons, devils, salamanders, and other fire-elemental-related beings
Languages: Common
Religion: unknown
Resources: hotsprings, medicinal herbs, fishing
Currency: mixed
Technology Level: High Middle Ages

A small settlement in the southern foothills of the Hellsgate Peaks near a sheltered natural harbor, Hotpools was built on the site of a destroyed stone temple to some forgotten deity. The great stone head of the deity, much worn by time, sits forlornly beside the long-shattered remains of the rest of the statue, and near an altar carved with weathered runes in a forgotten tongue. These mysterious remnants lie covered in moss and vines, only a few of them recognizable for what they are. Beside them is a cluster of five hotsprings, three of which have been surrounded and covered by columns and roofs of forest marble, open to the air on all sides.

The marble shelters were built during the reign of King Lertis Tevoy of Castorhage, as were a few surviving marble buildings in the nearby town. Some have said that Hotpools was King Lertis' primary reason for his bizarre fixation on building the Great Road. In one version of the tale, a courtier visited the Hotpools' baths and brought back a piece of the deity's statue as a souvenir for Lertis. The young man developed an obsession with the eldritch writing on the stone until he became possessed by the forgotten deity of Hotpools and was thus driven to carve a road into the forest — perhaps to recover some ancient treasure of the destroyed temple, or perhaps to specifically provoke a war as vengeance on the forgotten deity's enemies.

Most historians agree that Castorhagi rulers do not need forgotten deities and mysterious writings to inspire them to make bad decisions, but what is interesting about Hotpools is that all contact with the work crews building the settlement ceased sometime during the Forest Coast War. By the time the place was investigated by Castorhagi soldiers, it was deserted. The building project was put aside for after the war, and ultimately abandoned. The Castorhagers never again attempted an official settlement there.

The history of Hotpools is lost for centuries after that, though evidence suggests that several groups at least attempted to form communities there before the current city arose. Missives back and forth between would-be settlers and their sponsors or loved ones in the Tycho Free States also support the assumption that attempts were made. Oddly little is known about the relative success of such ventures or why they failed.

The current community at Hotpools is less than a century old. Its buildings are constructed mostly of mud-brick and thatch save where they repurposed marble scavenged from the Castorhagi ruins. It is a small but bustling place, and its economy revolves around the pools themselves and the nearby Hellsgate Peaks. Visitors can purchase simply-crafted jewelry made of local volcanic stones, souvenirs — both real and fake — from (allegedly) deeper inside the Hellsgate Peaks, medicines and potions that at least claim to be made using rare volcanic ingredients, and other such marvels. Services available include two surprisingly nice inns for a town this size, both dedicated to the peace and relaxation of the pools, with a skilled herbalist on staff at one and two skilled masseurs at the other.

Whatever mysterious force led to the disappearance of the previous Hotpools communities has yet to make its presence known in this one. Some suggest this may be because the current leadership of the hidden city of devils within the Hellsgate Peaks is clever enough to realize that Hotpools makes good bait to lure travelers into the deadly mountains. It is true — and most decent guides will say so — that the majority of travelers who venture more than a day into the Hellsgate Peaks do not return. Hotpools' residents recommend that travelers simply stay and enjoy the pools, and then go. But if one insists upon entering the mountains, guides are available here, at varying levels of ability and honesty. The best guides turn back before things get too interesting. The worst guides are those who turn out to be literal devils in disguise.

Geographic Features and Points of Interest in the Green Warden Forest and Free Coast

Boiling Maelstrom

Between the central strong current of the Strait of Gehenna and the largest eddying harbor on its north shore, tucked between the skirts of two Hellsgate Peaks volcanoes, churns the ever-present Boiling Maelstrom. Here the swift Gehenna central current smashes into the rocky cliffs that outline the sheltered Giant's Harbor, forcing the powerful flow back upon itself, and thus into an eternal and deadly spiral at the mouth of the harbor.

Any craft entering the Maelstrom would invariably be sucked beneath the waves and smashed against the rocky sea floor, but — so long as no volcanic activity is disrupting its current — the Maelstrom is at the very least predictable. The fire giants who live on the nearby shore of Giant's Harbor regularly navigate their craft around the Maelstrom's edges.

To untrained outsiders, however, the Boiling Maelstrom is truly deadly. Though it is rarely literally boiling, it is always hot enough to be concealed by a thick cloud of steam. Unless one already has memorized the safe paths around the outer edge, there is no way to see through the steam well enough to navigate around the whirlpool. Fire giants from Giant's Harbor apprentice to veteran Maelstrom pilots for five years before they attempt the feat themselves.

Circle of the Wild

Deep in the tangled depths of the forest, the elves of Eloitan venture to worship and take counsel at this eerie circle of stone monoliths. They are similar to the menhirs of the Green Warders but smaller and seem immune to the ravages of time and nature. Three times the height of a man, these rough-hewn stones are carved with Eloitan ideographs, as well as other symbols that no one can decipher — possibly the iconography of the fey creatures who also dwell in the forest.

This site is known to be a powerful source of arcane and divine magic, and also appears to be a "thin place" where the creatures of the fey and the material world can meet and travel to each others' realms. In the past, the Circle of the Wild was used as a neutral location where the Eloitan tribes could meet, where weapons were forbidden, and rivals could negotiate without the threat of violence. The elves could also meet here with the creatures of the fey, as these otherworldly beings also respected the truce at the Circle.

In recent years, however, the Circle of the Wild has become a far more ominous place. Now, tribes meet here for war councils to determine how to respond should outsiders enter the forest. Worse, the elves discovered that they can use the Circle's magic to summon ferocious fey creatures or dire animals of the deep forest and compel them to attack intruders.

With the passing years, some among the Green Warden Nations have come to believe that the Circle may have been corrupted, possibly by the same fell energies that have affected the Eloitan elves and their forest. Eloitan shamans are rumored to have visited the Circle to openly attempt to treat with evil fey and use its power to summon demons and other foul creatures. And some suspect that wicked fey from faerie realms beyond may use the Circle to gain access to the forest. In all, though its purposes appear to have originally been benign, the Circle of the Wild is now a perilous place indeed for elves and non-elves.

The Circle falls in territory claimed by both the Eloitan and the Serpent's Coil elves of the Green Warden Nations. Verbal and physical confrontation between priests on both sides are growing more common, and open skirmishes have sometimes broken out, though the fights so far have not led to outright warfare. Other elves have expressed deep concern at the conflict, but to this point neither side seems willing to listen or to de-escalate tensions.

Eloitan Forest

The Eloitan Forest is the name for the northwestern portion of the Green Warden Forest, closest to the eastern frontier of the Xha'en Hegemony. Here, after the destruction of the Green Warder Tyriem, the forest has become hostile, wild, and perilous, with a dark heart that troubles even the wild elves of the Green Warder Nations. It is home to the Eloitan tribe of wild elves who are insular and shun even the company of their fellow elves.

Forest Coast

The Forest Coast makes up almost 3000 miles of Crescent Sea coast, from the Hellsgate Peaks in the north all the way to the Mud Coast in the south. The northern portion, the Free Coast, is home to the Tycho Free States. There, the humans and wild elves of the Green Warden Forest maintain a watchful truce, careful not to encroach on the lands of the other. South of the Ilber Nole peninsula, the Forest Coast is largely uninhabited, a condition enforced by the wild elves of the Green Realm who have no desire to share their forest with others, particularly the kingdoms across the Crescent Sea who would plunder their resources and colonize their virgin woodland. To this end the elves keep a watchful eye on the coast and have established the fortresses of Linn Tark and Linn Meriku to watch the seas from the Mud Coast to Tandril Island.

In any case, much of the southern coastline is rocky and inhospitable to easy human settlement though it provides many safe havens to pirates and other seagoing vessels with a reason to hide from the navies of the Crescent Sea powers.

Giant's Harbor

The largest of the steam-hidden, eddying harbors that define the north coast of the deadly Strait of Gehenna, Giant's Harbor is the only place along the Gehenna coastline that truly teems with life. Always as hot as a hotspring (with subtle variations, depending on season and nearby volcanic activity), Giant's Harbor is home to a wide variety of unique, magical, and heat resistant sea life. Here can be found rare volcanic minerals, magical sea plants brimming with medicinal or dangerous properties, and some say the most beautiful population of starfish and sea anemones in the world.

Here is also the one place in the world where one can find the elusive ruby mussel. Ruby mussel shells are a dull, near-black red on the outside, barely distinguishable from typical blue-black mussels, albeit somewhat larger than average. Inside, their flesh is strangely metallic-tasting and can be toxic in large quantities, such that they are rarely eaten. However, the mother-of-pearl lining a ruby mussel's inner shell blazes in the wild oranges, pinks, reds, and yellows of a glorious sunrise, and when ruby mussels form pearls, they are brilliantly variegated red or orange.

Ruby mussels rarely form pearls (especially in captivity), and when they do, they are never perfectly round. A smooth, oblong ruby mussel pearl (often called a ruby pearl, lava pearl, blood pearl, or hell pearl), the size of a grain of rice, would be worth a thousand similarly-sized perfect rubies. Even ruby-mussel shells are worth extravagant sums, which is the primary reason why attempts have been made to keep them in captivity in heated pools, albeit with little long-term success.

Of course, one reason the ruby pearls are so precious, even aside from their rarity, is the near-impossibility of obtaining one from Giant's Harbor. To the south of the harbor lies the infamous Boiling Maelstrom and beyond it the deadly-swift waters of the Strait of Gehenna. To the east and west, the harbor is sheltered by unscalable volcanic cliffs. To the north, the harbor is guarded by the fire giant village of Kreglarran, which is populated by fiercely territorial warriors. Some say that even the waters of the harbor itself are guarded and the mussel beds tended by a race of intelligent octopods with whom the giants have a treaty. If so, only the Kreglarran fire giants have ever seen them.

The Great Forest Coast Road

The Great Forest Coast Road runs from Hotpools in the north to Ilber Nole and the ruins of Fort Toofar in the south. Originally laid by the Castorhagi to connect their penal colonies along the Forest Coast, it was carefully engineered with meticulous stone paving and clever drainage systems.

As Castorhage lost control of its colonies, many sections of the Great Forest Coast Road fell into disrepair. Over the years since, as the Tycho Free States have gained in economic strength, they have rebuilt and now maintain many stretches of the road. However, the fragmented nature of the Free States means that the road is typically in best repair wherever it is nearest to large current settlements. The places in worst disrepair include the last few dozen miles before Fort Toofar, where the final layer of the road's paving was never finished, and the section between Timbertown and Bogsweat, which washed out in a freak storm after having been damaged by several lightning strikes (some say a pair of wizards must have dueled there considering the extent of the damage).

Leading from Fringe into the Green Warden Forest are the remains of the Great Road that King Lertis Tevoy of Castorhage attempted to build to pierce the secrets of the Green Realm. Work on the road was abandoned during the Mortgage War with the elves. Ironically, this portion of the road may be the most beautiful. The wild elves chose not to dismantle the road's remains within their territory. Instead, they leave it as a reminder of past sorrows and betrayals, as well as to warn travelers what becomes of those who violate wild elf territory. Druids coaxed the forest to regrow around — or even through — the crumbling pavement. Many portions of the road here feel like a haunted, green cathedral, at once holy and terrible. Travelers in the region have often sighted ghosts or similar shadows working or fighting on the forest road or weeping beside it.

Green Warden Forest

The Green Realm once referred to all of the remains of the Akadonian Forest west of the Crescent Sea. Differences between the southern and northern wild elves, however, ultimately led to their sundering. The forest lands south of the Ilber Peninsula continue to be known as the Green Realm. The northern portion of the forest has come to be called, by its elven inhabitants, the Green Warden and extends northeastward past the Green Warder monoliths to include everything south of the Westwood and west of Hollow Mountain (though the elves of the Eloitan region, in the northwest portion of the wood nearest Xha'en, would not agree they are within the Green Warden).

The Green Warden is a strange and haunting forest, full of cathedral-like clearings and glens, ghostly sighing of breezes, fearless and often-magical wildlife, and occasionally hostile trees. Even outside the immediate vicinity of the discomfiting Green Warder monoliths, there is a sense throughout the Green Warden of being watched.

North of the monoliths, the Green Warden Forest is literally haunted in certain places, as the mystical ramifications of the ritual that created the Green Warders made it possible for the dead to remain so long as they are loyal to the forest and its living denizens. Though the wild elves are not entirely comfortable with this state of affairs, they tolerate their undead allies and avoid the haunted areas since it serves to protect the elven lands (and, in any event, the elves know of no way to alter this consequence of the ritual). The occasional stone or partial foundation of Warder Forts can also be found in the lands north of the monoliths, the last line of defense where the elves held back their enemies, human and other, while the year-long Warder Ritual was completed.

South of the Warders and east of the Eloitan, the Green Warden is an idyllic paradise for those who live there and understand its many secrets — and for any they invite as friends. For unwanted intruders, however, the Green Warden tends toward the brutal and nightmarish. Though the reasons are poorly understood, even to most of the elves, the trees and plants here are often fully awakened and intelligent. Perhaps one in every 500 plants and one in every 300 trees is sentient and able to move. Some even evidence druidical power, awakened by the elven druids of the region.

Monsters in the Green Warden are usually neutral or unaligned in outlook and are never harmful to the larger ecosystem. Indeed, many are either allied with the elves in protecting the forest or instinctively territorial toward all but the elves who learn from birth how to safely live alongside such beasts.

Green Warders

These massive, moss-covered monoliths loom 50 or more feet tall, peeking their bald stone heads up from the trees around them. Now covered by thick moss and vines, the stones were erected by elven might in a great ritual that lasted a full year.

Early in the eighth century I.R., humanoid incursions across the Crynnomar Gap threatened the Green Realm, which then extended nearly to the gap. The wild elves began a defense there that lasted until 725 I.R. When at last the humanoids were forced back into the steppes, the elves discovered that Reme had settled much of the northeastern part of their forest. Exhausted and tired of ongoing threats from their neighbors, the elves vowed to create a barrier across which none could pass. They withdrew farther west in what became known as the Third Exodus of the Elves.

The elves set a new border of seven great monoliths in a line across the northern part of the Green Realm and began a ritual that took an entire year to complete. Feeding into the ritual was the power of an ancient ley line linking the Impossible Peaks with the Hellsgate Peaks to the south. To complete the ritual, a powerful spellcaster was required to merge permanently with each of the seven monoliths and leave behind their elven selves forever. For this reason, each of the stones has its own name — the name of the elf whose spirit forever inhabits and empowers it. Three druids and four other casters volunteered for this eternal duty. In order from the Impossible Peaks to the Hellsgates, the stones are named Tyriem the Bard, Lysseia the Shapeshifter, Cryssien the Sorcerer, Piriel the Wizard, Meniera the Plant-Speaker, Kemmel the Healer, and Shinaia the Storm-Lord.

It is said that when the final climax of the year-long ritual spell was cast, every enemy of the elves or the forest within a hundred miles of any of the Green Warders was struck instantly dead. And thereafter, any who would wish harm to the Akadonian Forest or its wild elven inhabitants were said to fall violently ill when they stepped within the bounds of the legendary rite's range. If they retreated, they might recover, or they might not. But if they advanced despite their illness, death was said to almost certainly follow.

Despite what some histories claim, the ritual was not targeted against humans or any specific species. The power of the rite could even harm wild elves, should they approach the Warders with a wish to harm the forest or its wild elven inhabitants. Green Realm histories even record one instance where this power of the Warders is suspected to be the true cause of death of one notoriously wicked elven warrior.

It is unknown to what extent the Warders still retain the ability to sense the ill intent of the intelligent minds around them. It is not impossible that as the stones age they may have grown to see even humanoid creatures as simple animals, acting only on instinct. Cases of illness near the Warders are rarely recorded in current times, and no known recent cases have led to death. That being said, no ill-wishers in living memory have pressed on once ill, so perhaps the stones have not grown weaker but merely more merciful. It is difficult to say, and few with ill intent desire to approach the stones close enough to test them.

Those who do approach the monoliths — especially those who step close enough to see the deep-etched ancient runes buried beneath the millennia of moss and vines — can feel their thrum of power. No intelligent creature, to this day, can sleep restfully within miles of the Green Warders. The histories say that, in the early days, the stones' chosen Warders could project emotions to those around them and even send messages in dreams. Now, after nearly 3,000 years, it seems that the minds of these ancient elves-turned-monoliths have grown too vast and alien for the comfort of an ordinary consciousness, such that communion with the stones can cause outbursts of uncontrollable emotion, unshakable trances, and incomprehensible nightmares.

Each of the stones also seems to affect the area around it in ways that differ among the monoliths. Around Shinaia, the weather can be unpredictable or seem almost sentient. Near Kemmel, any who do manage to fall asleep may not awaken for days or weeks, though they will awaken in perfect health once they do, assuming nothing kills them in their sleep in the meantime. In the area about Meniera, the plants can all move of their own accord and exhibit animal-like intelligence. Piriel's monolith can drive visitors permanently mad without warning or apparent pattern, and Cryssien's is shrouded constantly in shadow and mist that interferes with magic cast in its vicinity and weakens most spells but rarely strengthens them beyond all control or causes the opposite of their intended effect. And around Lysseia, some unknown percentage of the otherwise-ordinary forest creatures are able to speak several languages and sometimes cast spells.

Tyriem's patch of forest was once full of haunting and sad melodies, woven into the breeze, the movement of leaves, the birdsong, and the babbling of every stream. However, many centuries ago, Tyriem's monolith was broken and thrown down — although no one knows how. As if still in mourning after all this time, the forest around his ruined monolith is eerily, uncomfortably silent.

All seven Warders are sites of wild elven spiritual pilgrimage, though few pilgrims can stand to remain in their presence for long. Kemmel, Meniara, and Lysseia are the most commonly visited Warders, while Piriel is treated most warily, and Tyriem is only accessible to those able to survive and defend themselves in deadly Eloitan territory.

Ever since Tyriem's destruction, the might of the Green Warders has lessened. Malevolent creatures have become emboldened within Eloitan, the northwestern region of the forest, and the wild elves of the Green Warden Nations grow ever more concerned that, any year now, the other six Warders will begin to fail. Wild elven magical scholars are researching what little record remains of the original ritual, both to ascertain the extent of the danger and to learn if it might be possible to restore Tyriem or — if the need grew sufficiently dire — to choose a new volunteer to stand with the other six as Warders of the forest.

Of course, since most threats to the forest now come from the Xha'en wilderness or the Crescent Sea, the relative tactical utility of fully restoring the Green Warders is debated. As is particularly obvious to those wild elven nations living closest to the Tycho Free States, the Green Warders' magic can extend only so far. It cannot protect the forest from every angle.

HELLSGATE PEAKS

This volcanically active mountain range (of which Infernis Isle is technically an extension), is home to many fire-loving creatures. Fire giants, red dragons, salamanders, and many other elementals of fire can be found here. In addition, it is well known that the Hellsgate Peaks host perhaps the largest population of devils in permanent residence on the Material Plane. The exact location of their city is unknown, but escaped slaves describe its terrible grandeur built deep inside the walls of a volcanic caldera.

The volcanoes of the Hellsgate Peaks, along with those of Infernis Isle, pour near-continuous ash and lava into the Strait of Gehenna, substantially altering nearby weather patterns and wildlife populations. The seabirds that roost in the Hellsgate Peaks along the coast are unique in all the world, and some are unusually large and dangerous compared to others of related species.

The peaks themselves are of similarly unique ecology, and even more dangerous than the coastal cliffs. All plants and animals are adapted to life in extreme heat, and many are magical. While some passages through the Hellsgate Peaks are traversable, other regions are too hot for humans (and most other natural creatures) to survive without magical assistance. Maps of the Hellsgate Peaks are difficult to acquire and are often rendered inaccurate by new outpourings of lava, ash, and boiling mud, such that a knowledgeable local guide is a necessity for travel through the region, a fact that enterprising devils have been known to exploit in order to acquire fresh slave labor for their city, often by disguising themselves and posing as guides.

HOLLOW MOUNTAIN

Suspected to be a dormant volcano, the appropriately named Hollow Mountain has long been left alone by natives of its region, though evidence shows it was inhabited by certain pre-human reptilian races long ago. Given the unusually high volcanic activity of the Hellsgate Peaks to the south, some scholars believe that Hollow Mountain is certain to erupt again and is thus best treated with great caution.

For a long time, Hollow Mountain was thought to be uninhabited. Recently, however, a secretive cult has arisen in the area around the Hollow Mountain, and rumor suggests that the cultists may have made the mountain into their base or temple. Everywhere that this cult has spread experiences strange disappearances and kidnappings, and members of the cult behave very differently than they did before becoming members. In any event, there is a growing concern that something bizarre and terrible is going on inside Hollow Mountain.

INFERNIS ISLE

An extension of the Hellsgate Peaks in the Crescent Sea, Infernis Isle is divided from the mainland by the perilous Strait of Gehenna. While the island, like the rest of the peaks in the range, is home to several unusually active volcanoes, regularly spitting lava and ash in large quantities, it is different from the rest of the Hellsgate Peaks in several respects.

Surrounded by the waters of the Crescent Sea, Infernis Isle is much cooler than the rest of the Hellsgate Peaks, which allows for natural creatures to exist on its slopes, particularly on the isle's eastern coast. Though the plant life is too sparse and the territory too steep and too dominated by volcanic rock to make Infernis Isle habitable to humanoids (not to mention the ever-present stink of sulfur), many seabirds and mammals survive there by fishing in the well-stocked, often bathwater-warm waters near the shoreline.

The highest points of the isle are more mysterious, however. Shrouded continuously in smoke and ash, the peaks are said to be impossible to climb. Tradition along the Free Coast claims that a very old red dragon makes its home near the top of Infernis Isle. But while smaller red dragons are often observed near the Hellsgate Peaks, none is large enough or powerful enough to fit the description of the legendary Infernis Isle Wyrm. Perhaps the creature is slumbering in its lair. Perhaps it is long dead or never existed. In any case, local sailors and fishermen approach the Infernis Isle coastline only in times of direst necessity, and none ventures up the isle's steep sides to explore the peaks above.

ONTHENLIAN RIVER

Some distance north and east of the Hellsgate Peaks runs the Onthenlian River. Named millennia ago by wild elves fighting to defend their forest homes, in the elvish of the era "onthenlian" meant "waters of bereavement." No record remains as to why the river was given such a grim designation, though some suggest it references the ash-gray color of its waters due to natural sediment in the region.

The mouth of the Onthenlian pours out into the volcano-heated, northward-running current at the upper end of the Strait of Gehenna and significantly cools the seawater and allows it to return to a more sea life-friendly temperature. The meeting of the hot strait with the cool river, however, plays havoc on local weather, and rain and thunderstorms are almost constant above that stretch of coastline. These "weeping skies" (as one old poem says of the region) have been postulated as another possible reason for the river's sorrowful name.

Whatever the ancient reason, fey and elven residents of the area recently began to identify more strongly with the "onthenlian" sentiment in light of a rash of kidnappings and disappearances. Taking place just barely outside the range of the Green Warders, where the river runs closest to Hollow Mountain, the disappearances seem to have arisen in tandem with a violent new local cult dedicated to something they call "the true nature."

Queensribbon River

Called the Ilian by the wild elves, after a silvery blue flower that grows in the region, the Queensribbon River is best known at its mouth in Timbertown, where ships come from all over the Crescent Sea to purchase lumber from the excellent Queensribbon tree farms the elves permit Timbertown to keep on the edge of the forest. East of the forest's eaves, especially in the late summer, the river's length is devoted to log-driving and lined on either bank by hypnotically row-planted trees or fresh-cut stumps.

A short distance into the forest, an ever-hidden contingent of wild elves guards the river and disallows all passage any farther into their domain. The guardians always include archers and at least one druid, and the river is lined with various traps and deterrents designed to hamper boats without disrupting wildlife. Timbertown officials are careful to never cross the elves in any way, to the extent of enacting several strict river-protection policies in their use of the Queensribbon waters, despite the Timbertown obsession with profit above all else. Residents who defy local law in this regard are commonly disavowed by the Timbertown authorities and are left to the elves to punish as they see fit.

It is said that no human has ever seen the source of the Queensribbon.

Saeriel River

The largest tributary of the river the elves call Ilian and the humans call Queensribbon, the Saeriel river runs mostly northeast in a narrow, tight meander, wriggling through the forest like the pretty creeping vine for which it was named in the local tongue. Between all the winding banks, several short waterfalls, and some jagged whitewater patches, the Saeriel River is rarely traversed by humanoids. It is, however, the spawning ground of the nalendrien, a rare breed of salmon that the local wild elves prize over all other fish.

It is lucky for the humans of Timbertown that the practice of log-driving does not hamper the annual runs of this culturally-important fish. Nalendrien swim upstream under the Timbertown logs and fight their way unerringly through the Saeriel-Ilian confluence, always turning up the Saeriel to spawn. Once they begin to leap up the rapids and waterfalls of the swiftly-winding river, the sight of their coppery orange bodies, glittering against the water in the sun, has inspired some of the most renowned of wild elf religious poetry in all the land.

Nalendrien is a corruption of a phrase meaning "flame in the water", and several parts of this magical fish can be used as spell components or medicines. The flesh or oils, prepared correctly, can increase wisdom. The powdered scales are said to be of use in crafting lightning-producing magical items, incidentally also turning the lightning that is produced a fiery orange in color. Finally, the roe can increase or restore one's hope in the face of despair, or one's courage to fight when frightened. The local wild elves closely guard their methods for preparing the fish for magical crafting and are impeccably moderate and respectful in the harvesting of their bounty. Outside their modest, ritualized harvests, they guard the fish as fiercely as if they were fellow elves, and many celebrations and songs are offered up during the annual nalendrien run.

Strait of Gehenna

While the swift flow of tidal waters through the Strait of Gehenna did allow it to carve a gap in the mountain range that includes the Hellsgate Peaks and Infernis Isle, even the inexorable patience of water has been unable to defend the strait from the constant effects of the region's volcanic activity.

At least once per month, and sometimes even several times in the same week, lava, hot ash, and boiling mud are known to pour into the strait from volcanic activity of the Hellsgate Peaks and Infernis Isle, oftentimes lasting for days at a time. But the current between the mainland and the island is so fierce that even this continuous influx of sediment and volcanic rock cannot clog up or dam the Strait of Gehenna. Instead, volcanic detritus is spread over the seafloor all the way to the northernmost and even the easternmost coasts of the Crescent Sea.

Between the powerful current and the constant heat, the Strait of Gehenna is entirely impassible by nonmagical crafts, and nothing nonmagical is known to live here. In the protected heat of eddying harbors, however, many heat-loving magical creatures can be found, including one sauna-like seaside village of fire giants in the largest of these harbors.

In addition, rumors persist of strange, alien species making homes cut into the smooth, volcanic stone that lines the central strait's narrow walls and deep floor. These rumors have been difficult to verify due to the strait's unusual weather patterns. The constant influx of superheated materials into the water fills the strait with an ever-present cloud of steam. This uncomfortably warm fog does at times drift southward or northward with the wind, or wear thin at the edges along the coastline, but it has been seen to fully dissipate only during the most violent of storms. For this reason, visibility into and within the Strait of Gehenna is all but nonexistent. If something alien does make its home in these fast-flowing waters, no one has ever seen it and lived to tell the tale.

Strange creatures, however, are not required to make the Strait of Gehenna impassible. The fierce current is difficult to steer against and likely to smash boats against the strait's rock walls, and after every lava flow new jagged teeth of broken volcanic rock are left behind to claw the undersides of craft that attempt the voyage. Such spears of rock are always worn away to smoothness in time, but since new hazards appear with every eruption, the only constant is the absolute unknowability of where it is and isn't safe to steer one's boat. Even the fire giants who live on the strait's shores do not put craft into the central current and instead trek by land to and from their village through the Hellsgate Peaks for any needed trade.

Toofar

When this ruin was still a Castorhagi fort, it was named Fort Tevoy after King Lertis Tevoy, the force behind the ill-fated Green Warden forest incursion. Tevoy was the last of such forts to be built, and by the time it was commissioned, every single one of King Lertis' military and economic advisors was telling him not to waste resources on extending the road down to yet another fort in what by then already looked to be a losing investment in lives and resources.

After three different generals found excuses to avoid participating in the military campaign that would be required to make King Lertis' new fort a reality, the king finally found a fourth, General Balgon, so blindly loyal he not only led the campaign to hold the fort's territory long enough to build the thing, he also named it Fort Tevoy after his beloved king.

The fort was finished in 2367 I.R. In 2369 I.R., General Balgon was slain in the battle of Tevoy, which also saw the destruction of the Castorhagi royal army garrison for the region and the sacking of Fort Tevoy by a wild elf warband. The fort was only in full operation for 19 months.

Now nicknamed "Fort Toofar," the ruins are used as an informal reconnaissance outpost by the corsairs of Ilber Nole.

Tranith

As King Lertis Tevoy's forays into the Green Realm began to anger the wild elves, Castorhagi settlers built several small forts facing the woods to defend themselves from their elven neighbors. Tranith was neither the largest of these nor even the farthest inland, though it is the farthest inland that survives today as discernible ruins.

Unlike most other such forts, Tranith did not even survive to the end of the war with the elves and the abandonment of the Great Road. Instead, it was destroyed in an earthquake relatively early in the war. What makes its tale particularly tragic is that it so happened that a group of settlers had taken shelter there just before the earthquake. These settlers had been making their homes somewhat deeper inside the Green Warden Forest, but when hostilities broke out between them and the elves, their warriors were defeated, leaving behind only the children, elderly, and a few caretakers.

This tiny band made its way through the forest back to the fort at Tranith and holed up there waiting for help and supplies to arrive. Unfortunately, the earthquake hit before help or supplies ever came, and the surviving refugees were trapped inside the damaged fort, many of them injured. At the same time, an escalation of violence between elves and humans in the area forced the humans to retreat and cede the fort to elven control. When the elves took possession — perhaps in an act of monstrous cruelty, or perhaps mistaking the refugees for soldiers still guarding the structure — they burned what remained of the broken little fort to the ground with the huddled, injured noncombatants still cowering inside.

Ever since that incident, the ruins of Tranith have been haunted. Travelers through the region are harassed by dangerous apparitions, and those who (usually unknowingly) take shelter in what is left of the ruins tell tales of terror and peril after fleeing for their lives — assuming they get out at all. In addition, those who die inside the ruined fort have been known to rise again as undead possessed by the restless ghosts of the abandoned refugees.

POLITICAL SUBDIVISIONS OF SOUTHWEST AKADOS

THE GREEN REALM

Capital: Solis Alunaris

Notable Settlements: Sataama Vassen, Sataama Vierta, Linn Syldryll, Linn Kothkaan, Linn Tark, Linn Meriku

Ruler: High King Riar Harwood, Royal Council

Government: tribal monarchy

Population: 500,000 (480,000 wild elves, approximately 20,000 centaurs (near Syldryll Vale and the Verdant Plains), small number of grey elves)

Monstrous: dire or giant animals native to the region (including but not limited to local breeds of monkeys, apes, brown bears, wolves, foxes, many snakes, birds, tigers, leopards, plant-type creatures native to the region (any, but especially treants, shambling mounds), arboreal dinosaurs, wood giants, awakened plants/trees, awakened animals, satyrs, pixies, centaurs, lycanthropes (various) dryads, unicorns, nymphs, quicklings, korreds, sprites, fauns, satyrs, owlbears, wyverns, pseudodragons, incursions of green dragons, drakes, elementals, and other temperate and sub-tropical forest creatures native to the region

Languages: Elvan, Sylvan, Druidic, Draconic, some Common

Religion: Arialee, the Green Father, animism, to a lesser extent Darach-Albith (some elves)

Resources: steel and weapons (Northern Steel Tongue Mountains), gold (Southern Steel Tongue Mountains), elven ponies (Syldryll Vale), magic, information (Emerald Mountains), wine.

Currency: Green Realms coin, mixed

Technology Level: Dark Age (wild elf villages), Renaissance (Solis Alunaris, Linn Tark, Linn Kothkaan, Linn Syldryll, Sataama Vassen, Sataama Vierta)

The Green Realm originally referred to all of the remnants of the Great Akadonian Forest west of the Crescent Sea, reaching from the Crynnomar Gap in the north to the High Barrens in the south. Since then, incursions of humans have reduced the extent of the forest, particularly in the lands of Reme, and nearly a thousand years ago, the northern wild elves seceded to form the Green Warden Nations. Since that time, the Green Realm encompasses only the forest south of the Ilber Peninsula. But even so reduced, the Green Realm constitutes well over one million square miles of subtropical and temperate woodland, the largest remaining extant of primeval forest in the world today, and the home of the largest nation of wild elves on Akados.

The wild elves of the Green Realm seek to keep their primeval paradise as pristine and unmolested by the taint of man, dwarf, goblin, and orc as possible. As such, they have built a tightly-knit bulwark around their realm made up of hidden woodland fortresses, awakened plant life, prehistoric beasts, and brutally ignorant neighbors that would dissuade incursions by their human neighbors, or the more complex threats from their dark elf kin based in the ever-shadowed walls of Vilik Strad.

HISTORY AND PEOPLE

The first elves arrived on Akados over 10,000 years ago, voyaging from their homeland in another plane of existence. Some event there eventually led to great numbers coming to live on the continent in what is now called the First Exodus of the Elves. Eventually, the elven forest realms grew to encompass most of the Great Akadonian Forest, which then covered nearly all of the southern half of the continent.

For thousands of years the elves lived in harmony with one another and with the creatures of the great forests. They roamed freely across Akados from the polished wooden halls of Solis Alunaris, the Sylvan City, in the west, to glorious Parnuble and Arendia in the east. Wherever they went, they learned the names and names of things around them and gave name and life to other things as befit their wild imagination. Always they stood against the terror of troll and giant, of ogre, and goblin whenever such creatures crawled down from the mountaintops or up from the chasms of the earth. They largely ignored the humans, who were mainly rustic farmers and ranchers, then populating the continent.

The Green Realm extended far to the south on the west coast of the Crescent Sea, but it never reached into the Talanos Peninsula, which then was a jungle plateau teeming with monsters and covered in a darkness that the elves feared. Then in −201 I.R., fires were seen behind the dark walls of Vilik Strad. The Lords of the Green Realm were alarmed and took counsel with the grey elves in the Emerald Mountains. Together, they began formulating a plan to halt the advance of their drow cousins, who were now observed in the deep shadow of the jungle canopy even in the brightness of day. Then came the event that changed elven history on Akados forever: the invasion of the Hyperboreans in −109 I.R. The elves of the Great Akadonian Forest gathered their strength and fought against the invaders, initially with great success, but in −91 I.R. they were betrayed by the mountain dwarves of the Stonehearts and their main host was massacred in an ambush at Lake Crimmormere.

The power of the elves was broken, and they faded back into the forests. But the Hyperboreans followed up their victory at Crimmormere and pressed on into the forests where they attacked and destroyed now-defenseless elven settlements. A byproduct of the evils visited on the elves by the Hyperboreans was a sudden increase in half-elven births among the elven remainder. After the loss of so many at Crimmormere, many among the elves saw the swift-maturing half-elves as a blessing. But others shunned the half-elves, calling them in elvish the "war-dead." In −27 I.R., a half-elven leader named Valenthlis rose and demanded a place of honor for half-elves in elven society. A civil war broke out between the elves who welcomed their half-brothers and those who did not, ending only when Queen Vaissilune was killed in the conflict. As a result of this tragedy, the elves that rejected the half-elves decided to withdraw to the west and migrated to the Green Realm in −26 I.R. in what became known as the Second Exodus of the Elves. They began calling themselves the wild elves to denote their complete denial of humanity and their civilization. The elves that remained behind and supported Valenthlis began calling themselves high elves, the ancestors of the elves who live today in eastern Akados.

There in the Green Realm, the elves withdrew from the world and for a time were at peace. This was broken in 52 I.R. by an incursion across their southern boundaries of armies of goblins, ogres, orcs, and bugbears driven by the dark elves in Vilik Strad. Emissaries were sent seeking advice and aid from the grey elves of the Emerald Mountains. Working together, Queen Talith Harwood of Solis Alunaris and King Reithon of Suomen Gron performed a great ritual at the edge of the Talanos Plateau, tearing a rift in the floor of the world. There they raised the Cinderhame Mountains from the edges of the planes of Earth and Fire, burning the dark jungle of the plateau to the ground and blocking the routes between Talanos and the Green Realm. King Reithon is said to have passed from the world of Boros as he infused the ritual with the last spark of the soul of the Eldest he held within his heart. His sacrifice was the price required to be paid for such a horrid violation of the natural order.

The dark elves of Vilik Strad who survived the rending of the ground and the scorching of their jungles returned to the safety of their shadowed fortress. It is said that they have licked their wounds since that day, plotting and waiting for an opportunity to blot out the sun and wreak revenge upon their cousins in the Green Realm. Meanwhile, bands of homeless

Legend

- ● Town or Village
- ◉ City
- ✪ Capital or Free City
- ✵ Imperial Capital
- ■ Fortress or Citadel
- ⁘ Ruins
- ▲ Place of Interest
- ～ Road
- ╱ Trail or Unused Road
- ⋯ Mountain Pass
- ✕ Battlefield

SOUTHWEST AKADOS

An ogre, hobgoblins and goblins venture forth from Vilik Strad into the High Barrens.

humanoids were left to wander the waste, cannibalizing one another and warring on their kin, until it is believed they finally settled on the shores of the Crescent Sea under the leadership of a prophet of Orcus, who forged the wanderers into what would become the "free" city-state of Braktu. Their land now protected from much of the rest of the world, the elves of the southern Green Realm grew ever more isolated, even from their kin in the northern parts of the forest. When the north felt threatened by raids from the Xha'en plains or from Castorhage, and even when one of the Green Warders fell, those in the south saw such events as far away, seeming indifferent to the plight of their northern cousins. As is told elsewhere, this estrangement ultimately led the northern wild elves to secede from the Green Realm and become the Green Warden Nations. And so the Green Realm remains isolated to this day, even from its kin to the north. Whether the rest of the world permits them to continue to enjoy their isolation remains to be seen.

Religion

Like all wild elves, the tribes of the Green Realm venerate the teachings of Arialee and sing the songs of the Fey Lands and the love and protection of the never-ending circle of life. Equally, the tribes follow the animism and naturalism of their elders and claim heraldry from the beasts of the wild and the living trees and plants that they call friends. Among the Unified Tribes are Oaks, Pines, Foxes, and Bears. Elders of the Green Realm are often skilled in druidic traditions and combine the shamanistic teachings of nature with the legends of Darach-Albith, the god-creator of all elves.

Trade and Commerce

The Green Realm is a land rich in natural resources. Food is abundant in the verdant forests, and the wild elves lack for little. They are careful curators of the ancient wood who carefully manage animal populations and clear dead wood in solemn ceremonies whose traditions stretch back more than 10,000 years. Trade items include rare jewels gifted them by the Hidden Ones of the Emerald Mountains, steel for weapons and armor that are drawn from the depths of the Northern Steel Tongue mountains, and gold drawn from mines in the Southern Steel Tongues. Elven-made steel tipped arrows and spears are much sought after by the tribes of centaurs who dwell in Syldryll Vale. The centaurs trade fine horses to the elves in exchange for such steel and the promise to defend the southern entryway to the kingdom from any outsiders. Like their cousins to the north, the masters of the Green Realm are well versed in the enchantment of magical items and the knowledge of spells, occasionally offering information, education, or magical items in trade. It is known that many among the human kingdoms of Akados covet timber from the Green Realm. Talk of trade in such things is laughable to the wild elves, who would just as soon dismember a child of their own upbringing as slaughter one of their kinfolk of wood and leaf.

Loyalty and Diplomacy

King Riar Harwood keeps ambassadors among the Green Warden Nations, just as they keep ambassadors within his own court. Though the northern and southern kin of the elves have been sundered, they remain deeply aware that the blood of the ancients, back to the time of the First Exodus, flows through all of their veins. Were a great threat to arise, the elves would be expected to join their forces to face it. In the meantime, King Riar prefers that the Green Warden Nations keep a watchful eye on the doings of the Xha'en Empire while the true High Lords of the Green Realm remain unknown to imperial spies and generals of that populous nation. He is uncomfortably aware that, should Xha'en decide to march into the beloved woods of the Great Akadonian Forest, they would surely take them, should they have the will to sacrifice millions in the endeavor. For this reason, the king encourages nationalistic tendencies among the Green Warden Nations and ensures they receive such weaponry and other aid they might need to act as a buffer.

The Green Realm also maintains good relations with the Five Clans of the Hoof in Syldryll Vale. But other than the centaur nation, the Green Realm has no other allies or relations with any other kingdoms or peoples.

GOVERNMENT

The Green Realms is a monarchy ruled by a king or queen with the guidance and assistance of an Elder Council. This council consists of tribal nobles elected by the heads of each tribe. Most councilors are elected to serve a term of 20 years though some are voted continuous terms by their individual tribes. Final authority is vested in the monarch based on the findings of the Elder Council, though in the majority of cases decisions are consistent with the council's suggested course of action. Under certain circumstances when the need is particularly dire, the monarch may dispatch emissaries from the Halls of Suomen Gron in quest of further advice from the Hidden Ones who dwell there. For themselves, the tribes are mostly autonomously run, with their own chieftains relaying information to the Elder Council of happenings in their portion of the Green Realm, making requests for aid in the form of magic, weapons, or reinforcements as needed. Tributes sent by these chieftains to the High King of the Forest include documents obtained from prisoners and samples of technology and magic seized from pirates and raiders.

For himself, King Riar Harwood is nearing the end of his reign and is expected to select his successor sometime in the next 20 years. Riar is incredibly old even for a wild elf. In the last several decades he has begun the process of becoming one with the great forest as his body begins to meld into the tree from which his throne has grown. As one with the tree he can sense immediate threats to the forest and direct resources to the source of those threats as far as the edges of the Green Realm's roots allow. Riar's eldest children Prince Sima and Princess Orovaki serve in effect as co-regents to the throne, standing at each side of their father as he receives advice from the Elder Council. The prince and princess act as intermediaries and ambassadors of the king in their dealings with the Green Warden Nations, and in the rare occasions when the advice of the Hidden Ones of Suomen Gron is sought.

For their part, the monarchs in the line of Harwood have sought fairness and neutrality in their rule, seeking little in the way of tribute but much in the way of respect. They allow the general autonomy of the tribes so long as each tribal chieftain remembers their purpose in protecting the sanctity and purity of the last great forest on Akados. Potential royal heirs spend years among the various tribes learning each particular tribe's customs and strengths. For example, an heir may spend years learning the stealth tactics of the Fox clan, or the pack hunting tactics of the Wolves. They may train their bodies in endurance running among the Elks, or in observation and sniper techniques of the Hawks. This personal interaction with the various members of the kingdom helps to ensure the tribal support of the Harwood line. By ensuring that his heirs develop a deep understanding of the other tribes, Riar hopes to avoid the misstep his ancestors made in not fully supporting their northern relatives at a time that they perhaps needed it most.

NOTABLE TRIBES

Although there are many tribes among the Green Realm, including some very small ones, the major tribes of the Green Realm are the Fox, the Elk, the Bear, the Eagle, the Leopard, the Wolf and the Red Hawk.

The Fox Tribe is a dedicated clan of scouts who roam the lands between the east and west coasts parallel to Tandril Island. They are sharp-eyed and sharp-witted, with golden-brown skin, hazel eyes, and reddish hair. They are experts at evasion and ambush, leading foes deep into the forest where they are dispatched by hidden traps. The Fox Tribe has the most trade with the Green Warden Nations, though they are still deeply loyal to the ancient bloodline in Solis Alunaris. The Elk Tribe ranges from the coastal plains of the west to the deep forests that parallel Bitter Island on the east, and are a strong tribe whose chieftain, Prince Jalaba Vui, is a respected leader known for his speed and strength. The Elks do more than take their name from the majestic beasts of the forest, as most are bonded with great dire elk of the wood and ride the beasts as their southernmost cousins who dwell near the Syldryll Vale ride horses. Living in the forests around the Karthu Mountains, where it shares territory with the Eagle Tribe, the Bear Tribe is known for its bravery and ferocity. The Bear Tribe maintains some of the most barbaric traditions of the wild elves. Their berserkers have fought at the forefront of every war ever waged on behalf of the Green Realm against its foes. Their villages are built in caves and they spend their days questing for challenges to prove their bravery.

The Eagle Tribe lives among the mountain cliffs of the Karthu range, traveling on the backs of great eagles. A small number of Eagles also live high among the trees close to Solis Alunaris where they offer aid in swift transportation and as eyes in the sky soaring above the majesty of the Green Realm. The Leopard and Wolf Tribes live deep within the woods. The homes of the Wolves are built close to the ground like the beasts whose name they keep and whose dens their villages emulate. The Leopards build their villages within the branches of the trees, their surefooted step, patience, and gold green eyes making them deadly stalkers of the deep arboreal gloom.

The Red Hawk Tribe lives among the coastal trees of the Crescent Sea. They are one of the most populous and powerful tribes of the realm and are tasked with watching the kingdom's safety and security from the castle of Linn Tark and for 500 miles to the north. Members of the Tribe of the Red Hawk are renowned archers and strategists whose raiding parties harry pirate camps and burn their ships when encountered. Like the Green Warden Nations, many of the other tribes are more nomadic in nature and keep small villages throughout the forest where they stay sometimes for a week, month, or even a few years before wandering deeper into the woodland. They let the voice of the forest speak to them, and if danger calls, all tribes are alerted and send their emissaries to the Elder Council for further instruction.

MILITARY

The armies of the deep forest are more varied than those of the Green Warden Nations to the north and have a mix of traditional and non-traditional troops to call on in times of need. Western territories bordering the broad plains and that have made alliances with the nomadic tribes of centaurs dwelling there possess a mounted light cavalry that can be called upon to harry and harass foes if necessary. Their numbers are small, so that between the western coastal plain and Syldryll Vale their numbers are under 5,000, though when bolstered by the wild centaur, the cavalry muster could potentially be much greater.

The cliffs of the Steel Tongues and the Karthu Mountains farther north are homes to tribes known for their tamed and ready giant eagles, with each region accounting for nearly a thousand air cavalry. Typically, these great birds are ridden by sorcerer knights, rangers, or druids who rain down thunder and lightning from the skies. The forest's interior is home to a host of rangers as well as sure-eyed archers of note, druids, sorcerers, and the alliances of treants, friendly forest giants, and fey creatures whom the elves call forth to reckon the terms of old alliances dating back to their mutual ancestors' origins in the Fey Realms. The eastern coast along the Mud Coast, the Forest Coast, and the Cinderhame Mountains contain more organized military forces with garrisons built along the timberline and hidden in the sides of hills. These forces are drawn from a mixture of tribes and train together for years in preparation of a human armada bent on invasion and conquest.

MAJOR THREATS

The deep forest holds its secrets, and some locations in the forest are dark and rotten. In such places, unclean spirits sometimes rise from the pit of hell to challenge the sanctity and security of those around them. There are monsters in the depths who claim their home among the shadows of the trees. Trolls and ogres are found in the deep forest, as are chimera, dangerous dinosaurs, carnivorous apes, harpies, hags, and other folk who remain dangerous and hidden in their own steadings.

When threats arise from the shadowy parts of the forest, the guardians of the wood band together to thwart the threat. Rarely, they have been known to quest forth beyond the borders of their ancient kingdom in search of aid for things that they admit that they cannot vanquish on their own. Less common though still dangerous threats to the Green Realm arrive in the occasional appearances of exploratory missions sent from Xha'en that are quickly turned away at the western coast. Other common dangers include pirates who pierce the veil of the forest in search of fabled elven treasures. Rarer still are encounters with legendary green dragons said to sleep in the depths of the deep timber or from one of the spawn of Qoatl Boax that slithers across the Mud Coast to test the resolve of the wood's defenders.

In recent centuries, ogres, hill giants, fire giants, trolls, bugbears, and gnolls have taken up holdings in the Cinderhame range. Bloody skirmishes have been fought that have set the elven sages to searching for the crumbling scrolls that detail pieces of the old ritual that would break open the earth to devour their enemies once more. It is speculated that these monstrous foes have been driven across the High Barrens to take their home there by their shadow-walking overlords in Vilik Strad.

WILDERNESS AND ADVENTURES

Like the Green Warden lands of the north, the elves of the Green Realms use magic and illusion to hide their villages from outsiders, preferring to direct them into traps and capture if they seem to be a mild threat. Strangers who enter the outskirts of the forest as often as not find themselves standing along the coast several days later, relieved of all but basic survival equipment but otherwise no worse for wear.

SOLIS ALUNARIS, SYLVAN CITY OF

(Sol-Iss A-LuNar-Iss)

Ruler: High King Riar Harwood, he who is one with the trees; Elder Council of the Green Realm; Caraeith Helias, Hierophant of the Sylvan City; Illieha the Star-treader; and Lord Sorceress Milathiu Velhei

Government: monarchy

Population: 90,000 (wild elves)

Languages: Elven, Sylvan, some Common

Religion: Animism, Arialee, Darach-Albith, lesser and fey deities.

Resources: magic, cultivated natural resources, fine art.

Currency: Green Realms coin, mixed

Technology Level: Medieval/Renaissance

Solis Alunaris, the Sylvan City, is the greatest wild elven city remaining in the Lost Lands. The folk of the great city, though not necessarily as wild as they once were, take pride in their naturalistic heritage and have grown the city from the seeds left by their ancestors, cultivating and nurturing its trunks and boughs into the spectacle that it is today.

To an uninformed observer, little would be seen of the great city from the ground. Comprising 20 square miles of 3,500-year-old trees that reach more than 500 feet into the air, the city is nestled among intertwining living boughs that have been shaped to the needs of its denizens. Hollows within trunks form entire apartments for elven families, and reclaimed wood of the forest has been built into thoroughfares and platforms that support the various shrines, temples, and lodges of the Elder Council of the Green Realm.

The forest city towers over other surrounding trees that stretch for hundreds of miles in every direction. The primeval woodland within view of the city is well guarded by awakened trees, treants, and patrols of wild elves who race among the broad tree limbs as easily as one would stroll across a green carpet of rolling turf or sail the winds on the backs of giant eagles.

LODGES OF THE TRIBES OF THE WILD

Each of the Tribes of the Wild are represented with their own great lodge within the city. These lodges are built onto platforms high in the boughs of the most sacred and ancient trees of the primeval forest. Each lodge is kept by a druid initiated in the deep arts of nature. Warriors of each tribe born to the line of chieftains and chieftesses serve an honorarium of several decades within the lodges. Here, they are often engaged in challenges and games against other tribes to keep their skills sharp while learning diplomacy and respect for the other tribes of the Green Realm. Lord General Yerrian Giath, the supreme war chieftain of the Kingdom of the Green Realm and member of the Elder Council, oversees their training. Yerrian Giath is taller than most of his kin, and like Riar Harwood, shows obvious descendance from the old lines of Suomen Gron in his violet eyes and silvery hair that is striking in his rich chestnut face.

It is Yerrian's job to ensure that the young nobles of the lodges comport themselves as noble warriors, heroes, and guardians of the Green Realm against all threats.

HIGH TOWER OF SOLUS ATRALIIS

Arcane instruction is sought by those who are born with the touch of the ancient fey magic at the High Tower of Solus Atraliis. Grown from a massive redwood, the tower of Atraliis is kept by Lord Sorceress Milathiu Velhei, a nearly 300-year-old wild elf and a seeker of mysteries and keeper of arcane secrets. She and her initiates train those young elves born to the mark of the sorcerer to wield their power in protection of the forest and the unified tribes.

RELIGION

Within the city of Solis Alunaris stand great temples to Arialee and Darach-Albith. Arialee's temple is formed among boughs of an enormous white khooma tree. A statue of the goddess shaped from the living wood of the tree and crowned with hair of leaves of pure gold stands within a natural archway formed by entwined branches. The temple is kept by Caraeith Helias, priestess of the goddess and hierophant of the Sylvan City. Her circle is charged with the life and health of the eternal trees of the Sylvan City. She instructs the princes and princesses of the tribes in the care of the forest beyond the city, in listening to the life that it shares, and in the physical and metaphysical stewardship of the forest.

Directly across from this holy place is the open-air temple of Darach-Albith tended by Illieha Star-treader. Illieha is one of the last of his kind, a cleric of the old faith descended directly from the priests of the creator-god in the First Exodus. Faith in the ancient religion of Darach-Albith has dwindled greatly among most of the elves in the ages since the migration, but homage is paid as is its due. Illieha seems almost an albino to the young wild elves, save those who have had the honor of being allowed to visit the halls of Suomen Gron, who recognize in Illieha a likeness to the first born of the Elders. Illieha tends to few acolytes, and to those few who arrive every few decades in search of religious knowledge. Illieha serves on the Council of Elders, though he is prone to travel the astral plane battling on behalf of his god, and like others, ever searching for the lost goddess. Many of the nobles dwelling within the city also keep a shrine to Rialae-Aibaru, the lost goddess who forever searches in anguish for her missing child.

LOYALTIES AND DIPLOMACY

The various tribes of the Green Warden Nations keep embassies in the Sylvan City, for despite their differences of opinion, King Riar is committed to reconciliation with the northern nations. He knows that if Castorhage rises to prominence again, and the rumblings in the Cinderhame Mountains prove true, that it may require a unified kingdom to ensure the survival of both forest and elf alike.

GOVERNMENT

Despite being the seat of power for the Green Realms, the Sylvan City itself is administered by Mayor Varenth Illuene and is divided into administrative districts that ensure the care and protection of the trees and the folk who dwell among them. As has long been the tradition, the king appoints the mayor of the city from among the commoners of the tribes who gains the rank of noble upon completion of their century long term of service. Varenth has served for nearly 50 years and is popular among the lesser magistrates of the city's districts and the common folk. He is more frequently the face of the city than the king himself, though this has much to do with Riar's slow transition from elf to forest spirit. Due to the importance of his work, though not a noble, Varenth serves on the Council of Elders.

The mayor and district magistrates who still bear the honorific title of chieftain from the purely tribal days of the past manage the homes and shops of the common folk. Within the trunks are districts filled with artisans and crafters who prepare food, tool leather, and weave fine linen fabric. Others carve great works of art from the fallen wood of the forest. There are also bowyers, fletchers, vintners, perfumers, and confectioners among the ones who live in the various districts that line the trunks of the great trees.

MILITARY

Beyond the civilian districts that fill the trunks and line the branches are the more military districts, such as the Root District on the forest floor where the Knights of the Burled Crown keep watch along with the treants and other sylvan beings who are allied with the Throne of the Green Realm. Higher in the branches are the nests of giant eagles and hippogriffs in the Bough District. These beasts are ridden by elite Knights of the Wind who serve as scouts and bodyguards of the king.

MAJOR THREATS

There are currently few immediate threats to the city of Solis Alunaris due to its location deep within the forest and the layers of protection that the forest and the various elven fortresses provide. It therefore serves as a solid training ground and center for culture and debate among the various of the Unified Tribes.

LESSER CITIES AND FORTRESSES OF THE GREEN REALM

The forest is dotted with small settlements, too innumerable to mention. The most important castles of the kingdom are located at points where danger to the forest is recognized, or where a watchful eye must be kept over wild allies of the fey who have occasionally proven to be difficult friends.

SATAAMA VIERTA (SAH TAM AH VI-EER-TA)

The river port of Sataama Vierta rests on the western banks of the Gold Wine River in the shadow of the Emerald Mountains. The city is well defended and is one of the few outward signs of wild elf might outside of the actual shadows of the Great Akadonian Forest itself. The port is closed to most visitors and serves in a mostly coastal military capacity. There is a growing voice among the local pirate confederacies to band together and sack the city and establish it as a port of ingress to the Green Realm and its rumored wealth of magic and untapped natural resources.

Sataama Vierta was established as a naval outpost at the suggestion of the Hidden Ones in the Emerald Mountains. The grey elves pointed out to the rulers of Solis Alunaris that it was only a matter of time before pirates or forces loyal to the Brotherhood of Skulls based out of Braktu would someday find a way to spread their depravity across the sea or under it.

The wild elves set forth establishing the port and building a navy with plans and technology afforded them by their grey elf kin. The ships they built were of a sleek outrigger form that allowed swift travel along the southern coastline. The wild elves for their part are not overly fond of the sea, preferring the glens and meadows of the deep forest to the rage of waves, and so typically stay close to the shore. Their navy is supplemented by friendly fey water creatures and alliances with tritons of the southern waters and water elementals. Sataama Vierta is ruled by Lady Hennith Tonkhala, chieftain of the Swordfish Tribe. She is conversant in Sea Elf and the Aquan tongues and has a strong relationship with the fey folk of the sea. The port has a population of 4,000 with roughly half of the denizens serving aboard ships and a quarter more who serve as defenders of the city.

SATAAMA VASSEN (SAH TAM AH VASS-EN)

Ruled by Lord Otaha Mikkvalla and the Lady Rovanna Delfii on behalf of King Riar, the port of Sataama Vassen has a population of 5,000 and is a relatively new settlement in terms of the ages of the wild elves. It was established in 530 I.R. after riders of the Verdant Plains encountered an exploratory surveying party from Xha'en. The survey party was slaughtered, and their boats sunk before they could return to their homeland. The queen of the Green Realm at the time decreed that a port would be established that would protect the Green Realm from any new incursions on their western shores by the race of man. Called the Blue Eye of the Sea by the elves, Sataama Vassen is well hidden in the shadow of the North Steel Tongue Mountain Range. Like its sister settlement Sataama Vierta, this small naval port houses scout ships used by the elves to watch the coastline and warn of incursions of pirates or attempted encroachment from Xha'en or the Utterends into the lands claimed by the Green Realm. Sataama Vassen is maintained by the Dolphin and Whale tribes. The noble chieftains of Sataama Vassen have a treaty with sea elves and merfolk of the Caerulean Ocean who have agreed to warn them should any invading navy set its sights for the relatively calm shores of the Verdant Plains.

A small fleet of 20 fast and elegant warships calls this port home. These stealthy vessels patrol the coastline from south of the Utterends to Syldryll Vale. The ships of Sataama Vassen avoid interaction with the navies of Xha'en but attack any pirates who enter the Caerulean Ocean on sight.

LINN KOTHKAAN, CASTLE OF THE EAGLE

Linn Kothkaan is located in the northernmost point of the Northern Steel Tongue Mountains and serves as the ancestral tribal hold of the Eagle Tribe who are charged with observing the wide plains to the west of the Great Akadonian Forest and keeping a watchful eye over the northern coasts from any potential threats from Xha'en.

Linn Kothkaan is well fortified and was carved with the help of magic, elementals, and earthbound creatures to mimic the natural surroundings of the mountainside. The castle is garrisoned by 2,000 elves with an aerie containing several hundred giant eagles who serve as mounts and brethren to the tribe.

LINN TARK, CASTLE OF THE WATCH

Built to be indistinguishable from the surrounding forest, this castle sits on a wooded butte that overlooks the vastness of the Mud Coast.

Linn Tark is administered by the Hawks and houses 3,000 wild elves of the tribe. There are 200 winged hippogriffs stabled at the fortress whose riders roam the forest coast south of Linn Meriku and observe the lizard folk of the Mud Coast from afar to ensure they continue to focus their attentions to their own kinfolk in the Crescent Sea to the east and avoid any curiosity over the doings of the forest dwellers to the west.

LINN SYLDRYLL, CASTLE OF THE VALE

This castle stands at the north end of the Syldryll Vale between the Emerald Mountains and the Southern Steel Tongue Range. Linn Syldryll is the last line of defense in the vale before entry into the heart of the forest. The fortress, built like other wild elf castles to resemble the local terrain, also serves as the center for trade with the nomadic centaur tribes of the vale who have long allied themselves with their wild elf neighbors.

Linn Syldryll is maintained by Lord Laaksion, a member of the Horse Tribe and second cousin of the king. The fortress houses 2,000 wild elf knights who ride the powerful elven ponies that are raised for them by the centaur clans of the valley. Laaksion is a renowned horseman whose family has maintained the centaur and elf alliance for hundreds of years.

LINN MERIKU

This hidden castle 500 miles northeast of Solis Alunaris is a purely military facility built in the last century to maintain a vigilant eye on the Forest Coast, serving as a waystation between Linn Tark and the coastal elves of the Green Warden Nations to the north. The fortress has proximity to Bitter Island and informs the Council of Elders whenever that cursed island rises from the waves.

The castle keeps a small naval dock where sleek elven galleys ply the waters 50 miles out to sea, dissuading pirates and reporting on the navies of Castorhage and the Low Country. The fortress houses 2500 archers, 1500 cavalry, and a contingent of 150 sorcerers trained to burn the ships of sea born invaders. Land patrols roam the coast and stay with coastal tribes on a fairly regular basis.

THE EMERALD MOUNTAINS

Ruler: King Semmjon and Queen Adosha of the Emerald Mountains

Capital: Suomen Gron

Government: monarchy

Population: 4,000 (excluding seasonal pilgrims) (3,500 grey elves, 300 wild elves, 200 gnomes)

Monstrous: dire or giant animals native to the region (including but not limited to local breeds of bears, wolves, leopards, birds, tigers), giant eagles, non-evil plant-type creatures native to the region (any, but especially treants), pixies, satyrs, other non-evil fey, centaurs, unicorns, pseudodragons, rocs, perytons, silver, and gold dragons, and other temperate or subtropical forest-dwelling non-evil creatures.

Languages: Elven, Sylvan, Gnome

Religion: Arialee, Darach-Albith, Rialae-Aibaru

Resources: gold, silver, precious gems, magic.

Currency: barter and trade

Technology Level: Medieval/Renaissance

Blanketed by high alpine forests at the southern end of the Green Realm are the Emerald Mountains, which are known to the elves as Gora Harmyth. Here is the home of the near mythic grey elf kingdom that shares the mountains' name. The magnificent halls of their capital of Suomen Gron are seldom visited by denizens of the Green Realm, save for rare pilgrimages by nobles who would seek advice from their ancient forebears in times of travail. The grey elves of the Emerald Mountains are quiet free spirits when left to their own devices. Being more closely related to the pure essence of the Fey Realms than other elves, they have become near legend even among their own kin, who refer to them as the Hidden Ones or the Shining Ones. Indeed, they are rarely seen anymore because they have so deeply attuned themselves with the world of spirit, fey, and magic that many of them are on the verge of becoming one with the fey essence of the cosmos. Some of the Shining Ones spend centuries dwelling among the glades of fairy folk, only seldom taking time to return to the gleaming fortresses of the Suomen Gron to observe the happenings of the mortal realms or to take action against the resurgence of Vilik Strad. The Hidden Ones have a natural capacity for wielding the chaotic forces of raw magic and shaping it into the natural world around them as easily as a potter shapes clay. It was with the help of the grey elf wizards of the Emerald Mountains that the wild elf high lords of the Green Realm were able to raise the Cinderhame Mountains from the crust of the world and thwart the advance of their dark elf adversaries across the Talanos Peninsula in year 52 I.R.

HISTORY AND PEOPLE

The grey elves were the first of the children of Darach-Albith to voyage from their ancestral homeland on another plane to Boros, even before the First Exodus of the Elves. More arrived in the First Exodus in roughly the year –6484 I.R. along with others of their kin, ancestors of the wild elves and high elves. What drove the elves to cross over to Boros in this wave remains a mystery of which the grey elves — who alone of the elves may know the truth — will not speak. After coming to Boros, the grey elves and their progeny were little changed. But, particularly after a few generations had passed, the other elves seemed to take on aspects of their new homeland. Their strong skin and flashing eyes came to reflect the colors of their native forests, of which their spirits quickly became a living part. As they

matured and married, they conceived more quickly by the standards of the Shining Ones but lived shorter lives than the grey. Their lives were just as deeply in tune with the natural order of the world but were perhaps richer for the shorter time they had upon it. These changes to their kin were at first considered quaint and primitive by the grey elves, who loved them all the more for it. But their new differences did result in the two groups of elves growing apart. The Shining Ones for their part largely left their exuberant cousins to their own devices and relocated to a new home in the Emerald Mountains, only interfering when advice was asked or when their society was threatened with destruction. In these days, sometimes princes and princesses of the grey would marry into the rising noble houses of the other elves to enhance the richness of the Eldest bloodline among their kinfolk. The other elves quickly spread throughout the Great Akadonian Forest, which then spanned the length and breadth of the continent, and tended the ancient woodland as wardens and protectors. In the east, they built cities indistinguishable from the primeval forests. Unfortunately, many of those cities were destroyed or abandoned following the Hyperborean invasion and the massacre at Lake Crimmormere in – 91 I.R. As many elves fled west in the Second Exodus, they were welcomed by the grey elves into the Green Realm, who helped re-establish noble lines and serve as mediators as new lands were settled and tribes formed. From this time forward, the elves of the west who rejected Valenthlis became known as the wild elves.

The wild elves of the west came to enjoy a close relationship with the grey elf kind, which proved critical when they were forced to call upon grey elven aid to prevent an invasion of the Green Realm by the dark elves of Vilik Strad.

But after many years, once the survival of the wild elven lineage was ensured with the establishment of the Harwood line, the host of the grey elves at last retreated into the alpine peaks of the Emerald Mountains and their secretive palace fortress of Suomen Gron. For their part, they were happy to withdraw from the ambitions of elves, dwarves, and men. The grey elves now spend a majority of their time re-attuning themselves with the power of the Fey Realms. They may cross into the lands of the fey and dance with the faerie folk, or spend centuries focused in the deep study of arcane magic. Still others take to traveling unseen through the lands of their children as they survey the world as it has become. Over the last centuries, the Shining Ones have turned their eyes once again to the deeps beneath Vilik Strad and rumors of dark powers growing there in strength.

GOVERNMENT

The grey elves of Gora Harmyth are ruled by an ancient monarchy led by Semmjon and Adosha, king and queen of the Emerald Mountains. The pair are descended from the eldest lines of grey elven royalty from before the First Exodus and are loved and admired by their people. The duo has been married for over two centuries and are nearly 400 years old.

RELIGION

On the surface, the grey elves of the Emerald Mountains don't seem to truly have any religion at all, until one realizes that these long-lived beings believe themselves children of the divine, descended from the god Darach-Albith and the lost goddess Rialae-Aibaru. A marble temple to Darach-Albith stands in a mountain vale not far from Suomen Gron, as does another small shrine to the fey deity Arialee. Here on midsummer and midwinter the barriers to the Fey Realm become thin and allow the grey elves to refresh their living spirit through contact with their original homeland. In these festivals they are reminded of the Eldest and the day when all shall join again, dancing at the feet of Arialee in the land of the fey when none shall need take up bow or wand in defense of life and freedom ever again.

TRADE AND COMMERCE

The denizens of the Emerald Mountains have little need of trade as they sustain themselves with magic and the bounty of the forests, rivers, and mountains. They receive infrequent though valuable tribute from the lords of the Green Realm as is tradition and return tenfold the gifts they receive from the wild elves in the form of wisdom and magical reinforcement. They have been known to disguise themselves as young wild elves and to trade for ponies and grain from the tribes of the vale.

MILITARY

The grey elves of the Emerald Mountains are known for their exceptional skill at ancient wizardry. They make use of summoned forces to absorb attacks and use explosive invocations to blast through enemy ranks. In addition, many of the Hidden Ones are skilled swordsmen, and their knights are remembered in antiquity for their bravery and deftness of blade strikes. A unit of grey elves is adorned in supple armor and wields bows and thin-bladed swords of exceptional strength and balance. They are fearless in the face of supernatural foes. Were it not for their small numbers and their languorous spirit, the grey elven combination of powerful wizardry and dizzying blade-craft would undoubtedly grant them dominion over any of the lesser mortal races in the world. Of the population of the Emerald Mountains, three-fourths are capable of taking up arms or wands to combat any threat. Their equipment is considered fine to excellent and has a good chance of being enchanted. A cadre of well-trained knights who ride the winds on the backs of pegasi form the royal guard known as the Tuul Rasaja. These riders of Suomen Gron serve as messengers, scouts, and protectors of King Semmjon and Queen Adosha.

The grey elves forged alliances over the millennia with younger gold and silver dragons who make their homes in the roots of the Emerald Mountains, though they call upon their aid only in extremis, for even kindly dragons charge high prices for their services, and not all of their bills may be paid in gold and jewels.

MAJOR THREATS

The most imminent threat to the Emerald Mountains is its proximity to the Cinderhame Mountains. Riders of the Tuul Rasaja have noted movement in those old volcanic cones of fire giant fortresses, as well as signs of hobgoblins and trolls. Already, the wizards of Gora Harmyth wonder if the ancient magic that was once used to raise the mountains from the earth may need to be called upon again to collapse them to dust. Time will tell. What is known is that the dark elves of the high walled city of Vilik Strad have had thousands of years to plan their revenge against the Hidden Ones and their cousins in the Green Realm.

WILDERNESS AND ADVENTURE

The mountains are dangerous to those who are not welcome there. The Hidden Ones have earned that name for a reason. They keep a watchful eye over the passes and are well aware days in advance of any incursion into their sanctum. Should travelers manage to find one of their hidden tunnels or mountain passes, they are met first with conjured weather followed by summoned beings and magical constructs designed to turn interlopers away. Should unwelcome visitors be persistent, they are next met with a force of grey elves intent on dissuading any further exploration of their land.

THE FIVE CLANS OF THE HOOF

Capital: None
Notable Settlements: Linn Syldryll
Ruler: Five Clans of the Hoof
Government: Tribal
Population: 24,000 (20,000 centaurs, 4,000 wild elves)
Languages: Elvan, Sylvan, Druidic, some Common
Religion: Arialee, Cavacendo
Resources: horses, wool, bison
Currency: Green Realms coin, mixed
Technology Level: Stone Age to Medieval

HISTORY AND PEOPLE

The centaurs of the Five Clans of Hoof have dwelt among the Syldryll Vale grasslands that skirt the Green Realm for as long as they can remember. Their oral tradition dates back to the time before meeting the first elves when they were taught the language of the elven folk by the Shining Ones, who were kin and friend to other beings that had once dwelt together in the realm of the fey in the time before time. The first encounters between centaur and elf were not without their own conflict, as the elves were giving birth to their own customs and traditions, which were not always compatible with the untamed primal passions of the centaur clans. The centaur folk, in turn, were fascinated by these new forest lords and sometimes approached them inappropriately, especially when filled with the heady wine that the elves offered them as gifts of gratitude and friendship.

Festivals of peace and friendship occasionally ended in bloody skirmishes. Ultimately, the high lords of the Green Realm held a council with the chieftains of plain and prairie. Arialee and the Green Father were themselves called upon to intercede on behalf of the conflicting parties. A treaty was arranged between the clans of the hoof and tribes of the wood whereby the hoof lords would be master of the prairie and plain, and the wild elves would be master of the forest glen. They would trade in kind, but the hoof lords would promise to drink their wine only among their own folk and keep their hands to themselves whenever they were found in mixed company. In exchange, the elves would provide access to weapons of steel, wine (in moderation), and protection in time of need from raiders from the sea and the beast folk who wandered into their lands from the bowels of the mountains. This truce remains in force to this day. The wild elves learned much from the culture of the Hoof Clans and took up horsemanship and riding with the centaurs as their nomadic families crossed the plains from their ancient homeland in Syldryll Vale to as far north as the foothills of the Karthu Mountains. Boisterous and competitive, the centaurs of the vale have a deep love of the heady forest wine vinted by the wild elves and a desire for arrowheads and weapons of the lightweight steel forged at the foot of the Northern Steel Tongue Mountain range by the skilled elven craftsmen.

GOVERNMENT

Governance of the Hoof Clans of the Syldryll Vale, to the extent one can call it that, consists of a loose confederation of tribal councils. Each clan has a chieftain who is elected from among the tribal members. Typically, the clan chieftain is responsible for the safety of the clan and for mediating between clan members in the case of conflict, setting scouts, and negotiating with the wild elves or strangers encountered in the grasslands. Each chieftain is assisted by a tribal shaman, who is usually the strongest spellcaster from among the tribe. This shaman may be a druid, cleric, sorcerer, or warlock. Below the chieftain are a number of sub-chieftains, each of whom is generally responsible for 4–6 hunters, herdsman, or warriors from the clan. In addition, a sub-chieftain may a have specialized job such as hunting, gathering, scouting, or security.

A chieftain may be challenged by others of the tribe at any time, with each Hoof Clan choosing its own method of election. In some clans it is by vote, while in others it is determined by a race, and still others choose unarmed combat to resolve leadership issues. In times of war, a war chief may be nominated by a clan. This is typically the most experienced and fierce warrior that the tribe has, which may or may not be the clan chieftain.

During threat of a broader conflict, several of the Hoof Clans may join together and nominate a war chief as their general to command them in battle.

TRADE AND COMMERCE

The tribes trade horses, cattle, sheep, wool, grain, pottery, and ale among each other and to the wild elves. Luxury items and commodities sought by the centaurs are elven wine, steel weapons, and elven horn bows. The center for trade in the Syldryll Vale is located around Linn Syldryll, the fortress of the wild elves at the southern edge of the forest. The different Hoof Clans make general migratory stops at the fortress throughout the year and bring their trade goods to the elves and compete in contests of archery and engage in various games with their elven hosts.

RELIGION

The centaurs of the Hoof Clans follow an animistic religion with additional veneration of Arialee as mother of the fey races and Cavacendo, the god of the fire horses who taught their race the power of the torch and flaming arrow against foes from forest and from the sea.

MILITARY

The centaurs of the Hoof Clans are adept lancers and archers who are particularly skilled in light cavalry activities. They pursue hit-and-run tactics. They avoid bunching up in mass waves that could be defeated by magic until they whittle their enemy's numbers down to a point where they stand little chance of failure.

Their more advanced units would be best described horn bow armed archers or barbarians armed with lance and weighted club. These units are supported by naturalist spellcasters such as druids, sorcerers, or warlocks.

MAJOR THREATS

Major threats to the vale come from its proximity to the Cinderhame Mountains, where incursions of ogres, trolls, and hill giants have become more commonplace, as has the appearance of hobgoblin raiding parties that appear to have discovered a mountain pass from the High Barrens. To the west, occasional threats from young stone giants striking out from the deep mountain interior have been known to occur in the shadows of the Steel Tongue Mountains.

The centaurs raised awareness of these incursions from the Cinderhame to their elven allies in Linn Syldryll and scouts were dispatched to investigate. It seems to many that the long sleeping forces of Vilik Strad have awakened once more and that the drums of war will once sound in the Vale.

TANDRIL ISLAND

(Tan-Drill)
Capital: Trinidar
Ruler: Lord Commodore Levassier Elian
Government: high council
Population: 90,000 (with an additional 20,000 transient population passing through) (55,000 Castorhagi human, 20,000 Rhemian, 6,000 halfling, 5,000 half-orc, 3,500 half-elf, 500 other)
Monstrous: ogres, hobgoblins
Languages: Common
Religion: Loa
Resources: fishing, coffee, sugar, trade
Currency: Castorhage, Rhemian, Mixed
Technology Level: Medieval/Renaissance

HISTORY AND PEOPLE

Tandril Island was colonized in 2284 I.R. by the City-State of Castorhage as a forward base for expansion and colonization into the Great Akadonian Forest.

The city of Trinidar, once known as the Jewel of the Crescent Sea, was founded at a natural harbor on the north coast of the island. Trade brought foreigners from other seafaring nations as well as indentured servants and slaves from the Castorhagi's wars of expansion. Within 40 years, using Tandril Island as a base of operations, Castorhage began the settlement of the Forest Coast through the establishment of penal colonies and work camps. In the end, the colonization of the mainland proved disastrous for the rulers of Castorhage, who were summarily defeated by the wild elf defenders in the Forest Coast War (also called the Mortgage War) that ended in 2373 I.R.

Despite the eventual loss of the Forest Coast colonies, Tandril Island and the port of Trinidar remained critical to the power structure of the Castorhage throne. Repeated attempts were made by Trinidar nobles and governors to increase their share in the wealth created through the island. These entreaties were most typically ignored by Castorhagi monarchs, who as usual demanded absolute fealty on the part of their colonies. Over time, the island's leaders found more and more ways to thwart Castorhage's efforts to collect taxes and otherwise command obedience from their colony, becoming increasingly wealthy in the process. By 2854 I.R., Trinidar was independent of Castorhage in all but name only. Efforts on the part of Castorhage to regain control were repeatedly thwarted by the Grand Duchy of Reme. When Castorhage lost the Short War with Reme in 3240 I.R., Trinidar took advantage of the situation and formally declared its independence. This resulted in the arrival of a new generation of Rhemian settlers who mixed with the local population and produced a folk who are as distinct and different as Rhemians are from the folk of Castorhage.

TRINIDAR AND THE INTERIOR

The city of Trinidar makes up 70% of the island's population. The port proper is the focus of the city, with the Governor's Keep standing on a bluff that overlooks the harbor. The naval garrison occupies the north side of the harbor and a lighthouse stands on the south side that guides shipping to the civilian docks. The city's architecture reflects the South Coastal style, being made from wooden timbers with grand shuttered windows and colorful stucco. In the time since it was founded, Trinidar has grown as a center for trade in the Western Crescent Sea, affording Rhemian naval ships and merchants a ready and welcoming port. The rest of the inland is rich with volcanic earth that lends itself to the growth of lush native crops. A number of Trinidarian nobles own various plantations located inland along the slopes and shores. These plantations typically house several hundred workers and a personal complement of guardsmen and overseers numbering 20–30 heavily armed individuals.

RELIGION

Tandril shares some of the darkness of its original founding homeland, and many of the gods of Castorhage continue to be worshiped here, along with the (sometimes unsavory) festivals dedicated to those gods. As an island whose lifeblood is trade, however, it has a fairly liberal view on religions, and many gods of folk from afar also have temples in the city. The city of Trinidar, in fact, possesses the only known major public temple on Akados dedicated to the worship of Loa of the Aizanes-Tulita, an island group west of Libynos far to the east.

TRADE

The Port of Trinidar holds a special place in the area of trade along the western Crescent Sea. The city is known as a place where ill-gotten gains can be exchanged with few questions. Smuggled items are quickly re-branded for a "fair" excise fee and immediately placed on merchant vessels that often return them to their port of origin. For this reason, the city is popular with pirates plying from as far off as the Razor Coast and the Utterends to those closer to home based in the foul city state of Braktu. Rhemian nobles turn a blind eye to the less savory aspect of Trinidaran trade and religion so long as the sliding scale of profit and geographical power remains in their favor and puts Castorhage at a disadvantage.

The Port of Trinidar is also home to a chapterhouse of the Imperial Mercantile League, where its mercenary members plot out risky ventures on the high seas in search of plunder and wealth at any cost. The league's offices are in an otherwise nondescript warehouse at one end of the docks and houses a private club for members as well. Denoted by their Sphinx of Boros tattoos, the league's locals constitute a small but critical percentage of non-military sailors who claim Trinidar as their home port. Their power in the city comes less from their numbers than their wealth and knowledge. The island's rich plantations produce foodstuffs — including sugar, rum, and rich coffee grown in its mountainous interior — that are much sought after on the eastern mainland and provide cash crops and a steady stream of homegrown revenue for the denizens of Tandril.

Government

The Port of Trinidar is ruled by a high council that is presided over by the Lord Commodore of Port Trinidar and attended by the Tradesman's Guild of Tandril. The high council seats 10 members, including seven nobles descended from the ancient families of Trinidar and three Rhemian transplants who are careful not to overexert their positions, though they do tend to vote in a unified block. The Tradesman's Guild is composed of shopkeepers, landlords, wholesalers, shipwrights, and tradesmen, including a representative of the Imperial Mercantile League who owns his position largely through intimidation of other members of the Tradesman's Guild. Membership in the guild requires fairly hefty dues, meaning the poorest of local businesses often group their coin together to back a single member who works for all of their collective interests. The lord commodore is appointed by the high council, though bribes from the Tradesman's Guild and the league go a long way in influencing the vote. The requirement for appointment is that the candidate be of blood descendancy from the original noble founders of the island. Furthermore, the lord commodore must have been a captain in the Trinidaran Navy with no fewer than 10 years of experience on the high seas.

The current lord commodore is Levassier Elian, a middle-aged, square-jawed man with iron gray hair, the scarred hands of a swordsman, and the eyes of a hawk.

Military

The Trinidaran military trains at the Naval Academy of the Crescent Sea, which offers training in seamanship, close-quarters combat, and a school of magic emphasizing crowd control tactics. Most sailors, marines, and magic-users are required to perform six months to a year of training before being sent out on their first patrol.

Trinidar's navy serves two purposes. It is first and foremost designed to intercept and destroy warships that would invade or otherwise threaten the port itself. Its secondary purpose is to serve as military escorts for wealthy merchants who pay a high premium for the protection provided by their heavily-armed warships.

Trinidaran marines wear studded leather and carry light crossbows and cutlasses. They are adept at close-quarters fighting and are trained in the use of the most modern ship- and land-borne siege equipment. These units are backed by wizards who pay off their training in service to Trinidar. There is usually at least one wizard per 20 standard marines.

Trinidaran soldiers work mostly in seeing to the defenses of the port from invaders and threats both monstrous and magical. Their shore patrol is renowned for its toughness and holds a long tradition of maintaining order among the various sailors who make port there, be they navies of visiting nations, pirates, or merchant marines looking to burn through their pay in the city's many taverns, gaming parlors, and pleasure houses. Entrance to the shore patrol requires a minimum of a year at sea in the service of the Trinidaran fleet.

The Trinidaran shore patrol wear chainmail hauberks, and are armed with saps, longswords, and shields. They swap weapons depending on the threat they face. Shore patrolmen who keep watch on the walls trade their clubs for heavy crossbows.

Major Threats

Trinidar's major threat comes from Castorhage. The royalty of the Blight would very much like to see Tandril back in its colonial empire, though they recognize that such an event would never be tolerated by Reme. As a result, their competition with Trinidar can be fierce and merciless, and many would, if they can't have Tandril, prefer to see it left in ashes. Other threats include the wild elves of the Green Realm and the Green Warden Nations, who would strike the denizens of Tandril Island from the map before it could again be used as a point of invasion against their beloved forests.

Reference Source: The Blight

The Mud Coast

Capital: Ajsak Telek
Ruler: High Priest Yax Telek, servant of Qoatl Boax
Government: tribal
Population: 300,000 lizardfolk, 25,000 (?) tsathar
Monstrous: dire or giant animals native to the region (including but not limited to local breeds of insects, snakes, birds, dinosaurs, crocodiles, alligators, catoblepas, hippopotami, fish, plant-type creatures native to the region (assassin vines, shambling mounds, gallows tree, witch trees, awakened plants/trees, awakened animals, bog men, black and green dragons, marsh jelly, wyverns, swamp trolls, green hags, locathah, sahuagin, frog, froghemoth, fen witches, hags, and other temperate and sub-tropical marsh, swamp and sea creatures native to the region
Languages: Draconic, Aquan
Religion: Tiamat; some Behemoth
Resources: fish, medicinal herbs, rare spices, pirate treasure
Currency: barter, gemstones
Technology Level: Stone Age (villages), Bronze Age (Ajsek Telek)

History and People

Long ago, the vast salt swamp that makes up the majority of the interior of the Mud Coast was at the bottom of the Crescent Sea until some unknown event caused the waters to recede. During what came to be known as the Age of Dragons, lizardfolk moved into this region and established temples and cities within the swampland. Some came to worship the Mother of Dragons while others sought guidance from Behemoth. They made pacts with great and powerful beings who granted them access to sorcery and power over the very fabric of the world. Eventually, those of the Cult of the Mother of Dragons became twisted by the powers they had summoned, and in the name of the Mother commenced the wholesale slaughter and sacrifice of intelligent life around them. At first, this meant any of their distant kin serpentfolk who wandered into the swamps and locathah who laid their eggs upon the muddy shores. But in the end, the lizardfolk turned upon themselves in a mass sacrifice of their own folk that left their civilization in ruin toward the end of the Age of Dragons some 400,000 years ago. Fallen into barbarism, the descendants of the original lizardfolk remain in the Mud Coast and dwell among the ruins of their fallen civilization. They harry ships foolish enough to weigh anchor off their coast and continue the ancient tradition of tormenting the locathah. Until recently, the greatest threat to the lizardfolk has been themselves. Eking out a brutal existence, the various tribes have long warred with each other, taking slaves of their own kind and practicing cannibalism in order to steal the life essence of their enemies. But less than a hundred years ago, a new Cult of Tiamat arose among the lizardfolk in the swamps, and new rituals to the Queen of Dragons have been wrought. The cult's prayers were heard and recently Tiamat sent her draconic emissary, Qoatl Boax, to the ruins of the ancient city of Ajsak Telek to serve as god-king of the lizard folk in her name. Upon his arrival the priests of Tiamat set about unifying the disparate tribes of the scale and tooth, slaughtering those who would not swear allegiance to the new rulers of Ajsak Telek. Qoatl Boax has overseen reconstruction of the city's defenses. He has also ordered exploration of the ruins of the ancient cities in search of forbidden artifacts and ancient hieroglyphs that — once deciphered — may reveal long-lost secrets. Unified and with newfound strength, the lizard folk venture as far inland as the edges of the tree line where their expeditions die in a rain of arrows or they find themselves beset by packs of wolves, prides of leopards, or picked to the bones by waves of giant hawks. Undeterred, the sorcerer priests of Ajsak Telek are merely testing the strength of the elves, much like a tiger tests the bars of its cage.

The lizardfolk are not the only race that calls the Mud Coast home. Tribes of tsathar hide deep in the swamps and worship their dark god in areas so desolate that even the lizardfolk don't venture there.

GOVERNMENT

More than half of the lizardfolk who dwell in the Mud Coast live in the swampland in one of a dozen or so tribes, each led by a powerful chieftain who is usually a barbarian, warlock, druid, or sorcerer. They live lives not so very different from other rustic folk, with the majority of chores involving the gathering of food and protecting the tribe from trolls, catoblepas, shambling mounds, vegepygmies, hags, and other dangerous denizens of the swamplands known to prey upon the lizardfolk. Closer to Ajsak Telek, governance is far more organized, with Qoatl Boax as the supreme authority and Yax Telek, the Mouth of the Dragon, as the wyrm's second in command. Below those two, various chieftains are given authority over territories near the capital (or, in a few cases, more distant areas of strategic import or that contain ruins to be explored), including the semi-settled lizardfolk in their area. The chieftains also act as military leaders with a certain number of warriors under their command. All positions of authority, including subchieftains and warrior leaders, are appointed by those directly above them, though Qoatl Boax has the authority to appoint or remove anyone at his whim.

RELIGION

The lizardfolk in the far-flung tribes along the fringes of the Mud Coast practice a form of animism that is very reptile-centric in nature, looking to crocodilians, monitor lizards, and similar beasts that resemble themselves. Increasingly, however, the Cult of Tiamat has spread, and the influence of the Queen of Dragons is growing by the day. This is particularly the case near Ajsak Telek where Qoatl Boax brooks no challenge to his mistress. Some few lizardfolk look to Behemoth but do so largely in secret.

The worship of Tiamat demands sacrifices, and the altars of the newly rebuilt pyramids of Ajsak Telek run with the blood of the lizardfolk's victims once more. Bands of hunters from the city now stalk the coastal waters for locathah and anchored merchant or pirate vessels. Others hunt along the edge of the timberline delineating their territory from the Green Realm in search of unsuspecting wild elves. In lieu of prisoners, the lizardfolk are known to slaughter unaffiliated tribes in mass sacrifices or even volunteer members of their own brood to ensure the favor of the Queen of Dragons.

TRADE AND COMMERCE

The lizardfolk of the mud banks seldom trade with anyone. Much of their gear is made up of stone and leather, metals that such as bronze and copper that resist rust, or sharpened bone. This is not to say that equipment possessed by the dwellers of Ajsak Telek are not sophisticated in other ways and means, or that their weapons are any less deadly in skilled hands.

Upon the arrival of Qoatl Boax, weapons and technology have taken on a decidedly more advanced nature, as vaults are uncovered from the ruins filled with weapons of the ancients. These weapons have been awarded to Qoatl Boax's most faithful servants. These include axes and maces of sturdy bronze, and javelins tipped with a rust-less iron alloy that supplement the churt missiles hurled by the atlatl of their coastal brethren. Still, the denizens of Ajsake Telek dig deeper as their excavation continues, bent on finding the fabled war bows of the ancients. The lizardfolk are aware of more advanced weaponry, having been subjected to it by pirates and navies that have assaulted their coastal villages, and would certainly be interested in acquiring such weapons should the opportunity present itself.

MILITARY

Since the ascendency of High Priest Yax Telek and the arrival of Qoatl Boax, the lizardfolk of Ajsake Telek have been organized into military units and have begun training in advanced combat techniques.

Below each chieftain are a number of expert warriors called kochatl. Each kochatl commands four experienced soldiers called popatl, each of whom in turn commands eight fighters known as tzitzi tmati. In addition, 100 kochatl (along with the corresponding number of popatl and tzitzi tmati) directly serve Qoatl Boaz in Ajsak Telek.

Ajsak Telek itself is further protected by the Chosen of Tiamat known as the qoatl tmati. These elite knights are fighters and sorcerers trained in more orthodox methods of combat than their barbarian cousins who dwell in the outer villages. They are often heavily armed with bronze weapons and enchanted items, and mix potions from the abundant resources of the swamps around them.

Thus far, the newly organized forces of the lizardfolk have only been tested in lesser combat where they move against villages or raiding parties into the Green Realms in search of weapons and magic.

MAJOR THREATS

Thick sludge and muddy swamps, with their clouds of mosquitos and biting flies, make for an unattractive locale to most not otherwise native to the Mud Coast. As such, the largest threats to the Mud Coast are internal, from the hidden enclaves of tsathar, or beasts and other hazards found there, such as dinosaurs, flesh-eating bacteria, piranha, stirges, and the hags who keep their covens among the muddy backwaters.

WILDERNESS AND ADVENTURES

The Mud Coast itself is a vast wilderness of thick mud and a mangrove swamp that is home to a variety of threats and challenges. There are still many ruins that have not yet been uncovered, and it is believed that a gate to the Styx is hidden there where the waters run directly from the Mouth of Tsathogga. A rumored temple to this malevolent Frog God is believed to be kept by tsathar monks somewhere in the trackless wastes. The masters of Ajsake Telek would like to see it conquered and its secrets stolen for the greater glory of Tiamat.

EARLDOM OF BORSS

Capital: Borss
Ruler: Earl Harald Borss-Evey
Government: Earldom
Population: 61,000 (50,000 Foerdewaith, 5,500 mountain dwarf, 5,000 halfling, 500 half-elf)
Monstrous: bears, sea lions, wolves, dire wolves, wild boars, lizardfolk, possible dragons
Languages: Common
Religion: Foerdewaith pantheon
Resources: mercenaries, fishing, shipping, dairy, privateers
Currency: mixed, Foere
Technology Level: Renaissance

The Earldom of Borss is the farthest land that still swears fealty to the Foerdewaith crown at Courghais and consists of the southern portion of the island of West Talon. The Earldom, and specifically its capital of Borss, are recognized as a safe haven by Foere merchants who ply the southern Crescent Sea and the waterways feeding trade along the southwest portion of the continent.

HISTORY AND PEOPLE

Originally the Hyperborean Province of West Talon, Borss became an earldom of Foere in 2812 I.R., as that kingdom expanded throughout Akados.

Though the Kingdom of Foere diminished long ago, the earls of Borss continue to find it favorable to remain loyal to the Court of Courghais to avoid interference from Castorhage. This makes Borss a favorable port for those who seek to avoid the dangers of Castorhagi influence in the southern seas.

A small but well respected and wealthy population of mountain dwarves dwells within their own enclave in the city of Borss. Many are descendants of the army that King Col of the Ironskull Great Mountain Clan from the Blackrock Mountains brought to the island in a failed assault on the Dread Dragon Temple. Many still long to avenge the death of the king and are known to hire adventurers with the purpose of testing the strength of the Dread Dragon Temple and seeking a way to destroy it.

The earls of Borss, for their part, leave the Dragon Heights alone. They have not felt the breath of a dragon in centuries and have no interest in stoking the fires that burn in the belly of old wyrms.

The city of Borss holds a small population of halflings from the Low Country, transplants who work as merchants and sailors to negotiate trade between the two regions and beyond. Other populations of note include a group of half elves feeling the pull of their elven side who long to catch a glimpse of the Green Realm, though to their sorrow they are not welcome among the wild elves of the deep forests. Many of the half elves serve in Borss as sailors, scouts, interpreters, and guides.

Religion

Natives of the earldom are generally members of the High Church of Foere, and temples to Stryme, Tyre, and Sefagreth in the city are well-attended.

Bishop Otto VanDeurer, a worshipper of Sefagreth, is the ranking ecclesiastical leader in the earldom and has the ear of Earl Harald. His advice has been crucial in helping the earl rapidly build his fortunes. Common folk of the earldom pay their respects to the Foere gods during their various seasonal rituals, with congregations of warriors paying homage to Tyr and Stryme and demonstrating their skill at arms in seasonal tournaments that are popular among the locals.

Trade and Commerce

The economy is largely based on shipping, fishing, and providing escort to ships plying the waterways through the Mouth of Akados onward to the southwestern coastline. Local merchant houses and foreign merchants who seek to establish a presence in Borss must execute a contract with the earl, who grants a charter in return for a percentage of the profits from any shipping venture.

The earl has banned the Imperial Mercantile League from operating within the earldom. The earl has begun to charter private captains with their own ships as privateers to hunt and destroy members of the Brotherhood of Skulls. This has brought the ire of the buccaneers who have alerted the brotherhood's other strongholds, making a war between the two forces increasingly likely.

Loyalty and Diplomacy

The earldom is on friendly terms with the Grand Duchy of Reme, the Kingdom of the Vast, the Principality of Olduvar, the Duchy of Mains, Bottomborough, and most of the coastal cities south of Castorhage. They are openly neutral to Castorhage, though secretly unfriendly, and work to avoid Castorhagi influence from creeping into their port.

The earldom's proximity to Vilik Strad, Braktu, and the Mud Coast is of increasing concern. Their warships seem to fight an unending battle against the fleet of Brotherhood of Skulls' pirates operating out of Braktu, who keep hidden bases in Treachery Bay. Quietly, the earl is investigating the cost and potential for success of an assault on Braktu to destroy the port and degrade the city-state's ability to harass trade.

Government

The earldom is a domain of the Kingdom of Foere, and all Foerdewaith laws apply here. As the local vassal of the Court at Courghais, Earl Harald rules, with the advice of his inner council which consists of his son Harald Borss-Evey II, Bishop VanDeurer, and Vice Admiral Anslaugh Vanwyken, known as "Iron Arms" for his thick forearms. Viscount Dejark Seablade, ruler of Kamis, affords his fealty to Earl Harald, and is the second-wealthiest and most powerful man in the earldom, after only Harald himself.

The earl also claims the fealty of four sea-lords who have chartered holdings within the earldom.

Military

Soldiers of the earldom are led by Earl Harald himself, while his fleet of a dozen armed carracks and twice that number of support ships is led by Vice Admiral Anslaugh. Half of the warships are out to sea at any given time providing merchant escort, with the other half plying the waterways close to port in patrol capacity or in drydocks for repair.

The city watch is administered by the harbormaster of the city watch, who has a keep near the docks that serves as the watch headquarters and city jail.

Major Threats

The Earldom of Borss is far from the center of Foere power in Courghais. As a result, it has to maintain local strength to protect itself from threats, since any assistance from the rest of the kingdom would be long in coming. Also for that reason, relationships with those who might be able to aid Borss, such as Reme, are nurtured by the earl. The greatest threat to the earldom comes from the denizens of the Talanos Peninsula, and in particular Braktu and the Brotherhood of Skulls, with whose ships the earl's navy does frequent battle. Other pirates on the Crescent Sea pose risks to those who use the port of Borss. And Castorhage remains a continuing concern, as the ruler of the Blight finds the presence of this outpost of Foere to be a thorn in his side.

Kamis, City of

Ruler: Viscount Dejark Seablade
Government: feudal
Population: 8500 (6,000 Foerdewaith, 2,000 mountain dwarf, 500 halfling)
Technology Level: Renaissance

Viscount Dejark Seablade is directly descended from Jarkun Seablade, a famous reaver and privateer who was granted the holding by the seventh earl of Borss after singlehandedly sinking three Castorhagi warships that were attempting to blockade the city of Borss.

Jarkun made good use of the money he made from privateering and investing, and his holding became greater than any of the other sea lords who served under Earl Hervesti. Soon a walled town rose up around his ever-growing keep. The Seablade clan has proven its loyalty to the earls of Borss time and again and were granted a viscounty within the earldom for their service. The viscounty has been given semi-autonomous status within the earldom out of respect for the Seablades (and also due to the fact that a conflict with the Seablades would be at best costly, and at worst disastrous, to the earldom).

Dejark's lords command four warships and have a contingency of 10 support ships. At least one warship is in Kamis' harbor at any given time with others participating in patrols on behalf of the earldom or on privateering assignment in behalf of the viscount.

Braktu, City-State of

(Brack-Too)
Ruler: High Horn Docefris
Government: theocracy
Population: 70,500 (30,000 goblin, 15,000 orc, 10,000 half-orc, 5,000 mixed-ethnicity human, 5,000 half-ogres and ogrillons, 500 drow)
Monstrous: various undead, hill giants, ogres, ogrillons
Languages: Orc, Goblin, Giant, Troll
Religion: Orcus
Resources: mercenary armies, piracy
Currency: mixed
Technology Level: Dark Ages

The city-state of Braktu sits on the Barren Coast of the Talanos Peninsula beneath the looming escarpment of the High Barrens, some 500 miles away from the shadowy walls of Vilik Strad. Those approaching the city from the sea are met with the terrifying sight of a series of monolithic demon faces carved into the side of towering rock walls. The largest of these carved demon faces is over 120 feet tall and can be clearly seen from nearly two miles out to sea. The face bears the likeness of a fiendish horned goat with its mouth outstretched as if it vomited forth the chaotic tumble of fortresses, buildings, towers, crumbling walls, and destitute hovels below it and surrounding the foul-smelling harbor. Braktu is ruled by a mad theocracy of death worshippers dedicated to the Demon Lord Orcus. It is surmised by some that the dead within Braktu outnumber the living, and if that is true, the High Horn of Orcus and his priests may command one of the largest armies of the dead in all of the Lost Lands.

HISTORY AND "PEOPLE"

The city was founded sometime between 500 and 700 I.R., but by who and for what reason remains largely a mystery. The city has a large population of orcs and ogres, as well as humans and humanoids of blended heritage descended from captured shipwreck survivors and a slave market maintained by the Brotherhood of Skulls, as well as migrations of people back and forth to Carcass on the Razor Sea. It is possible that independent tribes who broke away from Vilik Strad's sphere of influence after the cataclysm that brought the Cinderhame Mountains up from the bowels of Boros settled here as well. None know the truth, and few truly care.

Regardless of its origin, the city has flourished after its own fashion as a center for piracy, slave trade, and other darker mysteries on the southern coast of the Talanos Peninsula since its inception.

Braktu keeps an uneasy alliance with Vilik Strad. Neither trusts the other, yet both know a war between them would be disastrous for their goals, many of which share several of the same ends.

At one point in time, the High Altar of Orcus was located in Braktu, though that season has long passed, and the favor of the Lord of the Dead has moved back to Rappan Athuk, the legendary Dungeon of Graves on eastern Akados. As a consequence, a fierce rivalry exists between those of Orcus' priesthood that were trained in Braktu and those who rise from the pits of Rappan Athuk. Indeed, High Horn Docefris refuses to acknowledge emissaries from Rappan Athuk as authentic to the cause of the Lord of the Dead.

Braktu is overrun with hordes of undead. Entire districts are populated with ghouls, ghasts, and zombies (infectious and otherwise). It is believed that one of the city's many charnel houses is in fact a gateway to Styx where the Necropolis of Ankev itself can be accessed. The less intelligent undead are subservient to the living in all ways, and a steady stream of captives brought in by boats captained by the Brotherhood of Skulls ensures that the more intelligent dead have a fair amount of fresh flesh to feast upon.

RELIGION

Braktu is steeped in the worship of Orcus, though some tribes of hobgoblins and goblins in the city also pay homage to their paternal deity Snuurge and keep altars to him within their lairs. Within the city, the chief priests and necromancers of Orcus maintain retinues of dozens of zombies or other lesser undead, with stronger undead such as ghouls and their ilk as household thralls and guardians.

Monthly mass sacrifices to the Lord of the Dead take place during the ritual of the horned moon. There prisoners brought on ships of the Brotherhood of Skulls await their cursed fate. Some are executed by the priests of Orcus before his altar and raised immediately as fresh fiends of the undead. Others are led like cattle through stockyard pens to slathering masses of ghouls and other creatures where they are torn asunder for the entertainment of the living denizens of this municipality of mayhem.

TRADE AND COMMERCE

Braktu's economy is principally based on trade in the sale of undead armies and the importation of living prisoners. Would-be warlords and necromancers from around Akados seeking ready-made warriors to fill

out their armies or defend their strongholds know that such forces can be had for a price in the city of Braktu. Other revenue is generated from the mining of bitumen and phosphorus from the walls of the plateau. Among thriving ventures in the City of Ten Thousand Skulls are a chapterhouse of the Underguild, the Brotherhood of Skulls' Slave Market, the Necromancers' Market, and various mercenary tribes of orcs, hobgoblins, and humans of the plateau willing to sell their swords to well-paying would-be generals.

UNDERGUILD CHAPTERHOUSE

Undead allies of the Brotherhood of Skulls, the Underguild keeps a chapterhouse in the city of Braktu. The Dead Prince Evoine of Cailin Lee presides over the chapterhouse, which is a gaming hall popular with pirates, slavers, hobgoblins, bandits, and other generalized scum of the High Barrens who come down to the shore for a good time. Dead Prince Evoine has been a vampire for 400 years, having been chased from Olduvar after rising from the grave and slaughtering several of his kinfolk. With naught but a coffin of dirt from his own grave, he booked passage to the Duchy of Borss. Before the ship could make Borss, he caused it to wreck in sight of pirates, who brought him (and the other survivors of the wreck) to Braktu. Before long, Evoine managed to acquire enough coin to buy an interest with the Underguild and has run the chapterhouse ever since.

NECROMANCERS' MARKET

Necromancers from across the Crescent Sea often make a pilgrimage to the City of Ten Thousand Skulls for training in the dark arts of the dead. Several powerful necromancers call the city home and accept apprentices from among these pilgrims. Material components required for casting a variety of necromantic spells can be found in the city, as well as such components needed to craft permanent necromantic magic items. The market also provides access to permanent common undead for those who would have use for their services.

BROTHERHOOD OF SKULLS' SLAVE MARKET

The Slave Market and a portion of the docks of the city are managed by the pirate confederation known as the Brotherhood of Skulls. The brotherhood accept death as a part of their daily business and as such pay homage to Orcus, though not all of their number are outright worshippers of the Bloated Goat. The Brotherhood of Skulls ply the Strait of Praeis, the Mouth of Akados, Treachery Bay, the Barren Coast, and as far off as Tywyl Bay. They seek out merchant ships, transports, and small, lightweight warships that they can outfit and add to their pirate fleet.

The brotherhood brings their prisoners back to Braktu for sale to the high horn and his priests or to be bid over by the various factions of orcs, hobgoblins, and goblins who call the city home.

Captain Griego Aiello is a burly half-orc sorcerer that now manages the slave pits for the Brotherhood and sits upon their captains' council. The brotherhood keeps a half-dozen ships near harbor and has a dozen more out to sea plying the straits at any given time.

LOYALTY AND DIPLOMACY

Braktu is a self-contained city-state owing no particular loyalty to anyone save its rulers' blind devotion to the Lord of the Dead. The city does, however, have diplomatic ties to Vilik Strad due to their proximity to one another. Braktu's priesthood does not fear the dark elves of the walled city, as they have an army of undead at their beck and call, and nearly as many demons on retainer to do their bidding should the dark elves contemplate an invasion.

GOVERNMENT

Braktu is a theocracy dedicated to Orcus. The high priest of Braktu is High Horn Docefris, and the Horned Hierarchy ordain rules from the Demon Temple-Tombs carved into the rock face of the plateau wall. Most business with the Brotherhood of Skulls or the Underguild is assigned via personal contract with Docefris' inner circle of bishops. Decisions begin and end with Docefris, who serves as patriarch and

High Horn of Orcus in Braktu. Docefris claims to confer directly with Orcus (which he does … in a manner of speaking) on all matters.

MILITARY

Death-priests of Braktu command squads of common undead and units of orcs, hobgoblins, and, depending on their rank and power, ogres and trolls. These priests are organized in a hierarchy of deacons, protopriests, bishops, and metropolitans ending in Docefris himself. The bishops and beyond command their own demonic hosts in battle when needed. Despite his city's alliance with the Brotherhood of Skulls, Docefris recently commissioned several triremes each capable of carrying a complement of 200. His intent is to fill the holds with infectious undead and beach the ships near the shores of civilized lands where the spread of the undead may hasten the re-entry of Orcus, resurrected in Arvonliet's Apocalypse.

The city is unsure if it can count on the Brotherhood of Skulls as an ally against any seaborn invasion. They know that the brotherhood can be paid to ferry mercenary forces to other locations. Docefris' bishops expect that the brotherhood will do whatever it can to ensure its own survival. As a result, the priesthood garrisons their own mercenary armies of orcs, hobgoblins, and more powerful monsters in a manner that prevents the brotherhood from cutting and running if faced with a serious threat against the city.

MAJOR THREATS

Though an uneasy alliance exists between them for now, the dark elves of Vilik Strad could pose a serious threat to Braktu were they to find a reason to attack. Additionally, the growing naval and financial might of the earl of Borss and his allies could someday be turned against the City of Ten Thousand Skulls in the form of a new crusade. Should any such threat materialize, the priesthood of Braktu would be forced to empty their tombs of the dead, and in the mind of Docefris, begin the doomsday his visions have always promised. For the time being, the ships of Sataama Vierta and the Green Realm are no match for the pirates of the Brotherhood of Skulls. Were the elves of the Green Realm to become a threat to the port of Braktu, they could seek assistance from Vilik Strad, though the priesthood would be very reluctant to do so. Any such assistance would come with a price, and that price could affect the hierarchy of power not only in the Lost Lands, but also in the far reaches of the dark planes.

VILIK STRAD, THE DARK CITY

Capital: Vilik Strad
Ruler: Her Unholiness Queen Arabella Nightweave
Government: theocratic monarchy
Population: 1,751,500 (300,000 orc, 300,000 goblin, 250,000 drow, 200,000 gnoll, 200,000 hobgoblin, 200,000 kobold, 200,000 ogres, 100,000 bugbear, 1,000 hill giant, 500 fire giant)
Languages: Dark Elf, Under-Common, Abyssal, Common
Religion: demon worship
Resources: precious metals, jewels, mining, slaves, magic
Currency: mixed
Technology Level: Renaissance and other

This massively fortified citadel on the eastern tip of the High Barrens has a long and malevolent history. Its hundred-foot-high walls are carved from smooth black basalt, but it is said to be the citadel's heart that gives it its name as the Dark City. Vilik Strad is the only known major surface enclave of drow in Akados. The shadows of its high walls and the general miasma that hangs over the High Barrens shields them sufficiently from the sun to operate on the surface. Said to be an actual dark elf remnant of the Age of Strife, Vilik Strad has stood on this clifftop for as long as even the wild elves of the Green Realm can remember. It is entirely possible that it is the remains of one of the Doomspires from the time of the Gods' War.

Vilik Strad is home to thousands of drow, but they are substantially outnumbered by a vast host of slave and servant races. Orcs, ogres,

bugbears, gnolls, and giants are abundant in the city as are many other Under Realms' races that the drow have recruited to their cause.

It is said (incorrectly) that the powerful sorcerers of Vilik Strad caused the sinking of the Foerdewaith fleet of the Third Great Crusade in 3173 I.R. It is also said by some that Vilik Strad sent the Singed Man who took over the Duchy of Kear and created so much carnage in western Foere.

The high walls of the city's Overworks are heavily guarded by bands of ogres, giants, trolls, and bugbears, with entire towers set with reserve forces of hobgoblins. Its many gleaming, razor-like spires are said to bristle with weapons crafted from dark sorcery. A great central keep serves as the entrance to the Underworks and serves the needs of surface-dwelling dark elves who oversee the martial operations conducted above. These shadow dwellers wrap themselves in fine spider-silk robes and wear visors made from thin shards of dark violet crystal to protect their eyes even from bright moonlight.

HISTORY AND PEOPLE

The drow are believed to have held Vilik Strad for almost 15 millennia, reputedly having seized it from dwarves who had, in turn, wrested control of the fortress from its original serpentfolk builders that then ruled the Jungle of Shadows.

Once they became masters of Vilik Strad, sorcerers and priestesses of the dark elves (known as Matrons of Shadow) discovered the Underworks in the darkness below the citadel, where they found arcane machinery and learned secrets of the cosmos from denizens of the lower planes. Slow to breed and slow to move, the dark elves consolidated their power. Pacts with demons and knowledge of sorcery allowed them to enslave many of the fierce tribes of the Under Realms. Their thousands of years within the Underworks and the city built atop them have granted the dark elves of Vilik Strad a greater resistance to daylight than other drow, so that they do not suffer as much from the ill effects of bright light. To the west, they explored the deep dark of the Talanos Peninsula, building fortresses in the Jungle of Shadows with the purpose of expanding their empire from below to one that would rule the land above it as well. To the east, they built the Port of Ruin, as it has become known, with plans to seize islands throughout the Mouth of Akados.

Even as their influence spread in the realms below and across the Talanos Peninsula, the dark elves of Vilik Strad became aware of the arrival in the Green Realm nearby of groups of their Alfheim kin who were fleeing from wars in the east. As elves spread across the southwestern portion of Akados, the drow feared that it would not be long before these warped tree worshippers would find their way to the Jungle of Shadows. Deciding to act before their enemy was prepared, the dark elves sent an army of orcs, giants, hobgoblins, and gnolls to the very edge of the Jungle of Shadow with the intent of conquering the cities of Solis Alunaris and Suomen Gron in one fell swoop.

Their plan was shattered when the grey elves and wild elves of the Green Realm performed a mighty ritual in 52 I.R. that raised the Cinderhame Mountains and shattered the dark elven armies and turned the lush Jungle of Shadows to ash.

The drow were forced to retreat to Vilik Strad. There they have slowly rebuilt their strength and recently settled outposts in the Cinderhame Mountains themselves. They watch the Green Realm and bide their time before they have the might to move again against the forest and bring ruin to their hated alfar cousins.

RELIGION AND GOVERNMENT

The drow consider themselves to be near equals of lesser demons and fiends, and as such they have created pacts and alliances with several demon lords and similar dark powers of far planes. They favor the Queen of Spiders above others, and despise Orcus, who in one incarnation is said to have shown disrespect to the Lady of Webs.

The hierarchy of their empire is matrilineal, with noble born queens heading the government and the high priesthood of their demonic faith. The current ruler is Queen Arabella Nightweave, leader of the House of Nightweave. Arabella is thought to be around 200 years old and a high priestess of the Queen of Spiders. The House of Nightweave is one of the oldest and most feared families of dark elves in the Under Realms and is recognized among the inner and outer planes. Some whisper that Arabella may actually be an avatar of the Queen of Spiders herself, though this may be a rumor spread by her house to ensure obedience from other families in Vilik Strad.

Loving intrigue and trusting no one, Queen Nightweave sets the members of her court against each other, encouraging sabotage and even murder in efforts to prove their worth to her. Subversive civil wars have often been manipulated for the amusement of the queen. While preventing the accumulation of enough power by any of her courtiers to threaten the ascendency of House Nightweave, these types of machinations go a long way to explaining why it has taken the dark elves so long to grow in sufficient strength to again pose a threat to their neighbors.

The priestesses of the dark elves, known as the Matrons of Shadow, also hold many of the important administrative positions in the city. The matron known as the Sister of Jewels runs mining operations deep below the peninsula; the Sister of Slaves sees to the collection, imprisonment and training of slaves; the Sister of Death supervises the training of assassins; and the Sister of War commands the armies and directs the martial training of males and females. The Matrons of Shadow are assisted by a sorcerer caste of males.

Trade and Commerce

The drow of Vilik Strad are enormously wealthy, owing to hordes of soldier slaves, demonic pacts, and deposits of jewels and rare minerals mined from deep beneath the Talanos Peninsula. As a result, much of the actual economy of the dark elves is based on favor. He or she who has the favor of the most powerful demon, most unscrupulous efreet, or highest-ranking sorcerer shines most brightly in the avaricious eyes of Her Majesty Arabella.

Such things as gold, silver, and jewels therefore are a commodity among the wealthy, and are used primarily to pay for their personal armies and to entreat with demonic beings or dragons who might have an appetite for such treasure.

Loyalty and Diplomacy

The dark elves of Vilik Strad owe no loyalty to anyone save their patron demon lords and their queen. And even those loyalties are not complete. The Dark City keeps a fortified embassy in Braktu to keep an eye on the followers of Orcus and allows a surface embassy of Braktu in the Upper Works. These embassies are purely a charade and barely disguise the enmity the two groups have toward one another.

Military

The military strength of Vilik Strad is organized in cadres of humanoid warriors who are ruled by their own chieftains, but subservient to a regimented core of dark elf task masters. Hordes of goblin and kobold warrior slaves with spears and light bows are often sent forward into any attack, followed by cadres of more disciplined troops.

The cadres are typically divided into numbers of 500 to 1,000 hobgoblins, orcs, or gnolls, who bring a subchief per 25, a chief for every 500, and a major war chief for every thousand. In this mix are typically shamans and sorcerers working in support of the main hosts. Above these are shock troops of 100 to 200 bugbears set with whips and chains to ensure that the orcs and goblin hosts do not run and to keep the gnolls from eating the cowards.

When the dark elves venture forth in war themselves, they are typically organized into companies of 50 to 100 warriors wielding deadly weapons and wearing lightweight finely-tooled armor, with one or more sorcerers and Matrons of Shadow to provide magical aid. When the cause of battle calls for it, the matrons may bring forth bound demons ranging from vrocks to hezrou, or perhaps swarms of dretches. Within the city proper (both the Overworks and the Underworks), dark elf troops predominate, with the queen herself maintaining a royal guard of 10,000 shock troops, 100 sorcerers, and 100 priestesses of the Lady

of Webs, including subservient demons alleged to include nalfeshnee and glabrezu among their numbers.

Major Threats

The dark elves in truth have little to fear, save perhaps an invasion from the inner planes through an unmapped planar gate in the Underworks or the accidental release of some undiscovered arcane threat of the legendary serpentfolk from the depths below the city. Braktu is watched closely, but not thought of as a great risk. On the other hand, while the elves of the Green Realm do not have any intention of invading the Talanos Peninsula, the drow continue to perceive their distant cousins as some sort of existential threat, and plot and plan in the darkness of the citadel to end that threat forever.

Geographic Features and Points of Interest in Southwest Akados

Barren Coast

The southern coast of the Talanos Peninsula is more than 1,000 miles of inhospitable, rocky shoreline with few stunted trees and mosses surviving the ash that rains down from the Cinderhame Mountains to the west and the storms that Mother Oceanus drives up from the south. There are few places of safe harborage on the coastline other than at Braktu, which is perilous for entirely different reasons. And with sahuagin stalking the waters, only the desperate attempt to anchor anywhere near the Barren Coast.

Bitter Island

A few hundred miles off of the Forest Coast, Bitter Island has been claimed for hundreds of years by the monarchs of Castorhage, and has over the years been a royal residence, a hermetic retreat, and a place of exile. It also is a temporary island whose appearance and disappearance remains a mystery to sages. Some believe the island is transported by supernatural methods, perhaps as some form of trap laid by Dagon or another sea god to draw mortals to their doom. Others believe the island rises to the surface and is lowered again by mechanical means through vast undersea pumps constructed by a long-forgotten civilization that once called the island home. All that is confirmed is that the vast palace complex found upon the island, believed to date back to Phoromyceaen times, has been on the island since its discovery. Many visited the island, and many of those were lost when the island disappeared again. And whenever the island reappears, no evidence remains of any of those who occupied it when it disappeared. Nevertheless, the island continues to be sought out by explorers seeking to uncover its secrets and explore its lost history.

Reference Source: The Blight

Cinderhame Mountains

Raised from the crusts of the world by powerful rituals wrought by the mightiest among the grey elves and wild elves in 52 I.R., the creation of the volcanic Cinderhame Mountains decimated the then-rising drow empire of Vilik Strad, from which it has taken that citadel thousands of years to recover.

Their volcanic floes now cooled, and their cones frozen into great spires of obsidian, the mountains slowly became populated with various humanoid tribes, many of whom now swear their allegiance to Vilik Strad, which once again turns its attention to the verdant forests of the Green Realm. The mountains are home to fire giants, hill giants, bands of ogres, trolls, gnolls, and more.

East Talon

East Talon, located just off the northern coast of the Talanos Peninsula and 60 miles east of West Talon, is a mountainous wilderness island dominated by high peaks and thick forests. The island has no natural harbor suitable for building a port as its few rocky beaches are small and dominated by hundred-foot cliffs of sharp volcanic rock. From the sea, a single white spire several hundred feet tall can be seen rising from one of the cliff faces. None know for certain its purpose or who built it. It is surmised that the spire may be an ancient relic of a bygone age or perhaps the home of an archmage who does not wish to be bothered.

The island's interior is home to a number of dangerous beasts, mostly Pleistocene megafauna and primitive humanoids that are not averse to cannibalism, at least according to the few pirates and adventurers who managed to pierce the interior and return. The island's coastline is littered with shipwrecks, and it is common practice of the Borss Navy to check the shoreline for survivors after tropical storms blow through the region.

The Emerald Mountains

Situated at the southern end of the Green Realm, the Emerald Mountains (known as the Gora Harmyth to the elves) are steep, rugged peaks blanketed by alpine forests often deeply shrouded in mist. These mountains are dangerous to those who have not been invited. There are many natural threats, from wild animals and perilous fey to treacherous paths and sentient plant life, but most importantly, the grey elves of the heights do not like visitors.

Gold Wine River

The Gold Wine River runs 450 miles north to south through the heart of the southern forest. The river teems with an abundance of fish, waterfowl, and the fey folk of the water who keep their homes in the backwaters of the bubbling brooks and streams that feed the river.

The Green Realm Forest

At one time, the Great Akadonian Forest covered most of southern and central Akados, from the western coast of the continent almost to the shores of the Sinnar Ocean in the east. Now only the deep woodland west of the Crescent Sea remains of this massive forest. The southern extent, south of the Ilber Nole peninsula, is the home of the wild elves of the Green Realm. The elves protect much of the forest against intruders both human and otherwise. But in the darkest reaches, there are places even the elves are loath to go. After all, these woods are older even than the elven courts that call them home.

High Barrens, The

Once covered by the vast Jungle of Shadow, the upper world homeland of the burgeoning empire of Vilik Strad, this massive plateau on the Talanos Peninsula was turned barren and desolate when the elves of the Green Realm raised the Cinderhame Mountains and rained down volcanic ash and altered the local weather pattern to divert moisture to the north and south. So severe was the consequent drought that most of its original population perished, and the numerous cities and settlements built by slaves of the dark elves fell to ruin and were eventually consumed in dust. The broken, sometimes volcanically active land is sporadically inhabited by ogres, trolls, giants, drakes, and worse. Vilik Strad still considers the Barrens its own territory and has begun funding expeditions of its humanoid forces into the hinterlands where they have established bases in the Cinderhame Mountains. Patrols rarely extend into the ashen interior, however, where choking dust storms are still known to swirl.

Karthu Mountains

The Karthu Mountains, rugged, heavily wooded peaks rising from the western Green Realm Forest, are home to the Eagle Tribe of the Green Realm and their legendary great eagle mounts. In the forests of the foothills are the members of the Bear Tribe, renowned for their ferocity in battle and barbaric traditions. Few humans have ever seen these heights, and most of those who have, have never returned.

The Mud Coast

The Mud Coast comprises 500 miles of muddy coastline and 62,000 square miles of warm, swampy interior that borders the Green Realm to the west and the Crescent Sea to the east. This land is ancient, as primeval as the nearby forests of the Green Realm, and in a constant state of growth and decay for uncounted millennia. This land had once been at the bottom of the Crescent Sea until some unknown event caused the waters to recede ages ago. Today, a growing nation of lizardfolk and tsathar dedicated to the worship of the Mother of Dragons calls this salt swamp home. The coast is largely avoided by sailors and is generally shunned by the guardians of the Green Realm, who maintain outposts along their borders with the Mud Coast to protect against any incursions by lizardfolk into their forested kingdom.

Northern Steel Tongue Mountains

Though home to one of the major wild elf tribes, these mountains hold a largely unexplored interior whose jagged peaks and sheer cliffs face the ocean to the west. The elves seldom venture farther than the forested escarpments of the east where their mines and castles are held against any threats to come down from the mountains, including trolls, giants, wyverns and other lesser dragon kin that have been known to roost there.

Port Ruin

Vilik Strad once had a port city at the tip of the Talanos Peninsula whose true name is long since forgotten. It is now called Port Ruin by the navies of Castorhage, Reme, Foere, and the Earldom of Borss. None know when it first came to ruin or why the Dark City abandoned it. While the port seems to be deserted, rumors abound of dark ships at the docks in port, which are said to seize or sink ships that come too close. Whether or not this is true, more ships seem to go missing in the Mouth of Akados than can be explained by bad luck or weather, and the blame often falls on this port. As a result, it has been attacked several times by ships of each nation in retaliation. Naval captains are loath to land their marines on its shore, however, as they tend to not come back or, if they do, come back changed — unhinged and murderous. Such poor souls usually end up imprisoned or slain by their own comrades. Interestingly, the port never seems to be rebuilt after each attack, the port always appearing a virtual ruin and deserted, with no ships at the wharves, when the avenging ships bombard it with catapult, ballista, flaming debris, and spells from the water. Yet Port Ruin also seems to never be destroyed no matter the number and extent of the attacks, with the same buildings in near ruins and the same debris-choked but still recognizable streets each time. There is, in fact, no evidence that Vilik Strad has made any attempts to repair the port, or even enter it with their troops. No one is quite sure what is going on with this port city, but most mariners consider it cursed and avoid it at all costs.

Southern Steel Tongue Mountains

The mountains to the southwest of the Green Realm that form the western side of Syldryll Vale are called the Southern Steel Tongues. From these mountainous domains, the wild elves call upon mighty elementals to draw iron ore from the depths of the earth and smelt the ore with carbon from naturally fallen trees into a fine lightweight, high carbon elven steel used for the arrows, spears, and fine blades of the wild folk.

Syldryll River

The headwaters of the Syldryll River are deep in the Emerald Mountains and flow some 400 miles to the sea.

The river is rich in fish and waterfowl and is a source of fresh water for many of the herds that roam the grasslands of the Vale. The north fork starts in a mountain spring high in the Emerald Mountains where it erupts and cascades 1,000 feet to a shimmering lake below known as Arialee's Mirror. On the southern fork, Hidden Ones from Suomen Gron sometimes sail pleasure boats and survey the vast prairies of the vale, often obscured by illusion and hidden from the watchful eyes of the centaur clans.

SYLDRYLL VALE

Syldryll Vale makes up 125,000 square miles of native grassland located between the cliffs of the Southern Steel Tongues to the northwest and the Emerald Mountains of the east. The vale, like the Verdant Plains, is home to tribes of wild and free centaurs, the Five Clans of the Hoof, as well as wild elves who have taken up the horse culture from their hooved allies.

TALANOS PENINSULA

The Talanos Peninsula extends more than 1,000 miles from the base of the Cinderhame Mountains to the Mouth of Akados, nearly cutting off the Crescent Sea from Mother Oceanus. Once covered by lush jungle, the peninsula today is almost entirely barren and inhospitable, shrouded by layers of ash spewed forth from the Cinderhames. The interior is dominated by the plateau of the High Barrens. The only permanent settlements are Braktu on the Barren Coast and Vilik Strad, on the eastern end of the plateau.

TANDRIL ISLAND

Tandril Island is a green, verdant island about 50 miles off of the Forest Coast in the Crescent Sea. Once a colony of Castorhage, it is now independent of that nation-state. The port city of Trinidar is on the northern coast of the island. The interior is rich with volcanic earth that lends itself to the growth of lush native crops. Plantations owned by Trinidarian nobles produce, among other things, sugar, rum, and rich coffee grown in the mountainous interior.

TREACHERY BAY

Treachery Bay is bounded by the Mud Coast on the west, the Talanos Peninsula on the south, and the island of West Talon to the east. So sheltered, these waters are fairly calm and safe, though there are no ports other than those of Borss and Kamis on West Talon, and any sane sailor avoids the shores of either the Mud Coast or Talanos. As a result, the bay is seldom traveled by ships. It gained its name during the Short War between Reme and Castorhage, when a Castorhagi captain switched sides and assisted in the destruction of a Blighter naval squadron in these waters.

VERDANT PLAINS

The Verdant Plains make up 82,000 square miles of swaying grassland, home to the Gazelle and Buffalo tribes of the Green Realm. These tribes keep a friendly rivalry with one another as they ride the plains in search of adventure and excitement. The Buffalo and Gazelle tribes live for sport, holding races across the prairie and inviting their woodland kin to camp among the open skies of the plain.

WEST TALON

West Talon is the larger of two islands north of the Talanos Peninsula. The northern portion of the island, known as the Talonmoor, is rocky, wild, rainy and windswept, and is home to sea lions, seals, grizzly bears, black bears, red deer, wild boar, and elk. Nobles from Borrs in the southern part of the island sometimes sail here for hunting expeditions and to train their soldiers in survival skills. The mountainous central portion of the island, which divides the Talonmoor from the settled south, is called the Dragon Heights, where can be found the fabled Dread Dragon Temple.

The southern half of the island is quite hospitable and includes the Earldom of Borss with its orchards of fruit trees and vineyards, and the semi-autonomous city of Kamis.

REFERENCE SOURCE: DREAD DRAGON TEMPLE FROM QUESTS OF DOOM

DRAGON HEIGHTS

In the center of West Talon are three mountains that create a barrier between the Talonmoor and the fields of the Earldom of Borss. This mountainous terrain is the Dragon Heights. Climbing here is strenuous and dangerous, and many who attempt it fail to return. Dragons are said to lair in caves in the mountains, and lizardfolk prowl the slopes. In addition, here is found the ancient and massive Dread Dragon Temple, which has served as a holy site to the primordial dragons Tiamat and Behemoth since at least the Age of Dragons. The temple is said to be the hiding place of the fabled staff of the dragons. Legends hold that the dwarven King Col of the Ironskull Great Mountain Clan from the Blackrock Mountains was lost attempting to assault the temple with his army. The earls of Borss have always left it alone but use its dire reputation to protect their lands from invaders.

TALONMOOR

The Talonmoor is a wet, cool, and nearly treeless windswept wildland of nearly 10,000 square miles in the north of the island of West Talon. The Talonmoor serves as a hunting ground for the Earls of Borss, one of whom was lost to a bear on a hunting expedition more than a hundred years ago. The Talonmoor is an occasional site of shipwrecks on the island, and unusual items sometimes wash up on its windy shoreline.

THE HAUNTED STEPPES

Capital: none
Ruler: none
Government: clan chieftains (khans)
Population: 620,000 (607,500 Shattered Folk, 7,500 halfling, 3,500 half-elf, 1,500 wild elf)
Monstrous: goblins, gnolls, orcs, centaurs, hobgoblins, kobolds, axe beaks, ankhegs, hill giants, ogres, minotaurs, banshees, dire wolves, bugbears, perytons, worgs, skeletons, zombies, basilisks, revenants, cyclops, blood hawks, shadows, owlbears, wraiths, griffons, harpies, ghosts, nightmares, wyverns, lamias, manticores, mummies, bulettes, hippogriffs, chimeras, specters, trolls, wights, cockatrices, hell hounds, vampires, blue dragons, copper dragons
Languages: Kirkut (various dialects), Common
Religion: Ethtuwate
Resources: grain, livestock, horses, mercenaries,
Currency: barter, various coins
Technology Level: Dark Ages

The Haunted Steppes are a vast plain stretching from the Deepfells in the south and the Stoneheart Mountains in the east to the shores of Great Ocean Ûthaf in the west. The Lost Mountains and Lake Hali mark the end of the steppe to the northwest, but to the northeast they continue ever northward into frozen lands of increasing darkness known as the Shadowlands.

Once home to a powerful empire that challenged the might of the ancient Hyperboreans, these vast plains are now a cursed land of shadow-haunted horror and broken peoples. A place of fear and apprehension, the Haunted Steppes have borne the tread of hordes of murderous humanoids and the terror of the shadow-walkers, known to the Nørsk as the Scaedugenga. For long centuries, outsiders have avoided the steppes, praying that the fearsome things that dwell there never emerge again. Only in recent years have explorers from the City-State of Castorhage, Gtsang and Reme returned to these lands and discovered surprising truths about the region and those who call it home.

Almost all humans of the Haunted Steppes belong to the Shattered Folk tribes, distant descendants of the once-mighty Hundaei Empire. Most now live in the western portion of the steppes, south of the crook in the Devil's Tail. Elsewhere, nomadic tribes roam the greater expanse of the steppe, but in smaller numbers, never stopping anywhere for long. All Shattered Folk particularly avoid the lands near the Lost Mountains and Lake Hali, and quickly cross the central corridor known as the Road of Sorrows making signs to draw the blessing of their gods, fearing it is cursed and home to demons and other foul things.

HISTORY AND PEOPLE

In the distant past, this region was known to the nomadic folk who lived here as the Kayma-ura-mat (in archaic Kirkut, literally, "Mother of Grass"). They tended their herds of goats and followed the buffalo, antelope, and other game animals that migrated with the seasons. The people lived in family-based clans and roamed their ancestral lands under the leadership of chieftains known as khans. None today knows when they first arrived in these plains or from where they came. In their language of Kirkut, they referred to themselves as the "Hundaei," meaning "far-riders." And alongside the Hundaei were their chosen companions, greatest of the horses of the Lost Lands known as the Hu-Soncala ("mighty horse-lords"). The Hu-Soncala, it is said, were blessed with human intelligence, could speak their own language, and were masters of the magic that dwelled in the land itself.

Roaming across thousands of miles of open steppe — a land of bounty but also peril from terrifying storms and deep, cold winters — the Hundaei and the Hu-Soncala were undisputed masters of the plains. But danger lurked in the northwest where fearsome beasts, living shadows, and ancient slumbering devils were said to prowl beneath the ice and in the windswept crags of the Lost Mountains. Lake Hali in particular was forbidden — even catching a glimpse of its bleak shores was said to curse the viewer with madness and death. Tribal priests and soothsayers warned the clans against venturing near any of these places, an admonition that the clans were easily able to obey, for their own lands were rich and life was good. Unbeknownst to most of the clansfolk, however, their safety from the horrors of those mountains and the dark lake was not secured just by happenstance. An order of priests consisting of humans and their humanoid neighbors moved among the clans in secret, performing at set times ancient rituals that bound the evil that dwelt in the north. These priests were known as the Asran, or the Guardians.

This golden age on the steppes came to end, the Hundaei storytellers relate, when an evil god called Ocru-ca cursed the people for refusing to worship him, surrounding the plains with a wall of stone. Some scholars suggest that Ocru-ca may refer to the demon-god Orcus, and that these legends recall the raising of the Stoneheart Mountains in the distant past, an act that shattered much of the continent and disrupted rivers, seas, and the climate for thousands of leagues around.

After this catastrophe, game and fodder on the plains grew scarce. Many rivers dried up or flowed only during the rainy season. Even the mighty Ethtuwate-cala-Tun (meaning the "Gods' Ride River") was affected — where once it was at the center of a network of rivers that flowed throughout the steppes, after the disaster it grew broad and slow as its tributaries vanished or dwindled.

The consequent decline of the grasslands and reduction of water forced the Hundaei clans to wander farther afield. Herds grew smaller, seasonal crops became scarcer, and — worst of all — the Hu-Soncala lost their mystical abilities. Though still magnificent, sturdy, and powerful animals, within a century or two of the disaster they became mere shadows of their old selves. Stories told around the campfires do say that, even today, when the need is great, true Hu-Soncala are born to bear great warriors and cast powerful spells, but such tales may be little more than the wishful thinking of a diminished people.

As the years stretched on and the bounty of the steppes diminished, the tribes of the hills, mountains, and steppes — gnolls, goblins, centaurs, orcs, hobgoblins, and others — were also forced to struggle for resources and turned on each other and on the Hundaei clans for control of the best lands. Soon, the plains were ablaze with conflict and soaked in blood as human and humanoid clans fought for dominance. The Asran struggled for decades to maintain the rituals that kept the chaos of the Lost Mountains, Lake Hali, and the Shadowlands at bay, but eventually conflicts between Hundaei clans disrupted the performance of the ancient magics. The wards that protected the steppes wavered and weakened, and fearful things began to stir.

The events that followed are almost unknown among the scholars of the Lost Lands, but songs and tales of the Shattered Folk still recall the dark tragedy and epic heroism of this ancient time. Around –450 I.R., more than three centuries before the arrival of the Hyperborean legions on Akados, the first incursion of the Shadow on the steppes began with a strange darkness spreading outward from the Lost Mountains. Some unlucky Hundaei caught a glimpse of a column of inky blackness rising from the surface of Lake Hali and were struck blind or driven mad or, in some cases, died of horror from what they saw within the darkness. Clans that had ventured too close to the forbidden Shadowlands or the cursed lake were visited by strange, frightening dreams and visions, and a few even fell under the sway of the Shadow as it grew and spread. Such folk captured by the darkness came to be known as the Naduk-Taak or "Fallen Ones," if they are spoken of at all; for it is believed that even talking about them constitutes a bad omen.

The Haunted Steppes

The Fallen Ones, as well as many groups of non-humans — among them the goblins, ogres, centaurs, and hobgoblins — joined together under the banner of the Shadow and began to drive the Hundaei from the northern plains. Frightened rumor claimed that they were led by fearsome beings of shadow mounted on dark steeds and crowned with darkness. The clans who lived in the perilous lands just south of the Lost Mountains were the first to fall, slaughtered without mercy in a place that came to be called simply the Killing Ground, where their cursed bones still lie and are shunned by those who dwell in the Steppes.

Faced by this terrible threat, the Hundaei khans met in an urgent gathering and heard tales of survivors and the opinions of priests, soothsayers, and holy folk. The Asran themselves finally came forward. A power not of the earth threatened the steppes and — if it was not stopped — the entire world beyond.

On the fifth day of the gathering, a strange band of emissaries presented itself. Alone among the humanoids, only the gnolls resisted the siren call of the Shadow. A vicious, carnivorous and intensely xenophobic people, the gnolls nevertheless saw the omens, read the signs, and realized that the Shadow would swallow them whole along with their human foes. Though some gnoll clans refused to participate, the majority decided to band together and offer common cause with the Hundaei.

For their part, the humans were intensely suspicious, and many sensed treachery and called to reject the gnolls' emissaries. But the auguries were favorable, and all signs suggested that the beast-folk were telling the truth. When the khans selected the warrior-chief Utai as their supreme leader, Utai consulted with his advisors, allowed his priests to perform one more round of auguries, and then decided in the end to accept the gnolls' offer and go into battle with them.

Great battles were fought then on the steppes between the shadow-driven humanoids and the Hundaei and their gnoll allies. But a greater, and unseen, battle was fought in the Shüdar, or Shadow, the adjacent plane of reality that harbored the soul-essences of the shadow creatures. Little can be said about this other struggle, and the songs and stories are largely poetic. But the handful of scholars who have studied Hundaei stories and culture believe that the Asran used powerful and very old magic to cast their own spirits into the void. There they advanced through nightmarish landscapes to face down their foes — whether demons, gods, devils, or something utterly beyond comprehension is not known. Few Asran returned from the Shadow, and of those, some had had their sanity shattered. A few tales suggest that some of the Guardians were trapped in the Shadow and may perhaps remain there today.

Eventually, after long years of war, whatever goal the Asran sought in that darkened realm was achieved. At the height of a great battle where an army of humans and gnolls fought side-by-side against a horde of the north, a chorus of fearsome howls arose as the shadow-things were drawn away, dragged back across the threshold that they had crossed and exiled to the depths of the Shüdar.

Bereft of leadership, the humanoids fell back. The Fallen Ones, irrevocably changed and twisted by their alliance with the Shadows, fought mindlessly until they were scattered. Victorious but on the verge of exhaustion, the defenders dragged themselves north where the last six of the Asran guardians recast the wards to seal the Shadowlands and ward the Lost Mountains and Lake Hali. What dwelled there was not killed — for it may well have been impossible to kill by mortal means, no matter how powerful — but banished. The wards the Asran set were strong, and long years passed before the darkness again stirred and came to once more threaten the world.

The remaining Asran passed their knowledge on to a new generation and once more faded into Hundaei society, conducting their rituals and rites in secret, away from the prying eyes of the world. The gnolls and Hundaei swore oaths of peace and went their separate ways, and to this day will not war on each other. The Hundaei gradually returned to their old ways as decades stretched out into centuries.

Sometime around 5 I.R., Khan Jaganga of the Sukeken (or Leopard) clan had a fearsome and portentous dream. He saw strange men and women clad in strange armor, bearing spears and marching across the land, consuming crops and killing livestock in their path. In his dream they built a great stone table that encompassed the entire land, shutting out the sun and reducing the mighty Hundaei to servitude and slavery. Consulting his oracles, Jaganga became convinced that this dream was a prophecy. Although it is possible that the story of Jaganga's dream is apocryphal, there is a remarkable coincidence: at almost the same time, the Polemarch Oerson is said to have been granted a vision by the goddess Muir, showing him the location of the Sacred Table in Libynos, and bidding him to found there what became the sacred city of Tircople.

For many years the Hundaei had known that a new people had arrived on Akados to the east beyond the Stoneheart Mountains, but the newcomers were leagues distant and the steppe folk had their own affairs to worry about as the clans migrated, fought their own wars both petty and great, and saw to their own economic and spiritual needs. Safe for millennia behind the Deepfells and the Stonehearts, the Hundaei gave little thought to the outside world. They did trade with the mountain dwarves, however, and Jaganga learned that many dwarves had been displaced by the invaders — humans in bronze armor who had sailed in great oared ships with painted sails and called themselves the Hyperboreans.

Daring scouts from the Sukeken clan slipped through the mountain passes, surreptitiously observing the distant lands to the east and confirming Jaganga's greatest fear — that the Hyperboreans were on the march and determined to expand their empire.

By this time, Jaganga was already well on the way to uniting the clans through a cunning combination of diplomacy and conquest. A league of Hundaei khans still opposed him, but as he gained more confirmation from his priests and diviners, Jaganga grew more determined to weld the various tribes into a single nation, not only for his own glorification, but also to save his people from extinction.

Jaganga called for a great gathering of the Hundaei and there told the khans of his dream. Others affirmed the vision and spoke of their own. Priests and soothsayers confirmed the legitimacy of the visions. True, some priests counseled caution and suggested that the dreams were actually warnings against hasty action, but Jaganga believed that only aggression under his unified leadership would forestall destruction and set their cautious words aside. The choice that he presented to the remaining independent khans was simple — join his empire or be destroyed, either by his armies or by the Hyperboreans. In the end, either out of true conviction, or out of simple pragmatism, the dissident khans were convinced, and for the first time the Hundaei were united under a single ruler.

Though there was much to do to forge his new empire, Jaganga's primary focus was on the Hyperborean threat. The Great Khan decided to strike first. Guided by allies among the mountain dwarves, Jaganga's riders made their way through the seemingly impassible ramparts of the Stoneheart Mountains and emerged into the Sea of Grass and swept south, descending without warning in the heartland of the Hyperborean Empire in 12 I.R.

The effect on the Hyperboreans was devastating. It was as if the very ground had opened up and disgorged an army of devils, and the undermanned garrisons of the Xircos River region were quickly overrun by the fearsome riders whose style of warfare was well-suited to the endless plains on the Sea of Grass. Even the walled settlements that marked the northernmost extent of the Hyperborean Empire, utterly unprepared for war, fell before the Hundaei. Every warrior believed that they were fighting for the very survival of their people and saw their merciless slaughter simply as a pre-emptive act of self-defense.

The Invincible Horde, as it came to be known both by its members and its enemies, was finally stopped at the walls of Apothasalos, where the Polemarch Gnassus waited with two crack Hyperborean legions. It had taken months to gather the scattered legions but now at last the Hyperboreans were ready to make a stand.

This was a new form of warfare for the Hundaei. The serried ranks of bronze faced them from behind bristling masses of the long deadly pikes known as sarissa. Uncertain for the first time, the Hundaei pelted their foes with arrows, only to see the Hyperboreans form into a sturdy chelonae or tortoise formation to ward off the vast majority of their missiles. Frustrated, the Hundaei chiefs ordered their warriors to charge the enemy phalanxes, but most of their horses — possibly showing more sense than their riders — steadfastly refused to impale themselves on the bronze points of the enemy spears. Those that did manage to charge discovered the full effectiveness of the Hyperborean formation and fell back in disorder.

Counterattacks by the outnumbered but still effective Hyperborean cavalry nibbled away at Hundaei numbers, and with supplies and reinforcements funneled directly through Apothasalos the Hyperboreans showed no sign of weakening. Soon, the Hundaei commanders received word that more imperial legions were on their way, and finally decided to abandon the field. Though it was far from an overwhelming defeat, it was a defeat nonetheless, and the battered Hundaei withdrew in good order, retreating back through the passes and limping home.

This inconclusive campaign was only the beginning of a long conflict between the plains' riders and the Hyperboreans that would scar the psyches of both peoples for generations. Raids continued for many years, with various groups of Hundaei forces emerging from the mountains to cause havoc and widespread panic before withdrawing. Hard-pressed by a mobile and seemingly limitless enemy, the Hyperboreans were unable to pursue or take the battle to the Hundaei, or the Huns as they came to be known.

War between Hundaei and Hyperborean became a sad fact of life, and soon no one on either side could remember a time when the two peoples were *not* at war. Years grew into decades and decades into centuries. The Hundaei's entire existence began to revolve around the terrible conflict, and for their part, the Hyperboreans spent mountains of treasure to keep their frontier well-guarded. Legions stationed there became seasoned veterans, well-versed in warfare against the horse-lords. Hyperborean cavalry evolved to meet the threat, which led to the creation of entire mounted legions whose sole purpose was to patrol and protect the endless plains on the Sea of Grass.

In the end, the Hyperboreans broke the stalemate through the arrival of a new technology. From the dwarves of Irkaina, they learned the secrets of iron and steel. Many years passed before the new knowledge spread throughout the empire, and more before entire legions could be equipped with steel arms. But eventually, superior weaponry enabled the Hyperboreans to finally gain the upper hand and press through the mountain passes that had once served as highways for the Invincible Horde, until they finally broke through onto the Great Steppes.

Now, the darkest fears of the Great Khan's prophecy were coming to pass. Desperately the Hundaei pushed back, throwing themselves against the imperial legions with near-suicidal bravery. Some battles were won, but most were lost, for the Hyperboreans had learned much and counteracted the Hundaei with sturdy ranks of ironclad infantry and their own skilled light cavalry, which was sufficient to chase down and engage the nimble Hun riders.

But now, fighting across a mountain range and far from home, the Hyperboreans faced the same challenges as the Hundaei once had. Mountain supply lines were unreliable, and the steppes were unsuited to fortifications or permanent settlement. Hyperborean activity on the plains consisted mostly of counter-raids and a long-term attrition strategy intended to settle the region once the Hundaei were finally pacified. Despite these limitations, the empire met with some success, and pressure from the legions pushed the Hundaei westward, farther and farther away from the Stoneheart Mountains. And, entirely by accident, this pressure began the final downfall of the Hundaei.

Deprived of some of their most fertile and hospitable grazing lands, the Uken and Chabaike clans withdrew to the northwest. Lake Hali and the Lost Mountains had remained strictly forbidden since the coming of the Shadow, but memories had faded, and the displaced clans demanded the right to hunt and graze within sight of the taboo lands, well away from the troublesome Hyperboreans. When the Great Khan Ogedane forbade the migration, the two clans defied him, riding north in the year 680 I.R. and daring him to stop them. It was the greatest act of defiance directed against a Great Khan in generations, but Ogedane, pressed by the Hyperborean threat to the east, was unable to respond.

After the Great Khan's twin humiliations at the hands of his traditional enemies and his supposed vassals, confidence in Ogedane wavered and in several cases broke altogether, as more clans began to defy his authority. The Uken and Chabaike clans, from their new homes in the forbidden lands, raised the banner of revolt and demanded Ogedane's head and the election of a new Great Khan. To some, it seemed that those clans were driven by more than anger or resentment; their fury reminded some of the Fallen Ones, the long-ago Hundaei who were possessed by ill-omened spirits from the shadow.

Pressed on two sides, Ogedane gathered loyal clans and faced down the renegades. Battle was joined, and tens of thousands perished and entire clans were annihilated. In what may have been the bloodiest war in Akados' history, the Hundaei essentially committed collective suicide. By 683 I.R., the once-mighty empire was no more. Small bands of survivors still roamed the plains, and those who had made new homes in the Sea of Grass escaped the war. Some, it is said, went so far as to flee Akados entirely and make the long journey to far Libynos. But for all intents and purposes, the Hundaei as a people were gone forever. The surprised Hyperboreans suddenly realized that, through no actions of their own, their enemy had vanished.

Today, the descendants of the survivors who roam the Haunted Steppes are known as the Shattered Folk, a folk haunted by memories of ancient greatness. They bitterly recall the prophecy of the Great Khan Jaganga, and retell his story, a warning about the potentially tragic cost of fulfilled destiny.

Ironically, though their greatest enemy no longer roamed the Steppes, the Hyperboreans chose not to settle there and spent their treasure on expanding the empire elsewhere. But the void was not left unfilled. The humanoids of the steppes exulted at the downfall of the Hundaei. Within just a few years, hordes of humanoids swept across the steppes and through the Crynnomar Gap to threaten the northernmost reaches of the Green Realm. As is told elsewhere, the elves were forced to abandon their lands to the south to make a stand in the gap. Eventually, the humanoids were repelled, at great cost to the elves. In their absence, the folk of Reme felled trees and settled farms and legions to carve the new realm of the Northmarches from the former elven lands. The elves, tired of conflict, fled west, and established their new and inviolate boundaries of the Green Realm.

Alone among the humanoids of the steppes, the gnoll tribes mourned the Hundaei's passing, for they still recalled the days then human and gnoll stood together. To this day, the gnolls and Shattered Folk will not fight each other.

Despite the slaughter of the Hundaei, the Asran — who refused to fight in a civil war of clan against clan — survived and continued their vigil in the north to keep the Shadow contained.

For long years, the rest of the world gave little thought to the steppes, assuming it a savage wilderness. But by the 2800s I.R., the Kingdom of Foere was ascendant in Akados. Ambitious and practical, the Grand Duke Prince Cale — who had spared the kingdom from civil war by renouncing his claim to the throne — cast his eyes to the north and saw there a region ripe for the picking. Long ignored, the Great Steppes seemed largely depopulated, home to bands of disorganized humanoids, nomadic centaurs, and the last pitiable remnants of the Hundaei empire. The Great Colonization had begun.

At the call of the grand duke, great caravans of settlers gathered in the Northmarches of Reme and then moved north through the Crynnomar Gap and into the lands north of the Deepfells. They founded settlements there in what became known as the Caleen lands, which began to grow and thrive. Outposts were built north of the settlements, and the Foerdewaith then advanced into the Ethtuate-cala-tun basin, the old heartland of Hundaei civilization.

Within 70 years, a string of settlements sprang up along the base of the surrounding mountains and in an unbroken chain across the steppes to the western coast more than a thousand miles away. The Shattered Folk retreated and refused battle, hoping to preserve their numbers and retain their independence. Many chieftains and petty khans chose to negotiate and accepted payment for their lands or agreed to treaties that allowed for continued grazing and migration through the settled regions.

However, the Caleen colonists also discovered that humanoids existed on the steppes in much greater numbers than first believed. The many humanoid tribes had scattered and gone feral after their defeat at the hands of the wild elves, but an unbroken remnant had settled on the shores of Lake Hali in the shadow of the Lost Mountains. Here they regrouped and began to grow strong again. Priests and soothsayers among the Shattered Folk issued dire warnings to the Foerdewaith, cautioning them against going too far north or disturbing the terrible powers that slumbered there. To their later regret, the Foerdewaith saw these as reflections of the superstitions of a simple folk and utterly ignored the warnings.

When the colonists reached the shores of Lake Hali by 2931 I.R., they encountered better organized and more aggressive tribes of humanoids. Where before there had been only sporadic marauders, suddenly the floodgates opened. Hordes descended from Lake Hali onto the Great Steppes. The widely scattered Caleen settlements were ill-prepared and many were sacked and burned before the Foerdewaith were even aware of the threat. By the time they were able to regroup and prepare for war, they found themselves encircled by hostile tribes that had seemingly sprung up from the steppes themselves. Though hard pressed, the colonists managed to fortify their settlements and steadings while receiving additional military assistance from Courghais that allowed them to push back the humanoid marauders. The lands they controlled were consolidated and protected, but now a tense stalemate existed with roving bands of the hostile humanoids.

But the stalemate did not last. After 16 years, some event disrupted the rituals of the Asran, and none know the cause. The Shadow was freed, no longer contained by the ancient magics. With no warning, in 2947 I.R. the Scaedugenga burst forth from their place of exile and unleashed armies of humanoids and creatures of darkness in a renewed assault on the Caleen colonies.

Grand Duke Cale called to Reme and Foere for aid and, despite his advanced age, went north to personally command the defense. A body of troops called the Caleen Legion was raised and initially met with some success in battle, driving off humanoid armies and relieving several colonies from siege. The victory was short-lived, however, as more humanoids, in what seemed unending numbers, continued to pour forth from the shores of Lake Hali, from the mountains, and from the Shadowlands, welded into a single force by the dominance of the Scaedugenga. While the overking sought to raise a force to relieve the colonies, Cale was forced into battle south of the Everfar Hills. The Foerdewaith fought bravely, but in the end they could not overcome the might of the magic of the shadow and sheer numbers. Grand Duke Cale, his honor guard, and his legion fell there in battle. To this day, the battlefield is called Cale's Doom, where it is said that Cale's spirit and those of his legion wander each night, endlessly contending with the forces of shadow.

The story of the Shadow War's end is well known — the desperate race to the Crynnomar Gap, preparations for a doomed last stand, the return of the ancient wizards Margon and Alycthron and their raising of the Wizard's Wall. And there the tales of Reme and Foere end, with the armies of Shadow beneath the unscalable heights of the wall. But missing from those tales are what happened next in the steppes.

Staggered by the titanic magical forces marshaled to raise the Wizard's Wall, the Scaedugenga reeled back, initially seeking another route to the southern kingdoms. But unknown to the folk of Reme and Foere, the Asran still lived, and behind the wall they worked to save the rest of Akados from the horrors of the north. Gathering together with the priests of the Shattered Folk and tribal shamans from the gnoll and centaur tribes, the Asran again invoked the ancient rites and entered the Shadow plane, doing renewed battle with the Scaedugenga and their dark minions.

Though they were not as powerful as they once were, the magical forces that had raised the wall had also battered and weakened the Shadow, and after a long and costly struggle, the Scaedugenga were once more thrown back behind eldritch wards. Yet the defeat was not complete, and the new wards were weaker than those of old, and the Shadow continues to extend its dark tendrils from the far north even today.

To the rest of Akados, the Great Steppes were a place of tragedy and loss where sad spirits wandered. They were the Great Steppes no longer — after the defeat of the Shadow horde, the folk of Reme and Foere did their best to forget the lands beyond the Wizard's Wall, which they now called the Haunted Steppes.

Now ignored by the rest of the world, over time the steppes themselves returned to something approaching a normal existence. Remaining Shattered Folk clans returned to their ancient migratory routes and, in some cases, even created semi-permanent settlements. Some of the folk of the Caleen colonies also survived. Now trapped behind the Wizard's Wall, they settled into independent communities — intermarrying with some Shattered Folk and incorporating dwarves, halflings, and even some humanoids into their villages — and developed a new, unique society. Humanoid tribes bickered and fought each other. All came to shun certain lands where the shadow forces that had been unleashed had left a lasting mark, where ghosts, spirits, and undead roamed. The Asran, though diminished, continued to maintain their rituals, and now also wielded powers to repel and guard against the undead.

And so the steppes remained, forgotten, until the fateful year 3262 I.R., when the Castorhagi trader *Provision* made landfall at the mouth of the Devil's Tail. There they encountered and established a cautious friendship with a group of nomadic riders and soon learned that the descendants of the ancient Hundaei still lived on the plains, and that the local groups had banded together into the Confederacy of the Elitan-i-pan. The Haunted Steppes' long isolation was finally at an end as the wily and profit-minded Castorhagi established trade posts along the coast and expanded their contact with the locals.

Gtsang traders who ventured into the steppes in 3360 I.R. had some success with the Campacha tribes, another confederacy of Shattered Folk, who proved to be open to foreign trade. In the course of their expedition, the Gtsang reached the small community of Chesmire, located on the southern bank of the Tabur River, one of the villages of the survivors of the Caleen colonies. They soon realized that other small villages in the region appeared to have similar populations.

Then in 3439 I.R. the Conroi Expedition, a group of explorers sent from Reme to determine the extent of any threat from the Haunted Steppes, carefully crossed the Wizard's Wall at Durgam's Folly. They first made contact with the Campacha folk, who roamed not far from the wall. To the expedition's surprise, the Campacha proved to be a strong and well-established people who had pacified much of the southern steppes. Shortly thereafter, they confirmed the few rumors that had reached Reme from Gtsang and arrived at the villages where lived the descendants of survivors of the Caleen colonies.

Word of the survival of some of the original Caleen colonies shocked Reme and Foere. These communities, soon dubbed the Conroi Settlements, are only now making full contact with the outside world, visited by merchants and agents of Castorhage, Foere, and Reme. Rumors about these settlements continues to spread throughout Akados, much false, including the beliefs that they were actually founded by the Conroi Expedition, or had been on the verge of extinction before their rescue by the expedition's arrival.

For their part, the folk of the so-called Conroi Settlements (who generally refer to themselves as the Caleen) are uncertain about these foreign interlopers, and largely distrust a world that abandoned their ancestors long years ago.

The Shattered Folk of today are divided into countless clans ranging in size from a few dozen to a thousand or more, and still practice many of their old traditions. Many still hunt and graze, following the seasons across the steppe, and engage in skirmishes with neighboring clans as they fight over prime grazing land. Some are known to be utterly ruthless with their enemies and outsiders who enter their territory, while others, such as the Campacha and the Elitan-i-pan Confederacy, are open to outside contact and have made tentative moves to a more settled economy and lifestyle, actually building a few semi-permanent settlements and tending farms on the steppe.

For the most part, however, the folk of the plains continue to live on the Haunted Steppes in the same manner as they have for millennia. The outside world has come knocking, but so far, their influence is minimal, and there are still herds to graze, crops to grow, and battles to fight. And among the Shattered Folk, and among some of the other people of the steppes, including the centaurs and the gnolls who continue to remember the old stories, dwell the Asran, still dedicated to resisting the influence of the Shadow that lingers and bides its time in the far-away frozen north.

RELIGION

The tales of the Hyperboreans and their descendants make of the Hundaei the great enemy of civilization, brutal warriors interested only in conquest and bloodshed. In actual fact, the Hundaei were (and in their present incarnation as the Shattered Folk, are) a subtle and sophisticated people with a far more complex culture than their enemies wished to admit. Nowhere is this more evident than in the Ethtuwate faith, which is still practiced across the Haunted Steppe.

The ancient Hundaei were a varied people, and each great clan had its own traditions, beliefs, and legends. Their common faith was a highly adaptable and tolerant one, having evolved to encompass all of the Steppe folk. Ethtuwate practitioners believe that the universe was created when the primal deity Tunkaku, the Great Giver, split apart, with some of its elements forming the stars and celestial bodies and others forming the deities and powerful beings of law, chaos, good, evil, and neutrality. While Tunkaku no longer exists, its energies are suffused throughout the cosmos, and all living things contain a small spark of the Great Giver's spirit. Thus, many Hundaei continue to give thanks to the Great Giver for its sacrifice and its continued influence on the world. This attitude contributes to the Shattered Folk's tolerant faith, its great adaptability, and acceptance of other gods and goddesses.

Tunkaku gave birth to the two primary gods of the Ethtuwate mythos — the sun-deity Thaka, who rides across the sky on a great pegasus, and the moon-deity Drethra, who rules the night astride a mighty nightmare. While Thaka is most often portrayed as a god and Drethra as a goddess, they are actually androgynous (as are all deities of the pantheon), incorporating both male and female characteristics. Of the two Thaka is by far the most popular, as he is the good-aligned god of the sun, harvest, and life who rides the pegasus Hloctaw, while Drethra, usually portrayed as a creature of evil — pale and sickly with jet-black hair, steely-gray eyes, and parched, angry red lips — mounted on the nightmare steed Calcetrix the Malevolent.

In addition to these two supreme deities, the Ethtuwate faith includes a host of lesser demigods and spirits: Srishwa the Queen of Beasts, goddess of the hunt; Soncala the Horse Lord, god of war; Ugutis the Sin Master, the chaotic god of vice; Zuxaca the Serpent Trickster; and even a god of comedy and mischief named Cajusta, who is believed to have once been a mortal jester elevated to divine status by Thaka. While most of these are usually portrayed as male or female, these are only considered guises of genderless divine beings who can appear or act in any way they deem appropriate.

These gods are only the core pantheon however, for while the Hundaei worshipped many common traditional deities, their diverse and wide-ranging culture made room for local spirits, heroes, and demigods. The old clans' nomadic lifestyle brought them into contact with each other, which led to an exchange of gods, beliefs, philosophies, and ideas. The resulting Ethtuwate faith is therefore highly flexible and adaptive, easily adopting outside gods and faiths without conflict or question as needed.

The resulting laissez-faire attitude toward the divine makes the adoption of new gods and faiths comparatively easy, though missionaries often find the Shattered Folk to be incredibly frustrating, as they eagerly embrace foreign gods like Thyr and Jamboor while remaining faithful to the Ethtuwate pantheon. In fact, the Shattered Folk have often been more successful at converting foreigners to their openminded faith than the missionaries have at getting them to abandon their old beliefs.

That being said, most Shattered Folk draw the line at the worship of demons and evil gods, however, for they are not so naïve to believe that there is not true wickedness in the world. Some priests teach that the gods of evil exist to show the folly of selfishness and cruelty, and that even demons serve a purpose in the great schema of the cosmos. As the whims of nature and the changing character of fate are tools of the inscrutable divine, so too are the creatures and gods of evil.

Priests, soothsayers, diviners, and fortune tellers play an important role in Shattered Folk society, providing guidance and interpretation of omens, signs, portents, and dreams. Numerous methods of divination are used on the steppes, including the casting of bones, the flight of birds, and the examination of entrails. However, soothsayers insist that they are merely messengers, and that their interpretations are merely feeble mortal attempts to interpret the mystical. The final interpretation of signs and portents is up to the person for whom the signs are read. And priests and soothsayers remind anyone seeking guidance of the tragedy of Great Khan Jaganga, of his war with the Hyperboreans, and the role of prophecy in the destruction of their empire. One should not allow oneself to be led or deluded by dreams and visions.

TRADE AND COMMERCE

For nearly their entire history the Haunted Steppes have been isolated from the rest of the world. In the distant past, the Hundaei established a friendship with the dwarves of the Stoneheart Mountains and engaged in a small amount of trade, but this was the exception rather than the rule. It was not until very recently, when the ships of Castorhage made landfall in the Devil's Tail and established relations with the Elitan-i-pan Confederacy, that any real trade existed between the Haunted Steppes and the rest of the world.

Today, thin threads of merchant traffic connect the Elitan-i-pan Confederacy with the traders of Castorhage, and the Campacha with Gtsang, Reme, and Foere. Exotic foodstuffs, steelwork, jewelry, liquor, fine cloth, and lumber flow into the Haunted Steppes in exchange for fine steppes' horses, handcrafts, textiles, and herbs. For their part, the Shattered Folk also provide some of their local intoxicants and narcotics, including fermented mare's milk and the dried seeds and resin of the wild dreamleaf plant, which is harvested in the early fall and has begun to prove quite popular in the dens of Castorhage and Reme.

LOYALTIES AND DIPLOMACY

As with trade, the Haunted Steppes have always been a world apart. Since the end of the Shadow War, they have had little contact with the rest of Akados.

Today, the Shattered Folk remain fiercely independent, though some clans prove to be open to contact and even positive relations, as the Elitan-i-pan folk have with the Castorhagi. The discovery of the Conroi Settlements has brought further attention as diplomats from Reme and Foere have approached the colonists' descendants. For the most part, however, the folk of the steppes keep to themselves, free on the plains, living in the old ways among the ghosts of the past.

GOVERNMENT

No unified government exists on the Haunted Steppes. Each of the peoples who live here govern themselves in such manner as they see fit.

Clans of the Shattered Folk are governed by khans, who are usually either accomplished warriors or high priests. The status of khan varies from clan to clan — some are absolute rulers whose word is law while others are essentially figureheads with a council of wise men or women actually ruling the clan. Though most khans are male, it is not unusual

to encounter a female leader who gained the position through skillful leadership or martial accomplishment.

The folk of each of the Conroi Settlements are typically ruled by one or more elders or senior families chosen by such means as the settlement determines.

MILITARY

The ancient Hundaei were peerless warriors, skilled in the arts of mounted warfare. Each warrior bore a short horn bow, arrows and a pair of light lances which were used to deadly effect. The clans' nimble hit-and-run style of warfare frustrated many a Hyperborean commander, and while the Hundaei were rarely able to break the impregnable fortresses of the Hyperborean phalanx, they were never decisively defeated either.

Today's Shattered Folk continue many of the same traditions, including military training from the age a child can ride and the deadly use of the mounted shortbow and lance. Fewer opportunities exist for military glory these days, of course. No sane outsiders would attempt to invade the steppes, with endless miles of empty plain, mounted warriors without peer on such open spaces, and the land's reputation as haunted; and the Shattered Folk themselves have no interest in conquest any longer. Fights between clans tend to be short and relatively bloodless, often ending after only a handful of casualties. But the old ways remain strong, and twice-yearly gatherings on the plains bring together dozens of clans for games, drinking, gambling, and sport, including contests between lancers, bow-armed riders, and nimble, acrobatic trick-riders. The Hundaei may be a mere shadow of their former selves, but at times they shine quite brightly.

MAJOR THREATS

Today, no kingdoms of Akados have any desire to attempt to seize lands within the Haunted Steppes, the tales of old deterring any but the insane from such foolish endeavor. And those who dwell here have little or no interest in the goings-on beyond their plains. Whether either view could change with the new contacts between the Shattered Folk and Castorhage, Gtsang and Reme remains to be seen.

Clans bicker, and skirmishes occur with the humanoid tribes, but that is just the ordinary way of life here and poses no real threat to the inhabitants of the steppes.

Though now quiescent, the darkness of shadow continues to loom in the north. The Scaedugenga are held at bay by the magical barriers raised and maintained by the Asran, but even the most optimistic guardian knows that the wards are not what they once were and that the Shadow is constantly probing, seeking to return once more and spread across the mortal world.

WILDERNESS AND ADVENTURES

The Haunted Steppes are nearly all wilderness and continue to be a world unto themselves, isolated behind mountainous ramparts and the mystical barrier of the Wizard's Wall. While the Campacha and the Elitan-i-pan Confederacy have settled and pacified significant sections of the steppes, they remain vulnerable to raids from humanoids and other hostile Shattered Folk clans.

The rest of the plains are a vast and seemingly endless sea of grass broken here and there by rivers, especially the God's Ride River. The only significant heights in the steppes are the rugged Pin-i-Pinjhami Hills, home to hostile humanoids and largely avoided by the plains-dwelling clans.

Elsewhere, travelers are likely to encounter many challenges, some of which can be deadly to those who are inexperienced or unprepared. Fierce winds scour the plains, especially in winter, when they accumulate massive drifts that can strand and isolate travelers. Summer weather is also hazardous, as the temperature may soar to deadly levels. Great droughts also affect the plains in summer, drying rivers and reducing them to treacherous stretches of mud. Massive rain- and hailstorms pound the steppes during spring, causing flashfloods that can sweep away encampments or entire traveling groups.

In addition to the hazards of weather, the plains are also home to many marauding bands of goblins, orcs, hill giants, ogres, and others who like nothing better than to prey upon unwary travelers. Not all encounters are hostile, as the Shattered Folk, the centaurs, and (surprisingly) gnolls of the plains are sometimes willing to approach outsiders for trade or assistance. The gnolls are an especially interesting exception, as some have maintained good (or at least tolerant) relations with the Shattered Folk since the first Shadow incursion and are not inclined to simply attack humans on sight. Naturally, not all of these groups are always friendly, or even neutral, as many centaur tribes are very warlike and some of the clans of the Shattered Folk, such as the fearsome Ognari, are highly protective of their home territories.

And here and there can be found remnants of the incursions of the Shadow upon the Haunted Steppes, wandering undead and even the occasional demons or outsiders biding their time until the Asrans' barriers fall again. Rumors among the Shattered Folk also tell of strange beings of shadow that still stalk the plains, possibly Scaedugenga who avoided banishment by the Asran, hunting in the dark and seeking ways to break the wards and allow their fellows to return again to mortal lands.

Yet now, for the first time in generations, the Haunted Steppes are opening up to the outside world, as Castorhagi, Remans, and Foerdewaith reach out to the Shattered Folk. Trade caravans and diplomatic expeditions require experienced adventurers for protection. Scholars from the south, especially in Reme, seek more knowledge about the history of this highly isolated and in many ways, unknown region, particularly the history of the Shattered Folk in the wake of the Hundaei Empire's collapse, the nature of the Shadow Horde and the Scaedugenga, and the history of the surviving Caleen Colonies — how they survived and the challenges that they faced in doing so. Some enterprising adventurers have even set out to the plains on their own to investigate mysteries such as the Tangjan College, the Tav'chul, and the Cursed Ruin of Stone (though this last is extremely dangerous and risks the murderous rage of the Shattered Folk for violating a strict taboo). At the same time, ruins of the old colonies still molder amid the vast grasses. Some are entirely gone save for a few piles of stone, while others may be haunted by lonely spirits or inhabited by the creatures of the steppes. These battered settlements may provide shelter to travelers, or they may yet hold some remnants — for good or ill — of their original residents.

REFERENCE SOURCES: FIELDS OF BLOOD, THE BLIGHT

POLITICAL SUBDIVISIONS OF THE HAUNTED STEPPES

CAMPACHA PLAINS, CLANS OF THE

Capital: none
Notable Settlements: Thian, Petyan
Ruler: Khan Boro'ul Ikres, Khan Oqotur Tarkut and Khan Tolun Campacha
Government: tribal confederacy
Population: 109,700 (103,500 Shattered Folk, 2,700 Gtsang, 1,500 Rheman, 1,250 half-elf, 750 wild elf)
Monstrous: goblins, gnolls, orcs, centaurs, hobgoblins, kobolds, axe beaks, ankhegs, hill giants, ogres, minotaurs, banshees, dire wolves, bugbears, perytons, worgs, skeletons, zombies, basilisks, blood hawks, owlbears, wraiths, griffons, harpies, ghosts, nightmares, manticores, mummies, bulettes, hippogriffs, chimeras, specters, trolls, wights

Languages: Kirkut (Campacha dialects), Common
Religion: Ethtuwate
Resources: foodstuffs, grain, horses
Currency: barter or miscellaneous coins
Technology Level: Dark Ages

When the Conroi Expedition first crossed the Wizard's Wall past Durgam's Folly in 3439 I.R., they did not know what they would find. Though some rumors from Castorhage and Gtsang suggested that remnants of ancient peoples still lived there, most in Reme believed that the Haunted Steppes would prove to be nothing more than a vast charnel house, its inhabitants slain and lying silent beneath the eternal skies.

The rumors proved true, for the plains were not empty. Quite the contrary, the descendants of the Invincible Horde lived on and had spent the intervening centuries rebuilding. Fortunately for Conroi and her expedition, the first group they encountered were the united clans of the Campacha, powerful, but not unwilling to host and deal with these visitors from the south.

The Campacha Plains are still wild, and roving bands of humanoids can make the region hazardous. The old magic of the Shadow Horde still lingers even after centuries, sometimes opening doorways to other realms or compelling the ancient dead to rise and trouble the living. Just the same, the plains are a rich and relatively peaceful place where the Grand Duchy of Reme has tentatively begun to establish trade and learn about the history of the Haunted Steppes since the days of Cale's downfall.

HISTORY AND PEOPLE

The remaining Shattered Folk after the raising of the Wizard's Wall and the banishment of the Shadow by the Asran were few and scattered, but survivors there were. Those in the southern steppes had suffered such losses that they no longer needed to fight one another for territory. However, though the barriers in the north had been restored, many tribes of orcs and goblins remained on the plains to threaten the survivors. To avoid destruction, the Shattered Folk of the region were forced to band together.

The leading clan of the area was called the Campacha, and within a few generations the alliance transformed into a true confederacy named for its founding group. The humanoid threat was largely eliminated by coordinated defense, and the creation of the confederacy taught the Campacha the benefits of diplomacy. They also discovered that trade with the nearby Caleen colonies was to their advantage and enhanced their own security and prosperity. As a result, the fear and distrust of outsiders was far less among the Campacha than many of their more-isolated kinfolk. When the Conroi Expedition arrived, they found a well-established nation in the Campacha, one secure and willing to trade and even befriend those from the south. They tolerate the Reman missionaries, incorporating the foreign gods into their pantheon, and some among the Campacha have even considered forming settlements, farming, and tending herds rather than wandering the plains. Conservative Campacha are disdainful of this suggestion, but the idea is gaining popularity, and the Campacha may join the Elitan-i-pan Confederacy in founding permanent villages and farms.

Some time ago, a Gtsang scholar by the name of Tiblu Ottika arrived with the seemingly mad notion of establishing a major college in the midst of the Campacha Plains. Somewhat puzzled, the Campacha agreed, and the college was built near the town of Petyan. After initial success, the grand experiment collapsed as a horde of chaos-creatures emerged from the college, forcing a desperate defense by the Campacha wizard Tunicamna. Though the battle against the creatures was won, repercussions from the disaster have continued over the years, and the college remains abandoned and shunned.

RELIGION

Most Campacha practice the Ethtuwate faith of their ancestors. Since adherents of this faith can incorporate other deities, even imported gods such as Thyr and Muir, into their religion, missionaries from Reme, Foere, and elsewhere ventured onto the plains seeking converts.

Initial reports from these missionaries told of success and the conversion of entire communities, leading to the mistaken belief that the Campacha are somehow spiritually deprived and seeking new enlightenment. In reality, the easygoing Campacha listened to the stories of Thyr, Freya, Jamboor, and others, and simply added these "new" gods to their existing faith, even while continuing to remain faithful to Thaka and the other Ethtuwate deities. As this has become more apparent, the priesthoods of the other gods have come to find the Campacha maddening, for their demands that they abandon all other faiths to pursue a single pantheon are invariably met with mocking laughter and bafflement.

TRADE AND COMMERCE

For many years the Campacha were content to trade among themselves or with the Caleen. Occasionally, Campacha would venture into the Stonehearts to contact the dwarves and return with iron weapons, works of art, or tools. For the most part, however, trade and commerce played little role in the Campachas' life.

The arrival of the Remans, the Foerdewaith, and the Castorhagi changed that somewhat, as merchants from all three groups made contact with the Campacha and brought gold and finished goods in exchange for horses, grains, and other foodstuffs. Trade is a small but growing concern at this point, for though the Campacha have little to offer now, many foreigners see vast opportunities in the wide-open steppes.

LOYALTIES AND DIPLOMACY

Once an alliance of fiercely independent nomad clans who wished to be left alone and to see to their own security, the Campacha have been made aware of the outside world, and many seek to expand their contacts with Foere, Reme, and Castorhage. So far, the relationship consists of minimal diplomatic presence and trade, but this seems likely to expand.

GOVERNMENT

Like the Elitan-i-pan, the other major assembly of the Shattered Folk, the Campacha are a confederacy of several clans — the Ikres, Tarkut and Campacha — and after decades have come to be known by the name of the most prominent of these. The independent nature of the old Hundaei society has led to a fairly loose state with minimal organization. Each of the three federated clans is led by its own khan and elder council, and these three khans meet each month in the Tae'kon encampment to administer and oversee the Campacha region, settling disputes, making laws and overseeing relations with the Caleen and other outsiders. Most decisions are made by consensus, but the presence of three khans makes tie votes unlikely.

MILITARY

The old warrior traditions are still practiced by the Campacha, and every clan member is trained from birth in the arts of riding, shooting, and combat with lance and tulwar. All members of the federation, even many young and elderly, are highly capable warriors and in times of conflict can be called upon to defend their folk. The warriors of each clan are under the command of their respective khan, but should an outside power threaten the region, the khans would almost certainly select one of their number to be supreme leader.

MAJOR THREATS

Orcs, ogres, and hill giants of the region are a constant threat and raid Campacha lands in the spring and summer. These incursions are opposed by the nearest clan, which sends mounted warriors to intercept incoming raiders or pursue those attempting to escape. Battles between the Campacha and wolf-mounted goblins or orcish worg riders are also a frequent event in this portion of the steppes.

REFERENCE SOURCE: FIELDS OF BLOOD

PETYAN, VILLAGE OF

Ruler: Elder Priest Quanata
Government: clan
Population: 168 (104 Shattered Folk, 22 half-elf, 18 wild elf, 24 others)

Like most settlements on the grasslands of Campacha, Petyan has a sizable transient population. The village lies a few miles west of a migratory buffalo route and grazing area, making it a popular destination for nomadic people during the spring and summer months.

In addition to its ideal hunting location, the underground rivers and aquifers that bisect the area are also perfect for sedentary farmers. Lush crops of corn and other food staples dot the landscape in every direction. The farmers who tend to these fields dwell in earth lodges built into the sides of small hills or excavated from the ground. These permanent structures feature a wooden dome covered by dirt, reeds, mud-bricks, and similar materials. Because they are partially underground, these homes are better suited for the extreme temperatures encountered during the hot summers and the frigid winters.

Petyan's residents are entirely self-sufficient, so commerce in the traditional sense is far less prevalent than in conventional communities. It is possible to purchase goods and services within the settlement, though barter is the preferable method of acquiring valuables within Petyan. Its permanent and even temporary residents all share some degree of kinship. Naturally, those belonging to the full-time population are more closely related to one another than its transient settlers, who are typically first and second cousins several generations removed from the permanent residents. Still, the bonds of blood run strong, and even the most-distant relations respect the authority and wisdom of the village's patriarch. The patriarch is revered as a titular authority figure that provides wisdom and guidance, though he wields no real political and military authority. Instead, leadership is determined on the battlefield and the hunting grounds. The bravest and fiercest warrior from among the patriarch's immediate family assumes autonomy over the village. Hintah fulfilled that role in Petyan until the centaurs killed him. After his death, Quanata, the resident cleric, reluctantly accepted the role as the village's leader.

REFERENCE SOURCE: FIELDS OF BLOOD

THIAN, VILLAGE OF

Ruler: Chieftain Angarzhu the Wise
Government: clan chieftain
Population: 330 (Shattered Folk)

Thian is an especially sacred place for the Shattered Folk, as it is the site of the Mound of the Sun, the primary temple of the god Thaka. As its name suggests, the temple is a vast and ancient earth mound that dates back to the earliest history of the Hundaei clans. Inside, a series of rough corridors and chambers lead to a vaulted central chamber where a round opening in the roof frames the sun perfectly at noon on midsummer, a time of especially solemn ritual.

A scattering of permanent settlements — rubble or sod with attached farm plots or animal pens — surrounds the temple. Beyond the settlements lie seasonal encampments where nomadic Campacha spend the warmer months hunting herd animals and engaging in trade.

Though inns and rooming houses are normally rare in the steppe lands, this town also boasts housing for pilgrims and visitors, as most of the Shattered Folk, regardless of their clan, wish to visit the Mound of the Sun at least once in their lives. Travel here is heaviest at midsummer, and the crowd that is here to witness the moment when the sun passes directly overhead frequently overflows the mound completely.

REFERENCE SOURCE: FIELDS OF BLOOD

TAE'KON ENCAMPMENT

This fertile, picturesque grassy spot lies near the middle of the Campacha lands. It is here that the Campacha khans meet each month to make decisions regarding their peoples. Usually these meetings are small and sober gatherings that feature a huddle of tents and lean-tos around a central pavilion, but the Great Meeting that takes place on the summer equinox each year is a more festive occasion with thousands of Campacha gathering, raising colorful banners and erecting wildly-decorated tents, engaging in games and contests, feasting, drinking, and celebrating the founding of the confederacy.

CASTORHAGI COLONIES

PORT KINSAL, COLONY OF

Ruler: Governor Josep Mantral
Government: colony
Population: 1,194 (620 Castorhagi, 326 Elitani, 150 Rheman, 98 halfling)
Languages: Common, Kirkut
Religion: Castorhagi pantheon, Ethtuwate, Mick O'Delving
Technology Level: Medieval

The smaller of the two Castorhagi trade settlements, Port Kinsal is located on the site of the first Castorhagi landing three centuries ago. Situated on a cold and fairly bleak stretch of the Elitani coast, the climate is harsher here along the Devil's Tail, and the settlement is more vulnerable than Port Mandei, having endured several humanoid raids over the past years. Kinsal is protected by a strong wooden wall reinforced with stone here and there, and many buildings are stone. Like Mandei, the settlement includes port facilities, trading centers and inns that cater to a wide range of visitors.

Though the Elitani will certainly help defend the settlement if possible, they are not as strong in this region as elsewhere. As a result, the Kinsal folk know they can't necessarily depend upon the nomads and must defend the settlement on their own. About 250 Castorhagi and mercenary warriors are stationed here, as well as 50 elite halfling archers. In addition to the archers, Kinsal is also home to a branch of the Lightbody Trade Alliance, a halfling mercantile group based out of Courghais.

PORT MANDEI, COLONY OF

Ruler: Governor Alexa Wolsten
Government: colony
Population: 1,605 (875 Castorhagi, 350 Elitani, 220 Rheman, 160 Foerdewaith)
Languages: Common, Kirkut
Religion: Castorhagi pantheon, Ethtuwate, Thyr, Jamboor
Technology Level: Medieval

Located on the shores of Tabur Bay, Port Mandei is one of two Castorhagi trading ports along the Elitani Coast. Founded nearly two centuries ago, it has grown into a substantial settlement, with well-equipped docks and repair facilities, warehouses, trading establishments and inns that cater to Elitani and foreign traders. The town bustles with activity as ships and trade caravans arrive and depart along with their attendant crowds of sailors, traders, Elitani clansfolk, mercenary guards and, in recent years, adventurers who have begun to venture into the steppes.

Port Mandei boasts sturdy stone buildings and a wood-and-stone wall and a small group of 200 professional mercenaries who keep the place safe from humanoid attacks. This threat has faded in recent years as the nearby Elitani secured the plains and usually intercept humanoids before they get anywhere near the outpost.

ELITAN-I-PAN CONFEDERATION

Capital: none
Notable Settlements: none
Ruler: High Khan Yalbaq Alchi-Tarqut
Government: Confederacy
Population: 87,000 (85,750 Shattered Folk, 750 half-elf, 500 Castorhagi)
Monstrous: goblins, gnolls, orcs, centaurs, hobgoblins, kobolds, axe beaks, ankhegs, hill giants, ogres, minotaurs, banshees, dire wolves, bugbears, perytons, worgs, skeletons, zombies, basilisks, revenants, blood hawks, shadows, owlbears, wraiths, griffons, harpies, ghosts, nightmares, wyverns, manticores, mummies, bulettes, hippogriffs, chimeras, specters, trolls, wights, cockatrices, hell hounds, vampires, blue dragons
Languages: Kirkut (Elitan-i-Pani dialects), Common
Religion: Ethtuwate
Resources: grains, leather goods, horses
Currency: barter
Technology Level: Dark Ages

As the Campacha of the south have gathered together the surviving clans into a single confederacy, so have the Shattered Folk of the Elitan-i-pan region drawn together for mutual defense. More religious and mystically-minded than the Campacha, the Elitan-i-pan folk have continued and expanded the old traditions of divination, soothsaying, and the analysis of omens. Castorhagi explorers and merchants contacted the confederation in 3262 I.R. and maintained steady and largely friendly trade with them since then.

HISTORY AND PEOPLE

For several years after the raising of the Wizard's Wall, the Shattered Folk of the Elitan region of the Ethtuwate-cala-tun (Gods' Ride) basin struggled against the humanoid tribes left on the steppes after the banishment of the Shadow. Each clan faced the threat alone, and some clans were annihilated when they were overwhelmed by the orcish or goblin tribes.

In 2955 I.R., Khan Elanghus of the Elun-koro (Thunder Rider) clan called upon the other khans, suggesting that they would all be better served to set aside the old hatreds and band together for mutual defense and benefit. A few clans rejected the proposal and struck out on their own, but a core of a dozen clans agreed and swore common cause. An attack on one would be an attack on all, and the allied clans swore to never fight or shed each other's blood again, submitting to a council of chiefs to mediate disputes. Clans would be strengthened by arranged intermarriage, and priests would likewise move from clan to clan to share their specific wisdom and spiritual guidance, further joining the clans into a single entity.

The omens for the alliance were good, for within a few years the clans that had rejected Elanghus' proposal were either wiped out or reconsidered their refusal and joined their fellows. Within three generations, the confederacy was well established and while its member clans retained their independence, they all thought of themselves as a single related people.

The new confederacy was tested over the following years as waves of humanoid migration and invasion swept through the Ethtuwate basin. Had they not declared common cause, many clans would surely have been annihilated, and the wise counsel of Elanghus was fully recognized by his descendants. The worst of these invasions came in 3130 I.R. when the orcish warlord Hazhgol Swordhand united several orc clans, conquered several goblin clans and turned them into slave warriors, and began a crusade to claim the entire Gods' Ride River basin and its rich lands. Hazhgol's deadly worg-chariots swept into the river lands and descended on the Elitani-i-pani.

Over generations, the Elitan-i-pan had grown into a highly religious people devoted to the Ethtuwate faith and its pantheon. While the confederation's warriors rode out to face the warlord, their priests remained behind to seek guidance and wisdom and to read the omens and cast their various objects of divination. Even powerful spells brought mixed and ambiguous results, and initial engagements with the orcs and goblins proved unsuccessful. The old Hundaei mobile tactics of hit, run, withdraw, then attack from a different direction were frustrated by goblin wolf-riders and ended, at best, in bloody draws with casualties on both sides. Still, Hazhgol's horde advanced despite the Elitans' best efforts to resist him.

Consensus came to the meditating priests when a common thread developed in their visions and omen readings. All signs pointed to the old ruins at Pan-ni-Rikam-Po (the Cursed Ruins of Stone), the remains of the only great city ever built by the Hundaei, the place that had served as the capital of the Great Khans in the glory days of the Invincible Horde and the endless wars with Hyperborea. Dreams revealed that a great weapon lay there, one sufficient to defeat Hazhgol and shatter his horde. It seemed imperative that some hero venture to the old city, brave its dangers, and retrieve the weapon, whatever it was.

There was one problem — after the city had been devastated in the great Hundaei civil war, it was declared cursed by the surviving khans. Entry was absolutely forbidden on pain of death to both Hundaei and outsiders. This prohibition remained even so many long generations after, and all knew that anyone who ventured into the ruin would do so at the cost of his or her life.

Nevertheless, it seemed that the only answer to the crisis lay at the heart of the forbidden city, and a call went out to the warriors of Elitan to volunteer.

Despite the tolerant nature of the Ethtuwate faith, breaking ancient tribal taboos was a difficult, if not impossible, task for even the boldest warrior. Only a handful responded, and of these, the omens and divinations favored only one — a young man named Tahtona from the Mua-chae clan. When the council of priests announced that he had been chosen, Tahtona spent the next day fasting and meditating upon what lay ahead. He was not an experienced warrior and had fought in only a few skirmishes, but he had felt a compulsion to answer the priests' call and now faced his fate with stoic resolve.

Alone, Tahtona ventured into the forbidden ruins. What took place in Pan-ni-Rikam-Po is not known, for he did not share his story with anyone. All that is known is that after nearly a fortnight Tahtona emerged clad in the lacquered armor of a chieftain, polished and gleaming, backed with fine silk, looking new and untouched. He bore a black horn bow, a quiver of arrows that seemed to radiate dark energy, and a pair of lances with heads of strange glassy material. He spoke little but assured his friends that he was still the young and vital Tahtona. He had, however, seen his destiny, and he emphasized that the ruins were still forbidden.

The young warrior, now somehow transformed into a mighty war chief, gathered the clans to him and called upon them to meet Hazhgol in battle. Soon the entire Elitan-i-pan Confederation rode forth to seek out the orcish horde. Hazhgol seemed drawn to them and eagerly responded, his chariots in the lead, supported by hordes of screaming goblin archers.

The battle that came to be called Bloody Grass was the greatest since the coming of the Shadow Horde. At first, the orcs had the upper hand as their chariots cut through the Elitani riders and the goblins held them at bay with volleys of small but deadly red-feathered arrows. But soon the tide began to turn. The chariots were stopped and cut to pieces, and the goblins fled, leaving Hazhgol and his worg cavalry to advance for the final confrontation. Cunningly, the orcish warlord sent his swift goblin wolf-riders around the flanks in an attempt to envelop the Elitani, but the Shattered Folks' own light cavalry countered, and the battle began to sprawl over the vast plains.

It was then that Tahtona advanced alone against the horde. Those who saw him claimed that as he rode, he grew in stature, and that the spirits of ancient Hundaei warriors rode with him, mounted on the shades of the old Hu-Soncala, the legendary horses of the old days. It was said that Tahtona's lance impaled dozens with each strike and that his black arrows slew hundreds with each shot. The Spirit Host, as it came to be called in legend, cut through their enemies. Mighty orcish warriors, renowned for their morale and fanaticism, fled in terror until only Hazhgol and his bodyguard remained. Tahtona rode at the orcish chieftain.

The battle that followed is said to have gone on for hours. Some stories say that the sun itself stood motionless in the sky as the two battled. Neither gave ground and neither asked for quarter, for they both knew that the outcome of the great battle hinged on this single fight. Swords and lances clashed, armor was battered, and blood was shed.

In the end, the two warriors stood dismounted, near exhaustion, weapons still clashing. Then it is said that a strange thing happened. Both combatants paused, their gazes locked, their rage transforming into an expression of acceptance, recognition, and — strangely — respect. As if by mutual agreement, the warriors raced at each other, simultaneously piercing each other's hearts and dying together, locked in eternal combat. The orcish warlord was overthrown, and the brave Tahtona paid the price for his violation of ancient taboo.

As expected, the loss of their leader disheartened the horde as subordinate chieftains began to fight for control and dominance. By the time the sun set, the orcs and goblins had been driven from the field of battle and, though they had suffered terribly, the Elitan-i-pan emerged victorious.

The confederacy recovered from their losses at Bloody Grass and slowly rebuilt its numbers and kept the plains relatively secure. As always, the steppes were never fully at peace, for raids and territorial conflicts continued. The ghosts and undead who trouble the rest of the region are present here as well, including shades and vengeful spirits called forth from the old battlefield at Bloody Grass, and clan priests or warriors must often be dispatched to deal with them. All the same, the union of the various folk prove successful, and the Elitani forged a secure and relatively stable nation.

Then in the year 3262 I.R., Elitani scouts reported making contact with foreigners on the shores of the Devil's Tail. It was the Castorhagi trader *Provision* on a mission to contact the indigenous peoples of the steppes to possibly establish trade relations. To the Castorhagi captain's infinite relief, these descendants of the fearsome Hundaei proved friendly, open, and willing to talk. Within a few years, Castorhagi trade settlements were established, and mercantile traffic began to flow.

While the years of isolation and persistent bitterness over the long war with Hyperborea hardened many of the Shattered Folk and reinforced their xenophobia, the Elitani had, in creating their confederacy, sown the seeds of forward-thinking diplomacy. While they retained many of the old traditions, the Elitan-i-pan were open to new ideas. In the years since contact, some clans have begun to transition to a more settled economy, building permanent or semi-permanent villages and farms in some of the more fertile regions of the God's Ride basin, and the inflow of foreign goods, ideas, and faiths has affected some of these communities. Foreign missionaries have visited the region but, as with the Campacha of the south, the Elitan refuse to forsake their faith and instead incorporate other gods and religious traditions into their complex and highly adaptable religious life.

Religion

One of the unifying factors of the Elitan-i-pan Confederacy is its religious practices. They are far more devout and mystical than their Campacha cousin to the south and revere the Sky-God under the name Nah-ki-at. Omens, prophecies, and divination by a number of means (spells, casting of dice or stones, entrail-reading, and the like) are practiced with great reverence and given significant credence by all, even the most powerful local chieftains. Priests wield considerable influence in Elitan society, but usually act as advisors, mediators, and counselors, and rarely get involved in clan politics or rulership.

Trade and Commerce

The Elitan-i-pan's primary exposure to the world beyond the Haunted Steppes is due to their trade relationship with the city-state of Castorhage. For nearly three centuries, goods have flowed from the two major Castorhage trade cities along the Elitani coast, exchanged for local goods, foodstuffs, and especially horses. Over the years, the sturdy steppe horses bred by the Elitani for export have grown popular throughout eastern Akados and recently found their way into the Xha'en Hegemony through the Castorhagi trade missions on the Bream Islands.

LOYALTIES AND DIPLOMACY

The confederacy maintains diplomatic relations with other clans and alliances of the Shattered Folk, including the southern alliance of the Campacha. Until the arrival of the Castorhagi, that was all that the Elitani needed. Today, they have taken tentative steps toward contact beyond the borders of the steppes, as a handful of Elitani have visited Reme, Castorhage, Foere, and the Xha'en Hegemony. So far, the Elitani maintain full relations with only the Castorhagi, but the other powers of the region have seen the city-state's successes and have increased their efforts to establish diplomatic ties.

For their part, the Elitan welcome the attention. Most feel that the old xenophobic attitudes are part of the past, since most of their ancient enemies are long since extinct. A few holdouts resist the encroachment of the outside world, but they are a distinct minority.

GOVERNMENT

More than a dozen clans make up the Elitan-i-pan Confederacy, each led by its own khan, chieftain or, in the case of the Mora-tahn (Storm Hawk) clan, a trio of high priestesses. The many different clans represent different traditions and practices, a factor that the confederacy's founder, Khan Elanghus, recognized when he first proposed the new alliance. Cultural and religious exchanges between the different clans helped lessen these differences, and though the various groups retained many differences, they also managed to forge a common identity.

Constructing a unified rulership was a challenge, for every clan felt it was best qualified to lead. In the end, the chiefs all came together and decided that the confederacy's High Khan would be a rotating office chosen once every five years from among the leaders of the various clans. A single khan could not serve two consecutive terms, and a new khan would be chosen by vote of the other khans. The khan thus chosen would be the confederacy's paramount leader, though in important matters that affect multiple clans, the khan's decisions must be ratified by a majority vote of the other khans. This system has persisted, with various modifications and adjustments, over several centuries and continues to this day.

MILITARY

The Elitani retain the traditional Hundaei values and, as with other clans, all are trained in the arts of war, and all able-bodied warriors are called up to serve should the region ever be threatened. Each clan has its own specialty — some are scouts, others are expert horse archers, while others serve as armored lancers capable of standing up even to the steel-clad knights of other nations. The High Khan traditionally commands the confederacy's military, but unless the khan is especially capable, he or she generally appoints an experienced veteran as general.

MAJOR THREATS

Conflicts still rage on the steppes — with smaller, rival clans of the Shattered Folk, with humanoid tribes, and with the undead or unnatural creatures that continue to stalk the plains in the wake of the raising of the Wizard's Wall. As always, the greatest threat still slumbers in the far north in the form of the vanquished Shadow Horde. No one can say whether the horde will one day return, but anyone who is familiar with the history of Akados knows that evil is never truly defeated, and that it is usually only a matter of time before it rises again.

REFERENCE SOURCE: THE BLIGHT

LOST COLONIES OF THE CALEEN

Capital: none
Notable Settlements: Cale's Hope, Fort Relian, Imar, Chesmire, Enua
Ruler: none
Government: clan confederacy
Population: 2,305 (1,890 mixed Foerdewaith-Hundaei, 220 halfling, 120 half-elf, 75 gnome)
Monstrous: goblins, gnolls, kobolds, ankhegs, hill giants, ogres, minotaurs, banshees, dire wolves, bugbears, perytons, skeletons, zombies, blood hawks, shadows, owlbears, wraiths, griffons, harpies, ghosts, nightmares, wyverns, lamias, manticores, bulettes, hippogriffs, chimeras, specters, trolls, wights, cockatrices
Languages: Kirkut (mainly Campacha dialects), Common
Religion: Ethtuwate, Muir, Thyr, Jamboor
Resources: grain, fruit, livestock, wool
Currency: barter, miscellaneous coins
Technology Level: Dark Ages

When the Shadow Horde poured forth from the north and swept the Great Steppes in 2947 I.R., it was believed that all of the Caleen colonies were destroyed. As a result, the folk of Reme, safe behind the Wizard's Wall, made no attempts to reach the lost colonies.

Yet when Gtsang traders began exploring up the Tabur River in recent centuries, they discovered intact settlements of folk of mixed Foerdewaith-Shattered Folk ancestry where some of those lost colonies had been. Later, the Conroi Expedition discovered even larger settlements to the east along the Deepfells and the old course of the Tabur, now known as the Ghost River. These settlements had in fact survived the Shadow Horde and continued through the years of isolation since then. The easternmost villages are popularly referred to as the Conroi Settlements, which has given rise to the myth that they were actually founded or delivered from extinction by the arrival of the Conroi Expedition.

HISTORY AND PEOPLE

The days of the Great Colonization was a time of great optimism and excitement. Colonists flowed by the thousands through the Crynnomar Gap, expanding northwards into the steppes. The Caleen colonies, named for the Grand Duke Prince Cale who had envisioned the endeavor, would spread throughout the north. Humanoids, monsters and the remnants of the once-great Hundaei Empire would be brushed aside and soon Reme would command vast new territories, rivaling even the ancient Hyperboreans in power. It was not to be.

Starting in 2861 I.R., colonists made their way past the gap, then turned northwest, taking the path of least resistance along the verdant lands surrounding the Tabur River. Small outposts were founded as they went, and some of these outposts such as Fort Relian and Cale's Hope grew into true settlements. Progress seemed all but inevitable, for at first popular belief was reinforced — the humanoids and human nomads of the region were either entirely absent or weak. The collapse of the Hundaei Empire was so complete that it had all but scoured the land of defenders. The colonists saw this as a sign from Thyr himself that their destiny was manifest, and that the plains belonged to them and them alone.

The colonies grew and dotted the land as the settlers' trails diverged, some founding new towns along the coast while others struck directly north past the Everfar Hills, across the Gods' Ride River, and into the heart of the steppes. Soon it became apparent that their initial optimism was somewhat misplaced, as the farther north they went, the greater resistance from the humanoids and the surviving Hundaei grew. All the same they pressed on, reaching the bleak shores of Lake Hali in 2931 I.R. It was then that disaster struck.

At first, very little news filtered down from the far north. The new colonies were facing resistance, but few expected it to amount to much. But soon the news turned dire. Something greater had stirred, and the humanoids were far more numerous than initially thought. Swarming from lairs in the Lost Mountains they descended on the small northern settlements, wiping them out and sending a wave of refugees fleeing south. The refugees brought even worse tidings, for it seemed that the humanoids were being led by shadowy, demonic creatures that emerged from the realms of the far north that the Hundaei had avoided with such superstitious fervor.

Grimly the colonists prepared to defend themselves.

The Shadow Horde advanced southward, and it soon became clear that their intention was to sweep humanity from the steppes. If that succeeded, there seemed little that could stand before them if they passed the Crynnomar Gap. One after another, the colonies between Lake Hali and the Everfar Hills fell to the advancing horde.

With regular Foerdewaith troops scarce and reinforcements months away, the colonists had no choice but to form their own army, dubbing it the Caleen Legion. The legion managed to hold the humanoids at bay for a time, but in the end even reinforcements from the Northmarches weren't enough. Grand Duke Cale, who had arrived to personally take command, perished in battle south of the Everfar Hills, and what remained of the Caleen Legion was scattered.

Only the Caleen Colonies along the Tabur River remained. Some fled toward the Crynnomar Gap while others grimly prepared for a last stand. To their shock however, the horde turned aside and marched directly toward the gap, leaving only a small contingent of humanoids to assault the Tabur River settlements.

The fight that followed was fierce, and in the end the Tabur River folk managed, after significant losses, to push back the humanoids. Though they had won a temporary reprieve, the Tabur River folk knew that it was only a matter of time before the horde, having defeated the Foerdewaith in the south, would return to finish the job. Only a miracle could save them.

The miracle came in the form of two ancient wizards who returned seemingly out of the mists of time to work one of the mightiest acts of magic in history — the raising of the Wizard's Wall that permanently sealed the Crynnomar Gap and caused devastating changes throughout the region. Walls and buildings crumbled. Rivers changed their courses. Lakes appeared where there had been none. But despite the upheaval, the Caleen colonies survived, though now the life-giving Tabur had permanently shifted, leaving them astride a dry riverbed.

But the Shadow Horde was frustrated, not defeated. It could still exterminate the last Foerdewaith survivors. Now a second miracle was delivered by the Shattered Folk and the secret society known as the Asran, who worked another great ritual and vanquished the fearsome Scaedugenga and sent them back to their shadowy homeland. The humanoids fell to bickering and retreated, leaving the battered settlements of the southern steppes in relative peace.

Slowly the settlements rebuilt. Walls were restored, structures repaired. New farming lands were established in the rich soil left behind by the Tabur River's diversion while irrigation was provided by wells and small streams from the Deepfells. The Caleen, as they now called themselves, formed a rough alliance of independent settlements and reached out to the Campacha nomads who had moved back into their traditional territories. Eventually intermarrying with the local Shattered Folk, the people of the settlements lived for generations, until they were rediscovered by the rest of the world through visits from Gtsang traders and the Conroi Expedition.

Religion

The original colonists came from all across Foere and brought their various faiths with them. Primary among their deities were the traditional religions of Thyr, Muir, Jamboor and a handful of other Hyperborean or Foerdewaith gods. When the Great Colonization collapsed into disaster and the Shadow Horde was on the march, the people of the colonies prayed to all their gods for deliverance. The diversion and eventual banishment of the Scaedugenga seemed to be an answer to these prayers, and the faith of the Caleen was bolstered and increased. As years went by, temples and shrines to their traditional gods were founded, while contacts, migration, and intermarriage with the nearby Caleen also brought the Ethtuwate faith, whose tolerant and inclusive culture allowed it to easily integrate into Caleen society.

Trade and Commerce

For most of their history, the Caleen Colonies have been largely self-reliant, though there has always been some amount of trade within the colony settlements and with the local Campacha. Over time, many of the colonies and farms have come to produce a modest surplus, which provides a solid basis for trade with the Campacha and, more recently, the Remans and Castorhagi. The old riverbeds have been converted to farming and produce oats, wheat, and rye. The Caleen have also cultivated significant fruit plantations where they grow apples, pears, and various nuts.

Loyalties and Diplomacy

Left on their own for centuries, the Caleen colonies have developed a fierce streak of independence, even from each other. While they are entirely capable of banding together in defense of the region, the settlements are all distinctly separate entities, each with its own leaders, government, and way of life.

Of necessity, the Caleen maintain good relations with the Campacha who helped them in the aftermath of the Shadow Horde and continue to aid the Caleen against monsters and humanoid raids. Campacha can ride freely through Caleen territory, and Caleen merchants, farmers, and even adventurers may be found throughout Campacha lands.

Recent years have left the Caleen in a state of flux, for after their rediscovery by the Conroi Expedition and the popular adoption of the term "Conroi Settlements" for the easternmost Caleen cities (a practice that has infuriated most Caleen), the region has become a popular destination for scientists, scholars, adventurers, and merchants. While the new visitors have brought contact with the outside world as well as goods and services long absent from the area, the Caleen have remained standoffish, suspicious of the descendants of those who abandoned them so many years ago.

Government

The Caleen do not have a collective government but instead act as a group of independent settlements that work together as needed for mutual protection, economics, and general welfare. The Caleen themselves are a singularly self-reliant people and the notion of banding together as a confederacy or — worse — a true kingdom is contrary to their independent natures.

Military

After surviving the horrors of the Shadow Horde, the Caleen were forced to see to their own defense. Fortunately, a number of veterans of the Caleen Legion survived the war, along with a small group of Foerdewaith regular soldiers, and these individuals formed the core of the militias who continue to defend the Caleen settlements to this day. Despite the Caleen towns' independence, they practice mutual defense out of necessity, with commanders selected from among the most accomplished and skilled warriors to command all Caleen troops regardless of their town of origin.

Caleen militia consist primarily of infantry armed mostly with spears and bows and armored with padded cloth or light leather armor. If mounted troops or scouts are needed, the Caleen can call upon the Campacha for assistance, and help is usually given except in very unusual circumstances.

Major Threats

The Caleen have always lived in a land of great peril, even in times of relative peace, surviving invasions, natural disasters, and raids from the humanoids of the plains and the Deepfells. Storms, floods, extreme winter weather, heat in summer, droughts, blights, and other natural disasters are every bit as perilous as the goblins, gnolls, ogres, and other hostiles who ravage the settlements. Though their greatest threat — the Scaedugenga — are gone, the Caleen do not forget and dread the time when the Shadow may again move on the steppes.

Wilderness and Adventures

The Caleen region is covered by significant wilderness — it is, in fact, almost all wilderness with small settlements dotted here and there. Some of the villages are connected by unpaved roads, but most are separated by wide open grasslands with occasional stands of trees that can provide either shelter or concealment for patient humanoid ambushers. Banditry is, thankfully, less of a hazard in the Caleen colonies than elsewhere due to the relatively low population and limited prosperity of the region.

The area does not contain much in the way of ruins, tombs, or other traditional adventuring sites. However, the presence of significant numbers of hostile species constitutes an opportunity for freelance adventurers. Heroes could end up hunting down raiders, patrolling travel routes, pursuing humanoids, centaurs, or other hostiles who have sacked settlements or taken captives.

CONROI SETTLEMENTS

The eastern settlements of the lost Caleen colonies discovered by the Conroi Expedition in 3439 I.R. are now commonly referred to, outside the villages themselves, as the Conroi Settlements. Since the return of the expedition and its acclamation by the public, a false belief has developed among the general public that the eastern settlements (Imar, Cale's Hope, and Fort Relian) were actually founded — or in some stories, rescued from extinction — by the expedition, leading to the popular name for the towns. In reality, they were well-established towns with significant populations for centuries before the expedition was even conceived.

CALE'S HOPE, SETTLEMENT OF

Ruler: Mayor Ambros Tyndar
Government: clan chieftain
Population: 925 (mostly mixed Foerdewaith-Hundaei)
Languages: Kirkut (mainly Campacha dialects), Common
Religion: Ethtuwate, Thyr, Muir, Jamboor
Technology Level: Dark Ages

The largest and generally the leading settlement of the lost Caleen colonies, Cale's Hope is located along a portion of the Tabur River that still flows. After the deliverance of the colonies from the scourge of the Shadow Horde, the surviving inhabitants of Cale's Hope rebuilt and established new farms and bred their depleted stock of goats and sheep with the help of the Campacha nomads who recognized the need for peace and good relations in the chaotic world of the post-horde steppes.

Like the other colonies, Cale's Hope retained a fierce independent streak and never formally joined their fellow settlements in any kind of confederacy or alliance. Just the same, Cale's Hope became a center for trade and a meeting place located conveniently between the eastern and western settlements. Today, the town continues to prosper, with partly-paved streets, several inns, and a wood-and-stone wall. Diplomatic missions from Castorhage, Reme, and Foere have all chosen Cale's Hope as their main location in the region, and outsiders — including merchants, explorers, and even adventurers — have become a more common sight. Mayor Ambros is a prosperous local farmer and is canny enough to recognize the potential advantages of contact with the outside world. However, he is adamantly against allowing any foreign influence and demonstrates his diplomatic cunning by playing the various visiting factions off each other.

FORT RELIAN, SETTLEMENT OF

Ruler: Marshal Nadea Charan
Government: garrison commander
Population: 760 (mostly mixed Foerdewaith-Hundaei)
Languages: Kirkut (mainly Campacha dialects), Common
Religion: Ethtuwate, Thyr, Muir, Jamboor
Technology Level: Dark Ages

A military fort built to defend the old colonies, Fort Relian has stood on the steppes since the first wave of the Great Colonization. When the Shadow Horde came rampaging out of the north, destroying colonies and slaughtering their fleeing inhabitants, Fort Relian became the base of the Caleen Legion, a scratch force made up of Foerdewaith regulars and colonist militia. As the horde advanced, the fortress swelled with

THE CONROI EXPEDITION

For generations, the lands north of the Wizard's Wall lay untouched and unexplored (at least by the humans of the south). Many legends and wild tales were circulated about the place, but for the most part the Haunted Steppes remained a cypher. Most believed that they were all but lifeless, possibly inhabited by a handful of humans or humanoids, scoured by the passing of the Shadow Horde and the magical upheavals created by the Wizard's Wall. Of the old Caleen colonies, nothing was known, and nearly everyone believed them to be extinct, slaughtered by the humanoids and the Scaedugenga.

Still, there were those who felt that there was knowledge to be gained on the steppes. If nothing else, explorers could learn the fate of those left behind and also possibly gauge whether the Shadow Horde still existed and, if so, whether it presented a threat. In 3439 I.R., Professor Ilene Conroi of the Grand Duchy of Reme proposed an expedition north of the Wizard's Wall. Her goal was to survey the Haunted Steppes and report on the region's current status — its land, flora and fauna, its people (if any) and, most importantly, the potential for threat to Reme. Obtaining modest financing from the grand duke, Conroi set out to recruit scholars from across Akados. She was joined by several prominent historians, geologists, biologists, and other scientists. Supplies were purchased and sent ahead to await the expedition. Professional caravan guards and adventurers were hired to escort the expedition. By summer, the expedition arrived at Durgam's Folly and was ready to cross into the unknown north through the mountain passes below the fortress's dark walls.

The expedition made its first discovery soon after entering the plains, for the Campacha people of the southern steppes had taken note of the caravan and approached the newcomers. To the surprise of Conroi and her fellow explorers, the Campacha proved to be friendly and helpful.

Guided by Campacha scouts, the Conroi expedition set out into the grasslands. Their perils and adventures are far too numerous to describe, but of note here was their discovery that some of the supposedly lost Caleen colonies had actually survived the ravages of the Shadow Horde. West of Shadowfell Lake, the great body of water that lay at the base of the Wizard's Wall, several settlements endured, inhabited by the descendants of the old Foerdewaith colonists and the Shattered Folk of the region. They told stories of their founding, many of which had evolved and changed until they barely resembled true events, and by this time they had nearly forgotten the names of their old kingdoms. Here they lived, adapted to the land, tending their herds and farming the harsh soil.

Though Conroi and her expedition made many discoveries in their two years of exploration, the rediscovery of the colonies was its most significant achievement. Upon their return, the expedition members were proclaimed as heroes and their exploits magnified by heroic chronicles, bardic songs, and popular legend. Today, popular belief holds that the eastern Caleen colonies were actually founded by the Conroi Expedition, a false notion that discounts the efforts and resilience of the colonists.

desperate refugees and came under siege by humanoids as the main body of the horde moved south to invade the Northmarches. Fort Relian's walls shook and some buildings tumbled as the Wizard's Wall was raised, but the citadel survived and kept countless refugees safe. Desultory attacks by the humanoids continued, but with the banishment of the Scaedugenga, these fled to the north and left the fortress battered but intact.

The fortress became the center of a new settlement, and today is the second most populous town in the Caleen region. Inhabitants are amused at apocryphal stories of how the Conroi Expedition "saved" the fortress and are somewhat annoyed at being referred to as one of the "Conroi Settlements," but they remain open to visitors and are interested in learning more about the world outside the steppes. Like the other former colonies, Relians are very independent. The current inhabitants are of mixed heritage, with Foerdewaith and Shattered Folk ancestry.

Fort Relian remains home to what is still called the Caleen Legion, a small contingent of about 150 veteran warriors, and the garrison commander, officially called the "marshal," is also the town's ruler. The current leader, Marshal Nadea Charan, is a tough, no-nonsense woman who lost an eye in a centaur raid several years ago. She rules with stern but fair hand.

The town itself is made up primarily of a stone keep surrounded by wood and stone buildings, and boasts a temple to all of the local gods (including Thaka and several other Ethtuwate deities), as well as a number of inns and general merchandise stores, a farmer's market, and a livestock yard where horses, sheep, and goats can be bought and sold.

Imar, Settlement of

Ruler: Mayor Axel Connor
Government: mayor and council
Population: 420 (mostly mixed Foerdewaith-Hundaei)
Languages: Kirkut (mainly Campacha dialects), Common
Religion: Ethtuwate, Thyr, Jamboor
Technology Level: Dark Ages

One of the lost Caleen colonies, and also considered part of the "Conroi Settlements" by outsiders, Imar is unusual in that it retains many very old defensive works that were erected by the old Caleen Legion. A great earth berm set with squat stone towers surrounds the town, making it an especially tough nut for attackers to crack. As a result, Imar has not suffered as many humanoid attacks as other Caleen towns, and some of its buildings are more than 200 years old. Inside the walls, Imar looks actually more like a town of Reme or Foere than a rough frontier settlement. Imar is considered the safest and most beautiful of the Caleen colonies, with several inns, stables, and a large merchant square where folk from all across the area come to trade on market days. Significant temples devoted to Thyr, Muir, and Jamboor can be found here as well, along with a stone council house where Mayor Axel and his advisors meet weekly. A few foreigners live here, mostly Castorhagi traders and members of the Reman diplomatic mission.

Imar once stood on the shores of the Tabur River, but with the geological shifts that took place with the raising of the Wizard's Wall, the old riverbed has been turned into orchards and farmlands to produce grains and fruit in sufficient quantities that they can sometimes be exported to other Caleen towns.

Chesmire, Settlement of

Ruler: Elder Sabratha
Government: village elder
Population: 115 (mostly mixed Foerdewaith-Hundaei)
Languages: Kirkut (mainly Campacha dialects), Common
Religion: Ethtuwate, Thyr, Jamboor
Technology Level: Dark Ages

A small community of 115 souls, Chesmire is the westernmost of the lost Caleen colonies. Living in relative isolation until its discovery by Gtsang traders in 3360 I.R., Chesmire's inhabitants had lived a precarious existence, growing just enough food to survive and tending to small herds of goats and sheep. A small amount of trade with Enua and other small villages also took place. The arrival of the Gtsang established relations with the outside world after many years and brought in much-needed goods. The later arrival of the Castorhagi who wished to trade with the Shattered Folk also aided Chesmire and its surrounding settlements.

Chesmire remains a very small settlement inhabited by the descendants of the original Foerdewaith settlers and Shattered Folk clansfolk. The village consists of a huddle of stone and sod houses surrounded by a wooden palisade. When danger threatens, Chesmire can call up about 60 able-bodied militia to defend it, and older folks tell stories of several ferocious fights with marauding goblins or orcs that were near-run things indeed. The town has few resources save the grains and vegetables that it grows and the goats and sheep that graze in the surrounding grasslands. The current leader is Elder Sabratha, a wizened old woman who claims to be more than 100 years old.

Enua, Settlement of

Ruler: Father Gedney
Government: theocracy
Population: 85 (mostly mixed Foerdewaith-Hundaei)
Languages: Kirkut (mainly Campacha dialects), Common
Religion: Ethtuwate, Thyr, Jamboor
Technology Level: Dark Ages

A tiny village that is home to 85 souls of mixed Foerdewaith and Shattered Folk ancestry, Enua is another of the lost Caleen colonies. Once boasting a population of over a thousand colonists, much of Enua's population fled as the Shadow Horde advanced. Those who remained behind prepared for their fate but were delivered when the horde turned to assault the Crynnomar Gap. Defending itself against an assault by horde-allied humanoids, Enua barely survived the onslaught and was again saved by the miraculous banishment of the horde by the rituals of the Asran, though no one in the village knew it. In the following generations, Enua grew smaller still, finally stabilizing at its current tiny population.

Like the nearby settlement of Chesmire, Enua survives on subsistence agriculture and the herding of goats, though a small stream of foreign goods and necessities has begun to arrive thanks to the traders of Gtsang and Castorhage. The village is led by the solemn-faced Father Gedney, a priest of Thyr and Thaka (a situation that the Enuans do not find at all odd, given their long association with the tolerant Shattered Folk).

Ognari, Lands of the

Capital: Castle of Skulls (?)
Notable Settlements: None
Ruler: Ognar the Awful (?)
Government: monarchy
Population: 22,500 (21,000 Shattered Folk, 1,500 mountain dwarves)
Monstrous: goblins, gnolls, orcs, ankhegs, hill giants, ogres, minotaurs, banshees, dire wolves, skeletons, zombies, hell hounds, bugbears, perytons, shadows, wraiths, griffons, harpies, ghosts, nightmares, wyverns, manticores, bulettes, hippogriffs, chimeras, specters, trolls, wights, cockatrices
Languages: Kirkut (Ognari dialects)
Religion: none
Resources: horses, mercenaries
Currency: barter or miscellaneous coins
Technology Level: Dark Ages

The Ognari nomads of the eastern steppe are greatly feared, even by the other Shattered Folk. A particularly wicked and violent group, the Ognari engage in the practices of headhunting and even (it is said by their enemies) cannibalism. Nevertheless, these violent nomads also do a booming business as mercenaries, especially with their fellow

Shattered Folk, who can overcome their fear long enough to hire them for especially unpleasant tasks. Today, some outside forces have taken an interest in the Ognari's services as well.

HISTORY AND PEOPLE

The nomads of the northern steppes were among the most ferocious of the Great Khan's opponents in the short but catastrophic Hundaei civil war of 683 I.R. Many of these tribes engaged in excessive brutality and were believed to have fallen under the influence of the fell shadow creatures and the madness that dwelled in the Lost Mountains and Lake Hali. Some had even degenerated into little more than violent warrior cults interested only in war and slaughter. These cultists filed their teeth and tattooed their faces to resemble demons, and some were said to eat the flesh of fallen enemies while others took their foes' heads as trophies. Though they suffered severe losses in the war and were scattered in its aftermath, the northern nomads survived as independent warrior bands that stalked the plains hunting both game and their fellow humans.

This situation persisted for many long generations as chaos and warfare spread, with humanoids and humans struggling for survival. It was not until the 3200s I.R. that a single leader rose and began to reunite the various northern bands.

The warlord named Ognar appeared to be just another brutal tribal chieftain, but he soon proved to be far more. While vanquishing rival chieftains and absorbing their tribes into his own growing horde, Ognar, who became known (to his enemies at any rate) as Ognar the Awful, took many wounds that would have normally been fatal, yet he always survived, though often with horrific scars. The source of this invulnerability was unknown, but undoubtedly unnatural.

Once Ognar subdued all of his rival chieftains, he summoned the conquered bands to a great gathering just south of the Shadowlands. There he gathered a thousand prisoners along with all of the surviving enemy chiefs, and sacrificed them in a long and bloody ceremony, piling their heads into a great pyramid. Once his gory task was complete, Ognar summoned a band of dark priests of Drethra, who spent an entire night inscribing a magical circle around the great pyramid while the gathered nomads, alternately fascinated or terrified, watched in grim anticipation. When the first rays of dawn struck the pyramid, a fearsome transformation began. The victims' skulls grew in size and stature and the entire mound became a vast, grisly structure. Ognar declared the place his Castle of Skulls and vanished inside.

Ognar has not been seen since that day, but the Castle of Skulls, which has the power to move about the steppes and is rarely in one place for more than a few days, continues to grow as Ognari warriors and mercenaries bring heads as tribute. These severed heads are absorbed into the castle's structure, which now towers over the Steppes. As for Ognar, most of the clansfolk believe that he still lives, for periodically a great booming voice issues forth from the castle, though none can truly say it is Ognar himself.

The Ognari now serve as mercenaries, selling their services to anyone who isn't squeamish about their violent practices. Fearsome warriors, the Ognari bedeck themselves in the severed heads of their foes and wear masks made to resemble skulls or demons. They are a profane and heretical people who shun the will of the gods and put war and the taking of heads before all other pursuits. They tell fantastical stories about taking the heads of gods, demons, and heroes, and are both feared and reluctantly admired throughout the Haunted Steppes for their martial skill and suicidal bravery.

RELIGION

The Ognari claim to worship no gods but instead venerate their ancestors and some of the spirits of the plains, which they call upon for aid in battle. They have no priests or temples, but some Ognari may serve as druids and cast nature-based magic and craft magic items such as rings, spears, and amulets from enemy skulls to provide protection and prowess in battle.

TRADE AND COMMERCE

The Ognari have no major trade routes, and mercantilism is not a large part of their culture. Some other clans of the Shattered Folk do visit Ognari territory to sell them foodstuffs and supplies, but the Ognari never offer anything save gold in return. Between raids, buying foreign goods, and tending their own herds and crops, the Ognari manage to take care of their basic needs. Their primary source of income is through service as mercenaries and though most folk of the Shattered Lands outwardly abhor the headhunters and their barbaric practices, few clans are so selective that they won't hire a few of them if needed, for a variety of reasons such as holding or claiming territory to ridding their lands of pesky raiding humanoids. For their part, the Ognari are not terribly picky either and serve any employers who can pay their price.

LOYALTIES AND DIPLOMACY

The Ognari shun diplomacy and maintain no relations with any outside kingdom or clan. They are highly suspicious and even hostile toward strangers in their lands, unless the stranger carries a blue banner to signify the intention to sell goods or negotiate with the Ognari for their services as sellswords. Otherwise, the Ognari stick strictly to themselves, though in times of shortage they raid neighboring clans for food, livestock, and other necessities. These raids satisfy the Ognari's cultural need for battle and heads, as do conflicts with the orc, goblin, and ogre tribes of the region. Though they reject many of the old Hundaei values, the Ognari oddly enough still maintain the old truce with the gnolls and generally the two groups avoid each other.

GOVERNMENT

Though technically a confederacy of numerous warrior bands and clans under the leadership of a single Great Khan, the Ognari are always simply called "the Ognari," and everyone on the steppes knows what that means.

The Ognari have little in the way of a formal government structure. Each of the various groups that makes up the Ognari has its own traditions, decorations, weapons, clothing, and armor, but as time has gone by, these various groups have evolved into essentially warrior societies within the greater Ognari clan. Each is led by its own chieftain and generally sees to its own needs while cooperating with the other societies. Chaotic and insular, the Ognari seem to function together out of mutual need and cultural identity.

Though no one has seen him in decades, the Great Khan Ognari (he is the only leader on the steppes who has the temerity to have adopted the old title) rules from his mobile Castle of Skulls which has over the years grown to be truly enormous. It creeps at a walking pace around the Haunted Steppe, sometimes in the foothills of the Stonehearts, sometimes at the edge of the Gods' Ride Basin, other times on the very edge of the cursed Shadowlands. Occasionally a great voice booms from the castle and issues orders to the Ognari, imparts wisdom, or simply babbles incomprehensibly. Tradition and true fear of the Great Khan and what he has become keep the Ognari coming to the castle to present their tribute in the form of heads before they depart, often quickly.

MILITARY

The Ognari military is one of the most feared and dangerous in all the steppes. Their numbers do not compare to the more numerous Elitani-pan and Campacha, but they make up for this deficiency in expertise and ferocity. Each of the Ognari's component warband/societies has a different style of fighting, along with different armor, weapons, and decorations, including tattoos, filed teeth, facial scarring, and other unique features. Currently, about a dozen different bands are among the Ognari and number from a few hundred to a thousand. All fight mounted on their fierce steppe horses, but some specialize in lance combat, others in mounted archery or close-quarters sword fighting, and so on.

Ognari are best known as mercenaries, usually in service to other clans of the Shattered Folk. Clients can hire anywhere from a score or so of warriors to an entire warband. Theoretically, the entire Ognari nation is available for hire but so far no one has met the headhunters' steep price for such services. As contacts with the Castorhagi, Remans, and Foerdewaith expand, the Ognari's reputation has spread, leading some foreigners to approach the nomads seeking their services. So far, only a few hundred Ognari serve as guards or raiders in other lands, but that number may be growing.

MAJOR THREATS

The Ognari experience the same threats as the other steppe folk — marauding humanoids and wandering undead created by the many magical catastrophes that racked the region, demons that appear from random rifts, and gates and even shadow creatures that emerge from the Shadowlands to the north. The Ognari are generally secure from other steppe tribes who avoid them due to their ferocious reputation.

WILDERNESS AND ADVENTURES

The Ognari themselves present a major challenge to adventurers in the region, for they are quite hostile to those who do not bear the proper blue banner that signifies a desire to trade with or hire the Ognari as mercenaries. The Ognari are quite merciless with such outsiders, seeing them as an opportunity to hone their martial skills and, of course, to take heads.

Besides hiring the Ognari, not many good reasons exist for visiting their section of the plains, but a few still make the attempt and make their way to the haunted ruins of Tay'chul or seek out the legendary Castle of Skulls as it moves across the plains of its own volition, seemingly at random. This last is particularly anathema to the Ognari, who hold their sacred ruler in high esteem and believe that he still lives, ruling his people from his morbid fortress. To date, no one — including the Ognari themselves — has seen the interior of the Castle of Skulls and lived.

REFERENCE SOURCE: LOST LORE: THE HEADHUNTER

GEOGRAPHIC FEATURES AND POINTS OF INTEREST IN THE HAUNTED STEPPES

BITTERWOOD

Rising from the shores of the icy northern ocean, the Bitterwood is a tangled mass of wind-tortured surf pines and tough undergrowth. Very little lives in the Bitterwood due to its inhospitability, but some particularly hardy birds nest among its trees. The wood is also a poor source of timber, for the trees are small and twisted, contorted by wind and cold. Some claim that trolls live among the tangled branches and point to a number of mysterious disappearances of humans and horses nearby, but this assertion has never been proven.

CALE'S DOOM

The Grand Duke Cale is a legend among the peoples of Reme and Foere — the noble prince who renounced the throne to prevent civil war then presided over one of the nation's greatest adventures. That the Great Colonization ended in horror and disaster seems to only add to Cale's reputation, for he died heroically in battle at the head of his troops, desperately striving to stem the tide of shadow and save the kingdom.

This bleak and weathered spot on the Haunted Steppes is considered ill-omened by the Shattered Folk, for it is where the Caleen Legion and Grand Duke Prince Cale fell, consumed by the Shadow Horde. It is said that ghosts wander the land, still refighting the battle, and that sometimes disembodied spirits driven mad by centuries of woe fall upon the living, driven by envy and rage. The truth of these stories isn't certain, for the Campacha and the Caleen avoid the place with superstitious zeal. It is known that creatures of shadow have sometimes been seen here, and that at least one party of eager young treasure hunters never returned. This has not quieted rumors that magic weapons, armor, and other plunder might be found here, but so far few have had the courage to brave the curse of Cale's Doom and search.

CLIFFS OF ODRAN-HI-NIM (THE END OF LIGHT)

These precipitous cliffs, visited only by lonely seabirds, extend from the northern portions of the Haunted Steppes to the uttermost north and form the western edge of the Nam-i-Budhani Mountains. The sun is never bright here, and many days it never rises at all or fails to break the dismal cloud cover. Far beyond the freezing iceberg-laden waters here lies the mysterious realm known only in whispers as the Ebon Shroud.

CRYNNOMAR GAP

See "Geographic Features and Points of Interest the Northmarches" in "The Lands of Reme."

DEVIL'S TAIL

The Icetongue empties into this great gulf at the northwest corner of the Haunted Steppes. Unlike the river, the Devil's Tail gulf is not considered especially ill-omened and is home to pods of whales and orca, as well as herds of seals, sea lions, and walruses. Legends speak of an enormous sea-turtle called the Father of Waters (or Kalam-eth-nar in Kirkut), who aids lost sailors and sometimes grants prophetic visions. The Castorhagi first made landfall here before meeting the Elitani clans in 3262 I.R.

ELDER FOREST

The forests of the Haunted Steppes are small and isolated. Some legends among the Shattered Folk claim that they were once far more extensive, but that they dwindled when the Stoneheart Mountains rose and cut the steppes off from the rest of the world. The Elder Forest is said to be one last remnant of the old woodlands. Stories tell of a hidden palace that is still inhabited by the beings who once controlled the woods (possibly high elves, deva, or other mystical beings) and that ordinary mortals will be struck dead or at least driven to madness if they set eyes on the palace and its unearthly beauty. Those few, brave Shattered Folk who have ventured to the edge of the woods report strange sylvan or aberrant creatures such as unicorns, owlbears, and fey of all sorts dwelling there.

ELITANI COAST

So named by the Castorhagi traders who have been coming here since the late 3200s I.R., the western edge of the Akados continent is a place of cold, uneasy seas and beaches of shingle or rough sand with little in the way of anchorages or sheltered bays. Nonetheless, the Castorhagi managed to carve out two rugged settlements at Ports Kinsal in the north and Mandei in the south. The Elitani-i-pan clans tend to avoid the seashore, finding little of benefit there, and leave the area mostly to the Castorhagi.

ETHTUWATE-CALA-TUN (GODS' RIDE RIVER)

This extensive river and its tributaries once formed a fertile network of rich grazing and farming lands and gave birth to the great Hundaei culture. The Shattered Folk's legends hold that long ago an evil god raised the Stoneheart Mountains to punish the people and cut them off from the rest of the continent, and after that the river lands grew more arid and less productive. Today, while the Gods' Ride remains a central feature of the Haunted Steppes, its flow is not as great or as easily predictable as in the past. Its lands remain ideal for grazing, but occasional droughts can cause deprivation, and some of its various tributaries are seasonal, dwindling to muddy trickles in dry seasons before swelling to floods when the rains come. The Elitan-i-pan Confederacy controls much of the western portion of the river basin and have begun to construct permanent or semi-permanent settlements in tentative steps from a nomadic culture to a more settled economy.

GHOST RIVER

Once the Tabur River flowed through this region along the northern edge of the Deepfells. The old Foerdewaith settlers built the Caleen colonies here using the river for irrigation and travel. The creation of the Wizard's Wall changed all that by permanently diverting the route of the Tabur and leaving its old river valley dry. The Caleen colonies, which in Foere were believed destroyed by the Shadow Horde, survived the disaster and managed to scrape by in the aftermath. The dry riverbed was nevertheless rich agricultural land, and today runoff from the Deepfells keeps the region irrigated and allows for the maintenance of modest farms. Many of these are subsistence operations that can feed only individual homes or communities, but some surplus is produced, which is sold to the Campacha nomads who come here to trade.

Icetongue River

This river system drains from the lower slopes of the Nam-i-Budhani (or Lost) Mountains. Its waters are considered cursed (with good reason, given that the Lost Mountains have on several occasions produced both humanoid invaders and shadow horrors that threatened to conquer the Steppes). The Shattered Folk never travel through this area, though young warriors are often sent to test their manhood in this region as their coming-of-age ceremonies. Many never return, and those who do are forbidden to speak of their experiences.

Kalist ka River

This narrow, swift river flows through a treacherous gorge to join the God's Ride River just south of the Zuxaca Canyon. Some travelers have reported that the canyon walls are covered in small caves or holes that harbor dangerous worm-like creatures. Some speculate that these might be the larval stages of some species of giant insect, but the distance and isolation of the region prevents further study.

Killing Ground

The region south of the Lost Mountains was once home to several Hundaei clans. Their proximity to the forbidden regions, including Lake Hali and the Shadowlands to the north, sometimes affected their lives and spawned strange creatures or induced madness in those who ventured too close, but for the most part these were just more of the normal challenges faced by the nomads in those days. All of that changed around −450 I.R. when the first incursion of shadow swept out of the north and corrupted some clans and destroyed many others. The shadows themselves killed and corrupted many, but most deaths were a result of clans turning on each other (and on themselves) in a maddened blood-frenzy. Legend holds that the grounds are so thick with the skulls of the dead that a traveler can walk for miles without ever touching earth. Among the Shattered Folk, the area is strictly taboo and even approaching the Killing Ground merits severe punishment. Undead in many forms lurk here, along with murderous remnants of the Shadow and (it is said) the shambling remains of the old corrupted Hundaei tribes, known as the Fallen Ones.

Lake Hali

The Shattered Folk of the Haunted Steppes regard Lake Hali with deep (and fully justified) superstitious dread. Not only is its very material substance cursed so that those who even view the place are said to go mad, but the lake was also central to the two great incursions of shadow that ravaged the steppes over the past millennia. Something dwells there, the priests and seers say — something utterly inimical to humanity and all other mortal creatures. Exactly who, or what, dwells in the lake is not known, and is certainly never spoken of save in the darkest of whispers.

The lake's proximity is blamed for the birth of the Fallen Ones — Hundaei clans that were corrupted by its strange energies and drawn into the terrible Shadow Horde. None of this mattered to the Foerdewaith settlers who ventured into the region during the Great Colonization, and their subsequent construction and exploration around the lake and in the Lost Mountains beyond disturbed something that responded with a wave of madness and horror. The second coming of the Shadow Horde is believed to be directly related to the colonists' settlement of the Lake Hali region, but some believe that whatever lives there was entirely distinct from the Scaedugenga. The shadows, they suggest, were merely a side effect and the real danger remains hidden, lurking and biding its time.

Few records exist of the Foerdewaith exploration, but several accounts claim that the ruins of at least three cities of some apparent advancement lie near the shores of these dark lake waters that cast no reflections. Who or what built them is a mystery, if they in fact exist. Even darker rumors claim that strange artifacts have been discovered in these settlements, and that some of them may actually have been brought south to Reme or nearby kingdoms, but so far there has been little evidence of this.

Miranda-Tun (Northstar River)

A prominent tributary of the Ethtuwate-cala-tun basin, the Miranda-Tun flows south from the Lost Mountains across the northern plains before joining the main river east of the Everfar Hills. Though the river has a somewhat dark reputation due to its origin, many generations of Shattered Folk and Hundaei before them have watered their horses in the Miranda-Tun without incident.

Nam-i-Budhani (Lost Mountains)

These bleak, eternally snow-covered crags located between the cursed Lake Hali and the fearsome Shadowlands are the northernmost mountains in all of Akados and have a dire, ominous reputation among the Shattered Folk. Known to be riddled with caverns and tunnels and crawling with savage humanoid tribes, the Lost Mountains are also rumored to contain gateways to the realm of shadow from whence came the terrible Scaedugenga. The humanoids — goblins, kobolds, orcs, hobgoblins, and others — seem to fall under the shadow's influence quite easily and have on at least two occasions swept out of the mountains in a seemingly irresistible flood to ravage the steppes in the name of their masters. Today, the mountains are forbidden by strict taboo, though many think it is only a matter of time before the wards set by the old Asran guardians weaken and allow the Shadow to emerge again.

Pan-ni-Rikam-Po (The Cursed Ruins of Stone)

The Hundaei were not well known as city-builders, but here in the middle of the endless steppelands, the Great Khan Jaganga built a permanent settlement of stone where he and his people could live, and where the other clans could come to meet and trade. In those days it was called Kolo-ba-thun, which means "Home of the Great Ones" in Kirkut. This capital city thrived for many generations, outlasting Jaganga himself. Completely destroyed in the Hundaei civil war of 681–683 I.R., the place was renamed Pan-ni-Rikam-Po (Cursed Ruin of Stone) and now exists as an abandoned ruin inhabited only by wild beasts and the restless dead.

The wreckage of the capital remains taboo to all Shattered Folk tribes, and none will enter its borders on pain of death. Only once was this taboo broken, by the young warrior Tahtona when he followed the guidance of the soothsayers and condemned himself to death by entering the ruins. He returned to lead his people to victory over their foes, but perished in the battle, thus fulfilling his destiny and maintaining the sacred taboo.

Pin-i-Pinjhami (Everfar Hills)

These highlands between the Tabur and Gods' Ride rivers are the highest prominences in the Haunted Steppes. They are avoided by the nomadic Shattered Folk who dislike hills and places that interfere with free movement, leaving them to various quarrelsome gnoll, hill giant, and kobold tribes.

Road of Sorrows

No longer a true road, this region was the path that was followed by the original Caleen settlers as they traveled northwest along the foot of the Deepfells, founding villages and forts as they went. It is also the path followed by a branch of the Shadow Horde as it advanced, destroying as it went. The northwestern end of the path is considered especially unlucky and is avoided by the Caleen and the Shattered Folk, for lingering bits of shadow and undead of all kinds have been encountered there among the ruins of burned-out and slaughtered settlements.

SHADOWFELL LAKE

The raising of the Wizard's Wall in 2947 I.R. shifted the geography of the entire region. Rivers changed their course or dried up, valleys became plains, even the mountains of the Deepfells shuddered and in places crumbled. The great Wanaheeli River that once flowed along the northern edge of the Deepfells was diverted, leaving behind a great lake at the northern base of the Wizard's Wall. Shadowfell Lake remains today, and the passing of the centuries has transformed it into a far more natural formation, with gentle shores and cold deeps. At some unknown time in the past, some enterprising Caleen colonists seeded it with fish, so various species of chad, trout, pupfish, and bass can be found in the lake. The Caleen sometimes venture here to fish, but the Shattered Folk generally shun such activities.

Despite its dire sorcery-ridden birth and its ominous moniker, Shadowfell Lake is a surprisingly peaceful and pleasant place. The Wizard's Wall rises to the south while stands of birch and elm have sprung up along its edge, with hazel, buckthorn, and wild roses growing beneath. Bear, puma, and wolves hunt along its shores. Though giants or hobgoblins from the Deepfells or gnolls and goblins from the plains may sometimes be encountered here, Shadowfell Lake is one of the most sedate places in all the Haunted Steppes.

SHADOWLANDS

This bleak, barren land lies at the northernmost end of Akados between the Stonehearts and the Lost Mountains. No one has explored this region, which is known to be home to the Scaedugenga shadow-walkers who have led humanoid hordes to invade the southern lands on numerous occasions. No one truly knows who or what the Scaedugenga are, nor what truly lies in the heart of the Shadowlands, though some dark and ancient rumors speak of something called the Ebon Shroud that lies beyond them.

SONCALA-TUN (HORSE LORD RIVER)

This major tributary of the Ethtuwater-cala-Tun is large enough that it continues to flow year-round, though in the dry season it tends to slow to a thin trickle. The Shattered Folk water their horses here and also harvest clay from the red earth along its banks. Trolls are sometimes encountered near the river when they come here to catch fish.

TABUR BAY

The great inlet that forms the mouth of the Tabur River was explored by Gtsang traders centuries ago, but never settled. Today it hosts one of the few permanent settlements in the steppes, the Castorhagi trade city of Port Mandei.

REFERENCE SOURCE: THE BLIGHT

TABUR RIVER

This river of the southern steppes once joined what is now the Wanaheeli River where it descends from the Deepfells at North Pass. However, the continental subsidence caused by the creation of the Wizard's Wall altered the course of the river so that one of its tributaries in the western Deepfells became its primary headwaters, and all connection with the Wanaheeli waters was lost. Now it flows directly from the new headwaters into Tabur Bay.

TANGJAN COLLEGE

Decades ago, the Gtsang scholar Tiblu Ottika braved the dangers of the Haunted Steppes and had a vision of a great institution of learning located in one of the most isolated places in all of Akados — the vast Campacha Plains. Though many thought him mad (at that point he was not), Tiblu overcame many obstacles to establish his institution, making friends with the bewildered Campacha and attracting hardy scholars who survived the difficult journey to the newly-founded Tangjan College. For a decade the place thrived, until Tiblu — who had grown increasingly irrational — abruptly closed the place. Tiblu's friends and family abandoned him and a few years later a horde of strange chaotic creatures emerged from the disintegrating buildings to devastate the surrounding Campacha lands, only to be defeated by the Campacha wizard Tunicamna and his band of veteran warriors. Today, the college still stands abandoned on the plains, haunted by madness and the protean creatures of chaos.

REFERENCE SOURCE: FIELDS OF BLOOD

TAV'CHUL (THE FIVE PILLARS)

In the midst of the cold northern plains, near the territory of the feared Ognari headhunters, stands a circle of five ancient pillars inscribed with runic symbols that no scholar has yet to decipher. This part of the steppes is especially hazardous, for in addition to the Ognari (who dislike outsiders who are not here specifically to do business with them), several orcish tribes lay claim to the area, and rumors persist that Scaedugenga shadow-creatures have been encountered near (or even within the confines of) the Five Pillars.

Who built the pillars, what they are for, and how they got to this place remain unsolved mysteries. When the Ognari can be persuaded to talk, they claim that the pillars date back to the ancient days of the plains, when they were used for the worship of the demon-god Ocru-Ca, who they believe raised the Stoneheart Mountains to isolate the steppes. With proper inducement, they may confide that the pillars are only the upper works of a vast network of underground passages that may or may not still harbor traces of the old magic, or evil artifacts used in sacrificial ceremonies. Whether this is true or not isn't known — the Ognari do take great pleasure in deceiving foreigners — and so far, no one is believed to have actually explored the pillars or determined what lies beneath them.

WANAHEELI RIVER

The raising of the Wizard's Wall caused massive shifts in local geography and essentially split the old Tabur River in two. The western branch remained and reformed around a tributary in the northern Deepfells, while the eastern half continued to flow from the Stonehearts but ended at the new Shadowfell Lake. Renamed the Wanaheeli River for a local chieftain who survived the catastrophe, the river continues to flow today, pouring down from its old headwaters.

The Wanaheeli is shallow but wide and quite wild, to the extent that wooden bridges don't normally last for more than a few years before collapsing or being swept away by spring floods. A few stone bridges span the river in places, but these are rare, and some were originally built by Foerdewaith colonists and remain today due to maintenance by the Campacha or the Caleen.

REFERENCE SOURCE: FIELDS OF BLOOD

WORGWOODS

Forests are rare in the Haunted Steppes, and those that do exist are thick, tangled, and hardy. The Worgwoods of the eastern steppes are typical, with old gnarled evergreens protecting a handful of open meadows and vales in the woodlands' heart. The region is named for the giant lupine predators that lair here and hunt the surrounding grasslands. The orcish tribes of the steppe breed their own black-furred worgs as riding beasts but sometimes venture here to hunt or capture new breeding stock.

ZUXACA CANYON

This extensive canyon system lies along the northern reaches of the Gods' Ride River. It is avoided by the Campacha, who consider it to be under the influence of the demigod of madness, Zuxaca the Serpent Trickster. It is true that there appear to be an unnatural number of serpents in the canyon, slithering through thickets of oak and scrub. The area is known to be infested with monsters of all sorts in fact, from giant spiders and insects to trolls, ankheg, shambling mounds, and similarly dangerous creatures. Legend holds that a secret temple to the Serpent Trickster is hidden somewhere in the canyon, but to this day no serious exploration of the canyon has been attempted.

THE LANDS OF REME

REME, GRAND DUCHY OF (DUCAL LANDS)

Capital: City of Reme
Ruler: His Far-Reaching Presence Iltobarus, Grand Duke (Kirkut: Great Khan) of Reme, Wave-Rider of the Crescent Sea and Wind-Rider of the Marches
Government: monarchy with a Loreclannic-feudal organization
Population: 4,341,000 (including only grand ducal lands) (2,186,200 Loreclannic, 1,738,500 Foerdewaith, 162,400 halfling, 71,100 mountain dwarf, 66,500 hill dwarf, 59,500 gnome, 31,400 half-elf, 17,300 high elf, 7,300 half-orc; 800 other)
Monstrous: hobgoblins and orcs (Deepfells), goblins, orcs, trolls, rocs and green dragons (Green Mountains and Quail Valley), dire hyenas and gnolls (Westwood and the Endless Hills), creatures of shadow (Haunted Wood), orcs (Ashen Hills), kobolds (High Downs), sabosan, greenskin orcs and ettins (Whiterush River region)
Languages: Common, Rhemish, Kirkut, Elven
Religion: Solanus, Dame Torren, Mithras (city); Archeillus, Sefagreth, Vanitthu, Belon the Wise, Muir, Thyr; Kamien, Freya, Telophus, Ceres (countryside)
Resources: wine, baleen oil, grain, lumber, salt, trade
Currency: Rhemish
Technology Level: Renaissance (City of Reme), Medieval (cities), High Middle Ages (rural areas)

The Grand Duchy of Reme is a vast realm: a network of well-settled river valleys running through enormous areas of almost-uncharted wilderness. To the west, Reme's territory extends to the Deepfell Mountains and the forbidden Green Realm of the wild elves. To the east, it reaches to the town of Fareme near the western edge of the Stoneheart Valley. Its northern border is the Wizard's Wall across the Crynnomar Gap, and to the south, the realm extends to the Whiterush River. The land borders of Reme do not tell the whole story, however, for Reme is also a seafaring nation, one of the most significant in the world. The grand duke has no colonial aspirations, but the nation has been focused on dominating trade on the Crescent Sea for centuries, and Rhemish ships venture throughout the known world from the city's great port.

In overall size, the Grand Duchy of Reme rivals the entire holdings of the overking of Foere and exceeds that of the actual Kingdom of Foere by quite a bit. However, most of Reme remains wild, inhabited by nomadic tribal clans known as Loreclans rather than agrarian settlements. With the exception of river valleys, Reme is almost entirely a vast grassland prairie, poorly suited to farming. The Frontier in the northwest is only nominally under the jurisdiction of the Northmarches, for the reach of the duchess at Ironfell only barely extends into this region. In the west, permanent agricultural settlements have only recently begun to form in the Windreft following the resolution of civil wars that have ravaged the Westmarch for the last several decades. The civilization of Reme is powerful, but the settled population is widely scattered in pockets and along the great rivers.

Given the uneven settlement and great distances within the wild territories of the Reme, the grand duchy has evolved into a number of marches providing for more local administration. Today, these are the Westmarch, the Northmarches and Waymarch, in addition to the central lands which are held directly by the grand duke. The origin of power of the dukes of Reme are as Loreclannic chiefs, and their authority, developed over the course of millennia, extends to ancient Loreclannic boundaries rather than feudal grants of the land itself. The distinction between Reme's Loreclannic traditions and Foere's feudal law is nuanced, but it is a key factor in understanding the history and the nature of the Rhemish people.

HISTORY AND PEOPLE

Reme is dominated by its various Loreclans: a social collective akin to that of a tribe but more complex in terms of internal organization. Loreclans usually have between 500 and 1,000 members, but there are smaller Loreclans that have fallen upon hard times over the years and the urban Loreclans in and around the city of Reme can number as many as 5,000. Across the vast Sea of Grass dominating Reme's central plains, vast differences exist between the cultures of the various Loreclans, with all of them respect an overarching tradition governing the rights of all of the Loreclans but with each clan having its own unique customs and practices.

Most Loreclans are led by a "baron," a word imported from the Hyperborean/Common tongue that in Rhemish is usually the word "tarkhan." Both titles are used throughout the lands of Reme. There is no permanent level of nobility between the barons/tarkhans and the dukes (or khans), which leaves a vast gap for any kind of administration of collective Loreclan traditions or interclan justice, or the mediation of interclan disputes.

This gap is usually filled by those appointed to the role of "pashtar," a temporary title for an individual who acts in the nature of an attorney, mediator, ambassador, or temporary chieftain for more than one Loreclan at one time, usually for a single purpose. Most of the Loreclan representatives at the ducal courts are pashtars given temporary authority by a group of barons to speak for their collective Loreclans. Anyone designated as a pashtar has an absolute right to the hospitality of tribes along the journey to a court — they are sacrosanct when acting in the capacity of pashtar.

PRE-HYPERBOREAN PERIOD

Pre-Hyperborean Rhemish history comes to us from the varied oral traditions of the Loreclans, although most of the commonly-told stories have been put to writing, expanded upon, and even turned into scripts for plays in the famed Rhemish theaters. At least as far back as such tales go, the original inhabitants of the Rhemish plains were nomadic and divided into numerous Loreclans, some of which no longer exist because they were destroyed in battle, merged with other Loreclans or, in some cases, simply vanished from the tales.

HYPERBOREAN ERA

The city of Reme was founded under the name of Remenos by Polemarch Oerson in the earliest years of the Hyperborean conquest of Akados, and since that time the lands of Reme have largely been governed from that city. Boasting an excellent natural harbor and central location on trade routes, Remenos quickly became the premier port on the Crescent Sea, and the lands under its sway expanded to the west and east. For many years, any expansion north was held in check by the wild elves of the Green Realm, whose domain then extended to forests north of the High Downs. Then in the early Eighth Century I.R., warbands from humanoid tribes in the Great Steppes poured through the Crynnomar Gap to make war on the elves. Fearing that the humanoids if not stopped would threaten their homelands farther to the west in the Green Realm, in 712 I.R. the elves moved up to the Crynnomar Gap to make it their line of defense, emptying their lands further south. Noting the withdrawal of the elves, the military governor of Remenos took the opportunity to move into the forests north of the High Downs. When the elves finally beat back the humanoids and returned from the gap in 725 I.R., they found Hyperborean legions entrenched and loggers clearcutting their former forest homes. Already disorganized and depleted after their war with the humanoids, the wild elves lacked the will for further battle and withdrew west deeper into the Green Realm, leaving Remenos in possession of the northern lands all the way to the Crynnomar Gap.

Grand Duchy of Reme and Environs

Hundreds of years of peace followed the withdrawal of the wild elves as Reme consolidated its hold on the lands south of the Crynnomar Gap. Then in 1548 I.R., hobgoblins raiding parties from the Deepfell Mountains fell upon the northern fringes of Reme. Survivors reported a new hobgoblin kingdom had arisen among the clans of Dragonbone Peak, which was led by a seemingly unbeatable warlord. The armies of the Northmarches were staggered by the onslaught, and by 1557 I.R. had fallen to the hobgoblin hordes. Everything north of the High Downs was claimed by the hobgoblin kingdom of the Deepfells. Reme set a defensive line between the High Downs and the Green Mountains. Several years later, a group of adventurers infiltrated Dragonbone Peak and discovered that the warlord of the hobgoblins was in fact the demigod Kakobovia.

In 1571 I.R., an army of Deepfell hobgoblins and allied orcs invaded Arcady in the Feirgotha Plateau in the midst of the Stoneheart Mountains, only to be destroyed in a magical attack the following year. Kakobovia survived, however, and gathered the remaining forces of Dragonbone to launch an all-out attack on the High Downs. At the Battle of Ironhill, the hobgoblin army was lured into a trap and destroyed by forces of Reme. Grand Duke Borell I of Reme himself led the army and is said to have personally banished Kakobovia from the Material Plane.

Rhemish nomads and settlers flooded back into the Northmarches after the Battle of Ironhill, harrying and destroying any remaining outposts of the hobgoblin horde, and quickly re-established their dominion over the homelands from which they had retreated.

For nearly a millennium, the lands of Reme remained largely unthreatened, a prosperous though thinly populated region of the empire. In 2496 I.R., the Hyperborean capital of Curgantium was destroyed in a wildfire that spread and burned the Plains of Suilley and Matagost Forest. Three years later, the imperial capital moved to Tircople in Libynos, and the Hyperboreans abandoned their western empire. The

harmost of Reme, Barthorios Deciandos, was ordered to march to Libynos with his legions, along with the dependent harmost of Panetoth.

Deciandos, who had spent the majority of his life in Reme and was in fact half-Rhemish, was disinclined to leave. He consulted with the Loreclannic dukes and the harmost of Panetoth and with the high priests and priestesses of Dame Torren, Mithras, and Solanus in a series of counsels known today as the Council of Deciandos. Deciandos argued that Hyperborean withdrawal from the region would cause tremendous upheaval, and that if it was necessary for the Hyperboreans to withdraw then something needed to be done to fill the ensuing power vacuum. At the end of the Council of Deciandos, the decision was made that the harmosts would resign their posts, and that Deciandos would be acclaimed grand duke in his own right by the Loreclans, accepting a sovereign position over Reme. In the end, only a very few of the Hyperboreans in Reme actually departed for the east, as the majority of the Hyperborean power structure simply changed its name — from the service of the imperator to the service of the grand duke. To reflect the new order, the name of the capital city was changed from Remenos (its Hyperborean name) to Reme

Foerdewaith Era

This period of independence barely lasted 200 years. In the early part of the 28th Century I.R., envoys of Macobert, king of Foere, came to Reme with a proposition: swear fealty or prepare for war. The canny Grand Duke Altharus III, recognizing the benefits that would come from allying with Macobert as well as the importance to Foere of a secure harbor on the Crescent Sea, sent diplomats to negotiate a favorable treaty. And a favorable treaty he obtained that granted Reme substantial independence in exchange for an oath of fealty, Foere's access to the port, and a small annual payment to the crown.

Then in the year 2858 I.R., Overking Paulus of Foere died. He left behind twin sons, Kennet and Cale, though no one knew which was the elder. Different factions of the empire supported each of the brothers, and the possibility of a civil war loomed.

A similar situation loomed in Reme where the childless Grand Duke Yajot Oersi Windflame suffered from a wasting sickness that would clearly prove fatal at some time in the near future. As in Foere (though due to a lack of obvious heirs rather than too many), a succession war threatened the Oersi rulership of Reme, with Loreclans beginning to form sides behind a number of possible successors.

The twin heirs of Foere, showing a wisdom beyond their years, chose a course of action that solved both problems. It is likely that the solution evolved slowly in the minds of the various nobles involved, but eventually someone must have noticed the opportunity inherent in the long Rhemish tradition of adopting outsiders into their Loreclannic structure. In preparation for the eventual death of Grand Duke Yajot Oersi Windflame, Cale Macobert entered the Oersi Loreclan as Cale Oersi Macobert, adopted by the dying grand duke as a son and heir. This gave the Loreclans of Reme time to accept Cale as their future leader, and for the Oersi to overcome (either by negotiation or by combat) the claims of other potential successors.

In Foere, Kennet was eventually crowned as the sole overking of the Foerdewaith. Cale, meanwhile, abdicated his claim to the throne, and succeeded to the title of grand duke of Reme. The arrangement served to unite the two realms more closely for many years to come and aligned the new Oersi dynasty in Reme with the royal lineage of Foere. Cale's adoption remained a point of friction for decades among many of the Rhemish Loreclans, but to deny its validity would clearly fly in the face of centuries of Rhemish Loreclannic tradition. So-called "conservatives" pointing to the fact that Cale had no Rhemish blood received little help from equally conservative Loreclannic leaders who sought to adhere closely to Rhemish traditions. Ultimately, the voices of opposition wavered and grew silent.

With the full support and resources of Courghais at his disposal, Cale of Reme began the Great Colonization, a mass migration of settlers through the Crynnomar Gap into the fertile and largely unoccupied grasslands of the Great Steppes. The Foerdewaith military provided all the protection that the colonists needed against the few bands of Shattered Folk and disorganized humanoid tribes that were occasionally seen upon the plains beyond Reme. Little was known in Reme of the battles that the elves had fought at the gap more than two millennia before, and such rumors as were remembered were generally dismissed — the Rhemish are quite aware that their campfire tales of valor and war contain a bit of poetic license. Unfortunately, in this case the dark fireside tales were fairly accurate.

Within 70 years, a string of settlements sprang up along the base of the surrounding mountains and in an unbroken chain across the steppes to the western coast more than a thousand miles away. The colonists then reached the shores of Lake Hali in the far northwest where they found better-organized and aggressive tribes of humanoids that suddenly descended in hordes onto the Great Steppes. The widely scattered settlements were ill prepared, and many were sacked and burned before the Foerdewaith were even aware of the threat. With additional military assistance from Courghais, the colonists fortified their steadings and slowly pushed back the humanoid marauders, until a tense stalemate settled in.

The stalemate did not last long. Less than two decades later, the floodgates opened once again in a horde that poured forth from the Lost Mountains in numbers not seen since the great elven defense of the Crynnomar Gap, and this time new horrors never seen by the men of Foere accompanied the horde, creatures of Shadow only whispered of in the old tales of the Northlands and the Ancient Ones. The horde descended in a tide that rolled south, burning and destroying settlements as it went. Finally, at a battlefield now known as Cale's Doom, the Caleen Legion and the remaining colonial irregulars met the humanoids and shadow-walkers. But against this new threat, the steel pikes and heavy cavalry of Foere proved little worth, and the legion fell where it stood with tens of thousands dead. Among the missing was Grand Duke Cale himself.

Refugees from the settlements poured into Reme, and the army of the Foerdewaith prepared to march north to try to stop the oncoming horde. In this time of Reme's greatest need, the powerful archmages Margon and Alycthron appeared out of legend, having vanished from the knowledge of men more than 10 centuries before. At the Crynnomar Gap, where the gathering legions of Foere stared across a field at seemingly endless numbers of humanoids, the wizards called upon ancient and forgotten magics. The ground before the legions broke and tilted steeply backward, creating a slope where only a flat plain had stood before. The hordes beyond the break watched as the tilted ground rose in a massive escarpment of earth and stone before them, rising hundreds of feet and stretching all the way from the flanks of the Stoneheart Mountains, across the Crynnomar Gap, to the flanks of the Deepfells more than 500 miles distant. With such an unscalable height — thereafter known as the Wizard's Wall — blocking their path into the human lands, the humanoid hordes were turned back.

Sorrowful even in victory at the loss of the colonies and anyone trapped below on the plains beyond the Wizard's Wall, the soldiers of Foere turned their backs upon the House of Cale and began the long march home. Garrisons were left along the length of the broken escarpment to ensure that no attempts were made to scale the wall and sneak into the human lands beyond, but never again, swore the folk of Reme, would they cross the Crynnomar Gap and enter what became known as the Haunted Steppes beyond.

Between 2960 I.R. and 3207 I.R., the Foerdewaith embarked on four great crusades to Libynos in efforts to control the ancient city of Tircople and the holy Sacred Table. Many of the forces sent on these crusades took ship from the port of Reme, and in the sinking of the Third Great Crusade's fleet both Grand Duke Tobiah and his son and heir Crown Duke Jesper were lost at sea. Ultimately unsuccessful, the aggregate effect of these crusades was to drain the resources of Foere, in both manpower and gold. By 3213 I.R., Ramthion Island declared its independence from Foere, marking the beginning of the Foerdewaith Wars of Succession.

Independent World Power

In 3233 I.R., the grand duke of Reme, with the concurrence of the Lords' Council of Reme, declared its independence from Foere. By this time, the overking was unable to do much other than complain and attempt, without avail, to pressure other monarchs not to recognize the grand duchy's independence. The young king Luceus of Castorhage, caught between the two, managed to offend both nations and soon found himself in the decisive Short War with Reme. In seven months, Reme soundly defeated Castorhage's navy, forestalling Castorhage's attempts to regain control of its former possessions: Tandril Island and the Forest Coast. In the next year, the Free States declared their independence in the Forest Coast, and the Grand Duchy of Reme became the first to recognize this new state.

Civil Unrest in the Westmarch

Over the last 500 years, various families have contested for dominance in the Westmarch, which has led to civil unrest and, in a few circumstances, outright rebellion against the grand dukes. Recently, the last of the disobedient families was brought to heel, leaving the grand duke in firm control of the Westmarch. As a result, areas under the domain of the duke in Eckland that were formerly largely inaccessible, such as the Windreft, have become fertile ground for new settlers.

Ethnicity and Culture

Roughly a third of the humans in the grand duchy have some degree of Foerdewaith ancestry, although these are clustered mostly in cities, towns, and other substantial settlements. Adoption of Foerdewaith culture is more widespread in Reme than actual Foerdewaith ancestry, for the cultural impact of Reme's alliance of convenience with Foere extended into the Loreclans of the plains as well as the cities. The common tongue is used as a trade language to overcome Loreclannic dialects of Kirkut, jewelry is heavily influenced by Foerdewaith craftsmanship, and — perhaps oddly, perhaps not — plays and music from Foere are performed enthusiastically by amateur troupes even deep in the plains, by purely nomadic Loreclans.

THE LORECLANS AND THE SHATTERED FOLK

Every 50 years, tribal families from the Shattered Folk beyond the Crynnomar Gap are permitted to petition for a right to settle in the Rhemish plains, and a lottery is held to determine who may immigrate. Those granted the right to cross the Wizard's Wall are usually incorporated into one of the Loreclans, for most tribes of the Shattered Plains have at least some relations, if distant, in the Rhemish plains that have been granted their own Loreclannic lands.

RELIGION

Although temples to many gods may be found within the walls of the city of Reme, Solanus, Dame Torren, and Mithras are the matron/patron deities of the city, and their worship is predominant among the residents. The worship of Mithras is almost exclusively limited to the cities and settlements, having been an import of the Hyperborean legions that did not catch on among the nomadic Loreclans.

In addition to the three most prominent deities, other gods (mainly of the Hyperborean or native Loreclannic pantheons) are worshipped throughout the grand duchy. Merchants and travelers pray to Sefagreth or Belon the Wise, many soldiers and city guards venerate Vanitthu, and throughout the countryside Kamien, Freya, Telophus, and Ceres have devotees. Given the dedication to Solanus throughout Reme, this is one of the few regions on Akados that has proven resistant to the growth of the faith of Mitra.

Many among the more nomadic Loreclans worship Halatra the Horse, while Loreclannic knights often pray to Bowbe, god of battle-ragers. The worship of Bowbe is more common in the eastern regions of the plains but is found scattered throughout the Loreclans across the country.

TRADE AND COMMERCE

The city of Reme sits at the western end of the Tradeway, a critical trade road that in the east passes through Bard's Gate, and thence to Freegate, a port city on the Gulf of Akados. The Tradeway has existed since the days of the Hyperborean Empire and provides a direct travel route that does not require a detour through the heart of the Foerdewaith empire.

The city of Reme also boasts one of the best harbors on the Crescent Sea, with merchant traffic arriving from and departing to all of the known ports of Akados and beyond.

As a result, nearly anything can be bought or sold in the markets of Reme. Most of the trade throughout the grand duchy is controlled by several powerful merchant houses, each of which has a representative on the Council of Merchant Houses and Guilds that, with a lord mayor, governs the city of Reme.

LOYALTIES AND DIPLOMACY

Reme has no colonies beyond its traditional, ancient borders. In part, this is due to a distaste for foreign conquest arising from the painful memory of the terrors that nearly overran the grand duchy from the Haunted Steppes after the disastrous attempt to colonize those lands during the reign of the Grand Duke Cale. But even without that impetus, with the excellent harbor at the city of Reme, vast lands providing ample food and other resources, and a central location in Akados unmatched by any other power, it really has no need to look elsewhere for conquest or colonization. Reme's entire political structure is based upon the ancestral lands of its Loreclans, and there are no ancestral lands that Reme has not already reached and protected. If Reme were ever to lose control of lands claimed by one or more of its Loreclans, however, the reprisal would be savage, involving hordes of mounted cavalry in numbers far beyond what most feudal leaders could possibly mobilize.

As a result of this general attitude of peacefulness beyond the borders, the grand duchy seeks to be on good terms with other realms of the Lost Lands, so long as they do not threaten the sovereignty of Reme's lands or the security of its trade. Stability is the primary goal sought by the grand dukes. As a result, it is on friendly terms with Foere, the Kingdom of the North Heath, the Kingdom of the Vast, the Principality of Olduvar, the Kingdom of Suilley, Bard's Gate, the Borderland Provinces and the Kingdom of Oceanus. It has particularly good relations with the Tycho Free States and has been instrumental in ensuring their ongoing independence. Reme trades with various cities in the Northlands throughout Libynos. Reme even has good — albeit wary — relations with Castorhage.

To protect its interests, the grand dukes have agents and spies in nearly every country and major city on Akados, and even in many locales in Libynos. The slow but steady deterioration of Foere is of great concern to Reme, particularly the growing chaos in the Borderland Provinces and Sundered Kingdoms. This concern is a large part of the reason that the grand dukes have encouraged the alliance between the Duchy of Waymarch and Bard's Gate, as this secures the Tradeway and the eastern border of the grand duchy.

GOVERNMENT

The Grand Duchy of Reme is a hereditary, feudal monarchy ruled by a sovereign known in the common tongue as the grand duke or grand duchess. In Rhemish, with its ancient linguistic roots in Kirkut, the title instead is "grand khan." For purposes of understanding Reme's structure of government, as opposed to its culture, the term "grand duke" is probably the better fit. The grand duke's powers are more limited than those of the khans of the Hundaei of old, subject to Loreclannic conventions and ancient ancestral promises, rather than a legal code of the type that restrains feudal rulers in other cultures such as Foere. Yet even beyond these conventions and ancestral promises, the grand dukes of Reme seldom interfere in the affairs of the dukes of the Waymarch, the Westmarch, and the Northmarches.

Local authority in the Marches is devolved to the respective dukes of the Northmarches, the Westmarch, and the Waymarch as the protectors of Loreclans that have sworn fealty to them as groups. Although the position of duke by tradition passes down to the predecessor's first heir, the grand dukes can remove and appoint dukes, a right that has been exercised by them on only a few, very rare occasions. Below the dukes (or, in the case of the ducal lands, the grand duke), settled regions are usually divided into baronies (a title now given to a Loreclannic chieftain), with some small communities held by "Loreclannic knights" — a close analogy to the status of knighthood elsewhere in the Lost Lands.

The grand dukes have long ruled with the guidance of a high council made up of the dukes of the Marches and a group of chosen advisors. The advisors generally include one or more of the ruling members of the prominent merchant houses such as Drenwall, Oron, and Gastone-Sheshek.

MILITARY

Given the size of the territory of Reme, it is unsurprising that the duchy maintains a sizable military contingent at all times. The grand duke draws forces from the grand ducal lands, and from the forces of the dukes, who are obliged to provide a certain number of warriors to their monarch each year. The navy of Reme also owes allegiance directly to the grand duke, and warships are continually venturing around the Crescent Sea and beyond the Mouth of Akados to protect shipping lanes and deter pirates. Command of the ships of the Reman navy is vested in the lord high admiral of Reme, a direct appointee of the grand duke.

Reme's military tends to focus on heavy infantry with large contingents of the light cavalry of Loreclannic warriors. Light infantry has little value in Reme's open interior. Given the vast distances involved, the most likely combat would be between light cavalry units. Heavy infantry would instead see use in battles against settlements or fortifications. The Rhemish tactic against invasions such as the great hobgoblin incursions or large-scale banditry focuses on cutting off supply lines, weakening opposing forces, and, in many cases, simply waiting until the invaders starve or become lost on the open plain, engaging in open combat only when the enemy is weakest. In foreign wars (such as the Crusades), Reme's most significant contribution has been in the form of mounted archers clad in light armor of high quality.

MAJOR THREATS

The major threat to trade seen by the grand dukes is the growing instability of the other kingdoms of Akados, particularly the deterioration of Foere.

In terms of actual political threats to the country, Reme has few concerns at this time in its history. The civil unrest historically seen in the Westmarch has recently been resolved in Reme's favor. There are, of course, tribes of humanoids in the realm, particularly in the Green Mountains and in the far north amid the Haunted Wood and the Deepfells. But none of those pose any real threat to the security of the Rhemish heartland. The Haunted Steppes beyond the Crynnomar Gap also poses a theoretical danger, but the Wizard's Wall continues to be an impassable barrier to those of ill intent who might wish to cross.

For more information, see **Grand Duchy of Reme**, forthcoming from **Frog God Games**.

REME, CITY OF (CAPITAL)

Ruler: Lord Mayor Aldus Artaxis
Government: mayor and Council of Merchant Houses and Guilds (appointed by and subject to the Grand Duke)
Population: 311,295 (104,200 Loreclannic, 90,295 Foerdewaith, 53,800 human mixed ethnicity, 18,500 halfling, 12,900 half-elf, 10,700 mountain dwarf, 9,400 hill dwarf, 6,200 gnome, 5,100 high elf, 200 other)
Religion: Solanus, Dame Torren, Mithras
Technology Level: Renaissance

The city of Reme is one of the two most important port cities on the Crescent Sea (the other being Castorhage) and is the capital of the Grand Duchy of Reme. At its docks, merchant ships arrive from and sail to all of the known ports of Akados and even Libynos. It sits on the western terminus of the great Tradeway, the merchant road that runs east to Bard's Gate and then to Freegate on the Gulf of Akados. As a result, Reme is one of the great trading cities of the world, where virtually anything can be bought or sold.

The city of Reme is also one of the oldest on Akados, dating back to the era before the founding of the Hyperborean empires. Originally, it was the location for trading posts where Loreclannic tribes would meet. When Polemarch Oerson and his legions arrived here on the shores of the Crescent Sea in the early years of their conquests, they united the trading posts and began to lay the foundations of a city they called Remenos.

The elegant walls of the city of Reme and the spires and towers rising from within can be seen for miles out to sea. There are several large market squares within the city, about which can be found merchants, traders, artisans, craftsmen, mapmakers, and scholars with few peers anywhere in the world. The city also boasts the Arcanum Collegium, one of the most prominent wizards' colleges on Akados, and several museums and art galleries. The Reman Theatre is recognized far and wide for its cadre of famous playwrights and arresting performances.

RELIGION

The city of Reme is one of the most cosmopolitan cities of Akados, and accordingly, temples to nearly every god known may be found somewhere within its walls. However, Solanus, Dame Torren, and Mithras are the matron/patron deities of the city, and their worship is predominant among the residents. The city boasts the High Altar of Solanus at the venerable Hospital of St. Jethra the Martyred, which maintains 1,220 beds and accepts the sick and infirm seeking healing from all over Akados. Prominent temples to Sefagreth, Vanitthu, Belon the Wise, Muir, and Thyr can also be found in the city, and are well-attended.

GOVERNMENT

The lord mayor of the city of Reme, charged with administering the city and enforcing its laws, is appointed by the grand duke, and serves at the sovereign's will. Laws are approved by a Council of Merchant Houses and Guilds, the members of which are also appointed by the grand duke. That said, each of the major merchant houses and guilds of Reme has traditionally had a seat on the council, and the grand dukes pay close attention to their proposals concerning foreign trade. Even in the city, the Rhemish tradition of consensus (relative to other cities of the world) and a flat hierarchy of government (again, as a relative matter) reflects the city's Loreclannic roots, even after millennia of urban existence.

Officials below the lord mayor are typically appointed by the lord mayor, though positions of substantial authority are often subject to approval by the council. The grand duke has the right to remove or appoint any of these officials at any time, though this has been seldom exercised over the years.

Certain crimes and matters are, under the laws of Reme, subject to punishment or enforcement by the applicable merchant house or guild, but usually only if others outside the house or guild are not involved. Other matters come before magistrates appointed by the lord mayor and approved by the council.

As a general matter, the city of Reme has been well-run for centuries thanks to the appointment of qualified administrators to the role of lord mayor. That being said, more than one thieves' guild is active in the city, as well as other groups that operate in the shadows.

GILBOATH, TOWN OF

Ruler: Mayor Aerin Sarporond
Government: mayor and town council
Population: 2,220 (1,104 Foerdewaith, 611 Loreclannic, 257 human mixed ethnicity, 225 halfling, 23 half-elf)
Religion: Muir
Resources: grain, wine
Technology Level: Medieval

Gilboath is a small town about 150 miles north of the City of Reme. Its main business, were it not for one fact, would be agriculture. Rich fields and vineyards can be found in the surrounding region. Farmers and vintners come into town to sell their wares and to buy goods from elsewhere.

The town's great claim to fame, however, is its most famous son, Gerrant of Gilboath, a Justicar of Muir, one of the last two members of that holy order. Gerrant was lost in the Battle of Tsar between the Army of Light and the Disciples of Orcus in 3209 I.R. Sometime after that, a shrine to Muir was established in Gilboath. The townsfolk spared no expense in building the temple, which is constructed of beautiful white marble and houses six falcons, Muir's sacred animal. It is said that the falconer can read portents from the goddess in the flights of his raptors. Pilgrims from near and far come to the shrine to worship Muir and seek the intercession of her holy paladin Gerrant.

QUINTAS, CITY OF

Ruler: Earl Darvel Arcunas
Government: feudal
Population: 21,378 (15,173 Foerdewaith, 3,120 Loreclannic, 1,211 human mixed ethnicity, 841 hill dwarf, 629 gnome, 244 half-elf, 160 halfling)
Religion: Freya, Telophus, Archeillus
Resources: trade (cattle), grain
Technology Level: Medieval

Quintas sits at the crossing of three important trade roads, one leading north to Ironhill and the Northmarches, one east to Broadwater, the gateway to Eamonvale, and the last south to Yalendir, and the rest of the grand duchy. Earl Arcunas has profited greatly from this location and the amount of tradegoods that pass through the city's gates. As a result, the earl is a very wealthy man. Fortunately for the folk of Quintas and the rest of the county, the earl is also a thoughtful shepherd of his wealth and ensures that his demesne is well run with as little corruption as possible.

Outside the city walls is a large open area called the Mustering Field. Although it would make for good farmland, it is always kept unsown. According to local legend, the field was used for the mustering of the armies of Reme in 1573 I.R. on their way to the Battle of Ironhill with the forces of Dragonbone Peak, and again of the Foerdewaith legions heading north to the Crynnomar Gap during the war against the humanoid and shadow hordes from the Haunted Plains in 2947 I.R. It is said that so long as the field remains available for the use of the Rheman army, the grand duchy will never fall.

Varazath, City of

Ruler: Commander Alforce Berallo and Baron Midiera Nais
Government: feudal
Population: 16,248 (10,935 Loreclannic, 2,956 Foerdewaith, 1,250 human mixed ethnicity, 811 halfling, 296 half-elf)
Religion: Freya, Telophus, Sefagreth
Resources: trade, cattle
Technology Level: Medieval

Varazath represents the northern extent of the lands of the grand duke. The city stands aside the relatively minor trade route between central Reme and the Frontier at the northern extent of the Road of Horses. The city is located on a small rise and consists of two sections contained within the city walls: the ducal city made up of the inner bailey and the ducal castle, which is held directly by the grand duke, and the larger baronial city, held by the local baron in fealty to the grand duke, which occupies the outer bailey of the city. The ducal castle is in reality more a fortress than a residence, given its primary purpose as a military installation protecting the territory of the grand duke from intruders from the mountains and the High Downs. Since the fortress is as isolated as one can get in the grand duke's lands, it is neither a desired posting nor particularly efficient. Slovenly, in fact, would be the word chosen by most of the duchy's commanders to describe the condition of the fortress and its garrison. The city reflects the relative poverty of its trade route but is by no means in the poor condition of the garrison that ostensibly protects it.

Whiterush, Town of

Ruler: Lord Breldin Greaves
Government: feudal
Population: 4,220 (2,104 Foerdewaith, 1,406 Loreclannic, 462 human mixed ethnicity, 225 halfling, 23 half-elf)
Religion: Kamien, Freya, Telophus
Resources: trade, timber, fishing
Technology Level: Medieval

Whiterush is a trade town located where the Poitres Road crosses the Whiterush River just above the Whiterush Falls. Lord Breldin Greaves holds title to the city and most of the nearby river valley. Lord Breldin spent his own youth enjoying wine, women, and sausages, and today is a doddering old man with a prominent paunch and a permanently addled expression on his wrinkled face. A local family, the Quinns, control much of the trade going through Whiterush. The land here is generally peaceful, although rumor says that a tribe of orcs lives nearby in the forests to the north of town.

REFERENCE SOURCE: ONS5 ONE NIGHT STANDS 5: SCORNED

Yalendir, City of

Ruler: Lady Belestra Vorns
Government: governor appointed by the Grand Duke
Population: 36,422 (18,671 Foerdewaith, 14,011 Loreclannic, 2,685 human mixed ethnicity, 944 halfling, 111 half-elf)
Religion: Freya, Telophus, Kamien
Resources: trade, grains, glass
Technology Level: Medieval

Yalendir is a key trade city located at the fork of the Remenos River and the River Eamon and astride the Trade Road from Panetoth in the south to Quintas and Broadwater in the north. As a result, a large portion of the goods heading to and from the Northmarches and the Stoneheart Mountains must pass through its gates.

Lady Belestra Vorns was granted the lucrative governance of Yalendir seven years ago after retiring from a highly successful career as a captain in the Rhemish navy. Having had enough of the sea for several lifetimes, she asked for a demesne far from the ocean and was thus vested in lands outside Yalendir and appointed as the city's governor. She is a thoughtful ruler with little experience in administration who relies heavily on her advisors. Perhaps too heavily, as several take advantage of their position, and a bit of corruption now plagues the city. Increasingly, bribery is required to get anything accomplished. There is little doubt that the Lady Vorns would put a stop to this behavior if she knew of it. So far, it is relatively confined, and, given the wealth that passes through the city, has not risen to the level where she might take notice.

Yalendir is recognized throughout Reme for the wonderful stained glass manufactured here. While the sand must be brought in via the river, certain plants found on the river's shore here are processed into dyes that produce magnificent colors in the glass. The secrets of the glassworks are closely held by the glassworkers' guild here and are never shared with anyone other than another master or one's apprentice.

Geographic Features and Points of Interest in the Grand Duchy

Remenos River

The city of Reme sits astride the Remenos River, which makes its slow, peaceful way through the fields of Reme from the Stoneheart Mountains, 1,000 miles to the northeast. The Remenos is navigable virtually all the way to the Stonehearts and is regularly used to transport goods both upriver and downriver.

Road of Horses

This road runs north from the Western Reme Road about 100 miles west of the city of Reme, through the heart of the grand duke's ducal lands, past Gilboath and along the eastern margins of the Green Mountains, until it reaches the town of Varazath, beyond which are the open plains of the Northmarches and the Frontier. Well-maintained along its southern portions, the road's quality deteriorates significantly the farther north one goes and is essentially a dirt track by the time Varazath is reached. Of old, Loreclannic tribes would follow the path now taken by this road to Reme, where they would bring their finest horses for trade or show.

Whiterush River

The Whiterush River flows through a lightly forested river valley running from the Old Tors to Rimeth Sound. It is navigable for most of its length and is economically important to southern Reme.

Waymarch, Duchy of

Ruler: Lucius Qellinroque, Harmost of Panetoth, Duke of the Waymarch, Voice of the Grand Duke in the East
Capital: Panetoth
Government: feudal
Population: 3,752,500 (1,330,100 Foerdewaith, 975,300 Loreclannic, 799,700 other human mixed ethnicity, 267,100 halfling, 133,400 half-elf, 111,600 mountain dwarf, 102,800 hill dwarf, 31,200 high elf, 1,300 other)
Languages: Common, Elven
Religion: Mithras and Mitra (primary), Quell (secondary as patron of duke's house)
Resources: horses, cattle, military
Currency: Rhemish
Technology Level: Medieval

The vast lands of the Duchy of Waymarch are mostly made up of rolling grassland, with limited water other than a few collections of lakes from spring rainstorms and winter snowmelt. No major rivers cross the Waymarch plains, so water shortages are common in summer. As a result, the plains are excellent for raising horses, sheep, and certain cattle, but make for poor farmland.

The region of the Waymarch has, since Hyperborean times, been governed by a military administrator called a harmost who is based in Panetoth, the regional capital. When the Hyperboreans left Akados, rule of the Waymarch was granted to a Loreclannic chieftain, who was given the titles of both harmost and duke. This combination of harmost of Panetoth and duke of Waymarch survives to this day.

The current duke, Lucius Qellinroque, of House of Qellinroque ("Rock of Quell"), is the great grandson of Duke Borell, who was named for the famous Grand Duke Borell I of Reme who defeated the forces of the Hobgoblin Kingdom of the Deepfells in 1573 I.R.

Under its charter with Reme, Waymarch is required to keep a large military force for the protection of the grand duchy. With its limited resources, however, the march has historically struggled to support such an expense. In the last century, the dukes of Waymarch hit upon a solution to their persistent lack of income. The city of Bard's Gate to the east was growing ever richer in coin, but not in the military presence necessary to defend its extensive interests. With the blessing of the grand dukes, Waymarch began hiring out its soldiers to the City of Lyres as mercenary troops. Such soldiers are only permitted to serve in regions geographically adjacent to the grand duchy in case a military emergency arises that necessitates their recall home. This requirement has imposed little by way of real limitation, however, as the lands of interest to Bard's Gate adjoin those of the Waymarch, even if the troops hired by the city are often deployed to posts as far away as the Binjerin River Valley in the Gulf of Akados or even deep into the Sundered Kingdoms.

Most of the folk of Waymarch are of Foerdewaith extraction, particularly in Panetoth and the other towns and cities of the March. The plains, however, are dominated by the nomadic Loreclans, who migrate throughout Waymarch, the lands of the grand duke, and the Northmarches each year. Some of the prominent Loreclans currently in the plains of Waymarch include the Grass Sailors, the Quick Knives, the Stone Faces, the Thunder Riders, the Stone Walkers, and Beast Takers.

Every 50 years, families among the Shattered Folk beyond the Crynnomar Gap are permitted to petition for a right to settle in the Rhemish plains, and a lottery is held to determine who may immigrate. Those permitted to settle usually join existing Loreclans in the plains of Reme, though occasionally they may form new clans with a direct grant of range lands to be held thereafter. The latter typically occurs only when an existing Loreclan is declared for elimination by the grand duke as punishment for egregious violation of ancestral tradition. This is on the verge of happening with the Quick Knives Loreclan, so there is a good chance that at some point in the near future a Shattered-Folk tribe might replace the (exterminated) Quick Knives in their Loreclannic territory.

Religion

The worship of Mithras (in the cities), Solanus, Kamien, and Dame Torren is widespread in the Waymarch, as is the case in the rest of Reme. Devotion to Freya is also common in the countryside, and Sefagreth has followers in many of the towns and inns along the Tradeway. Although Quell is the patron deity of the ducal family, the sea god is not otherwise a prominent deity in this landlocked realm.

Trade and Commerce

Waymarch is essential to the protection of nearly 3,000 miles of roadway from Bard's Gate in the east to Reme in the west. The duchy further patrols the road from the capital city of Panetoth to the trade city of Broadwater. These roads serve as arteries of commerce for the entire Grand Duchy of Reme and are of vast economic and territorial importance. Large volumes of cattle, sheep, horses, grains, wool, linen, and cotton are hauled along the Tradeway, as are finished goods brought in from the port of Reme and the broad river-markets of Bard's Gate.

To this end, cavalry waystations are frequent sights along the roads of Waymarch, and dozens of riders are tasked with patrolling and repairing the long tracts of the Tradeway so that commerce can keep moving at a steady clip.

Yet for such a large duchy, Waymarch itself produces surprisingly little in the way of commodities for trade elsewhere. The horses of its plains are renowned and can fetch good prices in town and city markets. Otherwise, Waymarch is primarily a crossroad of trade, its revenues coming from taxes and fees (in addition to the hire of mercenaries to Bard's Gate), and many of those in its cities and towns make their living catering to the needs of those traveling east and west.

Government

Lucius Qellinroque is the fourth of his line to hold the title of duke of Waymarch. He has been forced to be a creative administrator of his demesne, always looking for sources of revenue to help pay for his feudal obligations to the grand duke in Reme. So far, by hiring out a substantial portion of his military to Bard's Gate, he has managed to keep local coffers full and his vassals happy.

Military

Under its ancestral obligations to the grand duke of Reme, Waymarch is required to maintain a sizable military presence for the defense of the grand duchy. Of course, many of the soldiers of Waymarch are abroad at any one time in the service of Bard's Gate. Were an emergency to arise they could be recalled, but given the distances, it would take time before the bulk could make it back to Rhemish territory.

Major Threats

Few major threats to Waymarch exist other than the risk of severe drought, which occurs once a decade or so. It is on reasonably good terms with all of its neighbors, and though a substantial portion of its military is in the east in service to Bard's Gate, there are no true military challengers on its horizon. Of late, however, its soldiers guarding the Tradeway have been attacked, and rumors say that Duke Passur of Ysser may be involved in these events. Though the Tradeway would be a prize of incomparable value, any attempt by Ysser to annex any portion of that road would undoubtedly be met by the full military force Waymarch could bring to bear and could risk war between Reme and Foere. Any proven aggression by Ysser, or other events which might arise from the increasing instability of the northern provinces of Foere, could drag the March more deeply into the politics of its former sovereign in Courghais than either it or the grand duke may desire.

Panetoth, City of (Capital)

Ruler: Duke Lucius Qellinroque
Government: feudal
Population: 82,419 (47,297 Foerdewaith, 20,617 human mixed ethnicity, 11,241 Loreclannic, 1,256 hill dwarf, 941 mountain dwarf, 777 halfling, 199 half-elf, 91 high elf)
Languages: Common, Kirkut, Dwarven
Religion: Mithras and Mitra, Quell (ducal family)
Resources: trade, horses, military
Technology Level: Medieval

Panetoth is the capital and regional administrative center that oversees Waymarch and houses its main garrison as well as the ducal palace. Patrols of the Waymarch and the absence of many soldiers in service to Bard's Gate means that the military encampments on the plains north of the city are never full. The city is also a key trading center, as it sits on the Tradeway, the main road from Reme to points east as well as the center of the Kingdom of Foere. The Temple of Mitra in the city protects the dwindling water supply every summer from contamination to prevent outbreaks of dysentery and cholera.

Fareme, City of

Ruler: Lord Ostric Kensalius
Government: feudal
Population: 4,000 (2,850 Foerdewaith, 500 Loreclannic, 212
  halfling, 121 half-elf, 105 gnome, 212 hill dwarf); but swells to
  10,000 during in caravan season
Languages: Common
Religion: Sefagreth, Belon the Wise, Mithras, Mitra, Quell
Resources: trade, horses, military
Technology Level: Medieval

The Tradeway links the eastern cities of Freegate, Derinden, Arendia, and Bard's Gate to the lands of the Grand Duchy of Reme to the west. The farthest eastern extent of the Duchy of Waymarch, the city of Fareme lies on its border with the Suzerainty of Bard's Gate. Here, Fareme serves as a waystation for merchants traveling east and west. During the caravan season, which runs from the beginning of Eostre until the end of Blótmond, the population temporarily swells to roughly 10,000 souls, though its full-time permanent inhabitants shrink significantly shortly after the caravan season ends. The numerous transients passing through town often bring more than their provisions and wares with them. Countless days of monotonous travel wearies the mind and body, prompting many visitors to drop their inhibitions and indulge their wild sides for at least a few days in a rough-and-tumble town catering to such folks. Fareme boasts a disproportionate number of inns, taverns, brothels, and gaming halls to suit every taste in addition to meeting the caravans' practical demands including open-air markets, general stores, pastures, paddocks, warehouses, wheelwrights, and other services necessary to properly outfit traveling merchants.

Despite its hard-partying reputation, Fareme's authorities display little tolerance for bad behavior in public. Drinking, gambling, carousing, and haggling are accepted pastimes in Fareme, but its city guards do not tolerate fighting or thievery conducted out in the open. What happens behind closed doors, however, is none of the guards' business, especially when it comes to the city's thriving black market of stolen relics and evil magical objects supposedly salvaged from the ruins of Tsar and Tsen. In addition, large quantities of illegal intoxicants exchange hands here for final distribution to High Karst far to the north. While the city largely turns a blind eye to these clandestine affairs, murder, rape, and other violent offenses incurring bodily harm are severely punished regardless of where they occur. The city can call upon 150 mounted soldiers to assist in this endeavor, complemented by 350 pikemen who also serve as an auxiliary police force alongside 100 constables who keep the peace on the streets.

Though it is geographically on the boundary between Waymarch and Bard's Gate, Fareme is firmly under the political control of the duke in Panetoth. However, Bard's Gate exerts far more economic influence over the city, especially among its caravan workers who frequently find work from a sign posted at a tavern, an inn, or a place of ill repute. Although more than two weeks march from Bard's Gate, the Wheelwrights' Guild makes its subtle presence known throughout the city. No one hires onto a caravan without the organization receiving at least a small cut from the transaction.

No institution benefits more from the steady stream of new arrivals than the Temple of Sefagreth. His followers always pay homage to their patron deity before stepping out on the road again into the great unknown. An upstart church dedicated to Belon the Wise has also taken root in Fareme. Its worshippers include many travelers, but it appeals more to wizards and other arcane practitioners who dabble in the trade and exchange of rare mystical tomes and other curiosities. Many residents and visitors alike believe his priests control the distribution and sale of magical items within the city. Others speculate that the Church of Belon the Wise is merely a front for another more insidious organization because of their propensity for dealing with vile objects best left undisturbed. Regardless of the truth, the god's followers maintain a well-respected public façade.

Geographic Features and Points of Interest in the Duchy of Waymarch

The Dagger & Rose

A traveler's inn and tavern located at the intersection of the Tradeway and the King's Road, this establishment was opened 60 years ago by Tamalaine of Portia, an enigmatic elven woman rumored to be of noble birth. The Monfrad clan, woodsmen and rangers who have lived in these parts for hundreds of years, built the tavern for her and then later sent family members to work there. Throughout its history, the Dagger has seen all manner of travelers come through its gates, ranging from humble young aristocrats with barely a gold sovereign to their names to princes fleeing incognito to escape death at the hands of assassins. The region is also home to a band of brigands called the Highwaymen who assault travelers on the roads and are said to be led by a mysterious leader named Black Jack Cutter.

REFERENCE SOURCE: DM1 BOOK OF TAVERNS: THE DAGGER & ROSE

Fivestones

Not far from the Grimburg in the shadow of the Stoneheart Mountains on the eastern reaches of Waymarch is a partial ring of five standing stones (once there were seven), around which has grown up a small village of a few hundred souls. This is the site of an ancient settlement that once served to supply and support the Stoneface Clan of the Grimburg. The settlement's occupants have changed many times over the intervening millennia, but it has always been here. Perhaps some mysterious force draws certain folk to come here to support the svirfneblin fortress without even knowing why. The current village consists of a mix of humans and rock gnomes who conduct trade with the distant Tradeway and provide supplies to the Stoneface Clan. They have no knowledge of the purpose of the Grimburg, though they do enjoy sharing rumors among themselves.

The Grimburg

This massive stone fortress is ancient, predating the arrival of the Hyperboreans. A very visible part of the landscape of northern Waymarch, the Grimburg is often mistaken for a huge block of stone rising from the rolling green foothills of the Stoneheart Mountains. A closer look, however, reveals observation holes and arrow slits that are cleverly hidden into the crevasses of the stone, and cold-wrought-iron stapling pins running up one side of the huge rock. The fortress itself is seemingly constructed from a solid piece of granite that emerges from the natural bedrock here. The only entrance is a massive, concealed gate that is always guarded by surly, heavily armed and armored deep gnomes.

Known to only a few is that the Grimburg is a planar prison for holding the most dangerous and powerful of extraplanar fugitives, fiends, and godlings. Its interior gives access to many dimensional gates and cells. It has been manned by the Stoneface Clan of deep gnomes who were given their charge at the end of the Age of Strife, roughly 14,000 years ago, by the elemental Lord Mocham — who infused it with a portion of his power to enable it to hold its prisoners. It has had no verified escapes, with one possible exception. When the Wizard's Wall was raised in 2947 I.R. — when Alycthron and Margon called on the spirits of the Haunted Steppes and the Stoneheart and Deepfell mountains to move the very foundations of Akados itself — in that moment of siphoning power, a great crack appeared in the wall of the fortress. It has since been repaired, but rumors persist that one unidentified prisoner was able to make its escape. The Stonefaces deny any such assertion.

Since that time, however, observers of the earth-spirit in the Stoneheart Mountain Dungeon have noticed that it seems to grieve deeply.

The Ice Tower

Standing at the head of a great glacial flow that has broken free from the Stoneheart Ice Plateau is the Accursed Ice Tower of Kal-Tior. The tower serves as home and siege tower of Kal-Tior the warlock, herald of Count Perfidium of Kainus, a high prince in the Court of the Nine Hells.

The tower itself is guarded by a nest of soulless ice goblins and a tribe of frost giants who pledge their allegiance to Count Perfidium.

The flow of the glacier, with the tower at its head, moves slowly but surely, and has now nearly reached the plains of Waymarch. From here, Kal-Tior will turn the direction of his infernal tower toward the Grimburg. Once there, he intends to freeze the gnomish prison vault solid and smash it to pieces to free those held within.

The tower's movements are controlled by blood sacrifice, and thus far its progression has been fed by the sacrifice of ice gnomes and captured Rhemish plainsmen from the grasslands of Waymarch south of Eamonvale.

The last few hundred miles are going to require greater sacrifices, however, and Kal-Tior has called upon his master for the assistance of ice devils, more frost giants, and any other help that can be offered to begin his assault on Grimburg.

See *Cold as Hell*, forthcoming from **Frog God Games** for more on the Ice Tower.

The Plains

Most of the Waymarch, along with the northern extant of the royal domain of the grand duke, consists of vast plains of rolling hills covered by grasses and sedges. Across these plains ride the Loreclans, the mostly-nomadic, horse-riding folk native to Reme. In the Waymarch, the largest Loreclans include the Grass Sailors, the Quick Knives, the Stone Faces, the Thunder Riders, the Stone Walkers, and the Beast Takers. All of the Loreclans here in eastern Reme are subject to the duke in Panetoth in his capacity as Loreclannic chief, and are largely on good terms with each other, taking care not to interfere with the territory or rights of the other Loreclans — with the exception of the Quick Knives. That Loreclan has in recent years come into increasing conflict with its neighbors, with its horsemen visiting random and extreme violence on those they encounter. It is said that in the councils of the duke, the termination of the Quick Knives as a sovereign clan — the most severe punishment under the laws of Reme — has finally been broached.

Superb horsemen and virtually unmatched light cavalry, the Plainsmen are also great traders who are able to carry the goods of Reme much more quickly than traditional caravans, although in smaller quantities.

The Tradeway

This major trade road runs all the way from the city of Reme in the west, past Bard's Gate and to Freegate on the coast of the Sinnar Ocean. Some merchant companies exist solely for the caravan run on this road. A typical caravan takes roughly one year to travel the entire length, with seasonal stopovers in Panetoth, Fareme/Bard's Gate, and Arendia.

Westmarch, Duchy of the

Ruler: Duke Wylan Rogers
Capital: Eckland
Government: feudal
Population: 1,224,789 (604,844 Loreclannic, 470,839 Foerdewaith, 79,065 halfling, 45,209 half-elf, 11,176 hill dwarf, 8,211 mountain dwarf, 3,890 high elf, 1,555 other)
Monstrous: orcs, hobgoblins
Languages: Common, Rhemish, Elven
Religion: Quell, Mithras, Dame Torren, Halatra (plains)
Resources: cattle, grains, fish, pearls, emeralds
Currency: Rhemish
Technology Level: Medieval

The Duchy of the Westmarch has been a problem for the grand dukes of Reme for generations. At least four of the leading families of the March have fought among themselves for as long as they can recall over slights that no one remembers. These families each have the support of more than one Loreclan, and the pashtars have not been able to broker any sort of mediated peace among them. As a result, this region has been plagued with infighting that finally degraded over the last several decades into regular eruptions of outright civil war. Various grand dukes mediated or interfered in various ways, but without lasting success. Every tenuous peace was eventually followed by new acts of ever-escalating retribution for claimed or perceived wrongdoing.

Two years ago, Grand Duke Iltobarus brokered another new peace when he elevated Wylan Rogers to the ducal seat at Eckland. Duke Wylan — of Foerdewaith ancestry but backed by a number of influential Loreclannic pashtars — managed to pacify the competing families and restore order to the duchy once more, but much strife still lurks under the surface. Few believe that the Duchy of the Westmarch will see a lasting peace.

Most folk of the Duchy of the Westmarch live in the southern and eastern sections of the duchy, with a Foerdewaith-type feudal structure in the areas closest to Eckland. The farther north and west one goes, the wilder the land becomes, and the more the old Loreclannic traditions are entrenched. Warring groups of allied Loreclannic barons control less-populated territories in the Westmarch wilderness, each waiting for a show of weakness from the new duke and the opportunity to break the newly imposed peace.

Trade and Commerce

With peace established by Duke Rogers, trade is finally returning to the Duchy of the Westmarch. The port of Martyn's Nest sees seaborne traffic from around the Crescent Sea, most of which comes for the pearls obtained in the nearby coastal waters and for the emeralds mined from the Green Mountains and cut by the gemcutters guild based in the port. Cattle ranching can be found in the southern and western portions of the duchy, with sparser Loreclan herds occupying the rest of the duchy.

Government

Duke Rogers is making every effort to obtain and hold full control of the levers of power within Westmarch. He has appointed trusted friends and advisors to all of the positions of authority within the duchy, and so far, the vast majority of them appear competent and trustworthy. But he has a long way to go before he can claim to have excised all the decay and corruption that has taken deep root from decades of internal strife.

Military

The duchy's land military, directly controlled by the duke, primarily serves as a peacekeeping force. It is used to guard the countryside against bandits and monsters, as well as to minimize opportunities for feuding Loreclannic families to pick fresh fights with one another. That being said, the households of Loreclannic barons are permitted small personal guards for their own security, and a few towns without ducal barracks are permitted to organize semi-professional guard militias. Ducal barracks dot the outer Westmarch borders and are common in all major Westmarch cities as well as most larger towns. These enable the duke's own forces to keep most of the region safe for travel and trade.

Major Threats

Many internal and external threats to Westmarch exist. Duke Rogers is still in the process of consolidating power and pacifying the Loreclannic barons of the duchy, and any number of events could derail his efforts or even recommence the civil wars that have been the rule here for generations. Many dangers exist in the Green Mountains, Westwood, and the Endless Hills. And the eaves of the Green Realm are not far away, along with the shadow of Hollow Mountain, around which it is said a cult with unknown intentions has grown.

ECKLAND, CITY OF (CAPITAL)

Ruler: Duke Wylan Rogers
Government: feudal
Population: 37,811 (Foerdewaith 27,335, human mixed
  ethnicity 7,093, halfling 1,224, half-elf 1,002, hill dwarf 771,
  mountain dwarf 330, high elf 41, other humanoid 15)
Languages: Common
Religion: Quell, Vanitthu, Solanus, Archeillus
Resources: trade, grain, cattle
Technology Level: Medieval

Eckland is the capital of the Westmarch and is located at the end of
the Western Reme Road on the Quail River. The duke's castle sits on
an island in the middle of the river. Both banks of the river have docks
for barges going upriver toward the Green Mountains and downriver
to the Crescent Sea. Eckland is firmly under the personal control of the
duke. He has appointed a city administrant to run the operations of the
capital, as well as each of the various magistrates and the captain of the
city guard.

The major markets of Westmarch are found here in the city, and so this
is the endpoint for merchants and traders traveling the Western Reme
Road. The surrounding lands are fertile and well-watered, bringing
farmers and cattle ranchers into town to sell their wares.

GLONDARR, TOWN OF

This coastal town is about 10 miles west of Martyn's Nest.

MARTYN'S NEST, TOWN OF

Ruler: Council of Ministers
Government: Three duke-appointed district ministers
  (Vennelitia Shiningtide, Augusthir Megson, and Athlindra
  Penabi) and their appointed staff
Population: 5,672 (2,120 Foerdewaith, 1,737 Loreclannic, 682
  high elf, 567 half-elf, 341 halfling, 113 hill dwarf, 57 gnome, 55
  half-orc) (Note: The Martyn's Nest region includes as many as
  20,000 individuals)
Languages: Common, Elven, many others
Religion: Quell, Sefagreth
Resources: fish, pearls, emeralds, mercenaries, shipping,
  foreign goods
Technology Level: Medieval/Renaissance

The size of Martyn's Nest depends entirely upon where one chooses
to draw its borders. Many towns dot the western Reme coast, and as
Reme's population has grown over the generations, the towns around
Martyn's Nest in particular have bled together at the edges to form what
some consider to be a single sprawling town along the entire eastern
shore of Martyn's Bay, nearly two-thirds the acreage of the city of Reme
in total.

Officially, however, Martyn's Nest is a modest town on the southern
Baronswood Peninsula, just south of the Quail River's mouth. This is,
indeed, the best-organized and best-governed portion of the city, with a
population approaching 6,000 permanent residents and perhaps twice
that during peak shipping seasons.

REFERENCE SOURCE: K1 A FAMILY AFFAIR

TANNER'S GREEN, TOWN OF

Ruler: Mayor Rutiger
Government: elected mayor
Population: 309 (198 Foerdewaith, 101 Loreclannic, 10 halfling)
Languages: Common
Religion: Freya
Resources: farming, ranching, some trade
Technology Level: Medieval

Tanner's Green is a small town near the eaves of the Westwood,
not far from the borderland with the Frontier. It is governed by Mayor
Rutiger, a position that is chosen by the landowning citizens of the town
every three years. A temple of Freya is in the town, which relies mostly
on farming, ranching, and a small amount of trade.

REFERENCE SOURCE: K10 DEMONHEART

GEOGRAPHIC FEATURES AND POINTS OF INTEREST IN THE WESTMARCH

BARONSWOOD

This forest near Martyn's Nest is rumored to be the home of the green
dragon Aureensaador.

CAER DIRE

The ruins of an ancient castle, this is now a tavern and trademeet
for three tribes of ogres and orcs who live in the region. An ogre mage
named Brazzer Mandragore, whose standard is a rook and broken lance,
is said to reside in this area as well.

Some 500 years ago, this was known as Caer Dunaven, the summer
home of the Dunaven family, nobles in the court of the grand duke.
According to legend, the Dunaven family eventually fell out of favor
with the court in Reme due to the machinations of another local family
that sought to usurp them.

REFERENCE SOURCE: DM1 BOOK OF TAVERNS: THE QUINTAIN'S TOWER

DUNAVENWOOD

This region of forested land is located near Caer Dire, which of old
was known as Caer Dunaven. The woodland is protected by a group of
rangers known as the Wood Wards of St. Sophia. Wild forest buffalo
wander the Dunavenwood.

REFERENCE SOURCE: DM1 BOOK OF TAVERNS: THE QUINTAIN'S TOWER

ENDLESS HILLS

Officially a part of the Westmarch, the Endless Hills are unsettled and
wild, well beyond Reme's control. Hot in summer and cold in winter, the
hills are arid, rugged, and covered in coarse grasses that are interrupted
here and there by seasonal streams and stands of hardy oak, juniper, and
cottonwood. Hyenas, both dire and ordinary, roam the hills, and hostile
tribes of gnolls make travel extremely hazardous. In the distant past, the
gnolls were far more numerous and powerful, threatening the elves of
the Westwood and even raiding nearby human settlements.

THE GALLOWS

The Gallows is a teardrop-shaped island some 450 miles to the
southwest of Martyn's Nest in the Crescent Sea, with an extension on
the northern end that gives it the vague resemblance of a hangman's
noose. The island runs 20 miles north to south and eight miles east to
west. Light pine forest dots the entire island, except for the center, where
a craggy hill known as Dead Man's Head resides. The eastern beach
holds the remnants of a village and cemetery of unknown origin.

Previously known as God's Tear Island, for many years it was an
important trading port and safe haven for merchants in the midst of the
Crescent Sea. Though surrounding reefs make the waters around the
island perilous to navigate, the islanders learned the passages and would
row out to ships arriving at the island and lead them safely to the docks.

About a hundred years ago, however, the baron at Martyn's Nest
learned that the island was the haven of a group of fierce pirates that had
been terrorizing the sea lanes out of Reme. The baron mobilized a large
fleet and seized the island. The islanders mysteriously vanished before
he arrived. Four months later, the baron's fleet sank or captured each and
every one of the pirates' ships. It is said that, as they looted the vacant
island, the baron's soldiers reported seeing strange shapes lurking in
the shadows and hearing disturbing noises. At first, these reports were
dismissed, but then soldiers began to disappear in the night. Their
bodies would eventually be found with fearful expressions on their
faces, but no marks on them to indicate how they had died. By the time

the baron's soldiers left the island, rumors had spread that it was haunted by the ghosts of the dead pirates. The baron's soldiers returned to tell the tales to their families and the name of the island became known as the Gallows. To this day, the island remains uninhabited, and sailors refuse to go there, as they believe the island is cursed.

REFERENCE SOURCE: K1 A FAMILY AFFAIR

GREEN MOUNTAINS

The Green Mountains are a range of now extinct volcanoes northwest of the city of Reme in the Duchy of Westmarch. Caves dot the heights, which feature groves of aspen and other alpine trees. The range is divided into eastern and western arms by the Quail Valley, the origin of the Quail River that runs south into the heartland of the duchy. Dwarves of the Green Mountain Clan live in the western range and mine emeralds renowned for their brightness and clarity. Other parts of the mountains are less hospitable. Orcs, goblins, and other humanoids dwell amid the peaks, and rocs are said to migrate south from here every autumn. Rumors also abound that ruins of prehuman civilizations can be found in the roots of these mountains.

QUAIL RIVER

The Quail River runs south from a source high in the Green Mountains through Quail Valley and into the heartland of the Duchy of the Westmarch, past the march capital of Eckland, and eventually to a marshy mouth on the Crescent Sea.

REFERENCE SOURCE: G4 THE VAULT OF LARIN KARR

QUAIL VALLEY

Quail Valley divides the eastern and western ranges of the Green Mountains. The Quail River originates at the northern end of the valley, high in the mountain peaks. Within Quail Valley can be found the Nin Forest, a dense, old-growth woodland said to be home to a group of elves, and the lightly wooded Gaskar Hills, which is prowled by the White Fist orc tribe. The Gaskar Hills are also the location of the Thorfax Mines, which produce a steady stream of iron ore, a key source of revenue for the Westmarch. The valley hosts a few small towns, including Pembrose, Bostwick, and Twain. Rumor has it that entrances to the Under Realms, the deep caverns and twisting tunnels that underlie much of the known world, exist somewhere in Quail Valley. Hints of civilizations older than humanity are also said to be hidden in this valley.

REFERENCE SOURCE: G4 THE VAULT OF LARIN KARR

TOWER OF JHEDOPHAR

More than a thousand years ago, a great mage named Jhedophar built a school of magic at the westernmost edge of the Green Mountains. Some centuries later, he closed the school, drove his students away, and sealed himself within his tower, never to emerge. Though the tower has largely passed from history and memory, it does yet stand, only recently rediscovered by intrepid adventurers.

Inside, over the centuries, the tower has become a veritable labyrinth of terror packed with undead monstrosities, perilous eldritch mysteries, and a dragon who claims a portion of the tower for himself. Little else is known, as none has yet penetrated the tower's ancient heart — none, anyway, who has escaped to tell the tale.

REFERENCE SOURCE: K7 THE TOWER OF JHEDOPHAR

WESTWOOD

This tangled forest in the far western portion of the Westmarch borders on the Endless Hills. Currently home to wood elves and gnolls, it was once inhabited by an ancient race of elves known as the Trae'este (Shadows of the Forest). It is said that in the distant past, the Trae'este summoned outsiders to battle a gnoll invasion from over the Endless Hills but were forced to sacrifice themselves and merge their souls with the Westwood to vanquish an especially powerful demon-lord they inadvertently called up and were unable to dismiss.

REFERENCE SOURCE: K10 DEMONHEART

THE WINDREFT

The Windreft is a remote area of the Westmarch west of the Green Mountains that has long been wild and, until recently, unsettled. Now that Duke Rogers is in Eckland, however, the grand duke deems it worthwhile to see if settlers can be enticed to move there. The risks are not insubstantial, as orc tribes control much of the nearby foothills, hobgoblins camp in the north, boggards infest the waterwoods, gnolls hunt in the open plains, and trolls sometimes wander down from the Green Mountains. Recently, the tiny town of Glory was established in the Windreft. But rumor has it that the town may in fact be located directly over something that perhaps would best be left undisturbed.

REFERENCE SOURCE: LOST LORE: TOWN OF GLORY

NORTHMARCHES, DUCHY OF THE

Capital: Ironhill
Notable Settlements: Albion, Dreikeng and Harrowfar (in the Frontier), Ionkri Hall, Nerimar, Tanith
Ruler: Duchess Candrella Iskadar
Government: feudal
Population: 220,000 (subject to seasonal variation) (85,000 Loreclannic, 60,000 Foerdewaith, 19,500 half-elf, 15,000 other human mixed ethnicity, 12,000 gnome [High Downs], 10,000 halfling, 8,500 hill dwarf, 5,000 mountain dwarf, 3,000 wood elf [Haunted Wood], 2,000 other)
Monstrous: hobgoblins (Deepfells), goblins, centaurs, gnolls (the Frontier), trolls, creatures of shadow (Haunted Wood), orcs (Ashen Hills), kobolds (High Downs), dryad (Eisenwood, Haunted Wood), bugbears, ogres, ettercap (Haunted Wood), ankheg, banshee, basilisk, chimera, cockatrice, peryton, treants (Haunted Wood), cyclops, manticores (the Frontier), owlbears (Haunted Wood, Sternwood)
Languages: Common, Kirkut (among some Loreclannic visitors from the deep plains), Elven
Religion: Solanus, Dame Torren, Mithras (Ironhill); Kamien, Freya, Telophus, Ceres (countryside), Halatra, Solanus, Dame Torren (Loreclans)
Resources: cattle, sheep, iron, chalk, timber
Currency: Rhemish
Technology Level: Medieval

For most of Reme's history, the Northmarches constituted the effective frontier of the grand duchy. Though lands beyond have been claimed over the centuries, this March has always been the last line of defense, the farthest reach of homeland that must be protected at all costs. Those crossing the windblown plains occasionally stumble across bones or rusted weapons or armor half-buried in the thin soil, remains of ancient battlefields where the legions and Loreclans of Reme met humanoids and darker enemies from beyond the Crynnomar Gap or hobgoblin armies from the Deepfells. Fortunately, few such forces have threatened the lands of the grand duke for many centuries now, though a watchful eye is still maintained in Durgam's Folly and in watchtowers on the Wizard's Wall overlooking the Haunted Steppes.

The land here is lightly populated, with little agriculture possible. Horses and cattle graze on the plains, however, and several of the Plains' Loreclans range over the Northmarches on a seasonal basis. Iron and chalk are profitably mined from the High Downs.

On official maps, the Northmarches include the Frontier and the Haunted Wood, but the duchess ignores both, since any effort to settle those lands would end up costing more in lives and treasure than it could ever conceivably be worth.

The few settlements, other than the capital of Ironhill, are largely trading posts for trappers, cattle drives, and prospectors, or are logging towns along the forest edges. The folk dwelling here are hardy, proud of their self-sufficiency, and often suspicious of those from the south. The duchess also maintains the military outposts along Wizard's Wall, including the fortress of Durgam's Folly, and fields a substantial standing army that patrols the outskirts of the Haunted Wood and the Gryphon Hills to protect against incursions of humanoids and other threats. The army is well supplied with light cavalry from the Loreclans, and very little gets past their watchful eyes.

TRADE AND COMMERCE

Northmarcher livestock, iron from the western slopes of the Stoneheart Mountains, and chalk from the High Downs all make their way along trade routes to the rest of the grand duchy and to places such as Waymarch, Ysser, the heartland of Foere, and Bard's Gate, earning much-needed gold and silver. An equally small but vital trickle of trade returns, bringing textiles, grains, manufactured goods, and a variety of foodstuffs back to the Northmarches.

The nomadic Loreclans provide an especially vital link to the other duchies as well, for their yearly migration route takes them from the Northmarches in the summer to the ducal lands of the grand duke in the spring and fall, and their winter camps in the Waymarch, then back again. Skilled merchants, the semi-nomadic Loreclans trade as they go, obtaining goods that they need and items that they know will be needed in their upcoming destinations.

GOVERNMENT

Rhemish rule in the Northmarches is minimal out of necessity, for beyond the various military garrisons sparsely posted throughout the duchy, the vast distances and unpopulated lands provide little opportunity (or need) for the exercise of real authority. Fortunately for Grand Duke Iltobarus, Northmarchers maintain a strong sense of Rhemish identity, despite their isolation and distrust of outsiders.

A hereditary duchy, the Northmarches are currently ruled by Duchess Candrella, the fifth ruler in the Iskadar line. While she is ambitious and wishes to see the Northmarches become a fully-integrated part of the grand duchy, with new roads, palaces, fortresses and cities (she has familiarized herself with the region's history and longs for the old days before the Deepfells invasion), Candrella is also realistic and knows that such changes cannot take place within her own lifetime. With little in the way of support from a grand duke who has numerous other priorities, Candrella must content herself with less ambitious projects such as building a paved, raised road through the High Downs and providing some much-needed repairs to the walls of Durgam's Folly.

MILITARY

The military forces of the Northmarches are charged with guarding the Wizard's Wall, and thus garrison Durgam's Folly as well as the watchtowers built atop the escarpment overlooking the Haunted Steppes. They also patrol the outskirts of the Haunted Wood and the Gryphon Hills, as well as the border with the Frontier and the foothills of the Stoneheart Mountains. As a result, the army of the Northmarches is comparable in size to that of many nations on Akados. Troops are regularly shifted among posts to avoid boredom and complacency. Command is held by the lord high commander of the Northmarches, who reports directly to the duchess.

MAJOR THREATS

There are many and varied threats to the Northmarches. Humanoids and worse live in the Haunted Wood and in the Gryphon Hills, and often find their way into the Northmarches from the Frontier. Just 30 years ago, a goblin raid from the Gryphon Hills claimed the life of the duke at the time. There is also the looming presence of the Haunted Steppes to the north. Though nothing has threatened to breach the Wizard's Wall in generations, there is something unsettling about the lands beyond. No one who serves at Durgam's Folly or at one of the watchtowers on the escarpment can ever forget the sight of those barren and haunted lands, or shake the feeling that something there is watching and waiting for some unknown event or portent to once more bring forth a darkness against the lands of Reme.

More immediately, both of the duchess' sons are manifestly unqualified to succeed her on the ducal throne at Ironhill. In the absence of another obvious and legal heir, her passing may result in chaos and, potentially, civil war in the Northmarches.

IRONHILL, CITY OF (CAPITAL)

Ruler: Mayor Ingal Stellan and Duchess Candrella Iskadar
Government: ducal city; feudal
Population: 56,194 (24,677 Loreclannic, 21,481 Foerdewaith, 3,890 gnome, 2,111 hill dwarf, 1,841 mountain dwarf, 1,041 halfling, 912 half-elf, 219 high elf, 22 other)
Languages: Common, Kirkut (Loreclannic dialects)
Religion: Solanus, Dame Torren, Mithras
Technology Level: Medieval

The capital of the Duchy of the Northmarches is heavily fortified — hill dwarves aided in building its walls and other defenses — and designed to withstand attack from any foe no matter how strong. The final battle against the demigod Kakobovia in 1573 I.R. occurred in a vale amid the hills within sight of the city. Since then, Ironhill has grown significantly and is the only real urban center in the Northmarches.

Designed to be a refuge to the region in the event of war, Ironhill's walls encompass much more space than is necessary for its typical population. Several large greens on the southeast and southwest sides of the city can be converted into tent camps that could hold thousands of refugees if necessary. The northern half of the city is divided into several quarters, including a merchants' quarter and a gnomish enclave, overlooked by the massive Tower of the North, fortress of the duchess. Scores of military barracks sit in the shadow of the tower and house at all times a sizable complement of soldiers either returning from duty on the borders of the March or preparing for assignment. One of the largest temples on Akados dedicated to Vanitthu, god of the steadfast guard, is located in the western part of the city. Temples of Solanus and Dame Torren are also prominent in the city; both expanded recently to house larger congregations.

ALBION, VILLAGE OF

Ruler: Mayor Jorgin
Government: feudal
Population: 140 (50 Foerdewaith, 45 Loreclannic, 25 human mixed ethnicity, 15 gnome, 10 halfling)
Religion: Solanus, Freya
Resources: timber, trapping
Technology Level: Medieval

Albion is a small village north of the High Downs located on the road from Ironhill to Durgam's Folly. Situated relatively near the eastern eaves of the Haunted Wood, locals make their living with some logging and trapping in the forest and provide for those on the road heading south to the ducal capital or north to the Wizard's Wall. The level-headed Mayor Jorgin was appointed to his position by the baron of Tanith, whose domain nominally includes Albion, although villagers see little of their lord other than the annual tax collectors. Of late, a wizard from Reme has settled in the area and built a tower outside of town.

REFERENCE SOURCE: LOST LORE: EMBERS OF DOMIN'S TOWER

IONKRI HALL, TOWN OF

Ruler: Lord
Government: hereditary monarchy
Population: 11,500 (11,250 gnome, 110 Loreclannic, 50 Foerdewaith, 50 halfling, 40 human mixed ethnicity)
Languages: Gnomish, Common
Religion: Dre'uain the Lame, Hammer Mittelschmerz
Resources: mining
Technology Level: Medieval

This gnomish town sits in a valley in the western High Downs and is surrounded by a high wall that seems to have been made of a single seamless block of stone. Visitors are allowed into the mercantile quarter inside the main gate, where shops, taverns, and inns cater to traders and travelers. Only gnomes may enter the rest of the town, which is said to include homes aboveground as well as dwellings below. Several mines are located a few miles to the north and west of Ionkri Hall, and carts are regularly seen traveling the road to and from the town.

Nerimar, Town of

Ruler: Mayor Ganik Athranos
Government: democratic
Population: 1,583 (613 Foerdewaith, 520 Loreclannic, 218 other human mixed ethnicity, 144 gnome, 88 halfling)
Languages: Common
Religion: Solanus, Freya
Resources: timber
Technology Level: Medieval

Nerimar is a frontier town located a day's march south of the Haunted Wood. It is a bustling trade hub and the last stop before passing into western wilderness. The residents are a rough-and-tumble sort, mainly trappers and loggers, overseen by a mayor who appoints a small city council and is democratically elected every two years. The current mayor is Ganik Athranos, who also owns the leading local inn, the Wizard's Wall. However, many suspect that another secretive organization may truly be the power in Nerimar.

REFERENCE SOURCE:
ONS6 ONE NIGHT STANDS: CURSE OF SHADOWHOLD

Tanith, Town of

Ruler: Baron Silas Novar
Government: feudal
Population: 1,251 (766 Foerdewaith, 356 Loreclannic, 103 gnome, 26 halfling)
Languages: Common
Religion: Solanus, Arialee
Resources: grain, livestock, iron, copper
Technology Level: Medieval

The second-largest town in this region of the Northmarches, Tanith lies close by the Stoneheart Mountains. It is an important trade center for iron and copper from the dwarven mines to the east and a stopover point for troops going to and coming from the fortress at Durgam's Folly.

Tanith is a ducal territory with a hereditary Loreclannic chieftain who bears the official title of baron. The current baron is Silas Novar, a young Loreclannic knight who was forced to take the office only two years ago when his father perished while fighting marauding hill giants.

Geographic Features and Points of Interest in the Northmarches

Crynnomar Gap

The Crynnomar Gap is the 500-mile pass between the Deepfells on the west and the Stoneheart Mountains on the east, and constitutes the border between the lands of Reme and the Haunted Steppes of the north. Through this gap, dark armies of humanoids and worse have poured south several times in the long-ago past as they sought to conquer the lands of the elves and humans. Since 2947 I.R., the Wizards' Wall has sealed the gap.

Durgam's Folly

The mighty fortress of Durgam's Folly has long stood guard on the shoulders of the Stoneheart Mountains, serving as a bastion between the settled lands to the south and the wild steppes of the north. It predates the creation of the Wizard's Wall, having been founded by the military captain Durgam Volmsmer in the earliest years of the Great Colonization of the steppes by Reme. It was nicknamed Durgam's Folly by those who believed that it would never stand and expected it to quickly succumb to the evil creatures of the Stonehearts. Early attacks on the citadel by forces of orcs and goblins seemed to confirm these expectations, and the name stuck, despite all of the attacks invariably failing. It is now said that Durgam's Folly is in fact unconquerable, proof against any external threat. Such would be a good thing, as since the raising of the Wizard's Wall, Durgam's Folly now guards the eastern flank of the wall and the only passes through the mountains leading to the southern lands of Reme.

It is said that Durgam's Folly was originally built on the ruins of an older fortification of unknown provenance. Of late, the grand duke has sent one of his court's wizards to the fortress to develop new magical defenses that could be employed were a new attack to come from the Haunted Steppes.

The citadel is currently commended by Captain Evrik, a capable soldier.

REFERENCE SOURCE: G1 THE SIEGE OF DURGAM'S FOLLY

Haunted Wood

The Haunted Wood is a vast forest crossing northern stretches of the Duchy of the Northmarches from the Deepfells almost to the foothills of the Stoneheart Mountains. This woodland has always been considered fey and strange, and it is believed that large portions of it currently lie under a shadowy curse. It was never actually a part of the Great Akadonian Forest that once swathed much of the continent, always having been separated by the Green Mountains and chalky High Downs to the south. Tribes of reclusive wood elves still live in this forest but are largely confined to the settlement of Golden Oak as a consequence of the shadowy curse that besets the woodland.

Five thousand years ago, the Haunted Wood was connected to the Namjan Forest across the Gryphon Hills. It was then the domain of the elven kingdom of Alathanar, home of the Alathi tribe. These elves who worshipped the goddess Shalraei were advanced in arcane knowledge and lived in homes melded from the living trees and rocks of the forest. It is said that a king among these elves turned to dark powers, which led to a civil war that ultimately destroyed the kingdom. Since that time, the elven presence in these northern forests has diminished (particularly after the wild elves departed to the south and west in the Third Exodus of the Elves) and the Shadow increased. The forest has gradually shrunk over the years until it is now completely isolated from the Namjan to the west.

Somewhere in the Haunted Wood can be found the ruins of Shadowhold, the stronghold of the dark elven king.

REFERENCE SOURCE:
ONS6 ONE NIGHT STANDS: CURSE OF SHADOWHOLD

High Downs

The High Downs are a natural chalky highland area of central Reme between the Green Mountains and the Stoneheart Mountains. They are considered to be the southern boundary of the Duchy of the Northmarches.

The capital of the Northmarches is at Ironhill in the High Downs. This area is home to large numbers of gnomes and is the historic site of an ancestral rock gnome homeland, specifically the royal gnome Clan Granith.

The invasion of the Northmarches by the Hobgoblin Kingdom of the Deepfells was stopped here at the High Downs. In 1573 I.R., an army led by Grand Duke Borell I ambushed the remaining hobgoblin army at the Battle of Ironhill, forever ending their threat against Reme. In the battle, the grand duke also defeated the hobgoblin demigod Kakobovia and banished him from the Material Plane.

Wizard's Wall

The Wizard's Wall is a vast cliff escarpment more than 500 miles in length that runs across the Crynnomar Gap between the Deepfells to the west and the Stoneheart Mountains on the east. For well over half a millennium, it has been an impenetrable barrier protecting the Northmarches of the Grand Duchy of Reme from the Haunted Steppes to the north.

Approaching the wall from the Northmarches, the land slopes gently upward, almost imperceptibly, until it suddenly drops in sheer cliffs to a base on the Haunted Steppes, as much as 1000 feet below. Along its western end at the base of the escarpment, the shallow, swampy Shadowfell Lake formed from waters that collected from the redirected Wanaheeli River. The face of the escarpment is effectively impassible, the rock of its vertical walls brittle and likely to crumble in the hands of any who might try to climb them. Attempts to pass the wall on the west are thwarted by the sharp crags and high peaks of the Deepfells, while the fortress known as Durgam's Folly guards the only known trail through the Stonehearts at its eastern end. More than just a physical obstacle, the stony precipice holds power over the unseen as well and bars passage by dark spirits from the steppe that seek to cross into the southern lands.

After the destruction of the Caleen Colonies in the Haunted Steppes in 2947 I.R., the wall was raised through the use of ancient and powerful magics by the archmages Alycthron and Margon to block what otherwise would have been an unstoppable invasion of Reme by hordes of humanoids and shadow-walkers from the Lost Mountains far to the north.

In the long years since, Reme has kept a watch on the Haunted Steppes beyond the Wizard's Wall. In addition to the permanent garrison at Durgam's Folly, the Duchy of the Northmarches maintains a number of watchtowers along the top of the escarpment. Troops are regularly shifted among these watchtowers, Durgam's Folly, and other assignments in the Northmarches, including patrols of the outskirts of the Haunted Wood and the Gryphon Hills. While some smaller towers are not always manned, the six largest host permanent contingents of soldiers charged with watching over the plains beyond. From the west, these six towers are called Haldor's Tower, Granite Eye, Rilla's Watch, the Tower of the Rock, the Duchess Tower, and Coursguard.

THE FRONTIER

Although the lands called the Frontier are considered a part of the Duchy of the Northmarches of Reme, in truth it is wild and outside the control of the grand duke and his vassals. The land is higher, the climate is generally cold, particularly in the winter, and not favorable at all for crops. Flora and fauna are both hardy, with herds of elk, buffalo, and caribou migrating with the seasons.

The nomadic Vaeltaia centaurs scratch out a hard living here, moving from place to place following the seasons and the game that they require for survival. Old treaties with the centaurs limited settlements, but today small farms dot the territory, along with the occasional cottages of trappers, woodcutters, and hunters. There are also a few communal farms of religious fanatics who believe that someday these lands will become fertile, with well-cultivated fields. To the extent that there is an economy, money can be made from timber and the fur trade.

DREIKENG, VILLAGE OF

Ruler: none
Government: council
Population: 512 (256 Loreclannic, 181 Foerdewaith, 50 hill dwarf, 21 half-elf, 4 half orc)
Languages: Common
Religion: Bablukar, Solanus, Dame Torren
Resources: timber, trapping
Technology Level: Medieval

Dreikeng is a village of about 500 souls (the vast majority being humans, with a small number of dwarves, half-elves, and half-orcs) dedicated, for the most part, to woodcutting, hunting, trapping, and manufacturing. Located on the Aciier River, a council of three local merchants govern the village.

About 100 miles south of Dreikeng is the even smaller village of Gauldark, which is home to about 200 residents, principally humans and a few refugees — often half-orcs. For most of the year it is almost vacant, with its residents in the forest woodcutting, hunting, and trapping. Only during winter, when inclement weather forces the people to find shelter, is the hamlet full "of suffocating life," as the villagers say. The town contains an outpost of the local thieves' guild (known as the Silver Crown Society), a shrine to the god Bablukar, and tavern named the Stuffed Bear — despite having stuffed boar inside instead.

REFERENCE SOURCE: K5 THE SIX SPHERES OF ZAIHHESS

HARROWFAR, TOWN OF

Ruler: Mayor Alijah Drusk
Government: informal democracy, chartered by the grand duke
Population: 1,172 (304 Loreclannic, 237 Foerdewaith, 231 high elf, 165 hill dwarf, 127 halfling, 85 gnome, 14 half-orc, 9 other)
Languages: Common, Elvish
Religion: Solanus
Resources: subsistence only, basic needs
Technology Level: mostly Dark Ages, with some Medieval elements

Though ostensibly capital of the Rhemish Frontier, and thus under the jurisdiction of the Northmarches, the town of Harrowfar is located at the eastern edge of the Endless Hills, which are often also considered to be Westmarch territory. This confusion is, itself, indicative of the region surrounding Harrowfar, as no real control over these lands is maintained or presumed by any authority in Reme, though Harrowfar's mayor does occasionally receive instructions from the duchess of the Northmarches, the duke of the Westmarch, or from the grand duke directly. When she's lucky, these instructions do not contradict one another.

A rough border town, Harrowfar boasts steel-reinforced wooden palisades along with other defenses against the hostile gnoll tribes of the hills. Harrowfar's full-time professional guard is unusually large for the town's size and often provides protection for other settlers and travelers in the region. This guard force was originally funded by the grand duke as part of his sponsorship of the Harrowfar settling expedition.

GEOGRAPHIC FEATURES AND POINTS OF INTEREST IN THE FRONTIER

ACIIER RIVER

This river runs from its source in the Ashen Hills past Dreikeng and between the Eisenwood and the Sternwood, and thence around the Green Mountains into the fields of the Westmarch, until it reaches the Quail River some distance north of Eckland. Logs of Eisenwood red cedar are shipped by barge down the Aciier for sale in the markets to the south.

REFERENCE SOURCE: K5 THE SIX SPHERES OF ZAIHHESS

ASHEN HILLS

This area of rocky, largely barren hills east of the Deepfells contains no know veins of precious ores, though some of the gray stone here can be quarried for use in building. Tribes of orcs roam these hills. In addition, it is said that an ancient complex of tunnels, possibly dug by a prehuman race, can be found deep in these hills, which ends in a secret valley containing a magnificent temple.

REFERENCE SOURCE: K5 THE SIX SPHERES OF ZAIHHESS

DEEPFELLS

This mountain range, despite its isolation, has played host to a number of momentous events in the history of Akados. In −6484 I.R., the Obsidian Vault plunged into the range, creating the strange structure known as the Devil's Finger. In those days, dwarves inhabited portions of the Deepfells, and the arrival of the vault prompted some of them to begin worshipping the demon known as the Faceless Lord. The dwarves were largely displaced by hobgoblin clans who began moving into the region, and by 1548 I.R., under the leadership of the demigod Kakobovia, the Hobgoblin Kingdom of the Deepfells had grown powerful enough to threaten the Northmarches of Reme, eventually reaching its tendrils as far east as the Starcrag fortresses. Kakobovia was eventually defeated and banished at the Battle of Ironhill in 1573 I.R., and the hobgoblins were pushed back into the mountains over subsequent decades.

Today, the Deepfells remain a dangerous place. Communities of dwarves struggle to survive against the hobgoblin clans who still dwell in the mountains, leaderless but still deadly.

REFERENCE SOURCES: G5 CHAOS RISING; MOUNTAINS OF MADNESS

DEVIL'S FINGER

This bizarre tower resembles a great bony finger rising 750 feet above an isolated valley in the Deepfells. It was formed 10,000 years ago when the demon lord Juiblex's Obsidian Vault crashed into the mountains. Within the tower, a clan of dwarves built the citadel of Dwurschmiede. The dwarven god Dwerfater ultimately trapped Juiblex in the vault some 9000 years ago. Three thousand years ago, Orcus, rising in power in the Abyss after his humiliation by the Three Gods, sent forth an army of demons in an unsuccessful attempt to invade Dwurschmiede. Finally, some 1300 years ago, the citadel fell to undead legions of the necromancer Giltz after being betrayed from within by a dwarf priest follower of Orcus.

REFERENCE SOURCE: G5 CHAOS RISING

DRAGONBONE PEAK

This high peak in the midst of the Deepfell mountain range is honeycombed with caves and roughhewn passages, a citadel of the Deepfells' hobgoblins. Dragonbone today is a mere shadow of its former greatness, when it served as home to the demigod Kakobovia and his powerful hobgoblin empire. Kakobovia's power reached its zenith in the late 1500s I.R., but Grand Duke Borell I of Reme finally defeated the demigod at the Battle of Ironhill. Without a leader, the Deepfell hobgoblins splintered into competing factions and scattered throughout the mountains, though the Dragonbone clan remains the strongest and most influential due to its control of the citadel.

EISENWOOD FOREST

The Eisenwood Forest is regularly logged for its famous red cedars. The reddish wood is used to build most of the structures in the surrounding area and is sent on rafts via the Aciier River to the markets in the south for sale. Many animals also call the Eisenwood Forest home, including deer, squirrels, and the like, with the occasional dire boar falling prey to the hunters, and vice versa.

REFERENCE SOURCE: K5 THE SIX SPHERES OF ZAIHHESS

GRYPHON HILLS

The rocky, largely barren Gryphon Hills arise as foothills on the eastern end of the Deepfells, bounded by the Haunted Wood in the east and the Sternwood in the south. They are separated from the Ashen Hills by the Namjan Forest and the Fehlween River to the west. Hobgoblins, ogres, and hill giants are known to prowl the Gryphon Hills, which are also well-known for caverns harboring bears, griffons, large cats, and manticores. The occasional dragon may also be seen winging overhead. According to rumor, the tomb of Thajar Darkfrag, an infamous archmage, can be found somewhere in these hills.

REFERENCE SOURCE: K5 THE SIX SPHERES OF ZAIHHESS

NAMJAN FOREST

The Namjan Forest is an old growth forest of northern Reme located between the Ashen Hills and the Gryphon Hills. At one time, this forest was a part of the Haunted Wood, which then extended over the Gryphon Hills. In the intervening years, both forests receded, and today they are separated by several hundred miles. According to rumor, the Ancient One sorcerer-warlord Dyraxl Uhl-Kal-Totten, who killed himself in a sorcerous explosion in the face of a siege by his enemies, once controlled this region, which has been the subject of incursions from the Shadow Plane.

The Fehlween River begins in the hills north of the Namjan Forest and runs through the woods to the south until it joins the Aciier River above Dreikeng.

Thistlehill, a gnomish mine fabled for its rare sunbreath quartz, is found within the Namjan Forest.

REFERENCE SOURCE:
THE DARKENING OF NAMJAN FOREST FROM QUESTS OF DOOM

STERNWOOD

The Sternwood Forest has a very bad reputation because of the many people who have of late disappeared in its vicinity. The most accepted cause is the presence of a particularly ferocious and well-organized pack of wolves. Others believe that a band of thieves and refugees use the forest as a hiding place, and some even think that some terrible monster inhabits the forest. The last is the typical story told to newcomers in a tavern to get some free drinks or coin in exchange for information. In fact, a wizard of substantial power built a stronghold upon a small hill in the midst of the forest, from which he sets loose undead slaves to act as guardians of the forest.

REFERENCE SOURCE: K5 THE SIX SPHERES OF ZAIHHESS

EAMONVALE

Capital: Dun Eamon
Major Settlement: Broadwater
Ruler: Lord Arb Angus
Government: Feudal
Population: 46,505 (29,606 Uplander, 4,979 Foerdewaith, 4,226 mountain dwarf, 2,921 half-elf, 1,818 human mixed ethnicity, 912 gnome, 716 hill dwarf, 676 halfling, 401 high elf, 250 other)
Monstrous: wolves, great cats (including jaguars), bears, serpents, girallons, dire animals, smilodons, kamadans, dryads, sprites, oakmen, brownies, and buckawns
Languages: Common
Religion: Thyr, Sefagreth, Belon the Wise, Stryme, Kamien, Dre'uain, Pekko, Solanus, the Green Father
Resources: trade, timber, fur
Currency: Eamonvale (though Rhemian currency is widely accepted)
Technology Level: Medieval

Eamonvale is a long fertile valley through which runs one of the few trade roads across the Stoneheart Mountains. The valley, the forested mountain slopes that flank it, and its deep swamps and boggy moors are governed from the Grey Citadel of Dun Eamon. The authority of the Lord of Eamonvale extends from the mountain passes near the river's headwaters to the trading center of Broadwater at the edge of the foothills of the Stonehearts.

For reasons that remain unclear, the Grand Duchy of Reme has never laid claim to the lands of Eamonvale, even though it is the source of a major tributary of the river that at its mouth empties into the Crescent Sea at the city of Reme itself. Rumors suggest that Eamon Angus, the original lord of Eamonvale, performed some critical service to the grand duke centuries ago and was rewarded with a permanent writ to hold Eamonvale free of the authority of Reme. Whether or not that is the case, neither the grand dukes nor the dukes of the Northmarches have ever attempted to annex the valley, though that has not stopped Rhemish merchant houses from seeking influence over this key trading route.

HISTORY AND PEOPLE

In 3238 I.R., Eamon Angus founded a small trading post at a ford near the end of a valley in the western eaves of the Stoneheart Mountains, south of the High Downs. As it became apparent that the trading post and the growing community on the ford were in a position to influence trade across the mountains, the community attracted the attention of several merchant families from the heartland of Reme. As the number of caravans moving across the ford and stopping to trade within the walls of the city grew steadily, the merchants sought a toehold in the thriving economy. Angus and his descendants forbade their emporiums in the city that would become Dun Eamon, so the merchants were forced to barter their goods and collect their tariffs before the caravans entered the valley.

At the mouth of the valley where the River Eamon calmed and widened into a navigable waterway, the tent cities and caravan camps of the traders grew into the town of Broadwater. It was here that the powerful Rhemian merchant house of Drenwal was able to establish an emporium and dominate the smaller independent traders. With total control of the movement of goods up the valley, House Drenwal taxed goods so heavily that they became unmarketable in the frontier communities. The merchant dynasty bought out caravans of certain critical supplies to deny the settlers the tools for their survival. When Eamonvale had been weakened by their actions, a scion of the Drenwal empire led an army of mercenaries upriver to sack the Angus trading center at the ford and seize the lucrative position on the trade road for themselves.

Angus and his supporters raised an army of woodsmen and settlers and engaged the merchant prince with a ferocity and tenacity that surprised even the seasoned mercenary generals. The battles of the Frontier War were hard-fought and costly, but the people of Eamonvale drove the army of House Drenwal from the valley and secured their economic freedom and gained effective control over the trading center of Broadwater. House Drenwal withdrew from the economics of the region but has never forgotten the chagrin of their defeat in the campaign and still covets the valley's flourishing economy.

The frontiersmen of Eamonvale fought for generations to preserve their rights in the valley, first wresting their sustenance from the untamed wilds, then defending their homes against humanoid onslaughts and, most recently, dealing with the political machinations of greedy merchant empires. The people of Eamonvale are hardy and self-sufficient, hardships are taken in stride, and respect is reserved for those who earn it. Two dominant social groups exist in the valley and are usually at odds with each other. The woodsmen who people the fertile slopes and forested glens of the valley regard the merchant class as arrogant foreigners from pampered lowland cities; the merchants regard the woodsmen as savages whose uncouth lifestyle they tolerate only in the interests of profit.

RELIGION

Among the merchants, Sefagreth is worshipped, and a temple to this god can be found in Broadwater. The locals generally prefer Dre'uain (particularly among the craftsman), Kamien, Pekko, and Thyr. Many travelers also sacrifice to Belon the Wise, seeking protection as they travel into the wilds beyond the valley. The Angus family, rulers of Eamonvale, have typically honored Stryme, and Lord Arb Angus' brother, Cael Angus, currently serves as the Master of the Temple of Fortitude and High Priest of Stryme in Dun Eamon. Rumor has it that the Angus family adopted Stryme as their patron after a long-ago battle where they fought alongside dwarves who honored that god.

TRADE AND COMMERCE

Eamonvale is a key location on one of the few commercial trading routes over the Stoneheart Mountains. Caravans, traders, explorers, and more take the Eamonvale Trade Road, and Dun Eamon and Broadwater are the last safe havens before entering the deep mountains. This has made the valley a target of many merchant houses over the centuries, though the Angus family has fended off all threats to the independence of their domain. Other than trade, the valley also produces fur and timber that is sent downriver to Yalendir and beyond into the heartland of Reme.

LOYALTIES AND DIPLOMACY

Eamonvale is isolated, located on the very limits of civilization several hundred miles from the nearest Rhemian city of Quintas. It remains on friendly terms with the grand duchy, having apparently been guaranteed its independence around the time it was founded. On rare occasions, ducal patrols visit Broadwater or Dun Eamon on their way to assignments along the Stoneheart foothills, and they treat the locals with care and respect (which treatment is reciprocated by the Eamonvalers). The only real diplomatic challenge to the Angus family comes from Rhemian merchant houses, and particularly House Drenwal, which continually seek to influence or control the trade routes through the Stonehearts.

GOVERNMENT

For almost three centuries, rule of Eamonvale has passed by hereditary descent through the Angus family, beginning with Eamon Angus, the founder of Dun Eamon. The current ruler is Lord Arb Angus, a tall, robust man with thick brown hair and a well-trimmed beard. The region has developed well under his reign. He is young, having just entered his 30th year, and he rules with the confidence and vigor of youth tempered by the strict discipline and wisdom of his father. His policies on trade and tax ensure a place for the local farmers and craftsmen in the economy, and his strict prohibition on foreign guild influence has drawn much controversy. While many abroad would see him overthrown, he is well loved by his citizens.

Arb Angus remains unmarried, and it is well known in the valley that he intends to wait until later in life to take a wife. He has two younger brothers: Bron Angus serves as captain of the Mist Watch in Dun Eamon, and Cael Angus is master of the Temple of Fortitude and high priest of Stryme in Dun Eamon.

MILITARY

The maintenance of law and order in and around the Grey Citadel is the responsibility of the Mist Watch, which is over 200 strong. The force is made up of career soldiers, citizen militia, and wilderness outriders. There is no law of mandatory service for the citizens, but any man living within the city walls is subject to conscription in times of war.

Bron Angus, Arb Angus' younger brother, is the captain of the watch and has been highly successful despite his young age. His experiences as a young man in a mercenary company taught him to be intolerant of sloth, insolence, and drunkenness, and his strict orders have resulted in an elite fighting force. The members of the Mist Watch are trained to a basic level with all weapons and tactics, but many of them have additional areas of expertise. All the watchmen are rotated through various duty stations to avoid boredom and complacency.

Another 200 soldiers serve in the Broadwater Guard, a standing military force garrisoned at the Old Keep in Broadwater. These guardsmen, under command of sergeants and captains, are charged with safeguarding the town from external threats, a duty that includes manning the walls and gates, patrolling the immediate vicinity, and responding to any apparent threat in the small communities immediately outside the gates. As the largest armed body of troops in the city, they may also be called upon to respond to any large disturbance within the walls, but they do not operate regular patrols in the town (which is the province of the Broadwater Constabulary).

MAJOR THREATS

There are many threats to Eamonvale that require the continual vigilance of the Angus family. The mountains contain many perils, including the orcs of Og-Brethos to the north and the other monsters that call the Stonehearts home. But historically, the greatest threat to Eamonvale has come from the merchant families of Reme who continually seek to take control of this critical juncture on the trade road across the mountains. It is said that House Drenwal, in particular, holds a deep grudge against the Angus family for evicting them from Broadwater in the Frontier Wars several centuries ago.

REFERENCE SOURCES: G6 THE GREY CITADEL; K12 THE EAMONVALE INCURSION

Broadwater, Town of

Ruler: Council Chairman Alfgar (appointed by Lord Angus of Dun Eamon)
Government: town council
Population: 2,268 (1,022 Uplander, 811 Foerdewaith, 90 half-elf, 74 mountain dwarf, 68 gnome, 61 halfling, 58 high elf, 45 half-orc, 39 hill dwarf)
Languages: Common
Religion: Sefagreth, Belon the Wise, Pekko
Resources: trade, furs and pelts
Technology Level: Medieval

Broadwater, a thriving crossroads town of more than 2,000 citizens, marks the lower end of Eamonvale and the point where the River Eamon, having frothed and plunged its way down from its mountainous origins, finally becomes navigable by watercraft. The river, the Eamonvale Trade Road, and two other busy trade routes meet in Broadwater, bringing with them trade goods, foreign travelers, fighting men, ambitious merchantmen, fortune seekers, intrigue, and adventure. The walled town contains a maze of twisting streets, crowded markets, and whitewashed sandstone walls, and is divided into four quarters. Of late, additional communities have sprung up outside the gates.

The town of Broadwater also represents the extent of the influence of the Angus clan, where the rule of the Lord of Eamonvale gives way to the authority of the Northmarches of the Grand Duchy of Reme.

REFERENCE SOURCE: K12 THE EAMONVALE INCURSION

Dun Eamon, City of (Capital)

Ruler: Lord Angus of Dun Eamon
Government: Feudal
Population: 5,722 (4,323 Uplander, 312 mountain dwarf, 229 gnome, 209 half-elf, 183 human mixed ethnicity, 171 halfling, 115 high elf, 87 hill dwarf, 51 half-orc, 42 Foerdewaith)
Languages: Common
Religion: Stryme, Dre'uain, Belon the Wise, Kamien
Resources: trade, furs and pelts
Technology Level: Medieval

The city of Dun Eamon is the center of government for Eamonvale. Located high in the mist-shrouded mountain crags of the Stoneheart Mountains, it is a city like no other. Locally known as the Grey Citadel, it is an important trading city that sits on a broad ford at the base of one plunging waterfall and at the head of another. Midway across the ford, a huge slab of bedrock divides the river into two channels. On the island between, many generations ago, Eamon Angus staked a claim and founded a tiny trading post. Now, centuries later, expansion of the duchies and kingdoms on either side of the Stoneheart Mountains and development of trade between them have caused the tiny trading center and way station to grow into a heavily fortified citadel, with the lordship still in the hands of the Angus family. Three brothers of the Angus Clan currently rule over the city and valley with strictness and compassion, and they have seen it flourish under their authority.

The Grey Citadel is renowned as the location of some of the finest forges in the land. Nearly any tool, weapon, or other metal item can be crafted there, and the quality of their alloys and strength of their castings are unsurpassed. Due to its critical location at the ford and its safety relative to the perils of the frontier, the Grey Citadel is a popular stop on the route to the passes of the Stonehearts. It is a hiring point for caravan laborers and guards for the dangerous journey over the mountains to the distant kingdoms beyond. Many hunters and trappers pass through the gates every season to sell their pelts and to re-supply for another trip into the wild mountains beyond. Traveling minstrels, adventurers, and highwaymen all call the city home from time to time.

A rampart wall surrounds the entire island, with watchtowers evenly distributed along it, and a massive gatehouse guards each entrance where the road rises up from the ford. Where the divided channels of the river spill over the lower falls, the island rises steeply to a flat-topped promontory. On this slab of rock sits the upper city, which consists of the craftsman's district, the vast market, and the largest taverns. The stone buildings are quarried from the same gray basalt as the bedrock they sit on, as are the city walls and keep. The rest of the buildings are half-timbered two- and three-story structures, with roofs of thatch or shingle. The cobblestone streets and alleys are always shiny and damp, and everything in the city hosts at least a thin sheen of green moss, and many buildings have thick clumps of ferns growing on the roof. Amid the green-forested slopes and drifting gray rain clouds, the gray-green edifices of the citadel blend right in.

According to rumor, a network of caves and caverns and even an underground river lie beneath Dun Eamon.

REFERENCE SOURCE: G6 THE GREY CITADEL

Eamonvale Trade Road

Winding a course through Eamonvale's mountainous wilderness, this road is the chief artery of transit for the valley. It runs from the town of Broadwater, past several villages, through the gates of the Grey Citadel of Dun Eamon and beyond, until it slips into the snow-clad passes of the Stoneheart Mountains and eventually arrives at the Feirgotha Plateau. Beyond that, the eastern eaves of the Stonehearts are reached through the Southern Pass, to the Desolation of Tsar, or the Cobalt Pass. Traffic on the road includes mercantile enterprises ranging from large caravans to tiny farm carts, as well as travelers, military forces, homesteaders, pilgrims, and indigenous creatures.

River Eamon

The River Eamon flows down out of the Stoneheart Mountains, first through snow-fed mountain streams before crashing down through rocky gorges and finally calming and widening at the town of Broadwater, where it enters the plains of the Northmarches of Reme on its eventual way to join the Remenos River to the Crescent Sea.

South-Central Akados

Heartland of the Kingdom of Foere

Political Subdivisions of the Heartland of the Kingdom of Foere

Kingdom of Foere

Capital: Courghais

Notable Settlements: Croix, Demz, Farall Hold, Nains, Pentahs, Sion

Ruler: His Holy Radiance, Emperor of the Hyperborean Monarchy, Overking of the Foerdewaith and Heldring, Prince of Ynys Cymragh, Guardian of the West, Grand Admiral of the Oceans, Suzerain of Khemit, Protector of Tircople and the Sacred Table, Defender of the Faith, King Ovar I

Government: feudal kingdom

Population: 4,193,400 (including only royal lands) (3,061,900 Foerdewaith, 621,500 human mixed ethnicity, 323,400 halfling, 58,800 high elf, 46,400 mountain dwarf, 33,600 half-elf, 22,900 hill dwarf, 16,300 gnome, 5,900 half-orc, 1,800 orc, 900 other)

Monstrous: giant animal, wolf, goblin, hobgoblin, fey (plains); gnoll, forest troll, giant animal, owlbear, forlarren, dryad, green dragon (forest); hill giant, stone giant, giant eagle, hippogriff, cave moray (mountains)

Languages: Common, Gasquen, Halfling, Dwarven, Elven, Gnome

Religion: Archeillus, Mitra, Thyr, Stryme, Freya, Mick O'Delving, Dwerfater, Muir, Bacchus-Dionysus

Resources: grain, foodstuffs, gold, glass, metalwork, stonemasonry, manufactured goods, textiles, timber, trade hub

Currency: Foere

Technology Level: High Middle Ages

The Kingdom of Foere is the heir of the Hyperborean Empires of old and to this day maintains a claim to most of the lands of Akados as well as large portions of far Libynos beyond the Sinnar Sea. At one time, the overking's arm really did stretch that far. But today, Foere is now a mere shadow of its prior greatness. It still commands, at least nominally, the loyalty of the Duchy of Ysser, the County of Coutaine, the County of Roy, the Barony of Baldenar, the Duchy of Saxe, the Duchy of Mains, the Duchy of Listonshire, the Duchy of the Rampart, Aachen Province, the County of Vourdon, Exeter Province, and Cerediun Province. However, the domains east of the March of Mountains are in reality mostly semi-independent, as Foere has little ability to enforce its edicts at such a distance. And the lands no longer under the command of the overking far exceed those that remain. The breakup of the Foerdewaith Empire has left much chaos in its wake as the rule of law crumbles and new kingdoms have little reason not to go to war against each other.

History and People

Toward the end of the 25th Century I.R., the Hyperborean Empire in Akados collapsed. In 2496 I.R., a wildfire destroyed the imperial capital of Curgantium and spread to burn the Plains of Suilley and Matagost Forest. Three years later, the capital moved to Tircople in Libynos, and the Hyperboreans abandoned their western empire. By 2632 I.R., the last Hyperborean abandoned Tircople, and their age came to an end.

In the void resulting from the retreat of the Hyperboreans, wars raged between petty kings throughout Akados seeking to obtain and hold lands, wealth, and warriors. One such kingdom in central Akados was Foere. Their king, a half-elf named Macobert, had been a chiliarch (battalion commander) of the Hyperborean legion that faced the Cataphracts of Daan in battle decades earlier. Upon his return to Foere, Macobert overthrew his nation's king and instituted the military traditions he learned from his time in the legion. To this he added experience he gleaned from having faced the seemingly invincible Cataphracts of Daan and bred his own war mounts to create his own heavy cavalry. The expense of their mounts and gear was such that he recruited the members for this specialized unit only from among the lords of Foere, much like the old Hyperborean hippeis class. He trained these riders in cavalry tactics and the use of combined arms until he created the deadliest fighting force since the Cataphracts of Daan. He called them his Knights.

The Knights of Macobert served as the anchor for his army and allowed him to defeat and unite all of the petty kingdoms around until soon one Kingdom of Foere ruled in central Akados. He carried the standard of the lost glory of Hyperborea, and many vassal kingdoms flocked to his banner seeking his protection or hoping to share in the spoils of his victories. Soon the Foerdewaith, as his people were called, became recognized as the dominant authority and spiritual inheritors of the ancient Hyperborean Empire. And in his 260th year, King Macobert marched his vast host, led by his thousands of Knights, in a long pilgrimage across the Isthmus of Irkaina to distant Tircople.

There he found the city in near ruins, its few inhabitants left in the wake of the Hyperboreans' departure a mere shadow of their former masters. Macobert quickly claimed the city and at the newly cleared High Altar of Muir had himself crowned as Macobert I, Overking of the Hyperborean Monarchy of the Foerdewaith. He left a small garrison to refurbish the city and returned with his forces to the Foerdewaith fortress of Caene and set about rebuilding it into a capital to rival Curgantium. Upon its completion in the time of Macobert's son, Magnusson, the capital city was renamed Courghais — the "Heartstone" — to serve as the seat of the Hyperborean Monarchy of the Foerdewaith.

The Foerdewaith continued to consolidate their hegemony over Akados and maintained their control of Tircople as a distant client kingdom. The road between Occibolos (later known as Oxibbul) and Tircople was kept open as a pilgrim route, but the rest of the territory between was largely left to itself, being considered too far away from Courghais' interests to be of importance. A series of powerful Foerdewaith overkings expanded the control of Foere and brought the former Hyperborean lands of Akados under their banner as the legitimate heir of that empire. Overking Osbert II even took a large force of Knights of Macobert, supported by heavy infantry, over the Helwall and against the shieldwalls of the Heldring. The expert tactics of the Knights in flanking and engaging the rear of the Heldring shieldwalls while the Foerdewaiths' own shieldwall held them in place proved disastrous for the Heldring so that even that land of barbaric warriors finally tasted true defeat on its home ground and was brought under the sway of the banner of Foere. The Foerdewaith did not, however, attempt a crossing of the Straits of Daan. The losses suffered by the Daanites in purging the Hyperborean Empire of its corruption were still fresh in the memory of the Foerdewaith, and Osbert and his successors chose to leave the island of Ynys Cymragh and its people in peace, reckoning they had endured enough.

In 2843 I.R., Queen Beraia, wife of Overking Paulus, gave birth to twin sons, Kennet and Cale. The royal physiker was drunk at the time of the delivery, and Queen Beraia died in the childbirth. Overcome with grief, Overking Paulus summarily executed the physiker for his gross incompetence and only afterward realized that only Beraia and the physician had known which of the twins was firstborn. The overking had been in the chambers outside the birthing room, and the group of midwives attending the physician did not see which child was first since they assumed the physiker would tie a red string to the ankle of the first

SOUTH-CENTRAL AKADOS

Legend
Town or Village
City
Capital or Free City
Imperial Capital
Fortress or Citadel
Ruins
Place of Interest
Road
Trail or Unused Road
Mountain Pass
Battlefield

MOTHER OCEANUS

The Citadel of Caene in the city of Courghais, capital of Foere.

child at the moment of birth as was tradition in Foere. A pious man, Paulus dared not simply decree one child as the heir in possible defiance of the will of the gods, and as a result both brothers grew up as co-heirs to the crown in the tradition of Oesson and Oeric nearly three millennia before. While the brothers got along well enough, the land was troubled by the possibility of civil war upon the death of Paulus if the brothers did not choose to administer it peacefully as co-regents.

As the twins reached the age of majority, Overking Paulus died of an illness that had afflicted him for several years. Immediately, parties supporting one twin or the other stepped forward hoping to promote their choice to take control of the empire and bring more power to their own ambitions. Instead, the twins showed a wisdom beyond their years and chose another course. Kennet would be crowned as the sole overking of the Hyperborean Monarchy. Cale, meanwhile, abdicated his claim to the throne. Kennet rewarded him by giving him sole control of the rich port of Reme as well as all the nearby marches that controlled access to the Crynnomar Gap. Shortly after, Cale began the Great Colonization, an attempt to settle the fertile and largely unoccupied grasslands of the Great Steppes. As is told elsewhere, this led to great misfortune, and resulted in the death of Cale and the near-destruction of Reme.

In the year 2958 I.R., a Libynosian king declared anathema the infidels of the Foerdewaith and led his people, called the Huun, in a holy war against the Akadonian at the Sacred Table. The Huun swept over the mountains and slaughtered the inhabitants of Tircople and the valley basin. Fully half the Justicars of Muir fell in the onslaught, with the rest being abroad in their wandering duties. In addition, the pontifex and the first high lord were slain.

In Courghais, Overking Granicus learned of this attack and called for an immediate liberation of the Sacred Table in what became known as the First Great Crusade. Justicars who had formed chapters within lands across Foere raised armies for the cause. A great flotilla eventually sailed to land a crusader army on far Libynos. The crusader forces drove the Huun before them and recaptured Tircople and the Sacred Table. Ten years later, the Huun retook Tircople, and a Second Great Crusade was launched. The Foerdewaith again seized the Sacred Table, which they held until 3169 I.R. when the Huun overran the Crusader Coast and again sacked Tircople. A Third Great Crusade failed when the entire fleet was lost at sea, and 30 years would pass before a Fourth Great Crusade could be gathered, this time led by Overking Oessum VIII himself, a pious and devoted warrior of Muir. Eight years later, the Huun army was destroyed at the Battle of the Sickles when it was caught between the crusader army and allies the overking raised from the hill dwarves of the nearby Shamash Kush.

The Sacred Table and Crusader States were secure, and Tircople was once again in the hands of the Foerdewaith. Unfortunately, Overking Oessum VIII was killed in the final battle and died without an heir. The ensuing political struggles to put any one of a number of potential candidates upon the Hyperborean throne sapped the momentum of the victory in Tircople. Plans to ordain a new pontifex and renew the faiths of Thyr and Muir — which of late had been in decline since the loss of Tircople — failed. Finally, Graeltor, an aged uncle of Oessum who had served as administrator of the monarchy while the overking was on campaign, was crowned overking in Courghais.

The reign of Graeltor was not long. Shortly after his coronation, the patriarchs of Thyr and Muir in Courghais along with a delegation of many of the other good and neutral faiths approached him about a threat arising in the wastes north of Bard's Gate where the temple-city of Orcus known as Tsar was threatening all trade between Foere and the Isthmus of Irkaina. Though the temple-city had been there for many years, Graeltor, having been left in Akados while Oessum and his armies achieved glory in Libynos, decided to declare his own crusade against evil, which he dubbed the Army of Light. Under the command of Zelkor, Graeltor's trusted archmage advisor, the Army of Light gathered at Bard's Gate and fought its way through the outer defensives of Tsar. Among the many warriors who made up the Army of Light were Alaric of Tircople and Gerrant of Gilboath, the last two Justicars of Muir. After several months, the Army of Light finally laid siege to the city of Tsar itself.

The siege of Tsar lasted for over a year, during which many insidious weapons and tactics were unleashed to claim tens of thousands on both sides. Meanwhile in distant Libynos, swarms of invading Mguru tribesmen emerged from the Malagro Jungle and overran Tircople and the Sacred Table, reducing it to a burning waste. News of this atrocity rocked the morale of the Army of Light. Alaric of Tircople returned to the Sacred Table, where he and the third high lord perished in an attempt to retake the holy city. Back in Akados, Gerrant of Gilboath also fell outside Tsar. Shortly thereafter, the forces of Tsar suddenly retreated from the field and led the vengeful Army of Light on a long chase down the coast of the Gulf of Akados. At last, the Army of Light cornered the forces of Tsar in the Forest of Hope. The disciples of Orcus and the Army of Light entered the forest, and thereupon disappeared entirely. No sign of either has been seen since.

The shock of the loss of so much of the realm's nobility and greatest warriors shook Foere to its core. Uprisings spontaneously occurred across the kingdom, with few knights or noblemen to put them down. Graeltor died some years later in his bed and passed the crown of the Hyperborean Monarchy on to his largely unknown and untested grandson Oedwin, which brought about the Foerdewaith Wars of Succession. Ramthion Island declared its independence from Foere in 3213 I.R. Pontos Island did the same in 3215 I.R. and renamed itself the Kingdom of Oceanus. Two years later, a Foerdewaith fleet attempted to retake Pontos Island but was defeated by Oceanus at the Battle of Kapichi Point. Within a few more years, Endhome, Burgundia, and Suilley declared their independence from Courghais. In 3223 I.R., Suilley defeated a Foerdewaith army at the Battle of Bullocks Bale, and soon after, Southvale, Vast, and North Heath were independent as well. Finally, in 3233 I.R., even the Grand Duchy of Reme left Foere, an event that the overking by then had little choice but to accept. As the remnants of the Kingdom of Foere turned inward and became more decadent, many of the former Foere lands east of the March of Mountains and west of the Blackrock Mountains fought among themselves as law and order slowly disintegrated in the region.

Just three years ago, however, in 3514 I.R., a Huun army appeared on the northern border of the Desolation of Tsar past the ruins of Oxibbul and advanced into the kingdoms of Akados. In the Lyre Valley, they found their way blocked by Bard's Gate and lay siege to the city. The current overking of Courghais, King Ovar the Magnificent, hastily called for a new Great Crusade against the age-old enemy and rallied the nobles and men-at-arms of Foere and its independent neighbors in the defense of Bard's Gate. But first he unleashed a fleet of ships against the sambuks of the Huun navy in the Gulf of Akados. The Foerdewaith and Heldring ships delivered a crushing defeat to the Huun ships and forced them into a retreat back up to the coasts of the Sea of Spices.

With their supply lines disrupted by the loss of their naval support, the besieging Huun forces withdrew from the walls of Bard's Gate and marched back across the Desolation with the crusader army in pursuit. At last report, the Huun army had entered the wastes of the Irkainian Desert with the crusaders close behind, but nothing further has been heard for two years. With no word from the king of Foere nor any of the lesser rulers who marched with him, the Lost Lands are on the verge of turmoil as the rule of law is stretched by the absence of so many lords and men-at-arms. Now, King Ovar is said to have returned to his Throne Tower of the Citadel Caene alone at night astride his trained black dragon. The other lords of Akados who have heard this rumor are left to wonder how this could have happened and, if it is true, what became of the rest of the army that marched with the overking.

Loyalties and Diplomacy

Foere maintains good relations with Reme despite the grand duchy's declaration of independence, as well as with Bard's Gate. Foere and Oceanus continue to abide by the non-aggression treaty they signed in 3339 I.R. It has a substantially more complicated relationship with its other former vassals, particularly the Vast, North Heath, Olduvar, and Suilley. While not hostile, there is no love lost among the Foerdewaith for these realms and they will not go out of their way to aid them. That being said, Overking Ovar was able to muster support from many of the independent kingdoms that had once sworn fealty to Courghais to take part in the recent crusade against the Huun and lift the siege of Bard's Gate. However, tensions have increased among these realms because of the rumors currently circulating that the overking has returned — without those who followed him.

Trade and Commerce

Foere remains a center of trade and commerce throughout Akados. Given its central location, the kingdom lies at the crossroads of trade routes that reach to the farthest ends of the continent and beyond to Libynos. In addition, Courghais is a center of learning and manufacture known far and wide for its smithing, stonework, glassblowing, and textiles. If something cannot be found in Courghais, it can be made there.

Several trading houses of substantial antiquity are based in Courghais, and they hold mercantile interests throughout Foere and the rest of Akados, and beyond. The most notable are Houses Iskane and Tulius.

Government

Before he disappeared with his army while chasing the withdrawing Huun, Overking Ovar the Magnificent ruled Foere with a fist of iron. In many ways, he was a throwback to previous overkings, but he was also a ruler unfortunately born at a time when his kingdom was in decline. Reynald, the overking's son and the prince of Foere, frequently served as his father's liaison with other realms. In Ovar's absence, Reynald has been ruling the kingdom as regent.

Outside the royal demesne, nobles who serve as vassals of the overking possess the authority to govern on behalf of their lord. Dukes are the greatest of these vassals, followed by barons. Fiefdoms below the barons are known as cantrefs, and, before the rise of Macobert, were ruled by a prince. After the establishment of Foere, they came to be administered by lords and favored men-at-arms — frequently a member of the Knights of Macobert. Most vassalages are hereditary, but the overking may remove and appoint a successor to one of his nobles under certain circumstances.

Magistrates preside over courts throughout the kingdom and have certain jurisdiction even in the lands of the overking's vassals. The overking appoints most of these magistrates, who are known as Listeners. Where ecclesiastical law prevails (such as in the domain of a cathedral city), the local ecclesiastical magnate appoints the magistrates, who are called Lawgivers.

Military

Foere has historically fielded one of the largest armies on Akados, although it is scattered throughout the kingdom, a necessity given the sheer magnitude of the lands under Foerdewaith control. The overking commands a sizable personal army based in Courghais, and each of his vassals also maintains military forces and is obliged to provide a certain number of soldiers per year to the kingdom if the overking so demands.

Unfortunately, a sizable portion of the armed forces of Foere left with Overking Ovar in pursuit of the invading Huun two years ago and have not been seen since. In his absence, Prince Reynald and the duchies and baronies of Foere began conscripting soldiers from the towns and countryside since the threats to the kingdom persist. But the army remains seriously depleted, and the remaining commanders fear what might happen if a war were to break out or if an invasion were to occur.

Major Threats

The largest threat to Foere at the moment is likely its continuing disintegration. Each province that secedes makes it easier for the next one to do the same. While the lands owing fealty to Courghais have been stable for some time now, the absence of the overking and a sizable portion of the armies of Foere have left the country unstable and rife with rumor. If the tales of Ovar's return without the army are true, it is impossible to know what effect that might have on the vassals farthest from Courghais or even on the nobility of the city itself.

COURGHAIS, IMPERIAL CITY OF (CAPITAL)

Ruler: King Ovar I
Government: feudalism
Population: 221,341 (153,784 Foerdewaith, 41,200 human
mixed ethnicity, 17,643 halfling, 3,098 high elf, 2,861 half-elf,
1,243 gnome, 793 hill dwarf, 629 half-orc, 90 other)
Languages: Common, Gasquen, Halfling, Elven, Gnome,
Dwarven
Religion: Archeillus, Mitra, Thyr, Stryme, Freya, Mick
O'Delving, Dwerfater, Muir, Bacchus-Dionysus
Resources: grain, foodstuffs, glass, manufactured goods, trade
Technology Level: High Middle Ages

The Imperial City of Courghais (which means "Heartstone" in
Gasquen) is the seat of the overking of the Kingdom of Foere. Built
on a peninsula on the eastern shore of the Star Sea, it rises up on the
shoulders of a long hill overlooking the waters. The walls and many of
the towers of the city are constructed of a white granite originally cut
from the Rampart Mountains. During the day, the city shines white,
but at sunset over the Star Sea on a clear day, some odd property of the
granite transforms the slanting rays of the sun such that the city glows
a brilliant, golden-red color and gives rise to its Gasquen name.

Designed in a manner intended to mirror the ancient capital city of
Curgantium, Courghais is divided into several quarters. The Royal
Quarter, which sits upon the highest part of the landward portion of the
city, includes the Citadel of Caene with its Throne Tower that was built
in homage to the Tower of Oerson of lost Curgantium. At the other end
of the city, rising high above the waters at the end of the peninsula, is
the Cathedral Quarter and the Cathedral of the Tesseract. The Docks
are on the northern side of the city along the shore of the Star Sea,
with the Merchant Quarter rising beyond that. Other quarters within the
city include the Highborn Quarter (where are found the mansions of
nobility), the Minstrels' Quarter, and the Low Quarter. Each quarter is,
in turn, divided into wards.

The Kingdom of Foere has been in decline for some 300 years now
since the beginning of the Foerdewaith Wars of Succession. Province
after province declared independence from the overking, and of those
that remain loyal, the ability of the court to enforce its wishes grows
weaker with each passing year. As wealth and power fail, the intrigues
of the nobility in the city become ever more vicious and desperate.
Increasingly, Courghais has become a city that boasts a veneer of
virtue and respectability but covering a wicked and immoral heart.
And with the overking and many of his nobility — including almost
all of the Knights of Macobert — away on campaign against the
Huun, those remaining in the city are resorting to the darkest forms
of conspiracy and scheming to achieve whatever dominance they can
over their rivals.

RELIGION

High above the waters of the Star Sea, the Cathedral of the Tesseract
rises at the center of the Cathedral Quarter of Courghais. The cathedral
is the seat of the archbishop of Foere and is dedicated to the entire
Foerdewaith pantheon, although Quell, the original patron of Saint
Macobert, and Mitra, the patron of the overkings since the Battle
of Oescreheit Downs, predominate. It is by far the largest, most
magnificent cathedral in all of the domains — current and former — of
the Foerdewaith Empire. The cathedral is a massive temple of white
marble columns with a burnished copper roof and serves as a beacon
that can be seen for miles outside of Courghais — and even far out into
the Star Sea. All gods of the pantheon are venerated here, and many
of the bishops, deacons, and priests sent to minister to the peoples of
Akados are trained within its walls. Pilgrims from far and wide travel
to Courghais to visit the Cathedral of the Tesseract and to pray at the
holy shrines of the gods of Foere. For those wishing to bring home a
memento of their visit, sellers in the city's markets and on the streets
offer small statues of the gods and, so they claim, true relics of various
saints and the gods themselves.

GOVERNMENT

Though it constitutes the seat and capital of the royal domain of the
overking, Courghais is ruled directly by the lord commander of the citadel,
an appointee of the overking and usually a Knight of Macobert. The lord
commander also commands the overking's royal army that is based here.

A group of quartermasters, ward captains, and watch captains — all
appointed by (or with the approval of) the lord commander — administer
the city and enforce the city's laws. Justice within the city is overseen by
a group of magistrates known as Listeners appointed by the overking,
with each sitting in one or more ward or quarter courts. A city militia
separate from the royal army based in the city maintains order within the
walls and is the first line of defense in the event of attack (which would
be extraordinarily unlikely here in the center of the kingdom).

Many guilds are active in Courghais, but by tradition they have no
role in government, though the request of a guildmaster does carry some
weight with the lord commander. While not to the liking of most of the
guilds, their lack of any authority over the city goes back hundreds of
years, and the critical position of Courghais in the economy of Foere
makes it impossible to simply depart the city. As a result, however,
bribery (and, on occasion, blackmail) has long been a tool used by the
guilds to ensure that their voices are heard.

The Cathedral of the Tesseract is considered its own cathedral city
enclave within greater Courghais. As a result, the laws applicable in the
Cathedral Quarter are ecclesiastical and are enforced by the archbishop
or the mayor of the palace (or other ecclesiastical magnates appointed by
the archbishop). Similarly, clerics found to have broken any laws within
Courghais, even if outside the Cathedral Quarter, are usually remanded
to the cathedral for punishment, though in rare cases the overking has
exercised the right to supersede religious jurisdiction.

Since 3515 I.R., King Ovar and his Knights of Macobert have been
on campaign chasing Huun invaders who laid siege to Bard's Gate. He
took with him the well-regarded Lord Unstan Dary, the former lord
commander of Courghais. In the overking's absence, his son Prince
Reynald now rules as regent with the assistance of the less-well-
regarded Baron Pelorious Vandon (a younger son of a noble, and not a
Knight of Macobert), who is serving as lord commander.

Recently, rumors began swirling about the city that King Ovar
returned to the Throne Tower of the Citadel of Caene, flying alone
into the city at night astride his black dragon. If he has in fact returned
without the army, rebellion is a real possibility among many of the noble
families of Foere.

CHANTRY, CATHEDRAL CITY OF

Ruler: Her Grace Salashara Ofor, Archdeacon of Quell, God of
the Seas
Government: feudalism/religious (Kingdom of Foere)
Population: 8,705 (5477 Foerdewaith, 990 human mixed
ethnicity, 891 half-elf, 712 halfling, 433 high elf, 123 hill
dwarf, 59 gnome, 20 other)
Languages: Common, Gasquen, Halfling, Elven, Dwarven,
Gnome
Religion: Quell, Archellius, Solanus, Thyr
Resources: fishing, grain, foodstuffs, religious pilgrimage sites
Technology Level: High Middle Ages

Chantry is a city of memories and echoes of memories, of reminders
of past greatness, all now mere shadows of what once was the seat of
mighty kings.

Before the founding of Courghais, Chantry was the capital of Foere,
as it had been the seat of the petty kings of the tribes of the Foere for
dozens of generations. Here, in fact, is the birthplace of Macobert the
Great, where he first claimed descent from the Sea-God Quell. In 2744
I.R., Macobert was crowned the first overking of Foere in this city,
which remained the capital of the kingdom for his entire life. Even after
the court moved to the Heartstone farther north on the coast of the Star
Sea during the reign of Macobert's son Magnusson, Chantry remained
a place of importance. Macobert founded a cathedral to his patron god

within Chantry, the first of the Foerdewaith cathedral cities. After his death, it was renamed the Chancel of Macobert the Great, and for four generations, his descendants came here to receive the blessing of the Sea King.

Then in 2802 I.R., the god Mitra appeared to Overking Osbert II, Macobert's great-great-grandson, and promised the Foerdewaith victory over the Heldring in what became known as the Battle of Oescreheit Downs. Osbert took Mitra as his new patron, and the worship of Quell began a slow but inevitable decline in the lands of Foere. And with the decline of the Sea King, so declined his city of Chantry.

The city's walls of stone blocks remain strong, though most of the towers are unoccupied as Chantry has too few soldiers to man them. Much of the land within the walls is now a field for grazing sheep and cows, and long-unoccupied buildings have been razed, their stones harvested for other purposes. As a result, from the outside, Chantry appears to be a great city, but from within, it seems largely empty and provincial.

The archbishop ensures that enough funds are made available to Chantry to maintain the chancel in a condition befitting its history. Built in an archaic style quite distinct from the typical neo-Hyperborean temples, the cathedral is longer along its east-west axis. It is lower in the middle and rises in a series of stepped levels on each of its eastern and western ends, each of which is topped by a graceful tower clad in blue-white marble.

Archdeacon Salashara Ofor comes from a family with ancient roots in the region; her ancestors were Foere nobility from times even before the rise of Macobert. She is quite devoted to Quell and is an excellent cleric, though her disdain of politics doesn't help her city in the intrigues that roil the court in Courghais. Dunastan Reev, her mayor of the palace, is highly competent and does his best with the limited resources available to him. Some still make the pilgrimage to Chantry to visit the Chancel of Macobert the Great and to see the supposed birthplace of the first overking. Some travel from as far as Oceanus, though such visitors take great care to avoid attention given the current perilous relations between Courghais and Pontus Tinigal.

A circle of ruined marble columns can be found in a field about 10 miles east of Chantry. These columns surround a stone disk set in the ground that is inscribed with elegant elvish script that forms an inward-leading spiral to the center. Now ruined, this location once permitted transportation to and from a similar disk found at Elfingate in the Kingdom of Suilley.

CHÂLAIX, CITY OF

Ruler: Lord Darandaran Choly (currently absent)
Government: feudalism (Kingdom of Foere)
Population: 15,889 (10,996 Foerdewaith, 1,411 half-elf, 1,241 human mixed ethnicity, 1,011 halfling, 992 high elf, 119 mountain dwarf, 89 gnome, 30 other)
Languages: Common, Gasquen, Halfling, Elven
Religion: Archeillus, Mitra, Thyr, Muir, Kamien, Belon the Wise, Ceres, Dre'uain the Lame, Freya, Mick O'Delving, Solanus, Telophus, Yenomesh
Resources: trade, fishing, grain, wine, olive oil, manufactured goods
Technology Level: High Middle Ages

At the end of its northernmost arm, the waters of the Star Sea flow into the Great Amrin River and begin their long journey east to the distant Sinnar. For thousands of years, the hilltop just south of the juncture of sea and river has hosted settlements, the most ancient of which perhaps predate the arrival of humans on Akados. Today, the mighty Castle Châlaix commands the crest of the hill, its gray stone towers and flapping pennants visible for many miles, whether from over the waters or the rolling fields of eastern Foere. From the castle, the city spills down steep cobbled streets to the docks and warehouses jutting forth into the waters of the Star Sea.

All trade between the port cities of the Star Sea and the eastern provinces by way of the Great Amrin River must pass through the harbor of Châlaix. And for those preferring wagon to boat, the road from the heartland of Foere to Aixe also runs through this city. As a result, the coffers of Châlaix are always full from the various taxes and levies imposed on merchants traveling east or west.

In addition, the lands about Châlaix are known for their vineyards and olive groves, and many of the best vintages and oils of Foere are found here on the northeastern shores of the Star Sea.

Lord Darandaran Choly's family has held the city of Châlaix now for four generations. Like the three generations of Choly's before him, Darandaran is a Knight of Macobert. As a result, in 3515 I.R., he, along with nearly all of the others of his order, left on campaign with the overking in pursuit of the Huun invaders that had besieged Bard's Gate. In his absence, his wife, the Lady Escaril Choly, and his seneschal, the elderly Horam Pris, administer the city and countryside. While both are competent, many within the kingdom would like nothing more than to seize the Castle Châlaix, its robust revenue, and its rich lands. The longer Darandaran remains away, the deeper the intrigues that seek to wrest Châlaix away from his lady.

Many visitors come to Châlaix to see the famous catacombs that lie beneath the city hill. Most of the chambers and passages are restricted, but a number may be accessed by those wishing to pray at one of the underground chapels to various gods of Foere, several of which claim to hold relics of sacred power. Although now most burials occur in one of the cemeteries outside the city walls, some families still retain the right to interment in the catacombs. The exact age of the catacombs, and their full extent, remains unknown.

CROIX, CATHEDRAL CITY OF

Ruler: Lord Foran Solled, His Grace Amaril Basile, Archdeacon of Thyr, God of Law and Justice
Government: feudalism/religious (Kingdom of Foere)
Population: 9,264 (5,920 Foerdewaith, 887 halfling, 800 human mixed ethnicity, 745 high elf, 607 mountain dwarf, 193 half-elf, 67 gnome, 45 other)
Languages: Common, Gasquen, Halfling, Elven, Dwarven, Gnome
Religion: Belon the Wise, Ceres, Dre'uain the Lame, Freya, Mitra, Thyr, Muir, Mick O'Delving, Solanus, Telophus, Yenomesh
Resources: grain, foodstuffs, manufactured goods, trade hub
Technology Level: High Middle Ages

Judge's Road, which heads north from Malan and the Barony of Baldenar, ends at the tall, tan stone walls of the city of Croix where it overlooks the Star Sea. Those walls, as well as the docks and many of its stone buildings, are made from a tan limestone dug from quarries located 50 or so miles to the northeast on the shore of the Star Sea. A mix of new wood and wattle and daub buildings, as well as some newer stone structures, add color to the city. But none of these buildings compares to the beauty and elegance of St. Bannor's Church, the seat of power for His Grace Amaril Basile, Archdeacon of Thyr, God of Law and Justice.

From the docks, goods are brought in and out of Croix via ships crossing the Star Sea to or from Courghais, Sion, and Pentahs, while wagon trains travel via the Judge's Road to the south and beyond that along the King's Road to the east. The steady traffic in goods makes Croix an important trading hub, with numerous businesses aimed at entertaining and supporting the constant flow of merchants and goods. Judge's Road passes though the city's gates and travels all the way down to the docks with inns, taverns, shops, gambling houses, and brothels lining the entire route. Nearby fields provide corn, wheat, and sorghum, while the Star Sea is fished for a wide array of freshwater delicacies. Many of the fine wines, brandies, and other rarities shipped to Courghais can be found here, but usually at a hefty price.

Lord Foran Solled and the militia assigned to him control all the areas associated with trade within Croix, while the archdeacon and his ecclesiastical magnates administer the rest of the city as well as the surrounding area. Tensions exist between the two, but as both were appointed specifically by the overking, they try to stay within the bounds of their assigned duties. This essentially means that Lord Solled focuses entirely on ensuring that trade and goods move through the city quickly and efficiently while the archdeacon handles virtually everything else.

St. Bannor's Church

Dedicated to Thyr, but open to the worshippers and clerics of the other neutral and good gods of the Foerdewaith pantheon, this massive, elegant cathedral is a testament to rarely-witnessed architectural and engineering skill. Elegantly carved marble spires rise from four towers at the outer corners of the cathedral while a fifth, much-larger spire rises from the center of the roof. Each spire possesses abstract representations of all of the gods of the Foerdewaith and Hyperborean pantheons.

The archdeacon controls most of the city as well as the surrounding farmlands with the help of his ecclesiastical magnates and their retainers. All ordinary crimes within Croix are tried under ecclesiastical law. In effect, the church runs the city, although Lord Solled technically runs the docks, gates, and trade areas. However, any crimes found to be committed in these areas are turned over to the church.

Demz, City of

Ruler: Lord Oton Tarquin
Government: feudalism
Population: 6,512 (3,931 Foerdewaith, 910 human mixed ethnicity, 805 high elf, 653 halfling, 121 half-elf, 67 gnome, 25 other)
Languages: Common, Gasquen, Elven, Halfling, Gnome
Religion: Mitra, Thyr, Muir, Mick O'Delving, Dre'uain the Lame
Resources: grain, livestock (cattle), foodstuffs (cheeses), trade
Technology Level: High Middle Ages

Built on a low hill with a clear view of the surrounding fields, Demz has low stone walls that frame several gates that enter the sprawling city. Positioned above the surrounding terrain, it is exposed to high winds and storms that race across the nearby plains during the spring and summer, so the buildings here are generally squat, low stone structures, many of which have deep foundations and basements. The main trade roads from Nains, Poiretre, and Sion enter the city through broad gates and meet in a large central square that is surrounded by shops, taverns, gambling houses, and brothels. Corrals and parking areas for wagons take up a large portion of the square.

The high winds that often batter Demz force Lord Tarquin to maintain cobblestone roads for the main streets of the city and to lay down gravel on the side roads. Exposed dirt is torn up and spun around by the winds and spread throughout the city. The small military contingent here is often tasked with maintaining the roads as well as actively patrolling all the trade routes in and out of the city.

Rich farms and fields surrounding the city support a variety of crops and a large dairy cattle industry. Cheeses of all varieties from Demz are considered a delicacy by many. Most are exported through Sion to other parts of Foere, but some are preserved and sent much greater distances.

Farall Hold, Town of

Ruler: Lady Aral Gemlight
Government: feudalism
Population: 11,267 (7,635 Foerdewaith, 1,587 halfling, 925 high-elf, 423 mountain dwarf, 329 gnome, 210 human mixed ethnicity, 108 half-elf, 50 other)
Languages: Common, Elven, Gnome, Dwarven, Halfling
Religion: Archeillus, Mitra, Thyr, Muir, Mick O'Delving, Solanus, Telophus, Yenomesh
Resources: fishing, foodstuffs, trade
Technology Level: Medieval

The lovely terraced gardens and homes of Farall Hold are a sight to behold for any traveler. As welcoming as the small city appears from a distance, with its colorful buildings and statues arranged carefully on a tall hill overlooking the Star Sea, most of the city is off limits to visitors. Farall Hold is largely a retirement community for elite servants and advisors to the overking. The "retirement" is in many ways as much prison as reward, despite the lavish surroundings. By relocating former key advisors and servants with knowledge of the kingdom's secrets to Farall Hold, the overking ensures that those secrets are kept safe. The retirees are not allowed out of the city without a guard detail and are permitted visitors only from approved lists.

Arranged along roads circling up a tall hill rising from the shoreline with the Star Sea, the highest and most elegant homes and gardens stand behind a tall, heavily guarded wall with a single gate that allows access to the restricted portion of the city. Residents here refer to the homes of the elite as "above the wall" and to the rest of the city as "below the wall." Unwelcome visitors who are not on a proper list or who do not have papers allowing them access to areas beyond the wall are turned away. Anyone discovered above the wall without proper authority is arrested, investigated briefly, and, if not allowed access, executed.

Most of the retired elite are served by live-in servants and cooks, with a large number of additional services provided by those living below the wall, most of whom have special passes and are recognized by the guards. The docks here are small, suitable for fishing boats and the smaller boats that bring deliveries from Sion and Pentahs.

Lady Aral Gemlight runs the city for the overking and pays special attention to keeping the chosen former servants and advisors in luxurious living conditions while also restricting and monitoring their movements and interactions. While some goods are grown locally, most of the more expensive luxury items are brought in at the expense of the crown.

Nains, Cathedral City of

Ruler: Archdeacon Melijan Velon, Voice of Mitra, Lord-Captain Joucalt Chenare
Government: Religious/Military/Feudal (Kingdom of Foere)
Population: 21,632 (16,622 Foerdewaith, 1,569 halfling, 1,208 mountain dwarf, 791 high elf, 620 human mixed ethnicity, 563 gnome, 189 half-elf, 70 other)
Languages: Common, Gasquen, Halfling, Dwarven, Elven, Gnome
Religion: Archeillus, Belon the Wise, Ceres, Dre'uain the Lame, Freya, Mitra, Thyr, Muir, Mick O'Delving, Solanus, Telophus, Yenomesh
Resources: grain, livestock (cattle, sheep), foodstuffs, trade
Technology Level: Medieval

Broad walls of black stone surround this fortress-like city that sits on the main trade road from Reme and the Kingdom of the North Heath into Foere. The white stone pinnacles of the massive Cathedral of Saint Angeline rise from the center of the city, dominating its skyline and acting as a beacon to travelers as they approach the city walls.

While nearby lands supply cattle, sheep, and large amounts of corn, wheat, and sorghum, the main driving forces of the economy here are tourism and trade. The trade caravans traveling through provide ample opportunities for shops selling provisions as well as taverns, gambling houses, and brothels. Equal to those is the constant influx of pilgrims coming to see the cathedral and to worship in its holy halls.

Lord-Captain Joucalt Chenare is in charge of a significant military contingent here. He is responsible for patrolling the trade road and keeping it safe and in good repair, while his duties within the city are largely restricted to maintaining control of his troops. All other aspects of the city are under the rule of His Grace, Archdeacon Melijan Velon, Voice of Mitra, a man whose faith barely matches his charisma and forceful personality. The overking has chosen not to assign this city to any civilian lord, believing, justly, that a competition between the personalities of the archdeacon, the lord-captain, and a third party would be bad for the city.

Cathedral of Saint Angeline

By order of the overking, the cathedral must welcome clerics and pilgrims of all the neutral and good faiths, but the cathedral itself is sworn and dedicated to Mitra. The overking assigned this cathedral, as well as the city of Nains, to His Grace Archdeacon Melijan Velon, Voice of Mitra. Ecclesiastical magnates and retainers do most of the work administering the city and local region, while the clerics manage the cathedral.

The cathedral is constructed of smooth white stone and possesses niches and altars to the many gods of the Foerdewaith pantheon. While Mitra might be the main god worshipped here, Archeillus is almost equally represented in the images, statues, and paintings found throughout the stone hallways.

PENTAHS, CITY OF

Ruler: Lady Selicine Bonhil
Government: Feudalism
Population: 6,414 (4,070 Foerdewaith, 590 halfling, 489 high elf, 407 hill dwarf, 310 human mixed ethnicity, 291 half-elf, 167 gnome, 90 other)
Languages: Common, Gasquen, Halfling, Elven, Dwarven
Religion: Archeillus, Belon the Wise, Freya, Mitra, Thyr, Muir, Mick O'Delving, Solanus
Resources: fishing, manufactured goods, grain, foodstuffs, livestock (sheep, goats), spirits (ale, mead), trade hub
Technology Level: High Middle Ages

Known to some as the "Gateway to the North," Pentahs is a city of sprawling wood-framed structures that cling to the rocky cliffs above the Star Sea. Goods brought in by ship to the docks are raised to the city by an elaborate system of ropes and pulleys, while visitors must make a short but steep climb via a series of stairways and ramps. Possessing a large military contingent and surrounded by nearby farms and ranches, Pentahs is a well-established trade hub between the lands to the north and the main seat of the Kingdom of Foere.

Pentahs' claim to fame comes from a 250-year-old song made popular by the great bard Raeilha Redsong in which, somehow, the lamb stew and mead of Pentahs are used by a young maid to seduce a prince. The song was made popular by the overking of the time, perhaps in part because he was having an affair with the bard in question, and in the years since Pentahs has embraced this, with almost every inn and tavern providing a fine, spiced lamb stew and quality mead to their customers.

In truth, Pentahs is a crucial link to the north and is important for trade and the information networks that the overking maintains. Lady Selicine Bonhil was put in charge of Pentahs with the specific orders to maintain trade and the information networks with the north. Command of the military is held by a captain appointed by the overking. Troops stationed here usually do not stay long and are rotated out to other duties every three or four months or so.

While trade drives the economy in Pentahs and supports most of the shop owners, inns, and taverns, a series of powerful guilds also reside here, their members crafting well-regarded furniture, jewelry, and cookware. Nearby farms produce grains, corn, a selection of fruits and vegetables, as well as sheep and goats. Goats' milk and goat cheese are very popular in the city, as is mead that is brewed by multiple houses.

SION, CITY OF

Ruler: Lord Altral Galon
Government: feudalism
Population: 6,279 (3,565 Foerdewaith, 987 hill dwarf, 726 halfling, 380 human mixed ethnicity, 270 high elf, 197 gnome, 94 half-elf, 60 other)
Languages: Common, Gasquen, Dwarven, Halfling, Elven
Religion: Dre'uain the Lame, Freya, Mitra, Thyr, Muir, Mick O'Delving
Resources: livestock (cattle), foodstuffs, manufactured goods, fishing
Technology Level: High Middle Ages

Known to some as the "City in the Cliff," Sion consists of wood-frame and stone buildings built into and at the top of a cliffside overlooking the Star Sea. Most of the homes set into the cliff wall have ancient foundations, their true origins lost to time. Sion's importance comes from its natural harbor on the Star Sea and its well-organized docks.

While goods travel through Sion in a steady stream, merchants do not stay here long. The air near the waters below is tainted with the strong smell of fish and a hint of decay, while the atmosphere on the cliffs above is dominated by the stench of slaughterhouses and tanneries that only the local residents can endure for long.

In addition to trade, ranches near Sion provide a large number of cattle for the kingdom, many of which are slaughtered here with the meat preserved and sent on to other cities. Sion produces leather for a wide variety of products, including armor, saddles, clothing, shoes, and other accessories. The fishing industry provides fish to Courghais and other nearby cities. Lord Altral Galon would like to focus the city more on trade, having started his own gambling hall here, but he recognizes that the various aromas of the industries that originally made Sion important to the kingdom make it difficult to entice travelers into staying for long.

BARONY OF BALDENAR

Capital: Malan
Notable Settlements: Corvusrook, Nyham Chae
Ruler: Baron Gaitan Baldenar
Government: feudal barony (Kingdom of Foere)
Population: 499,470 (385,950 Foerdewaith, 26,200 human mixed ethnicity, 23,500 halfling, 21,200 high elf, 16,100 hill dwarf, 11,200 gnome, 6,700 mountain dwarf, 5,600 half-elf, 2,120 half-orc, 900 other)
Monstrous: giant animal, wolf, goblin, hobgoblin, fey (plains); gnoll, forest troll, giant animal, owlbear, forlarren, dryad, green dragon (forest); hill giant, stone giant, giant eagle, hippogriff, cave moray (mountains)
Languages: Common, Gasquen, Halfling, Dwarven, Elven, Gnome
Religion: Archeillus, Mitra, Thyr, Stryme, Freya, Mick O'Delving, Dwerfater, Muir, Bacchus-Dionysus
Resources: grain, foodstuffs, gold, manufactured goods, timber, trade hub
Currency: Foere
Technology Level: Medieval

The Barony of Baldenar stretches from an area 50 miles south of Corvusrook, north along Judge's Road to the intersection with the King's Road, and then east to Nyham Chae. Its principal farms and settlements are found in the well-watered lands between Malan and the Shadrack Forest, particularly along the Gilded River. On official maps, the barony includes all of the Shadrack Forest to the base of the Rampart Mountains. In practice, the forest is little patrolled.

HISTORY AND PEOPLE

Baron Gaitan Baldenar is a young, charismatic, and forceful leader that many consider a throwback to the first Baron Baldenar granted these lands by the overking in Courghais for his heroism in battle. But recent generations squandered much of the goodwill once granted the barony by the overking. The Baldenar family lineage is one of the longest continuous family lineages in the kingdom, with some throughout history having served with such distinction that the Baldenar coat of arms is displayed in the halls of the overking. As with all long lineages, there are sometimes less-effective rulers, as the past few barons of Baldenar have demonstrated. The crown has noticed Gaitan's hard work eliminating the corruption that grew in the province under his father's rule. While the light of the Duchy of Saxe may be fading in the halls of the overking, the Barony of Baldenar is rising.

Corruption and mismanagement grew over several recent generations until it reached a point where something had to be done. Gaitan had his father declared incompetent, with approval and encouragement from the overking, and took over the barony at the age of 24. Well-educated, driven, and disgusted by what he felt were the failings of his own family, Gaitan replaced all of his father's leaders and advisors with individuals who were both competent and trusted. Several of the new advisors were brought in from other parts of the kingdom but the initial distrust these advisors faced receded due to the startling changes in the barony under its new ruler. Additionally, nearly all of the mayors and other local city leaders were also relieved of duty and replaced with appointed mayors and staff loyal to Gaitan himself.

TRADE AND COMMERCE

Much of the barony's income is generated from control over the King's Road and Judge's Road and the trade these routes generate. Gold-mining operations near Corvusrook along the Gilded River are well-protected and owned by the Baldenar family. Recent generations spent income on opulent mansions and castles and large parties, but Gaitan ended this practice and focused on shoring up the reputation of the barony. Farming operations help support the larger cities while logging operations in the Shadrack Forest are relatively minimal and mostly restricted to areas near Nyham Chae.

LOYALTIES AND DIPLOMACY

Baron Baldenar is completely loyal to the crown. His goal is to become important and recognized enough to increase his position in the kingdom and to consolidate his control over the region he now possesses. He has an excellent relationship with Lord-Commander Lorant of the County of Roy and active trade agreements with the Iron Kingdom and the Duchy of Mains. He has a tense relationship with Duke Mercur Saxe, however, as Saxe believes that Baldenar's efforts to increase the use of the King's Road as a trade route to the east hurts the trade coming through Saxentry.

Tasked with the upkeep and protection of both the King's Road and Judge's Road from Corvusrook to Nyham Chae by the overking, Gaitan performed necessary repairs and upkeep to make merchant traffic smoother. Increased patrols reduced the number of brigands that moved into the area during past rule to the point that the trade roads are now largely considered safe.

GOVERNMENT

The baron's rule has been forceful, direct, and on occasion, violent. His swift punishment of the corrupt elite earned him the love and respect of the more common folk, particularly members of the various guilds. The court system is presently run with judges handpicked by Baron Baldenar with the approval of the overking. The baron's service in the Foere military began at the age of 14, with several years of education at the University of Mains in Arbo, through which he came to know a number of highly educated, dedicated, and loyal servants to the crown, from among whom he picked many of his advisors.

MILITARY

Officially, all military forces within the barony are under the charge of Baron Baldenar, although the military forces stationed in Nyham Chae are under Mayor Piers Touriq, who orders regular patrols near Shadrack Forest and the Rampart Mountains. The forces presently stationed at Nyham Chae come from regions outside the barony in hopes of reducing the corruption that was prevalent here recently.

MAJOR THREATS

Being near the seat of power of the kingdom, and the close proximity of the military forces in Ems, make this one of the safer areas on all of Akados, particularly now that the baron has eliminated the major abuses and corruption that were so prevalent before and taken steps to reduce or eliminate brigands along the major trade roads. Creatures from the Shadrack Forest and the Rampart Mountains still pose a threat but the newly invigorated barony is now taking steps to reduce them as well.

WILDERNESS AND ADVENTURE

The baron is still looking for knowledgeable people with no link to the past rulers and leaders to help investigate some of those who are still in power. Some who were already taken and convicted hid their wealth, and the baron is always seeking to recover such lost treasure as well. Shadrack Forest is largely unexplored, as there has been so little of value discovered there and few want to deal with the gnolls living within. Rumored ruins in the Rampart Mountains, as well as the hill giants and stone giants that are reported to live there, also attract explorers and treasure seekers.

MALAN, CITY OF (CAPITAL)

Ruler: Baron Gaitan Baldenar
Government: feudalism
Population: 23,205 (17,379 Foerdewaith, 1,633 halfling, 1,282 high elf, 1,050 human mixed ethnicity, 876 gnome, 578 hill dwarf, 234 half-elf, 113 half-orc, 60 other)
Languages: Common, Gasquen, Halfling, Elven, Gnome, Dwarven
Religion: Archeillus, Mitra, Thyr, Stryme, Freya, Mick O'Delving, Dwerfater, Muir, Bacchus-Dionysus
Resources: grain, foodstuffs, manufactured goods, trade
Technology Level: Medieval

As recently as 10 years ago, Malan had decayed into a city where the divide between rich and poor was extreme and appalling. Nobility, wealthy merchants, and the guardsmen who were supposed to keep the peace and protect the people held clear sway over the rest of the city and the surrounding area. Skilled craftsmen were taxed and harassed to the point that they could barely feed their families; less-skilled workers were even more hard pressed. Gaitan Baldenar usurped power from his own father and took over the city and the barony with the support of the overking. The anger and rage at this drove his father to an early grave, but the act of defiance gave this city new hope.

Corruption as deep and pervasive as that suffered here in Malan is difficult to overcome quickly but Gaitan's swift and decisive actions have, at least, driven any remaining malfeasance into the darkness. New leaders for every level of the guard were installed, and those accused and found guilty of corruption were convicted of "treason against the crown" and publicly executed. The guilds cheered these efforts at first, until guild leaders realized their own illegal fees and penalties made them subject to the same crimes. Craftsmen and honest merchants and traders are now free to ply their trades without interference or harassment.

Decaying tenements and buildings have been repaired, or are being repaired, using funds gained by seizing the properties and money of those convicted of corruption. Whispers say that Gaitan used the corruption scandals to eliminate business competitors or personal enemies and steal their wealth. Whether true or not, the general populace loves their new baron and the broad changes that have been made here. Where once caravans would make their way through this crossroads city as quickly as possible, now they pause to enjoy the taverns, inns, and various shops and trading opportunities. "Caravan Run," a broad section of cobblestone road in the city's center with guarded parking areas for large groups of wagons, is often filled now.

Ancient stone walls around the city are also being repaired, even if the threat of a military attack seems small. Gaitan considers it a matter of pride. The High Quarters of the city is home to opulent mansions and ornate, walled homes, but many of these homes are now owned by the baron and used to house his top advisors under the philosophy that if they are paid and treated well already, the temptation to resort to graft is eliminated. Other parts of the city are in various states of repair as years of neglect and mismanagement are slowly overcome.

CORVUSROOK, CITY OF

Ruler: Mayor Suavar Redmont
Government: feudalism
Population: 11,282 (6,760 Foerdewaith, 1,423 halfling, 947 mountain dwarf, 788 gnome, 592 high elf, 530 human mixed ethnicity, 187 half-elf, 55 other)
Languages: Common, Gasquen, Halfling, Dwarven, Gnome, Elven
Religion: Archeillus, Mitra, Thyr, Stryme, Mick O'Delving, Dwerfater, Muir,
Resources: gold, grain, foodstuffs, trade
Technology Level: High Middle Ages

Constructed on one of the safest crossings of the Gilded River, Corvusrook sits at the crossroads of several trade routes, including Judge's Road heading north to the Kingdom of Foere. Bridges built here make crossing the river easier, and the city is growing into a busy trade hub while still maintaining its original roots as a mining town. A number of rich gold mines are located nearby on the rocky shores of the Gilded River. Dwarves contracted by Baron Gaitan Baldenar now run several of those mines. The dwarves are expensive mine managers and workers, but their honesty and loyalty provide a welcome relief from the corrupt management of the past.

Simple but well-made wood-frame buildings dominate Corvusrook, which has no real city wall to speak of. Guard towers look over the trade roads in every direction with open terrain giving a clear view for a great distance. While small, the city is growing and bustles with energy of traveling caravans and miners coming in and out. Taverns, inns, and a wide variety of shops do steady business during the day while the evenings are often more sedate. Miners and the crafters and tradesmen take equally dim views of each other, but the elimination of corruption in the city government and the various guilds has begun to smooth things over.

Baron Baldenar appointed Mayor Suavar Redmont to oversee the city with the aim of ridding it of corruption within the guards and other government offices. The powers given the mayor are broad, and the additional troops he brought are loyal to both him and the baron, which gives him great latitude in his management of the city. Merchants and several of the guild leaders were upset at their sudden loss of power and became very nervous when Mayor Redmont ordered the first executions of corrupt guardsmen and tax collectors. But the mayor enjoys the full confidence of the baron, as well as support from the newly appointed mine managers and other dwarves working the mines.

NYHAM CHAE, CITY OF

Ruler: Mayor Piers Touriq
Government: feudalism
Population: 10,247 (5,610 Foerdewaith, 1,230 hill dwarf, 1,166 halfling, 928 high elf, 543 gnome, 370 human mixed ethnicity, 281 half-elf, 89 half-orc, 30 other)
Languages: Common, Gasquen, Dwarven, Elven, Halfling, Gnome
Religion: Archeillus, Mitra, Mick O'Delving, Dwerfater, Muir
Resources: timber, foodstuffs, trade
Technology Level: Dark Ages

Nyham Chae suffered the worst under the corruption and mismanagement of previous rulers. Ongoing repairs to the ancient walls around this small city, and to the King's Road winding through it, feel like a bandage over a deeper wound. Despite rebuilding efforts throughout the city, a sense of decay, a hint of darkness, clings to the atmosphere here. Seen best in the quiet countenance of its residents, there is an ongoing feeling that some dark calamity is on its way.

Mayor Piers Touriq battles against corruption here in the name of the overking and the baron. Where other areas of the barony were corrupt, Nyham Chae was a festering pool of darkness and decay. Rather than taking the time to investigate the crimes of those who had run the city, Mayor Touriq brought in his own guardsmen and rounded up the city leaders, previous guard members, and guild leaders in a single night. It was decided that, in Nyham Chae, there were no innocents in power and the previous leaders of the city were all executed over a period of several weeks. The purge and reclamation of wealth paid for the major building projects in the city, with repairs to the walls and the King's Road being of primary importance as they were directly ordered by the overking of Foere.

Wood-frame buildings here stand atop ancient stone foundations that predate even the stone of the King's Road. While foundations so old in other places hint at some previous greatness, here there is no sense of a greater past or more impressive history, just age. Freshwater springs in the center of the city support beautiful, if ill-kept, gardens but little else here could be described as beautiful. New efforts to clean and revitalize have done nothing to quell the stench of the tanneries or the smoke that hangs heavy in the humid air.

Nyham Chae, once a major stop on the King's Road between the main seat of the Kingdom of Foere and the Duchy of the Rampart to the east, became a place merchants and trade caravans avoid staying in for long. The overking of Foere himself ordered his new baron to ensure the city is brought back to its previous, if not glory, at least ability to support the needs of the kingdom.

BILTSCROUGH, CATHEDRAL CITY OF

Ruler: Archdeacon Peridor
Government: ecclesiastical
Population: 48,662 (46,561 Foerdewaith, 1,020 human mixed ethnicity, 671 halfling, 399 half-elf, 11 other)
Humanoid: halflings (some), half-elves (few)
Languages: Common, Gasquen, Halfling
Religion: Archeillus, Mithras, Dre'uain the Lame
Resources: pilgrimage, trade
Technology Level: High Middle Ages

Biltscrough is a cathedral city of the High Church of Foere and, despite being located at the border of the Duchy of Mains and the Duchy of Saxe, is independent of both. Situated in the middle of these two great Foerdewaith demesnes, the city sits in the center of trade and information within the southern Kingdoms of Foere. Though the principal business of Biltscrough is service to the gods, a vibrant community has grown up around the cathedral and temples, and many commercial interests set up shop in their shadows. The roads in and out of the city gates are bustling from sunrise to sunset. Traveling merchants, loggers, miners, adventurers, and pilgrims arrive with a plethora of tales and stories ranging from the mundane to the ridiculous.

In the center of the city is the magnificent Cathedral of St. Flail, dedicated to Archeillus. Constructed of stone clad in golden sheeting, the cathedral boasts a main central tower that rises almost 300 feet into the air and dwarfs seven smaller surrounding towers. Outside of the cathedral on the holy grounds are other temples to Foerdewaith gods, including Mithras and Dre'uain the Lame. The ecclesiastical compound is surrounded by high, white stone walls. Outside these walls is the rest of the city, itself now surrounded by a further set of walls.

The Cathedral of St. Flail is the seat of Archdeacon Peridor, who oversees the cathedral and the administration of the city and its nearby environs with the assistance of the ecclesiastical magnates under his supervision. As an independent city, issues of royal interest (such as taxation, defense, and the lay courts) are overseen by the mayor of the palace in the name of the overking. Representatives of both Mains and Saxe live in the city and are happy to provide advice to the archdeacon, but Peridor is an excellent diplomat as well as a cleric, and runs Biltscrough in the manner in which he sees fit.

COUNTY OF COUTAINE

Capital: Cantelburgh
Ruler: Count Eggar le-Gaunt
Government: feudal county (Kingdom of Foere)
Population: 2,922,900 (2,803,084 Foerdewaith, 61,955 halfling, 41,200 human mixed ethnicity, 11,121 half-elf, 3,719 hill dwarf, 1,091 high elf, 622 gnome, 108 other)
Monstrous: wolf, dire wolf, large animals, kobold (open areas), hill giant, orc, wyvern
Languages: Common, Halfling, Dwarven, Elven, Gnome
Religion: Archeillus, Belon the Wise, Dre'uain the Lame, Muir, Solanus, Mick O'Delving, Mitra, Thyr
Resources: iron ore, manufactured goods, grain, cattle, foodstuffs, spirits (wine)
Currency: Foere
Technology Level: Medieval

North of the Star Sea, the County of Coutaine is in the heart of old Foere and, to this day, a loyal domain of the Court at Courghais. The western boundary of the county is the Elderwood (which itself is within the overking's lands), and the eastern boundary is the Mons Terminus and the Great Amrin River. On the north, it shares a border with the Duchy of Ysser, and on the south it abuts the royal domain of Foere. The only wilderness is near the Elderwood and the Mons Terminus, with the rest of the county being primarily rich fields, farmlands, and vineyards.

HISTORY AND PEOPLE

Early in Macobert's conquest of central Akados, the future overking set his eyes upon the petty kingdom of Cantel north of the Star Sea. As Macobert's army approached, the king of Cantel went to the Cathedral of St. Oerson in Cantelburgh to seek the blessing of the archdeacon on the eve of battle. According to legend, while praying at the high altar, the king had a vision from Muir of a great empire that would be founded by Foere. Heeding the god's message, the king rode forth to Macobert's army and, holding high a flag of truce, came before Macobert and swore allegiance to him. Macobert accepted the king of Cantel as his first vassal and named him Count of Coutaine (a Gasquen word that roughly translates to "first land").

Since that time, the rulership of Coutaine has passed through various families of the original house of the kings of Cantel, which for the last 700 years has been the le-Gaunt family. The current Count, Eggar, is a robust man in his 50s and one of the few great nobles of Foere who did not follow Ovar on his campaign against the Huun. He walks with a noticeable limp, a reminder of a near-fatal injury he suffered in his youth.

Situated as it is in the heartland of Foere, the vast majority of folk in the county are of Foerdewaith extraction.

RELIGION

With the Cathedral-City of Cantelburgh as its capital, the County of Coutaine is heavily influenced by the traditions and worship of the old gods of Hyperborea, in particular Muir and Thyr. The le-Gaunt family has long been faithful adherents of Muir, and Count Eggar, no exception, is always happy to expound on the tenets of his faith to anyone who so much as makes a minor inquiry.

TRADE AND COMMERCE

Coutaine is in a most enviable location in the domains of Foere. Its lands are rich and provide good soil for farming and cattle. The county maintains iron mines along the southwestern slopes of the Mons Terminus. And its location astride the routes between the port cities of the Star Sea to the south and the duchies of Ysser and Waymarch to the north provides it a critical role in trade among some of the most populated areas of Akados. Cantelburgh is recognized for mapmaking (as it hosts the headquarters of the famed Guild of Cartographers and Explorers), casting bronze, and the manufacture of clocks.

The western reaches of the county are known for their vineyards, including the Le Chateau Gluant, a winery of repute near the edge of the Elderwood on the lower slopes of the Broken Mountains.

LOYALTIES AND DIPLOMACY

Coutaine is entirely surrounded by the royal lands and other domains of the Kingdom of Foere, to which it remains loyal. Count Eggar is troubled by the disappearance of Overking Ovar and, though he would not say so publicly, does not trust Duke Othon Passur of Ysser. But the count's main focus is on ruling his county, and he tries not to worry too much about other nations and their troubles.

GOVERNMENT

Count Eggar rules the county from his seat in Cité Coutain on the eastern edge of Cantelburgh. Outside the city, his authority is enforced by his various vassals, as well as by sheriffs and judges he appoints to towns throughout the countryside. He is advised by a small council that consists of his most important vassals and the archdeacon.

Within Cantelburgh, however, which is a cathedral city, authority is held by the archdeacon and, to the extent royal matters are implicated, the mayor of the palace (except within Cité Coutain itself). In other circumstances, this division of power might result in a great deal of political strife. However, Eggar le-Gaunt, a sincere devotee of Muir, and Archdeacon Artes Monfrier have for many years been good friends and always manage to reach mutual agreement in governance.

MILITARY

The count maintains a modest force of soldiers loyal to him and can call up a levy from his vassals. A goodly number of the county's professional soldiery went off with King Ovar to chase the Huun, though the lack of any substantial current threat to the county means they haven't been missed greatly. The count does keep a close watch on his northern border, however. His spies tell him that the duke of Ysser is looking to expand the lands of his duchy. While these aims at the moment seem likely focused on Waymarch, Eggar recognizes the wealth of his own lands and remains vigilant in case his northern neighbor decides to take advantage of the overking's absence and expand at the expense of Coutaine.

MAJOR THREATS

Bandits, humanoids, and other threats can be found along the eaves of the Elderwood and on the slopes of Mon Terminus. Few of these venture far into the lands of the county, however, which remains quite safe and peaceful. The greatest threat to Coutaine may in fact be its northern neighbor, the Duchy of Ysser, should the overking not return to Courghais and re-establish normal order.

CANTELBURGH, CATHEDRAL CITY OF (CAPITAL)

Ruler: Archdeacon Artes Monfrier, Mayor of the Palace Telifere Palogi, Count Eggar le-Gaunt
Government: feudalism/ecclesiastical
Population: 73,004 (68,459 Foerdewaith, 2,118 halfling, 1,300 human mixed ethnicity, 612 half-elf, 303 high elf, 167 hill dwarf, 45 other)
Languages: Common, Gasquen, Halfling, Elven, Dwarven
Religion: Thyr, Muir, Freya, Mitra, Mick O'Delving, Stryme, Dwerfater
Technology Level: Medieval

Cantelburgh is a Foerdewaith cathedral city and home of St. Oerson's Basilica. In addition, the seat of the count of Coutaine is on the eastern edge of Cantelburgh.

Other than in the Cité Coutain (where the count's authority is predominant), Cantelburgh is ruled by the archdeacon and his mayor of the palace. Wards are overseen by watch captains appointed by the mayor. The archdeacon has also chartered a guild of judges that consists of clerics who provide justice to the citizens of the city in dreams.

St. Oerson's Basilica rises high on a hill in the midst of the western half of the city and is dedicated to the "Three Gods of Hyperborea." Two of these gods are known to be Thyr and Muir, while the third god is, oddly, uncertain. Records from the times of the ancient empire are vague, and the identity of that third god is neither indicated in the magnificent murals and tapestries throughout the basilica nor spoken of by the clerics of the cathedral. In any case, it seems clear that the third deity must be one that is now missing or dead. As a result, most believe it was Arden, who perished in a battle with mighty demonic forces before the coming of the Hyperboreans to Akados.

In addition to being a trade city and market for the many goods brought from the countryside, Cantelburgh is known for its bronze casting and the manufacture of clocks. It is also the headquarters of the famed Guild of Cartographers and Explorers. Though based here, the guild casts its members in all directions in an effort to expand the known world. In backwater ports and seedy towns throughout Akados and beyond, one may find a guild house full of great beast hunters, brave explorers, and bookworm librarians.

Duchy of Mains

Capital: Arbo
Notable Settlements: Dundlend, Fornal, Carson's Mill
Ruler: Duchess Aeria Enserrat
Government: feudal, Palatine Duchy of Foere
Population: 2,965,800 (2,471,200 Foerdewaith, 210,540 halfling, 174,100 human mixed ethnicity, 38,600 high elf, 23,260 mountain dwarf, 18,980 half-elf, 12,220 gnome, 8,200 hill dwarf, 6,700 half-orc, 1,325 orc, 675 other)
Monstrous: giant animals, wolf, dire wolf, goblin, hobgoblin, ogre (plains); nixie, nymph, giant leech, giant turtle, dragon turtle (Mains River); gelatinous cube, lephane, mimic, water elemental, will-o'-wisp (Lake Escaurt); any forest creature or forest subtype creature in or near Harwood Forest
Languages: Common, Gasquen, Halfling, Elven, Dwarven, Gnome
Religion: Mitra, Freya, Mithras, Mick O'Delving, Stryme, Thyr, Muir, Dwerfater, Narrah
Resources: foodstuffs, grain, trade, timber, manufactured products, iron, ironworks, magical resources, spirits (ale, mead)
Currency: Foere
Technology Level: Medieval

The Duchy of Mains stretches from Dundlend to Lake Escaurt, south into Harwood Forest and southeast into the Wolf Hills. Official maps of the Kingdom of Foere have the duchy laying claim to large swaths of Harwood Forest, but the forest is more defended against than controlled. The fields, pastures, and orchards of the Duchy of Mains are rich, well-tended and extremely well protected.

History and People

Unquestioned loyalty to the crown of the Kingdom of Foere marks the history of this large duchy, and this fealty continues to this day. The aging duchess and her two sons are completely loyal to the crown as, historically, the crown has provided the duchy with the resources to defend and strengthen its hold on a land that is often beset by creatures roaming out of Harwood Forest as well as hostilities from the Principality of Olduvar.

During the early expansion and conquests of the Kingdom of Foere, the overking found an easy and steady ally when they came to "the Mains," where lived fierce, tactical fighters more concerned with monstrous creatures than the conflicts of men. Offered a way out of battle for a pledge of fealty, Jeorge Enserrat, the leader of the area at the time of Foere's arrival, saw an opportunity to offer his loyalty in exchange for the resources to better protect his people from the encroaching forest creatures to the south and the predations of nearby nation-states. Their first proof of loyalty was providing assistance in the conquest and "pacification" of the area now known as the Duchy of Saxe. That act led to the formation of the Duchy of Mains and Enserrat's elevation as a duke of the kingdom. It also earned the resources to significantly improve the defenses of Arbo against creatures from the forest to the south, allowing the city to prosper and grow.

Throughout the subsequent centuries, the Duchy of Mains has remained steadfastly loyal to the crown, providing some of its best captains, generals, and advisors. Always on watch for attacks from creatures from Harwood Forest, the militia and guardsmen of the duchy are highly trained in a wide variety of military styles and techniques. Forced at times to fight off dragons, ettins, giants, and other creatures, the hardened soldiers of the duchy are more than happy to face "ordinary" troops in more ordinary battles. Presently the lord-governor of Exeter Province is Benevic of Lortsbar, a knight-commander leading the defenses of Dundlend during one of the Principality of Olduvar's many attacks. The battles brought Lord Benevic to fame as he held off vast numbers of troops while losing very few of his own men. Many other generals and commanders assigned in other locations come from the Duchy of Mains, in part due to the schooling troops are required to go through here.

Loyalties and Diplomacy

The Duchy of Mains has a friendly, though "careful," relationship with the Iron Kingdom of Dorriden but remains hostile to the Principality of Olduvar that repeatedly tests their borders. Trade relationships with the Barony of Baldenar and the Duchy of Saxe are both friendly and active, with tariffs in all directions controlled by the overking of the Kingdom of Foere in Courghais. The duchy maintains a number of small fortresses and towers along the border with Olduvar and has towers overlooking parts of Harwood Forest. Officially, the Duchy of Mains extends into and claims large portions of Harwood Forest, though in reality only the outer edges of the forest are explored as few want to risk the creatures deeper within.

Forces from Dundlend formerly protected the farms of the Genev Gap from monstrous incursions from Harwood Forest. The recent move of the Barony of Baile to essentially revolt and declare its allegiance to the Iron Kingdom of Dorriden caused the overking in Foere to order troops stationed in the Duchy of Mains to no longer protect those farms. Some of the creatures coming out of the forest have even been harried and driven toward the barony. Tensions with the Barony of Baile run high, but trade relationships with the Iron Kingdom remain strong.

Trade and Commerce

Lumber from the Harwood Forest is sent to Arbo for eventual trade and transportation while farmlands north of Arbo toward Lake Escaurt provide rich harvests of wheat, corn, and a variety of other crops. Fish from Lake Escaurt and the Mains River provide additional variety to the tables of those who can afford them. While there have been numerous attempts in parts of the duchy to raise grapes for wine, these efforts have not succeeded. This said, Arbo boasts several dwarven-controlled breweries known for fine ales and meads that are traded throughout the kingdom.

Government

Duchess Aeria Enserrat is aging and soon plans to turn the duchy over to Sorar, her eldest son. While her loyalty remains intact, she is frustrated that some of her finest military leaders and advisors have been "taken" by the crown for services elsewhere. This has caused her to temper some of her reports to Courghais, in which she downplays the strengths and leadership of some of her best people, particularly her sons and, lately, her older grandsons. Her advisors are chosen for intelligence and loyalty. The duchess is considered a pleasant woman who is easy to work for, and her sons and grandchildren are highly regarded. Citizens of Arbo and Dundlend strongly support the ruling family as they see the benefits of their rulership in day-to-day life. More distant Fornal and Carson's Mill are only beginning to receive more attention, and taxation, and are not as thrilled.

Several generations ago, education was made a priority in the duchy, and the duchess continues that focus of trying to make certain that children learn to read and write and to do simple mathematics at an early age. Schooling beyond the age of 10 is not forced but is encouraged. Children under 10 must attend school three days per week. Carson's Mill and Fornal have only recently begun schools, but Dundlend and Arbo have well-established schools for all ages. The University of Mains in Arbo provides advanced education in military tactics, agriculture, languages, and mathematics. The duchess has made it her goal to expand the prestige and breadth of the university as she believes it will increase the duchy's standing with the crown even further.

Military

A large military contingent is stationed here, in part due to the border with the Principality of Olduvar and the nearby Harwood Forest. Lord-Commander Malcom Enserrat is in charge of all of Foere's military forces within the duchy. He keeps the majority of his forces in or near Dundlend and in small fortresses and towers along Harwood Forest. A large percentage of military officers throughout Foere have spent some time in training at the University of Mains in Arbo.

Major Threats

Harwood Forest provides a constant threat, with creatures coming out of the forest at random. The Principality of Olduvar has been known to attack about once a decade, though so far all such attacks have been easily defeated and thrown back by the military here.

While the interior of the duchy is fairly safe, the areas around the Wolf Hills, Lake Escaurt, and, of course, Harwood Forest, provide ample opportunity for adventurers to explore. The duchy actively encourages adventurers to delve into the depths of Harwood Forest and hope that this might reduce the incidents of creatures coming out of the forest to attack or harass its people. While maps might claim that large portions of Harwood Forest are under the control of the Duchy of Mains, the simple truth is that the forest is not patrolled or controlled in any way.

ARBO, CITY OF (CAPITAL)

Ruler: Duchess Aeria Enserrat
Government: feudalism
Population: 64,500 (40,650 Foerdewaith, 5,680 halfling, 5,150 high elf, 4,280 mountain dwarf, 3,200 human mixed ethnicity, 3,020 half-elf, 1,880 gnome, 430 half-orc, 120 orc, 90 other)
Languages: Common, Gasquen, Halfling, Elven, Gnome, Dwarven
Religion: Mitra, Freya, Mithras, Mick O'Delving, Stryme, Thyr, Muir, Dwerfater
Resources: manufactured goods, iron, ironworks, foodstuffs, spirits (ale, mead), timber
Technology Level: Medieval

White stone walls around Arbo are heavy, squat, wide, and studded with battlements and towers that face outward on all sides. Ballistae and a variety of catapults are set to target the surrounding lands and skies. At a distance, the walls and battlements look like a challenge, a fist raised against whatever might come. More than an appearance of strength, Arbo has in fact never been conquered. Dragons have burned parts of the city, giants have attacked its walls, and basilisks have tried its gates, but the city stood against them all and remains poised against any other threats that may come. The people here bear a fierce pride born of the challenges faced, and beaten, by the city as a whole. Ancient foundations and catacombs here are rebuilt or modified as needed without heed to their history as Arbo is more concerned about its future than its past.

While there is a district mainly populated by the poorer residents, most of the city is well mixed, with walled-off mansions standing amid homes, workshops, and stores. The center square of the city is protected with a second wall that encloses the palace, the main government buildings, and the growing University of Mains. Well-designed and cared for streets and sewage systems throughout the entire city — even in the poorer district — mark the city as forward-thinking and "modern" in spite of its ancient roots.

Officially, Duchess Aeria Enserrat rules from the capital city of the Duchy of Mains, but in reality, it is her son Sorar who controls the day-to-day activities of the city. The duchess concerns herself with promoting the schools and the developing university as she believes they provide a lasting impact on the future of the duchy. Sorar Enserrat is well-liked in the city and across the duchy; he is pleasant, charismatic, and generally finds pragmatic solutions to problems that might arise. Decorated military service during his younger years earns him the respect and admiration of the militia and guards, and that military background helps him maintain a strong defense for the city.

Generally, trade goods must follow the trade route through Saxentry in the Duchy of Saxe to the northeast, but as both dukedoms are sworn to the Kingdom of Foere, this generally doesn't cause any problems. Arbo exports some food items but its predominant exports and trade goods include luxury quality ales and meads and a variety of lumber and wood products. Much of the iron from the nearby iron mines is either used within the city or sent out for trade. Hunters and adventurers delve into Harwood Forest in search of valuable ingredients for magical spells and items that are sold here, often to the university. Dwarven stonemasons based here are often contracted for the construction of walls, castles, or other structures at costs far beyond the standard.

CARSON'S MILL, VILLAGE OF

Ruler: Mayor Reils DeVrilis
Government: feudal
Population: 581 (350 Foerdewaith, 64 high elf, 55 human mixed ethnicity, 52 dwarf, 31 half-elf, 16 half-orc, 12 halfling)
Languages: Common
Religion: Mitra, Freya, the Green Father
Resources: timber
Technology Level: Dark Ages

Located at the southeastern edge of the lands claimed by the Duchy of Mains, Carson's Mill is a bustling river valley community supported by logging and milling. Here, rough logs are cut into lumber for overland travel or to be loaded onto barges to be sent downriver to the heart of the duchy. Though Mains has long ignored the town, the recent decision of Durbenford to declare fealty to Suilley has made this location substantially more important strategically. Only recently have schoolteachers been sent here, and according to rumor, the duchess is now considering posting militia to the town.

A mill for cutting logs is built across the Hyon River and is the heart of the village. Many villagers work there or in the storage buildings beside it. Other shops that transport the cut logs have grown up around the mill. Logs are supplied upriver and beyond in the portion of Harwood Forest known as the Barren Forest.

Captain of the Watch Torcan Hald and his small security detail police the lumber town, with Mayor Reils DeVrilis acting as judge in disputes.

REFERENCE SOURCE: GLADES OF DEATH

DUNDLEND, CITY OF

Ruler: Lord-Commander Malcom Enserrat
Government: military/feudalism
Population: 29,993 (22,030 Foerdewaith, 2,140 high elf, 1,729 halfling, 1,290 human mixed ethnicity, 1,272 half-elf, 835 gnome, 647 hill dwarf, 50 other)
Languages: Common, Gasquen, Elven, Halfling, Gnome, Dwarven
Religion: Mitra, Freya, Mithras, Mick O'Delving, Stryme, Thyr, Muir, Dwerfater,
Resources: trade hub, manufactured goods, timber, foodstuffs
Technology Level: Medieval

Squatting on the east-west trade route between the Kingdom of Foere and the nations to the west, Dundlend provides control of trade to and from the kingdom as well as a focal point for the defense of Foere and the southern dukedoms. Construction of the walls and battlements here is similar to that of Arbo, with heavy white stone blocks that can be seen for miles during the daylight. However, the defenses here have been taken to another level and include three sets of walls protecting progressively smaller portions of the city, with the central portion encompassing land reserved for military barracks, government offices, and small fields and wells for fresh water in the event of a prolonged siege. Ballistae and catapults maintained on battlements of all of the walls are ready for any attack, whether monstrous or man.

Lord-Commander Malcom Enserrat is part of the leading family of the Duchy of Mains and a lord-commander of the militia of the Kingdom of Foere. At 60, he is the youngest son of Duchess Aeria and has children and grandchildren of his own. While not as attractive or outgoing as his mother and older brother, the lord-commander's military bearing, evenhanded justice, and pragmatic negotiations make him equally loved in Dundlend and by the troops who serve him.

Lumber contractors and woodworkers do a good business here, but Dundlend is mainly a stop for merchants and caravans, earning money both through trade and provisioning. Taverns, gambling houses, inns, and other services for those traveling through do well here. The strong military presence, largely paid by tariffs as well as an allowance from the crown, also provides strong income for the service businesses.

Fornal, Town of

Ruler: Mayor Hiergad the Red
Government: feudalism
Population: 1,142 (1,052 Foerdewaith, 35 human mixed ethnicity, 28 halfling, 19 gnome, 8 half-elf)
Languages: Common, Halfling, Gnome
Religion: Freya, Thyr, Narrah
Resources: timber, foodstuffs, gems
Technology Level: Dark Ages

Small enough to avoid notice for many years, Fornal has of late become important to the Duchy of Mains and the Kingdom of Foere. The recent declaration of Durbenford for the Kingdom of Suilley has forced the duchy to maintain a closer presence on its eastern borders. Little more than a community of loggers, hunters, and gem prospectors, the wooden walls of Fornal are barely a match for the rare monstrous creature from Harwood Forest or the Wolf Hills, let alone for any sort of military battle. The increased militia presence and new school — both forced upon the village by the duchess — are unwelcome but tolerated, as the taxes are low and the increased militia helps get lumber and furs to more lucrative markets.

Elderly Mayor Hiergad the Red holds the position mainly by default since he was the only one of the more important villagers willing to take the job. Angry at the duchy's recent interference, he was given the opportunity to speak to Duchess Enserrat personally. Impressed by her honesty and directness, he has since encouraged the villagers to make adjustments. The present population includes approximately 100 militia and 2 schoolteachers sent by the duchess. More troops and investments in the town have been promised, which has residents pleased and concerned.

Barony of Loup-Montagne

Ruler: Baron Ghislain Chaput
Government: feudalism
Population: 34,620 (32,577 Foerdewaith, 1,160 human mixed ethnicity, 821 halfling, 62 half-elf)
Languages: Common, Halfling
Religion: Freya, Thyr, Narrah
Resources: timber, foodstuffs
Currency: Foere, mixed
Technology Level: Dark Ages

The Barony of Loup-Montagne is a small holding of Mains in the eaves of the Harwood Forest. Its main town is Roulune, which is actually within the wood, and holds barely 500 people. The rest of its populace is spread throughout the forest and engages in hunting, logging, or trapping. Others are found in the fields east of the wood in widely scattered farms. The greatest threat to the region are wolves out of Harwood. The current baron, Ghislain Chaput, is only 19 years old and inherited the barony last year when wolves killed his grandfather Nicodeme, the prior baron. Perhaps coincidentally, Ghislain was next in line because his father and mother were both killed by a pack of wolves nearly 12 years ago.

A ruined abbey dedicated to St. Ulrich and the abandoned Castle Travers, former seat of the barons of Loup-Montagne, are somewhere in the forest to the west.

Reference Source: Bad Moon Rising from Quests of Doom

County of Roy

Capital: Ems
Ruler: Lord-Commander Norgrim Lorant
Government: military (Kingdom of Foere)
Population: 2,116,100 (1,866,400 Foerdewaith, 98,100 halfling, 68,200 human mixed ethnicity, 27,900 half-elf, 18,250 mountain dwarf, 17,300 high elf, 12,100 gnome, 5,670 half-orc, 1,200 orc, 980 other)
Monstrous: wolf, dire wolf, large animals, kobold (open areas); hill giant, stone giant, orc, dragon, wyvern, goblin, bugbear, hobgoblin (near Blackrock Mountains)
Languages: Common, Halfling, Dwarven, Elven, Gnome
Religion: Archeillus, Belon the Wise, Dre'uain the Lame, Mick O'Delving, Mitra, Stryme, Thyr
Resources: iron ore, manufactured goods, foodstuffs, military training, spirits (wine)
Currency: Foere
Technology Level: Medieval

Framed by Judge's Road to the east, the Blackrock Mountains to the southwest, and the main cities and roads of the Kingdom of Foere itself to the north, the County of Roy is a land of broad, rich fields and lightly forested hills. Farms, vineyards, and homes throughout this region are largely safe and well-protected. Not only are these lands close to the main seat of power of the overking in Foere but they are also under the strict control of the county's military, with its fields, mines, and businesses focused entirely on supporting the preparation, training, and deployment of the many varied military branches of Foere.

Walled mansions and castles belonging to some of the wealthiest merchants and nobility of the kingdom can be found in isolated parts of the County of Roy, though these residences are generally considered "summer homes" by those wealthy enough to keep and maintain them. The militia stationed within Roy do not usually interfere with the possessions of the wealthy or the powerful, even though the orders of the overking provide them the right to investigate or even take control of any home or building in Roy. Only those in favor with the overking are given leave to maintain holdings here.

History and People

The county of Roy was one of the first earldoms handed out by the overking of the kingdom of Foere to one of his loyal generals, Earl Corwin Geoth, and remained in that family for many generations. One of the most steadfast supporters of the crown during the early centuries of Foere's growth and expansion, the Geoth family and local nobility ultimately fell into sloth and decadence. When Overking Oessum was killed in battle in 3207 I.R. and Overking Graeltor took the throne, the decay in Roy was too much for the new overking to stomach. While calling his troops to arms, the overking not only discovered that the leaders and nobility of Roy were engaging in parties dedicated to bloodshed in which servants and commoners were being tortured, murdered, and abused, but also that money assigned from the crown for the maintenance of troops and arms for the defense of the nation was being embezzled and that troops were poorly equipped and poorly trained. While the first offense angered Graeltor, it was the latter that caused him to dissolve the title of the Geoth family and have the family, and all nobles involved, put to the sword.

The overking then put the County of Roy under military rule and placed control of the iron mines near the base of the Blackrock Mountains and the entire area at the disposal of his generals for supplying and training troops during the Foerdewaith Wars of Succession. During the hundreds of years since, the tactically important location near the Iron Kingdom of Dorriden and the Kingdom of the North Heath has remained under strict military control. Facing continuing decay of the eastern provinces and potential threats nearby, it is unlikely the overking will make a change here any time soon.

A vast body of militia are held here, kept as a reserve location for troops due to easy support with the nearby fields and vineyards. Horror stories of the time before military control keep the common folk satisfied with their place as they are well-cared for and Lord-Commander Lorant has firm regulations against any abuse of commoners by his troops. Iron ore from mines at the base of the mountains is transported to Ems for smelting and working into weapons and tools. Fields and grazeland near Ems provide food for the troops, and vineyards near central Roy provide a number of fine wines, much of which is transported to Courghais for the crown. Although slavery in Foere might be illegal, prisoners of war kept here are put to work in the fields and mines as virtual slaves with any attempt to escape bringing a swift execution.

Religion

In addition to a number of smaller temples and shrines dedicated to a variety of gods throughout the area, a massive cathedral dedicated to Stryme, God of Strength, is located in Ems. Many soldiers here follow Stryme as a result of the cathedral, with a number of others following Solanus or Archeillus.

Trade and Commerce

Most of the resources in Roy are used to support the military troops stationed within the county, with a substantial surplus available to be sent by wagonload to other locations of military importance. Fields here are largely dedicated to grains and other foods that can be easily transported, as well as feed for cattle and horses. While some of the surplus iron ore mined from the base of the Blackrock Mountains is sold or traded with other parts of Foere, most is reserved for weapons and armor. Vineyards in central Roy produce excellent wines with the best of these reserved for the overking's cellars in Courghais. A number of smaller businesses support the troops in various ways, particularly with regard to entertainment, but relatively few travelers or merchant caravans spend much time in Roy.

Loyalties and Diplomacy

The military leaders here are among the most faithful and loyal to the crown and are ready to respond to the overking's orders at a moment's notice. Trade caravans entering from the Kingdom of the North Heath to the west are allowed to travel through without harassment, but it is always clear that one of the reasons for the military stationed here is to remind the Kingdom of the North Heath, and even Reme farther to the northwest, that Foere is ready to go to battle. To the feudal baronies and principalities nearby, Roy serves as notice that they all serve at the pleasure of the overking.

Government

The entirety of the County of Roy, including the capital city of Ems, is under strict military rule. Military officers and judicial systems oversee all actions, including any crimes, of the military here. Lord-Commander Norgrim Lorant was assigned control of the County of Roy directly by the overking and is well-established in this position. One concession to the civilian population is a civil court system that handles any crimes or disputes between civilians. All law enforcement is handled by specially trained militia, as are all guard duties and training throughout the area. By law, the military can enter and investigate any home or building throughout the County of Roy at any time, for any reason. They can also examine any merchant goods traveling through and seize them if they see fit. In truth, it has been decades since any military official has taken advantage of these laws. Lord-Commander Lorant insists on evenhanded and steady enforcement of the laws of the Kingdom of Foere. Any officer violating or abusing the rules and privileges granted here is court-martialed.

Military

Troops stationed in Roy total almost 75% of the population, such that military troops are used during harvests and planting times for some of the fields. Assignment to Roy involves a great deal of training exercises but is generally considered a "good" assignment. Cavalry, infantry, artillery (ballistae and trebuchet), and specialized troops are all trained in different parts of the county. Most new recruits from the surrounding principalities receive their basic introductory training in Roy as well. This means that there is a mix of highly trained, experienced veterans and fresh new recruits. While senior officers look forward to closing out their service in Roy, junior officers prefer other assignments to increase their chance of promotion.

Major Threats

The constant military drilling and patrols throughout Roy make it one of the safest areas of the entire Kingdom of Foere. At one time, civilians could have expected the threat of soldiers taking advantage of them, but the present strict rule means that there is little likelihood of even that happening. Some fear the continuing decay of Foere's domains to the east might mean a major campaign using most of the troops that reside here, which would leave a power vacuum in the county, as well as leaving the area largely unprotected.

Wilderness and Adventure

Constant military patrols and training exercises make Roy one of the most heavily-guarded areas in Foere, leaving few opportunities for adventure. Adventurers might seek out excitement at the base of the Blackrock Mountains where some giants or orcs sometimes make an appearance. Military leaders here view adventurers with some caution as they are suspicious of possible spies.

Ems, Cathedral City of (Capital)

Ruler: Lord-Commander Norgrim Lorant; Archdeacon Roeder Steelgrace
Government: military/ecclesiastic
Population: 47,400 (33,435 Foerdewaith, 4,200 halfling, 3,980 mountain dwarf, 1,320 half-elf, 1,190 human mixed ethnicity, 1,105 high elf, 950 gnome, 720 half-orc, 500 other)
Languages: Common, Halfling, Dwarven, Elven, Gnome
Religion: Archeillus, Belon the Wise, Dre'uain the Lame, Mick O'Delving, Mitra, Stryme, Thyr
Resources: ironwork, manufactured goods, foodstuffs, spirits (wine), trade
Technology Level: Medieval

Transformed by years of military control, Ems is an efficiently organized city with wide cobblestone streets organized in a simple grid. Military barracks and apartments line the inside of the tall stone walls enclosing the city. Open city squares and parks separate many of the other buildings, including shops, apartments, homes, and government offices. Large metal smelting and metalsmithing operations are located in the southern portion of the city. Vast stables housing the cavalry, as well as the supply wagons, are located inside the northern wall away from the smells and sounds of the metal operations to the south. Training yards for all forms of military practice are found inside and outside the walls.

It is only the presence of a number of civilian shops, taverns, and other businesses that separates Ems from simply being a large fortress. The sturdy walls and potent defenses combine with the constant noise of the marching and training of soldiers inside the city walls to provide a constant reminder that this city is always prepared for war. In fact, by the overking's decree, this city's sole purpose is to provide for the training and provisioning of his military forces.

History and People

Corruption and abuses of the Geoth family caused the County of Roy and Ems to be turned over to strict military control several hundred years ago. Over time, Ems was transformed into a highly-organized city with advanced defenses, water and food storage, and an advanced sewage system. Garbage collection and disposal is also controlled by the military to keep the city streets clean and passable, as well as to cut down on vermin and disease.

All economic industries here are controlled by the military or, at least, are designed to fully support the military. While there are many ordinary citizens here plying their business, mostly in the form of taverns, eateries, gambling houses, and brothels, produce coming in from the surrounding fields and the iron ore and smelting operations are meant to provide for the military. While some citizens initially feared military control, most residents now enjoy the safety the strong military presence and order provides.

The western side of the city is devoted to massive warehouses for food and weapon storage as well as large barracks for housing soldiers. It is actually rare that all of the barracks are full, as most troops are rotated in and out of the city in part for training, but also to avoid overtaxing the resources of the city itself. In times of heavy troop rotations, the population of the city can grow by more than 50% for a period of several weeks.

Palaces and mansions of the noble families found guilty of crimes against the crown so many centuries ago can be found in the eastern section of the city. Most were transformed into housing for the top military officers and their families long ago, with some sold to the families that have taken over the mining and smelting operations on behalf of the kingdom.

ST. ELB'S CATHEDRAL

One of the few attractions that actually draws visitors to Ems is the massive cathedral found here. Dedicated to Stryme the Mighty, God of Strength, who is also known as Strym to the dwarves, the white marble structure has an iron roof and towers that remain free of rust or tarnish. Services at the cathedral are attended principally by human soldiers and laborers, but all are welcome. The priests here encourage hard physical labor and dedication to one's physical form, so the military leaders are happy to encourage their soldiers to worship Stryme.

The cathedral is considered a city unto itself, and it and the immediate surrounding grounds are subject to ecclesiastical law, ruled by His Grace Archdeacon Roeder Steelgrace, Loyal Servant of Stryme, in the name of the overking. The military and the church have historically had good relations in Roy, as it was originally members of the church that drew attention to the corruption and decadence of the Geoth family and other nobility that lead to military rule over the County of Roy. Archdeacon Steelgrace and Lord-Commander Lorgrant continue that tradition, and in fact get along well. Both leaders are loyal to the crown and do their best to manage their areas together for the betterment of the kingdom.

DUCHY OF SAXE

Capital: Saxentry
Ruler: Duke Mercur Saxe
Government: feudal, Palatine Duchy of Foere
Population: 3,155,700 (2,575,500 Foerdewaith, 243,500 halfling, 193,400 human mixed ethnicity, 43,800 high elf, 32,100 mountain dwarf, 27,900 half-elf, 19,800 hill dwarf, 12,800 gnome, 4,900 half-orc, 1,100 orc, 900 other)
Monstrous: giant animal, wolf, goblin, hobgoblin, orc, ogre, ogre-kin (plains); giant animal, troll, orc, stone giant, demon (mountains)
Languages: Common, Gasquen, Halfling, Elven, Dwarven, Gnome
Religion: Mitra, Belon the Wise, Muir, Archeillus, Freya, Mithras, Mick O'Delving, Dre'uain the Lame
Resources: grain, gold, iron, foodstuffs, spirits (beer, mead), manufactured goods, livestock (cattle, sheep), trade hub, timber
Currency: Foere
Technology Level: Medieval

Wedged between parts of the Kal'Lugus Mountains to the east and Lake Escaurt to the west, the Duchy of Saxe is relatively small, but it stands on a major trade route between the east and west. One of the earliest conquests in the expansion of the Kingdom of Foere, Saxe is well-established, wealthy, and of great importance to the crown. Saxentry is known for its architecture and ancient roots and has been used as an example for city planning in other areas.

HISTORY AND PEOPLE

Conquered and held by Foere early during its expansion, the Duchy of Saxe was named and granted in 2807 I.R. to one of the generals instrumental in the conquest of the eastern provinces. Recently, the Duchy of Saxe fell from favor with the overking in Courghais. Once considered a guiding light, a shining example of loyalty and service, recent losses of lands to the east of the March of Mountains have frustrated the overking and some of the blame has, perhaps unfairly, been placed on the Duchy of Saxe. Expected to maintain information networks and pass information to the overking, Saxe has allowed those networks to fade and break down.

In general, the people here are hearty, cheerful, and overwhelmingly loyal to the crown. The nobility and wealthier merchants do their best to prove their fealty to Foere, though the effort goes increasingly unrecognized in Courghais. In the view of the crown, Saxe's most important role is control over the trade routes heading to the eastern provinces. While the duke has ensured that the trade roads are carefully maintained and patrolled, other parts of the border are less well protected, and his agents have failed to provide important intelligence at key moments.

TRADE AND COMMERCE

Although smaller than some baronies, Saxe is a densely populated, wealthy province with control over a major trade route combined with rich farmlands and productive gold and iron mines. Craftsmen and crofter's guilds thrive in Saxe, and clothing, armor, weapons, furniture, and a variety of other trade goods are made here, with some craftsmen living in small, isolated communities to focus on their manufacturing.

LOYALTIES AND DIPLOMACY

The duke and his people are loyal to the crown. All male nobility of the Duchy of Saxe are required to perform a minimum of three years of military service to Foere as evidence of their loyalty and dedication to the overking. The duchy as a whole has good trade relations with the Duchy of Mains, the Iron Kingdom, the Kingdom of Suilley, Keston Province, and the County of Toullen. The personal relationship between Duke Mercur Saxe and Duchess Aeria Enserrat of the Duchy of Mains is somewhat tense. Duke Saxe believes that some lands presently assigned to Mains should belong to Saxe, as they did in the past, while Duchess Enserrat believes the duke is a bumbling incompetent, and she has made no secret of her assessment.

GOVERNMENT

Ruled for many centuries by the Saxe family, the leadership here has been surprisingly stable. Over the years, there have been few conflicts about succession and almost nothing in terms of scandal. While the term "boring as Saxe" has fallen from use, it is that stability and loyalty to the crown that made the Duchy of Saxe so highly valued. Alas, all families and nations have their ebb and flow, and Duke Mercur Saxe is neither bright nor charismatic. These factors, when combined with poor advisors — all friends of the duke from his childhood — have put Saxe's influence and power on a precipitous decline.

The court system is well-organized, although like most in Foere, it substantially favors the wealthy. The militia and guardsmen are also well-organized and equipped. Other parts of the government are controlled, at least officially, by childhood friends or longtime allies of the duke. Most of these are unfit for their jobs, and many try to take financial advantage of their positions when they can. The networks of spies and information gathering about the eastern provinces that Saxe was once responsible for have been poorly monitored, and this failure has angered the crown.

MILITARY

Because Saxe is a gateway to the east, particularly the Kingdom of Suilley and other areas that have broken away from Foere, there is a strong military presence here. Lord Marshall Bertrand commands all the forces of Foere stationed throughout the area while Captain Korwell commands the militia and guard forces of Saxe. All of the male nobility are required to perform three years of service for Foere and must be prepared to answer a call to battle from the overking.

MAJOR THREATS

Saxe, though fading from favor with the overking, is of major importance to the Kingdom of Foere, so troops, trade routes, and farmlands in the duchy are carefully defended and watched over. The overking and the duke openly fear possible attack from the east, though in truth this may likely be more of an excuse to increase certain taxes and troop deployments in the area. The true threat to Saxe at this time is the incompetence of its ruler and the growing corruption and ineffectiveness of the people he has appointed at several levels of government.

WILDERNESS AND ADVENTURE

Areas near the Kal'lugus Mountains and Shadrack Forest are poorly patrolled and subject to incursions of monsters. The deep catacombs beneath Saxentry, known as the undercity, are said to be haunted. Otherwise, much of the rest of Saxe is free from excitement as most of the area is well-settled. That being said, some adventure can be found here in the form of special jobs and investigations for some of the nobility, who are always seeking new forms of wealth as well as information.

SAXENTRY, CITY OF (CAPITAL)

Ruler: Duke Mercur Saxe
Government: feudalism
Population: 83,536 (57,170 Foerdewaith, 6,130 halfling, 5,980 high elf, 5,378 mountain dwarf, 4,110 human mixed ethnicity, 3,112 gnome, 960 half-elf, 463 half-orc, 133 orc, 100 other)
Languages: Common, Gasquen, Halfling, Elven, Dwarven, Gnome
Religion: Mitra, Belon the Wise, Muir, Archeillus, Freya, Mithras, Mick O'Delving, Dre'uain the Lame
Resources: grain, gold, iron, foodstuffs, spirits (beer, mead), manufactured goods, livestock (cattle, sheep), trade hub, timber
Technology Level: Medieval

Income from the nearby gold mines and longstanding presence on a major trade route have made Saxentry one of the wealthiest cities in the Kingdom of Foere. While new structures dot the city, many of the buildings are old, with some bordering on truly ancient. The stone of the city's foundations, as well as the stone lining the trade routes for several miles in either direction from Saxentry, is extremely old and predates the earliest histories of the area. Known entrances to the catacombs and tunnels beneath the city are filled in and regularly patrolled by guards as the undercity is known to be haunted. A well-designed sewage system is in place to route wastes and wastewater out of the city safely.

Nobility and the wealthier merchants display their wealth through the architectural designs and ornate decorations of their mansions, and the city itself proclaims its wealth in the display of three immense temples. The largest temple, dedicated to Mitra, is flanked by temples to Belon the Wise and Muir. While each temple is dedicated to its particular god and decorated appropriately, the massive marble structures are similar in their ostentatious display of art and gold leaf throughout their interiors. Each religious order takes the responsibility for guarding its own temple. The faithful are always welcome, and other visitors are allowed limited access when no services are taking place.

The temples look over a wide central plaza where the trade routes from Arbo to the southwest, Corvusrook to the northwest, and the route heading east toward the Borderlands all meet together. Wide enough to allow caravans to pass each other or to park and trade, the cobblestone square is filled with food and supply vendors ready to make a quick sale.

Tall gray stone walls encircle the city with smaller stone walls and gates dividing the inside of the city into smaller sections. Wide, tall gates allow entry to the largest wagon caravans to well-maintained streets providing straight passage through the central square. Taverns, inns, and shops carrying any goods one can imagine line the major streets passing through the central square. Guards patrol the entire city but the areas seeing the heaviest patrols are the northern area, which is devoted to the homes of the wealthy nobles and merchants, and the central square where caravans meet and the main government offices, military offices, barracks, and the ornate temples can be found.

DUCHY OF YSSER

(EE-sur)
Capital: Tourse
Ruler: Duke Othon Passur
Government: feudal, Palatine Duchy of Foere
Population: 2,226,847 (1,566,608 Foerdewaith, 388,909 human mixed ethnicity, 171,300 halfling, 29,207 high elf, 21,288 hill dwarf, 18,671 half-elf, 12,338 mountain dwarf, 9,140 gnome, 6,119 half-orc, 2,767 orc, 500 other)
Monstrous: giant animal, wolf, goblin, hobgoblin, orc, ogre, ogre-kin (plains), troll
Languages: Common, Gasquen, Halfling, Elven, Dwarven, Gnome
Religion: Archeillus, Mitra, Belon the Wise, Muir, Freya, Mithras, Mick O'Delving, Dre'uain the Lame
Resources: grain, foodstuffs, spirits (beer, mead), manufactured goods, livestock (cattle, sheep), trade hub, timber, ore, diamonds (Broken Mountains)
Currency: Foere
Technology Level: Medieval

The Duchy of Ysser consists of rolling hills and fields dotted with farms, cattle ranches, and small copses of woods. It is bounded on the west by the Elderwood, the Broken Mountains, and the Old Tors Road, and on the east by the Mons Terminus. Its northern border, by agreement with Reme, runs 50 miles south of the Tradeway. On the south, the border between Ysser and Coutaine has been the subject of dispute, and, on more than one occasion, hostility, for centuries, even though both are vassals of Foere. Though the matter was technically settled in 3011 I.R. by a writ issued by the overking, Ysser came to believe that the royal surveyor who set the border was in fact biased in favor of Coutaine, as it was later discovered that he was a member of the Guild of Cartographers and Explorers based in Cantelburgh. Since that time, the dukes of Ysser have coveted the richer lands of their neighbor to the south and have looked for any opportunity to expand their holdings.

HISTORY AND PEOPLE

Ysser was the last of the petty kingdoms about the Star Sea that Macobert conquered before he turned his eyes east to the plains beyond the March of Mountains. The capital of Tourse finally surrendered to Foere in 2741 I.R. after a two-year siege. The defeated king, his entire family, and the majority of his retainers were promptly executed, and their bodies were left to rot in gibbets hanging in the main city square.

Macobert awarded the newly created Duchy of Ysser to one of his knights, who, while his king was in the east, managed to lose his holdings in a game of chance. Since then, the duchy has passed through the hands of a number of noble families of Foere, with few lasting more than two generations. In this Duke Othon Passur is unusual, as he is the third generation of his family to hold the fiefdom.

Most of the folk of Ysser are Foerdewaith, descendants of the various tribes originally conquered by Macobert. However, its location astride and near trade routes that cross the continent means that many other people are traveling through, and often settling, in the lands of the duchy.

RELIGION

The oldest temple in Tourse is devoted to the worship of Archeillus, who is the patron of the current duke and his family. In fact, the duke requires all of his vassals to attend services there and has been known to frown upon those showing devotion to other gods. Nevertheless, a substantial temple to Mitra manages to maintain a body of worshippers. Solanus, one of the patron gods of Reme, is greatly disfavored here.

Smaller temples to Belon the Wise, Muir, and Dre'uain the Lame are also in the city, while the folk in the countryside often worship Freya, Mithras, or Mick O'Delving.

Some clerics visiting Tourse have of late returned with concerns about the temple to Archeillus in Tourse. Some of the devotions seem different from those performed elsewhere in Akados, and certain ceremonies are held in secret and only for the greatest nobles of the duchy, away from the sight of those of lesser rank. And the mutual, and near-fanatical, devotion shown by the duke and the clergy of Archeillus to each other seems oddly disturbing. Rumors question whether the priests of Archeillus do in fact honor that god, but any espousing such rumors had best not speak them in front of agents of the duke or they may find themselves in great peril.

TRADE AND COMMERCE

Astride the Northern Kingdom Road, the Duchy of Ysser is an important center of trade. Its own resources are a bit more limited. Some of its fields, particularly on the south, boast soil rich enough for farming various grains. A number of well-respected ales and beers are brewed in Ysser. In the north, the soil is less fertile, and in those lands are found ranches with cattle and sheep. Some logging and trapping occur in the portion of the Elderwood that borders the duchy. Ores are mined from the lower slopes of the Mons Terminus, and diamonds can be found in the Broken Mountains, where the mines are held by the Baron Denar Craldan of Vroulet, a vassal of the duke.

LOYALTIES AND DIPLOMACY

As a loyal vassal of Foere, the dukes of Ysser do not technically engage in diplomacy independent of the overking. This has not, however, actually impeded Ysser from meddling in affairs both domestic and foreign where an advantage can be found.

Of late, with the overking, many other nobles, and nearly all of the Knights of Macobert away campaigning against the Huun, Duke Othon Passur has seen certain new favorable opportunities arise. It is said that agents of the duchy have been seen in the Stoneheart Valley hiring gnolls to attack Waymark troops in service to Bard's Gate. Already critical to trade along the Northern Kingdom Road, Ysser would be in position to even further enrich itself were the duchy able to gain a foothold on the Tradeway, and dominion over commerce going east and west as well.

Perhaps the only thing more attractive to Duke Othon than incorporating the Tradeway into his demesne would be taking lands from the hated Coutaine to the south. His spies and soldiers probe the border, looking for any opportunity, but so far the watchful Count Eggar le-Gaunt has countered each move. If the authority of the Crown at Courghais is not restored soon, however, the duke may decide to take matters into his own hands and commence open hostility to gain what he wants.

GOVERNMENT

Ruling a palatine duchy of Foere, the duke is sovereign in the lands of Ysser and possesses within its bounds the authority of the overking. As with the rest of Foere, Ysser's government is feudal, with counts and margraves holding lands as vassals of the dukes. Ysser, however, has fewer such vassals than its peer realms. It is a poorly kept secret that Othon and his predecessors have over the years sought ways to arrange the forfeit of their vassals' lands, to the enlargement of those held directly by the dukes.

As a result, few of the vassals of Ysser trust their liege, with the dukes ruling by fear rather than love or friendship. Similarly, the dukes have historically appointed magistrates who sit in courts throughout the duchy, with the authority to investigate and dispense justice in the name of the duke independent of the local feudal lords. The duke's vassals are wary of interfering with a magistrate, unless it can be done without attribution; more than one such vassal has been banished or beheaded, their lands forfeit to the duke.

MILITARY

The dukes of Ysser maintain a sizable body of soldiers loyal only to them, often enhanced by mercenaries or sell-swords bought by the coin gained through the lucrative trade passing through the duchy. While the dukes also have the right to call upon levies from their vassals, the level of distrust between liege and vassal leaves such an action at best uncertain.

MAJOR THREATS

There are really no major external threats to Ysser. Both of its neighbors, Waymarch and Coutaine, would much prefer peace with the duchy than hostility. As a result, the greatest danger may in fact be the duke's ambition and whatever mysterious plans may be motivating the priests of Archeillus in Tourse. Additionally, though Othon has been deft at maintaining fear among his vassals, were he to show weakness or take a sufficiently outrageous action, a rebellion or assassination attempt is not entirely out of the question.

TOURSE, CITY OF (CAPITAL)

(tur-SAY)

Ruler: Margravine Cassandra Angot (subject to Duke Othon Passur)

Government: feudalism

Population: 54,112 (40,454 Foerdewaith, 9,864 human mixed ethnicity, 1,010 halfling, 959 high elf, 801 hill dwarf, 719 half-elf, 214 gnome, 91 other)

Languages: Common, Gasquen, Halfling, Elven, Dwarven, Gnome

Religion: Archeillus, Mitra, Belon the Wise, Muir, Dre'uain the Lame

Resources: trade, manufactured goods, finance, spirits (beer, mead)

Technology Level: Medieval

Tourse, a walled, wealthy city astride the North Kingdom Road, is the capital of the Duchy of Ysser. In the bustling markets of the city, goods from all over Akados can be bought and sold. The skills of the glassblowers, the gem cutters, and the smiths of Tourse are renowned and produce goods that are often sent by caravan for sale as far as the port cities of Libynos. The taverns of the city are always well-stocked with the famous ales and beers of Ysser, including the annual winner of the Brewers' Fest in Hogshead Bend.

Due to the duchy's location in the heartland of Foere in the midst of Akados, many of the noble families of Ysser have long been involved in mercantile businesses, with interests throughout the continent and, in some cases, beyond the seas. As a consequence, a few of those houses have become known for banking, providing letters of credit, safekeeping valuables, and lending through their chapters in key trading cities. The leading banking family in Tourse is House Angot, the head of which is the Margravine Cassandra.

Shortly after Ysser became a vassal of Foere, the dukes granted to a loyal noble family the title of margrave of Tourse, to rule the city proper in the name and on behalf of the duke. About 150 years ago, the title passed to the Angot family, which has used the secular authority so gained to enhance its mercantile interests. In 3510 I.R., the most recent margrave died in his sleep, and being without heir, his widow the Margravine Cassandra took the reins of the city. She is only 43 years old and has many suitors who would wish to gain her title and leadership of the Angot interests. As of yet, she continues to play them against each other while maintaining a firm grip on both city and family. Some have now sought the ear of the duke, suggesting that a successor to the margravine should be identified sooner rather than later. Those who know Cassandra well, however, would advise against underestimating her.

The oldest temple in Tourse is devoted to the worship of Archeillus, who is the patron of the current duke and his family. In fact, the duke requires all of his vassals to attend services there and has been known to frown upon those showing devotion to other gods. The city also boasts a substantial temple to Mitra and smaller temples to Belon the Wise, Muir, and Dre'uain the Lame.

While the Margravine attends services at the temple of Archeillus with the duke, she has been seen quietly worshipping at the temple of Mitra, a fact she has so far been able to hide from Othon.

HOGSHEAD BEND, TOWN OF

Hogshead Bend is a small town of about 200 souls that is built around a spring in the midst of the fields of eastern Ysser. It would be entirely unremarkable but for the fact that it hosts an annual festival on the date of Brewers' Fest, a day holy to the god Pekko. For the week before the holiday, the population of the town swells fiftyfold or more as travelers from far and wide come to taste (and, in the case of merchants, purchase hogsheads of) the ales and beers competing in the annual competition for best brew of Hogshead Bend. Whether it is the water of the village spring, the grains grown in the nearby fields, or some other unknown factor, the ales and beers of the six brewers in this tiny village are recognized as the best throughout Akados. After each year's Brewers'

Fest, the winning brew can often be found in taverns as far Kingsgardt, Castorhage, Bard's Gate, Brookmere, and the Tycho Free States.

TORWATCH KEEP

The Duchy of Ysser maintains this fortress, which was constructed after the destruction of the Black Monastery to keep an eye on the Old Tors for any resurgence of the dark cult that built the monastery. Those exploring the darker parts of the Old Tors or the Elderwood often use Torwatch Keep as a base of operations, where supplies, a safe rest, and healing can be found.

GEOGRAPHIC FEATURES AND POINTS OF INTEREST IN THE HEARTLAND OF THE KINGDOM OF FOERE

BROKEN MOUNTAINS

Though close to the Old Tors, the Broken Mountains are much more recent, likely raised as a result of the same forces that created the Stoneheart Mountains far to the northeast. Their peaks are high and sharp, with heavily forested deep valleys.

In the early years of the Hyperborean conquest of Akados, plans originally called for the Tower of Oerson to be built in a valley of the Broken Mountains. However, earthquakes repeatedly shattered the upland vale where the tower's construction had begun, killing hundreds of builders. The site came to be deemed cursed, and construction of the tower was moved east to the future location of the city of Curgantium on the Great Amrin River.

To this day, earthquakes regularly strike the Broken Mountains. According to legend, a restless dragon (or even larger beast) sleeps beneath the ruined foundations of the unfinished Hyperborean tower.

The Broken Mountains are home to the Senelast Clan of hill dwarves. The northern portions of the mountains fall within the domain of the baron of Vroulet, who owes fealty to the duke of Ysser. The baron's wealth largely derives from diamond mines located in the lower slopes of the range.

Le Chateau Gluant, a winery of repute, lies within western Coutaine, at the edge of the Elderwood in the rolling lower slopes of the Broken Mountains.

REFERENCE SOURCES: FGG2 STRANGE BEDFELLOWS;

THE NOBLE ROT FROM QUESTS OF DOOM

ELDERWOOD

The Elderwood is an old growth forest of northwestern Foere bordered by the Old Tors on the west and the Broken Mountains on the northeast. The Saymere Valley lies between the Elderwood and the Old Tors, part of the County of Barresque of Foere. The eastern portion of the forest is known for its towering redwood trees.

For millennia before the Second Exodus, the Elderwood was home to a number of clans of wild elves, including Clan Silverblossom. It is said that Elderis Thadell, the Silverblossom king, went mad while in the Elderwood and slaughtered his family and drank poison. Many of the elves' abandoned tree villages can still be found.

Three small villages were established in 3285 I.R. along the eastern edge of the forest: Harmony, which has a population of 227; Stone's Throw with 351 residents; and Thorbold, which holds 197 folk. All are within the small Barony of Kamlan, part of the royal demesne of Foere. Recently, the people of the three villages began clearcutting trees to expand the pastureland for their sheep.

The forest is home to several branches of an ancient druidic order, including the Druidic Order of Talanis. In addition, goblin tribes are known to haunt the Elderwood, and are reported to hold a dungeon stronghold somewhere in the forest deeps.

REFERENCE SOURCES: FGG2 STRANGE BEDFELLOWS;
THE COVERED BRIDGE FROM QUESTS OF DOOM 4

GILDED RIVER

The yellow sands and dirt along the shores of this wide, winding river gave rise to its name, and the discovery of gold in some of those sands near Corvusrook made that name last. Starting deep in Shadrack Forest, the Gilded River winds its way through the Barony of Baldenar and into the Duchy of Mains where it finally enters Lake Escaurt. Its shallow, sandy shores drop off quickly into a very deep center. The river moves slowly and calmly due to its exceptional depth and rarely floods. River trout and other fish are caught here, but fishermen are cautious as there are larger creatures as well, some large enough to make a meal of the fishermen.

JUDGE'S ROAD

Running at least four wagons wide in all areas, Judge's Road runs from Corvusrook up to Croix and is still considered one of the most important trade routes in the Kingdom of Foere. While maintenance of the road has been spotty at times, lately the road is well-kept and patrolled regularly by troops under Baron Baldenar's banner. Made of gravel and cobblestones, the road is raised above the surrounding area so water runs off the road and keeps it clear of mud and debris.

KING'S ROAD

This wide gravel and cobblestone road stretches from the Kingdom of Foere to the Duchy of the Rampart and is one of the main routes used when the Kingdom of Foere made its march eastward to conquer the eastern provinces. Decay of the road was once seen by many as a sign of the decay of the kingdom itself. As the eastern provinces were lost, the maintenance of the road fell away as well. The stretch of the King's Road between Nyham Chae and Judge's Road has seen extensive repairs and rebuilding, and even the construction of rest areas for travelers. These changes were ordered by the overking when the new baron of Baldenar was installed.

LAKE ELB

Known on some maps as the "Lake of Glass," this eerie, large, freshwater lake possesses a mystery that none has been able to solve. While the water is cold, refreshing, and perfectly safe to drink, not one fish or aquatic creature lives in the lake itself. Creatures can swim and bathe in the icy waters with no ill effect other than perhaps a chill from its frigid temperature. Windmill-driven pumps pull water into long irrigation ditches heading to rich vineyards to the north, and the plants and animals around the lake thrive when fed these cold waters.

A second mystery surrounds the surface of the lake, which is unperturbed by winds of any strength, always undisturbed like a calm mirror reflecting the sky. Ripples from anything landing in the lake or swimmers die out quickly, never traveling far enough to truly shift the surface of the lake. Sages and learned men have come up with various, sometimes wild, theories to explain the mysteries of Lake Elb but none can truly explain it. There is something disturbing about the lake, a disquiet that strikes any intelligent observer that comes from the deepest, most primitive parts of the mind. It is far easier to drink the refreshing water, refill one's canteen, and continue on, than it is to contemplate the mysteries of Lake Elb.

LAKE ESCAURT

Boasting deep, icy cold waters colored by glowing phosphorescent algae, Lake Escaurt is the subject of many tales and stories of hauntings, ghosts, and other supernatural or magical phenomenon. Swirling, glowing waters add an eerie feel to the usually calm waters at night, but those fishermen used to the phenomenon remain unperturbed, worried more about the larger, more dangerous denizens of the darker, colder depths. Bodies of strange and terrifying creatures are sometimes found floating in the water, as are remains of other large, but at least recognizable, animals. The center of the lake goes as far down as some of the deepest oceans and is rumored to be the location of one or more portals leading to and from different portions of this world, or even other worlds.

Past centuries have seen conflicts over Lake Escaurt, with competing claims by the Duchy of Mains and the Duchy of Saxe. These conflicts were solved when the overking of Foere declared it the domain of the Duchy of Mains almost 150 years ago. Fishing here is bountiful, but in truth not enough to compensate for the expense of maintaining a militia presence and boats nearby to protect citizens near and on the lake.

LYNOSSE

This heavily forested island of approximately 2,600 square miles has long been the exclusive province of the overkings of Foere. Fishing boats are permitted to cast their nets near the shore, but none are permitted ashore without authorization from Courghais. A few docks protected by a stone fortification are located on the small bay on the southeastern shore, perpetually manned by a garrison of soldiers. Most locals believe that the overkings use the island as their personal hunting grounds for large game otherwise extinct elsewhere on Akados. Whether there may be another purpose to the island remains unknown.

MAINS RIVER

Beginning in the Edriss Mountains near the southern coasts of Akados, the Mains River rolls through the Duchy of Listonshire and through the Harwood Forest, and then through the Duchy of Mains to Lake Escaurt. Wide and slow moving, the river provides an excellent source of water for farms and orchards of the duchy as well as a wide variety of fish. Stretches of the river closer to Lake Escaurt are marked with walled mansions and small castles used as vacation homes by the very wealthy. Beautiful as the scenery may be, disappearances near the river are a regular occurrence so it is best not to travel on or near the flowing water alone.

NORTH KINGDOM ROAD

This well-maintained and patrolled road runs from Pentahs on the north shore of the Star Sea, north through Cantelburgh and Tourse, until it intersects the Tradeway past the border with the Duchy of Waymarch. Much trade passes along this road, which is a key artery of commerce between Foere, Reme, and the eastern provinces. It is very safe, and inns along the road provide ready accommodation to travelers of all sorts.

OLD TORS

These ancient, craggy hills cover almost 60,000 square miles of northwestern Foere beyond the Elderwood. Some scholars believe these were the oldest mountains of all Akados (save perhaps the Lost Mountains of the far north), now weathered down over countless eons. The overking claims this land, with the northern and western edge of the hill country constituting the border of his kingdom with the Duchy of Waymarch.

A few enclaves of halflings make their homes in these hills. Some of their elders insist that their folk have lived here since time immemorial and suggest that this may in fact be the original homeland of the halflings in the Lost Lands.

While Foere patrols do keep watch along the margins of the hills and make occasional forays to ensure no other realm claims this land, much of the hill country is wild and populated by orcs, hippogriffs, and batfolk.

Somewhere in the Old Tors is the Hill of Mornay, on which the notorious Black Brotherhood built their monastery in 3272 I.R. As is now well-known, the Black Brotherhood served dark powers and sought to assassinate the overking of Foere. In 3314 I.R., Overking Osment sent an army to besiege the Black Monastery. Many perished in the attempt and at the end the monastery disappeared in a massive conflagration. Three years later, Torwatch Keep was built to keep watch on the Hill of Mornay to ensure that the brotherhood never returns. In recent years, however, at least five incidents have occurred in which witnesses reported finding the Hill of Mornay once again crowned with black walls and slate-roofed towers. In every case, the manifestation of this revenant of the Black Monastery has been accompanied by widespread reports of madness, crime, and social unrest.

REFERENCE SOURCE: THE BLACK MONASTERY

OLD TORS ROAD

This road runs from its juncture at the North Kingdom Road west to Torwatch Keep. Long ago, this was part of a longer road that ran as far as Nains in the south. This route eventually fell into disfavor, and beyond Torwatch Keep, only a rough track and occasional cobbles now mark the way between the Old Tors and the Elderwood. Today, most of the traffic on the Old Tors Road is heading to or from Torwatch Keep, though some merchants do travel this way to reach small logging towns in the forest's eaves.

SAYMERE VALLEY

This serene valley lies between the Old Tors and the Elderwood in the northern extent of the County of Barresque, a small county of the Kingdom of Foere. Long ago, this area was part of a barony held by the Loga family, which controlled a road through the valley between the city of Nains in Foere to the south and Panetoth in the Duchy of Waymarch to the north. Eventually, the road was abandoned, the Loga family lost influence, and the valley was annexed by the County of Barresque. The old Loga manse remains in the valley, along with a covered bridge over the Upper Saymere River (which is too small to appear on the continental map).

In the past, duergar have been spotted in some force in the valley, leading some to believe that there may be an entrance to the Under Realms here. A paladin of Thyr, Sir Varral et-Casan the Blessed, is said to have lived in this region at one time.

REFERENCE SOURCE: THE COVERED BRIDGE FROM QUESTS OF DOOM 4

SHADRACK FOREST

Ancient, old growth forests with tall, majestic trees traditionally grant a sense of awe and mystery to the viewer, triggering the imagination, but Shadrack Forest breaks with that tradition. The hemlock and twisted elm trees here are dotted with birch trees and, here and there, a tall pine. Those trees that might be useful for loggers are tucked amid thick, sometimes toxic, undergrowth and a collection of trees of no real value. Shadrack Forest is merely ancient, its awe and mystery replaced with darkness and foreboding. Gnolls, not elves, roam and control the forest, or at least those areas not claimed by larger and more dangerous creatures. Massive dire bears and packs of dire wolves roam the center of the shadowy forest where few challenge their domains. While claimed by Foere and officially part of the Barony of Baldenar, the forest is considered to be of little real value. The gnoll tribes are left to themselves so long as they do not make any move out of the forest.

STAR SEA

The Star Sea is a large freshwater lake in the center of the domains of the Kingdom of Foere. It is fed by rivers issuing from the slopes of the Cretian, Rampart, and Blackrock Mountains. From its northernmost arm, its waters flow past the hill of Châlaix into the Great Amrin River, on the long journey east to the Amrin Estuary and the Sinnar Ocean.

Boats of all sizes ply the waters of the Star Sea, bringing goods to and from the ports on its shores, and down the Great Amrin River to the eastern provinces. The Star Sea also boasts many varieties of freshwater fish.

With little topography surrounding it to block wind, the Star Sea is also known for brutal and terrifying storms that often arise with little warning in the spring and summer months (and evaporate just as swiftly). Each year, some number of vessels fail to return to port after encountering these infamous storms; though in some cases, boats disappear without others reporting any bad weather. In any event, the bottom of the Star Sea is thought to be littered with the wreckage of thousands of years of vanished craft, some perhaps holding treasures long forgotten.

WOLF HILLS

The Wolf Hills southwest of Durbenford are principally rolling grassland with some low brushland, but in the south become tree-covered in the outskirts of the Harwood Forest. While several packs of wolves are known to occupy the area, a strange stone outcropping that looks very much like the head of a howling wolf rising from one of the hills closest to Fornal gives this range of low hills its name. While claimed by the Duchy of Mains and home to the towns of Carson's Mill and Fornal, the hills remain dangerous and travelers must be vigilant. Ettins, hill giants, and several tribes of goblins are known to hunt the area, and creatures from the darker portions of nearby Harwood Forest are always a danger. Sole prospectors and small groups of adventurers claim to have found gemstones in these hills but without better protection from the creatures here it has proven too dangerous to try to establish any mines. Prospectors from Fornal do make regular forays into the hills, but with limited success.

KINGDOM OF THE NORTH HEATH

Capital: Bret Harth
Notable Settlements: Broten, Poiretre
Ruler: King Lytyr Reddrake
Government: hereditary monarchy
Population: 1,645,800 (1,180,900 Foerdewaith, 277,300 human mixed ethnicity, 102,400 halflings, 37,600 half-elves, 34,200 high elves, 6,100 hill dwarves, 4,700 gnomes, 1,950 half-orcs, 650 other)
Monstrous: goblin, hobgoblin, kobold, bugbear, hill giant, orc, troll, sahuagin (coast), roc (coast), dragon (coast and regions near Blackrock Mountains)
Religion: Ceres, Darach-Albith, Dre'uain the Lame, Kamien, Mick O'Delving, Mitra, Muir, Telophus, Thyr, Yenomesh
Languages: Common, Halfling, Elven, Dwarven, Gnome
Resources: trade hub, iron, gold, manufactured goods, fishing, livestock (cattle, buffalo, sheep, goats), grain, foodstuffs, breeding (horses)
Currency: North Heath, mixed
Technology Level: Medieval

Spread from the jagged coast of Norshore and Bret Harth all the way across the Plains of Eauxe to Poiretre, the Kingdom of the North Heath covers a broad spread of land and an even broader variety of people. The coastal sailors and fisherman along the Crescent Sea have a very different culture than the farmers along the Meander River who are equally different from the tribal plainsmen of the Plains of Eauxe. Now independent of the rule of Foere as well as the powerful influence of Reme, the Kingdom of North Heath remembers warfare all too well and maintains a vigilant watch over nearby nations and free states.

HISTORY AND PEOPLE

History tells us that kingdoms and nations rise and fall, with new nations formed from the remnants of older ones. The Kingdom of the North Heath is no exception. Most of the kingdom's territory includes broad tracts of land with poor rocky soil growing little more than moss and tough grasses fit for only sheep and goats to eat. Only along the Meander River can good farmland be found. The mouth of that river, the current location of the city of Bret Harth, has long been settled, with its access to fresh water, mines along the coast, as well as good, arable land for crops. No records remain of those first settlers, and some of the foundations and ruins in and near the city predate even the Hyperborean Imperium. Whatever the origin of Bret Harth may have been, the modern Kingdom of the North Heath first came to be when the sailor and privateer Captain Ayre Barbossa conquered the city to provide a base for his operations. At that time, the city and surrounding areas were in dire need of leadership, and the captain easily stepped in to take over and proclaim himself king.

Several generations later, the small kingdom began to expand down the Meander River and toward the plains where it met powerful resistance by the Horsemen of Eauxe. The true birth of North Heath occurred when

King Drake Barbossa took the unusual step of challenging the chieftains of the plains tribes to individual combat. He successfully defeated the champions of all the tribes individually over the course of almost a year. His courage and prowess in battle earned him the fealty of the fierce warriors. While most of the citizens no longer recall this event nearly 1,000 years gone, the tribesmen still tell the tale of Drake, and the dreaded Horsemen of the Plains of Eauxe remain loyal to the throne of the Kingdom of the North Heath. The royal family still sends all of their children to spend a minimum of three years living among the Horsemen as a sign of their loyalty to the tribes.

Recognizing the growing power of the fledgling kingdom, the ascendant Kingdom of Foere decided to add even these poor lands to its principalities. The fierce horsemen fell to Macobert's advanced tactics and weapons in 2729 I.R., and North Heath was defeated. The former king of the North Heath was forced to bend the knee to Macobert and receive his new title of margrave of Bret Harth. Over the ensuing centuries, the Foerdewaith settled portions of the Plains of Eauxe, going so far as to grant title to the lands to a marquis of Eauxe, much to the anger of the plainsmen.

When the Singed Man rose in Kear (now the Kingdom of the Vast) in 2970 I.R., his predations and destruction reached far into the territories now claimed by North Heath. Laws against necromancy and the undead here reflect the fear still raised from that dark time in history.

After the disappearance of the Army of Light in 3210 I.R., Foere began its slow disintegration in the Foerdewaith Wars of Succession. One year after Duke Oden of Kear declared his domain's independence as the Kingdom of the Vast in 3224 I.R., the margrave of Bret Harth did the same, having himself crowned the newly restored king of the North Heath. This began a lengthy war with Foere that eventually ended in 3245 I.R. when an armistice was signed in conjunction with Vast, negotiated with the help of the City-State of Castorhage. It was agreed that the Plains of Eauxe would be abandoned by the villagers and townsmen who had settled the region and be restored to the free run of the Horsemen of Eauxe. Only Poiretre would be left as a place of meeting for the tribal councils and for administration by North Heath. Otherwise, the lands would become a largely depopulated buffer between Bret Harth and Courghais.

RELIGION

Muir, Goddess of Virtue, and Thyr, God of Law and Justice, are the major gods worshipped in the lands of the Kingdom of North Heath. Worship of Mitra is growing lately at the expense of Muir. Other minor gods are also worshipped in some locations but the major temples in cities such as Bret Harth and Broten are to these gods. The Horsemen of the Plains of Eauxe worship far differently; they provide no name for their gods but claim to worship the land, sun, and sky. Sages argue that some god must answer their prayers as clerics among the horsemen are as powerful as those of any of the named gods.

TRADE AND COMMERCE

Regular flooding along the Meander River helps keep the nearby farmlands fertile and productive and grow various grains, corn, and cotton and support herds of sheep and goats. The broader plains are home to cattle, buffalo, and wild horses tended by the tribal horsemen. The heath itself stretches from Bret Harth across to Broten and down toward the Plains of Eauxe. Sheep and goats raised on the heath provide wool, milk, and meat but the majority of crops and food come from the areas close to the Meander River. The coastal regions are supported principally by fishing, though Bret Harth and Broten focus on fishing and trade. Several isolated mines along Norshore and the area near Bret Harth provide some gold and iron, although not enough to support the full needs of the kingdom. Bret Harth and Poiretre boast large numbers of extremely skilled craftsmen that take imported raw materials and turn them into manufactured products recognized far and wide for quality, including furniture, clothing, cookware, weapons, and other items. As a result, the many trade agreements the kingdom has made are the lifeblood of its cities, and the king does everything possible to maintain them.

LOYALTIES AND DIPLOMACY

Trade agreements and treaties with the Kingdom of the Vast, the Grand Duchy of Reme, the Iron Kingdom of Dorriden, and the City-State of Castorhage and the armistice agreement with the Kingdom of Foere have long ensured North Heath's safety and economic well-being, though some of the aspects of those treaties cause King Lytyr and his advisors some concern. Although their vigilance is not entirely unwarranted, in spite of its size, the Kingdom of North Heath is a relatively poor nation populated by fierce and hardy people, particularly among the Horsemen of Eauxe, which makes it a poor target for conquest.

Kingdom of the Vast to the south is an ally and steady trade partner, as is the City-State of Castorhage. The Kingdom of the Vast provides a buffer against the Principality of Olduvar for North Heath, while North Heath provides the same role against Foere and Reme for the Kingdom of the Vast. The City-State of Castorhage, at this time, is happy to keep these smaller kingdoms independent restraining Reme and Foere so that it can focus on some of its own internal problems. Relations with Reme also remain on reasonably friendly terms.

Presently there is an uncomfortable peace with the Tycho Free States after a rogue North Heath admiral seeking fame and a route to power began an unsanctioned naval assault in 3511 I.R. Poorly planned and carried out without knowledge or support of the navy as a whole, the young admiral and his forces were defeated. In addition to the loss of several major ships in the embarrassing defeat, the Kingdom of the North Heath was left in an unfavorable position regarding trade and diplomacy while trying to rebuild and strengthen its navy, a necessity to protect its trade in the often-dangerous waters of the Crescent Sea.

GOVERNMENT

The Kingdom of the North Heath is a hereditary monarchy presently ruled by King Lytyr Reddrake. The Reddrake family came to power in 3403 I.R. when King Aylyr Reddrake (Barbossa), who had taken the family name of his Eauxe wife, succeeded to the throne after his cousin, the king, and his family were lost at sea. While over the centuries the royal succession of North Heath has been plagued with difficulties from time to time, King Lytyr took the throne without dissension. He maintains a strong set of advisors who represent the interests of all major craft and trade groups as well as the nobility. He also maintains a close connection to the horsemen. As a general rule, King Lytyr has been able to keep the nobility happy, the crafting and merchant guilds satisfied, and makes clear his support of the farmers, ranchers, and horsemen of his kingdom. He is known to venture throughout the kingdom to visit farms along the Meander River or goat herders on the heath simply to ensure that things are going well for his people. King Lytyr has two brothers, Joural, who is older and abdicated his position as heir in order to serve as a cleric of Muir, and Brance, who serves in the kingdom's navy. Lytessa, a much younger sister, resides among the riders where she now intends to stay. The king's main residence is in Bret Harth but he spends one month per year in Poiretre and several weeks in Broten as well as additional time with the horsemen.

A court system is in place with a high court that adjudicates crimes of the nobility as well as civil disagreements between merchants and families, and a low court that handles all other crimes. Officially, laws are applied to the nobility and low born equally, though in practice the wealthy and powerful rarely see trial. The horsemen of the Plains of Eauxe have their own tribal laws and justice. Horsemen guilty of minor crimes against other citizens are turned over to their tribe; only in the event of murder or rape of another citizen do horsemen go to a regular court, and in such cases, it is always the high court where they are treated as nobility. Anyone questioning the outcome of a trial can appeal to the king. King Lytyr has never overturned a court ruling, though some kings in the past have favored nobles or friends.

The cities and communities of the heath and along the Meander River have elected mayors and city councils who are sworn to serve the crown and the people. The king remains focused on the kingdom as a whole, particularly in maintaining its navy, and leaves the day-to-day operations of Bret Harth to the city council and mayor.

MILITARY

The military consists of three parts: the Navy, which commands all the ships of war and the ports at Bret Harth and Broten; the General Militia, including all regular troops and traditional cavalry of the kingdom; and the Horsemen of Eauxe, who form their own specialized horseback units. Marines trained in sea and land combat are part of the navy and serve on ships and in some of the harbors. In defense of the kingdom, the Horsemen of Eauxe are led by a horseman who has received additional training and education in modern tactics as well as ways to better incorporate their strengths with that of the general militia and cavalry. Since the time of the Singed Man, North Heath has maintained a strong and steady training regimen for its regular troops and its officers. All officers must pass stringent physical tests before assuming their first command.

The military is led as a whole by a council chaired by the king that consists of two senior admirals, a general from the army, a general from the cavalry, and the senior horsemen in charge of the Horsemen of Eauxe. The council decides where troops and ships are to be stationed as well as the movement and rotation of troops during peacetime, and, of course, oversees mobilization of the military as a whole in the event of an attack.

MAJOR THREATS

Coastal threats include all of the dangers of the Crescent Sea, including piracy, storms, and certain beasts from the depths. While some military leaders fear attack from Foere or Reme, both of these nations have their own concerns. Reme, in particular, has little interest in seizing lands with so little to likely gain. Near the coast and in the area of the Blackrock Mountains, dragons sometimes attack settled areas or ships. Strange forms of undead, likely somehow left behind during numerous battles throughout parts of the kingdom, are found in some areas, though they are usually quickly eliminated.

BRET HARTH, CITY OF (CAPITAL)

Rulers: Mayor Lady Brianna Hearthtracker
Government: democracy (sworn to the monarchy)
Population: 42,670 (27,345 Foerdewaith, 9,350 human mixed ethnicity, 2,670 halfling, 1,290 hill dwarf, 815 high elf, 670 gnome, 320 half-elf, 120 half-orc, 90 other)
Languages: Common, Elven, Gnome, Dwarven, Halfling
Religion: Mitra, Thyr
Resources: fishing, foodstuffs, gold, grain, iron, manufactured goods, trade hub
Technology Level: Medieval

Standing on low cliffs near the ocean, Bret Harth looks over rows of piers and docks that can accommodate ships and boats of all sizes. One of the largest and safest ports along the eastern shore of the Crescent Sea, Bret Harth keeps its tariffs and docking fees lower than the other large cities to attract a steady traffic of merchant vessels. It is also the safest harbor for fishermen working the dangerous sea along Norshore. These factors combine with a wide variety of skilled craftsmen creating trade goods to ensure that Bret Harth remains a bustling city. As the capital city of the Kingdom of the North Heath, Bret Harth also hosts ambassadors of several nearby nations as well as the offices of a number of merchant companies.

Like most large cities, Bret Harth has distinct areas and neighborhoods. The docks and all of the buildings near the water at the foot of the cliffs are known as Oceanside and possess a series of stone towers looking out over the piers and the ocean. These towers hold troops and siege weapons tasked with protecting the city from any naval attack. The largest tower near the center of the docks also contains a barracks for naval sailors on shore leave. Ships of the navy dock at the central piers closest to this tower. Northern piers are larger and are close to the larger warehouses and are generally reserved for merchants and trading vessels. The southern docks provide spots for fishing vessels.

Roads climb from Oceanside past stone warehouses, inns, and other buildings to reach the main city on the cliffs above. The city center closest to the docks is known to residents as Center Harth and hosts a variety of stores, markets, and craftsmen. Sturdy stone buildings of Center Harth frame a number of open squares that contain wide gardens and provide space for open air markets. Ancient foundations here and deep catacombs beneath them predate any written history of the area. Several of the buildings are equally old and made of carefully fitted stone that has withstood millennia of harsh weather.

North of Central Harth is the Quiet District, which consists of ornate homes and gardens along the cliffs with views of the sea. The nobility as well as foreign ambassadors and wealthy merchants and landowners make their homes here. Roads stretch south from Center Harth along solid stone buildings that squat along the cliff line to form the Loud District, home to simple laborers as well as the stores and shops of craftsmen. To the interior of all these districts are the varied buildings of Heathhome, one of the largest districts but generally relegated to the poorer laborers and tradesmen. Buildings here are more sheltered from the coastal storms, so wood structures and wattle-and-daub buildings are mixed with older stone structures.

The present mayor of Bret Harth is Lady Briana Hearthtracker, an aging noblewoman with extensive interests throughout the city. Elections are held every five years but only property owners are allowed to vote. The mayor works closely with advisors to the king to ensure that the city is working smoothly with the military and the navy. Elected mayors must accept their role while making an oath of allegiance to the king in a public ceremony.

BROTEN, CITY OF

Rulers: Mayor Lithan Whalesong
Government: Democracy (sworn to the Monarchy)
Population: 36,090 (25,305 Foerdewaith, 5,250 human mixed ethnicity, 2,120 halfling, 1,310 hill dwarf, 835 gnome, 760 high elf, 205 half-elf, 185 half-orc, 120 other)
Languages: Common, Halfling, Dwarven, Gnome, Elven
Religion: Muir, Thyr
Resources: fishing, foodstuffs, livestock (sheep, goats), trade hub
Technology Level: Medieval

Climbing from a low, rocky shoreline, Broten meets one of the main trade routes heading east toward the Kingdom of Foere and is the main reason, and possibly the only reason, that Foere spent the time and energy to conquer the Kingdom of the North Heath so many centuries ago. Like Bret Harth, tariffs and docking fees are kept low here to help encourage trade. Some of the great merchant houses of the Grand Duchy of Reme do not like the amount of trade Broten syphons away from them, but the grand dukes have long valued the buffer that North Heath serves between them and the central Kingdom of Foere, which leaves the merchant houses with no choice but to grudgingly accept the status quo.

The protected confines of Rimeth Sound and the natural depth of the water make Broten an ideal place to dock and unload large ships. Mayor Lithan Whalesong directed the building of sturdy, well-protected docks and carefully positioned warehouses to help increase the use of the docks and to build traffic through the city. Most of the buildings here are built of stone, with some heavy logs used as frames and support. The docks are protected by large stone towers armed with a variety of siege engines, and chains carefully positioned across the harbor entryway can be raised in the event of an attack.

Lithan Whalesong is the elected mayor of the city and takes care of all normal city activities and planning. Elections are held every five years with only property owners and noblemen with business interests being allowed to vote. A substantial militia outpost here is largely maintained to remind the Kingdom of Foere and the Grand Duchy of Reme that North Heath values its independence. General Cruen the Tall is in charge of all militia activities, while the city guard remains under Lithan's control. Admiral Tareek Darkbreeze is in charge of naval and marine forces in the area but defers to General Cruen for activities within the harbor itself.

While fishing and trade with sheep and goat ranchers of the heath are major industries here, Broten's key to survival is trade and all of the money it brings through the town. As such, it caters to visiting merchants and sailors, providing as many amenities as possible, including fine food, drinks, and suitably comfortable inns.

POIRETRE, CITY OF

Rulers: Mayor Pog Waveheart, Chieftess Lythara Ghostdrake
Government: Democracy/Tribal
Population: 27,030 (13,030 human mixed ethnicity, 10,325 Foerdewaith, 2,085 halfling, 625 hill dwarf, 470 high elf, 215 gnome, 195 half-elf, 85 other)
Languages: Common, Halfling, Elven, Dwarven, Gnome
Religion: Mitra, Solanus, Horseman Faith
Resources: foodstuffs, livestock (cattle, horses), breeding (horses), trade hub
Technology Level: Dark Ages

Poiretre was always a major meeting place for the tribal horsemen of the Plains of Eauxe, but with the armistice with Foere limiting the size of settlements permitted on the plains, Poiretre has grown into the sole meeting hall of the tribesmen as well as a key center of trade at the intersection of several major trade routes. Most of the buildings are constructed of wood, with some of clay brick and a scattering of wattle-and-daub structures. Protective walls around the city are made of heavy stone and boast series of well-protected iron gates that, when opened, can allow hundreds of horsemen to pass in or out of the city at a time. Wide streets allow horsemen to ride through without causing any congestion. Although a significant militia presence is located here and the city walls are very sturdy, the best protection lies in the horsemen who consider this their special grounds. Any attack on the city would be met with a counterattack by skilled, fearsome horsemen likely numbering in the hundreds of thousands.

Trade caravans pass through Poiretre almost continuously and often stop and unload some goods while loading up others for wherever their destination may be. The horsemen bring horses and cattle for trade and sale. Horses of the plains are much sought after as they are stronger and have greater endurance than most other breeds. Cattle sold here are considered to be of the highest quality. Inns, taverns, and a variety of other establishments here cater to traveling merchants and the tribal plainsmen.

There are two rulers here: Mayor Pog Waveheart, who was elected by the property owners and merchants of the city, and Chieftess Lythara Ghostdrake, who was chosen by the plains' tribes to represent their interests. All standard city business is conducted by the mayor while Chieftess Lythara decides all matters involving horsemen. Tribal meetings are held here regularly, with different tribes coming to trade, or argue, with others throughout the year. A greater meeting including representatives of all tribes (usually tribal leaders and all unmarried adults) occurs every two years on the Winter Solstice. At those times, tents stretch away from the city walls for miles, and the city becomes so crowded that even the horsemen choose to walk the streets rather than try to ride through. Centuries ago, this meeting was marked with duels and blood battles. Now, though there will still be a number of fights, and gambling to go with them, the meeting is mainly a time for tribesmen to meet others from other tribes. It is best described as a five-day long drunken party punctuated with dancing and orgies. Those not of the plains who try to participate are dissuaded, usually violently.

HORSEMEN OF EAUXE

The Horsemen of Eauxe roam the plains in individual tribes, tending to their horse and cattle while collecting certain fruits and roots as they travel. Simple but fierce, the horsemen are all trained as warriors from the age they can walk, following traditions created thousands of years ago. Religion here is simple and involves the worship of the land and the sun, although they give no name to their "gods" other than "life and love." They have no temples or specific rites, but their religious leaders easily match the powers of some of the highest clerics of the named gods, so some power must indeed answer their prayers. Contrary to rumors, the horsemen accept and respect magic and support wizards of their tribes. They also treat and care for their wounded, crippled, and aged. Those who can no longer keep up with the tribe are left at an oasis or are settled in Poiretre where any tribes passing through check on them and provide help as needed.

Among the tribes of the plains, women hold authority, and control all the major decisions of a tribe, as well as most of its wealth. When a man marries a woman of the plains, he must take her name and move to her tribe. Any wealth he might have becomes hers and is shared with her tribe. Outsiders can join or marry into a tribe so long as they follow all the traditions of the horsemen. Those who live here for more than a few years tend to develop the same deep connection to the land that the plainsmen possess.

Thousands of years of warfare between tribes turned the Horsemen of the Plains of Eauxe into a greatly feared force that, to the great fortune of kingdoms nearby, never left the plains for more than raids or skirmishes. The plainsmen have a mystical bond to the land here, one that often makes them uncomfortable when leaving it. It is even said that, in ages past, plainsmen would get sick and eventually die if they remained away from the plains for more than a few weeks. Rumors about a great leader who could separate them from the land came true in the form of King Drake Barbossa, who, in an effort to expand the Kingdom of the North Heath, decided to conquer the plains. Initially, he was met with several bruising defeats through which he came to respect the strength and ferocity of the plainsmen. Learning that sometimes tribes avoided war through challenges of single combat, he put his size, strength, and skill as a master swordsman and warrior to the test through challenges to the champions of the individual tribes. When he defeated the final champion, a meeting of all the tribes was convened during which King Drake Barbossa was titled "Great Chief" and the tribes all swore their allegiance.

After the ceremony, the tribal leaders informed him that he had changed their bond to the land, and that the Horsemen of the Plains of Eauxe were now free to leave and conquer at his command. Temptation to expand his kingdom did weigh on him, but in the end, he told them that there could be no more beautiful land than the Plains of Eauxe, and that there was no reason for them to leave but rather he hoped they could live in peace with the rest of his people and work together for a stronger kingdom. Since that time, all children of the royal family are expected to spend at least three years living among the plainsmen to learn their ways and also to understand the mystical bond to the land. Over the centuries, some of the royal family have chosen to stay with the plainsmen, marrying into a tribe or simply remaining with one. The royal line is now mixed with that of the plainsmen, further cementing the loyalty that began when Drake Barbossa respected their traditions.

Leaders of war parties now receive training in modern military tactics and techniques, which makes them an even more dangerous fighting force capable of exploiting the weaknesses in others and enhancing their own strengths. Wizards are encouraged to receive formal training before returning to help their tribes. Religious leaders sometimes meet with clerics of other gods, but they maintain their own traditions regarding passage of knowledge and power of the land to future leaders. In short, the Plainsmen of Eauxe are now a powerful threat to any nearby nation kept in check by one simple fact: They have no desire to leave the plains and see no reason to do so.

GEOGRAPHIC FEATURES AND POINTS OF INTEREST IN THE KINGDOM OF THE NORTH HEATH

THE BRINE HEATH

This great, poisoned salt swamp spoils the coast south of Norshore in the southwestern region of the Kingdom of the North Heath. The oily, briny waters are inimical to life, yet still some plants and creatures struggle to eke out an existence. Some giants and several types of dragons and drakes have been sighted here, and the ruins of the early Hyperborean city of Almanass stand in the northern reaches of the swamp.

MEANDER RIVER

Winding its way through plains and heath, Meander River runs a twisting course from the Blackrock Mountains to the Crescent Sea. Springtime flooding helps maintain a rich soil while the river itself provides water for farming. The river plain extends for several miles in each direction from the river, and most of it is actively farmed. Tilled farmland extends as far from the river as possible, eventually hitting the rocky soil of the heath to the west or the thick grasses of the Plains of Eauxe to the northeast. The river itself provides a home to a variety of freshwater fish, predominantly large river trout, and, strangely, a large number of turtles, from small box turtles to large snapping turtles and even dragon turtles. While the spring floods bring rushing, dangerous waters, the rest of the year the river moves slowly, living up to its name.

The farmers here are a solid, easygoing folk, well in touch with the river and its "moods." While many of the fields begin almost at the water's edge, the farmhouses themselves are usually far away from the flood zone, often not even visible from the river shore itself. Farmers along the river raise corn, rice, wheat, and a number of vegetables as well as a significant amount of cotton.

While their fields grow, Meander farmers fish the river in flat-bottom boats, careful to avoid known territories of some of the larger and more dangerous river denizens. Fall harvest is transported by barge either to the trade route near the Blackrock Mountains or toward the sea to Bret Harth.

The Plainsmen of Eauxe are happy to allow farming along the parts of the river that pass through their plains so long as the farmers share part of their harvest in fair trade and provide clear paths to the river's edge to feed cattle and horses as tribes pass through. Equally, the farmers in these areas are glad to trade with the plainsmen as their simple presence provides additional safety.

NORSHORE

The inhospitable shoreline of the Kingdom of the North Heath is marked on maps as Norshore but sailors familiar with the area have other, far-less-kind names. Cliffs and jagged rocks provide no safe harbor for ships, and the wisest sailors know that even coming near the shore here is hazardous. The mountain range of the island of Lymossus (home of the City-State of Castorhage) to the southwest actually extends northward toward Norshore, but those mountains don't rise far enough from the ocean bottom to break the surface of the Crescent Sea. Alas, a number of those jagged peaks come close enough to the surface to damage the hull of a ship, particularly during large storms with significant swells. The underwater mountain range creates a variable depth in the area near Norshore with some peaks only a few feet below the surface and deep valleys extending thousands of feet down. As a result of differing depths, a wide variety of ocean-going creatures call the area home.

Captains of the fishing boats that work the waters off the coast of Norshore know the area, and its risks, well. The rich fishing makes the hazards worthwhile, but nobody chances sailing close to the coast in stormy seas. Pods of killer whales and other creatures hunt here as well, but only rarely harass boats.

PLAINS OF EAUXE

Thick grasslands extend from an area west of the Meander River to the east beyond Poiretre and north toward Broten. These rolling grasslands may look flat from a distance, but the tall grasses conceal numerous small hills and valleys, many large enough to conceal a number of cattle or horses or armed tribesmen. Thick, lush grasses here support a wide variety of life, all of which is put to use by the roaming tribes of plainsmen. The only real hazard to travel here is those riders, and if they see fit to let travelers pass, there are almost no other dangers to be seen. Any creatures that could pose a threat are taken care of by the wandering tribes. Larger threats merely cause tribes to band together, and even dragons typically do little more than snatch a single isolated horse or animal before being set upon by the fierce plainsmen.

Oases dot the fertile land, some fed by underground springs, others simply consisting of rock-enclosed pools of seasonal rainwater. Over thousands of years of roaming, the tribes of riders have slowly transformed these oases until almost all of the trees and bushes growing near these pools of water are fruit bearing. No tribe passing takes all of the fruits or wild vegetables; they simply acquire what they need and leave the rest for other tribes.

RIMETH SOUND

As one moves inland along Rimeth Sound, the shores to the sides of the inlet slowly lower from high cliffs to a more approachable rocky shore. The bay itself is quite deep and supports a variety of fish, several types of seals, and a number of whales. Merchant ships, fishing boats, and naval vessels belonging to the Kingdom of the North Heath are common sights here. In the past, these have been contested waters with merchant ships from the Grand Duchy of Reme and pirates interfering with some of the traffic. Lately this has not been a problem, but the Kingdom of the North Heath keeps a close eye on the sea lanes here.

KINGDOM OF THE VAST

Capital: Eber
Notable Settlements: Cailin Lee (fortress), Seilo Ford, Streeth Ferry, Tourne
Ruler: King Jior Vast
Government: hereditary monarchy
Population: 935,460 (600,200 Foerdewaith, 197,240 human mixed ethnicity, 79,800 halfling, 22,850 half-elf, 18,900 high elf, 9,350 hill dwarf, 7,120 gnome, 600 half-orc, 300 other)
Monstrous: giants, orcs, goblins, trolls, wyverns, dragons, occasional undead
Languages: Common, Halfling, Elven, Dwarven, Gnome
Religion: Mitra, Freya, Mithras, Mick O'Delving, Stryme, Thyr, Muir, Dwerfater, Telophus, Ceres, Yenomesh
Resources: manufactured goods, grain, foodstuffs, spices, spirits (wine, brandy), livestock (cattle, sheep, goats), ironwork
Currency: Vast
Technology Level: Medieval

Stretching from the fortress of Cailin Lee at the southern border past Seilo Ford to the north and wedged between the Blackrock Mountains to the east and the lands around the Worntooth Peaks and the Crescent Sea to the west, the Kingdom of the Vast — sometimes also referred to as Kingdom of Vast — is a lightly-populated nation with good farmland and reasonably productive mines in the Worntooth Peaks and the western Blackrock Mountains. Now mainly known for its skilled artisans, the Kingdom of the Vast and its people remain haunted by memories of a time just 400 years ago when the realm was overrun with the undead minions of the vampire-lord that had enslaved their lands.

HISTORY AND PEOPLE

Thousands of years ago, an ancient people known now to scholars as simply "the Vast" lived in these lands, and left behind intricate, abstract stone sculptures dotting the landscape that range from five to 15 feet in size, and which, despite the passing of ages, seem even today to be newly carved, untouched by time or attempts at destruction. Nothing of this forgotten culture remains other than these sculptures, no hint of how they were made, or what magic was used to preserve them for so long. Those living here now claim to be descendants of the Vast, though the truth of this remains uncertain.

In the days of the height of the power of the Kingdom of Foere, these lands were the Duchy of Kear, held in fealty to the overking. When the overking gathered the Second Great Crusade to retake the Sacred Table in Libynos from the Huun, a vampire-lord known as the Singed Man arose and took advantage of the absence of so many warriors taking part in the crusade to conquer Kear. He named himself its Infernal Tyrant in 2970 I.R. King Prudus II of Castorhage, who was traveling through Kear at the time, was captured by the vampire's forces and slain. But until the crusaders returned, there was little that could be done to dislodge the Singed Man and his undead army. Finally, six years after the Sacred Table was retaken, the overking charged Battle-Duke Ormand of the Rampart with freeing Kear from the Singed Man. In 2977 I.R., the Battle-Duke's forces met those of the vampire lord in battle. Taken by surprise by undead rising from the banks of the Meander, Ormand and his Foerdewaith army were crushed by the Infernal Tyrant at the Battle of Seilo Ford. Worse, the battle-duke himself was slain and turned into a vampire spawn, becoming the servant and general of the Singed Man. For more than 150 years, the vampire-lord and his servant terrorized the lands of Kear. The exhausted forces of Foerdewaith and Castorhage could do little but watch.

The reign of the Infernal Tyrant finally ended in 3128 I.R. when Sir Varral the Blessed slew the Singed Man and Ormand. Foere reclaimed the Duchy of Kear, and a nephew of the overking was appointed duke in Eber. However, Castorhage seized the port of Tarry as recompense for the loss of their king. Foere decided not to challenge this annexation, and Tarry remained a Castorhagi dependency ever since, leaving the Kingdom of the Vast without a port on the Crescent Sea.

Fealty to Foere did not last long, however. The Foerdewaith Wars of Succession began in 3213 I.R., and Duke Oden of Kear declared independence from Courghais in 3224 I.R., renaming the duchy the Kingdom of the Vast. By the next year, the Kingdom of the North Heath had also declared its independence, and both nations began their battle for freedom from Foere's rule. Years of battles and skirmishes came to an end with the signing of an armistice between Foere, Vast, and North Heath in 3245 I.R., negotiated with the help of the City-State of Castorhage.

In an attempt to separate themselves further from Foere and Kear's troubled past, the new royal family changed its surname to Vast and made a concerted effort to connect themselves and their people to the Vast of old. In truth, these efforts were made in large part to help the people forget the years of brutality under the Singed Man and the years of war with Foere and to usher in a new era of confidence and growth. Recently, these efforts seem to have had some success, and the population of the kingdom is finally starting to grow again, though it is nowhere near what it was before the reign of the Infernal Tyrant. But even now, the predations and destruction brought by the Singed Man are not discussed in Vast, at least not in public.

RELIGION

Eber is home to a temple and large university constructed by the monks of Yenomesh, while other temples throughout the realm are dedicated to various good or neutrally-aligned gods. Almost all of the active temples in Vast were constructed after the brutal reign of the Singed Man, during which most temples were desecrated and destroyed.

TRADE AND COMMERCE

The soils of the lands of Vast produce a variety of crops and other foodstuffs which, given the kingdom's relatively low population, results in a good surplus for sale to other nations. While its mines in the Worntooths and Blackrocks may not be extensive, there are enough gem, iron, silver, and gold mines to support steady industries. Artisans and craftsmen in the cities take these raw materials and manufacture finished products that are traded or sent by caravan to the kingdom's bordering nations. All such trade must pass through one its neighbors, however, as Vast lacks a port on the Crescent Sea ever since Castorhage annexed Tarry following the defeat of the Infernal Tyrant. While the king of the Vast would like to establish a new port, the only possible location on the coast north of the Worntooths would undoubtedly provoke the wrath of the Blighters. As a result, no moves toward settling such a port have yet been made.

LOYALTIES AND DIPLOMACY

The Kingdom of the Vast remains largely free of outside influence due to a combination of wise treaty choices, natural terrain, and the fact that their most hostile neighbor, the Principality of Olduvar, is for the most part badly managed and under constantly changing leadership. Periodic skirmishes occur on the border with Olduvar, but the defenses of Cailin Lee and Eber have been more than sufficient to protect the homeland. Right now, it is unlikely Olduvar will mount a major attack any time soon, but Vast remains prepared. The City-State of Castorhage pays close attention to the politics and policies of Vast because its main trade port, Tarry, is completely surrounded by lands claimed by the Kingdom of the Vast. A close, friendly relationship benefits Castorhage, as it can then focus on its own internal problems without being concerned about the safety of Tarry.

King Jior Vast maintains healthy and positive trade and political agreements with Castorhage, the Iron Kingdom of Dorriden, the Barony of Baile and the Kingdom of the North Heath. It has cautious, but fair, trade agreements with the Kingdom of Foere. No trade or political agreements exist with the Principality of Olduvar, however, as the leadership of that country is not trusted. Most citizens of Vast consider the leaders of Olduvar to be insane and beyond understanding.

GOVERNMENT

While known to be egotistical and self-serving, King Jior Vast's rule is marked by his ability to follow the good advice of his wise and experienced counselors and advisors. He maintains complete control over appointments to various positions of power throughout his kingdom but does his best to choose well-qualified individuals to govern his cities and villages. Military decisions are left predominantly to his top military counselors and generals. Minor government officials and offices are generally filled with nobles or wealthy merchants who support the crown.

The court system is complex partly due to old traditions and, in part, because it benefits the wealthier nobility and landowners. The courts are split into Low Court, Courtesy Court, High Court, and Lion's Court. Low Courts handle criminal proceedings against anyone not considered to be of noble birth. Courtesy Courts handle financial or civil disputes of all types, but generally it costs money to file a grievance in the Courtesy Court, which usually reserves its use to the wealthy. Poor citizens who believe they have a case can appeal to certain legal representatives in the hopes that those barristers will pay the costs of filing a Courtesy Court case with the plans of recouping their costs and expenses in a final settlement, though this is extremely rare and when it does occur, there is often a different sponsor in the background trying to inconvenience a rival. High Courts decide criminal complaints against nobility while the Lion's Court decides criminal complaints against the military and any accusations of treason against the crown. All decisions can be appealed to the king, who has been known to grant clemency to some nobility and certain friends.

MILITARY

When Duke Oden of Kear declared independence from Foere, he benefited from the Foerdewaith custom of a well-ordered military. To this day, the soldiers of the Vast maintain strong traditions with intensive training and education, and are very well-organized. While there are some political disputes within the military ranks at times, generals have a great deal of power and influence throughout the kingdom, arising from their uniform competence as well as King Jior Vast's preference to allow the generals complete latitude in running the military as they choose. Vast is land-locked and has no navy, but its infantry and mounted knights are said to be among the finest in the Lost Lands.

MAJOR THREATS

Vast is under constant threat of attack by the Principality of Olduvar and is highly vigilant in that direction. A threat not often recognized is that posed by Castorhage, which controls the only port on the Crescent Sea available to the Vasters. Fortunately, the Blighters tend to be highly focused on their own intrigues and show little interest in interfering with Vast. But were their commercial interests to diverge for some reason, the city-state could inflict a great deal of pain on the kingdom. Occasional incursions of humanoids and other creatures come from the Worntooths and the Blackrock Mountains from time to time, though neither has posed much of a threat to the central parts of the kingdom.

WILDERNESS AND ADVENTURE

Most of the kingdom is now relatively safe. The years of dominance by the Singed Man, followed by years of warfare, actually reduced the population of monstrous creatures in the region. Adventurers might seek out the ancient ruins rumored to be hiding the Worntooth Peaks knowing that these mountains are home to hill giants, orcs, dragons, and other creatures. Some areas south of Eber close to Olduvar are unpopulated and wild and act as a sort of buffer zone between the two nations. Ruins of ancient temples and villages dot the area, buildings and towns so thoroughly destroyed by the Singed Man that they were never rebuilt.

EBER, CITY OF (CITY OF SPIRES, SPEAR OF THE VAST) (CAPITAL)

Rulers: King Jior Vast
Government: hereditary monarchy
Population: 84,980 (45,040 Foerdewaith, 18,250 human mixed ethnicity, 6,220 halfling; 5,720 high elf; 5,150 hill dwarf; 3,090 gnome; 860 half-elf; 430 half-orc, 120 orc, 100 other)
Languages: Common, Halfling, Elven, Dwarven, Gnome
Religion: Mitra, Freya, Mithras, Mick O'Delving, Stryme, Thyr, Muir, Dwerfater, Telophus, Ceres, Yenomesh
Resources: manufactured goods, ironwork, spices, foodstuffs, trade hub, banking
Technology Level: Medieval

Colorful towers topped by wind-blown pennants thrust up from the center of the capital city of the Vast, contrasting strongly with the tall, black, glassy stone city walls, quarried from the Worntooth Peaks. Within those walls, Eber appears to be the happiest place in the world. Visitors and travelers — not just citizens — who come to the city are overcome with joy. This happiness pervades everything. The sunlight seems brighter in Eber, the sky bluer, flowers smell better and are always in bloom, food tastes better. Nobody can explain why this is so. Some claim it has to do with the ancient Vast sculptures scattered about the city, but others say it is something in the air or water, while still more entertain conspiracies or some sort of evil at work, or even some sinister holdover from the vampire lords that once ruled these lands. Whatever the case may be, Eber is a happy place, and the happiness even remains with travelers for some time after they leave.

Strange though it may be, the sense of happiness here does not affect people's work or habits; they are just happy doing whatever it is they are doing. Perhaps some might do their jobs even better than they would otherwise, but the work still gets done, products are still made and sold, the streets are still patrolled, and, yes, thefts, robberies, and other crimes still occur. Several sages claim that the wide diversity in architectural styles and building materials used in Eber is a side effect of the happiness here, but whatever the case may be, the city contains a variety of beautiful homes and buildings in every possible architectural style. Massive walled mansions belonging to wealthy merchants can be surrounded by smaller buildings and apartments that somehow all seem to fit together.

Eber has the highest concentration in the kingdom of the abstract sculptures left by the long-gone Vast, spread throughout the city seemingly at random. The most well-known is a bright orange monolith carved in the shape of a spire standing almost 20 feet tall at the very center of the city near the king's castle. It twists toward the sky in complicated spirals that most find difficult and even disturbing to look at closely, as if the geometry is somehow wrong. It has been nicknamed the "Sunsucker" which, some would say, is an example of why a seven-year-old prince should not be allowed to name things. Yet the name is somehow apt, as the twisting spire appears to absorb the light of the setting sun before then emitting it in a soft glow throughout the night.

As the capital of the Kingdom of the Vast, Eber is home to embassies from nearby nations. Craftsmen here turn out elegant jewelry as well as high fashion clothing and ornate furniture, while nearby wineries and distilleries provide fine wines and liquors for elegant dining. Trade and crafts are Eber's primary lifeblood, and the strange sense of happiness that overcomes its visitors helps draw them back, contributing to the growth and prosperity of a city once decimated by the brutal control of the Singed Man.

UNIVERSITY OF THE VAST

Monks of Yenomesh, God of Glyphs and Writing, set up a small university called the University of the Vast and dedicated it to advanced studies. They accept some students outside of their devotion for a hefty fee but provide advisors and counsel to the king at no cost. Origins of the university are somewhat clouded as nobody outside the monks seems to know exactly when it was formed, how long it has been here, or the extent of the renowned library within its broad stone walls.

One thing that is known is that the monks and all their books remained well-hidden throughout the years the Singed Man controlled this region, only reappearing several years after his defeat. How and where they were hidden is unknown to any but the monks themselves.

SEILO FORD, CITY OF

Rulers: Earl Jalen Touret
Government: feudalism
Population: 19,562 (10,713 Foerdewaith, 5,220 human mixed ethnicity, 1,322 halfling, 928 mountain dwarf, 716 high elf, 434 gnome, 169 half-elf, 60 other)
Languages: Common, Halfling, Dwarven, Elven, Gnome
Religion: Mitra, Freya, Mithras, Mick O'Delving, Stryme, Dwerfater, Telophus, Ceres,
Resources: grain, foodstuffs, livestock (sheep, goats, cattle), manufactured goods, trade hub
Technology Level: High Middle Ages

Seilo Ford stands at a broad ford over the southern branch of the Meander River on the crossroads of the main trade routes from Tarry and the City-State of Castorhage to the west, to the Kingdom of the North Heath and the heart of Foere to the east, and to Streeth Ferry and the rest of Vast to the south. Buildings constructed of massive stone blocks squat like toads along the roads coming in and out of the city and huddle over the central square. More recent wood-frame buildings and wattle-and-daub structures fill in some of the spaces in between. Designers and builders of the original stone buildings have long been forgotten, though some say they haunt the equally ancient cisterns and aqueducts of Seilo Ford.

Merchant caravan traffic here is steady throughout most of the year and makes this small city crucial to the interests of the Kingdom of the Vast. Earl Jalen Touret keeps careful control over the city and ensures the trade routes are well guarded and that the various craft guilds and merchant alliances pay their dues and stay in line. His active management of the city causes some to bristle, but he holds his position as a direct appointment from the king and firmly believes that his actions are in the best interest of his king and his country.

While some of the buildings in the city seem extremely ancient, there is little to distinguish them but age. Their design is plain, uninspired, and often repeated from structure to structure. No artwork or writing left behind indicates who originally built them, though the scattering of buildings and the series of aqueducts beyond the city walls suggests that at one point the city was far larger. Some speculate that these buildings, like the strange sculptures throughout the kingdom, may have been created by the Vast, though most scholars discount this theory since the wildly artistic sculptures seem inconsistent with such boring and uninspiring buildings. It has also been noted that none of the strange abstract sculptures found in other parts of the kingdom are found within the confines of Seilo Ford or anywhere nearby.

Nearby farms along the branch of the Meander River heading south along the trade route toward Streeth Ferry provide the city with a wide variety of fruits, grains, and vegetables and nearby grazing lands provide sheep, goats, and some cattle. Strict control of the guilds here by Earl Touret hasn't quashed the activity of the artisans due to the vast amount of trade flowing through the city, though several guild leaders have in fact penned complaints to the crown.

Two miles upriver on the west bank of the Meander is the battlefield where the Foerdewaith forces under Battle-Duke Ormand fell to the Singed Man. Only stunted grasses now grows where the battle was fought, and it is said that the cries of the fallen can be heard on moonless nights in the breeze over the river.

STREETH FERRY, CITY OF

Rulers: Lady Quereth Oden
Government: feudalism
Population: 28,919 (17,100 Foerdewaith, 6,100 human mixed ethnicity, 2,169 halfling, 1,506 hill dwarf, 983 high elf, 723 gnome, 248 half-elf, 90 other)
Languages: Common, Halfling, Dwarven, Elven, Gnome
Religion: Mitra, Mithras, Mick O'Delving, Thyr, Muir, Dwerfater, Telophus, Ceres,
Resources: grain, foodstuffs, iron and ironwork, gold, semi-precious gems, manufactured goods, trade hub
Technology Level: Medieval

Once merely a ferry station enabling travelers on the trade road to pass over the southern branch of the Meander River, Streeth Ferry has grown into a small city spanning both sides of the river and the massive bridge that now spans the river. Built high enough to conquer spring flood waters and wide enough to allow caravans across in both directions, the bridge is a marvel of engineering and design. Trade caravans and wagons must pay a toll to cross the bridge, while city residents and lone travelers do not. Those wishing to avoid the toll can still take a ferry but, in general, the fees are almost the same. Although the bridge was constructed more than 100 years ago under the king's command, city residents talk about it as if it was a recent accomplishment of their own.

Crafting guilds are very strong here as the various woodworkers, metalsmiths, smelters, leatherworkers, and textile workers have found Streeth Ferry to be an excellent place to ply their trade. A road north of the city leads to mines in the Blackrock Mountains that produce a modest amount of iron ore, gold, and some semi-precious gemstones. Traffic on the roads provide easy trade for raw materials and for the sale of goods. After a few growth problems, city leaders decided to confine all of the industries that might create smoke or foul odors to the northern shore where prevailing winds take the noxious fumes away from the city. Tanneries, metal working, smelting, and similar crafts are kept north of the river while most residences and other businesses remain to the south.

Lady Quereth Oden, an elderly dowager, provides a gentle but firm guiding hand to this rapidly growing city in the name of her king. Her love for her city and her king come through in her discussions with the various trade guilds, other nobility, and city workers. Focused on growing the city and its trade, she makes certain that merchants and travelers of all types are made welcome. A well-loved, caring, charismatic leader, Lady Oden has strong support throughout the city.

Streeth Ferry boasts a number of the strange abstract stone sculptures found in different locations around the Kingdom of the Vast. The city square is built up around several such sculptures, with benches provided for viewing them and a variety of street venders selling various snacks and drinks nearby. Proud as the residents might be of these sculptures, they are considered relatively minor when compared to others found elsewhere in the kingdom.

TOURNE, CITY OF

Rulers: Lady Sarina White
Government: feudalism
Population: 16,158 (6,397 Foerdewaith, 4,870 human mixed ethnicity, 1,478 halfling, 1,397 high elf, 1,108 gnome, 532 mountain dwarf, 293 half-elf, 103 half-orc, 50 other)
Languages: Common, Halfling, Elven, Gnome, Dwarven
Religion: Mitra, Freya, Mithras, Mick O'Delving, Thyr, Muir, Dwerfater, Telophus, Ceres
Resources: grain, foodstuffs, livestock (cattle, sheep), spirits (wine, brandy), manufactured goods, trade
Technology Level: High Middle Ages

While the main trade route from Eber turns north from Tourne toward Streeth Ferry, a second, equally wide and well-maintained road runs south toward the fortress of Cailin Lee, down which provisions for the garrison there are regularly sent. Tourne itself, however, is little more than a stop along the way, a provisioning spot for merchant caravans and military supply trains. Few craftsmen are here, and most of the area is involved in farming of some type, with some vineyards farther out near the base of the Blackrock Mountains. The few taverns and inns do a steady business catering to the merchants and soldiers on their way to someplace else.

Positioned on a high plain not far from the foothills of the Blackrock Mountains, Tourne is in one of those locations where it is either uncomfortably hot or uncomfortably cold, and seldom in between. When it rains, it does so for days at a time, and rather than light showers it is usually subject to driving storms. Nearby farmlands and grazing pastures do well enough in the mixed weather, but few merchants or travelers prefer to endure it for very long.

The buildings, and even the people themselves, are a mix of old and new. Several stone homes and warehouses here are at least centuries old, built from sturdy stone that must have been quarried from the distant Blackrock Mountains. Other structures are newer wood-frame buildings or small homes made with clay bricks. Citizens range from young children to the oldest of the old. It seems that, barring accidents, people living in Tourne can reach a very advanced age. Lady Sarina White does her best to talk this up among the nobility and visiting merchants when she can, attempting to attract more money to the region she now controls in the name of the king, but her efforts are generally laughed away. Alas, there is no real reason for the present number of aged in the city other than a combination of luck and the fact that many of the craftsmen that once lived here have since moved to Streeth Ferry where the trade and profits are better.

One of the few interesting features of Tourne is an ancient temple in the northern portion of the city. The ornate stone structure has features similar to the sculptures hailing back to the Vast, but somehow seems both older and younger. Enterprising clerics have tried to consecrate the grounds to their own gods but have all met in failure. Covered with decorations geometric and abstract in nature, it is impossible to determine what god this temple was constructed for, but those investigating it have sensed no evil emanations, so the temple is simply left alone. It is one of the few ancient temples left intact during the brutal rule of the Singed Man.

CAILIN LEE, FORTRESS OF

Ruler: General Moorkal Redmane
Government: military
Population: 18,793 (14,500 Foerdewaith, 1,400 human mixed ethnicity, 1,280 mountain dwarf, 825 halfling, 525 high elf, 127 half-orc, 86 half-elf, 50 other)
Languages: Common, Dwarven, Halfling, Elven
Technology Level: Medieval

Built to address the constant — and annoying — threat posed by the Principality of Olduvar, Cailin Lee is a massive, squat fortress on a large hill overlooking the lands to the south. The king and his advisors know that Olduvar is a constant threat and ensure that the fortress is well maintained and provided with the most modern of armaments and training. The City-State of Castorhage prefers a free and independent Kingdom of the Vast next door to them over any other conquering country and, to that end, provides Cailin Lee with the siege engines and protection it needs to ensure its success.

Dwarves of the Iron Kingdom of Dorriden constructed the walls and buildings of the entire fortress several centuries ago and added to the few structures that were already here. Now expanded to encompass wells, field lands, and even grazing areas, the fortress covers an area the size of many small cities. The tall, crenellated walls and towers provide a wide view of the surrounding area and are patrolled and monitored by trained militia. Both the towers and the walls have shielded placements for ballistae, trebuchet, and other engines of war. General Redmane keeps the fortress in an admirable state of readiness. Forces here regularly patrol the region but are under orders to avoid any conflicts.

Cailin Lee has repelled a number of assaults from the Principality of Olduvar over the years, both direct attacks upon its walls and incursions of forces that sought to invade the Vast though paths that avoided the fortress altogether. Since the dwarven improvements were completed, the fortress has never fallen.

WORNTOOTH PEAKS

This broken jumble of volcanic mountains on the coast of the Crescent Sea is actually part of a chain of mountains running beneath the water to the Isle of Lymossus. Years of wind and rain have worn down these glassy mountains without softening their sharp and jagged lines. A scrabble of bushes, grasses and trees cling precariously to the sandy dirt filling the valleys and low areas between the high peaks, along with some high lakes and streams. Strewn through these mountains are occasional green and peaceful areas, areas cultivated by the orcs and giants that make the valleys between the ragged mountain tops their home.

Ruins of ancient cities and buildings can be found within these jagged peaks, but some of these ruins now provide homes for hill giants, orcs, and various other creatures hiding from the dragons and rocs also making these mountains their home.

IRON KINGDOM OF DORRIDEN

Capital: Iron Hall
Notable Settlements: Grimm Fortress, Arlonne (Barony of Baile)
Principalities: Barony of Baile
Ruler: High Thane Thornir Ironskull
Government: clan leadership (special)
Population: 781,300 (626,900 mountain dwarf, 81,200 Foerdewaith, 63,990 human mixed ethnicity, 5,010 halfling, 2,720 gnome, 670 high elf, 490 half-elf, 150 half-orc, 170 other)
Monstrous: orcs, goblins, hobgoblins, trolls, giants, wyverns, dragons
Languages: Dwarven, Common, Elven
Religion: Strym; Dwerfater, Father of Dwarves; Vergrimm

Earthsblood, Keeper of the Mines; Dre'uain the Lame; Belon the Wise; other good or neutral-aligned dwarven gods

Resources: copper, gold, iron, lead, mithral, platinum, silver, gems, ironwork, metal work, quarry stone, stonework, foodstuffs, livestock

Currency: Iron Crown, mixed

Technology Level: Renaissance

Dwarves of the Iron Kingdom claim the full range of the Blackrock Mountains and the lands of the Barony of Baile and the Genev Gap as their own. In truth, the fertile lands of the barony and the mountain passes important for trade are the only areas actively patrolled and defended. Dwarves living within Iron Hall generally delve deeper into the ground rather than exploring the surrounding mountains. Through a series of treaties, they have also agreed to permit mining in the foothills of the Blackrocks by the County of Roy, the Kingdom of the North Heath, and the Kingdom of the Vast, so long as those mines remain relatively shallow and don't impinge upon the historical territory of the dwarves. Outside the area the dwarves patrol, the mountainsides are wild and often home to perilous monsters such as giants, rocs, and dragons.

HISTORY AND PEOPLE

The Blackrock Mountains are home to the Ironskull clan of mountain dwarves, the most powerful of the mountain clans commonly encountered by the humans of Akados. It is said their ancestors moved here in ages past, after the original dwarves arriving in the Lost Lands divided into the Great Mountain Clans. The Ironskulls are known as renowned giant fighters with noteworthy heroic sons such as Dramen Ironskull (who was among the first of the Akadonian peoples to encounter the Xha'en) and Grimmbold Ironskull (who battled giants among the Forlorn Mountains). Its most famous scion perhaps was legendary Old Thane Col, who ruled the clan for well over 250 years until the venerable thane disappeared at sea 100 years ago with a rare dwarven armada as he sought to plumb the depths of the fabled Dragon Temple of the island of West Talon.

The ancestral hold of the Ironskull clan is Iron Hall, located deep in the Blackrock Mountains. From here they rule what has become known as the Iron Kingdom of Dorriden (a corruption of a compound word that approximately means "dwarven citadel"). They ensure the safety of key mountain passes but otherwise leave most of the mountaintops and vales to the creatures that choose to settle there, so long as they do not threaten the dwarven realm.

The Barony of Baile is a recent addition to the kingdom, one made through treaty rather than conquest. Feeling abandoned by Foere and at the whim of the mad rulers of the Principality of Olduvar, the baron of Baile came to the dwarves seeking a treaty or other arrangement for his barony's protection. Recognizing threats to the Barony of Baile as a potential threat to their own trade, and impressed by the baron's concern for his people, High Thane Thornir and the clan council offered him an equal seat on the clan council in exchange for his oath of fealty to the Iron Kingdom, an oath he was more than happy to give.

The newly expanded kingdom suffered a few growing pains and some increased tensions, but as time has passed, the relationship between the established dwarven kingdom and its new, predominantly human "clan" has improved to the benefit of both.

Of late, a great red wyrm has been seen flying among the peaks of the Blackrock Mountains, circling near the entrances to the Iron Kingdom but never landing. A few fear that this beast may be from the legendary Dragon Temple of West Talon, come to avenge some insult given by Old Thane Col years ago.

RELIGION

The patron of the Ironskull clan is Strym (also known as Stryme) and accordingly the Great Chapel in Iron Hall is dedicated to the god of strength, but many dwarves choose to worship other gods, and accordingly temples or altars can be found throughout Iron Hall dedicated to Dwerfater, Vergrimm Earthsblood, and yet other dwarven

gods. Worship of any evil gods or demon lords is prohibited in the Iron Kingdom. Humans of the Barony of Baile worship Belon the Wise as the first Baron Baile appointed to oversee this area by the overking of Foere was a worshipper of Belon the Wise.

TRADE AND COMMERCE

The Iron Kingdom of Dorriden produces a variety of metals, metal items, and weaponry and armor as well as gems and jewelry made and mined in Iron Hall. Skilled stonemasons work within the kingdom but also are engaged by the royalty of other nations to build their most important castles, palaces, and citadels. The addition of the Barony of Baile expanded trade to include a wide variety of grains, fruits, and other food items. The kingdom supports a strong militia as well as the construction of new fortifications along trade routes out of the mountains and now to help protect Baile.

LOYALTIES AND DIPLOMACY

Trade agreements with the City-State of Castorhage, the Kingdom of the Vast, the Kingdom of the North Heath, and some of the principalities of the Kingdom of Foere keep the nation and its economy strong. Significant tensions exist with the Principality of Olduvar, and tensions are growing with the overking in Foere related in large part to the Barony of Baile joining the Iron Kingdom. Nearby principalities of Foere continue to honor their trade agreements and Olduvar has never been thought of as a trustworthy trading partner.

The dwarven nation has no need or desire to expand and the provisions from the barony combined with the size and military might of the dwarves make the Iron Kingdom a formidable opponent that few have any desire to get into conflict with. All dwarves — and now that the Barony of Baile has joined the Iron Kingdom, all human citizens of the kingdom (male and female) — must spend two years in training in the militia and be prepared to serve the nation in a time of war.

GOVERNMENT

The Ironskull clan in the Iron Kingdom consists of 11 subclans (the royal Ironskull subclan, Ironbreaker, Whitehelm, Axebreaker, Craghold, Hammerfist, ForgeFire, Goldenbeard, Wolfbane, Silvercliff, and Anvilbreaker), and now the Barony of Baile. Each subclan appoints a representative to the clan council, who is usually its clan chief. The clan chief of the royal Ironskull subclan is high thane, which usually passes by descent to the eldest child (whether male or female). The baron himself serves on the council as representative of Baile.

A host of guards made up of members of all subclans enforce the laws of the kingdom, and a single court system is used to adjudicate civil and criminal complaints. The clan council appoints nine judges to the senior court, who in turn choose the judges for 12 lower courts. Court cases can be appealed to the senior court, and then, ultimately to the clan council itself. Appeals are rare. Most small cases are handled within a subclan. The court system is reserved for larger disputes or crimes.

With the exception of the predominantly human barony, other races making their home in the kingdom have no direct representation in the government or military, but citizens and visitors of all races are treated equally under the law. While some individual dwarves do bear ill will toward other races, the Iron Kingdom as a whole is welcoming to other races under the philosophy that a unified kingdom can more easily defeat powerful creatures such as dragons and hostile giants, allowing all to prosper.

MILITARY

Each subclan is expected to provide "regulars" to the military based on the size of the subclan. In addition, all citizens, which for the Iron Kingdom means dwarves and humans of the Barony of Baile, must serve two years in the militia for training. All citizens are expected to come to arms in a time of war. The high thane or the clan council can declare war or declare a military emergency, which generally involves a dragon attack or some sort of attack on one of the passes in the mountains, which causes the generals to muster troops and prepare for action. The military is under the command of the high thane, who delegates various responsibilities to several generals. The two most senior are the Lord of Stone, who oversees tactics and training, and the Lord of Steel, who is placed in charge of the Grimm Fortress and is responsible for immediate defense of the realm. A majority of the active regulars reside at the Grimm Fortress with additional small forces at locations in the Barony of Baile and larger garrisons at Iron Hall where militia training takes place.

MAJOR THREATS

Treasure-hungry dragons are always a threat to isolated dwarven settlements and mines, but any attacks on the Iron Kingdom are met with an overwhelming response. The military technology and equipment the dwarves have allow them to mount successful attacks against predatory dragons and giants in the mountains. Reports from those who have seen the great red wyrm circling the entrances to the Iron Kingdom, however, tell of a dragon the size of which has not been seen for ages.

The Principality of Olduvar has always caused difficulty, forcing the Iron Kingdom to look toward other nearby nations for trade. The Kingdom of Foere is extremely displeased with the loss of the Barony of Baile to the Iron Kingdom, but the tensions it has with the borderlands to the east and the military might of the dwarves prevent it from acting directly.

WILDERNESS AND ADVENTURES

With the dwarves delving downward into the mountains and leaving the surface largely unpatrolled and uncared for, a variety of creatures can be found in the Blackrock Mountains. The Ruins of Tiro'en attract some attention, as do tales of lost dwarven cities (untrue) and mines (partially true). A number of dragons have hidden lairs deep in the mountains, some of which have simply been lost to time. Explorers discovering any treasures are wise to keep them secret as the Iron Kingdom taxes such discoveries at a hefty 50%.

IRON HALL, CITY OF (CAPITAL)

Ruler: High Thane Thornir Ironskull
Government: clan leadership (special)
Population: 544,000 (526,600 mountain dwarf, 7,220 Foerdewaith, 5,580 human mixed ethnicity, 2,340 gnome, 2,180 halfling, 80 other)
Languages: Dwarven, Common, Elven
Religion: Strym; Dwerfater, Father of Dwarves; Vergrimm Earthsblood, Keeper of the Mines; Dre'uain the Lame; other good or neutral-aligned dwarven gods
Resources: copper, gold, iron, lead, mithral, platinum, silver, gems, ironwork, metal work, quarry stone, stonework, foodstuffs, livestock
Technology Level: Renaissance

Carved out of the mountains, the broad halls and passages of Iron Hall stretch and wind their way beneath the surface. The city branches its way beneath the mountains where some massive caverns and halls demonstrate the skill of the dwarven stonemasons and architects. The Ironskull clan that calls this home possesses a diversity and a calm confidence that most other enclaves of mountain dwarves do not demonstrate. This has allowed all to prosper here, and that prosperity enables the dwarves here to deal with other races with the conviction that their knowledge, skill, and kingdom shall endure all challenges.

HISTORY AND PEOPLE

When the subclans of the Ironskulls initially joined forces to form the Iron Kingdom of Dorriden, they had many small settlements throughout the Blackrock Mountains, which made them easier prey for dragons, giants, and other creatures. The decision to move all of the subclans to the hold of the royal Ironskull subclan provided greater strength and safety to the fledgling kingdom. One underground city was easier to defend and easier for the dwarves to expand. Initially, the city was subdivided into different areas for each subclan, but as the centuries have gone by, they have become closer and work together on a more even basis so these divisions are often in name only.

Shafts extend in a variety of directions deep into the mountains and allow access to mining areas as well as providing venting for the various forges that are hard at work near the city center. The protection afforded by the underground city, and the peaceful conditions at work, allowed the city and the kingdom to flourish and grow. The underground nature and strange manner in which it has grown and spread into the mountain makes it almost impossible for outsiders to gauge the true size of Iron Hall, but it is undoubtedly one of the largest cities in the Lost Lands, something the dwarves prefer to keep a secret from outsiders.

The strange history of the formation of the Blackrock Mountains provides the opportunity to mine a variety of metals and gems. Most of the mines can be reached through tunnels, but some dwarves do still travel overland to mine more distant areas. Iron Hall is known for some of the finest weapons and purest metals throughout the land. The situation of relative peace here has allowed dwarven smiths and craftsmen to focus entirely on their art creating unequalled metalwork that others can only strive to match. Stoneworkers and masons here are equally skilled and often called upon to fulfil contracts in other nations while also expanding and supporting the ever-growing underground city.

While officially the city and the Iron Kingdom are welcoming to all races, almost all non-dwarves live in a region just off the central artery through the city in a neighborhood that was originally for the clanless. Other races receive very little outright discrimination otherwise and are allowed free passage through all safe areas of the city.

THE GRIMM FORTRESS

Ruler: General Kord Axebreaker
Government: military
Population: 45,600 (42,150 mountain dwarf, 2,100 Foerdewaith, 1,350 human mixed ethnicity)
Languages: Dwarven, Common
Technology Level: Renaissance

This massive stone fortress is a sign of dwarven ingenuity and skill as well as a symbol of the power of the Iron Kingdom of Dorriden. The fortress itself is constructed along a long mountain ridge and gives a long view over Genev Gap to the south and oversees the rich farmlands of the Barony of Baile. Nearby farmers are expected to flee to the safety of its walls in the event of any sort of attack, so the fortress itself has far more housing than its troops actually require. The militia here is made up entirely of dwarven and human warriors, with humans making up less than a tenth of the contingent.

The thick, imposing walls stretch along the mountain walls for hundreds of yards and are punctuated with tall towers armed with powerful ballistae and other weapons capable of taking down dragons, giants, or foreign armies. General Kord Axebreaker and his staff keep the troops on high alert with constant training drills that under many circumstances could lead to complaints and grumbling, but the general's charisma and friendly nature to all of his troops keeps them dedicated to their jobs.

GEOGRAPHIC FEATURES AND POINTS OF INTEREST IN THE REGION OF THE IRON KINGDOM OF DORRIDEN

BLACKROCK MOUNTAINS

Some cataclysm of the ancient past brought forth a cluster of volcanoes spewing molten stone and metal to form the tall and forbidding Blackrock Mountains. Though the volcanoes have been dormant now for thousands of years, the rock thrust up by the eruptions and the volcanic glass left behind form massive mountains and jagged cliffs that are difficult to traverse or explore. Millenia of erosion and earthquakes have softened the mountains some, but their imposing glassy rock stretches thousands of feet upward in ragged lines with strange, twisting valleys and passes winding through and around the larger peaks. Travel through the mountains, even on well-known passes, is unforgiving and dangerous, particularly for those unskilled in such adventures. The Blackrock Mountains sit in the midst of a number of human kingdoms and partially divide the Kingdom of Foere from its prior possessions: the Kingdom of the North Heath, the Kingdom of the Vast, and the Principality of Olduvar.

Only the hardiest of plants find purchase in small pockets of sandy soil collecting in the gaps and valleys amid the Blackrocks. These few plants support a menagerie of creatures that are as tough and unforgiving as the mountains themselves. Dragons are drawn to the metals and gemstones hidden in the rocks and regularly come into conflict over small caves and lairs. Several clans of hearty stone giants make their home in some of the safer valleys, and storm giants are drawn to the area around the ruins of Tiro'en.

The dwarves of the Iron Kingdom of Dorriden call these forbidding mountains home and claim the entire range as their own, but they delve into the depths of the mountains seeking precious metals and gems beneath the surface and generally protect only the passes to and from Iron Hall. The rest of the mountains are left to themselves and defended only if threatened by a foreign army. Even giants are tolerated and left alone so long as they do not harry the trade caravans moving in and out of Iron Hall.

Tribes of goblins are known to haunt some areas of these mountains, though they keep far from any dwarven settlements or mines. Orcs were driven from the mountains during a dwarven campaign against dragons at the birth of the Iron Kingdom and can be found only in isolated family units that flee at the possibility of conflict. Rarer creatures have been sighted but most intelligent creatures stay far from any dwarven trade paths or activities.

Tiro'en (Ruins)

A city of glowing spires and magnificent glass and stone buildings of varying sizes, shapes, and designs — some of human or even halfling size, some large enough for giants — stands in the caldera of a long dead volcano. A strange stone obelisk at the center of the city is carved with a variety of symbols and seemingly random words of various languages. The symbols and words change slowly over time, as if the stone rewrites whatever was meant to be written there — with one exception: the word "Tiro'en" carved into the base of the obelisk in a variety of languages and alphabets.

Dust and dirt stirred by the winds sweeping through at this high-altitude swirl and move along broad avenues, empty fountains, statues, and wide areas that might once have been parks or greenways, but today there is no life amid the ruins. No plants, animals, or even mosses or fungi find purchase here. Any animals that might pass by move away quickly, and even intelligent creatures find the eerie ruins unsettling and have no desire to stay or explore. Buildings stand open, yet are strangely hollow and bereft of any life or even a hint of who, or what, may have lived here in the past.

While the location of Tiro'en is known and even marked on some maps, little is known about its history or origins. Rumored to hold treasures and secret knowledge, adventurers have tried to explore the ruins, only to be turned away by storm giants, if they do not disappear altogether. Dwarves of the Iron Kingdom give the ruins a wide berth and claim no knowledge of its origins.

In truth, a clan of storm giants built Tiro'en long ago, back in an age when some of giantkind thought it wise to share knowledge with other races. They used powerful spells to bring forth this city from the volcanic glass of the caldera. There they built a library and invited visitors from other races to come to exchange ideas and knowledge within a collection of ornate, beautiful buildings and gardens created to encourage peaceful contemplation and study.

The city's doom came when one storm giant seeking knowledge best left unknown touched the mind of an elder god and was driven irrevocably mad. Flush with power from this deity of the void, she cleansed the city, slaughtering every living creature, animal, and plant within its confines. Only the empty buildings and a looming sense of fear remains of the beauty that once was Tiro'en.

Whether they acknowledge it or not, the true history of Tiro'en and its destruction is what drove storm giants to their more solitary existence and their extreme caution when sharing knowledge, or even interacting, with other races. The ruins remain unexplored, as anyone entering the barren city triggers a signal that draws several storm giants to the area to discourage investigation. If asked for an explanation, none is given, as even the giants themselves have forgotten the details of Tiro'en's destruction. They just know that they are to prevent anyone from exploring here and possibly repeating whatever disaster might have occurred.

Wytch Bog

The Wytch Bog, located south of the western arm of the Blackrock Mountains, is a desolate wasteland of several thousand square miles covered in stinking peat bogs, saturated earth, and hardy greenery. No political entity claims dominion over the Wytch Bog. Almost every vestige of civilization, regardless of how insignificant, abruptly stops at the first tract of boggy soil. However, a number of hardy families have settled this land for centuries and eke out a living as farmers, peat cutters, and eel hunters. The Nadi River finds its source among the waters of the bog. It is said that deep within the bog is a haunted realm populated by shambling corpses, vengeful undead creatures, and pathetic spirits.

Barony of Baile

Capital: Arlonne
Ruler: Baron Duran Baile
Government: feudalism/monarchy (see below)
Population: 139,900 (86,400 Foerdewaith, 42,540 human mixed ethnicity, 6,350 mountain dwarf, 2,830 halfling, 670 high elf, 490 half-elf, 380 gnome, 150 half-orc, 90 other)
Monstrous: goblins, orcs, giants
Languages: Common, Dwarven, Elven, Gnomish
Religion: Belon the Wise, Mitra, Dre'uain the Lame
Resources: foodstuffs, grain, spices, spirits, trade hub
Currency: Iron Crown, mixed
Technology Level: Medieval

Stretching from the southern base of the Blackrock Mountains to include Arlonne and the rich farmlands near and along the mountains and west to the outskirts of the Wytch Bog, the Barony of Baile has endured numerous name and leadership changes over the centuries, but for the better part of three centuries the barony has been in the hands of the Baile family. Baron Duran Baile is deeply dedicated to the safety and well-being of his people, as were his father and grandfather before him, engendering great loyalty but creating difficulties for his rule. The wide-open farmlands and orchards are difficult to defend and easily attacked. Over the past few years, the Baile family has increased what defenses they could and done their best to help the farmers living on open land have sturdy structures to withstand smaller raids.

History and People

The barony was granted to Jorah Baile by the overking of Foere for his loyal service in the battles that won Vast and North Heath their independence. It was not necessarily the choicest grant of land. With North Heath, Vast, and Olduvar now independent of Foere, the barony became the frontier of the kingdom in the west. And even before the Foerdewaith Wars of Succession, the overkings had difficulty with this area, particularly as a result of continual unrest within the Principality of Olduvar. Time and again in the past, the nobles of Olduvar rebelled against Courghais, which required the intervention of imperial troops who would cross the fields of the barony on their way to Mose. In truth, the overkings preferred that the barony remain unfortified, as they did not want any impediment to taking back the principality when they needed to.

Ten years ago, Olduvar attacked the barony and left behind burned fields and buildings without actually approaching Arlonne. Baron Baile became enraged when the overking attributed the attack to simple raiders and refused to respond or provide helpful compensation and defense. The young baron reduced his tribute to the crown while using some of the money collected to build more secure warehouses for grains and goods in Arlonne, and began to seek ways to better defend his land and people. With pleas for assistance to Courghais ignored, and continued chaos in the Principality of Olduvar, Baron Baile finally turned toward the Iron Kingdom seeking any sort of alliance he could muster to defend his people.

Baron Duran Baile is an enigma to many of the other rulers in the area, as his first duty and thought is actually for the safety of his people. It is this love for his people and desire to protect them that so impressed the dwarves of the Iron Kingdom that they offered him an opportunity to join the Iron Kingdom and granted full clan rights to the barony. This offer allowed him to throw off any allegiance to Foere and provide a steadier more reliable defense for his people. It also provided the Iron Kingdom with rich farmlands to support the miners and craftsmen. And with the might of Dorriden now supporting the barony, Foere was left with few options to punish their former vassal.

Religion

When he was granted these rich lands by the overking, Baron Jorah Baile found mostly burned out ruins and was tasked with rebuilding Arlonne and other smaller settlements nearby. A devout adherent of Belon the Wise, Jorah had several temples built, all of which stand to this day. While Duran Baile follows the dwarven tradition of allowing the presence and worship of other gods, and temples to a few other Foerdewaith gods exist, most of the people of Baile venerate Belon the Wise, whose clerics and temples are the ones most well known in the area.

Trade and Commerce

Rich farmlands and orchards of the barony provide ample harvests of wheat, barley, and other grains as well as a wide variety of fruits and other vegetables. Vineyards along the base of the Blackrock Mountains produce fine wines and brandies that are a sought-out luxury item in many nearby nations. Rich soil and favorable weather patterns allow many of the farms to have multiple harvests in a single year. While it has always had good trade with the dwarves of Iron Hall, the barony's new position in the kingdom has strengthened that relationship and provided strong trade partners for a variety of other items as well.

Loyalties and Diplomacy

As a relatively new principality of the Iron Kingdom, the barony has somewhat tense relationships with those domains still loyal to the Kingdom of Foere. But those relations are warm compared to those with the Principality of Olduvar, which seems ready at any moment to attack and loot the towns and villages of the barony. For all intents, a cold war that occasionally becomes hot exists between the two nations. Whether the risk of angering the dwarves of Dorriden has changed the calculus in Mose remains unknown.

So far, Foere continues to abide by trade agreements with the Iron Kingdom. As a result, trade goods from the barony have been allowed to pass through with only normal tariffs. Baron Duran Baile is completely loyal to the Iron Kingdom, as they provided him a way to defend his people and help them prosper. In addition, he feels he understands and can trust the dwarves of the Iron Kingdom at their word, a trust he does not hold for leaders of other nearby nations. He has friendly relations with the Kingdom of the Vast as well as representatives that have visited him from the City-State of Castorhage.

Government

While feudal in origins, the barony can now be viewed as more of a hereditary monarchy. Baron Baile is firmly in charge of all decisions within the barony and acts now as the equivalent of a clan chieftain, with his position due to be handed down to his eldest child. Duran Baile

was raised to have a profound concern for his people and their well-being, and he is raising his children to have the same concerns, while also having them spend significant time with the dwarves to learn their culture and ways as he believes the union with the Iron Kingdom will truly protect his people and allow them to grow and thrive just as the dwarves have done in Iron Hall.

Now that barony is part of the Iron Kingdom, there is a small court in Arlonne with a judge appointed by the senior court of the Iron Kingdom. Other smaller criminal and civil cases are handled by the courts that the barony already had in place before the union with the dwarves.

Military

The wide, rich farmlands of the barony are a blessing and a curse, as there is little in the way of protection for the many farms spread out through the barony, leaving the population subject to attack by creatures or armies that can easily cross the open fields. While a significant population is found in Arlonne, most of the citizens of the barony are spread throughout the region on various farms and groups of farmhouses that could not even be called villages.

The small militia maintained by the baron is now under the leadership and guidance of the Iron Kingdom. While most of the soldiers in the barony are human, the addition of dwarven soldiers and officers has made the militia more tightly organized. Small outposts and towers built throughout Baile are manned with groups of five to 10 soldiers that keep watch for monstrous and military incursions. Officers of the Iron Kingdom reviewed the widespread farms and made plans to provide better protection for the citizenry. In some cases, specific farmhouses were reinforced to provide protection for groups of farmers. In others, small forts were built for farmers to flee to in the event of an attack.

Major Threats

While there has always been the threat of small raiding parties of goblins or giants coming out of the mountains or the Wytch Bog, the predominant threat to the Barony of Baile lies in attack from the Principality of Olduvar or, possibly, the Kingdom of Foere. Increased defenses and the new status as part of the Iron Kingdom make these attacks less likely, but Olduvar has been known to send troops or mercenaries to do nothing more than burn fields and destroy croplands.

Farms of the Genev Gap suffer slightly different dangers as monstrous creatures from Harwood Forest make forays into the rich fields in search of food. The increased number of towers and defenses in the area have helped, but these random encounters are a constant danger to those toiling the rich soil of the Genev Gap.

Arlonne, City of (Capital)

Ruler: Baron Duran Baile
Government: feudalism/monarchy
Population: 42,400 (26,750 Foerdewaith, 10,660 human mixed ethnicities, 2,430 mountain dwarf, 1,850 halfling, 420 high elf, 170 half-elf, 90 gnome, 30 half-orc)
Languages: Common, Dwarven, Halfling, Elven
Religion: Belon the Wise
Resources: foodstuffs, produce, spirits, grains, spices, trade hub
Technology Level: Medieval

Buildings of Arlonne are so spread out that it often feels more like a large village than the city it has become. Some of the land within the city area itself is reserved for crops and is actively farmed, spreading buildings out even farther. The baron's home and a number of important buildings and warehouses are behind a single wooden wall that stands only 25 feet high. The rest of the city must depend on the new towers placed throughout the sprawling buildings for defense.

History and People

Arlonne and the Barony of Baile are mostly populated by humans of Foerdewaith descent who were settled here by the Kingdom of Foere when it initially conquered these lands. Left largely undefended, the city has fallen many times in battle, changing hands between Foere and whatever forces happened to be in control of the Principality of Olduvar. The allegiance to the Iron Kingdom is a recent development that has increased the stability and protection of the city to the point that the citizens here are pleased with the new situation and are beginning to prosper as new trade agreements and partnerships grow.

Knowledge that their ruler cares enough about his people to take the drastic step of changing his allegiance from Foere to the Iron Kingdom makes the citizens here love and respect Baron Baile. While there was some initial fear and trepidation at the changes made, the dwarves are now welcomed openly, and the changes to the defenses have inspired confidence.

Religion

The only full temple in Arlonne is dedicated to Belon the Wise, largely because the first Baron Baile was a devout worshipper of that god. Other religions are allowed here, but in truth, few people practice any particular faith.

Trade and Commerce

Arlonne acts as a storage location and clearing point for the grains, fruits, spices, and livestock that allow the barony to thrive. Several dwarven merchants set up warehouses for the temporary storage of some of the metals and items that Iron Hall exports to other nations. Warehouses behind the wall hold barrels of aged spirits and wines that are sought-after luxury items in a number of nations. Mismanagement of nearby Olduvar and the growing demand for food within the Iron Kingdom continue to create additional trading opportunities for the merchants of Arlonne.

Government

Baron Duran Baile has retained the title baron but is now considered by the dwarves to be a clan chieftain. His rule is slated to be handed down to his eldest son, and he has every intention of continuing to hold leadership of the barony within his family lineage. The courts and judges of the Barony of Baile are housed within Arlonne, as are the few government offices and aides to the baron.

Genev Gap

Rich soil of the broad, level land in the gap between the Blackrock Mountains and Harwood Forest has largely been turned into bountiful farmlands with small communities and farms spread along the trade route stretching from the area west of the Gilded River to the Principality of Olduvar. Officially claimed by the Barony of Baile and the Iron Kingdom of Dorriden, these lands pose few natural defenses to armies or monsters and force farmers to build sturdy structures to protect their families in areas far from any city or town. The Iron Kingdom has begun the construction of a series of towers and outposts to defend against monstrous incursions from Harwood Forest. In the event of an approaching army, farmers are expected to flee to the safety of the Grimm Fortress.

The flat, level land here has been the meeting place for many battles over the centuries. Spearheads, broken swords, and other items are regularly turned up by plows. The open nature of the fields provides no real advantage to any side, and there is no easy way to maintain control of territories that might actually be conquered. While still angered by the betrayal of the Barony of Baile, the overking of Foere listened to his advisors and concluded that the costs of trying to retake the barony exceeded its value, and so it would be better to force the Iron Kingdom to defend those lands and, at the same time, create an additional buffer between Foere and the Principality of Olduvar. As a result, Courghais ordered the Duchy of Mains to leave the areas north of Dundlend alone. But Dundlend was also ordered to allow monsters or other invading creatures from Harwood Forest to pass by into the gap.

Principality of Olduvar

Capital: Mose
Notable Settlements: Bottomborough, Loagwater, Newmire, Oakhall, Overlook, Tratai, Westfort
Rulers: Prince Anscul White, Lord Roese Bloodsight, Lady Agacia Crossthain, Lady Karyn Greenheart
Government: oligarchy
Population: 1,227,900 (677,300 Foerdewaith, 328,470 human mixed ethnicity, 157,200 halfling, 23,200 half-elves, 17,100 high elves, 14,580 wild elves, 4,390 gnomes, 3,100 hill dwarves, 880 mountain dwarves, 560 half-orcs, 450 orcs, 400 other)
Monstrous: hobgoblin, goblin, kobold, stone giant, hill giant, ogre, treant, troll, dragon (green in the Low Country, red in Upland Vale), roc
Languages: Common, Dwarven, Elven
Religion: Freya, Muir, Thyr, Mitra, Solanus, Hecate (secret), Demogorgon (secret)
Resources: foodstuffs, silver, gems, gold, manufactured goods, spirits (ale, wine, whiskeys), timber, trade hub
Currency: Olduvarian
Technology Level: Medieval

Boasting rich farmland, a number of small gem and gold mines, and control over a major trade route, the Principality of Olduvar is a wealthy nation that often acts on designs to expand and conquer neighboring cities and nations though with only moderate, and usually short-lived, success. Spread across a narrow strip of land between the capital of Mose in the east, to Bottomborough and towns to the west with a dip south to Tratai, the Principality of Olduvar remains under the control of the nobility given positions here by the Kingdom of Foere.

History and People

Conquered by the Kingdom of Foere during its initial expansion, Olduvar had to be reconquered multiple times over the centuries as the leaders of the principality repeatedly revolted or simply disregarded orders from the crown. Olduvar seems to have always been ruled by a committee of like-minded despots focused on enriching themselves on the backs of their people. Following each new conquest, Foere would install new nobles to take control of the principality, but inevitably they would fall into the ways of the previous rulers. The chaos of the Foerdewaith Wars of Succession left the Kingdom of Foere distracted enough to ignore Olduvar as it simply broke off again and refused the leadership of the overking. Once Vast and North Heath won their independence, Courghais lost the will to try to control the western lands and made no attempts to retake Olduvar. Present politics suggest this policy will likely continue, as any actions against the principality now could threaten Foere's relationship with the Iron Kingdom of Dorriden, the City-State of Castorhage, and other smaller kingdoms.

All of the noble families of Olduvar are descended from those Foerdewaith families granted holdings here by various overkings during their rule of the principality, but none has any affinity for the crown. The commoners are largely Foerdewaith but include some high elves and half-elves as well as some rare half-orcs. Although officially against the laws of the principality, slaves are fairly common here, particularly in Bottomborough where some of the slaves include hobgoblins, orcs, elves, halflings, and humans.

While the nobility may indeed be somewhat mad, the commoners and general citizenry are hardworking, determined individuals struggling to better themselves in the face of a corrupt government. While they know their government is a problem, they would rather stick with the government they know than with some foreign power, and would provide a stiff defense were Olduvar attacked. Most of the population is spread throughout the rich farmlands near Mose and Tratai with a significant and diverse population in Bottomborough.

The Low Country and the Dale, home to many halflings, are claimed by Olduvar, and occasionally tax collectors from Loagwater ride through and demand payment. As there are no substantial resources to be exploited there, however, the principality largely leaves the halflings to themselves, a happy circumstance for them to say the least.

Religion

There is no predominant religion in Olduvar, as most of the nobility here follow no particular gods and no money is spent on temples in this region. Some of the commoners worship Muir and Freya, and in fact an ancient shrine to Freya can be found at the outer edges of Tratai, though few visit it. Mitra, Thyr, and Solanus also have minor followings in some areas. Lady Agacia Crossthain secretly worships Demogorgon, and Master Adoril Longstaff of Newmire worships Hecate.

Trade and Commerce

In spite of its political isolation, the Principality of Olduvar commands a wide variety of resources and does a great deal of trading in silver, gems, coal, lumber, rare stone, and slaves, though most of the trade travels through Bottomborough and the port at Loagwater to avoid the tariffs charged by their neighbors. While the government itself is poorly managed, the nobility and leading merchants take great care in running their individual businesses, and as a result, Olduvar boasts some of the finest vineyards, wineries, and distilleries in the Lost Lands as well as a variety of high-end crafts, including jewelry.

Loyalties and Diplomacy

Politically isolated and not trusted by any of the nations around them, Olduvar is presently held in check by the Free City of Brookmere to the southwest, the fortress of Cailin Lee of the Kingdom of the Vast to the north, and Dundlend of the Duchy of Mains and the Grimm Fortress of the Iron Kingdom of Dorriden to the east. Most of its history is made up of being conquered by Foere and then simply ignoring its rule. Leadership changes happen swiftly in Olduvar, so neighboring nations view any agreements with distrust and fully expect them not to be honored for very long.

Government

Olduvar's governing class consists of little more than a loose confederation of small noble families, with minimal common purpose. Leadership changes as a result of blackmail, assassination, open revolt, and coups are a standard feature of the principality's history. These changes make it difficult for Olduvar to form any lasting treaties or alliances because other nations and city-states don't trust any treaty or agreement with Olduvar to last. Occasional plans by one or another noble family to conquer nearby areas inevitably falter due to internal political infighting. Such military successes as are achieved are usually sabotaged by either the corrupt military or the very nobles who ordered the activities in the first place.

Each of the nominal rulers of Olduvar represents a particular group or region within the nation, chosen by a mixture of backroom deal-making, blackmail, and bribery. Anscul White represents the nobility of Mose, the putative capital of Olduvar, and in such capacity acts as the prince of Olduvar (a title held by this particular representative, which is neither hereditary nor endowed with much in the way of actual authority). Lord Roese Bloodsight is the ruler of Bottomborough and represents the Olduvaran merchant and craft guilds that have their headquarters in that city. Lady Karyn Greenheart of Loagwater represents those nobles whose lands are near the mouth of the Nadi River and maintains her position with the wealth obtained from the small port there and her gem mines in the Briar Hills. Lady Agacia Crossthain of Tratai draws her influence from trade goods produced by the nearby farmers and loggers in the Harwood Forest, as well as the nobles along the trade road between Mose and the Free City of Brookmere. Each of the representatives does their best to undermine the others while trying to secure greater power for themselves. Prince Anscul White has held his position only for one year and is already paranoid and fears poisoning or assassination. In truth, a number of the wealthier noblemen and merchants are dissatisfied with the present rulers so any one, or all, could be replaced at any time.

Such disarray and corruption infect all levels of Olduvar's government, from the oligarchs at the top to local offices, courts, and the military. As a result, the populace views all officials with distrust and disdain. Olduvar's natural resources should make it a wealthy nation for a country of its size, but this wealth has been squandered or embezzled in a variety of foolish enterprises. Individual noblemen often maintain their own private troops and refuse to provide them for defense or support of the nation. Most high-ranking members of the militia are on the payroll of one or more noble families providing information and contracts in their best interest.

Unsurprisingly, the system of justice is particularly corrupt. Officially, the laws of the principality are derived from those of Foere, but the resemblance is purely superficial. Guilt or innocence in Olduvar is largely determined by wealth rather than actual evidence or guilt. Some judges publicly list the price to have certain crimes dismissed. The poor are left with little choice but to face whatever penalty a judge decides to mete out. Disagreements between noble families or wealthy merchants are sometimes reached through negotiation, but often only after a series of secret attacks against each other's financial interests or family members.

Nearby nations view Olduvar's leaders as simply insane or mad. Bards in the nearby Kingdom of the Vast sing songs and tell jokes that all involve a punchline that includes "the Mad Prince of Olduvar" who apparently needs no other name as all of the Lords of Olduvar are viewed as insane.

Military

Generals and high-ranking officers of the military in Olduvar are among the most corrupt in the nation, and that is certainly saying something. Almost all of them are on the payroll of at least one noble family and some are paid off by several. Conscription for the rank-and-file is held at random intervals when officers believe they need more soldiers. The vast majority of military units are inefficient, corrupt, and loyal only to their immediate officers and friends, to the extent they possess any loyalties at all. However, wealthier noble families usually maintain their own guardsmen, and many of these soldiers are highly trained and knowledgeable. In fact, effective military officers are usually hired away by noble families as soon as their skills are noticed. At this point, none of Olduvar's neighbors has any interest in trying to conquer the nation and take on its numerous problems. All recent actions by the military have involved little more than chaotic and largely pointless raids on lands of the Kingdom of the Vast or the Barony of Baile.

Wilderness and Adventures

Most of the areas near Tratai and Mose are relatively well-tamed farmlands with occasional monstrous attacks from Harwood Forest to the southeast. Portions of the Eldevere Forest and the Briar Hills are home to various monstrous creatures that generally stay away from the more populated areas. The main adventures in Olduvar involve the various intrigues between the noble families that are always trying to spy on and damage each other.

Mose, City of (Capital)

Ruler: Prince Anscul White
Government: feudalism
Population: 65,342 (49,220 Foerdewaith, 14,620 human mixed ethnicity, 1,125 gnome, 198 half-elf, 87 mountain dwarf, 54 half-orc, 38 high elf)
Languages: Common, Gnome, Dwarven, Elven
Resources: silver, gems, foodstuffs, manufactured goods, trade hub
Technology Level: Medieval

Mose stands on a major trade route and has been subjected to numerous attacks over the years. The nobility here spent wisely on massive walls, towers, and defenses focused on protecting the Noble Quarter. The rest of the city is split into discrete areas, all of which have their own walls and protections, though not nearly as extensive as that of the Noble

Quarter. The Crafters' Quarter houses a variety of craftsmen, including jewelers and gem cutters as well as blacksmiths and woodworkers. All craftsmen require a license purchased from the city to work and sell their products. The Joy District houses inns, restaurants, and trading houses as well as brothels and gambling houses, all of which are licensed by the city, paying variable fees depending upon their profitability and the social status of their owners. The ironically named High Quarter on the southern part of the city holds military barracks and a variety of ramshackle buildings housing the poorer laborers and workers.

Most of the structures in Mose are simple wood-frame buildings, with some larger wattle-and-daub buildings in the Crafters' Quarter and random stone buildings spread throughout. Ancient stone foundations lead down to catacombs beneath the city that are often flooded and reek of sewage and decay. The Noble Quarter possesses mansions of the finest construction and materials, some of dwarven make, as the different noble families do their best to outdo each other.

All of the most profitable businesses are controlled by the noble families, whether it is gem or silver mines, wineries, distilleries, or wide swaths of farmland. The difference between the rich and poor here is marked and appalling. The poor are kept at least somewhat fed and satisfied not due to any generosity but because the nobles fear any possible revolt.

GOVERNMENT

The nobility in Mose control nearly all aspects of life and elect their prince, adopt favorable laws, and appoint judges who happily accept bribes. Craftsmen and merchants send representatives to the prince and other nobles, but the only path to influence is through bribery and blackmail. Officially, the laws apply to all, but in reality, the nobility is not subject to the same laws as the lowborn. Nobles have been known to openly abuse and even kill servants and lowborn without any repercussion. Most of the noble houses are in regular conflict with each other, often for reasons that stretch back generations. While these frictions rarely end in open conflict, assassination, blackmail, and sabotage are popular pastimes among the nobility. Ordinary citizens of Mose generally consider the noblemen to be bordering on insanity and do their best to avoid and reduce their interactions with the highborn.

Mose — and the Principality of Olduvar as a whole — is led by Prince Anscul White, who is beholden to several of the other major noble families in Mose and is unsure of his power. Local laws are enforced by the militia with a highly corrupt court system that heavily favors wealth and power.

MILITARY

The military in Mose is officially split into the general militia, which includes the city guard and infantry, and the cavalry, which is made up of mounted soldiers and knights. The cavalry mostly consists of wealthy sons not directly due inheritance of their family businesses or holdings, and are known to be particularly corrupt. While the military could be called to arms to defend the city and nation in time of need, their dedication is highly questionable. Any defense of the city is certain to focus on protecting the Noble Quarter.

BOTTOMBOROUGH, CITY OF

Ruler: Lord Roese Bloodsight
Government: dictatorship
Population: 38,348 (21,280 Foerdewaith, 15,450 human mixed ethnicity, 133 half-elf, 127 mountain dwarf, 63 gnome, 879 human mixed ethnicity slaves, 245 half-orc slaves, 148 orc slaves, 23 high elf slaves)
Languages: Common, Gnome, Dwarven, Elven, Orc
Resources: foodstuffs, manufactured goods, timber, trade hub
Technology Level: Medieval

While some large cities boast a long, deep, complicated history, Bottomborough is a recent city, a relatively new addition to the landscape. Built from a small village on the banks of the Nadi River into a bustling city, Bottomborough benefits by being far enough from the sea to avoid storm damage yet close enough to the Eldevere Forest and rich field lands to have dependable, steady resources. Although now close to 100 years old, the city grew so fast (and is still growing) that there is no real city planning; shops, craftsmen, taverns, inns, gambling halls, and even guard posts and government buildings are randomly strewn about on curving, complicated roads and alleys.

Broad wood walls surround the city, while thick stone walls protect Noble Row on the western edge of the city. Gates to the main city are monitored; individuals may enter as they please, but wagons are inspected for items that might need to be taxed. Gates to Noble Row, where the wealthiest merchants and noblemen maintain their mansions, are guarded and patrolled, and only select individuals and laborers with the correct papers are allowed to pass those gates. Roese Bloodsight rules Bottomborough, as well as Oakhall and Overlook to the north in the Eldevere Forest, with an iron fist. Guards and militia overseeing the city report to him, and he treats them as his own personal guard.

Nearby resources make this an ideal place for craftsman to ply their trade so long as they are careful not to anger any of the upper class. The real reason for Bottomborough's growth, however, lies in its darker nature. Anything can be bought here for a price. Almost all business activities and other transactions are legal, though also regulated and taxed. Gambling, prostitution, and even slavery are all legal here. It is rumored that the city hosts the headquarters of an assassin's guild that is licensed by Roese Bloodsight himself. The official laws of the Principality of Olduvar outlaw many of these activities, particularly the slave trade, but in Bottomborough, money and wealth create their own laws.

While Roese is an elected leader chosen by the noblemen of the city, he acquired his power through blackmail, extortion, and sheer physical force through control of the city's guardsmen and militia. He maintains his position the same way, and is broadly disliked, but his firm control of the militia and the guardsmen is something that other noblemen and merchants can't break. The fact that almost all of the noblemen and wealthy merchants of the city benefit somehow by the lax laws helps cement his power.

LOAGWATER, CITY OF

Ruler: Lady Karyn Greenheart
Government: dictatorship
Population: 24,896 (15,240 Foerdewaith, 7,552 human mixed ethnicity, 1,724 halfling, 167 gnome, 98 high elf, 86 half-elf, 29 mountain dwarf)
Languages: Common, Halfling, Gnome, Dwarven, Elven
Resources: gems, foodstuffs, timber
Technology Level: Medieval

Loagwater sits at the mouth of the Nadi River, its city wall surrounding a collection of stone and wood buildings on both banks of the river. The docks, while not extensive compared to other major harbors, see steady traffic of fishing and merchant vessels. As the Nadi isn't navigable for much of its length, goods brought to or from Loagwater mainly travel by small caravans on the road to Bottomborough or by flat-bottomed barges. Other than a few taverns and inns near the docks, Loagwater maintains few amenities in spite of the merchant traffic.

The northern section of the city includes a massive tower surrounded by large, ornate homes separated by exquisite gardens. Tall stone walls separate the homes of the nobility from the barracks and other buildings of the city. While this area has no official name, most of the common residents call it Noble Row and consider it off limits to travelers. The wealthy here control the docks, the fishing along the nearby coastline, and the gold, silver, and gem mines in the nearby Briar Hills. The inland fields where cotton, wheat, and other crops are grown are also controlled by the nobility, many of whom also own massive plantation-style homes outside the city. The Greenheart family controls many of the richest mines, and the resulting wealth is the source of Lady Karyn Greenheart's dominance over the city and the surrounding countryside.

Loagwater's domain includes the northern portion of the Briar Hills claimed by Olduvar, the lands about the Nadi River about halfway to

Bottomborough, and the southern end of the Eldevere Forest, including Newmire. Loagwater also claims dominion over the Low Country and the Dale, but as there is little there of value, the nobles of Loagwater ignore it, and the halflings who live there largely return the favor.

On the surface, Loagwater appears brighter and friendlier than other cities and major villages in Olduvar. The common people here are well fed and in good spirits, but this appearance is deceiving. Lady Greenheart dominates virtually all aspects of Loagwater, including the other noble houses that have businesses here. Her influence among the nobility and wealthy merchant class extends throughout the kingdom due to an extensive network of spies that helps her maintain information about all of the other major power players in Olduvar. She is not above blackmail or even assassination to maintain her power.

Lady Greenheart maintains a close relationship with Adoril Longstaff of Newmire, but hates and despises Roese Bloodsight of Bottomborough, particularly the darker businesses there. She does not have the influence to do more than keep Roese in check.

NEWMIRE, CITY OF

Ruler: Master Adoril Longstaff
Government: feudalism
Population: 19,305 (9,350 Foerdewaith, 8,490 human mixed ethnicity, 1,214 halfling, 98 half-elf, 76 half-orc, 54 orc [dock-working slaves], 23 high elf)
Languages: Common, Halfling, Orc, Elven
Religion: Hecate (secret, see below)
Resources: gold, silver, gems, foodstuffs, fishing, trade hub
Technology Level: Medieval

Newmire is built upon a modest hill overlooking the Eldevere Forest to the north and the fields down to the Nadi valley to the south. Thick stone walls surrounding elegant stone buildings occupy a small portion of the city to the south, while the rest of the city, protected by a tall wooden palisade, consists of sturdy, but fairly nondescript, wooden buildings. Although the wooden structures of the main city are solid and well-constructed, no effort has been made to decorate or paint the homes and buildings there. On the other hand, the ornate buildings behind the stone walls are clearly planned with artistry in mind and without any care for the cost of the construction or the materials used.

The main buildings here are constructed from lumber harvested from the nearby Eldevere Forest with stone reserved for walls and buildings of the nobles. Newmire's wealth is derived from farming along the forest margins and logging within the forest itself. Several valuable types of wood can be found in the southern reaches of the Eldevere, particularly a dark cherry wood excellent for furniture and small craftwork.

Master Adoril Longstaff, a wizard of some renown and power, lives here in a home beside his imposing tower. An egotistical, driven man, he rules Newmire and the surrounding area by virtue of his magical might and the fear it induces in the rest of the nobility. The local nobility fully supports him, believing that they have no real choice in the matter. His rule of Newmire is merely a task that helps him support his quest for greater magical power and knowledge. Adoril acts as a sworn supporter of Lady Karyn Greenheart, mostly because she can blackmail him over his worship of Hecate and his penchant for sacrificing innocents to demons in exchange for knowledge.

The guardsmen of the town answer solely to Master Longstaff, with any arrests or judgments decided directly by him. If someone is accused of a crime when he is not in town, they are held in jail until his return.

The other nobility of Olduvar prefer to ignore Adoril in part because he ignores their activities, leaving those things happening outside Newmire without interference. Combined with his magical activities, his lack of interference with others keeps him safe from the machinations of most of the other noble families.

RELIGION

Master Adoril Longstaff keeps a private altar to Hecate but is also open to, and investigating, worship of certain other demon lords in an effort to increase his power. While he does not openly declare his worship, he does prevent the building of any other temples or altars within the city limits using the official excuse that he doesn't want to favor any particular religion.

OAKHALL, VILLAGE OF

Ruler: Kohavier Wolfbane
Government: military (special)
Population: 3,476 (2,140 human mixed ethnicity, 988 Foerdewaith, 321 high elf, 27 half-elf)
Languages: Common, Elven
Resources: herbs, timber, spices
Technology Level: Dark Ages

Massive oaks stand like evenly-spaced pillars throughout the confines of Oakhall. Houses and cottages have been built at the foot of many of these massive trees, with additional homes built into the branches above. It is clear that the massive trees were planted in a specific spacing and orientation for a reason, but that reason, and those who did the planting, have long since faded into history.

Oakhall once was a thriving community closely in tune with the forest and provided timber, herbs, spices, and medicinal plants for trade with nearby cities. Roese Bloodsight had difficulties convincing the town leaders to increase their production of timber for his growing city and, after some frustrations, brought in a small army to conquer Oakhall and place it more firmly under his control. The residents are forced to log and gather herbs and spices simply for Bottomborough to use and trade.

Kohavier Wolfbane acts as the mayor of Oakhall but is, in reality, the leader of the extensive militia stationed here to ensure the cooperation of the villagers. The village is maintained under strict martial law, and guardsmen have the power to demand pretty much anything they desire. Those villagers with the means to do so fled Oakhall, leaving behind those with few options or who are unable to leave for whatever reason.

OVERLOOK, VILLAGE OF

Ruler: Waeira Steelsong
Government: feudalism
Population: 2,883 (920 human mixed ethnicity, 860 Foerdewaith, 525 gnome, 380 wild elf, 198 half-elf)
Languages: Common, Gnome, Elven
Religion: Solanus
Resources: silver, timber, herbs
Technology Level: Dark Ages

Rising to form a small hill, the land on which Overlook was built allows a view of much of Eldevere Forest, if one is willing to climb high enough into one of the trees. The trees here grow in a wild pattern, completely unlike the carefully planted trees of Oakhall. Cottages dot the area, as do small, burrow-like homes belonging to some of the gnomes that live here. A small wooden palisade surrounds the majority of the homes, but there is little in the way of an organized defense. A simple, ancient temple to Solanus is managed by a traveling cleric who saw it in a dream and came here to serve the people of the area.

In addition to logging the sturdy oaks of Eldevere Forest, Overlook is also home to several small silver mines owned and run by the Steelsong family that also controls the village. The gnomish miners get along well with the other residents and provide steady, fair leadership. Waeira Steelsong and her son Khorin do not like Roese Bloodsight or the activities in Bottomborough, but they do not have enough wealth or military might to do anything about it. They give him their support and send their goods through Bottomborough (though they have little choice). One small act of resistance they perform is to support refugees from Oakhall by providing them work in the forest as they can.

Wilder and, somehow, more primitive, the forest here frightens the guardsmen in Roese's employ, so Overlook is largely free of their predation. Villagers do not wander too far into the forest because the deeper woods are home to a group of highly xenophobic druids. So far, the druids have kept to themselves and not interfered with the logging in this area. Waeira is wary of the threat the druids and the forest might carry but also the threat of being conquered the way Oakhall was, so she does her best to provide trade goods as needed to Bottomborough to avoid any conflict.

TRATAI, CITY OF

Ruler: Lady Agacia Crossthain
Government: feudalism
Population: 30,536 (18,920 Foerdewaith, 10,420 human mixed ethnicity, 1,056 halfling, 97 half-elf, 27 mountain dwarf, 16 high elf)
Languages: Common, Halfling, Dwarven, Elven
Religion: Freya, Demogorgon (secretly, see text)
Resources: cotton, grain, timber, trade hub
Technology Level: Medieval

Rolling hills covered with fields of corn, wheat, barley, cotton and other crops surround the city of Tratai, which is spread across the top of a wide, flat hill. The city stands on the main trade road between the Free City of Brookmere to the south and Mose and the heartland of Olduvar to the north. Crumbling stone walls and structures on the outskirts of Tratai hint of a larger city in the past. Many of the buildings here are ancient and reminiscent of some of the old structures found in Brookmere. Newer buildings stand atop ancient stone foundations and crumbling catacombs. The larger streets are well-maintained cobblestone, while smaller alleys and side streets are simply dirt or gravel.

The outer walls of the city are only indifferently maintained, though guard patrols man the towers and walk the tops of the walls, alert to any potential attack from the nearby Harwood Forest. The central portion of the city is also walled, these being tall, broad, well-maintained, and constructed of heavy stones clearly cut and dressed by dwarven masons.

The wealthy nobility of Tratai live in almost palatial mansions on the northern side of the city. Militia and guardsmen are quartered in clean, comfortable barracks scattered along the city walls. Laborers and the poor are generally relegated to poorly maintained buildings that receive little or no services from the city. The poor here are truly poor, and often desperate, but the militia and ruling nobility show little or no mercy to the lower classes. Due to the imposition of high tariffs (both official and unofficial), few merchants or artisans choose to live in Tratai, so there is little of a middle class in the city.

RELIGION

A small, ancient shrine to Freya stands just outside the outer walls of Tratai. While it has no active clergy, local women spend a great deal of time cleaning and maintaining the shrine either in hopes the goddess will bless them with a child or in thanks for children they have. Lady Agacia Crossthain is a bitter woman who lost all her children and grandchildren to accidents, disease, or violence. She turned to worshipping Demogorgon in secrecy. Several of her top assistants and advisors also worship Demogorgon, but their celebrations and rituals are kept very quiet and private.

TRADE AND COMMERCE

Produce from all of the nearby farms is routed through the city and all wood from logging in the Harwood Forest is expected to pass through Tratai. A combination of heavy tariffs and a high markup sees most of the money made here going straight to the nobility and city coffers.

Officially, there are no tariffs on goods that are simply passing through Tratai, but the simple reality is that there are always small "fees" to be paid when passing through the gates or simply parking wagons in the city. There is little in the way of skilled craftsmen in the city as most of them were driven away long ago by the heavy burden of tariffs and the constant corruption of the guardsmen. Those few who remain work for one of the noble families. Cotton, wheat, rye, and corn are the main cash crops here. While these don't sound exciting to some, the volume of produce from the nearby farms is enough to bring in substantial wealth.

GOVERNMENT

Although in theory elected as mayor by the nobles in Tratai, Lady Agacia Crossthain maintains her position through a combination of blackmail and simple raw power. Frankly disliked by most of the region's nobility, she is tolerated as a "necessary evil" because few would want to spend the amount of energy it requires for her to remain in power, and many fear the disclosure of the information she possesses on their family businesses. She exchanges some information with Lady Karyn Greenheart when it benefits her. Both women distrust each other but have different enough business interests and goals that they are willing to work together toward their own ends.

Guardsmen and government officials are under the strict control of Lady Crossthain. Judges, prosecutors, and guardsmen are all easily bribed, although Lady Crossthain is the final arbiter of any court decisions that involve a capital crime, crimes between nobility, or civil disagreements between nobility. Her decisions are considered final. The local nobility control all of the business operations here, whether it is stables, inns, farms, or warehouses.

WESTFORT, KEEP OF

Ruler: Commander Argo Shalls
Government: military
Population: 3,211 (2,750 Foerdewaith, 433 human mixed ethnicity, 21 high elf, 18 half-elf)
Languages: Common
Technology Level: Dark Ages

Westfort is a stone keep built on an island in the Nadi River about 30 miles south of where it emerges from the Wytch Bog. The northernmost outpost of Olduvar, the keep is garrisoned to protect against incursions from the bog or the mountains, and to provide a staging point should the principality decide to invade the Barony of Baile or lands beyond. It refuses all trade with Baile, relying solely on supplies sent up the Nadi or overland from Mose. Commander Argo Shalls maintains strict discipline among his troops and ensures the readiness of a mustering field off the east bank of the river, large enough for an enormous army. He is, however, under strict orders not to do anything to provoke Baile or the Iron Kingdom. As a result, travelers who might involve his troops in any way will not find much succor here, no matter the peril they might find themselves in.

REFERENCE SOURCE: MARSHES OF MALICE

GEOGRAPHIC FEATURES AND POINTS OF INTEREST IN THE PRINCIPALITY OF OLDUVAR

BLOODSTONE MOUNTAINS

The Bloodstones are a small range of low, weathered mounts, other than the dual-peaked Mount Bloodstone, dark red and jagged, that rises to an elevation of 15,000 feet. These mountains tend to be avoided by most folk, as inhabitants of the peaks include stone giants, wyverns, at least one roc, and a tribe of yetis in the highest altitudes.

REFERENCE SOURCE: FGG1 FANE OF THE FALLEN

BRIAR HILLS

South of the Nadi River, near where it empties into the Crescent Sea, the Briar Hills run from the coast to the feet of the Bloodstone Mountains to the east. The Principality of Olduvar claims the entirety of these hills, but maintains a presence only in the northern section close to the river where their gold, silver, and gem mines can be found. On the south, the town of Briarwatch also mines iron ore but claims little of the highlands. Lightly forested, the Briar Hills are surprisingly difficult to traverse, with the tall grasses covering rocks, ravines, and steep slopes. Caves dot the landscape, some being the habitations of humanoids and other monsters that make this area home.

The Dale

The Dale is a low valley between the eaves of the Eldevere Forest and a small line of hills that separates it from the coastal plain of the Low Country. Many halflings call the Dale home and live in small clusters of homes burrowed into the hillsides. They have no settlements of any size and no real government, and band together only when some threat appears that requires collective action (which has not happened in living memory). They live in peace with the nearby forest, though they seldom venture far into its depths. The druids of Eldevere discourage any exploration, and the halflings are happy to stay in the valley and grow their gardens.

When tax collectors from Loagwater ride through, the halflings usually collect what is necessary to pay them off. They do not worry about how much actually arrives in Loagwater, as opposed to remaining in the pockets of the collectors. Otherwise, the purported rule of Olduvar has little effect on the rustic folk of the Dale.

Eldevere Forest

Tall oaks and sturdy maple trees predominate here, with some beech and birch trees and, in the southern portion of the forest, black cherry. The forest floor is often covered with a wide variety of undergrowth that provides edible and poisonous berries. Parts of the forest are logged and harvested, but the central northeastern portion of the forest east of the Dale is home to an ancient circle of elven druids. Their purpose there is unknown, as they do not talk with travelers except to warn them out of this region of the forest. They are extremely hostile to anyone not heeding their warnings, and attack if a second warning is ignored. Anyone trying to meet with them or talk to them is simply ignored. They refuse to grant safe passage through this part of the forest, even to other druids.

The Low Country

The Low Country is a flat plain rising from the Crescent Sea coast to a line of inland hills and green fields interspersed with briny marshland. There are no good locations for a port along the shore, so this area has never been settled in any material way. On the fields above the lowlands are clusters of small, colorful homes, inhabited by halflings who know where plants can grow.

The halflings tend to avoid the marshy lowlands of the Low Country, which are too soft to support buildings and too salty to permit anything to grow other than marsh grasses, which wave in the coastal breeze and conceal numerous dangerous sinkholes, pits, and areas of watery, loose mud and dirt that act like quicksand to the unwary. Because of the dangers of the marsh, the halflings of the Low Country are generally left alone, even by Olduvarian tax collectors.

Nadi River

Stretching from the base of the Blackrock Mountains to the Crescent Sea, the Nadi River winds through the Principality of Olduvar and provides water for the rich farmland near its banks. Narrow and very fast moving for most of its length, the river is hazardous to boaters and not very useful for trying to move goods due to areas of dangerous, rocky rapids. Only between Bottomborough and Loagwater is the river navigable, and even there, only by flat-bottomed boats. Bony pike and other fishes found in the river are not particularly flavorful, so there is little fishing.

Upland Vale

While the Worntooth Peaks are claimed by the Kingdom of the Vast, Olduvar maintains that it possesses the hills south of the mountains known as Upland Vale. However, Upland Vale is also claimed by a large tribe of stone giants that call the region home and take any incursions by "lesser" races as an insult to be is met with immediate attack. Past leaders of Olduvar have led campaigns to rid Upland Vale of the giants and goblinoid races found there, only to be met with costly defeat.

Brookmere, Free City of

Ruler: Lord Thorbold
Government: limited democracy
Population: 21,022 (10,030 Foerdewaith, 7,335 human mixed ethnicity, 2,130 high elf, 680 halfling, 365 hill dwarf, 215 gnome, 132 half-elf, 105 half-orc, 30 orc)
Languages: Common, Halfling, Elven, Gnome, Dwarven
Religion: Freya, Muir, Mitra, Thyr, Mick O'Delving, Dwerfater, Dre'uain the Lame
Resources: foodstuffs, livestock, manufactured goods, magical resources, trade hub, silver, spices, spirits
Currency: mixed
Technology Level: Medieval

Governed with a motto of "High Walls but Open Gates," the Free City of Brookmere controls the trade routes between Mose in the north, Bridgeport in the west on the Crescent Sea coast, and other points south. Massive stone walls wind their way around the ancient city and provide sturdy protection against any attacks. Although ancient in origins, the walls are carefully maintained as the protection they afford allow Brookmere to maintain its status as a free city.

Brookmere itself is a bewildering collection of old and new stone structures mixed with wood-frame buildings and a collection of tree-lined parks and avenues. Taverns, inns, and gambling houses line the main trade routes as they enter and exit the city while street vendors are found on every major (and some minor) thoroughfare. The skilled observer can easily determine that the walls of the city and some of the oldest buildings within are the sturdiest structures here, likely of dwarven construction. With generally pleasant temperatures, attractive surroundings and lenient laws, Brookmere is a favored stop for merchants.

History and People

Unbeknownst to any but a few learned sages, Brookmere's ancient foundations stretch through thousands of years of history and predate the formation of the Hyperborean Empire, let alone its expansion. First built in a deep forest, the original city was constructed from rock and stone pulled up through the earth using dark blood magic and ritual sacrifices by a coven of elves seeking a connection to the darker gods and demons of creation. Eventually, other elven tribes joined together to destroy the city and the coven of dark elves, either killing or driving its inhabitants away. The walls and buildings were razed, leaving behind nothing but rubble.

The location was rediscovered centuries later, and another city was built using the stone left behind from the first. While the design of the new city was advanced, considering drainage and the springs of fresh, cold water, it was eventually overrun by creatures of the forest, potentially at the instigation of druids, and the population was forced to move out. It was another thousand years before tribal hunters discovered the stone walls and eventually moved to settle in, and still more time before a clan of dwarves driven from their homes by the Hyperborean invasions to the east came to settle here as well. These dwarves took it upon themselves to build and enhance the walls and buildings in the hopes of avoiding being driven from this new home as well. Some of these designs and creations have lasted to the modern day and protect a city that predates nearly every settlement in the region. While most of those dwarves eventually moved on, some dwarven families still make their home here.

Heavy logging by the inhabitants of Brookmere eventually stripped much of the surrounding area, most of which was given over to wide fields growing a variety of crops and a number of orchards producing a vast array of different types of fruit.

When the Kingdom of Foere expanded and conquered both nearby and distant lands, Brookmere did fall along with all the rest, but the repeated revolts of the Principality of Olduvar kept Brookmere isolated from the main kingdom and largely forgotten. As the Foerdewaith Wars of Succession raged, Brookmere was largely forgotten, unimportant to the needs of the Kingdom of Foere. The departure of the Foerdewaith, however, has allowed the growth of a number of tribes of orcs and goblins within the light forests nearby, further isolating Brookmere from its neighbors.

In recent years, the efforts needed to combat the humanoids moving into the region, while largely successful, began to drain the city's coffers to the point that Lord Thorbold realized it wasn't sustainable. He has turned to diplomacy in an effort to set his potential adversaries against each other. To this end, he entered into a treaty with the Irontooth Clan of orcs and some other humanoids that reside in some of the light forests nearby. While the treaty is viewed poorly by some, most realize that the city has little choice.

While Brookmere spends a great deal on its defense, its strong walls and defenses cannot protect the farmlands outside the city walls. The presence of one of the few open schools of magic, and the knowledge that wizards training within are involved in the defense of the city, provides additional incentive for their neighbors to leave Brookmere in peace.

Most of the human population here is of Foerdewaith descent. There is a fairly large population of elves for a city of this size, and a number of dwarves make their home here, descendants of those who built many of the city's walls and buildings. These dwarves are considered "clanless" and looked down on by other dwarves, which keeps them isolated from other dwarven communities. A small contingent of gnomes that migrated here several decades ago has become important in the mining of gems as well as the crafting of jewelry and other works of art. Recent peaceful relations with the Irontooth Clan have seen orcs and half-orcs move into the city, where they are largely accepted or at least left alone in peace.

Citizens of Brookmere are generally outgoing and friendly and accept others for who they are. The philosophy here is that if your activities don't harm or prevent mine, then you are free to do whatever you please.

Religion

Brookmere has no declared religious affiliation, and, at least officially, allows and welcomes individuals of all faiths. Construction of temples and altars requires city approval and permits as well as a yearly tax. At present, small temples to Freya, Thyr, and Muir exist.

Trade and Commerce

Brookmere focuses on protecting the nearby farmlands and several small silver mines that help support the city. Trade traffic is not extensive, but continuous enough to continue to support the city and its slow growth. Thriving orchards, vineyards, and farmlands lie to the south of the main city walls, all producing bountiful harvests for trade and support of the city. Craftsmen here are among the most skilled in the Lost Lands and produce refined, expensive goods for trade.

Boosting its importance, the Free City of Brookmere is one of few cities to openly house a school of magic, which gives it greater importance in the area and helps maintain its status as a free city. Wizards from the school are directly tasked with defending the city in the event of any sort of attack and provide additional aid in the construction and maintenance of its defenses.

Loyalty and Diplomacy

As a declared Free City, Brookmere has had some difficulties with the Principality of Olduvar and the Kingdom of Foere which both, at different times in history, controlled the city and its environs. Olduvar used to attack as often as once a decade but it is presently too self-involved with its own intrigues to pose an active threat.

Briarwatch, Bridgeport, and Kindler's Bell have all declared a form of allegiance to Brookmere, more in an effort to protect themselves from the predations of Olduvar than for any true loyalty. Whether or not Brookmere would truly come to the defense of these small towns and villages remains an unanswered question. There have been no attacks and, while treaties have been signed, no taxes are collected on them by Brookmere. The reality is that they are of little economic or military importance and are geographically difficult to get to.

Brookmere adheres to few laws, and city leaders allow most activities so long as they are taxed and controlled in a way that benefits the city and its leading families. Those in charge recognize that their status as a free city is grounded partly on their distance from major nations as well as their impressive defenses. They have no desire to pique the interest or rage of larger and more powerful nations, so they avoid any extreme tariffs or activities that might reduce the trade traffic that makes its way through the city.

Government

The major guild leaders of the city elect a town-commander, who at this point is Lord Thorbold. He has formed an advisory council with leaders of several guilds and organizations including the Merchant Guild (Guildmaster Shokri), Crafters' Guild (Lady Jian Fodril), the captain of the guard (Captain Dal White), and the headmaster of the Brookmere Wizard's College (Lady Aerlyn). Brookmere maintains stability by keeping its militia and city walls strong and by keeping taxes and tariffs low. Leadership changes only when leaders of the four main institutions change. The past 50 years have seen stable and peaceful changes in the city leadership, which help maintain a strong city.

The laws of Brookmere are lax. Most drugs, prostitution, and even slavery are legal here, although actual trade in slaves is frowned upon. Simply put, physical attacks against others are illegal, except in the case of self-defense, and almost everything else is legal. Nevertheless, the city is relatively peaceful and considered safe for most travelers. A single court system handles all civil disagreements and criminal complaints. Decisions can be appealed to the town-commander, but he usually lets the court decisions stand.

The ancient foundations here conceal a vast network of catacombs dating back to the elven creators of the first city to stand here. Those who know of the catacombs whisper that they lead to larger, deeper networks of caverns stretching far beneath the surface. City leaders are, quite honestly, frightened of the possibility of what might lurk in those catacombs and caverns so all entrances are kept sealed. Any time a collapse or construction reveals a new opening, it is promptly filled in, and guards watch over it until it is forgotten. Although not discussed officially, anyone found attempting to enter the catacombs or creating an opening to them is immediately arrested and brought before city leaders for punishment.

Military

The military consists of the general militia under General Reid Coldstone, and the city guard under Captain Lizette Raintree. Both groups work together to defend the city and the surrounding farms and mines. The general militia includes highly-trained infantry and artillery (ballistae and trebuchet) and man the defensive walls of the city as well as making continuing patrols of the surrounding areas. The city guard takes care of all policing of the city, including monitoring the gates, protecting valued clients and businesses, and investigating crimes. The city guard also assists in the defense of the city under the orders of the militia. General Coldstone has a detailed knowledge of the powers and abilities of the most powerful mages in the Brookmere Wizard's College and is able to call upon them in the event the city is attacked.

Brookmere Wizard's College

One of the few openly declared schools of magic in the Lost Lands, the Brookmere Wizard's College possesses an extensive library and a few powerful mages, but, in truth, most of the students here possess little skill and are often children of wealthy families sent to learn control over their meager powers and to bring some enhanced reputation to their family. Students here are required to take oaths of allegiance to the school, which, in turn, swears to aid the city when needed. While some of the students are not powerful enough to find apprenticeship with more powerful mages, the number of students here makes the school a formidable addition to the protection of the city as a whole. Lady Aerlyn presently controls the school and its faculty.

Rumors about Archmage Hariodolbus and the school that he began more than 2,000 years ago abound. Possessing magical knowledge and abilities far beyond any normal mage, he is said to have founded the school here as a way to spread his knowledge and to help other mages discover their true powers. Truth, as in many cases, is darker and stranger than the stories that are now told. Archmage Hariodolbus was beholden to a demon for the powers he was given and needed to sacrifice someone of magical talent once each year to maintain his powers and keep the demon at bay. The school was started simply to collect likely candidates so the archmage could find one that wouldn't be missed. Few know the truth behind the school, but the building itself contains many secret rooms, some tainted with dark and evil magic.

Brookmere Library

Originally constructed by Archmage Hariodolbus at the same time as the Wizard's College, the Brookmere Library is famous throughout nearby lands as one of the finest repositories of knowledge in the Lost Lands. In existence now for more than 2,000, the library contains and protects an extensive collection of ancient texts, including various scrolls and tapestries from ancient times. The head of the library, who is known only as the Loremaster, personally decides who may see the rarest and most valuable texts, but other parts of the library are open to visitors. Many sages make pilgrimages to Brookmere simply to visit and study in the Brookmere Library.

Reference Source: FGG1 Fane of the Fallen

Briarwatch, Town of

Ruler: Elder Eimhar Powel
Government: limited democracy
Population: 1,377 (840 Foerdewaith, 457 human mixed ethnicity, 47 half-elf, 33 mountain dwarf)
Languages: Common, Dwarven
Religion: Solanus
Resources: livestock (goats, sheep), iron ore, grain
Currency: mixed
Technology Level: Dark Ages

Once nothing more than a small village of goat and sheep herders in the Briar Hills south of the Nadi River near the Crescent Sea, Briarwatch is growing. Iron ore found in the nearby hills has attracted the investment of the Jouril family, a major iron smelter in the Free City of Brookmere. The family brought in supplies and materials, built barracks-style buildings for their miners, and has gone out of their way to support the present village leadership. The village does not produce enough food for all of the new miners, so the Jourils import additional food that is sold to the miners at cost. Raw iron ore is taken by caravan to the Free City of Brookmere once a week.

Presently, Briarwatch is run by a council of original inhabitants who have reached the age of 60, and who elect one of their own to act as the elder of the village. The miners are still considered visitors and do not have a say in government. There are so many miners now that the villagers are afraid of being overrun. There is no town watch other than some guards hired by the Jouril family to protect the mines and shipments of ore. All herdsmen are expected to rise to the defense of the village and the herds when needed. However, the influx of new people has Elder Eimhar Powel considering asking some of the sturdier herdsmen and experienced hunters to act as a regular guard for the village. He intends to charge the Jouril family a tax to support this, but has yet to act on the plan.

Bridgeport, City of

Rulers: Baron Goron Ulien
Government: Limited Democracy
Population: 38,400 (21,200 Foerdewaith, 9,425 human mixed ethnicity, 3,820 halfling, 1,890 mountain dwarf, 1,210 high elf, 370 gnome, 265 half-elf, 135 half-orc, 85 other)
Languages: Common, Elven, Gnome, Dwarven, Halfling
Religion: Belon the Wise, Sefagreth, Quell, Muir
Resources: agriculture, trade, shipbuilding, shipbuilding supplies, livestock, banking
Currency: mixed
Technology Level: Medieval

Modest fortifications and stone buildings hover over the rocky shoreline here, protecting the piers and docks that are the lifeblood of Bridgeport. Most of the shoreline stretching from the Falconmere Peninsula up to the Worntooth Peaks can't support the large structures needed to form a good harbor as the shoreline varies from high and rocky to soft and swampy. Bridgeport is the closest safe port for large merchant vessels arriving through the Strait of Praeis and, of course, the last safe port before departing the Crescent Sea, which provides it with very heavy shipping and merchant traffic that the city does its best to support and encourage.

For more about Bridgeport, see *Sea King's Malice* from **Frog God Games**.

History and People

Like many of the areas nearby, Bridgeport was once under the control of the Kingdom of Foere but that control fell away during the Foerdewaith Wars of Succession. The separation from Foere by Olduvar and the presence of nearby Brookmere help keep Bridgeport independent. Most of the citizens are human residents of Foerdewaith descent, but there is also a significant population of halfling craftsmen and a number of dwarves that migrated here from Brookmere years ago. A healthy mix of other races can be found here as well; Bridgeport sees enough merchant traffic through its harbor that visitors occasionally decide to stop here and take up residence.

The foundations here are deep and ancient. As one of the few areas able to support a sizable harbor along this stretch of coastline, there has been a city of some type at this place for thousands of years. Warfare, piracy, and even massive storms have changed the shape and form of the city over time, as well as its residents, but this location is ideal for traders and merchants, so even in the face of catastrophe the city has always been rebuilt. The present structures have stood for several centuries but the flooded catacombs beneath the city are from a distant, unrecorded past.

Religion

All religions are welcomed here as the city's leaders do not want to alienate any merchants or traders. The Temple District is inland from the Trademoot and contains many temples, some grand and others quite humble. The leading among these are temples to Sefagreth (trade), Quell (the sea), and Belon the Wise. A temple to Muir is smaller and has fewer devotees. The Green Father is also worshipped here with a well-maintained temple and altar.

Trade and Commerce

Trade is the lifeblood of Bridgeport. Whether it is agricultural goods traveling to the port to be transported out or goods from the ships docking here meant to be sent inland, most of the city is devoted to attracting and keeping merchant traffic passing through. After agriculture, fishing and ship building and repair are the next largest contributors to the city's coffers, with various smaller guilds following closely behind.

While shipping and trade are certainly the primary concerns of Bridgeport, running a not-so-distant second is farming. The entire region is known for its large plantations. These farms fan out inland around Bridgeport and line the trade way to Brookmere. A semi-tropical climate, fertile ground, and easy access to distant and eager markets make this region an agricultural hotbed. While there are farms that raise livestock, the vast majority of the plantations in the region produce cash crops, with the most significant being allspice, figs, cotton, gold melon, maize, millet, olives, oranges, and turnips.

Another of Bridgeport's primary features is that it boasts one of the few true shipyards on the Crescent Sea. Shipwrights here are capable of building craft of almost any size and capability, and the shipyard can also perform repairs on damaged boats. The one drawback is that the yard is small enough that only one large ship can be built at a time, and each ship takes a considerable amount of construction time.

Three major trade houses are in Bridgeport: Risen Star, The Tamil Group, and Zephyr Assimilated, which is also the largest. These three concerns, and others, are responsible for shipping the local agricultural products abroad as well as inland. They then return with a vast array of goods from far-flung points in the Lost Lands to sell locally in Bridgeport or the surrounding cities.

A robust guild presence supports the seafaring trades and ship construction as well as a variety of inns, casinos, and brothels. Banking services provided by the Rising Sun Coinhouse are recognized throughout many of the major trade cities in the Lost Lands.

The busiest part of the city is the Trademoot. Close to the docks, the Trademoot is a combination open-air market and auction arena. Locals sell their wares and produce in booths while the open-air auction house is where all manner of things are sold. Most of the influential guilds and finest shops in Bridgeport surround the Trademoot.

Loyalty and Diplomacy

Bridgeport has a mutual defense treaty with the Free City of Brookmere, but, in truth, it would expect any attack against it to come from the sea, making the treaty of little benefit. Trade agreements with the City-State of Castorhage, Brookmere, the Kingdom of the North Heath, and even distant Reme help maintain trade traffic through the city. No present agreements are in place with the Tycho Free States, but there is considerable trade traffic with merchant vessels from the far side of the Crescent Sea.

Government

Bridgeport is a barony, but not exactly in the classic sense. While the baron is the nominal ruler of Bridgeport, he is advised by a council of city leaders called the Seven who are the heads of powerful and influential families residing in Bridgeport. Most of the members of the Seven are either from one of the major merchant houses or are plantation owners, the two biggest industries in Bridgeport (trade and farming). The baron of Bridgeport is thus more of a mayor working with the advice and consent of the Seven than a sovereign ruler.

The baron serves an indefinite term, one basically determined by the confidence and support of the Seven. This means the baron is forced to consider his supporters in all the decisions he makes. Goron Ulien has made it his goal to become as important as possible to the livelihood of the Free City of Brookmere as he believes it can only enhance and protect Bridgeport's status. Lax laws and reasonable tariffs ensure that a great deal of trade runs through Bridgeport, but without the support of a larger city or nation-state, the baron and others of the local elite believe their chances of growing larger are limited.

A well-armed and organized militia enforces the law, but these laws are designed to encourage trade and visitors, not to turn them away. While the actual trade in slaves is outlawed, ownership and use of slaves is fairly common, especially on the surrounding plantations. Import laws with respect to drugs and other items are equally friendly. There is a single court system in town managed by judges picked by the baron, usually with the approval of various city leaders. Corruption in the courts is common, and wealthy patrons have little to fear in the court system.

Military

The militia here is officially under the control of Colonel Girese Longcoat, who commands the guardsmen of the city. While the militia is not very large, it is well-trained, which makes their defensive positions formidable in the event of an attack. Most of the work of the militia comes in the form of acting as guardsmen policing the city for violent crimes. Bridgeport also has a small but effective navy of one galley and three longships under the command of Captain Coral White that patrols the waters just outside the harbor and periodically makes rounds to watch over active fishermen and whalers.

Major Threats

Baron Ulien and the city leaders believe that Bridgeport's major threat comes in its dependence on trade. So the city makes a concerted effort to encourage more skilled craftsmen to come to the city and hopes to encourage the proliferation of its already robust agricultural sector.

Kindler's Bell, Village of

Ruler: Sister Nin
Government: theocracy
Population: 1,657 (910 Foerdewaith, 605 human mixed ethnicity, 87 halfling, 55 half-elf)
Languages: Common, Halfling
Religion: Ninkasi (Goddess of Beer and Desire)
Resources: fishing, grain, foodstuffs
Currency: mixed
Technology Level: Dark Ages

Ramshackle buildings sprawl randomly across these rocky hills clinging to the coast of the Crescent Sea. While some are clean, tidy, and painted with bright colors, the majority of the homes and buildings are in poor repair, with many evincing obvious storm damage. The vast majority of those living inside the village earn their livelihood fishing the Crescent Sea. The shallow rocky waters of the small harbor are unsuitable for larger vessels, and only smaller fishing boats can really dock here. Periodically, larger ships anchor farther out and send boats in to trade, usually for fresh water and dried fish, but there is little in the way of active commerce.

Villagers live under the philosophy, "Work Hard, Play Harder." The center of the village is taken up by a wide, well-tended square before a small temple to Ninkasi, Goddess of Beer and Desire. On all Akados, only two clerics venerate this almost-forgotten goddess, and both serve at this temple. Every evening, the square hosts a party where fish are cooked on open fires and other foods are brought in from nearby homes. The clerics provide their blessing, and the eating, drinking, and revelry begin. Outsiders are welcome to join in; those who bring additional food or beverages even more so.

The nearby farmlands grow wheat and other grains and send their produce into the village as offerings. The farmers come into town many nights to also enjoy the festivities. The village and nearby farms exist seemingly in a microcosm, too small and out of the way for others to be concerned with, and too consumed with its constant revelry and signs of faith to the obscure goddess who protects them to wish to bother with the outside world. Most of the food and fish is consumed during the nightly parties, but some fish is smoked and dried to provide lasting rations.

Sister Nin, as the senior cleric, is the unquestioned ruler of the village. Sister Asi, the junior cleric, is her second-in-command. Both women are exceptionally beautiful and charismatic and use their magic to aid villagers in need. The daily revelry is part of the worship of their goddess that the villagers are happy to participate in. In turn, the clerics provide ale and other items with their spells, as well as healing to those devout villagers who might require it. The clerics protect the villagers in times of powerful storms; in turn, the villagers hold true to the faith and worship of Ninkasi.

Castorhage and Its Dependencies

City-State of Castorhage

Capital: Castorhage
Notable Settlements: Tarry
Ruler: Her Royal Highness Queen Alice and three crown justices
Government: hereditary monarchy
Population: 4,800,000 (3,216,000 human various ethnicity; 241,000 mongrelfolk; 239,000 ratfolk; 192,000 gnome; 192,000 dwarf; 144,000 half-elf; 96,000 goblinoid; 72,000 half-orc; 62,400 briny; 57,600 orc; 48,000 elf; 240,000 other including halfling, swyne, tengu, inphidian, tabaxi, grippli, ghazaks, dhampir, and vishkanyas)
Monstrous: too numerous to mention
Languages: Common, along with most other languages found in the Lost Lands

Religion: Mother Grace, Mammon, Lord Shingles, Sister Shadows, Mithras, Geryon, Lucifer, Baphomet, Brine, the Green Father, Demoriel

Resources: trade hub, manufactured goods, banking, coal, pitch, cotton, cloth, spices, whale oil, spirits (beer, liquors), ironwork, shipbuilding, tin, alchemical reagents, glass, alchemy, magical resources, breeding (dogs, warhorses)

Currency: Castorhage, mixed

Technology Level: Renaissance

The City-State of Castorhage is a shadowy and storied land with a deep, dark history stretching back thousands of years. Predominantly made up of the city of Castorhage, the city-state includes colonies in Between as well as the more conventional city of Tarry that provides a port for Castorhage on the mainland. Any listener hearing the name thinks of the city as a nation, for the city alone is larger than most nations, and certainly more powerful than all but the greatest. Known to most simply as "the Blight," Castorhage has many other names, including the Canker, the Rot, City of Secrets and Lies, City of Golems, and for many, simply the City.

HISTORY AND PEOPLE

The isle upon which Castorhage sits has a history longer and deeper than even modern scholars know, with settlements stretching back more than 12,000 years, a history too deep to enter into here. What is known to scholars at this point is that the city-state's early formation began 5,000 years ago with the rise of the Hyperborean Empire, during which Strategos Oleus Castorhage was granted the right to establish and rule the island province of Insula Lymossus. As the military governor, Oleus established Citadel Castorhage, which overlooks the Great Lyme River.

The Castorhagi family ruled as faithful stewards of the Hyperborean Empire for more than 1,700 years, during which time they built a successful city on the banks of the estuary. This ended when a mysterious stranger known as the Eburnean Oracle found the ear of Demos Castorhage and eventually convinced him to declare independence from the Hyperborean Empire and title himself King Demos Castorhage I. Within a decade, skirmishes with Hyperborean forces grew into the Eleventy Years war. The war went poorly for Castorhage, until finally the Borxia, Tredici, Nightshade, and Castorhage families established the First Illuminati and called upon the archdevil Caasimolar to intercede on their behalf. With the archdevil's help, an agreement was made whereby hostilities ceased and the city-state would retain its independence, but the Castorhage family had to pass the crown to the Borxia family.

The Borxia family ruled for 222 years before the Castorhage family regained the throne, which it has now held for 1,500 consecutive years, excepting a trio of short periods when non-Castorhagi queens were on the throne. Castorhagi rule has brought the city-state into the modern era through the collapse of the Hyperborean Empire as well as the growth of Foere and numerous challenges along the way. The greatest, and possibly most dangerous, was the discovery of the Between. This strange echo-land that can be reached through special mirror-portals provided a different way for Castorhage to expand and an entirely new set of resources to exploit. Most of the true colonies and expansion of Castorhage is now in the Between, which has had a variety of effects on the city-state.

Castorhage has made discoveries and breakthroughs in a variety of areas that some might find disturbing and even immoral, including the science of creating golems and planar binding. If other nations knew the scope of some of the experiments taking place within Castorhage, they might wish to put an end to it, but would also fear the consequences if they attempted to do so.

The citizens of Castorhage are a mix of races and creatures not seen elsewhere, including ratfolk, mongrelfolk, as well as creatures unique to Castorhage itself. The simple hustle and bustle of the city is full of people from distant lands who came here and stayed, sometimes even by choice. The City-State of Castorhage is a dynamic, changing nation, largely concentrated in its main city, yet spread out into the Between and in small colonies that represent its interests throughout the Lost Lands.

TRADE AND COMMERCE

Castorhage's trade relationships are so vast that it is sometimes easier to list those nations it doesn't trade with. Presently, Castorhage enjoys open and free trade relations with the Aizanes-Tulita Islands, the Free City of Brookmere, the city-states of the Buntesveldt, the free city of Endhome, the Elitan-i-Pan Confederation of the Haunted Steppes, the cities of the Domain of Hawkmoon, the Kingdom of Khemit, the Southern Libynosi Paramountcies, the City of Mulstabha, Port Shaw and other colonial settlements of the Razor Coast, the City of Trinidar, the Kingdom of the North Heath, the Kingdom of the Vast, and the Xha'en Hegemony. Nations and cities with somewhat more cautious trade agreements include Bard's Gate, the Kingdom of Foere, Gtsang Prefecture, the Huun Imperium, the Empire of Oceanus, the grey elves of Sarefein, the native Tulita of the Razor Sea, the Tycho Free States, the Kingdom of Helcynngae, and the Grand Duchy of Reme.

Castorhage has also settled colonies around the world, including on the Bream Islands near the Xha'en Hegemony and on Libynos. Many of those colonies' neighbors view Castorhage with distrust and trepidation. The Empire of Alcaldar and the Pirate Confederacy of the eastern Razor Sea are examples of two nations that not only don't have good trade relations with Castorhage but are openly hostile to its interests.

LOYALTIES AND DIPLOMACY

The City-State of Castorhage enjoys a close and friendly relationship with the Kingdom of the North Heath and the Kingdom of the Vast, with somewhat more tenuous relationships with the Grand Duchy of Reme, the Kingdom of Foere and the Tycho Free States. While North Heath and Vast feel a particular loyalty to Castorhage for its part in negotiating the end of the wars for their independence from Foere, keeping those nations free and independent was a tactical move on the part of Castorhage. The independence of those nations allows Castorhage to focus on its own problem with fewer concerns about Foere or Reme.

The simple truth of Castorhage is that it is not known for getting along well with others; it has always been more concerned about itself and its own problems than with anyone else.

GOVERNMENT

Officially, Her Royal Highness Queen Alice is the ruler of the City-State of Castorhage with nine-year-old Princess Alicia "The Little Queen" her chosen heir. The simple truth is that Queen Alice is merely a puppet for the crown justices who are the true rulers of Castorhage. The three crown justices, known as the Illuminati Triad by those who serve them, covertly control all matters of the city-state. The queen is kept under control by the alchemy used to keep her upright.

The simple, and somewhat disturbing, fact is that almost every element of the government is actively plotting to move higher through the sabotage, destruction, and even outright murder of those above them. Thirteen justices oversee specific aspects of city law or municipal governance while the under-justices beneath them actively plot against others as well as the justice they serve. Each under-justice is the chief jurist of a city district with absolute power in their district and can only be overruled by a member of the royal family. Judicares are minor judges who handle court and criminal cases beneath the notice of an under-justice. Streetclerks provide legal aid and other services for the under-justice and sometimes fill in for them when they don't feel like hearing a case. Underclerks assist streetclerks. Each of these wants to move upward through the ranks, and how they accomplish that feat is of little concern.

The maze of constant betrayal, spying, and deceit that makes up the government of Castorhage is perhaps a saving grace for the rest of the world. If not for these constant distractions and the continuing exploration of the Between, the city-state might turn its eyes outward toward the rest of the world.

MILITARY

Although the City-State of Castorhage is unwalled and maintains a standing army within the city numbering only 17,000, Castorhage has seemingly grown too big to fall to external invasion. The stinking Lych Fen surrounding the city is only one deterrent; it is the sheer press of humanity calling the city home that gives pause to any thought of a military invasion. A greater danger would be a blockade that let the city starve, but its powerful naval fleet makes such an endeavor simply an exercise of thought.

The Royal Army is estimated to have more than 100,000 colonial auxiliaries stationed throughout its possessions worldwide. Such troops are trained in their native land but then moved to other possessions to prevent any chance of an armed uprising in their homeland. Officially, the Royal Navy is part of the army and makes up approximately a quarter of its troops. The navy possesses a fleet of 57 ships of war, some of which are of the most modern design and abilities of any in the world.

The Watch (known as Officers of the Watch or the Queen's Men) numbers just over 2,100 and is somehow expected to patrol and prevent crime in a city of millions. In essence, the Watch worries only about major threats to the city or to its most important personages, and ignores most other crime as minor enough to be handled by others. Poorly paid and monitored, bribery of members of the Watch is considered more a standard than a surprise.

MAJOR THREATS

Much could be said of the threats the city faces simply because of the Between, but the City-State of Castorhage's greatest threat is itself. The infighting and competition between various elements of the city royalty, government, and secret organizations is the most consistent threat to Castorhage. A nation this powerful, with this many resources, magic, and technology at its disposal can only be brought down by itself.

WILDERNESS AND ADVENTURE

The City-State of Castorhage is full of adventure opportunities, whether it is exploring the Between, getting caught up in the intrigues of the cults or city leaders, battling against (or for) the Illuminati, working with the guilds, or getting involved in the politics of the city. Danger lies just a few steps forward in the streets and alleyways of the Blight, but the stalwart adventurer should be warned that this is no ordinary place and those steps forward could change them forever.

REFERENCE SOURCE: THE BLIGHT

CASTORHAGE

Ruler: Her Royal Highness Queen Alice and three crown justices

Government: hereditary monarchy

Population: 3,284,990 (2,200,950 human various ethnicity; 164,250 mongrelfolk; 164,250 ratfolk; 131,400 gnome; 131,400 dwarf; 98,550 half-elf; 65,700 goblinoid; 49,275 half-orc; 42,705 briny; 39,420 orc; 32,840 elf; 164,250 other including halfling, swyne, tengu, inphidian, tabaxi, grippli, ghazaks, dhampir, and vishkanyas)

Castorhage is both city and nation. While the city-state includes colonies throughout the known Lost Lands and the Between, in truth Castorhage is the city-state. It is a city of excess, deceit, lies, and desperation in which any object can be found, any item acquired, and any sin committed. Each of the districts of Castorhage is as large, or larger, than all but the greatest of cities in the Lost Lands, and each has its own flavor, its own twist on the Blight that consumes and, really, becomes this whole place.

This is merely a taste of the rot, decay, and opulence that is the Blight. The following brief description of the districts in Castorhage are just a quick glance, a sideways look from the corner of one's eye, and ill-equipped to encompass the true majesty, and horror, of the Blight.

THE CAPITOL

Seventeen centuries of labor and the lives of more than 10,000 workers brought to life the dreams of hundreds of architects, politicians, and kings in the form of the Capitol. A thousand buildings crushed into one, it rises as a single building imposing itself upon the entire city. This is the home of Queen Alice, the royal family, the crown justices, and the 13 justices who assist them. Servants of all types serve here, as do countless clerks and other officials. Deceit, lies, and betrayal command here, as they do throughout the city, but here they are unequalled, existing on a scale only the most twisted mind could encompass.

THE ARTISTS' QUARTER

At the heart of the city, the Artist's Quarter provides home to artists practicing a thousand different forms of performing and traditional arts. The district is fractured with artists gathering by disciplines, with streets of puppet-makers running to alleys of glassblowers stretching toward courtyards of paint makers. Lurking in the shadows here are the fetch, whose vampire elders are drawn to the waking nightlife, the Triads of the Xha'en and Gtsang immigrants, and the rebels and anarchists. Between these powerful groups and the various artists struggling for fame and glory, the Artists' Quarter is a hotbed of anarchy, intrigue, plots, blackmail, and deceit.

THE BARNACLES AND GREAT DOCK

Built upon various levels of tunnels that link in turn to the outer buildings, this large island town is a dizzying stack of buildings rising from the ocean. Hundreds of buildings are variously tied, nailed, or bolted to the precarious cliff faces hovering over jagged rocks below. Tunnels weave through the rock, and a vast array of bridges links to a wall of warehouses, buildings, cranes, and ferries that serve ships docked here.

BOOKTOWN

Tall buildings and towers linked by bridges, gangplanks, rope bridges, and ladders create echoing canyons that smell of old books and ink. BookTown is a repository for tomes and grimoires of all types, maps, arcana and all manner of written works. Merchants, wizards, and even creatures from distant planes find their way here in search of knowledge. BookTown is home to the Seminary, home to the greatest universities and academies clinging to the foot of the Capitol.

Knowledge has its price, and in Castorhage, almost everyone is willing to pay that price, particularly those in power. The Seminary is a center of experimentation where the first breach into the Between occurred and where the first alchymic undead were raised, and now provides a home for countless other horrific, dangerous experiments.

While the Seminary has its own special type of fame, the most hated parish in the city lies in BookTown. The City of Golems found here is home to an area of cottage universities and charnel houses providing alchemists and physikers free range, and an endless supply of bodies, to experiment upon.

FESTIVAL AND THE GREAT FAYRE

Festival is a huge timber pier in the Lyme River built around a squat gray hill. Ruled by the Rat Queen, this is a metropolis of wererats and hidden lycanthropy. Rising some 200 feet through steep streets called the Skew to the Great Fayre at the summit, Festival is a shamble of buildings built upon buildings, groaning and threatening to collapse at any moment. Half of Festival is covered with the Crimson Lantern, the town's prostitution district where the darkest of excesses can be enjoyed.

THE GREAT LYME RIVER (SISTER LYME)

The foul waters of Sister Lyme cut through the heart of the city, keeping at bay the districts behind its docks and warehouses, yet somehow touching upon them all with its fetid stain. It is a place of false islands, smuggling, piracy, murder, and any who wish to cloak their deeds in shadowy darkness. Somehow there is life here; sough-eels and slop-sharks are just a few of the many creatures hungrily watching those above. A fall into these tainted waters is a sure death sentence.

Adding to the river's dark stench is the Bilges, the answer to the city's sewer problem. Nicknamed both "Stinktown" and the "City of Perfume," the Bilges is about the lowest a person can find themselves in the city. All of the unwanted rubbish of the city comes here to die and decay in one of the islands of waste. The decay creates a stench unlike any other, a concentrated form of rot that causes the islands of refuse to shift, move, and seemingly change form with a life of their own.

The Gyre also finds home in the river, a town of flotsam and jetsam that should not hold together, yet somehow does. Its ability to support a settlement complete with buildings, boardwalk streets, and piers is unbelievable. It is one more of the impossible wonders of Sister Lyme that is both interesting and yet disturbing to behold.

THE HOLLOW AND BROKEN HILLS

Tree-lined avenues and parks, cliffs, inlets and temples and places of worship fill the splintered land here. Miracles happen among the temples, grottoes, and altars. Sanctuary, home of the master of the church in Castorhage, stands here, as do various vast holes that have come to replace some of the churches that were once here before. Powerful clerics, bishops, archbishops and holy fathers rule this part of the city, but don't be fooled, their lust for power and propensity for intrigue and duplicity runs as high as anywhere else in the city.

THE JUMBLE

Known as the Cat's Cradle, the Madness, the Maze, the City of Thieves, and a few less-kind names, the Jumble is a vast, confusing maze of streets rising upward and outward in a vague, pale mockery of the Capitol itself. It is a place to get lost or to seek a richer life, a home to a variety of thieves and villains, as well as those simply trying to escape something. The Jumble has its own markets and laws. Vigilantes walk the streets at night, but foul things still easily find a home here.

Claiming to be the greatest market in the world, the Bazaar sits beside and within the Jumble. It is a thousand streets filled with countless shops, stalls, markets, and traders, where, purportedly, anything can be found. The air here is tainted with desperation as voices call out the goods they are selling and arguments can be heard echoing through the maze of buildings.

THE SINKS

The Sinks provide a sign of Castorhage's future. The city itself is built on clay and silt deposits, the ever-increasing weight of building upon building crushing those at the bottom into the ground. The Sinks began as the brainchild of King Branner. Planned as a new town for artisans, it was cursed from the beginning. Even as "Branner's Folly" was being built, it was sinking into the soft ground. What remains today is a twisted wreckage of leaning walls, broken battlements, and haunting arched bridges over canals that range between a few feet deep and seemingly bottomless. The Sinks are disturbing for visitors, the view inducing fits of vertigo and dizziness, but the disowned nobility making their homes here think of it as an elite domain. This is a home for true exiles, those who have committed crimes beyond what is normal in the rest of Castorhage.

THE ASYLUM

Only in Castorhage would there be an area larger than most cities dedicated to nothing more than hiding the less-fortunate. This walled off area of the city has its own laws and even its own currency. The walls and buildings are secured such that there is only one single huge doorway in or out. The inmates here are left to rot; once cast into the Asylum, no one ever leaves.

TOILTOWN (EAST ENDING)

Whether one calls it the East, East Ending, or the State of Sweat, Toiltown is hated by everyone, even the overseers and managers who run the endless manufactories and sweatshops, workhouses, and underground mills. The lowest castes of the city live here amid the dizzying array of unnamed streets and slums. Life is cheap here. East Ending has an unenviable history of murder, there being several every night. Beneath even this dark surface lies a darker trade in slavery, and worse, because anything can be bought here.

Hanging from East Ending near the Great Docks is Boattown. While there are other boattowns throughout the Blight, this fixed group of piers, riverboats, and planks carries the name like a banner. Halfling families control this, the nastiest of boattowns, where fisherman rub shoulders with briny and murder costs but a few coins, if that.

TOWN BRIDGE

Town Bridge takes advantage of curious laws that do not recognize the bridge as part of the city. Lodgings and traders on the bridge escape taxation. As a result, Town Bridge is a mass of trade and humanity crushed into the space between the Great East Bridge Gate and the Royal West Bridge Gate. Shacks can be lashed onto the side of a building or simply hung out over the edge of the bridge itself. Buildings here stretch upward and outward over the Lyme River.

UNDERNEATH

The Underneath is everything below the city, and it is vast and deep. Made up of caves, fissures, and ancient buildings that have sunk beneath the ground, the Underneath touches every part of the city, and, in truth, threatens it with the possibility of collapse. Streets and buildings have been known to disappear into massive sinkholes as the caves and openings below lose their integrity and fall in themselves. The city just fills in and builds over these holes, as progress must be made.

PEOPLE

Castorhage is a clearinghouse for the unwanted, a stopping point for travelers, and a waypoint for wanderers. The Blight taints everyone living here over time until they become a part of the city in a way no other city bleeds into its people. Humans of every type found in the Lost Lands reside here, as do dwarves, elves, halflings, and all the other races. They are joined by coprophagi (roach people), briny, ratfolk, mongrelfolk, all manner of undead, dragons (though they usually hide their form), night slugs, swyne, tabaxi and many others who call the Blight home. If an intelligent creature exists on this or any other plane, it most likely can be found somewhere in Castorhage.

TARRY, CITY OF

Ruler: Duke Talmas Odrecky, Lord of the Damps
Government: feudal colony of the City-State of Castorhage
Population: 38,762 (30,235 human various ethnicity; 1,550 gnome; 1,500 mountain dwarf; 1,162 half-elf; 458 half-orc; 387 high elf; 3,470 other including halfling, briny, ratfolk, mongrelfolk, swyne, tengu, inphidian, and tabaxi)
Languages: Common, Gnome, Dwarven, Elven, Infernal
Religion: Mother Grace, Mammon, Lord Shingles, Sister Shadows, Mithras, Geryon, Lucifer, Baphomet, Brine, The Green Father, Demoriel
Resources: trade hub, manufactured goods, coal, pitch, cotton, cloth, whale oil, spirits (beer, liquors), alchemical reagents, alchemy, magical resources
Technology Level: Medieval

Tall stone buildings stand out along the shoreline, hovering above the docks extending out into the Crescent Sea. Tarry is one of the few areas along the eastern shoreline of the Crescent Sea suitable for larger docks and ships, so, in spite of other drawbacks to the waters in this area, Tarry has stood here in some form for thousands of years. The ancient foundations beneath some of the buildings have sunk deep into the soft earth, and are now filled with mud, silt, and water and almost impossible to explore.

Taverns, inns, joy houses, and supply houses surround a broad square at the foot of the docks where ships and caravan wagons exchange goods before heading out on their journeys. Opulent mansions overlook the docks and ocean from hills located away from and above the shoreline. The rest of the city feels as if it was simply tacked together, a random assortment of buildings with mixed purposes held together by hope, luck, and, in some cases, dark impulses. Some of the creatures found here shock visitors, as they are rarely seen anywhere but Castorhage. These creatures are just one more reminder that this is now a part of the City-State of Castorhage.

Annexed from the Duchy of Kear after the defeat of the Singed Man, Tarry provides the City-State of Castorhage with a port on the coast of Akados, a needed trading site that allows merchants to send their goods throughout the continent. Virtually any goods can be found here, as can most services, if one is able to pay the price. The lax laws and even more haphazard enforcement found in Castorhage have spread to Tarry like a looming cancer. Deaths at night are generally ruled accidental; apparently falling and accidently cutting one's own throat is a regular occurrence.

The seas around Tarry are shallow and silty, and the area is known for the oil and sludge seeping from the seabed. The oil seep creates an oily, sludgy area of ocean known as the Damps. Workers from Tarry collect the oily sludge and use it to make pitch, asphalt, tar, alchemist's fire, and a variety of other things.

Duke Talmas Odrecky runs Tarry in the name of the queen and maintains its docks and its status as trade hub while focusing on the magical resources the Damps provide. He is also in charge of the mysterious Preterhouse, a well-guarded site on a small island in the Damps. Preterhouse is rumored to be the site of experiments conducted by the government of Castorhage that are deemed too dangerous to be performed in the city. Considering the experiments performed in the city, it is difficult to imagine experiments horrific enough to be considered so dangerous.

THE SOUTHERN COAST OF AKADOS

POLITICAL SUBDIVISIONS OF THE SOUTHERN COAST OF AKADOS

DARKHOLLOW, CITY OF

Ruler: Triela Redbough, Jorak Mural, Drogo Coldburrow
Government: oligarchy
Population: 8,630 (2,762 human mixed ethnicity, 2,630 halfling, 2,538 high elf, 478 half-elf, 192 gnome, 17 mountain dwarf, 13 half-orc)
Languages: Common, Elven, Halfling, Gnome, Dwarven
Resources: herbs, spices, rare woods, woodwork
Currency: Foere, mixed
Technology Level: Dark Ages

Deep in the Harwood Forest a tall wooden palisade surrounds a small city, one built in levels with some homes nestled into the branches of the larger trees, quaint brightly-painted cottages on the ground, and burrow-like homes within the roots of the trees themselves. The trees and canopy have been trimmed back inside the walls to allow light to reach the ground where small fields have been tilled and grow herbs, flowers, and even a few crops. Halflings make up around 30% of the population, with the rest of the residents split almost evenly between humans and elves, with half-elves and individuals of a few other races making up the difference. Most of the halflings live in underground homes tucked into the roots of the trees. As one would expect, many of the elven residents occupy the homes built in the upper reaches of the trees, with some of the elves and a majority of the humans living in the cottages.

Most of the residents here delve into the forest during the daylight hours either for hunting, logging, collecting herbs or food, and in some cases seeking out gems or other rare items. Others focus on woodwork or other crafts. In truth, most of the residents here are simply working and living here because it is the only life they have known. Others know that there are places where life would be easier but choose to live here for reasons of their own. A few rare individuals are hiding out to avoid being captured and charged with crimes committed elsewhere.

HISTORY AND PEOPLE

Darkhollow contains a strange combination of races that came together out of necessity in a bid for simple survival. Originally split into encampments and villages of their own, the races were driven together to form a larger, safer community by the foul predations of a coven of hags. The hags would easily overrun smaller communities and use the residents in their foul rituals before moving on to another small village. Banding together to form a larger, organized force under the nominal control of an elven ranger known as Kailee Redarrow, humans, elves, and halflings managed to defeat or drive away the hags. After the hags were defeated, leaders of the three groups agreed to stay together for mutual protection. After more than 100 years, problems are rare, with everyone working together simply to survive in the dangerous environs of Harwood Forest.

Rather than breeding a people as harsh and dangerous as the forest they struggle to survive in, the hardships faced by the citizens of Darkhollow have made them open to visitors and they are usually welcoming and friendly. Working together ensures the continued survival of the city and the people within, so most of the residents here are happy to help others and expect that others will help them if they are ever in a time of need.

TRADE AND COMMERCE

Only a few items from this area are actually sent from Darkhollow in trade, those mainly being rare herbs and fine, rare woods. There is some trade in pelts and other items from creatures hunted in Harwood Forest, but travel from Darkhollow to other cities or nations that might want some of these goods is difficult and sometimes very dangerous. Most of the commerce is between residents who trade food for other items.

LOYALTIES AND DIPLOMACY

Officially, the Duchy of Mains claims Darkhollow, but Darkhollow has yet to pay any tribute or taxes and nobody has ever come from the duchy to collect or provide any leadership. In truth, there is not enough wealth or strategic advantage to Darkhollow for any nation to spend the time and effort to truly control it. Residents here are fine with that situation, as they know that no large nation would provide them with any real benefit while trying to drain away their resources.

GOVERNMENT

The original agreement forming Darkhollow declared that each of the major races would choose one representative and that the city would be led by those three representatives working together. Triela Redbough, an elderly elven ranger, provides most of the leadership, as her knowledge and wisdom are often sought out by all members of the village, including Jorak Mural, a young human druid who is uncomfortable with his position as a leader of the village. Drogo Coldburrow provides leadership and advice to the halflings but stays out of village business, only coming to meetings to ensure no decisions are made against his people.

While there are guards and sentries, they are more focused on the threats from the surrounding forest than worrying about enforcing any laws within the city walls. Arguments and fights do break out at times, but these are usually solved through calm negotiation. If a crime is severe enough to require prosecution, the city leaders act as judges and the senior guardsman on duty acts as prosecutor. The most severe penalty is banishment to the forest without clothing, supplies, or weapons. This is widely considered a death penalty and is given only rarely.

A small boat sails along the southern coast of Akados.

WILDERNESS AND ADVENTURES

Entirely surrounded by dangerous wilderness, Darkhollow is constantly wary of the creatures of the forest. Many of its residents trek into the forest daily, but very few travel far. Rumors of lost cities and other treasures in Harwood Forest often draw adventurers here as a first step toward delving deeper into the unknown.

FARSHORE, TOWN OF

Ruler: Mayor Mourtil Rouvarche
Government: Dictatorship (Benevolent)
Population: 3,040 (2,540 human mixed ethnicity, 190 high elf, 110 halfling, 75 half-orc, 60 half-elf, 45 gnome, 20 merfolk)
Languages: Common, Elven
Religion: Kamien, Telophus, Mitra
Resources: trade hub, foodstuffs, fresh water, spices, fishing
Currency: mixed
Technology Level: Dark Ages

Wood-frame buildings and wattle-and-daub structures sit on solid stone foundations near the shoreline of the crescent-shaped harbor that is the lifeblood of this town. Floating wooden docks extend into the harbor and provide safe berths for large ships. The Barrier Islands to the west make Farshore the only reasonably safe port for deep draft boats and large ships to dock for food, water, and supplies when traveling Oceanus between the Sinnar Ocean and the Crescent Sea. While Tindledusk farther to the west can handle large ships, it doesn't encourage and welcome trade the way Farshore does, and weather and conditions make Farshore an easier port of call for large vessels.

The summer months bring extensive ship travel through the area that extends into early fall. Periodic storms from late fall through spring make travel dangerous for ships, however, and as a result, Farshore must largely survive on the trade that takes place during the summer months. During high times, there are as many as three large ships and three smaller vessels (the maximum its small docks can handle) as well as some ships anchored farther out. When the port is at capacity, the population can be as much as 50–60% higher than normal, as fishermen and craftsmen come to trade with the passing ships.

HISTORY AND PEOPLE

Originally little more than an island village supporting fishermen of the area, Farshore grew with the advent of larger ships making long journeys from the Sinnar Ocean to the Crescent Sea. Many of the humans here are descendants of the original travelers from Oceander who arrived thousands of years ago, while the rest are of Foerdewaith descent. The few half-elves and merfolk who make their home here tend to keep themselves hidden from travelers. The merfolk are those who were cast out of their villages for some reason and have been welcomed by Mayor Mourtil Rouvarche so long as they provide assistance maintaining the harbor.

TRADE AND COMMERCE

Farshore exists as a trading port, not for major items, but for the food and fresh water ships require to make the long journey to and from the Crescent Sea. As one of the only safe ports for large ships in this region, Farshore is a destination for fishermen and fruit growers from the mainland during the summer months when trade is at its highest point. The tariffs charged are used to promote the village and maintain the docks. Aside from the food and freshwater, pearls are also traded here as some of the oysters found in the Barrier Islands provide beautiful pink and white pearls. The island itself is home to a number of small farms and orchards that provide additional food and spices for trade.

GOVERNMENT

Mayor Mourtil Rouvarche is the unchallenged ruler of the village and leader of the small militia that controls the docks and all other aspects of village life. There is little crime in this small village due to a combination of draconian laws and Mourtil's support of the "true" citizens of Farshore. Mourtil acts as judge and jury for any conflicts and has a history of always ruling in favor of his citizens. Ship captains know to keep control of their sailors when on shore leave as any violence against a citizen of Farshore brings about a death penalty with little chance of a trial.

While Mourtil controls much of the trade and makes a great deal of money on tariffs, he puts a lot of effort into ensuring that his citizens are cared for and that the village and docks are kept in good repair. Mourtil is a good ruler who is well-liked by the citizens. This said, his word is law and he does not tolerate anyone disputing his authority. He banishes citizens who speak out against him in public but is more tolerant if someone brings a complaint to him privately.

MAJOR THREATS

While too out of the way for any nearby countries to try to control, Farshore is important to merchant traffic. So long as trade tariffs are kept reasonable, it is unlikely any nation will choose to attack or demand its fealty, though if such a thing were to occur, Mourtil would likely surrender quickly to avoid damage to his town. Storms, sea creatures, and occasional pirate attacks (which are more easily defended) do occur, and the town often has to recover from damage from such events. So far, the sahuagin farther to the west pose no threat though Mourtil keeps a cautious eye in that direction.

HAMPTON HILL, TOWN OF

Ruler: Mayor Strybyorn Arthand
Government: limited democracy
Population: 1,153 (1,027 human mixed ethnicity, 58 halfling, 35 high elf, 12 mountain dwarf, 11 gnome, 10 half-elf)
Languages: Common, Halfling, Elven, Gnome, Dwarf
Resources: foodstuffs, luxury trade items, timber
Currency: mixed
Technology Level: Medieval

Framed by rolling hills and light forests, the brightly-painted cottages and buildings of Hampton Hill pose a colorful contrast to the surrounding area. The town and surrounding region have become a popular vacation destination for the wealthy, with some families maintaining homes in nearby Horrik Forest. Not only is the climate here generally pleasant, the region is well-sheltered from storms and well-patrolled by guards from Hampton Hill as well as private guards employed by visiting nobility and merchants.

HISTORY

Hampton Hill began centuries ago as a mining community focused on pulling silver from the nearby hills to the west. After these mines played out, some workers turned to nearby Horrik Forest for lumber while others extended fields away from the village. Over time, the pleasant surroundings attracted visitors and travelers, particularly when the region was under the firm control of the Kingdom of Foere. When powerful, wealthy families began building vacation homes in nearby Horrik Forest, the area became much more secure as patrols began clearing the more dangerous creatures out of the forest and surrounding areas.

Officially, Hampton Hill is no longer a part of Foere, nor is it a part of any other kingdom at this time. Present independence is maintained in part by the fact that some of the wealthy visitors to this area come from Olduvar, Foere, and Vast, and it is considered to be in the best interest of all of them that this vacation area remains independent. The presence of Londar Brightrain, a wizard of great power and renown living in nearby Horrik Forest, helps support continuing independence as well as the safety of the surrounding area. Londar Brightrain's colorful displays of magic at the Fall Festival every year help draw in additional visitors at that time of year.

The presence of nobles from many different nations, however, can make Hampton Hill a hotbed of rumor and intrigue. But only the vilest noble would risk any action that would affect the neutrality of Hampton Hill.

TRADE AND COMMERCE

Although a small city, Hampton Hill does trade in some high-end luxury items that would normally not be found in an area this small. The demands of the wealthy visitors and travelers drives the trade in these items, which is usually restricted to expensive wines, liquors, and luxury food items. A variety of grains, fruits, and vegetables are grown in the fields along the rolling hills outside the city.

GOVERNMENT

Mayor Strybyorn Arthand is elected by the property owners of the city once every four years. He has been the mayor for some time now as he has generally done a good job and the trade and taxes here help support enough guards to keep the city safe. The city has no major defenses against an attacking force and would certainly surrender if an organized army attacked.

REFERENCE SOURCE: G3 THE HALL OF THE RAINBOW MAGE

LISTONSHIRE, DUCHY OF

Ruler: Roderick, Duke of Listonshire
Capital: Castle Liston
Government: feudal
Population: 190,500 (95,300 Foerdewaith, 61,800 human mixed ethnicity, 15,200 half-elf, 12,600 halfling, 3,100 high elf, 1,500 hill dwarf, 900 gnome, 120 other)
Monstrous: bandits, orcs, doppelgangers, goblins, worgs, dire wolves, ogres, drench, trolls, korreds, wyverns, ghasts, ghouls, green dragons, skulks, quicklings, hangman trees, centaurs
Languages: Common, Elven
Religion: Archeillus, Solanus
Resources: timber, iron, gemstones, foodstuffs
Currency: Foere
Technology Level: Dark Ages

The Duchy of Listonshire has long stood at the very southern reach of the Kingdom of Foere. For generations, even before the Foerdewaith Wars of Succession, the duchy functioned, for all practical purposes, as an independent province, a kingdom in miniature. Separated from the main part of Foere by the largely impassable Harwood Forest, few of the overkings have ever felt it worth their attention. The duke paid his yearly taxes to Courghais and was otherwise left to rule as he would. For the most part, this proved a most equitable arrangement. Listonshire has always been reasonably prosperous for its size. Its crops are healthy and abundant, providing more than enough to feed the people who live here with a surplus left every year for sale to other, less-fortunate territories. The Edriss Mountains in the southwest have always provided adequate veins of ores and repositories of gems to keep mining a worthwhile (if not fabulously enriching) proposition, and the duchy's many forests provided substantial timber for use locally and sale elsewhere.

Of late, however, a curse seems to have come over the duchy. Over the last decade, the veins in the Edriss Mountains seem to have been played out, and the Greentail has become perilous, with woodsmen and trappers vanishing without a trace. Odd illnesses plagued its villagers and farmers. Now, those who have been spared sickness are moving away to Brookmere or points farther north. Towns and villages are deserted. Even the duke's two vassals, the barons of Durneth and Shrievmar, have not been spared.

REFERENCE SOURCE: K3 THE DOOM OF LISTONSHIRE

Castle Liston

Rulers: Roderick, Duke of Listonshire
Government: feudal
Population: 6,700 (4,250 Foerdewaith, 1,020 human mixed ethnicity, 710 half-elf, 430 halfling, 190 high elf, 60 hill dwarf, 30 gnome, 10 other)
Languages: Common, Elven
Religion: Archeillus
Technology Level: Dark Ages

Castle Liston is the home of the dukes of Listonshire. The castle is surrounded by a stone curtain wall. The wall occupies seven sides of an octagon, with the wide castle gate occupying the southeastern side. It was built to withstand even a lengthy siege, with thick wooded doors and a heavy bronze portcullis. Beyond the castle walls, a town has grown, itself unwalled.

Novgorod, City of

Ruler: Morwenna, Queen of Novgorod, Chosen of Medhiba
Government: monarchy
Population: 7,310 (6,660 demonkindred; 300 demonkindred slaves; 150 goblin slaves; 120 orc slaves; 80 human slaves)
Languages: Common, Infernal
Currency: mixed
Technology Level: Medieval

The dark, forbidding confines of Harwood Forest open up into the streets and buildings of a massive city without any clear division or preamble. Buildings twist into the boles of giant, rotting trees, while the streets and alleys are carpeted with stinking moss and fungi. Novgorod is a hidden, dark city, as dark as the forest around it, and the secret enclave of the demonkindred banished here and cursed with mortality. From a distance, the citizens might appear elven, but here, in their greater numbers, the superficial resemblance is unconvincing. Though their appearances vary, the small horns, long canine teeth, and predatory expressions make it clear that these are no ordinary humanoids.

The forests in the vicinity of Novgorod are filled with many dangers and ruins. Stone circles, forbidden temples, and a great crater are all said to be deep in the Harwood Forest in proximity to the dark city.

History

The Kashverai, a race of demons, served Lilith, the Demon Queen, in Fortress Neëriel, her grand home in the hells. These loyal servants were tempted to betray their queen, an action considered so vile by this powerful goddess of chaos that she stripped the entire race of their demonic powers and banished them to the material plane where they were doomed to die, in time, of old age. The Kashverai did not die out, however, but bred new offspring, not as powerful as their parents, but still carrying the taint of demonic chaos in their bloodline.

After battles, infighting, and a mix of assassination and blackmail, Vargoth Novgorod, an exiled elf from the realm of Caer Myrrdin in Harwood Forest, took over the displaced Kashverai and, moving deeper into the forest, founded the city of Novgorod, which his bloodline has retained unstable control of ever since. Novgorod was founded here to avoid the eye of Lilith and any other punishments she might mete out on those who betrayed her. In truth, as time and generations have gone on, she has all but forgotten the Kashverai, who now call themselves demonkindred. If reminded of their presence and their hope to once again attain full demon status, she would undoubtedly find some way to torture and abuse them for further revenge.

Government and Politics

Morwenna, Queen of Novgorod, Chosen of Medhiba, is the Novgorod heir presently on the throne, but her rule, while strong, is somewhat tenuous. Numerous factions with varied interests in the demonkindred city and the infighting between them has resulted in assassinations, murders, and outright fighting in the streets. Some groups are aimed at simply removing the Novgorod family from power, while others are focused on the promises made by the demoness Medhiba to return the demonkindred to true demonic form and power. Still others want to ignore the demon lords and gods and simply go out to conquer the world outside Harwood Forest and make it their own. Needless to say, such infighting is a blessing to the outside world, which is largely unaware of the presence and threat the demonkindred could pose. If the demonkindred residing here become truly unified behind a single leader and purpose, the results for those nearby could be disastrous.

Places of Interest

Spread throughout the trees and twisted growths of this part of Harwood Forest, Novgorod has several areas of note, though it would take a truly bold adventurer to risk entering the demonkindred city.

Castle Novgorod

Castle Novgorod stands upon a small mountain within the forest, with a single road leading to the tower guarding a bridge over a ravine into the castle itself. The seat of power for the Novgorod rulers, the castle is a large, well-constructed, and well-defended building that has stood here since shortly after the Kashverai were banished.

Slave Market

The demonkindred actively seek out slaves from areas near Harwood Forest, as well as from among the less fortunate of their own kind. Slaves are actively traded here, and a few traders make the long and dangerous journey to sell humans, goblins, or orcs in the slave markets in Bottomborough.

Arena

Slaves are pitted against each other and against monstrous creatures in the sands of the Arena. The moss-covered stone of the Arena walls and seating are of the same type used in the construction of Castle Novgorod, as the Arena was constructed at almost the same time. Demonkindred wizards often cast spells into the Arena before, or even during combat, adding illusions or summoned creatures to make the fights more entertaining.

The Laughing Skull Theatre

Confined to their forest city, in part due to their own infighting and conflicts, the demonkindred demand entertainment beyond that provided by the Arena. The twisted, murderous plays and skits performed here provide that entertainment, often along with deaths, dismemberments, and outright torture of slaves as may be called for in the playwrights' scripts.

The Magic Quarter

Made up of small magic academies mixed in with the residences of those studying the magical arts and various shops selling magical components, the Magic Quarter trumpets its existence with bright, sometimes painfully garish, flags and banners. Spells, potions, and various items can be bought here, but only by demonkindred customers.

Temples and Shrines

Numerous temples to Medhiba are found throughout the city, as are shrines to the Demon Queen Lilith. Medhiba finds the shrines and prayers to Lilith entertaining, as she knows the Demon Queen doesn't even notice them, and that if she did, she would only visit more vengeance upon the descendants of those who betrayed her.

Reference Source: *FGG1 Fane of the Fallen*

Ravenscar, Town of

Ruler: Lord Mayor Harlyth Obraiun
Government: democracy
Population: 1,455 (1,150 human mixed ethnicity, 131 halfling, 73 half-orc, 43 gnome, 29 hill dwarf, 15 high elf, 14 half-elf)
Languages: Common, Halfling, Gnome, Dwarf, Elven
Religion: Revered Mother
Resources: grain, foodstuffs, livestock (sheep)

Currency: mixed
Technology Level: Dark Ages

A collection of quaint wood-frame buildings surrounds a town market and a series of small roads heading out toward the Shroudwood and various nearby farms and ranches. While there are no walls for the city, a single small stone tower marks the home of Arendil, an elven wizard who helps protect the town from any attack.

Now known as Ravenscar, the town that first stood here was known as Castleview. The powerful wizard Taosiir constructed a castle here, and, while doing so, cleared out most of the monstrous creatures and other dangers in the area, which helped attract farmers to the area. Those farmers needed services and a place to trade their goods, so a town gradually grew up around the castle. At some point — certain histories argue different times — the castle and surrounding town were all but destroyed by a magical green fire that rained down on them one night, leaving behind nothing but ruins. The nearby farmers rebuilt the town and renamed it Ravenscar after the raven-shaped patch of burned ground left behind by the calamity.

The burned-out ruins of Taosiir's castle provide a beacon that attracts adventurers to the area, but in truth, no treasures have been found by those delving into the ruins. The villagers and local farmers stay away from the castle ruins, convinced that they are haunted. Lord Mayor Harlyth Obraiun is happy to attract adventurers and treasure seekers to the town, mostly in the hopes of increasing the security of the town for his people, but also because bandits are in the Shroudwood and he hopes adventurers might solve that problem for him. The fact that he runs the general supply store in Ravenscar also makes him very open to visitors.

Villagers are happy to provide services to travelers, and even the clerics at the temple of the Revered Mother certainly provide healing services at a reasonable cost, but the village does most of its trade and service with the nearby farmers. A few loggers go into the Shroudwood, but most of the area is dependent on farming.

REFERENCE SOURCE: K2 THE DIAMOND FORTRESS

TINDLEDUSK, TOWN OF

Rulers: Hunter Whyte, Guildsman Jeet Siam, Sea Witch Ciarra
  Quill
Government: oligarchy
Population: 2,580 (2,240 human mixed ethnicity, 130 halfling,
  105 high elf, 65 half-elf, 25 half-orc, 15 orc)
Languages: Common, Elven
Religion: Hecate (practiced in secrecy), Mitra
Resources: trade hub, foodstuffs, fresh water, spices, fishing
Currency: mixed
Technology Level: Dark Ages

A natural rise in the coastline provides the small homes and buildings of Tindledusk a beautiful view out over the small docks along the shoreline below. Tindledusk has one of the few ports along this stretch of southern coast where farmers and orchard growers can bring their good for trade and sale. Most of these goods are taken by boat to Farshore where there is more active trade during the summer months. Boasting pleasant weather most of the year and sheltered from the worst of the ocean storms, Tindledusk seems, on its surface, to be quaint and attractive. However, it has never become a major destination, partly because its docks have difficulty handling larger ships, but largely because the citizens do not welcome or encourage trade.

HISTORY AND PEOPLE

Tindledusk began as a village devoted to witchcraft, but the witches soon learned how unwelcome their powers were as they suffered numerous attacks. Safety required that they hide the presence of their powers and come to agreements with the hunters, farmers, and fishermen of the area. Over time, these agreements grew stronger as the witches helped protect Tindledusk and the surrounding area from a variety of threats coming from the Low Hills as well as from the ocean itself.

While Tindledusk itself does not boast a large population, an extensive collection of farmers and fruit growers of the nearby inland areas call it home.

TRADE AND COMMERCE

The main trade here is in dried and smoked meat, and fish, fruits, and vegetables, and some pearls and a few crafts that include jewelry and glasses and plates made from a variety of shells and glass. Most of these goods are traded to fishermen or smaller traders that then move the goods to Farshore for trade there. The witches discourage trade traffic through the city, preferring traders take their goods to Farshore.

GOVERNMENT

Fishermen who fish the Barrier Islands and hunters who hunt the Mean Shore and Low Hills nearby form a collective presently led by Hunter Whyte. Guildsman Jeet Siam leads the few craftsmen of the village, and Sea Witch Ciarra Quill is the chosen leader of the nearby coven of witches that exerts the most control over the village. The witches are the primary driving force in convincing the other groups to conduct their trade with Farshore rather than allowing ships to dock here with the potential result of an influx of strangers. The simple truth is that Ciarra Quill and the coven are the main power here, and they prefer to keep the others involved in day-to-day decisions and in managing the city itself so they can focus on their own activities.

Strangers and visitors are unwelcome and viewed with suspicion. The witches are a well-kept secret that help defend the village and make it appear smaller and less interesting than it already is. Magic, however, plays a strong role in the area, and the power of the coven helps keep the sahuagin of the Barrier Islands in check. Unknown to the main population, lone travelers are often captured and used by the witches in blood sacrifices designed to protect the village from dangerous weather.

GEOGRAPHIC FEATURES AND POINTS OF INTEREST IN THE SOUTHERN COAST OF AKADOS

BARREN FOREST

See "Harwood Forest" below.

BARRIER ISLANDS

These rough, rocky islands of varying sizes shelter the inner coastline and stretch from Farshore to the Mouth of Akados. They vary in size, with most covered in thick vegetation and populated by a large variety of birds and small animals. Coral reefs around the various islands somehow move through the shallow, rocky waters, their random movements combining with the rough, jagged shorelines of the islands to make the waters unnavigable for larger ships and deep draft boats.

A wide diversity of fish and oysters are found in this area, particularly near the moving reefs, but only the local fishermen from Tindledusk or Farshore are willing to risk these waters in their smaller boats. These fishermen take the time to study the reefs and their movements, and find their own safe zones to ply their trade. None of these fishermen travels west of the promontory south of Greentail Wood. A clan of sahuagin claims the unnamed bay between the Southern Reach and the Greentail Wood, and so long as no fishermen or ships impinge on their territory, they make no move against areas around them. Nobody knows how many sahuagin are actually in the area, but the local fishermen are afraid of them and avoid their territory. So far, the sahuagin stay within the bay, but the fishermen and town leaders nearby keep a wary eye on the waters near Greentail Wood.

COREDOR BELT

The low marshlands stretching from Tuller along Tywyl Bay to the

Low Hills are known as the Coredor Belt. Although the soil here is rich, this area between Harwood Forest and the ocean floods regularly during the fall and winter storm season and remains soft and wet during the summer months. While most of the soft land is unable to support any large buildings, a number of small citrus orchards dot the area. The farmers tending these orchards are a hardy and independent lot, taking their oranges, lemons, limes, and other fruit to either Tindledusk or even Tulley for trade. The fruit is in high demand for ships making long journeys. But there is risk in farming these lands, as they are also a haven to outlaws and others who fled to this otherwise lawless region to escape the reach of one nation or another.

Deer, moose, elk, and other woodland creatures brave the soft land to feed on the lush grasses during the spring and summer months, only to retreat to the forest at the sign of predators or when storms begin to strike. Dragons, drakes, and other creatures from the nearby forest aggressively pursue all prey into the open marshlands and pose potential problems for travelers.

EDRISS MOUNTAINS

The Edriss Mountains are an old range, heavily weathered over the ages. For many years, they held adequate veins of ores and repositories of gems that made mining a worthwhile proposition (although not a fabulously enriching one). Recently, however, the veins of ore all seem to have been spent, and ogres and dark fey moved into the vales between the forested peaks.

FALCONMERE PENINSULA

Stretching south from Hampton Hill and Tranquil Bay to end at the Southern Reach by Mandible Isle, Falconmere Peninsula creates a large inlet to the east and borders the beginning of the Crescent Sea to the west. Most of the coastline ends in tall, rough cliffs that provide no real areas to safely dock or land a boat. The inland areas include several large, old-growth forests as well as Hampton Hill, an area popular with some nobles, and Ravenscar, which is known for its artists. The peninsula's main claim to fame is the wide variety of birds and other flying creatures that call it home. Wyverns, rocs, and dragons along with many species of falcons and eagles are found here, with some intrepid adventurers making a living seeking out the eggs of the rarer creatures, or the creatures themselves.

GREENREACH

Towering rock walls rise from the waters of the southeastern Crescent Sea to a high plateau covered with lush, but strangely twisted, vegetation supporting a strange collection of mutated animals and creatures. Flying creatures otherwise seen all over Falconmere Peninsula and regions nearby avoid Greenreach, as do sailors and fishermen. The land here is tainted by ancient magics, poisoned somehow during the Gods' War almost 15,000 years ago. Plants and animals from the high plateau are permanently altered, and no known magic or spell can return them to normalcy. High cliffs and the lack of any good place to make landfall leave Greenreach and its twisted, mutated wildlife unexplored. Rumors of the creatures here, and those few that can be seen from the waters below, are enough to keep all but the foolhardiest from wanting to climb the cliffs and explore further.

GREENTAIL WOOD

Once the source of lumber and game hunted for nearby communities in the Duchy of Listonshire, the Greentail — so named because it seems to protrude from the Edriss Mountains — is now as dangerous and horror-filled as anyplace else in the vicinity of the duchy. The Silvermane tribe of centaurs has long dwelt deep in these woods and until recently remained largely aloof from the nearby human communities. Of late, however, they have expanded their reach throughout the forest and for some unknown reason have begun to slay fey and other good creatures of the wood as darker things move in. Soon, they may pose a danger even to those who travel outside the forest's eaves. It is said that some have seen a witch in the deep woods who is served by blue-tinted fey of evil disposition. It is also said that the forest is not beyond hope, as allies of good may still be found within. The trees of the Greentail grow thick and slow those without woodland skills as they travel within the forest.

REFERENCE SOURCE: K3 THE DOOM OF LISTONSHIRE

HARWOOD FOREST

Extending from an area just west of the Kal'lugus Mountains to the Principality of Olduvar and the Genev Gap, Harwood Forest is the last great remnant of the Great Akadonian Forest in eastern Akados. It is ancient, dark, and dangerous like few places in the Lost Lands. The deepest depths of the forest possess an aura of primal energy and a sense of unyielding power, as if it has an intelligence and incomprehensible drive of its own. While men and elves have hunted and lived along its edges for as long as history recalls, and have braved its darker depths, all attempts to settle the untamed forest have failed. An unknown number of humanoids, dark fey, lycanthropes, and more sinister denizens live beneath the trees of the Harwood.

It seems that all types of woodland may be found somewhere in this forest. In some areas, the trees are widely spread, while in others the undergrowth all but makes passage impossible. Elsewhere are stands of tall, ancient trees with canopies so thick that no light reaches the ground. Some druids speculate that Harwood Forest is a vestige of the original wood where all trees originated, as it seems that any tree found throughout the world can also be found somewhere here, from tropical trees near hot springs to towering redwoods in the cool valleys.

While the Duchy of Mains lays claim to parts of the forest, in truth, there is no governance here other than simple survival. The secret demonkindred city of Novgorod stands only for itself, leaving the rest of the forest and its denizens to do what they please. Elves, humans, and halflings of Darkhollow live together for mutual protection and survival. Ruins of ancient castles and cities dot the forest, overgrown to the point that almost nothing remains. Adventurers regularly trek into its dark and forbidding confines in search of lost treasures, although most return emptyhanded — if they return at all.

In the western verges of the Harwood live a group of wild elves. They have a city in the midst of the trees called Caer Myrrdin, which is the name they use for their realm as well. Farther east is the cursed city of Novgorod, originally founded by an exile from Caer Myrrdin.

The eastern reaches of the forest, south and east of Carson's Mill, are now known as the Barren Forest. The northernmost extent of the Barren Forest is also called the Wyld Wood (or the Wild Wood). Over the years, it has been subject to much logging and parts of it are charred from a massive forest fire that occurred many years ago. It is said that this part of the forest is home to a circle of druids, as well as a tribe of goblins and a colossal, lifeless tree reaching 500 feet into the air. This region of the forest establishes the western border of the County of Toullen.

South and west of the Wolf Hills within Harwood is a swampy region known as the Dyrgalas Fens. A few stalwart humans live here and scrounge a living through hunting, fishing, trapping, and even some agriculture. In addition to those honest folk, however, the Dyrgalas has some less-savory residents that include black and green dragons, lizardfolk, trolls, hags, escaped criminals, and a host of lycanthropes. The Drijoc River originates in these swamps and wends its way south through the Coredor Belt to Tywyl Bay.

REFERENCE SOURCES: FGG1 FANE OF THE FALLEN;
GLADES OF DEATH; HUNTER'S GAME FROM MARSHES OF MALICE;
DEATH IN DYRGALAS FROM QUESTS OF DOOM

HORRIK FOREST

Horrik Forest is a pleasant, temperate woodland of maples, oak, and birch trees that has drawn the attention of a variety of wealthy nobles and merchants from around Akados who have constructed isolated mansions in different regions of the forest. The areas around these mansions, along with the region about Hampton Hill, are quite well-patrolled and safe. Loggers work the forest near Hampton Hill in search of tall oaks and maples to harvest, but are careful not to log the lands of any of the estates. Other areas in the forest, however, are known to provide homes to kobolds, trolls, lammasu, and even rarer creatures.

One notable arrival to Horrik Forest is Londar Brightrain, a wizard of great power and reputation, who built his home in the forest near the dirt trade road that heads west from Hampton Hill.

REFERENCE SOURCE: G3 THE HALL OF THE RAINBOW MAGE

LANDSGRAVE ISLAND

Of all the Barrier Islands, Landsgrave Island is well-marked on the charts of all sailors traveling through the region and justly feared. Wise captains give this island a wide berth. The large rocky mountain in the center of the island ends in a broad cliff that looks disturbingly like a tombstone. Sailors' stories claim that sirens call ships to their death against the island's jagged rocks and that the region is haunted by ghosts of the lost as well as the evil that brought them there.

And those stories are, in fact, true. The island is indeed haunted by the ghosts of sailors lost when their ships crashed onto its shores. And during stormy times, sirens call to passing ships, though the stories of the island are so widespread that only ships driven far off course would ever find themselves close to these shores. At night, the island glows with strange green and purple lights that are visible from miles at sea, which makes it even easier to avoid.

Locals do not come to the island for any reason. The few fishermen who in the past have done so report that the fish in the shallow, rocky waters are bony and unpalatable, and that the deeper waters are the hunting ground of several schools of sharks seeking whales pushed into the rocky beaches by storms or any other prey that may happen by. At least one will tell the tale of a group of explorers who were brought to the island, never to be heard from again.

LOW HILLS

The Low Hills between the Harwood Forest and the Mean Shore are blanketed with high, thick grasses and sporadic trees, and are home to several small tribes of hill giants. Hunters from Tindledusk stay out of the hills to avoid the giants, but travelers from the Duchy of Listonshire have been known to make the fatal mistake of wandering into hill giant territory from time to time. The deer, goats, and other animals living here provide ample support for the tribes, and they seldom venture outside the hills. They have little interest in risking the dangers of the Harwood Forest, and they avoid the area near Tindledusk, which they believe is protected by a group of dangerous hags. It is said that standing stones almost obscured by the tall grass can be found deep in the hill country, along with deep wells dug by some unknown folk in the distant past. But the hill giants do not like visitors, so such rumors remain unsubstantiated.

MANDIBLE ISLE

The "jaws" protecting the narrow Strait of Praeis include Mandible Isle to the east and its mate, Maxilla Isle to the west. The strait separating the two is deep and wide, but the islands themselves are hazardous to ships that come too close. Mandible Isle is little more than a very high plateau surrounded by steep, rocky cliffs that provide no easily accessible shore line. A number of rocs make their homes on the high plateau and hunt animals in the heavy vegetation on the plateau as well as prey found on the Southern Reach nearby. While the massive creatures are not known to bother passing ships, their shadows and distant flying shapes strike fear into the sailors.

MAXILLA ISLE

Making up the western "jaw" bracketing the Strait of Praeis, Maxilla Isle is flatter than its sister Mandible Isle and rises from the ocean to a maximum height of barely 100 feet. Volcanic glass and jagged sharp stone make up a shoreline that, while vastly different from nearby Mandible, is equally forbidding and dangerous. Plants of the island are twisted and discolored, and some odd ones are like nothing else found anywhere in the Lost Lands, though the animals living here seem normal and unaffected. Its foreign appearance and dangerous shores mean it is an unlikely stop for any reason other than a shipwreck. Those who have been unfortunate enough to spend a night (or more) on the island are said to have felt strange, unearthly vibrations. Some of these poor folk went irrevocably insane, gibbering about "emanations from beyond the stars" or "the eyes of yellow." A few are said to have been cured of this insanity, but only after months away from the insidious influence of this island. Whatever the source of the madness, it doesn't seem to affect the sea birds and mammals that perch or sun on its rocks.

THE MOUTH OF AKADOS

Choppy windblown waters south of the Strait of Praeis are known as the Mouth of Akados, an apt name given the shape of the islands and lands nearby. Large whales and, periodically, other creatures of the dark, deep oceans to the south come to the shallower waters here in search of food. Such beasts only rarely cause problems for ships making their way in and out of the Crescent Sea. Pirate vessels are a much more prevalent danger, particularly during summer months when milder weather brings the annual influx of merchant ships passing through the Strait of Praeis. The pirates prefer to attack in the Mouth of Akados as the location provides more avenues for escape and it is easier to sink ships unseen near the broad open ocean.

THE MEAN SHORE

The broad and rocky coast of the mainland west of Tindledusk is marked by jagged beaches and rocky cliffs that make landing even a small fishing boat hazardous. The Barrier Islands to the south protect this section of shoreline from some of the harsher weather and waves that would normally break down and smooth the surfaces of the rocks and cliffs of the shore. In addition, the witches of Tindledusk use their magic to make the shore seem even less hospitable, thus reserving the land inland for the hunters from their town.

Populated by a number of game animals, the Mean Shore supports the Tindledusk hunters and also hill giants from several tribes of the Low Hills. The giants stay clear of the Tindledusk hunters because they believe the hunters to be in league with hags (which are actually the witches of Tindledusk, traveling in disguise).

SHROUDWOOD

This dark and tangled forest is home to a variety of trees and underbrush that leave the few patches of clear ground cloaked in moving shadows. Only the areas of the forest nearest to Ravenscar have been explored and, in the absence of easy trade routes to transport lumber away from the forest, there is little logging. A variety of birds and other flying creatures call the high branches of the forest home, leaving the ground to creatures that thrive in shadows and rumored to include dragon horses and a thesselgorgon. One or two tribes of wild elves are said to occupy the westernmost reaches of the Shroudwood, but the only sure residents are bandits that plague the local farms and villages. The bandit lair is well-hidden and few have the courage to enter the forest to search them out.

REFERENCE SOURCE: K2 THE DIAMOND FORTRESS

SOUTHERN REACH

The southern extension of Falconmere Peninsula slopes gradually toward the water and ends in a soft, marshy wetland known as the Southern Reach. The Barrier Islands to the southeast and Mandible Isle to the south shield the coast from storms, leaving the marsh stagnant and stinking of rot and decay. A variety of swamp creatures, as well as a strange variety of undead, call this area home, as do several young green dragons that divide the Southern Reach into their own hunting areas.

Tranquil Bay

Ensconced between Greenreach, the island to the west, and the rocky cliffs of the Falconmere Peninsula, the deep, calm waters of Tranquil Bay provide a safe place to anchor during storms. The lack of high winds and rough seas also make for an active breeding ground for several pods of whales and a variety of fish, which makes fishing boats from Kindler's Bell and Bridgeport to the north a common sight.

Tywyl Bay

This peaceful bay is heavily traveled by fishermen and ships and boats that don't wish to risk the deeper, rougher waters of Mother Oceanus. Large numbers of fish make the bay ideal for fishing, though those vessels must be wary of the whales and sharks that also make this their hunting ground. While ample prey is here to satisfy the larger sea creatures, fishing vessels have been attacked on occasion. Rocs, wyvern, and dragons also hunt these waters, though such instances are rare. Those who ply Tywyl Bay tell stories of isolated small villages of merfolk who stay beneath the waters and avoid interactions with surface races.

Western Mountains

The Western Mountains are a truly ancient range of thickly forested rocky peaks and valleys, much weathered over tens of millennia. Several tribes of orcs live in the heights. Also within this range is Arn's Mountain, said to be an important location from ages ago, about which remnants of ancient roads can still be seen.

Wyld Wood (or Wild Wood)

See "Harwood Forest" above.

SOUTHEASTERN AKADOS

THE BORDERLANDS

The Borderlands of Southeastern Akados are described in detail in ***The Lost Lands: Borderland Provinces*** by **Frog God Games**.

POLITICAL SUBDIVISIONS OF THE BORDERLANDS OF SOUTHEASTERN AKADOS

EXETER PROVINCE

Capital: Albor Broce
Notable Settlements: Cairn Condor, Jambles, Whitsun Measow
Ruler: Lord-Governor Benevic of Lortsbar
Government: feudalism (vassal of Foere)
Population: 1,326,560 (966,500 Foerdewaith, 206,000 Heldring, 62,000 halfling, 39,000 high elf, 26,560 half-orc, 12,800 hill dwarf, 9,500 wood elf, 4,200 mountain dwarf)
Monstrous: wolf, goblin, giant animal, centaur, hobgoblin, orc, auroch, ogre-kin, ogre, corpse rook (plains); fey, ettercap, tangtal, wood giant, forest drake, lycanthrope, treant, corpse rook (Wiltangle Forest); orc, ogre-kin, undead, quickwood, witherstench, ogre, harpy, half-ogre, vulchling, minotaur, troll (highlands); orc, rock troll, hill giant, peryton, ettin, gargoyle (Forlorn Mountains foothills)
Languages: Common, Helvaenic, Halfling, Elvish, Dwarven
Religion: Ceres, Vanitthu, Freya, Frigg, Tykee, Odin, Hester, Mick O'Delving, Tyr, Mithras, Darach-Albith
Resources: foodstuffs, livestock, grain, trade hub, gems, tobacco
Currency: Foere
Technology Level: High Middle Ages, Dark Ages (some isolated areas)

Exeter is a loyal province of the Kingdom of Foere and is ruled by a lord-governor appointed by the overking. It is cut off from the rest of the kingdom, and for the last 10 years has been governed on the principle of defending the borders at all costs, without preemptive attacks against raiders, and without regard for the decline of law and order in the interior of the province. The population of the rural areas is under constant threat from roaming brigands and monsters of all kinds.

Exeter's capital is Albor Broce, which is built around the site of an ancient Hyperborean fortress. Its territory extends north to the Wilderland Hills, west to the intersection of the South Road and Provincial Military Road, south to the edges of the Wiltangle Forest, and east to the Cut Horn Gap.

HISTORY AND PEOPLE

Exeter Province once extended all the way down to the Helwall, built 83 years before the Imperial Record began to chart the years, and as a military frontier, played a major role in battling the Heldring raiders at the dawn of the Hyperborean Empire. In 2802 I.R., after the Battle of Oescreheit Downs and the final defeat of the Heldring, the lands now governed as Cerediun Province were divided away from the original, much larger Province of Exeter. The early history of Exeter is a long recitation of war and ruin: Heldring armies marching through the area to raid along the March of Mountains, Hyperborean and then Foerdewaith armies marching to bring them to battle, refugees, fire, and pillage. Ten years ago, Exeter Province was spared from the violence of the Wilderlands Clan War of 3506 I.R. that was fought almost exclusively in Keston Province and the Wilderland Hills of southern Suilley. This was an exception to the norm, however; over the course of history, vast numbers of incursions into the regions between the March of Mountains and the Forlorn Mountains have pillaged their way through Exeter Province,

skirting around castles and forts but ravaging the countryside unopposed by the province's much-weaker armies. Exeter Province has long held the uneasy position of serving as one of civilization's buffer zones.

As a result of this dismal and violent history, the province is not heavily settled. At present, the lord-governor keeps his troops carefully deployed in camps and small forts to watch for further incursions from the north in case of a repeat of the Wilderlands Clan War. A chain of signal fires has been arranged to warn the capital if battle is joined in the highlands. One unintended result of this caution is that the rest of the province is currently short on troops and patrols, with most of the soldiery concentrated along the northern border or walled up in Albor Broce. Ten years of this defensive strategy have caused burgeoning problems with beasts and monsters in the rural countryside, and unchecked banditry is on the rise.

TRADE AND COMMERCE

Exeter conducts and regulates overland trade with Hawkmoon to the east, which generates most of its revenue, and to some extent also trades with the Helcynngae Peninsula to the south (though this goes through Cerediun Province first, which takes the most lucrative cut of tolls and taxes).

LOYALTIES AND DIPLOMACY

Exeter maintains its loyalty to the Throne of Foere, though it has little contact with its liege state. The overking's court sends a new lord-governor once every decade or so, and the former lord-governor assembles his retinue, guards, and profits for the journey home to Courghais. The province has virtually stopped paying taxes to Foere after bandits annihilated more than one large shipment of silver while in transit. Small shipments of tax money are often sent, along with guards, with merchant caravans on their way to the County of Vourdon. The total of these sums, though, is a slight fraction of what the overking could normally expect if the province were not cut off from the rest of the kingdom.

In return, Exeter Province receives less help from the Royal Court in Courghais than it would ordinarily expect as a loyal province, even though it would send the taxes if it could.

GOVERNMENT

A lord-governor residing in the capital of Albor Broce administers Exeter Province on behalf of the overking of Foere. The current lord-governor is Benevic of Lortsbar, a knight-commander who rose to fame in Foere after successfully holding off a massive assault upon a border castle under his command in the Duchy of Mains. Unfortunately, Lord Benevic's military expertise and attitudes are entirely defensive; on behalf of Exeter and Foere, he created a brilliant system of defenses and fortified the borders against attack, without focusing on the problems created by emptying the province's interior of troops.

WILDERNESS AND ADVENTURE

The wilderness is creeping into Exeter Province like nightfall. Troops no longer make regular patrols, and rural garrisons have been bled of their soldiers to man the forts and castles along the edge of the Wilderland Hills to the north. The population of the province has never been large, and settlements tend to be isolated, unguarded, and ripe for the plucking. This area has the potential for all kinds of adventures, for there is wilderness between almost every village and hamlet except along the high roads.

ALBOR BROCE (CAPITAL)

(AL-bor BRO-chee)
Population: 14,830 (11,222 Foerdewaith, 2159 halfling, 830 high elf, 619 hill dwarf)
Ruler: Sir Rohnic Ort, Minister of the Capital
Government: appointed minister

Albor Broce is the capital of Exeter Province, built 69 years before the beginning of the Imperial Record. Built on the site of an early

SOUTHEASTERN AKADOS

Legend
Town or Village
City
Capital or Free City
Imperial Capital
Fortress or Citadel
Ruins
Place of Interest
Road
Trail or Unused Road
Mountain Pass
Battlefield

SINNAR OCEAN

A caravan is ambushed by bandits on the Burgundian road.

Hyperborean fort, the streets still run in the straight grid laid out by the Hyperboreans, though the city has long since outgrown the ditch that surrounded the fort. In some places in the city, the ditch and berm can still be discerned as a gentle, curving rise in the ground, and occasionally the citizens still find artifacts of old Hyperborea when digging for new wells or building foundations. The city is well-fortified with high stone walls, and Lord-Governor Benevic has personally supervised their repair and improvement. The Citadel of Broce, home and court of the lord-governor, is constantly abuzz with soldiers training at siege defense and with the comings and goings of his force of spies.

These spies are organized as the Squires of the Ferret, which does not grant its members the full status of knighthood (which the lord-governor awards only to those who are staunch warriors), but lends them approximately the same powers as a sheriff. The Provincial Order of the Squires of the Ferret is commanded by a knight by the name of Sir Ghendric the Terrier, who essentially functions as Lord Benevic's spymaster. Since the province actually contains only a very few subversive conspirators, the Terrier has to stretch a bit to justify his position, and has a long-standing practice of treating late tax payments as evidence of treasonous intent.

The troops stationed in Albor Broce are trained to perfection, although most are unbloodied in combat; they should be a formidable fighting force if challenged. They are efficient at keeping order in the city, and their informants are well paid; any sort of crime beyond petty thievery is extraordinarily rare within the city walls.

Unlike most cities in the Borderland Provinces, Albor Broce has no municipal government of its own; it is treated as part of the lord-governor's direct responsibility, and the lord-governor delegates most tasks to Sir Rohnic Ort, his "Minister of the Capital." Sir Ort is a capable administrator and an intelligent man. He is disturbed by the increasing lawlessness of the countryside beyond the capital, but he considers his role to be limited to the city and nothing but the city. Moreover, even if someone asked him for a solution to the problems in Exeter Province, he would have no answer. Sir Ort is trapped within the same defensive mentality as the lord-governor, unable to see that all the province's resources for keeping order are deployed around the borders instead of balanced between the borders and the countryside. To be fair, Sir Ort has a weaker perspective than the lord-governor, since he is not privy to the province's large-scale deployments. Sitting in the well-defended capital, he has no way of understanding that within 25 miles of his armories are villages utterly undefended from even the threat of a few lightly-armed ruffians.

All traveling merchants passing through Albor Broce are required to bring their wagons to a large customs house just inside the gate where the contents are tallied and then taxed at 2% of their value. The lord-governor's tax-assessors are not easily bribed, for they know they are watched carefully by the Squires of the Ferret, and accepting bribes is a capital crime.

Cairn Condor, Citadel of

Population: 729 (631 Foerdewaith, 41 hill dwarf, 36 high elf, 21 halfling)
Ruler: Sir Pernanz Avor, strategos of Cairn Condor and the Forlorn March
Government: military

Cairn Condor is a citadel built on the crest of a tall foothill at the base of the Forlorn Mountains. The fortress is manned by troops from the Lord-Governor's army, and is the base for all patrols along Exeter's 250-mile mountain frontier. Its walls are 40 feet high, and the great keep rises to a height of 80 feet. A huge farseeing lens called the "Condor's

Eye" is mounted on the keep's roof and allows the castle's defenders to see great distances along the mountain border and into many of the nearby mountain valleys where foes might be gathering. When weather permits, the lens is constantly manned, being rotated inch by inch to survey the landscape for enemies.

The garrison of the fortress is 400 infantry, 200 cavalry, and 25 knights, together with 3 "counselor-mages" of 6th level.

JAMBLES, TOWN OF

Population: 2,721 (2721 (2305 halfling, 396 Foerdewaith, 20 high elf)
Ruler: Mayor Totho Bellfeather
Government: autocracy (elected mayor)

Jambles is a small town walled with stone, located just by the Provincial Military Road about halfway between Albor Broce and the crossroad with the South Road. The area enclosed by the walls is unusually large for the town's population, and from the outside it looks like a small city. The town was originally a halfling village of burrow-houses and a few one-story structures, but its location on the road caused a slow influx of human traders and even a few elves. Now the area inside the walls is a strange mix of four-story human buildings alongside the burrow-houses and low-ceilinged buildings of the town's halfling population.

WHITSUN MEASOW, VILLAGE OF

Population: 253 (Foerdewaith)
Ruler: Lum Yandly, "King Lum"
Government: overlord

Whitsun Measow is an unwalled settlement with a few well-built houses at the center and a sea of huts, hovels, and tents surrounding them. Originally an ordinary village, bandits took it over in 3514 I.R. and converted it into a stronghold for outlaws and heretics. The "King" of Whitsun Measow is a bandit chief named Lum Yandly who accumulated a small army of 150 outlaws from dispossessed peasants, heretics, and ordinary bandits before deciding to set up a permanent base. The village is now host to all kinds of refugees from justice.

KESTON PROVINCE

(KEST-un, occasionally GAST-un)
Capital: Kingston
Notable Settlements: Aljun
Ruler: His Excellency the Lord-Governor of the Suilleyn Dominion of Keston Province, Baron Miltrin Cormien
Government: feudalism (vassal of Suilley)
Population: 477,280 (385,150 Foerdewaith, 42,700 Heldring, 23,500 halfling, 17,680 half-elf, 4,100 hill dwarf, 2,060 high elf, 1,300 mountain dwarf, 790 half-orc)
Monstrous: wolf, goblin, giant animal, hobgoblin, orc, aurochs, ogre-kin, ogres (plains); giant mosquito, lizardfolk, bugbear, shambling mound, undead, chuul, black dragon (Creeping Mire); orc, ogre-kin, giant bat, undead, mobat, quickwood, witherstench, ogre, harpy, half-ogre, vulchling, minotaur, troll (highlands); giant animal, orc, ogre, mammoth, frost giant, ice troll, thunderbird, demon (mountains)
Languages: Common, Halfling, Dwarven, Elvish, Orc
Religion: Dre'uain the Lame, Mitra, Freya, Mithras, Thyr, Pekko, Mick O'Delving, Muir, Pan, Dwerfater
Resources: wool, livestock (sheep), flax, foodstuffs (apples), grain, linen, quarry stone, coal, lead
Currency: Foere
Technology Level: High Middle Ages

Keston Province is no longer a province of the Kingdoms of Foere, having declared fealty to the crown of Suilley. It has always been sparsely populated and is still reeling from the devastation of the Wilderlands Clan War. The province is well-governed, but even before the war only the areas around the main roads were particularly safe, and at this point the province's interior is no more than a sparsely settled wilderness.

The southern border of Keston Province runs due east from the intersection of the South Road with the Provincial Military Road, with an eastern boundary at the Trader's Way, 150 or so miles to the north of Albor Broce in Exeter Province. To the west, the province officially includes the eastern slopes of the Kal'Iugus and the southern half of the Meridian mountain ranges, but these are wild areas unpatrolled save at the very edges.

Between the two mountain ranges, the Keston Border extends through the high saddle of land along the Gap Road and runs all the way to the Duchy of Saxe.

HISTORY AND PEOPLE

Keston is very lightly populated, with most of its folk living in the towns and villages along the length of the South Road and the Gap Road. Few settlements remain along the Trader's Way after the ravages of the Wilderlands Clan War of 3506 I.R. There has never been more than a scattering of hamlets and freeholds in the province's interior or along the edge of the mountain ranges.

Before becoming a province of the Kingdom of Foere, the lands of Keston were subject to waves of Heldring raiders over the course of thousands of years. As Foere expanded, it took steps to secure the region in 2803 I.R. and established a garrison town at Kingston and drew boundary lines for a royal province. Most of the area's inhabitants, scattered in their hamlets and tiny villages, remained completely unaware of this change in status. Local warlords were forced, one by one, to call themselves "knights" and to enter the feudal hierarchy of the Foerdewaith by pledging fealty to the same chieftains they had always followed. These chieftains, in turn, discovered themselves actually to be "barons" who paid small amounts of tax to a distant governor in exchange for not being attacked. Once the concept of "taxes" had been gotten across by the burning of a few motte-and-bailey forts, the isolated settlements of the province settled into their new titles, and life continued as before. In a very real sense, Keston Province was annexed by nomenclature rather than by armies.

In 3336 I.R., Lord-Governor Fenevic Jaounehelm (JOWN-helm) switched his feudal allegiance from the overking of Foere to the king of Suilley, following the lead of Count Catrebrasse of Toullen.

Keston Province's recent history is dominated by the events and effects of the recent Wilderlands Clan War. Some 10 years ago, early in the year of 3506 I.R., a great horde of raiders emerged from the Wilderland Hills and burned the village of Bynum and fortified it to use as a base for ravaging the countryside. The lord-governor of Keston at that time, a veteran of several petty border wars, began assembling his forces to counter the invasion and invoked the feudal duties of his barons to provide soldiers. The army of Keston, such as it was, consisted of a core of trained infantry with the various small cavalry units ordinarily responsible for patrolling the province's roads. Barons and their knights, accompanied by small levies of troops of varying quality, assembled in the mustering-fields around Kingston underneath the colorful pennants of the feudal lords. Their numbers were small, and the then lord-governor sent the faster-moving elements of the army forward without the levies, but ordered the less-organized and less-experienced militia force to follow behind the veterans and knights along the South Road to the Provincial Military Road and then north to the borders of the Wilderland Hills.

In the first contact between the forward elements of the army of Keston and the raider horde at the ill-fated Battle of Sontanne Hill, the Kestonfolk engaged a mixed force of hill barbarians, orcs, and ogres. Sontanne Hill might have turned out to be a decisive victory for the more-organized soldiery of Keston, but the humanoids turned out to have the unexpected support of several margoyles and their lesser gargoyle kin that flew over the human army, swooping in and out to the kill. Demoralized by the attacks from the air, the army of Keston retreated back to forested cover, leaving the raider horde in possession of the field. Perhaps even worse for morale, the lord-governor of the province was badly wounded in the rearguard action when his leg was crushed. The few prisoners taken from Sontanne Hill revealed that a clan of margoyles from the Forlorn Mountains had organized the army of raiders and hoped to seize a domain for themselves in the lowlands. Not particularly intelligent, for margoyles are not, this clan nevertheless managed to use a mix of bad ideas, persuasiveness, and brute force to raise a truly massive horde of reavers to sweep down into the settled lands.

When groups of lost or fleeing soldiers from the defeated regular army met the advancing militias and levies on the Trader's Way, and news spread through the militia, the second force evaporated in a panic and headed back to Kingston without officers. The few barons who had been leading the levies were unable to rally them, and the army of Keston was effectively destroyed.

Drawn by the successes of the advance force, new tribes and clans poured out of the Wilderland Hills, some coming all the way from the Forlorn Mountains to join the pillaging. The count of Toullen, always a good neighbor to Keston Province, immediately sent a contingent of his own knights and solders to shore up the collapsing defense of Keston. Too badly injured to take the field, the lord-governor appointed Sir Miltrin Cormien to reassemble and command the army of Keston, largely because the knight was related to all four of the province's leading noble families and had demonstrated great heroism in the Battle of Sontanne Hill. This turned out to be a lucky decision, for as the war progressed, Sir Cormien's blood relation with the great nobles of the province was far eclipsed by his unexpected military genius.

Making the correct assumption that his enemy was not a single army but rather a collection of independent clans, Cormien took the extremely unpopular step of ordering his knights off their prized Suilley destriers and out of their heavy armor and put them in much lighter armor and onto lighter riding horses. This new force — small units of heavily armed light cavalry — fanned out across the contested area in eastern Keston guided by locals. By locating isolated clans and combining together for the battle, then splitting up again, Cormien's small army managed to check the advance of the horde, although the largest of the tribes remained undamaged by the light cavalry tactics.

By 3507 I.R., a small army raised by the king of Suilley finished mustering outside of Manas and marched south along the Flatlander Road to assist in Keston's defense. With the arrival of these heavier troops, the war settled into a more traditional pattern, with the allied armies of Keston, Suilley, and Toullen attempting to bring the large tribes into a pitched battle where they could be decisively defeated. These attempts failed, mainly due to poor leadership of the allies by the commander of Suilley's army, the largest in the field. After a year of watching the army get beaten back in petty defeat after petty defeat, the king of Suilley recalled his general and placed Keston's Sir Cormien at the head of all the allied forces. Baron Nalsibert, the disgraced Suilleyn general, drank himself to death on the road back to Manas and capped off a long and incompetent military career.

With Baron Nalsibert removed from command, and with a new influx of Foerdewaith troops from Vourdon and Exeter Provinces joining the allied army as a gesture from the overking, Sir Cormien (now Baron Cormien) undertook a series of lighting advances against the horde and cut off the army of the large Wormaganth Clan in a hamlet called Onjoun and slaughtered them. The margoyle leadership of the horde now discovered that they actually had very little control over their "subjects" and were virtually unable to respond as Cormien severed and destroyed their army clan by clan. The final battle took place deep in the Wilderland Hills as the clans retreated farther into their home territory. At the ancient fortifications of Broch Tarna, the allied armies broke and crushed the remaining hill clans, bringing an end to the bloody, three-year war and sending the few surviving margoyles fleeing back to their haunts high in the Forlorn Mountains. Cormien himself fought in the vanguard of the army, losing his left arm to the infection of a wound inflicted during the battle. When the former lord-governor eventually died from the lingering wounds

suffered at Sontanne Hill, the king of Suilley elevated Keston's hero, Baron Cormien, to the position.

TRADE AND COMMERCE

The city of Kingston is well placed for trade, being at the crossroad of the Gap Road leading into the Kingdoms of Foere, the South Road which runs from Toullen to the Duchy of the Rampart, and controlling the Provincial Military Road leading to the Domain of Hawkmoon through Exeter Province. None of these routes is very heavily traveled, but together they make enough revenue to maintain the province well. If the province manages to rebuild the ravaged rural communities lost to the depredations of the Wilderland Clans, it will become a strong nation over time. At present, however, the province is still struggling with the loss of farmland, villages, and rural population from the war.

LOYALTIES AND DIPLOMACY

Keston was once a province of Foere, but in 3336 I.R., along with the County of Toullen, Keston Province rescinded its feudal obligations to the Court of Courghais and offered fealty to the crown of Suilley. The realm of Suilley has governed it indirectly ever since.

GOVERNMENT

Since declaring its independence from Foere, Keston Province has been governed as a feudal vassal to the Kingdom of Suilley, very much along the same model used by the Kingdom of Foere. The king of Suilley appoints a lord-governor for the province, but the feudal ranks below the lord-governor are hereditary. These nobles offer their fealty to the king of Suilley but report to the lord-governor as the king's representative. Hence, travelers in the province find the usual mix of barons and knights, all with greater or lesser landholdings. Four dukes make up the governmental layer between the barons and the lord-governor, and these four dukes are extremely powerful in the province and even in Suilley. These four families, along with the lord-governor at the time, are the ones who delivered Keston into Suilley's hands by seceding from the Kingdom of Foere. The lord-governor who engineered the secession became rich in land and titles himself, but his family is by no means as powerful as the dukes, and his descendants do not much involve themselves in the province's government other than as ordinary members of the nobility.

Keston's current ruler is the retired general Baron Miltrin Cormien, who was elevated to the position of lord-governor by Ulrich IX, the young king of Suilley. Cormien is a disciplined administrator and staunchly loyal to the crown of Suilley, related by blood to all four of the dukes of Keston and a figure of legend among the common folk after his defeat of the Wilderland Clans.

WILDERNESS AND ADVENTURE

Other than along the roads, there is very little in Keston Province that is *not* wilderness. In the eastern part of the province, many secrets lie buried in the charred remains of forgotten villages. Wolves — and far worse things than wolves — howl unchallenged beneath the night skies of empty, rural Keston. Farms lie fallow, and forests claw their way back into the long-forgotten grounds of their ancestral growth. A few hardy settlements remain in these newly crafted wilds, and some new villages are springing up almost like colonies in a foreign land. Many of these new hamlets disappear in time, but some persevere and prosper.

KINGSTON, CITY OF (CAPITAL)

Population: 15,612 (9,844 Foerdewaith, 2,340 halfling, 1,008 Heldring, 876 half-elf, 721 hill dwarf, 503 half-orc, 259 gnome, 61 high elf)

Ruler: Lord-Governor Baron Miltrin Cormien

Government: The Council of Listeners, appointed by dukes, citizens, guilds, and the lord-governor

Kingston is a high-walled city with a strangely lopsided appearance, for its foundations shifted slightly during the Fiend Rains. The citadel, in particular, leans visibly, and has come to be known as the Tilting

Citadel. As far as anyone can tell, the walls are still strong and stable, but entering the city with its crooked houses and uneven streets gives some travelers a distinct sense of vertigo.

Kingston is the capital of Keston Province and the seat of the lord-governor, currently Baron Miltrin Cormien. It is governed by a council of 10 citizens known as the Council of Listeners. Each of the four dukes of the realm appoints one listener, the citizens of Kingston elect two, the city guilds elect two, and the lord-governor appoints two.

Kingston boasts a sizable temple to Mithras, with the entrance made up of a massive stone bull's head, with the mouth forming the gateway. But many in the city and the surrounding countryside worship Dre'uain the Lame, who has become a symbol of recovery of the once-settled areas emptied during the Wilderness Clan War.

The largest open-air market in the city is the Sliding Scales, a circular plaza filled with tents and vendors' booths from dawn until noon each day. The plaza developed a distinct slope when the Fiend Rains damaged the city's foundations. A ball could roll down the entire length of the market from west to east if not for the uneven cobblestones. A few permanent shops surround the plaza, and the council hall of the listeners stands at the western end of the market. Kingston houses a number of semi-professional theater companies of widely varying quality. An odd, sinister building in Kingston's poor quarter is the headquarters of the Academy of Inquisitors, a guild of torturers and interrogators operating across many of the realms in the Borderland Provinces. Graduates of the Red Academy are hired by various governors, dukes, barons, and others who maintain dismal prisons, often traveling great distances to lucrative postings. The origin and history of the academy are cloaked in a good bit of mystery and are not spoken of by the Red Inquisitors.

It is said that the Grey Rooks, a criminal brotherhood based in Durbenford, have a presence in Kingston.

ALJUN, TOWN OF

Population: 4,237 (3,728 Foerdewaith, 322 halfling, 162 high elf, 25 hill dwarf)
Ruler: guild representatives
Government: council

Aljun is one of the few towns near the Wilderland Hills to have survived the Wilderlands Clan War without much damage to its buildings or surrounding farmlands. Spared by chance from the initial waves of the assault, Aljun became a mustering point for the lord-governor's knights and soldiery, which soon made it an unattractive target for casual pillaging. Once the war ended, Aljun prospered as the only surviving market in the area.

Aljun is ruled by a town council made up of representatives from the Wool-Merchants' Guild, the Weavers' Guild, the Dyers' Guild, the Brewers' Guild, and the Guild of Smiths, the main industries here.

DUCHY OF THE RAMPART

Capital: Troye
Notable Settlements: Metzel, Reliquary of Jamboor, Ristalt
Ruler: His Most Noble Lordship, the Palatine Duke Claud VII, Battle-Duke of Foere and Sword of the Foerdewaith
Government: feudalism (palatine duchy of Foere)
Population: 3,156,000 (2,850,000 Foerdewaith, 183,000 hill dwarf, 57,500 halfling, 43,000 high elf, 13,500 half-elf, 6,200 gnome, 2,400 half-orc, 400 other)
Monstrous: giant rat, giant ant, krenshar, kobold, kenckoo, giant boar, ankheg, owlbear, bulette (plains) dire wolf, goblin, orc, giant lizard, ogre, stone giant, bugbear, hill giant, wyvern, roc, dragon, yrthak (mountains)
Languages: Common, Gasquen, Dwarven, Halfling, Elven, Gnome, Orc, High Boros
Religion: Sefagreth, Vanitthu, Archeillus, Mithras, Vergrimm Earthsblood, Mick O'Delving, Thyr (declining), Mitra (rising), Darach-Albith, Jamboor, Muir, Solanus (declining), Quell

Resources: coal, iron, gems, wool, quarry stone, cloth, timber, ironwork
Currency: Foere
Technology Level: Medieval

The Duchy of the Rampart is a palatine dukedom, which means that the title is hereditary and that the duke holds his lands directly from the overking. It is a stable and well-guarded realm with a strong sense of chivalry and feudal obligations. But a certain decay is setting in, and strange things lurk in the shadows. The creeping advance of the darkness is subtle and isolated, but very much present. The people of the duchy know in the backs of their minds that the Rampart is declining, but they do not understand why, or how to counter the process.

On the eastern side of the March of Mountains, the borders of the Duchy of the Rampart extend roughly 200–250 miles from Troye to the south, southeast, and west. To the west, the border extends roughly 600 miles and includes all of the lands between the Cretian Mountains and the Rampart Mountains.

The duchy was once much larger than it is now, reaching as far east as the Gundlock Hills, and south almost to the Lorremach Highhills (though this latter was a mix of Suilleyn and Rampartine nobles and villages that had no real delineation until the secession of the Suilleyn king). Most of these lands were lost to the Kingdom of Suilley during the Suilleyn rebellion from the Kingdoms of Foere, and there is no credible expectation that they could be retaken.

HISTORY AND PEOPLE

The Duchy of the Rampart was founded in 2802 I.R. when Overking Osbert II raised Claud Oberhammer, a war hero and the overking's nephew, to the status of Duke of the Rampart, Battle-Duke of Foere, and Sword of the Foerdewaith. In accordance with the ancient Hyperborean custom of *dux bellorum*, the battle-duke is traditionally the marshal of the armies of Foere anywhere they fight. This custom has waned over the years, with overkings or generals often leading armies into conflicts and crusades that occur far from the Rampart.

The earliest beginning of this break from custom came with a tragic occurrence, perhaps the duchy's greatest shame. During the Second Great Crusade of 2970–2971 I.R., while the majority of Foere's military forces were engaged across the Sinnar Ocean in far Libynos, a powerful vampire-lord known as the Singed Man arose in the western Kingdoms of Foere and conquered a great swath of territory in the distant Duchy of Kear, far to the west of the duchy itself. The Singed Man formed his own enslaved domain and named himself as its Infernal Tyrant. By the time the crusader forces returned from the east, the Infernal Tyrant was already well entrenched and ready for the attack of the war-weary soldiers.

Responsibility for dislodging the vampire-lord from his hold and freeing the oppressed lands was given to Duke Ormand I, palatine-duke of the Rampart and battle-duke of Foere. Because of the scattered nature of the returning armies and the depleted resources of Foere, Duke Ormand had great difficulty raising a new fighting force and properly equipping and supplying it. It was 2977 I.R. before Ormand finally marched on Kear, and in all those years the Singed Man had been carefully planning and preparing a response to just such an attack. Duke Ormand's forces trudged across the Plains of Eauxe, enduring the constant harassing tactics of the Singed Man's defenses, but finally brought the Infernal Tyrant's forces to ground at Seilo Ford, trapped against the flooding Meander River. Unfortunately, it was also there that Ormand discovered the horrific preparations of the Infernal Tyrant: All the dead of Kear suddenly rose up from the ground on the banks of the Meander around the duke's army and attacked from all sides.

Duke Ormand's army was decimated at Seilo Ford, the survivors fleeing east back toward Foere. The battle-duke himself was captured and turned into a vampire, an unholy slave of the Singed Man. Duke Ormand became the Singed Man's general and devoted servant and used his military prowess and experience to expand the wasted realm of the Infernal Tyrant to ever greater bounds. Foere's own armies were exhausted and crippled, unable to do anything but watch as the Infernal Tyrant ran rampant in the west. It was not until more than 50 years later that the paladin Sir Varral the Blessed was able to destroy the Singed

Man, free the realm of Kear, and finally send the former Duke Ormand to his eternal rest. Ormand's name was stricken from the line of the Rampart by his grandson, Duke Claude III, and a taint lingered upon the battle-dukes in the eyes some of the Foerdewaith overkings due to the late duke's failure. This great shame only festered over the years, leading perhaps to an overly aggressive war doctrine among the line of battle-dukes that ultimately led to the duchy's second-greatest shame at the Battle of Bullocks Bale some 94 years later.

In the war between Oceanus and Foere, when the city of Endhome declared neutrality in 3217 I.R. and expelled its Foerdewaith garrison, the forces of the Rampart marched up the King's Road to retake the city, but sudden intervention by Burgundia caused the outflanked Foerdewaith army to withdraw to Troye without bloodshed. The lord-general of the army was dismissed in disgrace by the enraged battle-duke of the Rampart, but the event was the first real damage dealt to Foerdewaith military invincibility in the provinces.

Only five years later, the forces of the Rampart were directly engaged in the war of Suilleyn independence of 3222 I.R. An aggressive new lord-general led his Foerdewaith army into western Suilley to bring the rebel barons to heel. Unfortunately for the battle-duke who was returning from far afield in the battles of Matagost to the east, his Foerdewaith were virtually slaughtered at the Battle of Bullocks Bale, with only a few managing to escape. At this one stroke, the legend of the military power of the Duchy of the Rampart was ended. The Rampart maintains a powerful army in the present day, but it is no longer seen as the invincible force that at one time simultaneously threatened and protected the realms of the overking.

The people of the Rampart are solidly and traditionally Foerdewaith and very loyal to the overking in Courghais. Chivalry is still a strongly held value among the knightly class, although there are certainly many knights whose claim to chivalry is dubious at best and scurrilous at worst. The Order of the Swan, whose device is a white swan on a black background framed by a circle of plumes, is an ancient order of knights based in the Rampart. Knights of the Swan are generally knights-errant rather than in service to a feudal lord. They owe their loyalty to the order, although they have often ridden to the defense of the duchy when danger threatens.

However, a certain sense of ennui, decadence, and decay has been slowly creeping into the Duchy of the Rampart for many years. The tenets of chivalry are on the wane, roadside inns seem just a bit less well kept, and the pleasures of some of the nobility are a bit more jaded than in centuries past. Banquets sport increasingly elaborate dishes carried to the table by poorly fed domestic servants. Heresy in on the rise, and small and secret covens of demon-worshippers have been uncovered in the rural countryside, their cults festering beneath the mask of a cheerful peasantry. The occasional savage murder goes unsolved, leaving people to look over their shoulders when walking alone. The touch of evil and decay is subtle, but its gentle pressure can be felt.

TRADE AND COMMERCE

The capital city of Troye benefits from an excellent strategic location for trade, although the city itself is not particularly mercantile. Caravans ascend the King's Road from the Kingdom of Foere and enter Troye's gates from the west. Southern trade arrives from Toullen, Keston, and Vourdon along the South Road, and the King's Road brings cargo from Endhome's seaport and the farms of the Gaelon River Valley. Many of these shipments change hands in Troye as the various different merchants buy each other's goods to take back on the return journey.

In general, the folk of the Rampart are not traders or merchants, but the duchy makes efforts to foster trade and travel within its borders. In 3423 I.R., the Duchy of the Rampart acted in cooperation with Endhome, Sunderland, and Suilley to establish Grollek's Grove as a merchants' post on the Trader's Way to foster commerce among the four realms. Even though the Kingdom of Suilley tends to divert caravans onto its own Flatlander Road rather than the more-dangerous Trader's Way, the duchy makes no protest about reducing trade to Grollek's Grove. The Flatlander Road, after all, eventually leads to Troye itself from which it can continue down the King's Road to Grollek's Grove, enriched from

its time within the duchy.

LOYALTIES AND DIPLOMACY

The Duchy of the Rampart is the easternmost domain of the Kingdoms of Foere. The duchy has stood for centuries as the eastern defense of the Foerdewaith homelands and is fiercely loyal to the overking and the heartlands to the west.

GOVERNMENT

The current ruler is Claud VII, Duke of the Rampart, Battle-Duke of Foere, and Sword of the Foerdewaith. He has a long and bloody history in petty wars on the wild fringes of civilization fighting on behalf of Foere, with the duchy administered in his absence by the nobleman Traont, Baron Thulde under the title of Lord-Steward of the Rampart. In the recent campaign against the Huun in the lands of the Gulf of Akados and Irkaina, the overking decided to lead the armies personally rather than placing the duke in his traditional post of command, and Claud returned to his lands in the Rampart, clearly confused and insulted.

Having been established by decree, the duchy is not a wild patchwork of feudal divisions like the provinces to its east. It is segmented into a regular system of equally-sized counties. The counts appoint sheriffs and other officials and usually have at least four castled baronies in their lands, along with several knightly manors.

WILDERNESS AND ADVENTURE

The Duchy of the Rampart is well-settled, although pockets of wilderness are everywhere in between settlements. The southern verge of the Cretians is a wild and rugged place, much more sparsely inhabited, and correspondingly more dangerous for those who venture close to these strange peaks. Fewer settlements are along the margins of the Rampart Mountains, but this is an area where mining towns and villages of hill dwarves can be found in the rugged foothills. Patrols are at least occasionally undertaken by actual troops rather than a lone knight or a few volunteer yeomen with billhooks and crossbows.

TROYE, CITY OF (CAPITAL)

(TROY)

Population: 44,600 (36,760 Foerdewaith, 4,023 hill dwarf, 1,910 halfling, 860 half-elf, 437 gnome, 322 high elf, 160 half-orc, 128 other)

Ruler: Lady Yvonne Talaine, Lord-Mayor of Troye

Government: appointed lord-mayor and elected council of burgesses

The high granite walls of Troye are resplendent with banners, and lines of colorful shields affixed to the battlements represent the various noble houses of the Duchy of the Rampart. Great towers stand at intervals above the walls, some crowned with trebuchets and ballistae, others with high, pointed roofs. Over it all rises the vast citadel of the duke, the greatest and most formidable structure in a city designed for war.

Troye is the capital of the Duchy of the Rampart and was founded in the Hyperborean era. The city is a major destination for caravans, whose merchants sell their cargos here to buy goods from faraway places for the return journey. Merchants planning on making the whole trek from the Kingdom of Foere into the provinces and back (most likely to Manas, but sometimes to Endhome) stop here to enjoy one last taste of city comforts before heading off into the wild.

This great metropolis at the far reaches of the Kingdoms of Foere offers a vast array of interesting sights, sounds, cultures, clothes, music, merriment, purchases, people, and pickpockets. It is wise to keep one hand on the belt pouch when walking through crowds in Troye. Tourist attractions include the University of Subtleties, the Great Stone Rabbit in Lapin Square, the smoke-snorting iron bull atop the temple of Mithras, the great Marchantal market, the dried remains of the six tall thieves (at the Citadel's Gate), and the Court of Thespians.

In any of the city's hundred small markets, mostly temporary affairs blocking crossroads, one can find herb-crusted breads, baskets of the dark purple, dream-inducing apples grown in the Yolbiac Vale, puppets, trained cats, dwarf-crafted trinkets, colorful surcoats, stolen items available for quick sale, clay idols painted with symbols, and all manner of merchandise culled from traveling merchants of the world.

Shells are a particularly popular item of jewelry, a curiosity in a city so far from the sea, and are often seen adorning wealthy merchants and nobles when they ride through the city's narrow streets. Pearls are also much more highly prized than mined gemstones.

Troye is governed by a lord-mayor whose position is equivalent in status to a count (in other words, higher than a baron but not ranked as high as a duke). The duke-palatine appoints the lord-mayor, but a council of burgesses elected by the city's landowners handles most of the job of managing the city. In the past, lords-mayor who continued to make unpopular decrees were stopped in their tracks by the citizens who shut down the gates, blocked streets, and started arresting people loyal to the unpopular mayor. So even though the city is not technically self-governed, there is a practical limit to what the duke can impose upon his capital city without its consent.

Troye is the headquarters or an important area of operations for a number of different organizations. Principal among these, of course, is the city's government and city guard. Others include the Council of Guilds that regulates the city's commerce; the Most Honorable Guild of Thieves, which regulates the city's crime and underworld; the Church of Vanitthu and the Temple of Jamboor, both important players in the city's politics and spiritual life; the city chapterhouse of the Order of the Swan; and the Guild of Magisters.

Troye is a large city containing many secrets — and many dangers for the unwary. Decadence is setting in, which is giving rise to a much higher level of murders and lesser crimes than in centuries — and even decades — past. The worst of the symptoms is the growth of demon-cults hiding within the city's walls that are conducting secret sacrifices and engaging in vicious plots to undermine the forces of law and mercy. Heresies are whispered in the shadows, and criminal gangs roam the streets at night, disappearing into dark alleys and abandoned buildings if challenged by the guards.

If a party of adventurers asks around about strange events, especially among city officials, they may hear about the bizarre posters, pamphlets, and handbills that have been finding their way into the city over the last couple of years. The texts of these writings are nonsensical and disturbing: visions of the underworld, pointless ramblings, and deranged advice. The city's officials have grave concerns about what seems at first glance to be nothing more than one more quirk of city life. They have observed that the printed materials have a certain fascination to them, and many citizens seem to be collecting them, even quoting them from time to time in ordinary discussions. Each time a new batch of pamphlets arrives, the city suffers a spate of unusual and pointless crimes, most of them completely petty. Signs are removed, turned upside down, or switched with those of other establishments. Horses are stolen from one stable, only to appear in another across the city. Bakeries report a tripling or quadrupling of the ordinary rate of pilfering. There seems to be no direct connection to the pamphlets, but the correlation is precise.

METZEL, TOWN OF

Population: 2,876 (1,356 Foerdewaith, 920 hill dwarf, 313 halfling, 152 half-elf, 77 gnome, 58 high elf)
Ruler: Commander of the Watch Pietre Balmont
Government: council

Metzel is located 10 miles from the base of the mountain pass into the Yolbiac Vale, and also benefits from several nearby coal and iron mines. Its main industry is smelting iron, and sturdy wagons containing pigs of iron and sacks of coal make their way down from Metzel to the forges of Troye, along with various products from the Yolbiac Vale.

The town is chartered by the palatine duke, which allows it to be self-ruled, and is governed by a council of three: the guildmaster of the Iron Smelters' Guild, the trademaster of the Merchant Brotherhood, and the commander of the watch. Metzel has a bad reputation for crime and questionable behavior.

The guilds here are well organized, and have the feel of an extortion racket rather than a means of ensuring high-quality goods.

RELIQUARY OF JAMBOOR

Population: 2,274 (Foerdewaith)
Ruler: High Reliquarian
Government: religious

The Reliquary is high in the foothills of the Rampart Mountains, but there is an excellent dirt road leading to the heights where the Reliquary is found. It is a massive fortress built into the side of a cliff, looking almost as if the sheer rock face had suffered an avalanche of carved stone walls and buildings.

The fortress houses a large temple-complex to Jamboor, "He Who Hears the Secrets of the Dead," Hyperborean god of knowledge, magic, and death. The complex includes the main temple, a library, an academy of magecraft, and extensive burial catacombs in the depths of the cliff behind the cascade of buildings. It is the most significant temple to the god in the Borderland Provinces, and the high reliquarian oversees the church's activities in the Rampart, Vourdon, Suilley, Keston, Toullen, Exeter, the Gaelon River Valley, Eastreach, and the Amrin Estuary.

The Reliquary is also the center of a considerable intelligence-gathering operation monitored by another high official who bears the title of "high excriptor." The high reliquarian is considered senior to the high excriptor, but both are selected based on omens direct from the god: the excriptor's role is more of an independent advisor to the reliquarian than a subordinate.

RISTALT, CITY OF

Population: 6,781 (3,627 Foerdewaith, 2,895 hill dwarf, 251 halfling, 8 gnome)
Ruler: Mayor Sir Sorbat of Gulping Pond
Government: overlord

The small city of Ristalt is walled with stone and surrounded by short, squat drum towers. The round citadel looks to be newer than the walls, and is quite beautifully constructed with protective symbols and realistic-looking vines sculpted as massive bas-relief decoration all around the wall. A mayor appointed by the duke governs the city. The current mayor is Sir Sorbat of Gulping Pond, a courtier more than a knight, but an adequate administrator nonetheless

Ristalt is the first destination of most products from the western face of the Rampart Mountains. The city turns some of the products into manufactured goods and sends the rest northward to the King's Road and thence to Troye. Dwarves are a common sight on the city streets, usually traders who live on the roads rather than actually dwelling in the mountains. For unknown reasons (possibly the dwarves), elves are greatly disliked here.

KINGDOM OF SUILLEY

Capital: Manas
Notable Settlements: Alembretia, Cluin, Pfefferain, Stronghold Hjerrin
Ruler: His Most Regal Majesty King Ulrich IX of Suilley, Sovereign of Keston and Toullen, Protector-Regent of the Lorremach.
Government: monarchy
Population: 2,449,600 (2,152,000 Foerdewaith, 202,500 halfling, 47,050 half-elf, 36,700 high elf, 7,250 hill dwarf, 3,280 gnome, 820 other)
Monstrous: hobgoblin, bugbear, hill giant, troll, manticore, roc, dragon (mainly Lorremach Highhills)
Languages: Common, Gasquen
Religion: Ceres, Sefagreth, Freya, Vanitthu, Mitra, Thyr, Muir, Archeillus, Mick O'Delving, Belon the Wise, Solanus, Darach-Albith, Yenomesh, Bowbe, The Father, Mathrigaunt the Mad

Resources: foodstuffs, livestock (horses), trade hub, grain, flax, spirits (ale), glass, manufactured goods, quarry stone, banking, copper, opium, gems

Currency: Suilley

Technology Level: Medieval (cities), High Middle Ages (countryside)

Some 300 years ago, the Kingdom of Suilley declared itself an independent kingdom and seceded from the Kingdoms of Foere. Since this time, other large regions of the Borderland Provinces have declared themselves vassals of the Suilleyn king, which has increased the kingdom's power by an order of magnitude but strained its resources to the utmost. It remains a real possibility that Suilley could collapse under this pressure, in which case vast areas of the Borderland Provinces would be thrown into chaos.

The northern border of Suilley is the King's Road until it comes within 150 miles of the city of Troye; these 150 miles are within the Duchy of the Rampart. The western border with the County of Vourdon is roughly 100 miles east of Olaric, and although parts of it are disputed, it is considered to run due north and south along this line. The southern border runs northwest from the very southernmost extent of the Lorremach Highhills, with the Flatlander Road approximately 50 miles inside the border, then turning southwest 200 miles south of Manas to join a triple border-point with Keston and Vourdon 150 or so miles south of the city of Olaric.

HISTORY AND PEOPLE

In the year 3222 I.R., Ghienvais Pas, the lord-governor of Suilley, had himself crowned as His Independent Majesty Ghienvais I, King of Suilley, Marquis of the Lorremach Highhills, and Warden of the Plains of Suilley. This event is still often called the "Theft of the Kingdom" in Foere, and Suilley the "Stolen Kingdom," although three centuries have turned the Suilleyn secession into an accomplished fact of history, legitimated by the passage of time. The rebellion's background can be explained in relatively simple terms, although the details are by definition more complex as it occurred within the larger tapestry of rebellion and secession that afflicted the Kingdoms of Foere during the Wars of Succession.

Essentially, the majority of the Suilleyn nobles came to see themselves as a separate branch of the Foerdewaith but entitled to equal status with the nobility of the heartland kingdoms in terms of taxes and privileges. It is likely that many of them did not anticipate war at all, merely a long and ultimately successful wrangling of diplomats in the Court at Courghais. Thus, the noble class of Suilley united around the lord-governor, marshalled their legal arguments, sent a letter to the royal court explaining their grievances, and crowned a monarch who offered fealty to the overking.

Despite the peacefulness of the intentions, a small civil war immediately broke out among barons in eastern Suilley, with loyalists and monarchists engaging each other in the plains near the Gundlock Hills, no doubt influenced by the struggles for independence occurring in Burgundia to the east.

Hopes of a peaceful secession were dashed, however, when the overking, watching his empire slip through his fingers as first Ramthion Island, then Pontos Island, and then Burgundia entered into rebellion, declared the king of Suilley to be a usurper and traitor to the crown, and his nobles to be stripped of their lands in favor of new, more faithful, vassals. By doing so, the Court at Courghais transformed a peaceful and ultimately still loyalist modification of feudal rights into a battlefield war, with the Suilleyn nobles suddenly fighting for their lives rather than merely for lower taxes and greater social status.

With its back to the wall, Suilley stripped its fields of able-bodied peasants to form battalions of levied troops, mustered every knight who could straddle a horse and hold a lance, and prepared for an all-out war to the death. Blacksmiths' hammers rang through the night, couriers rode lathered horses from one manorial estate to the next, and even many of the originally loyalist barons came to realize that they would be executed alongside the rebels if Foere returned in victory to its

former province. Surrender was no longer an option, and a soft resolve hardened into iron.

King Ghienvais realized the futility of trying to fight ardently loyalist barons in the east at the same time as a Foerdewaith army to the northwest, and attempted to entice the loyalist nobles in the Gundlock Hills region and the surrounding plains with peace offerings of lucrative trade and influence, but to no avail. Many monarchist nobles of those areas soon fled to the Suilleyn heartlands as the jubilant loyalists held trials and burned accused traitors at the stake, which caused civil war to erupt in eastern Suilley even as the western portion of the nascent kingdom prepared for an invasion by Foere.

The muddy season greatly slowed the assembly of the forces of Suilley, for the barons and supply wagons for the inevitable siege of Manas had to fight their way down mud-soaked cart trails and sodden country lanes. But the new king also anticipated that the mustering of additional forces in the Duchy of the Rampart would take time, even though the higher lands of the Rampart did not face the obstacle of mired supply lines, since so many Foerdewaith troops had already been deployed to Matagost to put down the Burgundian rebellion and defend against Oceander invasion in the east. The new kingdom did what it could to protect the capital city in the meantime. Suilleyn troops occupied the nearby gatehouses along the Rampart without opposition from the garrisons, whose commanders elected to withdraw rather than die in a hopeless last stand, and the great road between the capital cities of Manas and Troye was turned into a fortification.

Authorized for battle by the overking, the aggressive general in charge of the army of the Rampart, Lord-General Baron Cavodeill, moved into action immediately, not waiting for the arrival of the battle-duke from his deployment in Matagost, and not waiting for a full mustering of the barons. While the Suilleyn nobles were still organizing themselves in their rural manors and distant castles, or on the mud-wallowed roads to Manas, the Foerdewaith army marched down the Rampart against a kingdom that had barely started its preparations.

With siege engines in its train and heavy infantry able to fight on the causeway far better than levied peasants or mounted knights, the Foerdewaith army crushed opposition at gatehouse after gatehouse along the Rampart, drawing nearer to the city of Manas day by day. Had the lord-general of the Rampartine forces continued on this relentless march, the city of Manas might possibly have been taken at the outset of the war, although such an outcome would have been unlikely against a fortified city waiting for significant reinforcements to arrive from the countryside. In any case, the assault took a radically different turn when Rampartine scouts stumbled upon the main force of the small Suilleyn army circling around behind the Foerdewaith advance along the causeway. Correctly judging that the objective of the Suilleyn general was to retake the Rampart behind him, effectively cutting off his forces from reinforcement on the fortified road and allowing a hammer-and-anvil assault from behind when he reached the walls of Manas, the duchy's general moved his cavalry and main forces off the Rampart to prevent encirclement.

The Rampartine army caught and engaged the smaller Suilleyn force not more than a mile from the fortified causeway. In the open pastureland, the Foerdewaith knights and soldiery rapidly broke the smaller, hastily assembled array of Suilley's local knights and levies and forced them back in disorder to a copse of trees near the pastures of Bullocks Bale. Unfamiliar with the muddy season in Suilley, the lord-general of the Rampartine army immediately followed up his victory and pursued the retreating Suilleyn into the muddy fields below the higher ground around the causeway. Suddenly bogged down in mud and threatened with holes dug by the Suilleyn troops to break the legs of horses, the knights and cavalry of the Rampartine army died in droves from the missiles of archers and slingers sheltering in the copse of trees. The knights of Suilley circled entirely around the battle in the pasture to shatter the still-disorganized advance of the Foerdewaith infantry behind their mired cavalry, keeping to the higher ground near the causeway where their own charge could be delivered over dry, even ground. The army of the Rampart was utterly destroyed, and Suilley's "theft" into an independent monarchy free of the overking's authority became an accomplished fact, though it ultimately withdrew from the civil war in its own eastern region and foreswore claim to any of the lands near the Gundlock Hills.

As the power of Foere continued to decline in the provinces and the newly minted District of Sunderland beyond, the emerging Kingdom of Suilley found its power increasing by default. Although Suilley was forced to fight several more battles with the Foerdewaith after the first one, the cost of these conflicts was partially subsidized by other opponents of Foere, namely Endhome, Oceanus, and Burgundia. Captured territories between Manas and the duchy were granted to many of the monarchist nobility of eastern Suilley who had been forced to flee the loyalists, and this area continues to harbor considerable ill will toward the Kingdom of Foere, remembering burning villages and executions by loyalist bands of marauders. This ill will is not directed at the Duchy of the Rampart, for the anti-monarchists were Suilleyn themselves, but the monarchists are quite hostile to any Foerdewaith from across the March of Mountains.

Two major provinces of Foere, the County of Toullen and Province of Keston, ultimately renounced their fealty to the overking of Foere in the year 3336 I.R. and pledged themselves to the king of Suilley as vassal states.

An example of Suilley's emerging power and authority is its participation in establishing a trading post at Grollek's Grove in 3423 I.R. in concert with the city of Endhome, the formerly hostile Duchy of the Rampart, and what representatives could be found to stand for the District of Sunderland (many of whom were former loyalists who battled against Suilley's secession).

The largest problem facing Suilley at this time is actually the result of its own past successes in war and diplomacy. It has inherited the realms of Keston and Toullen with all their problems, which means the king of Suilley now possesses, largely by default, a wide-ranging and disorganized feudal empire. The Suilleyn monarchy is being entreated from all sides to shoulder the burden of solving vast regional problems caused by the retreat of Foere. With a relatively independent nobility, the king of Suilley would have enough work just organizing his own domain. He is instead being forced into a constant juggling act trying to balance wilderness and depopulation in Keston; problems in the Lorremach Highhills; tax-rebels and petty wars among the barons of his own country; occasional tension with Foere over the King's Road or the Rampart border; and the task of turning his patchwork confederacy of feudal states into a functioning whole with unified laws and common defense. The core of Suilley, a hundred or so miles around Manas, is a very stable domain, but one cannot rule a vast empire from such a small base, and this is what the King of Suilley faces. The resources simply do not exist to protect, subdue, rebuild, and organize all the things in Suilley's far-flung domains that need to be protected, subdued, rebuilt, and organized. Very few people realize how tenuous King Ulrich's situation actually has become. The treasury is emptied as soon as it is filled, his personal wealth is tied up in maintaining the army, and his soldiery is stretched thin as a wire. Suilley is a growing empire that could falter and fail simply from a run of bad luck or any significant catastrophe.

TRADE AND COMMERCE

A great deal of caravan traffic passes through Suilley on the north-south Trader's Way from Exeter Province, the east-west route along the South County Road from Olaric toward Endhome, or on the Rampart Road to and from Foere itself. The Trader's Way route passes through wild and dangerous places, and the Flatlander Road diverts its traffic from a 300-mile stretch of the Lorremach Highhills, but the South County Road and the Manas-to-Troye Rampart Road are both well patrolled and served by towns and fortified inns along the way.

Although Suilley endures a season of rain and mud each year, farms are productive and pillaging is infrequent, especially in the regions up to 25 miles from one of the roads (with the exception of the Trader's Way). The uninhabited parts of the country's rural interior — and some wild regions such as the Lorremach Highhills — cannot be described as safe, but they are not unduly dangerous for those who travel in large, well-armed groups.

Suilley has recently been making great efforts to entice northbound merchant caravans coming from Exeter Province to take the Flatlander Road through Manas rather than the Trader's Way. Given the dangers of the Trader's Way, even the small incentives offered are enough to persuade many merchants to take the Manas route. The result has been to make the Trader's Way between Grollek's Grove and Pfefferain even more sparsely traveled and more dangerous, but Suilley's main concern is the kingdom's coffers, not the safety of a road far at the realm's eastern border nor the lawless lands of the Sundered Kingdoms beyond that might suffer from this reduction in trade.

LOYALTIES AND DIPLOMACY

Because the overking has never officially recognized the independent status of Suilley and the Court at Courghais continues to address the king of Suilley as "our subject," relations between Suilley and the Kingdom of Foere are uneasy, but both realms are aware that the Kingdom of Foere no longer has the wherewithal to successfully invade Suilley. Relations between the Kingdom of Suilley and the duke of the Rampart are actually quite friendly, for the trade route between Manas and Troye is an important source of wealth for the duchy and the kingdom. Whatever the overking and his court might think of Suilley, the Duchy of the Rampart would be exceedingly unhappy to find its trade relationship with Suilley impeded by war.

Many of the barons of northern Suilley have their eye on the periphery of the Gaelon River Valley, and a few freehold lords on the northern side of the King's Road have pledged fealty to the king of Suilley. But at this point, the incursion into the Gaelon River region remains small and scattered. The Kingdom of Suilley is aware that while the Duchy of the Rampart cares little about the Gaelon River Valley, it (along with Foere, beyond the March of Mountains) cares a great deal about who controls the King's Road. The one event that could lead to renewed hostility between the two realms would be if the Suilleyn border began to creep too far beyond the King's Road itself, putting the road firmly into Suilley's control.

Suilley's good relations with the County of Vourdon on its western border are a high priority for the monarchy. If there is ever another war with the Kingdoms of Foere, Vourdon would threaten Suilley's flank in a conflict with the Duchy of the Rampart, and although Suilley's army is strong, it is not strong enough to fight two separate conflicts on different fronts (as evidenced by its failure to curb the civil war in its own eastern territories at the time of its own inception). Keston Province is a vassal of the Suilleyn king, but is too weak to tie down the forces of Vourdon in case of a war. To this end, Suilley maintains an ambassador in the city of Olaric, whose task is to ensure that potential conflicts between the realms are quickly resolved.

GOVERNMENT

Suilley is a monarchy ruled by a hereditary king or queen who derive descent from Ghienvais I, the first king to bear the crown in rebellion against Foere. The realm has eight ducal houses, which makes the king relatively strong compared with many of his peer monarchs, since it is rare for the dukes to agree long enough with each other to unite against the king in any way.

Only one queen has ruled Suilley in its history, for the succession traditionally goes to the oldest male offspring, and to the oldest female only if there is no male heir. The reign of Queen Dacinthe I was initially plagued by her uncle, Prince Huelbert, who claimed that no female could inherit the throne at all, which would make him the rightful king. Eventually, one of Dacinthe's loyal dukes captured Huelbert in battle and sent his head to the queen in a large glass bottle. Dacinthe ordered the bottled head displayed as the centerpiece at her next royal banquet to the distress of many of the guests, especially those suspected of complicity with the would-be usurper. All ambiguities in the law were thus completely clarified.

The heraldry of the house of King Ulrich, and thus the device of Suilley, is a golden crown over two red lions rampant, back to back, on a green field.

WILDERNESS AND ADVENTURE

As with most of the Borderland Provinces, Suilley is far more settled, law-abiding, and prosperous in the regions surrounding its patrolled roads than in the rural areas beyond. Much of the interior resembles a thick scattering of villages and castles merging into an equally thick scattering of wilderness. Thus, there are always opportunities to find adventure, even in the country's heartlands. The Lorremach Highhills and the Wilderland Hills are large wilderness regions with virtually no protection whatsoever and can be very dangerous to those without armed escorts.

MANAS, CITY OF (CAPITAL)

Population: 28,420 (21,500 Foerdewaith, 3,030 halfling, 1,700 half-elf, 950 high elf, 680 hill dwarf, 400 gnome, 160 other)

Ruler: Mayor Laurenti Rizaal

Government: elected council of burgesses chooses mayor

Manas is a sprawling metropolis that has outgrown its city walls, with cottages and other buildings extending in all directions around the central walled precincts. There has been a project to build an outer wall around these settlements, but construction has been stalled for some time.

Manas is the capital city of Suilley and houses the court of King Ulrich at Palaz Terondel within the city walls, along with various other institutions of the country's government. The city prospers from trade and from the stability of the surrounding region, being at the very heart of the king's authority and power. At the same time, however, the treasury is badly strained as the city helps to fund the king's distant landholdings and vassal nations.

Like Troye, Manas is an ancient city that charts its history back to the days of the Hyperboreans, although it grew as a trading town rather than originating as a fortress. The city's stone walls are of great antiquity, but they were built to replace wooden walls that had protected the city for centuries before quarrying ever began for the stronger fortifications. Below the city is a vast Hyperborean-era series of vaults, passageways, and tombs. Why a tomb complex would require such a wealth of rooms, galleries, and winding tunnels beneath Manas is a secret lost with the Hyperboreans, for it is not a common feature of Hyperborean city-building. Throughout the city, a number of holes have been dug deeply enough to break into the vaulted corridors and labyrinthine tunnels below so that sewage and storm water can drain down from the city streets and be dispersed in the labyrinth.

Manas has the vibrant, almost frenetic, atmosphere of a place at the center of events, and this is indeed the case, for the kingdom more and more is becoming the main center of gravity in the Borderland Provinces. The kingdom's trade roads are safer than average, its guilds are less venal than many, its courts of justice are fairer and less corrupt than one might expect, its coins are well minted, its troubadours have little trouble finding wealthy patrons, and its nobility still considers chivalry to be something more than a fashionable lie. Demolition of old buildings and the construction of larger ones clog the city's thoroughfares with stone and lumber as the city continues to expand to fit its emerging role as a major power. New merchant houses, not only from within Suilley but from places as far as Bard's Gate and Endhome, are opening their doors for business. Famous troubadours and jongleurs travel to the city from as far as Troye and Vermis to seek audiences and noble patronage. Manas has even begun to export some of its court fashions, perhaps the most significant mark of any city's pre-eminence. There are limits, of course; when Manas fashions are worn in Troye, the days of the Kingdom of Foere in the east will truly be ended, but that day has not yet come.

At present, Manas has no formal college of magecraft but it is home to several wizards and sorcerers of note who live in formidable palazzi with arcane wards upon the doors and strange guardians prowling their halls by night. The sorceress Veril of Tourne lives in the crumbling Palaz Tourne, the former home of her now-deceased father, the sorcerer Beinad of Tourne, son of Ylaine of Tourne, the Courghais-born sorceress who advised Ghienvais I when he was still a mere lord-governor, and was

an early advocate of the Suilleyn secession. The family is long-lived and not entirely sane. There is also Ciosceppio, who seems to disdain any surname, and whose rune-tattooed bull is, by specific decree of the king himself, not allowed into the city streets any more. The mystical Pytharian and the notable Rhomenides also number among the city's great mages, both of them solemn and long-bearded, quite satisfactory to the expectations of the citizens of Manas in terms of how wizards should look and behave.

Various factions operate within the city of Manas, especially now that the kingdom has become a major power in the provinces. The trade embassies of Bard's Gate and Endhome are both making considerable numbers of allies among the city's mercantile classes. The thieves' guild supervises criminal activities and several small opium guilds are involved in a savage battle to control sales of opium from Pfefferain. A diplomat from Courghais, while never referring to Suilley as a kingdom, works diligently to ensure that Foere's interests are represented in the court at Palaz Terondel. Representatives from the vassal courts in Kingston and Tertry promote caravan trade to their countries and petition Ulrich for funds and troops to assist in the interests of Keston and Toullen. Temples of various gods jostle for influence with the citizenry (especially those who are wealthy and/or noble). The quantity of intrigue as all these factions interact is mind-boggling.

The city maintains a small standing garrison, mostly to watch and guard the walls, but also a ceremonial bodyguard for the king, a troop of ranger-outriders, and a few spellcasters to supplement the city's Wardens.

Additionally, units of the Royal Army are stationed in the citadel, a round tower called the Caerronde (which also contains the royal dungeon) and serves as the city's last defense. The standing army of Suilley is much smaller than in days past when the Duchy of the Rampart represented a real threat, and many of its units are constantly on dispatch in Keston and even as far as Toullen trying to assist these vassal realms with the daunting task of keeping order. The army also patrols roads and maintains small garrisons throughout the kingdom, so the king's force here in Manas is not much larger than the city's own army. It usually is composed of a levied force of 200 trained peasants, 50 men-at-arms, and five mounted knights representing the feudal obligation of one or two barons to provide the king periodically with troops. Additionally, there is one battalion made up of 100 archers and 200 lightly armored infantrymen, and a second battalion of 300 heavy infantrymen. The King's Cavalry is made up of five troops of 20 riders plus their officers, one unit of 50 heavy cavalry, and a third unit of 20 knights together with their soldiers (a number varying from 30 to 50). All of these forces are supplemented by the private standing forces of the eight dukes and by a small corps of more-powerful individuals who shift from unit to unit as needed. This corps is often referred to as the King's Scepters and includes sorcerers, powerful fighters, clerics, and often a paladin or two. It is a mixed and often-changing group, but the Scepters are in many ways the troubleshooters and backbone of an otherwise relatively weak army.

The king has the ability to muster a massive army by calling up barons and knights, so the size of the standing army should not be seen as a measure of Suilley's true power. This is merely the group of professional, full-time soldiers who are ready to respond at a moment's notice if the king or country is threatened.

The Corps of Wardens is a separate contingent of guards maintained by the city who patrol the streets and respond to disorder and crimes. As with the Royal Army, the Wardens are mostly no more than trained but ordinary individuals who answer mundane problems such as thefts and tavern brawls. For larger matters such as Ciosceppio's rune-tattooed bull, the Wardens have a small number of spellcasters and clerics who support the ordinary Wardens with considerably more unusual resources. The commander of the Corps of Wardens is currently the knight Sir Orlando Cormont.

The city's symbol is three white circles arranged as a triangle around a badger on a blue field. This is distinct from the king's royal arms and represents only Manas itself, and it is proudly displayed on banners flown atop the houses of the city's wealthy merchants, the towers around the city wall, and the House of Burgesses.

The burgesses are prominent leaders elected by the citizens for terms of two years. It is the burgesses who elect the mayor, pass municipal laws, and undertake specific responsibilities such as the minister of justicators (courts), minister of the curtilage (the walls and defenses), and minister of revenues (gate and sales taxes).

The city's greatest market is Damozel Square, with the great merchants buying and selling large lots in the center, and small vendors selling to ordinary shoppers around the square's periphery. Every oddment and tidbit of the world seems to be available here, from diamonds and opium to turnips and flax.

Manas is an excellent place to hear rumors, find employment, and ferret out interesting opportunities. Representatives of the eight dukes are often looking for mercenaries who can solve problems in the countryside such as dealing with dragons and mysterious events. The city's wizards always require tasks and travels that would be too dangerous for ordinary people. The temples extend their benevolent reach as far into the realm as they can, usually offering such rewards as raising the dead or removing curses instead of paying money, but even the temples dip into their coffers to handle truly strange and threatening events, whether inside or outside the walls of Manas. Caravans always need guards, and merchants always seek unusual items to sell. Even within the city, there are strange mysteries, secret cults, sabotage, bodyguarding, and other interesting chances for gold and renown. Manas is a place where many possibilities converge.

ALEMBRETIA, CITY OF

Population: 13,240 (10,575 Foerdewaith 1,085 hill dwarf, 740 gnome, 460 half-elf, 380 halfling)
Ruler: Riobert Nev, Grand Master of the Glassmakers' Guild of Alembretia
Government: council

Alembretia is a large city on the Flatlander Road some 10 miles from the base of the Lorremach Highhills and perhaps 50 miles from the crossroad where the Flatlander Road meets the Trader's Way in the highlands. The citizens of Alembretia's upper class are a rather unpleasant lot, greedy and somewhat cruel, and are known for wearing elaborate clothes. Anyone dressed in ordinary garb is treated as a rank commoner, and on no account taken seriously.

The city makes considerable revenue from travelers on the Flatlander Road, but its main product is blown glass. The sandy hills of the Lorremach include several deposits of colored sand that can be incorporated into the glassmaking process. Alembretia's glass-makers and glassblowers are thus able to produce glassware in a variety of beautifully rich hues, or clear glass with graceful swirls of color.

The city is self-ruled by a Council of Guilds which is effectively controlled by the Glassmakers' Guild, whose members elect the majority of the council seats.

CLUIN, TOWN OF

Population: 3,213 (2,730 Foerdewaith, 480 half-elf, 3 gnome)
Ruler: Mayor Oswalt
Government: overlord

Cluin is one of the main towns along the road from Manas to Grollek's Grove. An elected mayor governs the town, and all citizens are entitled to vote. The current mayor is Oswalt of Cluin, a prominent merchant who has managed the town diligently and well. Most of the town's basic industry is centered on producing manufactured goods for the wealthier members of the surrounding rural communities. Only a very small amount of trade comes from caravans passing to and from Manas, although many of them stop here for the night, and the town is not authorized to tax travelers on the road. Cluin is a major pilgrimage destination. Some 100 years ago, a rune-covered pillar rose in the local cemetery under mysterious circumstances.

Now known as the Rock of Yenomesh, the artifact is holy to followers of both that Hyperborean god of glyphs and writing as well as Thyr.

PFEFFERAIN, TOWN OF

Population: 4,712 (2,686 Foerdewaith, 754 gnome, 613 halfling, 377 high elf, 236 half-elf, 46 hill dwarf)
Ruler: Mayor Arellias auf der Henneschlieden
Government: autocracy

Known to its citizens as the "Crown of the Lorremach," the hill-walled town of Pfefferain is part of the Kingdom of Suilley but has a charter that allows it to govern itself rather than being ruled by a local lord. A justicator (essentially a magistrate) from the king's court in Manas supervises the town's court of law and serves as the voice of the king's authority if needed, but the royal court does not interfere with any matters other than law and taxation. Pfefferain is left to itself on all local matters.

In this generally inhospitable region, Pfefferain benefits from its position in the middle of a large plot of fertile savannah territory near a spring-fed stream. The tillable land nearby supports corn, wheat, flax, soybeans, vegetables, and fruit trees, and grasslands supply grazing for herds of cattle, pigs, sheep, and horses. However, its main trade product is processed opium from the poppies that grow wild in the surrounding highlands. The town itself does not manufacture the opium; this is done, for the most part, by the hillfolk who gather or grow the poppies then bring the paste to the town to sell.

The town is extremely friendly to users of magic and is home to the "Revered Sorcerers and Wizards Guild of Pfefferain."

REFERENCE SOURCE: F1 VINDICATION

STRONGHOLD HJERRIN

Population: 3,672 (3,120 Foerdewaith, 330 hill dwarf, 179 gnome, 43 halfling)
Ruler: Fortress-Commander Sir Oessum Keenblade
Government: military command

Stronghold Hjerrin occupies the tops of two adjacent mesas and is built up between them to create a stone tunnel through which caravans may pass without entering the stronghold itself. The fortress is a vast construction of drum towers and thick walls designed to pour destruction down onto the road below. It flies a huge banner of the Kingdom of Suilley over the highest tower.

In the vast, shaded underpass through the fortress, one finds two inns, stables, a store selling general supplies, and the forge of an experienced blacksmith, all to allow caravans a safe rest stop and supplies for the next leg of their journey. The long, arched tunnel is as ancient as the stronghold it passes through, but the stonework remains as sound as the day the Hyperboreans built it.

Only travelers of very high station or fame are admitted to the stronghold itself for reasons of security. Most visitors are limited to the small community in the huge, arched underpass beneath the fortifications.

COUNTY OF TOULLEN

(TOO-len, antique: too-lain)
Capital: Tertry
Notable Settlements: Tuller, Durbenford
Ruler: The Honorable Luthien I, Count-Palatine of Toullen, Protector of the Southern Marches
Government: feudalism (palatine county of Suilley)
Population: 1,292,000 (789,600 Foerdewaith, 198,000 half-elf, 93,700 halfling, 59,100 high elf, 54,000 hill dwarf, 42,550 Heldring, 28,000 wood elf, 19,800 mountain dwarf, 4,950 gnome, 2,300 other)
Monstrous: giant boar, kobold, giant weasel, goblin, dire wolf, goblin snake, swan maiden (plains); orc, hill giant,

troll, trollhound, winter wolf, mammoth, frost giant, chimera, thunderbird, red dragon, white dragon (Kal'Iugus Mountains); giant animal, worg, giant spider, fey, ettercap, tangtal, wood giant, forest drake, lycanthrope, treant (Wiltangle Forest)

Languages: Common, Halfling, Elvish, Dwarven, Gnomish

Religion: Freya, Thyr, Mick O'Delving, Muir, Pan, Darach-Albith, Dwerfater, Vergrimm Earthsblood, Quell, Sefagreth, Shae'loegn, Path of the Shattered Sword

Resources: timber, flax, linen, foodstuffs, livestock (swine), copper, furs, gems, fishing, shipbuilding supplies, shipbuilding

Currency: Suilley

Technology Level: High Middle Ages, Medieval (Tertry and Tuller)

Toullen is now a feudal vassal of Suilley, essentially a palatine realm ruled by the count who has pledged his personal fealty to the Suilleyn king. It is a very rural country that is still recovering from long-term damage caused by the Fiend Rains. The main attraction of Toullen for most people of the Borderland Provinces is the Tournament of Lilies and the highly competitive jousting competitions of the county. Most of the county's revenue comes from logging and mining operations on the western slopes of the Kal'Iugus Mountains.

The county is a narrow realm bordered to the west by the Kal'Iugus Mountains, although a small annex exists beyond the mountains in a forested area dominated by the city of Durbenford that is reached by means of a mountain pass. The county's eastern border is the Wiltangle Forest, and on the south it extends all the way to the city of Tuller on the Tywyl Bay coast, the only port within Suilley's domains. Its northern border with Keston Province is the crossroad of the Provincial Military Road and the South Road, 200 miles by road from the capital city of Tertry.

HISTORY AND PEOPLE

The County of Toullen was established in 2856 I.R. during the period of time when Foere made great strides in organizing and consolidating its vassal states beyond the March of Mountains. In that year, the overking raised High Baron Trosvoun to the rank of count, granted him the vast region of Toullen as a feudal realm, and charged him with the task of uniting the local warlords and petty chieftains into an organized system of vassalage and fealty. Count Trosvoun established his seat of authority in the small town of Tertry on the South Road, thereby allowing reinforcements and supplies to travel swiftly to his assistance from Foere, if need be. Over the years, the mandated system of vassalage and fealty slowly developed outward from Tertry as one warlord after another eventually chose to join the county's march toward unification and centralized power, represented by the count and his distant, omnipotent overking.

In the year 3336 I.R., Count Catrebrasse II of Toullen declared that he was retracting his feudal loyalties from the Kingdom of Foere and would pay fealty instead to the kings of Suilley. Emboldened by this development, the lord-governor of Keston Province similarly shifted his allegiance to Suilley not more than a month after the count of Toullen's decree. It is evident an agreement was made between the two rulers so Toullen's troops would help defend Keston across the Gap Road in case of a counter-invasion by Foere. A large contingent of knights of Toullen was already present in Keston Province with a battalion of crossbowmen when the town criers of Kingston began ringing their bells to announce that the king of Kingston had changed.

Most likely the first discussions took place during the Tournament of Lilies in Tertry, which the lord-governor of Keston Province attended to witness a much-anticipated joust between Sir Rolvin of Dwarnhold and Sir Corin of Kingston (the victor being Sir Rolvin). Thereafter, Count Catrebrasse and the lord-governor remained in contact, making use of a magic mirror known as the *Ormoulande* that allowed them to use two mirrors to speak to each other at a distance. As all know, the legendary thief Morwin, also known as the "Golden Crescent," stole the *Ormoulande* from the palace of the count of Toullen some months later.

The catastrophic year of 3439 I.R. brought the Fiend Rains, torrential downpours along the March of Mountains that flooded the easternmost of Foere's provinces, principally the Duchy of the Rampart, the Kingdom of Suilley, Keston Province, and the Counties of Vourdon and Toullen. Although the city of Tertry was spared most of the destruction by being on somewhat higher ground near the mountains, the entire realm became a shallow river with the regions north of Tertry draining toward Keston, and the regions to the south draining slowly toward Tywyl Bay. Count Rolomair, who was wavering and indecisive and already suffering the disrespect of his subject nobility, failed to marshal any sort of response to the disaster and has since been given the appellation "Rolomair the Wetself." The deluge thus affected Toullen somewhat worse than the other provinces, and set the county back by years. Many barons declared themselves freeholders rather than vassals of the Wet Count, and petty wars against these barons occupied Rolomair's successors for a decade thereafter.

In the interim between the Fiend Rains and the present day, Toullen has struggled to recover its prosperity. It is somewhat aided by its possession of Suilley's only seaport, even though most of Suilley's trade goes north to Endhome or Eastgate.

It might seem like a strange thing for a nation to have a separate entry for a sport, but in Toullen's case, leaving out mention of the sport of jousting would be a serious omission. In addition to hosting the Tournament of Lilies at Tertry, which is the most prestigious tournament in the provinces and brings contestants from as far away as Eastreach and even Courghais, Toullen is obsessed with the sport. From knights on their Suilleyn destriers in elaborate plate armor, all the way to peasants on donkeys riding at each other with quarterstaffs and barrel lids, the County of Toullen is universally addicted to the lists.

Under the auspices of Count Quelovic II, the first Tournament of Lilies was held in Tertry in 3119 I.R. as a melee tournament with 25 knights to each side, and was resolved in a single mock battle that resulted in two deaths and a number of serious wounds. Members of the victorious side received chaplets of lilies, and all the knights — save two — declared that the mock battle had been a tremendous success. The count's popularity greatly increased, and on the spot he declared that the tournament would be repeated the following year on the same day (the day before the first full moon) in the same month. From that time, the Tournament of Lilies has evolved to become more a competition of individual jousts rather than of the melee, and a system of qualifications developed to ensure that the tournament would not drag on for weeks due to the number of participants.

As with the Province of Keston, the County of Toullen is not greatly affected by the retreat of Foere's power. These vassal states of Suilley threw off the yoke of Foere relatively early, and Foere was doing little to benefit them in the first place. They experienced the rough edge of Foerdewaith culture far more than the civilized edge; other than a countryside interpretation of chivalric principles and an invader's language, they have little to show for their temporary role as vassal states to the overking in Courghais.

For the Toullenese, the changing times have more to do with growth and stability, building connections with Suilley to benefit their people, and reclaiming fens and marshes that have stood fallow since the Fiend Rains decades ago.

TRADE AND COMMERCE

Virtually all of Toullen's wealth comes from two sources: merchants on the South Road and the extensive mining and logging efforts in the Kal'Iugus Mountains. Caravans on the South Road are fairly common as they make short legs of the route between the port at Tuller through Toullen and then beyond to Keston, Vourdon, the Duchy of the Rampart, and Manas. Caravans along this route are often quite large, but carry cargoes of relatively low value compared with the riches that traverse the north. Toullen gains more of its revenue from the Kal'Iugus Mountains, mainly along the western flanks, which are reached through the Toullen Pass 100 miles to the southwest of Tertry. On the far side of the mountains is the region of Durbenford, an area that renounced its fealty to Foere at the same time as Keston and Toullen, but instead pledged itself to the count of Toullen. Durbenford has extensive logging and mining resources and has proven to be a great financial boon to the county's limited coffers.

LOYALTIES AND DIPLOMACY

Toullen has been subject to the Kingdom of Suilley since 3336 I.R. and is on particularly good terms with the Province of Keston to its north. The only connection between Toullen and Suilley is through Keston, and at present, no good road leads directly from the two vassal states to that kingdom, although the Court of Manas is definitely contemplating one. No one is hostile to the county, and the county minds its own business in the regional politics of the provinces.

GOVERNMENT

A hereditary count — currently Luthien, first of his name to rule — governs Toullen. Count Luthien is a fat, friendly man who is much loved by his subjects. His popularity is greatly enhanced by the independent fame of his younger sister, the Demoiselle Cyrilinde the Lance, a champion tournament jouster and grand victor at one Tournament of Lilies. She has finished among the top 10 jousters for the last three years and taken the laurel crown in two of the last three Tournaments of the Realm.

Below the level of count, Toullen has a stratum of nobility called high barons to whom ordinary barons pledge fealty, with most knights in turn pledging fealty to one of the ordinary barons. Fifteen high baronial houses form an advisory council of sorts to the count, but the council has no actual governmental powers. Of all the realms in the Borderland Provinces, the count of Toullen exerts more direct power over his subjects than the ruler of any other realm. For Toullen, a weak ruler means a weak county (see e.g., Count Rolomair "Wetself"), but a strong ruler can make dramatic improvements without facing much opposition from great noble houses serving their own agendas. Count Luthien is a strong and popular ruler, and the county is benefitting greatly from his reign.

The 15 high baronial houses are the Aulzevern, Caer Nor, Grellec, Saltfalcon, Gloun, Nantres, Hleen, Jormorel, Tauntirion, Mothcandle, Cascat, Porthiliot, Greenwine, Liscondel, and Vanj. In addition, Lord Durben of Durbenford has been campaigning hard for the elevation of a 16th high baronial house for the last several years.

WILDERNESS AND ADVENTURE

In general, Toullen appears to be quite well settled, with villages and hamlets throughout the county's narrow band of territory. Yet these settlements all have much-smaller populations than one would expect, for the Fiend Rains turned a great deal of the county's tillable land to marsh and fen, something from which Toullen's former vast fields of grain have yet to recover.

Depopulated as it is, the countryside has few broad expanses of primeval wilderness, which makes for fewer threats to civilization. On the other hand, the Kal'Iugus Mountains to the west, and the Wiltangle Forest to the east, are quite wild and dangerous, indeed. Adventurers seeking their fortunes in Toullen will most likely be seeking out treasure and fame in one of these two places and should be prepared for unpleasant surprises in the wilderness of Toullen's marches.

TERTRY, CITY OF (CAPITAL)

Population: 13,593 (10,003 Foerdewaith, 1,312 half-elf, 880 halfling, 526 high elf, 442 hill dwarf, 350 other)
Ruler: city council
Government: city council subject to the count's veto

The city of Tertry is a forest of small towers bounded by a strong stone wall, with a river running through the middle of the city. A large, permanent field of tournaments and jousting is laid out beyond the city walls.

Tertry is the capital of the County of Toullen, but far more importantly to the Toullenese, it is the site of the annual Tournament of Lilies on the great lists and fields beyond the city walls.

The count's palace is located in the city, and the count reserves the power to veto any decisions made by the city for its own government, although this feudal privilege is seldom invoked. Subject to the count's veto, a council made up of an unusually diverse group governs the city. The Master of Revels, who is responsible for the tournament, is one of the members of the city's council. The count's official jester is also a member of the council. More prosaic members are two council seats appointed by the city's guilds, one commoner popularly elected by the people, one member of noble descent also selected by popular vote, one representative of the king of Suilley, and the city's high priest of Thyr.

The annual Tournament of Lilies is the highest event in the calendar of all Toullen. The fields around the city begin filling up a month before the tournament with knights from all over the provinces and far beyond Toullen's own borders. Pavilion tents fly long banners proclaiming the heraldry and lineages of the knights within, minstrels compose songs extolling the skills of their patrons, bookmakers stroll from one area to another taking bets, and the master of revels employs twice his normal staff just keeping matters from devolving into utter chaos.

The tournament is composed of several different contests, divided into three categories. The first category allows knights from any realm to participate in the individual jousts and is the main event of the tourney. Winning the Crown of Lilies is a matter of pride for provinces as far as Eastreach. Foreign knights participate in a number of qualifying jousts to limit the number of contestants once the true tournament begins.

The second category is the least of the events, being competitions other than jousting, and is open to the peasantry. Such competitions include wrestling, archery, quarterstaff, pig-hurling, and horse racing, to name but a few.

The third category is often called the Tournaments of the Realm, for only the count's subjects may participate in these jousts. Patronage from one of the 15 high barons or from the count himself is required in order to allow a knight to enter the Tournaments of the Realm. The least prestigious of the Tournaments of the Realm is the Peasants' Tourney, once held for comedic value, but which has become so serious that the Toullenese high barons now sponsor talented rural jousters by providing loaned armor and warhorses. Victory in the Peasants' Tourney leads to immediate offers of employment from barons in their personal forces and represents a tremendous improvement in the life of whatever talented peasant managed to defeat all others.

The next most prestigious Tournament of the Realm is the Warriors' Tourney, which is limited to members of the class "at arms," generally professional soldiers of all kinds, from city guards to royal or baronial regular troops. The winner in this tournament is invariably knighted on the jousting field.

The third and most prestigious Tournament of the Realm is almost as important to the folk of Toullen as the Crown of Lilies. This is the "Count's Tournament," and it is open only to Toullenese of the noble or knightly classes. As with the other Tournaments of the Realm, the Count's Tournament requires patronage by one of the high barons of the realm and also requires that a contestant has placed high in the lists of a qualifying lesser tournament in one of the county's towns.

Victories and placing in the Tournaments of the Realm (including the lesser ones) has become a matter of incalculable prestige for the high barons. All the country perceives a high baron's sponsored contestants as a kind of team, even though they all compete separately. The audiences at the tournament carry flags of their faction, engage in brawls with followers of other factions, and generally show an almost-religious fervor. The importance of winning and placing in the tournament now translates directly into political power; barons have switched allegiances from one high baron to another based on consistently poor results in the lists. Moreover, the high barons whose sponsored contestants win first, second, and third place in a tournament each exempt all the high baron's vassals from one of nine taxes levied by the count. The tournament exemptions are generally divided among different high barons, for it is highly unusual for a single faction to sweep first through third place in all three divisions of the Tournaments of the Realm, but it has happened a few times in history. Thus, even the peasantry benefits when their high baron's faction wins one or more divisions of the tournaments.

DURBENFORD, TOWN OF

Population: 7,073 (5,446 Foerdewaith, 637 halfling, 354 high elf, 212 hill dwarf, 141 gnome, 71 half-elf, 53 half-orc, 159 other)
Ruler: Marcus Durben, Lord of Durbenford
Government: hereditary lord

Durbenford is primarily a lumbering town, but it provides a very significant benefit to the County of Toullen to which it declared fealty (seceding from the Duchy of Saxe) when Toullen changed fealty to the Kingdom of Suilley. Durbenford is the most remote possession of the Kingdom of Suilley, which the folk of Durbenford refer to simply as "the Northern Kingdom." The particular species of pine tree native to the Durbenford region grows extremely straight, making them highly desirable for ship's masts and other specific uses.

REFERENCE SOURCE: TROUBLE AT DURBENFORD

TULLER, CITY OF

Population: 6,840 (4,126 Foerdewaith, 1,854 Heldring, 833 half-elf, 27 other)
Ruler: Mayor Bendigond Lune
Government: mayor and town council

Tuller is a seaport city located on a small, deep harbor on Tywyl Bay. It has high walls of a green-tinged stone, and a round citadel that flies the flag of Toullen: a yellow jousting helm on a black field with a green fleur-de-lis in the corner. A small island lies in the harbor, its land area completely occupied by a pillared temple with attached outbuildings, all made of stone.

Though Tuller is the only seaport accessible to the Kingdom of Suilley, and a small flotilla is maintained there to fend off pirates on Tywyl Bay, the kingdom nevertheless conducts very little trade through the port. There is a modest stream of seaborne trade between Tuller and the western ports of the Helcynngae Peninsula to the east, and with some ports of the Southern Reach to the west, but the merchants of Manas generally prefer to send their goods overland to ports such as Endhome or Eastgate where prices are higher.

COUNTY OF VOURDON

Capital: Olaric
Notable Settlements: Shullcross
Ruler: His Excellency Peilorth Rhombard I, Count-Palatine of Vourdon, Earl of the South Rampart Marches
Government: feudalism (palatine county of Foere)
Population: 914,000 (768,000 Foerdewaith, 68,500 hill dwarf, 50,100 halfling, 21,000 half-elf, 6,400 high elf)
Monstrous: ankheg, goblin, fey, smilodon (valley); spider-eye goblin, giant stag and boar, smilodon, forlarren, forest troll, owlbear, dryad, green dragon (forest); cave lion, hill giant, griffon, giant eagle, cave moray (mountains)
Languages: Common, Gasquen, Dwarven, Halfling, Elvish
Religion: Telophus, Ceres, Sefagreth, Thyr (declining), Pan, Hester, Archeillus, Freya, Stryme, Dwerfater, Bacchus-Dionysus, Moccavallo
Resources: spirits (wine, brandy), flax, grain, foodstuffs (grapes, apples, pears), linen, livestock (sheep, swine), wool
Currency: Suilley
Technology Level: Medieval

The County of Vourdon is a vassal state of the overking in Foere, with a great deal of independence from the distant rule of Courghais. It is a peaceful and productive land that enjoys good diplomatic and trade relations with its neighbors on either side of the March of Mountains.

Vourdon extends through the gap between the Meridian and Rampart ranges, from the verge of the Shadrack Forest (just west of Shullcross) to approximately 100 miles east of Olaric, 100 miles north of Olaric, and 150 miles south of Olaric.

HISTORY AND PEOPLE

The County of Vourdon was established by decree of the overking in the year 2822 I.R., thus incorporating a region that had been a largely ungoverned expanse since the days of Hyperborea that lay between the Kingdom of Foere and the outlying Province of Suilley. Lords and barons with their bloodlines dating back to the Hyperborean Age were required to pledge fealty to the new count, whose seat of government would be Caer Sferic near the thriving market town of Olaric. When the Archmage Quaoule destroyed Caer Sferic in a fit of pique, the count's surviving retainers brought the Throne of Harts to the town of Olaric itself, eventually building the Comital Palace to house it properly. In default of living heirs to the countship, the overking appointed a new great house to the position, and so began the still-surviving dynasty of the House of Rhombard.

During the Fiend Rains of 3439 I.R., Vourdon was subjected to massive flooding, its rivers becoming deluges and its lower-lying pastures becoming stagnant lakes. Unlike the catastrophic failure in Toullen, the County of Vourdon, under the leadership of Count Lorn of House Rhombard, responded immediately to the catastrophe. All the great mages of the county were summoned to Olaric to hear the Edict of Rains, which ordered them to different tasks in accordance with their capabilities, knowledge, and prestige. By means of great magicks and an unprecedented level of cooperation, the mages excavated a number of deep weirs along the March of Mountains, raised ramparts and dikes around many of the larger towns, and bound earth elementals to the task of cutting massive drainage canals to channel the mountain runoff down to the lower-lying regions of Suilley and Keston. The wizards Thylimeles, Fernijan, and Xolobar worked together (reportedly using lost secrets of Alycthron and Margon) to raise the city of Olaric itself to an altitude 10 feet higher than its original standing. All but the owners of the numerous collapsed buildings considered this a small price to pay for such security. The mages also created great terraces carved from the mountain rock east of the capital (using the same unknown magic) to stop rockslides and to abate surges of water during the heaviest rain.

Due to this orderly and expansive reaction to the flooding, the Fiend Rains affected Vourdon considerably less than they damaged the surrounding regions. Some of the canals are still in use and connect towns by waterway. The artificial mountain terraces are now home to fertile vineyards that produce the mediocre vintages of wine for which Olaric is justifiably not famous but sells in great quantity across the continent to establishments and wine cellars less interested in quality and more interested in price and availability.

In the year 3222 I.R., when the lord-governor of Suilley declared himself to be an independent monarch, the count of Vourdon declined the overking's demand to send troops against the rebellious new kingdom, citing obscure matters of feudal law. As a result, diplomatic relations between the County of Vourdon and the Kingdom of Suilley have always been friendly and amicable.

Vourdon has not suffered excessively from the retreat of Foere's influence, although the demands of the overking are increasing as his tax base and military power wane. Large numbers of troops have been requested, although so far the count has avoided sending more than the bare minimum. The tax burden is a bit more serious and causes consternation among the nobles. Thus far, the county's status as an independent vassal has allowed it to dodge or reduce several tax levies, but demands from the Court of Courghais are becoming more strident and threatening.

At the same time, diplomatic overtures from the Kingdom of Suilley continue, offering potentially enormous benefits to the county if it were to throw off the reins of Foere and offer its fealty to the Suilleyn king. The concern, however, is that even as weak as the Kingdom of Foere has become, it could still potentially overwhelm Vourdon before any help could arrive from Suilley. The County of Vourdon is no warrior nation, much as its knights believe otherwise, and its peaceful lands provide a desperately needed flow of gold and food into the Foerdewaith heartlands. The count is justifiably concerned that if Vourdon shifted its allegiance, Foere might not just accept the situation as it did with the secessions of Keston Province and the County of Toullen. War would be a definite possibility, and Vourdon is not prepared for such a conflict. Even more vexing, if Suilley's power continues to expand, while that of Foere weakens, the friendly persuasions of the king of Suilley might change their tone into demands or threats.

Caught between kingdoms, given choices of an increasingly demanding overlord, the potential of ruinous war against that overlord, or possibly waiting too late to join with Suilley on good terms, the count of Vourdon bides his time. With good luck, some new event will arise to give him better leverage against the demands of the overking. With bad luck, some new event may force his hand and require him to rush to Suilley, risking bloody retribution from Foere.

Trade and Commerce

The County of Vourdon is an exclusively agricultural region and initiates very little trade beyond its borders other than linen, bad wine, brandy, and small quantities of flax oil. A number of merchant caravans pass through Olaric on the way into and out of Foere along the South County Road, which is a safe and pleasant route. The length of the road from Olaric to Shullcross, while very hilly, is a pleasant journey, lined with fields of flax that turn into a sea of blue during the flowering season. Orchards cover the hillsides, and great terraces carved into the mountains are overburdened with the yellow grapes of Vourdon. Fortified stone chateaux may be seen in the distance, usually on hilltops from which the owner can look over the lands and farms of the fiefdom.

Olaric and Shullcross are below the highland gap between the Rampart Mountains and the Meridians. Shullcross is a lumbering town, and Olaric is surrounded by fields of golden wheat. Other than farming, Olaric's main industries are manufacturing linen from flax, selling barrels of "cask-quality" wine, and distilling brandy. Distillation in Olaric is a primitive process of mixing grain alcohol into wine, then distilling the mixture. The brandy is consumed in sailors' taverns and questionable dives across the provinces, just as the wine is imbibed in the manors of impoverished knights and the houses of miserly merchants.

The linen industry in Olaric produces fabrics with a wide variety of quality, some of which are suitable to be worn by kings. The lowest-quality flax fibers are woven into rope and twine, and the long ropewalk in Olaric is always a hive of activity.

Loyalties and Diplomacy

The County of Vourdon is an independent feudal state, subject to the overking of Foere.

Diplomatic relations with the adjacent Kingdom of Suilley are extremely good, partially based on the fact that Vourdon never attacked Suilley during Suilley's war of secession, but also due to trade along the South County Road directly between the capitals, and the general sense that the two realms are quite similar in culture and outlook.

The King of Suilley constantly attempts to woo the count of Vourdon into switching his allegiance from Foere to Suilley, making lucrative trade agreements and bestowing gifts. Thus far, all diplomatic efforts in this regard have failed, albeit very cordially. Vourdon's status as an independent feudal realm under Foere's protection is a comfortable situation for the counts of Vourdon, and they have seen no need to go through the turmoil of changing fealty.

Of late, however, Foere has made some onerous demands upon the county, calling up a number of troops to join the overking's army and levying several new taxes. If the trend continues, too many demands from Foere might certainly cause the count to rethink his current loyalties.

Government

The countship of Vourdon is a hereditary title currently held by Count Peilorth Rhombard, second of his name. Below the rank of count, the country has high barons as in Toullen, with barons below the high barons and knights below the barons. The count of Vourdon has only five high barons in his council, which means that those nobles exert considerable power in the country. On one occasion, four of the high barons threatened a civil war if the count enacted a particular law, which forced the count to withdraw the proposal.

Wilderness and Adventure

Vourdon is safe enough that wandering the villages looking for adventure yields relatively poor results, although there are always small groups of bandits to chase and the occasional predator from the adjoining mountain ranges. Most adventurers in the country are drawn to the mountain terraces, for when these were carved from the mountainsides, some few of them revealed ancient catacombs that had been underground until the removal of countless tons of rock. There are not many of these, but a few expeditions into some discovered that many of the passageways are of worked stone, their origins completely unknown. Moreover, they are home to a number of dangerous predators and contain ancient treasures. Little organized exploration of these catacombs has been attempted; their terraces are left unfarmed, and the folk of the mountainsides avoid them. It is possible that some of these catacombs are the source of predators that emerge from the mountains, although the high peaks of the mountains certainly house a variety of fell beasts.

Olaric, City of (Capital)

Population: 19,297 (18,102 Foerdewaith, 995 halfling, 170 half-elf, 30 other)
Ruler: Lord-Mayor Margaine Fleur
Government: lord-mayor appointed by the count-palatine

Olaric, also often spelled Olaaric, is the capital of Vourdon and seat of Count Peilorth Rhombard. The city is quite provincial, but pleasant. Indeed, the royal family of Ulrich, king of Suilley, has on more than one occasion summered in the upland wine country of the county, and guested at the Comital Palace here.

A grand city today, Olaric was a major agricultural center even in the ancient days of the Hyperborean Age. Relatively stable after the Hyperboreans' departure, Olaric expanded and built, providing a marketplace and protection for surrounding communities. Incorporated into the Kingdom of Foere and made seat of the new County of Vourdon in 2822 I.R., Olaric continued to expand. In 3506 I.R., as the Wilderlands Clan War raged in nearby Keston Province, Olaric served as a staging area for troops from Foere and other kingdoms, which also helped to discourage the hostile clans from attacking Vourdon.

Olaric's walls are not high, but they are serviceable enough to protect the city against any attacks short of a true siege. Slender towers around the wall rise to dramatic, conical roofs where the banner of Olaric (a bunch of yellow grapes on a field of green) and the Rhombard family (a red lion on black and white) fly proudly over the city. Four gates lead into the city to admit the high roads from the realms surrounding Vourdon, which cross in the city center.

Olaric's main industries are wheat-farming, manufacturing linen from the flax fields of the West Country, and distilling low-quality brandy. A few merchant houses are based here, but the majority of buying and selling is conducted by factors from merchant houses in Troye and Manas. As a flax-producer, the city also boasts the largest ball of twine in all of Foere, which is likely an accurate claim. It is displayed in the hall of the Ropemakers' Guild for those who wish to see it; admission is free.

Shullcross, Town of

Population: 3,100 (2,763 Foerdewaith, 282 high elf, 55 halfling)
Ruler: Mayor Jormandh Sawyer
Government: mayor appointed by the count-palatine

Shullcross is a walled town where flowering ivy covers the walls and many of the buildings in the city. A medium-sized settlement at the western border of Vourdon, the city stands where the South County Road turns southward and becomes the Saxen Road to the Duchy of Saxe.

Shullcross has traditionally been licensed by the throne to conduct logging in the royal forest of Shadrack ever since the days of the Hyperborean Empire, with the tradition carrying on through the rise of the Kingdoms of Foere. The timber industry is the mainstay of

Shullcross' small economy, with some flax farming, and the remainder coming from merchants crossing the gap to and from the provinces.

YOLBIAC VALE

(YOL-bee-ak)

Capital: none (though Coelum is usually considered the First City of the Vale)

Notable Settlements: Coelum

Ruler: none (13 "ducal" families rule most of the area)

Government: decentralized feudalism

Population: 85,800+ (79,000 Foerdewaith, 3,800 hill dwarf, 3,000 half-elf, unknown number of wood elf)

Monstrous: giant wolf, fey, ogre, lycanthrope, wight, treant, dullahan, hag, hangman tree, groaning spirit, vampire (Yolbiac Vale and passes); lycanthrope, adlet, frost drake, lamia, nightmare creature, yeti, wind walker, Leng spider (high peaks)

Languages: Common, Gasquen, Elvish, Dwarven, Druidic

Religion: Narrah, Thyr, The Green Father, Cybele, druidism, Hecate, Bilis

Resources: livestock (swine), timber, foodstuffs (dream-apples), spirits (wine), alchemical reagents

Currency: Foere

Technology Level: Dark Ages

The Yolbiac Vale is a dark and forested realm, barely populated, ruled by independent barons and a scattering of local nobles claiming higher status than baronial. Villages are far apart, roads are dangerous, peasants are secretive, and dangers lurk in the omnipresent forests. The people of the Yolbiac Vale are considered to be strange and unpredictable.

The vale is a deep indentation in the middle of the Cretian Mountains that runs from Coelum to about a hundred miles south of the town of Elet. It has several wide river valleys extending to the west that curl into the deep heart of the mountains. The strange folk of the Yolbiac populate these remote areas. The territory comprises approximately 22,000 square miles. The majority of the region is heavily forested, but not with a single, contiguous growth of trees. Instead, the region has many primordial forests that run five to 10 miles across. Ridges of stone, or infertile ground, divide the forests, for this is high and broken terrain.

As the teaching rhyme suggests, the great forest of the Scal Farnu is a dominating feature in the Yolbiac Vale. Irregularly shaped, it has long, narrow extents that most certainly shift their locations by several miles each lunar month beneath the waning gibbous moons. Common folk avoid the Scal Farnu, not because it is inherently deadly as with the Mouldenarc, but because strange and unpredictable things — often life-changing — happen in the forest. Such events are by no means always maleficent, but peasants are conservative folk and choose not to risk the shifting pathways that entice travelers into the shadowy, green depths of the Scal Farnu. The Scal Farnu is said to contain the manse of Hautmarlune, a mysterious archmage. It is also thought to contain the sacred groves of the druidess Rowena of the Hounds (as distinguished from the famous Rowena of Greatstone Cairn). Two supernatural hounds, Aubrei and Simain, prowl the forest, apparently immortal beasts that may guide a party of lost adventurers back to the safer paths if they follow. The hounds travel separately, and mortal weapons and magic cannot harm them. They are patient and not vindictive, but they depart if attacked, melting away into the trees. According to legend, these are the hounds of Rowena, but none knows for certain.

In the deepest forests of the lower peaks surrounding the vale are known to dwell a reclusive tribe of wood elves known to the Valefolk only as the Eldest. What tragedy or turmoil this people may have suffered in the past is not known, but they are seldom seen by the folk of the vale and when they are spotted, they remain distant and quickly disappear into the trees. Attempts to make contact with them have universally met with stony silences and hasty withdrawals, but so far they have shown no inclination over the years for hostilities toward the humans of the vale. To most of the Yolbiac's inhabitants, they are simply one more evidence of the vale's fey nature. Hints at a tragic history of these elven folk can be found, however, in the few elven ruins in the lowland parts of the valley and in the unusual preponderance of groaning spirits that are known to haunt some of the surrounding mountain slopes.

HISTORY AND PEOPLE

The Yolbiac Vale is a land of dark alpine forests, independent villages, isolated abbeys, bizarre superstitions, and strange perils. Its people are widely varied in attitudes and customs, for few of them ever leave the environs of their home villages. Such wanderers are highly suspect, and even though they bring back fascinating news and tales of other villages, they might be doppelgangers or shape-changed faeries. It is best to always be careful; some returning travelers merely receive a sound thrashing before being sent back on their way.

Events in the Yolbiac Vale proceed unchanged since time immemorial. Stories accumulate and are forgotten, heroes live and heroes die, strange and supernatural events occur, others are warded off by the proper hand gestures and taboos. Darkness abides, and life goes on. Such is the Yolbiac Vale.

TRADE AND COMMERCE

The Yolbiac region produces many strange commodities such as a variety of dark-purple apples that induce strange dreams and a dark grape, almost black, from which they ferment a potent, bitter wine that stains the lips and teeth of those who indulge frequently. Fey items are often brought down from the vale and include twists of hair or painted sticks that have magical powers, or finely chased goblets of hypnotic beauty. Purchasers of such items are cautioned; occasionally, their original owners imbued them with unanticipated consequences.

The vale may be reached either through the Coelum Pass in the Duchy of the Rampart or by the Ghostwind Pass near Elet in Aachen Province. During the summer months, there is a considerable amount of trade with the folk of the Yolbiac Vale, but when the winter snows set in, they are left to themselves. The Ghostwind Pass is completely inaccessible during the depths of winter, and the Coelum Pass is treacherous at best.

LOYALTIES AND DIPLOMACY

Outsiders consider the Yolbiac Vale to be an annex of Foere, but it is strangely ignored and appears to have no ruling authority whatsoever. As such, the vale cannot be said to have any loyalties to, or diplomacy with, other nations. At one point, a baron of Aachen Province led a small army into the Yolbiac with the intention of seizing a fiefdom, but there is no historical record of the event beyond the army's departure from Elet.

GOVERNMENT

The vale is considered a part of the Kingdom of Foere, but no one seems to rule it; there is no capital and no governor, just the occasionally tyrannical law of a few barons, some of whom pay fealty to one of the 13 so-called "ducal" families, more commonly referred to as the "Old Families." Unruled lands separate the baronies and duchies, but the barons make no attempt whatsoever to expand their territories and stay strictly within their traditional landholdings. This is a general tendency in the vale: Strange traditions and odd customs are seemingly more binding upon the folk of the Yolbiac than any decree of authority.

Old writings refer to the vale as the "canton" of the Yolbiac, but even these records seem not to mention any sort of authority over the area, which is exceedingly unusual, perhaps unique. The folk of the Yolbiac Vale refer only to "Good King Oerson," as if the ancient Hyperborean emperor still lived and ruled. They smile and nod when hearing about the Kingdom of Foere, as if the entire sweep of post-Hyperborean history were a fairy tale for gullible children.

WILDERNESS AND ADVENTURE

There is essentially nothing but wilderness and adventure in the Yolbiac Vale. Many villages find themselves in times of crisis without the help of anyone, and monster lairs are virtually everywhere in the high crags and deep forests of the region. Off the top of one's head, one can list Ysoolte's Weir, the caves of Quarvel, the lair of Borovendal, the Tor of the Yellow Witch, and many others. Adventuring in the Scal Farnu is possible for those of stout heart, and fur hunting in the Ghostwind Pass could leave a group of hunters with a nice bag full of gold afterward. It is more difficult to avoid adventure here than to seek it out.

REFERENCE SOURCE: PERILS OF GHOSTWIND PASS FROM QUESTS OF DOOM

COELUM, TOWN OF

Population: 2,848 (2,602 human various ethnicity, 181 hills dwarf, 65 half-elf)
Ruler: High Mayor Riaundo Groon
Government: high mayor elected by regional dukes

Coelum is not a political capital, but as the main town in the Yolbiac Vale, it is where most of the trade goods go to market, and where the local nobles go for their larger meetings. The 13 "ducal houses" of the vale, which are the old noble families whose bloodlines date back past any recorded history, elect a high mayor for the town every 10 years or so. The high mayor oversees the town's trade, maintenance of walls, and a small (but extremely well-armed and dangerous) city guard called the Husjaegers.

As with much of the Yolbiac Vale, the town seems, to outsiders at least, to be ruled more by its customs and superstitions than by any sort of actual law. Many of the inhabitants practice druidism.

GEOGRAPHIC FEATURES AND POINTS OF INTEREST IN THE BORDERLANDS OF SOUTHEASTERN AKADOS

BROCH TARNA

This ancient edifice is thought to be the oldest still-extant fortification in all of Akados. The Daanites of Ynys Cymragh would argue that some of the mountain fortresses on their island are older, but these are not technically on the mainland, and no one can be entirely sure about histories reaching so far back. There is no record at all of the people who originally built the broch; it was already an abandoned ruin when Oerson led his legion through this area in –88 I.R. Since then it has been rebuilt, occupied, and abandoned many times; so many times, in fact, that the broch has gained a reputation for being cursed in some way. The Hyperboreans chose to build a new fortress at Albor Broce rather than claim this one in the highlands, and a goodly number of those who have occupied Broch Tarna have died either in battle or for seemingly entirely unrelated reasons (an outbreak of plague, treachery from within, a well gone bad to poison the occupants, or everyone simply disappearing one night). The last known occupants were the margoyle overlords of the human hill clans of the Wilderland Hills, who were defeated there in the final battle of that war. Lately, wandering rangers have reported that the walls are repaired once again, and that spearmen walk the battlements once more. But no banner flies above its ramparts, so who (or what) these new occupiers are, and what their purpose is in garrisoning the fortress, remains unknown as of now.

THE CREEPING MIRE

Once a stark and beautiful moor in the center of Keston Province known as the Hearthglen, this area is the lowest-lying region between the March of Mountains and the highlands of the Wilderland Hills and Lorremachs. When the Fiend Rains unleashed their 10-year deluge upon the eastern slopes of the March of Mountains, the surrounding lands for thousands of square miles drained into the Hearthglen, and though much of the water did slowly seep into the ground, the area became a vast, ever-expanding swamp nonetheless and swallowed an ancient shrine holy to pilgrims of the Church of Mitra. Lizardfolk and brutish swamp dwellers are rumored to lurk in the dark waters of the swamp, but they are seldom seen, and their true numbers are unguessed beyond the accumulated disappearances of travelers on the Swamp Road.

CRETIAN MOUNTAINS

The Cretians are the northernmost range of the March of Mountains, and also the largest. The peaks of the Cretians are unusually high, taller than any others of the highest mountains of the central Kal'Iugus range. Many dark rumors and superstitious stories surround the Cretians, from tales of ghosts, to invisible giants that fly on the wind. The Cretians completely encircle the heavily wooded Yolbiac Vale, an isolated and inbred country with strange attitudes and motivations.

The heights of the Cretians are virtually unknown to geographers, scholars, and cartographers, with the exception of the outermost few miles around the periphery of the vast mountain range. Few venture into the interior, and fewer return.

KAL'IUGUS MOUNTAINS

(KAL-eye-YOU-gus)

The Kal'Iugus Mountains are the second largest of the ranges of the March of Mountains after the Cretians. The meaning of the odd name Kal'Iugus is lost to history, but it is thought to predate the arrival of the Hyperboreans. The highest part of the range is its northern spur, where the massive Jerinot (Jair-i-no) Glacier lies over the peaks, and which is said to be the home of giants and reclusive tribes of barbarians who ride across its surface on sleds pulled by dogs. The king of Suilley is lately concerned with reports of a giantish invasion preparing to descend from these northern slopes into Keston and Toullen, but so far no solid evidence has been uncovered to confirm the danger.

LORREMACH HIGHHILLS

The Lorremach Highhills are a rugged, savannah highland, very dry and riven with uncounted gullies and canyons. It receives little of the rainfall associated with the lowlands to the west. Winds blow violent dust storms through the area that carve the rocks into strange shapes, many of which are somehow eerie, others of which are dramatically beautiful. Farming is poor, although corn and opium poppies seem to thrive, and there are many hidden fens in the valleys or shaded by cliffs the locals call "florelgartens." The Lorremach is home to numerous tribes and communities of very diverse types. Halfling villages surround shaded farmland in the dells, their goats grazing on the scrub and sparse vegetation on the higher ground. Gnomes also have many settlements in the Lorremachs and live in caves around the edges of a florelgarten region and fish in the deep wells and streams found in many of the cave systems.

March of Mountains

This is the name for the broken range of mountains made up of (from north to south) the Cretian Mountains, the Rampart Mountains, the Meridian Range, and the Kal'Iugus Mountains.

Meridian Range

In the year 43 I.R., the Imperial Court geographer Rasymius declared the central peak of this range to be the highest point upon the exact Prime Meridian of the world of Boros, based on a series of exacting calculations. The mountain was named "Primus," and the range containing it became the "Meridian Range."

Mourninghaven Sanatorium

A sanitorium on this site was first constructed by the Church of Mitra as a hospital for the advancing arts of medicine and healing. It was built on a spot traditionally held to have been visited by Mitra in ancient times and stood surrounded by the Hearthglen, a picturesque green moor. For many years it faithfully served its role at the edge of the province of Keston and catered to the rich and poor alike, turning away no one in need of its healing. But following the Fiend Rains, the Hearthglen became the Creeping Mire. Entire buildings began to sink, and walls buckled and cracked as foundations shifted and settled. The road to the sanitorium grew increasingly wild and hazardous, and people stopped going to the facility for the healing it offered. Eventually, the Church of Mitra sold it to a local baronet who repurposed the sanitorium as an incarceration facility for those who committed crimes under the influence of mental illness. Dark tales of what happened behind its walls led to the sanitorium becoming known colloquially as Mourninghaven. Eventually, Keston took control of the site, but its sinister reputation, and the dangers of the Creeping Mire about the facility, have only continued to grow.

Rampart Mountains

The Rampart Mountains are so named because the central peaks of the range are steep and uniform like a castle wall. The mountains have always served as a bulwark defending the eastern flank of the Foerdewaith and the Hyperborean Empires. The western verge of the Ramparts, entirely within the Duchy of the Rampart, has numerous mines that produce gold and iron. Many of these are dwarven excavations, but the mining towns serving them are predominantly human. The duchy also rules the northern part of the range's eastern flanks.

Rampart Road

The Rampart is a raised causeway running from Troye to Manas and resembles a broad and short wall of earth and rock with a road running along the top that averages 30 feet in width. Small stone gatehouses at irregular intervals of 25 miles or so can be used to block passage along the road, although the gates are kept open unless there is a serious threat that invaders may be on the road.

South County Road

The South County Road is well-patrolled, well-settled, and peaceful. Most of the journey from Manas to Olaric passes through orchards and fields of flax; farm wagons laden with produce are a constant sight as they make their way to the various market towns and inns along the road.

South Road

The South Road runs north and south along the eastern rim of the March of Mountains, originating in Tuller on the south coast of Toullen and then passing northward through the County of Toullen, Keston Province, Vourdon, and the Duchy of the Rampart before ending in the city of Troyes. In old documents, the road is called the "South Provincial Road," but common usage has shortened the name.

Merchants generally prefer taking the South Road rather than Trader's Way for moving their cargoes north or south through the Borderland Provinces, for the Trader's Way passes through many areas of empty wilderness, and the South Road is at least lightly settled along its whole length. Even those on slow wagons only have to spend one or two nights under the stars rather than finding a roadside inn. Not necessarily a clean, honest, or comfortable one, but an inn nonetheless.

Swamp Road

The Swamp Road is desolate and obviously poorly maintained, especially during the spring rainy season when provincial repair crews are unwilling to brave the dangers of the Creeping Mire. Although it is one of the ancient stone-paved high roads built by the Hyperborean Empire, there are gaps, sometimes miles long, where floods and mudslides washed out the stones. These have been repaired many times by log corduroys in the past, but each spring, sections are washed out anew and require additional repair.

Tower of Corredrix

The Tower of Corredrix stands at the edge of the Lorremach Highhills and is now named for its current occupant, the wizard Corredrix. The tower itself is much older than the wizard, who took it by force from a hobgoblin chieftain and his band of brigands. It is an isolated place, and travelers are very unlikely to stumble upon it unless they already know of its existence and approximate whereabouts.

Trader's Way

The Trader's Way, insofar as it concerns the Kingdom of Suilley, extends from beyond Suilley's southern border into Exeter Province, runs northward through the town of Pfefferain, through the Lorremach Highhills to Stronghold Hjerrin, and then forms the country's eastern border with the District of Sunderland until it reaches Grollek's Grove at the base of the Gundlock Hills.

This reach of the Trader's Way runs through wild and untamed regions, for neither Suilley nor Sunderland has many settlements in the area. A small number of fortified inns are along the road, of course, for caravans are willing to pay good gold for a safe night's rest, but these are few and far between.

Wennesalar

Wennesalar was an old village of the Highhills that was recently destroyed and its population scattered. A wizard known as the Darkmage is widely considered to be responsible for the destruction, and the garrison at the crossroads chooses not to investigate what happened.

Wilderland Hills

Although the Wilderland Hills are generally considered to be a part of the Kingdom of Suilley, no real attempt is made by anyone to lay claim over these wild, desolate lands, other than a few patrols in the western reaches that keep the Trader's Way from becoming utterly infested with bandits and humanoid raiders. It was the hill clans and humanoid tribes from this desolate region that invaded Keston Province in 3506 I.R., and it was at the ancient fortress of Broch Tarna at the center of the hills where the final, decisive battle was fought to end the war. Some scattered clan remnants are still known to roam the highlands here, so few travelers dare to intrude too closely in the area.

Wiltangle Forest

The Wiltangle Forest is one of the last eastern remnants of the Great Akadonian Forest that once covered most of the continent. The majority of the Great Akadonian Forest was slowly broken up by a series of catastrophes and by woodcutting intended to free up farmland or burn out monsters. The Wiltangle, unaffected by the fate of the rest of the continental forest, is primordial and wild, and only little explored. The folk of Toullen engage in very little woodcutting on their side of the forest, but there are a few villages and logging camps in Cerediun Province along the eastern reaches of the forest.

Deep in the forest, more than one stone circle dating back to antiquity remain as holy sites to many druidic sects. Villages along the forest's

periphery are almost universally druidic, although various gods are recognized and some even have small temples that live alongside the influence of the druids. All attempts to actually subdue the druidic faith have met utter failure in this area, not always peaceful and often mysteriously.

In the days before the coming of the Hyperboreans, several elven kingdoms were in the Wiltangle, and the Heldring referred to the forest by a name that translates to "northern woodland kingdoms." A fey and deadly place for intruders, the southern reaches of the Wiltangle restricted the Heldring to their peninsula until the arrival of the Hyperboreans. Even then, the Heldring took care never to enter the forest in force.

To this day, the Wiltangle is a forest of legends: a witch queen who ruled until being transformed into a tree; ancient ruins along the riverbanks of the interior; cairns and holds of some diminutive race; and fabulous jewels recovered from a few upriver expeditions. Such tales may, of course, be exaggerated. The question, however, is not whether ancient treasures are in the Wiltangle, for there certainly are; the question is whether they are ripe for the taking or whether they are a fool's errand for those fated to die beneath leaf-green shadows.

Sundered Kingdoms and the Sinnar Coast of Southeastern Akados

The Sundered Kingdoms and the Sinnar Coast of Southeastern Akados are described in detail in ***The Lost Lands: Cults of the Sundered Kingdoms*** by **Frog God Games**.

Political Subdivisions of the Sundered Kingdoms and the Sinnar Coast of Southeastern Akados

Cerediun Province

(Ser-eh-DEE-un)
Capital: Trebes
Notable Settlements: Sessilbridge
Ruler: Lord-Governor Bryntwis Carlarion
Government: autocracy
Population: 27,000 (20,000 Foerdewaith, 4,000 other mixed human ethnicity, 1,500 halfling, 1,000 mountain dwarf, 500 half-elf)
Monstrous: goblins, goblin dogs, hill giants, trolls, werewolves, will-o'-wisps, wolves, worgs, wraiths, various undead
Languages: Common, Dwarven
Religion: Arialee, Muir, Oghma, Thyr
Resources: foodstuffs, grain, livestock, timber
Currency: Foere
Technology Level: Middle Ages

Cerediun is the southernmost province of the Kingdoms of Foere, lying to the south of Exeter Province between the Wiltangle Forest and the Scar-in-the-Sky Peaks, and just north of the Helcynngae Peninsula. The province still maintains its loyalty to Courghais and Foere, although this is mostly lip service. The current lord-governor is clearly playing a waiting game until he can declare himself to be an independent king.

HISTORY AND PEOPLE

The province's history reaches all the way back to the dawn of the Hyperborean Age, when the fierce Heldring of the Helcynngae Peninsula halted the all-conquering legions of Polemarch Oerson's march in –88 I.R. The imperial legions fell back and established Cerediun Province as a buffer state and began construction on the Helwall. The capital of Trebes surrendered to the expanding kingdom of Foere in 2748 I.R. and was quickly absorbed, though the Heldring held back the Foerdewaith as they had the Hyperboreans, and the overking's advance stopped at the Helwall.

Cerediun has since had a long history of being the first line of defense against the invading Heldring, though after the Battle of Oescreheit Downs and the Heldring conversion to the faiths of Thyr and Muir it has since maintained friendly trade with the Heldring. It was primarily Ceredian monks and missionaries who carried the faith of the sibling gods to the Heldring in those fraught times, and more than one became a martyr to their faiths in the process.

Sparsely populated and quite rugged, most of the province's population lives in the capital city of Trebes, with the remainder scattered in small villages, the most notable of which is the town of Greybriar that is home to about 1,000 halflings and a few hundred humans. Peace with the warlike Heldring has reduced Cerediun's importance, and many feel that Foere has forgotten the province altogether.

RELIGION

The Ceredians are a sober and devout people, most of whom worship Thyr and Muir, though a significant number also revere Oghma, the patron of Bard's Gate. Halflings are more likely to be found with shrines to the nature-goddess Arialee, whose faith predates the human deities. There are persistent rumors that a secret cult of Demogorgon has adherents in the province and that these cultists meet on moonless nights to perform sacrifice and other forbidden rites. Most sensible Ceredians dismiss these tales as nonsense, but they are careful to lock their doors during a new moon nevertheless.

TRADE AND COMMERCE

A small frontier state, Cerediun is largely self-sufficient, growing crops and raising livestock in small farm communities, none of which could be considered larger than a village. In good years, the province produces sufficient surplus to be exported, and the new trade relationship with the once-hostile Heldring has opened new markets for Ceredian farmers and merchants. Goods such as fish, spirits, and copper have also begun to flow from the south, further cementing the two regions' new relationship. Increasingly, Trebes is becoming less a military citadel than an important hub of trade between the province and its southern neighbor.

LOYALTIES AND DIPLOMACY

Ostensibly a province of the Kingdom of Foere, Cerediun has always been something of an unwanted stepchild to the overking, existing primarily as a buffer between the kingdom and the violence of the Heldring raiders. With the Heldring's newfound faith and improved attitude, Cerediun has been largely neglected and left to its own devices, a situation that suits the easygoing inhabitants quite well. In recent years, the growing accord between Cerediun and the Helcynn Kingdom has in fact made many feel closer to their southern neighbors than to the distant nobles of Courghais, a situation that the lord-governor hopes to use to his advantage.

In addition, Lord-Governor Bryntwis hopes that the new trading relations with the Heldring can be leveraged into a military alliance with his realm's old enemies, and that the southerners could be persuaded to support his move to establish an independent state. He is no fool, however, and knows that the warlike Heldring may not be the best of allies, for a vulnerable new nation on their frontier might reawaken their martial spirit and inspire them to surge past the neglected Helwall to take Cerediun for their own.

GOVERNMENT

The Ceredians are not an especially nationalistic people, preferring instead to see to their own concerns before that of any greater kingdom. As a result, the rule of Foere is usually thought to have little in the way of either benefit or hindrance, but simply as a fact of life. Lord-Governor Bryntwis Carlarion, an ambitious Foerdewaith nobleman who was assigned here due to his political connections, is nowhere near as pragmatic as his people and seeks to one day be the ruler of his own kingdom. He is a patient man and hopes to play the Foerdewaith and Heldring against each other, winning him a crown in the process.

WILDERNESS AND ADVENTURES

The land between villages tends to be fairly rugged and undeveloped, with small stands of woods, lonely valleys, and cold streams — much like the lands to the south beyond the Helwall. It's said that some areas are plagued by undead such as ghosts, revenants, and draug — the remnants of the ancient battles fought in the region. More substantial creatures such as small goblin clans, lone trolls, ogres, and other humanoid threats can be found here as well.

The adjoining Wiltangle Forest, once controlled by royal foresters and patrols, has grown more perilous in recent years, and creatures there have grown bolder, forcing some villages and farms to see to their own defense.

Given its violent history, Cerediun is not without its various legends, the best-known of which was the Witch of the Valley, a hag said to prey upon travelers and spirit them off to her hidden cave where she and her half-hag sons kept them alive while devouring them one limb at a time. Said to have been slain by the hero Devisha Parneux (or others, depending on the story), the witch supposedly left behind a hidden treasure that remains unfound to this day, but is guarded by (once more, depending on the story) the witch's ghost or a host of her reanimated victims.

TREBES, CITY OF (CAPITAL)

Population: 15,800 (13,725 Foerdewaith, 1,100 halfling, 725 mountain dwarf, 250 half-elf)
Ruler: Mayor Ondorio Voon
Government: mayor appointed by lord-governor

The city of Trebes is the capital and, for that matter, the only city of any real significance in the entire province of Cerediun, the largely-neglected southernmost province of the Kingdom of Foere. Once a Hyperborean garrison built to help contain the Heldring, the city surrendered to the advancing Foerdewaith in 2748 I.R., bringing the remainder of the province with them.

In the following years, Trebes was fortified and built up by the overking, and the massive Heldenheight Citadel was home to hundreds — and in times of crisis, thousands — of Foerdewaith soldiers. Times change, of course, and today with the great kingdom of Foere in decline, Trebes stands as a tribute to the faded glories of two empires.

Well-situated on a large island in the middle of the small lake of Piorvorun, Trebes is surrounded by rolling, fertile plains dotted with numerous villages. Trebes' old fortifications, from the days when the province was wracked with warfare, still stand, but are in poor repair — a faint echo of the city's past as a military citadel in its new role as a center of commerce. The lord-governor no longer holds court in the Citadel of Heldenheight and now occupies a palace in the city center rather than the cold fortress that rises above the city's peaked rooftops. Merchants from many lands pass through Trebes' markets, buying and selling in the many pleasant wine-plazas that one finds everywhere in the city, even in unexpected and out-of-the-way locations.

SESSILBRIDGE, TOWN OF

Ruler: Mayor Tavour Palann
Government: town council
Population: 1,622 (785 Foerdewaith, 454 Heldring, 333 human mixed ethnicity, 50 dwarf)
Monstrous: orcish races from nearby Sky Peaks
Languages: Common, Helvaenic
Religion: Eostre and Tyr
Resources: farming, river-fishing and hunting

Currency: bartering primarily with some common currency accepted

Technology Level: Medieval on land

Sessilbridge is built on and around a massive bridge over the River Sess, a bridge that is often compared to Lyre Bridge in Bard's Gate for its size and scope. The bridge and the town are ancient, dating to Hyperborean times before the death of Oerson. Nominally within the demesne of the province of Cerediun, as the last town before the Helwall, it tends to be quite independent, with little supervision from Trebes, and pays a modest annual tax based on trade passing over the bridge. The town is a center of the trade between Cerediun and the Heldring to the south.

A diverse mix of races have settled in this river-village, which is known to be the last stop along the south road to the Helcynngae Peninsula. An ever-changing racial profile keeps the small town interesting; depending on the time, the number of Heldring, mixed-race humans, dwarves, and even elves vary in the makeup of its residents.

HISTORY AND PEOPLE

The small town and bridge were established in –69 I.R. to provide a crossing over the River Sess and a watchful eye north of the Helwall over the southern part of the continent as well as the northern plains and forests. As the last stop before the Helwall, military garrisons would stage in the town on their way north or south, and those few traders and other travelers with reason to be in this region would find a safe haven within the town's walls. Over the years, armies have moved through the town using the bridge, though it has largely been held by one or other of the northern kingdoms.

Of late, as hostility between the Heldring and Foere declined, more folks from south of the wall have taken up residence here, especially as trade with Cerediun Province increased. Now, the city is a mix of Foerdewaith, Heldring, and a potpourri of other races, including dwarves and the occasional high elves or half-elves. Lord-Governor Bryntwis Carlarion's desire to expand trade has been good for the town's economy.

RELIGION

The Foere residents of Sessilbridge generally worship Arialee or Muir, and temples to both gods can be found on the bridge. For the Heldring, a combined shrine to the sibling gods of Eostre and Tyr is found in the southern portion of the town and is often filled to capacity with god-fearing residents. Zealous priests of the two gods ensure that their benches are always occupied and that the coffers are overflowing with donations.

TRADE AND COMMERCE

As the last stop before the Helwall for southbound travelers, Sessilbridge is a welcoming settlement with plenty of merchants, inns, and taverns. Dreading the harsher trip into the more dangerous peninsula beyond the wall, travelers have been known to linger in the comfortable town for more than a few days. Prosperous from constant travelers eager to spend their wealth, the town is constantly adding more homes, businesses, and residents.

LOYALTIES AND DIPLOMACY

Nominally, Sessilbridge is governed from Trebes as a possession of Cerediun Province. However, in practice, the proximity of the Helwall and the presence of sizable numbers of Heldring leave the town largely independent, and in fact, some support comes from both nations to keep the town in a defensible state. Soldiers of both regions live in the town and can be found repelling raids from brigands or wayward humanoids, though the Heldring are more usually found in the southern part at the foot of the bridge.

GOVERNMENT

Under a charter from the Cerediun lord-governors, a ruling council of five men, led by the most senior of the group, presides over laws and decides town matters. Tavour Palann is the current senior-most council member, having served on the council for more than 30 consecutive years. Once selected to the council, nothing short of death or treason removes a member from the elite group of officials.

MILITARY

Although the town has its own guard that patrols the interior of the town, Sessilbridge's borders are protected by Cerediun and Heldring soldiers on the north and south, respectively. As a general matter, however, the soldiers are present only for external protection and do not have jurisdiction within the walls of the river-town.

MAJOR THREATS

Dozens of roaming brigands and gangs of murderous humanoids constantly seek easy prey along the river and plains. Sessilbridge at first seems an easy target until the well-trained soldiers respond to attacks. Although most small raids are dispatched quickly, the occasional coordinated attack from larger groups of goblins and orcs may seriously test the soldiers and town fortifications.

DUCHY OF DUQUESNE (ALSO, DUSQUESNE)

(due-KANE)

Population: 18,000 (14,300 human mixed ethnicity, 1,050 wood elf, 850 halfling, 700 half-elf, 650 hill dwarf, 450 other)

Ruler: Duchess Shalindra

Government: Monarchy

Humanoid: wood elf (some), halfling (some), half-elf (some), hill dwarf (some)

Monstrous: ankheg, basilisks, bugbears, bulettes, centaurs, chimeras, cockatrice, cyclops, ettins, fomorians, goblins, griffons, hags, hill giants, kobolds, manticores, minotaurs, orcs, ogres, pegasus, perytons, stirges, treants, trolls, unicorns, werebears, wereboars, wererats, werewolves, will-o'-wisps, wyverns

Languages: Common

Religion: unknown

Resources: trade

Currency: Foere, barter

Technology Level: Medieval

The Duchy of Duquesne is a small realm independent of Cerediun Province and Exeter Province and the Domain of Hawkmoon. Entirely contained within the Cut Horn Gap between the Forlorn Mountains in the north and the Scar-in-the-Sky Peaks to the south, the duchy is currently under the rule of Duchess Shalindra. The duchess keeps the pass well-patrolled in exchange for the payment of tolls by those traveling through.

The origin of this duchy is unknown, and its political allegiances are unclear. Some scholars assume that the folk of the duchy are descendants of the people who eventually moved to settle the Domain of Hawkmoon, or perhaps are part of lost Parma. In any case, the duchess has made plain on many occasions that Duquesne is not, nor ever was, a part of the Kingdoms of Foere. She has also refused every offer from the Kingdom of Suilley to join its ranks. Despite its rather enigmatic political status, the duchy remains the closest overland trading partner of the Domain of Hawkmoon, and the two domains are allied in mutual defense.

DOMAIN OF HAWKMOON

Capital: City-State of Hawkmoon

Notable Settlements: Fort Fodom, Leafton, Swordport, Yunn

Ruler: None

Government: none (officially a protectorate of Hawkmoon City)

Population: 25,350 (14,500 human [Hawkmoon ethnicity], 5,000 halfling, 2,500 mountain dwarf, 1,500 wood elf, 1,200 gnome, 500 deep gnome, 150 aarakocra)

Monstrous: ankheg, banshees, basilisks, bugbears, bulettes, centaurs, chimeras, cockatrice, cyclops, dryads, ettins, faerie dragons, fomorians, goblins, griffons, hags, hell hounds, hill giants, kobolds, manticores, minotaurs, orcs, ogres, pegasus, perytons, pixies, satyrs, specters, sprites, stirges, treants, trolls, unicorns, vampires, werebears, wereboars, wererats, werewolves, will-o'-wisps, wraiths, wyverns, zombies

Languages: Common, Sirrocan
Religion: Thyr, Muir, Freya, the Hawkmoon Pantheon
Resources: Fish, foodstuffs, iron, livestock, tin
Currency: Foere
Technology Level: Medieval

Encircled by the treacherous Scar-in-the-Sky Peaks and the Moonsilver Sea, the Domain of Hawkmoon is geographically isolated, its borders forming a natural barrier against invaders — as well as a wall to dissuade its inhabitants from leaving. The region is said to be a haven of footpads, a place of succor for criminals fleeing persecution. There is indeed a bit of truth to these rumors, as the domain was first settled 300 years ago by marauders seeking a refuge against the armies of those nations they'd plundered. Echoes of this grim legacy can still be heard today.

History and People

In its earliest years, the Domain of Hawkmoon was inhabited by the legendary Yaltic peoples who oversaw seven local dynasties in the area but were in decline when first encountered by outsiders in 1944 I.R. The last of the Yalts fled Hawkmoon in the face of raids and population pressure during the polar shift in 2491 I.R. Within five years, the last of the Yalts had departed the region by sea to establish the city of Coralis, leaving their realm to the newcomers.

The domain's new masters were a hardy and fractious mix of outlaws and refugees from the fires that burned eastern Akados after the fall of Curgantium, and with little outside authority the region degenerated into a state of anarchy and lawlessness. The domain's destabilizing influence grew in later years as bandits and raiders — protected by the forbidding peaks of the Scar-in-the-Sky and Forlorn Mountains — started to raid other nations by sea. When Hawkmoon corsairs plagued the Helcynngae Peninsula, the Heldring were forced into a frustrating defensive war.

Eventually, the Heldring had enough of what they called the "open sore" of Hawkmoon on their doorstep and set sail in 2801 I.R. to invade the region and install one of their own on the throne and establish the puppet state commonly called the Kingdom of Hawkmoon.

The following year, the Battle of Oescreheit Downs heralded the downfall of the Helcynngae Heldring, but the Heldring regime in Hawkmoon was too isolated and secure for the Foerdewaith to dislodge. In fact, Hawkmoon became a refuge for the Heldring who refused to surrender, and Heldring rule persisted for nearly four more centuries.

It was not until 3282 I.R. that the people of Hawkmoon, led by many heroes and joined by the mountain dwarves, threw off the Heldrings' yoke and reclaimed their territory. The rebels were led by Hanfred Vel, a paladin of Muir, and the general Bosworth, both of whom saw a future for Hawkmoon that was well beyond its confused and bloody anarchic past. The overthrow of the Heldring was followed by the so-called Great Purge, during which Hanfred and Bosworth led their forces in a merciless campaign to rid the land of brigands and outlaws.

The new nation envisioned by the two liberators regrettably did not come to pass. Bosworth took the crown of the domain when the Heldring were thrown out, but his dynasty did not endure long after his death. His son Vargha served as viscount for a time, but a series of plagues ravaged the nation, and eventually the individual communities of Hawkmoon largely went back to their own ways. Nevertheless, Bosworth is remembered as the founder of modern Hawkmoon and is canonized among its inhabitants as "the Great."

Today's Hawkmoons have retained their old rugged and individualistic spirit, the notion of a united nation never having taken hold. True, the old bandits and warlords are gone, but now the region's inhabitants remain stubbornly resistant to outside authority. While they would unite to oppose an outside threat, and frequently combine forces to hunt down bandits, monsters and raiders, the people refuse to acknowledge that Hawkmoon is anything more than simply their homeland.

The Hawkmoons are descended from a dozen different ancestries, to the point that they are their own distinct nationality that combines the cultures and characteristics of their numerous forebears. Most speak the Common tongue, but many are fully bilingual with the ancient Sirrocan language, which locals speak when they wish to keep discussions secret from outsiders.

Despite the domain's apparent anarchy, there is very little violence, as most inhabitants are focused on their own communities and families, with little desire to impose their will on others. This independence is a two-edged sword, of course, for while the Hawkmoons accept little or no outside authority, they receive virtually no help either, making the domain a wildly varied place — wealthier communities maintain their own roads and public works, and diligently enforce their laws, while poorer towns and villages have correspondingly poor roads, sanitation, and defense, or are ruled by organized criminals who masquerade as constables or civil leaders. Likewise, law varies significantly from town to town, with acts that are legal in one being strictly illegal elsewhere.

Banditry and murder are nevertheless surprisingly rare, though property crime, robbery, extortion and similar acts are sadly more common. Hawkmoon boasts a single thieves' guild that is led by ex-adventurer Sivian Ulphar, who is known commonly as the Lucre King. While the guild controls much of the organized crime in Hawkmoon, the land's independent spirit extends to its criminal endeavors, and many small brotherhoods and gangs are active on a local level, engaged in highway robbery, con games, burglary of all kinds, livestock theft, smuggling, and the like. These small groups do not compete directly with Ulphar's guild, but they are so numerous that they commit a large percentage of the domain's crime.

As Hawkmoon City provides little support to the Outfolk, it falls to the locals to defend themselves against criminals, bandits, raiders and the occasional warlord. A class of freelance bounty hunters known as the Trunchers has developed to serve this need. Hired by individual communities, Trunchers range from moral and reliable freelance law-enforcement personnel to amoral, violent mercenaries who are only a step or two above the bandits that they are hired to apprehend.

Other denizens of the Hawkmoon Domain include the Horselords of Kur, a tribe of fiercely independent centaurs who often trade with local merchants and may occasionally be hired on to assist with merchant caravans or to defend communities against bandits.

Wood elves are also frequently seen in Hawkmoon. Based in the various forests throughout the domain, they are led by the prophetess Zinaida Quespar.

Religion

While the Foerdewaith deities of Thyr, Muir, and Freya have made inroads in Hawkmoon and elsewhere, the region is most notable for its unique pantheon, which scholars believe was inherited from the Yaltic dynasties that preceded the domain's current inhabitants. Like the people of Hawkmoon, their gods are a widely varied lot numbering no fewer than 29 individual deities, the most commonly worshipped of which include Aletheia, Goddess of Wisdom and Protection; Majium, God of Mercy and Magic; Oon, God of Nature; and Quooembla, God of Wisdom. Other gods are worshipped by smaller and more specialized groups, such as Zahm, God of Money and Business — revered by merchants and businessman — and Ulremara, Goddess of Candles and Desire, who is popular in brothels and taverns.

Most inhabitants of the domain worship their many gods in private, usually with family and close friends, but there are some organized priesthoods and temples, though these temples usually include statues, altars, and worship facilities for multiple gods.

Many in Hawkmoon believe that the moon vanishes from the sky one day each month, at the time of the new moon. They refer to this event as the "Vanishing Moon." Scholars elsewhere have found no evidence for this event, and the origin of this belief remains unknown.

Trade and Commerce

The Domain of Hawkmoon is mostly self-sufficient, producing foodstuffs, livestock, and timber sufficient to keep its population fed and housed. Excess is sold to the city-state, and outsiders may venture into the domain through Cut Horn Gap to trade in Leafton and Hawkmoon City. Mines in the Forlorn Mountains and the Scar-in-the-Sky produce iron and tin, some of which is exported to neighboring kingdoms, including the Kingdom of Helcynn.

Fishing vessels out of Swordport work the Moonsilver Sea and provide their haul to the rest of the domain. Trade ships from Oceanus and other port cities on the Sinnar Sea have been calling at Swordport more in recent years, bearing finished goods, cloth, clothing, weapons, and tools in exchange for Hawkmoon's products.

LOYALTIES AND DIPLOMACY

Neither the domain nor the city-state of Hawkmoon owes allegiance to any other state or kingdom, though a few foreign trade officials and diplomats — the most prominent being those from Castorhage, Oceanus, and Foere — maintain facilities. Most such contacts are with the city-state however, as the Outfolk have little to no interest in diplomacy or contact beyond some basic trade.

GOVERNMENT

At the heart of the domain is the city of Hawkmoon, an independent city-state that answers to no foreign power. The land outlying the city is officially a protectorate of Hawkmoon, though not part of the sovereign state itself. In other words, though Hawkmoon troops patrol the land, the Outfolk (as those beyond the city walls are called) are not beholden to the city nor in any way obliged to follow its mandates. The Outfolk pay no taxes to Hawkmoon, though they do use the city as the primary base for selling of their crops and manufactured goods. This strange dichotomy is the result of the region's oldest and most revered tradition: "Our ancestors came here to escape authority's oppressive grasp, and we shall not dishonor them by submitting." The Domain of Hawkmoon, then, teeters on the brink of anarchy, though it never fully tumbles into the abyss.

MILITARY

The domain has no official military, leaving patrols and security to the city-state's armed soldiery. However, the folk of Hawkmoon are independent and resourceful, well able to unite into a potent irregular force. Looking back to their days as Heldring vassals, most Hawkmoons are skilled scouts, hunters, archers, and guerrillas. While they almost joyfully defy any kind of central authority, the region's inhabitants actively defend their realm against outside threats, with each community forming ad hoc military units and even — in an act that would normally be met with derision and shock — submitting to command from experienced leaders from the city-state. These units are mostly infantry, though a few mounted scouts and skirmishers may be present. These Hawkmoon irregulars have very light armor, or none at all, and fight with light melee weapons and missile weapons, which they wield to good effect, engaging in hit-and-run attacks before vanishing into the wilderness to strike elsewhere.

These irregular community-based units don't just appear in times of national crisis — they also come together in the face of banditry, humanoid raiding, piracy, and other local threats, sometimes with several communities combining resources to eliminate the danger before returning to their normal independent existences.

WILDERNESS AND ADVENTURES

Hawkmoon Domain is a mixture of settled areas — farms, ranches, towns, and villages connected by locally-maintained roads of varying quality — and wild lands that are often under the control of bandits or monsters. Travel is always a chancy proposition, and trade expeditions between cities must usually be strongly defended. The stretches between towns are often heavily forested, which provides ideal concealment for attackers and requires considerable vigilance.

The land is also full of various bizarre and dangerous locations, the most obvious of which are ancient Yaltic palaces, temples, and tombs, some of which still contain old magic, treasure, and even potent artifacts. These are sometimes defended by spirits, demons, or the undead remains of their old guardians. It is said that a city was founded on an island in a lake somewhere in the domain and was home to a council of wizard-priests, but it sank as a consequence of a failed ritual and is yet to be rediscovered. An ancient dwarven mine is also rumored to exist beneath that lake. Elsewhere in Hawkmoon is the fearsome realm known as the Bonegarden where the spirits of thousands of criminals slaughtered in the Great Purge are trapped.

REFERENCE SOURCES: G2 What Evil Lurks; G9 A Lamentation of Thieves; K9 Elemental Moon; Dead Man's Chest

HAWKMOON, CITY-STATE OF

Population: 10,200 (6,850 human [Hawkmoon ethnicity], 2,250 halfling, 875 mountain dwarf, 225 gnome)
Ruler: Administrator Burgrave Malva
Government: elected administrator

The city of Hawkmoon is an independent city-state that holds the rest of Hawkmoon as a loose protectorate without considering it to be the territory of the city itself. The current ruler is Burgrave Malva, essentially an administrator of the city's interests, both urban and in the surrounding domain of the city-state.

Built on the remains of far-more-ancient Yaltic settlements, the modern city-state of Hawkmoon became fully independent with the expulsion of the Heldring in 3282 I.R. Initially led by the legendary Bosworth the Great, Hawkmoon City soon became the leading settlement of the region but never exercised anything beyond general leadership and guidance to the fiercely independent Outfolk. Today, the city-state retains its role as first among equals and provides patrols and military assistance to, but exercises little real authority over, the rest of the domain.

Many consider the city-state a lawless place where a powerful thieves' guild — led by an individual known as the Lucre King — and other crime networks, such as that run by the Valder family, help make policy and act as the true power in the city. The patriarch Chistoff Valder is considered equal to Administrator Burgrave Malva in the establishment of general policies and laws.

CORALIS, CITY OF

Population: unknown
Ruler: unknown
Government: unknown

The city of Coralis was founded by Yalts fleeing the Domain of Hawkmoon shortly after the shift of Boros' poles in 2491 I.R. Not a part of Hawkmoon, Coralis is built entirely on a broad expanse of coral reef somewhere east of the domain in the midst of the Sinnar Ocean. Today, it is a haven of peace and knowledge, a city of legend, encountered rarely by wayward travelers and built up in mortal minds as the earthly abode of the gods.

REFERENCE SOURCE: Dead Man's Chest

FORT FODOM

Population: 500 (almost all human [Hawkmoon ethnicity])
Ruler: military governor
Government: military

Fort Fodom guards the eastern coast of Hawkmoon from the threat of invasion by sea and marauding pirates. The fortress harbor is a common stopping-point for galleys making the coastal journey from Swordpoint to the Helcynngae Peninsula.

LEAFTON, VILLAGE OF

Population: 850 (625 human [Hawkmoon ethnicity], 225 halfling)
Ruler: Mayor Kaun Solear
Government: elders elect mayor

Leafton is a village of 850 peaceful folk. It is a pleasant farming community at the edge of the Gaunt Wood, ideal for a respite from the dangers of adventuring.

SWORDPORT, CITY OF

Population: 3,855 (2,820 human [Hawkmoon ethnicity], 555 halfling, 250 mountain dwarf, 230 gnome)
Ruler: Oro Gullina
Government: loose oligarchy

Known as the City of Shrouds, Swordport is a rollicking coastal city, the gateway to the Moonsilver Sea. It is the second most important urban area in the domain, a natural rival to Hawkmoon. Intrigue between the two cities is rich and complex as they vie for power in the domain.

YUNN, TOWN OF

Population: 472 (almost all human [Hawkmoon ethnicity])
Ruler: Sheb Nikandur
Government: pre-eminent citizen's personal influence

Yunn (or Yuun) is a small town on the shore of a lake in Hawkmoon that operates a sawmill in the Gaunt Wood. It has a population of 472 and is led by Sheb Nikandur, its "first citizen."

REFERENCE SOURCE: K9 Elemental Moon

KILDREN POINT

Capital: none
Notable Settlements: Kaf Village
Ruler: none
Government: clan hetmans
Population: 7,800 (7,000 Kaf, 800 Foerdewaith)
Monstrous: crab swarms, hyaenodons, locathah, giant crabs (coastline); bat swarms, gnolls, hyaenodons, dire bats, giant insects, ankhegs, sandlings, paleoskeleton creatures (Sand Hills)
Languages: Kaf, Common
Religion: Halatra the Horse
Resources: livestock (sheep, horses), wool, glass, gems
Technology Level: Dark Ages

This lonely stretch of coastline is out of the way and little-visited by the caravans of the Soldier's Road and coastal traders. It is the exclusive homeland of the enigmatic Kaf tribe who dwell in small clan settlements scattered throughout the peninsula and even into the Sand Hills. The only other humans who risk the threat of gnoll raiders are a few hardy prospectors and traders that are known to the Kaf and serve as a point of contact for outside commerce. Visitors to the peninsula are forewarned. Sometimes the riders of the Kaf are friendly to visitors seeking trade and swapping of tales, but other times they simply attack, seeking to rob those they run across.

KAF VILLAGE

Population: 522 (Kaf)
Ruler: none
Government: the hetmen of Kaf

Little more than a camp, really, Kaf Village is constructed on the northern edge of the Sand Hills where its riders can easily make forays into the desert wastes to hunt the giant insects that dwell there for their valuable carapaces and delicate wings which are used in jewelry and adornments for dwellings. Many of the village's homes are tents of stiff leather that have stood for many years and whose lines must constantly be replaced and new patches added due to the omnipresent winds of the point. At least half of the homes, however, are constructed from ill-fitting wooden beams and logs, their chinks filled with mud and thatching. Despite the aridity of the location, the village streets seem perpetually muddy due to the pigpens along either side that constantly drain into them and the horses that continually churn them into a stinking morass.

LOWPORT, FREE CITY OF

Ruler: Tyrant of Lowport, Conqueror of the Waves, Despot of the Stony Strand, Baljulias the Great
Government: dictatorship
Population: 13,800 (6,610 human [mostly Foerdewaith], 3,035 orc, 2,700 half-orc, 790 hobgoblin, 520 mountain dwarf, 125 half-elf, 20 high elf)
Monstrous: goblins, monstrous jellyfish, sahuagin (coastline); krenshars, howlers, ogres, barghests (countryside); rock baboons, worgs, ogres, hell hounds, harpies, hill giants, dragons (Stony Strand)
Languages: Common, Orc, Goblin
Religion: Thursis, Grotaag, Kakobovia
Resources: plunder, slaves, coal, chalk
Technology Level: Dark Ages

At one time, the Lowport region was the easternmost portion of the Kingdom of Burgundia with several fortifications of ancient Hyperborea built along the coastline to guard against sea invasion and piracy. However, the territory changed hands several times after Foere quit its claims upon it, and it ultimately ended up under the jurisdiction of Penmorgh with orders to man the old fortifications. The Southvalers were unequipped to deal with the remote forts and failed to properly garrison or oversee them so that when the sea reaver Gathos the Cruel arrived in the city of Parthos in 3485 I.R., he was able to put the entire garrison to the sword and rename the place Lowport with himself as the tyrant. Lowport was declared a free city with a port open to all comers and became a bastion of pirates, smugglers, slavers, and every unsavory sort imaginable. With Oceanus wholly occupied with its wars of expansion, there was no one with sufficient sea power to dislodge the scurvy lot that had taken over. By the time things had calmed enough for the powers-that-be to turn attention toward the situation, they found Gathos and his recruited mercenaries well entrenched with a heavily defended harbor. With no land areas of real value nearby to be claimed and defended, it became more expedient to simply patrol the waters off the coast to reduce piracy rather than try to root out the entire rats' nest. Gathos wisely ordered his piracy conducted farther afield to avoid antagonizing nearby Oceanus, and Lowport became a fixture of the Sinnar Coast.

Gathos' rule was cruel and profitable until the old pirate was challenged and defeated by a half-orc gladiator champion. But if folk thought that the rule of Baljulias the Great would bring moderation and greater civility to the town, they far overestimated the conscience of the foul brawler. Under Baljulias, Lowport has sunk even further into depravity, getting much more heavily involved in the slave trade and beginning to conduct kidnappings for ransom of valuable targets in the nearby realms. The situation has not grown so bad to require a military response yet, but many folk suspect that it won't be too many more years before an Oceanic fleet carrying a sufficient number of marines arrives to sweep the riffraff into the sea.

Lowport's claim to the Stony Strand hills is almost completely spurious; the city's reach extends perhaps 100 miles inland beyond the city walls. Orc bands make excursions into the hills, but so far Lowport has made no attempt to establish any permanent presence there.

The city itself is, as one might suspect, a haven for all kinds of seaborne villains. The tyrant's orcish allies are permitted (in small numbers) in the city, making the atmosphere even more volatile than normal in a pirate stronghold. The original cityfolk are docile under the tyrant's rule, waiting for some brave group of heroes to dislodge Gathos and return the city to peace and freedom.

A group of fugitives from Lowport have gathered at the nearby ruins of the Hyperborean fortress of Salyos.

Matagost Peninsula

(MAT-uh-gost)

Capital: Oestre
Notable Settlements: Heldring's Cross, Highreach, Highsmyth, Tirigoth
Ruler: Governor-General Alphonse d'Tarrio Alejandros
Government: military dictatorship
Population: 122,000 (58,650 Foerdewaith, 23,600 Oceander, 17,200 mountain dwarf, 12,000 half-elf, 6,800 high elf, 1,650 halfling, 1,110 gnome, 990 other)
Monstrous: goblins, worgs, bugbears, duergar, aberrant giants, stone giants, giant eagles (Matagost Range); wolves, dire wolves, giant beetles, inphidians, decapi (woodlands); snapping turtles, crab swarms, giant eels, sahuagin, kelp devils (coastline)
Languages: Common, Dwarven, Elven, Halfling, Gnome
Religion: Mithras, Tykee, Sefagreth, Dre'uain the Lame, Thyr
Resources: shipbuilding supplies, coal, iron, quarry stone, ironwork, timber, livestock (goats, pigs), lead, gems
Currency: Oceanus
Technology Level: Medieval

The Matagost Peninsula protrudes like the blade of a cleaver from the eastern side of Akados, stretching almost all the way to Ramthion Island where the dark Dardanal Strait marks its easternmost point. The Matagost Range bounds its southern flank while the northern shore looks out upon Pontos Island and the Gulf of Akados far to the north. The discovery of vast iron lodes in the mountains led to its current state as a leading fabricator and exporter of ironwork. This is the position it now holds in the Empire of Oceanus, the latest sovereign to control the lands of the peninsula. No longer a great forest, Matagost is lightly wooded for much of its length and provides firewood along with coal mined from the mountains to light the forge fires of Highsmyth.

History and People

In the days of Hyperborea, the Province of Matagost long sought to be a shipping capital but was always eclipsed by Tsen and its holdings to the north. With the destruction of that land and the emergence of Endhome as a trade center, Matagost was relegated to a military status to protect against Ramithi pirates and other threats. Over time, it developed into a self-sufficient province in its own right through its emergence as a center for ironwork.

After the fall of Hyperborea, Matagost was absorbed into the burgeoning Kingdom of Foere in 2745 I.R. Over time, the appointed lord-governors in Oestre gained some slightly greater standing as Ramthion Island was brought into the kingdom and Matagost came to serve as a hub for what limited travel existed between Courghais and that distant province.

When the Kingdom of Oceanus rebelled against Foere in 3215 I.R., the Foerdewaith fleet gathered at the great sea fortress of Highreach to crush the rebellion. However, after Oceanus soundly defeated the Foerdewaith navy at the Battle of Kapichi Point, Matagost found itself in a precarious position as neighbor to a growing naval empire and without the military support of its own distant master. Nevertheless, Matagost chose to stay the course and maintained its allegiance to the Court at Courghais. They benefited from Oceanus being occupied by other, greater threats and managed to marshal their own defenses.

When the Province of Burgundia declared its independence from Foere in 3221 I.R., the magnate of Oestre, the ruler of Matagost Province, marched on Trevi. His route through the Moon Fog Hills avoided detection, and he was able to lay siege to the city before the Burgundian army reached him. Now forced to defend a huge area against a possible invasion from Foere, the Burgundian army had insufficient forces to break the army of Matagost at Trevi. The city and both armies settled in to what would become a long siege.

In 3222 I.R., the province of Suilley seceded from Foere, and in 3224 I.R. the magnate of Penmorgh was assassinated, and the province of Southvale became a duchy of Burgundy. In response to this new uprising, the magnate of Oestre landed an army loyal to Foere south of Wellesley and marched on Penmorgh. His army outnumbered the forces holding Penmorgh, but the magnate of Oestre had not reckoned on the numbers and training of the peasants who arose from the countryside to harass them nor the heavy infantry provided by the dwarves of Durandel. The army of Matagost soon found itself outnumbered and caught in unfavorable terrain. The army was routed and forced to retreat to the coast to be picked up by the ships that had transported it.

With Matagost reeling from its sudden defeat, the new duke of Southvale took the initiative and marched his now-blooded army up the Southvale Causeway toward Trevi. These reinforcements, combined with the surrounding army of Burgundia, broke the siege of Trevi and routed the Matagost host. At the same time, word came that ships carrying survivors of Matagost's southern army encountered a storm in Dardanal Strait and many had gone down, including the one carrying the magnate of Oestre. Pandemonium immediately engulfed the Matagost Peninsula. A new lord-governor appointed by the overking was murdered in his chair when he convened a council of the leading families. Though many of the lords of Oestre were rich and powerful, none was capable of defeating all of his rivals and exerting power over the entire peninsula, which resulted in a bloody civil war that lasted for more than eight decades.

Finally, in 3312 I.R., a fleet of ships came silently out of a night fog and landed on the shores of Matagost. Oceander marines stormed ashore and quickly took Highreach while transport ships deployed infantry and cavalry units. In only a matter of weeks, Oceander units swept through the war-torn remnants of the peninsula and brought its civil war to a screeching halt. The banner of Oceanus was raised over Oestre, and the maritime empire had its first mainland holding. Matagost's massive foundries now produce the weapons and armor for the Oceander war machine, and its cities are the staging point for its continental land armies.

In ages past, the peninsula was heavily forested and inhabited by elves. Hundreds of generations of timbering and the great fires of Curgantium did much to clear its lands, but they have recovered significantly over the years. Some high elves still call Matagost home, though most live in the more sparsely populated areas where the trees grow thickest among the foothills of the mountains. These elves are friendly with the lowland humans and their Oceander masters. They avoid the filth and soot of Highsmyth but are commonly seen in Oestre and frequently serve as guides and hunters for travelers or caravans headed for the dwarven mines in the mountains.

The population of the Matagost Peninsula is composed primarily of native Foerdewaith stock, many with the blood of the Heldring in them from their invasions of long ago, but there are also many folk of Oceanus (also Foerdewaith but with the olive skin common to the natives of that island) who have relocated here to find their fortunes since the peninsula fell under Oceander control.

Religion

The Piedmont of the city of Oestre serves as the location of the marble-columned chief temple of the peninsula. It has venerated many deities over the years, but switched from the soldier god Mithras to Sefagreth, God of Commerce, by order of the governor-general 13 years ago in order to promote the prosperity of trade over Matagost after the long specter of war that it faced for so long. With so many military forces present in the peninsula, however, Mithras remains extremely popular, along with Tykee, the Patroness of Luck. Dre'uain the Lame is likewise widely venerated, especially in the forge-city of Highsmyth. The courts of law are still dedicated to Thyr, but his presence has faded greatly from the old days. Rumors of cults of diabolical or demonic influence in Oestre have circulated for centuries, but to date no evidence of such has ever been discovered by the authorities. Lack of proof, however, hasn't kept the rumors from continuing to swirl.

Trade and Commerce

Matagostian timber builds and maintains the Oceanic fleet at Highreach and beyond, while coal from the Matagost Range feeds the forge fires in Highsmyth. The many forges and foundries in Highsmyth create a constant racket at all hours of the day and night as they produce the armor and weapons needed to feed the expansion of the Oceander Empire.

LOYALTIES AND DIPLOMACY

The Matagost Peninsula is an occupied land. Long a province of Foere, it suffered over eight decades of civil war before the Oceanders conquered the area 200 years ago. While some of the old families continue to resent the Oceander occupation, they recognize the stability and peace that it has brought and make no move to rise in rebellion against the lord of Pontus Tinigal. While the native folk of Matagost harbor no great love for the Oceanders, they elect to make no trouble for them either — and not entirely because of the proficiency and ruthlessness of the Oceanic forces that control their lands. Besides, with the effective disintegration of Burgundia, rival claims to the lucrative mines of the Moon Fog Hills have evaporated, and the avarice of Matagostian aristocrats inclines them to cooperate with their Oceanic overlords with the prospect of greater riches on the horizon.

GOVERNMENT

The mayor of Oestre is the highest-ranking civilian on the peninsula, but it is the military governor-general appointed by Oceanus who resides in the Lord's Palace and rules Matagost as a military dictatorship. The governor-general appoints mayors of Oestre and Highsmyth (often from among the Oceander gentry), and the smaller towns and villages are allowed to elect or appoint their own mayors or headmen, though these must answer to regional correctors appointed by the governor-general who serve as magistrates and auditors of the local municipalities under their authority. There is little unrest among the Matagostian population, but the ever-present Oceanic soldiers and marines means any such troubles that do arise are put down quickly and brutally.

MILITARY

Matagost has no real military of its own beyond the household guards of the more powerful aristocratic families, primarily found in Oestre. However, the land remains highly militarized as a military dictatorship with Oceanic troops keeping and maintaining order and a watchful presence over the land. The main concentration of troops consists of 5,000 Oceanic marines kept in a constant state of readiness at the ancient fortress of Highreach. At any time, scores of Oceanic naval vessels and crews are present as well, all kept on hand and ready to depart at a moment's notice to address some threat to the empire anywhere in the world. The rest of the forces found in Matagost are the 3,500 soldiers and light cavalry primarily billeted in Oestre and Highsmyth and charged with keeping the peace upon the peninsula. Some few patrols make their way down the Soldier's Road west of Oestre to scout the western reaches, but most remain more centrally located.

MAJOR THREATS

The Matagost Peninsula enjoys a sort of wary peace. In many ways, the civil wars of 200 years ago exhausted its stores of violence. The Oceanic occupation is well-ordered, and the enemies of Oceanus lie far away, leaving Matagost a region of little national intrigue. There remain giants and goblinoids in the Matagost Range, and the mysterious depths of the Dardanal Strait continue to spawn weird ichthyic threats, but these offer little overt threat as a whole. Even the barbaric tribes of the Moon Fog Hills and ravenous gnolls of the Sand Hills seem little disposed toward being more than an occasional nuisance nipping at the borders of the realm.

WILDERNESS AND ADVENTURES

The thin veneer of calm over the peninsula hides a land ripe for adventure. Giants and goblins still control major parts of the Matagost Range, and rumors of gray dwarves and vengeful restlessness among the mountain dwarf clans themselves have been heard of late. Slimy, scaly things crawling up from the eastern and southern coasts point toward untold dangers hidden in the briny deeps of the Dardanal Strait and Matagost Bay, and the mysterious Moon Fog Hills remain able to swallow entire companies of soldiers in their silent embrace, leaving no trace but the dripping leaves in the fog-shrouded Mistwood.

OESTRE, CITY OF (CAPITAL)

Population: 15,616 (10,054 Foerdewaith and Oceander, 1,800 mountain dwarf, 1,410 half-elf, 855 halfling, 630 high elf, 520 gnome, 347 other)
Ruler: Governor-General Alphonse d'Tarrio Alejandros, Mayor Padrick de Querne
Government: mayor appointed by the governor-general

As long as an organized nation-state has existed on the peninsula of Matagost, Oestre has served as its capital. Built with double concentric walls, first in earth and wood and later replaced in stone, the piedmont of the city still serves as the location of the Lord's Palace and the marble columns of the city's chief temple, currently dedicated to Sefagreth, God of Commerce. Other prominent temples in town include those dedicated to the soldiers' deities of Mithras and Tykee, the Patroness of Luck. The citizens of Oestre are primarily the native Foerdewaith stock, many with the blood of the Heldring in them from their invasions of long ago, but there are also many folk of Oceanus (also Foerdewaith but with the olive skin common to the natives of that island) who have relocated here to find their fortunes since the city fell under Oceander control. Oestre is open to trade and travel, but entry and exit are strictly monitored, and the watch is always on the lookout for spies from distant Foere.

HELDRING'S CROSS, TOWN OF

Population: 1,332 (976 Foerdewaith and Oceander, 251 half-elf, 105 halfling)
Ruler: Fray Compton D'Lac (Cleric of Thyr)
Government: Church of Thyr

The town of Heldring's Cross lies at the crossroads where the Soldier's Road from Endhome meets the Hollow Road from Old Burgundia and both turn east toward Oestre. The town is considered the westernmost part of the Matagost Peninsula and has historically been considered disputed territory between that province and Sunderland to the west. There is currently no organized government of Sunderland, so Matagost's claim to the town has gone unchallenged for many years. Despite this, it remains virtually ignored by the government in Oestre and is generally fine with that.

The small burg's one claim to fame dates back to the times of the Heldring invasions of a thousand years ago. One war band led by an unnamed jarl, who was among the first to convert to the gods of the Hyperboreans, made its way here through the Moon Fog Hills. The journey was harrowing, the dangers of the mystical hills taking a heavy toll on the warriors, and the end of their journey brought them into battle at this point with a host of local warriors gathered from Oestre in the east. The Heldring were victorious despite their many travails, and the grateful jarl built a church here to Thyr in thanks for his aid. The original church is long since gone, but the 12-foot-tall, rune-scribed stone cross that he erected next to the church still stands, time-worn and lichen-crusted. Its runic inscription of thanks and dedication is faded but still legible, and it has always been seen as an important shrine to the church. The leader of the town is always a priest of Thyr sent to tend the shrine, and the Oceander cleric currently serving in that role (Fray Compton D'Lac) is no exception. He preaches the will of Thyr weekly and calls on travelers to seek justice and leave donations at his small church.

HIGHREACH, FORTRESS OF

Population: 5,256 (almost all Oceander)
Ruler: High Admiral Novar Tellefiri
Government: Military

The Hyperboreans originally constructed this great fortress on the Sinnar Coast to defend against attacks by Ramithi pirates. The fleet of Oceanus has since converted it into their own military harbor and strong point from which to project their naval power across the region.

In addition to the many ships constantly anchored here and their crew complements of sailors and marines, an army of 5,000 Oceander soldiers is constantly kept stationed here and drilled to battle readiness in order to be transported to anywhere needed at a moment's notice.

HIGHSMYTH, CITY OF

Population: 7,827 (3,890 Foerdewaith and Oceander, 1,962 mountain dwarf, 1,075 half-elf, 655 gnome, 245 halfling)
Ruler: Mayor Carlo d'Brocce Alvamo and Master Ironworkers Guildmaster Ivan Gundris
Government: mayor appointed by the governor-general, with high local influence by Ironworkers Guild

Highsmyth is the great ironmongering capital of the Matagost Peninsula. It provided a great deal of iron ore in the days of Hyperborea and Foere and even now serves as the primary foundry for the Empire of Oceanus. Here ironwork of the highest caliber is exported to Pontos Island for use in even more refined manufacturing. A great black fog continually hangs above the city from its hundreds of forge fires, and on days when the wind is still, this miasma sinks to street level and covers the city with its smudge. The result of these black fogs and the soot constantly falling from the many smokestacks stains everything within the city a dismal gray, which the Oceanic mayor cheerfully calls "the new color of gold."

TIRIGOTH, VILLAGE OF

Population: 782 (756 Foerdewaith, 19 gnome, 7 half-elf)
Ruler: Mayor Limper Karl and Sheriff Callawagn
Government: mayor for life, highly corrupt elections

The fishing village of Tirigoth lies on the southern end of the Criehammer Pass through the Matagost Range. It is small and isolated, and tends to its own business, sheltered by the surrounding cliffs as it ignores the rest of the world. It has no interest in the politics of the rest of the peninsula, and so far Oceanus has shown no interest in this tiny burg. A few years ago, the mayor's compatriot Sheriff Callawagn stumbled upon a small dwarven mining claim in the nearby mountains that contained a promising gold vein. Together they murdered a villager and framed the dwarven miners. The miners were arrested and executed, which gave the mayor and sheriff sole control over the mine to be worked by their gnomish crew. But now the mayor fears dwarven reprisals and has set a ban on dwarves within Tirigoth. It remains to be seen if the mountain dwarves of the Matagost Range realize the crime that has been perpetrated and seek vengeance.

OLD BURGUNDIA

Capital: none
Notable Settlements: Emryl, Terrin Keld, Tyr
Ruler: none
Government: anarchy (Wildlands), feudalism (settlements)
Population: 33,800 (13,350 Foerdewaith, 11,200 Erskaelosi, 7,100 mountain dwarf, 1,300 half-elf, 450 half-orc, 400 other)
Monstrous: dire animals, ghouls, leucrotta, boggards, megafauna, perytons (Wildlands); dire animals, orogs, ogres, crag giants, hill giants, stone giants, wyverns, dracolisks, frost giants, cave giants, rocs, cloud giants, dragons (Forlorn Mountains)
Languages: Common, Erskin, Dwarven
Religion: Bowbe, Gromm, Dwerfater
Resources: furs, plunder, ivory, quarry stone, cinnamon
Technology Level: Dark Ages

Once the richest of the Sundered Kingdoms, Burgundia stood out as a shining example of prosperity and sophistication. From the much-lauded capital of Trevi, with its marble buildings, silvery fountains, and vaunted walls, the kings of Burgundia enjoyed great reputation among monarchs throughout Akados. The kingdom's finely crafted furniture and unique silver-veined marble were found among the richest across the known world, and even today antique furnishings of Burgundia remain the prized pieces in palace collections from Castorhage to Menefet.

The great city of Trevi was besieged twice, once for five years against the Foerdewaith armies of Matagost when the city stood firm, and once for three years against the armies of Oceanus. In the second case, the king of Burgundia was killed in battle in Southvale and his young son Marteir was forced to take the throne. Between the young king's inexperience and the Oceanders' siege engines, the city fell. The Oceanders laid waste to the countryside from Trevi to Parthos and left behind a decimated population and destroyed infrastructure. While many survivors emigrated elsewhere, some few remained behind, though the kingdom never recovered as anything more than a handful of independent towns.

EMRYL, TOWN OF

Population: 1,166 (1,011 Foerdewaith, 105 mountain dwarf, 50 other)
Ruler: Lord Ergimot Culruh
Government: hereditary lordship

The town of Emryl sits astride the Southvale Causeway just north of the Forlorn foothills on the road to Weatherall in the Duchy of Southvale. Emryl prospers off the trade on this road, and the local lord, Ergimot Culruh, lives well and has the luxury to grow cassia trees from which to export the famed Burgundian cinnamon of old.

TERRIN KELD, TOWN OF

Population: 3,286 (2,645 Foerdewaith, 328 half-elf, 213 mountain dwarf, 100 other)
Ruler: Lord Caraway of Dunish
Government: hereditary lordship

Ruled by a lord claiming to be hereditary nobility, Terrin Keld is a trade town that serves the overland route from Southvale to points north and west. Grown much since the fall of Burgundia, it took in many refugees and is now walled with an earthen embankment and a wooden palisade. Four gates, each flanked by two wooden towers and topped by a fighting platform, open in its four walls, and torches are kept lit atop these throughout the night to provide light for the crossbowmen who constantly man them. The Wildlands are extremely dangerous at night, and Terrin Keld is one of the few spots of civilization in the area. Lord Caraway rules from nearby Dunish Keep and tasks his men-at-arms with patrolling the surrounding roads for both creatures from the wilds and armed parties coming from Lowport. He fears an attack someday from Baljulias the Great, the tyrant of Lowport, and has several paid informants in that town to alert him of any news.

TREVI, RUINS OF

Once a beautiful city to behold with shining walls of white studded with domed towers, gates of silver-chased Libynosi blackwood, and an acropolis built in the indigenous silver-veined marble, Trevi is now a crumbled shadow of its former glory. The walls are little more than rubble piles where the ashlar facing stones were taken by the invaders, and its famous gates now lie in twisted shattered ruin from the impact of Oceanic catapult stones, the silver chasing long since stripped away by the invaders. The ruins have been picked over and looted for the last 175 years, and occasional pack trains still come to salvage marble from the palaces on the acropolis for trade. Lately, however, scavenging parties from Terrin Keld and Emryl have failed to return. A fiendish ogre mage warlord calling herself the Beautiful Contessa has assumed control of the city and gathered the dregs of the countryside to her banner. She plants the heads of intruders and those who displease her atop pikes outside the ruined gates. Recently, one of the princess of Tyr's favored consorts was among those lost, and a band of devoted Erskaelosi warriors from that city calling themselves the Blade of Vengeance are planning an attack on this upstart's new kingdom.

TYR, CITY OF

Population: 7,362 (6,221 Erskaelosi, 731 mountain dwarf, 213 half-orc, 197 other)
Ruler: Bridthotina, Princess of Tyr
Government: monarchy (principality)

The Erskaelosi city of Tyr stands on the plains just to the north of the Giantlands like a taunt. It has weathered more attacks from giants and their kin than probably any other place on Lloegyr, yet endured despite the constant danger. Its walls are low earthen mounds studded with sharpened stakes designed to withstand pounding from hurled boulders and to hinder the ability of giants to simply walk over them. The area in front of and behind the mounds are riddled with narrow trenches from which defenders can take cover and then strike at attackers with longspears when they try to cross. The buildings of Tyr are a combination of hide tents and awnings and wooden structures. The Erskaelosi know that structures are easily susceptible to the attacks of giants and build them so they can be easily reconstructed. The only stone structures in the city are the dark basalt construction of the great arena where gladiatorial tournaments and executions of captured giants occur, and the Heartsflame Palace where the princess of Tyr dwells. Even these bear the scars of giant attacks, though neither has ever fallen.

RAMTHION ISLAND

Capital: none (formerly Port Clar)
Notable Settlements: Farketh Knowe, Fort Kellstyn, Lambert Landing, Port Clar, Salt Tide, Tentbrean, The Damerhold
Ruler: His Excellency the Governor-General Altorius d'Ambrago d'Mediceno Thyriskos (lowlands); His Grace the Dux Bellorum, Ombarto Trullian (mountains)
Government: military dictatorship (lowlands), feudalism (mountains)
Population: 52,300 (32,800 Ramithi, 17,000 Oceander, 2,000 half-elf, 500 gnome)
Monstrous: blood hawks, spriggans, caterwauls, banshees, rift drakes, vampires (Caterwaul Mountains); crab swarms, bunyips, giant crabs, sahuagin (coastline); giant frogs, oozes, gnolls, gallows trees, zombies, vampires, black dragons (Southfell Glades)
Languages: Gasquen (Ramithi), Common (Oceander)
Religion: Telonius and Ythral (Ramithi), Quell, Mithras, Sefagreth, Thyr, Muir and the Mother (Oceander), Dagon (Oceander, rumored)
Resources: chalk, cloth, fishing, flax, foodstuffs, grain, pottery, wool
Currency: Oceander, barter, hyperborean currency
Technology Level: Dark Ages

Originally an island of small fishing villages and laconic river folk, Ramthion Island came to be known for its cash crop of sugarcane and its infamous pirate clans. With much of the island to the north and south covered by swamplands and mountains in the west, most of the towns developed along the coasts or on the banks of the island's major river. Bargemen poling their great rafts up and down the shallow Caney River were a common sight in times of peace. Unfortunately, times of peace are often few and far between as invasions have disrupted the populace many times in the past. The coming and eventual ouster of the Heldring created the impetus for the many disparate villages to identify themselves as a unified people known as the Ramithi. And it is this Ramithi unity that provokes the people of the island to continue to resist the current invasion of the Kingdom of Oceanus.

HISTORY AND PEOPLE

Ramthion Island was one of the first conquests by the Hyperboreans when they arrived around –109 I.R. The pugnacious Ramithi pirates of the Sea Dagger put up a spirited fight, but the Hyperboreans prevailed and quickly established several fortresses and naval bases, including the coastal city of Port Clar.

With a new Hyperborean governor and Hyperborean taxes to pay, the Ramithi chafed under their new rulers' thumb and proved troublesome subjects. Ramthion proved to be an onerous and sometimes terrifying place for the Hyperboreans as well, for (as other would-be conquerors such as the Oceanders would find out in their time) the island was thick with ancient and mysterious ruins, bloody and disturbing folktales, rumors of hauntings and monsters, as well as numerous sightings of unusual, unknown, and frightening creatures that unnerved even the experienced Hyperborean legionnaires. Unsurprisingly, Ramthion began to gain a reputation for being haunted, cursed, and worse. Service on Ramthion was considered especially undesirable and often used as punishment. Consequently, the island quickly fell to lawlessness as lax Hyperborean administration allowed extensive banditry and piracy. Ramithi pirates continued to operate from all along the Sea Dagger, raiding shipping as far north as Legions Bay and as far south and west as the Mouth of Akados despite the Hyperboreans' best efforts to stamp them out. Despite the Hyperboreans' lack of overall success, the old clans of the Ramithi began a steady decline, though they continued to be a thorn in their conquerors' side.

The disasters that began with the great polar shift in 2491 I.R. culminated five years later in the destruction of the Tower of Oerson and the wildfires that swept across the Plains of Suilley and the Matagost Forest, leading to a massive loss of life and population shifts. Refugees fled across the Dardanal Strait to Ramthion where the pirates welcomed them and helped maintain order in the face of the Hyperborean collapse a few years later. It seemed that the Ramithi once more had control of their own lands and destinies. By this time, only a few of the island's original clans remained, however, still practicing their piratical ways in the marshlands of the Sea Dagger. The refugees settled in the lowlands of the rest of the island, and for a while there was peace.

Unfortunately, Ramthion's respite did not last long, for in 2517 I.R. the bloodthirsty Heldring invaded, and the luckless islanders traded one oppressor for another. Heldring dominance was secured with the construction of the fortress of Farketh Knowe in 2523 I.R. The old Hyperborean fortress at Kellstyn was also expanded and renovated. It seemed as if the Heldring were planning on a long stay.

For nearly 300 years the islanders suffered under the Heldring yoke, and like the Hyperboreans before them, the occupiers came to fear the island and its mysterious inhabitants. Disappearances, strange bouts of madness and the appearance of many strange creatures plagued the Heldring, and the island's inhabitants proved even more troublesome than they had been with their previous conquerors. The common folk of the island, descended from various Hyperborean and Foerdewaith ancestors, declared common cause with the remaining Sea Dagger clans to forge a new Ramithi identity in the face of outside threats.

The pirate clans called for open rebellion in 2803 I.R., and the people responded, displacing the Heldring and smashing the fortress of Farketh Knowe. Despite their desire for freedom and independence, many wiser Ramithi realized that the realm would be unable to survive on its own, so the victorious islanders appealed to the overking in Courghais for admission to the kingdom of Foere. In 2805 I.R., the island was made an official Foerdewaith province.

Foere's administration was by far the least onerous yet. The populace was taxed lightly and generally left to their own devices by a sensible and experienced Foerdewaith governor. Life on the island continued at its old, leisurely pace, though pirates continued to operate out of their secret ports and friendly settlements along the Sea Dagger. In general, these corsairs steered clear of Foerdewaith vessels, and the governors largely turned a blind eye to their exploits. The Ramithi felt confident enough in their allegiance to Foere that in 3312 I.R. they rejected demands for fealty from the new kingdom of Oceanus, and resisted Oceander pressure for a century and a half.

New mysteries and legends were added to the island's already significant collection in 3422 I.R. when the entire town of Greenpool was devoured by an inexplicable combination of storm, wave, and earthquake. The Ramithi themselves heard the news, clutched their holy symbols and lucky talismans tightly, and prayed that the Doom of Greenpool would not take them. To this day, the region is considered cursed and is avoided by the (rightly) superstitious Ramithi.

Finally, in 3478 I.R., the Kingdom of Oceanus — weary after years of unrestricted Ramithi piracy with the winking approval of the Foerdewaith governor — launched a massive invasion of Ramthion. The island's newest conquerors stormed ashore and conquered much of the lowlands and constructed the fearsome fortress known as the Damerhold.

The Ramithi once more resisted, and the rebels gathered in the ruins of Farketh Knowe in 3483 I.R. and appointed a *dux bellorum* (war duke) to lead their armies against the Oceanders. The following year, the Oceanders sent an army into the Caterwaul Mountains to exterminate the rebels, but the operation ended in disaster with the Oceanders retreating to the lowlands and building a new stronghold at the site of Fort Kellstyn.

The Ramithi proved unable to follow up on their initial success, though they remained free in their strongholds in the Caterwaul Mountains. The Oceanders control the lowlands and use Port Clar as a major naval base and trading hub for their vast maritime empire, and their inroads into the island are maintained through their possession of the fortresses of the Damerhold and Fort Kellstyn. But so far, the armies of Oceanus have been unable to dislodge the Ramithi resistance from its mountainous foothold. An uneasy game of waiting and looking for opportunities to strike at the enemy has turned their war of invasion into a slow-burning pressure cooker.

Like the Hyperboreans and Heldring before them, the Oceanders have also found that the Ramithi rebels are not their only problem, for with their occupation they have discovered the island's rich history of folk tales and legends regarding disappearances and bogeymen that come in the night. They are discovering that at least some of these tales appear to have a basis in reality, as watchmen disappear from their posts and entire patrols are lost in the dark, leaving no clue as to the culprits or means. Governor-General Thyriskos believes that Ramithi partisans are to blame, but his closest advisor, the wizard Dom Alihsero d'Coba, fears something much older and more sinister is at work, something that even the local population fears.

Today's islanders count Foerdewaith and Ramithi ancestry but collectively consider themselves to be Ramithi. They remain fiercely independent, superstitious, and distrustful of outsiders. Strangers are usually not welcome in their villages, though most provide grudging hospitality so long as newcomers are not associated with the Oceanders. Most Ramithi still speak the old Gasquen tongue and feign ignorance of more common languages, though this is often a ruse by islanders to listen in on strangers' conversations.

Religion

While the Oceanders publicly follow more traditional deities such as the Mother, Thyr, and Muir, their worship of Dagon is an all but open secret on Ramthion. Temples to Telonius and Ythral have been hastily converted to Oceander use, with public services during the day and dark Dagonic rites at night. Worship of the dark sea-god has grown widespread among the Oceanders as a defense against the supposed forces that the Ramithi have mustered against their invaders.

The Ramithi have always worshipped their own gods — ancient deities that date from well before the arrival of even the Hyperboreans. Gods that, in fact, may be among the oldest still worshipped on Akados, for some religious scholars associate Telonius, Goddess of Creation, and Ythral, God of Destruction, with the gods of good who allied with the early Hyperborean deities during the Gods' War over 15,000 years ago. Shrines and sacred stones with extremely ancient symbols and indecipherable carvings are scattered across the island, and are often sites of supernatural activity — strange lights, extradimensional phenomena, strange creatures, and the like. Some very old temples and worship sites in caverns have literally been in use for millennia.

Telonius and Ythral represent the two poles of nature — one creative and one destructive — and together form a whole. Both priests and druids worship these deities, and lately have been directing the full force of their energies against the Oceanders, summoning ancient entities of chaos and madness to plague and distract the enemy. For their part, the Oceanders call the Ramithi priests "witches" and "warlocks" and ascribe all manner of wicked traits to them.

Trade and Commerce

As an official part of the Oceanders' kingdom, Ramthion serves primarily as a colony and source of goods, as well as providing bases for Oceanus' powerful navy. The common folk of Ramthion have always engaged in subsistence agriculture, producing very little beyond what is needed for survival, so the Oceanders' confiscation of crops and livestock has caused considerable suffering and deprivation.

The island once derived significant income from piracy, especially during its years as a Foerdewaith province when the governor allowed Ramithi corsairs to prey on other kingdoms' shipping with little or no risk of punishment. This situation in fact led to the Oceander conquest, for after generations of Foere-approved piracy, the kingdom's patience simply ran out.

Today, there is little trade in or out of Ramithi. The Oceanders import the goods they need to keep their occupation running and require the use of Oceander currency. The Ramithi in their mountain fastnesses, and those who are not directly under Oceander control, utilize barter or trade using a variety of coins from many lands, including many very old Hyperborean coins that have been in circulation for millennia.

Loyalties and Diplomacy

Ramthion is technically still a province of Foere, but the Oceander conquest changed that — most likely permanently given the decline of the Foerdewaith. As the struggle for control of Ramthion continues, the rebels have reached out to their old kingdom, as well as to other states such as Suilley, for assistance, but so far nothing has been forthcoming. The Ramithi remain a fiercely independent and troublesome people, but their isolation and the ongoing war makes outside relations difficult.

Government

The Ramithi have always lived in a sort of benign anarchy, with local communities governing themselves with an eye toward the general welfare, peace, and cooperation among islanders. The old Ramithi, who made their way as corsairs, were a surprisingly egalitarian society that nevertheless turned authority over to "captains" and "chieftains" in times of crisis. This model is followed when the Ramithi unite to face enemies such as the Heldring or the Oceanders — a single commander known as a *dux bellorum* (war duke) is chosen to lead all Ramithi forces. This war duke has great authority over all Ramithi and has absolute command on the battlefield, yet are always expected to act with the best interest of the people foremost.

The Oceanders serve under Governor-General Altorius d'Ambrago d'Mediceno Thyriskos, an especially prominent nobleman who hopes to quell the rebellion and thus earn greater influence in the empire. There are rumors that Altorius seeks to take the throne himself when the current ruler dies. He has instituted a two-pronged approach to the rebels, giving aid and support to lowland communities with one hand while launching a furious scorched-earth campaign against the Ramithi in the mountains. Oceander troops, backed by mercenaries, have begun to raid and torch Ramithi villages in an effort to deprive the rebels of their bases of operations. The campaign is bearing fruit, as the Ramithi rebels have retreated deeper into the mountains, but the Oceanders' have proved unable to dislodge them and remain stalled in the foothills.

Military

Two Oceander legions — the 15th and 22nd — serve on Ramthion, along with numerous mercenary regiments of various levels of quality recruited from all across Akados. Service on Ramthion is considered one of the most dangerous and onerous of duties, and the occupiers' morale is mercurial. The Oceanders generally believe that they are carrying out a sacred duty to their empire, while at the same time dreading the ghosts and bogeymen of Ramithi legend. When an Oceander patrol disappears or a lone sentry is found savaged by fearsome claws, their dread of the assignment grows. Ramithi ports are blockaded by the powerful Oceander navy, but smugglers constantly test the barriers, surreptitiously delivering food, supplies, and weapons to the rebels.

The Ramithi are organized differently in independent companies and regiments named for their region, their commander, or for various legendary creatures. These rough-and-ready units vary in size from a few dozen up to several hundred and can change in number and composition freely. The Ramithi tend to fight a guerrilla war, with few major full-scale engagements. Most battles in the mountains consist of raids, feints, or ambushes that usually end quickly with the Ramithi disappearing and the Oceanders left to count their dead. Today, 2,000 warriors form the core of *Dux Bellorum* Ombarto Trullian's forces based in the restored fortress at Farketh Knowe, with several thousand irregulars scattered throughout the rest of the island. Despite their retreat from the foothills, the Ramithi continue to gather strength, looking ahead to the day that they can all rise up and drive out the Oceanders, as they did the Heldring and the Hyperboreans before them.

Once skilled pirates, the Ramithi have little remaining in the way of naval assets, preferring instead to smuggle and raid with small, fast boats or mercenary naval units. As with land combat, Ramithi sailors shun set-piece naval battles and prefer to fight, inflict damage, and flee to hidden harbors or coastal villages.

MAJOR THREATS

Ramthion Island is an occupied land, conquered and colonized by the forces of the Empire of Oceanus. The ongoing resistance to the occupation represents the greatest threat to Ramthion's peace and stability, and some outside powers have taken advantage of the conflict to bleed and destabilize the empire. Smugglers regularly run the Oceander blockade to bring supplies and weapons from Foere and Suilley, as both powers find it in their interest to keep the Oceanders occupied and pinned down in Ramthion.

WILDERNESS AND ADVENTURES

Ramthion Island is a wild and rugged place. Its lowland regions from the Southfell Glades to the marshy areas of the Sea Dagger are dotted with small villages and farms with thatch-roofed stone huts, most with a population of a few dozen. Oceander legionnaires based at Fort Kellstyn and the Damerhold keep watch on main roads, river crossings, and strategic villages, but are naturally unable to be everywhere at once, which leaves the vast stretches between settlements unoccupied and unpatrolled.

These regions are mostly bleak moorland interrupted here and there by small stands of forest, crossed occasionally by cold, fast-moving streams. The island's two main rivers are the Caney, whose origin lies high in the Caterwaul Mountains, and the Lesser Reach, which flows from the stony-shored Lake Wealand. Largely unpopulated, the region around the lake is a source of many legends, and it is said that at least one and possibly more dragons or other fearsome serpents dwell in its chill depths, and can sometimes be glimpsed through the morning and evening fogs.

The barrows, cairns, and old places of worship are avoided by the Oceanders due to the dark and often entirely plausible legends associated with them. The spirits, undead, and dark fey creatures who inhabit their environs seem to be especially aggressive toward outsiders, and more than one patrol has vanished into the woods, dales, or moors never to be seen again.

Other beasts — shadowy, red-eyed, creeping through the darkness and haunting wild places — are said to dwell in the wild lands. Locals claim to know the charms and chants that ward off these mysterious creatures, but they keep these invocations and rituals secret, especially from the Oceanders.

Adventurers of only the hardiest and most daring (or foolhardy) sort are drawn to Ramthion Island to seek artifacts and treasures said to be hidden in old Hyperborean (or earlier) ruins. These ventures are inevitably fraught with peril, for both the occupying Oceanders and rebellious Ramithi dislike outsiders intruding: the Oceanders for disrupting the island and possibly associating with rebels; the Ramithi for the violation of their sacred places. From time to time, these adventurers do find their fortune, but they often find other things as well, including curses, disease, or the same ferociously protective unknown creatures that prey on the fearful Oceanders.

THE DAMERHOLD (FORTRESS)

Population: 5,260 (Oceander)
Ruler: Colonel-Commandant Obargria d'Havlina Chyri
Government: military

This massive stone-walled fortress serves as the strongpoint of Oceander power on Ramthion Island. Its construction was key to the pacification of the lowlands, and after many years it has seen the end of Ramithi resistance centered in the swamps of the Sea Dagger. The citadel's commander, Colonel-Commandant Obargria d'Havlina Chyri, has watched the core of the Oceander war effort shift westward to the vicinity of Fort Kellstyn to deal with rebels in the mountains, and he does not like to see the decrease in his influence upon the island. Unfortunately, since the governor-general likewise resides in the Damerhold and has authority over the commandant, there is little at this time that Chyri can do to directly determine Oceander war policy on the island. With a garrison of 350 heavy cavalry and 4,000 infantry, Lord Chyri awaits only the opportunity to once and for all squash the Ramithi resistance in a decisive battle.

FARKETH KNOWE (FORTRESS)

Population: 3,285 (Ramithi)
Ruler: Dux Bellorum Ombarto Trullian
Government: Military

The great stone fortress of Farketh Knowe was built by the Heldring to control the lowlands of their conquered islands. When the Ramithi pirates led the conquered peoples in rebellion against their Heldring overlords during the waning of the Heldring Expansion, the fortress was overrun and its walls thrown down. Its ruins remained formidable, however, and when the Ramithi refugees created a *dux bellorum* to lead them in their revolt against the Oceanders, that war leader chose the centuries-old ruins to serve as the focal point of their resistance. The walls and towers of Farketh Knowe stand strong once again with repairs continuing on sections that had crumbled and warriors once again filling its halls. Dux Bellorum Ombarto Trullian has gathered 2,000 Ramithi warriors here and continues to put the call out among the mountain refugee towns. His plan now is to continue a guerrilla campaign through the mountains until he can gather sufficient forces and determine the right location for a decisive battle against the invaders.

FORT KELLSTYN

Population: 950 (Oceander)
Ruler: Captain Garos d'Lamaya
Government: military

This small fort only recently sprang up within the last 30 years. After the lowlands were subjugated from the fastness at the Damerhold, the Oceanders realized that they needed a bastion against incursions from the Ramithi forces gathering in the mountains. The wooden palisade of the fort is augmented by stone towers that are being constructed at each of its corners, and the roof of the keep within has been replaced with tile to guard against the fire arrows of the rebels. The garrison is under the authority of Captain Garos d'Lamaya, who commands an Oceander force of 25 light cavalry and 267 infantry. In addition, another 100 Ramithi auxiliary infantry conscripted from among the conquered lowlanders live in a tent town outside the walls of the fort and serve to reinforce its troops when needed.

GREENPOOL, RUINS OF

Population: 0

The village of Greenpool stood for centuries on the rocky cliffs overlooking the ocean at the southernmost tip of Ramthion Island. Not exceedingly prosperous, it nevertheless made a fair trade on its local saltworks and fishing until 3422 I.R. In one night, the waves rose and crashed over the cliffs, though no storm blew them; the earth cracked and opened, though no earthquake shook them; and men fell dead where they stood, though no hand slew them. An unknown doom had come to Greenpool, and when dawn rose red over the town the next morning, not a living soul remained. Over the years, the town has been avoided as cursed, and what few buildings remain have fallen into ruins. The only thing that remains to easily identify the town is the green tidal pool from which it took its name. That strangely deep pond still exists, its waters occasionally rippling even when no wind touches its surface.

Lambert Landing, Town of

Population: 573 (mostly Oceander)
Ruler: Lord-Mayor Antoin Lambert VI
Government: hereditary mayor influenced by church leaders of Thyr and Kamien

This settlement lies where the muddy waters of the Lesser Reach branch off from the Caney River and head toward the mires of the Southfell Glades. Despite its small size, this town boasts a curtain wall and two stone churches, one to Thyr and one to Kamien, Goddess of Rivers, though none of these constructions is in particularly good repair. At one time, the town served as the central shipping point of the vast Toussant sugarcane empire, though it has fallen on hard times since the disappearance of that family a century ago. Now it exists by minor trade with river traffic to the north, as well as the shipment of fresh frog legs for the tables of the Oceanders in Port Clar (considered a rare delicacy among the new Oceander elite). There is also a significant trade in fools looking to enter the glades for hunting — or more likely, to find the lost treasures of Toussant House. Currently, only about half of this latter group ever return, and those who do have all returned emptyhanded.

Port Clar, City of

Population: 8,673 (almost all Oceander)
Ruler: mayor appointed by Governor-General
Government: dictatorship

Formerly a large trade town that sprang up around a Hyperborean fortress, Port Clar has seen a sudden expansion to a small city since it serves as the primary port of call for the Empire of Oceanus on Ramthion Island. The people still go about their business as normal, but now they make way for constant supply trains and columns of troops marching to or from the fortresses built farther inland. A small Oceanic naval base has been established with a fleet of five ships, and a contingent of 1,500 Oceander marines are likewise stationed in town for rapid deployment inland or upon the sea as necessary. The port has been opened to a greater expansion of contact due to the Oceander occupation, but the folk remain insular and tight-knit among themselves, waiting for the day when the occupiers leave.

Salt Tide, Village of

Population: 321 (270 Ramithi, 51 Oceander)
Ruler: Village Headman Natch Prumble
Government: village headman appointed by office of the governor-general to enforce absolute rule

The village of Salt Tide consists of a half-dozen families, all of whom work in the extensive saltworks that lie along the shore. Many other saltworks are located along the coasts and in the swamps of Ramthion Island, but Salt Tide is renowned for producing the whitest and most uniform crystals. The villagers of Salt Tide were long considered to be tenants of the principal clan-chief of the Ramithi, but they are now in the employ of the island's Oceander governor-general. They make a pittance for their backbreaking labor, but consider one tyrannical lord much like another, and go about their business in isolation save for the weekly ships that arrive to pick up loads of salt.

Tentbrean, Village of

Population: 626 (Ramithi)
Ruler: Savilara Barthee
Government: elected "village elder," not necessarily old

Tentbrean is a large village on the eastern coast of Ramthion Island. For some reason, merfolk find the people of Tentbrean to smell unusually trustworthy, and the village does a brisk trade with Port Clar in unusual deep-water shells and underwater salvage.

Duchy of Southvale

Capital: Penmorgh
Notable Settlements: Border Keep, Bradfield, Guildford, Southreach, Stonebridge, Weatherell, Wellesley
Ruler: The Honorable Lem Mastlan, Mayor of Penmorgh; Guildmaster Berezon of the Merchant Guild of Penmorgh; Deputy-Governor Alvoria d'Alvoros (of Oceanus), the self-styled "Duke" of Southvale
Government: oligarchy
Population: 165,000 (67,500 Foerdewaith, 51,000 Heldring, 26,500 mountain dwarf, 8,300 halfling, 5,000 half-elf, 3,700 high elf, 2,200 Erskaelosi, 800 other)
Monstrous: dire animals, orogs, ogres, giants, wyverns, dracolisks, rocs, dragons (mountains); kobolds, dire bears, goblins, fey, quickwoods, bugbears, undead, dracolisks, treants, behirs, demons, dragon horses (woodlands); goblins, buckawns, fey (countryside); skum, scrags (coastline); annis hags, medusas, dracolisks, serpentfolk, hydras (Black Marsh)
Languages: Common, Helvaenic, Dwarven, Halfling, Elven
Religion: Muir, Thyr, Freya, Herne
Resources: ambergris, chalk, fishing, foodstuffs, livestock, rare woods, shipbuilding, shipbuilding supplies, spirits, timber, trade hub, whale oil, wool
Currency: Southvale
Technology Level: High Middle Ages or Medieval (countryside), Renaissance (city of Penmorgh)

The Duchy of Southvale has existed in some form or fashion for more than 1,500 years since the city-state of Penmorome was established by Perigorn the Conqueror in 1930 I.R. Sheltered by the nearby Forlorn Mountains, the climate of the vale is milder with more rainfall than that of the rest of the Sundered Kingdoms. As a result, as long as there has been a fortification on the site of Penmorgh, the surrounding lands have been jealously guarded.

History and People

The city of Penmorome was established in the later days of the Hyperborean empire, well after the end of the Pax Hyperborea. Located near a tangled remnant of the old Akadonian Forest, the new settlement was from its founding subject to raids by goblins, hostile fey, and even vengeful treants. Despite the construction of massive walls about the city, the growth of Penmorome was severely constrained by the continual conflict from the Fae Copse. Eventually, occasional raids and punitive expeditions grew into open warfare. By 1943 I.R., the citizens of Penmorome had had enough and, with the assistance of soldiers from Parthos, razed the surrounding forests with fire and iron axe in a terrible campaign known today as the Great Conflagration. The evil treants and other fey were driven out, forced to flee to the Fae Copse and Black Wood.

With the threat from the forest eliminated, more Hyperboreans moved into Southvale and established more settlements, farms, and castles, finally establishing the Duchy of Southvale in 2002 I.R. with Penmorome as its capital.

The end of Hyperborean authority in the west following the destruction of the Tower of Oerson was a signal to opportunists and empire builders. In 2517 I.R., the land-hungry Heldring landed in Southvale and swept across the duchy and put Hyperborean towns to the torch. Penmorome's stout walls resisted the Heldring's most ferocious assaults, however, and Duchess Irylia declared the Edict of Sealing that barred entry to all foreigners. Soon, Southvale was effectively split. Hyperboreans retained control of the city, while the Heldring held the countryside.

The Heldring raiders found the forested lands of Southvale — which were spared the worst of changing climate and fire ravages — to be rich and fertile. They built settlements of their own among the ruins, including the cities of Wellesley, Weatherell, Freeport, North Bay, Penn, and Pike Point. Soon the surviving inhabitants of Southvale outside of Penmorome were living in these new Heldring settlements, intermarrying and assimilating with them.

The dominance of the Heldring began to break when the Polemarch Daan defeated the Heldring at the Battle of Agedium and began his legendary march to overthrow the corrupted Hyperborean Court at Tircople. Then in 2762 I.R., Overking Macobert, marching along the Sinnar Coast and bringing lands within his new Kingdom of Foere, approached Penmorome in force by land and by sea. The Heldring settlements provided little resistance as a few warbands were swept away and the rest quickly learned to lay down their arms at the king's approach. As Macobert's siege lines were put into place around Penmorome, the city's gates suddenly opened with a fanfare of trumpets. Out of the gates marched the primus of Penmorome and his entire family, complete with attendants, courtiers, and entertainers. Given leave to approach the great king's tent, the primus laid the keys of the city and a wreath of golden laurels as Macobert's feet and swore fealty to him on the spot.

Overking Macobert raised the primus to his feet. He said that Penmorome had stood in opposition to his rightful rule, but Penmorome stood no more. He said that before him he saw only the city of Penmorgh. He named the primus as magnate of Penmorgh and placed the entire Province of Southvale in his hands to rule with justice in the king's name.

Membership as a state within the Kingdom of Foere brought new prosperity and trade to Southvale. Centuries of relative peace passed, and dwarves from the fabled mines of Hazad-Burgh in the Forlorn Mountains discovered gold and silver in Southvale. With the permission of the magnate of Penmorgh, the dwarven city of Durandel was founded. Soon, precious metals flowed across the Blackflow River and out from the wharves of Penmorgh, bringing evermore riches to the guilds of that city. However, with the death of Overking Oessum VIII on the Fourth Great Crusade a mere century later, the beginnings of cracks in the provinces' foundations began to appear. In 3213 I.R., the Foerdewaith Wars of Succession began. Within a decade, Ramthion Island, Pontos Island, Burgundia, and Suilley all declared their independence from the Court in Courghais.

The Province of Southvale, secure in its out-of-the-way corner, watched the chaos engulfing its neighbors with great trepidation. But the walls of Penmorgh remained manned by trained troops and the local militias were raised in the town, so the vale felt ready for the approach of any external threat. It was not ready for a threat from within when one of the province's local barons, Tarler Traverthal, led a coup within the city and assassinated the magnate of Penmorgh. Traverthal gained the support of the guilds and, therefore, had the support of the local garrison. The Guild Council quickly raised Traverthal to the position of duke of Southvale and allied itself with Burgundia.

In response to this new uprising, the magnate of Oestre deployed the troops he brought to Highreach and, within a few months, a new army loyal to Foere landed south of Wellesley and marched on Penmorgh. The army outnumbered the forces holding Penmorgh, but the magnate of Oestre had not reckoned on the numbers and training of the peasants who arose from the countryside to harass them nor the heavy infantry provided by the dwarves of Durandel. The army of Matagost soon found itself outnumbered and caught in unfavorable terrain. The army was routed and forced to retreat to the coast to be picked up by their ships.

With Matagost reeling from its sudden defeat, Duke Tarler took the initiative and marched his now-blooded army up the Southvale Causeway toward Trevi. These reinforcements, combined with the surrounding army of Burgundia, broke the siege of Trevi and routed the Matagost host.

Southvale, little bloodied by the worst of the fighting, settled into something close to prosperity as the guilds jockeyed for power and control of trade in and out of Penmorgh. However, in the time of Duke Tarler's son, trouble came to Southvale. The giant tribes of the Giantlands in the neighboring Forlorn Mountains noticed the violence going on among the puny humans of the plains. But other than occasional raids into southern Burgundia where they encountered companies of heavily armed soldiers as often as they encountered spoils for the taking, they did little to get involved. With normalcy returning to Southvale, they now saw a land of accumulating riches that did not have nearly the numbers of armed troops as nearby Burgundia. So on one moonless night in the fall of 3306 I.R., a howling horde of hill giants led by their larger cousins stormed down from the mountains in western Southvale.

A call for help immediately went forth from Penmorgh to Trevi. However, the guilds of Penmorgh — in their unending loggerheads over primacy within Southvale — had recently backed a measure to undermine the Guild of Ironmongers, which had signed a lucrative agreement with the Royal House of Burgundia. The move cost the Burgundian king a great deal of money when his investment fell through and soured relations between him and Penmorgh. When King Guillerm received word of the attack on Southvale, he rashly ignored his court advisors and instead had his keeper of accounts tally the financial losses suffered as a result of the guilds of Penmorgh. He then estimated the number of days that a giant raid could ravage Southvale before Penmorgh suffered the same economic loss. When that number of days expired, King Guillerm the Petit (as he became known) gathered his army and marched on Southvale. But he was already too late.

The invading giants hit Southvale hard, ransacking many towns on its forested western border. The giants continued pushing forward as the militias and army were unable to get organized. They finally formed a defensive line at Guildford that held. A stalemate ensued for several days as the giants probed for weaknesses along the Guildford front as they continued ravaging the countryside they had already crossed. Things looked bleak for the defenders of the vale until a new army entered the field.

The gates of Durandel opened, and a dwarven host marched to war for the first time since the dwarven city's location, overlooked them as defenders of Southvale. The giants, unaware of the dwarven city's location, overlooked them as defenders of Southvale. When the dwarven army slashed into the rear flank of their hated enemy, the giants held only moments before breaking in a panic. Hundreds of giants fell in the space of a few hours, and hundreds more fled westward, back to the mountains. But on the field of battle, the duke of Southvale lay dead. When the army of Burgundia marched in a few weeks later, they found the giant threat averted and the battle-scarred populace turned against them. The guilds of Penmorgh had elected a mayor to oversee the city, and he became the de facto ruler of the entire duchy as a result.

King Guillerm quickly withdrew his forces to Trevi and only beat the messengers bearing news of Southvale's secession from the Kingdom of Burgundia. The outraged king threatened war, but this time cooler heads among his advisors prevailed. The army did not march again, and the Court of Burgundia hoped to normalize relations with Penmorgh through peaceful means in order to once again welcome them into the kingdom. Their hopes of consolidation never came to be. Six years later, Oceander marines captured much of the Matagost Peninsula, and Oceander diplomats were dispatched to the courts of Trevi, Port Clar, and Penmorgh to demand immediate fealty to Maximilian d'Horatius Pontos II of the Kingdom of Oceanus and Emperor of the Oceans Blue. Southvale, seeing a way to gain support against the hated King Guillerm of Burgundia (and with insufficient naval forces to effectively resist anyway), immediately swore fealty.

In 3350 I.R., King Phillipe of Burgundy traveled to Penmorgh on a diplomatic mission. Unfortunately, not all saw the visit of the sovereign of their former kingdom in a positive light, and some folk still remembered what they saw as the betrayal of the Burgundian throne during the giant invasion two generations earlier. It was just such partisans who plotted the assassination of King Phillipe at the aptly named King's Head Inn in Penmorgh. The plot was discovered, and the king escaped with his life and a serious injury that his court clerics healed, but the injury to his soul was not so quickly resolved.

The formerly friendly and outgoing Phillipe withdrew and became increasingly paranoid. Only a year later, the outriders of Weatherell reported a Burgundian army marching on their borders. A call for aid immediately went forth from Penmorgh, and a fleet was dispatched to land at Parthos and assist the defenders of Southvale. The Oceanic fleet successfully took Parthos and pinned the Burgundian king on the causeway between the mountains and Stony Strand. At the same time, an Oceander army marched forth from Oestre. Once again, little more than a century since the last time, Trevi found itself besieged. This time, however, its king was not inside to lead it. Trapped on the causeway, the Burgundian army was defeated at the Battle of Weatherell Moor, and King Phillipe was slain.

Since then, Southvale has been largely blessed with stability and prosperity, though the occasional attack by giants or treants does occur.

In 3392 I.R., a strange Tower of Bone suddenly appeared in the Fae Copse of Southvale and the dwarven city of Durandel was destroyed.

Consisting of a mixed population of old Foerdewaith (principally in Penmorgh) and descendants of Heldring invaders (in the surrounding countryside), Southvale is fairly cosmopolitan and enjoys the benefits of its inclusion in the empire of the Oceanders.

Religion

Foerdewaith-descended Southvalers revere Thyr and Muir, the traditional faiths of their ancestral kingdom. For the most part, the Heldring followed the example of their brethren in the Helcynngae Peninsula and also adopted the Foerdewaith faith, but there are persistent rumors of Heldring cults who still practice the worship of bloodthirsty Hel in the spirit of their savage ancestors.

Trade and Commerce

Conquest by Oceanus has had surprisingly positive effects on the province. Trade with the home empire has grown and, unlike in some other provinces, the Oceanders have made sure to apply only light pressure in the form of low taxes and minimal tariffs on goods.

Southvale has long been home to a wealthy merchant class. Goods such as livestock, rare woods, and timber from the remaining woodlots of the province, fish, and sheep's wool all flow through the ports of Penmorgh and Wellesley, while manufactured goods, metal, ironwork, and textiles are shipped in from the empire. Shipworks at Penmorgh provide repair and construction, and send ships to sea as merchants or in service to the Oceander navy. Wellesley is home to a thriving whaling industry and sends whale oil and ambergris to Oceanus and beyond.

Loyalties and Diplomacy

After a long history of conquest, independence, and assimilation, the Duchy of Southvale seems to have found some stability as a province of the growing kingdom of Oceanus. The inhabitants of the city of Penmorgh, originally Hyperborean but now largely of Foerdewaith extraction, are among the most loyal (or at least the less troublesome) inhabitants, as Oceander gold and goods flow through the docks. The Heldring of Wellesley and Southreach are similarly passé regarding the Oceanders and generally look the other way while enjoying the benefits of the province's status.

In the countryside, the Heldring are, unsurprisingly, less enthusiastic about Oceander dominance. Tax collection in the hinterlands is sometimes an onerous job, as Oceander officials sometimes disappear mysteriously and require armed escorts that further degrade their reputation. The Oceanders often respond harshly to attacks on their officials — arresting and executing the perpetrators, or at times displacing whole villages. The Oceanders have also tried to counteract their bad reputation by building roads, public works, and inns, but this does not seem to have mollified their critics. Dissatisfaction with Oceanus in the countryside has been growing for years and shows no sign of lagging.

Government

The duchy hasn't had a duke since the death of Artimus Traverthal during the giant invasion, and the mayor of Penmorgh has served as the primary decision maker for the entire vale since then. With the emergence of the Merchant Guild in Penmorgh as the true power behind the throne, it is now the guildmaster of this organization who wields the real power, though edicts are still issued in the name of the mayor.

Individual towns elect or appoint their own mayors, but these are all subject to the rulings of Penmorgh. Deputy-Governor Alvoria d'Alvoros of Oceanus, who resides in Penmorgh, has begun to style himself "the duke of Southvale," and he is consulted by Guildmaster Berezon and Mayor Mastlan on all policy decisions involving the region as a whole.

Military

The Oceanders keep a single legion stationed in Penmorgh, as well as a small fleet of warships. So far, though dislike of the Oceanders has grown in the countryside of late, they have seen no need to further reinforce their garrison, and service here is usually considered especially pleasant. The legion's primary occupation is patrolling the roads and keeping villages safe from monsters, bandits, and natural disasters, though from time to time a squad or platoon of warriors is tasked with escorting a tax collector or government official into a hostile area.

Punitive expeditions against local villagers are considered particularly onerous and unpleasant, as most Oceanders are fond of Southvale and consider it to be fully a part of the kingdom despite its essentially colonial status. Elsewhere, the legion has been called to counteract giant raids in the eastern half of the duchy, but so far, their response time has been slow, and most of the raiders have escaped back to the Giantlands.

Major Threats

Though Southvale is stable for now, and the city dwellers enjoy their status as a prosperous Oceander province, the country folk chafe under Oceanus' rule — either openly rebelling or complaining in private. Organized outside threats are few, but the adjacent crags of the Giantlands have always held dire threats to the folk of Southvale, especially those in unprotected villages and farms. The Giant War of 3306 I.R. began when well-organized tribes of hill and stone giants under the command of a powerful fire giant chief came down from the mountains and overwhelmed village militias and stole crops, livestock, and treasure. To the horror of the Southvalers, it seemed that this was no temporary raid; the giants intended to stay and were evicted only with the aid of the dwarves of Durandel. Today, Durandel is gone, and the giants remain in the mountains, and while raids are rare, they appear to be increasing in number and severity. Recently, a major raid interrupted traffic along the Southvale Causeway for several days before order was restored. Some witnesses reported that fire giants are once more leading the attacks. The Oceanders have directed their legion to defend against the attacks, but so far they have been unable to catch the giants in the act. Governor d'Alvoros has begun to contemplate hiring mercenaries or adventurers to counteract the raids.

Wilderness and Adventures

Much of Southvale is settled, and the region around Penmorgh is free of monsters and banditry. Other portions of the country, especially those that border on the Giantlands and the Stony Strand, are subject to attacks and threats from bandits, ogres, harpies, hill giants, and (it is rumored) even dragons and drakes. The Southvalers regularly venture into Stony Strand to harvest chalk and come into conflict with the orc bands dispatched by Baljulias the Great, the Tyrant of Lowport, and often require escort.

Elsewhere in the duchy, legends speak of pre-Hyperborean ruins hidden in the mountains of the Giantlands where it is said treasures from the Age of Kings may be found. Most scholars consider these rumors to be exaggerations and that what ruins exist are simply evidence of the duchy's pre-Hyperborean inhabitants — an alternative that might not be as lucrative for adventurers but which would be extremely valuable to historians and researchers.

The towns along the frontier of the Giantlands are also under threat, with giant activity increasing and the Oceander military so far unable to counteract it. Some town elders have begun to organize militia or have appealed to outsiders to help repel the raiders when they come. This call has been heeded by some adventurers who have engaged in their own counter-raids, attacking giant strongholds and bringing back stolen plunder (though the adventurers are always careful to take out their own cut of the proceeds).

PENMORGH, CITY OF (CAPITAL)

Population: 23,454 (18,529 human, 2111 mountain dwarf, 938
   halfling, 910 high elf, 704 half-orc, 235 half-elf, 27 other)
Ruler: Mayor Lem Mastlan, Guildmaster Gebhardt Berezon,
   Commander of the City Watch Montforte de Guise, Deputy-
   Governor Alvoria d'Alvoros "Duke of Southvale," and Lady Astrid
   Dugganey, a paladin of Muir, Mistress of the Order of Iron
Government: mayor appointed by deputy-governor

Southvale has always existed as one of the richest provinces of whatever
empire it was a part of, and the trade city of Penmorgh at its heart is where the
riches flow to and from. A century ago, the Merchant Guild gained control of,
consumed, or crushed all other guilds in the city to become its single driving
economic force. Known to most simply as "the Guild," the Merchant Guild
pulls the strings on a mercantile empire spanning most of its own continent of
Akados and even onto Libynos. Seen as the first city of Southvale, Penmorgh
has always dominated the rest of the duchy (other than during the Heldring
invasion) even when there has been no sitting duke. As goes the mayor of
Penmorgh, so goes the Duchy of Southvale — and for those in the know, as
goes the Guild, so goes the mayor. Even now as a territory of the Empire of
Oceanus with a new self-styled duke, it is still the Guild of Penmorgh that the
imperial authorities look to for principal local control.

In addition to a healthy city watch, militia, mercenary guild, and a
contingent of imperial Oceanic marines, Penmorgh boasts the headquarters of
a militant holy order dedicated to Muir known as the Order of Iron. This order
of paladins, based out of a stone fortress within the city, is the most militaristic
order of Muir west of the Temple Militant in Alcaldar. They see it as their duty
to bring the faith by sword to where it is needed most and frequently make
incursions into the Giantlands to forestall any threats that might emerge from
there. The Guild, the city, and even the Temple of Muir look askance on these
grim holy warriors, but none doubts their ability or dedication to defend the
city should the giants of the mountains threaten once again.

BORDER KEEP

Population: 2,070
Ruler: Colonel-Commandant Usario d'Sparoza Détienatos
Government: Military

Built following the giant invasion of two centuries ago, the Border Keep
was intended to repel raids by the giants of the Forlorn Mountains. The
giants' natural fear of the eerie forests of western Southvale (the Black
Forest and the Fae Copse) ensured that their primary route of invasion
was through the pass defended by Border Keep. The keep's walls were
built especially thick to withstand the thrown boulders of giants, and
its heavily reinforced roofs had to be replaced after every sortie by the
giants. After Southvale became a part of the empire of Oceanus, the keep
was rebuilt as a star fort with low, thick walls and bastions complete with
glacis to more effectively deflect the heavy missiles of attackers.

Under the command of Colonel-Commandant Usario d'Sparoza
Détienatos of the Order of the Lion and manned by 500 imperial soldiers
of Oceanus, a full town sprang up around the keep and provides support
and services to the garrison. Called Giant Fodder by the keep's troops,
the success of the Border Keep in repelling giant invasions in recent
decades has discouraged further attacks so that the town has never been
razed as most assume would happen in short order. However, it has been
some time since the last giant invasion and the memories of giants tend
to be short, so the next attack could come at any time.

BRADFIELD, CITY OF

Population: 4,223 (4,054 human, 84 mountain dwarf, 43
   halfling, 42 other)
Ruler: Mayor Mikaelah Bastich
Government: mayor appointed by Oceander deputy-governor

Bradfield stands on the Blackflow River where a lucrative toll bridge
spans the waterway. The city's reputation for thievery exceeds that of

even the larger cities of the duchy. But in the past 10 years, its new
captain of the guard, Lars van Leuwan — a retired adventurer and
national hero for his battles against giants in the mountains — brought a
great deal of order back to its streets. The town was almost completely
destroyed during the giant invasion, but ever since has hired extremely
competent mercenaries and experienced warriors to fill out the ranks of
its town guard. Those who visit Bradfield always make a point to stop at
the Red Dragon to sample some of the finest ale in Southvale.

DURANDEL, RUINS OF

Durand Strong-Arm founded the Targ Clan mountain dwarf city of
Durandel in 3190 I.R. after the fall of Hazad-Burgh. It began as an iron
mine but expanded into a full city after rich veins of silver and gold
were discovered. Durandel endured for 202 years and served as a major
participant in events of Southvale during the giant invasion and its war
for independence until the mysterious Tower of Bone appeared on the
surface above it and destroyed the dwarven city. The Tower of Bone's
lower levels broke through into the dwarven city, and the tower's ability
to create unique varieties of undead began a siege on the city from its
own catacombs. The city actually endured for several years after the
tower's initial appearance, though most of its surviving inhabitants fled
in the first few months. It was through the efforts of dwarven heroes such
as Dagfa Durbhis and Branwyr that the city lasted for as long as it did
and allowed as many dwarves to escape to safety, though ultimately they
were unsuccessful and a dwarven city of more than 30,000 inhabitants
was destroyed.

GUILDFORD, CITY OF

Population: 14,245 (9,456 human, 2,801 mountain dwarf, 722
   half-elf, 560 halfling, 493 high elf, 213 other)
Ruler: Mayor Harlan Mizerschmidt and Guild Representative
   Andressa Triff
Government: mayor appointed by Oceander deputy-governor
   (but effectively appointed by the Penmorgh Merchant Guild)

Built on the road connecting Penmorgh with the Southvale Causeway
where it crosses a minor branch of the Blackflow River, Guildford is
the second great trading city of Southvale. Firmly under control of the
Penmorgh Merchant Guild, the guild representative in town commands
more influence than anyone other than the Oceander deputy-governor
when he makes his frequent visits to the imperial hunting lodge kept
there by the Oceanic Court. While the deputy-governor is thoroughly
corrupt, the Merchant Guild actually sends its most valuable honest
representatives to Guildford where they can work in the financial
interests of the Guild without the risk of discovering the Guild's darker
doings. Representative Andressa Triff is a shining star in the Guild for
her financial acumen and incorruptibility, but she has begun to notice
minor discrepancies in some of the Guild's books so her days before she
must be quietly removed may be numbered.

The city walls of Guildford are strong and kept in good repair by a
full company of imperial troops that augment the city guard. But these
walls are scarred and show the tests of battle. It was here that the giant
invasion was finally halted and turned back with the aid of the dwarves
of Durandel in 3306 I.R. Since then, the city has maintained a watchful
eye on doings from the Giantlands that some would say borders on
paranoia. Regardless, Togus van Wellton, the captain of the guard and
a paladin of Muir, vows that should the giants come again, Guildford's
walls and defenders alike will not break.

SOUTHREACH, VILLAGE OF

Population: 960 (912 human, 31 halfling, 17 half-elf)
Ruler: Mayor Parmen Urgeni
Government: elected mayor

A small fishing village at the southern tip of Southvale, this settlement
was once considered the southernmost part of the Foerdewaith Empire.

Now it has little of interest to offer other than occasional sightings of the legendary Moonsilver Beast from the Moonsilver Sea to the south.

STONEBRIDGE, TOWN OF

Population: 1,768 (1,715 human, 35 halfling, 18 mountain dwarf)
Ruler: Mayor Edgar Fritch
Government: mayor appointed by Oceander deputy-governor

Built at the very northern edge of the Black Marsh, the town of Stonebridge sprang up around the great stone span constructed by the dwarves of Durandel to move supplies and goods to and from the humans of Penmorgh. The town has been razed several times by various fires and calamities, but the dwarven stonework of the bridge has withstood every disaster and allowed the town to be rebuilt. With little to offer as the location of a settlement, the tolls from the bridge and the river below it truly are the lifeblood of the town.

WEATHERELL, CITY OF

Population: 3,888 (2,527 human, 715 mountain dwarf, 483 half-elf, 102 high elf, 61 halfling)
Ruler: Inspector General Olthobol d'Charosa
Government: inspector-general appointed by Oceander deputy-governor

Known as the Doorway to Southvale, this Heldring city serves as the first line of defense against all land invasions of the duchy except those from the mountains. It is built as a palisaded fortification that crosses the Southvale Causeway, with the rest of the town built upon an elevated mound that overlooks the surrounding moors before they give way to the foothills between the Forlorn Mountains and the Stony Strand. Any army hoping to march into Southvale from the north must plan on overcoming this strongpoint or cross the marshy fens on either side. A motte and bailey keep raised above the center of town serves as the abode of Inspector General Olthobol d'Charosa, who inspects, issues permits, and taxes all trade caravans entering the duchy.

WELLESLEY, CITY OF

Population: 4,320 (4,121 human, 199 half-elf)
Ruler: Mayor Jorgen Jorgenson
Government: elected mayor

After Guildford, Wellesley is the largest city of Southvale outside Penmorgh. During the time of the Heldring invasion, the Heldring lord Jarl Ragnar kept his hall here atop a knoll overlooking the bay. The remnants of that hall still stand, its beams blackened by centuries of mold and lichen and its thatched roof long since carried away by winter winds. The population of Wellesley remains primarily Heldring to this day, and one walking its streets would not find longships pulled on the shore of the bay at all out of place, though the town boasts a fine set of wharves and the barbarians of yore are primarily fishermen and traders now. The old Heldring spirit still lives on to some extent, though, for offerings are still left on the blót nights to the old gods of the Helcynngae in the ruins of Ragnar's hall.

Notable citizens in Wellesley are Mayor Jorgen Jorgenson, Chief Constable Dryus Felthem, and Soothsayer Mmeld the Aglaecwif.

DISTRICT OF SUNDERLAND

Capital: none
Notable Settlements: Billockburne, Cat's Wife, Coburn, Dimmelhill, Fairbridge, Grollek's Grove, Malthlyn, Soldier Stone
Ruler: local town councils, magistrates, and mayors
Government: varies
Population: 220,000 (172,000 Foerdewaith, 22,000 Oceander [Foerdewaith], 11,000 half-elf, 6,500 halfling, 4,000 mountain dwarf, 2,100 high elf, 1,300 gnome, 1,100 other)

Monstrous: goblins, bat swarms, worgs, giant beetles, bugbears, dire bats, ogres, athachs, mutated creatures (Gundlock Hills); kobolds, orcs, stirges, trolls, hill giants, carrion moths, gray renders, slime crawlers, troglodytes, tsathar (Moon Fog Hills); wolves, blood hawks, lions, dire lions, giant spiders, wolfweres, leucrotta, lycanthropes, ebony horses (plains)
Languages: Common, Elven, Halfling
Religion: Kudrak, Freya, Mithras, Sefagreth, Stryme, Thyr
Resources: foodstuffs, wool, livestock (horses), wine, timber, copper, tin, silver, gems, mithral
Currency: Suilley
Technology Level: Dark Ages

Considered by Courghais to comprise everything between the Trader's Way and the sea, the District of Sunderland proper primarily encompasses the plains and hills between the Gaelon River to the north, Old Burgundia to the south, and the Matagost Peninsula to the east. Hundreds of villages and farmsteads are scattered across the district, most with no more than a few dozen inhabitants and many without even a name. The folk are primarily native Foerdewaith, though the Oceanders have moved in from the Matagost Peninsula and influence much of the northeastern parts of the district, primarily along the Soldier's Road. They do not extend their reach north of Soldier Stone because they do not wish to agitate Endhome, whom they see as a valuable trading partner. To the west, Sunderland extends to the King's Road and Trader's Way, and it reaches the Burgundian Road in places to the south. These lands are under no sovereign in general, though mercantile interests from other lands have made forays in some strategic locations.

Most of Sunderland is dry, rolling plains covered in low grasses and rocky outcroppings. Rivers are usually seasonal and appear during the rainy springs and dry up over the summer. Winters can be harsh with no mountains and few trees to break the bitter north winds. Horses are still bred on these plains as they have been for hundreds of generations, though it is no longer the primary source of horseflesh as it once was in the days of Foere. Shepherds and their flocks are frequently seen on these grasslands. The plains' two chains of hills are low but rugged in places, and often tree covered. On the gentler slopes of these hills, the soil is often good for vineyards and orchards.

HISTORY AND PEOPLE

Sunderland has always been a sparsely-populated, sleepy backwater. In fact, the Hyperboreans did not even exercise control here, preferring instead to simply patrol the roads to keep them clear of dangers. Since the departure of the Hyperboreans, the district has fallen under the influence of Foere and Burgundia, but with Foere's decline and Burgundia's destruction, the region has returned to a largely ungoverned state, with villages managing their own affairs. Merchants from Oceander, Foere, and Suilley have been visiting the region lately, seeking horses, wine, and other goods. Beyond this, Sunderland is usually simply a region that travelers pass through on the way to Eastreach, Southvale, or Suilley.

RELIGION

Most Sunderlanders worship the gods of Foere and Oceanus, primarily Muir and Thyr. The district has a small temple located in Malthlyn overseen by an aging priest and priestess, and a shrine in the midst of the Lonely Moor.

TRADE AND COMMERCE

Trade represents Sunderland's major contact with the outside world, as traders from neighboring lands regularly stop in small villages to barter for the district's various goods. In general, Foerdewaith coinage is used, though most Sutherlanders aren't particular and accept any currency that contains the right amount of gold, silver, or copper. Besides these small trade expeditions, there is little activity in the region besides travelers along the Burgundian and Hollow Roads, which has led to the establishment of several small inns. Of these, the Black Crow between Malthlyn and Terrin Keld is the most famous.

Wilderness and Adventures

Sunderland is a largely empty and uneventful place, though it is not without its potential challenges, particularly in the south along the borders of the Wilderlands and the ruins of Old Burgundia. The Erskaelosi barbarians of the Wildlands sometimes advance over the Burgundian Road seeking plunder and blood and force farmers to flee into the safety of local stockades or the village of Malthlyn.

Farther south, the ruins of Old Burgundia and the city of Trevi have become a haven for outlaws and humanoids, including ragtag orc bands, goblin gangs, and Erskaelosi barbarians who fight with each other but often venture into Sunderland. In the north and perilously close to Malthlyn, the creatures and supernatural forces of the Moon Fog Hills represent a danger to the Sunderlanders and an opportunity for adventurers.

Billockburne, Village of

Population: 165
Ruler: Sheriff Tom Gorn
Government: sheriff

Standing in the heart of Lonely Moor, Billockburne is one of the oldest extant settlements of Sunderland. The community was established to support the nearby shrine of Thyr, which is now known as the Chapel-on-the-Moor. The village consists mainly of herdsmen and peat cutters with a single blacksmith and some small trade with surrounding hamlets. The local public house serves as the center of society for the entire Lonely Moor area and draws folk from farms and thorps as much as a day's walk away.

Cat's Wife, Village of

Population: 74
Ruler: Bailiff Hans Krecher
Government: consensus of village notables

This quaint little village lies not far down a little-used side trail off the King's Road midway between the Gundlock Hills and the Gaelon River. It is a pleasant farming community that does some small trade with the travelers of the King's Road. It also has a small local river that happens to be one of the few stretches of waterway in the region capable of supporting fishing year-round. The villagers proudly point out that their village is named for the well-known fable about Cat seeking a wife and take great delight in putting the image of a cat in all of their decoration. Some scholars who have studied local folklore, however, think that the tale refers to actual incidents involving some sort of werebeast and is connected to a string of disappearances of young women that occurred in the area over two centuries ago. Whether the villagers know anything about that matter is open to conjecture, but if so, they do not let on about it.

Coburn, Village of

Population: 918
Ruler: Reeve Sylas Orth
Government: reeve elected by boatowners

Coburn is a fishing village and the only permanent settlement on Kadalon Bay. The docks are small, however, and boats longer than 30 feet or so need to anchor offshore. Visitors must be ferried to and from shore on dinghies or smaller boats. Few merchant ships come by, however, due to the somewhat sinister reputation of the bay. The boats of the Coburnese seem immune to whatever swallows up ships in these waters, and they stay at sea for days at a time seeking the renowned silver sea bass and red-billed swordfish. Some of the choicest fish is salted and sent inland to the Dancing Gnoll, a well-known inn and tavern on the Soldier's Road, and occasionally is sold to merchants who make their way to the village.

A single chapel overlooks Coburn from a nearby hill, but non-residents are not welcome to visit it, let alone worship there.

Dimmelhill, Village of

Population: 131
Ruler: Magistrate Arbel Threethumbs
Government: elected magistrate

A small village, Dimmelhill is a lone outpost amid the barren, windswept eastern reaches of the Gundlock Hills. Packs of violent humanoids, including goblins, ogres, and bugbears, roam these hills and threaten isolated farmsteads. When raids occur, locals flee to the village and the protection of the stout wooden palisade surrounding it.

Every three years, the local farmers and residents of Dimmelhill gather to elect one of their number to act as magistrate, with the authority to manage the village and nearby farms and to act as judge. Arbel Threethumbs, the current magistrate, is mainly known for having two thumbs on one of his hands, and for little else. He has served a bit over two years now, and he and most of the villagers are looking forward to the end of his term.

Unknown to most of those in Dimmelhill, the village is also home to a coven of witches dedicated to Cybele. The coven is led by a local midwife called Mother Tidwel, who has overseen the births of almost every babe in Dimmelhill and the surrounding farms for more than three decades. She checks each newborn for a mark that might indicate whether the baby has been chosen by Cybele. She notes these marks so members of her coven can settle near the children and keep an eye on them until the day when some unknown fate the Magna Mater has in store for them is revealed. The coven believes that somewhere nearby is a center of power holy to Cybele, though they have yet to find it.

Fairbridge, Town of

Population: 2,212 (1,354 human, 628 half-elf, 230 halfling)
Ruler: Magistrate Pythoras Kroon
Government: local magistrate

The town of Fairbridge stands where the Trader's Way crosses a small muddy river called the Granis by the locals, though it does not appear on any maps. The bridge is maintained and repaired every few years by workers out of Grollek's Grove to keep it sturdy and to repair washouts. The town's magistrate collects tolls for crossing the bridge from travelers who look as if they can be intimidated, though he has no authority to do so since the town does not maintain it. A crow cage next to the bridge usually contains the picked-over skeleton of some petty criminal that the locals like to point out to discourage miscreants.

Grollek's Grove, Town of

Population: 853 (785 human, 34 halfling, 17 high elf, 9 mountain dwarf, 8 half-elf)
Ruler: Magistrate Miriam Kriel
Government: local magistrate

Established a century ago by a consortium of merchants out of Endhome led by a shipping magnate named Beval, Grollek's Grove controls a key crossroads between the Trader's Way and the King's Road. The Beval family still resides in Endhome under their patriarch Alistair Beval but maintains extensive orchards in and around the small town. Branches of other families, including the Morricks and Eldorans, relocated to the town and own extensive vineyards from which they produce several of Endhome's fine selection of wines. The magistrate of Grollek's Grove is appointed by a vote of the shareholder merchant houses, and all have a vested interest in seeing the town continue to prosper. Tragedy struck the town five years ago at the wedding of Lord Beval's scion and few of the guests survived. The estate at nearby Morrick Mansion where it occurred has been considered cursed ever since.

MALTHLYN, TOWN OF

Population: 278 (194 human, 42 mountain dwarf, 15 high elf, 13 half-elf, 6 halfling, 5 gnome, 3 half-orc)
Ruler: Acting-Sheriff Cignor
Government: hereditary lord

Originally a land grant to a Foerdewaith knight by the overking five centuries ago, Malthlyn found prosperity through a silver mine established in the nearby Mistwood. Unfortunately, after several years the original Count Mathen went insane and murdered his family before killing himself at the family estate. The mine was closed, and the town sank into obscurity for centuries. Only recently has an heir to the Mathen name moved back in and re-established lordship over the town and mine after mithral was discovered within. A consortium of merchants in distant Bard's Gate provided the Mathen heirs the funding to reopen the mine and their ancestral estate. Because of the ominous reputation of the Moon Fog Hills and the dangers in transporting the mithral ore to the nearest ports, the consortium contracted Wayriders from the duke of Waymarch to provide security in and around the town. When shipments failed to arrive as expected, a company of Lyreguard from Bard's Gate was dispatched to investigate the problem. The merchants have yet to hear back from these troops.

SOLDIER STONE, TOWN OF

Population: 520 (310 human, 105 half-elf, 78 halfling, 25 high elf, 2 mountain dwarf)
Ruler: Sheriff Croweye and Curate Madderson
Government: ecclesiastical

This small town straddles the Soldier's Road west of the Sand Hills. Its location marks the site of a major battle in the wars that have raged across the plains in the past millennia, though no one quite knows which war or exactly who was fighting. The only thing to mark the site was a standing stone raised beside the roadway with a crude engraving of the image of Mithras, the Soldier God. Numerous arrowheads and bits of rusted armor and weapons have been found in the fields surrounding the area, indicating that the battle was large in scope and must have involved thousands of men. Digging around the base of the Soldier Stone unearthed 12 graves of warriors slain in that battle. They were reburied, but grave robbers stole anything of value they may have once had. To protect the site, the Church of Mithras built a shrine nearby, and a village sprang up around it shortly thereafter. The curate for the shrine, appointed by the church, holds authority over the village, though a sheriff is usually appointed by the curate to enforce civil laws.

GEOGRAPHIC FEATURES AND POINTS OF INTEREST IN THE SUNDERED KINGDOMS AND THE SINNAR COAST OF SOUTHEASTERN AKADOS

BURGUNDIAN ROAD

This roadway runs from the Trader's Way in the west to Lowport in the east by way of the trade town of Terrin Keld. It sees little enough traffic other than caravans out of Southvale, and much of its length is rutted and washed out. Bandit encounters are frequent occurrences.

CANEY RIVER AND THE LESSER REACH

The main artery of trade on Ramthion Island, the Caney River flows wide, muddy, and shallow down from the Caterwaul Mountains and across the plain before draining into the Sinnar Ocean at Port Clar. Named for the numberless sugarcane plantations along its length and the patches of wild sugarcane that grow along its banks, the river has been the lifeblood of the Ramithi for generations. Now in addition to the slow-moving cane barges that plod up and down its length, keelboats manned by Oceander marines patrol from Port Clar to the base of the mountains looking for Ramithi insurgents.

CATERWAUL PEAKS

Rising on the western end of the island as an extension of the Matagost Range beyond the strait, the Caterwaul Mountains serve as a foreboding natural fortress in the heart of Ramthion Island. Ruins from the time of the Ancient Ones still dot the peak, and the great fortress of Farketh Knowe stands on the high precipice of Mount Marvel. Many small Ramithi villages have sprung up in hidden dells and valleys as refugees from the lowlands seek to escape the Oceander invaders. These stubborn people have appointed a war leader to lead them in their rebellion against the invaders centered at the ancient Heldring fortress.

The peaks themselves are steep and jagged, broken by many narrow, high-walled valleys and precipitous waterfalls. The terrain is perfect for a guerrilla war against the conventional armies of Oceanus, and the Oceanders appear to be no closer to flushing the resistance out than they were when they began. A mountain village culture has developed among the Ramithi, and anyone who knows their hidden ways can find communities prospering, with children playing among the women who go about their business of weaving, building, and trading while the able-bodied men continually train for battle. At night, the fires are lit, and dancing and feasting take place in the streets while the folk forget their troubles for the moment and remember their lost homes on the rivers.

CUT HORN GAP

The Cut Horn Gap is a pass between the Forlorn Mountains in the north and the Scar-in-the Sky Peaks to the south, through which the Hawkmoon Road runs. The gap is not considered a part of Exeter Province, for it comprises the small Duchy of Duquesne, an enigmatic regime independent of its neighbors. The duchess keeps the pass well-patrolled in exchange for the payment of tolls by those traveling through.

DARDANAL STRAIT

The narrow strait between the Matagost Peninsula and Ramthion Island was once called the Narrow Sea. Though scholars have found artifacts to show that early inhabitants of the region navigated it in hide coracles and canoes, it has been impassible to such craft for thousands of years. In fact, after the activation of the *Obelisks of Chaos* some years ago, the influence of the demon lord Dagon fell heavy on these waters and made them dark and turbulent and filled with all manner of malevolent creatures. No less than two sahuagin cities, clusters of kelp devils, and multiple sightings of scyllas and charybdises are attributed to this befouled stretch of water. During the great flight of 2496 I.R., when wildfires forced refugees to attempt the straits in great numbers, the predators of the strait fed well. One Hyperborean ship captain called Dardanal the Navigator became legend after crossing the strait no fewer than 12 times with full shiploads of refugees. It was on his 13th trip across that he and his ship, the *Wayfarer*, vanished and allegedly fell to the creatures of those waters. The strait was renamed in his honor and is largely avoided. Men-of-war out of Highreach patrol the northern and southern end to prevent the vile things that lurk within from emerging in numbers. So far, they have successful kept the creatures contained, but no one knows how long this détente might last.

DEHARI RIVER

As the Domain of Hawkmoon's largest water channel, the Dehari plays an important role in the land's economic wellbeing. Even the most sizable of barges are capable of navigating much of the river's length, from its mouth in the Miasmoor to its headwaters north in the Forlorn Mountains. Being a major byway for merchants moving large quantities of heavy goods, the river sees a high degree of pirate activity. These river-robbers favor the marshes of the Miasmoor for their hideouts and ply their grisly trade from small, agile rafts that are easily hidden in the tall reeds and sawgrass of the swamp. The river is nearly a half-mile wide at its broadest point, which makes it very difficult for would-be lawmen to curtail the pirate enterprise.

DUSKMOON HILLS

The Duskmoon Hills are a large range of tall, jagged hills to the north of Endhome through which runs the last stretch of the Trader's Way. Endhome patrols the road through the hills, but the city has no particular interest in wasting time, gold, and people to tame these wild lands. Once travelers stray from the road, they are on their own.

REFERENCE SOURCE: The Lost Lands: The Lost City of Barakus

FLATLANDER ROAD

The Flatlander Road, unlike the various stone-paved high roads of old Hyperborea, turns and wanders, with much of it nothing more than a wide dirt trail. During Suilley's mud season, parts of the road are almost impassable, and bandits come out of the woodwork, some of them sponsored by local knights who desire a bit more revenue.

FORLORN MOUNTAINS

This vast mountain range is one of the largest other than the Stonehearts, and once served as the ancestral home of the Great Mountain Clan of Targ, although these dwarves are now widely scattered after the fall of the citadel at Hazad-Burgh in 3160 I.R. to giant invaders. Giants haunt the eastern reaches of the mountains in great numbers on the far side of the range, but Exeter Province is spared from the worst threat the mountains offer. Nevertheless, the province still has to cope with giantish raids from time to time, for the entire mountain range is rife with them. In recent years, the lord-governor of Exeter Province has done an excellent job of staving off the giant incursions, although some of the local nobles have voiced the opinion that rooting out trouble at the source might do more to stop the problem.

Legends speak of a strange and powerful wizard called the Mechanician who is said to have a fortress in the southern Forlorn Mountains where he keeps one of the fabled *Bells of Heaven*, though no one has been able to confirm this rumor.

GAP ROAD

The Gap Road is an old stone-paved high road between the Duchy of Saxe and Keston Province that runs through the hilly lands between the Meridian Range to the north and the Kal'Iugus Mountains to the south. It is relatively well-maintained, with milestones and a few places where the paving stones have been replaced. Much of its route passes through pleasant countryside.

A number of small roadside inns are found along the way, along with villages out of sight of the road but marked by cart trails that lead to the thoroughfare. As long as wayfarers do not push on too aggressively, it is possible to spend each night of the journey at a coaching inn. It is a safe assumption that rooms are available unless a caravan or mule train happens to be present already. Lone travelers are seldom seen on the road, although this is not so much due to highwaymen as to the pure length of the journey. It is more than 200 miles from Kingston to the western side of the gap, a long trip to make without companions. There are incidents of brigandage, of course, and monsters do come down from the cold southern heights to hunt, but this is one of the few areas that Keston Province can truly be said to govern, and it is well-patrolled.

GAUNT WOOD

Gaunt Wood occupies much of the northwestern portion of the Domain of Hawkmoon. As forests go, it is not particularly deadly, but caution is certainly advised, for the forest contains ogres and even the occasional hunting wyvern.

GIANTLANDS

A stretch of the Forlorn Mountains played host to the Storm Kings of old, great storm giants who possessed castles that floated upon clouds and fortresses atop the highest peaks. The Ancient Ones of the lowlands knew of their legend and gave homage when the great storms swept down from the mountains. But these despots of old disappeared long before the arrival of the first Hyperborean scouts, and little remains of that legendary kingdom save for a stretch of peaks in the Forlorns called the Giantlands.

This range still serves as home to an inordinate number of giants. Other than deep in the Stoneheart range, there is perhaps nowhere else in Lloegyr that serves as home to a greater concentration of giants than these peaks. Only the hardy dwarves of the Targ Mountain Clan dared live close to them, and Old Burgundia long reinforced its southern border with companies of heavily armed knights and Erskaelosi mercenaries. Giants of many sorts still live in the Giantlands, though it is believed that all of the storm giants left and few enough cloud giants remain. Strangely, fire giants have never been known to be found in this region. These giants live in various holds, steadings, and caves in conditions ranging from comparable of that to the Heldring of the lowlands to absolute squalor. They hunt in small bands but rarely leave the mountains themselves in any numbers. Not in two centuries has a powerful-enough chieftain arisen to unite the various groups into an organized invasion, though some fear that another one cannot be far off. Recently, giants have been raiding into the Duchy of Southvale with increased frequency, often led by fire giants, which many consider an especially alarming event, suggesting that a new chieftain may be emerging.

GNARLHEIM

The fortress of Gnarlheim stands against the side of one of the peaks of Mount Therosabad in the northern Forlorn Mountains. Its massive ramparts of crumbling stone and leaning towers are the remnant of an ancient storm giant citadel that crashed into the mountaintop long ago and was abandoned. Two decades ago, a powerful frost giant calling himself the Thunder-Caller rose up and inhabited the ruin with his band of giants and enslaved ogres. Since then, this self-styled king has attracted more giants of all kinds to his banner and is the closest thing to a true monarch among the Giantlands. The barbarians of Tyr fear that if a powerful giant does rise to unite the giant bands of the mountains, it will be King Graccus Bonesnapper. A bounty of a great weight in gold has been placed upon the giant king's head, but the walls and newly tunneled caverns beneath the fortress of Gnarlheim have proven to be a tough nut to crack for even experienced giant slayers.

GUNDLOCK HILLS

Much of these sprawling hills of Sunderland are considered comparatively safe, particularly the western portion. A fair number of villages are here in proximity to the Trader's Way and King's Road. This area boasts orchards and is fine vineyard country, though many of these are overgrown, having been abandoned after wars and skirmishes in the past. Bats can be a nuisance at night due to their occasional tendency to swarm, and the dire bats and mobats that hunt the more desolate regions that are capable of carrying away a goat or peasant are much more of a problem. The eastern portion of the Gundlocks, however, is much less populated and wilder. Violent humanoids roam these eastern hills in small packs, though they have yet to gather into groups large enough to pose a threat to anything other than isolated farmsteads.

HAZAD-BURGH, RUINS OF

The Great Mountain Clan of Targ created the kingdom of Hazad with its primary mines and citadel at Hazad-Burgh. Their mines were wealthy and one of the few sources of ironstone, but were under constant threat of attack being built so close to the Giantlands. When the defenses finally fell in 3160 I.R. after many years of declining population, the surviving remnant scattered into the mountains to the west while many migrated east into Southvale. It was this migration that led to the establishment of Durandel and the creation of the second great Targ citadel. Today, the empty halls of Hazad-Burgh are stalked by giants, undead guardians, and worse, and are avoided by all but the bravest. The most interesting tales of late speak of a blue dwarven ghost drifting among the corridors. However, there are also always tales of lost treasure caches within to convince the foolhardy to tempt their fate.

The Helwall

The Helwall is a 150-mile-long wall and string of defensive forts the Hyperboreans began in –83 I.R. to contain the wild tribes of the Heldring within the Helcynngae Peninsula and to keep them out of the continent's mainland. The fortifications were maintained by garrisons in some form or fashion until after the Battle of Oescreheit Downs, which broke the Heldring once and for all. Upkeep was sporadic over the years, and the fortifications have not been maintained by the northerners since the final defeat of the Heldring at Oescreheit Downs in 2802 I.R.

On the other hand, the ancient wall now serves to protect those in the Helcynngae Peninsula from invaders and raiders from the north. A small garrison of volunteers hand-selected from Kingsgardt serve one year of duty at the Helwall to maintain peace, protect the lands to the south, and reject entry of less-desirable northerners.

Hollow Road

The Hollow Road is an old track running between Terrin Keld in Old Burgundia and Heldring's Cross on the Matagost Peninsula. It had some significance in the old days when shipments of silver from the Mistwood Mines in the Moon Fog Hills were sent over its rugged course. But the road fell into disuse when the mines shut down over the intervening centuries. With the reopening of the mines in recent years, traffic has picked up again somewhat, and at times patrols of Waymarch cavalry and Lyreguard from distant Bard's Gate and its environs have been seen, though of late even these are absent.

Kadalon Bay

The waters north of the Matagost Peninsula and east of the Sand Hills and Kildren Point are known as Kadalon Bay. Relatively sheltered and with calm seas, this would seem to be a safe place for ships to anchor. Few, however, voluntarily choose to enter the bay, other than the fishermen of the village of Coburn, the only settlement on these shores. Sailors tell of ships that sail into these waters, never to be seen again. Worse, it is said that sometimes a deckhand from a lost ship will be found in a far city, gibbering and dirty, staring blankly at former friends. Whether or not there is truth to these tales, most captains prefer to avoid Kadalon Bay.

Kapichi Point

An ancient fortress of the Ramithi pirates once stood upon this lonely, rocky point that reaches into the Sinnar Ocean. For long years, treacherous sea rocks beneath its ramparts, which only the pirates knew how to navigate, protected them and their fleet from attacks by those who would end their piracy. However, in the Battle of Kapichi Point 300 years ago, the Ramithi clans in the fortress watched the Oceander navy brilliantly defeat the navy of Foerdewaith and send the overking's sailors to watery graves upon the very rocks beneath the fortress. They then looked on with horror as the Oceander fleet somehow navigated those self-same rocks and converged upon the Ramithi ships at dock in the harbor. In that one day, Oceanus destroyed the only two naval forces in western Akados capable of threatening their own fleets. The fortress of Kapichi was destroyed, and the surviving Ramithi fled into the swamps to the south to escape the slaughter. The piles of rubble that stand at the end of the point and the jagged rocks in the waters beyond the harbor serve as reminders of the Ramithi fortress and Foerdewaith navy that were both sent to their ruin here by the Oceanders.

King's Road

Originating in distant Courghais, the King's Road has carried the king's messengers to distant courts and armies to war for a thousand years and more. Now it is used mainly for trade as it ends in the mighty trading city of Endhome in the east. A bridge of wood and brick crosses the Gaelon River 100 miles west of Endhome. It is that city's duty by contract to see to its maintenance, and it has been repaired or replaced many times over the years after being destroyed in war or washed out in floods. A tollhouse now stands on either bank and collects tolls from travelers and traders. Southbound tolls go to the coffers of distant Courghais while northbound tolls feed into nearby Endhome.

Lesser Reach

Actually called the Lesser Reach of the Caney River, this languid flow trickles south into the glades and the scum-covered surface of Lake Latrouche in the heart of the swamp. The town of Lambert Landing lies just beyond the initial fork in the river.

Lonely Moor

East of the Gundlock Hills and north of Dimmelhill is the Lonely Moor, a vast stretch of verdant wetland where most of the rainfall collects after it drains from the hills. The land of the moor is lower than that of the coast to the east and north, so no rivers carry this drainage out to sea. As a result, a large moorland developed west of Stone-ring Knoll. The aridity of the area keeps this from becoming a true swampland, but grasses and heather grow thick in this region, and deadly bogs lie hidden beneath mossy patches that look like solid ground to the unwary. The paths that run across this region are known to be safe, but anyone venturing off of them risks disappearing among the unforgiving mires, both horse and rider alike. To aid travelers, the clerics of Thyr who once inhabited the moor erected stone crosses along the path. These ancient stone monuments are weathered and broken — and many are missing entirely — but those that remain still mark the safe trails and continue to guide those who would travel the paths of the moor known collectively as the Monk's Way.

Matagost Range

Rising along the southern edge of the peninsula, the Matagost Range runs from the Moon Fog Hills to the Dardanal Strait and are a part of the same range that makes up the Caterwaul Mountains on Ramthion Island. The peaks of this range are stark and knife-edged, and the highest peaks remain covered in white even during the summer. Many mountain dwarf clans, long friendly to the human lowlanders, work mines in this range and provide ore to the great foundries of Highsmyth. Though the roads to these mines are good, ore caravans are always heavily guarded because goblin worg-riders and their bugbear cousins are known to inhabit the lower slopes and gray dwarves have raided a few mines in the ridges above in recent years.

Miasmoor

The Miasmoor is a dangerous, marshy region in the Domain of Hawkmoon where the Dehari River empties from its sources in the Forlorn Mountains. Quicksand is a particular threat in this area. The Miasmoor is home to sawgrass, mangrove, sedges, cattails, reeds, water buffalo, and tribes of trolls.

Mistwood

See "Moon Fog Hills" below.

Moon Fog Hills

These sinister hills rise from the eastern plains of Sunderland and form the foothills of the Matagost Range. Much of these hills are covered by the Mistwood, a light forest that is much wilder than the copses and orchards that cover the rest of the plains. These hills are also quite rugged, with many hidden vales and isolated ridges where small villages and homesteads have existed for centuries, largely cut off from outside contact. There have always been many disappearances of travelers within the Moon Fog Hills, and not all of them are from monstrous or natural hazards.

These hills gain their name from the strange misty iridescence that rises from the treetops of the Mistwood at night to give the moon an ominous hazy halo that creates disorienting shadows beneath the trees. This strange phenomenon, combined with the lurid coloration that paints the sky during nights of the full moon, is thought to be the cause of a schizophrenic condition locally known as "moon haze." Cases of moon haze are fortunately infrequent, but when they do occur, they often lead to madness and murder. Unbeknownst to most of the inhabitants of the region, these strange manifestations are, in fact, a direct result of an unusually high concentration of *Obelisks of Chaos* in the area of Malthlyn.

In addition to these unique dangers in this region, the Moon Fog Hills also have an unusually high number of openings into the Under Realms from which foul subterranean denizens have been known to come forth in the night to wreak their own brand of havoc. More than one disappearance in the region has actually been the result of the unfortunate being dragged to realms below and whatever unimaginable fate awaits them there.

Moonsilver Sea

The waters of the Sinnar Ocean off of the eastern eaves of the Forlorn Mountains are known as the Moonsilver Sea. The magical lung leaf tree grows in scattered underwater groves on seabeds far below the surface. This area is also home to the (perhaps merely legendary) Moonsilver Beast that is said to occasionally be sighted from the shore.

Old Kingdom Road

Once the main road of Burgundia that brought traffic through Trevi, the Old Kingdom Road was largely destroyed by the army of Oceanus, which pulled up many of its paving stones to take back for building projects at Matagost and Parthos. It is now little more than a pitted lane that has a tendency to break cart wheels and bring animals up lame. The little-used cart track that brought travelers to the town of Terrin Keld became a bypass for this road and now carries all of the substantial traffic of Old Burgundia.

Provincial Military Road

This ancient road was built in the days of Hyperborea's war against the Heldring to connect the South Road with a direct route to the Helwall so that reinforcing armies were not faced with grueling overland travel. Despite the antiquity of its construction, the original paving stones remain in place, and the road is wide and level, which makes it easier to travel than many of the royal roads in the heartland of Foere. Once quite safe, the road is no longer adequately patrolled and is becoming more dangerous by the year.

Sand Hills

These windswept dunes rise in terraced formations on the western shore of Kadalon Bay south of Kildren Point. They are composed of a coarse yellow sand unique to the Sinnar Coast, and scholars speculate that they are all that remains of a time when an ancient inland sea covered much of the Sundered Kingdoms. This is supported by the vast skeletal remains of ancient sea beasts that are occasionally uncovered by the near-constant winds; sometimes these ancient bony remains crawl to life on their own and attempt to swim through the dunes or make a meal of curious onlookers. The hills are now home to a smattering of gnoll bands that hunt the giant insects that reside among them and domesticate the native hyaenodons.

Scar-in-the-Sky Peaks

The Scar-in-the-Sky Peaks form the southern border of the Domain of Hawkmoon and the eastern border of Cerediun Province. These mountains are inhabited by barbarian clans, rocs, griffons, giants, white dragons, and yeti, and is the home of the Stormbreaker cloud giant clan.

The Sea Dagger

The northern peninsula of Ramthion Island, the Sea Dagger got its name from its characteristic shape jutting out into the Sinnar Ocean as well as from the proclivity with which the rocks at its northern tip cut into the hulls of ships unfamiliar with its waters. Most of the peninsula is swampy and difficult terrain, which made it ideal as a barrier to guard the Ramithi pirate clans when they dwelt in their fortress on Kapichi Point. Despite the ominous terrain, these marshes don't share the same sinister reputation as those at the island's southern end, and for many years after the Oceander invasion they served as a hiding place for Ramithi resistance fighters. With the construction of the Damerhold, however, any patches of resistance that once resided here have largely been rooted out.

Sess River

The Sess River valley is generally a peaceful area dotted with small villages.

Soldier's Road

This military road starts in Endhome and wends its way to the southeast through Heldring's Cross and Oestre before finally ending at the fortress of Highreach. In the past, it felt the tread of mighty armies at war, but of late sees little use beyond local farmers and trade caravans.

Southfell Glades

The southern end of Ramthion Island is a swampy morass despite the fact that it lies far enough above the sea that it should be able to drain. Scholars speculate that some catastrophic deluge of old must have occurred to create the anomalous conditions, but no one knows for certain. The Lesser Reach of the Caney feeds into the swamp and Lake Latrouche at its center, and from there muddy fingerlets of water spread out to saturate the entire area of the glades. This area has been considered haunted since the earliest known times on Ramthion, and the ruins of the ill-starred Toussant family's house still rest somewhere within their dank embrace. Disappearances have always been common among villages that lie near the swamps and are usually attributed to alligators or the gargantuan frogs that haunt its depths, but the graybeards just shake their heads and know better. In addition, an undeniably large number of mindless undead wander the watery ways, so even the most skeptical have to consider that something supernatural may be at work here.

Southvale Causeway

This road runs south from Terrin Keld, passes the town of Emryl and the northern eaves of the Forlorn Mountains, and then after Weatherall crosses the moorlands before it heads into the heartland of Southvale on the way to its terminus at Penmorgh. Much of the road's length, especially in Southvale, is a raised causeway built up on an earthen mound to avoid the fens and hidden bogs along its route. Boggards are occasionally sighted along these marshy stretches, but they have yet to attack any sizable groups of travelers.

Stone-ring Knoll

This low grassy mound rises from the plain east of the Lonely Moor in Sunderland and is topped by a ring of nine ancient standing stones. There were originally 12 but three fell and two have long since been carted away for use as building material in a keep east of Billockburne. One of the fallen stones still lies sunken partially into the ground and can just be seen in the tall grass. The locals consider the knoll either a sacred or a cursed site. Those who spend the night upon it are said to experience visions of either paradise or madness, and more than one person has disappeared from the area, though this could easily be a result of the predators that roam the plains. Nonetheless, no village has ever been constructed too near the hill because of the superstitious fear the locals have of it.

In truth, Stone-ring Knoll is actually the site of Bryn Calun, the Holy Hill of Sull eons ago. Tribal shamans called dark powers here and laid a curse upon the whole region sealed with their blood. If anyone were to systematically dig up the top of the hill, they would find the remains of a great fire at its center with bits of charred bone, now mineralized from their long years of internment. Likewise, 50 feet below the surface of the mound is the first and greatest of the *Obelisks of Chaos*. This one is sacred to the demon lord Pazuzu and attempts to tamper with it cause blood hawks, giant wasps, air elementals, and vrocks to appear to defend it. If in danger of destruction, its caretaker nalfeshnee appears with reinforcements to destroy the interlopers.

STONY STRAND

This stretch of desolate, rocky coastline is little visited even by the inhabitants of Lowport. Too many wild or deadly creatures run amok to make travel within this area worthwhile for any but the most desperate. Nevertheless, Baljulias the Great, the Tyrant of Lowport, sends orc bands out into the hills semi-regularly to scrape the chalk above the sea for blocks of the stuff for export when his treasury begins to run low.

THOMKURN HEIGHTS

The Thomkurn Heights are a low mountain range overlooking the Moonsilver Sea. They are filled with isolated glades and valleys, most of which are inhabited by monsters of one kind or another.

TRADER'S WAY

Perhaps the longest road in Akados, this road carries trade from far to the south in Cerediun Province all the way to Telar Brindel in the north. Along this route, it serves as the western border of the District of Sunderland and is one of the trade routes passing through the crossroads village of Grollek's Grove.

THE WEIRWOOD

The Weirwood is located in the isolated Domain of Hawkmoon. Well removed from any trade roads, the forest of Weir has for centuries grown ungoverned by druids and uncharted by woodsmen. This isolation — and perhaps a bit of dark magic from a long-forgotten curse — allowed the Weir to become a crucible for all sorts of lifeforms that are usually kept in check by the hands of man. In particular, poisonous flora abounds in this dense and murky wood.

The treetops are so thickly entwined as to cover the ground in continuous shadow, permitting the rampant growth of lichen, fungi, and myriad mosses, many species of which are quite inimical to human life. As a result, few mammals stalk the forest, save those immune to the various natural toxins. Certain creatures adapted over the years to flourish in these environs and represent new genetic strains of common fauna: Deer, rabbits, and several types of vermin in the wood evolved into species entirely different from the ordinary members of their kind.

WILDLANDS

This desolate stretch of dry wastelands and blasted hills stretches across Old Burgundia south of the Burgundian Road from the Trader's Way to the Stony Strand. Once miles upon miles of lush, irrigated farmland, orchards, and copses of the native cassia trees, the Oceander invaders laid waste to the entire countryside and destroyed what they could not carry off. Rivers were dammed with brush and rubble, irrigation canals were allowed to silt in, and windmills that plumbed water wells were left to slowly succumb to time and the elements until this is now a dry and barren place home only to scavengers and creatures that hunt among the wastes looking for hot blood to drink. Bands of Erskaelosi barbarians roam these lands, eking out a living on the few resources it possesses and bringing to battle any fell creatures they find. Many Erskaelosi tents bear the horns and scales of the foul denizens they have bested, but just as many bleached bones of Erskaelosi warriors lie unburied in the unforgiving landscape where the hunters became the hunted.

WORTHAM FIRTH

This bay south of Cerediun Province lies at the eastern end of the Helwall and has been contested by pirates and freebooters from time immemorial as the mountains of its north coast provide innumerable fjords, inlets, and sheltered harbors where they roll down to the sea's edge. Trading ships ordinarily do not venture into the Firth, which represents a barrier to coastal galleys unless they are deep-keeled and sturdy enough to cross the open water around the Firth.

THE HELCYNNGAE PENINSULA AND YNYS CYMRAGH

KINGDOM OF THE HELCYNN

Capital: Kingsgardt
Notable Settlements: Aethelham, Berrocburh, Bournedon, Burcestor, Burh Weider, Durwent, Lichfield, Lymnester, Oxwain, Suthgardt, Uthelgardt, Warsley, Wellford, Wirric Bury
Ruler: His Pious Majesty by the Grace of Tyr, the Hledwalda Aethelmark, King of the Helcynn
Government: hereditary monarchy assisted by Witan (noble advisory council)
Population: 2,087,900 (1,954,300 Heldring, 75,800 Foerdewaith, 43,900 dwarf [mostly mountain dwarf], 9,200 human mixed ethnicity, 4,000 firbolg, 700 skinwalker)
Monstrous: wolves, bristle boars, goblins, goblin dogs, fey, quickwoods, wereboars, wights, bog hags, forester's banes, fachens, wood giants, will-o'-wisps (lowlands); goblins, goblin dogs, ogres, ogrens, wayangs, worgs, firbolgs, veds, ettins, werewolves, will-o'-wisps, trolls, nilbogs (mountains)
Languages: Helvaenic, Common, Dwarven
Religion: Tyr, Eostre, Odin, Thor, Frey, assorted other Ése, Hel
Resources: grain, fishing, pitch, livestock (cattle, swine), shipbuilding supplies, spirits (beer), quarry stone, copper, ships
Currency: Heldring
Technology Level: Dark Ages

The Helcynngae Peninsula extends from the southeastern coast of Akados for 1,000 miles and divides the Sinnar Ocean from Mother Oceanus and the deeper waters of the south. Dominated by high, rugged mountains, swift streams and rocky meadows, the peninsula has given birth to a people as hardy and, often, as unforgiving as the land. Though located on the southern end of the continent, the odd impact of the Tropic of Arden results in a much cooler clime along the peninsula than its latitude might otherwise suggest.

This harsh land is the home of the legendary — and feared — Heldring.

HISTORY AND PEOPLE

No records tell of a time before the Heldring lived on the Helcynngae Peninsula. Their own legends say that they were born in these lands, a warrior people in service to the ancient gods of their ancestors. According to their lore, long ago they were divided into seven different clans: the Baerroc (hailing from the region around Berrocburh), the Aelrich (from around Lichfield), the Uthael (near Uthelgardt), the Ochs (near Oxwain), the Waershael (about Warsley), the Woerc (near Wirric Bury) and the Suthca (near Suthgardt). Proof of the existence of such clans is limited since there are no written records from such days, though many noble families do claim long family trees showing descent from one cyning of a clan or another. Today, long years and intermarriage among the Heldring have made clan membership largely irrelevant to daily life.

Whatever the truth of the origin of the Heldring may be, they first enter the reckoning of history when the Hyperborean legions of Oerson, flush with their victory over the elves at the Battle of Crimmormere, swept the length and breadth of Akados as its new and unrivaled masters. In the barbarian tribes of the Helcynngae Peninsula, the polemarch met his match. The legions were unable to breach the neck of the peninsula, where they were faced with hordes of battle-hardened Heldring. The Hyperboreans ultimately decided that the cost in lives and treasure to take this land — particularly given the expanse of the empire already conquered — was too high, so they instead built a string of forts across the neck of the peninsula, connected by a wall called the Helwall, to contain the barbarian threat.

The Hyperboreans did not initially abandon their dreams of dominion over the peninsula, however, and from time to time sought to make inroads beyond the Helwall. Then in 288 I.R., the Heldring destroyed Strategos Verin and his legion in the Peninsular Campaign. Fearing that the barbarians would take the initiative and surge out to attack the newly settled Hyperborean lands, militias were raised from Helwall to Apothasalos, coastal forts were erected south of the Matagost Range to guard against sea invasion, and the forts of Albor Broce and Sylvos were expanded. Fortunately for the Hyperboreans, the Heldring did not attempt to move past the Helwall, and both sides settled into a status quo. And thereafter, for so long as the Hyperboreans ruled the rest of the lands and the seas, the Heldring remained behind the wall, living among their mountains, largely ignored by the rest of the world.

Then in 2496 I.R., the Tower of Oerson was destroyed, and wildfires ravaged Curgantium and spread across Akados, burning the Plains of Suilley and Matagost Forest. Within 20 years, the Hyperboreans withdrew to Libynos. In the chaos that followed, the Heldring finally crossed the Helwall in force and overran much of southeastern Akados. In 2516 I.R., their longships seized Ramthion Island, and the next year they invaded Southvale where they quickly took all of its lands other than the city of Penmorome (now known as Penmorgh), whose stout walls stood between the invaders and its inhabitants. Over the ensuing years, the Heldring settled lands as far as the Plains of Mayfurrow, and built new villages and towns and raised fortresses to protect their new domains. Some areas remained independent, such as the city of Freegate and the Forest Kingdoms (and the Ramithi of Ramthion Island were never pacified), but without any real threat to their dominance, the Heldring settled in as conquerors of an empire. In many places, they came to assimilate with the local populace, and to this day, many folk of eastern Akados claim descent from Heldring bloodlines.

The Heldring also turned to their neighbors on the island of Insula Extremis (known to the locals as Ynys Cymragh), whose population had long been protected by Hyperborean triremes and galleys. With no one to challenge them at sea, the Heldring landed on the shores of the island to seek land and plunder. Initially held off by warriors of the local tribes, the Heldring eventually seized a small kingdom when a chieftain hired them as mercenaries in a battle with his rivals. Using this foothold, the Heldring slowly increased their lands on the island until Daan, the son of a local chieftain who had served in the Hyperborean legions and a minor Hyperborean noblewoman, returned to Insula Extremis. Daan himself had been a hipparchos of cavalry officer in the legions and served for long years in the Irkainian peninsula. Employing the skills he learned in service to Hyperborea, he united the petty kingdoms and broke the power of the Heldring in 2576 I.R. at the Battle of Agedium when he drove them back to the sea. Later, when Daan marched to Tircople to free the Sacred Table, he was able to rally many Heldring warriors to fight alongside him. But after his death, the people of Ynys Cymragh withdrew back to their island, and the alliance with the Helcynngae Peninsula collapsed. Whether due to the strength of the Daanites or out of respect to Daan, the Heldring have never since made a serious effort to invade Insula Extremis.

At a time when the cult of Hel, the Goddess of Death and the Lady of Pestilence, was waxing among the Heldring, one thegn by the name of Swein Sigurdson turned his back on the wicked ways of Hel and sought an escape for his people. In 2731 I.R., he and his folk began the trek along the so-called Neimbrall Trail, eventually coming to settle in the Northlands of Akados.

In the meantime, on the mainland of Akados, the Heldring remained largely unchallenged until the rise of Foere, which claimed the mantle of the Hyperboreans of old. As the Foerdewaith realm expanded, it came into increasing conflict with the Heldring settlements and territories along the Sinnar coast. In 2801 I.R., armies of Heldring from the peninsula began a series of attacks on Foere holdings along the March of Mountains, burning settlements and slaughtering inhabitants as they went. In response, Overking Osbert II gathered a large force of Knights of Macobert supported by heavy infantry and marched south from

Courghais to meet the Heldring in battle. In a story now well-known, the god Mitra is said to have appeared to the overking while he was in the Heathglen and predicted that Foere would have victory over the Heldring. In response, Osbert built a shrine to the Sun Father, and in 2802 I.R. crossed the Helwall and met the shieldwall of the barbarians at Oescreheit Downs. The knights' expert tactics in flanking and engaging the rear of the Heldring as the Foerdewaith shieldwall held the front of the lines in place proved disastrous to the Heldring, who fell in huge numbers on the field of battle. Although some skirmishing continued for a period, the Helcynngae Peninsula was for all intents and purposes pacified and brought under the banner of Foere.

The Foerdewaith did not, however, attempt a crossing of the Straits of Daan. The losses suffered by the Daanites in purging the Hyperborean Empire of its corruption was still fresh in the memory of the Foerdewaith, and Osbert and his successors chose to leave the island of Ynys Cymragh and its people in peace, reckoning they had endured enough.

Following the Foerdewaith conquest, many of the Heldring were converted to the worship of Thyr and Eostre (their name for Muir). However, not all Heldring renounced their old ways, and a significant sub-kingdom of Heldring who still follow Hel remain in the Cumorian Mountains. Shunned by others of their countrymen, they now exist as a bloodthirsty monotheistic theocracy with their primary stronghold at Thunderhelde.

During the Foerdewaith Wars of Succession, the overking's representatives withdrew from the Helcynngae peninsula, presumably with the intention of returning once order was restored. They have yet to return. The Heldring have never felt it necessary to officially renounce their allegiance to the Court at Courghais, but they have in fact been independent now for several centuries.

In recent years, the ancient hostilities between the inhabitants of the Helcynngae Peninsula and their neighbors to the north have been replaced with a cautious détente, and trade is growing between the Heldring and Cerediun Province, and with many other ports on the coast of the Sinnar Ocean and even in the Crescent Sea. As a result, enclaves of Heldring can be found as far afield as Bard's Gate, Freegate, and Castorhage.

RELIGION

Since time immemorial, the Heldring worshipped their own pantheon of gods. According to rumor and legend, the Heldring people's unique ability to resist incursions by the Hyperboreans was the direct result of a pact they made with Hel, the Goddess of Death and the Lady of Pestilence, from whom their common name derives.

As a result of the Foerdewaith conquest, however, the faiths of Thyr and Muir (whom the Heldring refer to as Eostre) were introduced to the Helcynngae Peninsula and began to take hold as the major religion of that people, supplanting the worship of Hel and many of the older gods. Today, the Heldring have developed an almost-theocratic society devoted to Tyr and Eostre, to the extent that their hledwalda petitions annually for the High Altar of Thyr to be moved from Bard's Gate to Kingsgardt. To date, Thyr's clergy have remained silent on the subject of relocation, though patience wears thin among the Heldring nobility.

Some deities of the older Heldring pantheon, such as Odin, Thor, and Frey, continue to be worshipped — particularly in the countryside — but to a much lesser degree. The only ancient god whose worship is outlawed is Hel, though she remains venerated among the Heldring of the Cumorian Mountains around Thunderhelde.

TRADE AND COMMERCE

The conversion of the Heldring to the worship of Thyr and Eostre, and the decline of the veneration of Hel (except among the Cumorian peoples around Thunderhelde), have led to a substantial reduction in hostility between the Helcynngae Peninsula and the other folk of Akados. Regular caravans head north and south through Sessilbridge north of the Helwall as trade with Cerediun Province grows. Heldring longships are now common sights in many ports of Akados, particularly those on the Sinnar Coast that, as a result of prior Heldring conquests, have substantial populations that claim Heldring descent.

The Helcynngae Peninsula boasts many resources that form the basis of such trade, including copper, grain, fish, pitch, livestock, and the famous Heldring beer. The Heldring are also skilled shipbuilders, and the white pines of the Cumorians and Hatlus are highly sought after for their use as ship masts.

Loyalties and Diplomacy

For most of their history, the Heldring have been a people apart. This isolation started to break down following the departure of the Hyperboreans and the Heldring conquests of the eastern Sinnar Coast. Even then, however, they were little more than invaders and colonists, and disdained diplomatic entanglements. But after Oescreheit Downs and the introduction of the Foerdewaith pantheon, the Heldring were forced into interactions with other nations and peoples. Thus, the years following the disintegration of Foere saw a Heldring people much more open to trade and other relations with those beyond their borders.

Today, the kings of the Helcynn maintain good relationships with Cerediun Province and Exeter Province, and regularly trade with Southvale (where many of the people have Heldring blood), Freegate, and Bard's Gate. Heldring longships can be seen in many of the ports of the Sinnar Coast, and as far as the Crescent Sea. Similarly, merchant vessels from around Akados make calls in the ports of Warsley and Suthgardt. The current king, the Hledwalda Aethelmark, has seen that commerce can be just as valuable as conquest, with a lot less risk. As a result, he has sent delegations to many of the provinces and kingdoms that trade with his folk, though he has established no permanent embassies outside the peninsula.

The Ramithi, however, have never ceased despising the Heldring for their years of occupation and would attack a longship on sight were one to attempt a landing on Ramthion Island.

The dwarves of Erodgrimm in their citadel in the Eorec Heights refuse any and all embassies and merchants from outside their realm, other than rare humans in Suthgardt who have performed some service for the dwarves. As a general matter, the Heldring are happy to leave the dwarves to themselves.

The Heldring continue to look longingly at Insula Extremis, but they have not been willing to try the defenses of the inhabitants of that island for many years. Occasional raids do occur, however, and it may only be a matter of time before hostilities once again rise to the fore.

Government

The king or queen of the Helcynn is known as the hledwalda, a position of authority both secular and religious, holding legal power as a hereditary monarch and also as the Heldring high priest of Thyr (if a male) or Eostre (Muir) (if female). The title of hledwalda passes to the eldest child of the prior hledwalda able to wield a sword and shield, whether son or daughter. If no such person exists, either a cousin, nephew, or uncle of the previous hledwalda is chosen by the Witan.

It is said that in the distant past, the folk of the Helcynngae Peninsula were divided into seven clans. Each clan was led by a cyning, a kingling, and many Heldring nobles to this day boast genealogical tables that show their descent from one such ruler or another. Other than that, the concept of clan holds no power in Heldring society. Instead, most cities and towns (and the surrounding countryside) are now held by landed nobles known as ealdorman (or sometimes earls) who owe fealty to the hledwalda under a complex set of traditions defining their co-dependent relationship. Rulership of local shires is usually granted by the related ealdorman to a reeve. All such positions of nobility are usually hereditary and pass down to the eldest child. In certain circumstances with the consent of the liege, a domain could be split among siblings or other heirs. On rare occasions, the liege may strip a family of its inheritance to enable a supporting noble or other worthy individual to acquire the lands.

The lowest class of nobility among the Heldring are thegns, sometimes landed and sometimes landless warriors, who may serve a reeve or ealdorman, or may be granted rights directly by the hledwalda. Some thegns are based in coastal cities and instead of land count their holdings in longships; which, depending on the nature of the thegn, may make their coin either in trade or through raiding the lands of other folk.

Above the power of the Heldring nobility, including the hledwalda, is the authority of Thyr and Eostre. Church law on the Helcynngae Peninsula is supreme. The hledwalda is the high priest of one of these gods, depending on whether he or she is male or female. But for ecclesiastical purposes, the high priest or priestess of the other god is granted pre-eminence over the hledwalda. In part, this makes sense since the kings and queens are seldom educated to the extent of a true priest, but more importantly this ensures that at least some division of power is maintained.

Other than the hledwalda, those who swear themselves to the service of Thyr or Eostre are deemed removed from the domain of the nobility and become solely subject to the authority of the church. Monasteries and shrines are held in the name of the gods and are also outside the control of any nobles. The most senior priest or priestess assigned to that location holds religious and secular power over that location, as well as certain surrounding lands.

The greatest of the ealdormen, along with several members of the Heldring clergy, sit on the Witan, a council that meets in Kingsgardt four times a year and provides advice to the hledwalda concerning issues of importance. The opinions of the council are only advisory, however, and the decision of the hledwalda is final. However, many traditions in effect place boundaries on the scope of the king's or queen's authority, as does the fact that many of the nobles on the Witan have substantial holdings as well as warriors at their command.

Military

The Heldring continue to maintain a strict military tradition handed down to them over millennia. To this day, their bards sing songs of their ancestors' defeat of the Hyperboreans and the conquests of the Sinnar Coast, a standard to which all Heldring aspire. All children are taught to fight from a young age, and most also spend a number of their adolescent years onboard longships, even if they have no intention of becoming sailors. As a result, nearly the entire population of the peninsula can fight or man a ship if necessary.

Each ealdorman maintains a sizable house guard and can call upon the folk of their domain (including reeves and thegns) at any time in a moment of need. The hledwalda, who also boasts a large house guard, has the right to demand service from the ealdormen, though the traditions and customs around doing so limit such circumstances to either defense of the realm or for the purposes of raiding or conquering the lands of others. Since the Foerdewaith conquest of Helcynn, no king or queen has called upon the nobles for either purpose.

Major Threats

No nations of Akados pose any real threat to the Heldring. Their reputation as fierce and indomitable warriors remains, despite their defeat at Oescreheit Downs. There is some limited risk of piracy to their longships, but most sensible pirates avoid taking on Heldring ships, both because their sailors are uniformly excellent warriors but also because any gain would almost certainly be outweighed by the consequences of incurring the wrath of the Heldring.

The Helcynngae Peninsula itself, however, harbors dangers to those who venture too far from lands controlled by the various settlements. Orcs, goblins, trolls, and worse inhabit the Cumorian Mountains and the Hatlu Peaks, the latter of which are also prowled by dangerous lycanthropes. The depths of the forests and fens harbor creatures that thrive in darkness, and dragons and other wyrms are known to fly out of the Eorec Heights.

Kingsgardt, City of (Capital)

Ruler: His Pious Majesty by the Grace of Tyr, the Hledwalda
    Aethelmark, King of the Helcynn
Government: monarchy
Population: 27,770 (26,000 Heldring, 1,220 human mixed
    ethnicity, 550 mountain dwarf)
Monstrous: giants to the north, orcs and goblins to the west

Languages: Common, Helvaenic
Religion: Eostre and Tyr
Resources: merchant trade, precious metals in the mountains to the north
Currency: Heldring, though many Akadonian currencies are accepted
Technology Level: Medieval

The largest city in the Helcynngae Peninsula, Kingsgardt has been the capital of the Heldring and home to their rulers since the time of legends. Dozens of kings have sat the throne here, negotiating treaties, subjugating regions, and declaring war on enemies. Five hundred of the best-trained soldiers of Aethelmark's house guard — called the Kingsblood — are based in the royal keep within the city to protect the king and his family with their lives.

Built upon a massive granite rock amid the southern foothills of the Hatlu Peaks, Kingsgardt is a truly imposing edifice that stands watch over the road that runs the length of the peninsula. The city bustles with life and trade. The royal keep is clad in a dark blue stone with red-golden slate tiles on its roofs. Nearby, the Temple of Thyr and Eostre is constructed of white marble that the Heldring imported from Courghais.

HISTORY AND PEOPLE

Each of the original seven clans of the Heldring was centered in a different town or village in the peninsula. The mythical king who united the Heldring was named Thurbald the Great and was said to have been of the clan Uthael. When he became hledwalda, he chose to establish a new city as the capital of all of his people, which became Kingsgardt. He was not the first to build on this site, however. It appears that a fortress, if not a city, has been located here for as long as humans have occupied the Helcynngae Peninsula. No one today recalls the first builders on the rock of Kingsgardt, though it is clear that the foundations are truly ancient.

The vast majority of the population of Kingsgardt are Heldring. Many live here in the city, but many are those who are merely passing through, merchants looking for trade or nobles, great and minor, seeking an audience at the hledwalda's court. A small population of mountain dwarves has also settled in the eastern quarter of the city, and the southern quarter, near the market squares, hosts a modest number of folk from elsewhere in Akados.

RELIGION

The Temple of Thyr and Eostre, near the royal keep, is the center of all worship in the Helcynngae Peninsula, where the high priests of the two gods sit in ecclesiastical court and lead services attended by thousands. Priests, monks, and adepts are trained here, and then sent forth into the countryside to minister to the Heldring.

Smaller shrines of Eostre and Tyr can also be found throughout the city, perpetually filled with devoted worshippers of all races. Several services are offered each day and provide residents near-limitless options for worship day or night.

TRADE AND COMMERCE

Although the capital city is toward the southern end of the peninsula, merchants and caravans make the long trek down the road to trade with outstanding craftsmen and one-of-a-kind artisans. Kingsgardt has one of the largest open-air markets in southeast Akados and boasts more than 500 merchants in the maze of colorful tents and awnings. It is said that if it can't be found in Kingsgardt, it doesn't exist.

GOVERNMENT

The hledwalda has personal authority over all of Kingsgardt, but administration of the city is usually granted to a reeve, often a relative of the king. The reeve then appoints such offices as are necessary to see to the city's orderly management.

MAJOR THREATS

Although well protected by the king's personal house guard, the city is not without threats. Hill and frost giants from the Hatlu Peaks, filled with the desire for the fabled treasure within the vaults of the kings, occasionally descend from the tall mountains to invade the city. Never has a single giant made it past the outermost city walls, with the ballistae and catapults from the towers that loom over the open fields surrounding the city ready to strike them down.

AETHELHAM, TOWN OF

Ruler: Ealdorman Garth Ovunweld
Government: feudal
Population: 8,872 (8,550 Heldring, 322 mountain dwarf)
Monstrous: dragons, goblins
Languages: Common, Helvaenic
Religion: most worship Eostre and Tyr with some devoted to the goddess Hel (in secret)
Resources: grain, copper, livestock, woolen garments
Currency: Heldring, although barter is common
Technology Level: Dark Ages

This fortified town is located at the southern end of the old defensive earthwork known as the Wealdyke near a spur of the Cumorian Mountains. Now one of the larger towns of the Heldring, Aethelham is of comparatively recent construction. None of the ancient clans called this locale home. Instead, the town was likely built to hold the southern flank of the Wealdyke. But its location was fortuitous, with a commanding position over wide fields and access to mines in the nearby mountains.

In the fields nearby, farmers grow wheat, barley, and corn, and in the mountain foothills shepherds tend flocks of sheep. The wool-spinners in Aethelham are some of the best of their craft and produce well-made garments for their own use and for sale in the markets of Kingsgardt. Several dirt roads lead off to the Cumorians to several active mines (and some abandoned).

The family of the current ealdorman has held Aethelham in fiefdom for generations. It is said that one of his ancestors was responsible for building the Wealdyke, and tales of his battles with the Daanites are legendary.

The worship of the sibling gods Eostre and Tyr dominates in Aethelham, though many of the farmers and shepherds continue to venerate the old gods. Unknown to most, a few older families have connections to Thunderhelde in the mountains and continue to worship Hel in secret.

BERROCBURH, TOWN OF

Ruler: Ealdorman Bijeorn "Longbeard" Arjenstal
Government: feudal
Population: 2,117 (1,998 Heldring, 64 Foerdewaith, 55 human mixed ethnicity)
Monstrous: sea-raiders, orcish races from the Cumorian Mountains
Languages: Common, Helvaenic
Religion: Eostre and Tyr
Resources: fishing, farming, livestock
Currency: Heldring, barter
Technology Level: Dark Ages

A remote town in the far northwest of the kingdom, Berrocburh is secluded from much of the traffic through the central part of the peninsula. Though now largely a backwater, the town is proud of its history as the ancestral home of the Baerroc, one of the original seven, semi-mythical clans of the Heldring.

Most of the Berros make their living through farming or herding, though some fishing is done off of the nearby western coast of the peninsula. There are no good harbors in this area, which leaves the fishing vessels to launch off shores of rocky scree. It is easy to land boats there, however, and as a result, raids from western pirates and slavers have nearly decimated Berrocburh dozens of times throughout the town's history. In order to protect themselves, the Berros became formidable sailor-soldiers. Nearly every man, woman, and child in Berrocburh is capable of fighting, their tough existence hardening their will for survival. Children are taught archery as soon as they can hold a small bow, and women are equals to their husbands and fathers with sword and shield. Intruders are met with surprising tenacity and often flee after realizing their error in choosing the town as their target.

Capable shipbuilders and fishermen, Berrocburh's residents maintain a meager yet comfortable lifestyle. Though wary of strangers entering their town, the surprisingly good-natured Berros are willing to trade fairly for supplies they lack. Salted fish, clams, and shellfish are traded for tools, vegetables, and beer. Though the Heldring currency is accepted, many in the town prefer to barter for luxuries.

The town hosts a small temple to Eostre and Thyr, though attendance is meager except during the festival days.

The Berros have a unique tradition concerning their ealdorman, which due to its antiquity is honored by the hledwalda in Kingsgardt. The position is not hereditary. At an annual rite on the eve of the spring equinox, any Berros who feel their current ealdorman has lacked the proper skills or nerve to run the town may challenge the ealdorman to ritual combat, the winner taking or retaining the seat. Only one challenger may attempt to win the seat, elected by town vote if more than one steps forward. The current ealdorman may elect to step down at the spring equinox, vacating the seat willingly without any disrespect or dishonor.

Pirates and slavers are the most common threat to Berrocburh. However, raids from the west are becoming less frequent as the stories of the ferocious and unrelenting Berros reach foreign ears. Unfortunately, while the sea-raids have lessened over several decades, orcish stirrings within the Cumorian Mountains have increased. Orc tribes have probed farther north and west, hoping to gain a foothold beyond their dark holes. The northern end of the vast range is teeming with numerous orc clans, each vying for the rumored wealth of human villages.

Bournedon, Town of

Ruler: Iken Forewolden, Chieftain of the Long Road
Government: feudal
Population: 2,311 (1,625 Heldring, 348 mountain dwarf, 338 human mixed ethnicity)
Monstrous: orcs from the western hills and giants from the Hatlu peaks
Languages: Common, Helvaenic
Religion: Eostre and Tyr
Resources: traders, sheepherders, and some farming
Currency: Heldring, some Foerdewaith, and bartering for goods with travelers
Technology Level: Dark Ages

A central point in the peninsula and astride the Long Road, the bustling town of Bournedon sees a fair amount of traffic each day. It seems nearly every resident has something to sell or trade — homes along the main road all have storefronts open to travelers as they pass. Clothes, food, weapons, armor, supplies, and trinkets are found in plenty along the wide, stone road. Dwarves from the Cumorian Mountains have been allowed to bring their wares to sell at the northern and southern ends of town, displaying well-crafted weapons and armor at reasonable prices.

The town of Bournedon was formed around a temple to Hel long ago, bringing acolytes and worshippers to the central plain village where three dirt paths intersected. Over time, the village grew into a town boasting two great taverns (both still exist, the Rolling Mug and Broken Wheel) and several merchants with access to excellent wares. Although the temple of Hel was eventually destroyed, the town continued to thrive from its constant traffic. As a hospitable location on the Long Road, Bournedon has become a welcome stop for most travelers heading north or south.

Most of the people make their living trading and selling goods to travelers. Although nothing like the markets of bigger cities, travelers can find common supplies at affordable prices, whether they wish to pay in gold or silver, or trade an unwanted item or two. Nearly every merchant in Bournedon is agreeable to a reasonable deal. About a fifth of the town's residents still herd sheep along the hills and plains and provide the much-needed wool for many of the clothing shops on the town's main road.

Shrines for several deities have been erected within the town's borders, though the vast majority of its residents worship the common gods of the Heldring, both Tyr and Eostre. A small pocket of believers still pay homage to Hel although their practices are quiet and in secret. Most travelers can find a shrine serving a god or goddess from their homeland as they pass through this town.

Iken Forewolden, the ealdorman of Bournedon, also holds the traditional title of the chieftain of the Long Road. He has now been providing leadership over the slow-growing town for two decades. More businessman than warrior, the chieftain ensures that the families of Bournedon continue to prosper by limiting growth of new homes and businesses. Although Forewolden listens to the advice of many, he is the lone voice of leadership in the town. He makes and changes the rules, administers punishment to criminals, and negotiates deals with merchants and dwarven clans.

Although a score of lightly trained soldiers protects the inner portion of the town, Forewolden enlists the services of sturdy dwarves of the Bloodbeard clan and pays them in much-needed supplies. Nearly a hundred dwarven veterans, each with years of battle experience in the depths of the Cumorian Mountains, devoutly protect the borders of Bournedon. The stout Bloodbeards have quickly thwarted several orc and goblin raids from nearby hills.

The town's hired forces can easily contain and quash most humanoid raids from the west, but when hill and frost giants descend down from the eastern peaks of Hatlu, the town seeks reinforcements from dwarven clans and Heldring settlements from the north. Hundreds of mounted and armored dwarves often rout the slow-witted giants before they can do much damage to the town.

Burh Weider, Village of

Ruler: Thegn Haandol Weider, Council Spokesman
Government: feudal (Council of Elder Fishermen)
Population: 511 (Heldring)
Monstrous: pirates at sea, humanoid creatures from nearby mountains
Languages: Common, Helvaenic
Religion: Eostre and Thyr; worship of an unnamed sea god
Resources: fishing, light farming
Currency: Heldring accepted, but bartering preferred
Technology Level: Dark Ages

The village of Burh Weider, situated on the eastern coast, is one of the newest settlements in the Helcynngae Peninsula and was formed only three decades ago. Named after its original founding family, the settlement has grown as regional fishermen learned of the abundant sea life found off its shores. The secret to catching the long, delicate fish that reside off the coast is known only to those who have lived in the village for some time and is never shared with outsiders.

Yeolder Weider, a landless thegn, was granted the right to establish this village by the ealdorman in Uthelgardt about 30 years ago. He chose this coastal location after discovering the sea nearby to be teeming with strange, slender fish. Thinking he could catch and trade the long fish with neighboring settlements, he quickly set to the task of fishing the eastern coastline. However, he soon learned that the fish were more intelligent than other aquatic creatures and was unable to catch them. It took many months for the Weider family to discover the correct method for ensnaring the cunning fish. As the only fisherman able to catch the delicious sea creature, the Weider family and trusted villagers trade for supplies with frequent merchants who arrive by land and sea.

As with the rest of the Helcynngae Peninsula, the worship of Eostre and Thyr is prominent in Burh Weider, and a temple to the sibling gods is found on the western side of the village. However, local fishermen and their families quietly worship an unnamed sea god whose image has been passed down through stories from the original inhabitants of the area. Fisherman say prayers of thanks and reverence while at sea when successful capture of their bounty occurs. While no shrines, priests, or totems to this god can be found in Burh Weider, the people's devotion to their protector and judge is strong. So far, the church ignores the worship of this sea god so long as it remains largely hidden from view, and so long as the pews remain filled on holy days.

Although Thegn Haandol Weider has title to the village and surrounding lands, he governs with the advice (and usually, consent) of a council of elder sailors. At least half the council are his relatives from the Weider family, their voices being the most respected among the group. The elder sailors of the council are the only men and women who know the full secrets to fishing for the silvery delicacy.

Pirates and sea-raiders have been known to harass the small fishing vessels from the village on occasion, though the Burh Weider fishermen are always on the lookout for foreign ships and quickly slide their small boats into a well-hidden harbor if a threat appears. In addition, a local militia is maintained to protect the fishermen and farmers of Burh Weider from the threats of the sea and neighboring mountains. Several dozen well-armed men and women patrol the area, keeping an eye out for trouble from every direction. The small village is rarely a target and is avoided by most who pass by the hidden coastal locale. Occasionally, fisherman from other nearby settlements attempt to catch the cunning fish of these waters, but inevitably become frustrated, though this never stops new fishermen from arriving and trying to discover the secret to landing the rare sea creature.

BURKESTON, TOWN OF

Ruler: Ealdorman Orlan Fjordson
Government: feudal
Population: 4,750 (3,989 Heldring, 511 Foerdewaith, 250 human mixed ethnicity)
Monstrous: goblins, orcs, and trolls of the Cumorian Mountains (and some thrydreg)
Languages: Common, Helvaenic
Religion: Eostre, Thyr, Wotan the All-Father
Resources: trade, steel, sheep and goat herding, some farming
Currency: Heldring, though most common Akadonian currencies are accepted, as is barter
Technology Level: Dark Ages

Protectors of the Helwall and the northern peninsula, the people of Burkeston consider themselves the first line of defense to any invaders from beyond the ancient wall raised by the Hyperboreans. Ever vigilant and serious about their military prowess, the Burks are a fierce people with little tolerance for visitors who seek to disrupt the peace of the town. Many travelers have found themselves quickly dispatched by even the youngest of militia-men and in need of the healing services of the local clergy. Nearly three-quarters of the men of Burkeston can be ready to march to battle within a few moments and always seem more than willing to search out conflict and war.

Though there has been little conflict along the Helwall in generations, the people of Burkeston remain a tough and, to outsiders, an often mirthless folk. They are devoted to their families and livelihoods, holding these and their combat prowess above all else. It is mandatory that all Burks participate in daily training with sword and shield, lance, and longbow. Even children of five or six years of age can take down a bird in flight with a longbow.

As trade continues to grow between the Heldring and Cerediun Province (and the lands beyond), the road across the Helwall has seen a substantial increase in merchant traffic and other travelers in recent years. As the northernmost Heldring town on the Long Road, Burkeston has profited off of the trade by providing services to those passing north or south, collecting tolls for use of the road, and occasionally hiring themselves out as guards for caravans or others seeking protection in the peninsula.

The blacksmiths of Burkeston are renowned for their speed and quality of work, often drawing comparisons to dwarven skills. Excellent bowyers and fletchers can also be found in the village, though most are unwilling to trade their wares to outsiders.

Burkeston maintains a strong relationship with the smaller village of Berrocburh to the west and lends soldiers to assist in driving growing goblinoid clans back into the Cumorian Mountains from time to time. In return, the Berros supply their allies with small amounts of a rare fish egg found along the western coast that the inlanders consider a delicacy.

Ealdorman Orlan Fjordson rules Burkeston alongside a council of 13 elders elected by all residents of the town able to wield a sword. No Burk may run for council until they are of 30 years of age and may not hold a council seat for more than 10 years in total. By tradition, the vote of the council is to be accepted by the ealdorman (who holds a double vote on the council), though on rare occasions its decision can be overruled.

The town of Burkeston is always under threat of raids from the Cumorian Mountains, and occasionally from bandits seeking to attack traffic on the Long Road. However, the town is always in a state of preparedness and eager to meet any conflict head-on.

DURWENT, CITY OF

Ruler: Ealdorman Aelfric Dorgorson and Olagaard Bronzehand, aka "Ha'Dwarf"
Government: feudal
Population: 11,179 (7,222 Heldring, 3,005 dwarf, 952 human mixed ethnicity)
Monstrous: none
Languages: Common, Helvaenic, Dwarven
Religion: Thyr, Eostre, Dwerfater
Resources: shipping, trade, farming, sod-farming, sheepherding, some mining
Currency: Heldring, barter, raw gold, silver, or gems
Technology Level: Dark Ages

The city of Durwent stands upon a promontory on the eastern shore of the Helcynngae Peninsula. The Heldrings' largest port on the Sinnar Ocean, Durwent is the gateway to Kingsgardt and the central towns and farmlands of the kingdom. Ships from around Akados, and even from far Libynos, can be found at dock in the harbor alongside large numbers of Heldring longships. The city bustles with merchants and craftsmen, mercenaries, travelers, and vagabonds.

Ealdorman Dorgorson maintains a strict peace in the city and surrounding countryside, his house guard being large and well-paid. Docking fees and other tariffs keep his coffers full, but he is wise enough to know that overzealous costs would impair the trade that flows through the city. Corruption is much less prevalent here than is the case in other port cities.

The city walls, and much of the foundations, are of dwarven construction, and in fact predate the arrival of the Heldring to this locale. According to legend, when the ancestors of the Heldring first came to the promontory, they found the place already built, home to a small number of dwarves, unlike any others to be found in Akados. Where they came from, and how they might be related to their kin, is unknown. But to this day, the Durr dwarves are found only here, in Durwent and its nearby lands. Their differences with mountain and hill dwarves are noticeable. Although stocky and bearded like other dwarves, the Durr are blond and bronze-skinned. They enjoy swimming in the sea and sailing (to a small degree) and prefer the sun on their faces to the darkness of the underground. They are decent farmers and have just recently discovered their hidden talent for mining, scouring sea caves along the coast for hidden pockets of precious stones and metals. Though gregarious and happy to partake in trade and commerce, they keep their private lives to themselves, and show no more familiarity with other dwarven clans than they do with humans.

Of late, some substantial deposits of gemstones have been found in some of those nearby sea-caves, which has drawn attention (not all welcome) to Durwent and its unusual dwarven residents. Pirates harassing ships out of the port and brigands on the road to Wirric Bury, once unheard of, are becoming increasingly common.

The ealdorman usually leaves issues concerning the Durr dwarves to their hereditary chieftain, currently the generally well-regarded Olagaard Bronzehand, also known as "Ha'Dwarf." A number of traditions have developed to address those circumstances where matters arise between human and dwarf.

Most of the Heldring in Durwent worship Eostre and Thyr. Some of the Durr dwarves have come to venerate Thyr as well, though the majority pray to Dwerfater. If there is a shrine that the dwarves visit, however, it is unknown to their human neighbors.

Erodgrimm, City of

Ruler: Lord Grisselfire V
Government: Governing Council of Lords
Population: unknown (guesses of 5,000 to 10,000 mountain dwarves are possible)
Monstrous: all manner of dark-dwelling humanoids
Languages: Dwarven; some Common
Religion: Dwerfater
Resources: mining, trapping
Currency: Erodgrimm
Technology Level: Medieval

No greater population of dwarves exists on the peninsula than the number found in Erodgrimm, a mountain citadel carved into the Eorec Heights. Thousands of the stout folk work to remain both independent of the realm of the Heldrings and completely self-sufficient. From windows carved high on the mountainsides, one can see the southern plains of the Heldring to the north and the isle of Ynys Cymragh across the Straits of Daan to the southeast.

Erodgrimm was founded relatively recently, as the dwarves count the years, by a small group of survivors of the Great Mountain Clan Targ fleeing the destruction of Hazad-Burgh in 3160 I.R. As a general matter, the folk of the city rarely trade with any other than their own race. Until very recently, their citadel remained closed to the Heldring in neighboring settlements. With the exception of a few trusted humans in Suthgardt, not a single Heldring has been able to secure any of the exceptional swords, axes, shields, or armor that the expert craftsmen of the citadel create.

Numerous shrines to the dwarf-god Dwerfater are found throughout the citadel, on street corners, roofs, and fountains. The father of the dwarves is revered and respected in this mountain refuge. Several small temples are found at the outer edges of the city and are mainly attended by young dwarves and those not wishing to travel across the city to the main shrine at the citadel's center.

A governing council of 20 lords of the original families oversees the day-to-day and long-term needs of the community. Each family is responsible for a single craft or duty within the citadel, with their lone representative attending the council on their behalf. The council works to ensure that the citadel and its residents prosper. They elect one among their number to act as lord of the citadel, though the powers of this individual, absent war or other crisis, are more ceremonial than substantive.

Five hundred well-trained soldiers protect the citadel from harm and easily drive off small raids of goblins or orcs, and sometimes greater threats of ogres, trolls, or giants. Many of the surrounding humanoid tribes avoid crossing paths with the fearless dwarves as they know their survival is unlikely during any battle.

Recently, rumors have reached Erodgrimm that dwarven ruins have been found in the Cumorian Mountains. No tales tell of dwarven folk in those peaks, so the origin of those ruins — or the veracity of the rumors — remains unknown.

Lichfield, Town of

Ruler: Ealdorman Frolgar Frostboar
Government: feudal
Population: 3,665 (3,285 Heldring, 210 human mixed ethnicity, 170 Foerdewaith)
Monstrous: orcish races from the Cumorian Mountains
Languages: Common, Helvaenic
Religion: Thyr, Eostre
Resources: farming, trading, herding (livestock)
Currency: Heldring, barter
Technology Level: Dark Ages

Lichfield stands amid rolling plains on the Long Road between Burkeston and Lymnester. The town holds little in the way of wealth, earning nearly all of its income from trade along the road, along with some farming and livestock. But the people of Lichfield are proud folk of old stock, their town the ancestral home of the Aelrich, one of the legendary clans of the Heldring. Most have lived their entire lives in the town or nearby farms. The locals are average craftsmen at best, their only exceptional ability seemingly in animal husbandry.

Visitors rarely stay long in Lichfield, moving on after a few hours or a day at most. There are a few inns in town with comfortable beds, fine fare, and great dwarven ale. But there is little else here to divert a traveler's attention.

A town militia protects the residents from infrequent raids from the Cumorian Mountains to the west. Twenty armed men patrol the village day and night, banishing non-believers and repelling would-be troublemakers.

Lymnester, Town of

Ruler: Abbess Gunnfrith
Government: feudal (religious)
Population: 780 (632 Heldring, 111 human mixed ethnicity, 37 mountain dwarf)
Monstrous: orcish races from the Cumorian Mountains
Languages: Common, Helvaenic
Religion: Eostre, Tyr
Resources: farming, trading, herding
Currency: Heldring
Technology Level: Dark Ages

Lymnester is home to Leofric Abbey, a convent of 30 priestesses of Eostre led by the imposing Abbess Gunnfrith. The charter granting the town and surrounding lands to the church is one of the oldest, dating to shortly after Oescreheit Downs. The Warders of St. Leofric, a small order of holy knights, is based here to guard the abbey and the surrounding countryside.

With Leofric Abbey providentially located at the intersection of roads leading to Lichfield, Uthelgardt, and Bournedon, a small town has grown up around its walls to cater to merchants and travelers making their way through the peninsula. While those passing through are not required to pay any tolls, it is long tradition to make a donation of a portion of the value of one's goods to the abbey to ensure the gods' favor. After all, the roads here can be perilous, threatened by orcish raiders from the mountains or brigands seeking to separate coin from those traveling unawares. The abbey and the walled town are a welcome sight to many braving the empty miles in the midst of the peninsula. And tales certainly tell of greedy merchants who failed to pay a proper tithe to the priestesses, only to vanish after leaving Lymnester, never to arrive at their next destination.

Oxwain, Town of

Ruler: Ealdorman Ealdric Mundgard
Government: feudal
Population: 5,736 (4,852 Heldring, 811 human mixed ethnicity, 73 mountain dwarf)
Monstrous: humanoid races from the Cumorian Mountains
Languages: Common, Helvaenic
Religion: Eostre and Tyr; some worship of Hel in secret
Resources: trade, farming, herding, mining
Currency: Heldring
Technology Level: Dark Ages

The legendary home of the Ochs, one of the original Heldring clans, Oxwain in recent years has found itself increasingly dominated by the nearby capital of Kingsgardt. A proud folk, many Oxwains chafe under what they consider the overbearing rule of the hledwaldas. This has made the town a ripe target for intrigue by its mountain neighbor, the heretical city of Thunderhelde. More than a few nobles and leading citizens of Oxwain are rumored to have become initiates of the Lady of Pestilence.

Situated on the Long Road, much trade moves through the town of Oxwain and brings a not insubstantial amount of wealth to the residents. The nearby farms and fields are productive and provide a decent surplus that can be sold to merchants passing through or brought to the larger markets in Kingsgardt. Several lucrative mines are also maintained in the nearby Cumorian Mountains. It is said that some of the mines employ professional laborers from Thunderhelde, a folk particularly experienced with the craft of carving ores and gems from the mountain rock. Such allegations are unproven, however, as commerce with the excommunicated residents of that city is illegal among the Heldring.

Ealdorman Ealdric Mundgard does his best to convince his people of the value of being loyal servants to the crown. He makes a point of honoring all of his obligations to Kingsgardt to the letter and ensures that the hledwalda in turn honors all of his obligations to Oxwain. So far, at least among the other nobles, these efforts have silenced any talk of rebellion.

Ealdric, though married, has fathered no children as of yet. As a result, the current heir to Oxwain is his younger brother, Earrim Mundgard, who serves as the captain of the city guard. A few have noted Earrim's unusually frequent visits to the mines in the Cumorian foothills where he meets with locals living in the mountains. Moreover, tongues wag that Earrim never seems to attend services at the temple of Eostre and Thyr in the city.

Goblins and orcs from the Cumorian Mountains are always a threat to Oxwain, as are other dark creatures that live in the peaks and valleys. But the greatest threat may be the one recognized but left unspoken, the gradual infiltration of the influence of Thunderhelde and the worship of Hel into the city. What plans that mountain citadel may have are unknown, but a rebellion in Oxwain, which would undoubtedly bring down the wrath of Kingsgardt, would certainly be welcomed there.

SUTHGARDT, TOWN OF

Ruler: Ealdorman Forgwolfe Cavatral
Government: feudal/military
Population: 10,786 (9,110 Heldring, 835 human mixed ethnicity, 499 Foerdewaith, 342 mountain dwarf)
Monstrous: sea-raiders; humanoids, giants and wyrms from the Eorec Heights
Languages: Common, Helvaenic
Religion: Thyr
Resources: fishing (rare crabs and shellfish) and farming, trade
Currency: Heldring, barter
Technology Level: Dark Ages

The southernmost town of the Helcynngae Peninsula, Suthgardt is the ancestral home of the Suthca, one of the semi-mythical original clans of the Heldring. The town boasts a sizable presence of soldiers and armed longships, all under the command of the ealdorman, who also holds the Heldring title of helm of the south. Under the charter from Kingsgardt, Suthgardt is charged with guarding against invasion from Ynys Cymragh and protecting the nearby sea-lanes (particularly for the smaller coastal towns of Wellford and Warsley).

Many ships venturing between the Crescent Sea to the west and the Sinnar coast of Akados pay call at the port of Suthgardt to resupply. As a result, the town does a brisk trade, and many establishments cater to the needs of sailors and merchants. Many fishing vessels at the docks leave each morning to scour the small, southern bay for rare white crabs and pygmy shellfish, delicacies in other parts of the Lost Lands.

Nearly a fifth of the town's population are professional soldiers or sailors under the respective command of a chief of the Shieldwall

and a lord captain, each appointed by the ealdorman. A small council consisting of the chief, the lord captain, and representatives of several of the larger guilds in town advise the ealdorman, proposing laws and regulations for Suthgardt and the areas under its protection.

Suthgardt maintains a cautious relationship with the dwarven citadel of Erodgrimm in the Eorec Heights. The dwarves care little for issues of concern to humans, but some trade has proven beneficial to both. Most of the trade occurs, however, in Suthgardt; almost no humans are ever invited to, or permitted in, Erodgrimm. As a consequence, some items of dwarven handiwork of spectacular quality can be found in the more exclusive shops in town, though they are never on display — one has to know where to go and whom to ask.

It is said that the ealdorman and Lord Grisselfire have exchanged quiet embassies, and have agreed to aid the other in the event of any external threat that could pose a risk to the entire region. In fact, soldiers of both cities have repelled a few incursions of ogres and giants. If the rumors of a large dragon somewhere in the Eorec Heights prove true, then this alliance may prove critical.

Due to the dominance of the military in town, the worship of Thyr is predominant here, though there is a shrine to Eostre. Some of the sailors, conservative in their ways, continue to worship Njördr, the old god of seafarers and the winds.

THUNDERHELDE, CITY OF

Ruler: Hel's Regent, High Thegn of the Helcynn and Köenig of the Helite Council, Östric the Gaunt
Government: tyrannical theocracy with Helite Council (religious noble advisory council)
Population: 10,321 (9,601 Heldring, 341 ogrekin, 212 troll-blooded, 167 half-ogre)
Monstrous: goblins, goblin dogs, ogres, ogrens, worgs, firbolgs, ettins, will-o'-wisps, trolls, nilbogs
Languages: Helvaenic, Common, Giant, Goblin
Religion: Hel
Resources: coal, iron, ironwork, plunder, gems
Currency: none (though most coinage of precious metals are accepted)
Technology Level: Dark Ages

With the Foerdewaith defeat of the Heldring army at Oescreheit Downs in 2802 I.R., the Foere pantheon was introduced to the Helcynngae Peninsula, particularly the worship of Thyr and Eostre. When the hledwalda himself was converted, the veneration of the older gods started a precipitous decline. Shortly thereafter, the worship of Hel, who had previously been the matron deity of the Heldring, was outlawed.

Not all Heldring willingly gave up the ways of the Lady of Pestilence. After several armed conflicts, the Hel worshippers were driven into the Cumorian Mountains where they built stone-walled forts in the heights and forested valleys. Several attempts to exterminate them ended in disaster, and eventually the lowland Heldring decided to leave their former kin alone in the mountains.

Today, perhaps 35,000 Heldring live deep in the Cumorian Mountains alongside allies consisting of goblins, ogres, troll-blooded, and half-ogres numbering in the thousands. Their largest settlement, and the capital of their realm in exile, is the fortress city of Thunderhelde. From here, the Helfolk of the Cumorians are ruled with an iron fist by their high thegn, a high priest of Hel, alongside a council of priests and nobles known as the Helite Council. The folk of Thunderhelde seek to spread the worship of the Lady of Pestilence to their humanoid allies in the mountains, and eventually to their lowland kin. They live for hardship, battle, and purity, dreaming of the day when they will sweep the entire peninsula free of the invader gods and return the exclusive worship of Hel to their ancestral lands.

Within Thunderhelde and any lands under its control, the worship of any deity other than Hel is punishable by death (preferably by fire). Nearly every building and structure in the city displays the grim visage of the goddess, her blue and white face glaring at all who look in her direction. Those who die gloriously in battle are given large tombs in a mountainside overlooking the fortress and bestowed with all honors and respect of one who went to willingly serve their goddess.

Due to its isolation and the laws of Kingsgardt that prohibit commerce with Thunderhelde, its folks are self-sufficient and independent, only rarely trading with outsiders. The one exception is a growing, underground trade with the miners of Oxwain, the nearest Heldring settlement. The High Thegn has spies among those miners and is said to have agents in Oxwain itself. While he doesn't appear to be ready to provoke a general war with the Heldring, a rebellion by Oxwain would be an interesting — and likely useful — development.

UTHELGARDT, TOWN OF

Ruler: Ealdorman Brunhilda Harkeness, First Hunter of Uthelgardt
Government: feudal
Population: 5,707 (4,776 Heldring, 810 human mixed ethnicity, 121 Foerdewaith)
Monstrous: brigands and raiders of the plains
Languages: Helvaenic, Common
Religion: Eostre
Resources: trade, farming, mining
Currency: Heldring, barter
Technology Level: Dark Ages

The ancestral home of the Uthael, one of the original clans of the Heldring, Uthelgardt's most famous son is the semi-mythical Thurbald the Great, the first hledwalda of the Heldring. Once Thurbald finished his conquest of the Helcynngae Peninsula, however, he chose to establish a new city to be his capital, which became Kingsgardt. To this day, the Heldring of Uthelgardt, with their long memories, view the capital as a younger sibling, and themselves as the true, original first city of the peninsula. Whatever the true history may be, this hilltop city has long been home to thousands of folk, including artisans, merchants, and warriors.

Part of the reason for Uthelgardt's loss of influence is undoubtedly the fact that it lies off of the Long Road, the main route through the Helcynngae Peninsula. Moreover, the population is rather thin along the south coast of the Bryon Firth. As a result, while there certainly are opportunities for trade in Uthelgardt, there is simply not as much money to be made as in those cities on the Long Road.

In addition to trade, some mining is done in the nearby Hatlu Peaks, and farming and cattle are raised in the nearby fields.

There are those in the ealdorman's family who harbor dreams of the ancient glories of Uthelgardt, and in the dark whisper about what it might take to overthrow the predominance of Kingsgardt. Brunhilda Harkeness herself, however, seems to discourage such thoughts.

The folk of Uthelgardt, particularly those outside the city walls, are subject to the occasional raids of humanoids from the Hatlu Peaks such as goblins, orcs, and ogres, as well as brigands on the roads.

WARSLEY, TOWN OF

Ruler: Ealdorman Raegan Althorne
Government: feudal
Population: 3,470 (Heldring)
Monstrous: goblins, orcs, and giants from the Cumorian Mountains
Languages: Common, Helvaenic
Religion: Eostre and Tyr
Resources: trade, fishing, grains (wheat, barley, oats, potatoes)
Currency: Heldring, barter
Technology Level: Dark Ages

Warsley is a small burh and shire west of the Cumorian Mountains. Passage over the mountains being difficult (due to both physical barriers and the humanoid and other residents of the peaks), the town is largely isolated from the rest of the Helcynngae Peninsula other than by sea travel. Said to be the home of the Waershael, one of the original seven clans of the Heldring, the town today plays little part in the politics of the peninsula. It makes its way hosting ships traveling the southern coast of Akados at its docks, doing a decent business in trade and providing services to sailors and merchants; the Tangled Rigging, a dockside tavern, is a particular favorite among those who frequent the docks in Warsley. Fishing vessels leave from its port each morning and bring home their catches in the evening, and various grains are farmed in the fields between mountain and coast. As long as Warsley continues to pay its taxes to Kingsgardt, the rest of the Heldring mostly ignore the town, a state of affairs quite satisfactory to Warsley as well.

There have been the occasional troubles with the denizens of the Cumorian Mountains, however, and Warsley fought a mountain war with the goblins 20 years ago. Giants can also be a threat to outlying communities, and the fyrd has had to be raised in defense more than once in recent years.

The Althorne family has held the shire for many generations. The current ealdorman, Raegan, succeeded to the title last year after the ship his mother was on sank in a storm.

The Vale, a small idyllic valley, lies north of the town.

*REFERENCE SOURCE: DEEP IN THE VALE FROM **Quests of Doom***

WELLFORD, VILLAGE OF

Ruler: Lord Arlid Ansgaar
Government: feudal
Population: 931 (843 Heldring, 88 human mixed ethnicity)
Monstrous: sea-raiders, orcish races from the Cumorian Mountains
Languages: Helvaenic, Common
Religion: Eostre and Tyr
Resources: fishing, some farming
Currency: Heldring, barter
Technology Level: Dark Ages

Wellford is one of the oldest fishing villages on the western coast of the peninsula. Only a few small piers jut out into the water but they are suitable for nothing larger than a modest fishing vessel. No roads lead to Wellford, just light trails that are easily found by experienced trackers and those familiar with the route. As a general matter, those who live here have lived here for many generations and support themselves by fishing or farming. They receive little notice from the larger cities of the Heldring. In recent years, however, as Suthgardt's longships have chased away pirates and others who might threaten Wellford, the town has seen some small growth.

Wellford's residents worship Eostre and Tyr in a temple that overlooks the ocean in the western edge of town. A single priest ministers to the villagers and is replaced only upon death or sickness.

Lord Ansgaar, the fifth of his line to hold title to Wellford, has been trying to increase his trade options by sending merchants to some neighboring settlements to offer fish, crabs, and other sea creatures for much-needed supplies not found in the coastal village. He would eventually like to raise enough funds to expand the docks to permit larger vessels to make port in Wellford.

Although the village primarily consists of fishermen and farmers, nearly 50 men and women have experienced enough battle along their settlement's borders to be able to protect their town from small raids or single pirate ships. In the event of any major threat, however, the villagers look to Suthgardt for protection. Luckily, their remote location keeps them safe from marauding hordes and large fleets of sea-raiders.

WIRRIC BURY, TOWN OF

Ruler: Ladies Evelynn, Astrid, Agraat, Yniss, and Ulaarta
Government: matriarchal council
Population: 7,500 (7,000 Heldring, 500 human mixed ethnicity)
Monstrous: humanoids from nearby mountains
Languages: Helvaenic, Common

Religion: Eostre and Thyr
Resources: farming, cattle-herding, and exceptional artisans
Currency: Heldring
Technology Level: Dark Ages

This large town at the northern end of the Wealdyke — located on the road between Kingsgardt and Durwent — is a well-organized and efficient settlement primarily controlled by five noblewomen who form a matriarchal council. Although men and women share common rules throughout the town, Wirric Bury has had only women in the role of leadership for many years. Since their initial appointment decades earlier, the town has known only success and prosperity.

Under the watchful gaze of the capital city to the west, the small town of Wirric Bury has steadily grown to become one of the largest settlements in the region. While hardworking residents farm and herd cattle in the open space surrounding the walled settlement, an emerging group of artisans and their work has been growing in popularity, with sculpting, pottery, and music gaining renown in the region. Recently, leaders of the community commissioned the construction of a large theater that is rumored to seat 1,000. Neighboring settlements and even the nobles at the Kingsgardt court are said to be eagerly awaiting the completion of the theater.

Although shrines dedicated to Eostre and Tyr are found within the sprawling town, worship services, like attendees, have been declining substantially of late. With their focus on the newly emerging arts, many residents pay less attention to the gods. Priests turned to the church in Kingsgardt for help but have yet to receive a reply on the matter.

Although Wirric Bury once only traded cattle and crops with merchants and neighboring towns, their recent development and advancement in the arts has attracted rich and wealthy collectors. Inns and taverns received face lifts to meet the needs of those used to more comfortable and attentive service. The new influx of wealth entering the town stimulated the economy, which drew more merchants, business, and residents at a faster rate than ever before. Wirric Bury will no doubt grow into a city in the coming years.

The matriarchal council — which collectively possesses the right and title of an ealdorman — controls every aspect of the growing town. Each council member has authority over one of five matters: economy, art, defense, religion, and law. Although all five members get an equal vote with respect to proposed changes or additions to the settlement's governing doctrines, each member is an expert in her own area of responsibility.

Ynys Cymragh

(IN-is KIM-rah)
Capital: Dunkelding and Demetae
Notable Settlements: Caer Cadwin, Caer Cwm, Luggbroch
Ruler: none, though Daan was recognized as polemarch (ardrigh/high king) in centuries past
Government: loosely allied petty kingdoms
Population: 177,099 (118,300 Daanite, 20,100 Heldring [typically slaves], 14,100 wood elf, 9,950 gnome, 7,900 Foerdewaith, 3,700 half-elf, 1,600 wyvaran, 999 mountain dwarf, 450 changeling)
Monstrous: kelpies, selkies, fey (coastline); bog hounds, bog horses, fey, dire animals, fachans, hags, will-o'-wisps (lowlands); goblins, hobgoblins, kobolds, bugbears, firbolgs, ogres, trolls, veds, wyverns, mist dragons (mountains)
Languages: Common, Ogham, Elven, Sylvan, Druidic, Dwarven
Religion: Mithras, Old Way, Thyr, Heldring Pantheon (some), Fey Pantheon, Bilis, Crom Dubh
Resources: livestock (cattle, sheep), wool, fishing, horses, tin, iron, ironwork, gems
Currency: Daanite
Technology Level: Iron Age

Ynys Cymragh, a windswept island of high mountains, deep forests, and green fields, rises out of the waters at the end of the Helcynngae Peninsula across the Straits of Daan. It is a realm apart, home of the legendary people of Daan, liberators of Tircople, who have withdrawn to their isle and suffer few to set foot upon their shores.

History and People

There are no tales of a time before the people of Daan lived on Ynys Cymragh. Their oldest legends tell of their ancestors coming forth from deep caves within the mountains to spread over the peaks, hills, and valleys of the isle. Here they lived in a time of myth, worshipping the gods of the Old Way, until the coming of the Hyperboreans.

Then in 128 I.R., the Hyperboreans landed upon its shores. They quickly colonized the island and renamed it Insula Extremis. Over the ensuing centuries, the original folk of Ynys Cymragh adopted many of the practices of the Hyperboreans, including the worship of Mithras. For long years, the island was a province of the empire and at peace. But in many ways, the ancient traditions remained unaffected by the conquest.

With the disintegration of the Hyperborean Empire in the years leading up to 2500 I.R., the people of Ynys Cymragh again broke into squabbling, petty kingdoms. At the same time, the void left by the departing Hyperboreans led others to exploit the new chaos. One such folk, the Heldring of the Helcynngae Peninsula, began a series of conquests on the mainland of Akados. They also turned to their nearby island neighbors on Insula Extremis. Initially, the kingdoms repelled their attempts at invasion. But then an unnamed lesser king (believed to have been a king of Caer Cadwin) imported Heldring mercenaries in 2521 I.R. to supplement his own army and allowed them to settle in some areas of lower Gwynmet as part of their payment. Caer Cadwin was successful and briefly conquered a large portion of the island, but within two years the Heldring settlers expanded beyond their allotted boundaries and illegally brought in more of their folk across the strait. Soon, the mercenaries who had been invited in overthrew Caer Cadwin and most of its lands, and the rest of the island found itself in a war against the Heldring tribes.

The folk of Ynys Cymragh held fast for years, creating a virtual stalemate at the Strathclyde Mountains. But the greater numbers of the Heldring took a toll as more of the invaders arrived from across the strait and raided the island's coastal settlements, steadily taking more ground each year.

The stalemate finally broke when Daan, a native of Ynys Cymragh who had served the Hyperboreans in far Irkaina, returned to his homeland with his cavalry of heavy cataphracts. A commander with surpassing military skill and a near-unstoppable force of armored knights, he rallied the petty kingdoms of the island and drove the Heldring back. In 2566 I.R., the kings granted him the Hyperborean title of polemarch and he was named ardrigh (or high king) with absolute authority over all the folk of Ynys Cymragh. In a series of victorious battles, Daan broke the back of the Heldring armies and drove them to a few coastal settlements. In 2576 I.R., he defeated the last Heldring thegns at the Battle of Agedium and expelled the last of the invaders from the island.

For a period of time after that, Ynys Cymragh knew peace, but word of the spreading corruption in the Hyperborean court of Tircople compelled Daan (who still considered himself and his people loyal subjects of the Hyperborean Empire) to raise his standard as polemarch and rally his people to march upon Tircople and overthrow Trystecce, the corrupt empress who had taken over the throne and the church. In 2580 I.R., Daan's fleet landed at Durwent and swept through the Helcynngae Peninsula, utterly defeating any Heldring who rose against him. As he continued his march north, the warriors of many Heldring tribes flocked to his banner and swelled his ranks. Daan spent the next four years marching the length of Akados and across the Isthmus of Irkaina, rallying thousands upon thousands to his cause.

In 2584 I.R., his march ended at Tircople, and he besieged the imperial city. He finally managed to destroy the lich-queen Trystecce but was slain in the process. With the empire liberated but in tatters, Daan's loyal men of Ynys Cymragh carried his body back home. Upon their return, the island forever cut itself off from the rest of the world and called all other realms "Lloegyr" (meaning the "Lost Lands"), and took up the practice of calling themselves Daanites. Daan's body was

After Daan's return from Irkaina, a number of Hyperborean deities took root on Ynys Cymragh, nowhere more so than here at Caer Cwm. A follower of Daan's took holy vows to Thyr while on campaign, and before departing on the crusade to free Tircople, founded in the citadel an order of holy priests and warriors to the god of law. Those orders remain based in the fortress to safeguard several holy artifacts of their god and send forth their best to protect and preach throughout Ynys Cymragh and beyond. Statues of Thyr are found throughout the town, and it seems that not a single soul intentionally skips worship services.

The residents of Caer Cwn fish along the small peninsula to the southeast and bring back their daily catch to the docks where they trade with other Daanite merchants for goods such as fruits and vegetables from elsewhere on the island. Many blacksmiths of Caer Cwm are extremely talented, but they are rarely willing to trade their wares to outsiders. They spend most of their time working on gear for their paladins and warriors to ensure their protection with well-crafted armor. Work and trade are all performed in the name of Thyr to ensure that the monks and warrior-priests of the citadel are well-fed and equipped. In return, the paladins of the fortress patrol the region and dispatch raiders and skirmishing humanoids.

Cantrefs under the protection of Caer Cwn are spread over the coast and into the Powyn Mountains. The paladins of the citadel take their responsibility to their folk seriously and do not tolerate any threats to the peace of their lands.

A council of seven natural-born residents of Caer Cwm who have taken vows to Thyr uphold laws, try criminals, and decide matters of varying importance. By tradition, three paladins, two priests, and two monks hold seats on the Council of the Seven, with each chosen for a period of seven years by signs and portents shown to the council by Thyr himself. One of the paladins is also chosen as lord of the citadel and serves until the portents declare a successor.

More than a third of the settlement's residents can take up arms, from the paladins and soldiers of the citadel down to the battle-seasoned fishermen within the village. Surrounded by 30-foot-high, five-foot-thick walls at the top of a high cliff peak, the town is nigh impregnable. Each paladin is trained in lance and sword, and is an expert at fighting upon horseback. Any small group facing 50 to 100 Caer Cwm paladins in full armor baring down on them is likely to bolt.

Luggbroch, Town of

Ruler: Queen Brisen Gwenog
Government: kingdom and council of five senior craftsmen
Population: 5,985 (5,289 Daanite, 696 human mixed ethnicity)
Monstrous: giants, orcs, and ogres
Languages: Common, Ogham
Religion: Old Ways, Mithras, Thyr
Resources: fishing, shipbuilding, ironwork, furniture and manufactured crafts, some mining
Currency: barter primarily, some common currencies accepted
Technology Level: Dark Ages

Luggbroch, the southernmost settlement of the Daanites on Ynys Cymragh, is the capital of Noduminia, the island's harsh and barren southwestern coast and upland vales in the Strathclydes. Despite its remote location, the locals have made the town a warm and welcoming place to those brave enough to descend the trails to the shoreline or ride the violent waves of the southern Sinnar Ocean.

Were it not for the stands of mighty pines found in the nearby mountains that are ideal for shipbuilding, this town would likely have never grown larger than a hamlet. But its renown for building vessels of legendary seaworthiness led many craftsmen and merchants to make a home here at the far end of civilization on Akados. The town's attraction is enhanced by a few mines in the mountains where deposits of coal and the occasional diamond can be found.

Today, in addition to fishing and shipbuilding, Luggbroch boasts some of the finest craftsmen in the Daanite lands. With few passes through the Strathclydes, most trade is via the ocean with other towns on Ynys Cymragh, and particularly with Dunkelding to the north, the only market on the island open to outsiders.

Many residents of Noduminia continue to follow the Old Ways. Others, however, find solace in the hands of Tyr, bravest of the gods, who understands the trials of folk so remote from their fellows, including their sacrifices in the harshest of terrain and most unforgiving of elements.

The eldest member of five of the leading families of artisans sits on a traditional council and advises the king or queen and approves all major changes in local law.

Luggbroch maintains a modest militia that guards the town walls and patrols the small villages of Noduminia inland. But in the event of a real threat, they would likely need to look to the neighboring city of Dunkelding and the citadel of Caer Cwm. Every once in a while, giants or other humanoids seek to raid from the mountain fastnesses. Most settlements hunker down in those circumstances and wait for the invaders to depart. Luggbroch itself, mostly at the base of high cliffs overlooking the sea, is too hard a target for any but the most-organized bands. Occasionally, sea-raiders and pirates unfamiliar with the southern shoreline have thought to plunder the town. However, swift and punishing retribution from Dunkelding sailors has become common knowledge to those who travel the southern shipping lanes, with less-reputable ships usually avoiding the shoreline town.

Geographic Features and Points of Interest in the Helcynngae Peninsula

Bryon Firth

This is the largest firth of Helcynngae Peninsula. Historically, this has been the primary launching point of invading fleets of Heldring longships in the last thousand years. The Oescreheit Downs lie along its west coast.

Cumorian Mountains

A massive range of tall peaks and jagged mountains cascades through the entire western edge of the peninsula, effectively cutting off villages and hamlets on the west coast from aid from larger settlements in the central plains. Those separated by the dense ridge have learned to survive on their own with little support from their distant kin.

Countless tribes and clans of humanoid races populate the inhospitable mountain range. Goblins, orcs, ogres, trolls, and giants are found in large numbers throughout the Cumorians, which makes travel through or under the range a deadly proposition. The Heldring of Thunderhelde, with their veneration of Hel, pose a threat to any who might pass near their lands.

Rumors of ancient dwarven mines and tunnels made of gold beneath the Cumorian Mountains are unfounded but widely believed by the Heldring people. Numerous expeditions have resulted in failure — they either never find the legendary locales or never return.

Eorec Heights

The towering mountain range at the end of the Helcynngae Peninsula once provided natural protection from the Daanites of Ynys Cymragh years ago. The steep cliffs and near-vertical peaks make the Strait of Daan a windswept, choppy waterway that tests the skills of even the most experienced sailors.

Giants and various humanoids call these peaks home. In addition, the dwarven citadel of Erodgrimm is located here, though visitors are not welcome.

Small dragons have been known to lair in the Eorec Heights, primarily fighting among themselves to dominate the highest mountaintops. Wyrm sightings below the clouds are rare, and the beasts are only briefly witnessed as the large lizards grab up sheep, cows, or other cattle for a quick meal.

HATLU PEAKS

The eastern mountains of the Helcynngae Peninsula provide natural protection for the central plains and the great city of Kingsgardt. Raging storms along snowy peaks of the range are far away from the herders and farmers of the plains below.

Typical deep-dwelling creatures roam the mountain range and battle with other foul foes over a few hundred feet of rock. Tribes of goblins clash with orc clans while trolls and ogres butcher each other for better lairs. Luckily for the Heldrings on the plains below, the dimwitted and vile humanoids of the mountains are preoccupied with each other and their own greedy needs. However, lycanthropes are also known to roam these heights, and they are less easily fooled.

THE HELWALL

See "Helwall" under "Geographic Features and Points of Interest in the Sundered Kingdoms and the Sinnar Coast of Southeastern Akados."

MON MAGNI

The highest point on Ynys Cymragh, this mountain is considered sacred and is home to a powerful druidic order that protects a large ancient cromlech at the summit's peak. From this location, the evil ardrigh (high king) Crom Dubh ruled the island for a short time centuries ago. Mon Magni is also believed by some to hold the tomb of Daan.

OESCREHEIT DOWNS

This highland down, riddled with old stone circles of the Ancient Folk, is where Overking Osbert II of Foere defeated the Heldring and finally brought about the conquest of the Helcynngae Peninsula by the Foerdewaith. It is guarded by an ancient druidic order that use the local quail as spies.

POWYN MOUNTAINS

This small secondary mountain range is an offshoot of the larger Strathclyde Mountains on Ynys Cymragh. The mountain cantrefs of Caer Cwm occupy its northernmost portions.

RHOS BAY

The isle of Ynys Wair is in the midst of this bay on the west side of Ynys Cymragh, on the shores of which is also the port city and old Daanite capital of Demetae.

STRAIT OF DAAN

This narrow waterway separates the island of Ynys Cymragh from the mainland of the Helcynngae Peninsula. It has long been considered hostile waters infested by sea serpents and worse, though it is true that invasion fleets from Helcynngae and Ynys Cymragh have crossed its waters.

STRATHCLYDE MOUNTAINS

This primary mountain range of Ynys Cymragh serves as a natural barrier between the western kingdoms and eastern kingdoms of the island. Foothills and nearby vales are often settled by those who give allegiance to one of the nearby towns with their petty kinds. Most of the range, however, effectively lies outside the control of any kingdom. Mon Magni is claimed by Gwynmet. Many unusual creatures call these mountain peaks home, including fey, mysterious mountain dwarves, giants and goblinoids, wyverns, and an unusual concentration of mist dragons around certain peaks.

WEALDYKE

This manmade raised causeway and ditch running between Wirric Bury and Aethelham was constructed in the middle of the last millennium to provide a line of defense (which was ultimately unsuccessful) against the invasions of the Daanites from Ynys Cymragh. Remarkable in the swiftness of its completion, rumors say that it was raised upon the remnants of a much older fortification. The histories of the Heldring, however, do not tell of any earlier invaders of the peninsula, so if this is the case, it is unknown who might have built it or for what purpose.

YNYS WAIR

This island in the Straits of Daan is shrouded in mystery. Traditionally, it is considered one of the petty kingdoms of Ynys Cymragh, but in reality, it has had little to do with the larger island. It is said that many fey live on Ynys Wair, and that a stronghold of druids can be found there as well. Some connection with the druids of Mon Magni in the Strathclydes on Ynys Cymragh certainly exists, but the nature of that connection is unknown. Despite the various wars and conquests fought on the lands about the island, no navy has ever landed on its shores, nor has any army ever attempted to seize its ground. Some legends say that the tomb of Daan himself lies somewhere on the island. Whatever else may be said about Ynys Wair, it is certainly a place of great — though hidden — power.

EASTERN AKADOS AND THE STONEHEART MOUNTAINS

CENTRAL SINNAR COAST OF EASTERN AKADOS

The central Sinnar Coast of eastern Akados is described in detail in *The Lost Lands: Borderland Provinces* by **Frog God Games**.

POLITICAL SUBDIVISIONS OF THE CENTRAL SINNAR COAST OF EASTERN AKADOS

AACHEN PROVINCE

(AWK-in or AH-khin)
Capital: Vermis (32,500)
Notable Settlements: Aixe, Becqueril, Dlante, Elet, Gretspaan Citadel, Taundre
Ruler: Lord-Governor Theriven the Leopard
Government: feudalism (vassal of Foere)
Population: 2,238,000 (2,100,000 Foerdewaith, 105,000 halfling, 24,000 high elf, 9,000 hill dwarf)
Monstrous: goblin, giant animal (bear, dragonfly, wolf, stag), bugbear, fey, ankheg, gnoll, ogre, basilisk, cockatrice, giant, manticore, peryton (near Cretian Mountains), tiger, undead, treant, wyvern (Cretian foothills), unicorn
Languages: Common, Halfling, Elvish, Dwarven
Religion: Ceres, Freya, Thyr (declining), Mick O'Delving, Archeillus, Darach-Albith, Jamboor, Solanus (badly declining), Telophus, Belon the Wise, Kamien, Yenomesh
Resources: grain, wool, cloth, manufactured goods, cotton, furs, gems, silver
Currency: Foere
Technology Level: Medieval (cities), High Middle Ages (rural areas)

Aachen Province remains loyal to the Kingdom of Foere and is ruled by a lord-governor appointed by the overking. It is a relatively peaceful province, but potential revolution is brewing among the nobility. Order in the province is beginning to decay as outside trade dwindles due to high taxes at the border, and the pressure of this decline is already affecting the farmers and peasantry.

Aachen Province is found immediately to the west of Eastreach Province, in the Aachen Gap between the Mons Terminus range and the Cretian Mountains. Its boundaries are relatively well-established, with the exception of the rural boundaries with Eastreach Province. Starting clockwise from the Great Bridge, Aachen's border cuts southeast in a generally diagonal line to just south of the Estuary Road's intersection with the Wain Road. It is this boundary that gets vague as it circles around farms and villages in the countryside. Thence, the line naturally follows the edge of the Cretian Mountains westward through the town of Elet and eventually to the city of Aixe. It is here that the boundary line crosses the Aachen Gap and continues northwest to reach the southern extent of the Mons Terminus just north of the ruins of Curgantium. The western border is demarcated by the upper run of the Great Amrin River, where it hugs the edge of the Mons Terminus Range northward to the Great Bridge.

These boundaries correspond closely to the older concept of "the Aachenland," although the old Aachenland culture extends a bit farther south into Foere than the administrative boundaries of the province.

HISTORY AND PEOPLE

The native Aachenlanders were absorbed into the Kingdoms of Foere when King Macobert established the province in the year 2720 I.R. At the time, the Aachenlanders were a loose affiliation of tribes having been previously united under the Hyperborean Empire, sharing a common language and trading among each other fairly peacefully. The original language of Aachen has entirely died out, first replaced by High Boros and then by the common tongue, although it has left the Aachenlanders with a still-recognizable accent in their Westerling speech, and several idioms not found elsewhere, such as expressing "don't wait too long" by saying, "don't let fish eat you."

Vast wildfires spawned by the explosion of the Tower of Oerson in 2496 I.R. devastated the entire region south of the city of Vermis, with the wind-blown wave of flames eventually spreading all the way to the Matagost Peninsula thousands of miles to the east. The city of Aixe was spared only due to its huge, lake-fed moat, and might still have starved to death in the ensuing famines if it were not sited directly upon a road leading to areas not affected by the fires. Untold thousands died from fire and famine in the rural areas of what would become the Province of Aachen; scholars estimate that the population of the area took 300 years to rebuild to its original numbers from before the fires.

Lord-Governor Theriven the Leopard is the veteran of several feudal wars and the younger son of a noble Foerdewaith family, born in Troye. Without any prospect of an inheritance, Theriven took service as a mercenary and distinguished himself on the battlefield as a staunch supporter of Foere. He is a grim and unflinching man, intolerant of dissent and difficult to read. As a widely-traveled warrior, he is enough of a realist to see that even in the close province of Aachen, the Court in Courghais is no longer offering much support in return for the revenues it collects, and that the prosperity of "his" lands is slowly dwindling. He is unnervingly quiet on this subject, a complete cipher.

A vast number of the landsgrafs in Aachen resent the unequal bargain being given to them by the overking, which is to pay high taxes in exchange for slight assistance. They hear of the power of the nobles in free Suilley and look across the borders to see the riches of a predatory nobility in Eastreach Province, and they compare it to their own role as providers to a hungry, desperate, foreign empire. To most of them, the reason for the difference is obvious: It is the hand of Foere that keeps them weak. More and more they are talking behind closed doors, and training their men-at-arms in case the need arises to take one side or another in an armed resolution. So far, the situation cannot be described as a volatile one, for most of the landsgrafs consider themselves to be hereditary Foerdewaith, even if they are angered by their brethren nobles to the west.

A few nobles, predominantly barons but also a few landsgrafs, have begun to call their heritage "Fairdevaine" rather than "Foerdewaith," reflecting the local Aachenland dialect of the Westerling common speech. These are the nobles to watch the most closely, for if the nobility of Aachen begins to sever itself from the bloodlines of the Kingdom of Foere, rebellion is nigh. At the moment, though, most of the nobles perceive the situation as more of a family squabble among Foerdewaith lords in the same empire, not as a dispute between two different nationalities. In short, lines are being drawn, but they are still faint. The pot simmers, but the heat remains low.

TRADE AND COMMERCE

As with the western region of Eastreach, Aachen is fairly well populated, with numerous farming towns and trading villages. A fairly

The Central & Northern Sinnar Coast

Eastern Akados and the Stoneheart Mountains

Legend
Town or Village
City
Capital or Free City
Imperial Capital
Fortress or Citadel
Ruins
Place of Interest
Road
Trail or Unused Road
Mountain Pass
Battlefield

extensive network of passable roads in the province allows even the smallest settlements access to large markets, so farms are generally large and prosperous in the Aachen heartlands. Moreover, Aachen's internal governance is much better organized than its rather corrupt northeastern neighbor Eastreach, with fewer so-called "tolls" being extorted from travelers by petty nobles and pocket fiefdoms. Many of the small towns in Aachen hold great "fayres" during which peasants from the surrounding regions and traveling merchants from other towns congregate to buy and sell all manner of goods. Such fayres are often held three or four times per year.

Unlike its neighboring province of Eastreach, Aachen does not enjoy a lucrative financial relationship with Bard's Gate (for which the lord-governors have been more than a bit resentful in the past). For this reason, the lords-governor of Aachen charge fairly extortionate taxes on foreign caravans heading to and from Bard's Gate — which is in turn one of the many reasons Bard's Gate conducts so much traffic by riverboat through Eastreach, skirting Aachen entirely.

Loyalties and Diplomacy

Aachen is connected by high roads almost directly to the overking's capital at Courghais and remains loyal to the Kingdom of Foere. As such, a lord-governor administers the province on behalf of the overking. The current lord-governor is a somewhat frightening individual by the name of Theriven the Leopard.

Government

The lord-governorship is not a hereditary title, being an appointment granted in the Court of Courghais by the overking. Thus far, no lord-governor has refused to surrender the office or establish a hereditary succession; most of them are, in any case, anxious to return to the civilized center of the Kingdoms of Foere once they accumulate a modest fortune in the provinces.

As a general rule for understanding the government of Aachen:
• If it is a high road, a bridge, or a court of law, a regional governor is in charge of it.
• If it is a city, the mayor reports to the lord-governor and to no one else (although the regional governor still runs the court system).
• If it is a town, it either reports to the lord-governor as a city (a "free town") or is governed by a noble as part of the feudal system, although the courts remain under the supervision of the regional governor.
• If it is a piece of land, a wagon-trail, or a village, a noble of some rank is in charge.

The province has seven major partitions ruled by regional governors who are appointed by the royal court in Foere in the same manner as the lord-governor, each of whom administers the roads, courts, and some of the towns across a wide region. Within the regional governorships, but reporting directly to the lord-governor, are well-defined feudal landgraves, each ruled by a noble lord bearing the title of "landsgraf," who administers the countryside (but not the courts or roads) over an area roughly 50 miles across. Local barons, in fealty to the landsgrafs, govern at the lowest level of the hierarchy. Most barons have the double responsibility of maintaining a court for the governor while owing military and tithe duties to the landsgraf. These baronies can be of wildly varying sizes; many are little more than a small castle surrounded by a mile or so of dreary wilderness; others might encompass a small town and several miles of fertile farmland.

The seven governorships of Aachen are: Aixe (containing nine landgraves), Vermis (containing 13 landgraves), Gretspaan (containing six landgraves), Tremonde (containing eight landgraves), Dlante (containing four landgraves), Sauv Lar (containing seven landgraves), and Basivaine (containing five landgraves). At present, no landsgraf holds more than one landgrave, so there are 52 landsgrafs ruling the land of Aachen, in fealty to the office (but not specifically to the person) of the lord-governor.

Wilderness and Adventure

The relative stability of Aachen as a province should not be understood to suggest that the countryside is nothing but a placid expanse of fields and cheerful peasants, although many such places exist, especially in the heartlands. Many forests spread through the region harbor beasts dire and strange, and there are countless areas in Aachen that have either never been tamed or that have been allowed to return to the wild. In particular, the lower reaches and foothills of the Cretians and the Mons Terminus mountain ranges are home to bandits and monsters alike. Settlements in these remote areas cling grimly to their existence in the face of these threats, receiving only sporadic, halfhearted support from those who boast of the province's stability.

The wilder parts of Aachen are home to tigers, which can be a threat to herding communities. The tigers of Aachen (often referred to as "leopards") are spotted rather than the striped varieties more commonly found in lands of the East, most likely a strain that has survived from the days when the land was covered with great forests.

Reference Source: The Lost Lands: Borderland Provinces

Vermis, City of (Capital)

(VIRM-iss, sometimes WIRM-us)
Population: 32,500 (28,200 Foerdewaith, 3,000 halfling, 870 high elf, 385 hill dwarf, 45 other)
Ruler: Mayor-Palatine Landour Sebat
Government: overlord

The great city of Vermis is the capital of Aachen Province and the seat of the lord-governor of all Aachen. Vermis stands on the ruins of the old Hyperborean city of Lecinium, which was burned and abandoned in the wave of catastrophes that followed the planetary pole shift in the late 2400s I.R. Survivors began to rebuild the ruins in the early 2500s, and the town — later, city — of Vermis was officially founded around 2575 I.R. Using building materials and wealth salvaged from the remains of Lecinium, Vermis erected a sturdy wall to defend against bandit attacks and increased its influence over nearby commotes and farms. While most Aachen communities remained independent, Vermis exercised considerable influence over the settlements along the western branch of the Great Amrin River, while Aixe grew influential in the south.

The city's northern location meant that raids by the Bandit King Rinos fell most heavily on Vermis and its surrounding commotes. Vermis' militia grew into a professional and well-seasoned army, but its numbers and mobility limited its effectiveness against Rinos. Like the leaders of Aixe to the south, the mayor and other Vermis city officials realized that some sort of union with the neighboring kingdom of Foere was all but inevitable. When the time came to negotiate, the mayor-palatine swore fealty to the overking in exchange for a fair amount of autonomy, as well as status for his city as capital of Aachen, the newest fiefdom of Foere.

Vermis is a river-port city with a deep harbor in the Great Amrin River protected from river-pirates by an island-tower in the river known as the Harbor's Bite. Vast quantities of food and trade goods travel down to Vermis from the upriver farms and villages to feed the city's population. Trade goods find their way onto the city's riverboats, their great yellow sails proudly marked with the city's black dragon to boldly warn pirates not to incur the city's wrath.

Two hills dominate the city: The High Mercha, crowned by the white-walled College of Vermis, and the Groldhill, dominated by the grim citadel of Vermis Grold.

Notable temples in Vermis include the Chapterhouse-Crypt of Jamboor below the High Mercha Hill; the aging stone cathedral of Solanus; the newly expanded temple of Mitra; the Twin-temple of Thyr and Muir; and the Great Mill-Temple of Ceres.

Vermis is a diverse city that hosts folk from all across Akados. Merchants, travelers, diplomats, explorers, and adventurers rub shoulders along the city's docks, inns, and streets. Goods from all corners of the continent and beyond pass through the city, making Vermis a major trading crossroads. Many major trading houses maintain a presence in Vermis due to its vital location — Houses Drenwal and Gastone-Sheshek of Reme have major offices, while the influential Foere houses of Iskane and Tulius have made Vermis their eastern base of operations. Business for caravan masters and guards is especially brisk, giving rise to several agencies providing assistance and freelance work to those with the proper skills.

The King of Oceanus

AIXE, CITY OF

(ECKS, or ah-YEEKS-uh)
Population: 8,600 (7,650 Foerdewaith, 570 hill dwarf, 380 halfling)
Ruler: Bertolde Kavre, Mayor-Palatine of Aixe, Baron of Tharhold and Kavredal
Government: autocracy

The city of Aixe is a pleasant sight with its walls whitewashed and its towers fluttering with colorful banners, surrounded by a lake-fed moat 100 feet across. Drawbridges lead over the moats to the city gates, each of which is crowned by a painted portcullis-and-key symbol. On the far side of the moat from the city, buildings cluster near the drawbridges like small villages outside the city walls.

The fortified city of Aixe describes itself as the "Gateway of Foere," and the rather self-important title has some basis in fact, for it is within the walls of Aixe that the high road from Foere branches into the province's three main highroads: The Cross Cut, the Estuary Road, and the Royal Vermis Road. Most of the province's trade with Foere passes through the gates of Aixe going one way or another.

Aixe is an old city dating back to the Hyperborean era, although it has long outgrown the small area originally enclosed by the Hyperborean walls (now torn down). Its prosperity from trade allowed it to build new walls over a century ago, but the city has again outgrown them and relies upon the open grounds beyond the city to provide needed space for new housing and for assembling caravans.

Originally, the landsgraf of Peridor denied the city any taxes on the lucrative business of providing open space to caravans, but some years ago the mayor-palatine's guardsmen hauled the current landsgraf's father from his residence in the city and declared him guilty within the hour. They summarily beheaded him in the city center and placed his head on a pike outside the merchant camp. The city then sent an apologetic letter to the lord-governor claiming that the entire affair had been a case of mistaken identity; they had thought the man was a pig thief named Boden. In order to prevent future cases of mistaken identity, the Peridors now pay the city a share of their profits.

Boden Bristleback, the actual pig thief, was never captured. He escaped the city, despite being grievously wounded, and fled to the Alder Zerin Forest, where a large pack of feral pigs attacked his pursuers. Routed by the porcine assault, the guardsmen were forced to retreat back to the city in disarray: emptyhanded, wounded, and deeply embarrassed. The mayor-palatine died later in a mysterious hunting accident near the Peridor lands, and the Peridor family sent a large basket of overripe pomegranates to the city as a token of their respect.

As far as visitors are concerned, the city of Aixe is pleasantly friendly to foreigners. An entry toll is collected by the governor's guards at the city gate, a small fee of 1 silver coin per non-citizen entering the city, and since merchants absorb the city's transaction taxes, visitors who wish to sell gems or other treasure in the city can do so at good prices.

As described, all four of the entrance gates have small "outer cities" on the far side of the drawbridges where buildings have been built to avoid the crowding inside the walls. And within the walls, it is indeed crowded. Half-timber buildings press close against narrow, twisting streets, overshadowing them in many cases with built-out balconies. Caravans and travelers passing through the city must force their way through a pressing crowd of local wagons and citizens. To avoid crowding, many arriving caravans are admitted through the city in the early hours of the morning to begin their journeys before dawn breaks and the city wakes to life.

The crossroad where the four high roads divide toward their respective city gates is a vast market fronted by the Court of the Governor of Aixe and the Hall of the Mayor-Palatine, as well as the city's guildhall. The city's guilds are not as powerful as they are in free cities, for they are ultimately subject to laws and decrees of the lord-governor in Vermis. Rather than having much political power in the city, they serve mainly to ensure that the city's products are of high quality, and that citizens are not cheated. However, there is a constant drumbeat from the guildmasters that Aixe should seek the status of a chartered city under its own government. The overkings have thus far utterly forbidden the lord-governors from granting such a charter, so the efforts of the guilds have had little effect.

As with the other major cities of Aachen, the area within the walls is ruled by a mayor-palatine who reports directly to the lord-governor over the head of the regional governor. Just outside the wall, the situation is a bit complex. The surrounding roads (and the city's courts) are maintained by the regional governor of Aixe. However, the lands off the roads are part of the feudal system, held by the landsgraf of Peridor. The Peridors maintain two "merchant camps" outside the city walls, wooden-walled palisades where caravans can assemble without trying to do so in the chaotic, crowded streets of the city.

BECQUERIL, VILLAGE OF

(BEK-er-il)
Population: 172 (Foerdewaith)
Ruler: Baron Jauntir of Becqueril
Government: overlord

Becqueril is a village built around the ancestral castle of Baron Jauntir of Becqueril, whose domain extends approximately five miles in all directions from the castle. There are 15 knightly manor houses in the barony, and two other villages about the same size as Becqueril: the village of Oton and the village of Cthayr. The rest of the barony's population is scattered throughout the area in isolated hamlets.

DLANTE, TOWN OF

(de-LANT)
Population: 5,329 (5,223 Foerdewaith, 106 halfling)
Ruler: Regional Governor Baroness Azile de Palaintre
Government: overlord

Dlante is the seat of the governor of the region of Dlante, which reaches to the border of Eastreach Province 50 miles to the east along the Wain Road. The regional governor is Azile de Palaintre, a noblewoman of Foere appointed to her post by the overking's court in the city of Courghais. She is ill-tempered and rude to those of lower social status, but she has the redeeming quality of being less rapacious than any of the other regional governors in Aachen Province. She benefits greatly from local taxes and from her share of judicial bribery, but she keeps these sources of income to a modest sum rather than amassing whatever she can get. As a result, Dlante has managed to keep itself in good condition despite the slow decline of trade on the Wain Road. This section of the road is relatively well-patrolled, the milestones are maintained, and roadside inns are careful not to charge exorbitant prices to travelers. Dlante is well-regarded by the caravan merchants of Bard's Gate, and they always make stopovers here to re-provision and rest their horses.

White-painted stone walls surround the town, with five pointed towers, their conical roofs painted a bright red. The townsfolk of Dlante are universally heavyset, and the wealthiest of them have a definite tendency toward corpulence. By custom, the town citizens (and only the town citizens) wear blue cylindrical hats with a very slight taper, essentially a fez without a tassel. The higher a citizen's social status, the taller the fez. Rich merchants strut around town in hats more than a foot tall, spangled with semiprecious stones and decorated with ostrich feathers, sometimes trimmed with blue-dyed fur. Ordinary laborers wear a modest fez decorated with a guild badge or a decorative copper button.

ELET, TOWN OF

(EL-et)
Population: 1,540 (1,434 Foerdewaith, 73 hill dwarf, 33 halfling)
Ruler: Mayor Alisce Elevard
Government: overlord (Karlat of Krevin, absentee landsgraf)

Elet is a small, stone-walled town on the Estuary Road roughly halfway between Aixe and Eastgate. It lies at the base of the Ghostwind Pass into the Yolbiac Vale, a dangerous crossing utterly impassable due to snow and terrifying winds during at least two months of the year. Trade with the strange valefolk on the far side of the mountain pass is sporadic at best, and most of Elet's wealth (such as it is) comes from travelers on the Estuary Road.

The town is relatively insignificant other than for its strategic location at the base of the pass into the Yolbiac Vale; it is no larger than several other towns along the Estuary Road. Elet sees traveling druids from time to time on their way to pay respect to one or another of the druidic holy sites in Ghostwind Pass.

GRETSPAAN CITADEL

Population: 1,167 (926 Foerdewaith, 102 halfling, 79 half-elf, 60 hill dwarf)
Ruler: Baron Auricard, Regional Governor of Gretspaan
Government: overlord

On the south bank of the Great Amrin River, just within the border of Aachen Province, stands the fortified citadel of Gretspaan, seat of the regional governor of Gretspaan. The citadel serves as a strong border fortress, and also quarters the various customs officials who collect their own tariffs on merchants entering the Province from Bard's Gate. Travelers are welcomed into the town, but are not permitted in the citadel unless they have business with the regional governor or the garrison.

TAUNDRE, VILLAGE OF

(TAWN-druh)
Population: 467 (433 Foerdewaith, 34 halfling)
Ruler: Mayor Norman Gant
Government: secret syndicate

Taundre appears an unremarkable village with sagging stone walls and a sleepy, countryside atmosphere. There is a small market fairground outside the walls, and a single guard lounging by the entrance gate. It contains no temple or any other unusual feature to distinguish itself from dozens of other small country villages. The ordinary appearance is deliberate, for the village is actually the headquarters of perhaps the most far-flung criminal empire in the Borderland Provinces, a group called the Friendly Men.

AMRIN ESTUARY REGION

Capital: none (Bard's Gate controls both major cities)
Notable Settlements: Amrin Ferry, Eastgate, Telar Brindel
Ruler: none
Government: semi-autonomy (suzerainty of Bard's Gate who controls the cities, the land is loosely governed by a League of Estuary Lords, all freeholders)
Population: 420,000 (378,000 Foerdewaith, 33,000 halfling, 6,300 half-elf, 2,700 high elf)
Monstrous: giant snake, goblin, boggard, green hag, ogre, cockatrice, catoblepas (coastal swamps); giant eel, giant gar, koalinth, kelpie, scrag, sea hag (estuary); crab swarm, sand snake, bugbear, giant crayfish, gremlin, sandling (shoreline)
Languages: Common, Halfling, Elvish
Religion: Freya (countryside), Dame Torren, Pekko, Thyr, Sefagreth (Eastgate), Vanitthu (Telar Brindel), Mick O'Delving, Tykee (shipboard), Quell
Resources: trade hub, fishing, foodstuffs, shipbuilding
Technology Level: Medieval (cities), High Middle Ages (rural)

The city of Bard's Gate dominates the economic and political landscape in the Amrin Estuary region. The giant metropolis effectively controls the two major cities located here: Eastgate and Telar Brindel. However, the cities' authority barely extends beyond their walls, with the exception of patrolling the major trade roads. Instead, the task of safeguarding the balance of the Amrin Estuary other than the estuary's northern bank, which falls under the jurisdiction of Eastreach Province, has been delegated to the local nobles who form the League of Estuary Lords. These administrators operate with complete autonomy, provided of course, that their actions do not adversely harm the interests of the area's two major cities or by proxy, Bard's Gate.

Despite its proximity to a major body of water, the wetlands surrounding the estuary only extend a few miles from shore with the exception of the Half-Pickle Marsh on the northern bank. Otherwise, much of the untamed grasslands have been transformed into farmland. The temperate climate encourages the growth of numerous grain crops, though the wild animal population in the region is surprisingly low. By and large, the terrain remains level throughout the area with only mild inclines and gradual swales.

AMRIN FERRY, VILLAGE OF

Population: 228 (203 human [103 local Foerdewaith, 100 Waymark cavalry], 25 halfling)
Ruler: Commander of the Amrin Ferry Garrison, Falzar Kennick
Government: autocracy

Bard's Gate established the settlement of Amrin Ferry primarily to protect river barges ferrying local produce for sale in Eastgate. The village boasts several fortifications, including stone walls, a ballista, and a catapult to repel invaders. A lone frigate from Bard's Gate safeguards the waters around the docks and piers that can simultaneously accommodate four cargo barges. Peasants from the area east of the Great Amrin River haul their crops, livestock, and timber to this waystation for safe transport to various seaports along the Amrin Estuary and beyond rather than risk an overland journey on the perilous Lowwater Road, even though the 100 strong detachment of Waymarch cavalry stationed here periodically patrol the hazardous thoroughfare. Amrin Ferry is exclusively human save for the 25 halflings who live here.

EASTGATE, CITY OF

Population: 18,900 (3,700 in winter) (15,350 Foerdewaith, 1,700 halfling, 800 half-elf, 620 hill dwarf, 430 high elf)
Ruler: Commissary, Lord Lurmis Vergen
Government: overlord

The city of Eastgate is Bard's Gate's avenue to the sea and effectively a distant annex of Bard's Gate itself. It is a major market and clearinghouse for upriver and downriver traffic to and from Bard's Gate, being the place where outgoing cargo is taken from riverboat to ship, where goods from Telar Brindel are loaded onto riverboats or sold to intermediaries, and where ship cargos from distant ports are sold or consigned to merchants planning to make the extended journey to Bard's Gate.

The city is managed on behalf of Bard's Gate by an administrative commissary appointed by the high burgess of Bard's Gate, and is responsible for overseeing the logistics and scheduling of shipments on barges upriver, overland caravans, and the veritable fleet of coasters and galleons that trades here during the spring, summer, and autumn.

During these months, Eastgate's walls are packed with merchants, rivermen, ship captains, and traders of every conceivable kind of commodity. Bills of lading for goods held in warehouses are traded back and forth in shouted auctions, wagons piled high with vegetables creak their way in from the countryside to collide in vast entanglements in the streets, and the city's year-round citizens drive themselves to exhaustion looking after the needs of all these arrivals, making money hand-over-fist in the process.

In the winter, when the river sometimes ices over and the tidal waters of the estuary become violent, the population drops to a fifth of its summertime high, deprived of most of its waterborne trade in both directions. The only mercantile activity in the winter city is the overland caravan trade going east and west.

Despite the distance separating the two settlements, Eastgate feels more like an exurb of Bard's Gate than a community in its own right. The laws of Bard's Gate apply here as if Eastgate were merely a distant part of Bard's Gate itself. Many of the city's traditions, institutions, and religions closely mirror those found in Bard's Gate. The Temple of Sefagreth is the largest religious structure in the city, and the most widely worshipped deity, though shrines dedicated to other gods and faiths from Bard's Gate can also be found in other quarters of the city. The guilds who dominate commerce in the large metropolis to the northwest also ply their trades in Eastgate's markets, docks, warehouses, and factories. The powerful Wheelwrights' Guild from Bard's Gate and the Friendly Men, the homegrown regional criminal organization, operate different rackets within Eastgate, thus avoiding any conflicts of interest between the competing entities. On those rare occasions when they cross paths, they adhere to strict professional courtesies to avoid escalating a minor disagreement into a major gang war.

As part of the Suzerainty of Bard's Gate, Eastgate's defense falls upon a small cavalry unit from the Waymarch and the impressive stone walls surrounding its districts. In a pinch, the city can summon reinforcements from Amrin Ferry to bolster its mobile-yet-undersized military. A small volunteer militia drills outside the city gates once a week, and a permanent "Towerguard" of soldiers keeps watch from the towers of the city walls and guard the gates.

Sheriffs and constables handle actual law enforcement within the city, organized the same as their counterparts in Bard's Gate. The "sheriff of Eastgate" is also considered an "undersheriff of Bard's Gate," and the "Eastgate chief of constables" is technically a "deputy chief of constables of Bard's Gate." Of course, these are fine distinctions when seen from the perspective of an accused criminal facing prison, but vital for arranging a banquet table by social rank. The sheriffs are responsible for making arrests under warrant, and for maintaining jails and prisons, but they do not investigate crimes; essentially, they work as instruments of the courts rather than being ordinary police. The constables are a true police force; they make arrests in the course of their duties, and without a sheriff's warrant. The constables are responsible for the investigation of crimes, being the law-enforcement arm of the city's government rather than of the courts.

The installation of Meliandor Gane as the chief of constables has significantly decreased crime, presumably because of his tremendous talents in the arts of divination and deductive reasoning. Chief Constable Gane is unorthodox in his methods and enjoys the intellectual challenge of hunting down criminals. The constabulary holds him in a certain degree of awe, and so do many of the city's current prisoners. Many believe his presence alone has caused spies and criminals from rival Endhome to hastily pack their bags and return to their city, while simultaneously forcing the Friendly Men and the Wheelwrights' Guild to deliberately maintain a low profile. Rumblings in the underworld suggest one or both entities may be contemplating violently ending the chief of constables' tenure in Eastgate if his investigations significantly impact their operations in the city.

Telar Brindel, City of

Population: 8,800 (7,200 Foerdewaith, 850 half-elf, 437 hill dwarf, 189 halfling, 73 high elf, 51 gnome)
Ruler: Admiral of Telar Brindel, Sir Gowan Maulwin
Government: overlord

Lacking direct access to the sea, the city of Bard's Gate realized it needed a naval presence somewhere on the coastline of the Sinnar Ocean to protect its interests abroad. In the aftermath of Oceanus' founding and rapid ascension to its status as a naval superpower, the opportunistic representatives acting on behalf of Bard's Gate pounced upon Foere's inattention toward the important seaport of Telar Brindel. Left to its own devices, the city and its leaders quickly acquiesced to the metropolis's overtures and fell under its sway, becoming a member of its suzerainty, much to Foere's dismay. Bard's Gate revitalized the rundown installation that now supports the fleet of fighting ships defending the vessels flying under the city's flag from pirates, aquatic monsters, and aggression from the Kingdom of Oceanus.

Almost every industry within Telar Brindel supports the mission of securing and maintaining the city's fleet. Its imposing walls and artillery pieces defend the harbor against incursions from sea, while its ground forces of 500 Free Defenders and two full companies of Waymark cavalry secure the installation and patrol the surrounding land areas, especially Trader's Way. Telar Brindel's shipbuilding and repair facilities enjoy a stellar reputation throughout Akados, far superior to those at Eastgate, where the harbor is devoted to trade. In addition to constructing and maintaining the fleet for Bard's Gate, the shipwrights also build merchant vessels and repair damaged ships. However, captured ships or those suspected of engaging in piracy who seek repairs in Telar Brindel's famous shipyard face a battery of inquiries from the local authorities if the captain cannot provide a letter of marque from the admiral granting the skipper permission to legally hunt pirates.

The admiral of Telar Brindel has the final word on all civic matters within the naval station, but he delegates its daily management to the city's council of elected burgesses. He prefers focusing his keen attention on the men and women under his command. A stickler for details, Sir Gowan gets involved in every facet of his naval operation, regardless of how trivial it may be. Nonetheless, his marines admire the revered knight for his sailing prowess, military mind, and local roots as the second son of a landholding family only four miles away from Telar Brindel. Despite the admiral's diligence, rumors about saboteurs and spies from Oceanus and Endhome abound in the shipyards throughout the city.

Bard's Gate Region

Capital: Bard's Gate
Notable Settlements: Byrn, Crimmor, Darnagal, Derindin, Fairhill, Freegate, Glendovel Close
Ruler: High Burgess Cylyria and Bard's Gate Council of Burghers, local mayors and government bodies
Government: oligarchy
Population: 5,296,200 (4,940,000 Foerdewaith, 83,000 Plainsman, 55,500 Oceander, 49,000 half-elf, 37,700 hill dwarf, 33,800 halfling, 26,200 Riverfolk, 21,500 Heldring, 17,500 high elf, 14,000 gnome, 8,200 Erskaelosi, 3,600 mountain dwarf, 2,250 wood elf, 2,050 street dwarf, 1,900 other)
Monstrous: stirges, gnolls, orcs, worgs, ogres, undead, trolls, manticores, owlbears, hill giants, ettins, dragons, gibbering orbs (Stoneheart Valley); stirges, orcs, giant spiders, gnolls, giant animals (badgers, bears, wolves), dryads, ogres, chike, manticores, owlbears, fey, undead, treants, dragons (green, black) (Stoneheart Forest); stirges, manticores, hoar spirits, stone giants, revenants, lantern goats, banshees, murder-born (Lost Boy Mountain); ant swarms, ankhegs, giant animals (badgers, bison, wolverines), stirges, orcs, plague ghouls, will-o'-wisps, hippogriffs, axe beaks, perytons, kamadans (Plains of Mayfurrow); bat swarms, giant bats, giant ants, chokers, spiggans, rock trolls, cave fishers, wyverns, destrachans (Glimmer Gorge); giant eels, giant gars, koalinths, kelpies, scrags, sea hags (Amrin Estuary); crab swarms, giant snapping turtles, giant eels, kelp devils, sahuagin (coastline); goblins, orcs, giant animals (beavers, otters, and snapping turtles), hobgoblins, ratfolk, lizard folk, giant crayfish, river trolls (Binjerin River Valley); giant sharks, giant animals (squids, octopi, fish), sahuagin, sea spiders, merrow, nisps, scrags, sea hags, coral giants, deck devils, undead, storm giants, sea serpents (Gulf of Akados)
Languages: Common, Kirkut, Dwarvish, Halfling, Helvaenic, Elvish, Erskin, Gnomish
Religion: Oghma, Dre'uain, Tykee, Sefagrath, Vanithu, Telophus, Freya, Ceres, Mick O'Delving, Thyr (declining),

Belon the Wise, Pan, Darach-Albith, Orcus, Muir (declining),
Jamboor

Resources: trade hub, grain, wool, banking, manufactured
goods, livestock, timber, quarry stone, copper, wine, tobacco,
dyes, silver

Technology Level: Renaissance (Bard's Gate), Medieval
(cities), High Middle Ages (rural areas), Iron Age (Freegate)

The giant metropolis governs the lands and settlements in its
suzerainty as a calm, rational parent trying to placate a petulant
child. It uses reason, patience, and cajoling to bring its subjects into
line rather than brute force. Although the city boasts a professional
army that includes a small unit of skilled adventurers known as the
Lyreguard, its military forces are singularly devoted to defending
Bard's Gate rather than expanding its territory through military
conquest. The men and women dedicated to this critical task are
primarily stationed atop and within the city's walls and in two
critical strongholds — the Citadel of Ravens just beyond the walls,
and the Citadel of the Griffon in the neighboring valley. In addition
to the massive city, numerous smaller settlements and other points
of interest exist outside its stone walls, especially in the Lyre Valley.
This region features some of the Lost Lands' most seminal locations
such as Stoneheart Valley, the Stoneheart Mountain Dungeon, and
the underbelly of Bard's Gate itself.

The Bard's Gate region has some of the most diverse terrain in
Akados. The city proper sits atop a hill overlooking the valleys
beneath it. The Stoneheart Mountains to the metropolis's north cast
a dark shadow across the foothills and the iconic valley beneath it.
West of Bard's Gate lies the fearsome Stoneheart Forest, while the
road east crosses through the Forest Kingdoms. The region's moderate
climate supports a vibrant savanna warm and humid enough to support
crucial food staple crops and herds of domesticated animals. Despite
the presence of civilization throughout the area, orcs, hobgoblins,
goblins, and other aggressive humanoids and monsters pose a constant
threat to the region.

The region of Bard's Gate is described in detail in *The Lost Lands:
Bard's Gate* by **Frog God Games**.

BARD'S GATE

Ruler: Cylyria, High Burgess and Mayor of the Council

Government: council (council of burghers)

Population: 125,000 (87,750 human [79,500 Foerdewaith, 2,800
Riverfolk, 2,500 Plainsmen, 1,300 Heldring, 1,000 Erskaelosi,
650 Ashurian], 14,000 half-elf, 8,000 elf [6,200 high elf, 1,800
wood elf], 6,000 dwarf [4,100 hill dwarf, 1,100 mountain dwarf,
800 street dwarf], 3,000 halfling, 2,250 gnome, 2,000 ratfolk,
1,750 half-orc, 250 other)

Monstrous: small populations of wererats and ratfolk within
the sewers

Languages: Common, Kirkut, Dwarven, Halfling, Helvaenic,
Elven, Erskin, Gnome

Religion: pious, tolerant

Resources: trade hub, banking, manufactured goods, wool,

Currency: mixed

Technology Level: Renaissance

Bard's Gate is one of the epicenters of trade in Akados. Merchants
travel here from far and wide to peddle their wares to buyers from
distant markets in perhaps the most business-friendly environment in
the world. Bard's Gate projects its favorable commercial image through
its cadre of emissaries and diplomats who travel across the high seas
and trek over the network of overland highways traversing the whole of
Akados to forge economic ties with long-distance trading partners. The
city occupies several islands within the Stoneheart River and both sides
of the riverbank adjacent to the islands. Bridges connect the islands to
each other and the nearby mainland, while a massive wall surrounds the
entire metropolis.

HISTORY AND PEOPLE

Like most major settlements, Bard's Gate owes its creation more
to circumstance than intentional design. Its story began with a river,
several islands within that river, and the great mountain range stretching
across the spine of Akados. The swath of ground that would become
Bard's Gate stood at a critical juncture in the route between the lucrative
markets of Remenos and Curgantium to the south and the marvels of
Tsen to the north. The island chain within the Stoneheart River was
easily the most fordable location across the waterway. In 2717 I.R.,
Rinos, the self-proclaimed bandit king, arrived at the Stoneheart River
crossing and constructed a bridge spanning from the western bank of the
river to the main island. Rinos naturally named the structure the King's
Bridge in honor of himself. However, his reign and legacy were short-
lived. The bard Turlin, whom Rinos previously condemned to death,
swept across the King's Bridge with his peasant followers and wiped out
Rinos' defenders in a surprise attack in the middle of the night. Rinos
soon met the same fate he reserved for Turlin, though unlike the latter,
the bandit king's name quickly faded into obscurity. In the aftermath
of his revolt, Turlin commissioned the construction of the Lyre Bridge
connecting the central island to the eastern bank of the Stoneheart
River. To finance the construction and protect the fledgling trademoot,
he struck an accord with the churches of Thyr and Muir granting them
the authority to lay the foundations for their churches on the river's west
bank. In short order, the Foerdewaith Monarchy also decreed Turlin's
new settlement as a free township unhindered by tax or fealty to the
Foerdewaith Monarchy.

Within 150 years, the trademoot had grown to be a sizable town for
merchants and vendors. East-west trade increased as Reme's status
increased, and the churches of Thyr and Muir constructed temple
halls to meet the populace's demands. The King's Bridge, as the town
was called at the time, taxed every good passing through or across its
bridges. To circumvent these levies, canny merchants dug canals to
bypass the bridges. These canals remain to this day and give the city part
of its distinctive character. The trademoot continued to transform from a
trading center into a civic entity with government works and plans over
the intervening 300 years. During this time, the city officially adopted
the name Bard's Gate in honor of Turlin. It established a formal military
known as the Lyre's Guard, and created a town council of merchants to
run the city and the elected office of Burgher to oversee the settlement's
defenses and negotiate trade arrangements with foreign states. This
newly founded government came to the town's defense when demonic
creatures began to appear in the Lyre Valley. Many adventurers and
citizens answered the call, including the bard Duquaene of Penmorgh.
Duquaene organized the resistance and defeated the threat, amassing
a great treasure in the process. With his newfound wealth, he founded
Bard's College on North Island.

The college attracted the finest minds and talents to the city as
well as adding to its affluence. Its founder soon ascended to the title
of high burgher during which time he uprooted corruption within the
mayor's office and enforced the rule of law within the city. Duquaene's
reforms set the stage for the metropolis's ascendency into the upper
echelon of Akadonian cities. Bard's Gate played a prominent role in
the grand crusade against the temple-city of Tsar. The church leaders
of Thyr and Muir encouraged citizens to join the Army of Light in its
march against the demon prince and his minions amassing in Tsar.
When the army vanished into nothingness, the calamity left many of
the city's sons and daughters orphans and took a significant toll on the
metropolis's treasury. Naturally, many residents directed their anger
toward the church leaders who endorsed the campaign against Orcus
and his legions. In the aftermath of the Battle of Tsar, Bard's Gate
underwent tremendous internal turmoil as various factions pointed their
fingers in multiple directions. The disputes led to profound reforms,
including the formation of the Wheelwrights' Guild from the remnants
of the Teamsters' Accord, the construction of the Citadel of the Griffon
outside the city proper, and the creation of the free company named the
Lyreguard to defend the city.

Over the last 20 years, Bard's Gate has faced several crises. Gnolls
descended into the Lyre Valley from a hidden fortress in the valley's

northern reaches. Only the concerted efforts of the griffon riders and Lyreguard turned the tide of battle in the city's favor. In light of these attacks, city leaders voted to establish a small professional military force including a formal River Watch. However, the military proved useless during the next tragedy to befall the city. A mysterious, black fog swooped down upon the city from Rogue's Island and caused the inhabitants of Slip-Galley's Abbey to disappear along with several random citizens. A few years later, the military force proved its mettle when a strange foreign army appeared in the Lyre Valley. The army of men known as the Huun had sacked Tircople on multiple occasions. While the Huun swept through the valley with little resistance, the walls of Bard's Gate proved a worthy opponent. The Huun besieged the city for 14 months until relief came in the form of a massive flotilla and a combined army of Akadonians led by King Ovar that smashed the Huun fleet and forced them to abandon the siege. The army pursued the fleeing Huun for two years, pushing them as far north as the Vast Desert. Their fate remains unknown.

The city's eclectic demographics demonstrates its diversity. Humans of multiple ethnicities make up the majority of the population, with those of Foerdewaith descent accounting for the largest group by a vast margin. Half-elves and elves constitute a significant minority within Bard's Gate, giving these races increased clout among the city's leadership and upper classes. Dwarves trail behind them, followed by halflings, gnomes, half-orcs, and a tiny segment of other assorted peoples. The city's ratfolk predominantly dwell in the city's sewers, out of sight from the general population.

Religion

The devotees of numerous faiths may freely worship their chosen deity within the city's tolerant walls. However, it comes as no surprise that the city's primary religion is the worship of Oghma, God of Bards and Protector of Bard's Gate. His faithful gather in the Auditorium of the Silver Hall, which functions more as a performance center than a formal church. Dre'uain the Lame, God of Crafts, and Sefagreth, the official patron of the trade upon which the city is built, closely follow Oghma in popularity. Other religions boast widespread followings among certain segments of the population. Young people gravitate toward the worship of Freya, Goddess of Love and Fertility, while many members of the various city watches venerate Vanitthu, God of the Steadfast Guard. The college crowd and the abundant arcane community belong to the church of Yenomesh, the God of Glyphs and Writing. Tyree, Goddess of Luck and Good Fortune, appeals to almost everyone in the city. Non-human residents also keep their traditional faiths alive.

Some outsiders refer to Bard's Gate as the City of a Thousand Gods and with good reason. If one looks hard enough, it is possible to find a temple or at least a shrine dedicated to almost every deity imaginable. Despite the city's tolerant views toward religion, its leaders prohibit the open worship of deities who espouse evil ideals such as murder, treachery, or thievery, or who partake in outlawed rituals, especially human sacrifices. Nonetheless, these banned faiths endure in the city's nefarious underbelly. Some believe the Cult of Orcus has taken root here, while rumors about the Cult of Set constantly circulate in the bars and taverns scattered throughout the city.

Trade and Commerce

Bard's Gate owes its existence to its humble beginning as a trademoot. Strategically located on the Stoneheart River, the independent city avoided falling under the aegis of the Kingdom of Foere, which made it an ideal stopover for states hostile to Foere who took advantage of the shortest land route between the eastern and western seas. With the nearly impassable Stoneheart Mountains looming to the north, the ford at Bard's Gate also served as the most expeditious means of reaching the eastern continent while once again circumventing scrutiny from rival nations. To ensure the safe passage of goods along these roads, the city regularly patrols the Lyre Valley in an effort to prevent brigands and monsters from harassing overland traffic that could jeopardize their lucrative enterprise.

In firm command of overland trade, Bard's Gate turned its expansive eyes to the seas. To further its maritime ambitions, the city established a naval base at Telar Brindel while controlling major ports in Freegate, Eastgate, and at Cantyn Light. The metropolis' ships receive a warm welcome in every major port on the Gulf of Akados and the Sinnar Ocean — with the exception of Endhome where they garner an indifferent reception. Although its ships travel far and wide on the high seas, the city first and foremost facilitates trade among numerous commercial partners. While Bard's Gate exports its fair share of manufactured goods and locally produced commodities to distant lands across its roads and aboard its ships, its economic fortunes depend upon providing a safe, neutral ground for people of all types to exchange goods and services without political considerations or national identities coming into play. Its army and those of its allies safeguard the network of roads connecting the city to far-off lands, while its navy and the ships under its flag defend the waterways against pirates and offer a reliable mode of transportation to reach any port of call.

Multiple guilds keep the commerce humming throughout the city. The Wheelwrights' Guild, formed from the wreckage of the Teamsters' Accord, may be the wealthiest and most influential. Duloth Armatige leads the organization through a combination of coercion, intimidation, quick wits, and fast talking. The union of wagon builders and freight haulers has never been more prosperous, providing ample fuel to power Duloth's grand ambitions to take an even more prominent role among the city's leadership cadre while simultaneously keeping his greedy fingers in multiple pies. Other guilds operating within Bard's Gate exert lesser degrees of sway over the city's affairs. The Beggar's Guild hears every word uttered on the streets. They trade their information and secrets for the right price, much like the Harlots' Guild which obtains its sordid stories in a more compromising manner. The Gem Cutter and Jewelers' Guild, the Scribes' Guild, and the Glassblowers' Guild deal in more conventional fare buying, selling, and creating items in their specialized fields.

Diplomacy

Bard's Gate flexes its muscles using coins and courtiers instead of the more conventional cacophony of marching boots. Its diplomats command respect wherever they travel, for they bring with them the promise of great riches to those who share their mutual interest to spread the wealth throughout the world. The metropolis' diversity also allows its ambassadors to appeal to foreign powers on a personal level because its representatives may share the same lineage, language, customs, or religion as their people or leaders. Whereas the members of a homogenous society must learn the nuances of dealing with people different than them, the city's diplomatic corps practically hits the ground running when its emissaries first set foot in a new court.

In addition to drawing upon an eclectic population, the metropolis also affords its diplomats a top-tier education. While Bard's College enjoys a stellar reputation as a premier university for the study of music and the arts, the learning institution also teaches oratory and diplomacy. Many of its graduates go on to become great leaders and statesmen. These pupils also receive a background in the study and application of the mystical arts. In many respects, the city's diplomatic envoys, spies, and agents are better equipped to cow a hostile foe to their will than the ranks of its small yet elite military forces.

The august and powerful Dominion Arcane also lends its guidance and support to the city's diplomatic corps, though its expenditures in time and resources reflect its mutual interest in seeing the city prosper rather than being wholly altruistic. With this body's backing and the goodwill earned from the city's massive treasury, the ambassadors and negotiators make for formidable opponents when brokering deals. Many foreign negotiators fearing the legendary prowess of the city's orators come to the negotiating table armed with dweomers to dispel and detect any charms and magical influences that may be in effect. However, their efforts are in vain. The representatives of Bard's Gate are too sophisticated to resort to magically charming those interacting with them. Magic and the discipline and training required to harness and master it have far more subtle applications than crudely attempting to directly enchant a prospective partner. Indeed, those who deal with diplomats from Bard's Gate often repeat the axiom, "Keep your eye on your purse, not because they'll steal it but because you'll end up giving freely." This expression best captures the negotiating expertise of those seeking a trade deal, a defense pact, or any other relationship with the Suzerainty of Bard's Gate.

GOVERNMENT

The engine of enterprise powers the government of Bard's Gate. Regardless of its size or strength, the head of each guild who is commonly called a burgher or burgess occupies a seat on the Council of Burghers that controls the city's purse strings. The burghers and burgesses select one of their own to serve as the mayor of the council, who functions as the group's leader. Although the average citizens exercise no control over the selection of burghers and burgesses nor the mayor of the council, they directly elect the city's political leader who assumes the title of high burgher or high burgess. This peculiar power sharing arrangement has sown more dissention than order. Throughout its history, the pendulum has swung back and forth multiple times as the Council of Burghers and the mayor of the council have vied for supremacy with the high burgher. Weak high burghers often fall prey to the council's machinations, as the collective heads of the guilds subjugate the people's elected leader to a subordinate role. Adept high burghers assert their dominance over the guilds and often simultaneously act as high burgher and mayor of the council. Cylyria, the current high burgess, has accomplished the latter feat. The city's highly capable ruler simultaneously enjoys widespread support from the populace and control over its robust coffers. Nonetheless, some within the Council of Burghers, most notably Duloth, chafe under her regime. They seek to once again separate the offices of the mayor of the council and the high burgess, preferably with someone of their choosing taking her place as the mayor.

For their part, the citizens of Bard's Gate seem content to watch this struggle unfold provided their government performs one critical task — it ensures their personal safety. While those empowered to act on the people's behalf adopt a "live and let live" attitude, their retinue of law enforcement personnel work diligently to eradicate street crime and safeguard property. Of course, the populace expects the city's sheriffs, constables, and judges to administer the civic code in a fair and just manner rather than use their authority to suppress the people of Bard's Gate. Despite their intensive efforts, some sections of the city remain dangerous, even during broad daylight.

MILITARY

The elite Lyreguard and its standing army, the Free Defenders, whose numbers dwindled to 1,500 after the recent crusade, protect the city. The former entity numbers around 250 specialized troops and includes the Griffon Riders, an aerial cavalry unit, the Gentlemen, the high burgess's personal bodyguards, a dozen war wizards, and 30 clerics of various goodly faiths. The Free Defenders man the city's outer defenses, most notably in the towers, gatehouses, the keep, the walls, and the metropolis's two citadels — the Citadel of the Griffon and The Citadel of the Raven. Three hundred men-at-arms, 20 heavy knights, and 90 light cavalry troops of the Duchy of Waymarch reinforce the Free Defenders. As the names suggest, the 75 Gatesmen and 150 Wall Watchers defend the city's gates and walls. The city divides its navy into three branches, the Admiralty of Telar Brindel stationed at that distant port, the Admiralty of the Fleet, anchored in the waters around Bard's Gate, and the River Watch, a small fleet charged with the task of protecting the city's commercial interests on the Stoneheart River.

Bard's Gate can certainly field a highly-skilled and well-trained fighting force, but its sheer numbers appear to be disproportionate to a city of its immense size. The metropolis' status as a free city-state and the epicenter of trade throughout Akados and Libynos reinforce its importance to the global economy as exemplified by the unified response to the Huun invasion. Too many people have too much to lose if Bard's Gate fails. When faced with imminent danger, Bard's Gate can reliably call upon its numerous allies and business partners for aid.

MAJOR THREATS

The gnolls and orcs of the Stoneheart Valley pose a constant threat to Bard's Gate and the lands beyond. The gnolls under King Ga'awootarr's leadership grow more aggressive by the day. They recently sacked several small villages and farmholds. The high burgess fears the gnolls could directly assault the city in the near future if they secure a powerful ally to support them. The orcs massing in the valley present an even greater problem. Over the years, black orc tribes from Rappan Athuk have poured into the area in increasing numbers. Although the chaotic humanoids lack centralized leadership, powerful despots currently vying for control over the disorganized hordes could unite them under a single banner that would effectively signal an imminent invasion.

The city's walls and outer defenses may repulse external invaders, yet mortar and stone cannot protect Bard's Gate from itself. The guilds and their masters frequently clamor for a greater say in the city's administration or subtly hint at a change in regime when their demands fall on deaf ears. These legitimate entities predominately operate within the parameters of the current system, though some also partake in illicit and underhanded activities to further their cause, Duloth being first among them. The city's illegal and secretive groups lurk in the shadows, proliferating their schemes and machinations behind closed doors. The most active and dangerous of these is the Cult of Orcus. Its agents attempt to infiltrate positions of critical importance within the city and then wield their influence to corrupt it. Rumors circulating in the taverns and shops speak of other depraved cults practicing their vile acts and venerating their malevolent deities. Assassins, spies, and thieves also ply their nefarious trades everywhere from the halls of power to the city's seedy underbelly.

The preceding threats have plagued Bard's Gate for many years, but the most imminent danger suddenly appeared on the metropolis's doorstep a few years earlier. The Huuns seemingly materialized out of nowhere, besieging Bard's Gate for 14 arduous months. The city dug in until an allied Akadonian force repelled the invasion and pursued the fleeing Huuns into the desert far from the city walls. Yet many believe the Huuns placed clandestine military units in strategic locations surrounding Bard's Gate. With the allied army at least hundreds of miles away, a surprise assault from these guerrilla regiments would pose a significant peril to the depleted forces currently defending the city. Furthermore, it seems doubtful that the metropolis's allies could quickly raise another force to beat back the Huuns again.

CITADEL OF GRIFFONS

This fortification 30 miles northwest of Bard's Gate serves as an important buffer against an attack from the Lyre Valley. A moat surrounds the impressive installation's 30-foot-high and 20-foot-thick walls connected to four guard towers, a gatehouse with massive doors, and a central keep. The Citadel of Griffons houses the crème de la crème of the city's military units. Sir Imril commands these crack troops who stand on the frontline in their struggle to tame the unruly Lyre Valley. A dozen Lyreguard Griffon Riders occupy the central keep along with 60 Lyreguard members, 200 Free Defenders, and a contingent of troops from the Duchy of Waymarch. These brave men and women patrol the surrounding area and man some of the siege engines positioned atop the walls. The Griffon Riders perform aerial reconnaissance missions and can warn Bard's Gate of impending danger heading its way. During the Huun invasion, the marauders put the citadel to the ultimate test, which it passed with flying colors after withstanding four months of a prolonged siege.

CITADEL OF RAVENS

Situated atop a craggy hilltop just north of the city, this fortified tower overlooks the Stoneheart River and the valley beneath it. The stronghold functions as the city's last line of defense, forcing the aggressor to defeat the fortress' defenders before making a run at Bard's Gate proper. While the Citadel of Griffons survived the Huun advance, the Citadel of Ravens fared much worse. The invaders threw everything they had at the citadel's walls for two weeks until they finally reduced the reinforced structures into a smoldering heap of sundered stones. Two years later, the citadel appears reborn. Built from newly cut stone, the revitalized keep stands upon its original foundation where it soars above the surrounding countryside. One hundred Lyreguards, five Lyreguard Griffon Riders, 200 Free Defenders, 100 Waymarch men-at-arms, and a contingent of war wizards and clerics maintain a vigilant watch over the untamed wilderness beyond the complex's walls. In light of recent developments, most notably the Huun threat and massing humanoid tribes in the valley, the citadel's war wizards experiment on innovative magical wards and weapons designed to stop attackers in their tracks. Some rumors claim they possess long-lost tomes salvaged from the ruins of Oxibbul or even Tsen. Armed with the knowledge presumably gained from these forgotten works, the war wizards allegedly push the boundaries of mystical power to new heights in their attempt to safeguard Bard's Gate and its people.

Byrn, Town of

Population: 123 (78 Plainsman, 45 Foerdewaith)
Ruler: Lord Faragast Bronwasser
Government: autocracy

The small town of Byrn embodies Waymarch's pastoral lifestyle. Sheep are the town's lifeblood as its industrious residents rely on the beasts to produce some of the finest cheese and wool products in the entire region. Indeed, the town's residents never sell their flocks nor slaughter their animals for personal consumption because a living sheep reaps a far greater return on their investment than a butchered one. Lord Faragast Bronwasser, the town's ruler, leads a cavalry corps of 15 dedicated and experienced riders to safeguard the settlement's livestock from thieves and poachers as well as defend the community against attacks from humanoid marauders descending from the nearby hills and mountains. While the people of Byrn are generally kind and friendly, their warm hearts instantly freeze for rustlers and aggressive humanoids. The lord personally amputates the transgressor's fingers, toes, and tongue with an intentionally dull blade for a first offense. Those foolish enough to attempt a second offense forfeit their wretched lives after several days of horrifically painful torture. However, Byrn's residents most fear a creature of legend who supposedly inhabits the prairie. The horsemen refer to the monstrosity as "The Two-Faced Man." No one has seen the creature for more than a generation, though most people blame every disappearance on the fabled abomination.

Crimmor, Village of

Population: 226 (178 Foerdewaith, 22 halfling, 11 Riverfolk, 8 half-elf, 4 gnome, 3 high elf)
Ruler: Flendon (Wistus)
Government: secret syndicate

Formerly a friendly competitor and rival of Fairhill, the small village of Crimmor has experienced a sharp decline over the past several years. The fishing village farther east of Fairhill along the banks of Lake Crimmormere welcomes few travelers from the Tradeway, even though it is only six miles south of its outskirts. The only exception applies to wagons in desperate need of repair. In these dire circumstances, the caravan leader may divert from the road and visit Stipish, the town's resident wheelwright whom many consider to be the finest mechanic in the area. Otherwise, Crimmor has undoubtedly seen better days. The lake, once renowned for its abundant stock of largemouth bass, appears to be utterly depleted of the tasty fish and any other marine life for that matter.

Fortunately, local residents still derive sustenance from the land and can also purchase provisions from the occasional merchant who ventures into town. When these rare visitors stop in Crimmor, Flendon, the leader of the local merchant's guild, races out to meet them. The haughty gentleman passes himself off as the town's ruler, though he exercises no true authority within Crimmor. Instead, Wistus and the thieves' guild control Crimmor through their puppet Flendon. Wistus and his underlings have their hands in every pie within the corrupt town. To keep up the ruse, Wistus kicks back a tiny sliver of his profits to the cowardly and overmatched Flendon. Although crime is pervasive in Crimmor, the guild's illicit activities may be the least of its problems. The fishermen speak of strange creatures inhabiting Lake Crimmormere. To make matters worse, stirges beset the town every evening. No one

knows where either of these menaces dwells or what these creatures seek, yet Wistus and Flendon seem disinterested in getting to the bottom of these mysteries.

Darnagal, Town of

Population: 1,225 (985 Foerdewaith, 115 hill dwarf, 100 halfling, 25 Heldring)
Ruler: Lord Mayor Holger the Gray
Government: mayor appointed by Bard's Gate

Two trade routes — the Coast Road and Shepherd's Crook — converge at the coastal town of Darnagal. It is in a perilous neighborhood, between the Shorsai Forest and the realm of Acregor to the north and the Great Salt Marsh to the south. As a consequence, Darnagal maintains a standing militia of over 100 soldiers and at need can call upon another 200 armed members of its citizenry. The town is surrounded by 10-foot-thick earthen and wooden palisades standing between 15 and 20 feet tall.

In addition to caravans arriving and departing via the Coast Road and Shepherd's Crook, trade passes through Darnagal's modest but well-maintained wharves.

Lord Mayor Holger the Gray is regularly required to placate the squabbling merchant houses that jockey for political and economic advantage in the town. His hold on power is a delicate balancing act between currying their favor without harming the competition, while keeping the peace within the town.

Derindin, City of

Population: 7,720 (6,555 Foerdewaith, 655 half-elf, 310 high elf, 200 halfling)
Ruler: Commissary Vronton Tweege
Government: commissary appointed by Bard's Gate

Like many other settlements on the Tradeway, Derindin owes its existence primarily to geography. The waters of the Glimmrill Run gouged the earth and stone to create a wide and deep canyon separating Bard's Gate from Freegate. At some unknown time in the distant past, the elves erected a wondrous suspension bridge made from magically reinforced cords that spanned the entire length of the intimidating chasm. When they abandoned the crossing, bandits filled the void and controlled the bridge for several centuries until the combined forces of elves and Freegate's phalanxes severed the structure's supports, simultaneously wrecking the bridge and the brigands who controlled it. With the bandits out of the way, the city of Bard's Gate swooped in to rebuild the span with the indigenous elves' permission and assistance. The engineers who designed the successor bridge recreated many of the span's original features as well as fortifying its ends to prevent another entity from duplicating what the elves and Freegate had done to sabotage the structure. Today, the city of Derindin occupies the bridge itself as well as the land adjacent to each end of the crossing.

Much like the bandit lords of old, Commissary Vronton Tweege watches over the shops, tenements, and structures from his lofty perch atop the tower at the bridge's center rather than dwelling on solid ground or at one of its secure ends. Although the span no longer sways like its first incarnation, some observers believe the commissary tempts fate by duplicating the error of its last bandit leader Ootmar the Short-Sighted who plummeted to his death in the canyon when his adversaries literally cut the bridge's cords on one end. Vronton believes his personal safety relies more heavily on facilitating commerce in Derindin and ensuring the safety of the Tradeway in his neck of the woods rather than taking up a strategic position on the city's bridge. Although firmly part of the Suzerainty of Bard's Gate, the commissary wants to transform Derindin into more than just another stopover on the Tradeway. To attract merchants to the city, Vronton discreetly encourages the city's manufacturers to produce knockoffs of valuable goods and commodities that they intersperse among the genuine articles at a discount price. The creation of fake diamonds and other gemstones made from glass and other worthless minerals has risen to such a level that jewelers deride a poorly cut gemstone as a "Derindian trinket." Metallurgists also get in the fun, forging counterfeit weapons purportedly made out of legendary steel. Those manufacturers and merchants who partake in this pastime frequently worship the treacherous god Moccavallo in his temple not surprisingly constructed on the moderately unstable northern precipice of the bridge. Of course, not everything on Derindin's shelves is a fabrication. The real deals are out there for educated customers who can spot the difference between the genuine article and a phony one.

The notion of dangling precariously above a chasm instills a sense of bravado among its citizens who realize it only takes a hard shove to send someone into a headfirst freefall into the canyon below the bridge. The self-reliant residents take matters into their own hands rather than foist their grievances onto the apathetic civic authorities. Obviously, they also expect the same of those visiting their city, especially when it comes to someone who was cheated in the unregulated marketplace. In Derindin, dueling resolves every dispute. The parameters of this personal contest must be agreed upon beforehand by both parties, including the types of weapons used, the lethality of the affair, and the specific date and time for the potentially deadly rendezvous. Newcomers soon discover that Derindin's laws allow for the selection of a champion to take the combatant's place in this match. Not surprisingly, the city's influential Champions' Guild fiercely lobbied for this exception, which almost all of Derindin's business owners happily invoke when faced off against an angry customer.

On those rare occasions when the commissary has no choice but to intervene in a civic matter, he relies upon the settlement's 43 handpicked marshals to amicably resolve the situation, if possible. In keeping with Derindin's customs, those who refuse to come along peacefully or disrespect the marshals' authority get ceremoniously pushed over the side of the bridge and into the canyon 110 feet beneath the span. The fortunate few who survive the plunge face a lifetime ban from Derindin, but no further retribution from Vronton and his marshals unless they return. The city's military forces include 10 Lyreguard officers who command a volunteer force of 370 bowmen, spearmen, and men-at-arms. A contingent of 40 elven knights from Arendia and a phalanx of 64 legionnaires from Freegate complement Derindin's army, which ultimately answers to its true masters back in Bard's Gate.

FAIRHILL, TOWN OF

Population: 420 (340 Foerdewaith, 30 mountain dwarf, 25 halfling, 15 high elf, 10 other)
Ruler: Arlen the Magistrate
Government: autocracy

The small town of Fairhill occupies the largest in a cluster of gently sloping hills roughly 10 miles north of the Tradeway linking Fareme and Bard's Gate. The town's residents are predominately human with small pockets of elves, halflings, dwarves, and a handful of other races. Its diverse population lives off the land farming in the fertile fields beneath the hills as well as providing goods and services to merchants and other travelers venturing to either of the larger settlements on the nearby trade route. Two taverns, an inn, a central market, and several boutique shops cater to these visitors' needs. Arlen the Magistrate, a retired captain in the Lyreguard and former adventurer, rules the town with a just and even hand. Shandril, the resident priestess of Freya, lends her aid when needed to Fairhill's capable leader. The cleric embraces her role as the townsfolk's spiritual guide and the earthly representative of the town's patron deity. Although she personally founded Fairhill 90 years earlier at Freya's direction, she happily defers all secular matters to Arlen as she wants no part in governing over her congregation's daily affairs.

Arlen entrusts Fairhill's defense to Baran the One-Handed and his company of 25 guards. These soldiers primarily occupy the stone watchtower in the town's square, which gives them an ideal vantage point to monitor activity within the settlement and beyond. The balance of Fairhill's military forces are stationed at other strategic locations scattered around the town. At Shandril's insistence, Fairhill lacks any walls or other fortifications and instead relies upon Freya's blessing to keep its people safe. Her passive defensive strategy represents one of the few bones of

contention between Arlen, Baran, and the revered priestess. A recent spate of orc attacks on the Tradeway and the outlying farms and homesteads suggests a greater enemy may be coordinating these raids for an unknown purpose. Some townsfolk believe a vampire dwelling in a ruined keep outside of town may direct their activities, whereas others blame the recent killings on a witch Shandril exiled shortly after she founded Fairhill.

FAREME

See "Fareme" under "The Lands of Reme — Grand Duchy of Reme — Duchy of Waymarch."

FOREST KINGDOMS (FOREST OF PARNA)

Population: 173,200 (72,744 high elf, 60,620 wood elf, 21,400 half-elf, 18,236 Foerdewaith, 200 other)
Ruler: none
Government: varies

Centuries of human colonization and the great wildfires of 2496 I.R. were not enough to deforest this swath of the Great Akadonian Forest that once covered most of central and southern Akados. High elves and wood elves still hold sway within these woods, leading scholars to deem it the last true remnant of the great elven kingdom despite the numerous schisms and infighting among the high elven houses and wood elves who control the area. For many centuries, the indigenous elves tenaciously beat back humans trespassing into their lands until they came to the stark realization that they could not win a war of attrition against such a prolific foe. They retreated deep into the twilit depths of the forest and established the fabled Kingdom of Parnuble, while maintaining wary eyes on the invaders. Much to their surprise, the humans treated the land they settled with dignity, prompting the half-elves among them to reach a peaceful accord with the newcomers, though some elves still clung to their isolationist beliefs. The queen of Parnuble ultimately ended the conflict by allowing the wood elves to maintain their own clans in the forest's interior. She also granted them the legal right to forcibly resist human incursions. Conversely, the high elves entered into an era of increased cooperation with their human neighbors.

The Kingdom of Parnuble, governed by Queen Tuiliar, controls the city of Arendia, the forest areas bordering the length of the Tradeway, and large interior portions of the woodland. Several smaller high elven houses rule their own fiefdoms within the realm, the most noteworthy being the High House of Jarlax, which claims sovereignty over the northern section of the forest at the headwaters of Glimmrill Run. These high elves hold the queen and her house in contempt, deeming them to be traitors to their race for collaborating with the humans. Their warriors occasionally raid the Tradeway to express their displeasure, though their activities never rise above the nuisance level. The emissaries of the queen and Bard's Gate remain committed to amicably solving these problems.

Several self-proclaimed baronies and counties have taken root in the forest's southern and western edges near the Unclaimed Lands, while free settlements, brigand holds, and at least one full-fledged bandit kingdom occupy the woodland's eastern fringes. These human-dominated territories avoid interfering in the affairs of Bard's Gate and the Kingdom of Parnuble. They instead focus their ire at the wood elf clans scattered throughout the forest's interior. Despite the wood elves' fierce independent streak and their dislike for humans, many still claim allegiance to the high elf queen. The clans frequently clash with the brigands and bandits in the region, accounting for the lion's share of blood spilt upon this lush green tapestry.

ARENDIA, CITY OF

Population: 7,230 (5,725 high elf, 810 half-elf, 670 Foerdewaith, 25 other)
Ruler: Queen Tuiliar
Government: monarchy

The trade city of Arendia simultaneously unites buyers with sellers and the humancentric culture of Bard's Gate with the high elven

Kingdom of Parnuble. Queen Tuiliar who also rules the Kingdom of Parnuble within the surrounding Forest of Parna founded Arendia to serve as the official meeting point between the two cultures. Arendia seamlessly fuses elements of high elven architecture with traditional building techniques incorporated from conventional human cities. Towering spires and narrow arches combine forces with treetop bridges and staircases arranged in a loose grid system occupying both sides of the Tradeway, which passes directly through the heart of Arendia. High elves outnumber human and half-elf residents by a ratio of roughly five-to-one, yet the majority graciously accepts the minority's traditions, cuisines, and religions despite some difficulties understanding less refined and sophisticated ideas. Nonetheless, there is no mistaking Arendia's distinctly elven character. The elven builders deliberately constructed the Temple of Darach-Albith in such a manner that its central courtyard incorporates the Tradeway into its design, forcing travelers using the route to pass through the holy site's gardens, fountains, and statues depicting the Father of the Elves' wondrous countenance. The architects also placed more emphasis on celebrating their natural surroundings than focusing on worked stone. Precisely manicured trees, shrubs, and other vegetation grow freely, while the city intentionally incorporated natural ponds, brooks, and streams into its extensive public works and water distribution system.

Despite the tranquil surroundings, resentment still persists in some pockets of the elven community. Queen Tuiliar sees the inclusion of humans into Arendia's society as an opportunity for the human settlers to reciprocate the favor and grant the elves greater influence among the elite of Bard's Gate. Some of her subjects strongly disagree. They view their human and half-elf neighbors as a contagion contaminating the sanctity of elven culture. Although no one publicly expresses these opinions within earshot of Queen Tuiliar or her supporters, the underground movement known as the Pristine Harp appears to be growing and gaining important allies. They predominately target human-owned property and businesses through intimidation, vandalism, and arson. While no one has died at the hands of the Pristine Harp, even the queen and her counselors demonstrate genuine concern that the organization seems poised to add violence to its repertoire. The intelligence gathered by her network of spies and informants tells her the group is homegrown, but a nagging hunch leads her to believe someone outside of Arendia instigates the Pristine Harp's actions and funds their operations. She personally suspects one or more of the guilds in Bard's Gate lends a helping hand to the Pristine Harp. However, she lacks any evidence to support this conclusion.

Despite her inklings, the commercial, cultural, and most importantly economic ties between her city and Bard's Gate remains strong. Cylria, the current high burgess of Bard's Gate, originally hails from Arendia and is a distant cousin of Queen Tuiliar. The women cooperatively work together to further each of their jointly shared or individual ambitions. The Fellowship of Note deploys at least 12 covert agents within Arendia. The operatives report their findings directly to Cylria, who in turn shares some of her information with her elven counterpart when appropriate. The pair also conduct joint patrols of the Tradeway sections passing through the Forest of Parna. For this task, Queen Tuiliar calls upon roughly 100 of the city's 1,100 mounted knights to partake in this vital endeavor. These fiercely loyal soldiers are equally adept at fighting in the saddle or on foot. In addition to monitoring activities on the Tradeway, her troops must also defend the city against incursions from rivals within the Forest Kingdoms and fend off monstrous incursions from the wilderness's indigenous inhabitants.

Freegate, City of

Population: 18,600 (18,175 human [Freegate natives], 310
  Foerdewaith, 45 halfling, 30 hill dwarf, 25 half-elf, 15 other)
Ruler: Praetor Julius Marcinius
Government: imperial

Founded 3,500 years ago, the city of Freegate lies on the coast of the Gulf of Akados at the mouth of the Talamerin River, making it a vital seaport and an important trade hub for the sprawling metropolis of Bard's Gate to the west. While known as Freegate in most circles, some residents still retain the title of *Porta Librum* as it is referred to in High Boros. Freegate remains true to its Hyperborean roots, as evidenced by the organization of its armed forces. The City Legion numbers 4,096 soldiers, roughly 1,000 men and women short of a full strength, classical legion, but in times of all-out war, the city can levy additional troops from the populace to form new legions with colorful names such as the Death's Head Legion. Praetor Julius Marcinius leads the City Legion, making him the de facto commander-in-chief of Freegate's ground forces. Freegate's fleet of six triremes under the command of the navarch with a ploiarch captaining each individual vessel, protects its interests at sea along with a small flotilla of ships from Bard's Gate. These forces came to the aid of their western ally during the Huun invasion a few years earlier. High walls surround the city and provide an added measure of protection against invasion.

In keeping with its Hyperborean traditions, citizens still speak High Boros, and the city maintains an active arena district with a gladiatorial circuit. Hyperborean currency also circulates among the populace, though coins minted in Bard's Gate are also commonly exchanged for various goods and services within the city. Marble fountains sculpted into the likenesses of historical figures and revered deities abound throughout the settlement, fed by the waters from a subterranean tributary coursing through an extensive network of underground cisterns and pipes. People routinely gather around these water distribution centers to discuss daily gossip and also stump for political office. Each fountain represents an individual electoral district from which residents select a local magistrate and a member of their ruling council, a legislative body of 28 individuals who govern the city. Praetor Julius Marcinius presides over the council's meetings and serves as the deciding vote in the event of a tie. Although he technically serves as an administrator and advisor to the group, the undying support of his troops lends great power to his voice and gives him tremendous influence over their decisions. The praetor remains dedicated to the principles of the republic. He maintains a healthy respect for vigorous debate and the right to disagree with his viewpoint, regardless of how misguided it may seem to him. For their part, praetors negotiate trade agreements with Bard's Gate and other partners, appoint diplomats to project the city's interests in strategic settlements throughout the region, and codify the city's laws and doctrines. Commissary Helios Pousalaki, an aging wine merchant and member of the council, holds the critical post of ratifying all trade transactions for the city. On most nights, he can be found at The Trireme outside the city. The 725 members of the city watch enforce the council's edicts within Freegate. Because of their close ties to the Suzerainty of Bard's Gate, outsiders erroneously relegate Freegate to colonial or commonwealth status, yet Freegate retains its unique identity of indigenous and Hyperborean culture. The city shares a reverence for Thyr and Muir, though its people also worship Zadastha, the goddess of love in her temple, which also houses a magnificent winery.

The consuls currently have their hands full dealing with the lingering effects from the unexpected Huun invasion. Intrigue always festers in Freegate's sewers, and rumors about wererats, snake people, and other boogeymen from children's stories hiding in the dank tunnels below the streets circulate practically everywhere.

Glendovel Close, Town of

Population: 2,170 (1,675 Foerdewaith, 300 halfling, 85
  mountain dwarf, 50 half-elf, 35 hill dwarf, 25 high elf)
Ruler: Sheriff Beauregard Dufresne
Government: elected official

Small streams pouring down from the heights of the Stoneheart Mountains wash water, sediment, and other nutrients onto the fields that make up Glendovel Close. This fertile soil yields an abundance of grains including wheat, barley, rye, rice, and oats that these farmers harvest for their own sustenance as well as export to Bard's Gate to the south and Darnagal to the east. In addition, vast herds of livestock graze on the lush pastures adjacent to the expansive farmland. The sprawling community stretches across thousands of cultivated acres with isolated homesteads separated by great distances from their closest neighbors. These parcels of tilled earth have belonged to the same families for many generations, which simultaneously forges the bonds of deep-seated friendships, often solidified by arranged marriages, and bitter rivalries between fierce competitors. Bard's Gate has a vested interest in maintaining stability within the boundaries of its northernmost ally and veritable bread basket. Therefore, the metropolis garrisons 20 Waymark cavalry troops at the site to help its homegrown militia of 120 men and women defend the crucial agricultural hub against internal and external threats.

Sheriff Beauregard Dufresne, the town's elected leader, and the 32 deputies under his direction, discreetly and delicately keep the peace within the farming community. They rarely interfere in personal disputes or even patrol the outlying areas. They focus their attention on the town's bustling market district where farmers sell their crops to purveyors from Bard's Gate, Darnagal, and even distant Freegate. While they keep a wary eye out for thieves and pickpockets, they primarily strive to ensure fast-talking merchants offer the genteel folk under their charge a fair price for their crops. They immediately notify new traveling wholesalers about this simple rule and the repercussions for disobeying it through permanent expulsion from the town's market square or several nights of lackluster accommodations in a prison cell.

Glendovel Close sits at the terminus for roads leading to and from Bard's Gate as well as Darnagal. For much of its existence, it functioned as a mere provider and distribution center for foodstuffs heading to these settlements. However, recent talk of reopening the Old North Road through the Desolation and the lands beyond have rekindled interest in expanding the town into a trading center linking the giant metropolis with underserved markets in Apothasalos and the landlocked Northlands. The great distances separating it from Acregor, the Desolation, the Azure Mountains, and the Dragon Hills keep those dangers at bay for now, but the sudden influx of newfound wealth and prosperity could potentially usher in a wave of envious outsiders seeking to claim a piece of the action for themselves. In this case, Sheriff Beauregard and his underlings would turn their gaze southward to Bard's Gate for protection against these combined menaces. At the moment, Glendovel Close retains its bucolic existence, though the question of how long it can remain out of the spotlight depends upon developments in the Desolation.

EASTREACH PROVINCE

Capital: Carterscroft

Notable Settlements: Drownboat Crossing, Eastwych, Florin's Cross, Oxmulch, Renderby, Zelkor's Ferry

Ruler: Lord-Governor Meridiac of Courghais

Government: feudalism (vassal of Foere)

Population: 1,222,000 (1,110,000 Foerdewaith, 73,000 halfling, 15,300 high elf, 9,800 half-elf, 6,050 wood elf, 4,200 gnome, 3,650 hill dwarf)

Monstrous: giant animal (bear, wolf and stag), kobold, bugbear, stirge, giant insect, worg, fey, giant spider, ratfolk, treant, trolls, undead, decapus, wyvern, green dragon (Forest of Hope); goblin, blood hawk, ogre, undead, ankheg, kenku, gnoll, green hag, fey, manticore, basilisk, copper dragon, bulette, (plains); giant snake, goblin, boggard, marsh jelly, hag, cockatrice, will-o'-wisp, black dragons (coastal swamps)

Languages: Common, Halfling, Elvish, Dwarven, Gnomish

Religion: Sefagreth, Solanus (declining), Freya, Pekko, Kamien, Telophus, Mitra (rising), Archeillus, Tykee, Thyr, Darach-Albith

Resources: grain, foodstuffs, trade hub, livestock, fishing, salt, shipbuilding, timber

Technology Level: Medieval (Carterscroft, Eastwych), High Middle Ages, Dark Ages (some remote areas)

Eastreach Province is still loyal to the Kingdoms of Foere and is governed by a lord-governor sent from the overking's court. The province has always suffered from fragmentation and decentralization in a complex feudal system, and the social order is now suffering very badly from corruption fueled by bribes from Bard's Gate. Internal travel is grinding almost to a halt due to tolls charged by petty barons, and as rural settlements become more isolated, the wilderness is beginning to creep back into civilized areas.

The official boundaries of Eastreach are defined as follows, beginning with Eastwych in the northeast. From Eastwych, the border runs south along the Sinnar Coast and the north shore of the Amrin Estuary. From here, it runs north of the Amrin Ferry by some 50 miles, thence along the Estuary Road to the crossroad with the Wain Road. From here, all agree that the border extends somewhat diagonally northwest to the Great Bridge over the Amrin, but the exact line has never been properly established. From the Great Bridge, the boundary line follows the banks of the Great River Amrin downriver to the southeast, then travels north along the Glimmrill River almost to the coast, then eastward along the shoreline back to Eastwych. Bard's Gate controls the Amrin River Ferry, all of the waters of the Amrin Estuary, and the Estuary's entire southern bank.

The lands north of the Great Amrin River, from the Glimmrill Run to the Great Bridge, are an unsettled wilderness all the way to the edge of the Stoneheart Forest, an expanse occupied by monsters, outlaws, and others who choose to live beyond the reach of established authority. Neither Bard's Gate nor Eastreach claim these lands, as they are dangerous and offer no measurable likelihood of tax revenues. From time to time, a lord-governor has offered minor patents of nobility for anyone willing to establish a freehold in the area beyond the Great Amrin. None of the resulting settlements has lasted more than a generation, and most came to a rather bad end.

The central and western lands of Eastreach are relatively populated and stable, with several farming and trading towns along the major roads. The northeast portion of Eastreach is likewise fairly well populated, with the frequency of villages increasing as one draws nearer to Eastwych. By contrast, southeast Eastreach is but lightly populated, and in the Forest of Hope and along the coast of the Sinnar Ocean, there are virtually no settlements at all.

HISTORY AND PEOPLE

In the year 2765 I.R., heralds at the Foerdewaith Court at Courghais issued the royal "Decree of Full Provincial Status to the lands of Eastreach, in Vassalage-Perpetual to the Overking in Foere." A hundred copies of the long document were painstakingly written to parchment, seals were affixed, and Foere had officially launched a privately funded invasion of the lands all the way from still-fledgling Aachen Province to the shores of the Sinnar Ocean. In essence, the so-called "Eastreach Decree" granted patents of nobility over lands not yet actually taken. Responsibility for "pacifying any unlawful resistance to the overking's decree by subjects in such lands" was left to the knights and barons "upon taking possession of their lawful demesnes in the province." In other words, if a Foerdewaith noble, or even a mercenary leader, could carve out a piece of Eastreach, they owned it. However, and unbeknownst to the overking of Foere, the Decree of Eastreach was accompanied by a second, unwritten law: the law of unintended consequences. The disorder and corruption of Eastreach Province clearly have their roots in the decree.

In the same year as the Eastreach Decree, Foere also established Pontus Tinigal on Pontos Island to form a base for the new Foerdewaith navy. This was a long-planned maneuver Macobert had organized years before, and already involved a decree that an admiral of Foere and a town senate would govern the salt-producing town of Eastwych, thus ensuring that the navy would have a supply port on the mainland. Annoying as it might have been for the citizens of Eastwych to learn they had been given away to a foreign navy, the town's special status as a naval possession spared it from the plunder and chaos the Eastreach Decree caused in the rest of the province. Refugees from the countryside streamed into the town during the invasion, and the admiral happily pressed them into service and shipped them off to Pontus Tinigal where they began reluctant careers as unpaid oarsmen on the poorly constructed galleys of the new Foerdewaith navy. It is to be noted that the shipbuilding skills of the Foerdewaith navy improved quickly over the years, but due to this incident, its popularity among the native Eastreachers took some time to repair.

Corruption and internal division are slowly eroding Eastreach Province, although the process is too gradual to be obvious. The flow of money from Bard's Gate pays the nobility well for their cooperation with Bard's Gate commerce, but little of the wealth makes its way into the lives of the common folk of the province. The rich grow richer; the poor grow poorer. As more of the petty nobility try to get a place at the trough, they are creating more little borders within the realm, all of which charge tariffs on farmers and traders passing through. The result is a slow withering of overland journeys in the areas not served by the official high roads. As an example, trade down the Canyon River is on the increase, with merchants and traders becoming more willing to risk a long, dangerous circuit around the much-shorter but exorbitantly expensive overland trek through the country roads.

With the intense focus on money, the nobility is coming to see the peasantry as a resource, instead of perceiving themselves as guardians of the peasantry. More wilderness is encroaching upon the province as the commonfolk lose their optimism and drive in the face of irresponsible feudal lords, who are far more interested in collecting taxes than in supporting the welfare of their tenants. Land is beginning to go fallow in some places, forests are no longer patrolled, and the risky business of smuggling is becoming more common than ordinary trade. To foreigners, the creeping rot in Eastreach is fairly apparent, but the solution is much less clear.

TRADE AND COMMERCE

Eastreach Province, although it remains loyal to the Kingdoms of Foere, is on extremely good terms with the mercantile and political emissaries of Bard's Gate. Gold flows into the coffers of the province (and of the lord-governor) to ensure that overland trade between Telar Brindel and Bard's Gate remains unmolested. The high sheriff of internal revenue in Carterscroft oversees a force of sheriffs at the three main road-crossings into the province, where they document the number of wagon axles, people, and animals passing in and out, so the tax can be billed to Bard's Gate in the following year. Bard's Gate travelers are given a special token when they cross the border from Aachen on the Wain Road or the Cross Cut, and at the Estuary Road just north of the Eastgate crossroad. The same office operates taxing-posts along the internal roads to levy tolls upon anyone not holding one of the Bard's Gate tokens handed out at the borders. The position is a lucrative one, and an honest person has not held the post in centuries, as far as anyone can tell.

While actual troops from Bard's Gate are not allowed to travel the Eastreach roads (oddly, military forces of the Duchy of the Waymarch under contract with Bard's Gate are a notable, if infrequent, exception due to long-held treaties between Foere and Reme), river traffic down the Amrin is neither stopped nor inspected by officials of the province under the general trade agreements in place. This allows Bard's Gate to move soldiers and cargo down the Great Amrin River between the Estuary and the Stoneheart River branch. In Eastgate, merchants and river captains pay Bard's Gate for access to the river, and these tolls are used, in part, to fund the payments made to Eastreach Province.

Along the eastern coast, the Coast Road and Lowwater Road are far worse maintained than the three great roads that intersect in Carterscroft. Although Eastreacher patrols ride the northern half of the coast, and Bard's Gate sends riders from Eastgate along Lowwater Road, these patrols are sporadic and unenergetic. The forces of Eastreach use the duty to train junior officers, and Bard's Gate uses it as punishment duty for disgraced officers, so the patrols are particularly ineffectual.

LOYALTIES AND DIPLOMACY

Eastreach Province loosely maintains its status as a province of the Kingdoms of Foere and gives fealty to the throne in Courghais. As such, Eastreach marks the northeastern-most extent of the Foerdewaith realms.

GOVERNMENT

A lord-governor appointed in the Court of Courghais in Foere rules Eastreach on behalf of the overking. Most governors serve for five years and then resign or are recalled to Foere. The position is a lucrative one, for the lord-governor takes a share of most of the province's rampant corruption. There are no regional governors below the rank of the lord-governor, as there are in Aachen. Rather, all of Eastreach Province's governance beneath the lord-governor is (theoretically, in any case) a feudal pyramid with the overking of Foere at the top, dukes below the overking, barons pledging fealty to the dukes, and knights, in turn, whose feudal obligations are due to the barons. The lord-governor's role is to be the voice and proxy of the distant overking, which allows him to call upon the dukes in the same way as the overking himself. A vast number of barons captured their lands independently, however, and thus do not report to any higher noble such as a duke. These highly-independent nobles must be called upon individually by the lord-governor, which is a monumental task for the central government. This highly unstable, volatile arrangement is a holdover from the original frontier land grants made to the nobles who led armies into the area, and the throne has never successfully reorganized it. In consequence, Eastreach is a patchwork of fiefdoms and freeholds, with only marginal interference by the greater nobles in the affairs of their vassals. The lord-governor maintains a royal court of law only in the city of Carterscroft, although the courts hear appeals from the judgments of ducal and baronial courts that administer most of the criminal and civil cases of the province. As one might expect, the application of the laws varies wildly from one barony to another.

The system works poorly, is riddled with corruption and graft, and is the direct result of the original "Eastreach Decree" of 2765 I.R., which granted lands in Eastreach based on the vagaries of military conquest. When the dust of that conquest settled, it became apparent that the Eastreach Decree had created a province carved into an impossible number of fiefdoms with overlapping and disputed borders, no provision for maintaining a centralized government, and no means of changing the system. Another factor that tended to protect the new barons and lords of Eastreach was that the Eastreach Decree assembled a particular sort of noble in the province. These were not parade-ground soldiers or tournament knights who had responded to the overking's offer of lands that were not his to give. Rather, every siege-battered stone castle and fortified manor house in Eastreach now housed a complement of battle-hardened veterans: armed, trained, blooded, and considerably more loyal to their commanders than to the overking. The overking wisely decided that sweeping changes to the prerogatives of this particular group of nobles could wait a generation, and each overking has made the same decision since.

As a province of the Kingdom of Foere, Eastreach is required by the overking to maintain and shoulder most of the expenses of the Royal Navy of Foere, whose principal port on the eastern coast of Akados is the port city of Eastwych. The fleet prevents any maritime advances that might be made by the Empire of Oceanus onto the mainland. As a part of the agreements made between Eastreach Province and Bard's Gate, the city of Eastgate maintains a second fleet, funded and commanded by Bard's Gate, to patrol and defend the Amrin Estuary on Eastreach's behalf. Courghais does not care for this perceived violation of their sovereignty, but Eastreach makes sure that a significant portion of the Bard's Gate payments make it back to the royal treasury each year to keep the overking's court appeased.

WILDERNESS AND ADVENTURE

Eastreach Province is no longer as productive as it once was under the rule of Foere, and the wilderness is beginning to encroach even upon areas once deemed completely safe. The eastern half of Eastreach Province was never particularly safe to begin with, and small communities in the east are actually finding themselves isolated from trade and protection, left to fend for themselves. This is particularly true in the belt of land between the Great Amrin River and the Forest of Hope, but the newfound phenomenon of the "widowed hamlet" is growing more common in the entire region from the central rivers all the way to the eastern seaboard. In addition to the obvious adventurers' destination of Rappan Athuk, the whole of eastern Eastreach offers plenty of scope for wandering adventurers to fight monsters, rescue villages, and even for higher-level characters to take a village under their wing as a freehold. New castles are needed, for the old ones lie neglected and crumbling as beasts prowl their walls; bandits are rife, and predatory tax collectors often arrive with armed soldiers to take even more than the bandits would. It is an area that cries for heroes, and finds none to answer the call.

REFERENCE SOURCE: RAPPAN ATHUK

CARTERSCROFT, CITY OF (CAPITAL)

Population: 17,721 (14,130 Foerdewaith, 2,025 halfling, 1,463 half-elf, 82 gnome, 21 high elf)
Ruler: Former Lord-Governor of Eastreach, now styled as Mayor Lord-Governor Hormengarde the Fat
Government: mayor elected by landowners

Carterscroft is a large walled city at the intersection of three main high-roads. A fourth major road, the Tantivy, leads from the city gates to the northeast, but it is an ordinary packed-dirt thoroughfare, not one of the stone-paved Hyperborean roads. The city towers fly the banner of Eastreach, a black flag showing a scroll and four coins below a purple crown.

The city of Carterscroft is the capital of Eastreach. This is the headquarters of the provincial government's corruption, engineered by the merchants of the city of Bard's Gate for their own safe passage through the region.

HISTORY AND PEOPLE

Carterscroft emerged as a large trading town in the days of Hyperborea, a staging ground for traders and armies preparing to make the long journey between the core of the empire to the distant lands of the Isthmus of Irkaina, and even to distant Libynos beyond. The city is named for the massive fenced crofts that have always been set aside to form and organize caravans that often number a hundred or more travelers.

GOVERNMENT

A mayor elected by the city's landowners governs the city of Carterscroft. While it is unusual for a Foerdewaith Provincial Capital to be self-governed, the law dates back to the original invasion of Eastreach by the Kingdoms of Foere. When the ragged but energetic invasion of Eastreach began in 2765 I.R., the mayor of Carterscroft impounded all caravan cargoes inside the city walls to provide a large emergency store of food to withstand a siege. By the time the vanguard of the Foerdewaith invaders arrived at the city walls, they found a well-defended and well-provisioned stronghold facing them. For a while, the Foerdewaith barons and their forces contented themselves with seizing the lands around the city, but without a large army to invest the city, food supplies continued to be smuggled in, and it became clear that any siege would be prolonged and costly. Eventually, some of the more influential Foerdewaith nobles struck a deal with the city: In exchange for surrendering, Carterscroft would remain self-governed by its own citizenry, and only small numbers of Foerdewaith soldiers would be allowed in the city walls at any given time. The second part of the agreement was mutually forgotten once the province's lord-governor was installed in Carterscroft; even the worst of the invading barons would hardly pillage the lord-governor's own capital city. The first part of the agreement, entitling the city to elect its own mayor, has remained in place.

Any offense committed in the city walls, even treachery to the crown, is tried by the city's urban courts. The lord-governor also has a Court of Justice in the city that adjudges all crimes and offenses committed outside Carterscroft from anywhere in the province. Because the lord-governor's Court of Justice is the highest in the land, it is actually considerably busier than the urban courts.

The Province of Eastreach is filled to bursting with tiny baronies owing their allegiance directly to the overking instead of to a higher noble, due to the expansive "take-it-and-you-rule-it" provisions of the Eastreach Decree. Such barons are entitled to bring their grievances and squabbles directly to the lord-governor for resolution. If the lord-governor attempted to address all these petty issues directly, it would utterly paralyze the government of the province, burying it in local disputes. Fortunately, the tool of bribery is available to the government, and offers a quick and convenient way to resolve otherwise-thorny legal questions.

The urban and the provincial court systems are eminently bribable, so wealthy individuals are unlikely to face any sort of energetic prosecution as long as enough silver crosses the right palms. This has drawn the ire of the priesthood of Thyr, as further described below.

Carterscroft is the seat of the high sheriff of internal revenue, a lucrative posting appointed by the lord-governor to oversee payments from the merchants of Bard's Gate for safe passage through the province. A significant portion of this money flows into the hands of the lord-governor and the high sheriff, who take advantage of their short terms in office to amass personal fortunes before returning to Foere. The current high sheriff is Sir Croaten Gui (pronounced "gwee"), a pleasant man who has hanged more than a hundred peasants for failure to pay taxes.

RELIGION

Most of rural Eastreach Province worships the Hyperborean gods and goddesses rather than the divine patrons of invading Foere, or the fashionably newfangled deities whose worship is spreading from Bard's Gate. There is a developing split between the faiths of the peasantry and the patron gods revered by the nobility and merchants, and this split is reflected clearly here in the capital city. Archeillus, a god of nobility imported by the Foerdewaith invaders, has gained considerable traction among the nobility, and the worship of Sefagreth has begun to supplant the worship of Tykee among the merchants. The peasantry continues to worship Kamien, Freya, Solanus, and Telophus.

As a large city, Carterscroft is home to all sorts of small temples and shrines, including all of the above and others, but the predominant faiths are those of Archeillus, Tykee, and Sefagreth.

In recent years, the high priest of Thyr in Carterscroft has begun an active campaign to fight bribery and favoritism in the courts, issuing stern sermons and dire warnings. The government and wealthy citizens of the city have fought back actively against the high priest's campaign, cutting back or eliminating their donations to the temple, and even levying special taxes on Thyr's festival-days.

DROWNBOAT CROSSING, TOWN OF

Population: 4,287 (3,027 Foerdewaith, 961 halfling, 230 half-elf, 68 high elf)
Ruler: Baron Owen Foundofter
Government: overlord

Strategically located at the intersections of Glimmrill Run and the Great Amrin River, Drownboat Crossing specializes in ferrying passengers across the wide river. Numerous cart tracks and dirt paths converge at this point, which is one of the few upriver crossings in Eastreach Province. The Tantivy Road, the only thoroughfare connecting the provincial capital of Carterscroft with Florin's Cross and other portions of northern and eastern Eastreach Province, runs close to Drownboat Crossing. Humans account for roughly 70% of the large town's total residents, followed by a significant percentage of halflings with half-elves and elves combined making up less than 10% of the population.

Four large boats sailing under the town's flag shuttle farmers and merchants alike back and forth at a reasonable cost. The town's previous ruler, the father of current leader Baron Owen Foundofter, handsomely bribed the lord-governor for the exclusive rights to operate a ferry at this critical river juncture. The concession put almost every ferry operator within several miles of Drownboat Crossing out of business save for two who duplicated the baron's feat. For now, the baron tolerates the presence of another operator in close proximity to the town, though some of the town's unscrupulous citizens claim the Foundofters have solicited the services of several known saboteurs and provocateurs to disrupt their rivals' operations. There are no overt signs of trouble on the waterfront, but the chatter about these clandestine activities continues to increase with each passing day.

Like most noble families in Eastreach Province, bribery played a critical role in the Foundofters' rise to power. In addition to purchasing a virtual monopoly of the river ferry service, the family's control of Drownboat Crossing rakes in enormous profits from taxes and tolls levied on goods passing across the river. The Foundofters intentionally keep these fees reasonably low to retain popular support for their corrupt regime, while still generating enough income to support their lavish lifestyle. The baron openly offers favorable treatment to anyone willing to pay him for the privilege of being spoiled, with one crucial exception: Bribery is unacceptable when it pertains to the care of the town's ferry fleet. The Foundofters pride themselves on Drownboat Crossing's exceptional safety record, which contradicts the settlement's curious name whose origins have been lost to the annals of time.

EASTWYCH, CITY OF

Population: 26,204 (14,420 Foerdewaith garrison and sailors, 7,232 other human, 2,100 halfling, 1,862 half-elf, 580 high elf)
Ruler: Baron Teonj of Thovre (Grand Admiral), various city councilors
Government: council (for the city); grand admiral (for the naval base)

Eastwych is a major port for the Kingdom of Foere and principal headquarters of the Foerdewaith navy. The seaport is heavily fortified, with massive towers overlooking a deep harbor crowded with armed sailing galleons and long war-galleys, as well as merchant caravels and cogs. Trebuchets are mounted atop the larger towers, and the smaller towers bristle with mangonels and ballistae.

In addition to serving as the headquarters for the Foerdewaith fleet, the bustling trade hub also hosts numerous merchant cogs and caravels that import and export goods to and from countless destinations throughout Akados. The city predates the Hyperboreans' arrival and has been a major producer of salt and brine springs throughout its long, illustrious history. The metropolis also boasts a large garrison of Foerdewaith soldiers and marines charged with the task of guarding the port itself, patrolling the neighboring coastline, and serving as ships' companies for any naval expedition authorized by the overking. Indeed, these soldiers and marines make up more than half of the seaport's total population. The remaining residents are predominantly human, with roughly 2,000 halflings and half-elves and several hundred high elves rounding out the city's numbers.

The Foerdewaith navy's presence saddles the metropolis with a complex set of laws governing civilian and military jurisdictions. Eastwych's elected municipal senate oversees a city court known as the regular court. The 63 senators elected to this legislative body alternate presiding over cases falling under their purview. The Citadel of Troops operates a military court, while the admiral of the fleet oversees a court dealing with maritime legal matters. These judicial institutions are not as brazenly corrupt as most governmental offices in Eastreach Province, though those wealthy enough to hire one of the city's renowned attorneys can purchase virtual immunity from prosecution if they keep the severity of their offenses within reason. This concept abides with Eastwych's overarching philosophy that "anything that happens for the sake of having a good time is fine in our books."

Eastwych's numerous soldiers and sailors suffer from months of sheer boredom interrupted by several compressed minutes of tremendous stress while on the high seas or in combat. The pendulum swing between the two extremes causes much of the city's garrison to spend their free time and loose coins numbing their senses in one of the metropolis' seemingly infinite taverns or pursuing more expensive vices in the city's seedier quarters. The influx of visitors and traders from other lands adds to the intrigue. Drunken brawls, gambling disputes, and jealous arguments are common sights on Eastwych's streets and alleys. In the absence of any serious injuries, deaths, or significant damage to property, the city's officials generally allow the offenders to sober up or amicably resolve the situation without further incident. This approach frees the court system to address more pressing issues and also boosts the troops' morale knowing they will not get court-martialed or disciplined for a good time gone awry.

Admiral Treston Artraguis, commander of Eastwych Naval Base, oversees the facility's day-to-day operations and is responsible for keeping the soldiers and ships under his command highly motivated and battle ready. His counterpart, Baron Teonj of Thovre, the grand admiral of the Foerdewaith fleet, technically outranks Admiral Treston, but has no real authority over the military installation by intentional design. The overking refuses to commit the same mistake his predecessor made centuries earlier when local nobleman Grand Admiral Maximilian d'Varago Pontos successfully absconded with Courghais' fleet and declared himself Emperor of the Oceans Blue. Baron Teonj, a local Eastreach noble, serves at the overking's whim and is subject to the crown's orders in all matters concerning the fleet. Admiral Treston, on the other hand, has no ties to Eastreach Province or its local aristocracy. His loyalties lie solely with his superiors' best interests. The overking tasks him with protecting his fleet against incursions from the neighboring Kingdom of Oceanus and preparing his ships and soldiers to take back the renegade island at a moment's notice, though such ambitions are currently beyond the military's capabilities.

FLORIN'S CROSS, VILLAGE OF

Population: 526 (480 Foerdewaith, 31 hill dwarf, 11 half-elf, 4 gnome)
Ruler: Lord Crothian Barne
Government: overlord

The small town of Florin's Cross lies at the terminus of the Tantivy Road and a mere few miles from the more heavily traveled Coast Road. The settlement is an official possession of the lord-governor of the province, administered by the lord bailiff of Florin's Cross. Lord Crothian Barne currently holds this appointed position, which allows him and his family to reside in the castle known as Florinfort. The fortified keep has a small outer bailey and is manned by a force of 10 archers and 15 footmen who always remain safely ensconced inside its defensive outer walls. The aloof ruler and his men rarely venture outside the secure confines of the keep that feels as if it were a world away from the townsfolk who established their own militia and town watch without any aid from their disinterested Lord Bailiff.

Eastreach Province's lack of oversight has allowed a flourishing smuggling operation to take hold within the sleepy settlement at the intersection of two commercial roadways. The residents use the small and shallow yet navigable Scaramouche River to hustle convicts, heretics, and outlaws to safety, while also safeguarding large cargoes and crops from inspection and taxation at the hands of Eastreach Province's greedy robber-barons and corrupt tax collectors. Although these illegal activities are punishable by death, the townsfolk believe the province's onerous tax burden and oppressive policies leave them with no other choice. Worse still, rumors suggest the Friendly Men, a local criminal syndicate, wants their piece of the action as well.

Indeed, the seeds of rebellion sown in this small corner of Eastreach Province have given rise to rumblings about taking more aggressive and direct actions against the land's most tyrannical knights and even its barons. Such talk can sometimes be heard in the Beard Inn, the town's only tavern and inn where a group of local mimes known as the Tongue-Tied Fellows frequently entertain the crowd. The troupe of players with strange mannerisms and foreign customs seems oddly out of place in this establishment. Moreover, the men, who presumably traveled here from a distant land, stammer to explain why they came here or where they were going.

GUMSPUR, VILLAGE OF

Population: 363 (290 Foerdewaith, 45 halfling, 15 half-elf, 10 hill dwarf, 3 high elf)
Ruler: Reginald Reed
Government: overlord

At the confluence of the Great Amrin River and Glimmrill Run lies the village of Gumspur in the southeastern corner of the Unclaimed Lands only a few miles away from the substantially larger town of Drownboat Crossing. The town earned its name from the abundance of blackgum trees along the riverbank, but it is more well known for its two brands of pottery made by the Reed and the Larch families. Although competitors, the rivals have a friendly working relationship. The Reed family patriarch, Reginald Reed, functions as the village's mayor with the assistance of his constable Strom Levy and his two deputies.

OXMULCH, VILLAGE OF

Population: 98 (97 Foerdewaith, 1 hill dwarf)
Ruler: Reeve Charlo Monteague
Government: overlord (the absentee baron appoints a village reeve to oversee the village in his stead)

This small village built along the Cross Cut would remain anonymous if not for the byproduct of its resident herds of oxen. The grass growing within and around the village contains an anomalous quantity of nutrients. The oxen devouring the organic matter defecate an incredibly foul-smelling manure with exceptionally vigorous fertilizing properties. The village transports and sells this literally homegrown product by the cartload to the outlying farms and neighboring settlements. The manure generates significant income for the otherwise innocuous town, yet its prosperity comes with an added price. The terrible stench lingers everywhere, clinging to the clothes and bodies of anyone who spends even a few hours in Oxmulch. Nothing can remove the awful smell except for leaving the area and then thoroughly cleaning one's body and destroying any garments worn during the brief stay. Even in that case, the aroma persists for at least another 24 hours before finally dissipating.

RENDERBY, TOWN OF

Population: 2,640 (2,422 Foerdewaith, 136 half-elf, 57 high elf, 25 halfling)
Ruler: Mayor Barth Lottenbandry
Government: overlord

Renderby is the only significant settlement in the rural highlands upriver from Zelkor's Ferry at the mouth of the Canyon River. Its prolonged isolation has allowed several quirky beliefs and practices to take hold among its people. Through some misinterpretation of church doctrine, the townsfolk believe a person's sins are transferred to the goods they produce and then by extension to anyone who buys their products. Eager to cleanse their souls, these individuals offer discounts based upon the severity of their transgressions to visiting merchants who wear distinctive orange coats and have acquired quasi-holy status within the community. A person desperately seeking penance for a grave crime may even abduct a merchant and force that person to purchase their products for virtually nothing.

In an even stranger twist, Renderby conducts most financial transactions using chickens as a form of substitute currency. Records are kept of partial chicken transactions, and the mayor has even crafted wooden half-chicken tokens to facilitate purchases made using this bizarre system. The town is so odd, even the lord-governor and his barons ignore it, preferring to forfeit their tax revenue than to try to make sense of this weird place. Some merchants and residents alike speculate that those who created these unusual ideas may truly be "crazy like a fox." Although their methodology leaves visitors scratching their heads, they avoid the onerous tax burden foisted upon the rest of the province.

TURPIN, VILLAGE OF

Population: 812 (422 Foerdewaith, 196 Erskaelosi, 123 half-orc, 37 hill dwarf, 24 half-elf, 10 high elf)

Ruler: Count Jonas Ranquin
Government: overlord

This walled town inside the Unclaimed Lands lies on the banks of a small, navigable waterway named the Dwellerflow. The fortified keep inside these 20-foot-tall stone walls serves as the county seat for the self-styled "Count" Jonas Ranquin, a megalomaniac with delusions of grandeur. He makes his fortune masterminding and financing piracy on the Great Amrin River with his fleet of several small keelboats. The ships under his flag board any vessels they encounter on the bustling waterway, taking exactly half of their cargo and allowing their captain and crew to sail onward unharmed if the skipper immediately surrenders without a fight. Those who resist their peaceful overture forfeit their entire hold and face their full fury. The loot seized during their sea raids inevitably appears on the shelves in Turpin after the count takes his ample share of the booty. The authorities in Bard's Gate and Eastreach Province know Ranquin's name and his general whereabouts, but have been unable to pinpoint Turpin's exact location. So far, the count's naval forces have beaten back expeditions launched by the two states to eradicate the river pirates. For now, the count's operation qualifies as a nuisance rather than an immediate threat to either power's lucrative trading enterprises. Any escalation of his activities may warrant a more potent response from either or both of the aggrieved parties.

ZELKOR'S FERRY, SETTLEMENT OF

Population: 24 (Foerdewaith)
Ruler: Mayor Odo Bristleback
Government: autocracy

Adventurers heading to Rappan Athuk frequently stop over at this small fortified settlement surrounded by a stone wall and defended by two guard towers. The Bristleback family founded the settlement roughly 300 years ago, well before Bofeld and his companions discovered the mausoleum. The remote locate is a more popular destination for adventurers aspiring to test their mettle within the Dungeon of Graves because the nearby Mouth of Doom entrance is generally deemed to be less dangerous than the more harrowing opening Bofeld and his comrades found.

Zelkor's Ferry proper consists of an inn, a smithy, a ferry for crossing the adjacent river, and a trading post. Despite being so close to a place of unimaginable evil in the proverbial middle of nowhere, the settlement of Zelkor's Ferry offers safety and refuge to explorers endeavoring to find fame and riches inside the nearby dungeon. In addition to allowing adventurers to restock their supplies before heading across the Canyon River toward their destination, the settlement bristles with rumors about Rappan Athuk brought back by heroes who miraculously returned from their expedition to the deadly site. Ships venturing down the treacherous Canyon River periodically stop at Zelkor's Ferry to offload their cargo for transport down the nearby Coast Road. The captains of these vessels and caravan leaders also make a detour to the small town to hire seasoned mercenaries to safeguard themselves and their precious commodities. Naturally, these brave mariners and travelers also arrive at Zelkor's Ferry with tales of their own about the fabled dungeon and its inhospitable surroundings.

GAELON RIVER VALLEY

Capital: none (though Endhome exercises the greatest influence)
Notable Settlements: Beetlebridge, Deadfellows, Endhome, Gaelon River Bridge, Grimmsgate, Mirquinoc
Ruler: local village leaders and family heads (the Endhome senate holds great sway when it wishes to do so)
Government: varies
Population: 1,815,840 (1,265,000 Foerdewaith, 301,000 Gaeleen, 135,500 halfling, 61,000 wood elf, 28,800 hill dwarf, 21,660 high elf, 1,900 river giant, 980 Erskaelosi)

Monstrous: wolf, water moccasin, giant animals (beaver, otter, and snapping turtle), lizardfolk, giant water strider, ratfolk, gnoll, merrow, vulchling, lycanthrope, undead, rusalka, water orm (river valley); goblin, kobold, giant scorpion, orc, ogre, manticore, hippogriff, dragon (Duskmoon Hills); bugbear, tiger, flind, dire wolf, undead, ogre, troll, wyvern, cave giant, bulette (Cretian foothills)

Languages: Common, Gaeling, Halfling, Elvish, Giant, Dwarven, Erskin

Religion: Kamien, Telophus, Tykee, Pekko, Darach-Albith, Solanus, Vergrimm Earthsblood, Mick O'Delving, Jamboor, Narrah, The Horned God, Neriad

Resources: trade hub, fishing, foodstuffs, grain, pottery, timber, sugar, furs, dyes, gems, gold

Technology Level: High Middle Ages (major population centers), Dark Age (rural areas), Bronze Age (river giant settlements)

The Gaelon River Valley is a large area including the river's tributaries as well as the valley of the main river. It is a free land unclaimed by foreigners, with no central government. Many of the river valleys are inhabited, but the area also contains a considerable quantity of completely untamed wilderness. The great trading city of Endhome sits at the river mouth where it empties into the Sinnar Ocean.

The river and overland trade between the city of Endhome and the balance of the Gaelon River Valley defines this region. The coastal settlement's economic influence reaches deep into the entire area, though its potency wanes in proportion to the settlement's distance from the river or another well-traveled overland route. Travelers generally refer to these remote locales as the hinterlands. Regardless of location, the neutral commercial powerhouse keeps its nose out of local politics and allows these communities to govern themselves without interference from Endhome. Although the large metropolis garners much of the attention in the region, adventurers who travel here often focus their interest on the Duskmoon Hills, the alleged site of a lost city.

The many streams and tributaries branching off from the Gaelon River carve a circuitous path through the rolling grassy hills and wide valleys between the uplifted land masses. The elevation along the Gaelon River steadily decreases from the waterway's origins in the western mountains until the end of its journey in Endhome. The river valley's main geographic feature is the Duskmoon Hills.

BEETLEBRIDGE, VILLAGE OF

Population: 422 (human)
Government: council of elders

This small town near a bridge crossing the river Windyforth, a tributary of the Gaelon River, would be unremarkable if not for its unusual livestock. Outside the town's gates, its residents raise and breed massive giant beetles that they train to work as draft animals. In a clever twist, the townsfolk use trained dire badgers to root up and gather the beetles' eggs before they hatch. They train these vermin, which are larger than a horse, and then sell them to small villages in the countryside to perform the tasks normally assigned to traditional beasts of burden. The creature's carapace functions as crude armor, giving it natural protection against attacks and injuries sustained in the field. The beetles can certainly hold their own in a fight, yet the council of elders seems edgy. They recently learned a plot is currently afoot to steal the unhatched eggs from the breeding ground next season. They only know scant details about the plan and nothing about the conspirators, prompting some in their ranks to actively recruit investigators to unravel the mystery.

DEADFELLOWS, TOWN OF

Population: 1,240 (862 human, 316 hill dwarf, 62 halfling)
Government: anarchy

Anarchy reigns in the frontier settlement of Deadfellows, the highest upriver community on the Gaelon River. West of the town, the waterway transforms into rapids and shallows only navigable by small, highly mobile craft piloted by an experienced sailor. Like the turbulent waters outside its wooden stockade, the people who live and work here can be highly unpredictable and dangerous, as is evident from the three heads impaled on pikes outside the town's main gate. Rugged outdoorsmen rub elbows with an assortment of shady characters in Deadfellows' disreputable and lawless saloons. Sawdust spread across the floor in these establishments soaks up the blood, bodily fluids, and drinks spilt onto the wooden surface during the frequent barroom brawls. The most trivial incident or clumsy phrase can trigger a free-for-all, which almost always spills out into the alleys and streets where more of the participants' friends and enemies join the melee. With no one legally empowered to stop the carnage or punish the offenders, the donnybrook usually ends when one or more of the combatants lies dead in a pool of their own blood. Samuel Wesley Miller, a psychopath and professional assassin who carries himself as a gentleman and devout worshipper of Bowbe, is the most feared person in Deadfellows. Father Headbreaker, the resident cleric of Bowbe, has futilely tried to rein in the vicious man's murderous inclinations, but to no avail. Anyone who runs afoul of this calculating killer always winds up in a coffin much sooner than they intended.

ENDHOME, CITY OF

Ruler: Governor Ranlan Poole and 50-member senate
Government: autocracy
Population: 34,950 (22,000 Foerdewaith, 6,000 Oceander, 1,750 halfling, 1,750 half-elf, 1,750 hill dwarf, 1,000 wood elf, 700 other)
Monstrous: carrion crawlers, gargoyles, ghosts, ghasts, ghouls, goblins, golems, mummies, otyughs, shriekers, skeletons, vampires, violet fungi, wererats, zombies
Languages: Common
Religion: Jamboor, Da-Jin, Solanus, Thyr, Muir
Resources: alchemical reagent, ironwork, linen, magical resources, manufactured goods, shipbuilding supplies
Currency: Endhome
Technology Level: Medieval

The port city of Endhome is surrounded by a 20-foot-high stone wall with parapets and towers that is split in two by the Gaelon River. Many sailing ships are docked here or moored in the river awaiting cargo.

Endhome does not engage in the sort of far-reaching political machinations that Bard's Gate does, and over time, it seems likely that Bard's Gate will eclipse Endhome for the role of the continent's trade capital. It is already possible, and even quite likely, that Bard's Gate's far-flung network of investments and businesses, seen as a whole, represents a larger role in commerce than Endhome's role as a center of trade.

This independent seaport conducts business with whomever it chooses regardless of their political leanings or affiliations. Its bustling docks and warehouses teem with all manner of goods ranging from foodstuffs and livestock imported from the surrounding countryside to exotic materials shipped or hauled to the seaport from distant lands. Endhome makes it fortune assessing a small tax on every product entering the city regardless of whether it arrived here in a merchant's purse, in a caravan wagon, or in the hold of a massive barge. Nothing hits the shelves until the city gets its fair share for providing a neutral forum for trade.

HISTORY AND PEOPLE

The city of Endhome was originally a small trading post on the eastern coast of Akados, founded by the Hyperboreans at the site of a native fishing village. A sleepy and relatively quiet place for much of the Hyperborean

Age, Endhome endured storms, pirates, and the occasional monster raid to grow into a significant port by the end of the long Pax Hyperborea. By this time, the city had gained the (possibly self-applied) moniker of the "Trading Capital of the Continent," and ships from a dozen realms made landfall here to load and offload their cargos.

Endhome experienced a streak of uncommon luck in the following years as it survived the disastrous pole shift, the destruction of the Tower of Oerson, and the massive fires that followed.

The departure of the Imperial Court in 2499 I.R. left Endhome without any superior authority, and the nobles who were left behind agreed to form a 50-member senate to govern until the Hyperboreans' expected return.

Of course, the Hyperboreans did not return, and the senate became a permanent fixture, electing a governor every six years and managing a still-successful and prosperous port city. Endhome's importance to the sea trade helped keep it independent as King Macobert expanded the Kingdom of Foere into a continent-spanning empire, and played an important role as a transportation and supply hub from 2900 I.R. to 3100 I.R. as the Huun threat to Foere grew and the four great crusades were declared. The fourth and final crusade that succeeded in freeing the Sacred Table and Tircople in 3207 I.R. set sail from Endhome's harbor. Endhome's cooperation and friendship helped save Foere and cemented the city's independence. All the same, the city was not entirely free of Foerdewaith influence, for a garrison and fleet were permanently stationed there, ostensibly to protect the eastern coast from invasion and to keep the region's three vital roads — the Soldiers Road, the King's Road, and Trader's Way — free from banditry.

The situation did not trouble Endhome unduly for a decade or so, until the Foerdewaith Wars of Succession erupted. When the grand admiral of Pontus Tinigal rebelled against Foere and founded the Kingdom of Oceanus with him at its head as "Emperor of the Oceans Blue," Endhome was caught between warring factions. The disastrous Battle of Kapichi Point made matters worse, increasing Oceanus' influence in the region. After long and bitter debate, the Endhome senate declared its neutrality in 3217 I.R. and expelled the Foerdewaith garrison.

It was a slight that the overking could not ignore, and the following year Foere marched on Endhome, intending to besiege and conquer the city. Faced with destruction, Endhome entered into desperate negotiations with the Kingdom of Burgundia. As the Foerdewaith army drew near Endhome, a massive Burgundian force appeared on its flank and forced its withdrawal. The "siege" of Endhome was over before it began, and without bloodshed.

Unfortunately, the respite proved brief, and the Oceanders exploited the chaos, occupying Endhome and declaring it subject to the emperor's law. Fortunately, the Oceanders' occupation proved brief, and an uprising in 3221 I.R. forced the withdrawal of Oceanus' garrison. Occupied by the Burgundian revolution, the overking of Foere had no stomach for a two-front war and agreed to allow Endhome its continued independence.

Endhome has remained in its role as a trading hub ever since, joining with Sunderland, Suilley, and the Duchy of the Rampart to establish the trading post of Grollek's Grove in 3423 I.R.

One of the city's most famous institutions — the Endhome Academy of Wizardry, Alchemy and Arcane Knowledge — is almost as old as the city itself and has grown along with Endhome. Founded in the earliest days of the Hyperborean Age by the wizard Basil Strom, the academy's influence has much to do with the city's continued neutrality, for its doors are open to all who wish to learn the ways of arcane magic, and many arcane practitioners make the equivalent of a religious pilgrimage to acquire mystical knowledge and peruse its collection of tomes and rare writings. Many consider the renowned magical institute to be the finest training program for wizards on the continent, though its vaunted library rarely lives up to the hyperbole surrounding it.

Outside the academy, Endhome remains a wealthy and influential city, though some fear that the governor and the system that keeps him in place may be evolving into an effective oligarchy. Several influential families, including the Quinchinos, the Gaspars, and the Pulantis, have kept Governor Ranlan Pool in office for many years, though many rumors circulating about these families accuse them of everything from banditry to demon worship and everything in between. Much of Endhome is indeed corrupt and decadent, but this corruption has yet to significantly impair the city.

RELIGION

Endhome's religion is complex, with some following the teachings of the Foerdewaith deities Thyr and Muir, whose priests maintain small temples. Many Endhomers devote themselves to the neutral Jamboor, God of Death, Knowledge and Magic. Jamboor's is not an especially morbid faith despite its god's domains, for most adherents see death as a part of the normal cycle of life. Spellcasters and scholars are especially devoted to Jamboor's worship. Solanus, the Gentle Goddess of the Sun and Healing, is also venerated in the city, and her clerics are in many of the communities surrounding Endhome. Solanus' clerics are often found as adventurers or accompanying the army into battle. Last of Endhome's deities is the fearsome Da-Jin, God of Death — though of neutral alignment, this god has many evil worshippers, including necromancers and assassins. Da-Jin has his good and neutral followers as well, especially among morticians and even some doctors.

TRADE AND COMMERCE

The city of Endhome proclaims itself "Trade Capital of the Continent." Even though Bard's Gate is obviously a contender for the same claim, the fact of the matter is that Endhome, as a seaport, moves more trade through its docks on a daily basis than Bard's Gate. Endhome merchants scour the world for bargains, make long-term contracts, and jostle with the sharpest traders in the Lost Lands, and by doing so they still manage to remain ahead of Bard's Gate as a trading hub.

LOYALTIES AND DIPLOMACY

Endhome maintains its historic neutrality, refusing to ally or officially endorse any other kingdom. The closest it comes to this is in the establishment of Grollek's Grove along with Rampart, Sunderland, and Suilley, a trading city that is maintained jointly by the three kingdoms. Otherwise, Endhome remembers the consequences when it grew too close to Foere and Oceanus, and today maintains distant, if relatively friendly, relations with both kingdoms. Endhome's military is small but professional and strong enough to make any potential enemy think twice before attacking.

Diplomatically, Endhome tries to preserve good relations with every other nation, keeping the peace through a network of beneficial trade agreements. Endhome diplomats are present in Foere, Oceanus, Suilley, Sunderland, Rampart, and Castorhage, and have actually begun to make inroads even farther west, launching trade missions to the far lands of Xha'en.

GOVERNMENT

Endhome is best described as an autocratic republic, with a 50-person senate selecting governors from among their own numbers, and deciding every six years whether the governor should continue in office or be replaced. Replacement rarely occurs, however, for the senators, who almost exclusively hail from the merchant class, are not chosen democratically — rather they are appointed by the governor, who invariably selects political allies and toadies to fill vacancies. From time to time, even this self-perpetuating system fails and the senate removes a governor in what is commonly called a "coup." Nonetheless, the citizens seem satisfied with their civic officials' performance, which causes most people to overlook these warts and contently move on with their daily lives.

For the most part, however, the senate and governor function relatively well, overseeing Endhome's internal affairs and managing its diplomatic and trade relationships with other nations. Endhome's government invests heavily in its infrastructure to maintain its popularity. Clean-running water, a luxury in most communities, flows freely through the city, while its state-of-the-art sewers safely discharge waste from the elaborate water distribution system. Although the city routinely maintains the tunnels and pipes, animals and creatures drawn to refuse populate the subterranean passages and chambers. Rats, wererats, and other scavengers infest portions of the sewers, forcing the city's leadership to address these menaces. Aboveground, the city encourages private investment to cater to its affluent visitors and residents. Taverns, inns, and a host of other establishments service the needs of their clientele, while buyers and sellers alike flock to its fabled open-air bazaar, where an astute customer can buy practically anything if the individual knows where to look.

MILITARY

As an independent republic, Endhome must see to its own defense, and the city's wealth makes it a ripe target for foreign invasion and criminal activity. It maintains a 3,500-strong professional army of mostly infantry and archers, with a small but elite core of cavalry. These soldiers occupy posts atop the port's 20-foot-high stone walls, man its artillery pieces, patrol its streets, alleys, and roads, and keep the peace within Endhome. Conscription can swell the regular army by more than 6,000, and the addition of the spellcasters from the Wizard's Academy makes Endhome's military a significant threat. Endhome's navy is similarly small but professional, and can be supplemented with corsairs, armed merchant vessels, and mercenaries all paid for from Endhome's wealthy coffers.

Despite the city watch's diligent efforts, violent gangs still extort and abuse its poorest citizens, while rumors of nefarious deeds committed by the rich and famous circulate throughout the taverns and inns scattered around Endhome.

MAJOR THREATS

Endhome has in the past run afoul of Foere and Oceanus, and maintains a delicate relationship with both kingdoms, sometimes even managing to play them off against each other to maintain the city's neutrality and independence. In the rest of the world, Endhome plays it equally safe and does its best not to make enemies while keeping a neutral stance. Its friendly relations with Rampart, Suilley, and Sunderland also help keep the Foerdewaith at bay.

Beyond these rival kingdoms, Endhome faces no major threats, though banditry and monster raids in the surrounding countryside — particularly those centered on the ancient lost city of Barakus — continue to plague the city and its military.

WILDERNESS AND ADVENTURES

Endhome is a place of intrigue and double-dealing, as trade houses seek to outdo each other and steal each other's secrets, while the Wizard's Academy provides facilities and learning to arcanists from across the continent and beyond. The sewers beneath the city are a marvel of advanced design but sections are also ancient and labyrinthine, rumored to harbor hordes of ferocious rodents, wererats, slimes, and other fearsome creatures. Work patrolling the sewers is among the most onerous in the city.

The lands beyond the city walls are hazardous and frequently plagued by bandits and raiding monsters, but the most notable aspect of Endhome's environs is the ancient Lost City of Barakus. Built 12,000 years ago by the ancient Phoromyceaen civilization, the city's remains lie beneath the Duskmoon Hills. Most of the city's depths remain unexplored, but the Old Tusk orcs, followers of Orcus, were driven out of the place 20 years ago. Terrible rumors surround Barakus, including tales of demons, powerful undead, and powerful magical artifacts — more than enough to draw adventurers from far and wide, though so far it has swallowed up those who hope to plumb its secrets.

GAELON RIVER BRIDGE

Population: 3,251 (3,110 human, 68 half-elf, 48 hill dwarf, 25 halfling)
Ruler: Mayor Darius Bittersby
Government: autocracy (elected mayor)

Ancient dwarven engineers constructed the massive stone bridge that fords the width of the Gaelon River at the Trader's Way crossing and bisects the town bearing the same name. The dwarves who built the span left the area long ago only to be replaced by humans with a smattering of half-elves, halflings, and a few dozen hill dwarves. These people reside in an unwalled settlement of timber homes, stone warehouses, inns, and tanneries centered around an impressive wharf of wooden docks along both riverbanks. The town's tanneries enjoy a stellar reputation for producing exquisite leather and vellum products, which are sold in Endhome. The city's bookbinders and scribes in the Wizard's Academy covet these materials for their texture and durability.

The bridge's location on a major shipping intersection for river barges and overland caravans brings a steady stream of merchants and traders into the bustling community. For the most part, the docks of "Riverbridge," as it is locally called, run barges and keelboats up and downstream, including some of the nearby tributaries, to collect grain from the many granges lining the riverbanks and deliver it to Endhome for sale abroad. The waterborne traffic predominately ships grain from the local granges lining the river to Endhome for sale abroad. The captains and owners of the vessels engaged in this enterprise joined forces to create the "Keelcaptains' Guild," an organization that maintains warehouses and flophouses for their ships' cargo and crew. When a competing entity from Endhome attempted to establish a rival guild, the buildings owned and operated by the Endhome outfit burnt to the ground on three separate occasions under inexplicable circumstances. The newcomers apparently got the message, and they wisely abandoned the endeavor.

Nonetheless, Endhome officially maintains a military and economic presence in Gaelon River Bridge, even though the town elects its own mayor to manage local matters. The current incumbent, Mayor Darius Bittersby, settles minor disputes among the residents and handles small administrative matters, but Pivion Partridge, the emissary of Endhome stationed within the town, makes all major decisions. He and three of his subordinates regulate the market to prevent price gouging and other scams from disrupting commerce. Meanwhile, the 50 soldiers and several engineers under his command maintain and protect the bridge, the riverbanks, and the Trader's Way to ensure the free flow of trade through the area. When his troops cannot disprove rumors circulating through town, Pivion sometimes turns to adventurers for help, asking them to check out the latest story making the rounds in the community. Right now, Pivion seems concerned about a series of alleged vulchling attacks in the area.

GRIMMSGATE, VILLAGE OF

Population: 46 (human)
Ruler: none
Government: none

Grimmsgate is an isolated settlement on the now-unused trail that ran between the Free City of Mirquinoc and the Town of Keot, before Keot was destroyed in an earthquake. Now there is no more trade to sustain Grimmsgate: What was once a village has shrunken to a mere thorp of deteriorating buildings and dispirited inhabitants. According to rumor, an old, abandoned temple is located somewhere near the settlement.

REFERENCE SOURCE: GRIMMSGATE FROM QUESTS OF DOOM 2

MIRQUINOC, FREE CITY OF

(MER-qwin-ock)
Population: 7,647 (6231 human, 853 high elf, 233 half-elf, 187 gnome, 104 halfling, 39 hill dwarf, unknown number of fey)
Ruler: Mayor Gandar Golson
Government: autocracy (elected mayor)

The Free City of Mirquinoc stands just beyond the borders of Suilley, roughly a mile north of the King's Road. A walled city, Mirquinoc has been conquered several times in the wars that have swept through the area, but no one has held it for more than a day or two without retreating in disarray. Mirquinoc is located at an ancient, pre-Hyperborean crossroad, so old that neither of the original roads can be seen. However, the conjunction of these roads fixed the city of Mirquinoc squarely into a shifting co-existence with the realm of a faerie queen and her fey court. Throughout the city, the fey are often visible for a few moments out of the corner of the eye, but seem to disappear when looked at directly. Humans cannot cross the boundaries into the fey realm for the most part, although it can happen by accident if a person trips off some fey spell, or happens to walk into just the right place at just the right moment. Many of the fey, on the other hand, are able to step through the barrier into the human world of the city. For the most part, only the sprites of Mirquin Shee actually come through the border, although on occasion a korred appears in town to purchase or sell things.

The sprites of Mirquin Shee are unpredictable and capricious, considering themselves as the protectors of the city. Unfortunately, their view of what constitutes protection is frequently not the same as that of the city's ordinary residents. The sprites are haughty and proud, and on occasion they react badly to what they perceive as rude behavior to themselves. The city tries to minimize these misunderstandings by requesting that visitors completely ignore the sprites when encountering them.

Mirquin Shee is ruled by the faerie queen Twylinvere, a tall, slender figure with dragonfly wings who can occasionally be seen as a colorful but ghostly figure moving around in the city. She occasionally enters the human world to make agreements with the mayor or complain about certain humans that are behaving improperly.

Kingdom of Oceanus (Pontos Island)

Capital: Pontus Tinigal
Notable Settlements: Tros Zoas
Ruler: Roderigo d'Velas, Emperor of the Oceans Blue
Government: monarchy
Population: 458,160 (Pontos Island) (388,200 Oceander, 41,100 Foerdewaith, 18,800 halfling, 6,200 half-elf, 2,150 high elf, 1,010 hill dwarf, 700 other)
Monstrous: wolf, water moccasin, giant frog, rusalka, manticore, hippogriff, dire wolf, undead (inland); crab swarms, bunyips, giant crabs, sahuagin, sea hags (coastline)
Languages: Common
Religion: Quell, Solanus, Jamboor; Dagon (in secret)
Resources: trade, fishing, manufactured goods, foodstuffs, grain, pottery, dyes, gems, gold
Technology Level: Renaissance (Pontus Tinigal, Tros Zoas), Medieval (elsewhere)

The Kingdom of Oceanus practically sprang into existence overnight when the grand admiral of Pontus Tinigal thumbed his nose at his former king in far-off Courghais and absconded with his fleet in the process. Despite the overking's efforts to reclaim Pontos Island from his upstart rival, the wily naval commander soundly defeated the Kingdom of Foere's fleet on the open seas. With its victory, Oceanus catapulted to the status of naval superpower rivaled only by Bard's Gate and Endhome.

Using diplomatic and military maneuvers, the Kingdom of Oceanus expanded its foothold in Akados and now controls the Matagost Peninsula, Southvale, much of Sunderland, and the lowlands of Ramthion Island. In addition to its formidable fleet, it maintains the peace through non-aggression treaties with its enemies and friends alike.

Pontus Tinigal, City of (Capital)

Population: 26,023 (23,133 Oceander, 1,250 Foerdewaith, 825 halfling, 450 half-elf, 230 high elf, 100 hill dwarf, 35 other)
Ruler: Emperor Roderigo d'Velas
Government: autocracy

Located at the northern tip of Pontos Island, the city of Pontus Tinigal serves as the political capital of the Kingdom of Oceanus. It began its ascendency to prominence in 2765 I.R. when the ruling Kingdom of Foere established the province of Pontus Tinigal on the island, declaring the city bearing the same name as its provincial capital. Shortly after issuing the declaration, resources poured into the previously underdeveloped settlement. Teams of architects and artisans constructed public works, tenements, temples, and a host of other structures to reflect its lofty status as a representative of the kingdom. Endeavoring to use Pontos Island as a crucial port for its oceanic naval ambitions, the Foerdewaith Navy expanded its shipyards and harbor to accommodate an immense fleet within the safety of an inlet. The port's increased capacity was put to the test in 2970 I.R. when the crusader fleet and army gathered at

Pontus Tinigal and Tros Zoas before setting sail for Khemit. Because of the great distance between Pontus Tinigal and Courghais, the overking granted the grand admiral of Pontus Tinigal tremendous autonomy to act independently of the Foerdewaith monarchy. This lapse in judgment would come back to haunt the overking in 3215 I.R. when Maximilian d'Varago Pontos, the grand admiral of Pontus Tinigal, withdrew from Foere and declared himself Emperor of the Oceans Blue. He retained his seat of power in the former provincial capital, and after a series of naval engagements against his former Foerdewaith overlords, the newly proclaimed ruler of the Kingdom of Oceanus crushed his adversary at the pivotal Battle of Kapichi Point, ensuring his kingdom's survival for at least the foreseeable future.

Despite his resounding victory, the newly crowned emperor refused to sit still and bask in the glory. Virtually overnight, he increased Pontus Tinigal's shipbuilding capacity threefold, reinforced its already formidable 20-foot-high walls and solid iron gates, laid down concealed obstacles in the waters around the port to impede or puncture enemy vessels attempting to navigate into the harbor, and conscripted thousands of able-bodied men and women into its vaunted marine corps. Three hundred years later, almost 10,000 marines and sailors inhabit the city, though a spate of non-aggression treaties and unofficial truces have eased tensions among the rival naval powers allowing the city to no longer remain on a constant wartime footing. Nonetheless, its shipyards operate around the clock to build galleons, galleys, frigates, and other seafaring vessels for military and merchant fleets alike throughout Akados and far-off Libynos. The empire forbids guilds, yet the skilled craftsmen and laborers who toil on the docks function as an unofficial labor organization policing their own ranks and periodically demanding better pay and working conditions from their disinterested emperor who detests the entity's existence.

Emperor Roderigo d'Velas oversees his dominion from atop the Helmsman's Throne within the heavily fortified Almanza Citadel in the city's central quarter adjacent to the outwardly influential Temple of Quell. Oceanus' middle-aged emperor of 14 years seeks to maintain the status quo for the time being on the international front, though he has rolled out aggressive domestic reform policies during his tenure. The city has made numerous long overdue infrastructure upgrades and improvements over the last several years in a deliberate effort to distract the common people from noticing the emperor's harsh crackdown on personal liberties within Pontus Tinigal and his increasing efforts to confiscate private property for real and fictional crimes to finance his lavish expenditures and lifestyle. In addition to pleasing the expensive tastes of Empress Luna Coralona, the philandering husband supports 13 mistresses in Pontus Tinigal alone. The shrewd Luna, the daughter of a Southvale noble, leverages Roderigo's affairs to her advantage by feigning her love for the hopeless romantic while secretly detesting him.

To a casual observer who looks past the bustling docks and seedy wharfs, Pontus Tinigal more closely resembles a tropical resort city than a military compound. As part of his beautification efforts, palm trees fill many courtyards and streets, while decorative wrought-iron tresses and gates adorn most homes, windows, and outer walls. Yet behind the attractive façade lies an ugly secret. Dagon, the demon prince of the sea, works behind the scenes in Pontus Tinigal to further advance his alien causes. His worshippers often abduct strangers from the city's streets and sacrifice them to their diabolic lord in bloody rituals carried out in the sewers or an isolated stretch of beach. Some stories even claim the sahuagin join in with them to consume the victim's warm flesh. While Roderigo and his court publicly profess their faith in Quell, they secretly pay homage to the foul being who allegedly aided Oceanus in its hour of greatest need.

Tros Zoas, City of

Population: 16,562 (16,247 Oceander, 220 Foerdewaith, 40 halfling, 25 half-elf, 15 high elf, 10 hill dwarf, 5 other)
Ruler: Grand Admiral Lucrecia Lacibeles
Government: autocracy

This fortified seaport holds the distinction of being built on the foundation of the oldest known city-state in Akadonian history —

Xantallan. The famed explorer and military conqueror Koshag of Ur came to this island roughly 18,000 years ago aboard his flagship and founded his capital on what would later be known as Pontos Island at the site where he and the 1,200 soldiers who accompanied him aboard 18 warships first landed. From this launching point, the merciless warlord and his troops routed and enslaved the island's small population of indigenous humanoids. Koshag reigned over his new kingdom for 19 tumultuous years. After his death and interment on the mainland of Akados, the stronghold Koshag founded descended into chaos and disrepair. A series of powerful storms leveled most of its stone fortifications and flooded portions of the surviving buildings beneath seawater. Less than a century after its creation, the citadel, whose original name has been lost to the annals of history, was virtually uninhabited save for a handful of stragglers occupying pockets of the ruined fortress.

When the Hyperborean fleet set sail across the Pontine Straits to bring Pontos Island under its heel, it encountered sporadic, disorganized resistance. The remnants of Tros Zoas almost immediately succumbed to their new conquerors who appreciated the value of a fortified seaport on the island's southern coast. They rebuilt the crumbling coastal fortress in short order, bolstering its defenses and harbor in the process. After the Hyperboreans left Akados, the Kingdoms of Foere stepped into the breach and gained control of the citadel in what felt like a seamless transition of power from a political and cultural standpoint. Tros Zoas stamped its place in history when Overking Yurid gathered his crusader fleet in the port in 2970 I.R. to set sail for Khemit. After Maximilian d'Varago Pontos took command of a large portion of the Foerdewaith fleet in 3215 I.R., and declared himself Emperor of the Oceans Blue, Tros Zoas took a prominent role in the Kingdom of Oceanus' future ambitions.

The seaport's location on the southeastern coast of Pontos Island granted the emperor's newfound state easy access to the Sinnar Ocean near the Matagost Peninsula. Tros Zoas rapidly expanded from a fortress of a few thousand to a heavily fortified naval installation boasting more than 16,000 permanent residents, half of whom are sailors and marines in the Oceanic navy. In addition to housing its naval forces, a garrison of 1,000 infantryman, archers, and cavalry rigidly maintains order within Tros Zoas' imposing walls and in the largely untamed wilderness outside its 30-foot-high walls and outer moat. In keeping with the kingdom's maritime roots and traditions, the laws of the high seas also prevail on land, especially in its most populous seaport. The captain of any ship in the Oceanic navy has the legal authority to mete out justice regardless of where the perpetrator committed the punishable offense, even if the individual is outside the captain's chain of command. However, in a strange twist, Tros Zoas grants safe harbor to a handful of pirates the Kingdom of Oceanus clandestinely finances for a share of their ill-gotten booty. These discreet and savvy privateers predominately operate in the Pontine Straits or on the open seas far from Oceanus. To ensure their silence and loyalty, the kingdom requires their families to reside within Tros Zoas under the veiled threat that some harm would come to their loved ones if they betray their ties to the kingdom.

Grand Admiral Lucrecia Lacibeles administers the fortress's civic and judicial branches as well as nominally commanding the portion of the Oceanic fleet stationed here. She also occupies a religious position as the Divine Mistress of the Seas. In this capacity, she serves as the titular leader of the Church of Quell, Tros Zoas' patron deity, whose temple serves a dual role as a shrine dedicated to the sea god and a fully functional lighthouse at the edge of the harbor. While Lacibeles openly worships Quell, she secretly venerates Dagon in a small shrine tucked away in a dark corner of her secure keep built above the city's infamous dungeons where prisoners languish and suffer under some of the most unspeakable conditions in Akados. Despite the settlement's emphasis on crime and punishment, smugglers seeking to export Oceanus' high-tech equipment to foreign states frequently ply their trade on the docks and wharfs alongside Tros Zoas' longshoremen and shipwrights.

Geographic Features and Points of Interest in the Central Sinnar Coast of Eastern Akados

Amrin Estuary

The freshwaters of the Great Amrin River combine with the saline waters of the Sinnar Ocean to form a churning pool of brackish water within this long, narrow inlet on the southern coast of Eastreach Province. While the waves constantly pound the beaches facing the Sinnar Ocean, the estuary's geography lessens the tidal impact on its shorelines. However, the same circumstances protecting it from the angry crests also intensify the impacts of storm surge pouring into the estuary from high winds and major weather events. Fortunately, the Half-Pickle Marsh on the north shore absorbs much of the excess water spilling into the sheltered inlet diminishing the threat of flooding but not the dangerous rip currents swirling beneath the surface. The seemingly calm waters can easily lull inexperienced sea captains into a false sense of security, causing them to capsize or run aground in the shallow estuary.

Bard's Gate under the auspices of Eastgate and its naval installation at Telar Brindel dominates this body of water, though its ships allow those of rival nations to freely pass into the neighboring ocean or upriver on the Great Amrin. Although no longer as unruly as it was in the past, some privateers still ply their nefarious trade on the open waters preying on slow-moving barges and small vessels they easily outgun. Sea hags also plague the Amrin Estuary, with most residing close to the coasts to hunt fishermen on land and sea.

Barakus

Long before the Hyperboreans swept across Akados, a prehistoric people known as the Phoromyceaens dominated portions of the continent during the Age of Kings. While primitive by today's standards, the Phoromyceaens were remarkably advanced for their time. Although many of their people still farmed and hunted on the land above the surface, they were renowned for building sprawling subterranean cities ruled by potent sorcerer-kings and occasionally priest-kings, many of whom refused to accept death as a predetermined outcome. To defy the constraints of mortality, these power-mad rulers became liches or another form of sentient undead. Despite their efforts to live forever, the Phoromyceaens disappeared from Akados at the dawn of the Age of Silence. One of their great abandoned cities, Barakus, lies beneath a network of caves in the Duskmoon Hills outside of Endhome.

Prior to 20 years ago, the Old Tusk orc tribe infested these caverns until Endhome's military forcibly expelled the evil humanoids who worshipped the Demon Prince Orcus. After their removal, other monstrous denizens moved in to inhabit the cave system's upper levels, though the "Lost City of Barakus" beneath the caverns remains largely unexplored and undisturbed. Ancient legends predating recorded history suggest great mysteries and treasures lie in the presumably abandoned ruins deep beneath the caves. Tales spread among Endhome's academicians claim that a legendary magical blade still resides within its unhallowed halls, while logic would suggest its undead rulers may linger on in Barakus' forsaken depths.

Canyon River

Water runoff from sources in a highland range of scattered hills gathers steam as its flows through several shallow canyons before beginning its trek through the Forest of Hope and ultimately ending its journey as it empties into the Sinnar Ocean. Although several small villages and hamlets are in the surrounding area, only two settlements of note lie on the banks of this scarcely traveled river — the village of Zelkor's Ferry within the Forest of Hope and the town of Renderby in the highlands. The latter produces a sufficient quantity of gems and furs to warrant some merchants risking the dangerous downriver journey through the unruly Forest of Hope to transport these commodities for offloading on the docks at Zelkor's Ferry or a longer sea voyage to ports on the Sinnar Ocean. Teamsters who make this choice must decide whether the added danger of the sea route compensates for avoiding the extra financial cost of paying numerous taxes to a patchwork of baronies and governors while traveling on the overland route. Those who opt for undertaking this harrowing trek down the Canyon River speak of many hazards along the way, especially a great troll mound near a gorge deep within the Forest of Hope.

COAST ROAD

As the name suggests, this highway hugs the coastline from the town of Darnagal through Freegate and Eastwych into the Forest of Hope past the fabled dungeon of Rappan Athuk before merging into the Lowwater Road culminating at Amrin Ferry. It is the primary overland trade route linking the preceding settlements together, and it surprisingly offers a safer alternative than sailing across the stormy seas and the pirate-infested waters of the Pontine Straits. Nonetheless, merchants and travelers trekking over the Coast Road always stick to the well-worn thoroughfare rather than stray into the surrounding wilderness. Small villages and inns line the sides of the road at regular intervals, offering shelter, security, and a warm meal to anyone willing to pay a handsome price for these valuable amenities. Seasoned explorers make haste while the sun shines and wisely hunker down when night falls. Only Eastwych and Amrin Ferry routinely patrol the stretches of road under their jurisdictions; otherwise anyone walking along the Coast Road must go it alone. For this reason, caravan leaders typically hire experienced adventurers to accompany them on the long slog down the Akadonian shoreline.

Brigands are a recurring nuisance on the Coast Road. Concerted efforts to permanently eradicate the threat proves useless, as two ruffians spring up to take their deceased or captured predecessor's place. Worgs and ordinary wolves plague the route as well, especially when darkness falls across the land within the confines of the Forest of Hope. Meanwhile, ogres and their bugbear minions pay little attention to when and where they attack creatures moving across the Coast Road. Various bog dwellers stalk sections of the highway close to the Great Salt Marsh, while rumors about a vampire haunting the stretch of road through the forest circulate through every inn and tavern along the way.

CURGANT (RUINS)

The ruins of the city of Curgantium, once the magnificent capital of the Hyperborean Empire, are found on the southern tip of the Mons Terminus, just southwest of Vermis. Now known as Curgant, the site is a vast desolation of broken stone, overgrown with strange flowers and long grasses. The history of the ruins dates back a thousand years to when the city was destroyed in the explosion of the Tower of Oerson, which housed the imperial throne. The inconceivable power of the blast and the subsequent conflagration utterly eradicated the city and gave rise to raging wildfires that devoured their way across the dry plains, killing countless more by flame and famine.

Curgant is well known as a cursed place, and all give the ruins a wide berth. Rivermen passing down the Great Amrin past the ancient stone wharves of the city spit and cross their fingers to ward off bad luck. Many swear that the river waters around Curgant sometimes run red as blood or as black as night. No boat docks there even in the most inclement weather.

It is unknown to the world at large that the sewers beneath Curgant are still intact and serve as the headquarters for the continent-spanning master thieves' guild of vampires known as the Underguild. Such matters are given more detail in the adventure *Sewers of the Underguild* in *Quests of Doom Volume 1*.

DEEP WAKE

Sir Eldrad Lassetter built this castle 240 years ago after retiring from Endhome's navy. When he died intestate six years after the castle's completion with no living spouse, parents, or children, his surviving aunts, uncles, and cousins squabbled over the castle's ownership. Nineteen years of vicious fighting finally settled the thorny legal issues surrounding the land's title. The damage had been done by then, however. Nearly 20 years of neglect and pillaging by roaming bands of evil humanoids left the property in shambles. Unwilling and unable to pay for the costly repairs, Eldrad's heir walked away from the castle emptyhanded, condemning it to its current state.

The castle's walls almost entirely lie in ruins with none measuring more than three feet in height. Only a single tower survived mostly intact, though portions of the crenellations from its flat roof now litter the area around the tower's base. However, the damaged structure remains stable and now serves as the lair of the self-styled "Carrion King," an intelligent vulchling who has forged an alliance with a manticore and a small band of gnolls. These monsters and the Carrion King's vulchling cohorts conduct coordinated attacks on rafts and fishing vessels sailing on the Gaelon River 10 miles from Deep Wake. The local authorities identified the vulchlings as the culprits, but their investigation has not revealed where the vulchlings are hiding. Worried officials now seek adventurers to locate the vulchlings' hideout and destroy them.

DRAGONSPIRE

The red dragon Bezzalt has lived in this conical-shaped hill within the Duskmoon Hills for centuries. Although he covets Endhome's riches, the shrewd monster fears the Wizard Academy's tremendous magical might. For this reason, he always heads north when he ventures out of his lair to hunt. On those rare occasions when he leaves his treasure behind, the massive beast leaves his home through a 30-foot-wide flue that extends from the top of his cave. A natural angled lid on top of the flue keeps water and snow from penetrating into his abode. Seventy-five years ago, a contingent of industrious dwarven miners and thieves attempted to circumvent the stronghold's lone access point by boring a tunnel into the hill's eastern face. However, the greedy burglars came to blows over how to divvy up Bezzalt's treasure hoard. The wild fight left several of them dead and forced the group to abandon the endeavor before they could complete the passage. No one has mounted a serious expedition to Dragonspire since the dwarves' aborted attempt. Adventurers contemplating a trek to the locale frequently hear rumors about the dragon's purported minions, which include a fire giant, an efreet, or an elemental being wreathed in flames.

DUSKMOON HILLS

Clusters of trees and shrubs cover the tracts of relatively flat ground in these high, jagged hills reined with small creeks due north of Endhome. A portion of the Trader's Way carves a path through this natural impediment. Patrols dispatched from the city of Endhome ensure the safety of merchants and caravans traveling along this thoroughfare. A narrow, seldom-used shortcut known as the Fool's Road carves a more direct route through the obstacle than the popular Trader's Way, yet as the name appropriately implies, expediency sometimes comes at a hefty price. The city's military units never set foot on the Fool's Road or anywhere else in the Duskmoon Hills other than the Trader's Way, leaving explorers to fend for themselves in a hostile environment bristling with savage orcs, hobgoblins, goblins, grimlocks, and other monstrosities. Many of the adventurers who trek to these hills search for a network of caves previously inhabited by a band of orcs whom the city forcibly removed 20 years earlier. Although new horrors moved into the vacated premises, rumors suggest greater treasures and foes lie somewhere beneath the complex. The infrequent discovery of ancient pottery, bronze weapons, and primitive jewelry from a bygone civilization lends some credence to this theory.

ESTUARY ROAD

This road, which intersects with the Wain Cut, Trader's Way, and the Cross Cut among others, denotes the southern boundary of Eastreach Province. While it may fall within the borders of Eastreach Province, the Waymark cavalry stationed out of Eastgate regularly patrols the moderately traveled thoroughfare. Because of their diligent efforts and the financial investments made by Bard's Gate, the sections of the road closest to Eastgate and the other settlements along the route are reliably safe and well-maintained. More isolated portions of the road far from civilization are most commonly subject to attacks from bandits, gnolls, or goblins. Local baronies may also set up toll collection centers in remote corners of the road, though their builders quickly disassemble these makeshift barriers when confronted by soldiers from any established city-state along the route. Inns, taverns, general stores, hamlets, and small villages appear at semi-regular intervals for the majority of the journey, especially near Eastgate. One such inn, The Leavened Baker, serves a delicious sourdough bread with a homemade cheese spread that makes it a popular stopover for traveling merchants, cavalry officers, and dignitaries.

FOREST OF HOPE

Few places bear a more inappropriate name than this insidious cluster of gnarled trees and overgrown shrubs. The forest earned its moniker not based upon its disposition, but rather in honor of a long-forgotten princess named Hope. Most believe its original name, the Forest of Horrors, feels infinitely better suited for this swath of hellish wilderness. "Flirting with Princess Hope," given her association with the forest, is a widely used expression used to indicate that a person is about to do something not only stupid but also highly dangerous. Since this is exactly the province of many adventurers, they may hear it quite a lot.

Three hundred years ago, the Army of Light pursued Orcus' demonic minions into this forest from which they never emerged. Despite the efforts of numerous adventurers and expedition parties, their ultimate fate remains a mystery to this very day. The handful of fortunate souls who return from such excursions occasionally retrieve rusty equipment, moldy leatherware, tarnished talismans, and other gear left behind by a human army and diabolical hordes, but they never come back with a viable explanation for their sudden disappearance.

In an event that seems inextricably linked to the Army of Light's presumed destruction, explorers searching the forest's eastern edge near the Coast Road stumbled upon Rappan Athuk, the dreaded Dungeon of Graves, in 3400 I.R. Since its discovery more than a century ago, many adventurers have ventured to the remote site to plunder its fabled riches and test their mettle in one of the deadliest locations in all of Akados. The forest's deserved reputation for mayhem fails to dissuade everyone from entering into its terrible, woody embrace. The depths of the forest are choked with dens of giant spiders and other deadly predators such as trolls, stirges, and worgs. Outlaw bands take refuge in the tree-shadowed reaches, and each year ushers in a new hatching of young green dragons to plague the scattered settlements of the forest's western verge. Dragon season along the forest edge is a common testing-ground for young knights of Eastreach hoping to prove themselves, offering up battles with very small dragons whose size will necessarily be exaggerated in later retellings of the heroic tale.

FOREST KINGDOMS (FOREST OF PARNA)

Centuries of human colonization and the great wildfires of 2496 I.R. were not enough to deforest this swath of the Great Akadonian Forest that once covered most of central and southern Akados. Now the Kingdom of Parnuble, high elves and wood elves still hold sway within these woods.

FORTUNATE TOWER

This ordinary tower stands atop a hill where nothing stood less than 50 years ago. Despite being made from earth and stone, no one in the surrounding villages can recall laboring on the project or even hearing anything about its clandestine construction. Indeed, the local residents know nothing about its alleged inhabitant other than the name Lord Tyberis. Unbeknownst to them, the purported nobleman is a rakshasa who traveled across the land robbing anyone who piqued his interest. Several decades of getting the lay of the land has now taught the avaricious creature that he can amass a greater fortune through landholding and peasant labor than simple larceny. To test this theory, the ambitious Lord

Tyberis has bewitched several knights in neighboring manor houses to determine whether his subjects and their minions can trace his treachery back to him. If the experimentation phase proves successful, he plans to roll out his ambitious pilot to controlling the minds of the local barons in addition to the minor nobility.

GAELON RIVER

Stretching from the Sinnar Ocean near the city of Endhome to the mountains far west of the city, the Gaelon River is a vital trade route between the sprawling metropolis at its mouth and the smaller settlements lining its banks. These farming communities along the water's edge trade their crops, livestock, and other locally produced goods for more exotic fare imported from distant Endhome. The slow-moving, wide river can easily accommodate keelboats and river barges until it reaches the town of Deadfellows west of Gaelon River Bridge. At this juncture, numerous cataracts and shallows cause watercraft larger than a rowboat to run aground or crash into the rocks protruding from the rapids. In addition to the river basin, numerous small tributaries and streams branch off from the main body of water, though these waterways are typically too shallow and narrow for vessels larger than a fishing boat to navigate. The well-stocked river supports a wide variety of marine animals such as pike, catfish, bass, and some crab species that are prized for their sweet, tasty meat. One local fish tale claims a prehistoric turtle as large as a typical residence dwells in the deepest part of the river. However, no one has reported seeing this oversized reptile for more than 50 years. Nonetheless, residents playfully refer to the mythical beast as the Great Shell.

GLIMMRILL RUN

This tributary of the Great Amrin River runs almost due south from the edge of the Forest Kingdoms, through the gorge beneath Derindin, before emptying into its larger counterpart on the western boundary of Eastreach Province. The Unclaimed Lands form much of its western bank south of the Tradeway, while minor baronies and fortified estates connected by a patchwork of neglected roads litter the eastern bank. Piracy plagues almost the entire length of the waterway south of Derindin. The buccaneers significantly curtail trade along the river as Eastreach Province is either unwilling or unable to dispatch vessels to patrol the river. A few towns along the banks take matters into their own hands and arm their ships with a small contingent of mercenaries. While these precautions safeguard their cargo and crew, no one has mounted an organized offensive against the brigands who receive safe harbor from petty landholders along the river's edge in exchange for a share of their ill-gotten loot.

GRAYWASH RIVER

Fed by the countless tributaries tumbling off the northern slope of Mons Terminus, this waterway winds a circuitous path from Lost Boy Mountain toward the Tradeway followed by a sharp turn southeast where it ultimately converges with the Stoneheart River. The river, which is forded only near the Tradeway and a few other isolated locations for a lack of demand, predominately serves as a political boundary separating Bard's Gate from the Duchy of Waymarch. Hill dwarves reside in the foothills overlooking the waterway; otherwise, large stretches of the Graywash are deserted or sparsely inhabited. The river derived its name from the high sediment content in the water undoubtedly accumulated during the opening foray of its mountainous journey. The mineral concentration keeps fish populations low and gives the water a foul taste that discourages humanoids from settling around its banks. Some prospectors pan for gold and other precious metals in the shallow waters near Lost Boy Mountain. The occasional discovery of a large nugget of gold or copper sparks moderate interest in the river, but the enthusiasm soon wanes when the lucky strike turns out to be an anomaly. Local legends claim a rare species of fish acclimated to the conditions in the Graywash River roots out and eats metal fragments found on the riverbed. Because the fish cannot digest the particles, the material accumulates in its digestive tract. To date, only two specimens of this unusual carp known as the shiny carp have ever been caught and examined. Each contained several ounces of gold and copper in its distended belly.

GREAT AMRIN RIVER

Beginning in the Star Sea, the Great Amrin River winds a course through the Kingdoms of Foere's heartlands, where it eventually joins forces with the Stoneheart River for its final march to the Sinnar Ocean. Although it falls under the overking's territorial jurisdiction, treaties forged with representatives of Bard's Gate give that metropolis' ships unfettered access to the waterway from its confluence with the Stoneheart River to Eastgate and the Amrin Estuary. The wide, slow-moving river is naturally conducive to river traffic, though the seemingly placid nautical route deftly conceals several sections of rapids and undertows that have wrecked the vessels of many novice river captains.

Numerous small fishing hamlets and villages along the water's edge haul in sizable catches of pike, bass, and other freshwater fish they cook to feed their families or sell to wholesalers who frequent their docks and piers. These settlements also cater to the needs of the crewmembers and passengers of the ships sailing on these waters. They offer provisions, accommodations, entertainment, and many other services typically found in a maritime community to these transient visitors. The village of Pluffton on the southern bank north of Carterscroft is a popular stopover for river barge traffic as it offers one of the fanciest inns, The Ravenous Mariner, and the services of Madame Jocelyn Prudeau, a gorgeous fortune-teller renowned for her accurate readings and matchmaking success. Many lonely sailors beseech their skippers to make a brief detour to her establishment.

While most of these dockside enclaves operate legitimate enterprises, some petty fiefdoms and baronies on the Great Amrin's northern banks engage in river piracy to fatten their coffers. These brigands use their sleeker and faster keelboats to pursue and commandeer the slower unarmed merchant barges. If they succeed in this endeavor, they share the loot with the nobleman who harbored them before moving upriver or downriver to enter into a similar arrangement with another lord or lady in the area. Bard's Gate occasionally deploys troops to burn down the manor homes and crops of aristocrats sponsoring these activities, but their token efforts only make a small dent in the problem. Likewise, adventurers hired to root out the pirates merely displace them for a short time rather than eradicate them.

THE GREAT BRIDGE

An early Hyperborean imperator built the massive construction known as the Great Bridge to accommodate the movement of the legions northward.

Since the rise of the city, Bard's Gate has maintained the Great Bridge, which remains in excellent repair.

Two fortresses stand on the north and south banks of the bridge. To the north is Amrinbridge Fortress, an outpost of Bard's Gate. On the southern bank stands the Gretspaan Citadel, Foere's most distant possession on the Royal Vermis Road, the far edge of the overking's empire.

THE GREAT SALT MARSH

This stretch of coastline between Darnagal and Freegate has been a salty marshland for thousands of years. Within are trackless miles of peat bog, deep mud, stagnant water, and high, thick grasses. The smell of rotten eggs hangs like a shroud over the marsh.

Within the marsh can be found stone structures with elegant arches that are nearly submerged in the muck. These are the ruins of the ancient elven city of Varagost. When that city fell, the tales say, the magics used to bring it down also caused the land here to sink, which allowed the gulf waters to flood in, thus creating the marsh.

A tribe of lizardfolk successfully carved out a small piece of territory in the southern portion of the Great Salt Marsh, keeping an uneasy peace with a young black dragon and a spirit naga dwelling in the north. Other aquatic monsters and animals such as crocodiles, alligators, giant frogs, and hags also dwell within the bog. No humanoid settlements are within the Great Salt Marsh, though adventurers and explorers occasionally venture into the festering wetland to harvest peat or search for treasure within Varagost's submerged ruins.

HALF-PICKLE MARSH

When noted cartographer Abner Thornswallow drew his first map of Eastreach Province, he spontaneously commented that a narrow marsh on the province's southeastern coast greatly resembled a halved pickle. The curious name oddly stuck, though most travelers just refer to it as "The Pickle." Most travelers swear the expression to "be in a pickle" stems from getting caught in this malodorous and perilous wetland from where few ever return. When the Lowwater Road is the safest place in the Half-Pickle Marsh, that tells most people everything they need to know about the forsaken landscape. Bloated, shambling corpses wander aimlessly through the mud and vegetation seeking to exact revenge on the living, while hosts of demented creatures that include multiple flights of harpies and several prides of manticores hover above the muck preying on creatures bogged down in the damp soil. Bandits and fugitives seeking refuge from the authorities in Amrin Ferry and Eastgate sometimes take refuge in this festering marsh, though most outsiders quip that a lengthy prison stay is more accommodating than a single night in this disgusting place. These fearsome inhabitants share one common characteristic — they all avoid the marsh's apex predator, Deathroll, a spiteful, temperamental old black dragon who dwells in a submerged aquatic lair a few miles from the Amrin Estuary. Despite the allure of tremendous riches, no adventurer has so far dared to tangle with the malicious reptile on his home turf.

LAKE CRIMMORMERE

This roughly circular lake encompasses a 40-square-mile area directly northeast of the town of Crimmor in the Stoneheart Valley. For much of its history, the townspeople of Crimmor came to this lake to cast their lines and nets into the water to retrieve the bountiful largemouth bass who flourished here. However, the fishermen's luck appears to have run out as of late. A catch is extremely rare these days, and the handful of fish hauled back to shore are universally much smaller than normal. Some locals now believe the lake may be haunted by the spirits of fishermen who drowned in its waters or died in boating accidents. The true culprits behind the decline in the fish population are a band of freshwater locathahs who reside in an underwater lair on the northern end of the lake. Residents who have seen the creatures mistake their dark silhouettes for apparitions or other ghostly beings. The locathahs cautiously befriend any surface dwellers who approach them in a peaceful manner. On the other hand, humanoids openly brandishing weapons receive a chilly reception. If the locathahs are outnumbered or appear overmatched, they flee beneath the surface. Otherwise, they fight back against anyone who attacks them.

LOST BOY MOUNTAIN

At the northern tip of the Mons Terminus, towering more than 6,000 feet over the foothills below, Lost Boy Mountain is a place of great natural beauty, its flanks marked by cold streams cascading down rocky, forested glens from snow-capped heights. Such appearances are deceiving, unfortunately, as the tales told of this peak suggest that something sinister is present amid the trees and crags.

The earliest confirmed story about Lost Boy Mountain is from the 13th Century I.R. A cousin of the Hyperborean imperator was exploring the northern Mons Terminus with his family and a retinue of soldiers. One evening, they camped on the shoulders of the peak. In the morning, the youngest son of the noble was missing. His bedding was undisturbed, and no tracks could be found. A week's searching turned up no sign of the boy, though a few of the soldiers claimed to have heard the sound of a laughing child echoing from the mountain. This event might have otherwise been forgotten, except that some 80 years later, an old man arrived at the gates of Curgantium, claiming to be the lost child. He had, however, no memory of how he had become lost, or even of his life over the intervening decades. Eventually, he was sent to a monastery in what is now Cantelburgh to live out the rest of his days. It is said that he finally recalled what had happened to him, but would only tell the archdeacon at the cathedral. Upon hearing the tale, the old priest saddled a horse and rode out of the city, though no records tell of what then became of him.

Strange and inexplicable events continued to occur at what was thereafter referred to as Lost Boy Mountain. Over the ensuing centuries, many others have vanished from the slopes and valleys here, never to be seen again. Others say that an ancient civilization of dwarf-like beings lives under the mountain, and that Oerson himself lives with them. In a recent story making the rounds in Bard's Gate, it is said that an adventuring party came upon a group of Hyperborean soldiers taking shelter in a cave on the mountain's side who claimed to be on their way to a battle at Lake Crimmormere.

As a result of these tales, few locals are willing to brave the mountain's flanks. The folk of Byrn occasionally travel the paths they know, but always make sure to make proper prayers before venturing forth. Some prospectors pan for gold in the region, but they usually do not stay the night.

In addition to whatever power exists in Lost Boy Mountain, other more mundane perils also live in the region, including stirges, manticores, stone giants, revenants, and banshees.

Lowwater Road

The Lowwater Road hugs the northern edge of the Amrin Estuary where it passes through the Half-Pickle Marsh until it turns into the Coast Road farther north. Waymark cavalry stationed in Amrin Ferry occasionally patrol the unruly thoroughfare, yet their minimal efforts make no difference at all. This overland highway may be the most perilous in Akados. Many portions of the neglected road are buried beneath mud and marsh water, especially when heavy rains saturate the land. The ghost stories and legends pertaining to the Lowwater Road tally well over 100, which is far fewer than the number of unexplained disappearances that have occurred during its long history. The tale of Bartholomew the Blasphemer ranks among the most famous. In this story, a down-on-his-luck paladin who recently experienced a spate of horrific tragedies culminating in his young son's murder renounced his faith in Thyr and pledged his loyalty to a being he called The Whisperer. In short order, he realized the terrible consequences of his impulsive act. Unable to carry the burdens of his guilt and grief, the fallen servant of good leapt into the marsh and drowned himself in his heavy plate armor. The story also claims that the sound of sobbing heralds the arrival of his angry ghost. To ward off his spirit and bestow any modicum of good luck, travelers foolish enough to embark on the Lowwater Road traditionally spit three times and dance a few steps from a lively jig before taking their initial step onto the road.

Monastery of the Standing Stone

The serene Monastery of the Standing Stone lies nestled within a valley surrounded by foothills. Master Kala of the Yellow Robe is the master of this domain and leads the brothers and sisters under his tutelage toward the path of enlightenment and oneness with the universe. She teaches her pupils honor and duty are the ultimate expressions of a living creature, while suppressing their emotions. One's achievements are not measured by the outcome of their actions, but by their faithfulness to the preceding tenets. Through meditation, the monk communes with the inner being, placing integrity and obligation above personal satisfaction.

The monastery's pastoral setting encourages such introspection. Its décor and accommodations represent an exercise in simplicity, from its dirt-floored dojo where Kala and her fellow monks train, to the caves housing the remains of deceased monks and honored ancestors. The monastery derives its name from the perfectly-aligned standing stone in the midst of a grove surrounded by foothills. A small garden planted around the stone enhances the locale's serenity. Visitors who make their way to the monastery receive an aloof yet respectful reception from Kala and the resident monks. A pervasive myth in the region claims the stone has a special connection to the divine forces that created the neighboring Stoneheart Mountains. The exact nature of this link remains unknown, but its precise alignment to the surrounding foothills and trees lends a modicum of credence to this popular belief.

Mons Terminus

The Mons Terminus mountain range is the southernmost point of the Stoneheart Mountains beyond the Stoneheart Valley. The old imperial capital of Curgantium was built just to the south of the Mons Terminus on the Great Amrin River to symbolize the city's position as the core of the empire. The haunted Lost Boy Mountain is at the northern tip of the Mons Terminus.

The lower reaches and foothills of the Mons Terminus are home to bandits and monsters alike. Settlements in these remote areas cling grimly to their existence in the face of these threats, receiving only sporadic, halfhearted support from those who boast of Aachen's stability.

According to rumor, the dark elf city of Thoth Kathalis lies underneath the mountains of Mons Terminus. At least one avenue from that Under Realm city exits into the tunnels beneath Bard's Gate, with other points of access in the Stoneheart Forest and southern foothills of the valley.

Old Pirate Fortress

Seven hundred years ago, an upstart Foerdewaith baron defied the might of his nation's royal navy and extended his reach into the coastal waters bordering his fiefdom, where he annexed a tiny island in the Sinnar Ocean. The ambitious noble then built an imposing fortress on the small tract of land in the middle of the water. In an even bolder move, he doubled down on his aggressive wager by declaring his self-proclaimed right to engage in piracy on the high seas. His royal navy superiors in Pontus Tinigal begged to differ with his misguided opinion. They dispatched a flotilla of galleons and, off the shores of his island, the king of Foere taught him a fatal lesson. The baron and his vessels sank to the bottom of the ocean that day, never to be seen again. After his demise, several new generations of pirates occupied the fortress until the royal navy routed them from the premises. The old, crumbling fortress has sat abandoned for many years now. The neglect has taken a significant toll on the walls and interior buildings, which are now in a state of terrible disrepair or ruins. Some stories claim the baron buried his larcenous treasures in a secure vault somewhere on the island. However, no one has found any evidence to substantiate these fanciful tales.

Penprie Forest

Excessive logging reduced this deciduous forest that once stretched from the Gaelon River to the edge of the Duskmoon Hills to a fraction of its former size. Humans eventually abandoned the site, leaving its wild beasts and monstrous denizens to establish firm control over most of the woodland with the exception of the areas abutting the well-traveled Trader's Way, which passes close to the forest's eastern edge. The armed patrols defending this commercial thoroughfare make occasional forays into the forest's perimeter to ferret out meddlesome creatures or bandits conspiring to attack traveling merchants and their caravans. Naturally, their efforts keep the forest's perimeter comparatively safer than its rowdy interior. In the heart of the forest, giant spiders weave their webs amid the trees in the hopes of ensnaring an unfortunate victim, while gnolls, ogres, and goblins fight for dominance within the forest. Endhome's soldiers and adventurers are currently searching the Penprie Forest for a notorious local band of highway robbers known as the Green Tree Bandits who supposedly take refuge here alongside their presumed monstrous allies. The former do-gooders once sought to redistribute the city's wealth from its well-to-do citizens to the downtrodden but greed got the better of them. They kept their ill-gotten gains and now solely commit their crimes to benefit themselves. The resourceful cutthroats have robbed a dozen different merchant trains over the last six months, making their capture a priority in Endhome's merchant houses.

Plains of Mayfurrow

Numerous hamlets and villages flourish in the roughly rectangular swath of prairie delineated on all sides by a road or forest. The towns of Glendovel Close and Darnagal respectively occupy the northwestern and northeastern corners of this four-sided boundary, while the metropolises of Bard's Gate and Freegate respectively sit atop the southwestern and southeastern corners of this geometric shape. The influence of the preceding cities spreads far and wide across the vast grassland as many small towns and villages fall under the Suzerainty of Bard's Gate to varying degrees. The settlements scattered throughout the region almost exclusively rely upon currency minted in Bard's Gate.

Although no individual settlement produces anywhere near the output of agricultural products as Glendovel Close, their combined yields vastly outnumber the preceding community's harvest. Many refer to this stretch of peaceful countryside as the Gulf of Akados' breadbasket. Its prosperity may be attributable to its rich soil, temperate climate, and long-term tranquility. While armies have crossed the Plain of Mayfurrow in the past, it has been long years since any such event occurred, leaving the folk of the region in peace.

Nonetheless, roving bands of gnolls, orcs, goblins, and hobgoblins sometimes raid farming communities or assault travelers and explorers traversing the verdant landscape, mostly humanoids from Acregor or the Shorsai Forest looking for an easy target. In addition, vast herds of bison, deer, horses, and sheep roam the wilderness, leisurely grazing on the plentiful grasses and grains protruding from the ground. These game animals inevitably attract humanoid hunters as well as other predatory beasts, most notably foxes, coyotes, and mountain lions.

PONTINE STRAITS

This wide body of ocean separates the Akadonian mainland from Pontos Island. Its notoriously shallow, choppy waters have claimed many ships over the years, littering the seabed with numerous wrecks still bristling with their lost treasures. Nonetheless, the Pontine Straits keep their secrets well hidden. With an average depth of only 50 feet in most spots, it would seem the briny deep's riches would be ripe for the taking. However, the murky water beneath the surface limits visibility to only a few feet in many locations, which makes it difficult to spot the wooden skeletons concealed beneath thin layers of silt. To make matters worse, sea hags and the waterlogged, animated corpses of deceased mariners lost at sea plague undersea explorers at every turn. On the surface, pirates frequently menace ships sailing through the Pontine Straits, though some may grant safe passage to vessels flying under certain flags who grant them safe harbor or provide logistical assistance with their illicit operations. Surprisingly, none of the major naval powers in the region regularly patrol these waters for various reasons. Some may clandestinely support the privateers, while others wish to avoid giving any pretense to their enemies to respond to a perceived attack or imaginary incident if ships under both flags somehow meet on the open waters.

PONTOS ISLAND

Prior to Koshag of Ur's arrival more than 18,000 years ago, Pontos Island was a virtually uninhabited feral wilderness dominated by wild animals and a small population of megafauna. Sea hags freely roamed its coastline, while other aquatic and amphibious monsters dwelt along its beaches and rolling grasslands. Its few humanoid inhabitants lived along its shores in small, isolated fishing villages. Although his settlement at the present-day site of Tros Zoas was short-lived, the ambitious conqueror indelibly stamped his identity on the island. Humanoids who learned of the settlements began migrating from the mainland of Akados to the island in search of a better life.

Today, Pontos Island is a shadow of its former, wild self. Most residents live in small fishing villages near the lush beaches. While sea hags and other ocean dwellers still pose a hazard to these people, Oceanus' navy and marines keep these threats in check by routinely patrolling the waters around the island for all enemies. The sprawling grasslands still remain on many parts of the island's interior, but the Oceander people who live here have tamed large swaths of the unruly landscape, converting unkempt savannas and prairies into farmland and pastures for their livestock. The moderating effect of the Sinnar Ocean gives most of the island a temperate climate throughout the year except for the western shoreline, which experiences seasonal temperature variations. Despite their efforts at subduing the wilderness,

nature defies progress in some remote areas. Ancient legends speak of primordial, vaguely humanoid creatures who inhabit underground caves and feral lands overrun with vegetation. Some believe they are the undead descendants of Koshag who reverted to cannibalism to survive in the aftermath of his death. Others believe they are minions of Dagon who migrated to the island to perform their vile rituals long before Koshag's arrival.

RAPPAN ATHUK

Despite its enormous size and complexity, the dungeon known as Rappan Athuk, or the Dungeon of Graves in some vernacular, is a relative newcomer to Akados. Not coincidentally, the massive complex sprang up in the same general locale where the demonic minions of Orcus and the Army of Light vanished more than 300 years ago — the Forest of Hope. The disciples of Orcus who survived the battle against the forces of good came upon an isolated hillside that concealed a vast network of subterranean tunnels and chambers. They secretly began construction in earnest and repopulated the dank underground complex with hordes of demons, undead, and other evil monstrosities. For almost two centuries, the demon prince's servants covertly toiled in the darkness until 3400 I.R., when Thyr's high priest Bofred and his companions came upon the hidden entrance to a gargantuan mausoleum while investigating a rash of disappearances in the area. What he and his fellow adventurers saw in the labyrinth terrified him. Rappan Athuk's seemingly infinite layers of forbidden temples, crypts, tombs, and other horrors reminded him of the sinister Abyss where the fiendish Orcus and countless other demons revel in wanton bloodlust. Although some of Bofred's companions survived their trek into Rappan Athuk, they never set eyes on the priest of Thyr again. He was presumably lost somewhere in the catacombs within the cursed mausoleum.

Over the next century, the brave adventurers who journeyed to Rappan Athuk realized Bofred had found just one of many entrances into the Dungeon of Graves. Since then, numerous other adventurers have delved into the labyrinth seeking glory and riches or in pursuit of a nobler goal to rid the world of this terrible blight forever. Many have tried their luck in this endeavor, yet most failed in their quest, adding their name to the dungeon's innumerable list of victims. Those who survived the harrowing trek escaped with something perhaps more valuable than treasure: knowledge. Much to their dismay, they also discovered that the evil beacon lured numerous other sinister creatures into its disgusting embrace. The devotees of Tsathogga, the Frog God, slowly and steadily infiltrated the sprawling complex along with a host of other insidious beings from this plane of existence and from other worlds. To make matters worse, a handful of daring souls who ventured far into its depths also learned stranger, alien worlds existed in the bowels of the earth far beneath the desecrated cemetery.

REFERENCE SOURCES: RAPPAN ATHUK,
CYCLOPEAN DEEPS VOLUME 1 AND VOLUME 2

RUINED FORT

Before the Foerdewaith invasion, this fortification defended the intersection between the Coast Road and the Lowwater Road as well as monitoring coastal activities. However, during their war of conquest, the Foerdewaith pummeled the keep and its defenders into submission with their battery of siege engines. The stones and flames lobbed during their offensive reduced the formerly imposing stronghold into a smoldering mound of shattered stone and scorched wood. The lord-governor refuses to spend any money from his treasury to rebuild the badly damaged structure in such a remote and frankly underused corner of his province. In the absence of any state action, terrible creatures now infest the ruins. The most popular rumors suggest evil cultists have taken control of the sundered complex to perform their wicked rites and sacrificial rituals. Many believe they worship an unknown arch-devil seeking to restore a semblance of order to the chaotic forest around them.

Ruined Keep

Ninety years ago, the wizard Eralion used his burgeoning magical powers derived from newly acquired scrolls to conjure a stone keep into existence in the shadow of neighboring Fairhill. As he grew older, the good and righteous man let the fear of death seep into his soul. Mortality terrified him and, in his desperation, he beseeched Orcus to grant him a profane existence as an undying lich. The cruel demon prince knew the wizard lacked the mystical power to successfully complete the ritual, yet he deceived him into attempting it. In his final moments, Eralion realized Orcus had betrayed him, but it was too late. His life essence faded from him, resigning him to languish in the depths beneath his keep as a lowly shadow of his former self.

Upon his earthly demise, the magic holding the keep together slowly and steadily crumbled. Bandits inhabited the deteriorating stronghold for several years until a small unit of Waymarch soldiers expelled them from the keep. In the process, they dealt significant damage to the already decrepit structure. After their removal, the crumbling edifice remained abandoned save for its lone occupant holed up deep beneath its foundation. However, fresh tracks and other signs of activity confirm that the keep is no longer empty. Local rumors in Fairhill suggest a vampire dwells within the keep, though more reliable witnesses assert a band of orcs terrifying the area now take refuge in Eralion's former abode. It remains uncertain whether they are aware of the keep's past history or whether its undead host knows of the trespassers within his midst.

Shepherd's Crook

This sparsely traveled overland route connects the agricultural center of Glendovel Close to Darnagal with a stopover point in the tiny village of Palmer's Field. Stone mileposts erected along the sides of the well-worn path clearly delineate the road from the pervasive grasslands flourishing beside it. Despite or perhaps because of hosting only light traffic, the road remains relatively safe for nearly its entire length except for pockets of trouble close to the southern edges of the Shorsai Forest where bands of hobgoblins, gnolls, goblins, and orcs occasionally venture outside the woodland to try their luck at seizing a merchant caravan or butcher explorers traveling across Shepherd's Crook. Darnagal occasionally dispatches a small unit of mounted soldiers to patrol the area as a reaction to news of a recent attack or increased monstrous activity. According to legend, the road acquired its name when Cyril Wynbrush led his flock of 650 sheep from Glendovel Close to Darnagal. Some local residents who travel along the road swear they periodically hear a young lamb bleating, even though no animals are present. Many whisper silent prayers to Cyril when walking on Shepherd's Crook, hoping he watches over them and their companions during their journey.

Stoneheart Forest

Two major trade arteries, the Tradeway and the Stoneheart River, carve a path through the otherwise pristine wilderness. Traffic hustling across these thoroughfares rarely encounter any resistance from the indigenous denizens who have learned too many hard lessons about the severe consequences for disrupting the flow of goods to and from Bard's Gate. Those who stray from these patrolled and defended routes undergo a more harrowing ordeal. The section north of the Tradeway is less dense than its swampy counterpart to the south, but no less dangerous. Stirges, wolves, manticores, giant spiders, and several types of giants infest this portion of the woodlands. The stirges are so prolific in this area that many natives refer to the Stoneheart Forest as the Stirge Wood. Rumors insist an evil wizard living within the forest breeds and controls these creatures. The stirges and other indigenous denizens periodically leave the confines of the forest to descend upon the neighboring Stoneheart Valley or even make their way toward the more distant Lyre Valley. There is a long-standing belief that a group of elven rangers known as the Farseekers of Twilight maintains a hold within the forest's northern reach, though any concrete evidence of their existence remains elusive.

The region known as Kayden's Swamp is the most noteworthy feature of the forest south of the Tradeway. The wetlands developed around a cluster of islands in the center of the Stoneheart River. No one can say whether natural events or humanoid intervention created the malodorous, pest-ridden bayou, but all generally agree on one fact: The swamp's namesake dwells somewhere within its stinking confines. For the most part, the reputed necromancer allows river traffic to pass through his territory unharmed, provided they stay on course. Waterborne vessels deviating from the designated path encounter terrifying illusions, traps, mists, and other annoyances to keep the wayward traveler from venturing close to his secret island base. Those who refuse to turn back risk a personal encounter with the reclusive magician. For this reason, most ships sailing through the Stoneheart Forest hire one of the Riverfolk to lead them through the morass. The Riverfolk, who still dwell in small hamlets where they eke out a meager existence as eel hunters or peat harvesters, know the waterway's backchannels like the backs of their hands.

In addition to Kayden, the Stoneheart Forest also teems with oppressive mosquito swarms, crocodiles, alligators, frogs, and crocodilian humanoids known as chikes (croc folk). These bipedal horrors typically dwell in huts built onto soggy ground on the swamp's outskirts and the forest's interior regions near ponds and streams. Trolls, hobgoblins, goblins, and the assorted ranks of the undead as well as hosts of other malevolent creatures inhabit the forest's interior. While dimwitted, these monstrosities generally steer clear of the road and river and instead direct their anger and hunger at one another. Of course, travelers who veer away from the preceding thoroughfares are fair game in their eyes. According to some tales, an ancient green dragon named Weeping Cloud dwells within a tangle of thickets at the heart of the forest. The legends claim his lineage dates back to the bygone days when the Stoneheart Forest was a small parcel of the Great Akadonian Forest. The stories also say Weeping Cloud enforces the edict against attacking trespassers sticking to the road and the river. The dragon's perceived merciful stance derives from the annual tribute he reputedly receives from a consortium of interests affiliated with the various guilds and merchant houses reaping the financial rewards of Akados' international commerce. Less prevalent legends also claim a hidden portal within the Stoneheart Forest leads to a subterranean drow city, though these myths remain unconfirmed.

Stoneheart Mountain Dungeon

In the foothills of the Stoneheart Mountains, just north of Bard's Gate, lie the ruins of twin shrines dedicated to the virtuous deities Thyr and Muir. During their heyday, pilgrims traveled from far and wide to visit these holy sites. Yet over the passing centuries, the gods' popularity steadily waned as new gods captured the hearts and souls of eager followers. The shrines fell into neglect and then disuse after Abysthor, the last of the shrines' great priests, vanished 20 years ago. The absence of good creatures in the area allowed the forces of evil deep beneath the forgotten shrines to surge back to the forefront.

The devotees of Tsathogga, the vile Frog God, long inhabited a religious complex far below the ground. There in the darkness, his deranged tsathar servants conducted their wicked blood rituals and paid homage to their chaotic, demonic entity. However, after centuries of isolation and solitude, they learned they were no longer alone. Ten years ago, the followers of Orcus joined them after the demon prince imparted a vision to his high priest commanding him to also erect a temple in the depths of the Stoneheart Mountain Dungeon. The competing forces quickly struck an uneasy truce as both sought the same end. Each set out to locate the Black Monolith, a potent construct with the power to open a permanent gateway to the Abyss. However, unbeknownst to either party, the dungeon also contains another secret. Even farther below the temples, the spirit of the Stoneheart Mountain can be found in a chamber of earth blood. A lone guardian vigilantly defends both locations until the time comes when other righteous beings stand beside him to forever eradicate the evil infesting the Stoneheart Mountain Dungeon once and for all.

Those who dare venture to the Stoneheart Mountain Dungeon encounter a multi-tiered complex. The dilapidated shrines occupy the uppermost level and are accessible from the surface. Undead and carrion feeders took the place of clergy members and worshippers on this level. A network of caves connects the shrines with the temples and chambers beneath the Stoneheart Mountain Dungeon. At its lowest depths, many believe the tunnels and passageways in its allegedly bottomless pit connect the dungeon to Rappan Athuk and the Cyclopean Deeps.

STONEHEART RIVER

The waters filling the Stoneheart River begin their journey in the upper elevations of the mountain range bearing the same name. Rainfall and melting snow winds its way down the peaks and collects in the waterway bisecting a critical gap in central Akados. The water escaping the mountain tumbles in great falls and rapids until it calms down north of Bard's Gate where it widens and deepens at a significantly slower pace. The river's gentle demeanor facilitates the transportation of goods between Bard's Gate and destinations along the Great Amrin River and distant seaports on the Sinnar Ocean. Despite its dimensions, engineers forded the river at the site of the great metropolis, giving the city mastery of the overland route connecting east and west as well as direct access to the Stoneheart River.

The river is navigable from Bard's Gate until it reaches the northern edge of the Stoneheart Forest to the south where it narrows and transforms into shallow rapids again. Even the Riverfolk who were intimately familiar with the river's hidden sandbars and unpredictable currents could not overcome a series of cataracts known as the Stoneheart Falls. To circumvent this daunting obstacle, city administrators expended tremendous financial resources and amounts of manpower to construct and maintain portages around this location. More recently, the dwarven engineer Karling constructed an ingenious boat-lift using hydraulic pressure harnessed from a massive waterwheel. Embraced wholeheartedly by the Riverfolk who initially resented it, this device known as Karling's Contraption plucks the vessel completely out of the water and moves it past the cataracts to safety in a matter of minutes.

From here, the Stoneheart River widens to a breadth of one mile and deepens to 120 feet at its lowest point as it meanders a slow, dangerous path through the Stoneheart Forest. The trickiest and most perilous spot is a stinking morass known as Kayden's Swamp. The patch of mosquito-infested wetland acquired its name from the archmage of questionable character who allegedly dwells in this forsaken realm. Travelers making their way through this uncompromising stretch of the waterway typically hug what passes for the eastern bank of the river to avoid becoming hopelessly lost among the stagnant bog waters and marshy islands convoluting the correct route through the clusters of trees, shrubs, and other aquatic vegetation. Crocodiles, giant frogs, and other horrors lurk in these secluded spots. Almost every ship negotiating these confusing waters hires a Riverfolk guide or pilot to safely lead their vessel through the confounding network of dead-ends. Despite these difficulties, the Stoneheart River remains a relatively safe and reliable means of transportation due in large part to the interests who benefit from the river trade.

STONEHEART VALLEY

Foothills, swales, and nadirs mark the buffer zone between the massive Stoneheart Mountains to the north and the flatter grasslands and forests to the south. The valley is a study in flux and transition. Where the soil is fertile, lush grasses, pine trees, and other vegetation flourish. In regions dominated by exposed stone, the land appears lifeless and barren. The rocks embedded into the earth often feature sharp edges and jagged protrusions that make travel through the region slow and tedious. Despite its desolate appearance, the valley boasts a reliable water supply fed by frequent precipitation and runoff from the snowcapped summits of the neighboring Stoneheart Mountains. Small hamlets and lone farmsteads dot large portions of the landscape, though most residents dwell alongside the Tradeway running through the heart of the valley as well as the larger towns of Fairhill and Crimmor.

Hawks, falcons, eagles, and other birds of prey nest in the rocky nooks and crannies atop the foothills. These predators frequently circle the clear skies while scanning the bare stone for their next meal. Rodents such as mice, rats, squirrels, and other small mammals are their typical fare. Wolves are the dominant land-based predator species in the region. Their larger and more vicious worg relatives frequently accompany the pack during their hunts for deer and other game animals. Gnolls are the dominant disruptive force in the region, spreading havoc wherever they go. Orcs have also begun to make inroads into the area, most notably in the Ruined Keep and the wilderness surrounding Fairhill. Rumors even claim wormholes in the northern section of the valley burrow into the earth, where they ultimately lead to the Cyclopean Deeps.

REFERENCE SOURCE: THE LOST LANDS: STONEHEART VALLEY

STORMSHIELD

When Captain Aldrin Shaw deserted the royal navy and absconded with one of its cutters in 3436 I.R., the city of Eastwych saw fit to seize Stormshield, his private estate, as recompense for his traitorous actions. After decades of legal wrangling and bureaucratic delays, the city finally auctioned off his property to the highest bidder. However, the purchaser and every subsequent owner thereafter soon fell upon financial ruin or suffered a terrible tragedy almost immediately after buying Stormshield. The spacious residence is now considered to be cursed by bad luck, leaving it neglected and unoccupied for more than a decade. Indeed, the property's title became so clouded, even Eastwych lost track of who currently possesses a deed of ownership to the property. Those in the know claim a notorious swindler named Romar Sourwine may have acquired Stormshield's deed through some nefarious scheme or subterfuge. The wily confidence man was last seen embarking on a vessel heading up the Stoneheart River.

TALAMERIN RIVER

This gentle, languidly flowing river diverges from Glimmrill Run just outside the border of the Forest Kingdoms and empties into the delta overlooking The Trireme and Freegate. Merchants from the latter city transport goods to and from the elves dwelling within the last vestiges of the Great Akadonian Forest. Small fishing villages line the riverbank near well-known fishing holes coveted for their reliable supplies of catfish, walleye, and bass. Freegate's elite residents flaunt their luxurious pleasure crafts on this calm waterway rather than risk a rendezvous with pirates or a vicious storm on the open seas. These magnificent yachts must navigate around the numerous fishing kayaks, rafts, and rowboats clogging the congested waterway. Fortunately, the Talamerin River can accommodate the traffic with an average depth of 30 feet and an average width of 70 feet. Only a bridge built into the Coast Road just north of Freegate fords the river. In ancient times, the river cut a path through the Great Akadonian Forest that covered large swaths of the continent. Divers and salvagers scavenging on the riverbed occasionally retrieve elven objects from the distant past, which they sell to collectors and historians for further study.

TANTIVY ROAD

This long trail of packed dirt and occasional corduroy where the ground frequently becomes soggy is the only viable overland route from the capital of Carterscroft to the northern and eastern sections of the province. Despite offering a fast and reliable means of reaching remote locations, the prohibitive costs make Tantivy Road a less attractive option. As with most of rural Eastreach, numerous local barons and nobles demand tax money for entering their lands. In addition to contending with the rightful owners of these areas, travelers must also confront countless hucksters posing as tax collectors who impose levies of behalf of a real or imaginary landowner. According to a popular idiom, "one could leave Carterscroft with a full wagon and a full purse of gold and arrive at the road's terminus with nothing but a single shoe." In addition to being plagued by greedy local authorities, bugbears, gnolls, tigers, and even manticores periodically harass travelers making their way along the Tantivy Road. Needless to say, the real and alleged landowners take no actions whatsoever to address the monstrous denizens freely moving across their property.

The Trireme

Established 180 years ago in the woods on the outskirts of Freegate, this renowned tavern caters to epicurean tastes and serves some of the finest wines in the known world. During its illustrious history, the two-story building has changed owners on four occasions and it has incredibly burnt to the ground seven times only to be rebuilt almost immediately afterward. Local dreamers and nascent philosophers make up the bulk of the business's clientele. On most nights, these gregarious fellows vigorously converse about mundane and esoteric topics in the tavern's common room, though on some nights the burgeoning thinkers take over a private drinking room or engage in stimulating debates in the famous symposium provided the participants generously spread their wealth and knowledge with the servers and elite patrons. Foremost among these may be Helios Pousalaki, an influential commissary from neighboring Freegate. The older gentleman fancies himself as the quintessential intellectual on any subject. He speaks with such authority and dignity that depending on the mood every word parting from his lips feels as if it were the most profound or wittiest utterance ever.

With so many characters in play at the bustling enterprise, the Trireme is the place to be seen and heard not only to gain exposure to Freegate's rich and famous but to also pick up some interesting pieces of information. The current rumors circulating among its patrons mention an ancient bottle of wine stored somewhere on the premises, the haunting of the upper levels by one of the Trireme's former owners, a self-proclaimed priest of Bacchus challenging patrons to a drinking contest in exchange for a priceless wine goblet, and a story about a visiting wizard taking an acute interest in one of the staff members.

Unclaimed Lands

The Unclaimed Lands are the uncontrolled feudal lands north of the Great Amrin River and west of the Glimmrill Run until it reaches the Forest Kingdoms to the north.

When the Hyperboreans retreated from Akados, the forces of civilization abandoned this vast swath of territory bordering Eastreach Province. The region quickly descended into chaos as countless warlords, barons, and other self-professed nobles rushed in to fill the political and economic vacuum left in their wake. These despots ruled over their tiny fiefdoms from the safety of their castles and fortified manor homes. Inexplicably, the Foerdewaith stopped their advance into central Akados at the edge of the Great Amrin River, depriving the Unclaimed Lands of any stabilizing influence derived from the presence of a developed, centralized state.

From a technological and cultural standpoint, the people of the Unclaimed Lands underwent a slow regression from the lofty ideals of the Hyperboreans to the petty squabbles of backward boors fighting over a worthless tract of fallow earth. A sizable population of nomadic Erskaelosi also wander across the mostly untamed wilderness, though they are careful to avoid the more numerous small villages and hamlets inhabited by their Foerdewaith counterparts who greatly outnumber them. The influx of these displaced barbaric peoples adds further volatility to the Unclaimed Lands' muddy political situation. However, the Unclaimed Lands' humanoid residents, whether they are humans, half-orcs, orcs, or gnolls, universally agree on one thing — to avoid the Court of Loom Ché under all circumstances. The massive edifice constructed from dinosaur bones belongs to its denizen of Leng namesake. Within this compound, the enigmatic visitor from another world entertains an equally eclectic crowd of strange supernatural and alien beings.

Varagost

Ages ago, Varagost was a city of the elves, a magnificent citadel of towering pinnacles, graceful arches, glistening fountains, and courtyards of fruit trees. The sister of the city of Aranost to the northwest, Varagost was home to poets, singers, and musicians said to have been without equal in Akados.

But even among the long-lived elves, death eventually comes, and so it came to Varagost and Aranost. Each was sacked by the armies of Hyperborea as they sought to carve out an empire for themselves on Akados. The forests surrounding the cities were cut and burned to permit the legions easy passage. The cities were unwalled, since no enemies had ever before threatened their realms, but magic surrounded them, suffused them, and protected them. And so the invaders had to use magic as well, which brought down the foundations of the cities. In the case of Varagost, it also caused the lands about it to sink, which permitted the waters of the gulf to flood in and cover over the ruins of the elven city with a salt marsh.

Today, the Great Salt Marsh remains, and just the tops of a few towers of Varagost rise over the muck and water. Occasionally, adventurers enter the marsh to seek what treasures the elves might have left behind when they fled the destruction of their city. If any have returned with such treasure, no tale has yet been told.

The Wain Road (North-South Run)

Merchants traveling overland from Bard's Gate to Eastgate prefer taking this moderately safe highway, especially if they carry a token exempting them from paying local taxes while traveling along this road. Otherwise, the lord-governor's sheriffs collect tolls at irregular intervals from those who are not fortunate enough to benefit from one of the many trade agreements the metropolis of Bard's Gate brokered with the Kingdoms of Foere. Built by the Hyperboreans, the paved highway ideally suits wheeled vehicles as well as foot traffic. Like many roads in Eastreach Province, real and illegitimate landholders attempt to collect tolls from passing travelers. However, the lord-governor harshly addresses those poaching money otherwise destined for his coffers. When his sheriffs capture a scoundrel posing as one of their own, they mete out immediate justice by beheading the offender and impaling their decapitated head atop a pike imbedded into the side of the road as a warning to others inclined to follow down the same path. Bandits are the most common threat to travelers venturing along the Wain Road, though goblins, stirges, and other monsters also plague some isolated stretches of the Wain Road. For this reason, mercenaries typically accompany merchant caravans heading to or from Bard's Gate or Eastgate.

Wild Edge River

A vast triangular stone pedestal in the southwestern corner of Eastreach Province bifurcates the Great Amrin River into a smaller channel known as the Wild Edge River. This waterway then carves a path into the Forest of Hope, where it once again splits in two at the triangular base of a huge stone idol depicting a presumably ancient forgotten goddess. Hundreds of giant water snakes unseen anywhere else in Akados dwell in a network of passages underneath the statue's stone foundation. When darkness falls, the nightmarish creatures emit eerie warbling cries throughout the night. Both stone statues at the forks on the Wild Edge River predate the Hyperboreans' arrival in Akados. Despite being partially submerged beneath running water for several thousand years, the stones still appear freshly cut and show no telltale signs of erosion. Although connected to one of the busiest waterways in Akados, few vessels ever purposely venture down the Wild Edge River. Its banks are largely uninhabited, and it is forded at only one known location on the northern fork near the mausoleum. According to legend, a righteous general perished in battle at this spot. His grieving troops interred his body in a tomb along the river's edge to commemorate his sacrifice.

Northern Sinnar Coast of Eastern Akados

Political Subdivisions of the Northern Sinnar Coast of Eastern Akados

Acregor

Capital: Aranost
Ruler: Sagriss Bloodfist, King of Acregor and the Dragon Hills
Government: absolute monarchy
Population: unknown (ogres, goblins, gnolls, trolls, orcs, kobolds)
Monstrous: wolf, giant animal (beaver, otter, and snapping turtle), lycanthrope, undead, manticore, hippogriff, dragon (southern Dragon Hills)
Languages: various humanoid tongues
Religion: none
Resources: raiding
Technology Level: Dark Ages

Various elven, human, and humanoid peoples have lived in this area of the Dragon Hills over thousands of years. The elves originally were here, but then the Hyperboreans sacked their city of Aranost and drove the elves south into the deeper forest. Then for a time the Hyperboreans were here, and they even rebuilt Aranost in their own style. Eventually, their empire fell as well so that by 2514 I.R. the city was again abandoned.

Over the next several decades, various bands of orcs, goblinoids, trolls, and ogres moved into the Dragon Hills. Although settlements of humans were in the region, other forces were also present, and the departure of the Hyperboreans left a power vacuum. The humanoids found the hills to be open and welcoming, and provided good, rugged land in which to hide and make their camps, and from which they could raid nearby farms, fields, and wayward travelers.

Then in 2740 I.R., a half-troll by the name of Acregor Ironclaw arrived in the Dragon Hills with a band of ogres. Finding the humanoids of the hills in disarray, he set out to unify them into a single nation. It was a propitious time: The Hyperboreans were long gone, and the Foerdewaith were just beginning their path to empire. Acregor easily brought all of the tribes of the Dragon Hills under his banner, and for another 80 years, they became the terror of the plains. In this time, he reoccupied Aranost as his capital and built an enormous tower to act as his burial monument so that even when he was gone, he would continue to watch over his realm.

It is probably no surprise, however, that as he finally reached old age, Acregor's grip on his nation (which by then he had named after himself) began to break. Challengers arose until eventually he was assassinated in 2822 I.R. After three years of internal fighting, one of Acregor's ogre lieutenants claimed the mantle of Acregor and named himself king. The so-called Kingdom of Acregor has existed since that time, sometimes under an aggressive king who sought expansion and other times under weak rulers who faced continual civil war. But none has ever held the Dragon Hills as tightly as did the original Acregor, nor has any had his vision. Which is certainly something the neighboring human realms can be thankful for.

Today, Acregor is an annoyance and, at times, a grave danger to those passing near the Dragon Hills, but at least for now poses no real threat to Darnagal, Glendovel Close, or the other major settlements of the Plains of Mayfurrow.

The humanoids of Acregor are wary when they are in the southern Dragon Hills, as the family of blue dragons living there does not always take kindly to intrusions, whether accidental or intentional.

Aranost, City of

Population: 3,178 (mostly orcs and half-orcs, with varying numbers of other humanoids)
Ruler: King Sagriss Bloodfist
Government: absolute monarchy

Ages ago, Aranost was a city of the elves, a magnificent citadel of towering pinnacles, graceful arches, glistening fountains, and courtyards of fruit trees. The sister of the city of Varagost to the southeast, Varagost was home to poets, singers, and musicians said to have been without equal in Akados.

But even among the long-lived elves, death eventually comes, and so it came to Varagost and Aranost. Each city was sacked by the armies of Hyperborea as they carved out an empire for themselves on Akados. The Hyperboreans cut and burned the forests surrounding the cities to allow the legions easy passage. The cities were unwalled since no enemies had ever before threatened their realms, but protective magic surrounded and suffused them. And so the invaders had to use magic as well, which brought down the foundations of the cities.

Afterward, the Great Salt Marsh covered Varagost, making it uninhabitable. The Hyperboreans, however, decided to rebuild Aranost in their own style, and they held it until 2514 I.R. when it was abandoned along with the rest of Akados as the Hyperboreans withdrew across the sea to Libynos.

When Acregor Ironclaw finally took control of the humanoids inhabiting the Dragon Hills, he decided to make a capital on the ruins of Aranost. When he learned the city's original name, he retained it, thinking it amusing that a half-troll was now the lord of an elven city.

Today, Aranost remains the capital of the humanoid Kingdom of Acregor and sits atop a hill overlooking the ridges, valleys, and crags of the Dragon Hills. From here, generations of kings have looked out over the Plains of Mayfurrow and planned ways to seize the lowlands. As of yet, all such plans have come to naught. In the meantime, what was once a magnificent city of the elves is now a bleak, crime-ridden settlement of overcrowded shanties, ramshackle hovels, and omnipresent filth. The predominately orcish and half-orc population adequately adjusts to wallowing in this disgusting squalor festering with death and disease. They survive on a meager diet of grains, wild berries, and game foraged from the surrounding wilderness or sold in Aranost's cutthroat markets.

The Camp

Population: 355 (244 human, 36 orc or half-orc, 21 dwarf, 18 goblinoid, 11 halfling, 10 gnome, 7 elf or half-elf, 7 other, 1 hill giant)
Ruler: The Usurer
Government: anarchy

The Camp sits on the edge of oblivion overlooking the barren wasteland known as the Desolation. While it technically qualifies as a settlement, it completely lacks any sense of community. The riff-raff, ne'er-do-wells, and miscreants who live here personify the axiom, "every man for himself." Desperation rather than opportunity drove many of these individuals to this forsaken place. They live here by the seat of their pants, devising schemes to get ahead, usually at the expense of someone else. The Camp's residents live in ramshackle buildings cobbled together from salvaged scraps of wood, loose branches, bundled thatch, and practically any other material suitable for construction. In many respects, they merely survive instead of truly live.

Although the Camp has no formal government, some individuals enjoy more status than others. The Usurer stands out above all others. Many believe he founded the Camp, as he has always been here to the best of everyone's knowledge. This cunning man performs multiple functions within the Camp and serves as the settlement's moneychanger, blacksmith, and de facto leader. The Usurer exclusively mints the only recognized currency in town: iron bits. Therefore, anyone wishing to purchase food, drink, livestock, or equipment must first exchange their money for his iron bits. For an otherwise lawless society, this is the only regulation the locals universally enforce. None of the Camp's establishments accept any other form of currency.

The Camp may offer shelter and services, but it cannot guarantee safety, especially at night. Those who wander outdoors during the evening tend to disappear with alarming regularity, while those who stay indoors almost always awaken the following morning barring some unforeseen tragedy. Residents attribute the disappearances to the activities of a death church, though there is no credible evidence to support the assertion. For many years, no one outside the Camp cared about the town's missing people, but a new effort to reopen the north-south trade route through the Desolation has rekindled interest in the remote town. The locals warn visitors never to travel into the Desolation without a guide, and that the Camp itself presumably harbors many secrets not meant to be discovered. Some believe intelligent undead creatures walk among them, while others speak of strange folk walking abroad also seeking to venture into the Desolation. Most residents candidly discourage newcomers from setting foot in the barren wasteland at their doorstep. Those who openly talk about going to Tsar mysteriously vanish shortly thereafter, regardless of whether they freely walked about the settlement or hunkered down in one of its fragile buildings.

REFERENCE SOURCE: THE SLUMBERING TSAR SAGA

CANTYN LIGHT, TOWN OF

Population: 1,550 (680 Foerdewaith, 310 other human
  ethnicity, 190 half elf, 150 hill dwarf, 100 halfling, 85 gnome,
  35 other)
Ruler: Sea Lord Sir Argus Hamille
Government: sea lord appointed by Bard's Gate

Cantyn Light refers to the 170-foot-tall lighthouse overlooking the entrance to the Binjerin River as well as the town of Cantyn Light nestled in the shadow of the limestone tower. Experienced mariners recruited from Bard's Gate's navy operate the lighthouse under the direction of a representative from the city's Wizards' Guild. These individuals serve Sea Lord Sir Argus Hamille, the town's ruler. The blowhard naval officer constantly toots his own horn, regaling bored listeners with his fanciful accounts of his daring exploits on the high seas. The young man in his mid-30s attributes his premature retirement from active naval duty to the amputation of his lower right leg from a wound suffered during a sea battle. However, truth be told, he lost the limb to gangrene after neglecting to care for an infected toe. Furthermore, the sea lord's stories only took place in his imaginative mind. After less than six months in command, the high admiral grew tired of Hamille's cowardice and incompetence. He relieved him of his duties and relegated the braggart to his current backwater assignment.

Bard's Gate maintains a significant naval presence at the mouth of the Binjerin River. At any time, at least one frigate patrols the waters around the important harbor. The metropolis also stations a sizable contingent of ship's marines and Waymark cavalry in the town. Cantyn Light serves as the port of call for oceangoing vessels as well as the scows and swoops in the River Watch that patrol the Binjerin River. In keeping with the town's maritime tradition, the town of Cantyn Light has numerous warehouses, fish markets, ship repair facilities, taverns, and less-reputable establishments that cater to these professions. The town also boasts an ancient library that pales in comparison to the one found in Elise, yet still attracts its share of scholars and researchers. In another local cottage industry, stories about ghost ships sailing on the waters beyond the lighthouse and shipwrecks littering the sea floor spur sales of souvenirs, memorabilia, and guided tours of these areas. *The Blue Mermaid*, a caravel that vanished 250 years ago during the Night of the Deathly Fog, is the most famous and celebrated of these haunted vessels. Sculptors sell miniature replicas of this ship to curiosity seekers and collectors alike. According to legend, the ship appears on the horizon on moonlit nights when the ghostly spirits aboard the vessel walk atop the sea as they presumably search for lost crewmembers or the lighthouse's obscured beacon.

REFERENCE SOURCE: THE LOST LANDS: BARD'S GATE

CARTER'S FERRY, VILLAGE OF

Population: 42 (26 Foerdewaith, 8 half-elf, 6 halfling, 2 dwarf)
Ruler: none

The Carter family found itself between a rock and a hard place. When hordes of hobgoblins and orcs overran Oxibbul, Jeremiah Carter, his wife Eva, and their six children followed in the frenzied footsteps of countless others toward the Fingers. At some point during their harried journey, their paths diverged, leaving the Carters to go it alone for the rest of their trek. As they approached the riverbank, wild, bloodcurdling screams rose up behind them. Jeremiah, a devout worshipper of Freya, offered a silent petition to his beloved deity while he and Eva cradled their children in their arms in a final act of parental love. The frenetic war cries drew closer. At that moment, a ferry boat suddenly appeared at the edge of the riverbank. The vessel's pilot calmly beckoned the family to come aboard. With a single sweep from his oar, he pushed the family to safety as a throng of befuddled orcs helplessly watched them escape. The pilot never spoke, and each family member's description of this person wildly differed. Some swore he was a man, while others stared upon a woman. Eva and her daughter testified they saw an angel's face; Jeremiah and the others claimed the pilot was an ordinary man.

When the Carters finally joined the others in Elise, their fantastic tale of hope and salvation quickly spread far and wide. A simple stone shrine sculpted into the likeness of an oar now stands at the spot where Jeremiah and his family stood roughly 1,600 years earlier. A small town — better described as a waystation for merchants and caravans traveling along the Frenzied Crossing — also grew up around this locale. The 42 permanent residents of this tiny settlement make a living offering a variety of goods and services to these travelers, including a ferry service across the river. Taverns, inns, general stores, and other shops selling specialized equipment cater to the whims and needs of visitors and adventurers, especially those heading to the ruins of Oxibbul to unearth previously undiscovered treasures. A popular rumor circulating through the bars and common rooms claims that a renegade wizard from faraway Ghue Island spends his days poking around the rubble in Oxibbul searching for an abandoned relic left behind by a wizard from the Gray Tower.

ELISE, TOWN OF

Population: 605 (320 Foerdewaith, 90 other human ethnicity,
  80 half-elf, 45 halfling, 30 gnome, 20 hill dwarf, 10 high elf, 10
  other)
Ruler: Elisa
Government: autocracy

When Oxibbul fell to goblinoid marauders roughly 1,600 years ago, its surviving residents fled across the Fingers where they founded the sister settlements of Elise and Glaivr. Unlike its counterpart, Elise celebrates intellectual achievements and strictly enforces the numerous laws on its books. The wizard Elisa, the town's ruler, defers the adjudication of Elise's legal code to her three subordinates, Sarah, Joyce, and Sabrina, all of whom serve as judges and are also accomplished wizards in their own right. They and the 150 men-at-arms enlisted in the town guard keep the peace within Elise.

Although the sister settlements differ in their outlooks toward law and order, they remain on friendly terms. Elise exports its agricultural products to its larger trading partner, while Glaivr reciprocates with furs and timber. While Elise benefits greatly from its economic relationship with Glaivr, the same cannot be said about its romantic entanglements. Elisa continually rebuffs the unsolicited advances from Glaivr's leader

Lord Bertrand, whom she thoroughly despises. Elisa's blatant disinterest in marrying him fails to curtail his relentless interest in her.

Elisa instead focuses her attention on the town's renowned library, which contains many works from Oxibbul's repository of books and tomes. The library occupies a stone complex near Elisa's central tower inside the wooden palisade encircling the settlement. The library has acquired additional resources over the years to add to its already impressive collection and offers to purchase any noteworthy items that would interest Elisa or her apprentice wizards for a fair price. Visitors may access the library for a substantial fee or even hire a sage to assist with their research. The library may be one of the finest sources of esoteric knowledge in all of Akados. Adventurers considering a trek to Tsar or Tsen often stop here first to understand the history of these fabled locales and to get a preview of what horrors await them in these forbidden realms. Rumors also speak of a lost manuscript hidden or concealed in another tome somewhere within the library. The writing known as *Chaos Reigns* is supposedly the handiwork of none other than Orcus himself. Despite Elisa's extensive efforts and those of several other arcane practitioners, no trace of the document has ever been found, if it even exists in the first place.

REFERENCE SOURCE: THE LOST LANDS: SWORD OF AIR

GLAIVR, TOWN OF

Population: 2,073 (820 Foerdewaith, 308 other human ethnicity, 250 half-elf, 225 halfling, 220 gnome, 180 hill dwarf, 50 high elf, 20 other)
Ruler: Lord Bertrand
Government: autocracy

A large, log palisade surrounds a rough-and-tumble town of rowdy loggers, trappers, and adventurers who play just as hard as they work in the chaotic taverns and brothels. Not surprisingly, the copious tankards of alcohol and raging libidos fuel brawls that spill out of the establishments and onto the streets where they spread like a virulent epidemic. Lord Bertrand, the town's ruler, rarely interferes in these disputes, preferring to allow his citizens to sort these issues out for themselves unless the matter devolves into a full-scale riot. In that case, Bertrand deploys his 200-strong town guard to break up the donnybrook. Glaivr's wild and wooly character deviates greatly from its original laidback demeanor.

Founded in the aftermath of Oxibbul's collapse, the people who fled across the Fingers and into the lands beyond were predominately artisans and craftsmen rather than loggers and trappers. Over time, necessity and opportunity transformed generations of tradesfolk into lumberjacks and outdoorsmen. Glaivr's original settlers wisely chose the location for their new community at the intersection of two roads heading to Legion's Bay that also sat on the banks of the Binjerin River. Barges sailing to Bard's Gate and destinations farther inland load and unload their cargo and passengers on the massive wharf on the city's northern outskirts. These ships transport timber and fur from the neighboring Eng Wood and Kurz Wood to distant markets. The captains of these vessels frequently hire mercenaries and guards from the ranks of the town's burly woodsmen and rugged outdoorsmen. Many of these individuals worship the barbarian god Bowbe, who has a major temple in the city. The clerics in his service frequently tend to the injuries sustained during one of Glaivr's frequently melees, though they vehemently protest raising anyone killed in combat during one of these free-for-alls. Someone seeking those services must obtain them from the Temple of Freya that is also found in Glaivr.

As previously discussed, Lord Bertrand takes a hands-off approach to intervening in the affairs of others. He never metes out justice except in plainly evident cases of theft where ownership of the stolen item can be definitively proven, and obvious instances of premeditated murder. Glaivr's ruler prefers spending his days wooing Elisa from neighboring Elise and seeking bounty hunters to capture the fugitive Duncan who supposedly fled to the Hazed Canyon. To date, his efforts on both fronts have failed miserably.

REFERENCE SOURCE: THE LOST LANDS: SWORD OF AIR

GEOGRAPHIC FEATURES AND POINTS OF INTEREST IN THE NORTHERN SINNAR COAST OF EASTERN AKADOS

BINJERIN RIVER

The Binjerin River flows from the eastern edge of the Stoneheart mountains through the Stoneheart Foothills and the Black Forest and eventually into the Gulf of Akados. Barges transporting raw materials from areas farther upriver sail along this waterway on their journey to distant markets. In 2214 I.R., Glaivr and Bard's Gate established the River Watch to safeguard commercial traffic along this vital trade route. These armed patrols and troops from Bard's Gate work in tandem with the individual vessel's security forces to ensure the safe transport of goods and commodities. Fishermen drop their lines into the freshwater system, while crabbers, lobstermen, and mollusk harvesters troll the brackish estuary where the river meets the gulf. According to popular fish stories, the estuary contains oysters that produce green pearls while a seemingly immortal eight-foot-long freshwater bass named Big Jim swims in the Binjerin River.

REFERENCE SOURCES: THE LOST LANDS: BARD'S GATE,

THE LOST LANDS: SWORD OF AIR

THE BLACK FOREST

This deciduous forest boasts a wide variety of tree species, though it earned its name from the dark color of its iconic oak trees. The forest's thick canopy reaches a height of 200 feet in some places. The leaves prevent sunlight from reaching the ground, leaving the forest floor mostly barren, which allows creatures to move uninhibited across the forest floor in most areas. The Binjerin River carves a path through the western part of the Black Forest and allows loggers and woodsmen to easily transport timber downriver. These logging communities tend to be clustered around the river area as well as the forest's edges. Villagers and woodsmen fear to delve too deeply into the forest because many never come back. Folklore attributes their disappearances to a race of sentient spiders that purportedly dwell in a massive web complex. Woodsmen occasionally speak of an evil treant or an overgrown, sentient tree living within the forest. The only motivation to go into these remote reaches of the forest lies in the prospect of finding celestial cap mushrooms, an addictive narcotic illegally sold in Bard's Gate or legally purchased in High Karst.

REFERENCE SOURCE: THE LOST LANDS: SWORD OF AIR

DEARTHWOOD

The Dearthwood is a coniferous forest in the shadow of the Stoneheart Mountains. Brambles and briars grow in the thin, alkaline soil riddled with ponds and lakes tainted with lye. Contrary to popular wisdom, the safest drinking water comes from murky, bug-infested waters — provided the drinker first boils the liquid to kill any pathogens. The source of the toxic material remains a mystery, though some druids and rangers speculate runoff from the neighboring Stoneheart Mountains transports the metal hydroxide into the small streams and groundwater supply. Others counter that its roughly equal distribution throughout the Dearthwood confirms the lye leaches up to the surface from an underground source. Regardless of its origins, the contamination stunts the trees' trunks and needles, causing them to shed their spiny leaves at an accelerated rate. Because the trees and undergrowth grow close to the ground, moving through the Dearthwood often requires hacking through the brush with a sharp blade or other suitable tool. The proliferation of living and dead vegetation makes the forest vulnerable to forest fires from lightning strikes or carelessness.

The Dearthwood is sparsely populated by man and beast alike. The handful of villages scattered around the Dearthwood rarely number more than 100 individuals. Trolls and ogres prowl the woods searching for elusive game animals or wayward humanoids. Small populations of goblins, hobgoblins, gnolls, and orcs also paradoxically band together in search of prey. Adventurers periodically poke around the Dearthwood's hills, which some believe are wild elf burial mounds dating back to the age when the Great Akadonian Forest covered much of the land.

REFERENCE SOURCE: THE LOST LANDS: SWORD OF AIR

THE DESOLATION

For two years, two massive armies waged a titanic struggle in and around the city of Tsar. Thousands of creatures — good and evil, mortal and extraplanar, abyssal and celestial — perished in this epic conflict. Carnage of this unspeakable magnitude leaves an indelible mark on the land. To inflict such mass casualties, both sides unleashed horrific new weapons against their foes. Potent spells, supernatural abilities, experimental technologies, and godlike powers sundered flesh, bone, stone, and earth, laying waste to everything within their reach. More than 300 years have passed since the Battle of Tsar, yet even time cannot heal these wounds. The Desolation remains true to its name to this very day. It is an ashen, gray wasteland still desperately trying to recover from the hell rained down upon it.

The Desolation is bone dry save for the rare torrential downpour in late autumn. The breezes routinely whipping across the sere earth lift up tiny particles of dust and sand, leaving a noticeable gray haze in the air. Water is scarce, and the terrain is predominately flat and fallow. Any hills or other elevations were likely blasted into oblivion during the great battle, though the Stoneheart Escarpment to the Desolation's west remains intact.

Although the landscape seems monotonous, the handful of explorers who trekked across the Desolation divided it into four quadrants roughly corresponding to the east-west and north-south roads bisecting it. The southeastern quadrant is the bleakest of the four. Ash covers every square inch of ground, and undead monstrosities left behind from the battle freely walk the earth. A vast canyon fills the northeastern quadrant. Numerous caves cut into the walls of this obviously unnatural gorge harbor strange creatures and frightening abominations presumably summoned from the depths of the Abyss. The northwestern quadrant features a pockmarked landscape that witnessed the fiercest fighting during the Battle of Tsar. Countless geysers, craters, pits, and boiling pools of mud and sulfur scar this portion of the Desolation. Although water is more plentiful than elsewhere in the Desolation, toxins contaminate the overwhelming majority of water sources. Bizarre creatures formed from desecrated earth haunt this steamy domain. War reduced the formerly fertile southwestern quadrant into a hardened crust of dry earth teeming with the bones of the dead. It is nearly impossible to walk across the solidified ground without stepping on decomposed or mummified remains. While many still lie underfoot, a significant portion of the departed still walk the earth as vengeful apparitions or shambling corpses.

The only humanoid settlement of note within the Desolation is the Camp, a wild, rowdy place on the road passing through the barren wasteland. Before Tsar's fall, the vital trade route linked the isthmus with Foere. Indeed, the evil city reaped a tremendous windfall levying tariffs on goods and commodities passing through its territory. Once again, renewed interest in reopening this overland highway has rekindled interest in exploring the Desolation and clearing out any monstrous inhabitants who would threaten this endeavor.

REFERENCE SOURCE: THE SLUMBERING TSAR SAGA

DRAGON HILLS

The Dragon Hills span a section of the eastern coast of Akados south of Glaivr and Elise and north of the Shorsai Forest, and stretch from the ruins of Tsar and the Desolation to the west to the shattered remains of Oxibbul to the north. The hills are generally scrubland with a few trees dotting the slopes. Large rocky outcrops and eroded gullies pockmarking the landscape impede travel, especially vehicular traffic. The Dragon Hills derived their name from the two families of dragons who dwell here, one blue and one green. Fortunately for the hills' other inhabitants,

the covetous monsters spend their waking hours trying to steal treasure from their rival family or better yet, slay one of their adversaries in the process. Trolls, ogres, gnolls, goblinoids, orcs, and dire animals infest the Dragon Hills in surprisingly large numbers as well. Glaivr and Elise send out armed patrols into the hills to keep these creatures' numbers in check and simultaneously monitor the activities of the dragons who periodically raid livestock from the towns' farmers and ranchers.

The Dragon Hills contiguously stretch to the boundaries of the Shorsai Forest, yet the dragon's hegemony over the land roughly ceases just past the midway point between its northern and southern borders. The Kingdom of Acregor rules over much of the Dragon Hills, exerting its influence over its domain from the capital city of Aranost — other than the southern reaches, which are the hunting grounds of the dragons.

REFERENCE SOURCE: THE LOST LANDS: SWORD OF AIR

ENG WOOD

Loggers and trappers from the neighboring riverbanks as well as Glaivr frequently venture into this deciduous forest teeming with plant and animal life. Birches, oaks, and walnuts are the most common trees, though numerous other species flourish alongside these stalwarts. Game animals are also in abundance, with deer and rabbit topping the list. Small enclaves of orcs, hobgoblins, goblins, and kobolds also inhabitant the forest alongside a fiercely protective colony of elves, who defend the Eng Wood against any who would defile it. Fearful of the elves and unwanted attention from Glaivr, the badly outnumbered humanoids typically fight among themselves. They rarely attack woodsmen or hunters.

Although most people venture into the Eng Wood in pursuit of their livelihood, some trek into the forest seeking a mischievous leprechaun. According to the popular yet largely discredited story, the sly fey offers a lucky holy relic to anyone who can solve his riddle. In the tale, the trickster also claims the deity Mick O'Delving personally gave him the item for his assistance to a drunken halfling in need. The legend says the leprechaun lives in a small yet cozy cottage whose chimney bellows colorful orange smoke.

REFERENCE SOURCE: THE LOST LANDS: SWORD OF AIR

THE FINGERS

These tributaries of the Binjerin River subdivide into five smaller branches, thus earning the waterway its distinctive name. In like fashion, each bears the name of a digit on a human right hand. The Thumb portion points due south, followed in clockwise order by the Index, Middle, Ring, and Little Fingers. The predominately human population inhabiting this region dwells in small fishing villages and farming communities lining the banks of each of these shallow rivers. People living on the banks of the Thumb frequently venture into the neighboring Eng Wood or more distant Kurz Wood to harvest timber from these largely tranquil forests.

The Fingers' residents take great pride in their stretch of the river. They greet friends, family, and strangers alike by displaying the digit corresponding to the section of river they call home. For instance, a person dwelling along the banks of the Index Finger presents their index finger. Of course, gestures can have different meanings in other cultures. Therefore, these unconventional signals sometimes accidentally cause disagreements depending upon how the observer construes the outstretched finger. Despite their strong feelings about their homeland, most residents only playfully needle their rivals hailing from other tributaries.

Over the years, the Fingers have witnessed mass crossings, most notably when the surviving residents of Oxibbul fled across the rivers and established the towns of Glaivr and Elise to the south, and when humanoid tribes crossed the waterways several hundred years later to disappear into the Dragon Hills. Otherwise, the rivers witness little traffic other than loggers transporting timber down river for transport to distant markets and the occasional pleasure craft leisurely sailing atop the peaceful waterway.

FRENZIED CROSSING

This road once connected the Old North Road to Oxibbul, but after the latter's demise centuries ago, the thoroughfare turned southward toward the settlements of Carter's Ferry, Glaivr, Elise, and Cantyn Light, which were founded in the aftermath of Oxibbul's descent into chaos. The road primarily links the preceding settlements to the ports at Cantyn Light and the city of Apothasalos to the north. To protect their economic interests, Glaivr and Elise regularly dispatch patrols to protect overland commercial traffic and keep encroaching monsters and wild animals at bay. Despite their efforts, a band of outlaws sometimes dispossesses travelers of their goods and wealth. Locals refer to the group as the Dastardly Troupe, whom many believe originally hail from Glaivr based upon their expertise using trapping devices implanted just beneath the road's surface to ensnare creatures walking atop the Frenzied Crossing. A handful of residents even believe the bandits previously belonged to Glaivr's town guard. With the exception of these brigands, the road remains relatively safe save for the occasional rare encounter with orcs, goblins, hobgoblins, gnolls, or trolls.

THE GRAY FEN

Streams flow from the Stoneheart Mountains and drain into a low-lying basin east of the mountain range to create the Gray Fen, a dank wetland teeming with stagnant ponds layered with striated moss and clusters of hardy trees. The moderately alkaline environment supports numerous species of wild berries, carnivorous plants, and a healthy population of moose. The hobgoblins and dwarves from the neighboring strongholds sometimes venture onto the soggy terrain in pursuit of these massive beasts, though the Gray Fen's dangerous reputation dissuades many hunters from setting foot in this forsaken realm. Will-o'-wisps haunt these malodorous lands, feasting on the souls of the living who trespass into their territory. Marsh gas is also a constant menace along with mosquitoes and other insect pests who hound travelers at every turn in the Gray Fen. Humanoids who perish here often rise up from the muddy soil and assume an undead existence as partially mummified, waterlogged corpses.

The dwarves and hobgoblins alike believe many fugitives or conspirators fled into the watery morass to escape their pursuers and well-deserved justice. Rumors abound claiming these individuals founded a refuge within the fen for other individuals facing a similar predicament. Second- and thirdhand accounts describe the settlement reportedly known as Liberation as a wild, lawless mixed community of renegade dwarves, hobgoblins, and any other creatures seeking a new beginning far from civilization and the long arm of the law. Whether Liberation actually exists fuels heated debates in dwarven and hobgoblin circles, though no one has mustered enough courage to personally investigate the stories.

HAZED CANYON

Hydrothermal springs scattered around the base of a massive depression ringed by 300- to 600-foot-high cliffs continuously generate a hazy fog and keep temperatures within the basin at a balmy 90° Fahrenheit regardless of the season, time of day, or weather conditions. These warm waters form the river Harange, a swift-moving stream with dozens of small cataracts ranging in height from three to 12 feet. The water temperature in this hot river fluctuates between 100°–200° Fahrenheit. The Schindle River also courses through the area, but it is much cooler than its sweltering counterpart. The steamy vapors rising up from the springs and Harange obscure all vision in the area, especially along the rim, which is nearly impassable except for a treacherous path on the canyon's south side that ultimately leads to the bottom. However, few souls venture into the depths of the Hazed Canyon anymore. During its heyday, wealthy citizens from Tsen and Tsar visited the Tannesh Hot Springs and its reinvigorating baths for their reputed curative and rejuvenating properties. Loggers from Elise and even Glaivr ventured into the depression to hew the valuable teak and ironwood trees growing in the primordial forest in the Hazed Canyon's interior. Several citadels also lie at the bottom of the depression, though their architects and occupants are the subject of rampant speculation. Some believe the fugitive Duncan may reside within one of these complexes. Other stories claim a mad sorcerer built one of these towers to perform experiments

on steam technology. Legends also speak of two gargantuan beasts who skulk through the Hazed Canyon preying on the unwary.

REFERENCE SOURCE: THE LOST LANDS: SWORD OF AIR

ISLE OF THE BLESSED SERPENT

A warm southern current and the Tropic of Arden moderate the island's climate, keeping it constantly balmy and humid regardless of the season. These influences make the island's weather unpredictable and frightening. Torrential downpours can spontaneously erupt and roll across the sweltering forest in the blink of an eye. From shore, the Isle of the Blessed Serpent seems to be a tropical paradise with pristine sandy beaches, lush palm trees, swaths of arable farmland, and a dense jungle in its interior. Getting ashore can be perilous, however. The Great Serpent Reef surrounds the entire island save for a small breach in the living barrier on the northwest side of the island. The coral almost always tears through the hull or blocks the passage of any ship attempting to negotiate a path through or over the treacherous obstacle.

Those who reach the island encounter a primordial wilderness teeming with overgrown insects such as massive fire ants, beetles, dragonflies, and hordes of blood-sucking mosquitos. And, as the island's name suggests, many varieties of snakes, a substantial portion of which are poisonous. As a result, those few who do make the shore tend to spend little if any time on the island, which seems to be actively seeking to drive visitors away.

That being said, tales are told in the taverns along the wharves of Darnagal that lights are seen inland on the island at night, and sometimes, the ruins of stone towers can be seen through the forest canopy far inland.

Around the island, fish are plentiful, and many fishing boats come to the area to seek a full catch. If the winds begin to change, however, they head back to shore, since being blown upon the reefs would almost certainly be fatal.

KURZ WOOD

A mere stone's throw from nearby Glaivr, the Kurz Wood would likely qualify as the most heavily developed forest in the region. Sawmills line the Kurz Wood's northern perimeter, giving Glaivr's merchants easy access to its lucrative timber products. Trappers and loggers take up residence in small villages scattered throughout the forest's interior. Crude paths cutting through the undergrowth form a network of routes connecting the settlements to one another and the main road leading to Glaivr. The rugged men and women who live off the land in the Kurz Wood consider this stretch of wilderness safer than a typical city block in a bustling metropolis. Nonetheless, they are careful to avoid contact with the dryads who defend their sacred oaks and a band of centaurs who can be easily riled to anger. Despite peaceful outward appearances, some settlers have been expressing alarm over a rash of unsolved acts of sabotage against the forest's timber and fur industries. A growing number of trappers are complaining about someone or something destroying their traps, while the irate woodsmen gripe about missing equipment, dull saw blades, and frayed ropes. In each of these incidents, someone carved the likeness of a smiling rabbit with disproportionately large upright ears onto the nearby trees. The images perplex local residents and authorities alike who seem unsure what to make of these actions or speculate who or what could be behind them.

REFERENCE SOURCE: THE LOST LANDS: SWORD OF AIR

LONELY COAST

This stretch of shoreline on Legion's Bay earned its name after a wayward Boros trireme ran aground on the coast after escaping capture during the Battle of Hummaemidon. Other than this brief brush with history, the rocky, mostly uninhabited span of beach wallows in anonymity. Anglers who venture to this stretch of coastline hurl their baited hooks into the surf in the hopes of catching flounder or salmon bottom feeding on the sea bed. Divers occasionally visit the area searching for shipwrecks in the shallow waters around the Lonely

Coast. Those embarking in this risky endeavor must avoid the sea hags who dwell here, especially the wretch known as the Briny Mistress.

MERCHANT'S ROAD

Despite the name, the Hyperborean Empire built this ancient thoroughfare to facilitate military transport to the Pass of Hummaemidon and eventually to the Plains of Mayfurrow and Bard's Gate. The road fell into disrepair after the Hyperborean retreat but has experienced a recent resurgence since the proposed reopening of the trade route through the Desolation. The road links the city of Apothasalos to Bard's Gate via the Old North Road. Not surprisingly, the increased traffic along the long-abandoned route attracts attention from gnoll marauders and highwaymen looking for a quick score. Likewise, hucksters sometimes pose as soldiers from either city to collect tolls on the metropolis's behalf. Bard's Gate has been cracking down on this scam for several years, though frontier justice usually deals with this problem more effectively than the tedious court system ever could.

MOUNT MOFFAT

Nothing lives within 20 miles of this constantly belching volcano, which at 13,043 feet is unusually large for a cinder cone volcano. Mount Moffat continuously spews forth ash, toxic gases, and occasional lava, but its activity level presents a geological anomaly. It is too far from The Molten Flow or The Spine of Fire to be associated with those active volcanoes, which also differ in their structure and output. While the mountain could be a hotspot, scholars suspect the most likely explanation for its existence lies with an unnatural or supernatural cause. The general belief is that something stirs beneath the mountain, and it is likely associated with the forces that created the Stoneheart Mountains in the first place. The few souls who explored the mountain's inner workings found bizarre runes etched onto the stone walls and upside-down humanoid skeletons suspended from the ceiling by strange filaments wrapped around their ankles. Not surprisingly, these accounts dissuaded others from visiting the rocky behemoth. The tales date back several centuries. Therefore, it is impossible to tell whether the carvings and the killings represented current activities or were left behind by past civilizations.

THE NORTH CUT

This tributary of the Binjerin River has an average width of 30 feet and an average depth of 12 feet. Its crystal-blue waters cut a relatively straight path through the surrounding grasslands. Many species of salmon return to this river to spawn, which brings hungry predators such as bears and otters to these shores during these seasonal events. Numerous small fishing villages, wharfs, and piers also line the riverbank. These anglers compete with their bestial rivals for the proverbial catch of the day. The most prominent manmade structure on the largely pristine river is a bridge known as the Outstretched Hands. This unusual span crafted from cut stone and concrete resembles an arch with two interconnected, outstretched hands. Based upon its architectural design, most experts believe the Hyperboreans built the bridge. The most plausible explanation for its odd construction techniques lies with its intended purpose. Although obviously erected to span the river, its strange design suggests it represents a truce or a lasting peace between two forces on opposite sides of the river. While the forgotten ideals that birthed the bridge to life have been lost to the annals of time, it is still a popular destination for fishermen and most especially divers. Anyone who dives into the water and retrieves a scallop shell supposedly receives good luck for the next seven days. Only one in 50 tries ends in success.

OLD NORTH ROAD

Once a popular trade thoroughfare, the Old North Road hosts little traffic nowadays. It runs from Glendovel Close to the south and through the Desolation until it forks just past The Fingers into the Merchant's Road to the north and the Frenzied Crossing to the east. Naturally, the sharp decline in use has left the route in a state of neglect and disrepair.

Its popularity waned because of its passage through the dangerous and sparsely inhabited Desolation and its proximity to the hostile Kingdom of Acregor. Nonetheless, there has been some renewed interest in reopening the northern leg of the Old North Road passing through the environs around Tsar. A ramshackle settlement known as The Camp sits close to the road and acts as a gateway to the wasteland beyond it. These efforts aside, the Old North Road witnesses a disproportionate number of muggings, robberies, and attacks committed by a cast of characters ranging from bandits and orc raiders to Orcus' deranged minions and fantastical creatures rarely seen in Akados.

OXIBBUL

In 8 I.R., the Hyperborean legions founded the city of Occibolos at a strategic location at the convergence of the Binjerin River, the North Cut, and an overland roadway. The city rapidly expanded over the course of the next several years from a frontier settlement to a bustling trade hub. Occibolos' prosperity naturally attracted the interest of the invading Hundaei who poured across the Stoneheart Mountains and into Hyperborean lands. After withstanding several sieges, the city finally fell to the invaders in 494 I.R. The Hundaei burned the settlement and razed most of its structures to the ground. Occibolos sat vacant and unwanted for the next 1,000 years until 1494 I.R. when refugees from the surrounding area resettled the abandoned city. Its new occupants christened the settlement with a name — Oxibbul. Less than 10 years later, wizards fleeing the cataclysm at Tsen established the Gray Tower as a magical academy and guild hall. For the next three centuries, Oxibbul flourished in the shadow of the mystical structure. However, orcs and goblinoids from the Black Forest launched a wave of attacks against the city. The assaults continued almost unabated for the next century until even the mighty wizards could no longer hold back the surging tide. The remaining settlers and the wizards abandoned Oxibbul in 1915 I.R. Many retreated across the Fingers and established the towns of Elise and Glaivr.

The unenterprising orcs and hobgoblins rested on their predecessors' labors and allowed the town to slowly and steadily decay until it was no longer habitable, even by their lowly standards. By 2390 I.R., the utterly deserted Oxibbul lay in ruins. It remained that way until 2599 I.R. when the Kingdom of Foere rebuilt portions of the city while also temporarily restoring its original name of Occibolos. The revitalized town enjoyed a fleeting revival before petering out again when the Kingdom of Foere's power waned decades later. By 2880 I.R., Oxibbul regained its former name and status as a desolate, ruined settlement bereft of inhabitants.

Oxibbul's ideal location at the crossroads of several important trade routes would seem to bolster its fortunes as a settlement, yet time and again the city inevitably decayed into rubble. The descendants of its former residents now living in Glaivr and Elise swear the ruins must be cursed. Some ancient chronicles claim the Hyperboreans who first laid Oxibbul's foundations felt nervous and uneasy while excavating the site. An ancient tapestry depicts the first builders accidentally disinterring skeletal remains dipped into molten lead. According to legend, everyone depicted in the artwork mysteriously died less than one week later as blood relentlessly poured out of their swollen eye sockets. If the tale is true, the whereabouts and identity of the skeleton wrapped in lead remain unsolved. Likewise, its history and its relationship to the city are still shrouded in mystery.

PASS OF HUMMAEMIDON

On this hilly grassland, the legions of Hyperborea and Boros clashed in a climactic battle that forever changed Akados. After a titanic struggle, the Hyperboreans earned their independence and laid the foundations of their empire. On this day, the humans and the high elf descendants of the wild elves of the Green Realm reconciled. The alliance between men and elves put one old grudge to rest, but the actions of the Hyperborean legions gave birth to an enmity that still endures after 3,500 years. In an act known as the Great Betrayal, the dwarves' human allies turned against their former friends. The horrific slaughter ended only when the last mountain dwarf fell at the hands of their human betrayers. Although numerous generations have come and gone since this fateful day, the mountain dwarves never forgot nor forgave the traitorous act.

The passage of time has not erased these old memories nor the scars from the land. To this day, salvagers periodically unearth metal fragments, old bones, and other personal effects from the freshly tilled soil. Hobgoblins, hill giants, or ogres sometimes interrupt these excavations while hunting or scavenging for scraps themselves. Worse yet, the restless spirits of the mountain dwarves who perished in the battle refuse to let death inhibit their thirst for revenge. These angry souls take their ire out against any humans, half-elves, or elves who cross their path. While vengeance seems to be their primary goal, scattered firsthand accounts also report seeing these undead monstrosities actively seeking something buried underneath the ancient battlefield. Their objective remains unknown, though some of the witnesses claim to hear the apparitions utter the word "Dweram." No such word exists in the Dwarven language, which leads many to believe it may be a proper name or a contraction of two or more separate words.

SHORSAI FOREST

A remnant of the oldest forests in all of Akados, this primeval woodland once belonged to the Great Akadonian Forest in ancient times. A dense canopy of tightly-clustered deciduous trees keeps the forest immersed in twilight throughout the daytime hours while plunging the forest into pitch darkness when night falls. The tangle of protruding tree limbs, branches, and undergrowth covering the forest floor greatly impede travel through the woodland. Once, long ago, the ancestors of the elves, newly arrived in the world, lived in this area. While there may be remains in the deep forest of the elven domain, today the forest is given over entirely to evil humanoids and patches of forest haunted by dark things that even frighten the orcs and goblins.

Throughout the forest, various humanoid tribes, including bands of orcs and gnolls, vie for supremacy over their small fiefdoms. Recently, however, envoys from Acregor arrived in the forest seeking to bring the tribes under the banner of Aranost.

A small, 50-foot-wide waterway meanders through the Shorsai Forest from the Dragon Hills. It is never a swift stream, and it breaks into many small distributaries before finally reaching the shores of the Gulf of Akados in a boggy area of forest.

STARCRAG FOOTHILLS

The Starcrag Foothills, like the nearby Starcrag Range, fall outside the dominion of the great mountain dwarf clans who rule over the balance of the Stoneheart Mountains.

Instead of dwarves, roving bands of hobgoblins infest caves burrowing into this range of hills, some of which are oddly shaped. Some scholars speculate that the strange configurations may not be of natural origin. The most prevalent theory implies they are Hyperborean or Hundaei burial mounds, though several excavations in the region have yielded no evidence of any ancient tombs. The hobgoblins inhabiting the area pay titular fealty to the masters of Exor, Smashed Skull, and Bone Hollow in the nearby mountains. Although a handful of hobgoblin outlaws still roam the area seeking recruits to further their ambitions to reclaim their former glory or establish a new hobgoblin dynasty, the vast majority of these individuals are the descendants of deserters, fugitives, and mutineers. An aggressive and slightly unbalanced hobgoblin named Hroggar currently seeks recruits for just such a cause. The traitorous Hroggar foolishly attempted to stage a coup against King Teth Khan of Exor. The ill-conceived plot quickly unraveled and left the rebellious hobgoblin and his loyalists in a tricky spot. Hroggar fled in the aftermath of the catastrophe; his followers were not as lucky. The last sensation they experienced was the executioner's cold steel blade slicing through their outstretched necks.

REFERENCE SOURCE: THE LOST LANDS: SWORD OF AIR

STONEHEART ESCARPMENT

These sheer cliffs protrude from the Stoneheart Mountains in a roughly convex shape to form the backdrop for the temple-city of Tsar. Portions of the metropolis consist of terraces cut into the base of the mountain at varying elevations. The escarpment is surprisingly uniform for what is presumed to be a natural topographical feature with a consistent height of 5,500 feet and almost completely vertical, smooth surfaces. Even an experienced mountaineer faces a tremendous challenge attempting to scale up or rappel down these treacherous cliffs. The Southern Pass is the only negotiable path through the escarpment, though the route feels like a tricky spiral staircase in some stretches. Even worse, many believe any remaining guardians left behind in Tsar still keep a watchful eye on the formidable yet not impassable rocky barrier. According to the lyrics of *The Dirge of Gerrant*, a popular ballad, the Stoneheart Escarpment contains a secret passage that leads directing into the dungeons beneath where the Citadel of Orcus once stood in nearby Tsar.

TOWER OF ACREGOR

The Tower of Acregor was originally constructed for Acregor Ironclaw, the half-troll king of Acregor who first unified the humanoid tribes of the Dragon Hills. He intended it to be his burial monument.

Built of white marble, the blocks for the tower were scavenged from the ruins of the elven city of Aranost. Though now nearly 1,000 years old, it seems brand new. The tower itself is 50 feet tall and has no windows and only a single entrance — a pair of massive doors carved from ivory. No tales are told of what may be inside the tower. It is, in fact, unknown if Acregor is even buried here, as the chaos after his assassination left the fulfilment of any such plans in doubt.

TSAR

For centuries, Tsar embodied evil and hate. Orcus, the demon prince of the undead, delights in leading the righteous down the path of corruption, and the circumstances surrounding the genesis of Tsar are no different. The city began its existence more than 4,000 years ago as St. Harul's Hold, a bastion of good that housed the High Altars of Thyr and Muir. For centuries thereafter, the holy place, now known simply as St. Harul's, drew pilgrims from throughout Akados, including Polemarch Oerson who bestowed gifts upon its patriarch when the Hyperboreans first arrived in Akados. However, St. Harul's virtuous façade concealed a terrible secret. Over the course of several hundred years, the disciples of Orcus steadily infiltrated the shrine's political and ecclesiastical hierarchy like a malignant cancer. The end came in 2462 I.R. when Tam Xaverik, a clandestine priest of Orcus, became the Protector of the Hold. In less than 10 years, Tam successfully wiped away all remaining vestiges of Thyr and Muir including their clergy and followers, and renamed the debased city Tsarul.

Within a century, the small shrine and town expanded into a festering metropolis. Like a siren's call, the great temple city beckoned foul beings of all sorts into its diabolical embrace, including hordes of humanoid tribes from the Dragon Hills and hosts of evil men and monsters from every corner of Akados. There, in its wicked arms, Tsar sucked every iota of goodness and compassion from its subjects until only darkness and malevolence dwelt within the being's loathsome heart. At its center stood the great Citadel of Orcus, the epicenter of demonic worship in the mortal world. Within its wicked confines, the demon prince's deranged worshippers committed heinous atrocities and schemed to unleash even greater horrors against all who defied their master's baleful call.

Despite its stain upon the world, the great empires of Akados and beyond cast their eyes away from the terrible blight tainting their lands for hundreds of years. The Grand Cornu, Orcus' earthly representative, grew rich and complacent from their collective apathy and malaise. He levied stiff tariffs against goods passing over the roads crossing through his lands to the east. With the aid of the indigenous non-humanoid tribes, he established a foothold at a southern port to further expand his influence. It seemed no one would dare to challenge the Grand Cornu's machinations — until an opportunity for revenge reared its head.

Keen for a chance to settle the score for expelling them from St. Harul's centuries earlier, the weakened yet still potent churches of Thyr and Muir gathered a delegation of good- and neutral-aligned faiths to petition the newly-crowned Overking Graeltor to lead a crusade against Tsar. Buoyed by the success of his predecessor's crusade and Tsar's growing threat to the lucrative trade routes between the Isthmus and Foere, the new monarch assembled his own military force he dubbed the Army of Light. In 3208 I.R., Zelkor, a powerful archmage who served as Graeltor's most trusted advisor, led the Army of Light out of Bard's Gate to march against Tsar.

Zelkor's forces punched through Tsar's outer defenses, laying the land and the enemy to waste in horrific fashion. After a year of ferocious battles, the Army of Light now stood in sight of their goal — the depraved city of Tsar. The forces of good besieged the metropolis for months without any breakthroughs and a tremendous loss of life on both sides of the walls. Reinforcements from the depths of the Abyss continuously poured into Tsar, while celestial beings bolstered the ranks of Zelkor's demoralized army. Then without warning, the Grand Cornu and the entirety of Tsar's defenders inexplicably vanished from the city. When Zelkor caught sight of the force behind the Army of Light, he pursued Orcus' disciples into the Forest of Hope, where both sides were never seen nor heard from again.

Meanwhile, the paladin Bishu and a small contingent of knights entered the abandoned city, encountering only sporadic resistance on their way to the Citadel of Orcus. When they entered the demon prince's earthly stronghold, the structure inexplicably disappeared into nothingness, presumably taking Bishu and his cohorts with it. All that remained of Tsar and Orcus' minions were a handful of stragglers and the sundered ruins of a broken and abandoned city. While Graeltor could theoretically claim victory over Tsar, the heavy price in men and materiel left Foere in disarray. The Hyperborean monarchy of the Foerdewaith soon collapsed under the heavy weight of rebellion spurred primarily by the crusade's tremendous costs when measured in spent resources and lost lives.

Although Tsar technically had been defeated, few ventured to the shattered metropolis to claim the spoils of victory. The confrontation between the Army of Light and the minions of Orcus transformed Tsar and its surroundings into a desolate wasteland. Furthermore, many terrifying mysteries remained. No one could explain what happened to the Citadel of Orcus, the Army of Light, and the demonic hordes they chased into the Forest of Hope. For the most part, Tsar remains unchanged from that fateful day. Although some monstrous denizens streamed into the city to dwell amid the rubble and some guardians remain sequestered somewhere within the city, the settlement is now a far cry from its former, inglorious self. Rumors persist that many of Orcus' devotees still reside in the undercity below the broken streets and razed buildings. Others believe an even more ancient force predating all recorded history and legend played a role in deciding the battle's outcome for better or worse. Regardless of the truth, only the hardiest adventurers even dream of making the long, arduous slog to Tsar's desecrated ruins.

STONEHEART MOUNTAINS

Known as the Spine of the World in many circles, the Stoneheart Mountains stretch from the frozen Northlands to the north to the outskirts of cosmopolitan Bard's Gate to the south. Despite their impressive size, the mountain range is relatively new, having been magically raised atop the Keltine Barrier roughly 10,000 years ago. Most of the range's formidable peaks reach heights of 14,000 feet and higher, though the summits of many mountains in the northern and central portions of the range climb into the proverbial death zone of 26,000 feet, with the highest exceeding 30,000 feet. At these dizzying heights, temperatures routinely dip far below the freezing point. Few creatures can withstand the low oxygen levels and frigid temperatures in these areas, leaving them sparsely inhabited. Dense glaciers, sometimes hundreds of feet thick, cover the slopes and summits of the tallest peaks. Below these heights, sheep, oryxes, llamas, and other animals adapted to life at elevation thrive in this rocky, arid environment.

Mountain dwarves are the most dominant military and political force in the Stoneheart Mountains, though the hobgoblins occupying the citadels along the eastern edge of the Stoneheart Mountains and the neighboring Starcrag Mountains also vie for supremacy. Several dwarven clans hold sway over this vast region, with Clan Craenog being generally recognized as the strongest and most influential of these, though the other clans would certainly disagree. Although none of the mountain dwarves hold humans and elves in high regard, several of these clans at least tolerate their former adversaries.

In the northern regions of the Stonehearts, the only vestiges of civilization are a handful of small mountain dwarf villages, hobgoblin enclaves, and goblin cave complexes. Ogres, trolls, yetis, and other monstrous denizens also inhabit these tall, frozen peaks. Clan Tusov wields nominal control over the northern section of the Stoneheart Mountains, though its influence wanes significantly outside the friendly confines of their capital city of Icarros.

The more hospitable portions of the central Stoneheart Mountains host numerous mountain dwarf villages and goblinoid settlements. The territories of four mountain dwarf clans overlap across this area. Clan Duhnbeyl rules over the Spine of Fire and portions of the Vingotha and Telegotha Plateaus. After centuries of civil disturbances and political machinations, this resurgent clan's power is rapidly spreading from the epicenter of Halmarr, its political capital. Clan Koth wields its magical and technological might over the western Stoneheart Mountains. These dwarves seem content with their holdings, striving to maintain the status quo rather than confronting neighboring clans. Clan Craenog stands on the frontline against the hobgoblin citadels of Exor, Bonehollow, and Smashed Skull. From its strategic vantage point of Erod Flan, Clan Craenog boasts the largest and most experienced military force in the Stoneheart Mountains. They also claim the Feirgotha Plateau and most of the Eragotha Plateau for their own. After their expulsion from the Shengotha Plateau 500 years ago, Clan Krazzadak's foothold in the central Stoneheart Mountains has substantially diminished. Other than its capital city of Abad Durahai, the clan tenuously clings to a few isolated towns and villages scattered throughout the region. Despite Clan Krazzadak's decline in the central Stoneheart Mountains, this clan dominates the southern Stoneheart Mountains. Only the cities of Dun Eamon and Alesardin rival their power in this region. The former community on the western edge of the Stoneheart Mountains boasts a predominately human population while the latter city of Alesardin is almost exclusively inhabited by the svirfneblin.

Warfare is a near constant reality throughout much of the Stoneheart Mountains. Goblins and hobgoblins almost perpetually struggle against their mountain dwarf neighbors for supremacy. Although rival clans are apt to fight each other when an ideal opportunity presents itself, a loose alliance exists among the mountain dwarves. Secret "high-ways" carved into the highest elevations serve as clandestine networks to connect the cities and towns of opposing clans. So-called "low-ways" cut below the ground link the individual clans' citadels together. However, goblins and hobgoblins are not the only creatures to menace the indigenous dwarves. Old myths and legends claim the Stoneheart Mountains themselves are not just inanimate earth and stone. The tales say the mountains are living entities with minds of their own. Other stories speak of long-forgotten deities waging a titanic struggle against an unspeakable evil on the land that eventually became the Stoneheart Mountains. In this version, the divine being's dying essence coalesced into the rocks that form the chain. Not surprisingly, adventurers frequently scour the mountains searching for evidence to support one or more of these theories, though to date, no one has found anything to substantiate these accounts.

The Stoneheart Mountains
dowlands
Eastern Akados and the Stoneheart Mountains
Ognari Lands
Worgwoods
High Karst
Tanomir Fens
The Froz
The Hyperborean Way
Vindelsalven River
Blue Escarpmen
Grand Portage
Lake Hargos
Osen's Seep
Tribes
of K.
Shimmering River
Londhargo Tribes
Burgotha Plateau
Icarros
Kroaksenk
Zuxaca Canyon
Kallistrad
Mount Daergyd
The Molten Hook
Xanges River
The Black Fields
Telgotha Plateau
Halmarn
Vingotha Plateau
The Spire of Fire
Tanuil
Legionnaire Bridge
T'se
Mt. Moffat
Starcrag Range
Pass of Hummaemidon
Ghue Island
Bun
Gap
Coursguard
Wanabeeh
Durgam's Folly
ss Tower
Rock
d's Wall
Gap
od
Eagotha Plat
tha Plateau
Toth
Gray Fen
Exon
Smashed Skull
Bone Hollow
Deathmrook
Starcrag Foothills
Merchant's Road
rth Cut
Black Forest
Lonely Co
Legions Bay
Karedor

Legend
● Town or Village
◉ City
✪ Capital or Free City
✸ Imperial Capital
■ Fortress or Citadel
⋮ Ruins
▲ Place of Interest
〜 Road
⌢ Trail or Unused Road
⋯ Mountain Pass
✕ Battlefield

Political Subdivisions of the Stoneheart Mountains

Abad Durahai, City of

Ruler: Thorgrim Firebeard, the King in Exile
Government: monarchy
Population: 26,094 (25,684 mountain dwarf, 410 gnome) (city); 38,200 mountain dwarf in surrounding mountains
Monstrous: small populations of svirfneblin, minotaurs, and goblins (within the mines); dragons, giants, goblinoids, orcs, ogres, svirfneblin, wolves, wyvern (mountains)
Languages: Dwarven, Gnomish
Religion: Barator, Dwerfater (though many are agnostic)
Resources: mining, fungi
Currency: mixed
Technology Level: Medieval, Renaissance

Today, Abad Durahai is the capital of the dwarven Clan Krazzadak and the most populous settlement in the Stoneheart Mountains. For much of its existence, however, it was a bit of a backwater on the outskirts of the Shengotha Plateau. Then, 500 years ago, the snows came and buried the Shengotha Plateau and the old capital of Bryn Tuk Thull under a glacier of ice 500 feet deep. The dwarves were forced to flee what became known as the Stoneheart Ice Plateau, with many seeking refuge in Abad Durahai, the nearest Krazzadak settlement.

The architects who transformed the rapidly expanding Abad Durahai from a small community into a bustling city incorporated the cavern's natural stone walls into their plans, while using dwarf-made devices to further subdivide the space into smaller structures and buildings. Stone doors encased in bronze and embossed with mithral and silver grant access to the city proper. Networks of tunnels branch out from the main city and burrow into the rock and stone beneath Abad Durahai.

History and People

Abad Durahai was founded approximately 3,000 years ago by a family of Clan Krazzadak. Arriving from their nearby homeland in the Shengotha Plateau, they found a complex of natural caverns, and, more importantly, a vein of mithral. Many came here to mine, and soon it was a small but growing community.

When the glacier came to the Shengotha Plateau, Abad Durahai was a natural place for refugees to head. It was far too small to house so many, however, so architects quickly set to designing an expansion of the natural caverns, planning a much larger city and citadel. Tunnels and chambers were dug and soon filled with those seeking refuge, at first temporarily, but they soon settled in and became permanent residents.

The last king of Clan Krazzadak was lost with the coming of the ice, so a new king was declared from among the surviving royalty. The new king, Argrim Longhair, provided the leadership the shocked and stricken dwarves desperately needed, and soon their new capital was a thriving community. Argrim's grandson Thorgrim is the current king, or as the dwarves say, the King in Exile, as they intend one day to return to Bryn Tuk Thull and reclaim their legacy and homeland.

Despite the clan's perseverance, the many hardships heaped upon these dwarves give them a glum disposition and a suspicious outlook toward others.

Religion

The Battle of Hummaemidon and the destruction of their homeland on the Shengotha Plateau causes many of Abad Durahai's residents to take a lackadaisical approach to religion. Among trusted company, some dwarves sarcastically quip that "they will give to the gods, what the gods gave them — nothing." Nonetheless, roughly half of the city's dwarves still pay homage to their patron deities. Foremost of these is Barator, the God of the Forge. While this lost god has fallen out of favor with the other dwarven clans, the Krazzadaks maintain a strong affinity for him. Indeed, Abad Durahai hosts the god's exalted high altar.

TRADE AND COMMERCE

With hostile neighbors to the north and south, Abad Durahai's commercial partners remain limited. The city's mines produce significant quantities of diamonds and mithral as well as iron and silver ore that they export to other dwarven clans or to merchants in Bard's Gate. Unlike most of the great mountain clans, the dwarves of Clan Krazzadak deal directly with humans and other humanoids when absolutely necessary, though they still prefer dealing with non-human middlemen when possible. In addition to selling raw materials, Abad Durahai's craftsmen enjoy a stellar reputation among the buying public. Weapons and armor forged in the Temple of Barator rank among the most coveted in all of Akados. Many circles refer to these valuable items as "Durahai Steel." Genuine products fetch a handsome price in many cities and towns throughout Akados, though their value also spurs counterfeiters to manufacture cheap knockoffs of the real article.

DIPLOMACY

Over the past five centuries, Abad Durahai has engaged in multiple skirmishes with the svirfneblin city of Alesardin to the south and the barbegazi to the north. Some residents refer to this geopolitical stalemate as the "Gnomish Vice," a reference to being sandwiched between two factions of equally devious gnomish offshoots. Not surprisingly, the dwarves of Abad Durahai have no love for gnomes of any ilk and hold them in equal disregard as humans. While the dwarves can muster a far greater military force than either of their potential opponents, they are also reluctant to fight these foes on their terms in their own backyards. Abad Durahai's leadership is content to maintain the status quo on these fronts rather than go to war against either adversary.

King Thorgrim enjoys widespread popularity within Clan Krazzadak, though the same cannot be said for their ambivalent relations with Clan Craenog. The King in Exile endeavors to change this situation, but his diplomatic efforts have generated little progress on this front. A handful of voices within his court suggests normalizing relations with Bard's Gate. However, this tiny minority never presses the issue beyond a few comments about the potential economic benefits of such an arrangement. If the mood sours, the person immediately drops the matter. To date, the king shows no signs of softening his stances toward humans — or any other non-dwarves for that matter.

GOVERNMENT

Abad Durahai serves as Clan Krazzadak's capital city. From his seat of power atop the Mithral Throne, King Thorgrim Firebeard rules over the clan's holdings in the southern and western portions of the Stoneheart Mountains. His territory includes the range's southern tip as well as the lands due east and west of the Stoneheart Ice Plateau. Entering his 150th year, the charismatic and seasoned leader exudes a palpable aura of confidence and strength. He carefully deliberates on most decisions with input from the six-member council of appointed advisors and administrators known as the Mithral Seats. These individuals manage the city's daily affairs from its most vital operations to its mundane matters.

King Thorgrim governs in a stern yet fair manner. The monarch personally presides over all civil and criminal matters within the city. Thorgrim enjoys a strong reputation for honesty and impartiality. However, he rarely shows mercy when rendering a judgment or passing sentence. In his mind, logic, reason, and the letter of the law take precedence over personal feelings. His harsh attitude spurs some grumbling among the friends and families of the aggrieved, yet so far no one has openly spoken against the city's ruler.

MILITARY

For a city of its size, Abad Durahai's troop strength is comparatively small. In an emergency, the king can field an army of roughly 1,800 trained and experienced soldiers. However, only 600 soldiers are typically on active duty at any time. The city instead devotes much of its energy and industry to supporting each individual soldier with the best instruction and technological advancements rather than mass producing equipment and conscripting desperate young men and women. Clan Krazzadak believes one highly skilled, motivated, and well-equipped infantryman is worth more than 10 frightened, poorly-armed civilians pressed into service. Equally adept at close-quarters fighting with an axe or firing a crossbow from a distance, a dwarf in the king's service is a versatile killing machine. During their last major engagement with the svirfneblin in 3508 I.R. at the Skirmish of the Iron Intersection, King Thorgrim's charges killed 88 deep gnomes while sustaining only 14 casualties in a pitched subterranean battle.

MAJOR THREATS

Abad Durahai need not look far to find enemies at its gates. The svirfneblin city of Alesardin relishes an opportunity for revenge against their hated foes. Turning north, the dwarves would conversely jump at the opportunity to land a devastating blow to the barbegazi inhabiting their former homeland on the Shengotha Plateau or exact some retribution against the ice gnomes. Human incursions as well as territorial disputes with Clan Craenog also periodically challenge Clan Krazzadak's hegemony over the region.

ALESARDIN, CITY OF

Ruler: Council of Mystics
Government: oligarchy
Population: 5,596 svirfneblin
Languages: Gnomish (svifneblin)
Religion: unknown
Resources: trade, magic, mining
Currency: mixed
Technology Level: Medieval, Renaissance

The origins of Alesardin are known only to the deep gnomes who live there, and they do not tell outsiders. The dwarves of Abad Durahai say the city can be found in their records dating back at least 2,000 years.

Most deep gnomes, or svirfneblin, are of a relatively neutral outlook. Those of Alesardin are different, however. They are of a more sinister disposition, and it is said they worship dark deities in their mountain halls. They continually war with their dwarven neighbors and have been said to have sought alliances with other powers of evil in the world. Why the deep gnomes here are different is unknown, but some suspect something within the lowest reaches of their city is the source.

Fortunately, the numbers of svirfneblin in Alesardin are too small to pose a true threat to Abad Durahai, though this has not stopped them from the occasional raid or attack on a dwarven party in the mountains too close to their city. They also send agents to human settlements such as Bard's Gate for purposes that remain mysterious.

The city itself has portions both above and below ground. The architecture is elegant, though in a somber fashion. Dark colors with small, shining highlights, usually from gemstones, predominate. Trade is mainly with races found within the mountains, some far deeper than the halls of Alesardin. The city has a bustling central market, cosmopolitan residential districts, and a flourishing academy for magical research. There is great peril for outsiders, however; unless they have been invited, the xenophobic svirfneblin attack visitors on sight.

Rulership of the city is held by a council of mystics from the academy, where they use magic to divine portents and make sinister plans against the dwarves and folk of the surface.

BURVAADUN, GARRISON OF

This remote garrison lies on the frigid southeastern corner of the Feirgotha Plateau where it overlooks the Southern Pass. Although Clan Craenog publicly insists the installation serves a vital defensive purpose, the neglected fortress serves as a proving ground for exiles and misfits seeking redemption or anonymity. Its commander Foran Rockfeller oversees a meager force of 40 mountain dwarves, which includes 15 marginally-trained and equipped conscripts. Varus Broadshield, the garrison's resident cleric of Dwerfater, tends to the soldiers' spiritual and personal needs within the Temple of Dwerfater's welcoming confines. Varus' comforting words and divine inspiration could not come at a better time as the besieged garrison has witnessed an unexpected uptick of undead activity presumably originating from the long dormant Library of Arcady several miles away.

Erod Flan, Citadel of

Ruler: High Thane Kaelan
Government: monarchy
Population: 11,505 (11,200 mountain dwarf, 305 gnome) (city); 16,200 mountain dwarf in surrounding mountains
Monstrous: dragons, giants, goblinoids, orcs, ogres, svirfneblin, wolves, wyvern
Languages: Dwarven, Gnomish
Religion: Dwerfater
Resources: mining
Currency: mixed
Technology Level: Medieval, Renaissance

The dwarven citadel of Erod Flan functions as a military installation and the seat of power for Clan Craenog, the dominant political force in the region. The stronghold's first construction phase consisted of a fortified keep and a reinforced perimeter wall. The city rapidly expanded over the next several decades in response to the escalating threats from the neighboring Kingdom of Arcady to the west and the hobgoblins to the east. Fortunately for the dwarves, the two rivals turned against each other, ultimately resulting in their annihilation. Nonetheless, Erod Flan has successfully repulsed six hobgoblin assaults during its long, illustrious history, the most recent taking place shortly after King Kroma's disappearance at the Battle of Tsar.

Under the rulership of High Thane Kaelan, the clan's influence stretches across much of the central Stoneheart Mountains. The citadel sits atop an elongated mesa roughly 7,500 feet above sea level that grants its defenders an ideal vantage point for observing the area surrounding the secure fortress. In addition to its elevation and panoramic view, Erod Flan's defenses are impressive. Sheer rock walls and cliffs make up much of the slope surrounding the elevated structure. Two mountain passes grant access to the dwarven citadel through the rugged terrain, though these routes are intentionally winding with numerous tight turns, twists, and narrow stretches designed to prevent an enemy from lugging siege equipment close to its gates and walls.

To enforce his rule, the thane has an army of 2,500 disciplined professional soldiers at his disposal as well as an auxiliary force of 1,000 crossbowmen and swordsmen. In addition to asserting their authority over other mountain dwarf clans, Erod Flan's military also safeguards the region against the hobgoblins from Exor, Bonehollow, and Smashed Skull. While Kaelan's mind is up to the challenges, his frail body is in no condition to lead a campaign against the dwarves' many enemies. These tasks fall upon his older son Thron, who is also his likely successor, and Minchain Redash, the captain of Erod Flan's guards. Both men realize not all of the dwarves' threats are external. Matters of succession can be dodgy within the clan, as Kaelan's two brothers and Thron's younger sibling could lay claim to the throne when Kaelan passes into the next world. Kaelan's father Om experienced the same intrigue when he ascended to the throne following the death of his father Kroma two centuries earlier. Om's boorish cousin Garnock vigorously protested being passed over for his more capable younger cousin. Despite his brooding, the clan almost unanimously accepted Om as its leader. Still, the passage of time has failed to quell rumors of discontent simmering in some circles regarding Garnock's claims.

More recently, tales are swirling about clandestine activities in the sealed quartz mines beneath the city. Sixty years earlier, Kaelan himself led an expedition into the tunnels to root out the dark folk some say

may be making a resurgence along with their grimlock servants. The inherently xenophobic dwarves also cast a wary eye upon the small community of gnomes living within their capital. The dwarves respect their smaller humanoid counterparts for the remarkable ingenuity and technological prowess, though they never fully trust them.

In addition to its status as a military complex, Erod Flan also features many of the amenities found in a typical metropolis. Within its protective walls, farmers grow crops and raise livestock. Granaries store vast quantities of food in preparation for a protracted war or siege. Merchants, craftsmen, and professionals sell their wares and services in a bustling marketplace, while the soldiers sworn to defend Erod Flan reside in two massive barracks complexes on its grounds. Twelve taverns serve the needs of the city's population and provide accommodations for its infrequent visitors. Erod Flan's small gnomish quarter also produces and sells alchemical substances and a host of other curious odds and ends to various customers. The high thane and his family occupy a keep in the city's southeastern corner. Although primarily a residence, the keep also functions as an administrative and religious center. High Thane Kaelan also doubles as a cleric of Dwerfater, though his infirmity severely limits his ecclesiastical duties.

The dwarves inhabiting the small villages and settlements scattered throughout the region surrounding Erod Flan almost universally share some lineage with Clan Craenog. Although many of these common ancestors date back several generations, even the tiniest drop of blood from a distant, common relative cements the bonds of fraternity among members of Clan Craenog. These dwarves sometimes skirmish against the other dwarven clans surrounding them and the hobgoblin or orc marauders.

REFERENCE SOURCE: MOUNTAINS OF MADNESS

Halmarr (The Caldera)

Ruler: The Mountain Hammer Talcum Duhnbeyl
Government: autocracy
Population: 9,720 (9,600 mountain dwarf, 120 gnome) (city); 11,910 mountain dwarf in surrounding mountains
Monstrous: dragons, giants, goblinoids, orcs, ogres, svirfneblin, wolves, wyvern
Languages: Dwarven, Gnomish
Religion: Dwerfater
Resources: mining
Currency: mixed
Technology Level: Medieval, Renaissance

Sometimes, nature accomplishes more than the grandest schemes of humankind. Halmarr may be the greatest example of this principle. Instead of constructing massive walls and imposing fortifications, the dwarves of Clan Duhnbeyl built their capital city within the emptied magma chamber of an extinct caldera. The dead volcano's 8,673-foot-high steep slopes and unstable surfaces make it nearly impossible for a lone individual to scale. Any potential invader would be hard pressed to penetrate Halmarr's impressive defenses. Meanwhile, lava tubes and tunnels carved into the mountain's belly grant its residents access to the outside world beyond the mountain's exterior.

Since its last eruption expelled its fiery guts more than 8,000 years ago, Halmarr has remained stoic and silent. Although its magma chamber sits empty, fissures in the earth surrounding the city burrow several miles down into the rock where magma and steam still reside. These natural heat sources function as forges for the city's metalworkers and engineers who travel on primitive rail cars from their comfortable abodes on the surface into the sweltering caverns beneath the mountain. Halmarr's architects incorporate the metals forged in these volcanic furnaces into their building designs. Worked iron gates, trusses, and arches adorn homes, civic buildings, and temples.

The dwarves of Clan Duhnbeyl fled into the Spine of Fire in the immediate aftermath of the Great Betrayal. They settled in small, isolated villages along the slopes of the numerous stratovolcanoes bisecting the region. These first settlers farmed the fertile soil in the shadow of these smoldering behemoths while residing in caves carved into the sides of these stony behemoths. For much of its formative history, Clan Duhnbeyl remained scattered and leaderless until the first great Mountain Hammer Basal Duhnbeyl united the divided villages in 2045 I.R. Seven years later, he founded the city of Halmarr inside the lifeless crater. The first test of Halmarr's defenses came three centuries later in 2389 I.R. when an army of 1,000 orcs and ogre allies attempted to attack what they believed to be a defenseless city. The dwarves, armed with sophisticated siege equipment and explosive lava bombs, easily repelled their overmatched enemies. Clan Duhnbeyl experienced little difficulty crushing an external foe yet its internal adversaries proved more daunting. For the next 1,500 years, intrigues, scheming, and bitter family rivalries tore the city and clan apart in a series of brutal civil wars known as the Eruptions. The infighting finally died down one century ago, but the damage was already done. Near-constant warfare and strife relegated Clan Duhnbeyl to bit player status until Mountain Hammer Talcum Duhnbeyl rose to power six years ago.

Under his leadership, the clan experienced a rapid resurgence. Its industrial output tripled practically overnight, political infighting ceased, and its borders expanded into previously unclaimed territory. The previously downtrodden dwarves of Clan Duhnbeyl display a swagger not seen for centuries. Their newfound confidence comes with a price. Despite being blessed with boundless energy, a sharp tongue, and a keen mind, Talcum's amorality tempers some enthusiasm within the dwarven camp. The irreligious Talcum show no deference to Dwerfater's clergy who wielded tremendous influence over Felspar, his predecessor and inept older brother. The clan's former leader spent most of his days praying in Dwerfater's temple, solidifying the priesthood's control over the clan's temporal leader. Indeed, many dwarves viewed Halmarr's High Priest Garn Tousanem as their spiritual and secular leader. Not surprisingly, Garn and his subordinates suspect the ambitious Talcum played a role in his older sibling's sudden and unexpected demise.

In the current climate, even Garn fears to challenge Talcum's authority. The previously fickle military is now re-energized and fanatically loyal to their benefactor, who showers them with increased pay and improved equipment. His metalworkers secretly toil on a massive iron "firestick" in the fires deep below Halmarr. With this weapon, the ambitious dwarf allegedly sets his sights on expanding his kingdom into neighboring realms, most notably Clan Craenog's dominion over the Feirgotha Plateau. Sensing his growing bravado, rival clans and even the hobgoblins keep a wary eye on the smoldering furnace in the heart of the Stoneheart Mountains.

Hobgoblin Cities

Three cities of hobgoblins live — and fight — among the southern peaks of the Starcrag Range and the eastern eaves of the Stonehearts.

Reference Sources: Mountains of Madness, The Lost Lands: Sword of Air

Bone Hollow, City of

Ruler: Sahka Khan
Government: autocracy
Population: 9,482 goblinoid; unknown thousands in nearby mountains

Bone Hollow's greatest advantage in its wars against its hobgoblin and dwarven rivals is its strategic location. While Exor and Smashed Skull are sandwiched between two enemies, potentially forcing each citadel to engage two different foes on separate fronts, Bone Hollow's great distance from the dwarven heartlands significantly lessens the threat from the great clans. Furthermore, Bone Hollow boasts the finest fortifications in the region. Reinforced stone buildings, walls, and towers immediately test the mettle of any potential invader, while their contingent of ballistae and catapults challenges the attacker's fortitude. Despite these impressive bulwarks, the hobgoblins allow travelers and merchants to pass through their gates into the valley below Bone Hollow if they pay a hefty toll. Circumventing the toll is an offense punishable by death or worse. Non-hobgoblins may pass through the gates, but they are never allowed to enter the city proper or camp anywhere within its walls.

In addition to its impressive defenses, Bone Hollow can muster a mighty hobgoblin army 3,700 strong. Its warlords can call upon an auxiliary mounted force that includes a wyvern, a gray render, a six-headed hydra, two chimeras, four owlbears, four hell hounds, six cave bears, and a legion of wolves. The battalion's leader rides atop a fearsome blue dragon. Under the leadership of Sahka Khan, Bone Hollow either commits almost everything it has to a military campaign or its military stays safely ensconced behind its ramparts. Bone Hollow may not boast the largest army, but its cohesive force is the best-trained and best-equipped goblinoid army in the Stoneheart Mountains. To showcase its martial prowess and gain experience for its seasoned troops, Bone Hollow annually attacks its southern neighbor Smashed Skull in what feels more like a rite of passage than a realistic attempt to conquer the hobgoblin citadel. Sahka Khan's army routinely beats its adversaries into a bloody pulp on the field of battle, though the gains realized from these conflicts are minimal. Sahka Khan primarily participates in these exercises to satisfy his people's lust for carnage. Left to his own devices, he would happily bide his time and watch his hobgoblin adversaries and their dwarven rivals destroy each other.

The hobgoblins rely heavily upon slave labor to provide materiel and logistical support for their organized and disciplined military force. Dwarves and humans captured during one of their rare raids toil in the silver mines beneath the citadel, entertain the masses in gladiatorial games, or become unwilling sacrifices to their depraved deities. In turn, the hobgoblins use the silver ore to finance their wars of conquest. A handful of escaped slaves claim to have seen fleeting glimpses of dread horrors in the tunnels beneath Bone Hollow. Stories of tentacled monstrosities, amorphous mounds of blistered flesh, and skinless beasts represent just a sampling of these fantastical tales.

Exor, City of

Ruler: Teth Khan
Government: autocracy
Population: 15,043 goblinoid; unknown thousands in nearby mountains

The hobgoblin city of Exor sits between a rock and a hard place. The dwarves of Clan Craenog and their imposing citadels of Erod Flan and Tyr Whin loom to the south. To the north, Exor must contain the ambitions of Smashed Skull and Bone Hollow, their hobgoblin rivals. Nonetheless, Teth Khan and the roughly 10,000 hobgoblins under his command are up to the challenge and ready to take on any enemy. Tall, jagged peaks wreathed in ice surround Exor, which lies at the nadir of a mountain valley, 4,892 feet above sea level. A ring of coniferous trees along the city's perimeter encircles the massive citadel. Only a single road of Hyperborean origin leads past the forested tree line and into Exor proper. Instead of constructing a massive wall to protect their city, the hobgoblins constructed countless concealed pitfalls and other devious booby traps to ensnare potential invaders. Sentries posted at higher elevations also maintain a vigilant watch over the surrounding area.

Despite its more welcoming outward appearance, Exor feels more like a military base than a settlement. Barracks scattered across hundreds of acres offer its soldiers the crudest and most basic accommodations. The remainder of its population not under arms devotes its energies to feeding and equipping its troops in addition to cobbling together the settlement's overtaxed infrastructure. Vast mess halls, smithies, and other industries dedicated to manufacturing arms and armor operate day and night under the bleakest conditions. Even the hobgoblins' hardy constitution is no match for the virulent epidemics that constantly rage through the city because of the unsanitary conditions and overcrowding. Many hobgoblin commanders prefer to be in the field hunting game, conducting patrols, or skirmishing against their neighbors than languishing in squalor in Exor. The only assignment they would rather avoid is delving into the caverns beneath the city from which few ever return. The hobgoblins refer to these dark, foul passages as the Festering Chasm. Unearthly slimes, oozes, worms, and other mindless vermin infest the damp chambers and corridors. Ancient hobgoblin legends also speak of the Denizen, a mysterious, otherworldly being who performs grim blood sacrifices at the bottom of the Festering Chasm.

In the surface world, Exor's Teth Khan believes in quantity over quality. His massive army looks unstoppable from afar, but a closer look reveals that his malnourished, poorly-equipped, and moderately-trained soldiers look more impressive than they truly are. The hobgoblin king's complacency has filtered down through the ranks, though a newcomer aspires to shake Exor out of its slumber and smite its enemies once and for all. A young warlord named Grugdour sets his ambitious sights on the dwarven citadel of Tyr Whin. Accompanied by 3,000 handpicked troops, Grugdour plans to march across the Stoneheart Mountains and wrest control of the citadel from Clan Craenog. Rumors claim Grugdour has a network of spies and informants within Clan Craenog's capital city and frontier outpost.

SMASHED SKULL, CITY OF

Ruler: Gothar Khan
Government: autocracy
Population: 6,549 goblinoid; unknown thousands in nearby mountains

Smashed Skull is the least populous of the three great hobgoblin citadels in the Stoneheart Mountains. To compensate for their lack of hobgoblin manpower, the militaristic goblinoids open their ranks to hill giants, ogres, and even orcs. Gothar Khan views this alliance with these undisciplined barbarians as a necessary evil when considering their current predicament. Their hobgoblin foes to the north and south vastly outnumber or outclass their army. The inclusion of chaotic evil humanoids adds an unexpected wild card to the mix when combating their enemies. Although hobgoblins typically crave order and discipline, the weaker yet unorthodox adversary sometimes proves more dangerous than the marginally inferior but predictable opponent.

Gothar Khan recognizes the tempestuous nature of his newfound allies. Thus, he diverts much of his city's limited resources to maintaining their hedonistic and expensive lifestyle even if his citizens must ultimately pay the price for their loyalty. He makes sure the ale flows freely and the servants are comely in the orcish quarter of the city. Some sources claim his forces include a significant number of half-orcs as well as human mercenaries happy to extract a pound of flesh from their dwarven enemies. While some of his subordinates grumble about this situation, they realize Smashed Skull would quickly crumble without the giants and the orcish shock troops. Gothar Khan mainly fights on the defensive, falling back on the city's outer defenses of moats, palisades, and earthworks to keep their enemies at bay.

Gothar Khan is an average tactician. Instead, his abilities to motivate his troops and foster cohesion within the ranks of his diverse army prove to be his strengths. He also excels at reading his opponents, a skill he acquired playing games involving varying degrees of skill and chance. Gothar Khan willingly engages his adversaries in small skirmishes and minor battles, but when matched against a vastly superior force, the cagey hobgoblin boasts about his secret weapon — a otherworldly creature of terrible might and power contained within a magical prison beneath his citadel. To date, no adversary has ever challenged the wily Gothar's boast, leading many to speculate whether the being exists at all or is merely a figment of his vivid imagination.

ICARROS, CITY OF

Ruler: Her Exalted Highness Mother Edele Wargawn Tusov
Government: monarchy
Population: 5,280 mountain dwarf (city); 8,030 mountain dwarf in surrounding mountains
Monstrous: dire wolves, dragons, giants, goblinoids, orcs, ogres, wyvern, yeti
Languages: Dwarven
Religion: Dwerfater
Resources: mining
Currency: mixed
Technology Level: Medieval, Renaissance

Icarros differs greatly from the other dwarven strongholds scattered across the Stoneheart Mountains. Built atop the remnants of an ancient Hyperborean outpost, which in turn rested upon the ruined foundation of a shrine dedicated to a deity lost to the annals of time, Icarros lacks the thick walls and imposing defenses found in Erod Flan or Abad Durahai. Instead, the city entrusts its defenses to its elevation and the mountain's natural protections. The city's residents occupy a network of chambers and tunnels carved into the mountainside. At a staggering height of 19,223 feet, it takes most humanoids several weeks to acclimate to the dizzying altitude, making it impossible to simply march up the mountain, which is accessible by several well-worn passes. Constantly buffeted by strong winds and bitter cold, Icarros' residents rely upon their resourcefulness and cleverness to survive under these brutal conditions. For a few brief months during the mild summer, the dwarves farm the terraced landscape while making hunting forays in the valleys and foothills surrounding the mountain. For the remainder of the year, Icarros' inhabitants hunker down within their mountain halls, subsisting on their stores from the fleeting growing season as well as lichens, mushrooms, and other plants harvested from artificial greenhouses within the heart of their mountain.

Icarros is the northernmost bulwark of dwarven civilization in the Stoneheart Mountains and the political capital of Clan Tusov. Isolated from their dwarven brethren to the south, Icarros' residents share few of the cultural traits of their counterparts. Indeed, these mountain dwarves are slightly taller than average, which leads many of them to believe they possess some Nûklander lineage. They usually attribute their unique physical characteristics to the clan's brief interactions with the Hundaei, which makes them exceptionally wary of any Hyperborean resurgence in the area or settlements that emulate their traditions and practices.

The dwarves of Clan Tusov place more emphasis on loyalty and fidelity to their leaders than familial bonds. They live by the motto, "One's deeds outweigh their blood." The ideology stems from the fact that Icarros began its existence as a remote frontier outpost for dwarves who caused trouble within their own clans. In time, dwarves who fell out of favor with their clans and those seeking a higher status voluntarily migrated to the mountaintop settlement. The city's ruler, Her Exalted Highness Mother Edele Wargawn Tusov, rewards subjects who embrace this philosophy rather than tout their family's accomplishments. The prevailing outlook works hand in hand with her patronage of Grox who also extols the virtues of personal gain over the public good. Her exalted highness embodies these principles and uses her control of the legal system to funnel more riches into her coffers at the expense of others. Those who run afoul of her grand ambitions face her retinue of devious judges and fiery prosecutors, disparagingly referred to by many as the Immutable Gavels. To avoid her legion of solicitors, many dwarves quietly lead anonymous lives in what outwardly appears to be an oppressive society. Others see opportunity in a domain where talent supersedes birthright. The sky is the limit as long as one's interests do not conflict with those of her exalted highness.

Despite Icarros' impressive altitude, the mountain's summit towers an additional 12,000 feet above the city. Rumors insist yetis and an unknown offshoot race of humanoids live among the clouds at these dangerous elevations. While these tales circulate through the city like seeds on the wind, finding anyone who has seen either of these creatures proves nearly impossible.

KROAKSENK, CITY OF

Ruler: King Snogg
Government: autocracy
Population: 6,532 goblinoid

Tunnels boring into the base of a nameless mountain just north of the Telgotha Plateau lead into the overcrowded goblin city of Kroaksenk. The horrid stench emanating from the filthy streets and disgusting communal hovels filters through the passageways and out to the surface. The goblins and their handful of dwarven slaves live in utter squalor. They scratch out a miserable existence in the dark caverns far below the earth, where they primarily subsist on a diet of fungi and lichens scraped off the walls and ceilings of their malodorous abode. When the goblins crave fresh meat, they venture into the world in full force. At least 100 of them emerge from the ground to hunt fresh game, raid a nearby village, or scavenge for other predators' scraps. They occasionally tag along with their hobgoblin kin during one of their forays into a dwarven village or serve as auxiliary troops in one of their military campaigns, though the goblins' morale quickly breaks in the face of adversity.

For his part, King Snogg is content to safely manage his small fiefdom from the secure confines of his subterranean lair. The snarky monarch often quips that no dwarf or hobgoblin in his right mind would ever want to rule his underground cesspool of want and deprivation. Most tribe members decry their leader's deliberate efforts to worsen rather than better their lives, but all lack the courage to supplant the uncaring yet physically strong Snogg. Any revolution would require overthrowing him and also disposing of the King's Fists, his personal retinue of overgrown bodyguards, and a mysterious warlock in his service. Many believe the enigmatic figure known only as the Pall is a human or dwarf exile using the goblins as his instrument of revenge against his kin. Regardless of the stranger's motivations, Snogg's oppressed subjects believe he can see the future and thus snuff out any uprising before it even starts.

MINERS' REFUGE, TOWN OF

Rulers: Councilors Falgar Bazdag, Duurk Hammerfell, Haamman Dinzak, Maximilian Stroud, and Rosie Festmacher
Government: council
Population: 773 (387 mountain dwarf, 271 human [215 Uplander, 56 other human ethnicity], 56 hill dwarf, 39 gnome, 12 elf, 8 other)
Languages: Dwarven, Common
Religion: Dwerfater, Sefagreth
Resources: trade, iron, limestone, clay, some precious gems and metals, agricultural products
Technology Level: High Middle Ages

The town of Miners' Refuge lies near the headwaters of the River Eamon some 200 miles east of the fortress of Dun Eamon. Because of its location near the Eamonvale Trade Road, the town sees more commercial traffic than the typical mountain settlement. Though known predominately as a mining community, Miners' Refuge also produces agricultural products, especially food crops, textiles, and livestock. Streams fed by melting snows at the highest elevations of the neighboring mountain chain and minor tributaries of the River Eamon provide an ample supply of fresh water to support farmland, grazing animals, and a thriving humanoid population.

The majority of the folk of Miners' Refuge are dwarves of Clan Krazzadak who were displaced some 500 years ago when their homeland was destroyed when the ice covered the Shengotha Plateau and transformed it into the frozen wasteland now known as the Stoneheart Ice Plateau. Today, they mostly work as miners or merchants. The miners employed here make a comfortable living extracting mundane yet important commercial products such as rock salt, iron, limestone, and clay from tunnels bored into the sides of the foothills on the edge of town. They occasionally strike small veins of precious metals such as platinum, gold, and silver along with a rare, fortuitous deposit of rare minerals and gems. The town's smaller human population and a handful of gnomes, elves, and half-elves survive by tending the fields and raising livestock.

In spite of the perceived racial tolerance, Miners' Refuge is a segregated town in many respects. The mountain dwarves control all aspects of daily life within the community and own title to all of the land, even the land farmed by those of other races. A council of three mountain dwarves and two non-dwarves rules the town. This arrangement allows the humans to have a say in local affairs, though ultimate authority still rests with the dwarven majority. Dwarves appointed to the council serve a 20-year term, whereas non-dwarves are limited to spending 10 years

on the council. At the end of their tenure, the outgoing councilmember appoints a successor.

Over the years, the ruling dwarves have instituted several reforms aimed at lessening the racial hostility between the rival factions. The oldest of these is the "trustee" program. Humans can purchase this status on an annual or lifetime basis. A trustee may carry weapons, but the person must always wear an azure cloak while doing so. However, the cost to purchase this honor is beyond the limited means of most downtrodden humans. A more recent measure created a council of five people to rule the town. Of course, three of these individuals must be dwarves to ensure the dwarves retain the majority on all decisions. While these changes have bettered the lives of many humans, resentment lingers in some circles, especially in the human-dominated Silver Nugget Inn. Dwarves never venture inside the hotbed of intrigue and scheming. If a revolt were to take place, the seeds of the rebellion would undoubtedly be sown here. Nonetheless, most people have little time and energy for political wrangling. Most spend their days farming or exploring the surrounding foothills for gems and precious metals. Local folklore also speaks of a forgotten tomb hidden somewhere on the edge of town. However, the town is currently abuzz over a prophet who led a pilgrimage to reclaim the fabled Mithral Mountain from the mutinous dwarves who expelled Thane Ilger Ogradmek from his mountain stronghold roughly five centuries earlier.

The towering peak of Mithral Mountain — said to be the location of fabled dwarven mines — is east of Miners' Refuge in the Stonehearts and visible from anywhere in the town.

REFERENCE SOURCE: MOUNTAINS OF MADNESS

OG-BRETHOS, SETTLEMENT OF

Ruler: Drogg Thumbuster
Government: autocracy
Population: 1,402 orc and half-orc

The Stoneheart Mountains' orcs clearly play second fiddle to the more numerous goblin and hobgoblin adversaries, yet these aggressive and chaotic humanoids are more than capable of wreaking havoc throughout the region. Orcs under the command of Chieftain Drogg Thumbuster occupy the fortified settlement of Og-Brethos north of Dun Eamon and west of the Stoneheart Ice Plateau. A great earthen wall defends the residents' crude huts. The barbarous humanoids periodically attack merchants traveling to and from Dun Eamon as well as small, isolated dwarven and hobgoblin settlements on the sparsely-populated frontier. The orcs who serve under him include a substantial number of ghost-faced orcs and half-orcs. Despite Drogg's violent nature and bloodthirsty ways, he has proven to be a remarkably shrewd leader. He recognizes his people's limitations and makes sure not to undertake an action likely to provoke a concerted response from any of his more sophisticated neighbors. He believes his efforts are better served trying to locate a fabled lost orcish city supposedly buried beneath the Stoneheart Ice Plateau. His scouts recently found a crevasse in the ice close to the settlement's rumored location, spurring hope they may be close to finding the entrance to the fabled locale.

TYR WHIN, CITADEL OF

Ruler: Truvvan Blackgranite
Government: military
Population: 1,089 mountain dwarf (city); 320 mountain dwarf in surrounding mountains

Like Erod Flan, its larger counterpart, Clan Craenog built this imposing citadel more than 2,000 years ago in response to the growing threats from the Kingdom of Arcady on the neighboring Feirgotha Plateau and the hobgoblin strongholds of Exor, Bonehollow, and Smashed Skull in the Starcrag Range. Tyr Whin sits atop a small plateau surrounded by defensive earthworks and moats. A 30-foot-high, 1-1/2-foot-thick wall constructed from flat, interlocking stones reinforced by hardened gypsum completely encircles the military compound. Its artillery includes six trebuchets. Two gates guarded by towers and secured by massive iron doors grant access to the citadel's interior. The soldiers grow crops and raise livestock to feed and clothe the self-sufficient troops. Dwarves make up the entirety of the citadel's population.

As the clan's northernmost outpost, Tyr Whin witnesses more than its fair share of battle. Its current commander, Truvvan Blackgranite, the son-in-law of the clan's High Thane Kaelan, regularly leads patrols into the neighboring foothills to search for hobgoblin scouts, rival dwarven clan members, or human incursions. Skirmishes between the warring parties occur with frequent regularity. Dwarves who want to make a name for themselves within the clan often volunteer to serve at the distant fortress. Rumors of increasing hobgoblin activity abound within Tyr Whin's mighty walls, and some reports even suggest a full-scale hobgoblin attack is imminent. Furthermore, stories of human spies disguised as dwarves infiltrating the citadel also circulate among the troops, fueling rampant paranoia in many circles.

REFERENCE SOURCE: MOUNTAINS OF MADNESS

UHL RENNAL, CITY OF

Ruler: Grand Magister Arnuld Koth
Government: oligarchy
Population: 10,045 mountain dwarf (city); 18,620 mountain dwarf in surrounding mountains

Clan Koth's capital city in the western Stoneheart Mountains can be found inside of the tunnels and caves boring into a nearly-sheer terraced cliffside overlooking a mountain valley from a staggering vantage point of 11,750 feet above sea level. The clan's members use a bank of magical elevators at the mountain's base to slowly ascend to their virtually impregnable mountain stronghold. As an added measure of defense, the elevators are attuned only to transport dwarves to the complex's six entrances. These portals bore into the mountain and lead to Uhl Rennal's residential blocks, its religious center (the Temple of Crugas, the city's divine patron), and the city's focal point, the Academy of Arcane Arts and Sciences. This grand structure houses a vast repository of rare, mystical works, fabled magical weapons, and state-of-the-art technological wonders. Despite the mountain dwarves' profound xenophobia, the citadel's dwarven arcane practitioners often work in tandem with gnomish artificers to create these astounding objects. The dwarves' trove of magical wonders naturally piques the interests of thieves and adventurers alike. Therefore, Uhl Rennal's wizards safeguard their items with potent wards and defenses that reportedly include a sophisticated, mechanical draconic construct.

Grand Magister Arnuld Koth exerts ultimate authority over all events in Uhl Rennal and Clan Koth in general from the Hall of Mages. From his seat atop the Arcane Dais, the masterful wizard and his five-member Veiled Council oversee the city's daily operations as well as help direct magical research. In a unique twist, the Veiled Council members always use magical disguises to conceal their true identities. Each individual serves a 10-year term after being selected in a secret, random lottery. Anyone aspiring to be a member of the Veiled Council must use a specific spell that only wizards of extraordinary ability can cast to enter the drawing.

Uhl Rennal attracts prospective students and scholars from the clan's outlying villages and towns scattered across the western Stoneheart Mountains. Promising youngsters who display an affinity for magic must demonstrate their magical prowess before the Veiled Council. Those who pass the test enter into the academy, while those who fail must wait five years to try again. Although the system has been in place for centuries, a vocal minority insists that some human and elf moles walk among them as dwarves and gnomes. Fortunately for Clan Koth, real intrusions are exceedingly rare. The last occurred in 3487 I.R., when two rakshasa wizards fooled the city's defenses and stole an experimental prototype of an electromagnetic gyroscope. Although the object's purpose remains top secret, popular consensus believes the presumably magical item could theoretically alter the fabric of time and space in a localized area. Despite a frantic search for the culprits and the object, their fates remain a mystery.

The grand magister rightly fears the ramifications that could be unleashed if someone were to improperly use the magical device. Worse yet, he knows what terrors lie in the ruins deep beneath his city. Long ago, before recorded history, a Doomspire stood where Uhl Rennal now stands. From atop this towering fortress of burning skulls and calcified human remains, Osenkej the Witch King spread his baleful influence across the land. For 2,700 years, the Doomspire cast its vile shadow upon its people until an alliance of benevolent deities joined forces and destroyed the Doomspire within the city of Krezzel Dul. The dwarven deity Crugas entrusted the Koth Clan with the crucial task of safeguarding the razed city. In exchange for their service, the god also imparted the secrets of arcane magic to the clan, which they use to this very day.

GEOGRAPHIC FEATURES AND POINTS OF INTEREST IN THE STONEHEART MOUNTAINS

AZURE MOUNTAINS

Like the Starcrag Mountains, the Azure Mountains are technically part of the greater Stoneheart Mountains. These peaks along the southeastern edge of the range stretch from Alesardin to the eastern edge of the Stoneheart Ice Plateau. Giant eagles and griffons can sometimes be seen circling in the skies above the roughly 8,000-foot-tall peaks, which are often shrouded in fog. On the ground, the indigenous goblins vie with the mountain dwarves for supremacy in the region. Although the smaller goblinoids enjoy numerical superiority over their humanoid adversaries, the better organized and equipped dwarven villages still possess enough manpower to keep the unruly goblins in check.

BAEN'S KEEP

Named after the dwarven lord Baen, this heap of smashed rubble overlooks the pass that also commemorates the celebrated dwarven lord. Although it bears his name, Hyperborean conquerors laid the building's foundations roughly 1,500 years before Baen Halfhammer's demise. Throughout its history, the strategically located keep maintained a vigilant watch over the mountain route beneath it. The Hyperboreans and later the dwarves financed their operations by collecting tolls from travelers and merchants using the pass to facilitate trade with the gulf region.

In 1494 I.R., Aka Bakar and the Kingdom of Arcady seized control of Baen's Pass, slaying its caretaker Baen Halfhammer in the process. To eradicate any vestiges of the dwarves' influence in the region, the mighty wizard razed Baen's Keep to the ground, burying Baen's skeleton beneath the upturned stones and mortar. However, his death failed to relieve him of his solemn duties. His undead spirit stirs again each night at midnight and slays any creature who strays too close to the ruined stronghold he oversaw in life.

REFERENCE SOURCE: THE LOST LANDS: SWORD OF AIR

BAEN'S PASS

This pass across the Stoneheart Mountains begins in the foothills east of the range and ends at its intended destination on the Feirgotha Plateau. The gently-sloping mountain route passes underneath the shadow of the ruins of Baen's Keep and along the Silent Lake's southern shore. The dwarves of Clan Craenog still patrol the pass on an irregular basis, keeping a close eye on any human incursions into their territory or the activities of the undead monstrosities haunting both of the preceding locations. In addition to these dangers, the dwarves and other mountain travelers sometimes run afoul of ogres, trolls, and bandits hunting for easy victims. While the opportunistic monsters may dissuade some from traversing the pass, the alternative of tediously scaling steep mountains seems worse to most explorers. At its highest point, the pass only reaches an altitude just above 3,000 feet, where it gains access to the Feirgotha Plateau through a remarkably low gap in the otherwise formidable escarpment.

REFERENCE SOURCE: THE LOST LANDS: SWORD OF AIR

THE BLACK FIELDS

This expansive swath of land in the Vingotha Plateau earned its moniker from the black, volcanic soil covering the ground. Farmers covet the fertile earth deposited in the Black Fields, but the chilly conditions and thin air make the land less conducive to agricultural endeavors. Instead, the mountain dwarves quarry basalt from the site and use the cooled volcanic rock as a construction material and an artistic medium for master sculptors. Enmel Stoutchisel, a hermetic dwarf artist, maintains a studio adjacent to a partially exposed lava tube. The xenophobic eccentric and his six apprentices exclusively craft commissioned artworks for Clan Craenog, which likely represents the only organized commercial endeavor on the Vingotha Plateau. The High Thane's representatives travel to Enmel's studio once per year to pick up his completed artworks and give him the specifications for newly commissioned pieces. Despite his genius and his incredible skill, even the clan's interactions with the quirky and hot-tempered misanthrope may quickly go awry, as the old, cantankerous coot frequently instigates a heated verbal exchange with his rare visitors for no comprehensible reason. Nonetheless, the clan continues its testy relationship with Enmel for as long as his artistic abilities remain unsurpassed.

The mountain dwarves undisputedly wield absolute mastery over the Black Fields and the Vingotha Plateau at large, yet periodic disappearances in the area imply they are certainly not alone. Lava tubes cut into the bedrock beneath the fields are reputed to contain several communities of dark folk who harbor an ancient grudge against their dwarven adversaries. In a similar vein, dwarven folklore speaks of a clan of fire giants who built an extensive subterranean complex beneath the lava channels that empty into the Black Fields. Along with an efreet in their service, they purportedly travel to the surface on occasion to sift through the lava flows in search of an unknown anomaly in the discharged volcanic material.

BURGOTHA PLATEAU

The northernmost of the Stoneheart Mountains' great plateaus seems forgotten. At an average elevation of 8,000 feet, the Burgotha Plateau lies 10,000 feet and sometimes even 20,000 feet below the summits of the tall peaks surrounding it. The Hyperboreans and the Hundaei used the strategic location as a staging area during their wars of conquest throughout the region. Even today, salvagers have little difficulty finding relics such as a broken spear, splintered arrows, a rusty helmet, and archaic coins from this age. The ruins of abandoned garrisons, corrals, and military camps also litter the gravel-strewn landscape. Despite the obvious signs of humanoid habitation, these settlements were always transitory in nature. With the exception of a brief, summer thaw, the weather is generally chilly and raw. Snowfall is possible for roughly nine months of the year as runoff from melting snow and precipitation feeds the Xircos River. To make matters worse for permanent residents, pulverized stone and alkaline mineral make up its dusty soil and renders it incapable of supporting plant life.

At the present time, Clan Tusov and Clan Duhnbeyl claim hegemony over the barren plateau, yet neither exerts any effort to establish a permanent foothold on the mostly lifeless expanse. Even the Hyperboreans and Hundaei appeared hesitant to take up roots in this desolate land for reasons beyond the foul weather and the poor soil. The soldiers who camped here began experiencing an inexplicable unease after a few months on the plateau. Images of gruesome humanoid sacrifices and rivers of blood plagued their nightmares, causing many to experience long, troubling bouts of insomnia and depression. Some chose to stay awake and suffer the scourges of sleep deprivation rather than subject their weary minds to these terrifying thoughts. Most others either fled the area never to return or stayed and perished by their own hand.

COBALT PASS

Access to the Feirgotha Plateau from the east was long provided by the Southern Pass, which led over the Stoneheart Escarpment and thence into the mountains to the plateau. When Tsar fell into darkness, leaving the entrance to the Southern Pass in the midst of the Desolation, merchants and traders sought a different route to the plateau, and to the Eamonvale Trade Road beyond to the western eaves of the mountains. Thus the Cobalt Pass was carved through the high peaks. Named for some of the beautiful blue rock formations rising above the route, it is a treacherous road, often very narrow, with challenging switchbacks and substantial elevation changes, often running along precipitous cliffs that drop off into deep voids. Wyverns and other great airborne beasts seeking easy prey are known to hunt along the road. Were it not for the Desolation blocking entrance to the Southern Pass, few of right mind would use the Cobalt Pass.

ERAGOTHA PLATEAU

The westernmost of the plateaus of the Stonehearts, Eragotha stands alone and solitary, with no routes up its escarpment. No tales tell of any fortresses or settlements on its heights, nor have the dwarves, gnomes, or humanoids of the mountains ever settled here. There are no stories of caverns or other entrances here to places below the earth, or of any ores or gemstones to be found.

The top of Eragotha can be reached only by the most-experienced mountain climbers. Once upon the plateau, a visitor is greeted by what may be the oddest of lands in these peaks. Although the air here is cold and thin, stumps of petrified trees from a warm, wet clime dot the landscape. What appears to be the now-dry riverbed of a mighty river bisects the land, running from the northwest to the southeast right across the plateau. In places, bones of long-dead creatures of great size lie exposed to the elements. Some scholars theorize that Eragotha may be a relic of the land before the Stonehearts were raised, a region that, for some unknown reason, was not destroyed in that cataclysm, but instead was simply raised skyward as the earth heaved up. Why this land would have been preserved is the subject of some speculation, but no answers have yet arisen.

FEIRGOTHA PLATEAU

During its tumultuous history, the Feirgotha Plateau has been known by several names. Ancient texts sometimes refer to the frigid landscape as the Vastness, a moniker it earned because of its seemingly endless expanses of cold, alpine desert. The desolate wasteland experiences its most frigid temperatures closest to the escarpments surrounding the plateau whose elevation ranges between 5,000 feet at its nadir near Toh Kristael and 15,000 feet along the sheer, vertical cliffs surrounding the mesa. The nearly impassible rock walls, cliffs, and the pervasive threat of an avalanche make for an extremely challenging climb up the escarpments. Indeed, attempting to scale any of the escarpments demands tremendous mountaineering skill and experience. Fortunately, three mountain passes grant access to the elevated mesa. Pelivar Pass enters the plateau on the west, Baen's Pass provides access on the east, and to the south are the entrances to the Southern Pass and the Cobalt Pass. Those who reach the plateau encounter frigid tundra at its highest elevations and a cool alpine desert in its most hospitable spots. Strange rock formations abound throughout the Feirgotha Plateau. Some ascribe the creations to natural processes, though most scholars believe them to be ruined vestiges of past civilizations or feeble attempts at artwork by forgotten cultures or creatures. The most likely candidate for these pieces is the Kingdom of Arcady. However, several of these odd structures serve as the entrance to subterranean tunnels burrowing into the ground into manmade and natural abscesses beneath the ground.

During its brief halcyon days 2,000 years ago, the legendary wizard Aka Bakar transformed the Feirgotha Plateau into a vibrant, flourishing civilization known as the Kingdom of Arcady. Eighty years after its founding, hordes of orcs and hobgoblins swarmed onto the Feirgotha Plateau. Although they failed to conquer the nascent kingdom, their aggression and the acts of its deranged ruler plunged the realm into anarchy and chaos. Nearly all of the surviving residents abandoned the plateau and fled to neighboring regions, which once again returned the plateau to its former anonymity. By default, the Feirgotha Plateau fell under the sway of Clan Craenog, which monitors the activities in the wasteland from several outposts scattered across the sprawling landscape. Burvaadun, the most noteworthy of these defense installations, sits close to the Southern Pass and the presumably abandoned Library of Arcady, which is said to have been built by Thanopsis the Learned during the kingdom's heyday. Foran Rockfeller, the garrison's competent leader, commands a force of 40 troops largely composed of misfits and others who fell out of favor with Clan Craenog's most influential members. They closely monitor activities in the region, especially the library's rumored resurgence.

Although it has experienced a few renaissances throughout its existence, the Feirgotha Plateau, like its neighboring counterparts, today stands barren and nearly uninhabited. A few remnants of the orc and hobgoblin armies who marched against Arcady still linger in the harsh domain. Meanwhile, Clan Craenog periodically dispatches organized patrols to the area to seek out and destroy any burgeoning humanoid settlements attempting to take root in the parched soil, including those of their hated foes, the humans. The Feirgotha Plateau has a well-earned reputation for being inhospitable, yet there are some havens of life amid the pervading desolation. The handful of oases scattered across the wasteland boast clean, refreshing waters and palm trees during the condensed summer months. Naturally, the former inhabitants also sought out these refuges, where they sometimes left an indelible mark on these isolated lands in terms of discarded relics or abandoned sites.

REFERENCE SOURCES: THE LOST LANDS: SWORD OF AIR,
MOUNTAINS OF MADNESS

THE ICE FLOW

This enigmatic sliver of ice stretches from the Stoneheart Ice Plateau to the lowlands of the Waymarches. While glaciers normally move very slowly, this one is comparatively swift, having appeared only recently, with a tower of ice at the head of the flow. It has moved precipitously through a narrow pass of the Stonehearts toward the plains of Waymarch.

In fact, the Ice Flow is a magical flow of icy waters from the River Cocytus itself that broke through from , a realm of the Nine Hells. Created when the Ice Palace of Perfidium broke through into the mortal realms in the southern part of the Stoneheart Ice Plateau, the Ice Flow brings atop it the Accursed Ice Tower of Kal-Tior on a march down to the plains of Waymarch and, eventually, the Grimburg. The route of the Ice Flow is the only access from the plains to the Stoneheart Ice Plateau beyond, but it has become a hellish trek haunted by spirits escaped from the underworld, frost men, yetis, ice worms, and other horrors of the Icy Hell of , in addition to the threat of natural hazards such as jagged fissures and flesh-freezing Hell-borne winds.

For more on the Ice Flow, see *Cold as Hell*, forthcoming from **Frog God Games**.

THE ICE PALACE (ICE PALACE OF PERFIDIUM)

The Ice Palace, also known as the Ice Palace of Perfidium, is a towering fortress seemingly made entirely of ice that recently appeared atop the Stoneheart Ice Plateau. It is, in fact, an incursion into the material plane from , a realm of the Nine Hells.

Entry to the palace is indeed a step into a passage to Hell itself. The incursion was created through the summoning rituals of the warlock Kal-Tior as he called upon the strength of his patron Count Perfidium of , a high prince in the Court of the Nine Hells. On the spot of a collapsed ancient dwarven empire, Kal-Tior sacrificed more than 600 members of an ice gnome tribe upon the glacier. Their blood was mixed with the icy waters of Cocytus, which caused a thunderous crack heard as far away as Reme and Bard's Gate.

The rent in the fabric of reality allowed a mirror duplicate of Perfidium's Palace to break into the mortal plane. The palace is guarded by a contingent of ice devils, white dragons in service of Perfidium, ice mephits, frost giants, winter wolves, and an army of ice goblins formed from the soulless husks of the sacrificed ice gnomes.

The palace sits upon a vent of Hell itself and is both cold as ice and boiling with hellfire at the same time, giving the region around it an unholy glow. It appears in the form of a stack of massive snowflakes with crystalline edges of indescribable beauty silhouetted against the sulfurous nightmare glow of the Infernal Realms.

During the deepest coldest months of the year, Count Perfidium can gate a powerful avatar of himself onto the Stoneheart Ice Plateau and occupy the mirror throne. It is at this time that his servant Kal-Tior is at his most powerful.

Count Perfidium is sworn to free his ancient mistress from her prison in Grimburg and has influenced Kal-Tior to do his bidding in the execution of Perfidium's ancient quest.

For more on the Ice Palace, see *Cold as Hell*, forthcoming from **Frog God Games**.

ICE TOWER

See "The Ice Tower" under "The Lands of Reme — Grand Duchy of Reme — The Duchy of Waymarch."

MITHRAL MOUNTAIN

As one of Clan Krazzadak's most influential vassals, Thane Ilger Ogradmek and his ancestors ruled over Mithral Mountain for more than 1,000 years. However, a fateful event 500 years ago ended the Ogradmeks' control over the mountain. The surviving accounts claim the thane and his supporters perished during an uprising inspired by a new deity named Dwer-Bokham, a name that translates to "dwarf of mithral" in their native tongue. The dwarves who fell under the divine being's sway have mithral-colored skin and eyes. Over the years, the surviving Ogradmeks and their descendants have mounted numerous expeditions to retake the mountain from its upstart occupiers. However, every effort ended in failure. Over time, the dwarves came to realize the futility of their cause. They ceded dominance to Dwer-Bokham's servants and allowed Mithral Mountain to fade into legend. Some dwarves believe the deity is a cobaltog, a creature from ancient dwarven folklore who resembled living mithral and could exercise mental control over other creatures' minds. Many dwarves attribute the mountain's name to its rumored cobaltog resident as the mountain's mines predominately contain salt and coal rather than the priceless metal. However, the mountain's reputation for containing rich veins of the valuable material was reputedly enough to spur the alleged huckster Bargus Farmud to lead another assault against the mountain.

REFERENCE SOURCE: MOUNTAINS OF MADNESS

THE MOLTEN FLOW

The lava runoff from Mount Daergyd in the northern Vingotha Plateau rolls down its southern slope, where several tubes and channels funnel into a single river of lava known as the Molten Flow. The viscous liquid material meanders a circuitous path across the plateau until it disperses into a cluster of tributaries before finally pouring into the Black Field where it eventually cools. Some metallurgists and blacksmiths who call themselves the Brotherhood of Magma often venture to this isolated open-air forge to craft armor, weapons, and other metallic objects. This reclusive band of mountain dwarves dwells in tiny villages and caves dotting the plateau. They claim the magma imbues their handiwork with special properties, including the ability to wreath its metallic surface in bright red flames on command. Chas Delacroix, the group's founder, allegedly forged the Steel Flame in the fiery soup, though the blade's purported abilities as well as its very existence remain speculative at best. Despite the brotherhood's convincing boasts and wondrous yarns about their accomplishments, there are no verifiable accounts confirming their stories. Indeed, the mountain dwarves who also trek here from more "civilized" areas scoff at their metalworking prowess, telling potential customers the brotherhood is too incompetent to fashion a hole in a ring.

To add insult to injury, they allege the band's bloodline is contaminated by some human ancestry, which they assert can be confirmed by their slightly taller stature and untrustworthiness.

MOUNT DAERGYD

Lava continuously flows down multiple channels along Mount Daergyd's southern slope, while glaciers still coat the highest elevations of its northern and western faces. The 28,450-foot-tall shield volcano encompasses an area of roughly 125 squares miles, while its gargantuan magma chamber extends miles below the surface. The approach to the constantly shifting summit is steep and perilous. Climbers must dodge the copious outflow of lava to scale the peak's southern route or negotiate treacherous glacial outcroppings to reach the top of the smoldering cauldron of lava beneath it. Although none disputes Mount Daergyd's current classification as an active volcano, Hundaei and dwarven historical accounts indicate the mountain exhibited no signs of volcanic activity until it first erupted roughly 2,000 years ago in sudden and spectacular fashion. The prevailing myth claims that Dargoth, a wizard who fled Tsen, came to this remote site to open a gate to the Plane of Fire to summon a fabled salamander army from the realm's fiery depths. Dargoth successfully opened the portal but with disastrous consequences. Intense heat poured through the fissure, instantly melting the mountain's rocky innards while also burrowing deep into the ground to puncture a hole through the planet's crust. The conflagration consumed Dargoth and immediately transformed Mount Daergyd into a roiling shield volcano, which may be the most active hotspot in Akados.

PELIVAR PASS

Pelivar Pass winds a circuitous route across the western portion of the Stoneheart Mountains before reaching the elevated Feirgotha Plateau. Although it offers a viable alternative to laboriously climbing over numerous treacherous mountains, the pass is not for the faint of heart. It features multiple switchbacks, terrifying precipices, and steep inclines, all at elevations of 10,000 feet and higher. Because the western stretch is incomplete and predominately uninhabited, few travelers use this route which leads to widespread neglect throughout the highway. Scree from falling stones covers portions of the pass, while conspicuously placed boulders still block the path at obvious yet abandoned ambush sites. The dwarves exert little influence in the area, concentrating their efforts on more valuable assets to the north and east. A small clan of hill giants led by their oafish chieftain Ah-uhm rules in their stead. However, the oversized humanoid displays no interest in the affairs of others while his drinking goblet and belly are full.

THE SILENT LAKE

Water runoff from the surrounding mountains and even the distant Feirgotha Plateau trickles down streams and brooks before finally ending its journey at the Silent Lake. The freshwater repository sits at the nadir of a confluence of mountains, yet it still rests 8,420 feet above sea level. The shallow lake encompasses a wide area, though on average it is only 20 feet deep in most spots with a maximum depth of 45 feet near its eastern shore. Long ago, freshwater bass and trout abounded in the virtually pristine lake until an adventurer's careless act altered the lake forever.

Fresh from their exploits in Rappan Athuk, a party of explorers could not help but wonder why legions of the walking dead constantly followed them. After some deliberation, they finally placed the blame on a piece of an evil stone they recovered from the Dungeon of Graves. To rid themselves of the vile fragment, the party's cleric hurled the chunk of stone from the dread artifact into the water here, where it lies roughly 60 feet from the northern shore at a depth of eight feet. Hordes of undead now coalesce along the lake's shores, drawn to the power of the *Zombiestone of Karsh* lying at the bottom of the lake. All of these lifeless monsters are of the corporeal variety, as the artifact exerts its influence over decaying flesh and bone rather than wicked spirits. Mindless zombies, skeletons, and other lesser undead, most notably ghouls, make up the overwhelming majority of the Silent Lake's deceased residents.

However, some of these creatures also serve the vampire siblings Carina and Edmund Lashae, the lake's latest newcomers. The pair dwells in a small cave near the western shore among a small herd of oryxes who serve as their mounts and defenders. Indeed, many believe they travel across the mountain disguised as one of these beasts.

REFERENCE SOURCES: THE LOST LANDS: SWORD OF AIR

THE SPINE OF FIRE

The cluster of four stratovolcanoes bisecting the Telgotha Plateau and the Vingotha Plateau as well as the Feirgotha Plateau represents a geological anomaly. Far from any subduction zone or any other prevalent volcanic activity, the four mountains making up the Spine of Fire appear to be an unnatural phenomenon possibly linked to the range's creation 10,000 years ago. The 12,560-foot-tall Mount Ezrabor is the southernmost peak, while the 14,329-foot tall Mount Helcor is the northernmost peak. The 13,543-foot-tall mountain Acramon and the 15,002-foot-tall peak Phoetton make up the remaining two peaks. Despite their variations in height, all four mountains share the same general characteristics. The volcanoes intermittently erupt twice per decade, spewing columns of ash and pumice into the heavens. The mountains release lava and pyroclastic flows only during their most intense episodes, which generally occur once per century. Phoetton accounts for the last major eruption during 3482 I.R., when the volcano buried the five-mile radius around the mountain in 10 feet of ash, while its columns of ash and pumice were visible from as far away as the hobgoblin citadel of Exor. Indeed, Phoetton's discharge even coated the fortress with a thin film of debris.

Some scholars and theologians believe the Spine of Fire functions as a gateway into the heart of the Stoneheart Mountains. The tremendous quantities of energy required to create the range vent through these four portals to the outside world. The theory contends the passages found in the Spine of Fire may lead directly to the Stoneheart Mountains' underbelly, where the mysteries surrounding its creation may lie. However, individuals who have tested the hypothesis by venturing into the volcanoes during their dormant periods rarely returned. The few who made it back to safety spoke of encountering a previously unknown race of goblinoids deep beneath the mountains.

STARCRAG RANGE

The Starcrag Range, as an offshoot of the Stoneheart Mountains, is relatively young, as evidenced by its razor-sharp peaks and steep, sheer sides. Passes through the mountains are rare, and only those knowing their way have a reasonable chance of crossing them. The mountains rise to 12,000 feet above the plains below, with an average of 8,000 feet. The greatest heights bear glaciers, while even lesser peaks are snowcapped for most of the year, with the tree line at about 6,000 feet. The range is intercut by valleys and rivers, all flowing out and away from the mountains. A misty haze often covers the Starcrags, and all fear the things found in this mist.

This spur of the Stoneheart Mountains is typically classified as its own chain, though largely for political reasons rather than geographical. The Starcrag Range and its foothills are outside the control of the great mountain dwarf clans who rule over the balance of the Stoneheart Mountains. While the mountain dwarves can hardly be considered a united entity, their hegemony over the region warrants a separate distinction between the Stoneheart Mountains and their lesser brethren, the Starcrags, which are instead dominated by the dwarves' hobgoblin adversaries.

SOUTHERN PASS

On the eastern eaves of the Stonehearts, the Southern Pass to the Feirgotha Plateau starts as a road that meanders across the Desolation of Tsar and the Stoneheart Escarpment before entering the Stoneheart Mountains proper. The first stretch across the plains and lowlands remains neglected and unused. The dwarves of Clan Craenog and others often refer to this portion of the route as the "Dark Path." Only the foolhardy and those with an unrequited death wish venture into this foreboding locale. Instead, most travelers link up with the Southern Pass at some location in the mountains or avoid it entirely and take the more treacherous Cobalt Pass to the south. After crossing over the Stoneheart Escarpment, the Southern Pass remains fairly level throughout the remainder of the journey, where it reaches a maximum elevation of 6,000 feet at the foot of the Feirgotha Plateau, literally a stone's throw away from the dwarven garrison of Burvaadun. Beyond the plateau, the route west continues with the Eamonvale Trade Road, which leads past Miners' Refuge to Dun Eamon, and eventually Broadwater on the western eaves of the Stonehearts.

The soldiers manning the isolated outpost of Burvaadun rarely venture more than 10 miles from their mountain stronghold onto the Southern Pass, leaving travelers to fend for themselves. Furthermore, the dwarves patrolling the area apply the same brand of frontier justice to humans that they mete out to their hated adversaries the orcs and goblinoids. Beyond the dwarves' limited reach, anything goes. Renegade dwarves and those unaffiliated with the ruling Clan Craenog ply their trade as highwaymen and bandits while fending off incursions from ogres, hill giants, trolls, and the occasional manticore. A creature known only the "Winged Death" is the most-feared denizen of the Southern Pass. No firsthand accounts exist about any encounters with this supposedly otherworldly being, though rumors and myths claim an impenetrable shroud of darkness surrounds the entity. The stories also trace the creature's genesis to the Battle of Tsar.

REFERENCE SOURCES: *THE LOST LANDS: SWORD OF AIR,*
MOUNTAINS OF MADNESS

STONEHEART ICE PLATEAU (SHENGOTHA PLATEAU)

The Stoneheart Ice Plateau is one of the highest and coldest spots in central Akados. Within the plateau, a massive glacier of ice covers more than 60,000 square miles to a depth estimated at as much as 500 feet. Surrounding the plateau, which lies at an elevation of roughly 9,000 feet, is rugged, trackless mountain, with towering peaks reaching up to 12,000 feet or more. The only means of access to the plateau, other than crossing the mountains, is via a narrow pass on the southwest, but that is now filled by the cursed Ice Flow, and is a route best avoided by the sane.

Toward the southern end of the glacier, bathed in an unholy glow, is the Ice Palace of Perfidium.

Despite the enormity of the glacier and the entirely barren wasteland that now fills the plateau, not long ago this was a fertile and hospitable place. Before 3035 I.R., this was known as the Shengotha Plateau. Despite the altitude, winters were chilly yet not oppressive, while summers were brief and warm. This was the ancient homeland of the dwarven Clan Krazzadak. They had built four strategically positioned strongholds known as the Four Siblings about the plateau to defend the clan's lands against human migration, orc and goblinoid invasions, and their dwarven rivals. Yet these fortresses paled in comparison to the splendor of their capital city of Bryn Tuk Thull which they raised on a small hill in the middle of the plateau, and which shined brighter than any other star in the dwarven heavens. Gold, silver, rubies, and other precious metals and gemstones poured into the cosmopolitan metropolis from the mining operations in the nearby mountains. At its zenith, the Shengotha Plateau was known as the Stoneheart's Precious Jewel. And then one day, everything Clan Krazzadak accomplished came to a sudden and calamitous ruin.

No one can say whether the dwarves excavated something not meant to be found deep beneath the earth or committed some other transgression. It is said that a great wizard imbued with nearly godlike powers cursed the homeland of Clan Krazzadak. An unrelenting storm of snows struck, and within days an unnatural glacier entombed Bryn Tuk Thull, the Four Siblings, and the rest of the high plateau beneath hundreds of feet of compressed ice and snow. The dwarves had no choice but to flee (most heading to their nearby citadel of Abad Durahai), leaving their cities and much within them behind. They were soon replaced by frost giants, winter wolves, gelid beetles, and other creatures of cold who found the new climate of the plateau to their liking. A tribe of barbegazi (ice

gnomes) also arrived. They established a strong niche atop the glacier and burrowed tunnels into the abscesses within the now-frozen world.

Surviving members of Clan Krazzadak periodically venture back to the Ice Plateau seeking to reclaim some of its lost glory. Undoubtedly, many great treasures of the dwarves remain entombed under the ice. In addition, Thull XII, the last king of Shengotha, was lost along with members of his household and personal guard when the ice covered the plateau. Though now more than 500 years have passed, some wonder whether some of those dwarves or their descendants might yet live somewhere in the Stoneheart Ice Plateau.

REFERENCE SOURCES: *THE LOST LANDS: BARD'S GATE,*
MOUNTAINS OF MADNESS

TELGOTHA PLATEAU

Winds chilled by ice as they swirl around the surrounding peaks constantly buffet this desolate plateau, scouring away the earth until only heavy gravel and bare rock remain, nearly incapable of supporting any but the hardiest plant life. As a consequence, the Telgotha Plateau is virtually uninhabited save for a few wandering bands of dwarf scavengers searching the abscesses carved into the exposed rocks for any artifacts from a past age. Over the years, salvagers have managed to retrieve Hundaei relics from their brief passage onto the plateau during their conflicts with the Hyperboreans, along with small objects of Khemitite origin along the plateau's southern edges, likely left behind during exploratory missions from the Kingdom of Arcady's fleeting heyday 2,000 years ago.

At an average elevation of 16,200 feet, the elongated mesa towers over its neighbor to the east, the much lower yet more viable Vingotha Plateau, and its neighbors to the extreme south, the Eragotha Plateau and Feirgotha Plateau. The escarpments surrounding the plateau's edges are littered with dangerous rockfalls and nearly vertical surfaces. A handful of mountain dwarves claim to have found an extensive tunnel system accessible through cave entrances carved into the sheer rock face, yet these individuals are virtually impossible to locate. Not even the dwarves know who excavated the underground network of passageways and chambers, though a popular theory suggests they existed before the Stoneheart Mountains sprang into existence eons ago. The only object ever purportedly brought to the surface from the subterranean complex was a small alder wood statue of a grotesquely pregnant mother with a demonic face and a pair of claws digging their way out of the woman's womb. The horrific totem is currently said to be in the possession of a collector of ancient artifacts in Bard's Gate. If any have delved back into the site to further investigate the discovery, no tales of their success or failure have yet been told.

TOH KRISTAEL

This saltwater lake at the heart of the Feirgotha Plateau defies most natural laws. No rivers, streams, or other tributaries flow into the lake, and the arid climate generates insufficient precipitation to replenish any water lost to evaporation. To further cement its unnatural origins, Toh Kristael is reputedly bottomless. Some believe the legendary wizard Aka Bakar magically created the lake shortly after his arrival in Akados. In further support of this theory, scholars point to the fact he erected his capital city of Deepharbor on the lake's northern shores. Unfortunately, after the city's ruination at the hands of orc marauders, Toh Kristael claimed the razed metropolis as its own, submerging the rubble beneath its waters. However, the dwarves of Clan Craenog vigorously dispute this hypothesis. They insist Toh Kristael was here long before the Kingdom of Arcady sprang into existence. Instead, the dwarves trace the lake's origins to the foundation of the Stoneheart Mountains themselves, claiming the forces that gave birth to the peaks beget Toh Kristael as well.

The lake's only possible purely natural effect is its moderation of the prevailing climate surrounding it. The air here remains crisp and dry, but the temperatures are milder than in most parts of the Feirgotha Plateau. Salt and gypsum formations protrude from portions of the lake's surface along its shallower edges, while the gravel and salt pan bordering the lakefront stifles almost all flora other than a few tufts of grass and cacti tenaciously clinging to isolated clumps of arable topsoil amid the infertile earth.

In 3343 I.R., the explorer J'acu Niimo assembled a salvage team to probe the depths of Toh Kristael to learn more about Deepharbor's fate and to recover valuable relics. The fabled human druid and his associates dodged the vindictive dwarves patrolling the plateau's perimeter and arrived at the site two months after setting out from Glaivr. To his dismay, the lake's saline waters took a heavy toll on the ruins, corroding metallic objects and damaging stone and wood. Disappointed, J'acu expanded his operation to the lake's southern shore, where he discovered a lone island dominated by a tower. To his surprise, thick vegetation and vines covered the structure's exterior. J'acu and four of his most able colleagues could not resist the opportunity to personally examine the only standing manmade building that presumably survived the cataclysm that laid waste to Deepharbor and the Kingdom of Arcady. They swam out to the island and were soon engulfed by dozens or perhaps even hundreds of animated corpses. J'acu barely escaped, but the undead monsters devoured his four friends. He abandoned the effort, though the autobiographical account of his expedition, *The Anomalous Lake*, survives to this day and may prove useful to adventurers aspiring to follow in his illustrious footsteps.

REFERENCE SOURCES: THE LOST LANDS: SWORD OF AIR

VINGOTHA PLATEAU

Nestled along the Stoneheart Mountains' eastern edge, this narrow plateau has an average elevation of roughly 13,000 feet. It sits in the shadow of the Spine of Fire along its southwestern edge and adjacent to the neighboring Telgotha Plateau on its western border. The Vingotha Plateau is home to Mount Daergyd, the Molten Flow, and the Black Fields. Although the air is thin at this elevation, the fertile volcanic soil from the neighboring peaks allows some plant life to grow in this challenging environment, including a hardy species of coffee plant with yellow flowers reputed to invigorate the drinker with increased energy and greater resistance to altitude sickness at these dizzying heights. Fauna, on the other hand, proves less resilient than their green counterparts in this difficult domain. Yaks are the dominant animal species in the area. The 36 small and remote mountain dwarf villages scattered across the plateau raise yaks as livestock and beasts of burden. The majority of these settlements are concentrated along the plateau's borders with the neighboring peaks.

Over the centuries, the hobgoblins who hold dominion over the citadels of Bonehollow, Exor, and Smashed Skull to the southeast have periodically attempted to establish a foothold on the Vingotha Plateau to expand their influence northward. Their most recent attempt in 3420 I.R. failed when the mountain dwarves repelled their invasion with the help of reinforcements from distant Tyr Whin. Fortunately, the plateau's impressive defenses and limited strategic importance may be sufficient to keep future hobgoblin incursions at bay.

XIRCOS RIVER VALLEY

This vast area stretches from the edges of the Stoneheart Mountains in the west to the Vast Desert to the east, and encompasses the ruins of Tsen, the Burning Wastes, the cities of High Karst and Apothasalos, the village of Tanuil, and a number of tributary rivers flowing into the main waterway of the Xircos River. Fertile grasslands support numerous small farming communities through the interior regions and fishing villages along the banks of the Xircos and its larger tributaries. These small communities also hunt for herds of game animals grazing on the abundant plant life. Several forests also dot the landscape.

POLITICAL SUBDIVISIONS OF THE XIRCOS RIVER VALLEY

APOTHASALOS, CITY OF

Ruler: Harmost Gaelanicus Prescis
Government: imperial
Population: 10,274 (7,199 human mixed ethnicity, 1,050 half-elf, 910 hill dwarf, 870 halfling, 105 high elf, 90 mountain dwarf, 50 other)
Languages: Common, High Boros, Elven, Dwarven
Religion: Hyperborean pantheon
Resources: trade, grain, livestock, manufactured goods, metalwork, armor and weapons, glass, stonework
Currency: Apothasalos, Bard's Gate, other common currencies
Technology Level: Renaissance

Once the northern regional capital of the Hyperborean Empire, the city of Apothasalos is now an independent city-state whose influence extends well beyond its heavily fortified walls.

Apothasalos sprang from humble roots as a frontier outpost on an ancient military road predating the Hyperboreans' arrival. When Oerson and his legions came upon the settlement in –90 I.R., he decreed the location to be the ideal site for a regional capital. Construction began in earnest, and within six years a team of masons and artisans erected the massive outer walls and battlements that became the city's hallmark. These impressive defenses faced their first test in 14 I.R. when the Hundaei besieged the city in an assault known as the Month of Raining Arrows. Despite suffering extensive casualties, the beleaguered citizens withstood the onslaught. Relief came after 40 days when the Hyperborean commander Gnassus arrived on the scene. His legions defeated the Hundaei in spectacular fashion and ended the immediate threat to the exhausted city.

The city witnessed steady growth over the next 1,500 years as its proximity to neighboring Tsen made it a popular waystation for the bustling City of Wonders. However, that metropolis's utter destruction in 1491 I.R. shook Apothasalos' walls and foundation to the core. Fortunately, the Barrier Hills absorbed the brunt of the blast that laid waste to Tsen, though Apothasalos did not escape the apocalypse unscathed. Frightened by what they had witnessed, the city practically emptied overnight as terrified citizens fled their homes in a mad scramble to safety. When the initial chaos finally died down one year later, Apothasalos' leaders returned to the badly damaged yet still standing metropolis. Over the next several years, its residents slowly trickled back into their homes and businesses to resume their former existence.

With the destruction of Tsen, Apothasalos once again returned to its roots on the frontier's edge, though the imposing citadel was now a far cry from its previous incarnation as a crude outpost. Apothasalos functioned as a vital cog in the Hyperborean military machine. Yet with the Hyperborean decline and retreat 1,000 years later, Apothasalos underwent another metamorphosis from a defensive citadel into a commercial center. Nonetheless, its citizens still maintained the Hyperborean traditions and considered themselves to be a continuation of that bygone empire rather than its successors. Today, the city maintains a significant standing army of 1,910 infantrymen and cavalry troops known as the Knights of Apothasalos. Despite retaining some of its former traits, the city is now more celebrated for its markets than its military prowess or Hyperborean character. The metropolis extensively trades locally produced goods and commodities with the distant cities of Bard's Gate and Endhome. Its drovers' guild brings livestock to the markets, while its mercantile guild buys and sells nearly every imaginable product. Indeed, Apothasalos' knights primarily serve commercial interests, defending caravans and trade routes against incursions from the gnolls in the neighboring hills and the K'Haln riders to the north. Apothasalos maintains peaceful relations with Tanuil, the nearest notable settlement to the south.

Apothasalos' fortunes depend heavily upon its economic might, setting the stage for a power struggle between its political leader Harmost Gaelanicus Prescis and the potent guilds who seek greater autonomy and a larger role in the city's administrative and civic affairs. In addition to its legal enterprises, the city's small yet influential underworld syndicates also aspire to keep the harmost and her subordinates out of their business. Although violent, Apothasalos' criminal elements enforce a strict code prohibiting killing or seriously injuring innocent civilians. These rogues burglarize homes and businesses, smuggle contraband into the city, and sell illegal goods, most notably illicit narcotics purchased or manufactured in distant High Karst. They also rummage through the ruined portions of the city that were never rebuilt after the cataclysm at Tsen. Firsthand accounts claim that mutated humanoids, animals, and monsters roam the unstable passages and chambers in the city's ruined underbelly.

TANUIL, VILLAGE OF

Ruler: council of six women and one man
Government: oligarchy
Population: 307 (282 mixed human ethnicity, 11 half elf, 9 halfling, 5 hill dwarf)
Languages: Common
Religion: Diana
Resources: trade in exotic items and creatures
Currency: mixed
Technology Level: High Middle Ages

Hundreds of gargantuan mushrooms grow on the outskirts of this small village located in a bowl depression amid fields about 100 miles north of the Legionnaire Bridge. The enormous fungi reach an extraordinary height of 40 feet and each weighs roughly 1,000 pounds. The mushrooms are harmless and radiate a continuous *protection from evil* aura while embedded in the ground. The mushrooms lose all their mystical properties once they are removed, however. Such an event is a rare occurrence indeed, however, since the women who inhabitant Tanuil execute anyone attempting to steal one of their prized fungi.

Tanuil is a matriarchal society where the women are trained in the sword, lance, spear, bow and riding horses as soon as they can walk. In fact, their riding prowess and accuracy with a bow are virtually unsurpassed, which leads some to speculate that some Hundaei blood must flow through their veins.

Kaylaa, the resident high priestess of Diana, and five other distinguished women sit on the ruling council along with a lone male representative relegated to the sole task of settling ties among the women. Although the society believes men to be inferior, by tradition they treat everyone, regardless of gender, in a just and fair manner. Their outlook derives from a belief that men cannot control their emotions and require protection rather than an inherent superiority complex. In their

NORTHEASTERN AKADOS
Legend
Town or Village
City
Capital or Free City
Imperial Capital
Fortress or Citadel
Ruins
Place of Interest
Road
Trail or Unused Road
Mountain Pass
Battlefield
Sea of Grass
Vast Desert
Burning Wastes
The Bunitesveldt
Ikinian Desert
Ayde Hills
Sea of Spices
Gulf of Huun
Gulf of Akados
Gulf of Wanna
Great Ocean
Principality of Pelshtaria
Kalithid Peninsula
Perkstaman Peninsula
Lonely Coast
Karedonn
Bliski
Shinvi
Morbong
Alkis Anvil
Stavropol
Landsport
Aberond
Irith Kei

minds, the man's place is at home. The women, meanwhile, defend the village from aggressors.

These ferocious warriors also keep the peace in the village's thriving marketplace. Under their watchful eye and within the aura of the magical mushrooms, some of the strangest and most exotic items and creatures change hands. Merchants dealing in such oddities venture here from great distances to find curiosities absent from the shelves of the largest cities in Akados. Visitors sometimes also pay homage to Diana, the village's patron deity, in the temple that honors her.

Geographic Features and Points of Interest in the Xircos River Valley

Although dominated by grasslands, the Xircos River Valley boasts an eclectic collection of biomes that include deciduous and coniferous forests, uninhabitable wastelands, a searing hot desert, and a formidable mountain chain.

The Barrier Hills

From a technical standpoint, the Barrier Hills, which once were known as the Piedmont Highlands, qualify as mountains. However, when compared to the soaring Stoneheart Mountains to their west, the Barriers, with maximum elevations ranging from 2,500 to 5,000 feet, seem much more like bumps in the landscape than full-fledged mountains. They became known as the Barrier Hills after the explosion that destroyed Tsen immolated and permanently defaced their eastern slopes. The range took the brunt of the blast, which helped spare the city of Apothasalos from certain destruction and thus earned the highlands their new name. Like the nearby metropolis, the western slopes rebounded relatively quickly

from the devastation. However, the eastern side remains rocky and barren. Few humanoids venture here. The intrepid souls who throw caution to the wind to explore these peaks trudge across a desolate landscape teeming with deranged cultists, ogres, trolls, and bandits. Furthermore, explorers also frequently suffer from puzzling burns and inexplicable hair loss after spending only a few days in the area. Some attribute these ailments to temporal anomalies caused by an unnamed monster that stalks the hills. The majority place the blame squarely on the ruined city of Tsen to the east, claiming that whatever force razed the city still possesses the same destructive power it had thousands of years ago.

Reference Source: The Lost Lands: Sword of Air

The Bent Wood

The thick weeds and undergrowth covering the heavily overgrown floor of the Bent Wood pose significant challenges for travelers who attempt to negotiate a path through the region. The dense foliage appears so monotonous that even the most skilled woodsmen sometimes get lost amid the tangled vegetation. The only vestige of civilization to be found in the Bent Wood is an unmarked path rutted almost to the axle by decades of passing carts. Otherwise, the wilderness here reigns supreme. Giant spiders, wolves, worgs, and other beasts dominate the forest's wildlife. Gnolls and trolls hunt alongside these animals within the forest, which is also known as the "Forest of Horrors" in some circles. Stagnant ponds scattered throughout the Bent Wood teem with mosquitoes, leeches, and other bloodsucking pests. A document of dubious authenticity claims the Grand Cornu of Tsar secretly constructed a temple of Orcus somewhere within or beneath the Bent Wood, though no one has found any trace of his clandestine structure or the demon prince's devotees within the forest.

Reference Source: The Lost Lands: Sword of Air

THE BLOODY RUN

The waters in this broad, shallow stream originate in the hills above Chlestea Lake at the base of the Howling Fortress before ending their journey in the Xircos River. The stream, which has an average width of 30 feet and a maximum depth of three feet, earned its name from the reddish tint in the water. Popular folklore suggests blood from the Howling Fortress stains the Bloody Run, though most people attribute the unusual color to high concentrations of copper in the streambed. However, no one debates that the crawfish inhabiting the stream are among the tastiest in Akados, a realization that lures fishermen and connoisseurs to the banks of this otherwise ordinary freshwater stream.

REFERENCE SOURCE: THE LOST LANDS: SWORD OF AIR

CHLESTEA LAKE

Water runoff from the neighboring Barrier Hills pours into two shallow lakes separated by a freshwater swamp overrun by shrubs and small trees. Although Chlestea Lake consists of two distinct bodies of water, locals refer to the entire water system as Chlestea Lake. Blood Clan gnolls from the Howling Fortress frequently hunt for game and potential sacrifices in the malodorous wetland alongside trolls, ogres, lizardmen, crocodiles, and other predatory animals. Pluff mud — otherwise known as quicksand — is a common feature in the swamp, especially in areas devoid of trees or tangled shrubs. Although only a few feet deep in most spots, Chlestea Lake is well stocked with an assortment of fish as well as crustaceans and aquatic insects. Even the hungriest beast avoids the lair of Helcraw, the ancient black dragon who lords over the area. This massive reptile dwells in an underwater cavern accessible only through a 200-foot-long submerged tunnel. The sadistic monster lines the walls of this passageway with grisly trophies from her past victims. Severed heads, dismembered limbs, and personal mementoes simultaneously function as dire warnings and macabre décor for Helcraw's prospective visitors. Some travelers believe the wily dragon also uses the pluff mud to trap her prey or drag them into her lair. A growing belief in some circles is that the Blood Clan gnolls now worship the ancient black dragon as a deity.

REFERENCE SOURCE: THE LOST LANDS: SWORD OF AIR

DELAMARRA SALT PAN

During the vernal equinox, wealthy camel owners from every corner of Akados gather at the Delamarra Salt Pan on the northern verge of the Vast Desert for an entire week of festivities centered on a full day of camel racing on the ultrafast racetrack. The event culminates in the grand El-Ashad Invitational Stakes Race with a 5,000 gold piece purse to the winner. Naturally, the revelry involves extensive gambling among owners and spectators alike who hail from many of the continent's most renowned families. Even the most conservative estimates place the track's handle at 50,000 gold, making the racetrack a hotbed for other illicit activities as well as a target for enterprising thieves.

The racetrack has operated since 3314 I.R. under the management of the Millazzi family. They provide security for the events, oversee all pari-mutuel wagering, and ensure the integrity of the races for the betting public. The Millazzis enjoy an impeccable reputation for being incorruptible, though they also indulge in hard living and wild partying. Ambitious people trying to make a name for themselves covetously seek an elusive invitation to one of the Millazzis' legendary and raucous celebrations. When the festivities finally end, only a skeleton crew remains behind to maintain the racecourse and keep unwanted trespassers at bay.

GHUE ISLAND

Despite its proximity to the coast, Ghue Island feels as if it is a different world from a bygone era. Dinosaurs and other megafauna, including giant condors and clubneks, freely roam across the mountainous landmass in Legion's Bay. Primordial grasslands and rainforests cover the slopes of its peaks, which include several active cinder cone volcanoes. Nestled atop one of these 4,500-foot-tall mountains lies the Unspoken City, a settlement said to house 888 human wizards who conduct bizarre experiments and magical research that would be deemed unethical in the vilest mystical academies. A race of gaunt, undersized goblins known as the Depraved serve their deranged masters without question. The prevailing evidence would suggest Ghue Island's arcane practitioners twisted these unfortunate creatures into their present incarnation through magical means, selective breeding, or a combination of both.

The secretive cabal of mages has lived on the island for countless generations. In fact, all of these wizards share some common heritage, though males outnumber females by a whopping five-to-one ratio. Ghue Island's human residents place some inexplicable significance to the number 888. Therefore, whenever their population exceeds this number because of a newborn's arrival, they sacrifice and devour their oldest resident to restore balance to their community. While the wizards devote much of their time and energy to expanding their eldritch knowledge and mastering new spells and incantations, the urge to commit ritualistic murders and indulge in cannibalism remain foremost on their disturbed minds. When they cannot butcher one of their own, the wizards periodically look to Legion's Bay for fresh victims. Most mariners steer well clear of the island's bloody shores, yet some invariably sail into the mages' devious nets.

Several decades ago, Ghue Island's mages commandeered *The Swimming Hen*, a cog sailing out of Ustran Pazeel. In typical Ghue Island fashion, the wizards mercilessly slaughtered the crew and passengers. They then devoured their raw flesh and gnawed on their bones in a sickening feast. When word of the atrocity reached civilization, Captain Madrock Fist led the mercenary Company of Severed Steel in an assault against the Unspoken City. The mages brutally beat back the invasion, killing and sacrificing more than half of the company's members in the process. Captain Madrock's troubled mind never recovered from the horrors he witnessed on Ghue Island. He swore the mages had stitched animal limbs and heads onto animated humanoid torsos, though he never produced any evidence to support his testimony. However, those who survived the ordeal confirm his statements regarding the physical deformities plaguing Ghue Island's human population and the gruesome cannibalistic rituals he saw the wizards perform immediately after their attack failed. Several survivors also recall seeing a giant golden egg atop a pedestal on the summit of the mountain where the Unspoken City stands. These accounts may explain the pervasive rumors about giant condors dwelling on the island as well as confirm these birds' importance to the resident wizards.

HOWLING FORTRESS

Near the headwaters of the Bloody Run, this ancient fortress is carved some 350 feet up on the side of a granite crag that rises 600 feet above the neighboring Bent Wood. From the ruins of a gatehouse at its base, a causeway runs from the forest floor up the side of the cliff to a gaping stone maw in the massive walls, all that remains of the fortress's once mighty gates. Through the opening and delving deep into the earth is a complex that, over long years, has been used as a dwelling place, a citadel, and a prison.

The site dates back thousands of years to the Age of Dragons when titans and their giant servants walked the land. These massive beings are thought to be the original builders at this location, dwelling in grand galleries far below the surface. No one now knows the titans' purpose in delving here, though it is known that the deepest halls lead to natural caverns and tunnels which, according to rumor, connect to the world-spanning depths of the Under Realms. They abandoned the site for some unknown reason, and millennia later, a group of paladins devoted to Muir repurposed the ancient abode and transformed it into a fortress they called Muirgaard. They built their cloister here and incarcerated some of their world's most dangerous creatures deep beneath the citadel. Villains, monsters, and fiends bided their time in the paladins' escape-proof cells. However, the construction of Muir's temple in the Stoneheart Valley eventually rendered the prison here obsolete. The god's disciples transferred the inmates elsewhere, leaving Muirgaard unoccupied once again.

Within a few years, creatures from the unending caverns beneath Muirgaard began to repopulate the forsaken site. At some point, the Blood Clan gnolls made the old citadel their new home. Recently, the clan fell under the baleful influence of a bloodthirsty wyvern they worship as a god they call Yulanupior. The monster's insatiable lust for carnage spurs the gnolls to perform nightly sacrifices to the vile entity. The sound that occurs during these ghastly rituals earned the Howling Fortress and its environs its current name. To meet Yulanupior's surging demand for fresh souls, the gnolls expanded their base of operations to include waylaying passing caravans and travelers from nearby Apothasalos. The city has taken keen interest in the recent spate of disappearances in the vicinity of the Howling Fortress, which has prompted some of the metropolis's business enterprises to urge the harmost to take decisive action to address the rising threat.

While the gnolls undoubtedly pose a significant menace in the region, legends speak of far greater evils in the depths below the Howling Fortress. Few believe the titans simply walked away from their former home countless eons ago without leaving some trace of their presence in the ruined galleries. Likewise, while the paladins never acknowledged any successful escapes, it seems plausible that at least one of their prisoners outwitted Muirgaard's security and made a dash to freedom somewhere within the apparently bottomless chasm beneath the fortress. And deeper still are the ceaseless tunnels that may lead to the Under Realms below Akados. It is safe to say that the gnolls and their erstwhile deity represent just the tip of the iceberg of what awaits adventurers who dare explore the depths beneath the Howling Fortress.

Reference Source: The Lost Lands: Sword of Air

Legionnaire Bridge

Few architectural wonders have stood the test of time as well as Legionnaire Bridge. Although records say that the Hyperboreans constructed it, some scholars speculate that the 600-foot-long stone bridge actually predates even that ancient empire. In any case, the structure vehemently defies the forces of entropy working to destroy it. Its material components show no signs of erosion and can even withstand the mightiest blows without sustaining a tiny scratch. Some individual stone pieces weigh 500 tons, leaving observers to wonder how the builders transported these massive objects to the site and how they moved them into place. Despite its durability and exceptional properties, traffic across the bridge is relatively light. Some attribute the low volume to the disproportionate number of suicides that occur at the bridge. The few merchants who venture across the bridge report hearing unsettling sobbing, crying, and screams while trekking across the span.

Xanges River

This tributary river branches off from the wider Xircos River toward the eastern edge of the Stoneheart Mountains. The shallow waterway sees little traffic or usage as its banks are sparsely populated. The few small fishing villages along the river live off the plentiful trout and bass swimming in the murky water as well as farming the fertile soil alongside it. Humans make up the majority of these settlements' residents. They welcome strangers into their homes, which sharply contrasts with their staunch territorial outlook toward their neighbors. Bitter, longstanding family feuds are common throughout the area, with the most famous being the Browne-Ravene conflict that has raged on for three centuries. No one can accurately remember how or why it started, though some claim the dispute erupted over something as trivial as a prized fishing hole. Despite the foggy memories surrounding the feud's origins, both sides distinctly recall the number 279 — the number of lives lost on both sides to the constantly simmering grudge.

Xircos River

The slow-moving waters of the Xircos River roll into the Gulf of Akados through this wide and deep waterway. The natural obstacle is forded only at Legionnaire Bridge. Otherwise, ferries and barges shuttle passengers across the barrier. The city of Apothasalos also uses the river to ship goods to and from Bard's Gate to the south. Although the areas around the Xircos River are well-populated, crocodiles, lizardmen, and aquatic trolls also reside in this area. The belligerent creatures primarily feast on the giant catfish and crayfish inhabiting these waters, but hunger or bloodlust sometimes drives them to taste humanoid flesh rather than their traditional prey. The settlers they target live in small villages scattered throughout the fertile Xircos River valley. Fortunately, the commercial traffic navigating the river keeps such attacks to a minimum.

The fishermen's nets occasionally snag pottery shards, cut stones, and other objects from the river. Most of these people attribute these artifacts to shipwrecks, but a growing circle of skeptics refutes these claims. They assert that the gray ceramic items and stones are not indicative of any known civilization. They speculate that an ancient, prehistoric settlement must lie somewhere beneath the river's brackish waters. This conjecture also posits the question as to how the settlement ended up at the bottom of the Xircos River. Did a natural event such as an earthquake alter the river's course and submerge the city beneath the water, or did a divine hand play a role in its destruction? To date, no one has found any trace of this lost metropolis on the riverbed, if it even exists at all.

Vast Desert and the Irkainian Peninsula

Sea of Grass Region

The Sea of Grass is a vast steppe land that stretches from the Northlands in the north to the verges of the Vast Desert and the Xircos River Valley in the south, from the Stoneheart Mountains in the west to Seagestreland in the east. The long, slow Vindelsalven River runs through its northern reaches and provides a means of transportation from the Stonehearts and Lake Hargos all the way to Seagestre Gulf in the North Sea.

Roaming the Sea of Grass are the K'Haln tribes, the Mongat tribes, and the Lundhargo tribes, the descendants of the Hundaei who once settled these lands during their campaigns against the Hyperboreans. Great beasts also traverse the plains, tracing ancient migratory paths. There are dangers within the Tanomir Fens, which are said to be the home of strange men with the heads of lizards, great black wyrms that can break a ship in half, and worse.

Political Subdivisions of the Sea of Grass Region

High Karst, City of

Ruler: Mayor Thanicles Aenimeus
Government: republic
Population: 5,274 (4,134 mixed human ethnicity, 345 half-elf, 290 halfling, 210 high elf, 165 mountain dwarf, 110 gnome, 20 other)
Languages: Common, Elven, Dwarven, Kirkut (Sea of Grass dialects)
Religion: Hyperborean pantheon
Resources: hallucinogenics, grain, livestock, composite bows
Currency: mixed
Technology Level: Dark Ages

Isolated and alone, High Karst has developed an independent spirit and unique culture unmatched almost anywhere else in Akados. High Karst benefits from a strategic location on the banks of the Shimmering River in a remote tract of land in the shadow of the Stoneheart Mountains to its west. It traces its origins to an unusual bargain between the xenophobic mountain dwarves and their human adversaries. In 478 I.R., Clan Tusov ceded a slightly elevated plateau to a band of Hundaei warriors in exchange for the horse warriors' support against the hated Hyperboreans. After fulfilling their end of the pledge in a battle against the Hyperborean legions, the surviving Hundaei pitched their yurts and took up what they believed to be temporary residence on the lush pasture. They and their subsequent generations peacefully remained in this remote corner of the world for the next 2,000 years, though over that time their Hundaei heritage became increasingly diluted as they adopted more Hyperborean customs and became acclimated to a sedentary lifestyle. Their transformation became complete when a mutinous cohort of Hyperborean soldiers joined forces with their old enemies to formally found the city of High Karst in 2390 I.R.

During the first few years of High Karst's existence, political wrangling between the Hundaei old guard and the Hyperborean commanders, particularly their leader Oeanicus, threatened to unravel the fragile alliance between the old foes. However, in shocking fashion, the headstrong Oeanicus agreed to a power-sharing arrangement with the Hundaei. The turmoil slowly died down, and within three generations the lines between the Hundaei and the Hyperborean blurred into nothingness. The influx of elven and Nûklander blood over several centuries erased any traces of the Hundaei's former lineage and created one of Akados' most diverse gene pools.

Today, High Karst revels in its eclectic traditions and origins. In homage to its Hundaei roots, the sprawling city has no defensive walls, fortifications, or battlements. Instead, 100 mounted archers stand at the ready to defend High Karst against any enemy. Another 645 professional spearmen and 300 cavalry troops complement this mobile unit along with four siege engines (three ballistae and one trebuchet). However, stone and wooden structures replaced the old leather tents centuries ago.

Although most of High Karst's 1,277 acres are devoted to agriculture and animal husbandry, the city is best known for the few small quarters catering to a seedier industry, the manufacture and sale of hallucinogenic agents, especially celestial cap mushrooms and peyote. These narcotics are legal and easy to find in High Karst provided they are used under the supervision of one of the licensed dealers scattered throughout the city. Mayor Thancles personally issues these licenses to merchants. In addition to passing the mayor's character assessment, these individuals must also undergo basic medical training. Because of these stringent requirements, some unscrupulous entrepreneurs who cannot pass muster attempt to illegally sell these products in back alleys and other discreet locales. Thancles' agents often successfully root out these illicit establishments and treat their operators to an extended stay in High Karst's notoriously brutal prison system. The punishment for transgressing Thancles' laws can be severe, but some believe the rewards outweigh the risks, even if they only engage in the highly lucrative business for short periods of time. Wealthy clientele from Apothasalos and Bard's Gate who make the trek to distant High Karst can spend ungodly amounts of coin indulging their appetites for such earthly pleasures for days or even weeks at a time. Indeed, the city's name is a double entendre referring to its elevation above the surrounding lowlands on one hand and the legal use of narcotics on the other. This perception is so pervasive that even the neighboring mountain dwarves refer to the humans inhabiting the city as unmotivated stoners who pose no serious threat to their hegemony over the Stoneheart Mountains.

Despite the laissez-faire attitude toward the use of hallucinogens, High Karst's authorities have no tolerance for most other vices. The city frowns upon prostitution and gambling, while tightly regulating the distribution and sale of alcohol. Visitors sometimes fret that it is easier to find a peyote den than it is to locate a tavern within the city. Those who seek the latter often venture here to acquire one of High Karst's renowned composite bows that are made using traditional Hundaei components and techniques. The bowyers who manufacture these weapons personalize each bow to their owner's height and weight specifications as well as their personality, making them a popular gift for Akados' elite warriors and citizens.

PLAINS TRIBES

When the Great Khan Jaganga of the Hundaei first crossed the northern Stonehearts to make war on the Hyperboreans, his folk soon discovered the vast Sea of Grass east of the mountains, a grassland plain of thousands of square miles that was much like their homeland on the Great Steppes to the west. Many Hundaei moved into these lands, where they found good grazing for their horses and other supplies for their armies as they fought their enemy. As is told elsewhere, the conflict lasted many years. At the end of campaign seasons, when most Hundaei returned to their homeland over the mountain, some chose to remain on the Sea of Grass. Over time, many came to view these plains as their new homes. The khans supported these migrations, as making permanent their presence solidified supply lines and ensured a northern threat to the Hyperboreans even during the winter months.

Between 681 I.R. and 683 I.R., the Hundaei of the Great Steppes fought a terrible civil war, at the end of which their empire for all intents and purposes ceased to exist. Some refugees fled over the Stonehearts and joined their kinfolk in the Sea of Grass, while others fled farther, even to Libynos. Fortunately, the strife left those in the Sea of Grass untouched. But now with their homeland in ruin, they were left to themselves in their new lands.

Over time, the descendants of the Hundaei in the Sea of Grass developed their own culture and way of life and divided into three main tribal groups: the K'Haln, the Lundhargo, and the Mongat.

K'HALN TRIBES

Ruler: none
Government: tribal chieftains
Population: 203,200 (human tribesfolk [Hundaei descent])
Languages: Kirkut (K'Haln dialects)
Religion: animism/ancestor
Resources: raiding, grains, horses, livestock, trade
Currency: barter (some currencies of precious metal accepted)
Technology Level: Iron Age

The largest of the tribal groups of nomadic horse riders on the Sea of Grass, the K'Haln range from Lake Hargos and the lands near High Karst all the way to the northern verges of the Vast Desert.

More so than their Lundhargo and Mongat cousins, the K'Haln recall their origins across the Stonehearts as the remnant of the ancient Hundaei. They carry themselves proudly and tell stories of the days when their ancestors brought terror to even the great Hyperborean Empire. They are scrupulous in adherence to their traditions and customs and consider the other tribes to be degenerate and far too forgetful of the old ways.

The K'Haln venerate their ancestors as exemplars of the ancient traditions, honoring their memory and seeking their advice through holy priestesses who act as oracles. Though chieftains and great warriors are now laid to rest in the Staked Lands, in ancient times the greatest of their leaders were buried in chambers in mounds on the plains. Anyone desecrating the Staked Lands or a burial mound will be slaughtered on sight without opportunity to explain or atone. In addition to their ancestors, the K'Haln honor the forces of nature and consider the One Tree in the Sea of Grass a place of unique holiness.

The K'Haln roam the plains in tribal groups of various sizes ranging from a dozen to a hundred or more. Many are connected via marriage, and chieftains will meet when the seasonal ranges of one or more bands brings them together. This often occurs at the Stones of Kashimir, where the ranges of many of the tribes intersect. If there is a need for all of the tribes to gather (to elect a chieftain of chieftains, for example), they gather at the stones. Even when separated by vast distances over the Sea of Grass, the chieftains maintain contact with each other through messages carried by trained plains hawks. As a result, in times of need the K'Haln can act in concert to a remarkably high degree.

The K'Haln are on good terms with their Lundhargo and Mongat neighbors and will travel to the former's settlements at the times when the markets gather. Others who encounter the K'Haln on the Sea of Grass will usually be attacked for plunder and, if captured, sold to the Lundhargo.

LUNDHARGO TRIBES

Ruler: none
Government: tribal theocracy
Population: 101,700 (human tribesfolk [Hundaei descent])
Languages: High Lundo (dialect of Kirkut)
Religion: animism/ancestor
Resources: horses, livestock, grain, trade (including slaves), raiding
Currency: barter (some currencies of precious metal accepted)
Technology Level: Iron Age

The least numerous of the people of the Sea of Grass, the Lundhargo are a nomadic folk who move with the seasons in a range that extends along the lower portion of the Shimmering River and the upper reaches of the Xircos River.

Unlike their K'Haln and Mongat cousins, the Lundhargo have established semi-permanent settlements. Always built near the banks of a river, each of these settlements contains several timber constructions upon stone foundations, including a great hall, several lodges, and temples where ancestors or the forces of nature may be venerated or placated. The only year-round residents are priests who tend to the needs of the ancestors while the tribes are upon the plains. At several holy times during the year the tribes return to their traditional settlements to make sacrifices and receive instructions from the priests. The Lundhargo arrive with their families, horses, and flocks, setting up vast fields of colorful tents around the settlements. Though gathering for religious service, these are also times for celebration as distant relations greet each other, and the people contest in horse riding and strength of arms, arrange marriages and engage in trade and commerce.

Lundhargo traders travel widely throughout northern Akados to bring their goods to market at these times. In addition, merchants from Pelshtaria, Apothasalos, Bard's Gate, and even far Libynos are welcomed into the sprawling and chaotic market area, where it is said most anything that can be bought or sold can be found. This includes some trade of the less-than-savory sort, including an active market in slaves. Some of these unfortunates are captured by Lundhargo raiders, while others may have been purchased from their K'Haln or Mongat kin.

The Lundhargo think of themselves as the most "civilized" of the folk of the Sea of Grass. Each tribe is led by a patriarch or matriarch who wields secular authority and a priest or priestess who was apprenticed at the tribe's traditional settlement. Ultimate authority resides in the priest or priestess, however,

MONGAT TRIBES

Ruler: none
Government: tribal chieftains
Population: 127,900 (human tribesfolk [Hundaei descent])
Languages: Kirkut (Mongat dialects)
Religion: animism/ancestor
Resources: raiding, grains, horses, livestock, trade (including slaves)
Currency: barter (some currencies of precious metal accepted)
Technology Level: Iron Age

The Mongat are a loosely related group of nomadic tribes that roam the Vastmir Plains, the portion of the Sea of Grass west of Seagestreland. They are feared throughout the Northlands, and frequently raid in search of cattle and gold, and take hostages either to ransom or to sell to the Lundhargo for their slave markets to the west.

While the K'Haln and the Lundhargo each possess something of a collective identity, the Mongat barely consider themselves one people. Two Mongat tribes are as likely to fight as talk should they meet on the plains. And while they possess herds of livestock and harvest wild grains, the preferred activity of the Mongat warrior class is raiding other people for their provisions and possessions.

PRANDAYA, TOWN OF

Population: 193 (human mixed ethnicity)
Ruler: Abaya Mael Tirkonian
Government: autocracy

For the overwhelming majority of its 1,200-year history, the isolated town of Prandaya languished in obscurity. The settlement lies near the northwestern corner of the Vast Desert, close to a deep aquifer that provides its thirsty citizens a semi-reliable source of potable water. The sleepy, remote community normally attracts no attention from the outside world, but a chance event recently thrust Prandaya into the limelight. According to scattered yet seemingly reliable reports, the armies of Bard's Gate and other powers in eastern Akados recently engaged in a battle or series of battles against the Huun invaders within or on the outskirts of the town. The conflict's outcome remains in doubt along with the fates of those who fought in and around Prandaya.

Not surprisingly, this news led some adventurers and military units to trek toward the Vast Desert to confirm or refute these reports. Those who reach Prandaya discover a small, organized settlement of farmers irrigating their otherwise parched land with water hoisted out of nearby wells and onto the arid soil. While innately friendly, the wary residents have little to share or sell to strangers setting foot in their lands. Abaya Mael Tirkonian agrees with their sentiments, and grants shelter and provisions only to those visitors who offer his people and, most importantly, him, far more than they receive in return. In addition to his being a shrewd bargainer, astute observers also sense that the abaya appears to be hiding something about his tiny enclave, a secret he seems absolutely unwilling to reveal to anyone under any circumstances. Logic would deduce that his coyness must pertain to the missing armies, but the shifty Mael appears capable of perpetrating almost any intrigue.

GEOGRAPHIC FEATURES AND POINTS OF INTEREST IN THE SEA OF GRASS REGION

BLUE ESCARPMENT

The Sea of Grass is not the featureless waste outsiders assume it is. There are a few places where the rolling plains give rise to other landscapes. The blue escarpment is one such place. In eons past, the Vindelsalven River cut a different course and sliced through the topsoil to expose the blue stone bedrock beneath. For millennia, the waters cut away, yielding the canyon that shelters travelers and bandits alike. When the course of the river changed upstream of the blue escarpment, the canyons were left dry. Seasonal showers, usually in the spring, combine with snow melt to create a ghost of the once-mighty river that flowed through here; a ghost with teeth, for spring floods can easily come up suddenly and carry away man and horse.

The blue escarpment poses other dangers than seasonal floods. Wild animals congregate here, as do people, both seeking some relief from the sun and the wind of the plains. Water pools here from time to time, but outside of the spring rarely forms anything but a trickle. In the summer months, the canyons of the blue escarpment provide shade, though that hot season sees little water on the surface. Besides the many wandering animals and monsters, bandits and K'Haln tribes visit the canyon lands from time to time.

GRAND PORTAGE

No permanent settlements exist in the Sea of Grass, but if one were to ever develop, it would likely be at the place of the grand portage between Lake Hargos and the Shimmering River. Merchants — mostly Northlanders — transport their ships or boats overland between these waterways, which permits trade between the North Sea and the Gulf of Akados. The feat is impressive and requires a certain flair for engineering as the ships are loaded onto framework beds and moved on rollers. The work is horrendously brutal, and few undertake it, yet one or two ships seem to make the journey every year. Livestock or slaves, both of which are abandoned once the goal is reached, pull the rolling cradles. A bold crew can save months of time reaching the rich lands of the far south, trading and plundering to their heart's content, and then simply sailing home.

The K'Haln roam the lands about the lake and river, and sometimes demand a payment for safe travels over the portage. They also tend to seize any livestock or slaves left behind once the ship achieves its goal waterway. Not all are scooped up by the mounted raiders though, and small bands of escaped slaves or herds of oxen live out meager lives along the path of the grand portage.

LAKE HARGOS

Lake Hargos is a body of chill water fed by ice melt from glaciers in the Stoneheart Mountains. The Vindelsalven River enters the lake in the north and exits in the east, where the water meanders through the shallow and boggy Tanomir Fens for 200 miles before resuming its way to the Seagestre Gulf.

Fish are plentiful in the lake and folk of the K'Haln tribes will often come here to supplement their usual diet of milk, meat and grains. There are no settlements, though in a few places ruins of farmsteads or the broken walls of buildings of unknown purpose rise above the grasses near the shore. Between the western shore of the lake and the Shimmering River to the west is the Grand Portage. Each year, one or more vessels will pass through Lake Hargos on their way to, or after having crossed, the Grand Portage.

ONE TREE

A lone tree on a small ridge might not seem like much, but when featureless grasslands in every direction surround you, this lonely tree stands out for all to see. The K'Haln tie prayer strips, small metal bells, and shards of mirror to the tree's branches. All of these make One Tree easy to find in the dark, during storms, and in the early morning mist. Since it serves as such a prominent landmark for its part of the Sea of Grass, One Tree has become a sacred place of hospitality to the K'Haln. No person may be murdered in sight of it; nor may fires be lit.

OSEN'S SEEP

The grasslands are not dry per se, but surface water is fairly scarce. The underground aquifer rises in places, usually where there is a basin of sand over a cracked rocky substrate. One such place is Osen's Seep, which is named after the Northlander who dwells there. Seeps are sacred places of hospitality to the K'Haln horse nomads, and it is forbidden to kill within sight of one. Each seep has its own set of restrictions specific to it, and Osen's Seep gained one that prohibits walking backward. For his part, Osen was captured along the Grand Portage, managed to escape, and fled to the seep. Despite his weakened condition, he fended off those who tried to take him and now lives here in a crude grass shelter. Some of the local K'Haln consider him a shaman of some sort and provide Osen with food from time to time. Meanwhile, Osen waits and bides his time, knowing he might be murdered if he leaves sight of the seep.

SEA OF GRASS

The Sea of Grass is an enormous prairie east of the Stoneheart Mountains that spans 1,500 miles across northeastern Akados. Tallgrasses dominate the western regions, where prevailing winds off Legion Bay bring moisture north, while the eastern areas, particularly those bordering the Vast Desert, are largely covered by shortgrasses. In places, the land undulates in gently rolling hills, while in others, the terrain is entirely devoid of features, a vast and flat plain stretching to the horizon.

Surface water is fairly scarce in these plains. Scattered throughout the Sea of Grass, however, are isolated spots of wetland formed around one of the many seeps that leak underground water up through sandy soil to the surface. Such seeps are sacred places of hospitality to the K'Haln horse nomads. It is forbidden to kill within sight of one, and most have some odd and unique restrictions applicable to those who visit there.

While most seeps are little more than pools surrounded by denser grasses and perhaps a few trees, some are larger, up to a few miles across. Never truly a bog or swamp, such seeps can give rise to fens supporting cattails, bulrushes, and other water plants as well as small pools filled with fish, turtles, and waterfowl. Many birds stop at these places on their great migrations north and south to feed on the fen's plant and animal life before taking flight in great flocks. The K'Haln hunt the margins of the fens but rarely venture into their depths. While there is wild talk that a water serpent lives at the heart of each of these wetlands, the trepidation of the horse nomads is more prosaic. While never more than a few feet deep at any one point, the fens can be quite muddy and wet, which makes it difficult for horses to traverse.

SHIMMERING RIVER

The Shimmering River flows from its source in the Stoneheart Mountains south along the eastern eaves of the mountains until it empties into the Xircos River, which in turn runs to Legions Bay and the Gulf of Akados far to the south. By taking this route, those wishing to travel between the gulf and the North Sea can cut off the months it would otherwise take to sail around the Isthmus of Irkaina.

Not all travelers on the Shimmering River are simply passing by, however, for it was recently discovered that the river carries gold down from its mountain origins. The local Lundhargo tribes — horse nomads related to the K'Haln — have long draped fleeces in the water to collect gold. Hedin Armondson learned this and tried it himself, dragging a series of fleeces behind his longship as he sailed for the distant gulf. It certainly worked, and the moderate amount of gold he strained out led others to come to the Shimmering River to fleece for their own fortunes.

STAKED LANDS

The most sacred of places to the K'Haln in the Sea of Grass, the Staked Lands lie near the center of the plains. The chieftains and great warriors of the tribes are laid to rest here on tall wooden platforms. Vultures are common in this area, as are other scavengers, and the smell or sight of the dead is never far away. Strips of prayer cloths snap in the wind and the normally hot grasslands seem to always be cool and overcast. Outsiders are often tempted to raid these burials as they are said to contain the greatest treasures these heroes bore in life. Those who contemplate such desecration should know that not just the K'Haln defend the Staked Lands, but the very spirit of the Sea of Grass is said to watch over it.

STONES OF KASHIMIR

Not far from the Staked Lands are seven stones cut from the distant mountains and carried in ages past far out onto the plains. These stones serve as a meeting place for the K'Haln tribes and is where they elect their chief of chieftains, when they have one. The post is currently vacant, and has been for generations. The stones are a sacred place, and no killing can be done within their bounds or in sight of them. Other taboos include a ban on sex, drinking blood, or drawing weapons. During the year, various tribes come here to meet and trade, lending at times a festival air to the stones. The rest of the time, the stones stand empty and forlorn amid the tall grass.

THE STUMPS

Not far from the edge of the Vastmir Plains lies a failed attempt by Northlanders to settle on the Sea of Grass. Twenty years ago, Jarl Erp Danson settled here with his family and a small band of followers. After building a stout stockade, the jarl gathered wild cattle to form a herd and cut the thick prairie sod for farming. The work was laborious, and Erp's followers slowly deserted him for better prospects. One night, the K'Haln came and burned the fledgling hall, killing all inside. All that remains is a part of the wall and a fragment of roof, as well as the charred stumps of the palisade.

TANOMIR FENS

As the waters of Lake Hargos empty to the east, they flow into a lowland known as the Tanomir Fens, some 200 miles of swamp and bog. The current is slow here, and interrupted by brackish pools and sandbars. During the short summers, those who choose to take a ship between the North Sea and the Gulf of Akados via the Grand Portage must take this route. With care, a knowledgeable captain can usually pick out a route to permit a longship to pass, but depending on the season and the amount of rainfall in the mountains, there may be no way to avoid bottoming out, which requires backtracking or disembarking and towing the ship forward by hand. Such a process can be laborious and unpleasant, as the fens breed hordes of mosquitoes and many varieties of incessantly biting flies.

In the winter, the Tanomir Fens freeze over and are covered by ice and, often, great drifts of snow. This makes travel here even more perilous, as the ice may not support the weight of a person, and those who break through the ice find themselves soaking wet in sub-zero conditions, and potentially stuck in the unfrozen muck beneath.

Eventually, at its eastern end, the waters of the fens coalesce into a single stream, and the Vindelsalven River reforms and continues its path to Seagestre Gulf on the North Sea.

The Tanomir Fens are home to the Bog Walkers, a tribe of Seagestrelanders who made it up the Vindelsalven generations ago and now eke out a meager existence here among the fens. In their watery fortress, they do not fear Northlander or K'Haln attacks. But that does not mean they are safe, and they pay a price for their security from attack.

Any captain — and even the Bog Walkers — passing through the fens know that they must always take care, for the fens host many dangers. Hags and wyrms hunt here, and it is said that a race of strange folk with the heads of lizards can be found in the deepest parts of the swamps. What these monsters don't slay may fall instead to one of a dozen diseases passed on by brackish water and biting insects.

VASTMIR PLAINS

The forests of Seagestreland slowly give way on the west to the Vastmir Plains, the eastern region of the Sea of Grass. Small clumps of trees grow where the aquifer rises, or along small streams wandering toward the coast. The Seagestrelanders sometimes hunt this region, seeking aurochs and giant sloths and other plains-dwelling creatures. They must take great care, however, as this region is also home to the Mongat tribesfolk, horse-riding nomads who are not above taking prisoners and selling them as slaves in faraway markets.

VINDELSALVEN RIVER

Arising on the eastern eaves of the Stoneheart Mountains, the Vindelsalven River first pours into Lake Hargos, then meanders through the Tanomir Fens, and finally flows east until it empties into Seagestre Gulf in the North Sea at the small trading village of Stavie. For the Northlanders, this watercourse is their main means of traveling out onto the Sea of Grass, and is easily navigable until it reaches the fens. Even so, travelers rarely stop along the way, for few make the plains their destination and instead seek the Grand Portage and passage to the Shimmering River and the rich lands to the south.

VAST DESERT REGION

The Vast Desert is a climatological anomaly. This hot and dry wasteland stretches across terrain neighboring the cold Northlands. According to Hyperborean records, in the past this land was merely a dry, steppe grassland. But upon the destruction of Tsen, the temperatures in the region began to rise and rainfall became even more scarce, which resulted in the sandy, arid landscape of the Vast Desert today.

Scholars who consider the matter largely believe that the event that destroyed Tsen and created the Burning Wastes interacted with the Tropic of Arden in a manner that caused these climate changes to occur. Others, however, speculate that an additional factor may be a heat source lying deep beneath the desert's surface.

The fine particles of sand in the Vast Desert are hot to the touch, as many travelers can attest (and prove by producing at least one pair of sandals or shoes scorched by prolonged contact with the searing ground). The explanations for this phenomenon run the gamut from natural occurrences such as a subterranean river of lava or an underground peat fire to the fantastical as exemplified by the legends of the sprawling efreeti city to the totally bizarre theory about a perpetually burning crematorium. Supporters of these theories point to the Vast Desert's temperature data. While daytime highs are fairly normal for the biome's standards (110° Fahrenheit during the summers and 80° Fahrenheit during the winter), nighttime lows rarely drop more than 20° Fahrenheit overnight, suggesting the dry air either retains more warmth than it should or an alternative heat source keeps the night air downright balmy.

Details of the Vast Desert region and Tsen can be found in ***The Lost Lands: Sword of Air***.

BURNING WASTES

When ruin came to Tsen in 1491 I.R., the Barrier Hills to the west partially absorbed and deflected the shock waves south and east, spreading the devastation across a vast swath of territory now known as the Burning Wastes. The blast seared the land, though the impacts incrementally diminish based upon the distance from the epicenter in Tsen. The areas closest to the razed city suffer the greatest. Virtually nothing grows on the outskirts of Tsen. The soil is dry, mostly gravel and dust, and supports little in the way of either animal or plant life. What survives in these wastes tend to be mutated animals, carnivorous plants, and strange creatures that seemingly thrive in this arid and toxic environment. Even humanoids are a rare sight in this rugged terrain.

The Dead Lake is the only reputed and reliable water source within the Burning Wastes. Many of the buildings surrounding this body of water withstood the devastation. Nonetheless, they remain abandoned and are almost certainly haunted. However, some historians believe more buildings may lie beneath the waves. Debates rage about whether the lake predates the city's founding, thus suggesting the presence of an older civilization in the region, or whether the lake is a byproduct of Tsen's utter devastation. It seems likely that centuries of erosion took a terrible toll on any stone structure in the briny deep, yet some believe an expertly crafted building could endure prolonged exposure to water.

TSEN, RUINS OF

At its zenith, Tsen was the undisputed crown jewel of the Hyperborean Empire. The Hyperboreans founded the city to commemorate the eradication of the Hundaei and celebrate their transcendence to superpower status. The victors built their grand metropolis in 689 I.R. on ground sacred to the faith of Arden, securely nestled in a valley surrounded by the Piedmont Highlands (as they were known at the time). Tsen rapidly expanded, swelling from a population of a few thousand souls to roughly 500,000 inhabitants within a few decades. Wealth and knowledge also poured into the city, elevating Tsen into rarified air among Akados' greatest marvels. To acknowledge its growing sophistication and ascendance onto the world stage, it became known as the City of Wonders. Tsen thrived for 800 years and kept the world continuously awed over the next arcane or technological breakthrough to emerge from its laboratories and classrooms. Yet eight centuries of unparalleled achievements and magnificent accomplishments were undone in a single day.

Even the wisest could not foresee Tsen's total annihilation. While bloodthirsty humanoid marauders and inhuman monstrosities seemingly sprung from the ground around Tsen during the decades before its collapse, the city's potent military easily kept the swelling tide in check. Yet despite one victory after another, the enemies' numbers never abated. Year after year, the relentless hordes kept coming, pillaging the estates and villages beyond Tsen's imposing walls and fortifications. Tsen's oblivious citizens took notice of the escalating conflict only when a force of giants and their war machines finally punched a hole in the city's outer defenses. In response to the breach, the city's leaders finally assumed a wartime footing to completely eliminate the monstrous threat once and for all. Within a matter of weeks, Tsen conscripted thousands of able-bodied men to bolster the ranks of its already impressive army. In glorious fashion to the bluster of pomp and circumstance, columns of troops poured out of the city to face the enemy in a climactic battle on the fields surrounding Tsen. And in an instant, these best laid plans were irrevocably foiled.

It began with a portent of a white, feathered serpent rising from the Gulf of Akados to the south and soaring into the skies above Tsen. The exact mechanism responsible for what happened next and the winged beast's role in these events remain enduring mysteries to this day. However, there is no disputing that shortly after the feathered serpent appeared in the heavens, Tsen ceased to exist in an apocalyptic blast that leveled everything for miles around it. Nothing survived the unspeakable carnage. The cataclysm transformed Tsen and the surrounding area into a forsaken wasteland. Those who fled Tsen before its destruction resettled in other areas, most notably the Gray Tower in Oxibbul.

Most people believe nothing short of a god — and an exceptionally powerful one at that — could have wrought the devastation visited upon Tsen on that fateful day. Some speculate that the city's scholars and arcane practitioners were on the verge of a profound discovery that would have altered the balance of power between mortals and the divine beings lording over them. Others believe the witnesses mistook the feathered serpent for a comet, meteor, or an asteroid that crashed into Tsen and utterly pulverized it. Whatever the cause, the effects still endure.

At the present time, Tsen resembles an abandoned ghost town seemingly frozen in time. Some of its grand stone structures withstood the devastation, though years of exposure to the elements further eroded their already scarred surfaces. The detonation reduced the remainder of its stone buildings to rubble, while the conflagration that followed the explosion transformed its wooden buildings into charred ash. Although the ground no longer trembles and the flames burned out long ago, Tsen remains inhospitable. The soil, the air, the water, and virtually everything else in Tsen is poisonous. The melted sand and fine rocks making up the ground retain almost no moisture and cannot support even the simplest form of plant life. Although short term or prolonged exposure kills most living creatures who venture here, those who can survive in this toxic environment mutate in ways sometimes beneficial and sometimes detrimental. Some change so drastically that they become unrecognizable, while others develop terrifying powers that make them far more dangerous than ordinary members of their species. Of course, the undead, constructs, and some other creature types suffer no ill effects from Tsen's toxicity.

It is speculated that the lucrative mines beneath the city may have also survived predominately unscathed from the cataclysm. Tsen's founders erected the metropolis on this site to provide the expensive city with a consistent source of lead, gold, silver, and other valuable metals to finance construction expenditures and as a commodity to export to its neighbor Apothasalos or distant Bard's Gate. Speculation abounds that some of Tsen's population, including its ruling elite or its researchers, may have fled into the mines at the first sign of trouble, bringing their riches or their wondrous discoveries with them. Nonetheless, anyone who escaped the initial cataclysm would have also had to adapt to living underground for an extended period of time with any other creatures that cohabitate the mines. To date, no one has ventured to the mines to confirm or refute any of these theories.

THE BUNTESVELDT

Capital: none
Notable Settlements: Alkis Anvil, Bliski, Capra, Karedorn, Morborg, Shinvi, Stavropol, Ustran Pazeel
Ruler: none
Government: loose confederation of independent (sometimes rival) city-states; each has seat on Veldtrada council
Population: 337,410 (288,000 Irkainian, 21,300 Foerdewaith, 12,700 Erskaelosi, 7,760 hill dwarf, 3,850 half-orc, 3,800 Ashurian)
Monstrous: wild dogs, bat swarms, orcs, ankhegs, blood hawks, gnolls, lions, ghouls, death dogs, worgs, giant scorpions, ogres, wights, apparitions, bog hounds, sword wights, mummies, will-o'-wisps
Languages: Common, Semuric, Erskin, Dwarven, Orc
Religion: Chernobog, Belun, Svarog, Matsyra, Morozko, Mah-Barek
Resources: foodstuffs, wool, horses, livestock (sheep, cattle), furs, pit fighters, mercenaries
Currency: mixed
Technology Level: High Middle Ages

The land known as the Buntesveldt stretches from the borders of Brounthia in the north to the coast of the Gulf of Akados to the south, and between the harsh Vast Desert to the west and Irkainian Desert to the east. In the local tongue, its name means "colorful grassland."

Most of the Buntesveldt is indeed grassland, primarily tallgrass prairie. Why it is fertile in the midst of two deserts is a bit of a mystery. No major rivers run through these lands, but it receives plentiful rainfall on winds blowing from the Gulf of Akados to the south. Most scholars who consider the matter believe that this weather pattern, so different from that in the neighboring deserts, is the result of interaction of the Tropic of Arden with the cold currents in the gulf heading east to west offshore.

The Buntesveldt has been a crossroads of wars for thousands of years, as armies ranged from the centers of Akados in the west to Libynos in the east. The grassland conceals many burial mounds, necropolises, and ruined hill forts; some of which are reputed to be inhabited by undead.

HISTORY AND PEOPLE

The lands of the Buntesveldt were originally the home of various tribal folk related to the Erskaelosi of Akados. These tribes roamed throughout the Irkainian Peninsula for thousands of years, likely only disturbed on those occasions when Hyperborean armies used the peninsula on their campaigns east and west through their empire. Some Hyperboreans undoubtedly decided to settle in this region, and many of the current cities and towns appear to have foundations that go back to those ancient days.

Over time, the folk of the Buntesveldt settled increasingly in towns and then cities, though many stayed on the plains, preferring a nomadic life like their ancestors. Eventually, five cities came to dominate the grasslands: Bliski, Karedorn, Morborg, Stavropol, and Ustran Pazeel. At various points in history, one or another of the cities managed to conquer one or more of the others, but such times were seldom lasted long as the folk of the Buntesveldt tend to be disorderly and often unwilling to accept outside authority (while, by contrast, often deferring without question to their city's leadership). Over the years, cities forged various alliances with the nomadic tribes in the region to either enforce or overthrow conquests, but the allegiance of the nomads can be a fickle thing, and anyone who relies upon it is likely to live a short life.

At various times, the folk of the Buntesveldt were forced to flee to other lands or otherwise saw their population plummet, particularly during the Great Darkness and at the time of Daan's campaign to Libynos when many of the warriors of the grasslands joined his legions. In each case, however, they returned to their ancestral homeland.

About a thousand years ago, following the fall of the Hyperborean Empire, the Ammuyad Caliphate of northern Libynos crossed the Mulstabhin Passage and seized lands in Pelshtaria. The caliph's representatives eventually found their way to the cities of the Buntesveldt, where they introduced the worship of their god, Mah-Barek, and suggested that paying tribute to the caliph would be a wise choice. The response by the cities varied, with some paying nominal tribute, while others tied up the foreigners in webs of delay. The preferred state of chaos among the folk of the Buntesveldt was infinitely frustrating to the caliph's people, and undoubtedly plans were being made for a military solution. But after 150 years or so, plague in the caliphate's capital city and rebellion in the Antioch City-States drew the caliph's attention away. When the Pelshtarians finally threw off the foreign yoke, some in the Buntesveldt breathed a sigh of relief that the threat from afar had passed; others failed to notice, as they had already gone back to the old ways of undermining other cities of the grasslands.

Outside of the cities, most of the settled folk of the Buntesveldt live in small fortified settlements, towns, or ranches that are generally called klaches.

Though nomadic tribes continue to roam the plains, over the years they have been driven back by repeated campaigns by the city-states. Caught between the two deserts and their settled cousins, many of the nomads have taken to trading more the raiding, and have even adopted foreigners into their ranks. Ironically, the comparative peace and the arrival of foreigners have seen the nomadic population grow, putting some pressure on the resources of the veldt. A critical mass is growing and there are those who fear that it may only be a matter of time before someone decides that becoming a warlord of howling plains nomads would be a good career move.

RELIGION

Most folk of the Buntesveldt revere a pantheon of gods unique to the region, likely the original gods of the tribes. These include Chernobog, He Who Schemes in Darkness, Belun the Comforter, Svarog the Fire in the Sky, Matsyra, the Mother, and Morozko, Grandfather Frost. They also venerate (or at least placate) various spirits of nature and the home. There are no organized churches for these deities; rather, smaller shrines can be found in settlements and in natural locations where the presence of the god is particularly acute.

The worship of the Ammuyad deity Mah-Barek took hold to some extent in some of the cities of the Buntesveldt. Particularly among certain people living in the port cities on the Gulf of Akados, taking a foreign religion can be seen as a sign of sophistication, which aids in matters of trade with the caliphate. Small temples of the Church of Fatimashan and the Church of Marwen can be found in most major cities. Their clerics remain frustrated, however, that even their adherents continue to placate nature and home spirits, at least in private.

TRADE AND COMMERCE

The port cities of the Buntesveldt do a bustling trade with merchants from all over the Gulf of Akados and the Sinnar Ocean. Foodstuffs, textiles and horses, and commodities (such as amber) brought from the Northlands are exchanged shipside or in markets for spices, silk, manufactured items, and other foreign goods.

LOYALTIES AND DIPLOMACY

Separated by deserts on the east and the west, and a plain inhabited by nomads to the north, the Buntesveldt is isolated, and as a result faces little in the way of foreign threat. It tries to remain on good terms with all of the nations with which it trades, including its neighbors on the Irkainian Peninsula, but also the merchants of Foere and Bard's Gate, Castorhage, Reme, the Ammuyad Caliphate, and even far Khemit. The relationship with the caliphate can be a bit tense at times, but local adherents of Mah-Barek act as middlemen to ensure that matters do not escalate.

Locally, the relations among the city-states of the Buntesveldt itself varies from time to time, even sometimes day to day. Alliances are regularly made and broken, threats are delivered and ignored, and occasional skirmishes even occur.

GOVERNMENT

No unified government oversees the Buntesveldt. Each city-state rules itself and its region (the boundaries of which are largely agreed upon through ancient tradition, though that isn't to say disputes never arise), with no input from outsiders. However, each of the five major city-states sends a representative to a body known as the Veldtrada, a council of the cities that normally meets at Bliski. It is not a legislative body in any sense and has no authority to make laws or bind any city-state or other residents of the Buntesveldt. Rather, it provides a forum for discussion so that the leaders of the city-states can peacefully meet for mutual planning, treaties, and the administration of Alkis Anvil.

MILITARY

Each city-state raises its own army (and navies in the case of the port cities) for its own protection. These armies are usually under the command of the city leader. The only exception is the citadel of Alkis Anvil, to which each city-state is required to send a complement of soldiers.

POLITICAL SUBDIVISIONS OF THE BUNTESVELDT

ALKIS ANVIL, CITY OF

Ruler: Field Marshal Velis Skander
Government: military governor
Population: 5,879 (human [Irkainian])

Alkis Anvil is a military city on the verge of the Irkainian Desert whose purpose is to defend against raids and other incursions by the dwellers of the desert, humanoid and otherwise. The city is supported and administered cooperatively by all five city-states through the Veldtrada, the council of the city leaders.

Alkis Anvil sits on top of a hill overlooking the desert to the east, and is surrounded by a high stone wall. It hosts more than 2,500 soldiers of the five city-states, and more than that in civilians who provide the various necessities required by the troops. While a town for many of the civilians has grown up around the citadel on the hill slopes, in times of trouble there is more than enough space for all to fit within the walls. A deep well provides good water, and supplies are held in sufficient amounts to permit Alkis Anvil to withstand a siege of many months.

As is tradition, a marshal from Bliski commands the forces within Alkis Anvil. The current commander is Field Marshal Velis Skander, a relatively no-nonsense soldier who views his post as a solemn duty. However, he has now served in Alkis Anvil for 13 years and is beginning to look forward to a reassignment (or, if necessary, retirement) back to Bliski. As a result, some note that his attention wanders at times, and discipline among the troops suffers accordingly.

As small village called Wadi Pradyma stands southeast of Alkis Anvil, where it provides some trade with outlanders. It also marks the beginning of the Sandrun Track, the old Hyperborean Road that crosses the desert and leads to the Isthmus of Irkaina.

BLISKI, CITY OF

Ruler: Herzog Volger Werbrüten
Government: hereditary lord
Population: 28,262 (23,412 Irkainian, 2,110 Foerdewaith, 1,030 hill dwarf, 900 Erskaelosi, 460 half-orc, 350 Ashurian)

Bliski is the second-largest city in the Buntesveldt. Much trade passes through its large and well-managed harbor, which hosts vessels from nations around the Gulf of Akados and the Sinnar Ocean. Bliski is also a convenient trading location for merchants from Morborg and Stavropol in the north, whether they wish to sell in the city's markets or to the ships at port.

The city's herzog (equivalent to a duke) is a hereditary ruler, though new laws require the advice and consent of a council of landed nobles that meets quarterly in the grand hall of the palace. Herzog Volger Werbrüten is the 11th of his family to hold the title, and in many ways sees Bliski as he might a child: to be nurtured, protected, and promoted. He is relentless in his efforts to make the city not just the finest in all of the Buntesveldt, but also a leading city on the whole of the Sinnar Ocean. He anxiously seeks out travelers from afar who can tell him of other lands, and of the sights and sounds of other cities and realms. Much more so than his conservative peers, Volger is prepared to adopt foreign ideas that might enhance his city and its prosperity and reputation.

The towns of Shinvi and Capra are vassals of Bliski.

The Veldtrada meets in Bliski, and by tradition the herzog serves as the council's speaker. Meetings have been increasingly tense of late as friction between Bliski and Ustran Pazeel grows. Fortunately, the Veldtrada decides few issues of import, and those that are within its purview are those where the interests of the two cities tend to align.

CAPRA, TOWN OF

Ruler: Burgrave
Government: burgrave appointed by the herzog of Bliski
Population: 3,122 (2,593 Irkainian, 330 Foerdewaith, 102 hill dwarf, 85 half-orc, 12 Ashurian)

Capra is a town of the Buntesveldt and a vassal state of Bliski inland from Shinvi. It sits on the main trade route north to Morborg.

At various points in its history, Capra has been independent of Bliski and, in fact, of all the other city-states of the Buntesveldt. The town's leaders are typically traditionally-minded sorts with fine estates who maintain a strong martial pride in having carved out a town in the midst of the steppes and nomadic tribes. They usually seek to take no part in the political maneuverings of the larger settlements.

About 60 years ago, the grandfather of Herzog Volger Werbrüten of Bliski found himself in one of his city's periodic disputes with Ustran Pazeel and sent representatives to Capra to ensure their support in the conflict. Content with his town's little corner of the world and the rights ceded to them by law and custom, the burgrave of Capra planned to weather this new storm as it had all others. Namely, by ignoring it and staying studiously neutral.

Unfortunately, several leading families of Capra attempted to make an arrangement with Ustran Pazeel, the terms of which eventually found their way via whispers to the herzog. Within short order, a military detachment from Bliski was at the gates of Capra demanding the surrender of the leaders of the plot. When the burgrave was not forthcoming, a siege was set that lasted about two weeks before the annoyed leaders of several of the more prominent families of Capra opened the gates and handed over the decapitated heads of the traitors.

Since that time, Capra has been held carefully under the dominion of the larger city on the coast. The herzogs now appoint the local burgrave, though they take care to select locals who can be expected to satisfy the leading families of the town as well as the demands of Bliski.

KAREDORN, CITY OF

Ruler: Graf Volya Naraden
Government: hereditary lordship
Population: 9,600 (7,700 Irkainian, 765 Foerdewaith, 610 Ashurian, 275 half-orc, 100 hill dwarf, 150 other)

Karedorn is a small city at the end of the peninsula at the southwestern end of the domains of the Buntesveldt. For all of its history, its leaders have come from a single, ancient tribe of nomads known as the Naraden that once lived on this peninsula. The genealogy of the current graf goes back more than a thousand years, and if one takes the semi-legendary names before that time at face value, for 2,000 years further back.

As a result, there is much about Karedorn that is both ancient and traditional. The various religious festivals are taken very seriously, as are a number of fairly archaic customs. Visitors to a home are expected to make a small sacrifice to the household spirits. The obligations of hospitality are strictly enforced. Wearing a red-colored item of clothing is forbidden, unless one is heading off to battle or is an executioner performing official duties.

On the other hand, in many ways the city of Karedorn is far more open, both to foreigners and new ideas, than any other settlement in the Buntesveldt. The large, well-kept port sees much traffic from around the Gulf of Akados and the Sinnar Ocean. A sizable population of foreigners resides in the city seasonally or all year round. In fact, several foreigners made permanent homes in the area around Karedorn, and two were granted landed titles and serve in trusted positions as advisors to the graf.

In addition to the sea trade, vineyards and olive groves cover the hills behind Karedorn and produce wines and oils sought in many other ports of call.

Graf Volya is currently seeking ways to attract ships to visit her port rather than Ustran Pazeel or Bliski farther up the coast, including offering tariff holidays and a certain amount of free maintenance from her shipbuilders. However, she is aware of the acquisitive glances toward her city by the atabeg of Ustran Pazeel, and so is careful to cultivate the friendship of Herzog Werbrüten as a counterbalance to her dangerous neighbor.

MORBORG, CITY OF

Ruler: Boyars, led by Town Burgher Tarl Redsson
Government: oligarchy
Population: 21,811 (18,011 Irkainian, 1,330 Foerdewaith, 1,250 hill dwarf, 820 Erskaelosi, 220 Ashurian, 180 half-orc)

Morborg is the third-largest city in the Buntesveldt and the primary settlement of the lands inland from the coast (at least until one reaches Stavropol far to the northeast). It boasts high, thick walls as it has had to fend off assaults by its nomadic cousins from time to time.

Unlike the other cities of the Buntesveldt, Morborg is ruled by a council of local wealthy landowners known as boyars who together are known as the oligarchs. They elect another person to be the town burgher, who administers the city and is granted full membership and rights as an oligarch. The current burgher is Tarl Redsson, a grandson of immigrants who came from the Northlands, who owns several taverns and warehouses in the city. Before being appointed as burgher, Redsson was a captain in the city guard, where he developed a reputation as an excellent pugilist, deadly with a sword.

A small woodland of oak and pine once stood outside of Morborg, one of the only forests of these otherwise grass-covered plains. Unfortunately, it was logged until almost no trees are now left standing. As with the rest of the region, wood now must be imported to Morborg.

Morborg is famous throughout the Buntesveldt for its dark beers, and in particular Darkdale Bogwheat Ale, which is named for a boggy lowland area east of the city.

SHINVI, TOWN OF

Ruler: burgrave
Government: burgrave appointed by the herzog of Bliski
Population: 2,018 (2,005 Irkainian, 9 Foerdewaith, 4 Ashurian)

Shinvi is a small fishing village that grew into a larger town partly because its harbor is not deep enough for large ships. The farms and ranches inland and along the coast as far east as the edge of the Irkainian Desert bring their goods to trade here. Small coastal lighters carry goods south to Bliski and bring cargoes back. Shepherds bringing their herds from Capra to the north come down the Fold Road and stop at Shinvi to fatten up a bit before the big push to Bliski.

For most of its history, Shinvi has been a quiet and almost forgotten town. It sees enough wealth pass through to keep it afloat, the fishing is good, and the farms outside of town boast groves of almonds and olives, fields of wheat and barley, and some small herds of sheep. The population has grown, but slowly, as most immigrants to the region seek out the larger cities.

Shinvi is also a vassal of the larger city Bliski down the coast and has been for as long as folks here can remember. That being said, they keep their heads down, pay just the amount that Bliski seeks, and in return are pretty much left alone. Recently, however, pirates and corsairs off the coast began troubling the ships and boats sailing in or out of Shinvi's harbor. The town has no navy and is thus a much easier target than the other fortified ports on the coast. As a result, some town leaders are thinking about sending a delegation to Bliski for aid. But they fear what the herzog might ask for in return.

Stavropol, City of

Ruler: Graf Ingevni Plutovsky
Government: hereditary lordship
Population: 7,580 (6,105 Irkainian, 620 hill dwarf, 400
Erskaelosi, 220 Ashurian, 135 half-orc, 100 Foerdewaith)

Stavropol, the northernmost city of the Buntesveldt, sits at the end of the long trade road from the port towns on the Gulf of Akados far to the south. The footprint of the city is much larger than needed for its resident population, which provides for ample room should the people of the countryside need to take shelter here. It boasts high, thick walls to defend against any nomadic marauders who might assault the city. Some 900 miles from the nearest city of Morborg, the people of Stavropol know that in the event of an emergency, no help will be able to arrive quickly, if it arrives at all. That fact has led to a high degree of self-sufficiency among the people here, in addition to the creation of careful alliances with nearby nomadic tribes and a different perspective on security than the other cities near the coast.

Outside the city, large estates held by boyars grow various crops and provide pastureland for sheep and cattle. Trade routes run from here to the north, and it is not uncommon to see traders from Brounthia, Monrovia, and even farther to the north arrive in laden caravans at the city gates.

Graf Ingevni Plutovsky rules the region with an iron will. He is well aware that the wealth that passes through his city via trade, which fills his coffers, also presents an attractive target to those with the ability to take it. He is constantly scheming to ensure that Stavropol gets the best of any arrangement. And in point of fact, he is not above exaggerating the risks and perils to the city in order to strengthen his grip on the reins of power.

The northern verge of the Irkainian Desert is not far from Stavropol, and occasionally creatures of the deep sands find their way this far north. A small keep is maintained close to the desert to watch for any incursions and to mobilize the army should such an event arise. The keep is also used as a base for certain explorers and adventurers who seek things that may be hidden in the desert, or who need a place to rest before continuing a journey farther to the east or up to the north.

Ustran Pazeel, City of

Ruler: Atabeg Viskar Kurgan
Government: hereditary lordship
Population: 73,021 (68,091 Irkainian, 1,280 Ashurian, 1,210
half-orc, 1,090 Foerdewaith, 1,000 hill dwarf, 250 Erskaelosi,
100 other)

Though a city of the Buntesveldt whose atabeg sits on the Veldtrada, Ustran Pazeel is different from any other city of the region. For one, it used to be known as Graffa. Some 200 years ago, the herzog of Graffa married a noblewoman from Pelshtaria, whose father was from the Ammuyad Caliphate. Their son became an adherent of Mah-Barek and in his youth traveled to the capital of the caliphate at Hava. Eventually, he took an Ammuyad name (including the new family name of Kurgan) and made the town welcome to merchants from Pelshtaria and the caliphate, many of whom ended up settling in the region. Eventually, its leaders chose to rename it Ustran Pazeel (Pelshtarian for "source of blue waters"), and for themselves adopted the title of atabeg.

Over time, the city has grown substantially, both from internal growth and from immigration, though unfortunately without much forethought. In addition, a number of its leaders ended up being less-than-virtuous, taking bribes and seeking ways to make gold, whether legally or illegally. As a consequence, today Ustran Pazeel is a sprawling mass of alleys, markets, and slums, with gladiator pits (a tradition taken from cities in southern Libynos) and other vices. It is also the largest port city of the Buntesveldt, with a large portion of the sea trade (particularly from the caliphate) passing through its harbor.

Ustran Pazeel and Bliski have a long-standing rivalry as the two largest cities. More than political, this can be personal, as many on the Buntesveldt treat the citizens of Ustran Pazeel as foreigners, no matter how long they or their families may have lived here. In addition, Bliski continues to host the Veldtrada, its herzog is the speaker of the Veldtrada, and a captain of Bliski is always commander of Alkis Anvil — all privileges that the atabegs believe should be shared with their city. So far, however, bureaucratic corruption has robbed Ustran Pazeel of the financial and military power to challenge Bliski, even though the latter is smaller.

Geographic Features and Points of Interest in the Buntesveldt

Desert Road

The Desert Road runs from Bliski to the edge of the Irkainian Desert and then heads north along the verges of the desert until it meets up with the Great Veldt Road. It knits together the many small villages, farmsteads, ranches, and fishing hamlets along the eastern edge of the Buntesveldt. The road is wide enough for two wagons to pass each other. It is constructed of dressed sandstone, and features road markers and a drainage system. Sadly, a century of neglect has led to broken stones, filled ditches, lost markers, and a pair of deepening wagon ruts in the soft sandstone roadbed.

Fold Road

Running from Morborg to Shinvi and connecting the Desert Road with the Great Veldt Road, the Fold Road brings sheep from the interior of the Buntesveldt to market.

The Great Veldt Road

Stavropol is where the road ends and begins. From here, one can journey south along the paved road as far as distant Karedorn on the Gulf of Akados. Going north is open grassland, though a couple of trodden paths show the routes taken by merchants and travelers heading to and from the nations to the north.

The Kurgan Way

A project of the atabegs of Ustran Pazeel, the Kurgan Way runs from that city to Bliski. It is somewhat surprising that it was ever completed, as it was undoubtedly intended by the atabegs to provide an easy route for a conquering army to take on the way up the coast. The herzogs of Bliski may have permitted the construction as it would make it easier to monitor troop movements from the south, and to outflank them if they chose to take a route more inland. In any case, it has proven a boon to trade, and has not yet been used for a military campaign.

The Witch's Tail

This lone mountain rises up out of the grasslands to a snowcapped peak that can be seen from as far away as the Irkainian Desert. Natural philosophers have long pondered how this unusual geographic formation came to be, for there is no reason there should be a mountain here. The plains do not roll up to it in foothills, there are no mountain ranges nearby that the Witch's Tail could be an outlier of, and the land lacks any great waterway that could have eroded down hills or mountains around the Tail.

Even before natural philosophers pontificated about the mountain's origins, the local people had stories to explain it. One tale claimed that a powerful witch lived there. This witch, who tradition says should never be named so that her wrath is never brought down, is said to curse people with illnesses. Those who know her name risk falling sick, but also may use that knowledge to bring her magical powers to themselves. Knowing the witch's name is a sure sign of complicity in witchcraft, and local witch hunters go to great lengths to see if their suspects know one of the 107 names of the witch of Witch's Tail.

The folk of Ustran Pazeel believe that the mountain is the product of a battle between two djinn. They fought to raise a mountain into the sky, with one bringing it up and the other bringing it down. As it would be unfair to do this where other mountains could get in the way, they chose the grasslands as a neutral stage. The pair struggled and fought, and the mountain rose up to touch the stars and was dragged down until it was a great hole in the ground. After many years of this, the djinn grew bored with their sport and abandoned the mountain where it was.

To local nomads, the story of the mountain is that it rose up one day out of the grasslands because it wanted to. The spirit of the mountain had lived underground since the world was made and had heard stories from gophers, moles, and other burrowing creatures about the sun. The mountain wanted to see this strange thing, but could not through all the dirt and grass of the plains. It pushed and pushed, wiggled and jiggled, and after much effort poked through into the sky.

PRINCIPALITY OF PELSHTARIA

Capital: Irith Kel

Notable Settlements: Abernord, Alton, Ezerdúrum, Imazon, Izmirtzaçg, Jem Karteis, Mérsíni

Ruler: Prince Adem and Princess Adelet, and locally elected councils

Government: feudal with a competent local bureaucracy and elected councils

Population: 2,592,000 (1,911,930 human Pelshtarian ethnicity, 221,100 hill dwarf, 110,550 other human ethnicity, 99,250 halfling, 71,120 Erskaelosi, 52,210 Ashurian, 41,200 Berrini, 34,990 half-elf, 26,200 half-orc, 18,650 gnome, 2,800 high elf, 2,000 other)

Languages: Semuric, Dwarven

Religion: Mah-Barek

Resources: trade, manufactured goods, stonework, artwork, grain (wheat, barley), cattle, textiles (woolen), gold, gems, olives, oil, fruit

Currency: Pelshtarian

Technology Level: Medieval (cities), High Middle Ages (smaller settlements), Dark Ages (outlying areas)

Once the distant western edge of the Ammuyad Caliphate — and still is today depending with whom you speak — the Principality of Pelshtaria is a contradiction. According to the records of the caliphate, these lands constitute their province of Irkaina, a loyal taxpaying part of their domains. Such is not the understanding of those who live in the Principality of Pelshtaria, which is ruled by princes who ignore the caliph, though diplomatically so as to avoid damaging trade.

Five centuries ago, the land that is now Pelshtaria was inhabited by nomadic tribes likely related to the Erskaelosi of Akados and their cousins on the plains of the Buntesveldt. For long ages, armies passed through these lands on their way between Akados and Libynos, but the arid plains, steppes, and deserts of the Isthmus of Irkaina were left largely unsettled. Caliphate traders crossing the Mulstabhin Passage and the Sea of Spice told tales of these empty lands, which drew the attention of the caliph. After the departure of the Hyperboreans, the caliphate began an expansionist period during which it seized lands in the Antioch plains of northern Libynos. Finally, they looked here to the far northeastern corner of Akados. An expedition landed, fought the scattered horse and camel tribes, and pushed on along the northern coast.

After 10 years of campaigning, the armies reached the mouth of the Ilanos River. Behind them they had left a series of fortified towns to protect the overland route and to serve as bases for further thrusts into the interior. At the mouth of the river they built a large city that they named Irith Kel. Decades passed, and colonists from the caliphate swelled the ranks of the soldiery, occasionally intermarrying with the remnants of the local nomadic tribes.

The land between the Büyük Dâg Mountains and the Irkainian Desert was fertile, and the population rapidly soared. Living on a frontier, far

from home, the people learned to be self-reliant, largely independent of their parent nation. Every year saw new farms and villages founded, the local tribes having been subdued through warfare, trade, and absorption.

Settlements were eventually founded as far as the shores of the Gulf of Irkaina and through much of the interior of the Isthmus of Irkaina. The satrap of Irkaina sent out further expeditions, reaching as far as the cities of the Buntesveldt beyond the Irkainian Desert, with which trade was opened (and at least initial moves toward a conquest were contemplated). This humble frontier province was turning into a wealthy and powerful polity, one that wielded disproportionate power in the caliphate. Other satrapies eventually became envious of the resources being diverted from their own projects to further the expansion and growth of Irkaina.

Fearing a revolt among his nobility, the caliph sent his youngest son to replace the satrap. This turned the province into a royal demesne directly administered by the caliph's family, and so removed it from the politics of the satrapies. Within a few generations, it became the traditional post for the youngest sons of the caliphs for whom no better assignment was available. Not all such sons had a talent for governing a far province, however, and a century of inconsistent administration took its toll. The expansion ground to a halt. In the meantime, the wealth of Pelshtaria passed directly into the royal treasury and more than a few princely administrators made sure to not only take their cut, but to surround themselves with friends and supplicants seeking little more than wealth and luxury.

Some 150 years after the initial expansion of the caliphate's empire, plague struck at cities within its homeland, including the capital of Hava. The Antioch city-states took advantage of the situation and declared their independence from the caliphate. As the conflicts continued, administration of far Irkaina became unbearably burdensome, especially now that the province no longer was the source of great wealth it once had been. In 2773 I.R., the prince of Pelshtaria died and named his eldest son as heir without consulting the caliph. The nobles of the Irkainian Peninsula held their breaths and waited for the arrival of naval ships or soldiers to enforce a different succession. The invasion never came; the caliph, facing other more pressing matters, barely noticed the events in the far province.

Over the ensuing centuries, rule of the principality has passed by descent to the prior monarch's eldest child. Contacts with the caliphate dwindled to a point that the only relationship between the two realms is one of trade. The caliph in far Hava continues to stylize himself suzerain of Pelshtaria, but all now know this is just a title.

Even with the effective independence of Pelshtaria from the caliphate, the comparatively poor and corrupt rule of the princes largely continued unabated. Fifty years ago, however, a new prince named Kemal ascended the throne with radical ideas. A younger son, he was not expected to become prince and had traveled to the caliphate to study at its schools, where he learned much about law and governance. Upon the death of his elder sister, he returned to Irith Kel. As one of his first actions, he swept out the complex system of tax farmers, bureaucrats, and other leeches that held hereditary positions of little work and great pay. He then replaced those officials with people he knew, even some he had met while at school in the caliphate.

Links with the sprawling western parts of the province were strengthened, and a standing army was built to replace the underfunded and ill-equipped border patrols that so often failed to protect towns in the countryside from nomadic tribes. For the first time in centuries, the Northlanders were fended off when they came south past Monrovia to raid and pillage the northern coast.

After 30 years of reform, Kemal died and left behind a thriving and growing principality whose riches were being used to build infrastructure, universities, and hospitals, and to fund the defense of the land. He also left behind two children, the twins Prince Adem and Princess Adelet, who elected to govern jointly.

For the past two decades, Adem and Adelet have ruled Pelshtaria. They managed to continue their father's work of good governance and investing in the nation, kept the barbarians safely beyond the frontiers, and are much beloved by the populace. The increasingly obvious wealth of the nation, however, has drawn attention from others, including some within the caliphate who note that the principality is, in fact, a province of the caliphate even though it pays no taxes to the royal treasury. Some in far Hava are beginning to speak openly about changing those circumstances, perhaps at the point of a sword. Others, particularly among the trading houses, see the peaceful and open principality as a source of wealth they wish to leave undisturbed.

Most localities, whether a city, town, or other holding, in Pelshtaria are governed in part by a Council of Worthies. These bodies are chosen by a vote of all landholding citizens of good standing. In practice, this means that the wealthy elect their own to serve on the council, using the middle classes to round out the vote. These councils have limited powers and must report to the local feudal lord, who more often than not has a few friends or retainers on the council. Their role is to administer to local issues, adjudicate non-capital crimes (murder, arson, rape, kidnapping, and treason being the primary capital crimes in the principality), and pass laws with the consent of the feudal lord.

The principality boasts a sizable population of hill dwarves. While some reside in the larger cities where they make a living crafting, smithing or trading, most live in small villages or communities in the Ágaç Hills. Under a longstanding arrangement with the princes, the dwarves living there are largely left to govern themselves. As far as anyone knows, none of their communities holds more than a few hundred dwarves. Scholars believe that the ancient Hyperboreans learned the secret of steel from hill dwarves who lived here in ancient times. As a consequence, treasure hunters are often seen hunting through the Ágaç Hills in search of lost dwarven cities. The hill dwarves themselves will not comment on such speculation, and watch any who scour the hills with a degree of bemusement.

POLITICAL SUBDIVISIONS OF THE PRINCIPALITY OF PELSHTARIA

IRITH KEL, CITY OF (CAPITAL)

Ruler: Prince Adem and Princess Adelet, and Council of Worthies
Government: feudal
Population: 279,410 (192,540 human Pelshtarian ethnicity, 22,780 other human ethnicity, 17,320 hill dwarf, 13,500 halfling, 12,230 Ashurian, 9,120 Berrini, 6,100 half-elf, 5,240 half-orc, 250 gnome, 180 high elf, 150 other)

The capital of the Principality of Pelshtaria and seat of power for the twin prince and princess, Irith Kel is one of the oldest cities in the region. It serves as a major port where merchants from the Ammuyad Caliphate, the Northlands, the Buntesveldt, Abernord, the interior of the Isthmus of Irkaina, and even the Sea of Grass meet. As a major governmental and economic center, Irith Kel is the main focus of the region and what happens here affects the fortunes and lives of the entire principality.

Built five centuries ago by an expedition from the caliphate, Irith Kel is a well-planned city. The center is dominated by the palace and the barracks of the royal guard, both of which are surrounded by an inner wall. Between this center and the first outer wall are broad avenues, plazas with fountains and gardens, the houses of minor nobility, the University of Irkaina, the massive edifice of the Palace of Justice and Administration, and the old souk where goods of the highest caliber are bought and sold.

The city's growth was a planned affair, and concentric walls enclose orderly neighborhoods that mimic the city center but on a less grand scale. Some of these quarters are reserved for foreign residents, some of whom have lived in Irith Kel for generations. There is a raucous Brounthian district, as well as districts that are home to folk with ties to other provinces of the caliphate. Yet other districts are devoted to a specific type of commerce, thus keeping the tanners on the edge of the city downwind of other districts, the metal workers' district (which also includes alchemists) where its fires can be contained, and the camel markets away from anyone with a nose. Sewers run beneath the streets of all the districts, and aqueducts bring water in from the distant Büyük Dâg Mountains.

Despite this good planning and (recent) good governance, Irith Kel is not without troubles. A thieves' guild operates within the city, and its tendrils stretch across the principality and into areas the principality once ruled. Revolutionaries are common, especially around the university and in the many coffee shops that dot the residential neighborhoods. Not everyone is happy with the open disloyalty to the caliphate. Street violence is not uncommon. Holding the wrong views and walking into the wrong coffee shop can be dangerous, possibly deadly.

ABERNORD, CITY OF

Ruler: Council of Worthies
Government: oligarchy
Population: 35,821 (21,111 human Pelshtarian ethnicity, 8,990 Berrini, 2,850 Ashurian, 1,475 other human ethnicity, 1,100 halfling, 285 half-elf, 10 other)

This city-state officially declared its independence from the Principality of Pelshtaria last year. It had never been tightly bound to the principality largely due to distance and cultural influence. The nearby Kingdom of Brounthia is often wracked by civil strife, and refugees from its internecine conflicts often flee south along the coast or make the perilous crossing of the northern plains of the Buntesveldt to reach Abernord. This has left the city-state with a large Brounthian population.

The city is a blend of local nomadic, Irkainian, Ammuyad, and Brounthian cultures. Architecturally, the old city shows the influence of the caliphate with its broad avenues, large open-air markets, and stonework. The outer city that grew beyond the old city walls is largely Brounthian in origin, with stone and timber buildings thrown up with little central planning, unpaved streets, and many tight alleyways. Fires are common in the outer wards, and the city watch despairs of keeping these boroughs in order.

While this merging of cultures is behind the split from the rest of the principality, internal divisions are also great. The wealthier merchants and older families live in the walled old city, while the descendants of refugees dwell in the warrens outside. The Brounthian population tends towards skilled artisans with a large class of urban poor. This has spurred more than one riot against the "foreign" higher classes in the city. It is the middle classes of petty merchants, artisans, scholars, and military officers who have successfully blended the two cultures and from where the impetus for independence comes.

Increasing the strife is the sheer number of impoverished and outcast Brounthian nobility who make the city their home. It seems that nearly every Brounthian can claim descent from one nearly extinguished noble house or another, and no small few pretend to have royal blood. Plots and intrigues abound that hope to put some distant claimant back in power. Many of these are little more than fantasies, but some manage to gather enough power to present trouble for the city and their neighbors.

ALTON, TOWN OF

Ruler: none
Government: none
Population: 6,390 (3,355 human Pelshtarian ethnicity, 1,560 other human ethnicity, 612 hill dwarf, 465 half-elf, 210 half-orc, 138 gnome, 50 other)

Less than a year old, Alton is a gold rush town that lies in unclaimed land deep in the Büyük Dâg Mountains. It is a wild place without law, and some locals say without mercy or other noble sentiments. In its short existence, it has burned down twice and been relocated to the confluence of the Kisa and Porphyra Rivers.

Alton is a polyglot town as the gold seekers come from across the world. Merchants followed them and nearly anything the rugged adventurers might want from tools, food, and supplies to liquor and prostitutes can be found here. Rumors that the pasha of Ezerdúrum plans to send a company of soldiers and a bey to take control of the town have been flying since the town was first established. So far, nothing has happened, but agents loyal to the pasha have been seen drinking, gambling, and taking long rides through the mountains to just look at things.

Ezerdúrum. City of

Ruler: Pasha Sohret Ozgen and Council of Worthies
Government: feudal and council
Population: 67,820 (30,425 human Pelshtarian ethnicity, 21,100 other human ethnicity, 7,725 hill dwarf, 3,300 halfling, 1,800 Ashurian, 1,625 half-elf, 1,350 half-orc, 350 gnome, 65 high elf, 80 other)

The city of Ezerdúrum lies at the mouth of the Porphyra River where it empties into the Gulf of Irkaina. A major trading port, Ezerdúrum has long sought to rival grand Mérsíni as the primary wool center for the principality. Cut off from the Ilanos basin by the Ágaç Hills, Ezerdúrum has only ever managed to draw in folks from the southeastern edges of the hill country. Despite this, or perhaps because of it, the nobility and merchants of Ezerdúrum are even more prideful and arrogant than the famed beys of Ágaç. Many of the beys who trade in Ezerdúrum run smaller farms than those to the north, but they claim their wool is of higher quality due to the nature of their south-facing hill country.

Gold was discovered last year in the neighboring Büyük Dâg Mountains. This led to thousands of fortune seekers flooding into the city, with some from as far away as Akados. This swelled the sleepy city's population and a large tent city grew up outside the walls. Pasha Sohret Ozgen welcomes the needed income as well as the boom in trade, and is collecting a tax on every ounce of gold that passes through the city. The Council of Worthies are less pleased by this turn of events and, although willing to make fortunes off of the gold rush, they do not hesitate to pass laws that hamper the newcomers. A growing feud between the locals and the gold rush followers is growing, and already a few physical altercations have occurred in the city's streets.

Imazon, City of

Ruler: Pasha Ceren Syfi and the Council of Worthies
Government: feudal and council
Population: 25,380 (20,695 human Pelshtarian ethnicity, 3,210 other human ethnicity, 500 halfling, 330 Ashurian, 265 half-elf, 200 hill dwarf, 150 half-orc, 30 other)

Of all the cities of Pelshtaria, Imazon has the Council of Worthies with the greatest power. Other cities might have influential councils, but in Imazon the pasha is clearly there to do little more than sign anything the council passes. The Council of Worthies appoints all officials, makes and passes all laws, and decides criminal cases by circumventing the courts and feudal rights in place of trying cases itself.

This does not mean that the old feudal system is gone, just that the power is now in the hands of the lower nobility: the beys. All the seats on the council are held either by the beys themselves or by their toadying hirelings. Even the powerful merchants' guilds of the city are beholden to the beys, for if those nobles decide not to sell their wool in Imazon, they might just ship it to another port.

It is the trade in wool, wheat, and other agricultural products that drives the economy of Imazon. The interior of the Pelshtarian Peninsula is rich land. There are few sources of mineral wealth, but there is plenty of room to ranch and farm, as well as centuries of farmsteads evolving into estates, and estates merging into larger affairs. Wool, both raw cloth and that cut and dyed by the city's artisans, is the main export, but wheat, barley, olives, oil, and fruit are loaded into waiting vessels for shipment around the Sinnar Ocean.

Izmirtzaçg, Town of

Ruler: Pasha Ozakar Vural and the Council of Worthies
Government: feudal and council
Population: 3,740 (3,285 human Pelshtarian ethnicity, 255 other human ethnicity, 100 hill dwarf, 65 halfling, 35 other)

Izmirtzaçg is the only major settlement on the Beyaz River, but even so it is a small town that offers little to visitors. Founded two centuries ago to serve the petty ranches along the river, Izmirtzaçg is laid out like other towns and cities in the principality with a clear urban area, surrounding wall, broad avenues, large plazas, and much planning and foresight. Sadly, the region never developed economically and thus did not attract many settlers. Izmirtzaçg does not even hold a wool market of its own, but instead ships its produce to Ezerdúrum for foreign trade.

As a result, the town is not fully occupied and whole neighborhoods lie unused by all save vagrants and vermin. The great plazas stand empty most of the time except for a few tired vendors or sun-toughened farmers in from the countryside. The beys of the region are equally poor, but hold their titles with great pride even if they have to work their pitiful estates themselves.

Mérsíni, City of

Ruler: Pasha Iltas Uçar and Council of Worthies
Government: feudal and council
Population: 159,341 (107,161 human Pelshtarian ethnicity, 15,985 other human ethnicity, 13,900 hill dwarf, 9,200 halfling, 4,350 Ashurian, 3,100 Berrini, 2,775 half-elf, 1,900 half-orc, 870 gnome, 100 other)

Spanning the confluence of the Ilanos and Çayusk Rivers, Mérsíni is the second city of Pelshtaria. The fertile Ágaç Hills provide much of the city's wealth, and outside the walls are hundreds of estates worked by slaves. These estates are the homes to the beys of Ágaç, minor nobility descended from the original pioneering settlers. Smaller farmsteads lie on the edge of the hill country on less-secure and less-fertile land.

Sheep are a main agricultural product of the region, and Mérsíni has become a major wool-producing and manufacturing hub. Every household maintains at least a small carding and spinning operation; even the wives of the beys traditionally spin some wool. Cloth is manufactured in large facilities inside the city and provides work for a large class of laborers. Wool merchants come from as far away as the caliphate to trade in the golden domed Grand Suk of Mérsíni, their cargoes easily floated down the Ilanos to Irith Kel.

Geographic Features and Points of Interest in the Principality of Pelshtaria

Ágaç Hills

This semi-arid highland runs between the Norwold Gulf and the Gulf of Akados. The western edge of the hills slowly slopes down into grassland in the north and the Irkainian Desert in the south.

In the north, the Ágaç Hills provide prime land for grazing, with small farms filling the valleys. Most of the principality's population of hill dwarves make their homes in this region, living in small villages or communities. Some legends suggest that one or more ancient dwarven cities were once located in these hills, where the ancient Hyperboreans first learned the secret of steel from the hill dwarves who dwelt there.

The south is a different story. As the Ágaç Hills run to the southwest, they become increasingly more arid until they are little more than a hilly extension of the Irkainian Desert. After crossing the Lesser Porphyra River, sheep ranches and farms become scarce and the land less inhabited. This part of the hills is an abode of monstrous creatures, many of whom make regular forays north to feast on sheep and shepherds alike.

Beyaz River

Along with the Ilanos and Porphyra rivers, the Beyaz River drains from the Ágaç Hills. A small river whose flow is shallow and sluggish at best, the Beyaz runs from the southeastern edge of the hills to the Gulf of Irkaina. It has seen little settlement or development aside from the town of Izmirtzaçg at its mouth. Along the river's course are small stands of cottonwood trees and willows, but beyond that the grasslands are dry most of the year. A few nomadic tribes roam the areas between the Ágaç Hills and the sea, though they steer clear of the Beyaz River.

A wild and rugged place, the Beyaz River is rumored to be the abode of a water serpent. Known as the Ejderha by the locals, this serpent is said to attack small isolated farmsteads as far as a hundred miles from the river. While there is some truth that outlying farms have been burned and their residents slaughtered in gruesome ways, there is no proof that the cause is a water dragon and not nomadic raiders or other bandits.

Büyük Dâg Mountains

The soaring Büyük Dâg Mountains dominate the southern coast of the Isthmus of Irkaina. The highest peak, Aryat, stands 13,400 feet tall, and a half dozen lesser peaks are barely 1,000 feet below that. The range is an extremely rugged land of high bluffs, knife-edge canyons, and snowcapped peaks. In the spring, streams course down the slopes and fill the valleys before feeding the Porphyra River. Winter brings powerful storms that blanket the mountains in snow and freezing rain, and thunder snowstorms are common.

The Büyük Dâg Mountains are uninhabited; at least they have been for the past thousand years. A millennium ago, the mountains were home to a kingdom of giants that have passed beyond memory, though there are some slight references to them in ancient tomes. These giants were never very numerous, and their kingdom was little more than a single fortress and outlying homesteads or wandering tribes. The last king, Hakality the Fell Eyed, sought sorcerous power to extend his life, but found only thralldom to a vampire. This led to the wholesale slaughter of his people. All that remains today of the kingdom are cyclopean ruins deep in the mountains and things that haunt the jagged peaks.

Now, gold seekers are flooding into the Büyük Dâg Mountains along the Porphyra and Kisa rivers, a few of whom report seeing ruins high on the slopes.

Çayusk River

A tributary of the Ilanos River, the Çayusk drains from the middle portion of the Ágaç Hills. It flows roughly northwest until meeting with the Ilanos at the city of Mérsíni. Like most of the central and northern parts of the hills, the banks of the Çayusk are fertile and lined with the estates of the wool beys. Water rights in the hills are a complex affair, and feuds between families tend to have their roots in access to water for irrigation and grazing sheep. This has led to a bizarre system of legal challenges and sanctioned dueling.

Forest of Orman

At the eastern end of the Isthmus of Irkaina, not far from the shores of the Sea of Spice between Akados and Libynos, is a towering forest of gigantic pines with heights reaching as much as 600 feet. By all rights this should not be here, since there is no break in the flat terrain and no body of water or other geographic feature that would support a forest in the midst of the grasslands, much less one composed of such enormous trees.

In fact, the Forest of Orman is not a natural feature, and would not exist but for powerful magic. A kingdom of elves and fey dwells within the forest, and their arcane rituals carved into standing stones lining the forest's edge keep it intact. This magic alters the climate in the region so that rain falls daily, though always in a light drizzle that provides enough moisture for the forest to remain. Cool breezes waft mists between the giant trees and deposit a glistening coating of jewel-like dew. Grass fires stop at the edge of the stones, unable to touch the trees beyond. The enchantment is so powerful that time passes differently within the forest: it is always midsummer, days pass in endless sunshine or under rainbow-producing showers before becoming equally long nights, and a day is as long as a month outside. This magic is ancient and beyond the ken of the free-spirited and wild inhabitants of the Forest of Orman.

Early in the days of the conquests by the caliphate, soldiers of the caliph heard stories of the forest from the local nomads. After a few expeditions were lost, the land within the standing stones was forbidden to the army and later colonists. This prohibition lasts to this day and is enforced by the forces of Pelshtaria, even though they do not fully understand the reason.

Gulf of Irkaina

This northern arm of the Sinnar Ocean is bordered by the mainland of Irkaina to the west, the Isthmus of Irkaina to the north, and the Pelshtarian Peninsula to the east. It is a quiet gulf that is well protected from winds and has a stable current that runs along its inner coast. The gulf does see a good deal of sea traffic as a result of the three large cities along its coast, Izmirtzaçg at the mouth of the Beyaz River, Ezerdúrum at the mouth of the Porphyra River, and Imazon at the mouth of the Nehir River. Ships come from the caliphate to the east, as well as travelers from the Buntesveldt and the cities of the Gulf of Akados to the west.

All of this trade attracts roving sea bandits, including Northlanders who either take the Mulstabhin Passage or float down the rivers of the Sea of Grass to reach the Sinnar Ocean. To protect against piracy, Pelshtaria commissioned a small fleet of ships to hunt down these vagrants. So far, they have had little success; the gulf is large and the merchants are too numerous to defend.

Ilanos River

Fed by hundreds of small streams from the Ágaç Hills and the smaller Çayusk River, the Ilanos River is the heart of the Principality of Pelshtaria. More people live in the vast grasslands of the Isthmus of Irkaina and the Pelshtarian Peninsula farther east, but the citizens of the Ilanos valley are far more concentrated. Here, urban life has developed, and the princes who have ruled the land have always had their capital at the mouth of the river.

The Ilanos itself is a slow but wide and deep run, languid in its course, and rarely overflows its banks even during the spring rains. This allows river barges to make their way from the interior to the sea to bring wool and grain to Irith Kel. The river's passage has cut a deep valley into the hills, and there are many places where the bluffs are too steep to get a goat down. The feeding streams tend to run off the high hills in wondrous cascades. Where the river can be reached, small towns have developed. The principality's troops regularly patrol the valley, and the Ilanos and the hills it passes through are some of the safest parts of the realm.

Irkainian Desert

The Irkainian Desert covers almost 500 miles of the Irkainian Peninsula, from the eastern edge of the Buntesveldt to the western eaves of the Ágaç Hills. This desert consists of a rocky arid highland amid the peninsula's mighty grasslands. There are few oases, and those that exist are heavily guarded by the desert nomads who roam these wastes. Travel across the rocky desert is difficult, as stony ground quickly shreds both feet and hooves, and the lack of water and burning sunlight soon sap all strength. The only safe routes are seasonal watercourses that have cut their way through the cracked rock, but these limit travel to the directions their courses run. During the summer, temperatures during the day can rise to more than 100° Fahrenheit. After the sun sets, the warmth quickly leaves the rocks, and the chilly air can plummet to less than 50° Fahrenheit. In the winter, the cold is severe enough that travelers without proper clothing risk freezing to death.

Despite this harsh climate, people do live in the Irkainian Desert. Local nomads eke out a meager living from the land by raising small amounts of crops and fruit in the few oases, and by herding sheep, camels, and goats through grass-filled valleys. This subsistence is augmented by trade, rare as it is. For the people of the Isthmus of Irkaina, it is far easier to send goods by sea around the southern edge of the desert than across it, but this has not always been the case, nor is it always safe. Certainly, bulk cargos sail out of the Gulf of Irkaina to the Buntesveldt or travel by wagon to Stavropol. Smaller, high-value cargos can, for appropriate consideration, be carried by the nomads from one oasis to another using routes and centuries-old tribal alliances. While the nomads themselves are vicious fighters (and once poured out of their desert homes to raid neighboring lands), many merchants seeking routes through or around the desert hire their own guards.

ISTHMUS OF IRKAINA

The Isthmus of Irkaina is the wide neck of land between the western half of the Principality of Pelshtaria and the Kalithid Peninsula, and the eastern half, which includes the Pelshtarian Peninsula. These lands are fairly well-settled by the folk of Pelshtaria.

KALITHID PENINSULA

Jutting out into the Great Ocean from the Isthmus of Irkaina, the Kalithid Peninsula has a rocky coast that slopes gradually toward where it joins with the isthmus and the Pelshtarian Peninsula.

Wandering over the lands of the peninsula are tribes of lion centaurs that refer to themselves as the Kalithi (thus giving the peninsula its name). The centaurs defeated the caliphate's soldiers in a series of battles early in the colonization of Irkaina, and eventually a border between the two was agreed upon. The princes of Pelshtaria have been careful to continue to honor the agreement, which lasts to this day. On occasion, a lion centaur leaves its lands and searches for adventure elsewhere in the world. One of the marshals of the principality's cavalry is a Kalithid warrior.

KISA RIVER

This short river flows from between two peaks of the Büyük Dâg Mountains to join with the Porphyra River in a hundred-foot waterfall. It is a fast river with many rapids that becomes a torrent of water in the spring as the snow melts off the mountains. Gold has been found nearby, and a small gold rush is growing, bringing people into the mountains and into contact with the giants and trolls that live there.

LESSER PORPHYRA RIVER

Draining from the eastern edges of the Ágaç Hills, the Lesser Porphyra River meets the Porphyra River at a small town on its northern bank. The Lesser Porphyra sees a fair deal of river traffic from its origin in the hills as it heads to Ezerdúrum. The river thunders through cataracts and rapids in places, and requires boats to be carried over a portage beyond the rough waters. Even so, along much of its length it is far easier to send goods down the river to the Gulf of Irkaina than over the hills to the Çayusk and on to Irith Kel on the Great Ocean.

NEHIR RIVER

Fed by two steams, the slow-moving and prosaic north fork and the enchanted south fork, the Nehir is a wide waterway that serves as the main means of travel from neighboring farms to the port city of Imazon. Where the two forks join, a great rainbow is thrown up and one can hear the sound of falls, though none can be seen. This is no doubt due to the enchanted nature of the south fork, and locals have grown accustomed to hearing not just the falls but strange noises coming from within the thundering waters. Below these "falls," the water of the Nehir is safe to drink, the magic of the south fork either being diluted or disappearing into the spectral falls.

NEHIR RIVER, NORTH FORK

Draining from the rich grasslands of the Pelshtarian Peninsula, the north fork of the Nehir River is a shallow, meandering waterway that does not have enough flow to supply irrigation, move large boats, or power waterwheels. All that it seems able to provide the people who live along it is a place to water their flocks and themselves.

NEHIR RIVER, SOUTH FORK

With its source somewhere in the Forest of Orman, the south fork of the Nehir river is an odd stream. Its flow is unpredictable, and sudden floods as if from snow melt or spring rains can come in any season. While it provides abundant water and moves with enough volume to float boats and enough force to drive waterwheels, the people who live along it prefer to get their water from deep wells.

The south fork of the Nehir is a magical stream. The water is not always enchanted, but one can never be too careful. A hundred buckets might have no effect, but one drink could be disastrous. According to local talk, drinking from the stream can changes one's hair or eye color or cause the growth of horns or other cosmetic alterations, or even result in changing the drinker into another creature entirely. People have been turned into sheep. Sheep have been turned into dragons. In one memorable tale, a passing dragon rampaging through the region drunk deeply from the river and turned into a squirrel. True, a fire-breathing squirrel that took three days to hunt down and slay, but a squirrel nonetheless.

PELSHTARIAN PENINSULA

It may seem odd that the Pelshtarian Peninsula is on the other side of the principality than the capital and the rivers that form the heart of the nation, particularly one that is lightly populated and consists mainly of savannah broken only by occasional watering holes and ridges. However, the people of this region are descendants of the earliest settlers from the caliphate, and the name of the peninsula in fact predates the use of the term for the entire principality.

Today, the beys, all descendants of the leaders among the original settlers, own nearly all the land. When the caliphate first began the process of colonizing the peninsula, it handed out huge land grants of hundreds of square miles. The lucky settlers who managed to land one of these grants became a bey overnight with a larger holding than many of the oldest noble families in the caliphate. These holdings were just rugged wilderness, and the process of turning them into subsistence level farms was arduous.

Yet they did this, for the soil was fertile, the local nomads easily dealt with, and the people of the caliphate had generations of experience growing crops in arid environments.

The peninsular beys live on large estates separated from each other by miles of dusty dirt roads. Each is its own little kingdom with the bey and their family ruling without oversight and with the backing of law and custom. They tend to be a fractious bunch much infatuated by their independence and thwart any attempt to build a city or found a town larger than the trading hub of Imazon on the Nehir River.

Between these scattered estates, or technically on them as the beys claim large tracks of land, are vast wildernesses of wild animals, lurking monsters, and the few remnants of the nomadic tribes that once inhabited the peninsula. For the most part, each bey maintains a sufficient standing army of men-at-arms, not to mention the mounted warriors of their family retinues, to keep these threats at bay. Even so, from time to time when some danger does threaten, it may be easier and more profitable to hire outsiders to take on the risk.

PORPHYRA RIVER

Thundering down from the Büyük Dâg Mountains, the Porphyra River drains from the mountains and races along their edge to the sea where it is joined by the Lesser Porphyra River at a small town. This river does not see a lot of traffic since the land it flows through is rugged and unsettled. Even if there were people living along it, the river flows over so many falls and through hundreds of cataracts that travel would be impossible for any large boat. However, thanks to the growing gold rush, some people are now using the river to enter the mountains, but they must do so in light boats that they can easily portage over or around obstructions.

MULSTABHA AND THE MULSTABHIN PASSAGE

Krivcycek Island sits in the middle of the Mulstabhin Passage, the gap between the northeastern-most corner of Akados and the northwestern-most extent of Libynos. The island is the homeland of the nation of Mulstabha, a mysterious folk unlike any other known people in the world in appearance or culture. They are the people of the Land of the Bull from the Sea, so named for their founder, a Libynosi minotaur and pirate who founded the citadel of Jem Karteis. Somewhat confusingly, the island is also sometimes referred to as Mulstabha, which is also the term for the leader of these people.

In addition to the Mulstabhins, nomadic bands of people known as the Ghazaks also wander Krivcycek Island. They are few in number, rarely seen, and bear no resemblance whatsoever to their neighboring Mulstabhins. Unlike any other people, for reasons unknown the Ghazaks are able to move unhindered through Mulstabhin territory with impunity.

REFERENCE SOURCE: THE NORTHLANDS SAGA COMPLETE

JEM KARTEIS, CITY OF (CAPITAL)

Ruler: The Mulstabha
Government: council
Population: 28,360 (17,010 Mulstabhins, 3,780 foreign slaves, 3,475 Huun, 1,680 common giants, 1,270 hobgoblins, 647 dwarves, 378 lizardfolk, 120 other)

The bull-shaped city of Jem Karteis — which is protected by stout walls and fortifications and sits in the middle of an island surrounded by swampland — has defied conquest by princes and caliphs for centuries. The city began as a simple pirate fortress but has grown over the centuries into a bustling, but bizarre, place where the people and goods of Akados and Libynos meet. The city segregates its residents and foreign visitors with physical walls and cultural taboos. The five castes interact under strict auspices, and their interactions with outsiders are equally controlled.

KRIVCYCEK ISLAND

This large island sits in the middle of the Mulstabhin Passage between the Great Ocean Ûthaf and the Sea of Spice. It comprises the island nation of Mulstabha, a hilly interior, and swamp lands along the edges, and offers few places for ships to land.

A rough stony path crosses the island which, at low tide, can be used to cross between the continents, skirting the worst parts of the salt flats. Though often in poor repair and in some places washed out by tides, the road — constructed long ago by the Hyperboreans to connect their eastern and western empires — remains passable.

MULSTABHIN PASSAGE

The Mulstabhin Passage is the only means for ships to pass between the Great Ocean Ûthaf and the Gulf of Akados and Sinnar Ocean beyond. At low tide, the water drains away leaving a vast saltmarsh surrounding Krivcycek Island. But at high tide the waters of the Great Ocean Ûthaf and the Sinnar Ocean rush in and mingle to turn it into a true island and create the legendary Mulstabhin Passage between those two oceans.

Even at such high tides, the ways are treacherous for any other than flat-bottomed boats, and vessels frequently find themselves grounded on mud bars. For this reason, the Mulstabhins have marked passages with withies — long, flexible willow rods — for generations. These long rods are stuck upright in the mud on either side of the deeper-water channels, and when high tide comes, the tops of the rods remain visible above the surface of the water. These serve as guides so that ships can pass between them and avoid grounding themselves in the shallows. A whole series of these withy channels extend between the island and isthmus, and between the oceans to the north and south.

THE NORTHLANDS

The Northlands are not one homogenous region of the world, but are instead eight separate regions united by common culture and history. To outsiders, a Northlander is a Northlander, but the people of heavily settled and peaceful Vale are a far cry from the hardy frontiersmen of Estenfird. To tell a Gat that he is the same as a Hrolf is to ask to be brought violently into their generations-old feud. This is especially true considering that not all of those native to the Northlands are Northlanders, for the Nûklanders and Seagestrelanders are different cultures entirely, and the Nûklanders aren't even humans! It is not just the people, but the terrain, even the environments, that are different. The frigid tundra of Nûkland is a far cry from the boggy forests and moors of Hordaland, and both are strange and alien in comparison to the rocky volcanic mountains of Vastavikland.

HISTORY OF THE NORTHLANDS

The first folk who lived in the Northlands are known to history as the Andøvan. Very little else other than their name is so known. They left behind only barrow mounds, earthen hill forts, and enigmatic rings of standing stones upon the heights. The ancients who once dwelt in the Northlands are still held in a mixture of awe and fear by modern Northlanders, their barrow fields still haunted by the specters of their civilization that walk the night-darkened hills and forests.

The next to arrive were the Nûk, a tribe of wild elves seeking refuge from the Hyperborean wars in the south. Their descendants live in the Northlands to this day.

Next came the Uln, a wandering tribe of Shattered Folk, remnants of the Hundaei of the Haunted Plains far to the west and south. They founded cities in the Far North, but it is said they fell under the sway of a demonic cult and eventually were destroyed.

Barely a century and a half after the rise and fall of the Uln in the Far North, a third migration of humans began for the Northlands. At the far southern end of the continent of Akados, on the aptly named Helcynngae Peninsula lived the Heldring, a people of feared warriors of great size and martial prowess who sold the soul of their people to the goddess Hel in exchange for might and protection from the invading legions of the Hyperboreans. This contract served them well, for the Hyperboreans were never able to conquer these tribes and ultimately had to wall off the entire peninsula with a defensive breastwork known as the Helwall. It was from this ruthless and bloodthirsty people that the final migration emerged.

Not all of the tribes among the Heldring were as devoted to the Lady of Pestilence and, at a time when her cult's power was waxing among the Heldring, one thegn called Swein Sigurdson turned his back on the wicked ways of Hel and sought an escape for his people. Swein gathered his family and related clans and headed north to cross the Helwall. The clergy of Hel, however, learned of his defection and sent an army in pursuit. Unable to reach the Helwall, Swein retreated into the Cumorian Mountains to find safety. The Helite council's army pursued doggedly and drove them ever deeper among the jagged clefts. Finally, Swein and his people were forced to seek shelter in a cave and await the arrival of their imminent executioners. However, even as the Helite raiders charged up the valley and Swein formed his shieldwall across the mouth of the cave, an earthquake struck the valley. The cliff face above the cave mouth collapsed, sealing it off and trapping Swein's people within while killing many of the charging Helite warriors.

Saved by seemingly divine intervention, Swein nevertheless despaired at the prospect of his people dying trapped within the collapsed cavern. However, when torches were lit, it was found that the back of the cave had likewise collapsed to reveal a series of natural tunnels that ran deep beneath the earth and into the Under Realms. For two years, the clans following Swein survived and forged their path through the darkness of the Under Realms on what they came to call the Neimbrall Trail.

At some point during that journey, the Æsir gods of their ancestors, long forgotten when Hel became the dominant deity of the Helcynngae Peninsula, reappeared to them. Swein received a vision from Wotan the All-Father of a distant land of snowy peaks and timbered forests far from the Helcynngae Peninsula, a land where they could hack their homes out of the wilderness and live as a free people.

Swein Sigurdson became the first godi and led his people toward this promised land. For nearly three years, the clans of Swein stumbled through the dark, being forged by the hardships they faced and tempered by the foes they fought until finally one day he led them into the light of day from beneath the chain of mountains in a wide valley they named Storstrøm. Across the vale at the foot of another mountain range they found the Stone of Andøvan, which gave cryptic clues to the people who had lived in the valley long before, and named these mountains for them as a result. Unfortunately for Swein's people, the lands they found were not unoccupied; a troll-blooded people known as the thrydreg held sway in the lowlands around the North Sea. But the Æsir favored Swein's people and provided them with a stone fortress built upon a river from which they could defend themselves and begin their own expansion. Thus, with the might of their faith in the Æsir behind them and the tempering they had endured on the Neimbrall Trail within them, Swein's clans made war upon the thrydreg. No longer as numerous as they had once been due to the faltering resources since the climate shift, and with most of their true troll overlords long since relocated into the mountains, the thrydreg fell before the onslaught of Swein and his people. In a few short years, the thrydreg had been driven from the Vale and the new society of Northlanders had been established.

Over the following decades, the Northlanders continued to push the thrydreg back. They mastered the art of crafting swift longships with which they could launch raids all along the coast, and soon the last pockets of thrydreg were destroyed or in hiding among the wildlands. Swein was named the first køenig of Storstrøm Vale, and what became the first modern nation of the Northlands was begun.

For more information on the Northlands, see ***The Northlands Saga Complete*** from **Frog God Games**.

POLITICAL SUBDIVISIONS OF THE NORTHLANDS

KINGDOM OF BROUNTHIA

Capital: Cymilard
Notable Settlements: Chadwick, Craghold, Cymilsport, Hesten Down, Landisport, Monrovia, Tylival
Ruler: Queen Ivérna IV
Government: feudal
Population: 976,900 (903,029 Berrini, 31,200 Foerdewaith, 14,220 Northlander, 11,955 other human ethnicity, 9,211 mountain dwarf, 4,100 halfling, 1,675 half-elf, 1,510 other)
Languages: Hibor, Common, Nørsk
Religion: Hyperborean pantheon
Resources: grain, fishing, gold, silver, iron, tin, coal, livestock, trade, timber, fruit, wine, honey
Currency: Brounthian
Technology Level: High Middle Ages

The Kingdom of Brounthia lies along the coast of the Great Ocean between the Northlands and the Principality of Pelshtaria to the south and the Sea of Grass to the west. Brounthia has enjoyed relative internal peace but has fought off numerous invasions from the north, east, and west. Northlanders raid the coast, though these attacks have been

The Northlands
The Seal Coast and the Far North
Principality of
Kalthid Peninsula
Isthmus of Irkaid
Buruk Osg Mountains
Eserdorum
Mérsim
Irith Kel
Inkaïnian Desert
Norwold Gulf
Abennord
Landisport
Craghold
World's End Cliffs
Mesten Down
Monrovia
Ceaster Pool
Tjylval
Cymillard
Silver River
Brunthid
Kingdom of
Chadwick
Stavropol
The Buttesveldt
Burgenheim
Oslen
Fair Yrsa's Rock
Trotheim
Jarvik
Tallsinki
Galvë
Alkis
Anvil
Three Rivers
Vöss
Ölmer
Straits of Wÿl
North Sea
Halfstead
Nakobin
Volskol
The Frozen Taiga
Neuberg
Nakland
Javik
The Jomsburg
Jomsburg Island
Wotans Grinders
Wyrm Fang Rocks
Smolsvard
Sniptingstead
Monbora
Great Veldt Road
Vastmir Plains
Mongat Tribes
The Stumps
Delamarra Salt Pan
Blue Escarpment
Stones of Kashimir
Staked Lands
K'Waln Tribes
Sea of Grass
The Hyperborean Way
Tanomir Fens
Lake Verglas
Osens Seep
One Tree
Grand Portage
High Karst

Legend
Town or Village
City
Capital or Free City
Imperial Capital
Fortress or Citadel
Ruins
Place of Interest
Road
Trail or Unused Road
Mountain Pass
Battlefield

decreasing thanks to a combined political strategy of appeasement and playing the Northlanders against one another, and a system of coastal watchtowers. The rule of Prince Kemal of Pelshtaria, the father of the current prince and princess, put an end to the border skirmishes that once plagued relations between the two lands. However, the K'Haln tribes of the Sea of Grass still raid the western marches and have in the past swept as far as Cymilard.

A series of queens have ruled Brounthia since its founding. The nobility is mostly male though, and most of the culture is male dominated. The queen is not just a monarch, but is seen as a divine figure, a living goddess. The cult of the queen is the dominant religion and worship of her as divine protector, and of past queens as a pantheon ready to intercede on the behalf of supplicants, is entrenched in Brounthian society.

The queen is always a relative of her predecessor, but as divine queens they do not lay with mortals, and thus do not produce daughters to ascend to the throne. Shortly after coronation, the queen selects a number of sisters, nieces, or cousins to form her court. Their ages do not matter, and sometimes an aunt is selected as well. Brought into the court, these aspirants to the throne are educated in politics, natural philosophy, religion, art, music, and magic. Those who pass a brutal series of exams and remain celibate can compete for the throne when it becomes vacant. None knows what happens during these competitions, for all qualified applicants are locked in the Tower of Testing until one exits as either the sole survivor or the one that the other survivors acclaim as the only one worthy to be queen. Those who fail and are not slain in the Tower often bear marked injures that are both mental and physical.

The current queen, Ivérna IV, was old when she ascended to the throne five years ago. Now nearly 70 years of age, she has seen three Tests of the Tower, always surviving but never coming out on top. Five years ago her niece, Autona III, broke her vows and laid aside her divinity by becoming involved in a sexual relationship with one of her knights. The scandal rocked the kingdom and led to a hasty round of final examinations of aspirants. The testing went on for 12 days, and at the end only Ivérna and three others survived, none of them unscarred.

Despite her age, the queen has taken an active hand in ruling her nation. Where younger queens often foster a courtly romance and many knights and nobles behave as lovestruck fools in their presence, Ivérna rules more as a wise and kindly figure. Less-pious knights push the bounds of blasphemy by referring to her as the grandmother queen, but the allusion is not without merit. Brash young knights who would scoff at listening to an old woman find themselves dreading attracting her disappointment.

The old courtly romance seems to survive only in the hearts of older knights, most of whom had retired but chose to ride out once more in service to Ivérna. These elderly knights make up a new order of chivalry, the Grey Guard, and commit their last acts of heroism in her name — though only if they have a chance to rest up from the long ride and maybe take a hot bath. A little mulled wine would not be refused. Maybe some liniment, for the joints are as creaky as the armor on these cold mornings.

Cymilard, City of (Capital)

Ruler: Queen Ivérna IV
Government: feudal
Population: 67,590 (54,495 Berrini, 4,950 Foerdewaith, 3,600 other human ethnicity, 1,900 halfling, 1,375 mountain dwarf, 900 Northlander, 250 half-elf, 120 other)

The grand capital of the Kingdom of Brounthia, Cymilard is a gleaming city that sits on an island in Lake Berring. The heart of the city is the Palace of the Queens, a soaring edifice that seems to float out of the lake mists. The palace and most of the older buildings at the city's center are composed of white dolostone mined from the nearby Andøvan Mountains. Every day, 100 peasants polish the stone of the old city to a gleaming sheen. Surrounding the palace and nearby buildings is the High Wall, a tower and bastion studded with red granite brought from the distant World's Edge Mountains.

The city has spread from its original walls to cover the entire island, forming the Lower City of tile-roofed houses and shops, paved streets, and open squares. A causeway links the island to the shore of the lake where sits the New City, the much larger unplanned metropolis of commoners who support the nobles, merchants, and burghers on the island. The houses here are made of wood, the nicer ones of stone for the first floor with wooden upper floors. The streets are not all paved, and the buildings tend to lean or cram together to form twisting alleyways and dead-ends. The New City is ringed by a wall of gray stone cut from the World's End Mountains and, although in good repair, it not nearly as pretty as the High Wall.

Cymilard is the personal demesne of the queen and a great source of her income. Lake Berring is rich in fish and the Upper and Lower Red Rivers bring trade, gold, and silver to the city. An overland road leads to Hesten Down on the Great Ocean, making Cymilard the kingdom's main trade nexus. The shores of the lake are rich farmland, and most of this is also owned by the queen.

As the feudal lord of the city and the kingdom, the queen has a great deal of power in Cymilard. She personally holds court to hear the concerns of her people and sit in judgment of crimes. Most criminals, being both violators of civil and religious law in Brounthia, face harsh sentences. Being a nation with a highly stratified class system, there are different laws for nobles and commoners. The former face the stripping of their titles and lands followed by public humiliation and execution. Commoners are simply sent to mines in the Andøvans or the World's End Mountains.

CHADWICK, TOWN OF

Ruler: Lord Paval d'Luc
Government: feudal
Population: 4,300 (3,570 Berrini, 310 Foerdewaith, 275 other human ethnicity, 95 halfling, 40 half-elf, 10 other)

The most southwestern of the kingdom's towns, Chadwick lies on the very edge of the Sea of Grass. A few generations ago, it was just a small village of pioneers willing to break the thick sod of the grasslands and face off with nomadic raiders. For a time, the town was even outside of Brounthia and beyond the bounds of feudal law. The first Lord d'Luc came 50 years ago and claimed the land for himself and his heirs, backing up these bold assertions with royal writ. He brought with him carts full of seed, tools, and his peasants, and soon displaced the freesteaders.

The freesteaders headed deeper onto the grasslands, setting up the next wave of expansion for the kingdom. Lord d'Luc gained land and established a large estate that specialized in rearing warhorses, and soon became the most famed horse rancher in the kingdom. His successes drew other young nobles who did not stand to inherit wealth and were unwilling to take up a life as a royal warden or knight errant. This pushed the freesteaders further back, but also attracted the attentions of nearby nomadic tribes. Today, Chadwick sits well within the settled and safe band bordering the kingdom, and new territory out on the grasslands is opening up.

CRAGHOLD, CITY OF

Ruler: Lord Vernet
Government: feudal
Population: 14,370 (10,680 Berrini, 2,050 other human ethnicity, 805 mountain dwarf, 450 halfling, 300 half-elf, 85 other)

Sitting at the confluence of the Silver and Ruby rivers, Craghold is one of the major cities of the kingdom. It is a walled city built on a bluff that towers over the confluence and provides a refuge when the local nomadic tribes attack, though with the border pushing farther out onto the Sea of Grass, these attacks are increasingly rare. Even so, the city remains ready to defend itself and the surrounding lands.

Craghold sends goods down the Silver River to Landisport and receives foreign goods for distribution to the nobles of the region as well as sending imports north to Cymilsport. The lords of Craghold traditionally levy a tax on all goods that pass through the city. Most of this wealth is spent supporting knights in the field to defend the border, while a small portion is set aside and donated to the Queen's Own Marchers (who maintain a barracks here), and the rest goes into the coffers of the lord. Even though the percentage kept in the city is small, the amount of trade passing through results in a city of splendor that nearly rivals the capital in its grandeur. Towers of polished stone rise up from nobles' homes, the streets are safe and clean, and the court is majestic in silk and samite.

All this wealth and the taxes that create it have led to crime. While the streets of the city are safe, smugglers have long used the many caverns beneath the Crag to hide and move goods. Blacked-out barges approach from the river and unload cargos in the dead of night. Hidden entrances lie beneath noble houses and merchant emporiums alike. For decades, the smugglers of Craghold have labored under the authority of the Purple Man, an underworld figure who makes sure that all illicit trade passes through his hands, and that crime never reaches the point where it hurts the city's income. To deprive your protectors of what they need to defend the realm would be bad business. Smugglers operating without sanction are often found in the river with their faces cut off.

CYMILSPORT, CITY OF

Ruler: Lord Andreu
Government: feudal
Population: 11,340 (8,850 Berrini, 1,640 other human ethnicity, 425 halfling, 200 half-elf, 135 mountain dwarf, 90 other)

Sitting across Lake Berring from Cymilard, Cymilsport is a fishing village that has grown into a city. Originally simply a place where river boatmen gathered to take on cargo brought overland from Craghold to the south, the natural harbor attracted free fisherfolk to settle here. Many of the bargemen came as well, and the village began to grow. Within a few generations, it eclipsed the other landing points along the southern shore.

Fearing one of the fractious nobles of the region would lay claim to this growing free holding, the people of Cymilsport petitioned the queen to become a royal demesne. For a century they enjoyed direct royal rule and an appointed mayor, usually a former aspirant to the throne who had retired and married.

Twenty years ago, a massive nomad raid broke through into the interior of the kingdom. Cymilsport had never had a wall, and the town lay directly in the path of the wild horsemen. Many panicked, and the mayor fled with her entourage. Andreu the Bold, one of the common boatmen, rallied the town's defenders and encouraged them to build a hasty barricade. As the assault came, this band of rabble were unable to hold back the nomads, but they did hold them off long enough for many to escape the city. As the day ran short, the barricades failed and Andreu led a desperate battle in the city's streets. Rumors flew that help was coming from the east, but the defenders could fight for only so long against experienced warriors. Driven to the docks, the citizens of Cymilsport readied for a last stand and died keeping the nomads away from the river barges. When the defense at last collapsed and only a few remained, Andreu set the barges alight, denying the enemy the chance to cross the lake to the capital. He died in the inferno, shooting arrows at the nomads even though pierced by a dozen of theirs, and was last seen yelling threats from a flaming barge. The next morning, a large force of knights arrived and easily dispatched the weary and now-drunken raiders.

In recognition of this heroism, the queen elevated Andreu's eldest child to the nobility, granting him the title for the city his father died defending. The people of Cymilsport supported one of their own as their new lord, even if the child was only 11 years old. Now approaching 40, Lord Andreu has proven to be well suited to the task, and the city has recovered from the calamity that took his father and changed his stars.

HESTEN DOWN, CITY OF (BARONY OF HESTEN)

Symbol: A tower on a black field
Ruler: Baron Hesten
Government: feudal
Population: 35,910 (31,970 Berrini, 2,700 other human
ethnicity, 1,065 mountain dwarf, 145 halfling, 30 other)

The second-most busy port of the kingdom, Hesten Down is also
the seat for the Barony of Hesten. As such, it serves as a major
governmental and trade hub for the Great Ocean coast for the kingdom,
especially as Northlanders so often raid the Duchy of Monrovia. Some
raids reach as far south as Hesten Down, but these are usually small
affairs that are seeking out easy pickings. They do not find any in the
baron's lands.

Much like the coast of Monrovia to the north, the coast of the Barony
of Hesten is lined with watchtowers. In the event of an attack, signals
would be sent along the line to Hesten Down to alert the nobles and
call out the militia. A good road, unpaved but well-maintained, runs the
coast and links up with a similar road in Monrovia. When longships are
spotted, a small army can be rapidly gathered and sent to intercept. At
the same time, Royal Galleys launch from Hesten Down and cut the
Northlanders off from escape to sea. Rarely does this result in a fight,
for the Northlanders are wise enough to see when they are outclassed,
and there just might be easier pickings elsewhere.

Hesten Down itself has never been attacked. The harbor is protected
by a long breakwater studded with towers that juts out into the sea. The
city defenses face the ocean, though a sturdy wall protects the landward
side as well. With the wealth he has accumulated from the trade that
passes through his city, the baron is able to maintain hundreds of men-
at-arms and scores of knights.

It is this well-protected trade that supports Hesten Down, and to a
lesser extent the entire barony. True, feudal rights and levies help
and the land is rich, but they are dwarfed by the amount of gold that
passes through the harbor. The current baron seeks to increase this and
has converted most of his holdings into cash crops. So far, the bound
peasants haven't starved, but their food supply is becoming precarious.

LANDISPORT, CITY OF

Ruler: Lord Lafôret
Government: feudal
Population: 52,780 (39,565 Berrini, 7,210 Foerdewaith, 3,300
other human ethnicity, 1,250 mountain dwarf, 995 halfling,
300 half-elf, 160 other)

Brounthia's main seaport, Landisport sits at the mouth of the Silver
River where it flows into the Great Ocean. While a great deal of trade
leaves Hesten Down, most of its imports come through Landisport,
up the Silver River to Craghold, and then overland to Cymilsport.
This might seem an awkward and laborious route, but it has the twin
advantages of saving days or weeks at sea and avoiding the worst of the
Northlander raiders.

The World's End Mountains create dangerous weather conditions in
the northern parts of the Norwold Gulf. When a storm blows in, ships
can be driven off course, or worse, lost entirely. The mountains run
down to the sea in a series of tablelands that do not permit any easy
landing and certainly no harbors. To run goods north to Hesten Down
can be a dangerous undertaking; sending those same goods up the river
and overland is safer, but slower.

The city itself is a bustling hive of activity. Products of the estates
along the Silver and Ruby rivers come from upriver. Goods from such
faraway lands such as the Ammuyad Caliphate arrive at the harbor.
This great wealth is used to support the Royal Galleys as one-fifth of
all commerce goes into the royal treasury. This steep tax keeps most
foreign goods out of the hands of the common folk, something the
nobles are more than happy to support. After all, how will you know
who is common if not by their dress?

The Royal Galleys are six warships crewed by trained sailors and
commanded by nobles holding hereditary rights to the position. While
this does allow for a great deal of nepotism, to the Brounthians this is
right and proper. A noble first learns war at the feet of their parents, and
to the largely land-focused people of the kingdom, naval warfare is such
a rare specialization that only those who grew up with it can be trusted
to serve as officers.

MONROVIA, DUCHY OF

Ruler: Duke Jean d'Auberville
Government: feudal
Population: 146,000 (122,710 Berrini, 18,100 other human
ethnicity, 2,950 Northlander, 1,100 mountain dwarf, 500
halfling, 350 half-elf, 290 other)

Monrovia is the northernmost duchy in Brounthia and the one most
often raided by Northlanders. Duke d'Auberville has spent tens of
thousands of coins on defense of the coast, establishing watchtowers
and maintaining knights in the field all through the summer and well
into fall. This has bankrupted him and caused much friction between the
duchy and the queen. Taxes have been raised, new fines implemented,
and many freemen and some petty nobles have seen their fortunes
disappear into the duke's hungry coffers.

This has led to a revolt by the southern nobles, most of whom do not
see the value in giving up so much treasure and blood to defend a coast
they hardly ever see. The duke has responded in force, even trading land
to the Northlanders to gain mercenaries to put down this revolt. That
this is a revolt and not simply a border skirmish between two rulers is
something the duke is trying to keep outsiders from realizing, especially
the Northlanders who might take this as an opportunity to raid or, worse,
colonize the coast.

The seat of the duke is at the city of Monrovia, which sits five miles
from the coast. Other than the watchtowers, the duchy no longer has any
ports to its name; just last year, the duke transferred the town of Ceaster
Pool into Jarl Magnus Hrolfson's hands as part of a payment for nearly
5,000 Northlander mercenaries who served in the duke's wars against
his southern nobles.

TYLIVAL, FORTRESS OF

Ruler: Lord Marshal Isarn de le Haché
Government: military
Population: 10,150 (Berrini)

Tylival is a massive fortress standing deep within the World's End
Mountains. It is owned by the queen and manned not by the usual feudal
levies but a combination of the kingdom's two standing armies, the Royal
Wardens and the Queen's Own Marchers. The fortress is the headquarters
of both forces and serves as the main recruiting, training, and logistics
center of the kingdom. The walls are high and strong, the troops stationed
there on alert, and most assume the fortress is impregnable. The walls
form a ring that encompasses not only the fortress but also fields and
pastures. With deep cisterns and sturdy bastions, Tylival is a difficult siege
prospect. The center of the fort is an unnaturally tall tower whose upper
levels are closed off to all but the lord marshal.

The Royal Wardens are the senior force at Tylival and their
commander, the lord marshal, governs the fortress. Charged with
patrolling the World's End Mountains and keeping the peace in the
region, the Royal Wardens are as much law enforcers as soldiers. They
are a heavily armed and armored force, the younger sons of nobles and
landless knights, and maintain a high level of readiness. If the kingdom
is ever threatened, nearly 3,000 knights and their supporting squires can
be called in to the field.

Standing as a direct opposite in nature and mission are the
Queen's Own Marchers. These light horseman patrol and defend the
southwestern border of the kingdom. Riding the edges of the Sea of
Grass, the Marchers fight nomadic tribes and monsters coming off the
steppe lands.

Membership is limited to those the queen personally selects, and a great selection feast occurs every spring. Mostly these are freemen of some kind, though foreigners who are willing to take and uphold their oaths are welcome. By long standing tradition upon joining the marchers, a person forsakes their name, heritage, and nationality, and adopts a new identity for the length of their lifetime oaths.

It might seem odd to station so many soldiers here, as well as base the Marchers so far from the border they are tasked with patrolling. The queens have long been aware of the danger beneath the World's End Mountains. However, the kingdom needs the gold, iron, tin, and coal found there. The fortress of Tylival was built in case something awakens. In dire need, the entire fortress can be turned into a weapon, with the tall lord marshal's tower serving as the focal point of a ritual to drain the souls of all within the fortress as it burns the rampaging horror to ash.

ESTENFIRD

Capital: Three Rivers
Notable Settlements: Nieuburg, Risør, Úlmer, Vöss
Ruler: Althing of Estenfird and local Things
Government: democratic
Population: 22,200 (22,200 Northlander, small number of dwarves and Nûk)
Monstrous: giants, drakes, wyverns, linnorms, dragons (Wyrm Fang Mountains); dire animals, barghests, worgs, fey, vlkodlak, megafauna, grimmswine, ajatars, erdhenne (woodlands); trolls, ice trolls (Troll Axe Pass); yeti, remorhaz, vlkodlak (Bloody Pass)
Languages: Nørsk, Common, Dwarven, Nûk
Religion: Æsir, Vanir, Ginnvaettir
Resources: timber, furs, foodstuffs, copper, gems
Technology Level: Dark Ages

As one of the newest Northlander colonies, Estenfird is a wild land on the frontier of what the Northlanders call civilization (and considering that the rest of the world thinks of the Northlands as the frontier, that is saying something about its ruggedness). Less a nation than a quarrelsome collection of independent-minded settlers, Estenfird does not have a kœnig or jarl, leaving the local Things and the Althing of Estenfird as the only semblance of government in the region. Estenfird ranges from the tip of the Skagerrok Peninsula northwest along the Ice River as far as Nieuburg. Few settlers have pushed beyond Nieuburg, as the climate becomes far too cold for agriculture and the Nûk, although not violent, have made it known that they do not appreciate people moving into their lands. Many brave words are said in the halls of Estenfird about pushing the Nûk out of the way, but so far none have dared to confront that enigmatic and mystical race.

The average Estenfirder is a rugged and forthright person inured to hard work and dangerous environments. They are often stern and taciturn, slow to speak, but quick to act. Few Estenfirders go a-viking, as they have plenty of adventure at home. In the southern portions of the region, along the many rivers and on the coast, agriculture takes precedence, and many Estenfirders are farmers or herdsmen. The rivers of Estenfird are rich in fish, but the surrounding waters yield only a poor catch, making this region one of the few that sees little in the way of maritime activity. Inland and in the mountains, fur trapping and logging are the primary industries. In the spring, fur trappers and hunters come down the rivers and gather at Three Rivers and Nieuburg to sell their season's catch. In the fall, the loggers come down in huge flotillas of cut timber to sell lumber to merchants from throughout the Northlands and beyond.

Estenfirders are notorious for their independent ways, a factor that causes worry in the more dictatorial jarls of other regions. There are no jarls in Estenfird, and to even suggest such a thing is to invite harsh words if not a duel. Many who come to the region do so to escape crimes or feuds or to live as free men and women beholden to and reliant upon

none. The local Things meet once a year, drawing in people from the scattered farmsteads and logging camps. The Things of Estenfird are unique in that they do not have a landholding requirement — there is so much unclaimed land in the region that all a person has to do to become a landholder is to point at a place and say "mine." Instead, to speak or vote in the Thing, a person must be free and have the sponsorship of anyone who has spoken before at that Thing. The Althing of Estenfird works in a similar way, only the requirement is that the sponsor has already spoken or voted in the regional Althing.

In addition to Three Rivers, Nieuburg, Risør, Úlmer, and Vöss, a number of permanent settlements are scattered throughout Estenfird. These include the seasonal whaling village of Bräcke on the eastern shore of the Skagerrok Peninsula; the settlement of Hörby, a logging camp established by a native of Storstrøm Vale; the village of Ørsa in the High Vale; and the village of Struer, which sits on the edge of the large pool of water in the Savage River beneath a steep waterfall known as the Maiden's Tears.

Estenfird suffers from several threats, in addition to the long cold winters and general ruggedness of the land. Giants are common in the Wyrm Fang Mountains, as are drakes and wyverns. The general lawlessness of the region promotes independence, but also encourages attacks by outlaws, bandits, and even Northlanders from other regions a-viking along the shore. The gravest threat to date has been the growth of the Beast Cult of Shibauroth, foul worshippers of a demon-god dedicated to bestial violence and mayhem.

THREE RIVERS, TOWN OF (CAPITAL)

Ruler: none
Government: council (Thing of Three Rivers, Althing of Estenfird)
Population: 1,640 (1,450 Northlander, 50 elf [Nûk], 40 dwarf 100 other)

The confluence of the Ice, Wrath, and Savage rivers forms a triangular peninsula of land that is the site of Three Rivers, the largest settlement in Estenfird. Most of the year, Three Rivers is an almost desolate town, but during the fur trade rendezvous in the spring and logging festival in the fall, the town swells to three times its normal population. Every five years the Althing of Estenfird meets here and brings in more people as the freeholders of the region gather to conduct trade, hear legal cases, and debate critical matters.

As befits a frontier settlement, Three Rivers is one of the better-defended towns in the Northlands. A stout wooden palisade blocks off the landward side, and the militia of the town hirth is one of the most active and best trained in the Northlands. In its short history, giants, werewolves, beast cultists, bandits, vikings, and even a wyrm have attacked Three Rivers. Although the town has been burned to the ground several times, the Althing of Estenfird has consistently voted to rebuild it each time, and even managed to collect enough donations to make it larger and stronger.

NIEUBURG, TOWN OF

Ruler: none
Government: anarchy
Population: 156 (150 Northlander, 6 elf [Nûk])

Sitting far up the Ice River, Nieuburg represents the farthest extent of Northlander territory. It lies on the very edge of the area claimed by Estenfird and the lands claimed by the Nûk and acts as a center of commerce and the major point of contact between these two peoples. Every spring, fur traders and trappers gather here to bring in the previous year's take and to pick up supplies for the next year. In the late summer, loggers gather their flotillas of cut timber to float downriver to Three Rivers. Nieuburg is a wild frontier town and shows it, with a transient population, ramshackle buildings, and a general ambivalence to authority of any kind. Some find it the freest settlement in the Northlands; others see it as barely contained anarchy.

Risør, Village of

Ruler: none
Government: anarchy
Population: 867 (832 Northlander, 34 dwarf)

Halfway between Vöss and Three Rivers, Risør is a walled village that is rapidly growing into a small town. It is a common stopping point for overland and river-borne trade, and its people have begun to make noise in the local Thing about building a permanent warehouse as well as housing for merchants.

Úlmer, Village of

Ruler: none
Government: anarchy
Population: 134 (Northlander)

This small fishing village enjoys a deep fjord that affords it a protected harbor. Although not as popular as Vöss, Úlmer does see some traffic. Most of these are adventurers and other heroes, and the village has become somewhat cosmopolitan in its outlook, assuming the strangers in question have plenty of money and don't cause trouble.

Vöss, Town of

Ruler: none
Government: anarchy
Population: 1,367 (1,009 Northlander, 302 other human ethnicity, 56 other)

As the main port of Estenfird, Vöss is rapidly growing from a small fishing hamlet into a town whose size may one day surpass Three Rivers. The local Thing has even voted to construct a breakwater in the Southlander fashion in order to encourage larger merchant ships from those soft (but rich) kingdoms. The people of Vöss are warm and inviting, knowing that only the trade of merchants, whalers, and lumberman provide the wealth their community needs in order to grow.

Gatland

Capital: Nakøbin
Notable Settlements: Javik
Ruler: Jarl Ljot Gatson
Government: Northlands feudal with an Althing and local Things
Population: 17,800 (16,900 Northlander, 900 Seagestrelander thralls; small number of dwarves)
Monstrous: giants, jotunt trolls, vlkodlak, dragons, linnorms, primal dragons, grendels, shantaks (Northern Olf Mountains); ogres, giant snapping turtles, draugs, dragonships, fjord linnorms (coastline); whales, reefclaws, trow, sea drakes, brine dragons (Virlik Bay)
Languages: Nørsk, Common, Dwarven, Seagestrelander
Religion: Æsir, Vanir
Resources: furs, coal, iron, plunder
Technology Level: Dark Ages

Three centuries ago when the tribal moots of the Northlanders evolved into the system of government known today as the Thing, not everyone was in favor of the change. True, the Things do not have much power per se, but their social might is very high, especially in Hordaland, Storstrøm Vale, and Estenfird. One of the leading groups that opposed the growing power of the Things was the Gat clan, who took themselves and their followers and settled a harsh and distant region, naming it Gatland.

Gatland is ruled by its jarls, all of whom are connected to the Gat clan in some way. Each jarl is a king in his own domain, the undisputed ruler of a piece of territory that contains only those who offer allegiance to him. Even Jarl Ljot Gatson, the eldest of the Gat clan, has no true authority over these petty tyrants, though his economic and military might means that his word is often heeded.

The land itself supports this sort of locally focused government. The interior of Gatland is dominated by the Olf Mountains, leaving only a coastal fringe capable of supporting farming. Even there, the soil is poor and rocky and forces the people of Gatland to rely on the sea for much of their sustenance. To the sea they have turned, becoming the best fishers and whalers in the Northlands but also crossing the whale road to trade and raid. In fact, trading/raiding is such an integral part of Gatlander life that some have entirely given up farming.

Nakøbin, Town of (Capital)

Government: overlord, council (Thing of Nakøbin, Althing of Gatland)
Ruler: Jarl Ljot Gatson
Population: 1,800 (1,780 Northlander, 20 dwarf)

Though the dispersed and complex political situation among the Gats means there is no true ruler or capital, the town of Nakøbin — since it is the ancestral home of the leading family of the Gats — is the de facto capital of Gatland. Originally merely the hall of the eldest of the five siblings who founded Gatland, Nakøbin has grown over the generations to become a thriving and prosperous town, complete with a wooden stockade and a permanent wharf/waterfront. The town has grown organically, spreading out from the old town centered on the Five Halls and the Field of the Althing. Merchants and travelers are welcome, and the town even boasts a few inns (actually little more than public hostels) to serve the needs of strangers.

The Althing of Gatland meets in Nakøbin every year at midsummer. Outsiders derisively call the Althing of Gatland the Allhen Thing, though never in the hearing of any Gats. This is because the Althing of Gatland is almost entirely composed of female representatives. Although the Gats have more than their share of spear maidens and other warrior women, it is the tradition for married women to give up their wandering ways and remain at home to tend their family's lands while the jarl and menfolk are off a-viking. As the best season for voyages is the summer, the laws of Gatland, as well as legal affairs, are nearly entirely in the hands of the women.

Javik, Town of

Ruler: Granny Æstrid
Government: overlord
Population: 1,850 (1,245 Northlander, 605 Seagestrelander)

Gatland's second city — though really just a large town — Javik is a fortified jarl's hall that has grown into a full-fledged settlement thanks to several generations of sound management by the sons and daughters (as well as grandsons, granddaughters, great-grandchildren, etc.) of the legendary Jarl Æstrid Gatsdottir. Granny Æstrid, as she is known, is still alive, though she does not take part in the day-to-day affairs of her jarldom. Decades ago — how many none really know — Granny Æstrid decided she was too old for going a-viking when she lost her last tooth in the sands of the distant Ammuyad Caliphate. Since then, she has turned her genius and energy to cultivating her domain, establishing trade and alliances throughout the Northlands, and watching her horde of progeny grow and, in many cases, grow old.

The town itself flows down toward a wide fjord from the High Hill upon which the sprawling Hall of Æstrid stands. Although the size of a town, and functioning much like one in many ways, Javik is governed as if it were a simple jarl's hall, and nearly everyone in Javik is related by blood or marriage (save the thralls of course). Merchants and other travelers are welcome, but find that the workshops are not storefronts and anything to be purchased must come from the jarl herself or one of her many, many representatives. The prices may be high and often in the form of barter, but travelers should take comfort that Granny Æstrid holds the laws of hospitality in high regard and will not turn away the needy, the honorable, or the desperate. There may be no inns, but there is always space for strangers in the hall's common room.

HORDALAND

Capital: Halfstead
Notable Settlements: Galvë
Ruler: Køenig Leif Ragison, Regent Gudrid Ragiswif
Government: Northlands feudal with local Things
Population: 78,200 (73,100 Northlander, 5,100 Seagestrelander thrall, small numbers of dwarf, giant-blooded, troll-blooded)
Monstrous: reefclaws, kelp devils, sea spiders, mudmen, trow (coastline); oozes, will-o'-the-wisps, wights, bog hags, shadows, devil dogs, witchfires, catoblepas, bog horses, bog hounds (moors); blood hawks, fey, dire animals, spriggan, grimmswine, vlkodlak, lycanthropes, tatzylwyrms, ajatars, woldgeist (Forest of Woe)
Languages: Nørsk, Common, Dwarven, Seagestrelander
Religion: Æsir, Vanir
Resources: trade hub, shipbuilding supplies, foodstuffs, whale oil, ambergris
Technology Level: High Middle Ages

Hordaland is a loosely governed kingdom that is on the brink of collapsing into warring jarldoms. The former køenig, Ragi Steinson, passed away last year after a lengthy illness, leaving behind a 10-year-old son as his heir. Young Køenig Leif Ragison rules through his regent mother, Gudrid Ragiswif. The jarls are divided as to their loyalty, with some supporting the køenig, some throwing their might behind Ragi Steinson's bastard son Amundi the Blond, and still others being courted by the Gats and Hrolfs.

The Hordalanders are more cosmopolitan than most of the other Northlanders, while remaining true to their Northlander ways much more so than the Hrolflanders. This is in large part due to the city of Halfstead, the Northland's largest settlement and biggest trading center. Hordalanders are used to seeing strange travelers from distant lands, many of which come and stay for an entire season before sailing off for home. It is not unusual for a Hordalander jarl to host one or more strangers from the Southlands or even the distant Ammuyad Caliphate for the winter, and to do so is often considered a great boon and sign of status.

However, the people who settled Hordaland came from the Storstrøm Vale, the very heart of Northlander culture. Hordalanders cling tightly to their traditions, seeing every freeholder as his own ruler and giving the jarls only enough power to organize the hirth and see that the kingdom is well managed. The local Things are very popular, and most Hordalanders treat the rulings of the Things as being more law than suggestion.

HALFSTEAD, TOWN OF (CAPITAL)

Ruler: Jarl Olaf Henrikson
Government: overlord
Population: 4,750 (4,050 Northlander, 400 Seagestrelander, 300 dwarf)

The capital of Hordaland, Halfstead sits on the end of the Hord Peninsula, practically in the middle of the Northlands. The town is a mixing pot of eastern and western Northlands, as well as one of the few places that dwarves can be seen in any number. The largest settlement in the Northlands, Halfstead is the primary destination for foreigners entering the area, and especially for merchants wishing to trade in furs and timber from Estenfird, amber from Seagestreland, linen and wool from the Storstrøm Vale, gold from Hrolfland, iron and exotic goods (often loot taken in viking raids) from Gatland, slaves from Seagestreland, or rare reindeer products from Nûkland.

Halfstead is the closest settlement to being a city in the Northlands. It is a walled warren of streets, shops, and houses that has grown organically and without any attempt at urban planning. Unlike the cities of the south, Halfstead has no urban poor or massive underclass; everybody here either works, starves to death, or leaves. What it does have is a large population of transient sellswords, wanderers, riffraff, and scum. These so-called "adventurers" flock to the town in the warm months to supply themselves before setting off across the Northlands in search of their fortunes. Those who make it back often spend their money at shops geared toward the adventuring trade before departing on another wild scheme to make it rich.

GALVË, TOWN OF

Ruler: Jarl Hrodi the Bald
Government: overlord
Population: 1,350 (1,250 Northlander, 100 Seagestrelander)

Halfstead and Trotheim are the two largest trading centers in the Northlands, and Galvë serves as a safe stopover on the Halfstead to Trotheim voyage. This small settlement is well protected with a stout earthen embankment and wooden palisade, and the jarl of Galvë often sends his warriors out to hunt the surrounding water for vikings, as opposed to raiding themselves. This serves to enhance the town's value as a stopping-over port, which brings in more-profitable trade. Galvë is a hospitable place, and the jarl is happy to feast merchants who come to visit and even sell goods back to them that were taken from them by vikings — and at fair prices as well. Hrodi is the father of the regent, Gudrid Ragiswif, the mother of young Køenig Leif Ragison. As such, he has a vested interest in seeing the child-køenig maintain his rule and has placed himself and his men at the køenig's disposal.

HROLFLAND

Capital: Osløn
Notable Settlements: Burgenheim, Ceaster Pool, Tallsinki
Ruler: Jarl Magnus Hrolfsblood the Bold
Government: Northlands feudal
Population: 76,000 (60,900 Northlander, 10,800 Seagestrelander thrall, 4,300 other human ethnicity; unknown number of other human in mountains)
Monstrous: giant crabs, bunyips, merrow, brine zombies (coastline); dire animals, leucrotta, giant pike, grimmswine, giants, trolls, bog hags, vlkodlak, bog horses, bog hounds, erdhenne (Fangerøm River Valley); giants, glacier toads, thrydregs, trollhounds, gargoyles, trolls, nachtjäger, dracolisks, yeti, thunderbirds, blood eagles (Andøvan Mountains)
Languages: Nørsk, Common, Seagestrelander
Religion: Æsir, Vanir, Southlander gods
Resources: foodstuffs, slave trade hub, gold, wool, timber, tin, manufactured goods, silver, quarry stone, whale oil
Technology Level: High Middle Ages (Stone Age in mountains)

The Hrolfs, one of the two most widespread and powerful of the many families of the Northlands, exert tight control over this area. The family is vast, and no one member has been able to convince the others to name him køenig and thus establish a third kingdom in the Northlands. Covering the entire Jarvik Peninsula from the Andøvan Mountains to the south to the Straits of Half, lies Hrolfland. The Hrolf clan rules this land with an iron fist, having either clan members or allies in every region in a position of power. Furthermore, the more powerful family members have begun attempting to institute more feudal systems of government and land management, even going so far as to dissolve local Things and outlaw the formation of an Althing of Hrolfland.

In order to shepherd their resources and stave off the land-greedy Gats, the Hrolfs have imported ideas and strategies from the Southlands, including employing Southlander mercenaries to fight fellow Northlanders. In Hrolfland, one can find the beginnings of a true feudal system, the use of crossbows and siege engines, and nobility who have taken to fighting from expensive (and imported) warhorses.

The common people of Hrolfland are little more than thralls at best, kept in bondage to the Hrolfs by vows of obligation. Even the townsfolk owe much of what they produce to their local jarl, who is always a Hrolf. The entire network of related jarls is officially ungoverned; however, Jarl Magnus Hrolfsblood is the predominant member of the clan and exerts a great deal of influence. Jarl Magnus fancies himself a king (not the less-powerful Northlander køenig), though he has yet to openly claim that title.

Osløn, Town of (Capital)

Ruler: Jarl Magnus Hrolfsblood and Jolier Magnuswif
Government: overlord
Population: 3,350 (2,500 Northlander, 850 other human ethnicity thrall)

Osløn is the capital of Hrolfland, and the home of the Hrolf clan. It is also a town rapidly growing into a city and in the process of changing its cultural makeup from that of the Northlands into a fusion of Northlander and Southlander cultures. A large fortification — called a "castle" by the Southlanders — is under construction just south of Osløn, though the process is slow and labor intensive. When completed, it will stand as tall as any Monrovian keep and be the strongest fortification in all the Northlands. The town itself is replacing its log palisade with stone walls, as well as paving its streets with cobblestones. A sewer is planned, but so far digging the necessary trenches has proven problematic in the sodden North Sea climate.

Nearly a dozen powerful members of the Hrolf clan live here, mostly in townhouses built to replace the more traditional halls and longhouses. Thralls abound and outnumber freemen two to one, an unusual proportion. In fact, the largest thrall market is here and accepts slavers from Seagestreland, as well as those from distant lands far to the south or across the Great Ocean. The Thing of Osløn still sits, but for the most part has lost what little power it had to the jarls of the Hrolf clan.

Burgenheim, Town of

Ruler: Lord Bothvar
Government: overlord
Population: 1,545 (1,200 Berrini, 250 other human ethnicity, 95 Northlander)

Halfstead may be the most cosmopolitan town in the Northlands, but Burgenheim is by far the most developed, at least by Southlander standards. The wooden palisade that surrounds the town is slowly being replaced by one of soaring stone in the Southlander fashion, the local Thing has been replaced by a council of lords (the local term for a jarl) overseen by Lord Bothvar, the jarl of Burgenheim. Serfs work the farms in the area, and freemen are limited to the craftsmen of the cities.

Trade is the major business of Burgenheim, and the Council of Lords hopes to attract all trade coming to and from the Northlands through their port, which they hope will eclipse Halfstead and the smaller trade moots or towns. Toward this end, they hired engineers from Monrovia to improve the port and docks, build warehouses, and even construct a stone house of worship to Wotan in the fashion of Southlander temples.

Ceaster Pool, Town of

Ruler: Jarl Nafni Hrolfsblood
Government: overlord
Population: 1,785 (970 Berrini, 615 Northlander, 110 other human ethnicity, 90 other)

Ceaster Pool, named for the natural lagoon formed behind the town's bay, was nearly raided and looted into oblivion before the Monrovians developed their watchtower and militia system. Faced with readied, massed crossbow-wielding peasants backed by armored knights, vikings set their sights elsewhere and the town was able to rebuild, becoming a popular stopover for longships heading for easier prey. Over the generations, the people of Ceaster Pool learned that trade with the fearsome Northlanders was beneficial and so came to welcome the sight of longships pulling into the bay.

In 3516 I.R., the Duke Jean d'Auberville of Monrovia transferred the town into Jarl Magnus Hrolfson's hands as part of a payment for nearly 5,000 Northlander mercenaries who served in the duke's wars against his southern nobles. Due to political infighting within the Hrolf clan, rulership of Ceaster Pool passed to Jarl Nafni, a rather traditionally minded Hrolf. Jarl Nafni has since set about turning the town and its surrounding lands into a Northlander jarldom, freeing some serfs, establishing a Thing, and in general upsetting the local culture — especially the local nobility. Rebellion is brewing among all the classes as Jarl Nafni has gone so far as to tear down the "womanly and weak" Southlander churches and build godi houses in their place.

Tallsinki, Town of

Ruler: Jorund, Jarl of Tallsinki
Government: overlord
Population: 560 (500 Northlander, 60 Seagestrelander thrall)

Facing Kulding Bay, Tallsinki is a small trade town largely ignored by the leaders of the Hrolf in favor of Osløn and Burgenheim. As such, it is the last bastion of traditional Hrolfs in the Northlands, people who prefer their own ways to that of the Southlanders and the freedom that being a Northlander provides. It is a town of dirt streets built around a central longhouse that is the home of the ruling Jarl Jorund and surrounded by an earthen rampart and palisade wall. The land around Tallsinki is not terribly fertile but provides enough to support a small community.

Nûkland

Capital: none
Notable Settlements: none known
Ruler: none known
Government: tribal
Population: unknown
Monstrous: dire animals, megafauna, adlets, taiga giants, cold fey, moss trolls, winter wolves, sasquatches, grimmswine, bandersnatch, forest drakes, vlkodlak, treants, humbabas, linnorms, ajatars (taiga forest); megafauna, dire animals, winter wolves, hoar spirits, linnorms (tundra); ice trolls, glacier toads, frost giants, cave giants, vlkodlak, yeti, frost worms, sleipnirs, linnorms, dragons, drakes, ajatars (Harfin Mountains)
Languages: Nûklander
Religion: nature spirits (primarily Landvaettir)
Resources: reindeer, gems, timber (unharvested)
Technology Level: Stone Age

Beyond the Northlands, indeed at the edge of the world, lies the vast evergreen forests and open tundra of Nûkland. How far it stretches north of its beginnings along a line running from the conifer forest of the Frozen Taiga just north of the Wyrm Fang Mountains to the far ice of the Endless Glacier, no one knows. Nûkland is at least several thousand square miles in extent, and likely more.

The taiga is home to a variety of large fauna such as saber-toothed tigers, giant beavers, cave bears, and huge palmate-racked deer. The trees of the taiga slowly give way from towering pines and spruces to stunted versions of these evergreens and eventually to clumps of dwarf trees sheltering in any nook or cranny the land provides. The terrain changes from soft pine needle-covered forests to boggy tundra, frozen throughout most of the year and providing fodder only in the short summer.

On the tundra itself, only the hardiest animals such as arctic wolves, musk oxen, reindeer, giant bears, and the legendary woolly mammoth thrive. Other megafauna have been reported, but many in the Northlands dismiss tales of tigers the size of horses, woolly rhinoceroses, and even giant sloths as just stories. What is known is that strange beasts unlike those found in more southerly climes can be found here, and returning with the claws, fangs, or pelts of such a great beast would put a hero well on the way to having his own saga sung in the mead halls of the Northlands.

In these lands roam tribes of folk known to the Northlanders as Nûklanders, despite their claims that this name is a mistranslation (a more correct translation would be "People of the Reindeer"). The Nûklanders are a different race than the human Northlanders, a race that foreigners would describe as elven.

The Nûklanders are hunters and herders of reindeer, and supplement their diet by gathering wild plants. They are nomadic, traveling as far south as Three Rivers in the winter and heading to the edge of the Endless Glacier in the summer. In addition to providing food and hides, their reindeer are also used as mounts and beasts of burden. Many of the tribes follow a migration route that takes them along the coast, where they prey on seals, walruses, and other sea life that spends its summer on land.

Although famed basket weavers and leatherworkers, the Nûklanders do not work metal, make pottery, or build permanent structures. Their tools are made from bone, wood, and stone, though trade with the Estenfirders and other Northlanders has introduced metal tools and ceramics into the Nûklander culture. Their homes are conical lodges made of hide with wooden supports, and a whole family from the youngest child to the most respected elder shares one dwelling.

It would be easy to say that the Nûklanders lack governments of any kind, and for the most part this is true. The idea that one person can command the obedience of many is foreign to them, as it is largely foreign to the Northlanders as well. There is no Nûklander equivalent of a jarl, much less a køenig. Decisions are made in councils that include all adult members of a tribe, and once a decision is made, it is up to the individual if they are going to follow it or not. Beyond the tribe, there is no higher authority, and no one speaks for the Nûklanders as a whole.

The Nûklanders turn to the spirits of the land for divine aid and spiritual comfort. To a Nûk, the gods turned their backs on them, but the simple spirits of the natural world will never forsake them. Animism is very strong in this faith, and every type of animal or plant, as well as natural features and events, have their guardian spirits. These spirits generally keep to their own spheres; a wolf spirit is concerned with wolf things, not bird things. The tribes' shamans are tasked with interceding with these spirits in order to placate them or request their aid, though every Nûklander knows some simple prayers (these are not spells, just minor forms of worship).

SEAGESTRELAND

Capital: none
Notable Settlements: Dnipirstead, Stavie
Ruler: none known
Government: tribal
Population: unknown (many Seagestrelander, few Northlander)
Monstrous: ogres, dire animals, winter wolves, lycanthropes, giants (coastal forest); giant crabs, giant vermin, quipper, carnivorous plants, hags, lizardfolk, trow, shambling mounds, ajatars (Dnipir Delta)
Languages: Seagestrelander
Religion: Seagestrelander tibaz
Resources: slaves, foodstuffs, gems (amber), furs, gold, timber (unharvested)
Technology Level: Stone Age

The southwestern coast of Seagestre Gulf is a wild region known as Seagestreland, the home to the savage barbarians known as the Seagestrelanders. These people are not Northlanders, and live by herding and farming in the rich forestlands along the coast. For generations, there has been a mixed relationship between the Northlanders and the Seagestrelanders. Longships come to trade, bringing iron tools and luxury goods to exchange for gold, furs, amber, and slaves. Sometimes the Northlanders arrive and just take what they want, which causes the Seagestrelanders to be very wary of the approach of a longship.

Numerous temporary trading posts along the Seagestreland coast are inhabited for a few weeks or months during the year. Only one of these is a permanent settlement that sees traffic year-round and, even then, the winter population is small.

DNIPIRSTEAD, VILLAGE OF

Ruler: Jarl Alvi Gyrdson
Government: autocracy
Population: 136 (125 Northlander, 11 Seagestrelander thrall)

For those embarking on a journey up the Dnipir River, Dnipirstead serves as the jumping-off point, the last Northlander settlement before the wilds of Seagestreland and the Sea of Grass beyond. The land around the village is very fertile, and several families have settled here, building small walled farmsteads and beginning the core of a growing colony. It is not just Northlanders and their thralls that can be found here, for the peoples of the Sea of Grass have learned that trade is better than being raided, and come here around at midsummer for a general trade moot. Some years, there are even travelers from the distant Ammuyad Caliphate, though as yet no true merchants have arrived from that far-off land.

STAVIE, HAMLET OF

Ruler: none
Government: council
Population: 45 (40 Northlanders, 5 Seagestrelander thrall)

Stavie is a poor, rustic affair of crude wooden buildings surrounded by a far-sturdier palisade and ditch. It is a jumping-off point and small trading post for merchants and vikings working the Seagestreland coast. During the summer, it is a bustling marketplace where fur, amber, and thralls are unloaded, bought, and loaded onto ships bound for larger markets, especially at Halfstead and Trotheim. Overseeing this activity is Knut the Lame, a Hordalander who had his left leg crushed by a giant bear in Estenfird many summers ago. Knut owns Stavie and takes a cut from all trade conducted there, but he also manages the trading post and, alongside his thralls, is the only winter resident.

STORSTRØM VALE

Capital: Trotheim
Notable Settlements: numerous villages, steadings, and jarldoms
Ruler: Althing of Storstrøm Vale with individual jarls and local Things
Government: Northlands feudal
Population: 119,000 (112,000 Northlander, 7,000 Seagestrelander thrall, unknown number of Mongat raiders along the Hardöen River, small number of dwarves)
Monstrous: giant crabs, gulper eels, reefclaws (coastline); giant pike, leshies, monstrous crayfish, bog mummies, bog hags, bog horses, bog hounds, erdhenne (Storm River Valley); giant scorpions, amphisbaena, giants, ogres, bhuta, nachtjäger, yrthaks (Waldron Mountains); dire animals, giants, thrydregs, glacier toads, trollhounds, gargoyles, trolls, nachtjäger, dracolisks, yeti, thunderbirds (Andøvan Mountains)
Languages: Nørsk, Common, Dwarven, Seagestrelander
Religion: Æsir, Vanir
Resources: foodstuffs, wool, Trondheim ponies, silver, iron, linen, chalk, ironwork, gems (primarily alabaster)
Technology Level: Dark Ages

The long valley of the Storm River runs from the lower slopes of the Waldron Mountains to the North Sea. It is the longest-inhabited and most heavily-populated area in the North, and as such is often considered the heart of the Northlands. There is currently no køenig of Storstrøm Vale, but in times past, one or another jarl amassed enough power to claim the crown. Today, Storstrøm Vale is divided into a host of petty jarldoms, each vying with the others to become powerful enough to claim the title of køenig. The local Things exert a great deal of authority, often challenging the jarl for power. Many of the Things' jurisdictions cross the boundaries of more than one jarldom. The Althing of Storstrøm Vale meets once every 10 years, and is the scene of some of the most heated political battles in the Northlands, for it is the vote of the Althing that decides who shall wear the crown. More than once over the years, these votes have resulted in spilled blood.

Storstrøm Vale is the cultural heartland of the Northlands, the place where the Northlanders' society as it exists today originated and where Northlander social mores find their greatest expression. While the coasts of the Hord Peninsula are nearly as densely settled, and the Gatlanders are the epitome of the viking ethos, the Vale-folk are the standard by which all others are judged. The largest godshouses and the burial cairns of some of the Northlands' greatest heroes can be found here, and it is the setting for many of the most popular ballads sung by the skalds.

A wealthy and industrious land, Storstrøm Vale is rich in good farmland and pasturage for their famed sturdy ponies, has plentiful fishing offshore and in the Storm River, and even has access to iron and silver in the Waldron Mountains. The land is deficient in only two things: true wilderness (though the foothills of the mountains are somewhat wild) and room. Every generation sees individuals or entire families leave Storstrøm Vale seeking their own land in less-crowded regions.

Several generations ago, a band of heroes fought a sect of the Beast Cult in the heart of Storstrøm Vale, defeating the vile cultists and freeing the upper reaches of the Storm River from the grip of the God of Blood and Beasts. The center of the cult's worship was a great stone idol depicting Shibauroth sitting atop a massive runestone, images of his bestial followers and their victims coiled below him like the scales of some huge wyrm. The totem disappeared after the cult leader was slain, but has since appeared time and again where the Beast Cult finds a new home. After a local sect of the cult is defeated, the totem again vanishes, only to appear again in some out-of-the-way location. Every appearance seems to draw in new cultists, calling to fell beasts and perverted souls alike.

Trotheim, Town of (Capital)

Government: jarl and council (Thing of Trotheim, Althing of Storstrøm Vale)
Ruler: Jarl Gyrthyr the Even-handed
Population: 3,980 (3,663 Northlander, 212 Seagestrelander thrall, 105 dwarf)

Sitting on an island at the mouth of the Storm River is the town of Trotheim. The second-largest settlement in the Northlands, Trotheim serves as the economic and political center of the Storstrøm Vale. Here, the Althing of Storstrøm Vale meets and, when there is a køenig, where he holds court. The Hall of the Køenig dominates the center of town, which although grand in scale, has fallen into disrepair over the decades. Every year the Thing of Trotheim brings forth a motion to have it refurbished, but each time the vote either fails to pass or no one acts on the decision. The remainder of the island is crowded with marketplaces, storehouses, and the "city" dwellings of the most powerful and influential people in Storstrøm Vale.

Although not as populous or cosmopolitan as Halfstead, Trotheim sees merchants from across the Northlands and beyond. The harbor is not the greatest, and the location is out of the way for most west-to-east traffic, but the economy is in some ways more robust. Storstrøm Vale is a rich agricultural land, shipping away a surplus of grains, fruits, processed foods, fish, and wool. Likewise, the many jarls are constantly squabbling and jockeying for social position. Having grander halls, finer clothes, and better retainers can elevate a middling jarl to greater importance, or bankrupt a social climber and force him back into the pack. These two factors — economy and wealth — bring in the merchants, and many who stop at Halfstead proceed on to Trotheim with their most expensive and luxurious goods.

The Hall of Jarl Anud Cursespear

Population: 1,550
Ruler: Jarl Anud Cursespear
Government: overlord

The hall is grand and well-placed. It sits in the Storstrøm Vale on the Ume River, a lesser tributary of the great Storm River. The hall also lies near the sea, and Jarl Anud's land reaches inland from the coast for a fair distance. It is a rich land, with many well-tended farms, expanses of wooded land, and prosperous fishing villages. The people are generally happy and content, and Jarl Anud is strict but fair and rules his people well.

The hall itself is a large and ornate affair, with the main hall and several outbuildings encompassed by a wooden stockade and surrounded by a shallow trench. The stockade is made from well-dressed timber brought from Estenfird at great expense, stands 30 feet high, and has a covered walkway around the outside. The stockade sits on a low earthen mound eight feet in height fronted by a shallow trench six feet deep with a bottom of mud and water. The water level is only filled by periodic rains or snow melts, and thus the trench is dry in the summer, contains approximately 15 inches of water most of the year, and becomes topped off by snow in the winter.

The main hall towers over the stockade, its central support a single ancient tree cut in Estenfird 20 years ago. The beam is nearly eight feet thick and runs from the front of the hall to the back, nearly a hundred feet in length. The hall rises 50 feet above the ground, a remarkable height for a building in the Northlands. The roof is of thatch, but the best thatch available, and is replaced twice annually. Every exposed surface is adorned with carvings of the gods, animals, the jarl's more honorable exploits, fantastical beasts (many of which the jarl has slain), and famous scenes from the sagas. The best of these carvings are accented in gold and silver, obvious displays of the jarl's wealth and power.

The hall is divided into four main sections, a main hall that reaches up through two stories and is surmounted by a balcony that runs the entire interior of the hall, several rooms off the main hall that are used to host important guests, rooms for servants to prepare food and drink, and finally the second floor, where the jarl, his family, and his closest retainers have their rooms. Such luxuries as private rooms are almost unheard of in the Northlands, and a sign of the jarl's wealth.

Beyond the Great Hall, the settlement consists of several outbuildings, barracks, workshops, and other assorted structures. Although only a jarl's hall, the population and industry rival that of small towns and forms not just the political center of the jarl's domain, but the economic as well.

The Hearth Stone

The Storm River splits into two branches roughly halfway along its length and reforms again several miles farther downstream. At the split stands a great stone of pitted black rock that is as hard as iron yet seems to float and bob upon the waters like a giant cork. This rock is known as the Hearth Stone, for legend holds that it was the home of the first Northlanders following Swein Sigurdson, the mold and forge from which the gods made them, and the center of the Northlands. If this is true, it happened so far back in the distant past that none can truly call it naught but legend, save those who come there to call upon the gods, and the godi who have built a mighty godshouse that spans the river.

The Hall of the Hearth Stone is the most sacred shrine of the Northlands. If Storstrøm Vale is the heart and guardian of Northlands culture, then the Hall of the Hearth Stone is the heart and guardian of Storstrøm Vale. It was here that the beginnings of Northlander culture took shelter as it fought off the troll-kin that inhabited the vale, and from here that the first køenig of Storstrøm Vale and eventually the first and only high køenig of the Northlands was acclaimed. It is said if there is ever to be a high køenig again, then it will be when a worthy hand wields the sword of Kraki Haraldson, entombed only a few miles upstream from this hall. The wyrd of the Northlands has always centered upon this place.

From one side of the mighty Storm River to another, a massive construction of wood, the only bridge that crosses that great river, straddles both forks of the waterway and brings pilgrims to stand directly above the Hearth Stone. A clan of godi whose ancestors spent 40 years constructing it manages this godshouse/bridge. Pilgrims are allowed entrance provided they give an acceptable donation. Once inside, they see one of the wonders of the Northlands, for every inch of the structure is carved with depictions of the gods, as well as monsters, villains, and heroes. The entire history of the Northlands can be seen here, and as new events of import occur, they are added, even if a new room needs to be constructed. Young members of the Hearthsons clan spend the early years of their adulthood traveling the Northlands to learn of — and often participate in — important events. Oddly, although so much of the history of the Northlands can be learned from studying the carvings inside the godshouse, the room that once held the origins of the Gat-Hrolf feud collapsed into the river and was washed away many, many generations ago, leaving that a mystery to the current generations.

The Tomb of High Køenig Kraki Haraldson

On a manmade hill overlooking the Storm River, not far from the Hall of the Hearth Stone, sits the tomb mound of Kraki Haraldson, the first and only high køenig of the Northlands. Well before the Northlanders expanded far beyond the borders of the vale — for in that time Hordaland, Gatland, and Hrolfland were the far frontiers — one jarl rose up and united the entire Northlands under his banner. Kraki Haraldson was a fearsome warlord, a feared sea reaver, and a brilliant politician. His might united even the feuding Gats and Hrolfs, as well as hundreds of independent jarls.

Not all were happy with this state of affairs and, following a decade of rule, a cabal of oath-breakers who styled themselves as freedom fighters assassinated the high køenig. The families of these assassins fled and settled the land that is now Vastavikland. The high køenig was laid to rest in a magnificent tomb that was in turn buried under tons of earth in order to keep his wight safe or, as some say, safely inside. To date, none has dared to open the barrow, despite the legends that speak of untold riches and, more alluring, *Kroenarck*, the sword of the high køenig — a weapon that some say would make its owner the second high køenig of all the Northlands.

Vastavikland

Capital: Smølsünd
Notable Settlements: Volskøl (varies)
Ruler: Kol the Redhanded, Køenig of Vastavikland
Government: Northlands feudal
Population: 22,400 (Northlander)
Monstrous: barracuda, devil kelp, sea hags (coastline); dire animals, fire giants, megafauna, mountain trolls, thrydregs, nachtjäger, thoqqua, devils, volcano giants, grendels, red dragons, blood eagles (Olf Mountains); whales, kelpies, trow, sea hags, dragon turtles (Bornhølm Sound)
Languages: Nørsk, Common, Dwarven
Religion: Æsir, Vanir
Resources: plunder, gold, gems
Technology Level: Dark Ages

Harsh, rugged lands breed hard, strong people, and no land is as harsh and rugged as Vastavikland. Estenfird may have its deep forests and tall mountains, and Nûkland its vast snow-covered tundra, but Vastavikland surpasses them all in natural wonders that can kill. The Olf Mountains do not so much roll toward the sea as march down to do battle, forming steep cliffs cut only by narrow fjords. Small holdings fill every habitable and arable inch of these valleys, but even so there are always more mouths than the land can support. Thus, the Vastaviklanders have developed a culture centered on raiding and trading the steady but tiny trickle of gold that flows down melt-water streams from the glacier-choked mountains.

To say that Vastaviklanders are violent is an understatement; jarls and køenigs are chosen by ritual combat. Men and women are raised to become warriors, and even the few thralls are trained to fight. Every spring, hundreds of longships set sail; those that come back bring much-needed supplies; those that don't reduce the number of mouths to feed during the winter.

Smølsünd, Town of (Capital)

Ruler: Kol the Redhanded, Køenig of Vastavikland
Government: overlord and althing
Population: 780 (Northlander)

This town is the largest settlement in Vastavikland and is the traditional seat of the køenig, as well as the Althing of Vastavikland. It is little more than a grand hall and supporting structures, all built on top of a great earthen mound originally constructed by the ancient Andøvan. A stout stockade surrounds the settlement, for in Vastavikland even the seat of the køenig is not immune to attack.

The current ruling monarch is Kol the Redhanded, a huge brute of a man who has spent the years before and since his ascension to the throne as one of the most-feared vikings to ever sail out of the North Sea. Kol does not so much rule here as he favors Smølsünd as his wintering port — when he does return for the winter, that is. This suits the people of Vastavikland, as they are not ones to accept an overly active or intrusive køenig.

In the absence of their monarch, most of the regular governance — what little there is — falls to the Althing. Like other lands in Northlands, the Althing of Vastavikland is made up of all freemen of the region and has very little authority to enforce its decrees. This suits the Vastaviklanders well, as most issues can be handled by duels or ongoing feuds. Even when a lawsuit or other issue is brought before the Althing, the coastal-dwelling freemen dominate attendance, and thus control the flow of debate.

Volskøl (Seasonal Trade Moot)

Ruler: none
Government: anarchy
Population: 1,000–1,500 (varies)

For most of the year, nothing is here but an open field and the remains of last year's Grand Festival. In the late summer months, people filter in and set up tents, and by harvest time, Volskøl becomes a thriving tent city of traders, farmers peddling their harvest, skirmishing bands of warriors, and vikings fresh back from the raiding season. All manner of folk come to Volskøl from across the Northlands and even far beyond. Like most of Vastavikland, the law here is based on force and might, though open theft and brigandage (at least within Volskøl) is generally met with violence from all and sundry. The Grand Festival ends with the first harvest moon and a huge bonfire party where the tents of this season, as well as a portion of every trade or deal made, is burned in offering to Wotan for his wisdom and might. This, of course, is followed by a three-day revel of drunkenness that sees many of the non-Northlander visitors quietly slipping away before the jovial mood changes, as well as the thorough destruction of the camp.

Geographic Features and Points of Interest in the Northlands

Andøvan Mountains

Separating Hrolfland from the Kingdom of Brounthia and its Duchy of Monrovia and from Storstrøm Vale, these tall mountains act as a natural barrier between the Northlands and the Southlands. At their eastern edge, they descend into rolling hills that permit some overland trade between the Hrolfs and the peoples of Brounthia and Monrovia. It is said that in ages past, the first Northlanders explored these mountains and fought wars against the tribes that held them. Ruins of the Andøvan peoples can be found in the mountains, as well as the remains of ancient battles and possibly the burial places of mighty heroes or powerful artifacts. The mountains are still home to some wild, savage humans, though no one has seen them in recent years. Giants and trolls abound, but have learned to give the slopes facing Hrolfland, Brounthia, and Storstrøm Vale a wide berth.

Bornhølm Peninsula

Most of Gatland lies on the Bornhølm Peninsula, a steep, cliff-faced peninsula cut by many small fjords. From the sea cliffs, the land rises sharply up to form the Olf Mountains, which leaves little or no room for flat or arable land. Small villages and halls can be found in nearly every fjord, and the headlands frequently house lookout towers. In general, the Bornhølm Peninsula is a dreary, fog-shrouded place of dangerous waters, hidden rocks, and small bays teaming with those who either are a-viking, returning from a-viking, or are soon to be a-viking.

Dnipir River

The Dnipir River, which flows down to the North Sea through the Sea of Grass and onward from a source far south, is the Northlanders' main highway into Seagestreland and beyond. It is a wide, lazy, and meandering stream, the mouth of which is a tangled delta of shifting islands and swamps. Strange creatures lurk here, including animals of great size and ferocity, hordes of flesh-eating frogs, and deadly snakes as long as three spears. The river itself is not without peril, for despite its broad expanse, it is very deep in the center and home to fish of extraordinary size. Among these fish is the famed river sturgeon, a monster of the depths that can grow to more than 300 pounds and whose salted eggs are considered a delicacy in the Northlands and beyond.

Deep in the marshes that form the delta of the Dnipir River is a simple cottage inhabited by a kindly, but somewhat mad, old woman. This woman, one of the three daughters of the Norn Skuld and a mortal hero, exists to offer aid and comfort to heroes on glorious quests. Those daring enough to brave the dangers of the swamp may find aid, information, or just a warm place to sleep — provided, of course, that she doesn't kill them first.

Fangerøm River

Thundering out of the Andøvan Mountains and plunging down a series of stony hills and steep waterfalls, the Fangerøm River was long thought to be too wild for travel and too unpredictable for agriculture. A generation ago, the Hrolfs hired Southlander engineers to come in and build dams, canals, and irrigation networks to allow the rich fields alongside the river to be farmed. These engineers are still at work, turning the lower expanses of this thundering river into arable land. However, the area has so long been uninhabited that it has become home to giants, trolls, and other monstrous creatures. In order to keep the project going, the Hrolfs must continually contend with the threat of attack, a prospect that threatens to drain the coffers of the Northland's wealthiest clan. Recently, the Hrolfs began offering hacksilver bounties on the heads of giants and trolls, encouraging would-be monster slayers from the Northlands and beyond to flock to the area.

Forest of Woe

Though much of central Hordaland is lightly forested, at the southern end of the Hord Peninsula is a deep, dark ancient forest that separates Hordaland from Storstrøm Vale. It is a haunted and dangerous place filled with monsters of every description, ruined Andøvan hill forts, and wild fey. The Forest of Woe is avoided by all sane people, and its existence cuts overland travel between the two neighboring regions. Despite a reputation for danger and evil, small handful of settlements are found along the forest's edge. Freesteaders cut and burned pocket farms, each surrounded by stout palisades and home to rugged and ever-watchful folk. Outlaws often flee into the forest, though few live long

enough to form permanent settlements. Rumor has it that a settlement of freeholding giant-blooded and troll-blooded outcasts exists somewhere in the depths of the forest, but its existence has yet to be verified.

Fortön River

The Fortön River flows out of the Waldron Mountains to join the Hardöen and thus form the Storm River. Its upper reaches are a series of cascades fed by springs and melting snow, but the river quickly tames as it descends into the vale proper. The mountain slopes it flows over are high in iron ore that tinges the river a reddish color. After the milky waters of the Öster join the Fortön, the combined water becomes a light pink. This odd coloration disappears shortly after the Fortön flows together with the Hardöen.

Hardöen River

One of the three rivers draining from the Andøvan Mountains, the Hardöen is a sluggish stream that provides fertile farmland along its widely space banks. However, it lies far from the heart of Storstrøm Vale and is a definite frontier. Bandits, fell beasts, trolls, and giants are not unknown, and the people are more rugged than the Valers from farther downstream. Five years ago, a large horde of mounted Outlanders called the Mongat found a pass through the mountains from the Sea of Grass to the southwest and terrorized the region until the hirth of the vale formed up and marched against them. A few survivors of these Mongat raiders still survive and harry the outlying farmsteads.

Harfin Peninsula

This unsettled peninsula juts out into the North Sea, shifting the winds and currents, and sending cold weather south into Hordaland and Storstrøm Vale. The Harfin Peninsula is covered in steep mountains, dotted with hot springs, and home to several volcanoes, among them Mount Helgastervän, which is also known as the Mountain of the Great Serpent. None live here, not even trolls and giants, and mad, wild beasts roam at will. Legends say that some of the beasts are so bizarre that they have flesh and blood of living fire.

Hord Peninsula

Centrally located on the North Sea, the Hord Peninsula is sometimes considered the heart of the Northlands despite the cultural prominence of neighboring Storstrøm Vale. The coastal areas slope gently down to the sea and are dotted with hundreds of tiny anchorages. These coastal lands are also very fertile and crossed by several small streams that flow from the interior. As a result, they are densely settled and cut up into nearly a hundred jarldoms, some rather petty, some grand (such as the jarldoms of Halfstead and Galvë). The central portion of the peninsula is lightly wooded, though only in the southern regions where lies the Forest of Woe can it be truly considered a forested area. As a result of the presence of this ominous woodland to the south, most of the settlements are concentrated in the central and northern areas or along the coasts.

In the center of the peninsula, the trees become sparse in a marshy upland that is called the Moors. A portion of these moors is dry with firmer footing and holds the area known as the Barrow Lands, which are generally considered a haunted and evil place. Beyond the settled lands, a thin fringe of forest, either not yet cleared or intentionally left wild, permits hunting and logging without venturing into the forest to the south.

Toward the northern end of Hordaland lies a series of low hills that resemble the knuckles of a gigantic troll pushing its hand out of the ground. These stony and barren hills are home to bandits and monsters. Lying outside of the boundaries of any jarl, the Trollfist Hills are often the refuge of outlaws cast out of Northlander civilization. A small path winds its way through the hills and leads to the Barrowlands beyond.

Ice River

Flowing out of its source somewhere in the distant tundra of Nûkland, the Ice River is the main artery of Estenfird. For most of the year, the river is a frozen sheet of thick ice that thaws for only a few months in the spring and summer before refreezing in early autumn. Even during the winter, the river serves as a means of transport as skiers, skaters, and sleds move up and down between villages. In the early spring, the river begins to thaw starting from the south and working its way north, with a simultaneous thaw occurring near Three Rivers as the Savage and Wrath rivers help break up the ice. During the thaw, the river is impassable as house-sized blocks of broken ice float toward the sea.

Jomsburg Island

The lair of the feared Jomsvikings, Jomsburg is a fortress-city perched high above the North Sea. Tall, thick walls surround the city, even on the seaward side, and the Jomsvikings spared no expense in the construction of their defenses, even going so far as to import priceless siege equipment from the Southlands. These siege engines throw stones large enough to sink a ship or shatter a shieldwall. The city proper is on the cliffs; however, a second city exists in a network of caves that lead from the main fortress through the cliffs to the sea caves below. It is in these sea caves that the Jomsvikings bring their longships and beach them in safety. The sea caves are strongly defended with underground fortifications and massive chains that can be stretched across their mouths in order to block attacking ships. A further defense is the nature of the caves themselves, for their entrances are difficult to spot and their passages are a maze of narrow winding watery tunnels. They are also allegedly home to the mysterious Jomsbeast.

The Jomsvikings themselves are notorious vikings and mercenaries who terrorize the Northlands and beyond with impunity. They are a tightknit brotherhood that swear blood oaths to each other and to their master, Jarl Ut the Fat. These pirates and cutthroats refuse to abide by any law but their own and live a life of debauchery and slaughter, taking what they want and crafting no goods, growing no food, and providing no useful services themselves — other than rapine and slaughter. Only the most desperate jarl would dare hire the Jomsvikings, and so most of the brotherhood spends at least part of the year in the service to the nobles of the Southlands or the distant Ammuyad Caliphate.

The Jomsburg is home to more than just the Jomsvikings and the Jomsbeast, for in a series of caverns on the southern cliffs of the island lives Old Meg, one of the three daughters of the Norn Skuld. Old Meg is a wizened, insane hag who offers deadly challenges to prove the mettle of those who come to her seeking aid. Those who pass receive information, items of magical potency, and respect from a half-divine entity. Those who fail are never heard from again, for not only do they lose their lives, but their very souls as well.

Kulding Bay

This large bay sees a great deal of shipping, and thus is prone to raiders and vikings. However, this threat is well known and the jarls that border its waters know to take precautions. Ships travel between Storstrøm Vale, Hordaland, and Hrolfland, the three most prosperous of Northlander regions. The presence of so many ships belonging to the Hrolfs draws in raiders from Gatland, and they do not always ask allegiance before attacking a vessel.

Sven Oakenfist was a notorious raider and viking of the previous generation who was slain in a raid by a stripling boy (the boy grew up to be Jarl Arnud Cursespear). The vikings buried their chieftain in a massive three-part barrow along Kulding Bay. Legends say that the wight of Sven Oakenfist sleeps uneasy, but they also tell of the great fortune buried with him.

Lake Berring

The center of Brounthia is the region around Lake Berring. This fertile land watered by the Red Rivers is divided into hundreds of noble estates, some not much larger than a farmstead in other nations. Bound peasants — commoners whose service and labor has been given to a lord in exchange for protection and care — work most of these. However, along the lake's edge are many small villages of fishermen who are by law and tradition freemen.

The fishermen of Lake Berring are a hardy bunch. The water is cold, and the lake often wracked by storms blowing in off the Great Ocean. No shallow puddle this, Lake Berring is as deep as the sea and large enough to produce large waves.

In addition to the natural dangers of working on the water, Lake Berring is also home to fish of gargantuan scale. Catching one of these deep-dwelling giant sturgeons is a battle worthy of song, a deed that makes the deep-water fishermen more like whalers than anglers. Should one bring up such a leviathan and get it safely to market, then one's fortune and fame are set, as are the fortune and fame of one's children and grandchildren.

Løln River

One of three rivers of Storstrøm Vale that drains from the Andøvan Mountains, the Løln River is also one of the fiercest. Dropping out of the mountains, it falls rapidly toward the Storm River over six high waterfalls that each form a deep pool at its base. Between these waterfalls, the river is swift but still provides more than enough water for the surrounding villages. Twenty years ago, the jarls of the Løln River gathered together with the local Things to bring in waterwheels from the Southlands to harness the power of the falls and the river. This led to a boom in the area as mills and other water-powered devices began to alter the local means of production. All the jarls and Things that invested in their construction own these mills jointly, and the cost of their maintenance is borne by a similar contract. Use is free to any of the signing Things or jarldoms.

Lower Red River

This long river winds down out of the World's End Mountains to empty into Lake Berring. The spring floods overfill the banks and spread fresh soil across the fields of the nobles who dwell here. It is on this great flood plain that the wars of the nobles are fought. These ceremonial and religious conflicts allow land to change hands, rights to pass from one to another, and disputes to be settled in an organized manner.

There are laws to the War of Banners, rules that define who may fight and who may not. The queen or her agents set numbers, equipment, date, and location. These are designed to make the fight fair, but also to limit the trampling of crops and destruction of the land. Most often, battles take place on prepared land set aside for the purpose, and many nobles maintain a small field just for the War of the Banners. On the day of battle, each side defends its banner against attacks. Should a banner be captured, the issue is decided. Often weapons are rebated for these conflicts; no sense in anyone getting killed, at least not any one important.

Mount Helgastervän

This towering volcano sends forth a constant cloud of smoke and ash that can be seen for miles out to sea. The land surrounding it is rent with fissures that pour forth colored smoke and steam, rife with hot springs bubbling with sulfurous water, and prone to earthquakes that level ridges and rend the earth. Legend says that the Great Serpent, a wyrm of enormous size and age, lairs somewhere in the mountain. These same legends tell of a great store of treasure taken from passing ships and the ancient Andøvan, but what hero is brave (or foolish) enough to venture into the Gates of Hell to retrieve it?

Mount Jurderheim

The tallest mountain in the Northlands, Mount Jurderheim is in the Olf Mountains, and is said to be unscalable by a mere mortal. Many heroes and would-be heroes have tried, and all died on its slopes, their frozen, wind-scoured corpses eventually found by the next group of fools. It is well known that some great wyrm lairs near the summit and does not take kindly to intruders into its domain. Still, the promise of fame and the chance at one of several lost treasures said to be either in the beast's lair or elsewhere on the mountain attract new victims every generation.

Mount Reik

Mount Reik, an active volcano in the Olf Mountains, while dwarfed by the nearby Mount Jurderheim, is still notable for the constant plume of smoke that rises from its gaping maw of a peak. The surrounding land is famous for its hot springs and sulfurous waters, as well as frequent earthquakes. Although other volcanoes exist in the Olf Mountains, Mount Reik is the largest and most active. It has rarely erupted in recent memory, but this just seems to mean that such an eruption is likely long overdue. The raw blood of the earth flows beneath Mount Reik's slopes and draws wizards and other less-savory types from across the world that seek to capture some of this lava for use in their magic. It is said that a great beast of living fire dwells within the mountain, but none has ever claimed to have seen it.

Northern Olf Mountains

Like the southern arm of the Olf Range, the northern arm is a rugged collection of steep mountains that slope precipitously down to the sea to form narrow fjords and high valleys. Unlike the southern range, the north is less prone to volcanism. The land is still dangerous and home to all manner of fearsome beasts as well as trolls, giants, and some of the largest wyrms seen in the Northlands.

North Sea, The

Part of no specific land, but central to all, the North Sea is the lifeblood of the Northlanders. The whale road of the Great Ocean Ûthaf and the infamous Northern Passage finds its terminus in the North Sea, and the waves that lap upon the rocky shores of the Seal Coast find their genesis in those same cold waters. For the Northlanders whose culture and sustenance relies upon the tradition of going a-viking, the North Sea is their highway and their escape route. The lives and livelihoods of a great portion of the population of the Northlands rides in longships upon the eddies and currents of the North Sea, and as its tides pull so too does their fate.

While the waters and cold are capable of quickly killing those that fall in for long, that is not the only danger that the dark waters hold. Storms are swift and sudden on the North Sea, and these gales have left the wreck of many a longship of doughty warriors upon some desolate shore or at the bottom of Rán's domain. As a result, ghost ships crewed by draug and worse haunt the campfire tales of many a stalwart sword brother, and it is not unknown for brine zombies to rise from the surf on a foggy coastal night. In the deeper waters, brine dragons, devilfish, grindylows, sea drakes, sea serpents, dire sharks, dragon turtles, gigantic specimens of octopi and squids, and even the legendary krakens pose hazards for the merchants, fishermen, and raiders alike that ply the sea's steel waves and freezing spray. The sea is a fickle mistress, from the secrets she holds to her deadly children, and even the mightiest køenig dares not forget to pay her homage.

Olf Mountains

These rugged mountains stretch from the forests of Seagestreland in the south well into Gatland in the north, and possibly beyond. For the most part, they are tall and steep, with tops capped with snow year-round. Between the mountains are thousands of small valleys fed by melt water and springs. In these dells dwell the hardiest of the Vastaviklanders, hardworking souls who don't mind living far removed from the rest of Northlander society. Each vale has its own jarl that gives grudging obedience only to the køenig in Smølsünd (if they give even that). The people of the mountains are freemen one and all, and often deride their coastal cousins for keeping thralls.

All of Vastavikland is subject to earthquakes and other seismic activity, but no part more so than the depths of the Olf Mountains. Hot springs are not unheard of, nor for one of the mountains to suddenly show itself to be a sleeping volcano, in addition to the many already-known volcanoes. This, combined with long winters (long even for the Northlanders), giants, wyrms, and other deadly creatures, makes the Olf Mountains one of the most-dangerous regions in an already deadly part of the world.

Öster River

The shortest river in Storstrøm Vale, the Öster is considered by many to be the least desirable of the rivers in the region. Its flow is rendered milky and opaque by the gypsum it picks up as it tumbles down out of the Waldron Mountains — that is, when it is flowing at all. A very seasonal river, the Öster River often dwindles to a trickle during the summer months, is a thundering tangle of trees and animal carcasses in the spring melt, and has been known to disappear completely during droughts.

Ruby River

Flowing down out of the southern end of the World's End Mountains, the Ruby River carries red-tinted silt down from those eroding heights to meet the broad flat gleam of the Silver River beneath the heights of Craghold. The Ruby is a small river whose rapid pace and low banks often lead to overflow during the spring rains and snow melt. This flood fertilizes the fields along its length, though at some risk of carrying away livestock and homes.

By longstanding tradition, the Ruby River is not divided up into noble estates. Instead, it has the largest collection of freeholdings in the kingdom. These small farmsteads have grown over the generations and although not true noble estates, marriages and outright purchase of land has merged many of the small farms into larger bodies. These are not worked by bound peasants, the owners are not nobles after all, but landless freemen.

Trolls, giants, and other monsters occasionally wander into the Ruby River valley from the World's End Mountains. Those living along the river have learned to be vigilant and to defend themselves as there are no knights ready to ride out, and the people tend toward hardy self-reliance. This sense of independence permeates all of the Ruby River freeholdings, and the people here never seem to be able to organize in any way that might put their common needs first.

Saudb River

Flowing along Storstrøm Vale's western border, the Saudb River is a quiet, peaceful stream whose banks are dotted with small jarldoms and freemen farmsteads. It can be said that the people living here have lost much of what other Northlanders consider the true nature of the Northlands, for the wilds of the Saudb have been tamed, the land is fruitful, and even the winters are mild. However, this region does tend to breed an unusual number of heroes and would-be heroes who find the contentment of the vale too much and thus leave to find new fortunes in more dangerous lands.

Sauøk River

This short river serves little purpose other than to fall out of the Waldron Mountains and feed the Storm River. Few people live along its length, for the river is too narrow and too filled with rapids and cataracts to be navigable. The surrounding mountains are still mostly wild and unexplored, home to fur trappers, hardscrabble farmers, and the occasional troll or giant band. Rumors of ancient dwarven cities and mines near the headwaters of the Sauøk have long drawn those seeking glory and fortune, but as yet, none have found anything other than tree-filled valleys and rocky slopes.

Savage River

Tumbling down from the Wyrm Fang Mountains, the Savage River lives up to its name with white-capped ferocity. Despite its speed and many rocky stretches, the spring floods tend to smooth out the rapids and allow loggers to float large rafts of timber down to Three Rivers. The rest of the year, the river is unnavigable but does have the distinction of being the only free-flowing body of water during Estenfird's long winters.

Seydiford Peninsula

A near twin of the Bornhølm Peninsula to the north, the Seydiford is a wild and rugged place largely unsuited to human life, and inhabited by giants, trolls, and worse. Of course, it is also the homeland of the Vastaviklanders, and few people call it by its proper name, conflating the entire Peninsula with Vastavikland. This is not quite true, as Vastavikland is much larger than just the one peninsula.

Siljøn River

This river runs from the Andøvan Mountains, through the fertile plains that make up the heartland of Hrolfland, and on into the North Sea in several lazy loops and turns. Along its route, it is fed by the Tynseid and Fangerøm rivers, gaining strength if not speed as it twists toward its mouth at the Bay of Osløn. Due to the Siljøn River's slow crawl and gentle nature, it is a favorite waterway for the interior of Hrolfland and also serves to bring stone and timber down from the Andøvan Mountains in order to feed the many construction projects underway in and around Osløn.

Silver River

Flowing from one of the larger seeps in the southeastern part of the Sea of Grass and fed by the Ruby River to the north, the Silver River empties into the Norwold Gulf at Landisport. Along its journey to the sea it passes by noble estates, small freeholds, and the city of Craghold. A wide flat river, the Silver sees many rover barges carrying the products of the land to Landisport and the goods from across the Great Ocean back up to Craghold.

Skagerrok Peninsula

Most of Estenfird lies on this peninsula bordered on the west by the North Sea and the east by the Great Ocean. High cliffs and rocky reefs protect nearly the entire coastline, allowing entrance into the interior only at three points. At the tip of the peninsula lies the mouth of the Ice River and the small village of Vöss. The seasonal whaling village of Bräcke is on the eastern shore. The eastern cliffs are broken by a long pass called the Gap that runs down from the valley of the Ice River to the sea at the village of Úlmer.

Storm River

The mighty Storm River, so named for its annual spring floods, is the heart of Storstrøm Vale, and thus in the minds of many, the true wellspring of the Northlands. It is along these banks that Northlander culture first developed, and today this river's banks are covered with the farms and fields of jarldoms and clans that are many centuries old. There is not one scrap of true wilderness along the entire length of the river, though carefully managed woods allow for hunting and the gathering of forest resources. Travelers are advised of two facts: First, the people along this river hold the customs of hospitality to a high standard and thus welcome worthy travelers into their halls and homes. Second, there is not a piece of land that does not belong to someone, and trespassers are not welcome — indeed, they are unworthy sorts who don't have enough honor to understand the rights of property. Stick to the roads or the river and be on your best behavior when you journey along the Storm.

Tynseid River

This tributary of the Siljøn is much like its master, slow and curving, and more than fertile enough by any standards. The entire length from the foothills of the Andøvan Mountains to the mouth of the river as it flows into the Siljøn is farmed. In generations past, the jarls of the Tynseid raided overland into Monrovia, but today they are content to enjoy the profits of their thrall-worked farms and the peace their clan enjoys with their southern neighbors. Most of the farms are large affairs, as the jarls of the Tynseid have absorbed lesser landholders over the years to create huge plantations worked by thralls bought at the market in Osløn.

Úme River

This small river flows out of the Andøvan Mountains and into the Storm River. It plunges rapidly down to Storstrøm Vale and ambles its way pleasantly through lush fields and small wooded lots until gently easing itself into the greater stream. Some of the prime jarldoms and holdings in the vale are here, especially along its northern banks, as one could easily lay claim to land that stretches from the Úme to the shores of the North Sea.

Upper Red River

The Upper Red River flows in a series of falls and cataracts down from the craggy Andøvan Mountains to flow a short rapid length into Lake Berring. It is much too fast of a river to make water travel easy for all but its last few miles. Those nobles who live along it have long been seen as somewhat rustic compared to the finery of the Lake Berring nobility of the cultured martial tempers of the Lower Red River nobles.

Despite lying well within the borders of the kingdom, the Upper Red River has always been a more rugged place. The nobility here often work their own land, and freemen farmsteads are common. Where the rest of the kingdom has strict class divisions, the Upper Red nobility are used to working closely with their vassals and often side-by-side in the fields.

Vindelsalven River

Like the Dnipir River, this river flows through the forests of Seagestreland and off into the Sea of Grass. Its source is far to the west across the Sea of Grass. Some Northmen and, in particular, Vikings from Vastavikland use the Vindelsalven and the Grand Portage between Lake Hargos and the Shimmering River to travel to the Gulf of Akados for trade or plunder.

Waldron Mountains

These great snow-capped peaks and the rain-deprived lands in their shadow act as a barrier between the Northlands and the Sea of Grass. They are also the source of the many rivers that flow through Storstrøm Vale, including the mighty Storm River that forms on their lower slopes where the Fortön and Öster meet. The mountains themselves are forested on their northern slopes, but the south-facing parts of the range fall within the mountains' rain shadow. Indeed, one of the wonders of the Northlands is that despite all the rain that falls upon the Waldron Mountains, it all seems to run off to the north, leaving the area beyond the range a desolate wasteland of cold desert until reaching the fertile lands along the Dnipir River.

Trolls and giants, as well as other monstrous creatures, inhabit the mountains. Long ago, before the coming of even the ancient Andøvan, the Waldron Mountains were home to a dwarven kingdom of some magnificence. According to Northlander legends, it is through this kingdom that some of the wandering tribes that were the ancestors of the Northlanders came, following a great tunnel beneath the mountains to the light of Storstrøm Vale at the other end. This tunnel, and all the lost dwarven holds and mines that are said to be in the Waldrons, have never been found.

WHALING BAY

Several varieties of whales can be found here during the summer months, and whalers from as far away as the Ammuyad Caliphate come to hunt the mighty beasts. A rare few Nûklanders have been known to take to the sea in their curious skin boats in order to harpoon a leviathan and drag it on shore, a feat many Northlanders view as being very brave (and which they have not managed to successfully emulate). In recent years, some small skirmishes between the Estenfirder whalers and interlopers from other lands have occurred.

WORLD'S EDGE MOUNTAINS

Legends hold that in the farthest extents of the north, far beyond even Nûkland or the fabled wonders of the Far North, lies the very edge of the world, a vast wall of mountains beyond which there is nothing. It is also said that if one were to travel to these distant peaks and cross them, one can take off and set sail among the stars, even to the very abodes of the gods. Of course, if one were to do this, one would rank among either the greatest fools or greatest heroes of the Northlands. Either way, no one known has made this journey and returned to tell of it.

WORLD'S END MOUNTAINS

These ancient and worn-down mountains stand at the southeastern edge of the Kingdom of Brounthia along the coast of the Norwold Gulf. The tallest of the World's End Mountains stands a mere 10,000 feet high, not nearly as impressive as the Andøvans to the north. Even so, these mountains present a rugged barrier that prevents overland travel to the Principality of Pelshtaria.

The mountains are rich in gold, granite, and other useful minerals. Iron mines delve deep beneath the mountains, as do others seeking tin and coal. These mines are owned by lords from Brounthia and worked by a mixture of condemned criminals and freemen. It is illegal under royal law to employ bound peasants in mining, and the Royal Wardens frequently patrol the area looking for transgressors, illegal mining operations, and dangerous monsters.

The World's End Mountains are not rich in monsters, though trolls, giants, and other threats can be found here. The true danger lies not on the surface but deep beneath the stunted peaks. In the earliest days of the world, the gods had many failures in their quest to create life. These failures were entombed beneath what was at that time the greatest mountain range in the world. As eons passed, these towering mountains slowly eroded. The terrors trapped there have not been released, and if left alone might not until the end of the world. However, the Brounthians mine deeper and deeper every year, and as mining technology improves, it is only a matter of time before one of these tombs cracks open and the world meets an early end.

WRATH RIVER

If the Savage River is furious, the Wrath River sets a new definition for angry water. At no time, and at no place, is this river navigable, from its source high in the eastern Wyrm Fangs until it reaches the Ice River at Three Rivers. This rapid-filled flow plunges down countless waterfalls, tumbles over several cataracts, and only occasionally forms small pools where the water slows from thundering to merely fast. Were it not for its remote location, the Wrath River would be an excellent location for Southlander-style water mills.

WYRM FANG MOUNTAINS

Estenfird is loomed over on all sides by the Wyrm Fang Mountains, towering snow-capped peaks that might as well have been carved out of gigantic blocks of granite and dropped onto the Skagerrok Peninsula. Below the perpetual snow is a wide band of windswept rock that drops steeply down to the mountains' shoulders. It is on these shoulders that a fortune in timber grows among the many hanging valleys and hidden dales formed by the interlocking lower slopes of the mountain range.

The forests also abound in game with red deer, moose, wolverines, bears, and other animals being common, as well as the rare megafauna that Estenfird is so well known for. These mountains are also home to wicked creatures such as giants, trolls, wyrms, and all manner of deadly and vicious monsters. Those foresters who hunt and lumber here are hardy souls, their bodies hardened by the harsh winters and steep slopes, and their hearts calloused by the deaths of so many friends and loved ones. It should be no wonder that the Beast Cult of Shibauroth has taken root in this isolated and punishing land.

WYRM FANG ROCKS

Sheer cliffs and the stony reefs of the Wyrm Fang Rocks protect the western coast of Estenfird. These reefs are large tooth-like rocks that just up above the high tide mark, or just below it. Many ships have been driven onto the rocks over the years, and rumors hold that brave men might be able to salvage great treasures from these frigid waters. Rumors also speak of undead and sea trolls populating the wrecks, so it would be wise to be wary and stout of heart in equal measures when exploring these locales.

BEYOND THE NORTHLANDS

YRSA'S ROCK

Out on the Great Ocean, not far from where the North Sea flows out to join the world sea, lies the fabled abode of Yrsa the Fair, one of the three Daughters of Skuld the Norn. Yrsa waits on this pillar of stone jutting out of the sea, chained at the summit and guarded by a fearsome beast. She lives as a test of the courage, heroism, and good manners of would-be heroes and rewards those who rescue her with boons and wisdom. Those who fail are consumed by the wyrm that guards her. Much is to be gained from rescuing Yrsa, but be warned, she only rewards those who come to her for the best of intentions and who treat her with utmost grace and respect.

The location of Fair Yrsa's Rock is not common knowledge, but those steeped in wisdom and learning maybe able to piece together its general location somewhere in the Cymu Current far south of the Cymu Islands but nearly due east of Halfstead.

CYMU ISLANDS

The Cymu Current is a warm-water current that flows past the mouth of the North Sea and heads northeast toward distant and unknown lands. The Oestryn Isles are said to lie in that current, but many hold them to be just a legend, or a confusion of the real Cymu Islands with a dream of fiction. The Cymu Islands are a small chain of volcanic islands that lie in the middle of the Cymu Current. They are lush gardens, heated from the warm waters of the sea and from the boiling rock within their hearts. Strange animals are known to inhabit these islands: lizards and snakes of grotesque size, birds that have no feathers, and even lizards that walk like men. The Northlanders rarely visit the Cymu Islands, though their location is well known and often used as a place of refuge for those blown far out to sea or who have chased whales or merchant vessels too far from more regularly traveled sea lanes.

BIG BAY ISLAND

Capital: none
Ruler: The Lizard Queen
Government: theocracy
Population: unknown number of lizardfolk
Monstrous: snakes, poisonous frogs, giant lizards, animated trees and plants
Languages: Reptilian
Religion: Worship of Lizard Queen
Resources: game, fishing, fresh water, anchorage
Technology Level: Stone Age

The Cymu Islands
Shipwreck Bay
Vasten's Hall
Dragon Mountain
Smoking Island
Pine Island
Sgird's Camp
T'Kumel
The Claw
Jasthij
Whitefish Bay
Wyrm Island
Thunder Island
Cymu Islands
The Spine
Big Bay
Harssst
Stinking Plains
Quiet Mountain
Joissik
Nathssst
Nathssik
Big Bay Island
GREAT OCEAN ÜTHAF
Legend
Town or Village
City
Capital or Free City
Imperial Capital
Fortress or Citadel
Ruins
Place of Interest
Road
Trail or Unused Road
Mountain Pass
Battlefield

The island that most Northlanders are familiar with, Big Bay Island is named for its large protected bay that lies along its eastern edge. The opening to Big Bay is deep and clear of obstruction, making it easy to navigate and nearly impossible to close off. A broad beach fills the interior arc of the bay and provides plenty of room to bring longships ashore and set up camps. Streams of fresh water runoff from the mountainous interior of the island, the jungles are filled with game, and fruit trees grow along the margins.

All in all, Big Bay Island is a perfect oasis for sailors. So fine is the anchorage that whalers often speak of making a visit part of their regular trade as opposed to an occasional place of refuge. However, something always seems to cause such talk to sputter out. No ship that has put into the bay has tarried longer than necessary, nor have merchants thought to set up even the crudest of settlements to see to the needs of Northlanders and other whalers.

Unbeknownst to the human visitors to the island, Big Bay Island is home to a group of lizardfolk.

Harssst Village

Ruler: High Priest Lorrsst
Government: theocracy
Population: 738 (lizardfolk)

Sitting at the base of the Quiet Mountain on Big Bay Island, Harssst is a small village of lizardfolk dedicated to the worship of the Lizard Queen, their ruler and deity. The village is situated on a large lagoon that connects to Big Bay via a narrow channel. This places them in fear of discovery by visitors coming to the bay, but so far, the thick jungle that the lizardfolk encourage to grow between their village and the bay has deterred investigation and concealed the village from casual view.

Ioissik Village

Ruler: High Priestess Gahssst
Government: theocracy
Population: 1,419 (lizardfolk)

This village lies deep in the jungles of Big Bay Island, far from the few trails that visitors frequent. It sits atop a small stream that rolls down from a fissure in one of the mountains in the island's heart. A peaceful village, the lizardfolk of Ioissik spend their days hunting the jungles, tilling their fields of cassava, and praying to the Lizard Queen.

Nathssik Village

Ruler: High Priest Ssirossik
Government: theocracy
Population: 1,312 (lizardfolk)

Not the largest village on Big Bay Island, but by far the most highly organized. Nathssik sits near the Temple of the Sinking Waters on the western slopes of Quiet Mountain. It is an outlier for the followers of the Lizard Queen, as it is both the westernmost of the villages and the one hardest to reach. A long spur of the mountain prevents easy travel, and only one pass is seasonal at best. When the rains come in the spring and fall, the pass is filled with rampaging water. During the winter, flash floods are common.

Temple of Sinking Waters

Ruler: The Lizard Queen
Government: theocracy
Population: 291 (lizardfolk)

The caldera of Quiet Mountain is home to a sprawling temple complex built by some long-dead civilization. The lizardfolk of Big Bay Island have long used the site as their capital, naming it the Temple of Sinking Waters after the extinct volcano's receding lakes. Only a small part of the temple is inhabited, while walls of rubble serve to keep at bay whatever strange things lurk in the shadowed depths.

The Lizard Queen rules her domain on Big Bay Island from a throne of giant reptile bones and other totemic trinkets. She is an old and powerful

sorceress, and her people worship her as a god. However, the Lizard Queen is getting long in tooth and fears one of her many children might try to move along their succession. To prevent such an end, she has begun researching a means to gain immortality, or failing that, lichdom.

Big Bay

This large protected bay sits on the eastern coast of Big Bay Island and provides a fine natural harbor. It is much frequented by Northlander ships in distress or those seeking a respite from whale hunting, or for those seeking a place to render their catch. Food and fresh water are plentiful, and the shore slopes well for pulling a knorr onto the beach.

Quiet Mountain

Quiet Mountain was once a volcano as active and fierce as any other in the Cymu Islands, but it has been millennia since the mountain last erupted. Few quakes rattle its slopes, and it is a rare and terrible day when gases or ash spew forth. The caldera at its peak holds a large lake that drains away in the dry season only to refill when the rains come. Where the water goes none knows, but to the lizardfolk who live there, this is as it has always been.

Stinking Plains

A massive break in the jungle formed by the Stinking Plains extends northeast from Quiet Mountain. A final eruption before the volcano went quiescent left a large lava plain that cut its way nearly to the sea. Beneath this field of broken igneous rock and scattered obsidian patches lies a new hotspot that boils waters from deep in the earth and sends them up as geysers of steam, sulfurous pools, and the occasional burst of lava. The lizardfolk of the island rarely visit here, but the same civilization that built the ruins they named the Temple of Sinking Waters dwelled in this land and stumps of their towers protrude out of the plains.

The Claw

Capital: Vasten's Hall
Ruler: Jarl Vasten the Fat
Government: overlord
Population: 23 (Northlander)
Monstrous: none
Languages: Nørsk
Religion: none
Resources: none
Technology Level: Iron Age

Nine years ago, Vasten the Fat was leading a deep-sea whaling expedition when a sudden storm of unprecedented fierceness blew his knorr far out to sea. Damaged and taking on water, the ship limped along back toward Estenfird, but a second storm came along and tossed the crippled ship onto the Claw, a Cymu Island named after its rough shape of a three-fingered hand reaching across the sea.

One of the lowest lying of the islands, the Claw presents a poor place to make a home. With their ship destroyed and the island lacking in tall trees suitable for crafting another, Vasten the Fat ordered his crew to set up a new home here. The living is poor, as the soil is unsuited for agriculture and passing storms regularly rip across the rocky island.

Vasten's Hall (Capital)

Ruler: Jarl Vasten the Fat
Government: overlord
Population: 12 (Northlander)

Jarl Vasten is mad. He rules over a hall that is not much more than a lean-to of driftwood timbers laid against a stony hillside. Those of his crew who remain are either as mad as him or captives to the terror inflicted upon them. Cannibalism is common, and the jarl and his followers are not above hunting the narrows and straits around the Claw for other castaways. These they take back to their refuse-filled home for torture and consumption. When no other meal is in the offing, they subsist on crabs, mussels, rats, and each other.

Shipwreck Bay

Tucked inside one of the peninsulas that give the Claw its name, Shipwreck Bay is a trap laid by the gods or some demon, at least in the minds of the sailors who have heard of it. From the outside, the bay looks inviting, deep, and not too narrow, with a stone shore that slopes gently up to a break in the cliffs that line the island. The deception is quickly discovered upon entering, for the current is swift and varies as it runs across the sunken boulders that line the bay's bottom. These boulders are well rounded by the currents, but nonetheless are massive enough to stave in the hull of any ship that attempts to make the passage. Even the beach is a trick, for the rocky slope lies over an underground stream and proves a treacherous purchase for foot or keel.

Pine Island

The most northern of the Cymu Islands, Pine Island is not warmed as much by the current as other islands in the chain. That being said, it is still much warmer than an island at its latitude should be, and sports a large forest of tall pines that covers all but the highest reaches of the towering Dragon Mountain. What visitors come to the island seek the tall pines or hunt the seals that rest on its gravel beaches. Several small inlets provide a sheltered anchorage, though none as deep or safe as Big Bay.

Sigird's Camp

Ruler: Sigird Bjorgsdöttir
Government: council
Population: 8 (Northlander)

Refugees from the hall of Jarl Vasten the Fat, Sigird's Camp on Pine Island is tucked into one of the valleys carved by small streams running off Dragon Mountain. It is a well-ordered camp, but just a camp, and the dwellings are log-and-canvas cabins that the residents are constantly improving. Sigird led a group of the jarl's crew away one night in a canvas and pitch-bottom boat. They hoped to make for Big Bay, but the waves and current carried them north. Landing at last on Pine Island, the small band moved inland to escape recapture and sought protection from the mighty storms that plague the islands. They established a small camp there with a few gardens but not much else. Sigird hopes to one day build a seaworthy vessel and escape back to Estenfird, but the rigors of simple survival leave little time for other projects.

Dragon Mountain

Named for the shape of its peak and the plumes of smoke that occasionally boil out of it, Dragon Mountain is an active volcano that sits along the northern edge of Pine Island. Taller than the other mountains that dot the Cymu Islands, Dragon Mountain can be seen from miles out to sea and is often used as a landmark for navigation. Old sailors say that if you can see Dragon Mountain you have gone too far, for past it lies the open ocean and the unknown of the Far North.

Smoking Island

All of the Cymu Islands have volcanoes, but many are either dormant or extinct. The one that stands above Smoking Island is neither, as evidenced by the constant plume of smoke and ash that rises from its summit. The slopes of this mountain are riven by cracks that spew forth hot, acidic water and occasionally rivers of lava. The island is subject to frequent quakes, sinkholes, geysers, and other seismic activity.

The jungles of Smoking Island are some of the richest and densest in the Cymu Islands. Strange creatures live here alongside giant reptiles, insects of incredible size, and primitive ape creatures. The Northlanders avoid the place despite tales of lost cities and great treasure.

T'Kumel, City of

Ruler: Prince Havrash
Government: overlord
Population: 23,491 (grey apes)

Smoking Island is home to more than just animals and primitive ape people. A civilization, said to be ancient, dwells in the interior and struggles to survive against eruptions, quakes, and the hungry jungle.

T'Kumel is the city of the gray apes, tall simian humanoids unknown elsewhere in the Lost Lands. Their city is composed of massive blocks of stone cut from ruins found across the island, polished to a smooth glassy surface, and then decorated with reliefs chronicling their culture, history, and gods.

The rulers of T'Kumel do not claim kingship, nor do they sit upon the gold and ivory throne that lies at the heart of their palace. Instead, princes chosen from among the great warriors of the people and proclaimed to be regents for the return of the king rule the city. Strangers are not welcome in T'Kumel, but legends and prophecies say that one with smooth hairless skin the color of the night sky will come and bring the king back from beyond the stars.

Jastrij, Ruins of

These ruins extend from the foot of the Smoking Mountain to Whitefish Bay on the southern coast. They are towering cyclopean buildings, towers, and walls of stone that date to a time before man, massive edifices whose size hints at architects larger and broader than any human could hope to be. While not continuous, the ruins run for miles in tumbled clumps with full or mostly intact buildings rising up out of the jungle canopy.

The King of Lost Minara

To the north of the Smoking Mountain is a valley formed by two high ridges of igneous rock that flowed down some time ago. This valley is rich in smaller trees, hot springs, and a few scattered small ruins, but the main feature is a 100-foot-tall plinth upon which rests a pair of sandaled simian feet. The feet end at the ankles, and no other remains of whatever gargantuan statue once stood there can be found. The gray apes of T'Kumel say the statue was their long-lost king and the valley once housed the city of Minara, but there is no proof to back this wild tale.

Whitefish Bay

This deep bay on the western side of Smoking Island is the breeding ground for certain species of pale whales. In the summer months, the whales swim in, battle, and mate. The white whales would be easy hunting during this time, but prudence keeps whalers away during the mating season less their greed destroy the catch of future years.

The Spine

Not one island but a chain of rocky protuberances that jut out of the sea like the spine of some sunken corpse, these islands present little of interest, at least on the surface. Each jagged rock is but a peak of a larger landmass that sank beneath the waves in ages past. Below the water, hundreds of feet down into Cymu Current, lies a sunken city whose scale and construction mimic those on Smoking Island.

Thunder Island

The wind and waves fashioned the remains of this extinct volcano into a series of arches and shoals. As water and air moves through these, they set up a loud humming that builds until it bursts with a cacophony of sound. The waters around Thunder Island are treacherous with many subtly-hidden currents, jagged rocks just below the tide, and underwater passages that suck at passing ships. A rare few Northlanders visit the island, for the arching cliffs are home to nesting seabirds, some of which are valued for their eggs and plumage.

Wyrm Island

Sitting in the middle of the Cymu Islands, Wyrm Island is feared by the Northlanders, and for good reason. Washed by the warm Cymu Current and home to three active volcanoes, landing on the island is dangerous in the extreme. The jungles here are teeming with life, nearly all of it predatory in some degree, for on Wyrm Island even the plants eat meat. Legends say that those who land here, all with ships wrecked by storms or otherwise desperate, never return. Most of these sailors' tales lay the blame at the foot of the rocky coast and high cliffs, though some speak of a great dragon that wishes not to be disturbed, or worse, seeks slaves for some insane task.

THE FAR NORTH

The Far North is a land little-known even by the folks of the Northlands, of ice and tundra that lies well within the Arctic Circle. It lies to the north and northeast of the Northlands, on the edges of the unknown continent of Boros.

Legends hold that somewhere northeast of Estenfird lies an arm of land that is rich in gold, silver, and ivory. A place where whales are plentiful, seals abundant, and the people weak and fearful. No one alive has sailed there, for the voyage across the Great Ocean is dangerous and the reward could merely be a myth. Also, the same tales tell of a land of verdant green and warm winters far across the Great Ocean, but again no living man or woman has been there and returned. In general, although great sailors, the Northlanders are not ones to travel far out on the lonely expanse of the Great Ocean, for there live monsters of great size, masses of seaweed that can swallow ships, and strange and fell currents. No one is afraid of making the journey, but none sees the profit in chasing down riches found only in tales.

THE SEAL COAST

This cold and rocky coast supports hundreds of thousands of seals, walruses, and seabirds during the summer months. Cliffs rise up along the coast, broken here and there by beaches that tend to be more rock than sand. The cliffs are home to hosts of seabirds, including gulls, ospreys, cormorants, frigate birds, puffins, and terns. Fur-bearing seals, as well as elephant seals, walruses, and sea lions, cover the shores. Fish, crabs, squid, krill, whales, and porpoises fill the seas.

A number of villages are perched on the shores of the Seal Coast, where folk descended from the original Uln live to this day, and so are sometimes referred to collectively as Ulnataland. These villages are called Alcanavt, Gualivik, Hranavik, Intulvik, Laquirv, and Norvagak. Long ago, the Cult of Althunak held sway over the Uln, but its grip was broken before the Heldring arrived in the north. Some say, however, that the cult's adherents remain somewhere even farther north, deep in the tundra, where they plot their return.

Some scholars believe that the Seal Coast is not in fact part of the continent of Akados, but instead the shoreline of lost Boros, the homeland of the Hyperboreans, lost under the ice for thousands of years.

TUNDRA

The interior of the Far North is a vast tundra dotted with small microclimates that support stunted and twisted trees and shrubs. The wind is strong and a constant force that man, beast, and plant must contend with. During the day, the temperature slowly rises to slightly more than 50° Fahrenheit, and at night, it dips into the upper 30° Fahrenheit (and approaches freezing by morning). Mosses, lichens, and heath cover the ground. These low-lying plants often grow in clumps separated by small rivulets of melt water. Boggy areas are common around the lakes and are often the breeding ground of all manner of nasty little flying things such as mosquitoes, black flies, and no-see-um (a very tiny biting fly).

WAILING MOUNTAINS

These high and imposing mountains are composed of gray stone and rise suddenly out of the tundra, inland from the Seal Coast (two weeks by dogsled, or so they say). There are no foothills or general upslope in the approach to the Wailing Mountains, just a sudden springing of towering masses of stone. The mountains themselves are sheathed year-round with a thick layer of ice from their peaks to halfway down their steep flanks. The mountains support no life, as the wind whips from the west and scours even the shale and scree from the stony slopes.

At one point, the Uln are said to have founded settlements on the slopes of the Wailing Mountains. If they did so, all must have been abandoned ages ago. The White Fields of Death are beyond the Wailing Mountains.

WHITE FIELDS OF DEATH

The White Fields of Death are a vast plain of snow and ice that extends from the Wailing Mountains to the far horizon. No living soul has ever been known to cross them, and their extent is unknown. It is said ruins of the Hyperboreans of Boros lie here, cities crushed by the onslaught of ice and buried by snows as the world changed.

From the eastern peaks of the Wailing Mountains, the City of the Lord of Winter within the White Fields is visible 50 miles away on the opposite horizon. This is the ancient home of the terrible Cult of Althunak. To the north beyond the city, the plains continue to unknown realms.

NORTHERN LIBYNOS

AMMUYAD CALIPHATE

Capital: Hava
Notable Settlements: Bhutan, Cordival, Ethbosy, Kullar, Salt Springs, Tarasunah
Ruler: Grand Caliph Rayan bin Azhar Al Ammu
Government: monarchy
Population: 2,986,255 (2,921,899 Ashurian, 8,137 marshfolk, about 50,000 desert tribespeople, 6,219 other human ethnicity)
Monstrous: gnolls (near the Painted Canyons), grippli (marshes), genies, girtablilu (desert)
Languages: Semuric
Religion: Churches of Mah-Barek
Resources: trade, spices, crops, fishing, mercenaries
Currency: Ammuyad
Technology Level: Medieval (cities), High Middle Ages (outlying settlements), Dark Ages (tribal areas)

The Ammuyad Caliphate is in northwestern Libynos, between the towering Zakros Mountains and the shore of the Sinnar Ocean. Most of the land is deep sand desert that is sparsely populated by nomadic tribes, while the rest of the population is concentrated on the large peninsula in the central part of the coast. The caliphate itself is nearly 3,000 years old and has been ruled for close to 2,000 years by various branches of the House of Ammu.

The desert is divided into the Western Erg and the Great Eastern Erg. The western desert is comparatively small; the Eastern Erg, on the other hand, is hundreds of miles in width and length and makes up the large majority of the caliphate's land area. The two similar deserts are separated by the Great Desert Wall, a range of mountains that curve completely around the landward side of the populous area of the caliphate. Other than the desert area, the western peninsula is hilly and semi-arid except along the western coast where the climate is excellent. The other exception is the low-lying tip of the peninsula, which has marshes.

The best way through the Desert Wall for most people is to travel along the bank of the Havari River, which makes its way through the mountains via a badlands area called the Painted Canyons. The river's route provides a road for the frequent trade caravans as well as individual travelers. The caliphate trades its own products and those that come by ship from the west, for items and materials from Jaati and the Crusader Coast, through the city-states of Istaflumina.

HISTORY AND PEOPLES

The caliphate has the privilege of encompassing the area in which the deity Mah-Barek first came to mankind, and where his four disciples walked with him on the earth. At that time, northwestern Libynos was under the nominal rule of the Hyperborean Empire but the area had been in dangerous confusion for centuries. Once a region of well-watered fields, a series of volcanic eruptions and a change in prevailing winds led to hot, dry winds that blasted the Ashurian Plains into the Ashurian Desert. Only the intervention of powerful genies enabled the people of the region to survive. They lived mostly in small villages, with nomadic tribes roaming in between, and warred constantly over resources and authority.

The Hyperboreans were little concerned with a new religion and did not object even when Karram, eldest grandson of Mah-Barek's First Disciple Fatimashan, founded a new realm in 534 I.R. and was declared caliph, the secular protector of the religion. However, the Hyperborean authorities did require Karram to swear fealty to the empire. Soon, worshippers of Mah-Barek flocked to the territory dedicated to his veneration, and cities grew and prospered in the Karramid Caliphate.

When Karram's line failed in 1610 I.R., the burden was taken up by the descendants of Ammu, another of the first disciple's grandsons. The caliphs of today continue to be of the line of Ammu, for whom the caliphate is named.

The power of the Hyperboreans waxed and waned over the centuries as the caliphate continued to grow. The end for the empire came quickly after the shift of the planet's poles and the destruction of the imperial capital of Curgantium in 2496 I.R. At first, the Hyperboreans withdrew into Libynos, abandoning all of Akados by 2516 I.R. When Polemarch Daan marched on Tircople in 2584 I.R., many soldiers of the caliphate were part of his force that brought down the undead Imperatrix Trystecce. The Hyperborean Age was over, and within 50 years, the last of that race abandoned Libynos as well.

Into this vacuum, the caliphate spread. It had long traded with its neighboring provinces of the empire, but now it saw the opportunity to make a new empire under the banner of Mah-Barek. The region of the Antioch City-States was the first to come under its sway in 2611 I.R. This was followed in 2619 I.R. by a colonization effort in the Irkainian Peninsula of northeastern Akados, where the caliphate founded the Principality of Pelshtaria.

Unfortunately, this period of expansion was not destined to last. After 150 years or so, the Antioch City-States became restless, wishing to form a league of independent city-states without the oversight of the caliphate. When a great plague struck the trade city of Bhutan and its vicinity in 2768 I.R. and the capital city of Hava in 2769 I.R., all resources inside the caliphate were engaged to deal with the disease and to maintain food production and such trade as could still go on. The city-states took this opportunity to sever their ties with the caliphate. The plague years also broke down communications with Pelshtaria. By the time those were re-established in 2772 I.R., the colonists had learned they could do quite well without the caliphate's assistance. In 2773 I.R., a new prince of Pelshtaria was chosen without the consent of the caliph and the empire of the caliphate came to an end.

In many ways, this was a good result for the caliphate, which was no longer required to devote resources to administering foreign lands. Instead, the government concentrated on the growth of trade, and messengers focused on proclaiming the religion of Mah-Barek. Wealthy nobles sponsored groups of settlers in the great Maighib Desert of central Libynos, which eventually resulted in the establishment of the independent Sultanate of Khartous and the spread of the worship of Mah-Barek to Caddesh and Guurzan.

RELIGION

All followers of Mah-Barek are welcome in the caliphate. While other worship is not forbidden, no other obvious temples are permitted. Although the churches of Hafaz and Koua have no public centers of worship, the Church of Marwan has active worship facilities in all the major cities and many smaller locations as well. However, the hearts of most people are given to the Church of Fatimashan and following in her path of benevolence.

TRADE AND COMMERCE

Trade is key to the prosperity of the caliphate. This is exemplified by Bhutan, where ships arriving from distant parts of the world meet caravans that made their way across the Great Eastern Erg with goods from northern and eastern Libynos. The Great Caravan Road is a true economic accomplishment; after centuries of work, the Ammuyad Caliphate developed caravanserais about a day's march apart for most of the more-than-900-mile journey from Bhutan to the Empire of Assuria. The caliphate maintains good trade relations with dozens of countries around the world and cautiously profitable connections with many more.

Northern Libynos
Pine Island
Spring Dragon Mountain
Jastri
The Claw
Whitefish Bay
Nathsak Hatasst
Island Big Bay
Thunder Island
Big Bay Island
Cymu Islands
Great Ocean Üthaf
Baragibra
Timabur R.
Tola
Hethuarp
Chilhem
Avagib
Nidusar River
Kreg
Lake Sura
Suvchel River
Enfama
Inurha Island
Oskhalen River
Chtta River
Semra River
Hrolfsberg
Vilir Shore
Giengbar R.
Jalebau
Khadthalaga
Gulf of Hoin
Elogong
Molstabbir Passage
Samundar Patranca
Junctkran Mountains
Goplakh
Rukmubir Peninsula
Khulen-p
Athrina
Majoor
Merchant's Bluff
Jem Kartele
Mulstabbir
(Krivegqek Island)
Ruzhan
Empire of Adenia
Tyrnos Island
Greshma
Qhathln
Pardiso Oul
Out
Sharpelin
Urani
Mithkethrin
Miroter
Kalakh
Masudtzyn
Asshor
Forest of Osonoy
Iball
Eropsar
Terezeinah
Putsana
Ruig R. Putheris
Mountains
Perga
Maahri
Channa Geosh
Kouda
Nisre Ruimz
Lawraqah
Laigun
Lake Amoni
Jburmu
Haskud
Khondeshlikur
Ibnath
Desert
Penmuyad Caliphate
Tarasunah
Great Eastern Erg
Parphelon
Perthelon
Yoseiph
Ippor
Innecht
Erethu
Ked
Salt Springs
Ethboq
Ashurian Desert
Western Erg
Beni Hadith
Painted Canyons
Tribal Lands
Bhotan
Gulf of Ur
Shamash
Rasti
Bay of Bhingol
Cordival
Hava
Hayan
Kullar
Sea of Spices
Krimsreth
Lake Vallumir
Mirsim
Shiloh
Zefrin
Elnathan
Antioch
Antioch City-State
Thretraz
Tarresh
Laishah
Turkad
Eshcol
Zephath
Bailfsloke
Mines of Azaadipor
Isle of Sarmad Yazdg-or
Perazim
Geedbau
Villu
Titian Isles
Isle of Winds
Ephron
Hamor
Quoork
Diblatham
Isle of Bliss
Ostegli
Ifishazz
Gammad
Daoaad
Hottebh Hills
Sea of Baal
Af-Ibbos
Island of
Kirtius
Ghobad-Ush
Celestean Sea

Legend
● Town or Village
◎ City
★ Capital or Free City
✹ Imperial Capital
■ Fortress or Citadel
⋮ Ruins
▲ Place of Interest
〜 Road
⌁ Trail or Unused Road
⋯ Mountain Pass
✕ Battlefield

The Great Caravan Road in the Ammuyad Caliphate of northern Libynos.

LOYALTIES AND DIPLOMACY

The Ammuyad Caliphate exchanges embassies with most of the countries of northern and central Libynos, as well as those along the Sea of Baal. Representatives from many royal or ducal courts in Akados can also be found in Hava. Although the kingdoms of the western Maighib Desert are co-religionists of Mah-Barek, no formal treaties of mutual defense exist with them.

GOVERNMENT

Grand Caliph Rayan bin Azhar Al Ammu is the hereditary monarch of the caliphate. He encourages court intrigue among his nobles, partially because as long as they are intriguing against each other, they will not be inclined to ally together against him.

In general, rather than the rule passing to a minor child, a caliph designates an adult relative such as a brother or even an uncle as his heir, and then changes his heir when his sons are grown. Several times the monarchy has passed through all of a family of brothers before being handed on to the next generation. Rayan bin Azhar himself caused some controversy when he took the throne. His father was the last of a generation of brothers but not the oldest, so some thought the throne should have gone to one of the current caliph's cousins. Caliph Azhar bin Husni clearly designated Rayan as his heir, though, and the inheritance was clearly within the law, so the situation was eventually resolved. However, the caliphate's authority was damaged among some of its more distant settlements, and Caliph Rayan bin Azhar faced a difficult few years with fractious tribes and lesser nobles before peace was achieved.

No woman has ever served as caliph, though women can be sultanas and amiras.

MILITARY

Much of the Ammuyad military is employed in defense of the caliphate's lucrative trade. The navy, headquartered at Cordival, actively patrols for pirates and keeps watch for any sign of an invasion by sea, however unlikely that may seem in this day and age. The most persistent pirates are the Northlanders, whose longships slip through the Mulstabhin Passage. Sometimes they come peacefully to trade or enjoy the amenities of the cities; other times, they raid the north coast or western extremities of the caliphate and dash back to their home waters.

A primary responsibility of the Grand Army is protecting the Great Caravan Road from bandits and from dangerous creatures of the desert that may be beyond the capabilities of caravan guards. Another is securing the border of the caliphate. However, since borders with neighboring areas are nearly all nebulous and drawn in shifting sand, this can call for diplomacy as much as vigilance.

Given the distances the army travels, it is understandable that there are no true infantry units. The common soldiers are camel riders, and a company's equipment is all planned to be transported by camel-back. The elite units ride strong, light horses that are also trained to fight, and the troops are some of the best cavalry in the world. Another notable achievement by the Grand Army is its development of high-quality crossbows that it issues to all its troops. All soldiers are trained to use the weapon, and some units develop exceptional skills with it. Some Ammuyad soldiers, after the close of their seven-year enlistment, join (or form) mercenary organizations where their skills command high prices.

MAJOR THREATS

The greatest threat at this time to the peace of the caliphate is the lightning raids of the Northlanders. When several ships attack together, they can threaten the food stores of a local area or even supplies intended to feed the population of one of the large cities. The navy deals severely with any Northlander pirates they catch to discourage others in the future.

Hava, Grand City of (Capital)

Ruler: Grand Caliph Rayan bin Azhar Al Ammu
Government: monarchy
Population: 253,785 (mostly Ashurian, but many other human ethnicities as well)

The grand city of the caliph gleams white in the sun, but the flowered courtyards and tinkling fountains hide a world of cutthroat competition for power and prestige. Nobility and the wealthy vie with each other in their clothing and their palaces, their entertainments, and their affectations. Sometimes they even compete in their charities, which means that the Church of Fatimashan wins as hospitals, schools, and other benefits are funded by nobles whose names they then prominently display.

Hava is on the east coast of the Bay of Bhutan near the mouth of the Havari River. It has good port facilities and a fleet of fishermen who supply sea delicacies for the tables of the nobility and cheap, common fish for the rest of the people. Those merchants who want to trade directly with the capital city put in here, as do diplomatic vessels from around the world. Some merchants also come south from Bhutan along the Coast Road, which diverges from the Great Caravan Road at Walbah. The proximity of the Havari River allows irrigated cultivation of crops and orchards for miles around the city of Hava, which supplies part of the food for the capital.

The Grand Army of the caliphate is headquartered in Hava, so the caliph can have his generals nearby. In fact, Commander of the Grand Army General Fadila ibnat Aamir is one of his closest advisors as well as having become a good friend of Calipha Jalila. The Grand Army's troops, however, are scattered in fortresses and desert outposts throughout the caliphate.

Beni-Hadith, Satrapy of

Ruler: Effendi Lutfi ibn Harith
Government: governor appointed by the caliph
Population: 249 (Ashurian)

This oasis town is a caravan stop just west of the Painted Canyons. Being so close to the badlands, the town has a strong wall and an alert guard force. The town is crowded inside the wall, as the population has grown since the wall was built; they have started to stockpile stone for a new wall but it will be several years yet before it is finished. The caravanserai is built against the outside of the town's west wall where caravans have good access to the oasis and a guarded gate directly into the town for any who desire to do business. The town and caravanserai walls are made of stone from the nearby Painted Canyons, so they are each a patchwork of color. Because many caravans hire extra guards in Salt Springs solely for the nearly 150-mile trip through the badlands, Beni-Hadith usually has several people looking to hire on with groups going the other way so they can make a little money on their trip home.

Bhutan, Sultanate of

Ruler: Sultan Qusay ibn Zaahir al-Bhutani
Government: monarchy
Population: 119,371 (almost all Ashurian)

Bhutan is primarily a market city writ large. It thrives on trade, and merchants of every stripe can be seen here from time to time. Those from Istaflumina or Jaati usually arrive by caravan, while those from Baalthaaz, Khemit, or the cities of the far south or west arrive by ship. The docks can accommodate many ships at a time, and workers for hire are always available. Very little of the city is beautiful, but instead of parks it has marketplaces, and instead of civic buildings it has merchants' guilds. Its crowded streets are confusing to the uninitiated, but logical to experienced buyers and sellers. The animal and meat markets are on the west, from the wharf out. Next come things such as wool and leather, which diverge into clothing or armor and weapons. So it goes across the city, with the things of highest value (such as the heavily protected Jewelers' Guild, or the Moneychangers' Hall where gold and silver are bought and sold) being to the east. Other nobles sometimes view the sultan of Bhutan as being slightly grubby for associating so closely with so much trade, but the wealth he demonstrates (received from his small share of every transaction in the city) is more than enough to show their criticisms are pure jealousy.

One flaw in this otherwise excellent city is the existence of the Zuma Qulldishi, a complex criminal organization. The Zuma mostly engage in smuggling operations and robbery, and occasionally branch out into banditry or take on contracts for murder. Any goods that arrive from less-than-reputable sources go into the Zuma's network and make money in the markets in the underside of the city. The rumor is that the "Shadow Sultan" of the Zuma claims he has nearly as many people working to make money for him and his organization as Qusay al-Bhutani has for him. As long as the Zuma Qulldishi are not too blatant about their operations, the sultanate troops generally leave them alone; attempts in the past to squash the organization did not turn out well, so for now an unrecognized, uneasy truce exists.

Caravanserais

Ruler: see below
Government: governor appointed by the caliph, either a bey or the more-prestigious satrap; some may also be pashas (military commanders)
Population: varies (from 250 to 1,000+ depending on day and season)

Each caravanserai on the Great Caravan Road has a solid stone wall, a large open courtyard, and covered areas where people and animals can crowd together in case of a sandstorm. Every caravanserai has a reliable source of water (whether an oasis, a deep well, or some magical source), and they work hard to keep supplies of food on hand for animals as well as people. The sole purpose of some caravans is to resupply the caravanserais.

Being separated from each other by a day's journey, and being separated from their titular lords by an even farther distance, the local rulers possess great leeway in the exercise of their authority. A caravanserai whose governor is also a pasha (military commander) has a unit of the caliphate's Grand Army stationed there to provide security against threats too large for the guards of a caravan or caravanserai to handle. These mounted units patrol up and down the caravan route.

Cordival, Sultanate of

Ruler: Sultana Masuma ibnat Ghufran al-Cordavi
Government: monarchy
Population: 91,595 (mostly Ashurian, but many other human ethnicity as well)

The city of Cordival sits at the very tip of the peninsula of the caliphate, surrounded by a half-circle of water. Its location at the entrance to the Bay of Bhutan makes it the ideal location for the caliphate navy's headquarters, as it protects the other cities against any sea-borne attack. Grand Admiral Faysal ibn Haidar Al Ammu keeps a tight rein on the navy's section of the city, including setting guards at its internal wall. This does not severely restrict interaction between town and headquarters; many people from the city work in support of the ships and sailors, and many sailors have families in the port, or other important people to visit when off duty.

Cordival's harbor also serves a fleet of fishing boats and numerous merchant traders. Many ships coming from far-off Akados put in at Cordival on their way to Bhutan, needing a day or two in port after so long at sea.

The Sultanate of Cordival controls some of the most arable land in the caliphate. North of the Bhethos Marshes and along the west coast,

CARAVANSERAIS FROM BHUTAN IN THE WEST TO MAAHRI IN THE EAST:

Caravanserai Name	Governor	Typical High Season Population	Notes
Tirwal, Satrapy of	Sharifa Nura ibnat Tabassum	400	
al-Laqant, Satrapy of	Sharif Burhan ibn Khalid	300	
Walbah, Satrapy of	Sharifa Rajiya ibn Zaahir al-Bhutani	400	Coast road goes south to Hava
al-Hadra, Satrapy of	Pasha Akram al-Hava	500	
Saris, Satrapy of	Effendi Ridwan ibn Umran	400	
Wasqah, Beylik of	Begum Nimat ibnat Rahat	400	
Martulah, Satrapy of	Pasha Khayrat al-Junayd	400	
Sammurah, Emirate of	Amira Fathiyaa ibnat Malak	5,000	
Beni-Hadith, Satrapy of	Effendi Lutfi ibn Harith	250	See "Beni-Hadith"
Gaiyan, Ruins of	None	0	See "Gaiyan"
Salt Springs, Satrapy of	Pasha Hari Abubakkar	3,500	See "Salt Springs"
Qunkah, Beylik of	Bey Esmail ibn Shahnaz	500	
Laridah, Satrapy of	Effendi Yunus ibn Dana	300	
Nagirah, Beylik of	Bey Shadi ibn Ilyas	350	
Uryulah, Satrapy of	Pasha Bassam Nurulrad	400	
Ethbosy, Emirate of	Emir Mehmet ibn Sayid	5,000	See "Ethbosy"
Basit, Satrapy of	Sharif Ikram ibn Irfan	350	
Sokolla, Satrapy of	Effendiya Ghada ibnat Afzal	325	
Marida, Satrapy of	Sharif Wafai ibn Sheddad	375	
Tutilah, Satrapy of	Effendi Qadir ibn Omar	200	
al-Yussanah, Satrapy of	Sharif Nabil ibn Hisham	475	
Kemaleddin, Beylik of	Bey Canim ibn Husrev	300	
Als, Satrapy of	Pasha Anisa ibnat Qamar	250	
Ubbadah, Satrapy of	Sharifa Fayruz ibnat Makram	375	
Garundah, Emirate of	Amira Izdihar ibnat Rasul	3,250	
Tarifah, Satrapy of	Sharif Amjad ibn Munir	250	
Rundah, Satrapy of	Effendiya Basira ibnat Shukri	425	
Istiggah, Satrapy of	Pasha Haroun ibn Akram	175	
Arnit, Beylik of	Bey Galal ibn Samad	300	
Qarmunah, Satrapy of	Sharif Jinan ibn Najim	350	
Tarasunah, Emirate of	Amira Zubaida ibnat Farah Al Ammu	4,750	See "Tarasunah"
Arkus, Beylik of	Bey Rifat ibn Ephrikan	300	
Turgut, Satrapy of	Sharif Parlak ibn Fahd	500	
Saqaban, Beylik of	Bey Topal ibn Solih	200	
Al-Bunt, Satrapy of	SharifaTahira ibnat Talib	400	
Lawraqah, Satrapy of	Pasha Mazin al-Rasheed	550	See "Lawraqah"
Liyyun, Satrapy of	Sharifa Nashwa ibnat Amani	675	See "Liyyun"

the land is watered by rain off the ocean. The clement temperatures allow for growing many types of fruit, grains, and vegetables. Despite the good land, Cordival alone cannot grow enough food for the entire peninsula although they do trade a large amount to Bhutan and Hava. The Bhethos Marshes also produce a good quantity of edible products as well as reeds and grasses for weaving baskets, mats, and more.

ETHBOSY, EMIRATE OF

Ruler: Emir Mehmet ibn Sayid
Government: monarchy
Population: 4,923 (mostly Ashurian)

Despite being located along the Caravan Road in the desert instead of in the more "civilized" western part of the Ammuyad Caliphate, the emirs of Ethbosy have long been known for being educated and wise. They are also well-traveled, the current emir having made a trip not only to Jaati but also to Khartous in his youth. This means Ethbosy is home to not just a prominent caravan stop, but also a schola where people seeking knowledge learn literally at the feet of many educated men and women. Ethbosy's cosmopolitanism extends outside the human realms as well; the deep pool that fills the fountain of the caravanserai is said to be the long-time home of a marid scholar who came to the schola once and appreciated the interactions so much that he just stayed. Caravans often stop here for a day or two, and those with more esoteric goods may display their wares in the marketplace and stay a week or more if their sales are going well.

GAIYAN, RUINS OF

Population: 0

This caravanserai stands empty, and caravans seldom stop nearby, even though it is mostly intact. Rumor says the place is haunted by the souls of all those who died here, though tellers cannot agree on the cause. Some accounts say sand giants attacked the building and tore the gaping rent in the back wall and ate the inhabitants. Others say a plague took the people and the wall fell apart later. Whatever the case, no one takes refuge inside except in dire need. The compound still has its well, but sand has sifted in despite the worn wooden cover on top. There is nothing with which to draw up the water.

KULLAR, SULTANATE OF

Ruler: Sultan Barakat ibn Tamid al-Kullari
Government: monarchy
Population: 67,921 (mostly Ashurian, but many other human ethnicities as well)

Kullar lies on the western coast of the caliphate where the Kula River runs down out of the mountains of the Desert Wall. One of the few rivers in the country, the Kula has one thing the others do not: freshwater fish. The quantity harvested is generally only enough to provide for the immediate area, but sometimes fish are shipped live to Hava for the caliph's table. Fishing boats also go out from the port to do the usual saltwater fishing, though they are troubled sometimes by pulling up strange, ugly fish that no one is willing to eat and which attack the hands trying to throw them back.

Being far from the trade route to Bhutan, comparatively few ships come specifically to Kullar. The sultan spends much of his time at the court of the caliph in the capital city of Hava. One thing that draws certain people to Kullar, though, is the wizards' consortium headquartered here. It is sponsored by the sultan himself, who is very interested in magic though seemingly he has no talents in that direction. This group doesn't mind being off the beaten track, and Hava is not too far if they need some esoteric supplies or information. They study the magic of the sea and the desert, and try to understand the strange magic of spellcasters of the Istaflumina region. Some members of the group also specialize in knowledge of genie-kind, and they have seekers from around the world wanting to learn from them.

LAWRAQAH, SATRAPY OF

Ruler: Pasha Mazin al-Rasheed
Government: governor appointed by the caliph
Population: 547 (Ashurian)

Lawraqah is at the eastern edge of the Ammuyad Caliphate. The caliphate's nebulous border with the Empire of Assuria lies somewhere in the desert between the satrapy and Liyyun. The pasha's troops actively patrol the area but avoid coming into conflict with Assurian units on the same mission. If the caravanserai of Liyyun calls for help, the garrison sends a small unit under the command of an experienced (and it is hoped, diplomatic) soldier. It is important to avoid offending the Assurians — who are rather touchy — but both groups know how important the Caravan Road is to their respective countries and do their best to keep the peace in the area.

LIYYUN, SATRAPY OF

Ruler: Sharifa Nashwa ibnat Amani
Government: governor appointed by the caliph
Population: 682 (Ashurian)

This is the last caravanserai before travelers arrive at the crossroads of Maahri in the Empire of Assuria. Technically, it is within the borders claimed by Assuria, but traders from the caliphate built it centuries ago and continue to maintain it. If military assistance is needed for any reason, the satrap calls for the caliphate's troops stationed at Lawraqah rather than contacting the Assurian authorities. Travelers here are a combination of those exhausted by weeks of traversing the desert and those who are just getting started on their long journeys west. The sharifa frequently makes herself seen and sets aside time to hear the complaints or compliments of the caravan masters, serving as the first (or last) representative of the caliphate to these travelers from many countries.

SALT SPRINGS, SATRAPY OF

Ruler: Pasha Hari Abubakkar
Government: governor appointed by the caliph
Population: 3,476 (mostly Ashurian)

This caravanserai is unusual in that it is a rough oval instead of a rectangle, and most of it is protectively roofed rather than just the perimeter. It is also built atop the Great Caravan Road rather than next to it, so caravans must perforce enter the town. Of course, nearly every traveler would do this anyway, as Salt Springs is the last place for a protected stop before more than 140 miles of dangerous journey, and it is also well known for providing almost anything a caravan could need. Situated as it is only about 40 miles east of the Painted Canyons, Salt Springs always has many guards looking for jobs as caravan escorts to the distant town of Beni-Hadith. The pasha also has troops that provide general protection in the area, but they patrol for bandits and watch for enemies attacking out of the badlands; they do not go into the canyons.

REFERENCE SOURCE: **ONS2** *ONE NIGHT STANDS: DEATH IN THE PAINTED CANYONS, DEATH IN THE PAINTED CANYONS FROM QUESTS OF DOOM 2*

TARASUNAH, EMIRATE OF

Ruler: Amira Zubaida ibnat Farah Al Ammu
Government: monarchy
Population: 4,887 (mostly Ashurian)

No simple caravanserai, Tarasunah is a sizable town built around several deep wells. It is an inconvenient distance from the caravanserais on either side, so people must start early and arrive late when traversing either of those sections of the Caravan Road. That also means caravans almost never arrive one day and leave the next; instead, they take this as an opportunity to rest for a couple of days before pressing on.

In addition to providing support for passing caravans, Tarasunah hosts a thriving marketplace of its own where those caravans can interact with townsfolk and the people of nearby tribes. The desert wanderers come from some distance to see the merchants here, and tribes stop on their way north or south to buy things they cannot glean from the desert.

TRIBAL LANDS

Population: unknown; perhaps 50,000 (almost all Ashurian)
Ruler: varies; usually a sheikh or sheikha
Government: varies; most at least pay lip service to the caliphate

Tribes of nomads wander throughout the Eastern Erg, their camels or horses transporting them from oasis to oasis, or on the hunt, in an ongoing endeavor to provide for their people and maintain their independence. These are primarily of the same ethnicity as the more settled people of the caliphate to the west but they do not care to settle down as farmers or take to city living. A few wanderers are bandits and prey on the caravans traveling the trade road, although both the caravans and the Grand Army patrols make that an uncertain method of profit. Most tribes are content to lay claim to an oasis for a few years or carry on in a routine of visiting specific oases at certain seasons. Each tribe is ruled by a hereditary leader or "sheikh." In some cases, several tribes with ties of blood are under the control of a "malik" or king.

Some of the nomads worship one or more of the deities of Assuria, but the tribes in general worship Mah-Barek and so honor Caliph Rayan bin Azhar Al Ammu as the secular leader of that religion. The people themselves almost never visit the cities of the western caliphate to pay their respects to their ruler in person, but the sheikhs are expected to pay a certain amount of tribute each year. This is usually handled by paying it to one of the emirs or the military pashas who are easily located along the Great Caravan Road. The wandering tribes prefer to visit at Tarasunah, where the caravans often stop for a few days and lay out their wares, and the Amira's people treat them with respect.

Once in a while, one of the desert tribes happens across ancient ruins temporarily uncovered by the wind, and those who are brave enough enter the structures and return with stories of what they have seen, or even samples of stones with unknown carvings. The caravan merchants always pay a good price for those, as do the wealthy city-dwellers in the west. No one has yet had any luck in getting the nomads to find the ruins again, though, because the wind brings back the dunes as fast as it swept them away in the first place.

GEOGRAPHIC FEATURES AND POINTS OF INTEREST IN THE AMMUYAD CALIPHATE

ASHURIAN DESERT

The Ashurian Desert is a deep sand desert between the Zakros Mountains and the Sea of Spices or the Ammuyad Caliphate's Desert Wall. In the southeast, it blends into the arid lands in the southwest of the Istaflumina region. Its primary inhabitants are nomadic tribes, though several permanent settlements exist around oases, especially along the Great Caravan Road across the caliphate.

The area is named for the ancient Empire of Assuria to the east, which held sway over the area thousands of years ago when it was fertile farmland. Following the creation of the Tropic of Arden 180 years before the arrival of the Hyperboreans, violent earthquakes and volcanic activity in the western Zakros Mountains drove the Assurians out of their cool mountain villas. On the plains, weather patterns changed and the rains ceased to fall. Within a generation, the entire area became as dry as dust, and the Assurians were forced to abandon the cities they had built and return to their protected homeland. Gradually the sand rose and covered the ruins and continued to rise until great dunes blow constantly. Sometimes when the wind is persistent in an area, enough sand moves to uncover the houses or ziggurats of the ancient ruins.

The dunes have dried out and covered all the rivers but the fast-moving Havari, which begins deep in the Zakros Mountains. However, some of these river beds still serve to transport moisture from mountain runoff or the occasional desert rainstorm into the earth where it provides water for oases or wells.

BAY OF BHUTAN

Focused on the city of the same name, the Bay of Bhutan is usually busy with ships: vessels of diplomats and pilgrims for the beautiful capital city of Hava, naval craft from Cordival on patrol, and of course the many merchant ships heading for the trading city of Bhutan itself. Three of the four major cities of the Ammuyad Caliphate are on the bay, and it protects both Hava and Bhutan from all but the worst storms of the Sea of Spices. Fishing in the bay is good, and fleets go out from all three cities as well as many coastal villages. Several spots along the bay also have oyster reefs; the caliphate's upper classes consider oysters a particular delicacy, so harvesting them can be lucrative if the harvester has good contacts. The water in the bay is deep, so it sometimes receives unwelcome deep-sea visitors, but the caliphate's navy has so far always dealt with them.

BHETHOS MARSHES

The low-lying area between Bhutan and Cordival is a salt marsh called the Bhethos Marshes, which are within the domain of the Sultanate of Cordival. This uninspiring landscape has gray-green grasses that go on for a hundred miles, with occasional spots of high ground indicated by clumps of spindly trees. Some of the high areas are large enough to support a few huts, and the marshfolk live on these isolated hills. They make a living hunting frogs, turtles, and fish in their flat-bottomed boats, taking marsh birds or their eggs, and catching crabs. All of these are sold into the great markets in Bhutan or, from the western marshes, into Cordival. Sometimes the folk bring in unusual specimens of strange plants or animals with odd markings and weird changes. They have trouble selling these in the food markets, but wizards or scholars are often interested in acquiring them. Some marshfolk are skilled with herbs and gather (or cultivate) healing and culinary herbs to be found nowhere else in the caliphate. Marshfolk are pale-skinned, tight-lipped people who keep to themselves and rarely interact with the "drylanders." They are more likely to have neutral relations with the little grippli — small frog-like creatures with the same intelligence as most humans — that also live in isolated communities in the marsh.

DESERT WALL

Separating the caliphate's populous western peninsula from its great eastern desert is the range of mountains known as the Desert Wall. It curves along the landward side of the peninsula, with high peaks in the middle and lower mountains toward the coast on both ends. The pattern of the islands near the caliphate in the Sea of Spices and Sea of Baal suggests the curved range continues out into the ocean for 100 miles or more. Many of the peaks show indications of volcanism in the past, though there is no evidence of any active volcanoes now or any suggestion of them since the formation of the caliphate almost 3,000 years ago. The easiest route through the Desert Wall is to follow the valley of the Havari River, and that is the route taken by caravans. Other passes do exist, though, for those who are willing to take a more difficult way.

GREAT CARAVAN ROAD

The Great Caravan Road of the eastern desert runs from Bhutan on the coast in the Ammuyad Caliphate and across the desert to Maahri in the Empire of Assuria in Istaflumina. From there, caravans travel south to the great city of Ur, where trade is done with merchants from all across the continent. The Great Caravan Road is well marked and has caravanserai (small walled communities that provide safe locales for the caravans to rest and resupply) at oases all along the route. Being separated from each other by about a day's journey and being separated from their titular lords by an even greater distance, the local rulers possess great leeway in the exercise of their authority. Most traders prefer to become familiar with one or two stages (which may be several days' journey) and keep to the area that they know, but sometimes merchants are concerned about being cheated or believe others are not adequately representing their wares, and so they make the entire journey themselves. Thus it is common to have merchants from Istaflumina or Jaati on the Caravan Road, and traders from even farther away are not an unusual sight.

GREAT EASTERN ERG

Part of the Ashurian Desert, this vast dune sea has waves of sand that are moved by the wind and interrupted only by the occasional oasis. The Erg may be as much as 400 miles wide, and perhaps 1,000 miles north to south, although no one has ever measured its true extent. The dunes begin near the southern tip of the Desert Wall, just north of the hill country claimed by the Antioch City-States, and continue nearly 200 miles past the north end of the wall. In the east, the Great Erg is limited by the Zakros Mountains, though part of it continues into the Empire of Assuria itself. On the west, the sand runs right down to the coast of the Sea of Spices, where it is not contained by the Desert Wall.

Only the fast-moving Havari River can keep from being covered by the dunes, and even it collects a great deal of sand on its way through the desert. Relics of an earlier empire are known to be buried beneath the sands, from a time when the area was farmland rather than desolation, but the wind seldom reveals them, and no one has been able to chart their locations. The Eastern Erg is dotted with oases, and a well-traveled caravan road follows the most-efficient selection of these. Other routes across the desert are possible but may be more difficult or dangerous.

GULF OF HUUN

In the northwest, the Ammuyad Caliphate meets Krivcycek Island across the Mulstabhin Passage. The body of water on the northern side of the passage is the Gulf of Huun, part of the Great Ocean Ûthaf. In contrast to the warm currents of the Sea of Spices south of the passage, the Gulf of Huun is primarily cold and it chills the extreme northwestern tip of Libynos, which the caliphate does not claim. Some of the caliphate's merchant vessels travel through the gulf on their way to trade with the strange Northlanders, but more often Northlander ships make their way south to bask in the warmth and the exotic (to them) locations and foods of the caliphate.

HAVARI RIVER

Starting as a great waterfall in the Zakros Mountains, the Havari River runs northeast to southwest across the entire Eastern Erg. It loses much of its moisture to the desert but continues to run strongly as it passes through the Painted Canyons and enters the Bay of Bhutan at the caliph's city of Hava. Few people have ever tried to travel the Havari; its canyon through the Eastern Erg makes it difficult to access, and nothing has been discovered around its headwaters that would make developing it into a water route worth anyone's while. Certain visionaries, though, are convinced the river could be a viable means of transportation if something valuable lay upstream, so explorers and prospectors keep looking.

Coming through the Eastern Erg, the Havari picks up a great deal of sand and carries it to the coast. It forms a wide, changing delta as the river drops the debris where it enters the ocean. Every so often the mouth of the Havari must be dredged to keep its channel from moving too close to the wall of the caliph's city.

PAINTED CANYONS

These badlands of torn, rocky canyons split the Desert Wall east of the city of Bhutan. The multiple colors of rock displayed in the deep ravines give the area its name. Although still dangerous, these low-lying canyons provide the only route through the mountains for most people. Travelers and caravans primarily follow the valley of the Havari River, which runs east to west most of the way across the badlands at a point where they are only about 100 miles wide. The canyons are said to harbor gnolls, bandits, and criminals hiding from the caliph's justice, so caravans going through the area need to be well-guarded.

Stories suggest that somewhere in the canyons one can find the ruins of the fabled city of Omlach Tur. Rather than being primitive, the cliff-dwellers of that ancient city are said to have been the rulers of an empire that predated the caliphate by thousands of years.

REFERENCE SOURCE: ONS2 ONE NIGHT STANDS: DEATH IN THE PAINTED CANYONS, DEATH IN THE PAINTED CANYONS FROM QUESTS OF DOOM 2

SEA OF SPICES

The Sea of Spices is the northernmost extent of the Sinnar Ocean. It gets its name from the trade in rare spices that crosses it from the Ammuyad Caliphate and Far Jaati. The sea connects the Sinnar Ocean to the Great Ocean Ûthaf through the Mulstabhin Passage around Krivcycek Island. A warm current flows north along the western coast of Libynos and into the Sea of Spices, bringing a clement or even hot climate to the caliphate and the Irkaina Peninsula. This warm water meets the cold water of the Gulf of Huun around Krivcycek Island and often causes rough seas and bad weather in the Mulstabhin Passage.

WESTERN ERG

The Western Erg, an area of moving sand dunes roughly 200 miles in each direction, lies at the foot of the Desert Wall. It starts a little north of the Caravan Road going to Bhutan and runs right up to the edge of the Sea of Spices in the north. If anything, it is more desolate than the eastern desert as the more-livable lands around it allow people to bypass and ignore the western desert in a way they cannot do in the Great Eastern Erg.

ZAKROS MOUNTAINS, WESTERN

The western mass of the Zakros Mountains is somewhat different in character than the sections farther east. Not only are they prone to small earthquakes, several peaks up and down the range are active volcanoes. Nothing more than smoke has been noted in centuries but the earliest records of the caliphate indicate that, several hundred years before the country's foundation, these mountains experienced large explosions of fire and ash. Some legends do say that once, long ago, the lands of the caliphate were rich and watered, not desert. Whether this was ever the case, and whether the volcanic eruptions so noted had anything to do with the change in climate, is the subject of much speculation.

ISTAFLUMINA

Istaflumina is a region of fertile river plains and rolling hills bounded by the deep Ashurian Desert on the west and the high Zakros Mountains on the east. Isolated by these barriers, this region has changed more slowly than other parts of Libynos. As a result, it is the location of some of the most ancient cities in the world, now developed into city-states supported by the plentiful agricultural resources of the area. The fertile plain around the central rivers combines with the protecting mountain range to yield bountiful harvests, enough to feed the heavily urbanized populations.

Being home to civilizations whose roots go back to ancient times, ancient stories are told here and, in several cities, records of long-ago ages are carefully maintained. They recall a time when the empire of the Assurians reached far to the west, including the lands now covered by the sands of the Ashurian Desert. In those days, these western lands were much wetter than they are now, with grasses and crops growing amid cities and settlements. But then, more than 3,600 years ago, the Tropic of Arden was created and the lands changed. The western Zakros Mountains exploded with volcanic activity. The winds also changed, and with that the lifegiving rains ceased to fall in those western lands. Those grassy plains where the Assurians forged an empire dried up and were covered with ash, and later, sand. They had no choice but to withdraw to their original homeland in the valley of the two rivers where conditions were much better.

The rivers there ran more strongly, with plenty of water to irrigate crops. In these new circumstances, fewer people were needed to farm and they were able to produce food for many more people. The city-states grew much larger, and the kings had people available to build beautiful civic buildings and strong walls, and to field large armies. The various kingdoms of the area rose and fell as empires: Zumarians, Assurians, Hakhadians, Adenians, Ealimites, Parphelonians, and more.

About 1,000 years ago, the poles of the world shifted, and the climate took another change. This time, Istaflumina became cooler, and farming became slightly more difficult. The land is still mostly good and well-watered, but crops do not grow as quickly and more hands are needed to grow enough food for everyone. This is probably part of the reason that no empire is currently ascendant throughout the region; more people needed for farming leaves fewer available as soldiers. However, the balance is always subject to change.

ADENIA, EMPIRE OF

Capital: Mithkethrin
Notable Settlements: Athrina, Majoor, Masadizyn, Merchant's Bluff, Ruzhan, Terezernah
Ruler: Emperor Daraya-vaus III
Government: monarchy
Population: 1,805,485 (1,287,311 Ashurian, 483,817 Jaata, 16,881 Zakros Mountains tribe, 15,431 ratfolk, 2,045 other)
Monstrous: lizardfolk (coasts), tigers and weretigers (northern provinces), giants (mountains), flying lizards (Tyrnos Island)
Languages: Hakhadian, Merruwhan
Religion: Annunaki pantheon
Resources: trade, wool, excellent woven rugs, crops, oak wood, almonds, wine, mining, iridescent lizard feathers
Currency: Parphelonian
Technology Level: Medieval (largest cities), High Middle Ages (other towns), Dark Ages (rural areas)

Adenia has its origin in the high plateaus of the Zakros Mountains, between the range's line of high peaks and the sea to the east. It did not have the advantage of warm climate and fertile land held by most of Istaflumina, but its people have always been strong and determined. Using the river valleys as guide and transport, the Adenians conquered the lowlands to the west but after 10 generations were forced out of the area. More than 800 years ago they spread north in the mountains and east down to the sea. This means the Adenians now control the entire eastern coast of Istaflumina. Their domain runs from where the Zakros Mountains meet the coast of the Sea of Tyre in the south, north past the Vistaspa River and into the southern part of Jaati, where they have ruled part of the area for more than 500 years and expanded into a new province as recently as 100 years ago.

Having learned the value of sea trade during their years of power along the Gulf of Ur, the Adenians were quick to move into oceangoing ventures of their own when they took control of the eastern coastal areas. The Adenian Empire has the strongest navy in northern Libynos and uses it to maintain communication and control in their empire, which reaches barely more than 200 miles from the coast but is more than 1,000 miles long. In addition, they explored east, motivated by ancient tales in the city of Ur which is named after a great explorer who supposedly traveled far to the east and eventually founded a city on the other side of the world. During their search, the Adenians discovered Tyrnos Island and a few others but were eventually turned back by the violent line of storms blocking passage across the sea and reaching as far north and south as they dared sail.

The capital of Adenia, formerly at the mountain city of Masadizyn, was moved about 400 years ago to a new city built along the coast. The new capital was named Mithkethrin after Emperor Kethmanis, the ruler at the time. Adenia has settled into a series of provinces, each with its own satrap, a viceroy of the emperor who has a great deal of power in his or her own area. Three of the provinces are in the region of Istaflumina and two are in the southeast part of Jaati.

While Istaflumina has a generally accepted set of deities, and Adenia itself focuses primarily on Mitra (god of the sun, oaths, and justice), Jaati has a conglomeration of hundreds of deities from dozens of cultures. In some cases, the cultures may be lost, but their gods are still worshipped by some in Jaati. In order to have a successful empire, though, the emperor traditionally expects satraps to allow subject peoples their chosen methods of worship as much as practicable. This results in a mixture of beliefs in Adenian provinces that is not seen throughout the rest of Istaflumina.

MITHKETHRIN, IMPERIAL CITY OF (CAPITAL)

Ruler: Satrap Trophernes of Capital Province
Government: provincial satrap under the direct supervision of Emperor Daraya-vaus
Population: 283,621 (272,189 Ashurian, 5,250 Jaata, 3,051 ratfolk, 2,090 Zakros Mountains tribe, 1,041 other)

This beautiful city was built specifically as an imperial capital, with avenues and approaches perfect for receiving foreign dignitaries and accommodating nobles of the empire who come to pay their tribute to the emperor. Its docks are large and easily accommodate many oceangoing vessels at once, including an area for diplomatic ships to put in far from the odorous fishing docks or the chaotic warehouse district. Satrap Trophernes handles the details of the city itself and its surrounding lands, so the emperor is free to focus on the issues affecting the entire nation, or progress to various provinces, or travel to his summer palace.

The capital city also features a well-designed temple district built around an impressive temple to Mithra (the same deity as the Jaata god Mitra). It includes temples to Tammuz and Ishtar, popular deities from Parphelonia, and a Shrine of All Gods as a courtesy to visiting diplomats. This round, pillared hall has a dozen niches with altars, where appropriate symbols can be placed and different deities venerated temporarily.

Mithkethrin is on the River Turperin, which comes from deep in the Zakros Mountains. This is useful for moving people and cargo from the coast to the foothills and for transporting things such as logs down from the mountains, but the river from the mountain plateau down to the lowlands is too rough for boats. Individuals and caravans traveling to and from Masadizyn must make their way on the winding track that runs generally along the river.

ATHRINA, CITY OF

Ruler: Satrap (viceroy) Parushti of Tazhmaspada Province
Government: Provincial satrap appointed by emperor
Population: 93,101 (55,392 Jaata, 35,248 Ashurian, 2,211 ratfolk, 250 other)

Athrina sits on the bank of the Khulen River in what is usually considered the southeastern part of Jaati. It has been the capital of the Adenian province of Tazhmaspada for the past century. Under the rulership of the Adenians, the caste system is not so strongly enforced as it is through most of Jaati, so many unsatisfied people find their way here. The province also has a wide variety of religious adherents, from those who worship some of the deities of Khemit to a few who honor ancient gods of the old Hyperborean Empire, whose influence can still be felt even though it has been dead for nearly a thousand years. The Adenians also expanded the worship of Mitra in the area, and other Annunaki deities; some citizens dutifully pay their respects to the new gods, but the religion has not really become popular.

One of the main products of Tazhmaspada Province — and an important moneymaker for the satrap — is the harvesting of sandalwood in the mountains in the west. Wood is shipped down the Khulen River. Some is left for craftspeople, but most is exported, either to Mithkethrin for use in the imperial city or for sale to other merchants.

MAJOOR, TOWN OF

Ruler: Shahrbain (lord mayor) Ali Ashar
Government: shahrbain (may be elected or appointed) who reports to the provincial satrap
Population: 4,582 (2,255 Jaata, 2,117 Ashurian, 210 other)

A large town in Tazhmaspada Province, Majoor is a respectable trading hub and port on the Celestean Sea. Its citizens aggressively recruit ship traffic as well as caravans from the province's farming areas. One focus of the city's trade is the bazaar, which features a changing selection of eager vendors. Majoor recognizes that Jaati in general and the southeast provinces in particular have residents with a variety of beliefs. The city's primary Temple of the Eternal Sun is dedicated to Mithra (Mitra) but also to deities of the sun from other cultures.

REFERENCE SOURCE: K4 THE COILS OF SET

MASADIZYN, CITY OF

Ruler: Satrap Ritvarziya of Zakros Province
Government: provincial satrap appointed by emperor
Population: 58,447 (54,250 Ashurian, 4,097 Zakros Mountains tribe, 100 other)

Once the capital city of the Adenian Empire, Masadizyn lost its title to the coastal city of Mithkethrin about 400 years ago and is now merely the capital of Zakros Province of the empire. The city is located not far from the River Acina (a tributary of the Turperin) in the eastern part of the Zakros Mountains, which gives travelers a good route to Mithkethrin. Although the emperor's official residence is in the new capital, the old palace is maintained as a summer home. It also still contains most of the historical records and government archives of the Adenian Empire, and scholars can now study here without being interrupted by government bureaucrats, which they consider an improvement. Another important edifice is the ancient temple of Mithra (or Mitra), who for centuries was the only deity worshipped by the Adenians although they came to revere a few other deities during their years of supremacy in the valley of Ur.

Despite these important locations, some city officials and area nobles feel that Masadizyn has become very unimportant to the empire since it is no longer the capital, and they resent their consequent lack of power. The common people tend to view themselves as the ones truly of Adenian heritage since they maintain the mountain traditions of the empire, and are therefore superior to the "lowlanders."

Wool is an important product of Zakros Province, woven into both cloth and into intricately patterned rugs that are in great demand as exports. Another big crop is pistachio nuts, which are harvested and exported in large quantities.

MERCHANT'S BLUFF, CITY OF

Ruler: mercantile council
Government: council of guildmasters approved by the provincial satrap
Population: 9,117 (4,583 Ashurian, 3,911 Jaata, 623 other)

Part of Fradavarenah Province, this city lies on the southern shore of an inlet of the Celestean Sea, on high ground overlooking lowland fields. By establishing a series of dams and accommodating for the occasional flooding, area farmers are able to regularly produce good crops; this is profitable for them as well as the traders in Merchants' Bluff. Lumbering is also popular, with valuable hardwoods in the area. Religion here emphasizes interaction with the ocean. One temple is dedicated to the pantheon of all gods on behalf of sailors who may be lost at sea. Another temple is to a very ancient sea deity, the god Poseidon.

Unfortunately, Merchants' Bluff has been having problems in the past year or two, both with respect to the friendliness to outside traders (in this case, the lack thereof) and in the failure to keep the docks in good repair. Some captains are talking about no longer stopping here, but so far the city seems to still be in business.

REFERENCE SOURCE: K4 THE COILS OF SET

RUZHAN, CITY OF

Ruler: Satrap Haxmanis of Aspacan Province
Government: provincial satrap appointed by emperor
Population: 87,159 (48,910 Jaata, 36,449 Ashurian, 1,800 other)

Ruzhan is an old city on the coast of the Celestean Sea at what is considered to be the southern end of the Jaati region. It fell to the Adenian Empire, which made over the core parts of the city in its own image. The architectural style of the public buildings and temples is certainly different than anything in Jaati proper, and the variations give the city a distinctive feel. The religious district of Ruzhan holds temples to Mithra and other deities of Istaflumina as well as temples to several holders of the Thirteen Thrones, noble deities, and guardian deities and spirits of the Gohtra pantheon.

A harbor and fortress constructed near Ruzhan serve as a northern port for the imperial navy. Ships patrol from here north past Athrina, south to Mithkethrin, and in the Celestean Sea in general. They discourage any possible pirates and keep an eye on the shipping of countries from outside northern Libynos, particularly Castorhage.

As part of Aspacan Province, the empire claims a large part of the northern Zakros Mountains along the River Vistaspa. Very few bother to challenge this, but every few generations the barbarous Zethian tribes try to move out into the lowlands along the coast and have to be taught a lesson. The province has large oak forests in the mountainous areas, and almonds also grow well. The area is also well-known for its wine.

TEREZERNAH, CITY OF

Ruler: Satrap Bycithras of Fradavarenah Province
Government: provincial satrap appointed by emperor
Population: 91,246 (87,955 Ashurian, 1,478 ratfolk, 1,813 other)

Terezernah, the capital of Adenia's Fradavarenah Province, sits at the mouth of the River Risma in the southern part of the Adenian Empire. Nothing but a small fishing village was here before the Adenian conquest, but its replacement has become a major city and home to the empire's growing navy. Ships from Terezernah patrol the southern approaches of the empire, the capital, and Tyrnos Island, while vessels from a secondary base at Ruzhan patrol in the north. Naval ships seldom go far into the Gulf of Ur, as Parphelonia regards them as a threat, but they do protect Adenian merchants as necessary against any pirates in the area.

Fradavarenah is more conservative in its religion than the northern parts of the empire. Although worship of other deities is not forbidden, in public Terezernah has only a temple of Mithra.

Mining is an important business in the province and much metal is shipped to Mithkethrin to help equip the empire's military.

TYRNOS ISLAND

Ruler: Naurapati (naval commander) Xinthra-tasim
Government: military dictator as appointed by the emperor
Population: 1,852 (almost all Ashurian)

The Adenian Empire lays claim to Tyrnos Island, which sits about 150 miles off the eastern shore of northern Libynos. It has forested lowlands around the coast, but a short way inland, all around the island, are mountains so steep that even the peak-savvy Adenians could not explore them successfully. Full exploration was not necessary, though, to discover the incredible flying lizards that lived among the peaks. Unique to Tyrnos Island, these lizards have iridescent feathers both beautiful and magical. Like many lizards, though, they molt their skins on a regular basis and then the feathers can be gathered in good condition if people with the necessary skills are on hand at just the right time. The valuable feathers are sold to a select few merchants and traded at high prices in northern and eastern Libynos, but are almost unknown in the rest of the world.

The Adenians have built fortresses at key places around the island to protect their interests from intruders. The Castorhagi Far East Company and the Alcaldrich Imperial Navy have encroached more than once in the past three decades, though now that Castorhage and Alcaldar are practically at war, they may leave Tyrnos alone. Adenian ships patrol around the island regularly, although it is possible a small boat might find a place to put in that would be unnoticed.

Vigilance against intruders has been increased dramatically in the past few years. After mining various metals in the outer mountains for centuries, a vein of adamantium was discovered and a mine is now in operation. Work there accidentally led to another discovery, one that is being held in even greater secrecy: It seems the mountains do not cover the interior of the island. Instead, they ring a deep, round valley.

The few sages aware of the valley's existence speculate that it could be the remains of the caldera of a truly ancient volcano. Whatever its origin, the valley is filled with plants and animals unlike any ever encountered by any of the sages. The hot, damp atmosphere has caused ferns to grow high above a person's head, with thick trees towering over those. The animals seem even less likely than the flying lizards: one type has a body as big as a house and a tail as long and thick as a downed cedar tree. Another has a protective ruff or frill to guard its neck and a pair of vicious long horns, plus a third on the nose with which it can gore or toss a creature it feels is threatening it, as unfortunate explorers discovered. Flying lizards have been spotted among the tall trees, but these are a dozen feet long or more, rather than three to four as the ones in the outer mountains. Explorers and sages are certain there must be a way to use this discovery to showcase the might of the empire or increase the wealth of participants, but they have not yet determined what it might be.

ASSURIA, EMPIRE OF

Capital: Asshur
Notable Settlements: Arbail, Channa, Dul-Tharrudin, Erappa, Kalakh, Kutsana, Maahri, Mineffeh, Pardisu, Perqa
Ruler: King Nabuzerukin II
Government: royal dictatorship
Population: 1,341,777 (1,312,978 Ashurian of Istaflumina, 13,817 Ashurian of the Caliphate, 14,237 desert and mountain tribe, 745 other)
Monstrous: gnolls (often raid farms), ant lions, lamias (desert)
Languages: Hakhadian
Religion: Annunaki pantheon
Resources: stone, sculptures, iron, tin, crops, trade, glass, horses, wool cloth
Currency: Parphelonian
Technology Level: Dark Ages, Medieval (Kalakh, Maahri)

Assuria is hilly throughout most of its area, running from the foothills of the Zakros Mountains to the fertile river plain south of the capital city of Ashur. Its golden age as an empire has passed, but it is still a collection of strong cities that work together in defense and trade. The Assurians are feared by all for their savage and bloodthirsty tactics on the battlefield, skills which led them to conquer the entire area of Istaflumina and hold it for 300 years.

Certain nomadic folk also reside inside the territory claimed by Assuria. In the northern hills, past the city of Kutsana, are the Thurrians. Southwest, toward the great desert, are the Arramians who attack from the desert at sunset, hit a city or caravan, and then fade back into the desert with their plunder. Important campaigns were carried on against the Arramians in the past, and some suggest they have strongholds hidden in the desert, which is how they are able to survive such assaults by the Assurians time after time.

ASSHUR, CITY-STATE OF (CAPITAL)

Ruler: King Nabuzerukin II
Government: bureaucracy under royal dictatorship
Population: 95,174 (almost all Ashurian)

As first among equals of the cities in the Empire of Assuria, the walls of Asshur itself are hung with the skulls and bones of defeated enemies. The city's highly skilled army consists of mailed archers, spearmen, and charioteers. A ziggurat temple to Ishtar in her aspect of goddess of war is in the center of the city. (She is also worshipped in her aspect of goddess of love, but in Asshur that is done in a smaller temple separate from the great ziggurat.)

King Nabuzerukin II has his court here, making the city the gathering place of influential people, and those who wish to be so. The king's court is the central location for the skilled astronomers and stargazers who use observations of the night sky and celestial phenomena to predict the future. The court astrologers advise the king on all matters of the state, and lesser astrologers are consulted avidly by the people for information on their own decisions.

ARBAIL, CITY-STATE OF

Ruler: Paehutu (governor) Sharrizukup
Government: governor appointed by king
Population: 30,193 (almost all Ashurian)

Arbail is a rather small city located where the hill country of Assuria becomes the steep foothills of the Zakros Mountains. It is the site of an important quarry, with flatboats carrying stone downstream to the River Saan where it is eventually transported on to Asshur. The city also has some notable sculptors, including Ibbi-Rimush, the master of his own carving school.

CHANNA, CITY-STATE OF

Ruler: Paehutu Libbisharamat
Government: governor appointed by king
Population: 48,298 (almost all Ashurian)

Channa is a typical city-state of farmers and herders. The land is not quite as flat and not quite as fertile as the area farther along the River Yugraetes, but the smaller towns and settlements which are subject to Channa still do well for themselves and their city. The city is surrounded by canals and irrigation channels that funnel water from the river out to the farmlands. Channa has a small but adequate dock area on the river; some traders stop here on their way downriver from Perqa or Maahri, but most elect just to go on down the river to the great city of Parphelon.

A professional guard force of several thousand troops is ready to protect the city-state, or join the army of the king under the leadership of the paehutu. The thick, mud-brick walls of the city are large enough to allow those from the surrounding lands to take shelter in case of an attack on the area. An inner wall surrounds a ziggurat temple to Tammuz, god of fertility and rebirth. A processional way (paved with stone, unlike most of the dirt streets) leads from the main city gates to the gate in the temple wall and on to the steps of the temple itself. Thousands of people line the processional way and thousand more participate in the regular festivals to celebrate Tammuz and his mate Ishtar, who has her own temple just on the other side of the great one to Tammuz.

DUL-THARRUDIN, CITY-STATE OF

Ruler: Paehutu Nasidrigira
Government: governor appointed by king
Population: 31,186 (almost all Ashurian)

Dul-Tharrudin was originally built as a fortress to protect the capital city of Mineffeh and other cities in the triangle between the River Pykeris and River Saan. Assuria has been threatened over the years by its rivals in Hurardu, and the most important city-states of that kingdom are in the mountains about 100 miles north of Dul-Tharrudin, so it maintains a strong army ready to fight. The city has also been used as a starting point for attacks into Hurardu. After the capital was moved to Asshur, Dul-Tharrudin was expanded to hold a summer palace for later kings, who found the foothills cooler in the hot seasons than the current capital city.

ERAPPA, CITY-STATE OF

Ruler: King Urbatushara, advised by Qepu (delegate) Ketti-ramat, representative of King Nabuzerukin II
Government: vassal state of Assuria
Population: 71,296 (almost all Ashurian)

Erappa has been allowed to maintain some of its independence from Assuria, primarily because it serves as a point of attack and defense against the barbaric Kouthian tribes in the nearby Zakros Mountains. It has a standing army of 5,000 troops and sends strong patrols through the foothills in its area to push back on any encroachments by the Kouthians. The other value of Erappa is that its people raise fine horses, many of which it sends in tribute to the Assurian Empire.

KALAKH, CITY-STATE OF

Ruler: Paehutu Pobanilassur
Government: governor appointed by king
Population: 34,588 (almost all Ashurian)

Kalakh was capital of Assuria for a time several hundred years ago, but eventually diminished in importance when King Sardanopoleser built a new capital at Mineffeh. It sits at the confluence of the River Saan and the River Pykeris and is sometimes troubled by flooding when both rivers run high. Kalakh is an important center of glass-making, known especially for pale green and deep blue glass. Vessels are sometimes cut from solid blocks of colored glass, a rare technique used thousands of years ago but still seen in Assuria today.

KUTSANA, CITY-STATE OF

Ruler: King Hadasnadinshi, advised by Qepu Iddin-resuwa, representative of King Nabuzerukin II
Government: vassal state of Assuria
Population: 45,996 (almost all Ashurian)

Kutsana does good business cutting valuable timber throughout its hilly area and sending it down one of the tributaries of the River Shapur to the cities downstream, partially for profit but also as part of its tribute to Assuria. Its professional army is well-drilled and alert, as this city-state's area is most vulnerable to attacks by the Thurrians. That tribe is often aided by Hurardu, a rival kingdom of Assuria to the north.

MAAHRI, CITY-STATE OF

Ruler: Paehutu Ishkunduramat
Government: governor appointed by king
Population: 87,863 (almost all Ashurian)

Maahri is the eastern anchor of the Great Caravan Road where it sets off into the desert of the Great Eastern Erg and on to the city of Bhutan along the shore of the Sea of Spices. Caravans come from the west across the Ashurian Desert or from the south (from Parphelon, the ports at Ur, or other cities) and meet here. Most desert travelers prefer not to make the trip all the way to the plains' cities; instead, they want to trade their goods and head back into the familiar desert. Likewise, the Istaflumina merchants prefer not to risk the dangerous journey all the way to the western sea. As a consequence, Maahri is the place for the transfer or trade of large amounts of goods. The people of the area facilitate these deals (with inns, markets, commodity exchanges, private meeting houses, and more), and the Assurian Empire receives a small amount from each transaction. In addition, Maahri's troops actively patrol the area within a day's journey to ward off any attacks near the city by any desert tribes that might be inclined to harass the caravans.

MINEFFEH, CITY-STATE OF

Ruler: Paehutu Esadurimin
Government: governor appointed by king
Population: 61,892 (almost all Ashurian)

Mineffeh is another former capital city, having been favored by Assuria's kings for several hundred years. At its height, it had more than 150,000 inhabitants, was the largest city in the region, and received water via an elaborate system of canals and aqueducts. Revolt by a group of subjugated cities resulted in Mineffeh being sacked and largely abandoned for centuries. It has been restored by the current dynasty of kings, though they have not made it their capital; common houses have been rebuilt, but ruined palaces and temples abound and the current population by no means fills the area inside the expansive walls. When King Humban-Sharruken ordered the ancient city repopulated 300 years ago, his representatives discovered the library of the last ruler, King Ashur-Shuleriba, was largely intact thanks to magical protections set by that king's seers. This library became a royal concern and is overseen personally by the paehutu of the city, currently Esadurimin.

One issue with Mineffeh is that it is prone to earthquakes, with memorable ones occurring every generation or two and large ones happening every century or so. (While it was the capital, one quake leveled most of the city and required massive rebuilding.) Currently, no large quakes have been recorded going back five generations, so the seers of Mineffeh are concerned that one could happen in the next few years. Mineffeh is a major center of worship of the goddess Ishtar, and her temple was the first thing to be rebuilt by Humban-Sharruken as he sought her favor for his later conquests.

PARDISU, CITY-STATE OF

Ruler: Paehutu Ashurmentarah
Government: governor appointed by king
Population: 29,106 (almost all Ashurian)

Pardisu is in the north-central part of Assuria in some of the higher hills near the Zakros Mountains, and the farthest north city-state on the River Pykeris. It lays claim to some mines that produce iron and tin, very valuable commodities for the Assurian Empire. Because of their location, the mines have been the subject of raids by northern enemies from Hurardu, so a small fort has been built near the mines, and troops from Pardisu are stationed there at all times. In addition, its extensive sheep herds produce large quantities of wool so it is known for its cloth.

PERQA, CITY-STATE OF

Ruler: Paehutu Ubibneshezer
Government: governor appointed by king
Population: 34,547 (almost all Ashurian)

Being the westernmost of the city-states of Istaflumina, Perqa and Maahri have been most subject over the years to depredations by desert tribes. As a result, both cities have allied themselves for mutual protection for thousands of years. To an extent, the raids from the desert decreased with the establishment of the Great Caravan Road, which is well-patrolled by the army of the Ammuyad Caliphate. However, since Perqa is not on that road, it has had to expand its own guard patrols to be sure aggressive nomads didn't consider it an easy target.

The city's location on the upper part of the River Yugraetes means local merchants can easily transport wares all the way down the river to the great city of Parphelon and even Ur on the Gulf of Ur. In addition, the city is near where the River Shapur joins the Yugraetes, bringing would-be traders down from the north to take part in the city's markets. The confluence of the two rivers also makes the area a good one for freshwater fishing, and many peasants put nets in the river and then sell their catches in the city. Perqa is an important center of worship for Dagon, God of the Deep; he is viewed in the city as a god of water and the underworld.

EALIM, EMPIRE OF

Capital: Shushin
Notable Settlements: Khundeshlikur
Ruler: Emperor Nakhante-Khushinak
Government: monarchy
Population: 1,435,392 (1,423,347 Ashurian, 12,045 other)
Monstrous: giants (mountains), lizardfolk (coasts), hippocampi, kelp devils (ocean)
Languages: Hakhadian
Religion: Annunaki Pantheon
Resources: trade, crops, fishing, scholarship
Currency: Parphelonian
Technology Level: Renaissance (Shushin), Medieval (Khundeshlikur), High Middle Ages (other settlements), Dark Ages (rural areas)

The Empire of Ealim lies at the foot of the Zakros Mountains and currently holds the land all the way to the eastern bank of the River Pykeris. It also claims the entire eastern side of the Gulf of Ur around to and including the Ghutirshan Peninsula. The Ealimite culture has produced great works of literature, architecture, and sculpture. The empire is divided into a number of powerful princedoms, with each paying lip service to the emperor in Shushin. The Ealimites are masters of diplomacy and manipulation, and play a complex game of vassalage, political intermarriages, intrigues, and assassinations. Such internal conflict has generally prevented Ealim from dominating its western neighbors.

SHUSHIN, IMPERIAL CITY OF (CAPITAL)

Ruler: Emperor Nakhante-Khushinak
Government: City-Lord Kutir-amar, advising the emperor
Population: 211,254 (almost all Ashurian)

Shushin is a beautiful city situated on the River Murrani as it runs toward the Gulf of Ur. Its region produces an abundance of crops to support the city's large urban population. As the capital of the Ealimite Empire, the city is full of palaces (both royal and noble), temples, gardens, markets, elite craftspeople, and everyday folks going about their business. After the royal palace, the greatest building in the city is the ziggurat temple to Shushinak. The patron deity of Shushin is known as the Lord of Secrets, an appropriate choice for a city full of political turmoil. The court itself is rife with palace intrigue and assassinations as people try to put themselves in positions of wealth or power.

GHUTIRSHAN, PROVINCE OF

Capital: Khundeshlikur
Ruler: Prince Lagana-Shilkhamru
Government: monarchy; vassal of Empire of Ealim

Ghutirshan is on the peninsula of the same name, east of the Gulf of Ur. It is an ancient realm with a long history of civilization, though not quite so long as the cradle of the two rivers of Istaflumina. Prince Lagana-Shilkhamru reigns from the capital city of Khundeshlikur, but rule of the city itself is given over to the city-lord. Being on the coast of the sea, the province is exposed to damaging weather from which Ealim proper is protected by the Gulf of Ur. However, the land is still abundant and supports a large urban population. It is also a good location for trade though the ships of Ghutirshan are coasters rather than seagoing vessels.

IBNATH, RUINS OF

Population: 0

Ibnath was once a city of wealth, full of temples to the gods, and more temples and shrines to strange foreign gods. It is said that the priests dwelt in such magnificence that the gods became angry and turned against them. The gods cursed the city and sent a demon to destroy it, killing the highest priests and turning the people out to wander in the desert. The ruins of the city are now lost to the sands, though some desert folk still tell its tale and claim to recall where it sat.

KHUNDESHLIKUR, CITY OF (PROVINCIAL CAPITAL)

Ruler: City-Lord Shukunde-Khutiru
Government: city-lord appointed by the prince of Ghutirshan
Population: 122,138 (almost all Ashurian)

This ancient city in Ghutirshan welcomes scholars from around the world to the great Academy of Khundeshlikur. It is a center of theological and scientific thought in Libynos, and also a key location for research into medicine, astronomy, and mathematics. Sadly, due to its distant location, and the narrowminded tendencies of the scholars of Akados to discount the wisdom of the eastern continent, the academy is little known west of Khemit. The prevalence of scholars in the city does not mean the city emphasizes the esoteric to the detriment of the material. It has a thriving sea trade with the city-states on the Gulf of Ur and up the east coast to Jaati, as well as having a sizable army to protect it from incursion by land or sea.

HURARDU, KINGDOM OF

Capital: Vurushma
Notable Settlements: Dusathir
Ruler: King Balatshinu
Government: monarchy
Population: 858,518 (830,361 Ashurian, 28,157 Zakros Mountains tribe)
Monstrous: giants, ogres, thunderbirds
Languages: Hakhadian
Religion: Annunaki pantheon
Resources: trade, fishing, highland crops
Currency: Parphelonian
Technology Level: High Middle Ages (Vurushma), Dark Ages (other towns), Iron Age (rural areas, tribal villages)

Hurardu is a mountainous kingdom without the food and water resources of the plains' cities. Its people are tough, however, and get along well with what they have. The kingdom is a long-time enemy of Assuria and makes attacks on that empire from time to time. (It has to deal with reprisals as well, although at least the famed chariots of Assuria are not useful in Hurardu's mountainous territory.) The kingdom is also bothered by attacks from the Kymmurean tribes to the north. A people of fierce warriors, the Kymmureans have to be beaten back on a regular basis to keep Hurardu cities secure.

DUSATHIR, CITY OF

Ruler: City-Lord Diuresu
Government: city-lord appointed by king
Population: 25,642 (almost all Ashurian)

Dusathir is located on a relatively quiet inlet of Lake Fahn. Its docks carry on a thriving lake trade. Its ships cross to settlements on the other sides of the lake and transport goods from one to another, as well as back to its own markets and to Vurushma. The city has a small dock area but does not really emphasize water travel. Fishing is another activity of Dusathir's ships. The city has a standing army to protect against roving mountain tribes, but it has been decades since the city (as opposed to some outlying settlement) came under serious attack, so the army has been allowed to decrease in numbers and fall out of practice in the past few years.

VURUSHMA, CITY OF (CAPITAL)

Ruler: King Balatshinu
Government: monarchy
Population: 38,876 (almost all Ashurian)

The capital of Hurardu, the city of Vurushma lies on the shore of Lake Fahn. Located in a valley of the Zakros Mountains, Vurushma has a much-cooler climate than the lowland cities, and there are seasons when little food grows. The people of the area cultivate different crops than those in the warm river valleys and do some trading for other goods. The royal palace is built on a series of terraces overlooking the lake. The other grand building in the city is the Temple of Sin, the god of the moon. The clear mountain air is excellent for observing the night sky, and astrologers travel some distance to make readings of the stars at the Temple of Sin.

PARPHELONIA, EMPIRE OF

Capital: Parphelon
Ruler: Kingpriest Apullunedizu
Government: theocracy
Population: 3,065,054 (2,923,182 Ashurian, 12,248 desert tribe, 128,324 other human ethnicity, 1,300 other)
Monstrous: jackalweres gray renders, marsh beasts (Black Marshes), girtablilu (desert), lizardfolk (coasts), hippocampi, reefclaws (Gulf of Ur)
Languages: Hakhadian
Religion: Annunaki pantheon
Resources: religion, history, magic, crops, fishing, logging, herbs, trade
Currency: Parphelonian
Technology Level: Medieval (Parphelon, Ur), High Middle Ages (Ippur, Vorsiphe, Zibur), Dark Ages (Erethu, Gessh, Irrech, Kuuda), Iron Age (rural areas)

The Empire of Parphelonia is led by Apullunedizu, who is at once king and also the archpriest of Tiamat. The entire empire is not as dedicated to her worship as is the city of Parphelon (nor does the kingpriest require that), but it colors all interactions with the kingpriest and the capital city. Currently, the empire consists of the countries of Hakhad and Zumaru, but it has been larger in the past, and the kingpriest has plans to make it be so again in the future.

HAKHAD, KINGDOM OF

Capital: Parphelon
Notable Settlements: Gessh, Kuuda, Vorsiphe, Zibur
Ruler: Kingpriest Apullunedizu
Government: part of Empire of Parphelonia

Hakhad is in the central part of Istaflumina where the Pykeris and Yugraetes run close together. It is a land of hills and fertile plains dominated by the grand city of Parphelon. Hakhad in the past ruled all of Istaflumina and more, and in fact its language is still the common tongue of the entire area. Now, however, Hakhad is joined with Zumaru as part of the Empire of Parphelonia.

PARPHELON, CITY-STATE OF

Ruler: Assistant Archpriest Ekurzakir
Government: theocracy under Empire of Parphelonia
Population: 502,230 (468,830 Ashurian, 31,200 other human ethnicities, 2,200 other)

Parphelon is the greatest of the Istafluminan city-states. The mighty city is famed for its towering blue gates guarded by sculpted dragons and winged bulls. It is thoroughly devoted to the worship of Tiamat, the dragon-queen of chaos, with all other deities being relegated to minor status. Parphelon is ruled by the blue-bearded priests of Tiamat, who in turn serve the kingpriest, mightiest of all rulers in Istaflumina.

Its urban population is supported by agricultural settlements from miles around, as well as supplies purchased from the nearby city of Vorsiphe. The streets of Parphelon are crowded with people conducting their business, engaging in trade, and visiting the great city. The court of the kingpriest is full of intrigue, but nobles and courtiers are a bit more cautious than most places because a seriously wrong step can result in not just banishment, but instead becoming a sacrifice to Tiamat.

GESSH, CITY-STATE OF

Population: 52,496 (almost all Ashurian)
Ruler: City-Lord Marappla-iddin
Government: city-lord under Empire of Parphelonia

Gessh is an ancient city, of such antiquity that only Erethu has a clear claim to being of greater age. It was once the seat of a mighty dynasty of kings, but now is a minor city of primarily religious significance. It is only a day's journey east of Parphelon and features an elaborate temple to Inanna (now known as Ishtar) as well as the remains of some of the earliest palaces and other buildings constructed in all Libynos, which bring many religious pilgrims and other travelers to the city.

KUUDA, CITY-STATE OF

Ruler: Archpriest Mushezibti
Government: theocracy under Empire of Parphelonia
Population: 45,638 (almost all Ashurian)

The center of a death-cult serving Nergal, Erishkigal, and other gods, Kuuda is said to be always shrouded in the gloom of darkened skies. It is dominated by huge mortuary temples aboveground, and endless black halls and maggot-ridden mausoleums underground, where the dark-hearted archpriest is rumored to command legions of the dead. The work of the city is done by low-ranking members of the cult because any non-members abandoned the area long ago.

VORSIPHE, CITY-STATE OF

Ruler: City-Lord Aregalshu
Government: city-lord appointed by kingpriest
Population: 99,306 (almost all Ashurian)

Vorsiphe is effectively the "sister city" of Parphelon. Only a few miles away from the capital, its business is mostly supporting the business of Parphelon. Even the temples are lesser than the temples in Parphelon; before the coming of the priests of Tiamat, the greatest temple in Parphelon was dedicated to Marduk, beneficent deity of strength and law. Vorsiphe's greatest temple was built to Utu, the sun god, who is a lesser god of law. A few generations ago, the aged temple of Utu was updated and ornamented with rich blue glaze, similar to certain buildings in Parphelon. Temples now mostly act as archives of legal, administrative, and astronomical texts and perform fewer ceremonies, as they are anxious not to attract attention from the priests at Parphelon. The villages and settlements around Vorsiphe send their products into the city, but from there, a large part is shipped directly to Parphelon to support its population.

ZIBUR, CITY-STATE OF

Ruler: City-Lord Gashansunu
Government: city-lord appointed by Kingpriest
Population: 127,863 (almost all Ashurian)

Zibur sits on the eastern bank of the River Yugraetes, at the point at which that river and the Pykeris most closely approach each other. It is a stopping place for caravans or travelers who are traveling between the rivers, and is a crossing for those who so far have been on the west bank but need to move to the east to go on to Parphelon. The city of Zibur is dominated by the great ziggurat temple of Ea, god of healing and knowledge, and also of magic. Many of the priests of Ea are also magicians, and his temple is a center of teaching in that area. It is also a place where petitioners come to beg healing from the deity, with gifts as rich as they can afford.

ZUMARU, KINGDOM OF

Capital: Ur
Notable Settlements: Erethu, Ippur, Irrech, Ur
Ruler: Kingpriest Appullunedizu
Government: part of Empire of Parphelonia

Zumaru is the site of the most ancient civilization in the world. The tales say that thousands of years ago, explorers from Zumaru traveled to other parts of the world and founded the first cities there. Lying primarily in the great delta of the Rivers Pykeris and Yugraetes, much of the country is a swampy jungle crisscrossed by subsidiary streams and channels. Having been the seat of an empire in millennia past, Zumaru is joined with Hakhad as part of the Empire of Parphelonia, and is now little more than a regional designation.

ERETHU, CITY-STATE OF

Ruler: Priest-King Iaazipaa
Government: theocracy under Empire of Parphelonia
Population: 149,817 (almost all Ashurian)

This ancient city claims to be the oldest in the world. Some say that when the first farmers, fishers, and herders gathered and built homes here, under the very first king of Zumaru, the god Ea came to them and taught them how to have a civilization. Others claim the city was founded by a mystic fish-man who crawled ashore from the deep ocean and taught the people about letters and sciences, and arts of every kind. From him the people learned to build cities, to found temples, to compile laws, and to master geometry and mathematics.

After the first fish-man returned to the sea, others of his kind came secretly and continued to teach select people things such as sorcery and powers of the mind. Originally built along the southern bank of the River Yugraetes, the city lost easy access to water when the river changed its channel hundreds of years later. Although the drier land requires more people to work it, Erethu is still able to have a large urban population through the power of magic; the city is known today as a realm of sorcerers and demon-summoners. These dark magicians live in tall towers of red stone that are visible from miles away and are a recognizable landmark of Erethu.

IPPUR, CITY-STATE OF

Ruler: Archpriest Numunia
Government: theocracy under Empire of Parphelonia
Population: 112,618 (almost all Ashurian)

Ippur is one of the earliest city-states founded in Zumaru, but its age had not led it to stagnate. The holiest of all Zumaran cities, Ippur is the site of the great ziggurat temple of Enlil, the deity who is now also known as Marduk, the divine general in the war against chaos. Other temples to beneficent deities fill the city center and are the site of much worshipful activity. Many soldiers come here briefly for religious ceremonies, but being in the army of Ippur is also considered very prestigious and it is larger than usual for a city of its size, with nearly 20,000 troops.

IRRECH, CITY-STATE OF

Ruler: City-Lord Nikanuur
Government: city-lord appointed by kingpriest
Population: 148,636 (almost all Ashurian)

One of the oldest cities of Istaflumina, Irrech is built around a core of temples. The oldest and greatest ziggurat is to Inanna (now known as Ishtar), goddess of love and war, but almost as great is the ziggurat temple to Anu, distant god of law and protection. Many other gods are also represented in the temple district, some of which have few worshippers these days. Irrech has a great archive, though it is not well known, that contains primarily legal and scholarly tablets (though the archivists keep almost anything given into their care), some of which were inscribed thousands of years ago.

UR, CITY-STATE OF

Ruler: City-Lord Enhedanu
Government: city-lord appointed by Kingpriest
Population: 321,483 (306,448 Ashurian, 14,210 other human ethnicities, 825 other)

One of the oldest cities of Istaflumina (though not quite as old as Irrech), Ur flourishes today as a port city on the Gulf of Ur. Merchants bring products from throughout the river valleys, as well as from far-away places such as the Ammuyad Caliphate, to Ur. Here they trade them for goods from Jaati, Khemit, or even the jungles far to the south. During one of its periods of empire, a mighty ziggurat was built at Ur that can still be seen today. From the apex of the Ur ziggurat, the ancient stargazers surveyed the night sky and observed the passing of comets, and the birth and death of stars. It is said that these astronomers chronicled their findings, and the esoteric knowledge they gleaned from them, on cuneiform tablets so that the knowledge could be passed on to later generations. If this was done, however, the tablets have been lost to the centuries. The ziggurat is now dedicated to the worship of Ea, the god of wisdom.

GEOGRAPHIC FEATURES AND POINTS OF INTEREST IN ISTAFLUMINA

ASSURIAN PLAIN

The central plain of Istaflumina is commonly called the Assurian Plain after the Assurian Empire, who used it to such great advantage in conquering the rest of the area many hundred years ago. It begins near the city of Asshur and broadens where the two great rivers approach each other only 50 miles apart. It increases to more than 200 miles wide as the rivers flow to the southeast, and surrounds the delta formed by the great rivers. The entire plain is very fertile; with water supplied by irrigation from the River Yugraetes and the favorable weather, the land is able to produce crops twice a year and so feed the large urban population of the region.

BLACK MARSHES OF NAMMAT

An offshoot of the Zumaran swamp delta, close to the great River Pykeris, the loathsome marshland known as the Black Marshes of Nammat is avoided by most travelers, even if it means traveling upriver to make the difficult crossing of the Pykeris. The marshes are known to be inhabited by giant poisonous insects and blood-sucking bats, and many claim they are home to tribes of dangerous jackalweres that worship the demon-god Baal-Zag. Unconfirmed rumors also speak of a sunken tower deep within the marsh that was once the home of a powerful wizard, no doubt long dead.

CELESTEAN SEA

The warm Celestean Sea is part of the Great Ocean Ûthaf, along the east coast of both the Istaflumina region and Jaati, and gets its name from its vivid sky-blue color. The warm current flowing north along the coast makes ship travel from the south convenient, though return trips are not as easy; a ship must either hug the coast or travel far out to sea.

GULF OF UR

The Gulf of Ur is a protected inlet of the Great Ocean Ûthaf that stretches north from the Sea of Tyre. It is most notable for being the access to the sea of the Istaflumina region and is the outlet of its two major rivers, the River Pykeris and the River Yugraetes.

KHULEN RIVER

The Khulen River (which is fed by a tributary, the Hema) runs from the southern part of the Jungteran Mountains into the Celestean Sea. It forms the northern border of the Adenian Empire, at least in the lowlands. The Adenians have fortifications along the southern side of the river and the small countries along the northern side have built their fortifications as well, but they are aware that if the Adenians decide to annex another new province (as they did a century ago), those defenses are unlikely to hold them back for long.

LAKE AMONI

West of the River Yugraetes and about 30 miles west of the city-state of Zibur in Parphelonia lies Lake Amoni. The lake is deep and perhaps fed by an underground source because the water seems to be perpetually cool. It supports several small fishing settlements around its shores.

LAKE FAHN

This large mountain lake sits in the Kingdom of Hurardu on the northern edge of Istaflumina, and in fact that kingdom's two major city-states, Vurushma and Dusathir, are on its southeastern bank. Travel on the lake is easier than travel through the mountains, so the cities and settlements on it use that method primarily. It is still dangerous, however, especially in the storm season when a storm come up quickly and roil the lake wildly. In addition, there are rumored to be two or three large creatures that live deep in the lake, though that may just be a tale to account for boats lost unexpectedly.

LAKE SHUMA

About 50 miles northwest of the Gulf of Ur, the steep bank of the River Pykeris has a break on the western side and waters flow into Lake Shuma. The lake's banks are low enough to allow the water to be used for irrigation, and many fish carried down the Pykeris on its long journey end up in Lake Shuma so some local settlements are able to support themselves by fishing.

LAKE TURMIA

Among the high crests of the Zakros Mountains is a long valley with a deep, cold lake. Fed by the river of the same name (which comes from the high mountain peaks), Lake Turmia is not home to any cities, but wandering mountain tribes such as the Nallaeans or Kouthians often spend months living in the caves to be found around its shores.

ORDABA RIVER

The Ordaba River runs from high in the southern Jungteran Mountains down to the foothills, where it joins the Vistaspa River on its way to the Celestean Sea. As its upper reaches are actually farther north than the upper part of the Khulen River, the Adenian Empire uses the Ordaba to delimit its claims in the mountains.

PLATEAU OF ONG

The frigid plateau of Ong is said to be located among some of the highest peaks of the Zakros Mountains. Stories trickling from some of the mountain tribes claim a huge building located there houses veiled, yellow-robed mystics. Some say they have seen it, but only from a distance and only when they discovered it by accident; no one knows where it is, or no one has ever been able to find a way back to it. More accounts exist of tribespeople encountering the mystics in high mountain passes, but they seem peaceable, going about their own unknown business.

RED WASTE

Located in the area of Ealim, the Red Waste is a desert area extending from the base of the Zakros Mountains almost to the edge of the River Pykeris. It is an expanse of red sand dunes and barren rock outcroppings, with a scattering of small but vital oases. The Red Waste is home to the Saramite tribe, desert raiders not numerous enough to threaten a city-state but who often trouble outlying settlements and caravans.

RIVER ACINA

This tributary of the River Turperin winds north and west through the eastern Zakros Mountains and past Masadizyn, the old capital of the Empire of Ademia. Much of the river is navigable until the confluence with the Turperin, with only a few places where rapids make travel a bit more treacherous. Many summer days, boats can be seen floating through the calm waters, bearing nobles from Mithkethrin escaping the lowland heat of the capital.

RIVER ALSIKARU

This river rises in the Zakros Mountains east of Ealim and flows through the lowland into the east edge of the Gulf of Ur. It has a lesser branch slightly to the west (known locally as the River Dasikaru) which roughly parallels the River Murrani for more than 50 miles before turning east and joining its parent river.

RIVER AZAMU

Istaflumina's southernmost river of any notable size is the River Azamu. It flows through the Zakros Mountains for some distance before dropping to the plain of Ealim until it empties into the eastern edge of the Gulf of Ur. South of this point, any significant rivers rising in the mountains flow south and join the ocean outside the gulf.

RIVER LESSER SAAN

The Lesser Saan is a tributary of the River Pykeris of Istaflumina. It flows about 50 miles south of the River Saan and joins the Pykeris south of Asshur. It is fordable at several points, allowing travel along the eastern side of the River Pykeris.

RIVER MINALA

The River Minala flows from the heights of the Zakros Mountains southwest into the River Pykeris east of Zibur. Its banks are not steep (as those of the Pykeris are) so it can be used for irrigation, although fewer city-states are near it than along the larger rivers. It can also be forded at places, so caravans can cross it if they want to travel the east bank of the Pykeris instead of the west bank.

RIVER MURRANI

Running from the high Zakros Mountains into Ealim, the River Murrani flows by the Ealimite capital city of Shushin before flowing directly into the Gulf of Ur. It is usable for irrigation and provides plentiful water to and around Shushin.

RIVER PYKERIS

This river has its source north of Assuria, at the edge of the Zakros Mountains, and zigzags over 700 miles through the lowlands of Istaflumina to the Gulf of Ur. It is a rough and fast-flowing river; its high banks make it difficult to cross and unsuitable for irrigation. Its major tributaries (the River Saan, the Lesser Saan, and Minala) run out of the Zakros Mountains. The great cities of Assuria are concentrated along the Pykeris, though fewer cities are on the river farther south.

RIVER RISMA

The River Risma is a comparatively short river with its headwaters in the southeastern part of the Zakros Mountains. It flows primarily eastward and empties into the sea at Terezernah, where a large harbor provides docking space for dozens of ships.

River Saan

The Saan is a relatively short tributary of the Pykeris that flows down from the edge of the Zakros Mountains and joins the larger river near Kalakh. It can be forded, thereby allowing caravans from the city-states on the eastern bank of the Pykeris to travel that side as far as they choose rather than being forced to cross the Pykeris at any specific location.

River Shapur

The River Shapur starts in three branches in the hills of northern Assuria, the main one being the west branch, near the City-State of Kutsana. (The others are known as the Middle Shapur and the Lesser Shapur by people who live in the area and need to refer to them.) It has a strong current and is useful for river transportation as well as having a good amount of fish. The River Shapur joins the River Yugraetes a few miles north of Perqa.

River Turperin

The River Turperin winds through the peaks and high valleys of the eastern Zakros Mountains for a few hundred miles before it drops quickly to the lowland and meets the Celestean Sea near Mithkethrin. The last hundred miles or so could be traversed by boat, but not enough people live or labor along its route to make that a frequent occurrence. River traffic does come from Masadizyn in the south up to where the tributary, the River Acina, meets the Turperin. It is feasible to take a boat or barge from Masadizyn to the confluence of the rivers, but from there down to the lowlands, the river is too dangerous for humans. Important travelers are met at the confluence by trains of litters and bearers for the winding trip down through the mountains to the coastal plain. Others must provide their own transportation or simply go on foot. Since the travel down would require transferring cargo from a barge to some type of animal train, many merchants forgo river transportation on the Acina in favor of just bringing a caravan the entire distance.

Logging is done along the mountain reaches of the Turperin and the logs sent down the river to the capital city. At the time Mithkethrin was being built, modifications were done to the river in several spots to make the traverse smoother and to remove large rocks or other impediments that caused snags. Regular maintenance along the river means even now intervention by loggers is seldom needed to get the trees down to the city markets.

River Vistaspa

This long river runs for hundreds of miles through the northern Zakros Mountains in a generally easterly direction before flowing into the Celestean Sea at Ruzhan. Most people who view the river on a map accept it as the line of demarcation between the Istaflumina region and that of Jaati. The situation on the ground is more complicated, but since exact regional divisions are of most concern to the mapmakers, no one in the area is likely to argue the issue.

River Yugraetes

The Yugraetes starts in the hill country of far-western Assuria and wends its way through Hakhad and Zumaru as well before emptying into the Gulf of Ur. It has lower banks than the River Pykeris, which makes it usable for the irrigation that provides water to the fertile fields of the Assurian Plain. It is also navigable by flatboats as far north as Perqa, which makes it useful for merchant travel. Only a few cities of Assuria sit on the banks of the upper Yugraetes, but most of the major cities of Hakhad and Zumaru are along this river.

Zakros Mountains

The Zakros Mountains form the eastern barrier of the valley of the two rivers, protecting most of Istaflumina from the wild storms and changeable climate of the Great Ocean Ûthaf. Some peaks near the Gulf of Ur rise more than two miles high. The mountains are home to several tribes of nomads and barbarians. Near the River Saan and the Lesser Saan live the Kouthi people, who eke out a poor living in the cold climate of the high mountains. From time to time, a chieftain rallies all the Kouthi clans to descend upon the decadent plains' cities to loot and plunder. East of the Kouthians, where the peaks are not quite so high and the valleys broader, live the Nallaeans in the vicinity of Lake Turmia. Farther south, the Empire of Adenia has its homeland, and they are able to protect themselves quite well against the wild warriors.

The mountains also form a barrier to the north and the northwest that stretches for hundreds of miles and reaches more than three miles in height. In the midst of the peaks are glaciers perhaps thousands of years old, which are the ultimate sources of many of the rivers that flow from the Zakros range.

Highland rumors talk about isolated strongholds found among the peaks — a handful of impregnable fortress-cities situated along the river valleys of the interior Zakros Mountains. These fortresses are supposedly home to exiled warlords, tyrannical princes, or strange cults, depending on who is doing the telling. When asked for specifics, though, the mountain people are unwilling (or unable) to provide details, so the people of the city-states tend to view these accounts as mere fireside tales. These high and hostile mountains might be avoided altogether by civilized peoples except that in season, the mountain slopes abound with rare and wondrous — and costly — herbs useful to healers or magicians.

Jaati

The region of Jaati occupies the northeastern corner of the continent of Libynos. It extends as far north as many parts of the Northlands (located far to the west), but the warm currents pulled up the eastern continental coast from the equatorial ocean, along with the mysterious effects of the Tropic of Arden, heat the climate far beyond what might normally be expected from its latitude.

Jaati is not one single country, though it has been in the past. Instead, its many domains are ruled by rajahs and ranees, lords and princes, human and otherwise. It stretches from the warm coasts of the eastern ocean to the steep mountains of the west, from deep forest to rolling fields of wheat. People crowd its coastal cities, and villages line the rivers, while much of the interior is sparsely populated. Because of its isolation from much of Libynos, not to mention the rest of the world, the land is called "Far Jaati" by almost everyone except the people of the caliphate and the Istaflumina region.

Many cultures have spread back and forth over the region through the millennia, and influences have mixed and changed each other. Some locations are still very focused in a single culture and others continue to be influenced by a specific heritage, but overall the areas of Jaati are more similar than they are different.

The people of Jaati usually appear exotic to people from other countries. Silk is produced and woven in so much of the country that it is the usual fabric for clothing, especially among women. What would be a luxury almost anyplace else is a colorful commonplace in Jaati. Jewelry of gold and silver is a symbol of status but also a way to carry one's wealth, so most people wear some all the time and even more on special occasions. Coins are often attached to chains or sashes or fastened to skirts or vests, and it is not surprising to see garments sewn with coins of empires of the past as well as many of the present kingdoms.

Some residents of the region truly are exotic, as they are not even human. For example, the ebony-skinned vishkanyas with their solid-white eyes are rarely seen in the cities; if they have villages of their own, the common person is unaware. Prevailing wisdom says that their skin is poisonous, though others refute this and say the vishkanyas merely craft poisons for assassins — or perhaps they are the assassins themselves. Many Jaata consider crossing paths with a vishkanya to be a sign of bad luck or possibly even impending death, and they change their route to avoid the encounter or completely look the other way to be able to say they never saw a vishkanya in their path.

Also native to Jaati are the ratfolk. Thought by many to have been created by the goddess S'Surimiss (Queen of Rats), others attribute the race's origins to uncanny experiments by some ancient master of magic. Although in some areas humans treat them as if they were no better than rats themselves, ratfolk are apt to be clever and quick, with a nose for acquisition that makes many of them good merchants. Ratfolk tend to live in large families in some of the warrens of alleys and buildings that make up the lower-class neighborhoods of Jaati's bigger cities, even living underground in places where that is a possibility.

In contrast to the ratfolk, the rakshasas of Jaati often live in luxury in large cities, being among people without anyone realizing it. Their ability to change shape and also to magically influence the humans around them allows them to come and go as they please while also having servants to see their needs.

One important cultural aspect of Jaati is its caste system. Although not obvious to outsiders with only short experience, the caste system exerts a strong influence on the living situations and career choices of the Jaata. In the Jaati region, people are born to a certain station in life (whether that be as a descendant of generations of warriors, part of a family of weavers, or a member of the nobility), and they are expected to spend their lives doing what their ancestors did before them. It is not impossible for people to rise in caste during their lifetimes, but it is not easy either.

Part of the reason for that difficulty is that the caste system is an important part of the religion in Jaati. According to their beliefs, it is the destiny of each soul eventually to ascend to godhood, but they must earn that ascension by actions in life: good deeds, works of charity, and self-sacrifice. To make this possible, each soul is born and reborn, hopefully each time moving farther up the coil. Eventually, the sufficiently ascended soul is welcomed into the Gardens of Heaven as one of the guardian deities. These thousands of spirits watch over springs, mountains, and rivers, villages, and city street corners. Such a minor deity may, over the long course of time, aspire to become one of the nobles in the Court of Heaven, or ultimately even one of the 12 who sit on the Thirteen Thrones.

Avunta, Castorhagi Colony of

Capital: Hethwarp
Notable Settlements: Chikheni
Ruler: Colonial Governor Thertina Lorwin
Government: The Far East Company of Castorhage
Population: 2,811,813 (2,057,111 Jaata, 326,515 Castorhagi, 408,726 ratfolk, 19,261 other human ethnicity, 200 other)
Monstrous: lizardfolk, river trolls (jungles), sea serpents, locathah
Languages: Westerling, Meeruwhan
Religion: Castorhagi pantheon, Gohtra pantheon
Resources: cloves, nutmeg, cinnamon, ebony wood, teak wood, rice, fruit, trade
Currency: Castorhagi, old Avunta
Technology Level: High Middle Ages (Hethwarp), Dark Ages (cities), Iron Age (rural areas)

Avunta is in the northeast part of Jaati, on the broad plain where the Dhobe River flattens out and widens. The country is entirely under the control of a Castorhagi mercantile group, the Far East Company, and has been for 57 years. Technically, Avunta is a royal colony of the City-State of Castorhage, but company people only bother with that detail in official reports. The company's main focus has been on some high-value spices that grow well in this area, as well as expensive hardwoods such as ebony and teak. The spices are more quickly renewable; the ebony especially is becoming scarce despite local foresters conscientiously replanting. Very little wood is designated anymore for local crafters; most of it goes back to cabinetmakers and woodcarvers in Castorhage or is sold at high prices in the large cities of Akados.

As for spices, cloves and nutmeg are those most emphasized by the factors, although cinnamon is also pushed where it will grow well. The

spice plantations are mostly worked by slaves, either debt-slaves or criminals. With the company in charge, there is plenty of opportunity for both those populations to grow.

The Far East Company has not bothered to interfere in the religious practices of the native Jaati. The locals are not in the habit of taking a holy day to rest every week, so even the frequent religious festivals amount to an improvement over work habits in much of the rest of the world. The company does maintain appropriate worship facilities for its own employees; just because they are far from home does not mean they should be deprived of the comfort of the Church of Mother Grace, for example.

Hethwarp, City of (Capital)

Ruler: Chief Factor Colethan Steard
Government: The Far East Company of Castorhage
Population: 124,928 (77,450 Castorhagi, 31,800 Jaata, 8,330 ratfolk, 7,283 other human ethnicity, 65 other)

The city of Hethwarp started out as a small port town, then became a trade mission, and then was built into a bustling city when the Far East Company took control of the country of Avunta. The most important parts of the city are the trade market, the harbor, and the walled Company Quarter where company officials from the colonial governor on her estate down to mid-level managers live in luxury (or at least comfort) brought about largely by the labors of closely supervised locals who live primarily in the warrens of the Native Quarter.

The trade markets deal in grains (especially the ubiquitous rice), fruit, hardwoods, fabrics such as muslins and silks, and many more things. Plantation managers negotiate tightly with ship captains or trade intermediaries for the best prices for their goods; they know they probably have only five or 10 years to accumulate as much as they can pinch from the commodities that pass through their hands before they might be rotated to another station and have to learn a new system from the beginning.

The harbor is a busy place, with large oceangoing vessels sailing out of Castorhage calling here and smaller ships running up and down the coast to other Castorhagi stations. Although most large ships do travel all the way to Baragibra (because after a ship has come all the way from Castorhage, why not sail another hundred miles or two), they use Hethwarp as their location for shore leave before heading out on the long trip home. Resources come here from capable, aggressive factors who have made inroads along the Dhobe, as well as some who have stations on the Tusora River to the west, and others who managed to establish themselves in villages on the west side of the Ukshauka Hills. Hethwarp has been a great success for the Far East Company and the business is actively exploring extending its official reach farther up the Dhobe and north along the coast into what is now the Kingdom of Tola.

Chikheni, City of

Ruler: Chief Factor Priseth Harnar, on behalf of Mehtar Shantinath Talarom
Government: The Far East Company of Castorhage
Population: 142,701 (93,300 Jaata, 27,320 ratfolk, 19,810 Castorhagi, 2,241 other human ethnicity, 30 other)

Chikheni, on the lower Dhobe River, was once the capital of the Kingdom of Avunta. With the country under the control of the Castorhagi Far East Company, the hereditary ruler (now a mere mehtar, or prince) is reduced to ruling his own estate and advocating for his people while the company's factor controls everything else in his name. Chikheni still has many beautiful temples, and wide marble steps lead down into the river so huge crowds of people can simultaneously immerse themselves in the water for the various holy festivals. Other than during the colorful spectacles of festival times, though, the city feels rundown and the people dispirited.

For three generations, many young people of Chikheni have gone to work in the Castorhagi city of Hethwarp (a name considered ugly by the local Jaati). Others, listening to the blandishments of the royal army recruiters, go to take training as warriors. For some, this provides a way to improve their lives, while for others, desperate enough, it means taking on the work of a lower caste. (As the saying goes, "you can't eat caste.") Of those who remain in Chikheni, the majority now are forced to work for the company for the benefit of Hethwarp or Castorhage itself. Few have been able to continue to live their lives in the traditional way.

For example, the city was once home to a lively community of expert woodworkers, but now only a handful are permitted to practice that trade anymore. The cabinetmakers of Chikheni once were renowned for their ebony pieces intricately inlaid with lighter woods and bits of ivory and mother-of-pearl, with the inlays in elaborate patterns of flowers and vines, or repeating geometry. Now only one or two such items are crafted a year on the entire Ebony Street; most of the wood goes to foreign carvers to make their own furniture.

KHADHALAYA, KINGDOM OF

Capital: Jalebas
Notable Settlements: Elogong
Ruler: Rani (Queen) Jaimathi Leporing
Government: monarchy
Population: 2,741,160 (2,283,117 Jaata, 334,581 ratfolk, 95,524 Castorhagi, 26,285 other human ethnicity, 1,653 other)
Monstrous: giant snapping turtles, reefclaws (coast), spider eater, jaculi (land)
Languages: Merruwhan, Westerling
Religion: Gohtra pantheon
Resources: crops, muslin cloth, teak wood, wood carvings, furniture, trade, silk
Currency: Khadhalayan, Castorhagi
Technology Level: High Middle Ages (cities), Dark Ages (rural area)

Khadhalaya is on the east-central coast of Jaati. Warm currents flowing from the south give this area some of the warmest climate in the region, which is reflected in the nearly tropical trees and crops that grow there. The small farmers of Khadhalaya grow plenty of food to support the cities and for export, along with cotton for fine muslin cloth. One of the country's most important products, though, is the teak wood grown on plantations around the Gengba River. It supplies the raw material for local craftspeople for the manufacture of furniture, chests, carved statues, and other fine products. The wood is also desired by builders and crafters outside of Khadhalaya. The easiest way to transport large pieces of wood or whole logs would be to send them down the river to Jalebas and on to Elogong. However, since all trade in Elogong is controlled by Castorhage's Far East Company, some producers do not believe they receive good prices there. The cost of land transportation to one of the smaller ports along the coast is also significant, though, so most end up just going through Elogong.

JALEBAS, CITY OF; CITY OF NINETEEN BRIDGES (CAPITAL)

Ruler: Nawab Hiranya Tolipur
Government: bureaucracy; city governor appointed by Rani
Population: 385,239 (258,670 Jaata, 105,230 ratfolk, 6,269 Castorhagi, 14,210 other human ethnicity, 860 other)

The capital of the Kingdom of Khadhalaya, Jalebas is one of the largest cities in Jaati. Within its walls may be found many temples and many marketplaces, with caravans from the north, south, and west passing through its gates.

Jalebas is built at the confluence of the Chetta River and its tributary the Gengba. Where they meet, the two rivers split into multiple streams before rejoining into the single Chetta past the city. As the city has grown, it has spread over the multiple islands formed by these streams, which has required 19 bridges to be built over the waters to connect the larger streets that run the length of more than one island. As this occurred over time, it is certainly unlikely that the pattern of bridges was conceived with any plan in mind. However, after the last one was constructed, a mapmaker discovered that it was possible to trace a path in the shapes of certain religious or lucky symbols by walking around the city and crossing the bridges in particular patterns. Since then, hundreds of pilgrims each week come to the city to "walk the symbols" in the hope of gaining favor from the gods, or to accrue luck, or to develop personal merit to advance on the coil in the next life.

This complicates the life of the city, because any obstruction on a street that is part of one of the "symbols" gives rise to angry complaints from the pilgrims. That in turn distresses the merchants who make good money selling food and remembrances to them. As a result, the administration has designated special patrols in different parts of the city to respond quickly in case a street becomes blocked. Repairs to the streets in the patterns must be done late at night (to avoid hampering the pilgrims) and most importantly, no more bridges can be built. When the city made plans to do just that about 30 years ago, people rioted in the streets because they claimed an additional bridge would ruin the patterns and bring ill luck for anyone who walked the streets. Since then, the city has continued to grow but residents must deal with any inconvenience in how far they must travel to cross the rivers.

ELOGONG, CITY OF

Ruler: Nawab (governor) Nephzu Laruri
Government: bureaucracy; city governor appointed by Rani
Population: 95,921 (68,900 Jaata, 21,100 ratfolk, 2,500 Castorhagi, 3,101 other human ethnicity, 320 other)

Elogong is a major port city at the mouth of the Chetta River in eastern Jaati. Due to the quantity of teak wood available from the interior of Khadhalaya, the city has many woodworkers who export many beautiful woodcarvings and furnishings. One specialty is pieces with inlaid patterns of ivory. Although their work is in great demand, the craftspeople of Elogong compete with the woodworkers of Chikheni for sales, and as a result both groups end up with prices lower than they might see otherwise.

The port of Elogong, and thus all its sea trade, is controlled (per contract) by the Far East Company of Castorhage. The company favors its own ships over those of other nations; traders from Khadhalaya do not even own ships because some previous rajah contracted all shipping of cargo — private as well as public — to the Castorhagi company. This policy has produced unrest before but, at least so far, without leading to any change. Recently, local traders, farmers, and craftspeople have become somewhat more agitated because they believe the Castorhagi are buying goods at significantly lower prices than others might be willing to pay, and charging much-higher prices for shipping. The second 99-year contract will be up in about three years, so the time for change may be coming.

However, some fear the Far East Company will attempt to renew its agreement by force. Sirdar Shardul Umswai, commanding general of the royal army, had been quietly conducting training exercises inland away from the notice of the foreigners, and increasing the number of recruits. Building his force has been a gradual process, however, as he also has to compete with the Far East Company, which recruits many young people of Khadhalaya's lower castes to train as soldiers and then travel to new and strange parts of the world as company guards. Since this experience could allow them to aspire to the caste of warriors upon their return, service to the company continues to attract many local youth.

KREY, PRINCIPALITY OF

Capital: Enfama
Ruler: Varambani Council currently led by Prince Ypaka Langlut, Defender of the Center
Government: council of five varambani (princes and defenders)

Population: 3,378,679 (3,226,218 Jaata, 114,832 ratfolk, 35,103 Castorhagi, 2,526 other)
Monstrous: lizardfolk, rakklethorn toad, giant owl
Languages: Merruwhan
Religion: Gohtra pantheon
Resources: cotton, muslin cloth, dyes, crops, livestock, trade
Currency: Kreyik, Castorhagi
Technology Level: High Middle Ages (Enfama), Dark Ages (rural areas), Medieval (Inurha Island)

The Principality of Krey is in northeast Jaati, north of the Surchal River. It is primarily agricultural country and grows many types of food and cotton for the production of fine muslin cloth. The country is ruled by a Council of five princes (called Defenders, or Varambani) in charge of the various geographic regions of the country. About 200 years ago, representatives of the Far East Company, a mercantile concern from the City-State of Castorhage, approached the council with a request to open a trade mission in the city of Enfama. Somewhat persuaded by the three heavily-armed ships in their harbor but not favorably impressed with the company's representatives, the Varambani Council declined their request to build their mission in the government sector of Enfama. Instead, with the excuse that the space would be too crowded for the company's needs, the council offered the foreigners space on the island of Inuhra.

Over the past decades, the Castorhagi Far East Company gradually took over all the land on Inuhra and for the past 10 or 12 years they have been pressing again for a plot of land — larger, this time — in the capital city of Enfama. Prince Hazzar-ash-Makesh, Defender of the West, is currently in Castorhage at the invitation of the Far East Company, ostensibly to conduct talks about an additional trade location. While Prince Hazzar usually goes to some lengths to keep his colleagues and the servants from becoming uncomfortable due to his appearance, he traveled to Castorhage in his true guise as a tiger-kin rakshasa with a retinue of his close relations. Apparently, this caused some consternation in the city and among the officials of the Far East Company, and the Varambani Council is waiting to hear how the negotiations are going.

Enfama, City of (Capital)

Ruler: Princess Kirana Naghavel, Defender of the East
Government: Varambani Council
Population: 148,632 (109,282 Jaata, 36,200 ratfolk, 2,050 Castorhagi, 1,100 other)

Enfama, the capital of the Principality of Krey, is a coastal city several miles north of the Surchal River in northeastern Jaati. Although not large as Jaata cities go, Enfama is a busy place and trades the area's agricultural products and livestock for transport to other cities in the region and to foreign merchants for export. Especially lively is the cloth market where spinners, weavers, and dyers of muslin make exchanges and purchasers bid on bulk sales. Enfama is also a religious center; sailors from the north and east coasts stop here to leave offerings at the temple of the noble deity Nagtel, god of rivers and oceans and the rains that fill them. Enfama has for centuries also been the meeting place of the ruling Varambani Council. This puts extra pressure on Princess Kirana, as she responsible for the welfare (and possible defense) of the city and for the safety of the council members and staff from other areas of the country.

Inurha Island

Ruler: Chief Factor Asonia Silvestre
Government: Castorhagi Far East Company
Population: 30,388 (24,100 Castorhagi, 4,820 Jaata, 1,220 ratfolk, 248 other)

Inurha Island is one of dozens of islands up and down the southeastern part of Krey and near the mouth of the Surchal River. At one time an additional dock area for trading ships, it is now entirely given over to the trade station of the Castorhagi Far East Company. The company has filled the island with docks, repair facilities, multistory warehouses, barracks, and elegant manor houses for the local company officers, all surrounded with defensive fortifications. The Far East Company uses the island as a primary trading facility and also as a storage and repair location for all the organization's ventures in the Jaati region. The docks at Inurha could hold more than enough vessels to entirely blockade the port at Enfama if that were the company's intention. The Varambani Council may or may not yet be aware of this risk, but the chief factor plans to point it out at an opportune moment.

Nyaslan, Kingdom of

Capital: Zuniu
Ruler: Shaasak Sesshaan
Government: dictatorship
Population: 1,860,838 (1,828,162 nagaji, 25,945 nagas, 6,531 other human ethnicity, 200 other [0 ratfolk])
Monstrous: tangtal, iron cobras, sepia snakes
Languages: Meeruwhan
Religion: Gohtra pantheon, especially Hassith-Kaa, The Great Serpent
Resources: crops, fruit, nuts, spices (no silk)
Currency: any country of Jaati
Technology Level: Dark Ages

The kingdom officially named Nyaslan is in the western part of Jaati in the thickly forested area between the Dhobe and the Mahur rivers. Almost no one outside the kingdom uses that name, though; nearly everyone calls it Nagaland. Ruled by the great Shaasak of Serpents, the country is an organized population of the magical, human-visaged snake-people. Sesshaan himself is unique in his country: a huge naga with five heads. Even those who disagree with him in many ways show him a great deal of respect.

Inhabited by many different types of nagas with different moral viewpoints and areas of interest, Nyaslan is as calm and united as most human kingdoms, which is to say, not all that much. The main topic on which the nagas do agree is that all nagas are superior to humanoids. Some view humanoids as useful servants; others consider them a source of food; while more benevolent nagas see them as lesser beings to be protected.

The most common servants in and around Nyaslan's cities are the ubiquitous nagaji, ophidian humanoids developed by ancient nagas specifically as a slave race. They venerate the nagas and even worship the Shaasak as a god. The nagaji do most of the work of the kingdom, generally only being allowed to pay enough attention to their own needs to continue to work efficiently for the nagas. Over the years, a few nagaji have broken away from their slavery and managed to escape, but those are few and far between. The nagas don't bother to hunt down escaped slaves, because they have plenty. Those who stay and upset the natural order, though, are dealt with harshly.

A few other humanoids also live in Nyaslan's cities and serve the nagas, though as servants or useful tools rather than as slaves. A few may even believe they are partners with nagas in something, but they eventually realize they are mistaken. Not all nagas have the ability to magically deceive or beguile humanoids, but the many that do have no qualms about using any means to gain the help they might need, or things they might desire.

The country of Nyaslan has good-quality soil and it is well watered, with many natural streams and pools for the convenience of the serpent-people. The nagas of Nyaslan do not confine themselves to the bounds of their country, either. Some travel through the thick forests to neighboring kingdoms to explore or to interfere. Others use the Mahur or Dhobe Rivers to swim far downstream to visit coastal cities or to travel elsewhere in Jaati.

Zuniu, City of (Capital)

Ruler: Shaasak Sesshaan
Government: dictatorship
Population: 124,055 (118,210 nagaji, 2,921 nagas, 2,844 other human ethnicity, 80 other [0 ratfolk])

The capital of Nyaslan, Zuniu lies just south of the Mahur River. The core of the city is constructed mostly of dark gray stone from the foothills in the western part of the country. The stone holds the warmth of the sun and many nagas bask on various ledges and perches much of the day. Paths are smooth, and upper levels are reached by ramps rather than stairs. Pools and canals are interspersed among the land routes for those nagas that prefer to travel by (or rest in) water. All these areas are maintained in top condition by the nagaji slaves for the enjoyment of their masters. Nagas generally transport themselves throughout the city, but some are pulled by nagaji in wheeled carts or carried in litters. Many nagas choose to live in buildings but others simply lair in grassy bowers or in ponds. The shaasak has a palace with public rooms that can hold crowds, but also private rooms with doors where he can store his valuable items or spend time in solitude.

Around the city's core is an area where merchants and craftspeople are allowed to trade with the nagas. Most of those trading in this area are humanoid, though a few nagas set up locations to offer knowledge or skills to other nagas. Outside that is the area where the humanoids live. This includes visitors, merchants, and servants on one side, and on the other side, the nagaji in their cramped wattle-and-daub huts. The entire focus of the city is on, first, the comfort and service of the shaasak and his people, and then the oversight of the entire country for the benefit of the nagas. The humanoids are useful tools that would be missed if they were unavailable, but their welfare is not considered in any plans by the nagas.

Six Pools of the Moon Maidens

In the deep forest outside Zuniu is a clearing. Here, a tower stands, apparently built for naga as it has a sloping ramp in front and no door. To this tower often come a group of observers: nagas with a fascination for the two moons, who study their movements and see in them indications of history or portents for the future. Even older than the tower are six pools in the clearing, outlined by circles of stone. The edges are cracked and overgrown with moss and weeds, and the pools choked with slime and algae.

Some of the nagaji, or perhaps one or two of the humanoids who serve the naga, may know the story: These six pools were made to honor six moon maidens. When the six pools each reflect the two moons side by side, the six maidens will return to dance again and grant the wish of any petitioner brave enough to join them.

Tola, Philosophical Kingdom of

Capital: Baragibra
Ruler: Scholar-Queen Yamini Onapurma
Government: monarchy
Population: 3,462,101 (3,042,386 Jaata, 418,337 ratfolk, 1,242 Castorhagi, 136 rakshasas)
Monstrous: lizardfolk, summoned outsiders, constructs
Languages: Merruwhan, Semuric, Westerling
Religion: Gohtra pantheon
Resources: silk, gold, platinum, other precious metals, knowledge, research, magic
Currency: Tolan, Castorhagi
Technology Level: High Middle Ages, Dark Ages (only isolated rural areas)

The Philosophical Kingdom of Tola on the northern coast of Libynos is a country that values the intellect above all things. Here, intelligent discussion and even lively debate are said to be always welcome. At least 11 colleges are located throughout the kingdom, and each city and town boasts a square where scholars and locals regularly meet to discuss issues of philosophy, science, ethics, and history.

On the other hand, the life of the mind does not put food on the table. The queen, although she prefers scholarly pursuits, is very realistic when it comes to ruling her kingdom. She knows that agriculture and trade, although largely physical, are crucial to the survival and well-being of her subjects. Fortunately, Tola is blessed with many natural resources, and the queen turns all of those — gold, platinum, other valuable ores, silk by the bale, and much more — to preserving her country, guarding it securely, and encouraging all the citizens to be educated enough that they can engage in research or experimentation of their own, no matter how rudimentary.

Diplomacy has also proven to play an important role in Tola, especially when dealing with representatives of the very down-to-earth City-State of Castorhage and its predatory Far East Company. The scholar-queen's chief minister, an unimpressive-looking fellow by the name of Eshaan Gabharu, has been able to outthink and fast-talk the Far East representatives in every encounter they have had in nearly 20 years. So successful has he been, in fact, that Queen Yamini has begun to worry that the company might try to have the chief minister assassinated so they don't have to deal with him anymore.

Baragibra, City of (Capital)

Ruler: Sages' Council
Government: council of sages (and other scholars), with consent of the queen
Population: 164,862 (134,735 Jaata, 29,690 ratfolk, 416 Castorhagi, 21 rakshasas)

Baragibra is well known as a home of sages and scholars, archivists and alchemists. Over the millennia, they have expanded the scope of the information they seek, from coveting all the knowledge of Jaati, to that of all of Libynos, to that of the entire world. Upkeep of the city tends to be a bit on the sloppy side, in part because the supervisors are more interested in their own personal research than maintenance, and also because the laborers themselves prefer to attend to projects of their own. This lack of attention extends to other mundane tasks as well; two eating houses have closed recently after patrons became severely ill, in one case because the cook tried an unsuccessful (and unwise) experiment with the food, and in the other because the cook failed to notice that the food being served was rotten.

However, the city takes fire very seriously. With so much valuable knowledge stored as paper or in other flammable forms, any out-of-control fire — even briefly — is a threat to everyone. Anyone who causes an accidental fire once is prohibited from future use of flames. The penalty for a second offense is exile. A third, should one ever occur, means death. Purposely setting an uncontrolled fire is punished by a long imprisonment; in that situation, death is the sentence for a second offense. Anyone with a treasured collection tries to get a magical fire suppressant of some type to protect their possessions in a worst-case scenario.

This fear of flames makes Baragibra's culture somewhat different than that of other Jaati cities. Businesses such as bakeries, blacksmiths, or laundries that use fire are all located in the "Stone Circle" — a district surrounded by stone walls where all the buildings are stone or brick and even the streets are paved. No trees or other plants are grown in the area. People who need to cook usually put something together in an iron pot and then pay a small amount to have it put in the side of the bakery's oven for the day. If one cannot afford the launderer's fee, one can at least rent a tub of heated water for an hour and so not need one's own fire. In another approach, some of the best inns for scholars have magical candles or stones that continually produce light or heat — one more way to avoid the risk of flames. In addition, for activities that might cause an explosion or have a strong risk of fire, a section of the ocean beach has been set aside. Small huts, constructed of stone transported for this purpose, offer experimenters a distant location as fire-resistant as possible.

The knowledgeable people of Baragibra worship many deities, but in general, a few are particularly revered by most of the population. One is Thindawl, a guardian who is the god of truth. Others are Jengpata, a noble deity who is the goddess of speech and wisdom, and the Istaflumina god Yenomesh, said to be the inventor of the written word, which is so important to the scholars of Baragibra.

The Academy of the Nine Great Wizards once stood inside the walls of Baragibra. The preeminent school of magic in the entire region, its training is restricted to those of the Great Wizard caste. It is run by a council of nine masters who hold chairs named for the academy's founders. It was not long after its establishment before the practice of certain spells and experimentation brought the masters and their students into conflict with the archivists and collectors of Baragibra. For several hundred years now, the academy has rejoiced in the ownership of an excellent, large stone building with surrounding gravel fields and stone walkways located just over two miles outside the west gate of Baragibra.

YAT-KIRMAN, KINGDOM OF

Capital: Goplakh
Ruler: Rao Indhragudem Zhawnvawn
Government: dictatorship
Population: 1,347,826 (1,342,266 Jaata, 4,871 rakshasas, 579 vishkanyas, 110 other [0 ratfolk])
Monstrous: cockatrices, pyrolisks, cobra flowers
Languages: Merruwhan
Religion: none
Resources: silk, crops, herd animals, spices
Currency: Kirmani
Technology Level: Dark Ages, High Middle Ages (Goplakh)

This country in the interior of the Jaati region is isolated by the deep gorge of the upper Dhobe River. Access appears to be completely cut off; from the east side of the river, all that can be seen are broken bridge abutments and mist rising from the river, obscuring the other side.

This is all an illusion, however, designed to better protect a kingdom that wants to be left alone. In reality, an elaborate stone bridge crosses the river, centuries old and narrow but strong. The far side of the bridge is heavily guarded, though the watchers are posted where they cannot be seen by those approaching. (After all, if the bridge is broken, there should be no need for armed guards.)

Yat-Kirman is ruled by a noble rakshasa who welcomes refugees from the caste system and even fugitives from "justice," as long as they can profitably contribute to the orderly welfare of the kingdom and the wealth of the rao. Thieves, brawlers, or others who would disturb the peace are not welcome and are ejected from the kingdom — though not necessarily at the bridge.

Citizens are expected to work hard to produce as much as possible to meet the kingdom's needs and to provide such trade goods as the rao may need to obtain things he desires that the kingdom cannot itself create. Although the residents of Yat-Kirman work hard, most are no doubt better off than they were in their homelands, and a lower population in Yat-Kirman means that the residents are not crowded together as much as in the great river cities. Even in Goplakh, most folk here have an opportunity to grow food for themselves, which is unheard of in the alleys and warrens of the large cities.

The power of the rao over the kingdom here is greater than what is seen in even the most dictatorial regimes in Jaati. For example, the rao has the right, over all residents of Yat-Kirman, to decide who is allowed to grow or make or buy or sell anything. He seldom interferes if all goes well, but if conflict arises, he often makes arbitrary decisions by which everyone must abide. Moreover, most religious activity is forbidden within the kingdom. Although the rao acknowledges the existence of gods and that they do have some degree of divine power, he rejects any authority they might have over himself, his domain, or his people. From the perspective of the rao, if his people wish to worship a divine figure, they may pray to him. The rao has not actually claimed himself divine, but there are those who point out that he has obviously ascended past the common souls still on the coil and thus must be a deity of some caste. (This is true, from a certain point of view.)

GOPLAKH, CITY OF (CAPITAL)

Ruler: Rao Indhragudem Zhawnvawn
Government: dictatorship
Population: 34,771 (33,286 Jaata; 1,330 rakshasas; 145 vishkanyas, 10 other [0 ratfolk])

The capital of Yat-Kirman, Goplakh sits not far from the Dhobe River gorge. It is a well-organized city with streets laid out in spokes with the royal palace at the center. Some residents live in houses made for only one family, though most live in multistory buildings with six residences or more. A market is distant enough from the palace that the rao is not disturbed by the noise. A few inns are allowed to operate, primarily for the convenience of locals acquiring prepared food and beverages. However, visitors do arrive from time to time, and the existence of inns quickly solves any question about where they may stay. Any work animals such as forest elephants or the rare horse are kept near the edge of the city in the direction that is usually downwind from the palace.

The people are reasonably happy, though the emphasis placed on keeping their rao satisfied at all times can cause them stress. One important responsibility of his people is keeping a supply of food for the rao to hunt when he gets hungry. He sometimes takes the form of a tiger to make his kills himself and then dines immediately. At other times, he orders a meal of 20 courses or more and eats with the sophistication of the greatest maharajah. Both of those options emphasize the power of the rao, though the first reminds local people of the likely negative consequences of ever angering their ruler.

Supplying servants for the rao's palace takes the efforts of many residents of Goplakh. In addition to food preparation, cleaning, guard duty, care of the royal menagerie, and other mundane tasks, he requires specialized servants such as archivists, translators, librarians, historians, musicians, artists, and others. Any who cannot be found already within his kingdom must be persuaded or, as a last resort, hired to do his bidding. Zhawnvawn also has a full complement of body servants for those times when he wants to be bathed or massaged, but several have scars, evidence of the rao's occasionally terrible temper.

The women of the rao's harem are technically not servants, though he often treats them as such. Most were brought from outside the country and may even have been slaves purchased for the rakshasa or kidnapped by his kinsmen. Zhawnvawn seldom chooses members of the harem from his own people, though some women persuade him to do so. It is known that one sure way to wealth and influence inside the kingdom is to bear one of his offspring and though his preferred mates seem to be other rakshasa, at least one or two women in every generation bear him children and survive to enjoy the prestige it brings.

GEOGRAPHIC FEATURES AND POINTS OF INTEREST IN JAATI

CHETTA RIVER

The Chetta River runs from the Ukshauka Hills southeast to the Celestean Sea, where the trade city of Elogong sits near the mouth of the river. Two tributaries draining from the same range of hills join it on its way to the sea: closer to the source (or to the north) is the Zema River, while the Gengba River flows into it farther downstream. The Chetta is the largest river in the Jaati region that flows east rather than north.

DHOBE RIVER

The Dhobe is the longest river in Jaati. It starts in the southeastern part of the Jungteran Mountains and flows north and a little east to the Great Ocean Ûthaf. In its upper reaches, the Dhobe runs through a steep gorge, but the rocky walls drop away as it is joined by the Laramis River and the land becomes lower and smoother, and also more easily flooded. The river itself widens a great deal in the lowlands and then divides and divides again into a number of distributaries as it approaches the sea.

The Dhobe is called the "Mother of Jaati" because it and all its little tributaries water so much of the region. In that way it is considered sacred to Eoya, the Mother, one of the thrones and fierce defender of her children. People dip themselves into the Dhobe River during rituals in the worship of Eoya. Also, as she is the Destroyer of Evil, submerging in the Dhobe is said to be a sure way to remove a curse. Towns and villages along its banks often have wide stairs that descend into the river to make it easier for people to dip themselves in the Dhobe.

Jungteran Mountains

The range of massive peaks running north and south on the western side of Jaati is the Jungteran Mountains, which are thought to be more than 1,000 miles long. The high altitude of the summits has given rise to several glaciers throughout the mountains; this permanent icecap on the range and moisture caught by the mountain peaks are the source of most of the rivers of Jaati. Many unusual species of animals are found in the high range and also farther south in the contiguous Zakros Mountains of Istaflumina. The Jungterans are so high and dangerous that the only people of Jaati said to have crossed them are the champions of the hero stories of old.

Laramis River

The Laramis River is generally considered to be the northern border of Yat-Kirman. The land drops abruptly at the river, which results in the south side of the river being a high, nearly impassible rock wall while the north bank is only a dozen feet higher than the river. (This results in flooding nearly every year during the spring thaw.) The walls of the gorge holding the Dhobe River also drop sharply at the confluence of the two rivers.

Mahur River

Flowing north through the foothills of the Jungteran Mountains, the Mahur is a strong river that travels nearly 400 miles before it pours into the Dhobe about 100 miles from the northern coast of Jaati. Its own tributaries, such as the Tusora, increase the water it carries. When the snow in the mountains melts in the spring, the Mahur and Tusora are the cause of many floods for at least 50 miles around its confluence with the Dhobe.

Surchal River

On the east side of Jaati, the Surchal River flows through the Principality of Krey to join the Great Ocean Ûthaf. It has its source in Lake Sura, the largest freshwater lake in Jaati.

Timabur River

The Timabur River is the most northern major river in Jaati. It runs east and a little south from the northern reaches of the Jungteran Mountains before turning to the north and flowing into the Great Ocean Ûthaf. The city of Baragibra sits near the mouth. The river's main tributary, the Mynsin, also comes from the mountains but runs northeasterly to join the Timabur about 50 miles from the coast.

Ukshauka Hills

This line of hills runs generally north and south, roughly 300 miles from the east coast of Jaati. It is responsible for sending the large Dhobe River on its northerly course, while providing a source for several smaller rivers that flow to the east. People who live west of the Ukshaukas, in the "shadow" of the high mountains or near rivers that run from them, generally consider the hills to be inconvenient to cross but not impressive. Coastal residents, however, who are used to the flatter lands to the east tend to regard the hills as a serious barrier and often do not consider crossing them for travel or trade.

Northern Wildlands

Bhitiram

On the west side of the Jungteran Mountains runs a long coastline 100 to 200 miles wide with towering trees, many over 300 feet high. They are so tall that shorter trees grow below them and small trees and bushes below those. The people of northern Jaati who have even heard of the area call it the Giant Coast because of the height of the trees. Tales told to children say the people and animals of the forest are as large as the trees. However, the area is generally considered to be uninhabited. People of Jaati do not travel there — a prohibition on traveling around the mountains is one of their oldest taboos — so that assumption has not been verified for many generations.

The climate to the west of the mountains is noticeably cooler than the climate of Jaati proper, and different types of trees grow well there. Giant redwoods are common in the moist, humid climate along the coast. Giant sequoia trees grow inland along the western slopes of the Jungteran Mountains. They are not so tall as the redwoods (though they can still reach over 300 feet), but in girth they far outdo the lower trees. Both types can live for millennia.

Unbeknownst to those on the eastern side of the mountains, the forests to the west are indeed inhabited, including by some humans. The people in Bhitiram are mostly worshippers and guardians of nature who for thousands of years have revered and cared for the giant trees. That is to say, they have assisted the giants living in the area to care for the ancient trees. These giants of the rainforest and woods generally stand two to three times the size of the human inhabitants, yet they are still tiny compared to the trees. Giants and humans live peacefully in villages near each other, or in some cases even in the same villages.

One strange thing about the populations of giants and humans in the area is that they tend to be shapeshifters. Many humans have the magical ability to change shape and use this to roam through the forests with more freedom than their two-legged forms would permit. Most giants, on the other hand, are some type of were-creatures. Werebears are the most prevalent, with boars also frequently encountered. Giants dwelling on the mountain slopes are often were-raptors and prefer the heights for their soaring wings.

Samundar Patranca

This coastline of northwestern Libynos, south of Bhitiram, is labeled Samundar Patranca on certain maps in the archives of the Ammuyad Caliphate, though the origin of the name is unknown. Neither those archives nor the records of the various seafaring peoples of the Sinnar Ocean seem to contain reports of visitors to these shores. Certainly, the desolate stretches between Samundar Patranca and the populated regions of Libynos discourage exploration. Perhaps the absence of information is due to the lack of travelers to this area, or the failure of any who have visited to return; or perhaps information has been suppressed for some reason as yet to be discovered.

The lands of Samundar Patranca are cooler and drier than in the rainforest to the northeast. The trees that are so prevalent along the coast and in the mountains toward the east become sparse, with little but patches of scrubland and rocks the farther one goes west.

Along these shores, colonies of penguins fill the sheltered bays. They can be heard for miles, if anyone is there to hear them. The waters offshore are often visited by sea lions and orcas, which come to feed on the penguins. The water birds do have allies, though; the coast is also home to many groups of selkies. The seal-people like to make pets of these birds that can swim with them, and frequently hunt the penguins' sea predators so the population is not threatened.

The selkies have enemies of their own at the border of their range. Farther to the west lives a great colony of crabpeople, and if the fishing becomes slim, competition for food may develop into open warfare.

On land, the landscape may be rough but it is well watered both by runoff from the mountains and by water from underground. Other than animals, the area is primarily populated by various types of water fey and some elemental creatures that live in the many freshwater pools and streams along the coast. In the hills and the mountains themselves are fey or elementals of the air, though they stay far from the great forests to the northeast; in no way do they want to come to the attention of the raptor shape-changers that live in the mountains there. This prevalence of fey creatures carries on farther south into the mountains; great disturbances of the past have uncovered molten lava there in open volcanoes. Far from the knowledge of any humans, twisted fire fey and elementals that enjoy the lava make themselves at home. These volcanoes have been quiet (but for a little smoke) for millennia, so hopefully the fire creatures will be content in their igneous homes and not feel a need to stir themselves to greater activity.

So far as anyone knows, no people have made homes along these shores or inland.

RUKMUBIR PENINSULA

The northwest corner of Libynos, stretching out to the Isthmus of Irkaina, this peninsula is a wild region with dry, stony soil; scouring winds; harsh, rainy winters; and parched summers. The soil is thin and sandy and does not support much plant life. Soldiers of the caliphate's Grand Army patrol here from time to time, but their horses will not eat the scrubby grasses of the area so they never stay long. The "dusty corner of Libynos," as they call it, has been largely uninhabited for as long as records have been kept in the caliphate. Explorers have reported the crumbled remains of ancient stone buildings, so there may have been some settlements made under the Assurians but the ruins are not enough for there to have been anything more than a few small towns. In recent years, some Northlanders have tried to settle in the extreme northwest corner of the peninsula but no one from the caliphate is aware of this.

HROLFSBERG, TOWN OF

Ruler: jarl appointed by the køenig of Hrolfland
Government: colony of Hrolfland
Population: 521 (Northlanders)

Hrolfsberg is a successful colony town on the Villr Shore of far northwestern Libynos, an important location for the Northlanders on a lucrative trade route.

REFERENCE SOURCE: NS10 THE BROKEN SHIELDWALL

VILLR SHORE

On the northwestern peninsula of Libynos, the most northwestern coast was named the Villr Shore (or "wild shore") by the Northlanders who explored and later settled it. The town of Hrolfsberg is located at its northwestern tip.

ANTIOCH CITY-STATES

Capital: none
Ruler: none
Government: varies
Population: 1,844,783 (1,835,017 Antiochian, 4,559 Ashurian, 3,694 Baalathite, 972 Khemitite, 419 other human ethnicity, 122 hill dwarf)
Monstrous: ravager beetles, giant ants (hills), gnolls, manticores (grasslands)
Languages: Antiochian
Religion: Hyperborean pantheon, Churches of Mah-Barek, Anumon
Resources: trade, fishing, hot springs, copper, iron, marble, sculptures, glass, porcelain, steel weapons, shipbuilding, tobacco, cabb'e,
Currency: Ammuyad, Parphelonian
Technology Level: Renaissance (Kinnereth, Mirsim, Shilon, Tarresh), Medieval (other city-states), High Middle Ages (rural areas)

The Antioch City-States are a league of trade cities in the warm plains and hill country between the northern shore of the Sea of Baal and the Scythirian Mountains to the northeast. The city-states have negotiated treaties and other mutual arrangements addressing such matters as the availability of raw materials, transportation, and the distribution of finished goods. The object of the arrangements is to coordinate the cities' mercantile activities and to minimize, as much as possible, the influence and control of outside countries or organizations. Internal conflicts are carefully concealed in order to better present a solid front to their trading partners and other outsiders.

For most of the Hyperborean era, these cities were a part of the empire and subject to its legal regime and trade policies. The empire's dominion over Libynos was broken when the undead Imperatrix Trystecce of Tircople was slain by Daan in 2584 I.R. Attempts by the cities at independence thereafter were only briefly successful, as the then-ascendant Ammuyad Caliphate quickly swept in to take advantage of the power vacuum left by the end of Hyperborea. After about 150 years, organized resistance began to grow in the city-states. Taking advantage of two years of plague in the caliphate, the cities ousted the local governors and installed their own leaders and defensive forces. At last, the Antioch City-States were free of outside domination and quickly arranged terms for an alliance for mutual defense and profit.

For the past several hundred years, the city-states have been renowned as leaders in the expansion and innovation of trade, from the sourcing of raw materials to the processes of refinement, as well as the manufacture and transportation of finished goods. Most people in the region learn to figure well as children, and the merchants have developed advanced methods of accounting for expenses and income in trade to be sure they maximize their profits. A large percentage of the population is literate, which fosters better communication over long distances as well as accurate recording of contractual agreements between parties. The money flowing into the region has also enabled some of the wealthiest merchants to sponsor musicians, artists, and philosophers, so the arts are flourishing in the city-states in parallel with its many crafts and trades.

The territory of the Antioch City-States extends in the northwest to where the Desert Wall meets the Sea of Baal, and in the southeast to the near shore of the Palena River, which defines the border with Baalthaaz. In the north and the east it reaches into the foothills of the Scythirian Mountains where the cities of Kinnereth, Mirsim, Shilon, and Shiamun hold sway. Somewhere beyond those cities is the border with the dwarven kingdom of Shamash Kush; while the boundary line may be ill-defined amid the hills, the dwarves firmly let trespassers know when they cross into dwarven lands.

The roads between the city-states are well-maintained and well-patrolled to ensure the safe and swift transport of raw materials and finished goods. The ships of the trading league are solidly built and well-armed, with plenty of marines for protection against the privateers of Numeda or the aggressive navy of neighboring Baalthaaz. As a general matter, the merchants of Antioch prefer to trade with other free cities such as Endhome or Bard's Gate but are willing to send their ships anywhere that is safe and profitable.

Most of the city-states are communal republics wherein the citizens of each city and its respective surroundings have sworn themselves to mutual defense. They also elect leaders or representatives to look after the business of the city-state, though this process takes several different forms throughout the region and sometimes wealthy families hold more power and influence than a strictly democratic system would suggest.

The primary religion of the Antioch City-States is the pantheon of the Hyperborean Empire, though some other deities of Libynos and even Foere also have a place. The desert religion of Mah-Barek, pressed strongly by the Ammuyad Caliphate during the period of its hegemony, continues to attract worshippers in the region. In particular, the low-key, charitable Church of Fatimashan is common, with its orphanages and hospitals in every major city and most towns. The more exuberant Church of Marwan is also accepted, though it has temples in few locations.

ANTIOCH, RUINS OF
Population: 0

The city of Antioch was named after Antiocham Solinius, an ancient Hyperborean trade official who first identified the cities of this region as being in a prime location for the development of specific commodities and goods and the expansion of trade, as a counterweight to the merchants of Khemit.

The city was built in a hilly area near an underground deposit of salt. Mining that salt was the basis for hundreds of years of prosperity until one day when a tremendous earthquake or possibly an explosion from somewhere in the mines rocked the city. It shook the foundations of the town and opened great rents in the earth. Much of the city literally crumbled into the salt mines below, and a huge portion of the population was killed. Many people simply fled, never to return. Eventually, a number of the more-determined survivors moved as a group farther into the hills to the little town of Peleth, where copper had recently been discovered. To this day, the ruins of Antioch are avoided as extremely dangerous, although other earthquakes in the past two millennia could have settled the loose stone by now.

ELNATHAN, CITY-STATE OF
Ruler: Podest Thuras Zinelloh of Ostegli
Government: podest and council
Population: 34,509 (almost all Antiochian)

Hot springs are common in the hill country of the Antioch City-States. Many towns and even villages among the hills boast a mineral spring if not an actual bathing house. Only the area of Elnathan, though, has genuine Hyperborean bathing houses built by the empire and conscientiously maintained ever since. The elaborate tile mosaics (both on the walls and in the pools), the steam rooms, and pools of various temperatures set the Great Baths of Elnathan far above those of any other hot springs of the region.

Millennia ago, a pilgrim road was built from the far west to the holy city of Tircople, and one of its last stages ran through the area that is now occupied by the Antioch City-States. After the growth of Elnathan, the pilgrim road was changed to pass through the city, which allowed tired

EASTERN LIBYNOS

Legend
Town or Village
City
Capital or Free City
Imperial Capital
Fortress or Citadel
Ruins
Place of Interest
Road
Trail or Unused Road
Mountain Pass
Battlefield

Four adventurers look upon the ruins of the holy city of Tircople on the Sacred Table.

and dirty worshippers of Muir a chance to rest and purify themselves before the final difficult trek into the mountains. Today, the pilgrim road is gone over most of its length, but the roads to Elnathan are of course still maintained as part of the city-states' systems. Modern travelers can easily get to the city itself to try the restorative properties of the mineral waters as well as other health benefits.

Under the Hyperborean Empire, Elnathan was a site where imperial merchants and officials in the area could go to relax. It was also a place for imperial soldiers to rest and relax during their long assignments far from home. It was an easy step from rest to recuperation, and the empire started sending injured soldiers (and sailors) here for treatments. Facilities were started to train more people to care for the affected personnel, which eventually developed into full-fledged colleges of healing. A single consolidated institution is active still, passing on thousands of years of accumulated knowledge. In addition, a line of healers began studying plants and herbal treatments from the local area, the Istaflumina region, and Jaati. They combined this research with the knowledge of Hyperborean specialists and expanded it even more. This Herbal House inside the Grand Academy of Life and Healing continues to collect information on plants in general and herbal remedies in particular from throughout the world, and those who know of it consider it one of the greatest repositories of plant information in Libynos, if not the whole world.

The highest authority in Elnathan is the podest (a title derived from the ancient Hyperborean word for "power"), who has nine elected consuls to advise her. The podest is most often nominated by the advisors but is voted on by the citizens. Given the podest's supreme power in the government, a neutral party is often desired and so the position frequently goes to a foreigner who is less likely to favor one guild or political faction above others. (Notable people from Ur are often chosen, as are people of Ifthaaz, for different reasons.) The podest serves a one-year term, though the position can possibly be renewed.

Religious observance in Elnathan is largely focused around deities of healing. In fact, at one time a great temple of healing was built where each deity could have a chapel and they could all be worshipped together. Even such compatible priesthoods still had significant differences, though, and it was not too long before individual temples were again built and the one-time temple became another building for the grand academy. The people of Elnathan worship such deities as Bablukar, Lord of the Golden Sword; Ceres, goddess of midwives as well as healing and home; Solanus, who gives the healing light of the sun; and Zadastha, a deity of Jaati who also embraces healing.

Near the Great Baths outside the city of Elnathan are some chapels devoted to other deities who do not focus on healing. One is to the goddess Kamien, the patron of both springs and travel. Another is to Muir, goddess of virtue, that dates back to when the pilgrim road was first diverted to Elnathan. Enameled copper medals with the name of the goddess, and miniature versions of her holy sword symbol, are still sold in the area to travelers.

KINNERETH, CITY-STATE OF

Ruler: Chief Magistrate Gregorio Luppi
Government: great council
Population: 44,916 (almost all Antiochian)

The northernmost of the Antioch City-States, Kinnereth is located in the hills to the north of the Gamberale River. It is best known for the beautiful porcelain made by its artisans. Not only is it fine and elegant, but due to the availability of special dyes from Jaati, Kinnereth porcelain is decorated with amazing colors seldom produced elsewhere, especially reds and purples. It is available in many shapes, from large tureens and pots for household use to dinnerware and flasks to tiles of various sizes to lidded boxes and tiny rouge pots. The various porcelain houses employ people not only to do the shaping and glazing of the many different items offered, but also scores (or even hundreds) of painters to decorate all those in a variety of patterns. Some craftspeople also produce heavier ceramics, but these are not shipped as widely as is the finer work; Kinnereth porcelain is found in wealthy households throughout the world. The long-time production and distribution of such fragile goods also necessitated the development of methods of transporting them safely over long distances. In conjunction with the merchants of Mirsim (who sell fine glassware), they have an excellent reputation for intact deliveries.

Kinnereth's government is handled by a great council consisting of 28 representatives elected from seven sections of the city and its area, with each section electing one person per year. The great council in turn elects a chief magistrate from among their number, usually for a four-year term.

The people of Kinnereth are not highly religious, but many do worship Sefagreth, god of trade and travel, as well as Yenomesh, god of knowledge, symbols, and magic. In addition, every town and village in this area has at least a shrine to Ceres as the goddess of community.

MIRSIM, CITY-STATE OF

Ruler: Caterina Cialdoni, Presiding Consul
Government: community council
Population: 43,674 (almost all Antiochian)

Sitting on the shore of Lake Valbruna, Mirsim is a colorful city with full windows of colored glass in civic buildings and the homes of the wealthy, and smaller hanging designs of bright glass in many windows. Some artists also seem to make a business of crafting mosaics of small glass chips, as they glitter from the walls of several buildings.

Glass-making is the focal business in Mirsim, and includes stained glass, mirrors, vessels, decorative items of many types, and, of course, window panes. The merchants have also devised excellent methods for shipping such breakable things, although debate still goes on over whether merely washed wool is best as padding or whether it needs to be carded as well.

Another related craft is enameling. The most popular items to enamel are those of copper from Peleth, such as jewelry and the iconic pot-and-cup sets used to prepare and serve cabb'e and other hot drinks. However, enameling is also done on glass items such as vases, containers, and decorative pieces, and of course on gold and silver jewelry and items. Enameled religious emblems from Mirsim were a traditional acquisition for travelers to the city of Tircople, and even though the pilgrim road is rarely traveled these days, devotional emblems for many deities are still made in the city.

Mirsim is governed by a community council of 18 consuls who are elected on a rotating basis of six each year to three-year terms. The presiding consul is elected separately to a four-year term, for a total of 19 council members.

The most-beloved deity in the area of Mirsim is Solanus, goddess of the sun, who shines on all the glass and makes the city beautiful. Also popular is the deity Rhiaan, goddess of air and travel, whose worship was brought from Jaati by merchant devotees. Others worshipped are Telophus, who has in his purview all the elements which go into the making of glass, and Thasizier, a god of protection as well as of magic. The Mah-Barek sect of Marwan has a temple here that is filled with color and song.

PELETH, CITY-STATE OF

Ruler: Banner Holder Orsina Torelli
Government: council of patricians
Population: 41,676 (almost all Antiochian)

The City-State of Peleth is best known for its production of copper and brass items. The area has a large open copper mine and other smaller mines that produce some copper and also zinc. The copper is used to make all sorts of items for trade from household goods to cabb'e pots and burners to pieces of jewelry. The brass made here is used for such things as musical instruments, locks and keys, astrolabes, vessels and fonts, and large cast decorative objects. In the past, metalmasters of Peleth have traded to places in Jaati for tin and thus made bronze, including casting monumental statues for the Hyperborean Empire. There has been little call for such monuments in the past millennium or more, though, so the current masters have no experience with that.

Although most of the initial smelting goes on nearer the mines, the city of Peleth is full of metalworkers, and the city usually smells strongly of smoke and hot metal. Despite the sometimes-uncomfortable atmosphere, the people are proud of their work and their city. Many buildings are ornamented with bright brass or rosy copper and fountains ring in metal basins. Some crafters work in partnership with enamelers in Mirsim to produce highly decorated base items (including jewelry) and then send them on to the enamelers to add color, thus increasing the value substantially.

The City-State of Peleth does have one quirk: for an area so full of fire and forges, it is remarkably intolerant of alchemists. Any person who seems to be an alchemist is likely to be met with remarks such as, "We don't serve your kind here" and "You'd be better off just getting out of the area altogether." If queried, citizens' responses include "They're just dangerous" and "Everyone knows they can't be trusted," although no one points to any specific proof.

The governance of Peleth is handled by a council of patricians. The various towns and guilds of the city-state nominate members who are educated, reliable, and local leaders or upstanding guild members, to a list of eligible persons. Every two months, nine people are chosen randomly from the list to serve as patricians. No one ever has to serve more than two months at a time, so this civil service is not too great a hardship on businesspeople. The list itself is refreshed every five years. The leader of the council is also chosen by lottery and is called the banner holder — literally the person in charge of the city's banner for the next two months. The banner holder has the right to represent the city-state by making proclamations, entering into agreements, and so on. Other offices are elected by the citizens.

The primary deity worshipped in the area of Peleth is Dre'uain, god of smiths and crafters. Another one is Note, who is a god of stringed instruments and music in general, and the instrument-makers often invoke him in their work and performances. The Church of Marwan (a sect of the Mah-Barek religion) also has a temple here that often features instrumental performances, both at the temple and impromptu ones in public locations.

SHIAMUN, CITY-STATE OF

Ruler: Marin Saltarellis, presiding member
Government: Consilium Sapientium
Population: 36,474 (almost all Antiochian)

Shiamun is located in the northwestern extent of the Scythirian Mountains. Its main source of wealth is iron found in several mines located in the area, and its top product is bars of processed iron traded to Tarresh for use by the steelcrafters in that city-state. As part of the price, Tarresh returns a certain amount of steelwork, so on average people in Shiamun are better armed than most. (This helps to keep people safe in a comparatively wild part of the city-states.) Shiamun does have some steel production of its own; while it does not turn out the high-quality weapons done in Tarresh, it provides the entire city-state area with good tools and affordable standard armor.

Transporting iron bars is easier than moving all the raw rock, so most of the processing is done near the mines rather than in the city of Shiamun itself. Most of those who work the iron or steel are in the city, so it has more than its share of forges and the sounds of the hammers ring out all day long.

The city-state is governed by the Consilium Sapientium, a council of the wise (the title was passed down from the Hyperborean Empire). The council has 27 members who are entirely re-elected every three years. Each year, the group elects one of its members to preside over its deliberations and, effectively, become the spokesperson for the city-state for that year.

The most prominent deity of Shiamun is Dre'uain, the gnomish god of smiths and metalworking. Along with him, shrines are built to the Libynosi elemental goddess Ninevah. Those more in the merchant professions, or in charge of relations with the hill dwarves, tend to worship Sefagreth, the god of commerce, and Anumon, a god of protection and travel whose worship was introduced from Numeda a few centuries ago. They may also call on Zadastha, who grants aid to those needing personal charisma or help in diplomacy.

SHILON, CITY-STATE OF

Ruler: Podest Tishri Vizqorseh
Government: podest and great council
Population: 39,511 (almost all Antiochian)

This city-state's area is primarily in the high foothills of the Scythirian Mountains, at the edge of Shamash Kush, where two large marble quarries are maintained. One is a surface quarry along the sides of several tall hills, where the revealed light marble stands out among the dark trees. Switchback roads allow workers and wagons to travel up and down to cut the great pieces of marble and then bring them down from their high locations. This is called the Kileab Quarry, after the village at the base of the earliest hillside quarry.

The other is called the Doffi Quarry, and it is entirely underground. It has the same switchback roads, and a village at the base of a hill, but little else on the surface indicates the existence of a quarry there. Underground, though, the quarry has branches, turns, and drops that take it over a mile deep inside the hill.

Given the proximity of all that marble, Shilon is also home to many sculptors. In the days of the Hyperborean Empire, some of the best sculptors in the world lived and worked in the city-state. They produced large statues, busts of kings, architectural carvings, and many other elegant works in marble. In fact, Shilon developed one of the few arts academies in the world whose teaching is primarily sculpture, with drawing and painting receiving less emphasis. The Antioch Academy of Sculpture and Arts also has a sculpture museum that includes examples of antique marble statuary and items from Khemit, Jaati, and other places. Today, in addition to plain marble as well as sculptures being sold around the world, marble from other places is transported to the academy to be carved by the master sculptors there.

Shilon is close to the dwarven kingdom of Shamash Kush, and the depth of the Doffi Quarry has fueled rumors of a connection between the two, though nothing certain has been proven. In general, relations with the dwarves are good, and from time to time the people of the city-states and Shamash Kush have been known to cooperate where their interests align.

The city-state is governed by a podest (or "power"). He oversees a great council of 17 representatives elected from various districts of the city-state to communicate and implement the podest's plans. The great councilors in turn elect six of their number to form a minor council that directly advises the podest. The podest serves a one-year term, though the position can possibly be renewed; he is most often nominated by the advisors but is voted on by the citizens. Given the podest's supreme power in the government, a neutral party is often desired, and so the position frequently goes to a foreigner who is less likely to favor one guild or political faction above others. Notable people from Ur or Ifthaaz are often chosen; the current podest is from Gibbathon in eastern Ifthaaz.

The people of Shilon worship several deities whose aspects include knowledge or art such as Yenomesh, Thyr, Jamboor, and Dre'uain. The Mah-Barek sect of Marwan is also very active here, worshipping with colorful paintings, displays of what they call "living sculptures," and even demonstrative dance.

TARRESH, CITY-STATE OF

Ruler: Banner Holder
Government: council of citizens
Population: 59,275 (almost all Antiochian)

The City-State of Tarresh is situated near the mouth of the Gamberale River. It is the most populous of the city-states and has the largest city. Outsiders sometimes consider Tarresh to be the "capital of Antioch," though anyone from the other city-states will disagree. Tarresh is known for its steelwork and weaponsmithing, especially the superb quality of its blades. Its only rival in Libynos is the city of Cadua in Alcaldar, which is also known to do some good work.

The city-state gets almost all its iron directly from Shiamun, and as part of the price returns a certain amount of steelwork to that mountain city. Most of what flows back is in common daggers and long or short swords, but those "common" weapons are of a quality higher than what many nobles in distant Akados can ever boast.

In addition to the weaponsmithing, Tarresh has a large and active harbor, the largest in the city-states. Ships from Akados and other parts of Libynos usually come here to trade unless their owners are more interested in agricultural goods, in which case they go to Turkad.

The government of Tarresh is handled by a council of citizens. The various towns and guilds of the city-state nominate members who are upstanding guild members, businesspeople, or leaders in their communities. They must also be educated, reliable, and financially sound. The names are placed on a list of eligible persons and, every two months, nine people are chosen randomly from the list to serve as council members. No one ever has to serve more than two months at a time, so this civil service is not too great a hardship on businesspeople. The list itself is refreshed every five years. The leader of the council is also chosen by lottery and is called the banner holder — literally the person in charge of the city's banner for the next two months. The banner holder has the right to represent the city-state by making proclamations, entering into agreements, and so on. Other offices are elected by all the citizens.

With so many weapon-makers, the city of Tarresh is also a center for warriors, with mercenary groups coming here to bargain and train, and many individual fighters coming and going. All these have made the temple of Mithras, the warriors' god, one of the most popular in the city. Vanitthu is another militaristic god with a good following and even the rough Thursis, god of destruction in battle, has enough devotees for a chapel in an out-of-the-way quarter. The merchants and traders, on the other hand, favor Sefagreth, patron of trade and commerce but also a god of travel, and of luck. Alongside him, they also worship Quell, the Akadian god of the sea.

TURKAD, CITY-STATE OF

Ruler: Chief Magistrate Psalome Sfondrati
Government: chief magistrate and great council
Population: 52,228 (almost all Antiochian)

The City-State of Turkad is the southernmost of the Antioch City-States, sitting a few miles north of the mouth of the Palena River that serves as the border with Baalthaaz, and controlling a large area inland. The main product of the Turkad region is tobacco. It is grown on great plantations and processed, then boxed or baled and shipped out of the city's port. Most tobacco produced here is the common type known locally as Libynos Blue. However, certain areas with favorable soils may instead grow the Numedan Blond or other varieties.

In order to produce this important crop as inexpensively as possible, Turkad enlists convicted criminals as workers. Citizens of the city-states are forbidden to own slaves, so convict labor is the next best thing. When criminals in the Antioch region are sentenced to hard labor, in some places it means hauling mine tailings or scooping and sorting stone chips. In Turkad, it means working the plantations. Convict labor is so valuable to Turkad, in fact, that judges are sometimes suspected of increasing (or decreasing) sentences to hard labor for the benefit of plantation owners.

Another popular trade good from Turkad is cabb'e. Cabb'e is made from tree seeds (known as "beans") harvested in Far Jaati, transported by ship to Ur then by dwarven caravan through the underground kingdom of Shamash Kush, and finally down the Palena River to Turkad. These beans are roasted by a process which the Brewers' Guild teaches to only a select few, and used to brew a dark, strong drink that is popular throughout the city-states and many neighboring countries. Surprisingly, Turkad's cabb'e is also popular in the City-State of Castorhage, which is almost all the way around the world. Castorhage is known to have colonies right in Jaati, and rumor says some people have been experimenting with roasting their own beans, but despite this they keep returning to Turkad to buy their cabb'e, as well as the mechanical grinders sold to reduce the roasted beans to an easily brewable state and the enameled copper pots, cups, and burners to actually boil the liquid.

Shipbuilding is another important industry in Turkad. The same tall trees grown in Baalthaaz and used for ship's masts and planking also grow in the southern part of the Antioch City-States. The great logs are transported to the Palena River and floated down to Turkad. Unlike in Baalthaaz, the wood is not traded outside the region. Instead, shipbuilders use it in great yards along the coast to build the merchant vessels and occasional other ships needed by the city-states.

The City-State of Turkad is governed by a chief magistrate and a great council of 25 members who serve for five years each. Council members are elected by the citizens from a slate of nominees proposed by the council. The chief magistrate serves until she is subjected to a vote of no confidence by the council members, at which time they elect one of their own to serve as the new chief magistrate.

In the area of Turkad, the god Telophus, Lord of Crops, is very important to the many products for trade. Other deities worshipped include those who favor travel, such as Kamien of the Rivers; Rhiaan, a Gohtra deity of birds and more; Sefagreth, the god of trade and travel; and Anumon of the Numedans, protector of travelers and the law.

GEOGRAPHIC FEATURES AND POINTS OF INTEREST IN THE ANTIOCH CITY-STATES

GAMBERALE RIVER

This river flows west and southwest from the hills of Shamash Kush through some of the most-populated areas of the Antioch City-States. It flows into the Sea of Baal, and the city of Tarresh sits on its north bank at the mouth of the river.

LAKE VALBRUNA

This large lake, biggest of the multitude of lakes in the Antioch City-States, is in the north-central part of the city-states; a small river connects the lake to the Gamberale River. The city of Mirsim is located on its southeastern shore.

PALENA RIVER

The Palena River flows southwest out of the northwestern part of the Scythirian Mountains into the Sea of Baal. It is the southern border of the Antioch City-States and divides that area from the Kingdom of Baalthaaz. The city of Turkad is on the northern bank of the river where it enters the sea.

SHAMASH KUSH, DWARVEN KINGDOM OF

Capital: unknown
Ruler: King Gedek VII, "The Hammer"
Government: monarchy
Population: unknown
Monstrous: gnolls, lupins (surface), lizardfolk (coast)
Languages: Dwarven
Religion: dwarven deities
Resources: trade
Currency: Shamish; Parphelonian used in trade
Technology Level: unknown

This strong kingdom of hill dwarves is located northeast of the Antioch City-States and southwest of the Gulf of Ur. They claim a large area of the northern foothills of the Scythirian Mountains and occasionally have border disputes with the city-states when those expand too far in the direction of the kingdom.

The dwarves are not entirely isolationist and do trade with the humans in the surrounding areas. For many generations, they preferred the humans to come to them, but just recently (in the last 200 years or so), dwarven traders have gone out seeking to buy and sell for themselves. In part, this is a response to a few unscrupulous humans who didn't give fair value for dwarven goods. More than that, though, it is a conscious policy to be more aware of what is going on in the world outside the dwarves' sturdy but rather restrictive walls.

The hill dwarves have two towns — locations where they allow humans to enter and trade. In the direction of Ur is the underground market town known as Ark-Nazm, and in the southwest toward Shiamun is Onz-Khadam. The towns are similarly constructed, with great defensive gates and fortifications, an entry cavern (with stabling for merchants' animals), and another strong inner gate. Through that is a long passage into the hill to an open area with booths and even wooden buildings — the trading town itself. Those going there, though, should remember that even when friendly, these dwarves are never off their guard.

One merchant, on his first visit, spent two days in cordial and profitable trading. As he described later, he was leaving when he was horrified to discover that the roof of the long tunnel — which appeared so solid from beneath — was actually nothing but a slab holding up tons of loose rock that could become a deadfall trap at any time. The dwarves of Shamash Kush made no effort to hide the trap from those in the market town; it was clearly visible from the inside of the trading cavern as he approached the tunnel again. It is details like this that remind humans that the dwarves can get along without them just fine and are prepared to do so at any moment.

BAALTHAAZ, IFTHAAZ, AND THE SEA OF BAAL

BAALTHAAZ, THE FIVE CITIES OF

Capital: Perazim
Notable Settlements: Eshcol, Laishah, Zephathel, Zeruin
Ruler: High King Zimri
Government: monarchy
Population: 1,663,331 (1,657,007 Baalathite, 3,297 Ashurian, 2,849 Antiochian, 178 Khemitite)
Monstrous: gnolls, pegasi (plains), giant ants, flame drakes (hills)
Languages: Baalathite

Religion: Kehna pantheon
Resources: crops, wine, fish, tobacco, cedar wood, finished cedar
goods, pine ship masts, shipbuilding, weapons and armor, trade
Currency: Baalathite, Ammuyad
Technology Level: High Middle Ages, Medieval (Perazim)

The country of Baalthaaz is on the warm eastern coast of the Sea of Baal, north of Ifthaaz and south of the Antioch City-States. Once a group of separate city-states, it has long been unified into a single kingdom but some of the previous independence persists. Together they are known as the Five Cities, and are ruled by the Five Crowns. In order of founding, the cities are: Perazim, Laishah, Eshcol, Zephathel, and Zeruin. The country is hilly but fertile, when plenty of rain comes.

In fact, the fertility and productive capability of the land (and sea) are the major focus of the Baalathite religious observances. Although many new deities have been introduced to the coast of the Sea of Baal in the past few millennia — the Hyperborean deities, Mah-Barek, Anumon — the people of Baalthaaz (and Ifthaaz) hold strongly to the ancient Kehna pantheon. They attribute the continued prosperity of their lands to this constancy and continue to make worship of their gods the center of their culture.

The people of Baalthaaz tend to make bragging claims about their ancestry, many of which can neither be proven nor disproven. They say they are descended from the Sea Peoples, ancient explorers who sailed the coasts of Libynos and beyond. This may be true; no records exist that would show this, but within the region the Sea Peoples are generally thought to have originated in the eastern part of what is now the Sea of Baal.

The Baalathites also claim that in ages past, angels and demigods found their men and women so beautiful that the divine beings left the palace of Illion, King of the Gods, and instead resided for a while on Boros where they took humans as their spouses. That may be truth or legend, but it is certain that from time to time people of Baalthaaz demonstrate exceptional height, strength, beauty, or aptitudes.

Baalthaaz is primarily an agricultural country, with some other industries. Many areas have excellent vineyards, so much wine is produced, some of which is exported.

The most important exports of Baalthaaz, however, are its trees. The eastern hills and mountains have tall pines grown specifically for ship masts and great cedars that are harvested for their strong and fragrant wood. The foresters of Laishah and Zeruin are very particular about the trees for masts; these take regular cultivation and years to develop, so only a limited number are available each year. The Five Crowns of Baalthaaz always have a list of countries or shipbuilding companies that are waiting to receive masts, and can sometimes be influenced to move one up (or down) the list.

Influence is a large feature of both business and government in Baalthaaz, and bribery and extortion are common. Officially, neither is condoned but it hard for an individual to raise a large enough fuss to have a minor government bureaucrat disciplined, much less a powerful person censured. Power, achieved by any means possible, is the general goal of individuals in Baalthaaz.

When the Hyperboreans conquered the five kingdoms that later became the country of Baalthaaz, they deplored the decadent way of life and what they saw as the personal immorality of the people of the area. The bribery and buying of influence were also offensive to the majority of the Hyperboreans, although even in imperial service there were always a few people willing to enrich themselves. Attempts to transplant the Hyperborean deities were a failure; temples were built, but no one ever attended them except the few Hyperboreans in the area. The Baalathites were willing to concede that the deities of the Hyperboreans were real; those gods simply had nothing to do with the people of the Five Cities, who stayed true to their own pantheon. With the building of Tircople, the Hyperboreans levied heavy taxes on the region in the form of foodstuffs to support the city, but in general the Five Cities experienced little hardship during the hegemony of the Hyperborean Empire. As the empire declined and abandoned fortresses in the quiet central areas of its jurisdiction, the various crowns took control. Those fortresses saw a great deal of use in the struggles for supremacy among the Five Crowns, but today mostly lie in ruins.

ESHCOL, CITY OF

Ruler: Queen Talmaia
Government: monarchy
Population: 46,681 (almost all Baalathite)

Eshcol is a port in northwestern Baalthaaz, a few miles south of the Palena River that marks the northern border of the country. The river between Baalthaaz and the City-State of Turkad is supposed to be a neutral area so vessels are (in general) allowed to pass unmolested. Cedar is transported from the area of Zeruin, both as planks of wood and as finished wood products, and logs for the masts of ships come down the Palena tied together as rafts. Sitting on the edge of a large farming region, Eshcol also ships out a lot of agricultural products such as food grown for export and wine from the central hills.

In the flat lands along the Palena River, farmers cultivate tobacco. Most is used inside the country rather than sold in foreign trade and locals are more willing to experiment so more varieties are grown, including some that have stronger or different effects than the plantation tobacco produced by the bale around Turkad to the north.

The city is home to several successful commercial fishing operations, and sells fish to interior towns as well as exporting many varieties of smoked or preserved seafood. The devout people of Eshcol attribute this to the presence in their midst of the high temple of Dagon, god of the sea. The temple is built on piles in the harbor and at high tide seems to float on the surface of the water. Inside, a great statue of the fish-tailed deity stands on a platform behind a bronze altar. Smoke from the burning of offerings rises through many small openings near the roof and wafts out over the city. These offerings are usually land animals, but may also be land birds.

Another method of sacrifice is to take a creature out on a boat into deep water, truss it up, and drop it into the sea; the larger, more intelligent, or more exotic the creature, the more it is hoped Dagon will value the sacrifice. When a fishing boat puts to sea with a dog or goat aboard, it is likely the crew is planning on this sort of offering. If the boat carries a sheep or calf, it probably means the owner has severely offended the deity and is trying to make reparations before a tragedy occurs. Foreigners do occasionally disappear from the dock area, but no one has ever proven one of the fishermen (or the priests of Dagon) is responsible.

Other than the large temple to Dagon, the city also has the usual temples to Baal and to Athera, and many shrines or small chapels to various of the Seventy Gracious Gods. The queen also has a personal shrine to Illion inside her palace.

Queen Talmaia rules her city and its area with a tight grip. Her beautiful speaking voice tends to make people want to agree with her, because everything she says sounds pleasing and reasonable. Even her own advisors sometimes have trouble disagreeing with her because her voice distracts people from their thoughts. The queen is known to be diplomatic, but also ruthless with enemies and competitors.

LAISHAH, CITY OF

Ruler: Queen Hacalia
Government: monarchy
Population: 44,985 (almost all Baalathite)

Laishah is a city in eastern Baalthaaz, up the Zanosh River from the capital of Perazim where the river is joined by one of its tributaries. The area around Laishah produces ship masts and cedar wood, and forestry is one of the region's most common occupations. Another is mining; the foothills of the high Scythirian Mountains have a great deal of mineral wealth. The city takes in the smelted metals or raw materials, and sends much of it downriver as finished products. The city of Laishah is known inside the country for producing good weapons and armor, but the wealthy prefer to purchase theirs from Tarresh, one of the Antioch City-States.

Laishah has its quota of temples to the major deities and shrines to many of the Seventy Gracious Gods, but it also has one most cities lack. In the hills outside the city stands a major temple to Agamid, god of fire, who in most places is represented only by a small, out-of-the-way temple or shrine. Rumor claims that Queen Hacalia is a devotee of this uncomfortable deity, and that this is one source of her personal influence and wealth. The motto of the priests of Agamid is that "great power requires great sacrifice," and Agamid demands blood — that of a thinking being and preferably with a long life ahead of it, which is cut short. Not many people are willing to make the sacrifices required by the deity, but in times of great trouble in Baalthaaz, the crowns have been known to come to Laishah ready to sacrifice whoever is necessary to protect the country.

Queen Hacalia has firm control of her region of the kingdom, but she is widely known for her beauty. Taller than many men, she has rare golden-blonde hair that falls in ringlets about her shoulders, and eyes the blue of gathering storm clouds. Rumor says that she is always on the lookout for a new man who can stand up to her, to replace her current fancy.

Perazim, City of (Capital)

Ruler: High King Zimri
Government: monarchy
Population: 84,222 (almost all Baalathite)

The capital of Baalthaaz, the decadent city of Perazim sits on the coast of the Sea of Baal at the mouth of the Zanosh River. The largest city in the country, it also boasts the largest harbor of the Five Cities, so much of the country's trade passes through its wharves. The harbor is also home to a series of busy shipyards; while most navies buy their raw material from Baalthaaz and build their ships themselves, commercial purchasers would rather just pay for a completed vessel and the shipbuilders here are happy to oblige. There are enough eager customers along the coast of the Sea of Baal to keep the yards full all the time.

Most of the produce from the agricultural region around Perazim goes to feed the people of the city and the sizable military forces stationed there. Ostensibly for national defense, the standing army first and foremost protects the capital and the high king against possible attacks by one or more of the other crowns. Baalthaaz has been unified for centuries, but the high throne does not always pass peacefully from parent to child. Perazim has wide gates to welcome trade and travelers, but its walls are high and strongly fortified. Unbeknownst to most, the city has extensive stores in case of a siege and quantities of simple weapons available to arm the citizens. The current high king actually listened to the history taught by his tutor and vowed not to make the mistakes made by the people his ancestors defeated for the high throne.

The navy of Baalthaaz protects Perazim against attacks from the sea, guards the country's shipping (against acknowledged pirates as well as the Numedan privateers), and collects a fee from other vessels to let them pass unmolested. The navy patrols up to about 100 miles off the coast and keeps the Numedans out of that area; in return, they feel entitled to a gratuity from any ships they find sailing in their area of protection. The fee is steep, but since it is still considerably less than the amount that would be taken by the Numedan privateers (which would be everything), most ships grudgingly pay it.

Within the city of Perazim is the high temple of Baal. It is a great pillared building entered up a long flight of wide steps, and each day at dawn and at sunset the great pairs of kettledrums ring out from the broad porch at the top, praising the god of storms and battle. However, Baal is also Lord of the Earth, whose rains water the ground and bring fertility to the land. Men throughout the country worship that aspect of the god by taking their turns in his temple; masked in the guise of the deity, they act as his representatives and engage in ritual prostitution with women who come to worship Baal, their own faces masked to emphasize the religious rather than personal nature of the interaction.

Illion, King of the Gods, also has a temple in Perazim. He is generally honored in shrines within each crown's palace, as rulers and judges are those who most owe him homage, but the city of Perazim has the one temple that anyone can attend to try to entreat a favor of the distant god. The tasteful building is made of gray stone in a reserved style. A few priests, generally known for their wisdom, live in the edifice and are in charge of the occasional sacrifices. They spend the rest of their time studying the books of the national archives, which are kept in the library of Illion's high temple.

The goddess Athera, of course, has a large and busy temple in Perazim but her high temple is actually in Zephathel. Dagon, god of the sea, is worshipped at a temple at the harbor. The building is surrounded by a moat connected to the ocean, so the waterway is usually full of fish. Rumor claims that the streets of smithies and metalworkers have a hidden chapel to Agamid, the evil god of fire, but he has no official temple in the city. Scattered everywhere, it seems, are shrines and chapels to various of the Seventy Gracious Gods. Ift (Last of the Seventy and the patron of Ifthaaz) actually has a temple, but it is located in the foreign quarter and so is out of mind to most people of the city.

Zephathel, City of

Ruler: King Reshiem
Government: monarchy
Population: 66,679 (almost all Baalathite)

The city of Zephathel is in central Baalthaaz on the Zanosh River about halfway between the seacoast and the Scythirian Mountains. Its region is the most productive of the entire country, with fields full of several types of grain and vineyards bursting with luscious grapes, source of some of the best wines in a thousand miles. Many bottles of wine are exported, most through the port of Perazim. However, some wine and foodstuffs are shipped upriver to Laishah, where they are traded with merchants coming down the Zanosh from the other side of the Scythirian Mountains who are willing to pay a premium for high-quality goods.

Zephathel has a prominent temple to Baal, a large temple to fish-tailed Dagon in his aspect of provider of grain, and of course chapels and shrines to many of the Seventy. The greatest feature of the temple quarter, though, is the beautiful high temple of Athera, consort of Illion and goddess of fertility. Her participation in the ongoing fruitfulness of the land is incredibly important to Baalthaaz, and accordingly all citizens are expected to actively engage in her worship. Garlands of flowers and ribbons wrap the tall freestanding pillars at the top of the exterior stairs and services are held each afternoon and evening involving entrancing singing in parts and exotic dancing by trained priestesses.

Outside the cities, worship of Athera throughout Baalthaaz (joined with that of Baal as Lord of the Earth) generally takes place in the countryside near such fields as the gods are asked to bless. A tall pole is erected on a hilltop or in a grove, and votaries kiss it, bedeck it with flowers, and leave fruits (such as apples, oranges, or pears) at its base. Couples — even married ones — frequently engage in personal offerings at these locations.

Reshiem, king of Zephathel, is somewhat taller than most men but broad and very strong; his highly muscled torso, arms, and legs are emphasized by his usual mode of dress in a golden pectoral piece, crimson cloak, and heavily-embroidered kilt. Such a man is obviously expected to be a warrior, which he is, but Reshiem is also a strategist and a diplomat; when his deep voice speaks softly, people listen to what he has to say.

Zeruin, City of

Ruler: King Shabbethai
Government: monarchy
Population: 39,553 (almost all Baalathite)

Zeruin is in northern Baalthaaz on the Dura River, a tributary of the Palena. It sits in the foothills of the Scythirian Mountains at a higher altitude than most of the country. Goods are shipped down the Palena River to the port of Eshcol, just a few miles south of the river's mouth. The Palena is the official border between the country of Baalthaaz and the northern city-states of Shiamun and Turkad and so (officially) neutral territory.

The most important products of the Zeruin region are trees — tall pines for ship masts and cedars for a variety of uses. Forestry is a much-honored profession, and the men and women who cultivate the great trees and select those for harvesting are generally considered both knowledgeable and wise. Sometimes the crowns try to influence them to increase the harvest, but except in times of war the foresters have not allowed overcutting in many generations. The area around Zeruin has many excellent carpenters and woodcarvers who craft finished products from the cedar, but much is also exported as lumber.

The lord of the earth and lady of fertility are worshipped in this tree-growing area as strongly as in any of the lower agricultural regions. The city and towns have the usual temples and shrines. However, the foresters raise a pole to Athera and Baal in every grove that is planted and perform fertility rituals to call the favor of the deities to the new trees. Dagon, as god of grain, has a small temple in Zeruin and is worshipped in the farming communities in the region; chapels and shrines to many of the Seventy can also be found throughout the area.

King Shabbethai appears fit for a man of middle age, but other than that he seems to be nothing out of the ordinary physically. People give him great deference, though, and the high king consults him frequently for his advice. King Shabbethai claims to be descended from angels and it seems this might be true, as his insight into people is almost frightening. He is said to be impossible to deceive, because even as one lies to him, the person's body shouts their falsehood in many tiny ways and he notices every one.

IFTHAAZ

Capital: Ostegli

Notable Settlements: Arbel, Bicri, Diblatham, Ephron, Gammad, Gibbathon, Hamor

Ruler: Sopira, Great Matriarch of Ifthaaz

Government: ruling council

Population: 1,447,097 (1,442,033 Baalathite; 2,785 Ashurian; 2,193 Antiochian; 86 Khemitite)

Monstrous: ankhegs (plains), gnolls, hobgoblins, velvet ants (hills)

Languages: Baalathite

Religion: Kehna pantheon

Resources: cork, wine, crops, herd animals, dyes, dyed cotton cloth, poppy syrup, bardic school, translators, mining, weapons, trade

Currency: Baalathite, Ammuyad

Technology Level: Medieval (cities), High Middle Ages (smaller towns and rural areas)

The country of Ifthaaz lies on the eastern shore of the Sea of Baal, north of Numeda and south of Baalthaaz. It claims all of the Nerodim Hills to the north, and to the south, the portion of the Taanach Hills north of the Erto River.

Ifthaaz enjoys some of the best climate in the area, with sea breezes warming and watering its fertile fields. This is essential to the country, because most of the inhabitants prefer to live in cities, and the fertility of the land makes it possible to support the population with fewer farmers than might be necessary in other places. Inland are the open lands where the cork oaks grow; the country of Ifthaaz produces the cork to stop the wine bottles of fully half the world. In the hills are vineyards where the Ifthazites produce the country's own wine and lay claim to a good share of those corks. To the east, the land rises to the high Scythirian Mountains, which provide mineral resources.

Ifthaaz is not necessarily a powerful country, but it is subtly supported by Baalthaaz, which sees it as a buffer against Numeda. The country's patron deity is a god of thieves and treachery, and most outsiders view the entirety of its people as liars and cheats. They don't cheat everyone, though; they are very reliable to their own groups. Family over others, countrymen over strangers; contracts are rare but inviolable.

All business here depends on the payment of gratuities. While it is considered rude to ask for one, it is very rude (or insulting, depending on the circumstances) not to offer. Only the crudest, lowest boors would demand a consideration, and if they did, a knowledgeable businessperson would probably turn them down. A slightly less rude person might hint. A powerful boss never even mentions it, but very likely refuses to treat with anyone not offering. A brash assistant might point out that gifting the boss is a good idea. A really suave assistant would get the message across without saying it. Ifthazites give foreigners a chance to learn the expectations, but they are expected to learn quickly.

Though Ifthaaz was certainly a part of the Hyperborean Empire while it lasted, the empire never managed to truly incorporate these lands into its hegemony. In Khemit, the Hyperboreans found people after their own hearts — lawful, organized, and bureaucratic. In Baalthaaz, they found people they despised — immoral, personally violent, and pirates. In Ifthaaz, the Hyperborean authority died the death of a thousand cuts as they were distracted, lied to, worked around, and organized against by a people with a strong code of honor that embraced almost everything the Hyperboreans opposed. The Hyperboreans never even bothered to recruit Ifthazites as troops; they considered them too underhanded to use.

The Ifthazites, for their part, despised the Hyperboreans for their hypocrisy. They told shining stories of heroes but their deeds were petty. Ifthazites are usually petty and they know it, but they do have stories of heroes who rise above being petty to have their shining moments. (These usually involve someone who risks life and limb to fulfill a contract, or who gets the better of an opponent after having made an unwise agreement; a smuggler who cleverly gets a needed or extravagant item past a watchful guard; or a person who goes to the utmost to obey a command of the family or clan leader.) Having rejected the Hyperboreans, the Ifthazites were no better pleased by their successors of Foere. Fortunately, being away from the land route from Curgantium to Tircople, and not a large power at sea, Ifthaaz was largely ignored by both empires, which allowed it to quietly prosper.

The populace in Ifthaaz is organized into various clans, some large and some small, a custom their cousins in Baalthaaz abandoned millennia ago. Ties of family are highly valued here, and form the basis of the code of honor (such as it is) that defines Ifthazite society.

Ifthaaz is governed by a ruling council that consists of representatives of its clans. Each great clan has a member on the council at all times. The lesser and minor clans have rotating representation according to a schedule that has been laid out for more than 400 years. In total, the ruling council has 15 members, from whom they elect their own leader, who is known as the great matriarch (or patriarch) of Ifthaaz.

Each clan — even the minor ones — has a clan fortress, a traditional stronghold. However, since the large clan wars are far in the past, most are now just the core of a town or area, rather than a fortress actually able to shelter the entire clan. (One exception is the immense fortress-city of the Noascai at Ephron, which guards the border with Baalthaaz.) A clan's area usually includes a town with a rural area around it, but even the farmers tend to cluster in villages rather than on isolated homesteads; most Ifthazites just seem to like being able to interact with people whenever they choose. The people of Baalthaaz look down on their cousins in Ifthaaz as being stiff, provincial, and generally boring because their lives are centered much more around time spent with clan and family rather than in the self-indulgent, licentious pursuits common among Baalathites.

Ifthazites primarily worship Ift, god of deception. They also actively worship other deities of the Kehna pantheon, with temples to Baal and Athera in the major cities, although those tend to be less busy than comparable locations in Baalathite cities. The coastal cities have appropriate temples to Dagon. (Agamid is worshipped only in secret in Ifthaaz, if at all.) Shrines to members of the Seventy seem to be everywhere, however; as their patron deity is Last of the Seventy (youngest and most favored of his divine parents), the people of Ifthaaz tend to look more to those than to the great gods.

Ostegli, City of (Capital)

Ruler: Sopira, Great Matriarch of Ifthaaz
Government: ruling council
Population: 65,779 (almost all Baalathite)

Ostegli is on the coast of the Sea of Baal, in the central portion of Ifthaaz's coast. Many of the civic buildings are made of white marble, some at the core dating back to the days of the Hyperboreans. After the rule of the western invaders dwindled away, the Ifthazites took a smug pleasure in repurposing the government buildings, fortresses, temples, and palaces for their own use. The harbor here is in good condition but not as large as those at Gammad or Diblatham, which handle more cargo. The small ships of the coastal patrol are based here and go out in pairs to try to keep Numeda's privateers away from merchants headed for Ifthaaz.

This is also the headquarters of the country's military, known as the Council's Guard; it has its own officers and is officially under the control of the council rather than the great matriarch (or patriarch). However, the great matriarch has her own personal guard consisting of the best of the best from throughout the country, each of whom is sworn to serve and protect the leader, even against her own clan or the council if necessary. (Members of the matriarch's guard tend to figure relatively frequently in the hero tales of Ifthaaz.)

Sopira, the current great matriarch, has served already for three years and is still a favorite among the council and clans, so she is likely to serve several more. She uses her elaborate hairstyles and colorful clothing to seem intimidating, or sometimes quite shallow, but is actually very down-to-earth and highly intelligent. Sopira is an excellent negotiator and something of a linguist, speaking several languages.

Arbel, City of Clan Tavilan

Ruler: Palmolis, Matriarch of Tavilan
Government: autocracy
Population: 29,318 (almost all Baalathite)

Arbel sits near the southern border of Ifthaaz in the Taanach Hills, at the confluence of the Erto River with its tributary, the Millo. The area is full of vineyards, and Arbel is home to the Wine Consortium, a multi-clan organization focused on exporting wines. The group works to increase the exposure of vineyards of small clans. It also acquires sample wines and vines from other parts of the world and analyzes them to improve local wines. The vine-growers here use advanced methods of crossbreeding and propagation to produce excellent vintages.

Being near the border with Numeda, the area of Clan Tavilan is used as a training headquarters for the troops of the council's guard. New recruits get some seasoning patrolling the southern border at the Erto River before they are assigned elsewhere. The northern part of Numeda is one of the few food-producing areas of the country and the people there are not normally inclined to cause conflict with the neighbors. However, on occasion some rowdy young people head into the hills looking for trouble. The first line of defense is a variety of traps along the likely routes, so most invaders call it quits before the guard has to get directly involved.

Matriarch Palmolis is a gray-haired, motherly type of woman who likes to have a cup of cabb'e with visitors to put them at ease for her seemingly casual questioning. She was also a trap specialist with the Council's Guard in the past and is always pleased to hear when one of the types she invented is put to good use around Arbel. People whisper that she upgraded the traps on the clan fortress after she became matriarch, but no one has actually attempted to verify that.

Bicri, City of Clan Magelah

Ruler: Jamnia, Matriarch of Magelah
Government: autocracy
Population: 47,621 (almost all Baalathite)

Located where the Calno joins the larger Fara River, Bicri is one of three cities on the north side of the Fara. It has issues with flooding when all the snow melts upriver, so buildings on the lower side of town tend to be built on high foundations.

Because of its convenient location at the confluence of the rivers, Bicri has become a trade city for goods flowing toward and from the Scythirian Mountains. The smaller clans in that area provide much of the metal used in the country, and a large portion of the metal weapons and tools.

Magelah, the first patriarch of the clan and the founder of Bicri, is said to have been a renowned bard. In the city, he also established a notable bardic school for music and performance, the only one in Libynos that specializes in teaching satire. At the school, bards (and sometimes other students) are taught how to gather intelligence from their audiences and the use of codes and cyphers, including the use of code words or songs to communicate information secretly to other bards. Musicians from this school are welcomed throughout eastern and central Libynos and usually well-received even farther afield, but they tend to travel to places of interest to their clan rather than just wandering.

Jamnia, the clan matriarch, always has musicians present on formal occasions and knows all the musicians' codes, though she is not herself musically inclined. She is very interested in codes and code-breaking, however, and has translated two coded messages from historical documents that had been unbroken for centuries. Matriarch Jamnia tends to be rather brusque with people she views as taking too much of her time, as she has a wide range of responsibilities and interests she could pursue instead. She believes life is too short to waste it in polite conversation.

Diblatham, City of Clan Guelmin

Ruler: Hacmon, Patriarch of Guelmin
Government: autocracy
Population: 52,657 (almost all Baalathite)

Diblatham is on the coast of the Sea of Baal at the mouth of the Fara River. It is one of the two largest ports in Ifthaaz, and large quantities of wine, cork, and other products are shipped from its harbor to many far locations. One specialty here is cotton cloth dyed in bright colors. Ifthazites tend to dress in combinations of these eye-catching fabrics, so that a group of people on a street appears more like a bouquet of flowers or a flock of bright birds. The seacoast between Diblatham and Ephron is the habitat of rock snails, from which the dye the Hyperboreans called "imperial purple" is made. Several villages along the coast make the purple dye, which became the foundation of a many-hued dyeing industry and made Diblatham an important location in the trade of dye itself as well as colored cloth.

A specialty of the local sailors is smuggling. Several of the merchant ships take on special cargo for delivery from and to various places along the coast of the Sea of Baal, from the caliphate around to Guurzan. They may even smuggle things back into Ifthaaz, although that is almost pointless; some do it just to stay in practice.

Diblatham is ruled by Patriarch Hacmon, a distinguished-looking man of middle years. He takes his responsibilities to his clan very seriously and has retained the leadership for over a dozen years. However, he also enjoys the occasional prank and has been known to do elaborate preparations taking weeks or months to set up a joke or a prank on someone.

Ephron, Fortress-City of Clan Noascai

Ruler: Zohar, Patriarch of Noascai
Government: autocracy
Population: 62,556 (almost all Baalathite)

The fortress-city of Ephron, on the coast of the Sea of Baal, marks the border of Ifthaaz with Baalthaaz. From Ephron, the border officially runs northeast along the northern edge of the Nerodim Hills and into the Scythirian Mountains to where it meets the upper part of the Fara River. Although the border was hotly disputed in the past, it has been in approximately its current location for centuries.

Ephron is located in a good farming area; rural hamlets beholden to the city raise plentiful food and the patriarch also encourages rooftop gardening by the fortress's inhabitants. The city does not have a port, despite being on the coast; clan leaders have long felt that would introduce an unnecessary vulnerability. Instead, two or three villages nearby have larger dock areas than the average fishing community, and any sea travel or trade is conducted through these.

The Noascai clan has held the border with Baalthaaz for more than 800 years. The clan's fortress has grown to a walled city, and the warriors of the clan are effectively the northern border army of Ifthaaz. They patrol throughout the Nerodim Hills to watch for encroachment or for smuggling attempts by foreigners. Any smuggling that is permitted in the area is done by fellow Ifthazites. The southern portion of Baalthaaz is not heavily populated, however, so to be really profitable smugglers must travel to one of the Five Cities, or through Baalthaaz altogether and into the Antioch City States beyond. Some smugglers manage to make their way to Shamash Kush to trade with the dwarves there, which can be lucrative indeed.

Patriarch Zohar was a captain in the border patrol until a decade ago, but resigned to pursue his intense interest in strategy. He is an acknowledged expert in the wars of northern and eastern Libynos over the past few hundred years (including the ultimately failing strategies of the western religious crusades) and has collected and preserved any material he could find on the Hyperborean military in the eastern continent. A man of but medium height, with a salt-and-pepper mustache and beard, he nevertheless has a commanding presence that helps him control his sometimes-fractious people.

GAMMAD, CITY OF CLAN REZIM

Ruler: Lisco, Patriarch of Rezim
Government: autocracy
Population: 42,353 (almost all Baalathite)

Gammad is at the mouth of the Erto River where it enters the Sea of Baal. It has a large trade port with an active fishing industry. Although not at the southern border of Ifthaaz, it is the closest coastal city. Gammad is well-fortified to protect against attacks by the privateers of Numeda, and against any attack by a Numedan land force. A large force of the Council's Guard is headquartered here, but most of the troops are stationed in the areas of lesser or minor clans farther to the east. The city has its own militia and a small naval force that patrols nearby waters against the Numedan corsairs. The warriors of Gammad have the reputation of being vicious fighters, so the cowardly corsairs generally avoid contact with their ships.

Clan Rezim also has other specialties, however. Many of its people seem to have a knack for languages and tend to pick them up easily, with good accents. Just listening to foreigners at the docks can be a good experience, but the clan also brings in teachers from many places and often arranges for the clan's students to travel and practice their speaking or to pick up new tongues. As a result, multilingual citizens of Gammad are often in demand as translators, since not everyone can afford magical translation and there are those who prefer to not employ magical means in any case. Some of the more talented clan members are even able to pick up the body language of other cultures. That makes it easy for them to blend in with foreigners in Ifthaaz or with the native culture when they are visiting other countries. Combined with training and practice in disguises and certain other techniques, this allows particular members of Clan Rezim to act as excellent spies.

Lisco, the patriarch of Rezim, is said to have been a sailor in his youth. A story is told that he sailed for two years as a Khemitite on a ship out of Akados and even made himself at home in the Khemitian community in the great western city of Bard's Gate with no one ever suspecting he was not what he claimed. Other stories whisper of secrets Lisco discovered while in that guise, and point to packages he receives from Khemit on a regular basis. If these rumors have ever reached the patriarch's ears, however, he has shown no sign of it. Instead, his greatest concerns seem to be his three granddaughters, the safety of ships coming into the area (for what city can carry on profitable trade if all its partners are attacked), and his elaborate formal garden, in that order.

GIBBATHON, CITY OF CLAN DORISIO

Ruler: Hamath, Patriarch of Dorisio
Government: autocracy
Population: 32,589 (almost all Baalathite)

Gibbathon is on the plain of eastern Ifthaaz, in the heart of the cork-producing area. The cork oaks require careful husbandry, with trees needing years of cultivation before any cork can be harvested and then more years before they produce top-quality material. A majority of the population of the eastern part of the country is involved in the cork industry in one way or another, whether in husbandry, harvesting, processing, or transportation.

Another important crop in the area of Gibbathon is poppies. Acre after acre of them are grown, and Clan Dorisio specializes in processing them, mostly into the syrup that is so popular in Baalthaaz. While some oldsters in Ifthaaz take poppy for joint pain, taking it just for pleasure is frowned upon because it dulls the senses. As a result, little of the syrup is sold inside the country; the majority is exported to be used by the hedonists of Baalthaaz, especially in the great temples. The clan processes other types of plant material as well and makes other medicinals for pain. However, a few knowledgeable alchemists also make plant-based poisons that are quietly sold into certain markets. These craftspeople take charge of many apprentices in the Dorisio clan so this knowledge will be passed down and always continue to be available to the clan.

Hamath, the patriarch of Dorisio, is unusually young for his position but he would not have come to it if he did not have the confidence of his clan. In one change from the policies of his predecessor, he is sending out clan personnel with samples of the poppy syrup. They are taking it to demonstrate to potential clients, especially in cities along the west coast of the Sinnar Ocean, to increase the market for the clan's high-quality products.

HAMOR, CITY OF CLAN NALCHIDEM

Ruler: Tebak, Patriarch of Nalchidem
Government: autocracy
Population: 27,452 (almost all Baalathite)

Hamor is at the edge of the hill country of central Ifthaaz, in a good wine-producing area. As the largest city in the region, goods such as wine and grain are usually collected in Hamor and then transported by road to Ostegli or possibly Gammad. In many ways, central Ifthaaz is a stereotypical farming area, and Hamor is the center of that, with sheep-shearing competitions, milking championships, and country dances to pass the time.

However, there is another side to Hamor. Being in a vulnerable area and tramped over more than once by invading foreigners, millennia ago locals opened up a cave system below what is now the city where the entire population could live for an extended time while fighting raged above. This hideaway is recalled only by a few sages except for one group: a very specialized organization that trains skilled assassins and sends them out in support of the clan or country. For the past few centuries, they have called themselves the Reapers, in a play on the bucolic area in which their facility is located. The order is almost entirely restricted to members of Clan Nalchidem; sometimes an outsider will be accepted for training, but only after the execution of an ironclad contract and the receipt of other sureties.

Tebak, the patriarch of Nalchidem, is whispered to have been among the assassins in his younger days, though he has been a staid part of the city's government for decades. Some claim he was even personally involved in a coup in Ammuyad nearly 40 years ago. If asked privately, Tebak neither confirms nor denies this rumor. If asked publicly, he roundly excoriates the scoundrel who makes such an accusation and makes sure the person has trouble doing business in Hamor henceforth.

Geographic Features and Points of Interest in Baalthaaz, Ifthaaz, and the Sea of Baal

Azaadipur, Mines of

Situated among the mountainous cliffs in the western Titian Isles, the mines of Azaadipur are old by even those who have studied the Hyperborean Empire, dating back to the earliest civilized human occupation of the region. Rumor says that more than five miles of twisting tunnels run beneath the surface of the largest island, some of which are so narrow that ancient Khemit used small demihuman and child slaves to be able to access them.

Freegate conquered the islands around the mines several years ago, and the mines have now been refitted and are actively being worked again, producing abundant copper.

Bliss, Isle of

In the eastern part of the Sea of Baal, about 100 miles south of the city of Perazim, the Isle of Bliss is the largest of a group of dozens of small islands. Perhaps 50 miles from tip to tip, the island is home to small fishing villages and not much else. The inhabitants are the descendants of island natives and the crews of ships that wrecked in the islands.

Calno River

A tributary of the Fara, the Calno River flows out of the Scythirian Mountains across the northeast part of Ifthaaz. A large part of the cork production of eastern Ifthaaz is transported to the Calno and shipped downriver to Diblatham for export.

Dura River

The Dura River runs from the Scythirian Mountains through northeastern Baalthaaz. It is a tributary of the Palena River, which serves as the border between Baalthaaz and the Antioch City-States. The Baalathite city of Zeruin lies on the Dura River

Erto River

The largest river in the southern part of Ifthaaz is the Erto, which flows out of the Scythirian Mountains and through the Taanach Hills to enter the Sea of Baal at Gammad. The Erto River is considered the border between Ifthaaz and Numeda to its south.

Groups of rash youth from Numeda will on occasion attempt to challenge the border by dashing on horseback out of the hills, crossing the river, and looking for someone to attack to prove they are helping their country. Ifthaaz uses the border area to train its new guard troops, so the young Numedans almost always encounter a patrol of soldiers better armed than they are and also more familiar with the territory. The Ifthazites are generally content with chasing the miscreants back across the river, and as long as neither side has to contend with actual troops crossing the border, tolerable neutrality is maintained.

Fara River

The Fara River is the main river in Ifthaaz and flows through the northern part of the country to the sea at Diblatham. Half its length runs through the Scythirian Mountains and foothills before it reaches the city of Bicri and is joined by its tributary, the Calno. The Fara and its tributaries water fully half of Ifthaaz, and the river also acts as an important trade route for goods from northeast Ifthaaz.

Free Main

A name sometimes used in Akados for the Sea of Baal. (See "Sea of Baal" below.)

Mare Librum

An archaic name sometimes used in Akados for the Sea of Baal. (See "Sea of Baal" below.)

Millo River

Flowing out of the Scythirian Mountains through southeastern Ifthaaz, the Millo River is a tributary of the Erto, which it joins near the city of Arbel. In the spring, when snow melts in the lower part of the mountains, both the Millo and Erto run high and the lower parts of Arbel have problems with flooding, as do other towns and villages in that area.

Nerodim Hills

This line of hills extends west from the foothills of the Scythirian Mountains to about 50 miles from the Sea of Baal. It is considered to be the northern border of Ifthaaz, which claims the entirety of the Nerodim. Although the terrain is rough, caravans of traders (or more likely smugglers) are able to make their way through the area.

Quorrk

In the midst of the Sea of Baal, this rough island's mountain peaks rise from dry, lightly-wooded land at their base. Located atop a windswept spur of rock among the mountains is a small settlement of vulture-like bird-men who can often be seen soaring and circling above the island. There are no reports of the vulture-men attacking ships, but sailors tell horror stories about what happens to people who land or are shipwrecked on the island.

Sarmad Yazdg-or, Isle of

In the Sea of Baal, about 200 miles south of Tarresh, lies the strange Isle of Sarmad Yazdg-or. Passing ships often avoid it due to the weird nature of the cult found there. Among the boulder-strewn hills of that isle stands the monastery called the House of Three Mysteries, where dwell shaven-headed seers with supernatural insights brought on by consuming the often-deadly purple lotus. The multistory building is surrounded by a 25-foot wall and the gate is guarded, but it is opened for those willing to pay for their far-seeing divinatory powers.

Sea of Baal

The eastern arm of the northern Sinnar Ocean is known in Libynos as the Sea of Baal. It is warmed by currents drawn up from the equatorial south so the climate around its shores ranges from balmy and pleasant to very warm. Major storms such as hurricanes are almost unknown. No one has actually measured the sea's distance, but those who have sailed it many times shrug and give a guess of about 700 miles from Al-Ibbos to Turkad, and more than 1,600 miles from the northern tip of Caddesh to the eastern shore.

Throne of Baal

The meaning of the name Baalthaaz is "Throne of Baal," and the country has a holy site with that name carved into a sheer mountain cliff in the western Scythirian Mountains, north and east of Laishah. While it was originally a natural formation, over many years, devotees have worked the surrounding rock into elaborate decorations such that it does indeed have the appearance of a gigantic throne, with arms that look like giant bear paws and a mass of misshapen demons writhing beneath the seat. The view is impressive; if Baal truly sat there, he would be able look right across his country to the sea that bears his name. A curse would supposedly come to anyone else who dares sit there, but people sometimes make the journey to pray at the throne's foot when beseeching their deity for a special favor.

Throne of Ift

As Baalthaaz means "Throne of Baal," so Ifthaaz means "Throne of Ift." A stone throne was supposedly cut into a mountain long ago as a mockery of the Throne of Baal. However, the Throne of Ift is now barely more than a legend. No one knows where it may be, and worshippers do not seek it, as it has no importance to Ift at all. However, some legends say that behind the false Throne of Ift, if one can find it, is a secret chamber with the true Throne of Ift, and one who can pass the guardians to the true throne will earn a great reward. Stories of the greatest thief who ever lived claim he "took a gem from the throne of Ift"; further tales claim a few others managed to emulate him since then.

TITIAN ISLES

Across a thousand miles, the Sea of Baal is dotted with islands referred to as the Titian Isles for their golden-auburn color. The majority of the islands are arid and volcanic in origin, though the volcanos that forced them from the bottom of the sea are long extinct. Sailors stop at the small ports throughout the isles to resupply, trade, and take on fresh water. Ownership of the islands has traded hands over the millennia as various powers sought to control the islands' mineral resources and strategic positions.

REFERENCE SOURCE: CITY OF BRASS

WINDS, ISLE OF

For centuries, a great storm has blown around the Isle of Winds, drawing in ships to wreck upon its shores and stranding sailors upon its rocky beaches. From a distance, a great tornado can be seen ever grinding against the barren stone beach, its vortex reaching into the lightning-shot blue-black skies that glower above it. Stripped bare of its vegetation and soil, the isle is a forbidding place. Those survivors who claim to have set foot upon the Isle of Winds were driven mad for their experience, or drink heavily in an effort to forget the things they saw there.

ZANOSH RIVER

The Zanosh River runs through central Baalthaaz, rising in the Scythirian Mountains to the east and running west and southwest through hilly country to the Sea of Baal. Perazim, the national capital, is situated near the mouth of the river.

CRUSADER COAST

Capital: none
Ruler: varies
Government: varies
Population: unknown
Monstrous: dragon turtle, renzer (aquatic), inphidians, nues, kamadans (Malagro)
Languages: Westerling, Bhanakhat, Alcaldrich (islands); tribal languages (Malagro)
Religion: Muir; Paramountcies pantheon (islands); tribal spirits (Malagro)
Resources: medicines, crops, tobacco, hand crafts, trade (islands)
Currency: Foere, Bhanakhiran, Alcaldrich, other (islands); barter (Malagro)
Technology Level: High Middle Ages (Ber Ga Ma, Lycania), Dark Ages (other islands), Stone Age (Malagro)

The Crusader Coast refers to a portion of the eastern coastal lands of Libynos, from the mouth of the Gulf of Ur in the north to the southern end of the Jungle of Malagro in the south. Bordered on the west by the Scythirian Mountains, the region includes the plateau of the Sacred Table where lie the ruins of the holy city of Tircople, as well as the chain of islands running along the coast, from the isle of Cyproean in the north to Lycania in the south.

At the time of the First Great Crusade in 2960 I.R., the Foerdewaith of Akados used what is now the Crusader Coast as a staging area for their attempts to retake the Sacred Table and hold it from the Huun. After that crusade, they built fortresses and established colonies that came to be known as the Crusader States. Over two and a half centuries, the Foerdewaith and the Huun clashed in four great crusades. Each time after the armies from Akados retook the Sacred Table, they eventually became complacent, which permitted the Huun to attack Tircople and put the coastal Crusader States to the torch. Finally, the Huun were definitively beaten in 3207 I.R. at the Battle of the Sickles by a Foerdewaith army aided by dwarven allies from Shamash Kush, yet even this victory would be short-lived.

Ironically, it was not the Huun who would drive Foere from the Libynosi mainland but the Mguru tribe from the Jungle of Malagro, who sacked Tircople and left it a ruin in 3209 I.R. With the beginning of the Foerdewaith Wars of Succession only four years later, no further crusades were declared. The coastal Crusader States, destroyed by the Huun in 3169 I.R., were never rebuilt. Tircople would remain uninhabited, and as Foere's internal dissension sapped its strength, one by one most of the island Crusader States fell from its control. Of their island fortresses, some have been repurposed, becoming merchant centers or pirate havens, and others have deteriorated and been abandoned. Today, only the island of Cyproean remains under even nominal Fordewaith control, and only the lone tower on Aretas still flies the banner of the church of Muir.

ARETAS, ISLAND KEEP OF

Ruler: Sir Tirath
Government: feudal
Population: 63 (mainly Foerdewaith)

South of Cyproean in the Sea of Tyre is the island of Aretas. A simple keep stands near the western side of the isle, with a floating dock extending from the rocky shingle out into the sea. The area around the keep is tended farmland and orchards but the rest of the island is wild jungle. From the highest peak of the tower flies the white and red flag of the church of Muir.

This isolated location is the home of Sir Tirath, knight of Muir, along with his family and their vassals. Sir Tirath is the latest representative in a longstanding line of knights who have held this watchtower as their duty. He came to the place through his marriage to the daughter of the previous knight, Lady Daria. That woman came to the island after dreaming someone needed her, and indeed the elderly knight then overseeing the tower had needed someone to take his place.

Muir has blessed the island with abundant water and fertile soil, so life is not too onerous for any of the residents. Lady Gerasa, who learned healing from her mother, oversees a large, long-established garden of medicinal herbs. She concocts many healing powders and teas, and her medicines are the most common reason ships stop at Aretas.

Although the crusaders have long abandoned the Crusader Coast, Sir Tirath carries on the tradition of his predecessors, maintains the knowledge of the goddess in the area, and keeps records of the history of her city and its environs. He hopes perhaps one of his own children will succeed him some day, but trusts that Muir will provide his replacement at the appropriate time.

BARKOS ISLAND

Ruler: Captain Lucien Delamain
Government: autocracy
Population: unknown

Lying in the Sea of Tyre off the coast of eastern Libynos, Barkos is a small island, yet has two small harbors, one on its north shore and one on its south. Each of the harbors is partially concealed from the sea by tall cliffs, and the approaches to each are rocky, making it likely that a captain unfamiliar with the island would ground his ship or rip its hull. These factors made the island difficult for the crusaders to use, although they did so anyway. On the other hand, they make Barkos an excellent base for pirates, and so it has been now for many years.

Pirate Captain Lucien "the Black" Delamain claims control over the south harbor and leadership over the pirate band that calls itself the Merry Marauders. They are more vicious than their name would indicate, and ships (and villages) go to great lengths to resist them because those taken alive invariably wish they had died instead.

The north harbor is controlled by Captain Romike Hildrsdottir and her Sea Rovers. They are an offshoot of the Marauders and formed when Captain Romike (as she prefers to be called) saw a diplomatic split as the best way to avoid bloody rebellion. The Sea Rovers plan their own operations and choose their own targets, but pay a portion of their take to Lucien the Black in order to be left alone. Ships from each group have the right to put into each other's harbor in case of emergency. The Sea Rovers almost never take advantage of this, though, while the Marauders do so more often than would seem necessary. Captain Romike just accepts that Lucien the Black has his people checking up on her, and keeps preparations for the Rovers' future plans well away from prying eyes in their harbor.

One drawback to the rocky entrances to each of the harbors is that just a few ships could bottle up those inside. To counter this risk, both harbors have placed siege engines in high places where they can strike ships at sea.

Over the years, the pirates have done some desultory cultivation of fruit trees and berry bushes (which were probably first started by the crusaders), so there is food on the island, and fish in the sea if they are inclined to catch them. Captain Romike encourages her group to smoke some fish and set it aside in case of future need, along with some of the dried or preserved foods from ships they take. This is one of the preparations the Sea Rovers don't report to Lucien the Black, who sees no reason for any such precautions.

BER GA MA, ISLAND OF

Ruler: Hexarga Sisak Roi Raichat of Gold
Government: Kachan Yala Inter-Faction Mercantile League
Population: 1,118 (mostly Bhanakhiri)

Known as Bergama in the records of Foere and the Crusader States, the pronunciation of this busy island's name has changed under its current ownership. Situated near the center of the Crusader Coast, it is claimed by the Kachan Yala Inter-Faction Mercantile League of Bhanakhiri, and the port welcomes merchant ships of all nations, for a reasonable fee. The harbor and docks were restored and upgraded when the league took over about 180 years ago.

The town of Amnas Chakaio has grown up around the old keep and provides for the needs of ships and their crews, from minor ship repairs to limited amounts of fresh food and water to taverns and shops for sailors who just want to be ashore for a few hours. Some trading is done here, by ships that might not cross paths somewhere else, but it is not a major activity as this is primarily a stopover for ships on their way elsewhere.

Since Amnas Chakaio was built as a town of Bhanakhiri, it seems strange to most of the crews who come here. Just the colors and styles of the townspeople's clothing are peculiar to them; the faction colors and markers, gilded spirit houses (with an especially large one outside the centuries-old keep), strange temples to unusual gods, and of course gladiatorial competitions in the arena, make the island seem very foreign and exotic to people from northern or central Libynos or distant Akados, and make it a popular calling place for those ships. (For more information on this culture, see "Southern Libynos — Southern Paramountcies — Bhanakhiri, Ottiarky of.")

The island's top authority is Hexarga Sisak Roi Raichat of the Gold Faction of Bhanakhiri, appointed by the Kachan Yala. The hexarga is a master merchant in her own right, so she understands the concerns and struggles of the traders who come to the island, but she was selected primarily for her skill in diplomacy and her facility with languages. She is ably assisted by several specialists in translation, but she speaks enough of several different languages to at least hold a polite conversation with many of the merchant captains who call on her. Sisak Roi Raichat is below average height, and less plump than her position

and wealth would warrant, but her staff and citizens treat her with great respect. Ship captains who have had the poor judgment to bring their quarrels into her presence also spread their esteem for her; many years of training in hand-to-hand combat have given the hexarga the ability to quiet a disagreement with a few sharp blows, leaving both sides to repent of their errors.

CRUSADER STATES, RUINS OF
Population: 0

The Crusader States were a group of domains under the auspices of the Hyperborean Monarchy of the Foerdewaith that were established to guard and support the holy city of Tircople. Records of the various states certainly still exist in some archive in Courghais, and perhaps even in the capitals of some nations in Libynos. However, the states themselves are now all gone and forgotten by all but a few scholars.

Originally established after the First Crusade, the Crusader States lie along the coast of the Sea of Tyre on several of the islands offshore and, on the continent, in the northern part of the Jungle of Malagro. The mainland states were the County of Rheguim, the Barony of Talbrimmon, and the Barony of Ithamar. On the islands were the Barony of Cyproean and the fortresses of Aretas, Bergama, Tyropean, Nevalla, and Lycania.

The Crusader States provided support to the holy city of Tircople, a place for pilgrims to arrive if traveling by sea, and bases for merchants of Akados optimistically seeking to trade with the nations of Libynos. Before the Fourth Crusade, the island barony of Cyproean became a staging area for the armies of Foere. The coastal States also kept watch on the nearby Jungle of Malagro, whose inhabitants were not friendly to the crusaders but were not overtly hostile either, perhaps being intimidated by their advanced armor and weapons. So long as the Foerdewaith did not venture too far into the interior, the tribes of the jungle left the crusaders alone. As a result, the Crusader States judged the tribes to pose little threat to their people, much less to Tircople itself.

Twice, the Huun attacked the coastal Crusader States. The first time, only 10 years after the First Crusade, the Huun were able to seize the fortresses and towns of Rhegium as they laid siege to Tircople. This led to the Second Crusade, which saw the Foerdewaith eventually retake the Sacred Table and the lands of Rhegium. The Crusader States were substantially strengthened, and for 200 years they prospered. Then in 3169 I.R., the Huun again attacked, overrunning the mainland Crusader Coast and burning to the ground the fortresses and towns of the three onshore Crusader States, before moving on and devastating the proud city of Tircople. Only the island Crusader States survived, and all they could do was watch in horror as their brethren cities ashore were fired to light up the entire coast at night in a ghastly spectacle. It took almost 40 years, including the loss of the Third Crusade at sea, before Foere retook the Sacred Table in the Fourth Great Crusade. By that point, the settlements of the coastal Crusader States had been lost to the jungle. Though some consideration was given to re-establishing them, the subsequent sack of Tircople by the Mguru tribe of the Jungle of Malagro just two years later and the beginning of the Foerdewaith Wars of Succession shortly thereafter meant that all such plans came to naught.

From the sea, however, the ruins of some of the largest of the fortresses of the coastal Crusader States can still be seen. Visible in the north is the fortress of Galbanum, which was part of the County of Rhegium; it stands at the edge of the Wasted Desert, just south of the Zoar River that falls from the heights of the mountains to the west. Next is the massive castle of the Counts of Rhegium itself, followed by the great tower of Mithredath. Farther south, one can make out the extensive remains of Castle Talbrimmon, once headquarters to the barons of that name. Farthest to the south, the substantial castle of the barons of Ithamar can be discerned from the top of a ship's mast at sea despite the jungle's attempts to swallow it whole.

All these fortresses are considered unpopulated by the officials of Foere and those western merchants who travel this way. However, such useful fortifications are unlikely to be completely unoccupied, even in their ruined condition.

Cyproean, Island Barony of

Ruler: Baroness Avvia Malthace
Government: protectorate of the Kingdom of Foere
Population: 10,743 (mostly Foerdewaith)

Cyproean is the northernmost, and largest, island of the Crusader Coast. It has high, rocky hills in the center and no fewer than three good harbors for ships. Each of these harbors has a protective fortress, with Fortress Aven on the harbor to the west being where most of the traffic arrives, now and historically. To the southeast is Fortress Shan, and on the north is Fortress Perath. Rivers run from the central ridge down to the sea in every direction, watering the land well. With the warm climate produced by southerly currents along the coast, growers on Cypyroean can even cultivate tobacco (or "pipeweed" as it is known in parts of Akados) and ship it west as an exotic type that brings a high price.

Cyproean is technically a protectorate of the Kingdom of Foere. The connection goes back to the Hyperborean Monarchy of the Foerdewaith, which claimed the island after the First Crusade on the Sacred Table and set up a fortress here to protect the holy city of Tircople. More fortifications were built throughout the Crusader Coast after the Second Crusade, which stood guard successfully for more than 200 years until the third Huun attack on not just the holy city but the Crusader States as well. The baron and knights at Cyproean could do nothing to help their land-borne comrades during that assault, or during the tragic loss of the laden ships of the Third Crusade. However, as the Fourth Crusade approached, they opened their fortresses and their island and played host to nearly all of the gathering crusaders, until their numbers were sufficient to finally begin the assault to retake Tircople. So much of the island was required for the assembled armies that some units of crusaders were forced to fortify and camp in caves in the hills, and isolated locations can still be found with remnants the soldiers inadvertently left behind.

After the success of the Fourth Crusade, some crusaders elected to stay on Cyproean and join those who had been part of the island barony for generations, though most of the soldiers from Akados returned home. With the commencement of the Foerdewaith Wars of Succession shortly thereafter, though, the influence of Foere waned and the hand of Courghais touched the inhabitants of Cyproean only lightly. Despite their great distance, however, the folk of the island still find a benefit in naming themselves loyal citizens of the kingdom.

Today, merchant ships from Foere travel to Cyproean and sometimes even beyond, making their way all the way to Jaati. A few ships headquartered at Fort Shan occasionally make trips down the eastern coast of Libynos to trade with the denizens of the southern part of the continent. Colonists from Foere boosted the island's population and it now raises enough food — and makes enough products — to trade for most of what it needs to be self-sustaining.

Lycania, Island of

Ruler: Exarch Ana-Paterna of Hacienda Almoster
Government: controlled by Empire of Alcaldar
Population: 947 (mostly Alcaldrich)

The southernmost island of what is traditionally considered the Crusader Coast, Lycania is now a colony of the Empire of Alcaldar. About 100 years ago, Alcaldrich explorers found the nearly intact keep on the western shore empty, abandoned by the Foerdewaith who had once inhabited the island. Seeing an opportunity, Alcaldar immediately sent engineers, masons, and settlers, even though the journey was long and difficult. With the opening of the Channel Lakes 18 years ago, however, and the growing population at the east end of the canal system, Lycania has become a perfect steppingstone for Alcaldar's increasingly lucrative trade with Istaflumina and Jaati.

The colony, small but growing, is governed by Alcaldrich Exarch Ana-Paterna of Hacienda Almoster and a staff of advisors and assistants. A company of imperial marines protects the island from pirates and other enemies, and also accompanies the island's naval vessel, the *Princesa Adrianna*, on patrols. (The pirates of Barkos sometimes give the small ship trouble, but they have learned to leave the island alone.) The small number of settlers has increased enough that there are now three small towns spaced around the island, each with a strong wooden palisade and a town hall where weapons are stored in case the locals need to protect their home while waiting for reinforcements. The harbor offers a sturdy dock that can hold as many as a dozen fishing boats, or four ocean-going vessels.

Exarch Ana-Paterna maintains a luxurious residence inside the keep, primarily to show passing merchants and officials of other nations the wealth and splendor of Alcaldar. In keeping with the tradition in the Channel Lakes area (and much of southern Libynos), the exarch always keeps a supply of gifts on hand for visitors. These are usually figures hand carved from wood produced on Lycania, in the form of one of the island's beautiful native birds or elaborate local flowers.

While the exarch's primary duty is to ensure the safety and growth of the colony on Lycania, almost as important is diplomacy and spreading a favorable impression of the empire. In support of the mission of diplomacy, the island's tiny navy actively patrols the area for pirates and will intervene anytime they see a ship attacked. The single vessel also does search-and-rescue operations; after large storms, the island's fishing fleet aids it in looking for damaged ships in nearby waters.

Fernán Giraldino of Iber, the leading priest of Muir on Lycania, looks after the religious needs of the people but is alert to opportunities to spread the worship of Muir — or at least knowledge of her — to travelers as well as the rest of the Crusader Coast. He puts particular effort into trying to convince Sir Tirath of Aretas Island that the Church Militans is the logical place for him and that oversight of Aretas by Alcaldar would increase the glory of Muir as well as improving the lot of everyone on that island. So far, Sir Tirath remains unconvinced but not to the point of being rude to the priest when they meet.

Nevalla Island

Ruler: none
Government: none
Population: unknown

An island of the Crusader Coast, Nevalla has a row of three mountains as its spine, one of which is a dead volcanic cone. On the western end sits a strong fortress, probably the largest along the coast after Fortress Aven on Cyproean. The front (western) side of the citadel has a high wall and strong gate that is approached by a road winding up from the sea, while the back wall is the sheer face of a towering cliff.

Although the fortress appears from a distance to be in good condition, the same cannot be said for the rest of the island. At the western shore, the remains of a small village are strewn about, and a few stone piers are all that are left of the docks. Elsewhere, the trees stand close and underbrush chokes the areas in between, broken only by the occasional stream finding its way out of the interior. And yet, the island is known to be inhabited — by a dragon.

Many ships sailing in the area have seen the dragon come and go from the courtyard of the fortress. Common wisdom is that the beast has taken over the great hall as its lair. It may have killed the former inhabitants, or driven them away, or simply found the island nearly abandoned and moved in; none now seems to know which may have been the case.

One detail upon which no one can agree is the color of the dragon. Reports include red, green, black (which some point out could merely be a silhouette of some other type against the sun), copper, brass, bronze, and even gold. No reasonable explanation has been offered for this discrepancy; certainly, multiple dragons would not be sharing the keep! All do agree that the dragon has been on the island for hundreds of years, that the few attempts to dislodge it in the past have been abject failures, and that it must be very old and powerful by now, making it even more dangerous. The dragon seems to mostly hunt in the Malagro Jungle or directly in the sea, and for whatever reason does not molest nearby shipping. As a result, none of the local powers has found any incentive to accost the dragon in its lair.

Unbeknownst to outsiders, the old dragon (which does indeed use the great hall as at least part of its lair) is a copper dragon in the habit of using illusion to cloak its true form in public. Also unknown is that the island has a humanoid population: a community of nagaji, escaped by ones and twos from their serpentine masters in Jaati. They have been able to live here with impunity due to the dragon's success in keeping interlopers away and spectators at a safe distance.

TIRCOPLE, RUINS OF

Population: 0

Located on a high plateau in the northern part of the Scythirian Mountains, Tircople lies ruined and abandoned. A broken road runs across the dry, rocky landscape to its shattered gates and tumbled walls. The view into the city is nothing but broken buildings. On a hill within the city are the remains of what may have been the high temple of Muir. Fluted columns rise far enough to be seen from the gate, but the entire roof is gone, and the walls are crumbling. Sometimes wandering folk of the desert come into the city for shelter, but since water is hard to find among the ruins, none stay long.

According to legend, this ancient city was founded by the brother of the very first imperator of the Hyperborean Empire. Built to honor the Hyperborean goddess Muir, it was for centuries a pilgrimage destination and a bastion for the cause of good in the world. A pilgrim road was maintained from the Hyperborean capital of Curgantium, all the way across the Isthmus of Irkaina to the Sacred Table, and thousands made the trek each year.

Tircople was the capital of the Hyperborean Empire for a time after the tragic destruction of Curgantium. Later, the Hyperboreans abandoned the city, and it was only restored when claimed by Macobert, first overking of the Hyperborean Monarchy of the Foerdewaith. Under that kingdom's auspices, pilgrimages resumed, much to the relief of towns and villages along the route who served the travelers.

Tircople was the focus of the various crusades by people of the western kingdoms against the Huun, who attacked the area for religious reasons. (See "Sacred Table" below.)

TYROPEON, ISLAND OF

Ruler: Sir Jules Tyropeon, owner
Government: autocracy
Population: 327 (275 Foerdewaith, 52 other human ethnicity)

Tyropeon Island lies along the Crusader Coast; it is the second-largest island in the chain, after Cyproean in the north. The fortress on its western shore looks like it has seen better days, but the nearby villages are well-kept, with good stone houses to stand against the ocean storms. The island is owned by Sir Jules Tyropeon, but he makes most of his decisions with input from a group of trusted advisors, so he is hardly the autocrat that rumor would make him.

Many people think Sir Jules is a charlatan and with good reason, as he spent many years at that occupation. However, "Sir" Jules really is the descendant of Sir Micah Tyropeon — who was granted this island by the monarch of Foere — and he has the old papers to prove it. Sir Jules decided to try to make a go of living in his distant ancestor's tower when things got quite hot for him in Foere and the surrounding area. He gathered up a group of settlers who likewise were seeking better fortune or needed to get out of Akados for an extended period, and set sail for the Island of Tyropeon. Life away from a city brought a lot of surprises to him and some of his settlers proved the value of their early training in hewing wood, starting fires, and setting snares for animals. Twenty years has given the group a chance to get on their feet, and Sir Jules really has proven to be a decent leader.

Their recent goal has been to start attracting ships to Tyropeon as a stopover on merchant routes along the east coast of Libynos. This is somewhat hampered by the Bhanakhiri town of Amnas Chakaio on Ber Ga Ma Island to the north, and the Alcaldrich fortress on Lycania Island to the south. However, while some western sailors find Amnas Chakaio exotic and attractive, others find it weird and repelling; Sir Jules and his people plan to capitalize on the latter. He convinced a bardic friend back in Akados to frequent some captains' taverns and places where merchants gather to sing of the joys of Tyropeon as a little piece of home in the strange waters of Libynos, and this is beginning to have an effect. The fact that most Akadian crops grow amazingly well in the much warmer climate of Tyropeon means the island has more foodstuffs to offer than the smaller Ber Ga Ma, and that also attracts some ships. The competition may yet become fierce, but Sir Jules and his people are determined to grasp some of the lucrative business for themselves.

One thing that has kept Sir Jules safe from some of his rougher settlers, and Tyropeon in general safe from the pirates in the area, is Sir Jules' wife, Lady Taerentym. A gray elf, her presence with Sir Jules increases the respect others have for him, and her sorcerous abilities strike fear in the hearts of area pirates. (The stone statue of one miscreant who was slow to retreat during an attack stands firmly placed near the dock as a warning to others.) Knowing that his half-elven children will be long-lived is one thing that encourages Sir Jules to build for the future.

GEOGRAPHIC FEATURES AND POINTS OF INTEREST OF THE CRUSADER COAST

MALAGRO, JUNGLE OF

The Malagro Jungle stretches along the east coast of eastern Libynos, between the Scythirian Mountains and the sea. At least three distinct major tribes are attested in the archives of the Crusader Coast, with many sub-groups said to exist. In the south is the Mintaya tribe, which is largely isolationist and seldom has contact with westerners. In the central part is the Mettubo tribe, a strong group with good weapons. Those are necessary to protect themselves against the more-numerous Mguru, which are in the north.

All the tribes are known to practice cannibalism, though whether it is done only as a sign of victory in battle or whether it is a regular habit is undetermined. All three tribes also hold to the practice of taking the heads of those they vanquish, removing the bones by some method only they know, and then shrinking the skin so that the whole head could belong to a child's toy but is still recognizable as that of a defeated enemy. Powerful warriors and tribal shamans often sport strings of these heads to show their prowess.

The Mguru tribe had the most contact with the Crusader States but generally left the settlers from Akados alone. It was only at the very end, when most of the crusaders had left Tircople and gone in search of glory elsewhere, that the Mguru came boiling out of the jungle and overran the city. They put all the inhabitants to the sword and finished the complete destruction of that once-mighty city. Why they did so remains a subject of much debate among scholars, and no satisfactory reason has yet been discovered.

Today, the Mguru and the other tribes of the Malagro carry on their lives in much the same way as their distant ancestors. Inhabitants of the islands of the Crusader Coast seldom go ashore near the jungle, and people of the tribes are seldom seen out from under the trees, so there is little conflict between the two. Occasionally, however, explorers or exploiters try to search for ruins of the Crusader States or acquire other resources of the jungle, and they are often in jeopardy because the tribes are alert for intruders.

SACRED TABLE

The Sacred Table is a high plateau in the northern part of the Scythirian Mountains. According to legend, it was once a green valley among the towering peaks, but today it is a desert, flat and hot in the glare of the sun with no shade except the shadow of the surrounding mountains. Toward the eastern part of the plateau are the ruins of the ancient and sacred city of Tircople. Near the edges of the plateau on the north, south, east and west are the ruins of four other fortresses built after the First Crusade to protect the holy city from attack from any direction. Their names are still recalled by a handful of priests, sages (especially in the Antioch City-States), and a few of the island inhabitants of the Crusader Coast.

In the west, overlooking what was once the eastern end of the pilgrim road, stands the ruined Tower of the White Lady. The Tower of the Silver Star — the most intact — guards the northern edge. In the east, the Tower of the Scarlet Hand appears almost intact when seen from the Wasted Desert below, but the western side is crumbled to a pile of rock. To the south, rubble is all that is left of the Tower of the Upright Deed; it was practically razed by the Huun when they held the plateau for almost a decade before the Fourth Crusade.

Also on the plateau stand the remains of the Yellow Keep. Built by the Huun during their siege of Tircople before the Second Crusade, it was not only the headquarters of their interdiction but also a way to taunt the frustrated defenders by torturing prisoners and hanging them from its ramparts. The Crusaders completely destroyed the walls but the foundations are still visible, although part seems to have fallen into some sort of pit or sinkhole below.

SCYTHIRIAN MOUNTAINS

The Scythirian Mountains dominate eastern Libynos. Their northeastern extent reaches nearly to the Gulf of Ur while the southern end touches the Ruby Sea between Numeda and Imya, over 2,000 miles away. Unbeknownst to most of the world, the mountains actually separate in the middle. There, the east and west ranges are little more than 50 miles wide, between which are more than 200 miles of wasteland known as the Desert of Oreb. Few are aware of the existence of the desert, and fewer still have seen it, as the height and ruggedness of the surrounding mountains discourage all but the most relentless, expert, and lucky mountaineers from even considering crossing them. The Huun, of course, live in the Desert of Oreb and know the routes — some over the mountains and some under — that permit them to travel to the Malagro and to Ifthaaz, whether for trade or for other purposes.

The eastern and western edges of the mountain range are high; perhaps they are not the highest in the world, but they cut off the moisture rising in the clouds. Consequently, the western slope near Baalthaaz and Ifthaaz gets a great deal of rain that waters those countries. The eastern slope along the Jungle of Malagro cuts off clouds from the ocean, giving the jungle plentiful moisture to go with the warmth provided by the southerly sea currents. The region between the two arms of mountains, then, is entirely in rainshadow and receives almost no moisture at any time of the year. It is thus a dry, sandy desert inhabitable only by the most adaptable of people and creatures.

TYRE, SEA OF

The Sea of Tyre lies off the coast of eastern Libynos, north of the Boiling Sea. The Gulf of Ur empties into it from the north. It holds the chain of islands known as the Crusader Coast.

WASTED DESERT

The Wasted Desert is dry and rocky, with the Sea of Tyre to its east where the stones and gritty sand run right down to the sea. To the west, a steep escarpment rises to the high plateau known as the Sacred Table and to the south runs the Zoar River, dropping down from the high mountains and running along a rocky path to the sea, barely moistening the ground along its high banks. Dry streambeds in the desert are prone to flashfloods during violent spring storms, but even when rain comes it evaporates quickly, giving little sustenance to the few plants that grow in this harsh climate. Those that do are tough, twisted, and thorny, and even the spiny cacti that are edible are terribly bitter to the taste.

Oral tradition among the natives of the Malagro Jungle to the south suggests this area was once green and growing. Whether due to a curse or a change in weather patterns, it is now a barren and unpleasant place. However, it has played an important part in the history of the Lost Lands,

as three of the crusades for the city of Tircople landed (or attempted to land) in the Wasted Desert to gain a foothold in Libynos.

The most obvious legacy of that history is the great Crusaders' Road that rises straight from the desert floor to the plateau of the Sacred Table high above. Its surface is smooth (or nearly so) even today, though its edges have become chipped and worn. Four horsemen side by side can ride safely, or eight if they go shoulder to shoulder in a thundering charge. Solid stone supports the road as it climbs higher and higher. Rather than being the creation of any Hyperborean technology, the road was fashioned through the power of great spells worked by the mages of the First Crusade. Calling upon ancient magics, they pulled stone and earth together into a causeway that allowed the crusaders to access the Sacred Table from an unexpected direction and defeat the Huun invaders.

After that crusade, towers were built near the top and bottom of the causeway to guard it. Both were taken briefly in the attacks before the Second Crusade but then stood their duty nearly 200 years before the fortifications were destroyed in the events that precipitated the Third Crusade. From the vantage of the desert floor, the high Tower of the Scarlet Hand appears heartbreakingly intact but is in fact a broken shell, and nothing but a circle of rubble on the desert remains of the Fortress of Parvalim that once guarded the lower extent of the road.

ZOAR RIVER

The Zoar starts high in the mountains and falls fast over a steep drop to the flatter land below. It forms the southern boundary of the Wasted Desert. When the snow melts on the lower slopes of the mountains, it runs very fast and cold and sometimes even overflows its lower north bank. During the rainy season, multiple dry streambeds throughout the desert fill with floodwaters, all pouring into the Zoar. Later in the year, when the snowmelt diminishes and the rains come to an end, the Zoar is much less full and can even be forded in spots.

HUUN IMPERIUM

Capital: Sin'shar
Notable Settlements: Paho't-mab, Shuul
Ruler: King of Kings Ossimandius the Undying
Government: autocracy
Population: 2,951,188 (all Huun)
Monstrous: karkadanns, sand giants, dune horrors (desert), crag giants, black trolls (mountains)
Languages: Huunic
Religion: Huun pantheon
Resources: limestone, sandstone, granite, marble, quartzite, iron, gold, silver, gemstones, medicinal plants
Currency: Huun (internal only), Baalathite, Ammuyad, Khemitian
Technology Level: Medieval, Dark Ages (villages and rural areas)

The homeland of the Huun Imperium is the Desert of Oreb, a high, isolated desert plateau in eastern Libynos. With rain-bearing clouds blocked by the high Scythirian Mountains to the west and the even higher Tirzhakah Mountains to the east, the Huun are largely dependent for water on sources in and from the mountains. The high mountains also have odd effects on the wind, which swirls strongly between the mountain ranges and can create powerful sandstorms that race across the desert with incredible speed.

The isolated location of the Desert of Oreb has resulted in the development of some strange plants and creatures found nowhere else, many of which have been adapted by the Huun to further their own needs. For instance, the plateau at one time had a small population of karkadanns, a muscular, rhino-like creature only rarely seen in other deserts of the world. The Huun increased the beasts' numbers and trained them for riding, giving the imperium an alternative to the camels they also imported for transportation across the hundreds of miles of desert they call home. Less easy to work with were the monstrous creatures the Huun now call "war beasts," but eventually ways were found to train them and methods developed to use them in warfare.

The Huun do not permit intruders to the imperium; those caught trespassing should best hope for an immediate death, as the only alternative is painful (and ultimately fatal) questioning regarding their business and intentions in the Imperium. Most who encounter Huun outside the high desert meet only armored warriors in battle. Very few (typically limited to merchants or traders from Ifthaaz or the Malagro) can claim any other relationship with the folk of the Imperium, and they do not discuss such things. As a result, the Huun have been able to remain a mystery to most of the world, and much of what is said about them is little more than wild speculation or unsubstantiated rumor.

History and Peoples

The Huun people are content to have outsiders believe that their origins are shrouded in myth and legend. Akadonian scholars have pieced together enough to conclude that year 1 of the Huun Chronicle corresponds with the year 2496 I.R., a year remembered for the fiery destruction of Curgantium and the beginning of the end of the Hyperborean empire. This seems to be the year the Huun organized the scattered settlements in and around the Desert of Oreb into a unified kingdom.

Many foreigners, based on little more than proximity, have assumed the Huun are an Ashurian folk. However, the history and stories of the imperium describe their descent from the ancient Hundaei clans of the Great Steppes of Akados, making the Huun the inheritors of an ancient legacy of enmity to Hyperborea. Physical similarities between the Huun and the other known descendants of the Hundaei make this claim quite plausible, though the same histories indicate some intermixing with other peoples of Libynos. How the Huun's ancestors found their way from the Haunted Steppes to the far reaches of Libynos is a topic of Huun myth little shared with outsiders, though the involvement of their great peacock deities is strongly implied.

For long years, the Hyperboreans occupied a plateau north of the Desert of Oreb, which they called the Sacred Table, and on which their city of Tircople was located. After the fall of their empire, they abandoned Tircople in 137 H.C. (2632 I.R.), an event greeted by the Huun with satisfaction. Unfortunately, the Akadonian kingdom of Foere, which viewed itself as the spiritual successor of Hyperborea, decided to lay claim to the Sacred Table in 249 H.C. (2744 I.R.).

In the year 463 H.C. (2958 I.R.), the god Nergal (who was then in ascendance) sent a vision to Ossimandius, the Huun king of kings, revealing the plateau as sacred to Nergal's faith: It conceals an entrance to the Underworld, the realm of Nergal's consort Erishkigal. Ossimandius duly declared a holy war against the Foerdewaith. The Huun armies swept over the mountains and slaughtered the inhabitants of Tircople and the plateau around it. Imperium soldiers were proud to say that they caught and killed both the pontifex, or religious leader of the city, and the purported first high lord of Tircople who was in charge of the military. They also put to the sword all of the Foerdewaith knights guarding the city, supposedly half of their total number in the entire world.

As is told elsewhere, this led to the so-called First Great Crusade and almost 250 years of warfare (and three further crusades) between the distant Foerdewaith and the imperium. The last such crusade ended with a Foerdewaith victory at the Battle of the Sickles in 712 H.C. (3207 I.R.), though it was only possible with the aid of an attack by dwarves of Shamash Kush on the Huun rear. This would likely not have been the final struggle between the two, but future conflict was preempted when fierce fighters of the Mguru tribe of the Malagro attacked the Sacred Table, slaying the entire remaining population of Tircople and destroying the city. The Mguru did not remain, and the Akadonians have never returned. Though the imperium has seen no need to reoccupy the plateau to date, Huun scouts patrol the area to ensure that future visitors do not believe it unprotected.

In addition to their homeland in the Scythirian Mountains, the Huun left a mark on other parts of Libynos, such as the Gulf of Huun off the continent's northwestern peninsula, so-called even on modern maps made in Akados. Yet other than the conflict over the holy plateau, the imperium has not openly sought to dominate peoples outside the Desert of Oreb for most of its existence. Recently, however, the priesthood of Nergal has been urging more active engagement with the outside world, following which an army of the imperium made a surprise attack into the heart of Akados. Marching to the very walls of Bard's Gate in 1019 H.C. (3514 I.R.), the army besieged the city for more than a year before making a calculated retreat ahead of the approaching forces of the overking of Foere. In addition, Huun warriors are now stationed at the great citadel of the Mulstabhins on Krivcycek Island in the midst of the only land passage between Libynos and Akados. Though the nuances of the plans of the priests and generals are not widely known even among the Huun, their armies — both in the desert and abroad — are prepared to bring glory to the imperium.

Throughout the years in their homeland, the Huun have spent much time traversing the sand and rocks of Oreb, and thus consider themselves people of the high desert rather than of the mountains. However, Oreb lacks the oases or wells usually found in hot sandy deserts (such as in Khemit or the Ashurian Desert), so the vast majority of the population is concentrated on the outskirts of the desert, near the mountains, rather than in the center. In addition, a sizable percentage of the Huun live and work in and under the mountains themselves.

Religion

The Huun worship a pantheon of gods, though the one most in ascendance today is Nergal, deathbringer and god of plague. His consort is Erishkigal, the gentle amasser of souls, who gives souls a place to rest until the destruction comes. Also venerated are Aku'te Selissa, the uncaring mother (called the White Lady); and the Peacock God Maas Tal'ek, destroyer of the universe and the end of all things.

Trade and Commerce

The Huun go to substantial lengths to be entirely self-sufficient, despite the harsh environment of the high desert. The imperium's engineers and wizards worked to make water supplies more accessible, creating and expanding channels for snowmelt from the mountains and tapping underground water sources. The courses of certain rivers have even been changed to flow toward the desert or at least to mountain valleys where the water is available to the Huun. This enabled the irrigation of terraces built along the mountainsides and furnished reliable sources of food for the nation.

Given the difficulties of travel over the mountains, exploration underground has sought to find usable routes to the lands beyond the peaks. This has been largely unsuccessful in locating easy means of travel north or south. However, several cavern systems were discovered that, with modification, opened routes east to the Malagro Jungle and west to the various nations along the Sea of Baal. Some trade occurs via these routes, primarily with the jungle peoples of the Malagro and with some discreet merchants in Ifthaaz and Baalthaaz. Only the most-trusted Huun are given the opportunity to travel to these lands outside the mountains. The routes themselves are kept secret even from most Huun and are zealously protected from any outsiders.

The mountains themselves provide many resources. Stone, of course, is readily available and many types have been quarried. The Huun have also been mining the mountains for hundreds of years, finding everything from iron ore to silver and gold to gemstones. Some miners believe such rare substances as diamond, adamantine, and even mithral may be found deeper under the Tirzhakah Mountains and exploration is continuing in that direction.

Loyalties and Diplomacy

The imperium has no embassies in any other country, nor do any other nations have formal relations with the Huun. Mutually cautious trading relationships, sometimes conducted at one remove, are maintained with a select group of countries.

GOVERNMENT

The imperium is ruled by an absolute monarch known as King of Kings Ossimandius the Undying. This happens to be the same name used by the king who first sacked the city of Tircople in 463 H.C. (2958 I.R.). As a result, outsiders are forced to speculate whether the current king of kings is indeed the same individual or if the name and title are always taken by the ruler of the imperium. The Huun are content to let them wonder.

MILITARY

The Huun are among the most feared warriors in all of the Lost Lands. The infantry is fierce and the cavalry are excellent in the saddle or dismounted, riding camels, horses, or karkadanns, as the situation demands. The infantry on foot are supported by mounted archers that fire clouds of arrows in swift attacks and then withdraw. The armies of the imperium are most renowned for their fury in combat and their nearly unbreakable morale.

Huun warriors typically wear steeply pitched conical helms of burnished steel that cover the back and sides of their neck with steel scales, and have bronze nasal guards. The lower part of the face is protected against blowing sand or dust by a veil of black silk and the small portion of the face that is still visible (namely the eyes and cheeks) is darkened with kohl. Opponents find this gives a sinister, otherworldly appearance that has shaken more than one foe facing the Huun in battle. Soldiers of the imperium use lamellar armor made of overlapping steel plates covered in black lacquer and trimmed in polished brass.

MAJOR THREATS

For hundreds of years, the sand giants in the southern part of the Desert of Oreb were the major threat to the Huun. In the past decades, the king of kings finally reached an accommodation with the leaders of all the giant tribes and despite a few incidents, the peace seems to be holding.

Although the risk of outside invasion is negligible, the Huun stay vigilant. However, the desert has its own risks, including various monsters of both sand and mountain. In addition, some places in the desert are said to be haunted by the dead or worse, and the Huun shun such places of ill repute. It takes knowledge and experience to read the signs of the desert well enough to know where such places are and to avoid them, though, and few other than the desert scouts have that skill.

SIN'SHAR, CITY OF (CAPITAL)

Ruler: King of Kings Ossimandius the Undying
Government: autocracy
Population: 84,759 (all Huun)

The capital of the imperium, Sin'shar lies along the eastern edge of the desert near a natural basin at the foot of Mount Zadak. A river has been diverted to fill the basin as a lake, and the city is built near and around it. A planned city, the main roads fan out neatly with the most important buildings near the center. However, the centuries have taken their toll on the intended organization; winding alleys, dead-end streets, and hidden courts can be found in Sin'shar just like in every other large city in the world.

The palace of the king of kings is of granite, sturdy and imposing rather than elegant. As with most Huun buildings, its large windows have carved screens to let in any breeze while keeping out most of the sun. The windows also have strong coverings and heavy hangings that are put in place in case of a sandstorm or when the temperature drops drastically at night, as it often does. Interior hallways have no windows, which makes them stuffy but also a possible shelter should a very bad storm blow up. Besides housing the palace staff and the assistants and guards of the king of kings, the building also includes enough bedrooms to accommodate the many people who might need to be at court at the same time. Despite being in the palace, these rooms are not luxurious, as luxury and softness have very little place in the life of the Huun. In addition, the rooms tend to be all very similar; the Huun have no nobility to expect special treatment, only those deserving of more respect due to experience, profession, or skill.

The public rooms of the palace are likewise less ornamented than most such edifices in other kingdoms, although the throne room itself is decorated around the edges with murals of peacocks in larger-than-life size. The throne of the king of kings is barely larger than an average chair, though its workmanship is exceptional and it is well-cushioned.

One feature of the palace known only to the most senior officials and quite well hidden is the Room of Travel. Set in the walls of this room are magical doorways to other cities in the imperium, guarded by a group of the Huun's best warriors lest some enemy ever access one and try to use it in an attack. Primarily for use by messengers and for the transportation of small cargo, they also are occasionally employed by the king of kings or other important government officials to visit other Huun cities.

Other civic buildings in Sin'shar are built of granite quarried nearby in the Tirzhakah range, and their architecture is primarily practical. Exceptions are the four temples in the city, which are each built of stone particularly chosen to please and represent each deity and which vary in style.

The most popular temple in recent years is the black basalt temple of Nergal the Deathbringer, who sends war, plague, and other forms of devastation. Some worship to pray for his wrath on their enemies, while many try to propitiate him and turn his attention away from themselves. His consort is Erishkigal, who allows the souls of the dead to abide in the Underworld so they are not forced to roam the earth after death. Her temple is built of marble, gray with swirls like the mists of the Underworld.

The Garden of the Mother holds the temple of Aku'te Selissa, the uncaring mother, who is also known as the White Lady. Using irrigation from the lake, a large garden area has been built with many exotic flowers, fruits, etc. An army of gardeners takes care of the grounds while a corps of beautiful young men and women play and perform for the delight of the goddess. Sometimes they learn and execute elaborate dances or musical pieces; other times they play the games of children, though often with an element of danger added.

In the center of the garden is a special area called the White Garden. It has only plants which bear white flowers and is built around a white marble statue of the goddess, with her hard eyes, aloof expression, and diadem, cloak, and train of white peacock feathers. Peacocks of all types roam the outer garden freely, but only white ones are allowed in the White Garden; others are violently chased out. Someone is on duty in the White Garden at all times, so a person is always near if the goddess desires to speak. Such a server always dresses in white, of course. Nearby is the actual temple to the White Lady. Made of pure white marble, it seems to have been inspired by certain ancient temples of Jaati; it has a clean, pleasing shape with the walls elaborately carved and pierced. Inside it includes living areas for the lady's priests and attendants as well as plenty of space for worship.

The final temple stands opposite the city on the far side of the lake, in a desolate, rocky area. A road to it is paved with black granite but it is impossible to tell what type of stone was used to construct the temple because it is entirely covered in colorful mosaics composed of bits of gemstones set in geometric patterns and in swirls of peacock feathers. Inside, the single great room is almost dark but the faint light shows more mosaics covering the walls completely. At the front of the room, lights illuminate a tall mosaic of a beautiful, blue-skinned man with solid black eyes. He wears a diadem of small feathers and is feathered himself, beginning at his cheeks. He has feathered arms, like a peacock's wings, and he wears a robe of feathers the same blue as his skin and a cloak with a long train of peacock feathers. This is the temple of the Peacock God Maas Tal'ek, destroyer of the universe and the end of all things.

PAHO'T-MAB, CITY OF

Ruler: High Administrator Perrizz Qos
Government: bureaucracy under the guidance of King of Kings
 Ossimandius
Population: 41,881 (all Huun)

This city is located near the headwaters of the Zoar River, some miles from where it cascades down a waterfall to the Jungle of Malagro far below. It is also the nearest Huun city to the plateau known to the people of Akados as the Sacred Table. This is the only Huun city that has ever come under attack by the foreign armies calling themselves crusaders, although several of their lesser fortresses and outposts have been destroyed. Paho't-mab is built around a palace smaller but more elaborate than that of the king of kings in Sin'shar, as well as a temple to Nergal in a stereotypical style. These and a few government buildings help convince outsiders that Paho't-mab is the capital of the imperium so that they don't venture into the desert to search for something more. The ground below the city is rock that is honeycombed with caves developed centuries ago into underground shelters to house most of the populace in case of attack. One cave beneath the false palace contains a Room of Travel connected to the real palace of the king of kings so that, in the worst situation, people could evacuate to Sin'shar. This has never been necessary, and only a handful of the most trusted people even know the room exists.

People living in Paho't-mab generally understand that they are decoys; it is either a great honor or a punishment to be sent there to live. On one hand, the city is still at risk even though it has been a few hundred years since any warfare has occurred in the region. On the other hand, residents of Paho't-mab have the opportunity to go down to the jungle and possibly even to the sea. Exposure to other people and places is good background for becoming a diplomat — a person chosen to represent the Huun in another nation, whether that is as a negotiator or as a stealthy observer.

While the king of kings is occasionally in residence at Paho't-mab, governing the city is left to High Administrator Perrizz Qos. Military units stationed in the city are part of the Northern Command under General Second Class Hulek Shar-Ishkun and decisions regarding trade issues fall to Master Tradesman Raba Shebitku. A significant percentage of the population spends most of its time farming small terraces around the city and one of the duties of the high administrator is to be sure the city has enough food and water stored at all times to sustain the entire populace through a year-long siege.

SHUUL, MILITARY CITY OF

Ruler: General First Class Uluk Zamzummin
Government: military bureaucracy under the guidance of King
 of Kings Ossimandius
Population: 83,839 (all Huun)

Located far to the south in the Desert of Oreb, Shuul is the military headquarters and training center of the Huun Imperium. Almost the entire present-day population of the imperium has passed through here in their youth. Those who were unfit may have spent only a brief time training in the desert, but it is still an experience that unifies more than it divides the people.

Since the dispersed nature of the resources of the imperium has resulted in towns and villages being scattered around the desert, many people grow up without ever meeting a person from more than a few miles away. Certainly, Eastholders near the Tirzhakah Mountains would almost never see a Westholder from the far side of the desert. Meeting during military training helps bring the various people into an appreciation for each other. It also provides a large trained force for the defense of the imperium, or to add to the active roster for an exceptional international foray.

The Fortress of Shuul has a very high, strong wall that was built for defense before the imperium concluded its peace with the sand giants at the south end of the desert. Most of its supplies are brought by caravan from villages on the outskirts of the desert but the fortress has a secret magical means to supply water if they are ever truly desperate. In addition, deep within the fortress is a Room of Travel with a doorway that connects it to Sin'shar. The training, though, takes place at a camp in the desert rather than inside the walls of the fortress; indeed, unless the sand giants abrogate the strong oaths their leaders swore, most military trainees at Shuul will never even see the inside of the fortress. The city and the training camp are entirely run by the military; the only civilians in the area are some who travel with the supply caravans.

GEOGRAPHIC FEATURES AND POINTS OF INTEREST OF THE HUUN IMPERIUM

OREB, DESERT OF

The Desert of Oreb lies between the two arms of the Scythirian Mountains, or between the Scythirian and Tirzhakah Mountains for those who use the name given to the eastern range by the Huun. This region, at a high elevation between the two arms of mountains, is entirely in rainshadow and receives almost no moisture at any time of the year. It is thus a dry, sandy, and cold desert.

Various creatures acclimated to such arid conditions make their home here, including several tribes of sand giants in the southern end of the desert. It is also the home of the Huun Imperium, which used technology and magic to find water, build cities, and make a life for their people in a place no one else wanted.

When the Hyperboreans first arrived at the Sacred Table, several expeditions were mounted to explore the mountains of the region, and at least one party is said to have made it to the Desert of Oreb. Their report indicated that they waded through the dunes for a handful of days, seeing no sources of water or sign of habitation, though they did catch distant glimpses of what they simply called "strange creatures." Eventually they turned back and reported that they found nothing more than desolation. No further expeditions were sent to the area and, until the sack of Tircople that led to the First Great Crusade, most memory of the land between the mountains was lost.

TIRZHAKAH MOUNTAINS

Tirzhakah is the name the Huun give to the range of very high mountains east of the Desert of Oreb. Most people other than the Huun believe the Scythirian Mountains continue all the way from Baalthaaz and its neighbors on the west to the Malagro Jungle on the east, and so call all those mountains Scythirian. As far as the Huun are concerned, the Tirzhakah Mountains begin south of the Zoar River and its waterfall and continue all along the east side of the desert. Where the desert ends and the two mountain ranges join again, the single range is the Scythirian Mountains.

IMYA AND SHABBIS

IMYA OF AXUUM

Capital: Saphar
Notable Settlements: Bahrkela, Fereshan, Namran, Talatem,
 Yamnat, Yuhaqbiz
Ruler: Nem-Mulya (royal governor) Mehadis
Government: royal governor appointed by the king of Axuum
Population: 956,225 (951,751 Merowen, of Imya and Axuum;
 4,474 other human ethnicity)
Monstrous: blood hawks, gnasher lizards (mountains), sea cats
 (coast), retch hounds
Languages: Khemitian; Imyan still spoken in rural areas
Religion: Pharaonic pantheon
Resources: gemstones, pearls, silver, gold, adamantium,

cane sugar, cocoa beans, spices, myrrh, frankincense, ivory, rosewood, cedar, wood products
Currency: Axuumite
Technology Level: High Middle Ages (Saphar, Bahrkela), Dark Ages (other cities), Iron Age (rural areas)

Imya is in eastern Libynos, on a broad peninsula between the Boiling Sea and the Ruby Sea. Separated from Numeda to the northwest by the Karaman Mountains, the country has very different terrain than its desert neighbor. The northeast has verdant woodlands while the central plain is well-watered and lightly-wooded savannah. Coastline makes up about two-thirds of the country's border, and sea industries provide a livelihood for many people.

For most of its history, Imya, secure behind the barrier of the Karaman Mountains, was left largely alone by the great powers of Libynos. It has long traded with other peoples, largely through the sea lanes via its major ports, but otherwise has been a bit of a backwater. Then, about 250 years, ships of the Kingdom of Axuum from central Libynos landed in Imya's coastal cities, bearing marines and siege equipment. The complacent Imyans had but a small army that the forces of the invaders completely overwhelmed. In less than a year, Axuum had secured all of the major settlements of Imya and began the process of stripping the land of as much wealth as possible.

Today, Imya is ruled by a royal governor (known as the nem-mulya) appointed by King Urtigaddi of Axuum. Governors (or mulyas) with authority over cities and regions within Imya are appointed by the nem-mulya at Saphar from the local population, but are expected in return to pay tribute to the nem-mulya and to pay the requisite tributes and taxes required by the king. Axuumite traders have a monopoly on exports; Imyan merchants or craftspeople can sell quantities of goods only within the country or to an Axuumite, not to any foreign traders. (Personal sales to foreigners are grudgingly permitted, though officials often check up on businesses that seem to attract a lot of foreign customers.)

Of course, the Axuumite monopoly has led to efforts to circumvent these restrictions.

Fishing villages line the Imyan coast, and a fishing boat during the day can easily become a smuggler's boat at night. This requires contacts outside the country, though, because a small boat needs to meet another boat or ship at sea, not try to sail hundreds of miles to the nearest country that is not Axuum. One place where smugglers have found good success is along the far northern coast of Imya. From a sheltered bay or cove, a small boat can transport cargo to one of the mountainous islands in Cinnabar Bay, where another boat can pick it up and carry it on to the markets in Shabbis. Such smuggling is dangerous, as the nem-mulya is known to employ spies, but some Imyans are sufficiently angry or desperate to take such risks, particularly if it allows them to strike back at those who are siphoning off the wealth of their country.

Other Imyans express their displeasure with the Axuum dominion by contacting Numedan corsairs with information on the day and time of the departure of richly-laden merchant ships, anticipating that the corsairs will be willing to reward such useful information, or at least pay something for it the next time.

In addition to establishing a trade monopoly, Axuum has made other changes in Imya to increase the amount of wealth taken from the area. For example, the criminal code in Imya was modified to ensure an adequate supply of convicts sentenced to serve in the adamantium mines in the Karaman Mountains. Also, about 30 years ago the king of Axuum decided to introduce great elephants into Imya's central savannah to increase the availability of ivory. Several towns and villages were displaced to give the elephants plenty of room to roam; now only the smallest villages are left in what has come to be called "Elephant Country."

At least outwardly, most of the people of Imya worship the deities of Khemit, which were introduced by the Axuumites with the conquest. In many locales, temples and shrines to the old gods were simply allowed to fall to ruin while larger, more elaborate temples to the new gods were built. Despite the risks of discovery, some Imyans managed to pass down knowledge of the old ways and continue to worship the old gods, though in secret. After two and a half centuries, however, fewer Imyans

recall the ancient prayers and rituals.

The changes imposed by Axuum have been backed up by a strong contingent of the Royal Army, which has been stationed in Imya since the conquest. (The king feels it does soldiers good to have a chance to be active outside the country, and it keeps them sharp in case Axuum should ever be threatened.) Each city has at least one company of soldiers billeted there in a fortress or reinforced barracks, and even some towns are required to host a contingent of Axuumite troops.

Saphar, City of (Capital)

Ruler: Nem-Mulya Mehadis
Government: royal governor appointed by the king of Axuum
Population: 28,921 (mostly Merowen)

Saphar is on the south coast of Imya at the mouth of the Seydi River, with an excellent harbor that was expanded and improved only about 20 years ago. It is an old city and, before the conquest, was the capital of Imya. Now it is the headquarters of Axuum's authority, and the old king's palace has become the luxurious residence of the nem-mulya, with Axuumite administrators and magistrates using the rooms that were once frequented by Imya's nobility. Since Nem-Mulya Mehadis believes anything worth doing is worth doing to excess, he also has a substantial country estate nearby and a villa at a beautiful location on the coast about a day's journey east.

Nem-Mulya Mehadis is a connoisseur of excellent food and takes advantage of his position in Imya to get fresh spices, and seafood directly from the ocean. He is always interested in hiring another cook who is the master of some new cuisine. (Currently, Mehadis desires the services of someone who can cook him genuine Kaldilooran food, which he has heard is distinctive.)

Despite the distractions of the table, however, Mehadis does not forget his duty to Axuum. He employs several regional experts who advise him on ways that Imya might produce even more income for the benefit of Axuum, and has his deputies (all of whom are from Axuum) look into any likely possibilities. Recently he has been mixing business with pleasure by having people experiment with ways to keep fish alive on board a ship for extended periods of time so that unusual types such as swordfish could be taken locally and sold to gourmands in other parts of the continent.

An important industry in the Saphar region is the harvesting and processing of myrrh and frankincense. Although those are also produced in certain other countries, the total yield in Saphar is greater than in other areas and is primarily of good quality.

In the city of Saphar, the Axuumite conquerors actually pulled down the temples to the country's previous gods, and in their place built majestic new edifices dedicated to such deities of Khemit as Ra, Osiris, Isis, Thoth, and Set. Those who objected were put to hauling great stone blocks for the building of the new temples; within short order, at least in public, the worship of the old gods vanished, and the veneration of these foreign gods became universal.

Bahrkela, City of

Ruler: Mulya (governor) Zergaz
Government: local governor appointed by Nem-Mulya Mehadis
Population: 10,382 (mostly Merowen)

Bahrkela is a port on the east coast of the Ruby Sea that predates the conquest by Axuum. Using gemstones and metal mined in the Karaman Mountains and brought to town via riverboat, the renowned craftspeople at Bahrkela produce cut gems, silver jewelry with set stones, worked pieces of silver, and plain silver ingots. The mountains in the area also yield some good-quality iron. The smiths here are not as skilled as those at Cadua in Alcaldar or Tarresh in Antioch, but they do produce sturdy steel tools and weapons that are sold by Axuum throughout the Central Kingdoms and into Khemit.

Most of the merchandise from Bahrkela, however, goes directly to Axuum to be exported through its trade network. The harbor here is busy with ships carrying goods to Axuum or directly to other destinations, alongside fishing boats going out to the Ruby Sea. Many Axuumite merchants have representatives here to look after their interests and it is a popular post, as the local seacoast has an excellent climate.

FERESHAN, CITY OF

Ruler: Mulya Lathial
Government: Local governor appointed by Nem-Mulya Mehadis
Population: 17,678 (mostly Merowen)

The city of Fereshan is located on the east coast of the Ruby Sea, about 150 miles from where that body opens into the great ocean, at the mouth of the small Tahir River. For many generations a small town with a mediocre harbor, Fereshan was forced to make many improvements to suit the needs of the Axuumites. As the Imyan port closest to Axuum's capital of Mazaber, it has become the base of the Axuumite military in Imya. Many people are employed transporting supplies for the Royal Army of Axuum, and in supporting its headquarters and camps. Not everyone is happy about the presence of the army in the area, but the Mulya has people alert for dissent; her spies usually ferret out troublemakers before they inconvenience the troops and cause difficulty for the entire city.

Fereshan is also the port where great elephants captured by Axuum for release in Imya's interior disembark. The king's animal speakers, who are able to command the cooperation of the huge beasts, prefer to let the creatures off the ships as close as possible to their eventual home. Most of the folk of Fereshan are in awe of the great beasts, and some are so enchanted that they follow the elephants out of the city to the savannah, where they settle in to watch them for long periods of time. A few have even sought to become animal speakers in Axuum, but at best have ended up as servants; they exchange the onerous task of keeping the transport ships clean for the privilege of caring for the majestic beasts for the short time they are in captivity.

In contrast, some residents of Fereshan are among those previously displaced from the country's interior to make room for the new herds of elephants. They resent the creatures and occasionally try to harm them, or advocate against cooperating with the animal speakers whenever they bring more. This has resulted in more than a little tension in the city, and the mulya and her officials work hard to keep the situation under control lest it come to the attention of the local Axuumite commander, General Fer'am of Jarmi, also sometimes known as Fer'am the Grim.

NAMRAN, CITY OF

Ruler: Mulya Hutar
Government: Local governor appointed by Nem-Mulya Mehadis
Population: 11,583 (mostly Merowen)

On the east coast of Imya, Namran sits at the mouth of the Yuhanem River where it enters the Boiling Sea. The surrounding region supplies primarily agricultural products, but among these are cane sugar, cocoa beans, and several types of spices, so it provides its share of wealth for Axuumite merchants. Mulya Hutar is often under pressure to increase production to meet the demand in various markets, but he is wise enough to realize that the land needs care in order to maintain its abundant yields for future years. He works with expert growers to find ways to mollify the traders without exhausting the land.

In addition, ingots and finished goods from the adamantine mines and smithies around Yamnat come down the river to the docks at Namran. These shipments are always accompanied by a contingent of royal soldiers and remain under guard whether at a warehouse or on the dock until they are loaded aboard a ship and on their way to Axuum. Most locals know to avoid the docks when a shipment is ready to be loaded, since the soldiers view anyone in the area as a likely thief and often take extreme action to defend the shipment from anyone they may suspect of ill intent, on even the slightest suspicion, and no matter the reasonableness of an offered explanation.

TALATEM, CITY OF

Ruler: Mulya Yazil
Government: local governor appointed by Nem-Mulya Mehadis
Population: 12,471 (mostly Merowen)

Talatem, on the southeastern coast of Imya, lies at the mouth of the long Damat River, which flows into and out of Lake Gevegi near the Karaman Mountains. The river provides a way to transport goods from roughly one-third of the country to the port of Talatem, where Axuumite traders purchase them at favorable prices to sell elsewhere at a good profit. This includes foodstuffs, wines, and raw cotton, as well as gemstones and gold from mines in the mountains.

One source of wealth available in the area of Talatem is the pearl oysters to be found up and down the coast. Talatem is at the edge of the Boiling Sea and something about the qualities of the water there means that oysters tend to produce more pearls with golden coloration, which are quite rare elsewhere, as well as many pink pearls. Authorities have a process by which only certain beds can be harvested in a year while others are rested, and pearl divers in the approved beds need to register with an administrator from the mulya's office. Of course, any enforcers will go only so far afield from Talatem, so any oyster bed more than about 10 miles from the city might be harvested by unapproved workers and not all the pearls might get back to an official trader.

YAMNAT, TOWN OF

Ruler: Mulya Ayzur
Government: local governor appointed by Nem-Mulya Mehadis
Population: 6,916 (mostly Merowen)

Built on a bend of the upper Yuhanem River on the shoulders of the Karanam Mountains, Yamnat is less than 20 years old, having been established for the sole purpose of controlling and supporting the adamantium mines in the nearby mountains. While the town is surrounded by a sturdy stone wall, its buildings are all constructed from rough-hewn local wood, and it lacks many of the amenities one might expect in a town of its size. This is partially due to a lack of demand, as most of the miners are convicts who receive no pay for their labor and have little time for leisure. However, enough others work in the area to sustain a modest number of establishments catering to their needs for drinking, gambling, and private recreation.

More than just a mining town, Yamnat has the facilities and craftsmen to process the ore from the ground into ingots and even to manufacture some finished goods. This avoids the labor of transporting the bulky ore to one location for smelting and another location to have it worked. To ensure the town's success, Axuum encourages experienced smiths as well as mine workers to move to Yamnat, though any sales must of course go through approved Axuumite merchants or agents.

The rare metal is much more time-consuming to mine than iron or gold, and more difficult to work than steel, so progress is slow. King Urtigaddi of Axuum takes a personal interest in the adamantium mines, and so Nem-Mulya Mehadis does as well. Mulya Ayzur paid a pretty penny for his governorship and sees this as his big chance to break into more lucrative levels of government service, as well as putting away something for himself from the profits of the mine. That means he is constantly pushing the miners to work faster and the smelters to get every bit of the metal out of the raw ore. He tried pressuring the smiths but that didn't go well, as any smith with the ability to craft adamantium can easily find work in other places. Ayzur was bluntly told to leave them alone or they would all quit and he would have to explain the situation to the nem-mulya, so he stays strictly away from the smiths except for inspecting their work and keeping the occasional dagger for himself "as a sample."

Ayzur is also a bully to others in town, constantly expecting free services and threatening anyone who crosses him. He is disliked by most and outright hated by a few, but the company of the Royal Army in place "protecting the mines" keeps him safe until he crosses a person with nothing left to lose.

YUHAQBIZ, CITY OF

Ruler: Mulya Germa
Government: local governor appointed by Nem-Mulya Mehadis
Population: 8,849 (mostly Merowen)

Yuhaqbiz sits at the mouth of the Zarik River on a protected bay on the north coast of Imya in the larger Cinnabar Bay. Once, the city was the capital of the independent kingdom of Yeera until it fell to the kingdom of Imya some four centuries ago, which of course was later conquered by Axuum. Mulya Germa can trace her lineage back to the Yeerian royal family. (She would not be considered the heir, though, as at the time of that kingdom's demise it still only let males inherit the throne. Her son, should she have one, would qualify.) Yuhaqbiz was once a much-larger city but has diminished with each successive conquest. The section of the city toward the sea has been maintained, but inland the buildings have been allowed to fall to ruin, including temples that predated the conquest by Imya, and the royal palace of Yeera, which was badly damaged when the city first fell over 400 years ago.

The well-watered woodlands of northeastern Imya produce rosewood and cedar as timber for export along with wood products produced by local craftmasters. However, the most valuable industry of Yuhaqbiz is pearl diving for the black oysters along the coast. Black pearls seem to occur more frequently in Cinnabar Bay than anywhere else in the world and provide a great deal of wealth to Axuum. On the other hand, they are easy to smuggle and a good quantity make their way eventually to Shabbis. There, certain Imyans have a standing arrangement to sell the black pearls to a representative of the Huun Imperium, which pays a good price for them.

GEOGRAPHIC FEATURES AND POINTS OF INTEREST IN IMYA

BOILING SEA

The Boiling Sea is part of the Great Ocean Ûthaf along the coast of eastern Libynos near Imya and the Jungle of Malagro. Although the water is warm due to strong currents from the south, it is not boiling hot. However, bubbles the size of a hand or larger rise from it as if from the surface of a boiling pot. No reliable witnesses have demonstrated any harm from being immersed in the water or eating fish taken from the sea, so experienced sailors treat it as a mere curiosity and as a basis for tall tales to credulous landlubbers.

CINNABAR BAY

Off the Boiling Sea just north of Imya, Cinnabar Bay is most notable for its large, mountainous islands. It is possible to sail through the maze of islands and rocks to the western coast, but the danger is too great for any but the most desperate merchants. The coast has a few villages containing folk who prefer to be left well alone, and who support themselves by fishing, only occasionally making the trip out through the islands to the larger bay. People in Imya and in the city of Shabbis tell stories about famous pirates of the past who sailed out of Cinnabar Bay and had refuges among the islands. These accounts could have a degree of truth to them, but it is more likely that they are merely local stories.

DAMAT RIVER

The Damat River rises in the Karaman Mountains, flows into and out of Lake Gevegi, and then flows east and south. Its many tributaries drain from about a third of the country, from savannah on the west and agricultural land on the east. It provides a transportation network south to the coast at the city of Talatem.

LAKE NASHA

About 50 miles in diameter, Lake Nasha has several small villages along its shore that survive by fishing in the lake as well as doing small-scale agriculture and raising animals such as goats and chickens for food. The area of Lake Nasha has also become home to several herds of elephants, which causes competition for resources. The villagers don't dare kill the elephants, as that would bring severe reprisals on all the settlements in the area. They are trying to find a way to convince an animal speaker (from somewhere other than Axuum) to come and lead the herds farther east and north away from the inhabited area. From Lake Nasha, the Veli River runs southeast and joins the Seydi River on the way to the sea, making it easy to travel from the lake to the coast.

LONG TEETH, THE

This group of islands in Cinnabar Bay is named for the jagged peaks that dominate most of them. The southerly currents swirling into the bay give the Long Teeth a warm climate, and the islands are covered with vegetation everywhere except the rockiest slopes. Although generally considered to be uninhabited, a few hardy souls might be living in splendid isolation without being noticed by the rare visitors. The west coast of Cinnabar Bay is cut off from the rest of the Boiling Sea by the Long Teeth, as few ships large enough to sail the ocean can get past the islands. Only fishing vessels from a few small villages on the western shore, or some who set out from the northern coast of Imya, regularly sail among the Teeth.

SEYDI RIVER

This river flows from the southeast side of the Karaman Mountains, south to the sea at Saphar, the capital of Imya. The river is large enough that it effectively limits the portion of the savannah used by the elephants imported to Imya. Since even the animal speakers never check up on the herds after transporting them to Imya, no one has yet realized this but it is beginning to be an issue as more elephants are captured from the Yingozi Woodlands and released here.

SHABBIS, GREAT CITY OF

Ruler: Rumina Vihode, First Lady of the Council of Merchant Lords
Government: oligarchy; run by a group of 14 merchant lords who control the districts of the city
Population: 266,232 (126,660 Jaata, 51,600 Numedan, 23,930 Antiochian, 20,560 Baalathite, 8,100 Reaping Coast, 6,390 Bhanakhiri, 3,510 Castorhagi, 1,020 Foerdewaith, 21,262 other human ethnicity, 3,200 other)
Languages: Meeruwhan, Bhanikhat, Westerling, others
Religion: Gohtra pantheon, Paramountcies pantheon, Castorhagi pantheon, others
Resources: trade, manufactured goods, gems, arms, slaves, crime
Currency: Shabbisian
Technology Level: Medieval

The Green City of Jasper, as Shabbis is poetically named, lies in the Gulf of Shabbis on the coast of the Boiling Sea, north of Cinnabar Bay. Three rivers converge at the city. The Laisong River runs along the north side of the city, and aqueducts from it provide water for most of the Upper Districts. To the south, the Chuba and the Jeikhan Rivers merge and spread into a mire of slow streams and muddy hummocks before they eventually ooze into the Gulf of Shabbis. Lower parts of the city are prone to flooding during the rainy season, or even at high tides.

This city of a thousand wonders is literally built of jasper, at least in part. Centuries ago, an earthquake exposed an amazing deposit of the material commonly known as Khemitian jasper in the Scythirian Mountains near the headwaters of the Chuba River. City engineers were able to quarry it like marble, and most of the palaces and civic buildings located on a hill in the center of the city are made of the lustrous green stone. Other important buildings or wealthy residences are at least faced with the material. In addition, the walls are another type of green stone and have been polished by hundreds of years of convicts and slaves, so they also gleam in the sun.

The walled holdings of the merchant lords who dominate the city are at the highest reach of land between the rivers. The government center of the city is slightly lower, with the Merchants' Hall claiming the most prominent place. Beneath that are the districts of merchants and markets, then the craftspeople, and then the warehouses and crowded tenements of laborers. Near the docks and outside the walls, along the rivers, are slums that teem with people trying to get along in any way they can. Each merchant lord controls a district of the city; some districts are also oddly shaped as a result of negotiations for control and profit. Merchant lords are almost sovereign in their own districts, as long as they do nothing to hurt trade.

Along with its "thousand wonders," the Green City is also known as the source of a thousand plagues. Its swampy lowlands and dismal slums are infested by swarms of rats and insects known to carry many types of diseases, which range from the common threat of malaria to the unusually virulent Shabbisian Plague. The rats are impossible to keep off the ships in the harbor, so most countries of Libynos refuse to do business in Shabbis or allow Shabbisian ships into their ports for fear of spreading the plague. Ships from distant Akados still call here, though; the governments of their distant countries have not heard about the disease threats, and the traders themselves choose to take risks for the sake of profit.

Originally started by settlers from the Jaati region, the citizens of Shabbis now claim ancestry from dozens of countries and many types of people, including some whose forebears were not even humanoid. Languages abound, although Meeruwhan is most commonly spoken, and much bargaining in the markets is done by gestures. Of course, with the din of people in the market districts, sellers and buyers are unlikely to be able to hear each other anyway. (The Upper Districts are slightly quieter.)

Religion in the Green City is a jumble of beliefs, calling on deities and powers from Jaati in the north to Bhanakhiri in the far south to the remote City-State of Castorhage in the distant west. Aside from a large temple to the combined Ghotran gods located in the city center, temples and shrines are crowded in wherever they can fit and may not match the average worshipper's expectations. Lacking the space for freestanding buildings, deities might have a shrine in an alcove of a workroom or tavern, or a temple in part of an upper floor of a mercantile building.

NUMEDA, KINGDOM OF

Capital: Kirtius
Notable Settlements: Balgrimmon, Dawaad, Saruca
Ruler: King Massini
Government: monarchy
Population: 1,195,281 (1,170,804 Numedan, 24,332 other human ethnicity, 145 dwarf)
Monstrous: hobgoblins, harpies (desert), bugbears (anywhere), lantern goats (mountains)
Languages: Khemitian
Religion: Anumon
Resources: crops, livestock, horses, gold, iron, gemstones, marble, trade
Currency: Khemitian and Baalathite; also silver or gold trade bars
Technology Level: Medieval (Kirtius), High Middle Ages (other towns), Dark Ages (tribes)

The country of Numeda may be the largest kingdom of the Greater Maighib Desert, at least by land area. Occupying over half of the Numedan Peninsula in the south part of eastern Libynos, it is bounded on the west by Tahmakht (a possession of Khemit), on the southwest by the Ruby Sea, on the south and east by the Karaman Mountains, and on the north by the Kingdom of Ifthaaz. Numeda is a country of many parts, from the dry coastal regions along the Sea of Baal and Ruby Sea, to the arable areas of the north, to the deep sands and rocky flats of the Eastern Maighib Desert, to the hills and mountains forming the country's eastern border. These different regions mean the folk of Numeda vary substantially in their lives and livelihoods, with large cities near the sea of Baal, tribespeople in the desert, and prosperous mining settlements in the Karaman Mountains. Certain features serve to keep them united, however.

The people of Numeda tend to be fiercely independent, since the country developed as a culture of nomads based on the camel and the horse. For hundreds of years they survived by relying on their tightly-knit clans, having no long-term, permanent cities but only a few settlements around strategic oases or important religious sites. Then, more than a thousand years ago, a prophet walked out of the desert and gradually changed their civilization. Significant populations are now gathered in a few cities and many villages, and even Numedans who still live nomadic lifestyles in the desert visit the cities from time to time.

Sulymon the Prophet has influenced Numeda for hundreds of years. As the primary advocate of the deity Anumon (god of gates and keeper of laws), he encouraged the people to move toward the acknowledgement of national laws and a way of life that accepts the need for the presence and cooperation of others rather than just one's own small clan.

Numeda has some excellent natural resources, though they are not evenly distributed throughout the country. The northern hill country has enough grass for cattle and supports other crops, and the foothills to the east get enough moisture to raise sheep and grow grain. The eastern hills also have a great deal of mineral wealth found in various places along their length. Towns or individuals who can afford to fund a mining operation have become very wealthy, and the government has received its share of the abundance. Just because Numeda is a country of riches doesn't mean its people are rich, though. The wealth is concentrated in the hands of a few powerful people or clans, so others may turn to banditry or piracy to try to get their share.

However, when the government sanctions the piracy (for a share of the proceeds, of course), then criminals become upstanding privateers, naval heroes to the lowly people of the country. This is the situation with the mariners of Numeda: nobles sponsor ships and crews who "patrol" the waters around Numeda watching for ships "encroaching on Numeda's sovereign waters." Westerners named these ships corsairs (from the Hyperborean term "coursaros," which meant pirate), but the crews proudly adopted the pejorative term as their own.

In their small, fast ships, the corsairs of Numeda can't stand up to most armed ships in a fight, but they can easily overtake a laden (and lightly armed) merchantman or run away from the heavier naval vessels. Several fortresses along the coast of the Sea of Baal provide bases for these vessels. A smaller fleet of corsairs is also active in the Ruby Sea to the west of Numeda. The greatest enemy of the corsairs of Numeda is the Royal Navy of Khemit; their greatest competition is the navy of Baalthaaz.

Although the involvement of the nobility (and thus the government) with the Numedan privateers is widely known, most countries in Akados are not ready at this time to get into a naval war with a power so far away, so they confine their protective efforts to vigorously guarding their own merchants against the corsairs. Some private merchant houses or trade organizations, however, have taken matters into their own hands and hired forces to stage attacks on individual privateer fortresses in Numeda. Occasionally, those making such an assault even land and move inland in an effort to interrupt supply lines for the privateers. Such actions risk falling afoul of Numeda's Royal Army, however, and thus are kept strictly limited in time and scope so the attackers may swiftly return to their ships before encountering opposition.

The Royal Army of Numeda is primarily occupied patrolling the coastal road that runs from Khemit north to Ifthaaz and beyond. It is not much of a road, physically speaking, but is a common route for caravans and travelers. It is to the kingdom's benefit to minimize the number of bandit attacks along that track so Kirtius (and the country as a whole) can profit from the fees and taxes levied on the caravans. There was a time when merchants and traders refused to traverse Numeda due to the extensive banditry, and the treasury (and the populace as well) suffered as a result.

The army does run patrols into the interior of Numeda but unless they are actually chasing a group of bandits, the chance of a military unit casually encountering a band of roving marauders is negligible. They do try to contend with the hobgoblin warbands that roam the desert, as those present an ongoing threat to any human villages or encampments. (Certain desert tribes have reached their own accommodations with hobgoblins in their area, in places where resources are scarce enough that all the tribes either need to share or fight to the death.)

As a result, caravans to and from the east and south rely on strong contingents of their own guards, sometimes even including magical support. For some parts of the country, transporting goods by sea is an alternative, but then travelers have to contend with the privateers. The corsairs might avoid Numedan ships flying the flags of certain powerful people but others tend to be considered fair game. Many merchants prefer to stay with a situation they can perhaps control and choose overland travel except for cargos with more bulk and less value.

KIRTIUS, CITY OF (CAPITAL)

Ruler: King Massini
Government: monarchy
Population: 52,212 (47,220 Numedan, 4,986 other human ethnicity, 6 dwarf)

Numeda's capital city of Kirtius is located midway up the coast along the Sea of Baal and is the country's largest port. As the focus of all the caravan routes from the interior of the country, Kirtius is a center for trade in the jewels and precious metals mined from the Murat Hills beyond the desert. Goods flowing the other way are picked up by caravans for transportation east or south, and trains of pilgrims seeking the Holy City of Dawaad often begin their travels here.

From the Sea of Baal, Kirtius is recognizable by its twin lighthouses. The harbor area is host to the warehouse market, which teems with throngs of travelers and visitors from other kingdoms. Foreign traders deal in silk, jewels, rare herbs, spices, and other sundries, while Numedans sell the production of their mines and craftspeople.

The walled foreign quarter of the city is dangerous at the best of times; the constant flow of new people in and out of the city makes it easy for crime to flourish. Sleeping quarters are often on upper floors above gambling dens, taverns, or hookah lounges. Other parts of the city are higher quality, especially as the streets approach the garden-like walled neighborhood of the nobles' quarter, with its palatial estates. The royal palace itself is on a private island, reached by a bridge from the nobles' quarter.

The throne room of King Massini is a marvel, with replicas of date palm trees crafted in red marble and hung with jewels as fruit. The floor is covered with an inlaid map of central Libynos, the Sea of Baal, and even part of the coast of distant Akados. The king is often attended by his son, Prince Nidjal, who is learning statecraft. Another frequently with the king is his personal friend Emir Yama, who is also the country's highest-ranking general. Yama started his career as an officer in the light cavalry and takes every opportunity to speak highly of the units. The Numedan light cavalry are considered some of the best light horse in Libynos, and King Massini occasionally hires out their services to other Libynosi countries or city-states as mercenaries.

Just outside the southern gates of the city is the Oasis Aljania. This is a common stopping place for caravans that reach the city after the gates are shut for the night, or for those who may want to get started before the gates open in the morning. In addition, people who are low on funds and don't want to pay for a place to sleep inside the city often make their way out to the oasis for the night. This can be dangerous, though, as thieves often target unwary sleepers so it is best to be part of a group for mutual protection.

BALGRIMMON, TOWN OF

Ruler: Emir Ratip
Government: monarchy
Population: 21,994 (20,641 Numedan, 1,345 other human ethnicity, 8 dwarf)

Located on the east coast of the Ruby Sea, Balgrimmon is the largest Numedan port on that sea and handles most of the cargo trade for the southern part of Numeda. Ships sailing in and out of Balgrimmon make sure to fly the flag of any powerful merchant group or noble patron they can claim to put off the unwanted attention of any corsairs. Ships with no such sponsor hire as many marines as they can afford and pray to the gods for protection.

Several wealthy noble families live in the southern part of Numeda, so Balgrimmon does receive visits by ships from Axuum as well as distant places such as Far Jaati and Ur, bringing exotic, expensive products for the palaces of emirs and the tents of sheikhs. From here, caravan routes run north and south along the coast as well as to many mining towns in the Murat Hills.

Balgrimmon has a prominent temple to Anumon, and many people from the surrounding area travel here to attend the rituals. The truly ancient building has tall pillars holding up the ceiling, which is carved inside and out with storm clouds and bolts of lightning, and a large hall for the devotees to chant together in community.

DAWAAD, CITY OF

Ruler: Sulymon, Prophet of Anumon
Government: theocracy
Population: 7,886 (all Numedan)

Dawaad, a city in the desert of Numeda a few days' travel from the capital of Kirtius, has stood for many centuries as the center of worship for the god Anumon. The prophet Sulymon, a mortal possessed of a lifespan beyond that of normal men, rules this as a theocracy with the help of trusted assistants to see to the mundane details of the city while he looks after the spiritual training of its people and the many visitors who come to learn from his wisdom.

A twisted ramp rises 300 feet from the desert floor and winds up to the gates of the city, which are guarded by a massive gatehouse and a pair of guard towers. Just inside the gates is the foreign quarter, with merchants' warehouses, casbahs, taverns, and inns for those who may not be in the city for religious reasons. Past that is the city's great souk, or open-air market. Farther in is a section with lodging for large numbers of visiting pilgrims, and a district just outside the temple grounds for the many priests of Anumon. Called the khoury, these priests primarily live contemplative lives reading the prophecies of Sulymon and the other sacred texts of their faith. They are also permitted to have families, with in some cases both parents being priests and children even following in the footsteps of their parents in the church of Anumon.

The high temple of Anumon is surrounded by lush gardens, and many people walk here for pleasure or for religious contemplation. The temple itself is a mighty edifice to the power of law and order, with its main feature being a large assembly hall for mass services of worship. The focal point is a large stone statue of Anumon himself, who appears as a noble king with a plaited beard, and bearing a huge bronze scepter.

SARUCA, TOWN OF

Ruler: Amira Piyala
Government: monarchy
Population: 3,963 (2,121 Numedan, 1,810 other human ethnicity, 32 dwarf)

Saruca is a mining town in a rich part of the Murat Hills. The mines bring in various types of gemstones, gold, and iron, while marble is also quarried in the area. Mines in some other areas have trouble finding people in Numeda willing to do the work, as many natives are uncomfortable underground. Amira Piyala avoided this by following the policies of her predecessors and hired people from other countries to work in the shafts. Mines around Saruca are staffed by laborers from Khemit, Aethiope, the Channel Lakes region, some of the Antioch City-States, and even dwarves from some underground kingdom near Ur.

Towns in the amira's area try to treat these foreign miners well; market stalls even stock foods from their own cultures to make them feel at home. Some Numedans from tribes of the southern desert sneer at the miners as "ground grubbers," but mining townspeople are quick to correct them. Rather than being mere diggers, these people are mostly specialists whose work produces wealth for the Numedans. The mines have connections with traders who have connections with merchants who have connections with gemcutters, sculptors, or others who can craft the raw materials into valuable items.

GEOGRAPHIC FEATURES AND POINTS OF INTEREST IN NUMEDA

EASTERN MAIGHIB DESERT

The terrain of the great Maighib Desert crosses the Ruby Sea and continues on into Numeda. The central part of the country has deep desert like that in central Guurzan or southwest Khemit. Like Khemit, it has a number of oases in the desert, which makes it possible for tribes or travelers to survive there. It primarily consists of sand dunes, but portions to the south and northwest are dominated by rocky desert or barren hills.

GHOBAD-USK, OASIS OF

About 35 miles southeast of Kirtius, this oasis is a strategic point between competing desert tribes and has changed hands many times over the centuries. It is currently occupied by the Ahishkali tribe, which has defended its claim now for three years. The oasis has a healthy supply of date palms, and other fruit and olive trees grow under the shade of the taller trees.

KARAMAN MOUNTAINS

This range of mountains runs across the center of the Numedan peninsula along the southeast edge of the nation of Numeda, separating it from Imya farther south. Geologically, it is an extension of the Scythirian Mountains, though separated from the northern part of the chain by Cinnabar Bay in the Boiling Sea. The Karaman peaks are much lower than the heights of the range farther north. The mountains have many buried resources such as gemstones, gold, and more. Some mines are located on the west side of the range, though the miners may be hired from foreign countries, as the descendants of the desert-dwelling Numedans usually do not take well to the mountainous terrain. On the eastern side of the range, Imya maintains a sizable number of mines, at least one of which produces high-quality adamantium.

MATI-ALAMUL, RUINS OF

This large statue of basalt has the body of a sphinx, but the figure's face has been blotted out by wind-blown sands, as if the gods had wiped it out. The 40-foot-tall statue is surrounded by the eroding remains of a low, crumbling wall. The figure is known as "The Moaning King" due to horrible, droning wails that emanate from within the ruin on certain nights. These harrowing moans carry across the silence of a desert night to frighten tribes camping miles away. No one has any idea how the ruin came to be here, but it is spoken of only in hushed voices, and the place is almost universally avoided. Only harpies or creatures such as death dogs are ever reported in the area.

MURAT HILLS

The Murat Hills run along the entire eastern side of Numeda. They are merely foothills of the mountains farther east, but the Numedans consider the hills to be part of their country, while the mountains in most places are thought of more as a border. Iron and silver are mined in the northern hill country, while gemstones and gold can be found in the south. The hills are less dry than the rest of the country, watered by rainfall and runoff from the Karaman Mountains to the east. The moisture is sufficient for grazing flocks of sheep as well as raising grain to provide food for most of the country. The moisture is not enough to produce rivers, though; the streams that do exist vanish underground in the desert, where they probably supply the water for various oases or wells.

TAANACH HILLS

These hills lie primarily in northern Numeda, although parts extend into Ifthaaz. The Erto River, which flows through the hills, is the border between the two countries. This area receives more water than the desert just a short distance south, so people can raise enough fodder to keep cattle and can produce other farming crops. One crop that does well in the region is tobacco, and the variety known as "Numedan Blond" is grown almost exclusively in the Taanach Hills.

KHEMIT, TRIPLE KINGDOM OF

Capital: Thybos
Notable Settlements: many
Ruler: Pharaoh Tuthmosis IX, third ruler of the 39th (Wahibren) Dynasty
Government: monarchy and bureaucracy
Population: 5,816,434 (5,618,146 Khemitite, about 150,000 Desertfolk, 48,288 other human ethnicity)
Monstrous: kobolds, dwarves (mountains), gnolls, ommoths, sand krakens, sphinxes (desert)
Languages: Khemitian
Religion: Pharaonic pantheon
Resources: crops, beer, wine, olive oil, gold, silver, copper, iron, salt, alum, natron, knowledge, history, sandstone, limestone, marble, granite, porphyry, semi-precious gems, antiquities, trade
Currency: Khemitian
Technology Level: High Middle Ages (metropolises), Dark Ages (other cities), Iron Age (rural areas)

The Triple Kingdom of Khemit is one of the oldest human countries, having been in continuous existence for over 5,000 years. It lies in the northeastern corner of the southern half of the continent of Libynos, where the two parts of the continent meet, with the Ruby Sea to the east and the Kingdom of Guurzan to its west. The majority of the country is desert, with ranges of hills and a central river (the Stygian) that waters a large part of the country in its annual floods. Khemit considers itself to be three kingdoms joined together; hence the term triple kingdom. Upper Khemit, which is farthest upstream on the Stygian River, is in the south; its capital is Elephantine. The Middle Kingdom (or Middle Khemit) is the central portion of the country and has its capital at Thybos, which is also the current royal capital. Lower Khemit (or the Lower Kingdom) is the farthest north, in the area where the Stygian fans out into a delta and then flows into the Sea of Baal. Its capital is at Menefet, one of the largest cities in the world.

HISTORY AND PEOPLES

The history of Khemit begins more than 8,000 years ago during a time when the nomadic tribes of the region first began settling into small agricultural communities on the banks of the Stygian River. Over time, those communities grew, and by about 6,800 years ago, petty kingdoms had formed throughout the area, engaging in trade, conflict, and colonization. More than 5,000 years ago (1,500 years before the birth of the Hyperborean Imperial Record), Narmer — the first pharaoh — united many of the small kingdoms into what became known as the Conjoined Double Kingdom of Khemit. This was the time of the building of the great pyramids, symbols of ancient Khemit to this day.

Over the centuries, different families founded dynasties, and times of trouble came and went. During the 10th Dynasty, most of the southern land of Nubara was added to what then became the Triple Kingdom of Khemit. The 13th Dynasty, under Menkamin I, followed a troubled period, and as a result the Triple Kingdom was unable to resist the conquest of the Hyperborean Empire in 4 I.R. Khemit ultimately became the cornerstone of Hyperborean power in Libynos, and the pharaohs were able to govern their people under Hyperborean leadership. The Canal of the Pharaohs was constructed in the 15th dynasty with the assistance of Hyperborean engineers. More land was even added in the 17th Dynasty, as the eastern peninsula called Peleshtia was brought into the kingdom and renamed Tahmakht. However, no country cares to be controlled by another forever, and when the weakened Hyperboreans finally withdrew from Libynos in 2632 I.R., Pharoah Amyrtalos V declared a new start to a modern Khemitian calendar with that year becoming year 1.

In 328 New Khemit Reckoning (2960 I.R.), a great fleet of ships from Akados came to the Canal of the Pharaohs and sought passage to the east in a crusade to liberate their Sacred Table and the holy city of Tircople from the Huun. After lengthy debate among his advisers, some of whom were concerned about antagonizing the Huun, the pharaoh eventually permitted the flotilla to pass. The delay, however, angered the Foere leaders, and when a second crusade was launched 10 years later, the Akadians landed in Khemit, intent on using the nation as a staging ground for their forces. Although the Triple Kingdom was much stronger than it had been in the past, it was not strong enough to resist the Foerdewaith. The harbor of Pyrameses was taken by the overwhelming force of the crusader navy and, after a massacre in the city, it was used as the major supply hub for the entire army on its march to the east. The invaders occupied the metropolis of Menefet and much of Lower Khemit for about six years. The pharaoh, then ruling from Elephantine, was never threatened by the invaders, but the incident remains a point of resentment among the Khemitites to this day. Though now more than 500 years in the past, the occupation is a frequent topic of stories, and foreigners who seem to be from Akados may face hostility as a consequence. The Huun are also a target of anger, however, as they endangered Khemit by using the area to spy on and plot against the western invaders. As a result, any suspected Huun are likely to be seized and taken to the authorities at once.

Khemit is a productive country with many large urban populations. The cities are supported by the annual inundation by the Stygian River, which provides the fertile soil and water needed for thriving agriculture. The vast majority of the population lives on or near the river, with some cities along the Ruby Sea or one of the lakes in the northwest, and the few remaining located at oases, on trade routes. Khemit has a structured, highly-organized society where people know their places and most agree on the importance of working for the good of society as a whole. Army units are a reassuring presence in every city but are especially important for those on the frontier.

RELIGION

Khemit follows its own complex religion, where good and evil deities are worshipped in their proper spheres and the pharaoh is considered to be nigh unto a god himself. Temples and shrines are found almost everywhere, with only the most prominent being listed here. People tend to be suspicious of those who worship foreign gods, but as long as they do not disrespect the pharaoh, the Khemitites are likely to just mind their own business.

TRADE AND COMMERCE

Trade is an essential activity of the Triple Kingdom as it is the crossroads of Libynos. Khemit has an avenue to the east coast of Libynos through the Ruby Sea, while the Sea of Baal gives access to the entire western side of the continent as well as the cities of Akados. Caravans can enter Khemit by land from the west, south, or northeast, and leave in any of those directions or deliver goods to a ship for ocean transport. Traders of other countries haul their goods through the kingdom, and merchants of Khemit do brisk business in imports and exports themselves. Nearly any type of good available in Libynos can probably be found for sale in Khemit, especially in the markets of Menefet. Khemit's suns-and-sheaves currency is used by several countries along the Sea of Baal and is generally accepted throughout Libynos.

LOYALTIES AND DIPLOMACY

Khemit has good diplomatic relations with most countries in Libynos and a few in Akados. Representatives are usually not available in countries that were part of the Hyperborean Monarchy of the Foerdewaith, although sometimes particular merchants may be able to facilitate communications with the Khemitian government.

CENTRAL LIBYNOS

Legend
Town or Village
City
Capital or Free City
Imperial Capital
Fortress or Citadel
Ruins
Place of Interest
Road
Trail or Unused Road
Mountain Pass
Battlefield

Archon Gelvira-Resuela of Hacienda Zapardiel rides forth from the citadel in Cadua in the Empire of Alcaldar.

GOVERNMENT

The Triple Kingdom is a monarchy governed by Pharaoh Tuthmosis IX. He is the third ruler of the 39th (Wahibren) Dynasty, following his father Wahibre III and his brother Rameses XVIII to the throne. The monarchy is supported by the able efforts of thousands of government bureaucrats, who see to all the details that keep the kingdom functioning.

MILITARY

The navy of Khemit has two primary bases in the Sea of Baal. One is on the Island of Karpathos, about 20 miles northwest of Rashad. The other is at Pharos where the navy makes use of the excellent berthing and repair facilities originally constructed for the Hyperborean navy. In the Ruby Sea, Ipret-Isus is the home port of a significant fleet that patrols not just inside the Ruby Sea but up and down the coast outside the mouth of the sea. The army has units stationed in Thybos near the pharaoh and in other major cities, but much of the military is scattered among the towns and oases of Khemit to provide protection against bandits and (in the desert) nomadic tribes.

MAJOR THREATS

The country of Numeda is usually considered the greatest threat to Khemit. Its navy, though mostly just privateers, often threatens trade in Khemit by attacking merchant shipping. A ground attack by the Numedan military is less of a concern, but forces stay alert in Ascalon and other cities of Tahmakht near the border with Numeda. To the southwest and west, nomadic tribespeople of the Maighib Desert sometimes attack caravans or even villages. However, attackers just fade back into the deep desert so unless troops are stationed in the locations that come under attack, it is very difficult to pinpoint the culprits and exact justice.

REFERENCE SOURCE: *ALTHOUGH MANY NAMES HAVE BEEN MODIFIED AND ADDITIONAL DETAILS ADDED, MUCH OF THE MATERIAL FOR THE **TRIPLE KINGDOM OF KHEMIT** IS DERIVED FROM **GARY GYGAX'S NECROPOLIS** BY **NECROMANCER GAMES**.*

AARTUAT, VILLAGE OF

Ruler: Fifth Lieutenant Hamephat, Khemitian military
Government: bureaucracy
Population: 158 (mostly Khemitite)

Aartuat lies at the halfway point of the caravan route from Farnoc to the oasis of Dakla-Amun. It is basically a large caravanserai with a few houses around it, though the caravanserai is strongly built and has a military presence to guard against bandits. (A village so small is not assigned an administrator, so the young military commander fills that function, assisted by the unit scribe.) Aartuat's most notable feature is what they call the Pool of Hapy, a pleasing little pool just south of the village that is filled by a small waterfall and supports intensive gardening by the locals.

ABYDOS, CITY OF

Ruler: Principle Administrator Hophra-anu-tep
Government: bureaucracy
Population: 44,865 (mostly Khemitite)

Abydos is a large city of Middle Khemit, which is known for its several major temples and burial grounds. The most important temple is the high seat of the temple of Isis, Khemitian mother-goddess of life and magic. Her temple includes an important school for kheri-hebu, or priest-mages. Also present is the high seat of the temple of Anhur, god of war and the hunt; many soldiers passing through the area take time to make a sacrifice at his altar. The city has a secondary temple to Horus (whose main temple is in Edefu) and a major temple of Thoth, though his high seat is in Hermopolis.

Although the high seat of Osiris was moved to Menefet several hundred years ago, the Osiris temple in Abydos is still much used. For one thing, it includes the symbolic tomb of Osiris, who according to Khemitian theology was killed and then resurrected and now dwells in the Underworld. When this temple was primary, the area was the burial place of many of the ruling class; nobles of the Middle Kingdom are sometimes still buried in the historic necropolis here, which is known as Umm Alkhah.

ADUN-HASTUR, TOWN OF

Ruler: Administrator Shaphat
Government: bureaucracy
Population: 1,172 (mostly Khemitite)

Adun-Hastur is located at an oasis on the southern edge of the Harh-Ahu-Ra Hills. Not far from the oasis is the remains of a serpentine quarry. The bits of stone left are not large enough to use for architectural purposes and not high enough quality to use as gems or fine carvings. However, a few people make a business of getting useful pieces out of the quarry. They either carve them into undetailed items (such as cups or bowls) or sell the pieces directly to the small caravans that pass the oasis.

AHUR-PTAH, TOWN OF

Ruler: Administrator Tappuah
Government: bureaucracy
Population: 1,731 (mostly Khemitite)

This small town is at an oasis on one of the most-convenient caravan routes to Bahaadur, the capital city of neighboring Guurzan, so many caravans (especially those coming from Middle Khemit) stop here. It has a large caravanserai that is well-supplied with last-minute items that might be needed before caravans turn west to cross part of the Khemitian desert on the way to Guurzan. Ahur-Ptah is also the location of a small temple of Geb, god of the earth and a protector deity. Although it is not impressive, many caravan masters make a brief visit to pray for the safety of their caravans before traveling into the desert.

AKHETATEN, CITY OF

Ruler: City Administrator Heptup-zur
Government: bureaucracy
Population: 25,298 (mostly Khemitite)

Akhetaten lies on the east bank of the Stygian in lower Khemit. It is important as the high seat of the temple of Min, a god of fertility and power. It also hosts a temple to Anumon, god of gates and keeper of laws, whose worship spread from Numeda. In addition, the city has another major temple to the foreign deity Mah-Barek. The temple is run by the sect of Marwan (an important teacher of antiquity), and the priests welcome all to walk in the extensive temple gardens and enjoy the singing and dancing that are part of the worship. It seems chaotic to most Khemitites, as people tend to break out in song or spontaneous dance at odd times, not only during an established ritual. Apparently, there are also other sects of Mah-Barek, and the priests are willing to direct visitors to a location of the sect of Fatimashan. That sect has calmer observances and emphasizes work of charity rather than art, although the priests of Marwan characterize the others as boring.

One group of devotees at the temple of Mah-Barek is a community of artists with a distinctive style. They avoid the strict formality of most Khemitian art and instead depict subjects more realistically and in informal settings. That style has affected other artists in the area around Akhetaten and is spreading farther afield.

AMUT, TOWN OF

Ruler: Second Lieutenant Balebuk-zobah, Khemitian military
Government: bureaucracy
Population: 1,537 (mostly Khemitite)

Amut is the farthest west of all the populated places in Khemit. It is near the acknowledged western border of the land, which is the edge of the Qarrasat Hills that lie in neighboring Guurzan. Caravans stop here for a last rest in relative safety before pushing through the long pass in the dangerous hill country and going on to Bahaardun, the capital of Guurzan. The town has a caravanserai that also serves as a fortress, as well as a strong town wall — something seldom seen in the peaceful eastern regions of Khemit. An army unit has been stationed here for many years to guard the caravans against bandits and to guard the frontier against the weird things that come out of the hills. Its commander acts in place of a civil administrator.

ANUBIS, CITY OF

Ruler: City Administrator Anath-lebo
Government: bureaucracy
Population: 10,962 (mostly Khemitite)

The city of Anubis is on the west bank of the Stygian near the second cataract. (See "Stygian River" below for more information on the cataracts.) River traffic moves north of the cataract to the place where the Astebera River joins the Stygian just south of the first cataract; small ships can make it up the Astebera to the towns there. There is also some river traffic south on the Stygian to near Suleb where the third cataract is located.

The largest structure in the city is the truly ancient temple of Anubis, the high seat of the jackal-headed god of the dead in Khemit since the 7th Dynasty and the only temple dedicated to him. Despite repairs over the millennia, it is still slowly decaying. A great well called the Jackal Well for the carvings around it is also dedicated to Anubis and sits in the plaza in front of the temple. It is a properly maintained public water source, available for city dwellers and for those who travel to visit the temple. A short distance from the temple itself is the underground necropolis known as the Dog Catacomb. This extensive set of narrow stone tunnels is used for the burial of mummified animals of many types — beloved pets, or sacrificial creatures intended to carry a worshipper's prayers to a deity. At least one prior set of tunnels had been filled and blocked off; no one is sure if there were earlier ones or not, or how many animals might have been buried here in the past 4,000 years.

ASCALON, CITY OF

Ruler: City Administrator Saadia Afdal
Government: bureaucracy
Population: 24,153 (mostly Khemitite)

Ascalon is a profitable port in the Khemitian Governate of Tahmakht, the eastern-most city along the coast. It is built on a bluff overlooking the Sea of Baal, with a huge semicircular fortification protecting it on the land side and the port at the base of the bluff. Ascalon's port provides an eastern location for launching Khemitian merchant or warships into the Sea of Baal, but it gives only a little protection against storms. This sizable fortress lies directly on the land trade route from Khemit to Numeda and points beyond. It is the headquarters for a large body of troops whose stated purpose is to protect the eastern trade from bandits. Their unstated purpose, however, is to protect the border of Khemit against incursions from Numeda. Having an excellent underground water source, Ascalon is able to withstand long sieges and held out for several months at the time Khemit fell to the Hyperborean conquest.

ASHMEMNON, CITY OF

Ruler: City Administrator Qandil-gad-arat
Government: bureaucracy
Population: 18,592 (mostly Khemitite)

Ashmemnon lies on the west bank of the Stygian River in Lower Khemit, at the end of the caravan road running through the nearby major city of Hermopolis. Ashmemnon is an important supplier of food for the population of Hermopolis and is also known for the beautiful temple of Mert, the goddess of music and song. This is a fairly new temple, built early in the 37th Dynasty, and it is always full of music. The priests actively work to create new music (to praise Mert but also the other gods of Khemit) and have a small school where they teach the traditional songs and musical instruments and also how to create new music. Many musicians in the courts of the pharaoh and the viziers are either priests of Mert or were trained in her school.

ATEN-SEYAL, TOWN OF

Ruler: Administrator Haluza Hadid
Government: bureaucracy
Population: 3,924 (mostly Khemitite)

This town lies in the curve of the Astebera River, separated from the Ruby Sea by the Geb-el-Mardikh Mountains. A system of canals provides water for agriculture, but the ground is not as fertile as the valley of the Stygian so more work is required to supply the needs of the area. Aten-Seyal is the headquarters and supply center of two different mining operations that mine for diorite (for statues, memorial vases, and similar carvings), and possibly other minerals in the nearby foothills. Materials are shipped downriver by barge but must be transshipped at the first cataract on the Stygian, just below the river's junction with the Astebera. Tales have been told for years about the riches that can be found in the mountains, but whatever may be there doesn't seem to be making its way into this small town.

AZUL-SEPTE, TOWN OF

Ruler: Third Lieutenant Mawas-heqt
Government: bureaucracy
Population: 1,183 (mostly Khemitite)

Azul-Septe is an oasis town in the western desert of Khemit, a crucial stop on the primary caravan route from Middle Khemit to Guurzan. Isolated as it is, the town is protected by a sturdy mud-brick wall and a military unit (stationed at the fortified caravanserai) whose commander also acts as the town administrator. In addition to producing the food they supply to the caravans, the people of Azul-Septe mine a nearby supply of alum, an important additive for the dye process, where it is used to fix color to fibers for cloth.

BAQI, TOWN OF

Ruler: Administrator Mudir Avva
Government: bureaucracy
Population: 9,818 (mostly Khemitite)

Baqi is near the northern border of Upper Khemit, southeast of Elephantine. It sits on the small North Branch of the Astebera River and is a nexus of caravan routes that run on the east side of the upper Stygian River. This convenient location has led to prosperity for Baqi, as it is the main supply point between Keruma and Nhut, a distance of about 400 miles. Although Elephantine could easily supply caravans, the rough terrain between the North Astebera and the Stygian makes traveling through that area difficult.

Between Baqi and the city of Luqsor to its west lies the Valley of the Gods, a deep sandstone canyon several miles long into which are carved massive temples and the tombs of many of the southern pharaohs. In Baqi itself is the high seat of the temple of Meretseger, the cobra-headed goddess who is the special protector of the Valley of the Gods. (See "Valley of the Gods" below for more information.)

BASTUS, CITY OF

Ruler: Principal Administrator Nabila-e-qamat
Government: bureaucracy
Population: 41,214 (mostly Khemitite)

Bastus is in Lower Khemit, on the easternmost branch of the Stygian delta. It is a thriving trading center, an important stop for caravans headed to or from the area of Tahmakht, and was the capital of Khemit in the 30th Dynasty. It is also near the beginning of the Canal of the Pharaohs, which runs from the Stygian to Lake Trophimus and then to the Gulf of Mafket, where it connects to the Ruby Sea. This increases the amount of trade in Bastus as boats from the south transship their goods for transit through the canal to the sea, and vice versa.

The feature most visitors to Bastus notice immediately is the multitude of cats wandering the streets, unmolested except for the occasional swat with a straw broom. The reason, of course, is that the city is the high seat of the temple of Bast, goddess of beauty and cats. While not the only temple in the city, that of Bast is the largest and by far the most beautiful. Canals run from the river along each side of the approach to the entrance and then around the temple and on through the city. Some cats are specifically raised within the temple grounds but all cats are welcomed there. The annual festival to Bast is one of the most popular in the country and draws hundreds of thousands of people to the city. The necropolis outside the city includes an area for cat burials, which at this point is larger than the area for burying people.

BUHEN, TOWN OF

Ruler: Administrator Thanuro
Government: bureaucracy
Population: 4,653 (mostly Khemitite)

Buhen is located on the west bank of the Stygian, between the river's second and third cataracts. It has been a source of copper, which is found in the southern Harh-Ahu-Ra Hills, since the 4th Dynasty. Its primary function now, however, is to defend against invasions from Qesh. The fortress of Buhen was originally built in the 7th Dynasty as a protection against Nubara. After the unification of the Triple Kingdom at the start of the 10th Dynasty, that possible enemy was (largely) neutralized and military commanders in Upper Khemit turned their attention to Qesh. Buhen is the northernmost in a line of eight fortresses along the Stygian toward Qesh. The fortifications have changed hands from time to time, but the frontier conflict has been mostly confined to skirmishes since the 32nd Dynasty. Even so, a large military unit stationed in Buhen aggressively patrols the hills and border area.

BUTO, CITY OF

Ruler: Principal Administrator Nin-khamen Nazlit
Government: bureaucracy
Population: 98,158 (mostly Khemitite)

The city of Buto is very proud of its great temple to the goddess Buto, cobra-headed protector of Khemit in general, but pharaoh (and Lower Khemit) in particular. The theme of the cobra is found throughout the city, in carvings and paintings and in personal jewelry. The people are not so welcoming of actual cobras, however. The creatures are considered holy here and few kill them except in an extreme situation; instead the snake-catchers pick them up and carry them to the temple where they are kept in special enclosures. The temple also houses the oracle of Buto, who gives prophecies from the goddess. In addition, the city has a major temple to Osiris located at some distance from Buto's holy place.

The city of Buto is located in the northern part of the delta of the Stygian where the main and eastern branches of the Stygian reconnect before moving on to the sea. It is not as large a port or trading center as some other delta cities, but it has major shipbuilding facilities. Huge logs of cedar imported from Baalthaaz are made into the seagoing vessels that guard the coast and carry on Khemit's trade with cities on both continents. Some logs are also used for the barges that ply the Stygian.

DAHRA, CITY OF

Ruler: City Administrator Paran-mot
Government: bureaucracy
Population: 14,852 (mostly Khemitite)

Dahra is a major port on the Ruby Sea, the closest to the large population of the Lower Kingdom. Many merchants transfer their goods to caravans here for the trip up the coast and over to Hermopolis and nearby cities. Those heading to the area of Menefet may choose to sail through the Canal of the Pharaohs and then travel south from Bastus, but that may also involve transferring goods depending on the size of the ship involved.

At one time, ships intended for use in the Ruby Sea were built near the Sea of Baal and sailed up the Stygian, then taken apart and carried to Dahra where they were reconstructed. Since the construction of the canal in the 15th Dynasty, any ships other than the largest can simply travel from one sea to the other. In addition, due to the increase in trade with countries farther south, appropriate wood for shipbuilding is available through trade there and the large oceangoing ships for the Ruby Sea and the Great Ocean Ûthaf are built at Ipret-Isus.

The area around Dahra is also the source of porphyry, a rare deep purple stone used in sculptures and architecture. The Hyperboreans called it imperial porphyry and used it in many of their important buildings and statues in Libynos. (It is unknown if they used it elsewhere; it has not yet been identified in any other areas.) The stone is used in special locations in Khemit, of course, but is also exported to Baalthaaz and even to Jaati. No other source of imperial porphyry is known.

DAKLA-AMUN, TOWN OF

Ruler: Administrator Fayruz
Government: bureaucracy
Population: 1,327 (mostly Khemitite)

Dakla-Amun is located at the oasis of the same name, west of the Harh-Ahu-Ra Hills. The town has a high mud-brick wall as protection against bandits from the hills, but such attacks are infrequent enough that Dakla-Amun rates only a single squad of soldiers under the command of a young sergeant. Some caravans choose to travel through the town on the way to the western oasis at Amut and on to Guurzan, but it is not the most popular route. One key aspect of the oasis is a large deposit of alum in the area, which is mined for use as a dye fixative for cloth. It is important not only in Khemit but also in trade.

DASAT, CITY OF

Ruler: Principal Administrator Maneth-a-zebib
Government: bureaucracy
Population: 49,351 (mostly Khemitite)

The city of Dasat is on the east bank of the Stygian in Lower Khemit. It lies almost opposite the teeming metropolis of Menefet, and that has been the single factor that most affected the growth and progress of the city. Wealthy people who wanted to be out of the crush of the metropolis built homes in Dasat, and gradually businesses grew to supply their needs. While no longer a small town nor housing only the wealthy, much of Dasat is still spacious thanks to the wide boulevards and plazas built by the city's architects. It is also a place used to thinking well of its citizens. This means that some criminals who enjoy the trappings of wealth (such as antiquities smugglers, for example) hide here in plain sight while their neighbors remain unaware, because they can't believe anyone from Dasat could do something like that.

DJANET, METROPOLIS OF

Ruler: High Administrator Lael Timnath
Government: bureaucracy
Population: 101,447 (mostly Khemitite)

Djanet is in the northwest corner of Tahmakht on Lake Trophimus. At one time, it had access to the sea because a distributary of the Stygian River flowed through the area, but the mouth of the river silted up and left only the lake. The construction of the Canal of the Pharaohs in the 15th Dynasty again opened the possibility of water travel to the Sea of Baal and also to the Ruby Sea and the Stygian. This made Djanet a major trade center, the crossroads of routes by land to Numeda, Baalthaaz, and Antioch to the north, and by sea along the Ruby Sea and to the eastern coasts of northern and southern Libynos.

The city was the royal capital of Khemit during the 22nd Dynasty. Djanet is now the capital of the governate of Tahmakht, though in times of tension with Numeda the governor moves the military headquarters to Ascalon. The primary temples here are a set of three dedicated to the triad of Amun, Mût, and Chons. (See "Thybos, Metropolis of" below for more information on these deities.) The city also has the high seat of the temple of Heru, the hawk-headed god of law and order and patron of the pharaoh.

DUNQAR, TOWN OF

Ruler: Administrator Nhu-Ahmose
Government: bureaucracy
Population: 1,641 (mostly Khemitite)

Dunqar is an oasis town in the southern part of the Western Desert, east of the Harh-Ahu-Ra Hills. It sits on a trade route that goes from Middle Khemit and Elephantine into Qesh, or up through the Western Desert into southern Guurzan. Troops patrolling out of the military headquarters at Buhen discourage bandits, but nothing can keep them away completely. Of course, Dunqar has its own small military unit stationed out of a fortified caravanserai, so the town itself is generally safe. The oasis area also has a population of wild sand cats that roam the area, similar to the oasis town of Kurkar. (See "Kurkar, Town of" below for more information.)

EDEFU, CITY OF

Ruler: Principal Administrator Qalanas-Iqbal
Government: bureaucracy
Population: 57,581 (mostly Khemitite)

Edefu is on the east bank of the Stygian, about 35 miles south of Thybos. The oldest part of the city is thought to date back to the 6th Dynasty, and at times it has been an important administrative center, especially for the Hyperborean Empire when it had a presence in Khemit. The city's most important feature, though, is the high seat of the temple of Horus, the falcon-headed god of law and war and protector of the pharaoh. A new temple was built during the 33rd Dynasty to replace one that had stood for millennia. The red sandstone building has been maintained in excellent condition, and many travel to see the carvings on the interior walls and the 50-foot-tall statues of Horus as a falcon wearing the crown of the triple kingdom. The temple's scale is impressive, with a 50-foot-high arched gateway leading into the 400-foot-long main building. The area is surrounded by a 20-foot-high wall that is probably superfluous in this civilized day but may not have been when the temple was built more than 1,000 years ago.

ELEPHANTINE, METROPOLIS OF

Ruler: High Administrator Intef Bakenamon
Government: bureaucracy
Population: 162,368 (mostly Khemitite)

Elephantine is the capital city of Upper Khemit and is located north of the first cataract of the Stygian River. It was also the royal capital during the 26th and 27th Dynasties, and again during the 36th Dynasty when pharaohs of Nubiar ancestry had the throne.

The city is built partly on a wide island in the Stygian and partly on the eastern bank of the river. The name of the city is thought to refer to a group of large gray stones on the island, which from a distance look vaguely like a herd of elephants. Legend says they were such creatures at one time, but they were too costly to feed so the great sorcerer who owned them turned them to stone until he had need of them again.

While various deities are honored with temples on the mainland, the island has one major temple to the god Khnemu, deity of creation and invention. Near his temple stands a clever ancient invention: a stygometer used to measure the height of the river at flood season. It is a stone corridor into which the river can flow; stone steps go down to low-water level with each calculated step numbered with both Khemitian and Hyperborean numbers. Elephantine also has a large university. While it gives the usual teaching in subjects helpful to Khemitian civil servants, its faculty includes instructors from the former area of Nubara, Meroë, and other parts of central Libynos. This means its philosophies and methods can be very different than universities in Thybos and northern areas of the country.

FARNOC, CITY OF

Ruler: City Administrator Nektnebe-hezir
Government: bureaucracy
Population: 10,620 (mostly Khemitite)

Farnoc lies 60 miles west by caravan track of the great city of Thybos. Centrally located among several important caravan routes, the city has a regiment of the army's cavalry posted to it as well as hosting an office of the Utchatu, the criminal investigatory arm of the government's security service. In addition, rough, rocky hills somewhat north of the town are a source of basalt. The dark stone is used for statues and vessels, and sometimes for paving stones in necropolises.

GARZUL, CITY OF

Ruler: City Administrator Shum-Ukin
Government: bureaucracy
Population: 29,327 (mostly Khemitite)

Garzul is on the northern coast of Tahmakht, between Raffe and Ascalon. At the shore is a port on the Sea of Baal, with some warehouses and other buildings around it, but the city proper sits about a mile inland. Garzul is well fortified, being only a few dozen miles from the nebulous border between Khemit and the country of Numeda. A strong army unit is stationed here for security and to provide support to the primary border units in Ascalon. The wind off the Sea of Baal brings the area enough moisture to support brewing and winemaking as profitable industries, for export to the rest of Khemit as well as other parts of Tahmakht.

GEARA, CITY OF

Ruler: City Administrator Zalmon Kebar
Government: bureaucracy
Population: 26,575 (mostly Khemitite)

Geara is located on the Heshbon River in southern Tahmakht. It is near the eastern extent of Khemitian control and, being subject to occasional attack by roving bands from Numeda, boasts a high, thick city wall. The strong military unit stationed here is responsible for protecting both the city itself and the nearby mines and their workers.

Despite having access to the river's water, the rocky soil about Geara makes for poor cropland. Many locals herd goats and sheep in the hills. Others work in the nearby copper and iron mines, which provide the region's major trade exports. The copper mines are quite old, and having been worked over hundreds of years, are on the verge of depletion. From the products of the iron mines, the Tahmakhtim produce various types of bladed weapons, breastplates, and tools. They are able to send goods by caravan to Djanet or ship them from Geara's small port on the Heshbon, which is served by small boats that come up through the Gulf of Tahmakht from the Ruby Sea.

Residents of Geara have a temple to Sekhmet and one to Menu, and some shrines to Khemitian deities such as Tuart for personal protection, but they are not a pious people. They do have a lot of superstitions, though, and invoke unspecified blessings or protections by their use. Close study would show that many of these superstitions seem related to the old gods of ancient Peleshtia. The Khemitian authorities are unaware of the old temples cut deep into the Jeshennin Mountains and are oblivious to the fact that some still worship there.

GEBIT, TOWN OF

Ruler: Administrator Ezek-minya
Government: bureaucracy
Population: 5,842 (mostly Khemitite)

Gebit sits east of the Stygian in Middle Khemit near the large easterly bend in the river north and east of Thybos. It is an important caravan stop at the intersection between the road along the east bank of the river and the route to the Ruby Sea at Mersa Gawasis. As such, a strong military unit is stationed here to protect the numerous caravans from bandits in the Ruby Hills. The city is also the headquarters for some mining expeditions into the Eastern Desert.

Gebit was an important religious center during the Old Triple Kingdom (14th to 17th dynasties), but was later overshadowed by Thybos. It was previously the high seat of the temple of Min, and although that seat has since moved (to Akhetaten), Min is still popularly worshipped here as a sky god as well as a fertility deity.

GETHE, CITY OF

Ruler: City Administrator Adni Rezin
Government: bureaucracy
Population: 22,594 (mostly Khemitite)

Gethe is in the interior of Tahmakht, which is located in an oasis area where canals are used to water its fields. As one of the cities on the border of Khemitian control, it has a high strong wall to protect it against incursions from Numeda. The declared mission of the military unit stationed here is to patrol against bandits, but everyone knows its real purpose is to scout the border and protect the city from Numedan raids.

Gethe has designated specific areas for industry and production in accordance with careful planning at the time the city was built. It is surrounded by huge olive groves and possesses scores of facilities for pressing olive oil and storing and sealing it in ceramic jars. The oil is shipped through Garzul to cities of the delta.

In the city is a temple of Isis, goddess of fertility and magic. Although the current priestess performs all the proper rituals for the land and crops, rumor has it that she is much more interested in esoteric types of magic than in more common kinds of service. The other priests at the temple would seem to confirm this, as they are constantly doing research and often unavailable to help any but the most generous patrons.

GHIZEH, CITY OF

Ruler: Principal Administrator Khersa-es-menre
Government: bureaucracy
Population: 41,787 (mostly Khemitite)

A dozen miles north of Menefet, Ghizeh (or, rather, its necropolis) possesses the most-recognizable monuments in all of Khemit. On a plateau west of the city stand several mighty pyramids of pharaohs from the 4th through 8th dynasties, making them more than 4,000 years old. The pyramids are surrounded by other tombs of royal family members and nobles. The largest tomb is the Great Pyramid of Udimu, founder of the 6th Dynasty. Not to be outdone, Pharaoh Teti of the 7th Dynasty built a pyramid and also a huge sphinx that is thought to have his face.

The pyramids and the sphinx have been depicted many times in artwork and seen by people thousands of miles away, who otherwise know nothing of Khemit. When conquerors from the Hyperborean Empire first saw the Great Sphinx, they were awed and adopted it as a symbol of faraway places. It was used as the official symbol of the Imperial Mercantile League, a worldwide organization of traders who designated it the "Sphinx of Boros." Although the Great Sphinx has nothing at all to do with the ancient northern continent of Boros (and it seems doubtful that area has ever been visited by a real sphinx), the widespread use of the symbol made the Great Sphinx probably the best-known monument in the world.

Ghizeh is not only a city of the dead, however. It has its share of markets and temples and one other thing that brings people to the city — a zoological collection. What began as a pharaoh's menagerie now includes creatures from all over Libynos as well as a rare few native to Akados. They are mostly housed in displays purporting to be similar to their natural environments, which are sustained by a combination of expert design and magical power.

HAATH-GENURIT, TOWN OF

Ruler: Fifth Lieutenant Sherr-avva
Government: bureaucracy
Population: 821 (mostly Khemitite)

Haath-Genurit, the westernmost oasis in Khemit, is located just outside the northwest edge of the Assal-Aat Depression. The suspicious, insular people of this fortified town (including many of the soldiers assigned to the local army unit) are more closely related to the tribes of southern Guurzan than they are to most Khemitites. The oasis is used infrequently by caravans; most choose the more easterly route through Dakla-Amun. When given the opportunity, the inhabitants trade in a very white, fine-grained salt.

HAMI, TOWN OF

Ruler: Administrator Antara
Government: bureaucracy
Population: 9,813 (mostly Khemitite)

This town in the Eastern Desert near the southern Ruby Hills is known as an excellent source of alabaster. Carvings dedicated to Bast have been especially popular over many years (and there is a small temple to her here), but alabaster is most often used for canopic jars and other burial objects, sometimes even things as large as a sarcophagus. It is mined in blocks, then cut and worked at workshops in the town and shipped throughout Khemit. Hami is also a military center for its section of the Eastern Desert and has been since the 3rd Dynasty, with several units headquartered here to patrol the caravan routes as protection against bandits. The high seat of Menu, falcon-headed god of war, is a small but elaborate building constructed and maintained over the years by the soldiers of the garrison.

HELIOPOLIS, CITY OF

Ruler: Principal Administrator Jeren Dar-mennas
Government: bureaucracy
Population: 96,676 (mostly Khemitite)

When the Hyperborean Empire conquered Khemit during the 13th Dynasty, they went about integrating it into their empire. The royal capital was moved to Menefet, and the Hyperboreans built a city for themselves nearby on the east bank of the Stygian. They named it Heliopolis and built a temple to Ra as well as those to their own gods. A century later, that temple started an academy to teach the youth of the Hyperboreans side by side with exceptional youth or nobles' children from Khemit to help develop understanding between the two disparate cultures. Seeing the success of the academy, the Hyperboreans founded a university in the city.

The Academy of Ra at Heliopolis and the Hyperborean University of Khemit remain in existence to this day. As it did in the days of the Empire, the academy continues to educate the children of foreigners and Khemitites side by side. The university, which is not affiliated with any temple, teaches a wide range of topics and accepts students from all over the world, though few attend from outside Libynos.

HERMOPOLIS, METROPOLIS OF

Ruler: High Administrator Rifa'a Kagemni
Government: bureaucracy
Population: 115,906 (mostly Khemitite)

The city of Hermopolis is located at a confluence of the River Stygian and the Bakhari tributary in Lower Khemit. During flood season, this convergence makes the river a muddy expanse more than two miles wide that attracts tens of thousands of storks and flamingoes. Their cacophony can be heard more than a mile from the river.

Hermopolis is widely known as a center of learning and sophistication. It has the high seat of the temple of Thoth, ibis-headed god of knowledge and magic. It is overseen by Shemsi Neteru-f, high priest of Thoth and also archpriest of all Khemit. The temple includes a major library called the Thocaenum, which claims to rival the one at Pharos in the size of its collection, though its content is more religiously oriented. The temple also runs a major university in the metropolis that produces scholars highly sought after by the royal court of Khemit and by administrators throughout the kingdom. In addition, Hermopolis is the high seat of the temple of Khnemu, god of creation and invention.

IKKOR, CITY OF

Ruler: City Administrator Mose-ky-nebu
Government: bureaucracy
Population: 17,665 (mostly Khemitite)

Ikkor is located on the west bank of the Stygian, just south of the confluence with the Astebera River and of the first cataract. It is the first stop on the westbound trade route out of Elephantine, but it is so close to the origination point that few caravans stop long enough to profit the city much.

The bucolic peace of Ikkor has been disturbed in the past year or so by an influx of strangers from the north and south. Many of them claim to be prospecting in the rough land around the cataract, but they don't seem to be showing any results for that. Given that strangers dressed in outfits of black have been seen slipping in and out of town after dark, citizens are suspicious but can point to no actual criminal activity; not even any chickens have gone missing. One rumor is that these dark strangers are assassins with plans to kill the pharaoh or perhaps just the vizier. Another is that they have a hidden temple to the evil spirit Aapep, the black serpent and destroyer, and it is only a matter of time before they start kidnapping people as sacrifices to their dark lord.

INHY, CITY OF

Ruler: City Administrator Shuna-wiris
Government: bureaucracy
Population: 21,472 (mostly Khemitite)

Located on the Stygian River just a few miles northwest of the royal capital of Thybos, Inhy is home to many of the people who specifically serve the pharaoh (such as craftsmen or laborers), and to the priests who tend the great Necropolis lying outside the capital city. It is also the high seat of the temple of Anqet, goddess of water and rivers — the Stygian in particular. Many Khemitites all along the great river pray to her for the fertility of their crops. The temple has an elaborate stygometer, a structure for measuring the level of the Stygian River during its flood season and predicting a coming famine or disastrous inundation. This involves a channel that runs from the river into a deep cistern inside the temple. Stairs descending along the inside of the well allow access to the measuring column set in its center. It is read by the priests of Anqet, though the pharaoh himself has been known to view it on occasion.

IPRET-ISUS, CITY OF

Ruler: City Administrator Hamat-silsa
Government: bureaucracy
Population: 27,727 (mostly Khemitite)

Ipret-Isus is a major port, the first reached by ships coming to Khemit via the mouth of the Ruby Sea. It is a transshipment location for materials going to and from Upper Khemit and much of the Middle Kingdom, as well as the major shipbuilding center on the Ruby Sea. The city is the home port of a significant force of the Khemitian navy, although few naval ships are in port at any given time. The force patrols inside the Ruby Sea to keep merchant vessels safe from Numedan pirates on the east coast. However, it also looks out for the safety of Khemitian ships and the pharaoh's interests along a lengthy part of the coast north and south of the mouth of the Ruby Sea.

Ipret-Isus sits on the shore of a sheltered bay, with the Isle of Scorpions offshore. The bay is home to a large group of dolphins that usually stay out of the way of moving vessels; they are thought to bring luck to ships, so few threaten them in any way. Individual dolphins do occasionally splash or otherwise annoy smaller boats, however.

Unseen by the foreigners who crowd the port and unknown even by most of the Khemitites traveling through, an ancient temple is hidden among the hills a short distance from Ipret-Isus. It is dedicated to the group of deities collectively known as the Okdo-ad, the personified essential forces of nature. Four male-female couples represent the primordial waters, the invisible powers of the air, darkness itself, and infinity. These forces, worshipped in what is now Khemit before the kingdom was founded 5,000 years ago, are acknowledged by few today except in times of natural crises. They do still have active priests, some of whom leave the temple here to wander the countryside of Khemit. These priests are not part of the official pharaonic religious hierarchy, and any powers they have seem to come directly from nature.

ISHANTAR, CITY OF

Ruler: City Administrator Caphtos-min
Government: bureaucracy
Population: 18,542 (mostly Khemitite)

The city of Ishantar is a prosperous community on the east bank of the Stygian about 35 miles south of Menefet. Few barges stop at its docks, however, and boatmen are very careful as they pass through its waters due to the high number of crocodiles in the river here. Ishantar is the high seat of the temple of Sebk, crocodile-headed god of water and evil, so merchants with goods for Ishantar generally transport them by caravan rather than going by river and risking a confrontation with the sacred crocodiles.

Much of the temple of Sebk is built with no stairs — only ramps — to make it easier for holy crocodiles to enter. Within the temple, however, are stairs behind closed doors, to lead priests and adherents to altars where they can worship without the presence of the god's hungry children. (In actual fact, the crocodiles around the temple are kept well-fed by the priests, and so, unless harassed, typically leave people alone.) The temple has been rebuilt and expanded over the years. The oldest portion was built on a rock foundation into which crypts have been carved for interring the remains of priests of Sebk. Also buried in the old section are the mummified remains of hundreds of sacred crocodiles, from those barely over a foot long, which rest in groups in lidded jars, to one that exceeds 12 feet.

The entire city seems to be affected by the presence of the temple and the example of its priests. The people tend to be callous and spiteful, and the soldiers of the local garrison are bullies. Even the city's administration is corrupt — something otherwise quite rare in the Khemitian bureaucracy.

KARPATHOS, CITY OF

Ruler: Lord Gyges Tefre, Admiral Governor of Karpathos
Government: bureaucracy
Population: 13,143 (mostly Khemitite)

The city of Karpathos lies on the bay at the east end of the Island of Karpathos in the Sea of Baal, and is the island's primary settlement. It hosts a critical naval base for Khemit and protects the nation's shipping and makes possible coordinated movement against enemy ships. The admiral who governs the island reports jointly to pharaoh and the marshal of Khemit (who is also the minister of war), and answers only to them. Although a few civilian fishing boats sail from the southern edge of the bay, and there is a provision for merchant ships in the northernmost piers, most of the facilities in the bay are directly in support of the navy.

KERENUS, CITY OF

Ruler: Principal Administrator Amenemope
Government: bureaucracy
Population: 31,507 (mostly Khemitite)

Kerenus sits on the shore of Lake Sekhem in the Makir Hills of northern Khemit. The primary industry here is quarrying and carving red sandstone for temples and monuments. The stone is shipped down the river on barges and used as far south as Elephantine and Luqsor. In addition, the area produces some celestite, an unusual mineral named for its pale blue color and used as a gemstone or for carvings. Kerenus is also the high seat of the temple of Geb, god of the earth and one of the most important deities of Khemit. His temple is constructed primarily of the local sandstone, but its architects also employed stone from other areas of Khemit, including white limestone from near Ghizeh, serpentine from the west, and marble, granite, diorite, and porphyry from the hills and mountains along the Ruby Sea.

KERUMA, TOWN OF

Ruler: Administrator Sennefer
Government: bureaucracy
Population: 7,482 (mostly Khemitite)

Keruma lies on the east bank of the Stygian River where it curves through the southern Harh-Ahu-Ra Hills. It is the most southerly town in Khemit proper. (Nampata, which is farther south, is officially in the Nubiar Oversight.) At one time, Keruma was the capital of the Kingdom of Nubara, but since that country was largely incorporated into Khemit almost 4,000 years ago, the city has been slowly but inevitably dwindling in importance. The old city was surrounded by a substantial wall that encompassed a palace and several nearby mansions, as well as houses and workshops for the common people. Today, only the northern part of the old city is still occupied. Most of the original buildings were made from mudbrick and, in the unoccupied sections, have deteriorated significantly over the ensuing millennia. The old palace and mansions were constructed of mudbrick on stone foundations, so large parts of them remain standing.

Outside Keruma are two unusual structures the locals call deffufas, large buildings once apparently used for religious purposes. One is southwest of the city, not far from the river, up against a cluster of hills. Built of mudbrick, though much better preserved than the smaller buildings in the old city, it looks as if it could be used as a fortress. Overall, it is about 160 feet by 80 feet, though it does not define a regular rectangle. In places, the structure seems to be only one story tall (about 20 feet), while elsewhere the roof is as high as 60 feet. Parts seem to have been built right into the hillside. The roof is flat and could have been used for either ceremonies or defense. No one in Keruma will admit to having been inside the structure; while an outsider might be eager to explore, the locals have an aversion to the place and try to hinder anyone who publicly discusses going there.

The second deffufa, smaller than the first and built east of the old city, appears to be in part one story tall and in part two stories, about 40 feet at the highest. It sits at the north end of an extensive necropolis that contains tens of thousands of burials. Some of these are truly ancient, being (as the locals claim) much older than the Kingdom of Khemit itself. The pattern shows large graves — apparently those of important people — surrounded by groups of smaller ones. The oldest ones are covered with mounds of black and white pebbles, while later tombs are surmounted by pyramids in the Khemitian style. At the southern end of the necropolis are four very large, elaborate mounds which the people of Keruma say are the tombs of the last four kings of the free Kingdom of Nubara.

KHARKHA, TOWN OF

Ruler: Administrator Agaw-begawe
Government: bureaucracy
Population: 1,432 (mostly Khemitite)

Kharkha is the largest of the oases in the western desert. The town is built around some of the dozens of springs within an area about five miles wide and 10 miles long, in a valley about 10 times that size. Kharkha is a major caravan crossroads, and the valley shows the results of millennia of use. One example is a ruined temple nearly 2,000 years old (possibly built for the worship of Amut, Mût, and Chons) with palm-frond pillars supporting what remains of the roof, walls shaped like papyrus scrolls and covered with ancient carvings, and a long hallway lined with statues of ram-headed sphinxes. A ruined fortress of the Hyperboreans sits on a raised plateau within the valley, its wall gradually crumbling but its numerous guard towers still mostly intact.

KURKAR, TOWN OF

Ruler: Administrator Hebt-Kefia
Government: bureaucracy
Population: 6,109 (mostly Khemitite)

Kurkar is located at an oasis in the Western Desert, between Elephantine and the Harh-Ahu-Ra Hills. It is the site of a former tributary of the Stygian that is now merely a series of shallow watering holes supplied by a slow underground spring. The land rises west of the Stygian, so Kurkar is on a plateau that continues to rise toward the hills to the west. The oasis area is well-supplied with date palms and other crops that can be grown in poorer soils. The town itself has a sturdy wall and a military unit to guard it, and a fortified caravanserai for travelers. The oasis attracts gazelles and other wild animals, including small rodents, and those rodents seem to have attracted the elusive small felines known as sand cats. These wild cats, barely larger than a domesticated cat, drink very little since they get most of their liquid from their prey. Having a ready source of prey close at hand is not something to reject in the desert, though, so the evasive sand cats have made themselves at home around the edges of the oasis. The town of Dunqar to the southwest along the trade route is also known to have a population of sand cats.

KURNEK, CITY OF

Ruler: Principal Administrator Enumahotep
Government: bureaucracy
Population: 39,130 (mostly Khemitite)

On the eastern bank of the Stygian, opposite the capital city of Thybos, lies the temple city of Kurnek. Begun in the 19th Dynasty, it has been expanded by nearly all of the 20 dynasties since until now the temple complex/city sprawls more than a mile in each direction. It is crowded with temples or shrines to nearly every deity of Khemit, plus pillared walks, rows of statuary, and other religious venues. If that maze of building wasn't enough, Kurnek is also a busy city with little markets filling up courtyards, rows of small houses built along the backs of noble temples, and people everywhere offering food, lodging, or religious trinkets to the thousands of visitors. Most notable of the religious edifices is the temple of Amun, with 70-foot-tall pillars in its great hall.

LUQSOR, CITY OF

Ruler: Principal Administrator Nefersekheru
Government: bureaucracy
Population: 42,284 (mostly Khemitite)

The city of Luqsor is south of Elephantine in the rocky desert east of the first cataract of the Stygian. Watered by canals, it is populated mostly by priests, artisans, and workers of the government in Elephantine. It is best known, though, for its temples to important gods of the Khemitian pantheon. Built of sandstone from the surrounding canyons, the dozen large temples that fill the city have a unified look despite having been finished over hundreds of years. Most are credited to pharaohs of the 26th or 27th dynasties, when pharaohs of Nubiar heritage first moved the royal capital to Elephantine. Deities honored are Ptah, Isis, Osiris, Ra, Nephthys, Thoth, Horus, Set, Amun, Geb, and Apis. (Due to superstitions surrounding the first god of the dead, Anubis has no true temples other than the ancient one at the city of Anubis.) Other deities, or lesser aspects of these primary deities, are represented at rock-cut temples in the walls of the sandstone canyons between Luqsor and Baqi.

MENEFET, METROPOLIS OF

Ruler: High Administrator Amte Numhotep
Government: bureaucracy
Population: 1,973,888 (mostly Khemitite)

Menefet has been the capital of Khemit several times over the thousands of years. In particular, when the Hyperborean Empire took control of Khemit, they established Menefet as the royal capital because it gave them easier access to the native government. Furthermore, as the capital of the Lower Kingdom, Menefet has been a seat of power even when the royal capital was elsewhere. It is a huge city, one of the largest in the world, and is the most likely place in Khemit to encounter people from throughout the Lost Lands. Its commercial port area is incredibly busy, as it is a primary distribution point for food and other goods entering and leaving the kingdom.

Menefet is the financial center of Khemit and the entire desert region of central Libynos. Markets exist here for the trade of commodities that will never pass through Menefet but are for delivery elsewhere in Khemit, in other nations of Libynos, or beyond. The city includes large markets in gems and other valuables, and trades raw materials as well as worked stones. It goes without saying that a city of this size has a huge underworld, and the black markets in Menefet thrive almost as well as the official markets. One big underground enterprise in Menefet provides for the trade in antiquities. Authorization to acquire the ancient relics of past dynasties and empires comes and goes based on the whims of the pharaohs, but the desire for them by collectors seems never to go out of season.

As might be expected for a city with such a distinguished history, several religious hierarchies have their high seats in Menefet. The most important of these is the god Ptah, creator of the universe and of the other gods, and the patron deity of Menefet. Great bulls are raised near the city and sacrificed during his ceremonies. Of second importance is the high seat of the temple to Osiris, lord of the underworld and judge of souls. Other deities of Khemit whose high seats are in Menefet are Amun, the ram-headed god of sky and sun; Hathor, the beautiful goddess of music, dance, and other arts; Seker, hawk-headed deity of light and dark, life and death; and Sekhmet, lion-headed goddess of war and retribution. The city also has temples of one size or another to the full pantheon of Hyperborean gods; a good-sized temple to the desert deity Mah-Barek; one to Anumon, god of gates, whose worship originated in neighboring Numeda; and religious edifices of various types to many deities from throughout Libynos as well other parts of the world.

The Necropolis of Saghara, a few miles south of Menefet, was the royal burial ground beginning in the 2nd Dynasty when Menefet was the capital of the Conjoined Double Kingdom of Khemit. These early burials took place in underground galleries, but in the 4th Dynasty, kings began to build pyramids here, first a step pyramid and then several others. (These ancient pyramids are in poor condition, so few people come to view them; most visit the slightly later pyramids at Gizeh, which are more impressive.) Later, nobles were also buried here, primarily in rectangular tombs called mastabas. During dynasties when the royal capital has been elsewhere, the necropolis has been used for burial of non-noble (but usually wealthy) people, and specialized religious ceremonies.

MERSA GAWASIS, CITY OF

Ruler: City Administrator Qattam-uk
Government: bureaucracy
Population: 23,919 (mostly Khemitite)

Mersa Gawasis is a port city on the Ruby Sea, but it is best known for its natural beauty and excellent climate, and so is a popular location for wealthy Khemitites (or even foreigners) to have a second home when they want to be away from the city or desert. The city stretches along the sea, with docks for pleasure boats to the north and those for merchant vessels and fishing boats more to the south. The water along the coast is very clear and such underwater sights as coral reefs and octopi can be viewed from the cushioned comfort of a hired boat. Many people from inside and outside Khemit come to spend time in one of the city's many guesthouses, enjoy the pleasant climate, and marvel at the splendors of the sea. The city has a beautiful, modern temple to Hamehit, goddess of water, fish, and the seas, and its carved fountains and tiled pools with their fish playing are considered a must-see for all travelers.

NAMPATA, CITY OF

Ruler: Principal Administrator Kemheribsen
Government: bureaucracy
Population: 75,063 (mostly Khemitite)

Nampata lies on the Stygian River, two days' travel east of the confluence of the Stygian and the Setesh River, west of where the Stygian curves around the northern margins of the Mutabar Hills. It is the capital of Khemit's southernmost possession, the Nubiar Oversight, and the royal seat of the prince who governs it. (See "Nubiar Oversight" below for more information.)

The city has a prominent temple to Amun and a temple to Hapy; the god of the waters is as important to Nampata as he is to other cities north along the Stygian. A university, sponsored by the pharaoh, provides the training necessary to be a successful government scribe or scholar as well as instruction in a wide range of general knowledge. Being, as it is, at the end of a very long communications chain, Nampata is well-supplied with military units to protect the city in case of incursions by Qesh or Meroë, or rebellion by the local population. However, Nampata has been mostly peaceful for almost 100 years. Under those circumstances, it has grown prosperous from trade, including gold mined in the southern portion of the Geb-el-Mardikh Mountains and exotic items from Meroë, Aethiope, and other parts south.

NAQT, CITY OF

Ruler: Principal Administrator Makkedah Geb-ibil
Government: bureaucracy
Population: 63,194 (mostly Khemitite)

The city of Naqt sits where a major distributary leaves the Stygian in the delta. The capital of Khemit during the 31st Dynasty, it is now the military center of northern Khemit and the headquarters of the units in cities along the Stygian, scattered throughout the Western Desert, and in Tahmakht. It also has the responsibility of overseeing the protection of the coast and delta from invasion. Military personnel make up a large proportion of the population, and many of the businesses cater to the soldiers. Temples in the city honor several different Khemitian gods of protection or war, plus Mithras, the soldiers' god of the Hyperboreans. Southwest of the city is an extensive necropolis that includes the burial sites of many high-ranking officers.

The Necropolis of Terenouti southwest of Naqt has been in use since about the 19th Dynasty. Many important military leaders are buried in the vaulted tombs here and some common soldiers as well, especially those of the Hyperborean Empire. During the time of its influence over Khemit, this was the official military cemetery for those who wanted to be buried in the place of their service. A temple to the goddess Solanus overlooks the Hyperborean section. Smaller temples to Isis, Tuart, and Bes are also found in the necropolis.

NEKHEB, CITY OF

Ruler: Principal Administrator Horem-Gerizon
Government: bureaucracy
Population: 75,176 (mostly Khemitite)

This bustling city stretches for more than two miles along the eastern bank of the Stygian, about 50 miles south of the capital city of Thybos. Steep sandstone cliffs border the city on the north and south, and the same sandstone is easy to recognize in Nekheb's temples and civic buildings. The city is dedicated to Nekhbet, the vulture goddess, a deity of protection and war, and the high seat of her temple is found here. This temple is home to the goddess's oracle, the oldest office of oracle in all Khemit.

Nekheb is an ancient city that dates back to before the founding of the conjoined double kingdoms. It has been a prominent administrative center during several dynasties, and many important officials are buried in the rock-cut tombs of its necropolis, including regional governors, archpriests of Khemit, and one well-known admiral whose ships saved the country from an invasion. Parts of the sandstone cliffs are covered with carvings, some of which seem to be very old and of uncertain origin. It has been several generations since anyone cared to investigate them, so there may or may not be anyone now who recalls the purpose of the carvings.

NEKHEFT, CITY OF

Ruler: City Administrator Tahpanhes
Government: bureaucracy
Population: 23,599 (mostly Khemitite)

Nekheft is in the Eastern Desert, on the trade route from Nekheb on the Stygian River to Ipret-Isus on the Ruby Sea. The city has an important temple of Horus, who is sometimes said to be the consort of Nekhbet, the region's preeminent goddess. The city is surrounded by a mudbrick wall some 38 feet thick that encompasses a space about three times the area currently occupied by its residents. This is the third wall built over the millennia the city has been in existence, and this one (set on a foundation of the previous walls) was intended to provide for plenty of growth. This has been quite convenient for caravans, as they are able to camp inside the wall without crowding any area of the city. As a result, Nekheft is a popular overnight stop, and the city's people have developed additional services to gain as many coins as possible from travelers.

Near the edge of the city is an ancient structure built during an early dynasty, though its original purpose has been long forgotten. In form it could almost be a fortress, 30 feet tall and about 250 feet square, with thick mudbrick walls pierced by only a few scattered openings high in the walls. None recalls who might have been its original inhabitants, but today this is the home of a group of monks calling itself the Monastery of Nekheft. They dress in plain clothing and spend their time in scholarly pursuits, though they occasionally hire themselves out as scribes to earn money to support their organization. In fact, and unknown to the residents of Nekheft, this monastery is actually a group from the Church of Hafaz, a sect of the religion of Mah-Barek. Representing the purely intellectual side of that religion, these adherents are residing in Middle Khemit in an attempt to learn some of the esoteric secrets scattered about in various Khemitian temples, and to find any connections between those and the origins and powers of the world as taught by Mah-Barek. The church of Hafaz is nonviolent though quite secretive; as most of the monks are native Khemitites, there is little evidence that they are anything other than religious scholars devoted to a native god.

NHUT, CITY OF

Ruler: City Administrator Hakkatan
Government: bureaucracy
Population: 10,728 (mostly Khemitite)

Nhut sits at the crossroads of two trade routes through the Eastern Desert — one from Nekheb on the river to Ipret-Isus on the Ruby Sea, and the other running south to the city of Baqi and beyond to Keruma at the edge of the Nubiar Oversight. Its location means its people can make some coin serving the needs of the caravans, and also that they often get an early look at what is soon going to be trading in the capital city of Thybos and the great cities of Lower Khemit.

Nhut is known for its magnificent double temple, the only one of its design in the country. The eastern entrance is dedicated to Nefertem, lion-headed lord of the sunrise and god of healing. The western entrance is given to Duamutef, the god of funerary rites, who appears as a tall, hawk-headed man. Each half of the interior of the temple has carvings and decorations appropriate to the applicable deity, with sun motifs and medical instruments on the east side while funeral barges and scenes of mummification are on the west. The entire arrangement of courts, rooms, and pillared halls is symmetrically duplicated, with passageways from one side to the other, and the novelty of it has attracted many worshippers.

ONA, METROPOLIS OF

Ruler: High Administrator Nuzi-um-resen
Government: bureaucracy
Population: 140,288 (mostly Khemitite)

Ona is an ancient city whose origins date back nearly to the foundation of the kingdom of Khemit. It was, and has been, the high seat of the temple of Ra, the hawk-headed god of the sun. Although there are many other temples to the Pharaoh of the Gods, the primary temple has always been here. The proximity of this powerful temple led the Hyperboreans to name their own city of Heliopolis, built nearby, after the sun.

Ra's temple is not the only one in the city; among others, Ona also holds the high seat of the temple of Atmu, a creator deity and god of the setting sun. Most who visit Ona come for the temples, and these visitors support many guesthouses, eating establishments, and other businesses. In addition to religion, Ona is also an important agricultural trade center as it aggregates crops from villages along both sides of the river for further shipment down to the delta.

PERMEJHED, CITY OF

Ruler: City Administrator Adyut-hobab
Government: bureaucracy
Population: 21,783 (mostly Khemitite)

Permejhed is about 25 miles west of the Stygian on the Bakhari River. The city is far enough from the Stygian that its agricultural production is watered by canals rather than by the river itself, and keeping those clear is a major duty of the town's leadership. Its river port allows caravans from the Western Desert to transship here and then travel a good part of their route by water — and similarly in the other direction — so it is an important hub of trade. Founded during the 20th Dynasty, Permejhed has also been an administrative center, both for the Khemitian government and for the Hyperboreans during their period of influence. According to rumor, 1,000 years of Hyperborean (and other) records were dumped and left to rot somewhere in the desert outside of town, but because the desert is so dry, they are still out there, merely covered by several feet of sand.

Within Permejhed is the high seat of the temple of Set, jackal-headed god of evil and night. Despite his evil reputation, Set still has his duties to fulfill in the pantheon of Khemit: Every day the Black Serpent, Aapep, tries to devour Ra's Sun Boat as it moves across the heavens, and it is Set's task to battle him. Each evening, the serpent finally succeeds and plunges the world into darkness. Set must then cut open the belly of Aapep to allow the Sun Boat to escape and dawn to come to the world once again. Every morning when the sun rises, the people of Khemit know that Set is still doing his duty, and so the god receives a share of worship from most people even though they are certainly not his followers. Most such worship takes place at small shrines, though, and few common people ever visit Set's primary temple, where poisonous serpents are allowed to roam free, and each priest carries a staff in the shape of a cobra, which (it is said) will bite an offender on command.

PHAROS, METROPOLIS OF

Ruler: High Administrator Manetes Hept-anathoth
Government: bureaucracy
Population: 401,926 (mostly Khemitite)

Although believed to have been founded in ancient times by the Sea Peoples and a center of learning for millennia, this city and its famous port were primarily built up by the Hyperboreans during the rise of their hegemony over Khemit in the 13th Dynasty. Located on the coast of the Sea of Baal in the Western Desert, near the border with what is now Guurzan, Pharos has long been a key part of Khemit's defense against tribes from west of the Qarrasat Hills. Its immense lighthouse, whose light can be seen for as much as 35 miles, was also the first and greatest of a line of smaller signaling towers along the coast to Rashad in the delta of the Stygian. The port itself is its own marvel. Entered just east of the lighthouse and oriented east and west, it has a straight portion that offers berths for merchant ships, with enough space for 50 ships on each side of the channel. Past that is the interior portion of the port, which the Hyperboreans constructed for their military ships only. It is circular, built around a manmade island, and offers covered slips for more than 200 ships around its outer perimeter.

The city itself is a cosmopolitan mix of standard Khemitian architecture with the elaborate stone structures of the Hyperboreans. This blending is also seen in religious edifices; the city has temples in the Hyperborean style to Osiris, Isis, and Horus, one of the powerful triads of the Khemitian gods. Of course, the Hyperborean gods are also well represented. The great deities have impressive temples, many of which are still active locations of popular worship. The minor gods also have their places, though; it is said that every deity of Hyperborea had a temple someplace in Pharos, and most still have someone to light their altar fires.

In addition to religious locations, Pharos is full of civic works. Even just providing water for the city is an engineering achievement and is accomplished through a series of very deep cisterns whose long sides are supported by worked stone. Another landmark institution was a school, started during the 5th Dynasty by priests of Seshat, goddess of writing and knowledge. That small school grew to be the massive University of All Knowledge, which claims to teach all branches of learning. Its growth eventually drew it away from its religious roots, but it is said that sculptures from the original temple still remain inside one of the university buildings (no one is quite sure which one). The high seat of Seshat is in a larger temple that was built during the 14th Dynasty, facing the Great Library.

More notably, those early priests began a collection of writings in honor of their goddess. They gathered writings not just from Khemit but from all over Libynos. By the time the Hyperboreans arrived, the Great Library of Pharos had become a separate institution, and the librarians were thrilled to discover the existence of more cultures whose writings could be collected. The Hyperboreans assisted the library by donating copies of all official documents and many personal items, which resulted in explosive growth of the collection and (of necessity) the building. These days, scholars from the Great Library travel throughout Libynos, and to other parts of the world to gather writings and to transcribe histories and lore where that has not yet been done.

PYRAMESES, METROPOLIS OF

Ruler: High Administrator Lerapekt Shahm-es
Government: bureaucracy
Population: 111,774 (mostly Khemitite)

Pyrameses is in the Stygian Delta between two branches of a distributary. It is Khemit's major trading port and capable of handling dozens of large ships at a time. It is also near the entrance of the Canal of the Pharaohs, which runs from the Stygian River to Lake Trophimus and then to the Gulf of Mafket, where it connects to the Ruby Sea. Oceangoing vessels transship their cargo to river boats or to smaller ships that can travel through the canal and then to the sea again.

The city is full of guesthouses, storehouses, and stables, as well as palaces and temples, and is the largest city in Khemit by land area. Pyrameses was also the capital of the triple kingdom during the 29th Dynasty. Just more than 500 years ago (in the 36th Dynasty), the Foerdewaith of Akados invaded and its inhabitants were forced to labor in support of a great religious crusade the overking was conducting in eastern Libynos. This incident lingers still in local legend, and foreigners who look like they could be from the hated Kingdom of Foere may be treated badly by some.

RAFFE, CITY OF

Ruler: City Administrator Maacah
Government: bureaucracy
Population: 10,196 (mostly Khemitite)

Raffe is on the coast of the Sea of Baal in north-central Tahmakht. It has some port facilities on the coast and supports a small fishing industry. However, the city itself is located about half a mile inland, with strong walls and a military force to patrol the trade route through the area. Watered by moisture from the Sea of Baal, Raffe has extensive vineyards and wineries, and also fields of grain and breweries for beer. Most of the production is sent west to the larger cities in Lower Khemit.

The city has a temple to Geb, Khemitian deity of the earth, and a few shrines to other personal-protection deities, but they are generally attended by only a small portion of the population. More popular is the temple to Anumon, god of gates and keeper of laws, whose worship spread from Numeda. Claiming authority over admitting souls to the afterlife, Anumon calls into question the authority of the many Khemitian deities with responsibility for some aspect of death. The personal qualities of the god's priests can seldom be faulted, however, so the religion receives grudging acceptance by the religious hierarchy of Khemit.

RASHAD, METROPOLIS OF

Ruler: High Administrator Melqa-at-umran
Government: bureaucracy
Population: 135,442 (mostly Khemitite)

Rashad is another important port in the Stygian Delta and exports foodstuffs from Lower Khemit and transships goods for Menefet and other cities from oceangoing vessels to river ships. The patron deity of the city is Hapy, god of rivers and seas, and the high seat of the temple of Hapy is in Rashad. It sits on a stone foundation overlooking the Sea of Baal and the Stygian Delta, and is elaborately carved with fishes and birds. Hapy is revered almost equally with Ra, because without his life-giving waters, the entire land of Khemit would die; consequently, his temple is wealthy and his priests influential. Farther inland, inside the city, Rashad also has an important temple to Horus, deity of law and retribution.

SALIS, CITY OF

Ruler: City Administrator Faras-keft
Government: bureaucracy
Population: 27,665 (mostly Khemitite)

Salis sits on a slow-moving branch of the Stygian in the delta. The people of the city take advantage of the brackish condition of the distributary by using the water to make salt by the evaporation method. This provides a local source of salt, rather than having to get it from some of the larger sources in the Western Desert.

Salis is also the high seat of the temple of Neith, the beautiful and ancient goddess of war and wisdom and arbitrator among the gods. In Salis, the goddess is also revered as a creator, and the one who gives birth to Ra (the sun) every day. Other places assign these roles to different deities, however, which sometimes causes strife at religious councils. Every year, a great celebration called the Feast of Lamps is held for the goddess, and the sky over the whole city shows the light all night in her honor.

SELLEH-FASHAR, TOWN OF

Ruler: Administrator Ateneru
Government: bureaucracy
Population: 1,552 (mostly Khemitite)

This isolated oasis, covered with miles of date palms, is part of the caravan route from Upper Khemit and other southern countries north to Pharos or to Guurzan. It trades in dates, olives, and oil, and the townspeople are said to know the locations of silver mines (in the southern Harh-Ahu-Ra Hills) they try hard to keep secret from outsiders. If queried, the locals say they get the silver from Qesh or Meroë, but oasis natives casually wear enough silver jewelry to make that claim very questionable. The small population here is closely related to the desert tribes of Guurzan, and a few don't even speak Khemitian but only their own obscure language.

A notable structure is a temple of the Oracle of Amun, the ram-headed god of sky and sun. Believed to have been built early in the 10th Dynasty, even leaders of the Hyperboreans could attest to the veracity of its predictions, for they were known to consult it from time to time. (Its existence was hidden from the hated crusaders, however, as the priests reasonably feared its destruction by those single-minded folk.) Consulting oracles is not much in vogue in recent centuries, though, and the temple has deteriorated from lack of support.

SHEIRBAH, CITY OF

Ruler: City Administrator Esh Tibni
Government: bureaucracy
Population: 14,982 (mostly Khemitite)

Sheirbah is on the west coast of Tahmakht along the Gulf of Mafket, but it is primarily a Khemitian settlement. Fishing supplements the available agriculture, as this part of the coast is fairly dry. The city features an ancient temple to Hathor, usually known as the goddess of music and other arts, but sometimes in the past also thought of as a patroness of miners, and a protector of desert regions. Sheirbah is the location of an important turquoise mine, one that has literally been worked for millennia. The mining had gotten trickier over the years because workers have to follow narrower veins and work in areas that are difficult to access. Two other mines are near enough that the mining companies are headquartered here. A fairly recent find of turquoise in a new location means a new mine is being developed about halfway between Sheirbah and Wadi Mafket, but farther into the mountains.

SINWORHET, CITY OF

Ruler: Principal Administrator Medeba-iz-ghufran
Government: bureaucracy
Population: 60,966 (mostly Khemitite)

Sinworhet is located in the Makir Hills of northern Khemit, on Lake Bakhari where the river of the same name flows out to the south. Although the hills are rocky in general, and populated mostly by herds of goats, fertile soil is found around the shores of the lake. Settlement at this location goes back to the time of the double kingdom (probably in the 6th Dynasty) but the population of Sinworhet grew significantly during the Hyperborean period, when soldiers who had spent their careers in Khemit decided to retire in the area. This lakeside city was a popular choice for retirees and much of the populace has at least some Hyperborean ancestry. Several temples to Hyperborean deities can still be found here, especially the soldiers' god Mithras, and Telophus, lord of crops.

SULEB, CITY OF

Ruler: City Administrator Neb-Kenamon
Government: bureaucracy
Population: 13,105 (mostly Khemitite)

Suleb is on the west bank of the Stygian River, just north of the third cataract on the river. It is the most southern city on the western side of the river and has a strong wall and organized city guard to protect against attacks from the country of Qesh and from the creatures of the Harh-Ahu-Ra Hills. The hills are not just a source of peril, however; they also produce beautiful marble that has been used in buildings throughout upper Khemit, and valuable iron ore.

During the 23rd and 24th dynasties, the pharaohs of Thybos built a large temple to Amun in Suleb as part of establishing the deity's superiority throughout Khemit, and several traveled to Suleb for ceremonies. The walkway approaching the temple is paved with patterned marble pieces and guarded by marble ram-headed sphinxes to honor the ram-headed deity of the sun. Inside, the corridor that shows the pharaoh deified, with ram horns, is warded by statues of lionesses — symbols of the goddess Sekhmet who protects the pharaohs. Two pharaohs of the 24th Dynasty are buried in Suleb's extensive necropolis, as are other members of the royal family, court nobles, priests, officials from the south, and wealthy commoners who could afford to be buried with the nobility. These subterranean tombs are topped by pyramids with those of the pharaohs of course being the largest, although the size still does not come close to the older funerary pyramids in the north.

TALAM-QEDISH, TOWN OF

Ruler: Administrator Baiti-shobi
Government: bureaucracy
Population: 1,512 (mostly Khemitite)

This oasis town is currently best known as the home of Numhotep Orsi'a, a popular modern writer of poetry and of history, especially that of the Lower Kingdom. A less exciting, but more important, aspect of the town's economy is its ongoing mining of natron, a key component in the mummification so crucial to all Khemitian burials. While natron can also be found at other sites, that of Talam-Qedish is easiest to extract and closest to the population centers of Lower Khemit. It is also a center of caravans from and to Pharos and the country of Guurzan, with several routes converging. A strong wall protects against bandits, and two military units patrol the area with the town as their headquarters.

TANI-TERU, CITY OF

Ruler: Principal Administrator Ater-Shebma
Government: bureaucracy
Population: 32,611 (mostly Khemitite)

Tani-Teru is southwest of Thybos on the caravan route that parallels the Stygian River to its west. A route from the oases of the Western Desert intersects the other here, going on to Nekheb on the east bank and farther on to points on the Ruby Sea. The city is a prominent military location, headquarters to units that patrol the southern portion of the Western Desert, between the Stygian and the Harh-Ahu-Ra Hills. Tani-Teru is the location of the high seat of the temple of Upuat, god of war and protection. This wolf-headed deity is often depicted with blue or gray hair to distinguish him from Anubis, and is said to go ahead of pharaoh in war or the hunt and be the "opener of the way."

Another prominent temple is one to the goddess Hathor. Although her primary worship center is in Menefet, the temple here (from the 23rd Dynasty) is also large and well-known. The ceiling in one of its shrines is carved as a circular zodiac and shows the positions of the stars at different times of the year and also allow astronomers to predict eclipses of the moons. A decorated obelisk stands outside the temple and serves as the pointer of a giant sundial; the courtyard in which it stands is inlaid with a pattern of bronze lines, which make it possible to tell the time of day depending on the season of the year.

TET, CITY OF

Ruler: City Administrator Ahmose-mot
Government: bureaucracy
Population: 23,750 (mostly Khemitite)

The city of Tet is on Lake Sekhem in the Makir Hills of northern Khemit, and the people of Tet gain much of their livelihood from the lake. They fish and make most of the papyrus in the hill area from the reeds in the lake. Tet is also the high seat of Tefnut, goddess of storms and rivers. She is one of the deities of Khemit's all-important water, along with her brother Hapy. The people of her city make sure to always pour out a libation of water to her before eating or drinking, and at least sprinkle some water from their fingers before going about an activity, to gain her favor in their undertakings.

THANY, CITY OF

Ruler: City Administrator Meketari
Government: bureaucracy
Population: 21,684 (mostly Khemitite)

Thany lies east of the Stygian River in Lower Khemit, roughly between Ishantar and Akhetaten. Located about 10 miles into the Eastern Desert, Thany is a training ground for military recruits. Not all new military personnel attend training here; some in distant parts of the country are trained by local units. However, those who do attend this military school are generally considered better soldiers and more professional, and some may even eventually be promoted to officers. Not surprisingly, the city has a major temple of Anhur, god of war and the hunt. In addition to priests who minister to and encourage the soldiers in training, the temple also has hunters who range the Eastern Desert and even into the Ruby Hills to keep predatory animals away from settlements. Sometimes the hunters are hired by wealthy people from Menefet or Thybos to lead them on thrilling expeditions in pursuit of dangerous game.

Thybos, Metropolis of

Ruler: High Administrator Ghadir Shamramut
Government: bureaucracy
Population: 503,446 (mostly Khemitite)

Thybos is the traditional capital of Khemit's Middle Kingdom and the current royal capital. It has been the royal capital since the 37th Dynasty, as well as other times throughout the history of the country. It is a huge, sprawling city that is sometimes referred to as the City of a Hundred Gates, and is built on the west side of the Stygian River where it makes a curve to the east. Many pharaohs have lavished their wealth on it, building plazas, shrines, civic buildings, a major university, and temples to its patron deities. The Royal University (founded during the 11th Dynasty) has the pharaoh as its special patron. Even when the royal capital is in a different city, graduates of this university are often selected for good positions in the civil service and for serving directly in the pharaoh's court.

The primary deity of Thybos is Amun, the ram-headed god of the sky and sun. He is depicted as having blue skin and being crowned with two ostrich feathers. Thybos holds the high seat of the temple of Amun, as well as the high seats of the temples of Mût, consort of Amun, and of Chons, their son, the hawk-headed god of the silver moon and knowledge. This trinity of deities has been venerated in Thybos for millennia. The worship of the Thyban Triad has been so strong throughout Khemit that at times the priests of Amun have rivaled the pharaohs in wealth and influence. This has caused tension when the royal capital was in other locations in the country. When the royal capital is in Thybos and the pharaoh can keep a personal eye on the priests, their influence is not so disruptive.

Mût is the great mother goddess and queen of the gods, and she is usually depicted as holding an ankh of life and wearing the triple crown of Khemit. Her temple lies in the curve of a specially-built lake shaped like a crescent moon, and the annual Festival of Mût includes placing one of her statues on a boat and navigating around the lake while celebrations take place. (Although priests can be involved in temple administration and may be oracles, all rituals in the temples of Mût are handled by priestesses only, with the duty of chief priestess belonging to the queen of Khemit or her eldest daughter.) Another important ceremony takes place during the festival of the New Year, when the great statue of Amun is carried in a procession through the long line of guardian sphinx statues to visit the statue of Mût in her temple, thereby ensuring fertility for the city and country for the coming year.

The city of Thybos is also the high seat of the temple of Tuart, goddess of fertility and protection. She is represented as having the head and body of a pregnant hippopotamus, standing upright, with the legs of a lioness and the tail of a river crocodile. Tuart provides the fierce protection of the deadly mother hippopotamus combined with the features of other dangerous predators. As a riverine goddess, she is also linked to fertility (of crops as well as people) and plays a role in the annual inundation of the Stygian. Her image is carved on household items (especially furniture) and is worn by mothers and children on protective amulets.

The massive Necropolis of Thybos is outside the city to the northwest. It includes large private cemeteries, royal cemeteries (which hold the tombs not just of pharaohs but also royal families and high advisors), and other buildings erected for funerary purposes. Numerous pharaohs

have built mortuary temples here and dedicated them to various gods of death in the hopes that their own afterlives would be easier. Khemit has at least 10 deities who oversee some aspect of death or guard the dead, and temples to all of them can be found in this necropolis. Many people who work in the necropolis in some way, or serve in the temples, live in the city of Inhy as that is actually closer for most than Thybos itself.

Um, City of

Ruler: Administrator Katenatin
Government: bureaucracy
Population: 8,424 (mostly Khemitite)

Um is a southern port on the Ruby Sea. When the capital of Khemit was at Elephantine in the Upper Kingdom (during the 26th and 27th dynasties), Um was a major trading location, and even today remains convenient for trading in the south. However, the city is much smaller than it was at the time and has not had the money to keep up its large docks, so most bigger ships go on to Ipret-Isus. Um is also much hotter than the coastal cities farther north, and during certain times of the year needs to get its water from sources in the nearby Geb-el-Mardikh Mountains. Because of how close the mountains are to the coast, Um is the southernmost port of Khemit that is larger than a fishing village. Several sources of gold are located in the rocky Eastern Desert between Um and Elephantine, so the city serves as headquarters for some mining groups. Um is also a frequent base of operations for people who explore into the mountains or the Ruby Hills looking for resources they could profitably extract.

Wadi Mafket, City of

Ruler: City Administrator Shu-amgar
Government: bureaucracy
Population: 10,569 (mostly Khemitite)

Wadi Mafket is a port on the Gulf of Mafket on the southwestern edge of the Governate of Tahmakht. It is a prominent fishing town and also a travel destination for people from Tahmakht who want to visit the coast, having similar climate benefits as the Ruby Sea. It is also a location where large oceangoing ships transship cargo headed through the Canal of the Pharaohs and eventually on up the Stygian or to the Sea of Baal. In addition, traders go from here in smaller river-ships to the Gulf of Tahmakht and up the Heshbon River to Geara. They are willing to risk encounters with the pirate ships of the Numedan corsairs to move Geara's metal goods to market more quickly.

The city has moderate weather, receiving rain from the Gulf of Mafket, and is watered by a seasonal river from the mountains. Wadi Mafket holds a temple to Anqet, goddess of rivers and water, and also one to Geb, god of earth. It is a Khemitian settlement, rather than native Tahmakhtim, and has been on this site since the time of the conjoined double kingdoms.

Mining turquoise from the western Jeshennin Mountains is the most valuable local industry. A nearby valley leads to two important turquoise mines on facing sides of different mountains. Called the Valley of Caves, the approach to the mines has been filled with monuments to various pharaohs from the 5th to the 33rd dynasties, and small shrines to deities such as Horus and Thoth.

Geographic Features and Points of Interest in the Triple-Kingdom of Khemit

Assal-Aat Depression

Assal-Aat is a teardrop-shaped lowland in western Khemit more than 50 miles long and about 30 miles at its widest point, whose bottom of salt pans, seasonal dry lakes, and salt marshes is more than 400 feet below sea level. The eastern side of the depression drops off 700 feet from a rocky plateau. In contrast, the western side gradually rises to the Great Sand Sea, a huge area mostly filled by wave after wave of sand that goes from here west to Olappo in Guurzan and southwest an unknown distance.

Astebera River

The Astebera River flows out of the Geb-el-Mardikh Mountains west into the Stygian River, joined by the Small Astebera (to the south) and the North Branch. It meets the larger river just south of the first cataract of the Stygian. (See "Stygian River" below for more information.) The town of Aten-Seyal lies in the curve of the river before it reaches the Small Astebera, and the town of Baqi is located on the North Branch.

Bakhari Lake and River

Lake Bakhari in the northern Makir Hills is the primary sources of the Bakhari River. It is fed by an underground spring powerful enough that water from the lake flows south and east over 150 miles to join the Stygian River. The city of Sinworhet lies at the juncture of the lake and river.

Baswun Dam

This massive dam is a feat of early Khemitian engineering. Locals say that it once controlled the flows of three rivers, staving off dangerous flooding and watering fields 50 miles from the Stygian. It was the center of a thriving population. Then the deserts changed, and the rivers were cut off. Now the dam stands alone in the desert, with rocks at its base where waters once flowed. Sometimes caravans use it as a landmark, in the distance.

Canal of the Pharaohs

This canal runs from the delta of the Stygian River east to Lake Trophimus and then south to the Gulf of Mafket where it connects to the Ruby Sea. Locks designed by Hyperborean engineers during the 15th Dynasty keep the seawater from contaminating the fresh waters of river and lake. However, the canal is still subject to silting and becomes impassable if long-term maintenance is neglected, as has happened several times over the centuries. Some large oceangoing vessels have too deep of a draft for the river and canal, and so transship cargoes at one end or the other. Pyrameses or Bastus are the usual choices at the Sea of Baal end; Dahra or Wadi Mafket in Tahmakht are the best options in the Gulf of Mafket.

Geb-el-Mardikh Mountains

This mountain range runs north and south along the Ruby Sea, along the east coast of Upper Khemit and on through the Nubiar Oversight. (See "Nubiar Oversight" below for more information on that area.) It has almost no passes through it, and none large enough for a caravan to travel, so the coastal villages to the east have contact with the rest of Khemit only by water. The mountains are full of caves and are said to be populated by many underground species, including dwarves who never come to the surface, and kobolds. Any deep dwellers very rarely venture out of the caves, although sometimes an isolated coastal village is found destroyed with no sign of the attackers. The range also has many dangerous creatures aboveground, of course.

The mountains have some valuable mineral resources, but the distant location makes them troublesome to mine. Silver, marble, and garnet are available, among other things. Gold and silver are found together in some rock; rather than trying to divide the two (a complicated task), the metals are simply combined into electrum and used that way, so electrum is more common in Khemit than most areas.

Gorge of Osiris, Ruins of the

The Gorge of Osiris is a small canyon in the Harh-Ahu-Ra Hills, so named for the temple of Osiris at its mouth. The walls of the gorge were once used for shrines and burial places, but they fell into disuse centuries ago and now only a small group of priests tends to the temple.

Great Columns

These two columns, each about 100 feet tall, are believed to date to the 1st or 2nd dynasty. They were supposedly built to commemorate the place where two angels touched their feet to the earth. One column is of brick, and the other is stone. A narrow exterior stair winds to the top of each, but the one on the brick pillar is crumbling and considered unsafe to climb. The tops of the pillars are now weathered and nondescript, but locals claim they once held altars to the angels (or whatever type of beings they were), or possibly to Thoth.

Gulf of Mafket

This narrow gulf of the Ruby Sea lies between Lower Khemit on the west and the Khemitian Governate of Tahmakht on the east. The cities of Sheirbah and Wadi Mafket are on the Tahmakhtim side while the port city of Dahra sits on the western shore near the mouth of the gulf, between the sea and the Ruby Hills. The Gulf of Mafket connects the Ruby Sea to the Sea of Baal through the Canal of the Pharaohs, which runs north to Lake Trophimus and then west to the delta of the Stygian River near the city of Bastus.

Gulf of Tahmakht

This short, narrow gulf lies between the southern part of the peninsula of Tahmakht and the Kingdom of Numeda. Tahmakht has no major cities on the gulf itself, though there is one on the Heshbon River that flows from the Jeshennin Mountains into the gulf. This occasionally leads to Khemitian trade ships skirmishing in the gulf with Numedan corsairs, but the pirates generally prefer the easier pickings on the Ruby Sea itself.

Harh-Ahu-Ra Hills

This line of rough hills and rocky plateaus runs more-or-less north and south through Khemit's Western Desert, with the southern end of the range curving and extending into Meroë. It is interrupted at several places by gaps of a few miles but is considered to be a single set of hills. The point where the Harh-Ahu-Ra meet the Stygian is generally considered the border between Khemit and Qesh. Caravans from Middle Khemit usually travel east of the hills while those from Upper Khemit, Meroë, or points south sometimes cross through one of the southern passes and travel west of the hills. Bandits threaten travelers on either side, though robbers in the Western Desert tend to be bolder as sources of authority are farther between. The Harh-Ahu-Ra Hills contain mineral resources such as different types of valuable stone (marble and granite, for instance), and possibly also silver or gold, depending on who one believes.

Heshbon River

The Heshbon River flows around the eastern slopes of the Jeshennin Mountains and into the north end of the Gulf of Tahmakht. It has an underground source, flows all year round, and is deep enough for riverboats to navigate up to the city of Geara. The Heshbon is generally considered to be the border between Khemit and Numeda. Since there is little but deep desert on the Numedan side of the border, it goes uncontested for long periods of time.

ISLE OF SCORPIONS

This island in the Ruby Sea off the coast of the city of Ipret-Isus is about 20 miles at its widest point and 35 miles long with a central peak that is a long-dormant volcano. The sea breezes keep the climate pleasant. It is home to a major temple to Maftet, goddess of protection and healing, and its supporting villages. The large temple complex includes houses of healing and of training for healers, and also specializes in providing antidotes for injuries such as snakebites and scorpion stings.

IZDIHAR LAKE AND RIVER

One of a group of spring-fed lakes in the rocky Makir Hills of northern Khemit, Lake Izdihar is the smallest and southernmost of the three lakes. From it the Izdihar River flows south into the Bakhari River.

JESHENNIN MOUNTAINS

This range covers about half of the Tahmakht Peninsula, from foothills on the eastern side to high peaks in the center and west. The mountains are a source of copper and tin (for bronze), as well as iron in the east, and copper, iron, and turquoise in the southwest. They provide pasturage for goats and sheep, but the isolated peaks are also home to dangerous animals and strange creatures that *may* be only stories.

KARPATHOS, ISLAND OF

Karpathos is a long, slender island in the Sea of Baal about 20 miles northwest of Rashad in Khemit. Its primary settlement is on the eastern end where there is an excellent bay; the rest of the island has a rocky spine and supports a few villages of farmers and shepherds, which in turn support the Royal Navy's base there. A few other rocky little islands are grouped around it, each with a tiny population. About 300 feet from the western end of Karpathos is a small island called Mikrin. When Khemit first established a naval base on Karpathos in the 29th Dynasty, the two were a single island but they split apart during a strong earthquake in the 33rd Dynasty. Now only a few dozen shepherds call the smaller island home, and they strictly avoid the ruined city there. Ancient already when the city of Karpathos was built, the remnants are said to be those of a city of the Sea Peoples, though that doesn't explain the taboo against it among the local people.

KHEMIT, LOWER

Roughly considered to lie between the Sea of Baal and the junction of the Stygian and Bakhari rivers, Lower Khemit is the most populous area of the triple kingdom. It is governed by a vizier who is a member of pharaoh's high council and is expected to manage the territory as its ruler, doing so in pharaoh's name. Lower Khemit was strongly influenced by the Hyperborean Empire during the centuries of its power, so the cities here tend to be more cosmopolitan, and aware of the world outside Khemit, than places farther south. This extends to religion; temples to the Hyperborean deities are still fairly common in Lower Khemit and are sometimes attended by locals as well as foreigners.

During the military event known in parts of the continent of Akados as the Second Great Crusade, Lower Khemit was invaded by the so-called Hyperborean Monarchy of Foerdewaith. Pyrameses and its harbor were taken by the overwhelming force of the crusader navy, and the city was used as the major supply hub for the entire army on its march to some location of religious significance in eastern Libynos. The invaders also occupied the metropolis of Menefet specifically, and Lower Khemit in general, for about six years. Having taken place barely more than 500 years ago (during the 36th Dynasty), it is still a frequent topic of stories, and foreigners who seem to be from Akados may face resentment on the topic of the crusade. Those stories also support hatred of the Huun for the way they endangered Khemitites by using the area to decoy and spy on the western invaders. Any suspected Huun are likely to be grabbed and taken to the authorities at once.

KHEMIT, MIDDLE

The area known as Middle Khemit (or the Middle Kingdom) is considered to lie approximately from the Bakhari River in the north to just north of the city of Elephantine, or about even with the southern end of the Ruby Hills. It is not as densely populated as the land farther north, but it contains several important cities, including the royal capital. It is also a crucial farming area. The region is governed by a vizier who is a member of pharaoh's high council and is expected to manage the territory as its ruler, doing so in pharaoh's name. During the centuries of Hyperborean ascendancy, military units and traders from that empire left their influence on Middle Khemit, though it is less strong than in the northern part of the country. Much of the underground wealth of the country — especially gold and semiprecious gems — can be found (with some difficulty) in the Eastern Desert of Middle Khemit.

KHEMIT, UPPER

The area known as Upper Khemit runs from the city of Elephantine south to the Nubiar Oversight, although its southern border is somewhat nebulous across most of the distance. It is much less densely populated than the northern parts of the country; the majority of the people live in or near the upper capital of Elephantine. However, the perimeter areas (such as the Geb-el-Mardikh Mountains) contain most of the valuable mineral resources of the region. Caravans travel through Upper Khemit from the south, bringing trade from farther south. Most of Upper Khemit was once part of the Kingdom of Nubara, which was conquered and largely incorporated as the third part of the triple kingdom. (The balance of Nubara now comprises the Nubiar Oversight.)

The region is governed by a vizier who is a member of pharaoh's high council and is expected to manage the territory as its ruler, doing so in pharaoh's name. During the centuries of Hyperborean ascendancy, traders and explorers from that empire traveled through Upper Khemit and other countries of central Libynos, but the area was never really occupied by its military or controlled by its extensive bureaucracy. Although the entire country of Khemit was an acknowledged part of the Hyperborean Empire, the empire's influence on the southern area was weak. The culture of Nubara has been much more influential on southern and even central Khemit, especially during periods under pharaohs of Nubiar descent.

LAKE TROPHIMUS

This lake, east of the Stygian River delta, is an integral part of the Canal of the Pharaohs. Djanet, the capital of the Governate of Tahmakht, sits on its northeastern shore. Lake Trophimus is named after the Hyperborean noble who took the canal from a vague idea of the Khemitites (for several hundred years) to a working water route between seas. A memorial obelisk to Aristides Trophimus is visible from where the canal enters the lake from the west. The reverse side of the obelisk memorializes Trophimus as well as Drusilla Phileta, the engineer who designed the lock system, and Casiphia Tartessa, the architect who oversaw the building of the canal.

MAKIR HILLS

These hills are a rocky upthrust in north-central Khemit. Underground springs form lakes among the hills and make it possible to raise food for cities. Rivers run from the lakes south and east toward the Stygian, but the hard, rough desert south of the hills supports only a small population outside the Stygian's river valley. To the north, the land slopes down sharply toward the edge of the Sea of Baal.

NUBIAR OVERSIGHT

The Nubiar Oversight is the portion of Nubara not incorporated into the Triple Kingdom of Khemit, but governed by it. The borders of the Nubiar Oversight are somewhat vaguely defined given its remoteness and the relatively thin populations in the region. The northern border, between the Oversight and Upper Khemit, begins somewhere south of Keruma (which is within Upper Khemit), includes the north bank of the Stygian as it heads east (including Nampata, the capital of the Nubiar Oversight), and continues to the east beyond the point where the Stygian turns south around the Mutabar Hills all the way to the shores of the Ruby Sea, including the Geb-el-Mardikh Mountains. The Uashta Hills, east of the Geb-el-Mardikhs, however, are held by Axuum. On the south, the border is generally accepted to be the north bank of the Stygian and its tributaries, the Lapis River and the River Aeth, through the southern end of the Geb-el-Mardikh range.

The area is governed by the prince of the Nubiar Oversight; the position is effectively that of a vizier but is traditionally held by the designated heir to the pharaoh. Currently, this position is held by Prince Tutemheb, oldest child of Pharaoh Tuthmosis IX. The position is not administratively onerous, but the fractious population can make the area difficult to manage. When peaceful, the Nubiar Oversight tends to be prosperous, being a key location for trade into the southern part of central Libynos.

RUBY HILLS

The Ruby Hills are named for their proximity to the Ruby Sea rather than any rubies to be found in them. They are rich in minerals, though, and at various places have copper, gold (at several locations), iron, assorted semi-precious gems, and such stone as granite, sandstone, limestone, marble, porphyry, and others. The hills run north and south along the coast intermittently for about 375 miles, and also separate the slightly better climate of the seacoast from the extremes of the Eastern Desert.

RUBY SEA

The Ruby Sea is a warm sea more than 1,000 miles long that separates North Libynos from South Libynos. The sea is 100 to 150 miles wide, with most of that distance being relatively shallow. However, it has a deep crevasse that runs approximately along the middle of the sea and in places is more than a mile deep. The country of Numeda lies along almost the entire eastern bank of the Ruby Sea. Khemit lies along two-thirds of the western bank, with the country of Axuum along the southern third. The Ruby Sea teems with life, having impressive coral reefs along the coast, hundreds of types of fish (including some found nowhere else), porpoises, sharks, octopi, giant turtles, and many other types of marine creatures.

SEKHEM LAKE AND RIVER

Lake Sekhem is a spring-fed lake among rocky hills in the northern part of Khemit. It is the largest of a grouping of three lakes in the Makir Hills, being about 35 miles at its longest point. The Sekhem River flows into the Izdihar River shortly before the latter joins the Bakhari. The cities of Tet and Kerenus are along the shore of the lake.

STYGIAN RIVER

The Stygian River is central to the life and society of Khemit. First and foremost, it waters a large part of the country in its annual floods, which is referred to as the "inundation." The Stygian also provides easy transportation north and south through Khemit; travel downriver (north) is carried by the current, and travel upriver (south) is powered by the strong winds that blow south from the Sea of Baal. Ships can sail from the sea to the city of Elephantine, but after that point the river experiences the first of its cataracts, where the river channel is dangerously shallow and rocky, and the water runs fast and chaotically. The cataracts are effectively impassable for shipping, though some smaller vessels can be carried via a portage around the rapids.

Cataracts are not just dangerous to ships; they have rocky shores for miles along the river so farming cannot be done in those areas either. On the other hand, places where the banks are high and cut by the river often provide easy access to different types of stone. In addition, temples have been cut into the stone faces along the river at various places to honor several major gods of Khemit. Some of the most ancient rock temples in the far south may originally have been built for other non-Khemitian deities, though their use was converted to the accepted pantheon long ago.

About 200 miles upriver of Elephantine, near the city of Anubis, the river passes through a second cataract, with a third another 100 miles farther south near Suleb. Beyond that is Keruma and the southern border of Upper Khemit. Farther to the south, the Stygian crosses the Nubiar Oversight, past Nampata and around the Mutabar Hills, upriver to the confluence of the Opal and Lapis Rivers. There is the beginning of the Stygian, and the effective limit of the triple kingdom. Farther south are the lands of Meroë and Aethiope.

TAHMAKHT

Tahmakht is a small peninsula east of Khemit and west of Numeda that links the northern and southern parts of the continent of Libynos. It has a small area of land in the northeast suitable for dryland farming, but most is either desert or mountainous. Politically, it is a governate of Khemit and has been since at least the 17th Dynasty. The current governor general is Lord Ergol Zigith; his rank is higher than the viziers of the three divisions of Khemit, though not as high as the prince of the Nubiar Oversight. For Khemit, Tahmakht represents a conquered area and an important buffer zone against any possible invasion from Numeda to its east. Olive oil is an important product of the northeast area, as are wine and beer. Although the Takmakhtim all speak Khemitian, some still keep their own ancient language alive. Likewise, Khemitian deities are worshipped throughout Tahmakht (which is no surprise, after 3,000 years in that country's control), but the old gods of the ancient kingdom of Peleshtia are still quietly venerated in small pockets, mostly in isolated rural areas.

VALLEY OF THE GODS

The rocky terrain that forms the first cataract of the Stygian continues through the approximately 35 miles to the North Branch of the Astebera River. This area provided plenty of sandstone for the temples in the city of Luqsor, and the stone canyons were also used for other, rock-cut temples and the tombs of the southern pharaohs and other officials. The Valley of the Gods is actually a series of canyons that contain the temples (to the west) and the tombs, which are toward the east. It is watched over by the goddess Meretseger; her primary temple is in the town of Baqi, but she is also represented by one in the valley. The Valley of the Gods has dozens of temples cut directly into the rock to honor even some fairly obscure deities. Some gods have more than one temple, being dedicated to different aspects of the deities' powers. For example, one temple venerates Neith as a guardian of the dead; another recognizes Chons as god of time; and yet another celebrates Anqet in her aspect of goddess of pleasure and mistress to all the gods.

When the annual inundation of the Stygian begins, the temples of all deities with a fertility aspect (including those in the nearby city of Luqsor) hold a huge festival together, doing their part to ensure the fertility of the rest of Khemit along the entire length of the Stygian.

In the portion of the valley given over to tombs are burials of pharaohs from the 26th, 27th, and 36th dynasties, plus many viziers who were given the rule of Upper Khemit, and some governors of the Nubiar Oversight. The area also includes lesser tombs of court officials, chief artisans, and overseers. Although small, some of the tombs of the artisans are as elaborate as those of the viziers and governors, showing their skill in the carving and decorating of their own eventual resting places.

THE DESERT KINGDOMS

The Desert Kingdoms is a collective name for the kingdoms of the western Maighib Desert: Caddesh, Khartous, and Guurzan. The people of the desert in central Libynos are most likely to worship Mah-Barek but may also worship Anumon (whose center of worship is in Numeda), local spirits, or other obscure deities. The Empire of Alcaldar (farther south along the west coast of central Libynos) is currently attempting to conquer the Desert Kingdoms and add them to its empire and convert everyone to the worship of Muir, but their progress has been slow. They began at the Gulf of Caddesh and are stalled in that area because of the mutual resistance of the three kingdoms more than 200 years ago.

CADDESH, KINGDOM OF

Capital: El-Marresh
Notable Settlements: Jebel, Lixus, Mogda, Zataftown
Ruler: Prince-Regent Adul VII, vassal of Queen Leonore-Alcia of Alcaldar
Government: ruled by the Empire of Alcaldar in the person of Sebastos (Imperial Governor) Gregoria-Teresa, Duquesa of Esterquel
Population: 1,328,640 (1,304,926 Ashurians of Caddesh; 22,917 Alcaldrich; 797 other human ethnicity)
Monstrous: eblis (islands west of Zataf), strangle weed (gulf), trolls, troll dogs
Languages: Alcaldrich, Semuric
Religion: Muir and Thyr; some secretly worship Mah-Barek
Resources: crops, fish, fruit, medicinal herbs
Currency: Alcaldrich
Technology Level: Medieval (El-Marresh), Dark Ages

The country of Caddesh is on the northwestern peninsula of central Libynos. Its most-heavily populated region is along the coasts of the Gulf of Caddesh, where moisture from gulf breezes brings needed water. In contrast, the interior of the country is dominated by rocky desert and high badlands. While the populous coastal areas lie under the sway of Alcaldrich governors, the parts of the country that lie east, near the Maighib Desert, or north toward the Jekkibet Hills, are effectively outside the empire's influence. Off the west coast are three islands, the largest of which — Zataf — is part of Caddesh. The other two combine coastal swamps with steep, rocky interiors, for conditions so inhospitable that Caddesh doesn't even bother to claim them. The northern border of Caddesh is roughly denoted by the Kader River and the Arahm Pass through the Jekkibet Hills; to the east of the hills, the border is less well-defined.

EL-MARRESH, CITY OF (CAPITAL)

Ruler: Abaya (governor) Yakub Delkrim, appointed by Prince-Regent Adul VII
Government: ruled by Empire of Alcaldar
Population: 63,879 (mostly Ashurian)

El-Marresh has been the capital of Caddesh for thousands of years. This can be seen in its well-developed Old City area and in the number of very old buildings tucked along tiny alleys. That history gives context to the impression visitors receive that the city has recently been conquered by the Empire of Alcaldar, even though it happened more than 250 years ago. A temple to Muir has had a prominent place in the city for two centuries, and people still speak of going to "the new temple." The venerable university Al-Ulasham, known for millennia as an important source of teachings on magic and philosophy (among other things), closed its doors and dispersed its scholars and their libraries rather than be threatened by the conquerors; people speak as if it has been closed for a few weeks and might open again at any time. The populace appears to give genuine service to Muir and Thyr (or hides any dissent well), but the occasional attitude that Muir's worship is just one more in a series of religions introduced by outsiders annoys some of the Alcaldrich church leaders very much.

Although the city has been known for generations for its scholarship and the creativity of its magic, with the closing of Al-Ulasham those have both severely diminished under the Empire of Alcaldar. There are still sages and scribes to be found in the city, but they are cautious about what topics they address, to avoid falling afoul of Alcaldar's Holy Ecclessia Inquisitorial.

JEBEL, TOWN OF

Ruler: Abaya Ghallab al-Fihri
Government: ruled by Empire of Alcaldar
Population: 3,972 (mostly Ashurian)

The town of Jebel lies at the mouth of the Karkkaru River. It receives some moisture from the ocean winds in the Gulf of Caddesh, but less than areas farther south, so the water carried by the small river is important for irrigation. Excess food produced by agriculture and fishing along the coast is largely traded inland for iron or rare medicinal herbs from the Jekkibet Hills.

LIXUS, TOWN OF

Ruler: Abaya Mehdia Hespren
Government: ruled by Empire of Alcaldar
Population: 8,075 (mostly Ashurian)

Lixus would be just another coastal village except for an accident of geography: It is due west of the city of Olappo in Guurzan. One day, centuries ago, a handful of explorers from the nation to the east rode out of the desert. They eventually established mutually beneficial trading relationships with various merchants of Lixus. Aside from an increase in the amount of goods traded and the arrival of the Alcaldrich conquerors, not much has changed in hundreds of years.

The trip from Olappo to Lixus is fairly easy to navigate, but the return trip is trickier. Going either due east or due west takes about the same amount of concentration, but missing the direction on the trip west means a caravan ends up at some other point on the Gulf of Caddesh and can then make its way to Lixus. Missing the direction going east, however, means a caravan must find the relatively small dot that is Olappo or be lost in the depths of the Maighib Desert. Caravaners travel the route many times before they become willing to risk their lives on their own skills, and anyone heading up an east-bound caravan is likely to be a very experienced guide.

MOGDA, TOWN OF

Ruler: Abaya Claado Mehrut
Government: ruled by Empire of Alcaldar
Population: 2,427 (mostly Ashurian)

Mogda is an old town originally founded by ancient seafarers from what is now Baalthaaz, but it lost its importance as a port over the centuries. Its people still do some sea fishing, but caution rather than exploration is the norm. Mogda sits at the mouth of the Kader River on the west coast of Caddesh and suffered from being largely isolated from the rest of that country. Once the Empire of Alcaldar discovered its existence, they established contact with Mogda by sea, and ships began to call there from time to time. As a result, Mogda is one town that has definitely been more prosperous under Alcaldar than before, and this shows in the generally positive attitude of its populous to the empire and to Muir.

SALA, RUINS OF

Population: 0

Built on the ruins of a walled city abandoned centuries ago, Sala holds the tombs of the royalty of Caddesh. Some say Sala was the original capital of Caddesh, which is why the kings were buried there. Others say it was merely the original hometown of the royal family or perhaps a religious stronghold. It was (variously) lost to enemy attack or depopulated by a plague. In any case, the ghost of an assassinated king, or maybe a wronged heir, definitely wanders the ruins — or perhaps not. The tombs are built aboveground inside the mostly intact city wall. The necropolis is not strictly limited to royalty; other noble or powerful people have also been buried here, as well as those whom the kings desired to honor. Since the conquest of Caddesh by the Alcaldrich, the church ecclesiast of Muir has tried to discourage burials here, ostensibly because of the rituals of other religions practiced in the necropolis in the past. So far, the royal family (now reduced to regency status) has refused to be persuaded and holds to their tradition.

ZATAFTOWN, TOWN OF

Ruler: Abaya Nat'an Reymuun
Government: ruled by Empire of Alcaldar
Population: 5,198 (mostly Ashurian)

The prosperous little town of Zataftown sits on the southern end of the island of Zataf. The residents harvest (or arrange to have gathered) the bounties of the island and ship them to towns in the Gulf of Caddesh in exchange for finished goods such as cloth or metal tools. Zataftown is one place that has significantly prospered since the conquest of Caddesh by the Empire of Alcaldar. Not only has the call for the island's products increased, but shipping has become much easier with the bigger and better Alcaldrich ships than with the shaky coasters previously used by Caddesh.

GUURZAN, KINGDOM OF

Capital: Bahaadur
Notable Settlements: Al-Ibbos, Khaajir, Olappo, Qiraam
Ruler: Queen Gathbiyya Nasur-fumin
Government: monarchy
Population: 2,197,892 (1,993,863 Ashurians of Guurzan and Ammuyad; about 200,000 Desertfolk; 2,837 Khemitites; 1,192 Merowen)
Monstrous: kamadans (Qarrasat Hills), genies, ant lions, sand krakens, sand dwarves
Languages: Semuric, officially; many desert tribes speak traditional languages
Religion: Churches of Mah-Barek
Resources: crops, herd animals, fishing, linen
Currency: Ammuyad
Technology Level: High Middle Ages (Bahaadur), Iron Age

Guurzan lies on the southern coast of the Sea of Baal. It is bordered on the east by the Qarrasat Hills, beyond which lies the kingdom of Khemit. To the west is Khartous, with whom Guurzan is able to maintain a moderately cordial trading relationship as they are separated by hundreds of miles of desert. To the south is the great Maighib Desert. Guurzan claims a large portion of the deep desert, at least in name, but doesn't pretend to control it all. The southern part of the Maighib is primarily given over to nomadic tribes that roam freely from southwestern Khemit to the Gulf of Caddesh and back, occasionally traveling so far north as the markets at Olappo to trade with the cityfolk. Oases exist but are less frequent than in the north, and harder to find. That makes controlling an oasis — or even knowing of one — an important instrument of power. A number of years ago, a tribe of sand dwarves undermined a group of oases claimed by the Sahoduin tribe. That led not just to warfare between that tribe and the dwarves, but to a conflict that eventually lasted 20 years and involved tribes throughout the desert.

The country as a whole officially follows the religion of Mah-Barek and has made common cause in the past with its religious fellows in Khartous and Caddesh. However, many people, especially outside the cities, still worship older deities or local spirits instead of (or in addition to) Mah-Barek. A large portion of the population, even among the upper classes, can trace their ancestry back to the Omaruri people who once lived in the northern Maighib Desert, which perhaps explains the general attachment to older forms of religion.

BAHAADUR, CITY OF (CAPITAL)

Ruler: Abaya (governor) Arrij Teret-hesen
Government: governor appointed by queen
Population: 98,275 (mostly Ashurian)

Bahaadur is the capital city of Guurzan and sits at the tip of Juurkelion Bay on the east bank of the Torilaan River. Using the system of irrigation introduced by the city of Khaajir, Bahaadur and its environs are able to raise a large quantity of food. The city trades the surplus to interior cities such as Olappo that cannot grow enough for their own needs. Bahaadur has a small merchant shipping industry, but its port is mostly used by foreign ships from Khartous, Khemit, or more-distant points. Most of its trade is done by caravan, to western Khemit and the interior of Guurzan.

The court of Queen Gathbiyya is much less formal than royal courts in other nearby countries, unless ambassadors from another nation come calling, in which case all involved try to be as ceremonial as possible. Some see this informality as dangerous, but the queen has a traditional honor guard of warriors from the deep desert (some say actual Omaruri, but others say differently) who have guarded her family for eight centuries with no injury to any member of the royal family, so she is unconcerned.

AL-IBBOS, CITY OF

Ruler: Abaya Ibtissam Fari-duluun
Government: governor appointed by queen
Population: 12,448 (mostly Ashurian)

Al-Ibbos is a small port city on the northern coast of Guurzan, but it is primarily important for being a stop on the trade route from the huge city of Pharos in northern Khemit to the Guurzani capital at Bahaadur. It sits on the southern bank of the Orrisniheccht River, and a ferry service is available for caravans to cross the river, if needed. However, the river is shallow enough near the mouth that most livestock can swim, if the drovers are willing to risk the crocodiles. Al-Ibbos is the one city in the country to have a significant amount of fishing, but a good portion of its production is consumed locally; certainly, very little makes it any farther away than Bahaadur.

DENYALLU, RUINS OF

Population: 0

Deep in the desert stands a fortress. It is almost as far south as Set's Kingdom, or farther, but perhaps more in the direction of what are now called the Nazarre Mountains, or perhaps not. There, the desert is rocky, and a plateau stands above it. Upon the plateau, a great stone platform has been built, said to be 100 steps high, and on this stands the fortress. Its towering walls are made of clay, but they have been reinforced with logs so they are still strong though they are ancient. The walls are high, but no one patrols them. Towers stand at the corners, but no one stands guard. In the front, a gatehouse stands ready, but no gate pierces it; no one may enter. The singers lament for Denyallu, the lost city where gold paved the streets and jewels grew like flowers, but no living person has ever found Denyallu and returned to tell the tale.

KHAAJIR, CITY OF

Ruler: Abaya Djamilla Fayru-iiz
Government: governor appointed by queen
Population: 18,229 (mostly Ashurian)

Khaajir sits on the seacoast where the Myonaardia River empties into the ocean. Using a series of canals for irrigation, and the plentiful water coming from the Qarrasat Hills, Khaajir and its associated villages are major agricultural producers for the country of Guurzan. This includes flax for cloth, and the city produces linen for making clothing in the manner of Khemit. Khaajir also has a port and ships often stop here on their way to or from Bahaadur, but much commerce just goes by caravan between the two cities.

OLAPPO, CITY OF

Ruler: Abaya Naziik Nuh-rhuuthan
Government: governor appointed by queen
Population: 6,366 (mostly Ashurian)

Olappo is the farthest south of the major cities of Guurzan. It started out as an oasis community, but the use of magic to construct several deep wells in the past means its area now can support a population in the thousands. Olappo is at the end of a caravan route from Bahaadur, and also one extending to Lixus in Caddesh. That means that through this isolated city pass goods from some of the largest communities in the world (such as Pharos, in Khemit, and other cities of the triple kingdom) to the villages on the Gulf of Caddesh, and then back. It is also the usual starting place for expeditions heading south into the deep desert, so its merchants and even individuals have items available for sale that are not usually seen except in much larger cities. Most of these are genuinely useful, but sometimes a fast talker with a good story is able to pass off something strange as an item of "important equipment."

QIRAAM, CITY OF

Ruler: Abaya Muuqin Hudeyythin
Government: governor appointed by queen
Population: 8,671 (mostly Ashurian)

About 100 miles southwest of the capital, Qiraam has become a minor center of trade. Merchants from Khartous were persistent about making a route for caravans from their Pesha River to Guurzan, and it continues to be in use. (Enough oases were found that livestock can even be transported this way.) Much trade between Khartous and Khemit goes by ship, but when political issues mean those navies are at odds, merchants can still move their goods by the desert trade route.

KHARTOUS, SULTANATE OF

Capital: Khartous
Notable Settlements: Qamara, Xamesh, Zakkesh
Ruler: Sultan Faud Umarr
Government: monarchy
Population: 2,342,919 (2,190,658 Ashurians of Khartous and
  Ammuyad; about 150,000 Desertfolk; 2,261 Khemitites)
Monstrous: genies, ant lions, sand krakens, sphinxes
Languages: Semuric
Religion: churches of Mah-Barek
Resources: crops, herd animals, silver, lead, trade
Currency: Ammuyad
Technology Level: Medieval (Khartous), High Middle Ages
  (Qamara and other cities), Iron Age (rural areas)

The Sultanate of Khartous was founded hundreds of years ago by the Khartisines, worshippers of Mah-Barek who came across the Sea of Baal and displaced the nomadic folk living here previously. They primarily claimed the area along the coast, but built trade routes through the interior wherever they could find water sources to support caravans. The fertile Pesha River delta supplies most of the food for northern Khartous. The northern cities and towns are generally prosperous, with even most villages and individual farmers being well off compared to their counterparts in other lands. Many city-dwellers have a sophisticated lifestyle with luxuries brought from distant places by the aggressive trade policies of the kingdom. Much of the rest of Khartous, all the way to the ocean on the west, is deep sand desert. Valuable resources such as lead and silver have been found along the coast and to the west, but the desert to the south is largely unexplored, at least by the kingdom's present inhabitants.

CHASS, RUINS OF

Population: 0

A large, oddly-shaped building sits atop a plateau in the desert. Dozens of small oases are located within a mile or two of its base. Despite seeming like a logical stopping place for travelers, caravans specifically avoid the area. Rumors say that the ruins are the home of many vicious monsters that attack any caravans that come too close, but a few knowledgeable people suggest it is instead home to only a single huge, very dangerous, creature.

KHARTOUS, CITY OF (CAPITAL)

Ruler: Abaya (governor) of Khartous Region, Jibril Waqar
Government: regional governor appointed by sultan
Population: 129,763 (mostly Ashurian)

The capital city of the sultanate of the same name, Khartous sits on the eastern bank of the Eastern Branch in the Pesha River Delta where it flows into the sea. The city is focused on two things: trade and the court of the sultan. Although supplies for the city come down the river, it is the ocean trade that brings exotic luxuries and more wealth to the already wealthy merchants and nobles of Khartous. Their acquisitions tend to the ostentatious side, and are mostly used in making displays of power and vying for influence in and around the royal court. While the upper class compete with each other, the rest of the city exhibits all the activities and vices seen in crowded cities around the world.

Most people know the capital city was built on the location of a city conquered by the first sultan, but few have any idea how old that city actually was or how deep it went. Strange occurrences in the city that are superstitiously said to be the work of evil spirits may actually have completely different causes.

QAMARA, CITY OF

Ruler: Abaya of Basuuma region, Salamun ibn Saddesh
Government: regional governor appointed by sultan
Population: 9,397 (mostly Ashurian)

This small city is the seat of the region's governor, but it is best known as the location of Hamsha University. The university's reputation for excellent scholarship and training in the medical and magical arts makes it a popular destination for upper-class youth who want to expand their abilities in these areas. Qamara sits at the western edge of the Pesha River Delta.

REFERENCE SOURCES: DUNES OF DESOLATION,
CHILD'S PLAY FROM QUESTS OF DOOM 3

RABAKKA, NECROPOLIS OF

Population: 0

More than 100 miles from the city of Khartous, deep in the Maighib Desert, is the large Necropolis of Rabakka. Its distance into the desert means that a burial requires an extensive processional, and thus it is usually the burying place only of the elite. Originally founded for the family of the sultan and other nobles of the kingdom, it became the necropolis of choice as well for people of wealth or those who want to do particular honor to their dead. This includes families from cities across the kingdom, not just those in Khartous. Common people, and those of less wealth, must make do with a minor necropolis only a day's journey or so from their hometowns.

RAMAASHTA, VILLAGE OF

Ruler: Administrator Aramses Ottama
Government: administrator appointed by regional governor
Population: 183 (mostly Ashurian)

This small village sits near the Pesha River, not far from where the Eastern Branch splits off in the Pesha River Delta on its way to the nearby sea. It is known for producing excellent grains and flavorful meats. Purveyors of gourmet beers, breads, and meats buy the products to serve to food connoisseurs in Khartous. Unfortunately for sellers in Ramaashta, most of its products go through middlemen located in the town of Xamesh, 35 miles downriver on the Pesha, for resale to buyers in Khartous or elsewhere. The village is not far from the beginning of the trade route from the banks of the Pesha to far Qiraam in Guurzan across the desert, but the leaders of Ramaashta have yet to find a way to take advantage of this proximity.

***REFERENCE SOURCES: DUNES OF DESOLATION,
KING OF BEASTS FROM QUESTS OF DOOM 3***

XAMESH, CITY OF

Ruler: Abaya of Yamun region, Iskandar Rahat
Government: regional governor appointed by sultan
Population: 15,444 (mostly Ashurian)

Xamesh is about a day's caravan travel upriver from Khartous on the Eastern Branch in the Pesha River Delta. The regional capital, it is a popular stopping place for travelers or caravans going to or from the capital city. Sometimes people who need to leave Khartous for whatever reason (getting low on money, needing to get out of sight for a while) but who don't want to go far from the city, move to Xamesh for an extended period.

ZAKKESH, TOWN OF

Ruler: Administrator Toufik Bulus
Government: administrator appointed by regional governor
Population: 8,684 (mostly Ashurian)

Zakkesh, about a day by boat upriver from Xamesh, is on the western bank of the Pesha River. A slightly smaller town than the regional capital at Xamesh, Zakkesh is an excellent place for craftspeople who need large establishments but don't want to pay the prices for places in Khartous, or even in Xamesh. A lot of products are finished here and then taken down the river from the extensive docks at Zakkesh to be sold in the markets of Khartous.

GEOGRAPHIC FEATURES AND POINTS OF INTEREST IN THE DESERT KINGDOMS

AL-MARAK, OASIS OF

This massive freshwater spring is the largest source of water for the Kingdom of Khartous. It lies about 75 miles east of the city of Khartous and is an important stop for any caravans traveling east from the capital — which means the vast majority of caravans.

***REFERENCE SOURCES: DUNES OF DESOLATION,
MY BLUE OASIS FROM QUESTS OF DOOM 3***

GULF OF CADDESH

The Gulf of Caddesh is an excellent fishing ground as well as providing the country of Caddesh protection from most ocean storms; only the worst roil the gulf's waters to an extent that might endanger ships. Unfortunately, the gulf also provides seagoing enemies excellent access to the most-populated areas of the country.

JEKKIBET HILLS

The Jekkibet Hills are a large region of high badlands that runs north and south through the western part of Khartous into north-central Caddesh. The Kader and Karkkaru Rivers in Caddesh have their sources in those hills, as does the Pesha River in Khartous. The Arahm Pass is a narrow but relatively easy path through the badlands. It is little traveled due to the sparse population in the area, but it does serve as part of the

casually accepted border between Caddesh and Khartous. Old stories tell of gold mines in the hills, but those were apparently lost before Alcaldar occupied the country.

JUURKELION BAY

An inlet from the Sea of Baal (and ultimately the Sinnar Ocean), Juurkelion Bay provides access to the sea for the major cities of Guurzan. Its east coast is fairly flat, with three rivers flowing into it. Its west coast rises rapidly just a few miles north of Bahaadur until it is almost 2,000 feet above the water, and it remains high and rocky some distance after again meeting the sea. The west coast takes a long turn to the west of almost 50 miles before again turning north. About halfway along this distance, it is interrupted by a powerful waterfall flowing from an opening in the cliff and thundering into the sea. As no river flows into the bay from this area, the source of water for the waterfall is unknown, but scholars attribute it to an as-yet-undiscovered aquifer deep below the earth.

KADER RIVER

This river runs from the badlands of the Jekkibet Hills west to the Sinnar Ocean. It is generally considered to be the northwestern boundary of Caddesh, where it meets Khartous. The Kader is a fast-flowing river that begins in a series of narrow waterfalls and runs most of its length through a steep canyon.

KARKKARU RIVER

The Karkkaru River is barely worthy of the name, being only a small river that trickles out of the Jekkibet Hills. However, it does manage to carry enough water to the coast to allow farming in the area of Jebel, which is much needed by the folk in the region since the ocean breezes here bring much less moisture to the northern end of the Gulf of Caddesh than farther south.

MAIGHIB DESERT

Extending from the Sinnar Ocean to Numeda, and south hundreds of miles inland from the Sea of Baal, the Maighib Desert in central Libynos is one of the great deserts of the world. While most is huge, shifting dunes of sand, some parts are rocky and others are salt flats. The whole area is dotted with lifesaving oases and a few strong rivers make their way through to the coast. The majority of the population lives around the edges of the desert — near the sea — or along one of the determined rivers. Nomadic tribes do wander the interior, oasis to oasis, following wild animals or leading herds of their own, but they are seldom seen by outsiders.

MYONAARDIA RIVER

Coming from high in the Qarrasat Hills in eastern Guurzan, the Myonaardia runs into the sea in Juurkelion Bay near the city of Khaajir. Its plentiful water used for irrigation allows the local inhabitants to farm extensively, providing much of the surplus of crops needed to support the capital city.

ORRISNIHECCHT RIVER

This river runs from the Qarrasat Hills into the Sea of Baal on the north coast of Guurzan. Al-Ibbos sits on the west bank of the Orrisnihecct, and some farming villages use its water for irrigation. There is very little river traffic, though, and the irrigation is done very carefully, because the river in known to be crowded with crocodiles.

PESHA RIVER

The Pesha River of Khartous gets its start in the high badlands of the Jekkibet Hills and runs through a canyon in the harsh, rocky waste nearby to where the land flattens out to open desert. It is a strong-flowing river, but where the land is very low, as it approaches the sea, it spreads into a delta. The current becomes slow and small streams trickle off and rejoin the main channel, but it still averages 80 feet wide and the channel is 20 feet deep, so it cannot be easily forded. It has one significant split where the Eastern Branch of the Pesha makes its own way to the sea. The fertile river delta is heavily farmed, with villages and towns scattered throughout, and is the main source of food for all of northern Khartous.

Qarrasat Hills

The edge of the Qarrasat Hills has been accepted for millennia as the western boundary of Khemit; the hills themselves are wholly claimed by Guurzan. The Qarrasats are steep and rough and riddled with caves. Aside from the caravan route to the north of the hills, and one through a pass near the center of the range, people do not travel in the area unless they are looking for trouble. The hills are inhabited by a strange array of monsters, some quite weird and all dangerous. Young warriors looking to make a name for themselves, or mature hunters looking for a rare prize, may hunt in the hills for what they seek. Some find it, and some even return to tell about it.

Rresh River

About two-thirds of the watershed of the western part of the country drains into the Rresh, which empties into the Gulf of Caddesh at the capital city of El-Marresh. Despite its volume, however, the Rresh is not deep nor is it particularly fast. It is useful for barges or small sailboats, but not larger ships. As a consequence, the Empire of Alcaldar was unable to use the Rresh as a pathway to the interior in its conquest of Caddesh, and so the empire's control is still largely confined to the nation's coastlines.

Torilaan River

Beginning in the southern portion of the Qarrasat Hills, this river runs down into the tip of Juurkelion Bay where the capital city of Guurzan sits. It provides plenty of water for the land around Bahaadur and allows some outlying villages to ship their crops to the city by barge instead of caravan.

Zataf, Island of

Off the west coast of Caddesh, the island of Zataf is rich in fruit trees and other woods. The center of the island, however, is a narrow chain of high mountains that includes a line of three volcanoes. The largest cone, in the center, has been dormant for a thousand years. The north and south volcanoes have been known to give off smoke for short periods every 20 to 30 years, not necessarily at the same time. Zataf is said to be populated by a tribe of reclusive people who worship the volcanos as deities. They have not been seen in the area of Zataftown for generations, though, so most locals assume the tribe has died out.

Zataf Sound

Running roughly 300 miles between Zataf Island and mainland Caddesh, Zataf Sound is deep but with large protruding rocks and many odd currents. It is tricky, but possible, to navigate in something the size of a fishing vessel and almost impossible to get through safely in anything larger. The rocks of the Sound, and the rocky mainland coast along it, are home to several colonies of seals. This draws sharks to the waters, making them even more dangerous.

Alcaldar, Empire of

Capital: Mhalta
Notable Settlements: Alicantato, Cadua, Iber, Perona, Ruente
Ruler: Queen Leonore-Alcia
Government: monarchy
Population: 1,983,808 (1,975,723 Alcaldrich, 4,614 Foerdewaith, 2,165 Ashurians of Caddesh, 432 Antiochians, 146 Khemitites, 592 other human ethnicity, 136 elf)
Monstrous: orcs (south), hill giants, ronus, griffons (mountains)
Languages: Alcaldrich
Religion: Muir and Thyr
Resources: iron, silver, alabaster, stone, blackwood, salt, crops, medicinal herbs, fish, cattle, horses, leather goods, parchment, wool, shipbuilding, high-quality weapons
Currency: Alcaldrich
Technology Level: Renaissance (Mhalta, Cadua); High Middle Ages (other cities, noble households); Dark Ages (rural areas)

Alcaldar is located on the west coast of central Libynos, separated by the sheltering Nazarre Mountains from the southern part of the Maighib Desert. Its largest cities are built on the shores of Iber Bay but its holdings go well inland. Alcaldar was founded as an early Hyperborean colony. The colonists mixed bloodlines with the local plains- and mountain-dwellers for thousands of years, though noble families (and especially the royal family) have more Hyperborean heritage than others. The Alcaldrich favor the traditions and mannerisms of their Hyperborean (and later Foerdewaith) forebears but have also picked up many Libynosi customs that are thought strange in Akados.

One thing that sets Alcaldar apart from its Libynosi neighbors is its intense and exclusive worship of the goddess Muir and her attendant deity Thyr; it is the official, and only, religion of Alcaldar. King Alcoa, who decreed the country's conversion, also established the Holy Ecclessia Inquisitorial to protect the integrity of the faith. Shortly after that, the high ecclesiast of the temple of Muir in Perona formed the Church Militans as the active hand of the church. The two organizations are enthusiastic in spreading the worship of Muir (and Thyr) and in upholding the beliefs of the faithful.

About 275 years ago, King Istobal-Alcacé began the series of conquests and expansions that took Alcaldar from a kingdom to an Empire. He saw Alcaldar as the natural successor to the Hyperborean Empire, since the Hyperborean Empire of the Foerdewaith had disintegrated into squabbling kingdoms after the end of the Fourth Crusade. This led to the subjugation of the Kingdom of Caddesh, north along the Sinnar coast, and the acquisition of the area now known as the Channel Lakes. Exceptional resistance in northern Caddesh stalled the Alcaldrich conquest of the Desert Kingdoms, but the exploration and development of the Channel Lakes more than made up for it. Opening a navigable water connection through central Libynos allowed Alcaldar to build a colonial empire on the east coast of Libynos as well as the west.

Though its monarch could legitimately call herself an empress, Alcaldar is modestly governed by Queen Leonore-Alcia. The queen is fairly young and still unmarried; after she took the throne, the council and noble houses nearly tore themselves apart jockeying for a chance to have her marry into their families. They finally agreed she should marry a foreign noble to avoid internal conflict. Now the factions are each looking for a wealthy noble who will favor their group. (Good-looking, diplomatic, wealthy knights-errant might also be good candidates.) The queen herself is looking for a spouse, not a co-ruler. The older men of her council already think she should be ruled by their opinions; she is not going to share the authority of her position with a consort as well.

Mhalta, City of (Capital)

Ruler: Archon Aven-Carlo, Marqués of Tamora
Government: archon appointed by monarch
Population: 35,924 (33,746 Alcaldrich, 1,022 Foerdewaith, 819 Ashurians of Caddesh, 101 Antiochians, 35 Khemitites, 186 other human ethnicity, 15 elf)

The city of Mhalta is on the east coast of Iber Bay at the mouth of the Luena River. The east end of the bay is relatively shallow, so the docks at Mhalta are able to handle many types of ships, but not oceangoing vessels with a deep draft. The city does have a good-sized fishing fleet whose boats have Iber Bay mostly to themselves, as the other cities on the bay host relatively little fishing.

Mhalta was the capital city of the Kingdom of Alcaldar for over 3,000 years, and has been the capital of the empire now for nearly 300 years. As the country has grown in influence and power, so the capital city has increased in population and activity. It has a beautiful temple to Muir, and a smaller one in the same style to Thyr, surrounded by a garden of flowers. (It also has smaller chapels in other neighborhoods, so those who attend at the principal temple do not have to rub shoulders with the entire city.) Mhalta has its own university, an expensive school attended mostly by scions of the noble families of Alcaldar and by students from very wealthy houses whose parents hope to see them serve at court rather than go into trade.

Mhalta's most important function is to house the palace and the imperial court. That means it also welcomes hundreds of foreign visitors and plays host to all sorts of pageantry. The imperial court of Alcaldar has always been very formal, so the Clothing Workers' Guild of the city (which makes most of the court attire for the nobles present) is extremely important and well-off. Another important group right now are animal trainers, as the court is experiencing a recurrence of the fad of nobles having exotic animals as pets. Whether it is a cheetah on a gold leash, one of the grassland cats called *pajeros*, a tiny monkey from the southern jungles, or a brightly-feathered bird that can be taught to talk, many nobles keep unusual pets in their homes and some even show them off in public.

The queen's court is full of gossip and rumor, as everyone — high and low — tries to get information to better their own position or find a way to exert a little power. Though some degree of dissent is tolerated (at least, in certain matters), with the high ecclesiast often at the queen's shoulder, those who disagree are very careful about it. For instance, some traditionalists in her court complain quietly that the queen favors women when appointing people to positions of authority, and that she gives overly much attention to the noble families of southeast Alcaldar where she spent many summers with her mother's relatives at Estancia Galdames. However, no one has had the temerity to bring these whispers to the queen's attention.

The common people of Mhalta may as a whole be a bit better off than most of the rest of the country; plenty of visitors means plenty of opportunities for folks to earn a little coin and possibly to have a little excitement in life. Even the poor have it slightly better; with many nobles in town eager to prove their piety, almsgiving is high and the churches are often able to help those down on their luck. (Residents of haciendas and estancias are discouraged from moving to the cities, though, so relatively few countryfolk come to Mhalta to try to improve their lot in life.) The holdings of the high-born and wealthy take up so much space inside the city that middle-class residents are cramped into small living spaces ringing the city center and the lower class is mostly located outside the wall entirely. The lower quarters stretch from the docks around the north and south sides of the city, but very few settle outside the city toward the east. Even though the Nazarre Mountains proper are several miles from the Mhalta, strange things are said to come down and prowl the inhabited area between the mountains and the city wall.

ALICANTATO, TOWN OF

Ruler: Archon Mereni-Raul of Hacienda Almoster
Government: archon (city governor) appointed by monarch
Population: 4,340 (mostly Alcaldrich)

The town of Alicantato lies south of the eastern edge of the Navarre Mountains, between the rich farmlands of western Alcaldar and the Grasslands of Wahm. It started as a trading center where merchants from the coastal cities could deal their wares and in return buy the products of the grassland tribes: cattle and sheep for meat, cow hides for leather and sheep or goat skins for parchment, wool, medicinal herbs, and most importantly, horses. Over the years, many crafters moved to Alicantato and produce finished goods there rather than shipping raw materials, especially since the plains' city has plenty of space to separate some of the messier professions from the town center.

Alicantato has the privilege of providing horses to the royal household. Every two years in late summer, the Great Equine Exhibition takes place involving Alcaldrich horse breeders and grassland tribes with their wild horses. The Equine Captains of Alicantato examine all the horses and then purchase the very best to be schooled and gifted to the crown. This includes a pure white horse when available to be the royal parade horse of the queen herself. The last three royal parade horses (over a 12-year span) were selected from among the wild horses brought by members of the Maqhawe tribe, and plans are now afoot by some of the empire's horse breeders to acquire pairs of these "moon horses" themselves to earn the prestige of breeding the most important horse in the empire.

The gathering is made more exciting by the tradition of young people from affluent families coming to select their own first horse of adulthood, one that they may break or train themselves, or at least oversee its training. Young men have done this for more than a thousand years; few young women came until the past two or three centuries. However, with the example of a warrior goddess before them (as well as valiant women among the founding knights of the Holy Ecclessia), many girls want to have a more active life rather than living as traditional pampered ladies. Youth from poor families seldom have the chance to participate in this gathering, but some work diligently to be able to afford a horse — any horse — and see this as giving them a start in a different life.

About 300 years ago, Alicantato was subject to increasing raids by evil creatures out of the Kufa Mountains and the Eberro Wastes. A knightly order (formerly from the Sacred Table) received a grant of land in exchange for their protection of the eastern region of the nation. The knights built a strong fortress near a saltmarsh outside Alicantato; they shortly discovered underground deposits of salt on their property, and also found opals in the area. Alicantato became a very prosperous city as local people were employed to mine, and the products were bought and sold in the town. Shockingly, after more than 200 years of local service, the order was accused of blasphemy and demon worship, with the Church Militans discovering proof of their perfidy beneath the order's primary chapterhouse in Perona. Some of the knights from Alicantato were arrested by the Church Militans and ultimately executed, but many were away at the time and avoided capture by going into exile. Locals are hesitant to say anything about "the vanished knights," but if pressed, people state that the knights hid their evil behavior from the town at the time. For some unknown reason, no one says anything bad about them.

The Church Militans took over the fortress and the salt mine, which has since been worked by penitents (religious prisoners) instead of employing locals. (Although the Church Militans has had people search extensively, the opals appear to be exhausted.) The salt mine still makes large profits, but they all go to Perona or Mhalta, and Alicantato has dwindled in size.

CADUA, CITY OF

Ruler: Archon Gelvira-Resuela of Hacienda Zapardiel
Government: archon appointed by monarch
Population: 12,397 (11,940 Alcaldrich, 220 Foerdewaith, 112 Ashurians of Caddesh, 31 Antiochians, 10 Khemitites, 72 other human ethnicity, 12 elf)

Cadua is located on the northwestern shore of Iber Bay and is well-known for producing high-quality edged weapons, especially various types of swords and daggers. Under the Hyperborean Empire, Cadua was one of the first places that not only produced iron (in the nearby Nazarre Mountains) but also other minerals that improved the alloy of iron into steel. These minerals were later found in or traded from other locations, but Cadua had a head start on developing better steel. Its smiths (many of whom could really be considered metallurgists) continued to experiment with making steel and forging weapons. The steel-makers and weaponsmiths of Cadua keep their proprietary knowledge safe through the 977-year-old Alliance of Steel, which requires oaths of secrecy and special training before their confidential techniques are revealed. The group's greatest competitors in Libynos are the weaponsmiths of Tarresh, one of the Antioch City-States.

Cadua is also known for its dueling academies. Once focused specifically on preparing people for success in the tradition of dueling for one's honor, or to prove oneself right, the academies have now branched out into teaching all types of blade work. This has been necessary since Alcaldar has expanded into an empire, because restless people are inclined to go out seeking increased opportunity in new places rather than stay home and look for excitement by taking umbrage at other people's remarks. In addition, dueling was always more a practice of the affluent — insults among the lower classes tended to be settled with fisticuffs or a blade in the dark — but over the centuries it has become ritualized in ways that have increased the cost. (For example, to correctly execute a duel, the challenger must rent an arena or dueling ground and hire a referee and at least a healer, if not a full cleric.) This means dueling is now largely restricted to the nobility and the wealthy, and they tend to have instructors come to them rather than attending an academy.

Many masters (such as the eminent swordsman Camos Gemarin) teach with no more than a studio and a handful of students. Of the major schools, the Meruelo Academy of the Crossed Swords is the most well-known; its dozen instructors handle probably 20 times that number of students. Of course, all these gallant institutions are the subject of much discussion and comparison, not to mention gossip. It is said that one of the larger schools (it varies which one in the telling) once had a temple to the war-god Mithras as part of its facilities. Obviously, that was closed when Alcaldar came into the worship of Muir 300 years ago, but rumor says there is a secret way that someone could again access it and look on the ancient altar built by the Hyperboreans themselves.

Encroached upon as it is by the Nazarre Mountains, Cadua has only a few haciendas surrounding it. These include the noble estates of the Duquesa of Esterquel and the Conde of Isavana.

IBER, CITY OF

Ruler: Archon Argilo-Lucia of Hacienda Rispanis
Government: archon appointed by monarch
Population: 23,120 (22,414 Alcaldrich, 350 Foerdewaith, 185 Ashurians of Caddesh, 52 Antiochians, 15 Khemitites, 99 other human ethnicity, 5 elf)

Iber is the oldest city in Alcaldar and has a strong Hyperborean feel in its aged stone buildings. It is easily accessible to the largest crop-producing area of Alcaldar proper as well as the ranching estancias of the southeast. Possessing an excellent deep-water port, it is a center of sea fishing and has dry-dock facilities for the repair of oceangoing vessels. It is also a place where passengers going to Mhalta or Cadua may change to a smaller ship that can fit right up to one of the shallower docks in those cities.

In the Hyperborean tradition, Iber has an ancient university that is now nearly 3,000 years old. Although it has some competition from the more-modern facility in Mhalta, the Universitas Iberensis is generally considered to be the leading educational center of the entire west coast of Libynos. Since the enthusiastic conversion of Alcaldar to the worship of Muir and Thyr three centuries ago, Iber has also become the home of two knightly orders: the Knights of Our Lady of the Sword, who are dedicated to the protection of the empire, and the Brotherhood of the Gauntlet, who specialize in bringing lawbreakers to justice.

Furthermore, Iber is a major trading city. Many wealthy merchant families such as the houses of Aldover, Meroma, Pezzuoli, Wreldan, and Ziruela hail from Iber. Noble estates in the fertile western area of Alcaldar ship their agricultural products and the other goods their haciendas produce through the port of Iber to Mhalta, or north to the dominion of Caddesh. Estates in western Alcaldar include those of the duquesa of Rebollar, the marquesa of Ophelo, the marquesa of Rispanis, the conde of Micia, and the condesa of Almoster.

PERONA, CITY OF

Ruler: Archon Eldonza-Isabel, Marquesa of Navalcán
Government: archon appointed by monarch; bureaucracy
Population: 7,562 (7,392 Alcaldrich, 120 Foerdewaith, 50 other human ethnicity)

Built on an island in Iber Bay, Perona was originally just a fortress to guard the sea approaches to the capital city of Mhalta. Later, the city of Perona grew around the fortress, but the city is mostly focused on the island itself rather than becoming a significant port. This is primarily due to the island being high and rocky with sheer cliffs on most sides — excellent for defense but poor for mooring ships. It does have a section of rocky shingle beach facing the mainland on the south that has docks for shallow-draft vessels. Oceangoing ships calling at Perona must lie at anchor in the deeper water and send their smaller boats in to shore.

Much of the stone for the fortress and the city's prominent buildings was quarried on the island. A number of now-spent quarries are now used as storage, or shelters in case of severe weather. Some are walled off for private use, such as the burial chambers beneath the temple of Muir. Because of the lack of coordination — and the existence of competition — among various stonecutters in the past, the underground quarries are a maze of spaces and narrow connecting passages, though at least the support of the city above does not seem to be in danger.

Perona is blessed to be the home of the Temple of Muir in Alcaldar and the seat of High Ecclesiast Aitona-Trevisse Pezzuoli. (The priestess is of the opinion that the temple here should actually be the high altar of Muir given the sad state of the goddess's church in Akados, but she feels the time for pressing that issue has not quite come.) Personnel handling administrative and temporal matters relating to the temple have largely been moved to Mhalta where the high ecclesiast spends most of her time at the royal court, although she returns to Perona for holy services on a regular basis. The gleaming white temple of Muir (including the sizable chapel to her attendant deity, Thyr) is a popular destination for pilgrims from all over Alcaldar. The city of Perona does its best to serve their needs, from providing plentiful opportunities for housing persons of all sorts, to crafting jewelry and other small items that make suitable mementos of such an important journey.

RUENTE, CITY OF

Ruler: Archon Toril-Enrique, Duque of Clariana
Government: archon appointed by monarch; bureaucracy
Population: 15,412 (14,508 Alcaldrich, 524 Foerdewaith, 210 Ashurians of Caddesh, 45 Antiochians, 14 Khemitites, 106 other human ethnicity, 5 elf)

Ruente lies on a natural harbor on the south shore of Iber Bay. Its port's configuration means that it can dock 40 to 50 vessels while still having room for no fewer than three shipbuilding companies along the water. The facilities are almost entirely given over to the manufacture of ships for Alcaldar's Imperial Navy, with any extra capacity taken up by building merchant vessels for the great trading houses. However, one of the companies has some dry docks it uses primarily for repairs and maintenance. It keeps a waiting list of clients, but a ship that needs urgent repairs can usually be worked into the schedule for an appropriate fee.

The extensive space for docking large ships means Ruente is the port of choice for landing large cargoes intended for Mhalta, or embarking those from the eastern part of Alcaldar. Specifically, this means horses from the estancias or from Alicantato are shipped out from Ruente, and any group of people arriving with their own mounts is very likely to disembark at Ruente and then travel overland to the capital city.

East of Ruente and south of the Navarre Mountains lie the large plains estancias of such nobles as the duque of Pinilla, the marquesa of Sorueno, the marqués of Tamora, the marqués of Vellone, the conde of Galdames, and the condesa of Urrimi. Their primary products are the long-horned cattle for which the Grasslands of Wahm are famous, as well as many types of leather goods, and of course the excellent plains' horses.

Geographic Features and Points of Interest in the Empire of Alcaldar

Eberro Wastes

This set of badlands is about 200 miles from north to south and about 100 miles east to west between the Nazarre Mountains of Alcaldar and the Kufa Mountains. Though it is possible to find one's way through, either from the Nazarre to the Kufa Mountains or from the Maighib Desert to Alcaldar, it is difficult even for one who knows the territory well. The narrow, dead-end canyons and rocky defiles can be very confusing, and it is easy for a traveler to become fatally lost. A few small streams and pools are supplied by underground water sources, but the area is generally very dry.

Iber Bay

The waters of this bay are protected from the worst vagaries of the Sinnar Ocean and allow for safer travel in small boats. It isn't quite deep enough on the north and east sides for oceangoing vessels to dock directly at either Mhalta or Cadua, although both ports can fit dozens of smaller boats. However, the depth at the south shore accommodates large ships, and towns along the coast have shipbuilding and repair yards. The bay usually has a good supply of fish and fishing is a significant industry. Other larger fishing vessels are based out of the city of Iber and fish out into the Sinnar Ocean.

Luena River

The Luena River has its headwaters deep in the Nazarre Mountains, and runs fast and cold along its entire length into Iber Bay, though it flattens out somewhat as it approaches the coast next to the city of Mhalta. Its rocky bed makes boating down the river perilous, but its upper reaches produce some very tasty cool-water fish so sport fishers stalk its banks in search of delicacies, either for their own tables or for those of the wealthy in Mhalta. The river also occasionally produces strange creatures from the mountains, which it spits out on its banks near Mhalta, much to the consternation of the city's guards and those living outside the wall on the north.

Nazarre Mountains

These mountains cover more than a third of Alcaldar proper and provide it with bountiful natural resources. There are minerals such as the iron and other metals found near Cadua, alabaster in the east-central area, and silver in the southeast. (The metallurgists of Cadua speculate that more of the same materials might be found in the Kufa Mountains because their similar appearance suggests both sets of mountains may at one time have been part of the same range. So far no one has cared to try to drive the humanoids out of the Kufas and explore for valuable metals.) The mountains also provide tall, sturdy blackwood trees for shipbuilding and stone for building in the cities, as well as being home to wild mountain goats and sheep and other more exotic creatures.

Grasslands of Wahm

Capital: none
Notable Settlements: Caaddan, Ubuka, Wahm
Ruler: none
Government: tribal
Population: unknown
Monstrous: orcs, kathlin, gambado
Languages: Alcaldrich, tribal languages
Religion: Father Sky, Mother Earth, and other grasslands spirits
Resources: horses, herd animals, leather, wool, crops
Currency: Alcaldrich, barter

Technology Level: Bronze Age (nomadic tribes), Iron Age (settlements)

The Grasslands of Wahm are wide open plains stretching hundreds of miles in each direction, extending from the Kufa Mountains in the north to the region of the Channel Lakes in the south, and from the Central Uplands on the east all the way west to the Sinnar Ocean. Though portions of southeastern Alcaldar and southwestern Meroë are also plains, they are not typically considered to be parts of the grasslands.

The largest river in the region is the Wambatu, which runs through the southern portion of the grasslands. Other rivers also flow through the area, of course, but none pulls from such a large area as the Wambatu.

Throughout the grasslands are rolling hills, some of which can be rather steep, dropping sharply into one river valley or another. Rivers and streams in the grasslands are fairly easy to locate, since among the fields of grasses reaching to the horizon, lines of trees follow along the edges of any water source. Some areas have rocky hills and occasionally entrances to caverns where underground water has worn away the rock, though these are not evident from the surface; they are usually discovered by accident if at all.

The grasslands are populated in the north by various nomadic and semi-nomadic tribes, such as the Maqhawe, Mkuntho, and Moglai, and by the more-settled Metwano and Mwandu tribes south of the Wambatu River.

In the south, the Metwano tribes are farther west and so they have had the most contact with the Alcaldrich near the Channel Lakes who explore north from their base at San Caseo. Many villages have set up profitable trading relations with the city, sending their wool and woolen goods, and getting leather from the Moglai and Maqhawe that they then trade to the merchants at San Caseo. The Mwandu tribes are farther east and tend to stay close to the Wambatu. They are prolific farmers and do some trading with people from across the river, but they prefer to let the traders come to them rather than seeking out opportunity in a strange area.

North of the river are the Moglai, who range along the Wambatu and some distance north. The Moglai are more proficient farmers than the two tribes farther north and tend to herd in a more restricted range, but they are considered to be among the semi-nomadic grasslands tribes as they leave their homes for months at a time to find good pasturage. Farther north, the Maqhawe in the west and the Mkuntho in the east range through huge areas with their flocks and herds. The Maqhawe especially come into contact (and sometimes conflict) with the Alcaldrich in their home country, particularly the city of Alicantato. The Mkuntho do trade at Alicantato, but they also range far to the east and trade with those in the country of Meroë.

All the tribes of the Grasslands of Wahm have some similarities. They tend to have close-knit communities, without entering into active rivalries with other related tribes in the area. They all enjoy a good song or story, with most of them being naturally good singers. Their basic system of belief is fairly simple: Father Sky and Mother Earth, Brother Horse, Little Pajero the trickster, and Hungry Fire who sometimes seems to threaten the whole world. To this the northern tribes have added a few deities they learned from the Hyperboreans, such as Kamien of the Rivers and Telophus, who turns the seasons.

The northern tribes differ from those south of the Wambatu in that they are much less settled. Although they have home territories, they travel widely with their herds and flocks and depend on their strong horses in many ways. Animals they herd include sheep as well as the longhorned cattle, and sometimes horses. Most horses run in wild herds, and the plains' tribes make it a point of pride to capture and tame horses for their own use and also to sell to appreciative buyers. Currently, the Maqhawe have the best reputation in this area, though many people from each tribe are excellent horse trainers. Given that most people of the tribes have a chance to ride horses even before they can walk, almost all are good riders and many are superb. Some horsemen from the estancias of Alcaldar may ride as well as the plains' people, but very few.

Caaddan

Ruler: Chieftain Stolen Tongue
Government: autocracy
Population: 154 (orcs)

At some time in the past, a few small tribes of orcs apparently migrated north to the central plains of the Grasslands of Wahm, where they live in comparative harmony with their human neighbors. One of their small settlements is Caaddan, though it is more in the nature of a gathering place than a permanent community. A circular earthwork surrounds its perimeter, while inside, residents live in huts or lean-tos. The exception to this is the chieftain's residence, which is a sturdy, wooden one-room house. This village is half a dozen miles from a human town and the two have managed to live with only occasional skirmishes for the 20 years it has been there. The orcs raise sheep for food and wool, and use the wool to make felt coverings for their meager houses, among other things. They also breed dire boars, but keep only a half-dozen or so adults at any one time.

REFERENCE SOURCES: FIELDS OF BLOOD, RED WEDDING FROM QUESTS OF DOOM 3

Ubuka, Town of

Ruler: Mayor Sukh Bittumur (11 years in office)
Government: annual elections for mayor; group of influential people may act as informal advisors
Population: 475 (Lagish)

This is a town of the Moglai tribe and is typical of many small towns of the grasslands. It has a handful of permanent buildings (in this case, an inn, a tavern, and a combination office and residence for the mayor) and several transient merchants who have set up shop in tents or wagons. The rest of the town consists of a score of large farms and a few dozen smaller residences spread over 15 square miles. The town has no established property lines but residents generally recognize which areas are farmed by which household, or where a family's animals are kept. Many owners take their flocks of sheep or herds of cattle far afield to graze, returning to the home area from time to time.

REFERENCE SOURCES: FIELDS OF BLOOD, RED WEDDING FROM QUESTS OF DOOM 3

Wahm, Village of

Ruler: Elders Baako Iwabu, Mosi Umagga, Uzoma N'Dou
Government: three elders acting as counselors and caretakers of tradition
Population: 85 (Lagish)

This Mwandu village is built around a core area (called the Square by residents, though the common area is not square at all) with a couple of shops, a bakery, an inn, and a meeting hall. This center is surrounded at a little distance by the homes of the villagers, most of whom are farmers. Although the houses are relatively close together, the farm fields stretch out all around the village and are planted mostly with various grains. Locals also raise sheep and goats, although they seldom raise the larger beef cattle herded by tribes to the north of the Wambatu River.

Wahm has the advantage of being just a few miles from the newest bridge over the Wambatu River, so the villagers have an easy way to travel north if they want to trade with tribes on the other side of the river. (Few care to get that far from home, of course.) Sometimes, itinerant traders from the Moglai or other northern tribes come south and set up shop temporarily in Wahm because of its convenient location. Also, people from neighboring villages and outlying regions must pass through the area of Wahm to get to the bridge, so that has made it a central village in the area though it is certainly no larger than the others.

REFERENCE SOURCE: FEAST OF FURY FROM FIELDS OF BLOOD

Geographic Features and Points of Interest in the Grasslands of Wahm

Iwakkaranda

Also known as the Field of Bones, this was the site of a bloody battle a century ago. People say those who fought the battle were horrified by what they had done and swore off combat forever. The battle was so large that it is easy still today to find remnants of armor or repairable weapons by just walking across the battlefield, and some have actually found coins or gems. However, they say if you try to take anything away, the spirits of the dead rise up to stop you. That is likely just a tale to scare children, though.

REFERENCE SOURCE: FEAST OF FURY FROM FIELDS OF BLOOD

Wambatu River

The Wambatu River stretches for more than 1000 miles from a spring high in the Central Uplands west to the Sangre Sea. For most of its length it is 80 to 100 feet across, rough, fast-moving, and surprisingly deep. The only way to cross is to use a bridge or to take one's chances with a small boat. Several bridges have been built over the centuries so that presently, bridges span the river every 45 to 55 miles. (The newest one is about 300 miles upriver from the coast and has armed guards on it at all times to prevent anything from happening to it.) Enterprising souls are also known to keep small boats near areas where there is no bridge or where the bridge might be restricted or inconvenient in some way. (For instance, one bridge is badly deteriorated in spots though much of it is fine. Some travelers would rather not take their chances on that bridge and would instead trust a stranger in a small boat.)

The river has a very different character in the last 100 miles or so before the sea. Instead of running in a narrow cut, it spreads out and its bed becomes shallower and smoother. The river can be forded there with ease, though it becomes wider as it becomes shallower.

Zabladai, Ruins of

The outlines of an exterior wall are still visible, though it has been reduced to piles of rock. Scattered remnants remain inside what was once the wall; they have apparently been subject to a century or more of neglect and erosion, but outlines of individual buildings can still be seen. Supposedly, this was once a mighty city of the orcs 100 years ago or more. Rumors are not clear as to what destroyed the city, but it is now considered to be haunted.

REFERENCE SOURCES: FIELDS OF BLOOD, RED WEDDING FROM QUESTS OF DOOM 3

Central Kingdoms

The Central Kingdoms of Libynos lie south of Khemit down to the Channel Lakes (now claimed by the Empire of Alcaldar) and west of the Ruby Sea. They include Qesh, Meroë, Aethiope, Axuum, and Kazania in the Central Uplands. Most of these kingdoms have significantly influenced and been influenced by Khemit over the centuries. However, they were little influenced by the Hyperboreans, who invaded Khemit for a time but had scant contact with the countries to the south.

Aethiope, Kingdom of

Capital: Adeffa
Ruler: Negus (king) Radem
Government: monarchy
Population: 1,665,938 (1,656,180 Merowen, 6,227 Khemitites, 3,021 other human ethnicity, 510 other)
Monstrous: dire apes, viper vines, couatls
Languages: Khemitian

Religion: Pharaonic pantheon, traditional deities
Resources: obsidian, copper, gold, platinum, jewelry, magicians
Currency: Axuumite
Technology Level: Dark Ages

Aethiope is a country of southern Libynos located south of Khemit. It is bounded on the east by the River Aeth, its border with the country of Axuum. On the other side, the west edge of the Hills of Strabo is generally accepted as the border with Meroë. Through the center of the kingdom flows the Lapis River, which floods after the summer rains in the Central Uplands, effectively providing water for the entire country. The Aethiopans use the Lapis to travel north and south inside their country and also to trade with Meroë and Khemit farther downstream.

Aethiope has both forest and cropland, and important resources in the Hills of Strabo such as obsidian, copper, and gold. Even more valuable, though, is platinum. At this time, the platinum mines are somewhat depleted and are not producing as much as they were even 20 years ago. Diviners and other specialists are seeking new veins, but until some are found, the kingdom's income is slightly reduced.

Many people in Aethiope, especially in the north, worship the deities of Khemit, though some do still revere the old gods of the area.

Adeffa, City of (Capital)

Ruler: Mulya (governor) Samet
Government: governor appointed by the king
Population: 42,372 (41,232 Merowen, 850 Khemitites, 235 other human ethnicity, 55 other)

Situated on the west bank of the Lapis River, Adeffa is still an easy distance from the mines in the south part of the Hills of Strabo. Although other towns on the Lapis have small docks, Adeffa is the primary location for launching or landing large river boats or barges. Jewelers of Adeffa are known for their pieces using ivory and obsidian in striking patterns of black and white, either set in platinum or with the obsidian set directly into carved ivory pieces.

Baobab School, The

Ruler: Senior Scholar Ezba Harbe
Government: believed to be run by a group of elderly magicians who have retired from active teaching
Population: unknown

Located a few miles outside the city of Adeffa, the Baobab School is known for training many magicians in the ancient traditions of Aethiope. Lectures are held in the hollow portion of a great baobab tree, one nearly 2,000 years old and fully 40 feet across. The academy has no walls outsiders can see, merely a ladder set up next to a low spot for people to climb up into the hollow of the tree. It is said, though, that without an invitation it is impossible to enter the tree. In fact, over the centuries, outsiders who have tried to attack the tree have had no real success; apparently, despite its lack of walls, the school (and its tree home) is well protected.

No one knows how many scholars and students belong to the Baobab School. Sometimes, no one comes out of the tree for weeks, with a single student receiving supplies at the ladder. Other times, the tree seems to be almost as busy as an anthill, with people coming and going in all directions. When asked, locals shrug and guess that a hundred people (or maybe a few more) live inside the tree. This would seem impossible even for so large a tree; again, locals shrug and simply say it must be bigger on the inside.

Magicians from the Baobab School frequently become important residents of towns and cities in the Central Kingdoms and areas farther south. With experience, some advance to become prominent advisors at the court of the negus in Adeffa and at other royal courts in the area. A few move to Khemit and may even rise to be influential in that royal court; rumor says that each pharaoh of Khemit has had a Baobab magician as an advisor for four dynasties now.

Axuum, Kingdom of

Capital: Mazaber
Notable Settlements: Jarmi
Ruler: King Urtigaddi
Government: monarchy
Population: 2,158,276 (2,151,566 Merowen, 4,623 Khemitites, 2,087 other human ethnicity)
Monstrous: bulettes, couatls, manticores
Languages: Khemitian
Religion: Pharaonic pantheon, traditional deities
Resources: gold, emeralds, salt, tortoiseshell, ivory, trade, grains, fruit, wine, herd animals
Currency: Axuumite
Technology Level: High Middle Ages (Mazaber), Dark Ages

The Kingdom of Axuum controls lands along the southwest coast of the Ruby Sea, from the Uashta Hills in the north to the southern end of the Tekle Mountains, and west to the banks of the River Aeth. The southwestern part of the country, between the western verges of the mountains and the river, is at the edge of the Central Uplands of central Libynos.

The entire coastal region is given a pleasant climate by the proximity of the Ruby Sea. Farmers in the Uashta Hills and the lowlands east of the Tekle Mountains raise large amounts of wheat and barley, and herd cattle and sheep. West of the mountains, farmers cultivate groves of fruit trees and vineyards, and herd goats and camels.

Axuum has a mountainous spine with its highest peaks in the south, but with plenty of valleys and passes allowing travel from east to west. Keeping roads in good repair is an important responsibility of each town and village, and one thoroughly enforced by the crown. The west side of the Tekle Mountains is drier than the seacoast but also generally higher in elevation, so the temperature is only slightly hotter than the coast.

In addition to its homeland on the eastern coast of central Libynos, Axuum also controls the southern part of the Numedan peninsula, an area known as Imya, which it conquered some 250 years ago.

Axuum is well-known for its trading. The country imports goods from the other Central Kingdoms and sometimes even southern Guurzan or Khartous, and sends ships along the coast of Libynos as distant as Far Jaati. The port of Sallavinera (at the east end of the Channel Lakes) receives ships from far-off Akados and Axuumite merchants trade there for exotic goods from that distant continent. Axuum mints is own currency and the gold "stars," silver "moons," and bronze "little stars" (or just "littles") are used extensively along the east coast of Libynos.

The bureaucratic structure of the government of Axuum is well-developed and hierarchically organized, though not as extensive as that of Khemit. Citizens are expected to do their part in accomplishing the work of the kingdom, and much government effort is expended to ensure that this is the case. Control over the conquered territories in Imya is quite a bit stricter, however; despite being part of the kingdom for nearly 250 years, Imya's people sometimes still fail to appreciate the benefits of Axuumite dominion.

Axuum enforces a monopoly on trade in Imya and requires all imports and exports be made through authorized Axuumite traders. This monopoly has long been unpopular among Imyans. Other colonial obligations, such as requiring towns to support units of Axuumite soldiers (for their own protection, of course), have also resulted in some unrest among the populace. Nevertheless, the low density of Imya's population, and its isolation behind the Karaman Mountains, has made it easier for Axuum to maintain its control over Imya.

Many Axuumites worship the gods of Khemit, though some (especially in the south, or far from the cities) continue to worship traditional deities of the region. This veneration of the Khemitian deities was spread to Imya after its conquest and is enforced strictly there while it is not in Axuum itself.

MAZABER, CITY OF (CAPITAL)

Ruler: Mulya (governor) Zaqarnas
Government: governor appointed by the king
Population: 56,691 (54,204 Merowen, 1,811 Khemitites, 676 other human ethnicity)

The capital of Axuum and the country's largest city, Mazaber is a port city on the west coast of the Ruby Sea less than 200 miles from where it joins the ocean. Most of the country's imports and exports pass through the docks in Mazaber. The most valuable exports are tortoiseshell, salt, and gold and emeralds from the Tekle Mountains. Ivory from the herds of great elephants in the Central Uplands south of Axuum and Aethiope is also brought to Mazaber by caravan for export. However, the local ivory trade has gradually diminished since Alcaldar seized the Channel Lakes and built the canal system through the continent, which has prevented the herds wandering their traditional north and south migratory routes. To counter this, Axuum has attempted to expand the herds under their control by transporting elephants to new ranges in Imya.

JARMI, CITY OF

Ruler: Mulya Nezana
Government: governor appointed by the king
Population: 22,978 (21,415 Merowen, 1,122 Khemitites, 441 other human ethnicity)

Located on the western border of Axuum on the River Aeth, Jarmi has a river port and is a primary location for shipping trade goods on barges downriver to Khiertuom and on to locations in Khemit. The country's access to the Stygian River and the Ruby Sea is one of the factors that has made Axuum a center of trade. Recently in Jarmi, competition between rival organizations of dockworkers and carters turned violent and threats were made against traders and boat captains who are or are not using particular groups to do their work. An alliance of warriors has been offering to protect nervous traders from both sides, for a stiff fee.

KAZANIA, KINGDOM OF

(kah-zah-NEE-uh)
Capital: Mussa
Ruler: Queen Bahati
Government: monarchy
Population: 2,326,267 (2,320,803 Merowen, 5,464 other human ethnicity)
Monstrous: bulettes, manticores, krenshars
Languages: Kazanian
Religion: ancestor worship, traditional deities
Resources: ivory, myrrh, incense, exotic animals, hides
Currency: Axuumite
Technology Level: High Middle Ages (Mussa), Dark Ages

Kazania is a nation on the east coast of central Libynos, south of Aethiope and Axuum and north of the Channel Lakes. The meandering Uphar River denotes the northern border with Axuum. The southern border is indefinite and could become an issue of dispute with the Empire of Alcaldar, which now controls the Channel Lakes. The kingdom's lands also include coastal plains (where the vast majority of its population lives) from the seacoast in the east to the escarpment of the Central Uplands in the west, along with an indeterminate portion of the Central Uplands themselves. As the plateau is only sparsely populated, the borders with the other Central Kingdoms in that region remain largely undefined.

Kazania is said to be a very wealthy country, and it exports many rare things, though the merchant ships and naval vessels of the country are not advanced enough to undertake long ocean voyages without putting into a port every few days. The country has relatively easy access to ivory, though most of that is traded through merchants of Axuum. Kazania also produces myrrh and other incense, and does a thriving business in the sale of exotic animals and their hides. Alcaldrich ships, in particular, often call at the port of Mussa to acquire exotic animals, because they are apparently a fashion right now in the cities of their empire.

The relationship with Alcaldar is somewhat tense, however, as there is no defined border between Kazania and the empire's lands around the Channel Lakes. Due to the tension, Kazania has been growing its army in size for many years, and Queen Bahati has given standing orders to increase the numbers of soldiers on the walls of the city and on the walls of the palace fortress to show the country's vigilance. Patrols along the southern border area remain infrequent, however, as the army does not have enough troops to regularly monitor the area.

Unlike the other Central Kingdoms — or perhaps any other country in Libynos — Kazania is a matriarchy with the crown going to the eldest daughter of the queen and nobility, and property in general passes down from mother to daughter. It is possible these days for a son to inherit noble status, or even the crown, but only if the family has no daughters. Fortunately, Queen Bahati has three healthy daughters so having a male inherit will not be a problem in this generation.

The people of Kazania revere the spirits of their ancestors and leave spirit-gifts regularly on tombs to placate them, and also generally worship the traditional deities of the Central Kingdoms region.

MUSSA, CITY OF

(MUU-suh)
Ruler: Queen Bahati
Government: administrators under the direction of the queen
Population: 63,298 (61,055 Merowen, 2,243 other human ethnicity)

Mussa has a good harbor that accommodates many fishing boats and also has plenty of room for trading ships. The docks were expanded 12 years ago in anticipation of increasing the number of Kazanian ships going out from Mussa, but that has not actually occurred due to the outmoded local shipbuilding capability. On the other hand, the expansion has made room for many large merchant vessels of other nations to come to the city to trade, including ships from Alcaldar, Far Jaati, and even the distant city of Castorhage.

MEROË, KINGDOM OF

Capital: Meroë
Notable Settlements: Khiertuom, Kur
Ruler: Kandake (queen) Maleqora
Government: monarchy
Population: 2,908,955 (2,877,661 Merowen, 25,315 Khemitite, 4,179 Lagish, 1,800 other human ethnicity)
Monstrous: krenshar, hobgoblins, gnolls
Languages: Khemitian
Religion: Pharaonic pantheon
Resources: ironwork; iron or steel weapons, armor and tools; gold
Currency: Axuumite
Technology Level: Dark Ages, High Middle Ages (Kur)

The Kingdom of Meroë is in central Libynos, south of Khemit. To its east is the Kingdom of Aethiope, where its border is the western edge of the Hills of Strabo. To the west are the Khael Hills, and beyond that the lands of Qesh. Meroë's northern border is the south bank of the Setesh and Stygian rivers. To the south, it claims the territory as far as Lake Targania in the Central Uplands, the source of the Opal River. The Opal runs through the midst of Meroë's territory, past the city of Kur and the capital Meroë and thence to Khiertuom, where the Opal and Lapis join to form the Stygian River.

The northern part of the country is generally dry, similar to southern Khemit, but the central part is lightly wooded. In the south are the Central Uplands and vast grasslands that stretch hundreds of miles to the west and south.

The Khael Hills on the western edge of Meroë are rich with iron and gold and are therefore sometimes disputed between Meroë and Qesh. The people of Qesh are fierce but undisciplined, whereas Meroë has an excellent, well-trained army that has been able to defend the hill border now for more than 300 years. The kingdom possesses a strong and sophisticated iron industry that supplies iron and limited amounts of steel for most of the Central Kingdoms.

Nearly all the people of Meroë worship the pantheon of deities from Khemit, though a few still pay homage to the old gods of the area. For generations, the rulers (and sometimes other nobles) have been buried in pyramids similar to the rulers of Khemit, although the style of pyramids has changed over the centuries. The oldest style is the step pyramid, which was used much longer in Meroë than in Khemit. Eventually, the slant-sided pyramid was adopted but with a flat top, similar to the top of a step pyramid. In the past 300 years, the fashion has been to use a pyramid with a pointed top, but with a base much smaller than is usual in Khemit. This results in a steep-sided pyramid that appears tall for its width. Since the kings and queens of Meroë have seen no need for the wide spaces required by most pyramids in Khemit, all these types of pyramids can be seen in relatively close proximity in the royal burial areas a few miles outside of Meroë. The burial site of the qores (kings) is northeast of the city, while that of the kandakes (queens) is to the southeast.

MEROË, CITY OF (CAPITAL)

Ruler: Princess Sakaye
Government: administrator reporting directly to the kandake
Population: 46,286 (44,756 Merowen, 1,230 Khemitite, 300 other human ethnicity)

The city of Meroë is on the Opal River about 100 miles south of Khiertuom. It functions very much as an administrative center for the kandake, who prefers to make as many decisions as possible for her country. She is willing to delegate to trusted subordinates, but only after she hears a thorough explanation of a situation and gives careful instructions on the actions she wants carried out. There is no doubt that sometimes Kandake Maleqora feels that a situation could be handled better if she could only deal with it herself. Her servants (which is what they all are, even those who are quite important in their own right) go to great lengths to avoid disappointing the kandake. She does not resort to anything so crude as execution (or has not yet done so), but she has ways of making her displeasure strongly felt.

Meroë has a river dock, though it is not as large as the one in Khiertuom. It has a separate section for diplomatic visitors and for deliveries to the palace of the kandake so that such arrivals need never be delayed due to common traffic in the area. The city also has a wide stone bridge to allow caravans to cross the Opal River even during the annual river floods.

KHIERTUOM, CITY OF

Ruler: Prince Kernabes
Government: administrator reporting directly to the kandake
Population: 53,027 (49,092 Merowen, 3,110 Khemitite, 450 Lagish, 375 other human ethnicity)

This city is an important trading center where the Lapis and Opal rivers join to form the Stygian River. Boats go down the Stygian to the city of Nampata in Khemit and even farther north, as well as upriver on the Opal and Lapis. This benefit of Khiertuom's location, however, is offset by the flooding that occurs during the summer rainy season. Many of the buildings in the city are built on raised foundations to keep from being inundated every year, and most storage areas are up under the roof instead of at ground level to keep everything dry.

Khiertuom also receives caravans traveling south, either from the north through Khemit's Nubiar Oversight or ones from the northwest that may have crossed the Stygian at Nampata. In either case, these caravans nearly always want to stop in the great city of Khiertuom, so the city has ferries that operate across the rivers during all daylight hours. Some enterprising boatmen also take people across in the dark, but they charge a much higher fee for their cooperation in doing so.

KUR, CITY OF

Ruler: Prince Harsiotef
Government: administrator reporting directly to the Kandake
Population: 23,719 (almost all Merowen)

Kur is the center of ironworking in Meroë. A good road leads from the important iron mines in the Khael Hills to the city, and a strong bridge across the Opal River allows heavily-laden drays to cross directly without having to unload onto a barge. Many ironworkers have smelting facilities on the north side of the city, and some have the knowledge and expertise to make steel.

Smiths in the area turn out iron tools and weapons and ironwork such as gates, scrollwork to cover windows, and more. In addition, some of the smiths use the steel to make good weapons and armor and high-quality tools. The ironwork and goods are traded throughout the Central Kingdoms and some end up even farther away.

TEMELPA, RUINS OF

Population: 0

Once a bustling trade city built around the burial ziggurat of an important vizier and wizard to Qore Ergamenes of Meroë, about 200 years ago Temelpa gained a reputation as being a dangerous area for merchant caravans. When the trade routes moved elsewhere, the population did as well. The city was eventually abandoned and has fallen into ruins.

QESH, KINGDOM OF

Capital: Tungul
Ruler: Qore (king) Naqrin
Government: monarchy
Population: 1,473,428 (1,441,336 Merowen, 2,092 Khemitites, about 30,000 Desertfolk)
Monstrous: leucrotta, dust digger, gambado
Languages: Khemitian
Religion: Pharaonic pantheon
Resources: gold, stone, herd animals
Currency: Axuumite
Technology Level: Dark Ages, High Middle Ages (defense and weapons)

Qesh is a nation of poorly defined borders located in central Libynos south and west of Khemit. In the north, its land continues beyond the Setesh River for an uncertain distance into the wastes of the Maighib Desert. Its eastern border is at the Khael Hills, over which Qesh occasionally enters into armed disputes with Meroë. In the south, its folk occasionally travel as far as the northern plains of the vast Grasslands of Wahm. The kingdom also claims the Kufa Mountains to the west as part of its territory, but the prevalence of violent humanoid tribes there make it impossible to exercise any control except at the periphery.

Qesh is a land of warriors, many of them semi-nomadic, who move their various herds from place to place. A few settled towns sit along the Setesh River, but most population centers are around oases. In most ways, the government of Qesh is at best loosely organized. Clan chieftains acknowledge the authority of the Qore, pay due tribute, and come readily to any call to war. On small matters, though, the clans may disregard royal statements if they conflict with how the clan wants to handle things.

One matter on which the clans are united, however, is the need to keep the humanoids of Set's Kingdom confined in their mountains, ideally deep enough that the miners of Qesh can maintain safe access to the gold deposits known to be in the northeast part of the Kufa Mountains. The exceptional archery of the Qeshites (aided by their unusually keen eyesight) has been useful in this over the years. Forts with good wells have been built at oases with deep groundwater (in addition to such pools as may be on the surface) as rally points in case of an attack by the humanoids. Maintenance of the forts is given over to the local clans, so the quality is not uniform, but all know someday that their lives could depend on them so the strongholds are generally in good condition.

Despite maintaining a relationship with the country of Khemit that swings from ally to adversary and back again over the course of years, most of the citizens of Qesh worship the Khemitian deities.

Tungul, City of (Capital)

Ruler: Qore Naqrin
Government: officials reporting directly to the qore
Population: 22,846 (almost all Merowen)

Tungul is located on the south side of the Setesh River in the eastern part of Qesh. The palace of the qore is here, and much of his clan tends to stay in the northern part of the country either north or south of the Setesh. The city is old and made primarily of stone quarried from the Kufa Mountains and floated downriver on barges. Carvings and sculptures are gilded or inlaid with colorful mosaics, but most of these are many years old. Recent generations of qores have put less emphasis on the palace and more emphasis on their tombs. Royalty in Qesh are buried in tombs marked with pyramids; the bases are much smaller than those in the Khemitian style but the pyramids are nearly as high, which results in a tall, slender appearance.

Monastery of Light, Ruins of

Population: 0

For thousands of years, the reclusive monks of the Monastery of Light practiced their secret disciplines deep in the Maighib Desert. For the past century, though, the monastery has fallen completely silent. In the absence of any actual knowledge, the consensus among those in the region is that the monks must have fallen victim to some plague. Difficult to find at the best of times (because the monks located themselves in the desert specifically for the isolation and did not wish casual visitors), its location is now completely lost. Any marking on a map has to be speculation at best, but it is known that the monastery was located somewhere in the deep desert between Qesh, Khemit, and Guurzan.

Reference Source: Pyramid of Amra from Quests of Doom

Set's Kingdom

Capital: none
Ruler: varies; usually none
Government: none
Population: unknown
Monstrous: hill giants, cave giants, gnolls and flinds, ogres, orcs, bugbears
Languages: Khemitian, humanoid languages
Religion: Set, humanoid deities
Resources: unknown; possibly gold
Currency: Khemitian, Ammuyad, Alcaldrich
Technology Level: Iron Age

The evil humanoid groups of the Kufa Mountains are commonly referred to as Set's Kingdom, though in reality they are usually far from unified. Set's Kingdom has at times been an organized kingdom, sometimes for hundreds of years. During those times, it swept across parts of Qesh and Meroë, the southern Maighib Desert, and even sections of Khemit. Ultimately, though, the kingdom has never been able to grow into a continent-wide empire, as any organization among the humanoids typically dies with any leader able to unify them.

One challenge facing anyone who would attempt to claim dominion over Set's Kingdom is the eventual opposition of all of the human

nations surrounding it. Each time such a unification has occurred, the folk of Qesh, Alcaldar, Meroë, and even Khemit have intervened, usually killing the unifier and bringing an end to the new regime while simultaneously inflicting enough casualties on the humanoids to discourage any new attempts for several generations at least.

Moreover, the various groups in the mountains — orcs, gnolls, ogres, hill and cave giants, and more — tend to be innately chaotic and difficult to control as a group. They may want an evil kingdom, but not if they have to work together to achieve it. More than a few efforts by powerful leaders to seize control have floundered in the face of the chaotic tendencies of those who dwell among and under the mountain peaks.

What is not widely known outside the mountains is that the name of the kingdom is not merely colloquial. In fact, priests of Set have a large temple within the Kufas and are one of the forces that have attempted to unite the humanoids. The priests adhere to the principle of lawfulness, as does their deity. (Though evil in nature, Set has a responsibility in the cycle of the gods, which he faithfully fulfills every day.) Unfortunately for them, the chaotic monsters of the mountains have proven highly resistant to the institution of any semblance of organization or order.

Geographic Features and Points of Interest in the Central Kingdoms

Central Uplands

The Central Uplands are an enormous plateau of eastern central Libynos, more than 600 miles from its western edge to the Tekle Mountains on the east, and at least as far from its northern extent to the south. Meroë and Kazania lay claim to most of the territory in the plateau, with Aethiope and Axuum each claiming a small portion. Within the Central Uplands are Lake Targania and Lake Sulys, the sources of the Opal and Lapis Rivers, respectively. The Wambatu River, which runs south and west through the Grasslands of Wahm, also has its origin in a spring high on this plateau.

The Central Uplands are covered with savannah and open woodland, and are the home to such creatures as the great elephant and the giraffe. These animals tend to avoid the lower grasslands because there are too few of the trees and plants on which they like to graze. More of the populations are found in the Yingozi Woodlands on the south side of the Channel Lakes, but the groups are unable to mix now due to the deepened rivers and canals in that system.

Hills of Strabo

This stretch of hills is in Aethiope, and its western edge is usually understood to be the border between that country and Meroë. Among the hills are two or three long-extinct volcanoes where prospectors have found obsidian. Also located in the hills are deposits of gold and copper and a mostly depleted vein of platinum for which a replacement is most urgently being sought.

Khael Hills

Acting as the border between Meroë and Qesh, the important resources in the hills have also made them a source of contention. The two most prominent are gold and iron. While the gold is very valuable, the iron is the base of a significant industry in Meroë, especially around the city of Kur. A rough road runs north and south along most of the east side of the hills but a good road runs east to Kur to allow easy delivery of raw materials to the smelting facilities there.

Kufa Mountains

The Kufa Mountains of south Libynos are located south of the Maighib Desert, north of the Grasslands of Wahm and northeast of Alcaldar, and separated from the Navarre Mountains by the Eberro Wastes. The range is primarily inhabited by monsters and humanoids and is home to the so-called Set's Kingdom. The humanoids of the Kufas do not often raid into Alcaldar, having been taught the danger of doing so over many years by Alcaldar's Royal Army and more recently the Church Militans. It does happen from time to time, however, so those who live anywhere near the mountains are always on watch.

LAKE SULYS

This lake in the eastern half of the Central Uplands is the source of the Lapis River. It is smaller than Lake Targania, its counterpart. Whether it is deep or shallow has not been confirmed, as a local nomadic tribe views entering the waters of the lake as taboo and attempt to kill anyone who so much as approaches its shore. It has been noted — from a distance — that the waters of Lake Sulys seem to rise and fall with those of Lake Targania in some sort of pattern, as if they are connected in some way deep underground.

LAKE TARGANIA

This lake in the western half of the Central Uplands is the source of the Opal River. While not the largest lake in south Libynos, it is reputed to be the deepest; in fact, several expeditions have plumbed its depths but none have been able to confirm a bottom. The clear waters of Targania are particularly cold, especially once one descends to a point below which sunlight can penetrate.

During the rainy season, the lake rises considerably, though some scholars note that the rise seems, in fact, out of proportion to the amount of rain that has fallen. As a result, it is believed that an underground source to the lake contributes to the waters that ultimately cause the inundation in Khemit. In some years, a greater rise in Lake Targania seems to correspond to a lesser rise in Lake Sulys, while in other years both seem to exhibit a consistent rise, which leads some to speculate that there may be an underground connection between the two.

LAPIS RIVER

The Lapis River runs through Aethiope and has its source in Lake Sulys in the Central Uplands. Groundwater combines with the summer rains to flood the Lapis, which joins with the Opal near Khiertuom to become the Stygian River of Khemit. It is generally navigable, though less easily so than the River Aeth farther to the east.

MUTABAR HILLS

These rolling hills are largely covered in dense grasses and stunted oak trees and interspersed with rocky outcroppings. The Stygian River passes around the northern margins of the hills on its way to Nampata. The Mutabar Hills see few travelers and, as far as anyone knows, no people make their permanent homes here. Starting at nightfall, great flocks of a species of large, carnivorous bat pour forth from cavern openings among the rocks and rise into the dark sky to wheel over the hills in search of prey.

Scattered throughout the Mutabar Hills are enormous, cyclopean blocks of worked stone of obvious antiquity. The presence of the blocks gives rise to rumors that a city of giants was once located deep in the hills, in the extremely distant past.

OPAL RIVER

Flowing from Lake Targania in the Central Uplands, the Opal River is the main tributary of the Stygian River. The Opal and the Lapis River, which join at Khiertuom, together are the source of much of the floodwater that causes the Stygian's annual inundation, which in turn provides the fertility of Khemit. The Opal is navigable along much of its length as it runs through Meroë, which allows that country to use it as a corridor for trade down into Khemit.

RIVER AETH

Marking the border between Aethiope and Axuum, the River Aeth flows from the western margins of the Tekle Mountains into the Lapis River and ultimately into the Stygian and north toward the

sea. This connection allows Axuum to trade goods from the Central Kingdoms and places in southern Libynos hundreds of miles down the river into Khemit.

SETESH RIVER

The Setesh River has its origins deep in the Kufa Mountains. Little is known of its source, as anyone wishing to explore it must contend with the humanoids and other monsters of Set's Kingdom. Legend says that the waters of the river emerge from a cave high on a sheer cliff that is flanked by enormous carven statues of solid gold.

After passing out of the mountains, the Setesh flows east through the verges of the Maighib Desert of northern Qesh, and then north of Meroë, where it joins up with the Stygian River on its way north to Khemit.

TEKLE MOUNTAINS

This line of mountains runs through the middle of Axuum, from the coastal Uashta Hills in the north down south to the northern reaches of the Kingdom of Kazania. The southern part of the range, with the highest peaks of the range, is well inland from the coast and abuts the eastern side of the Central Uplands. The range is broken by several valleys lined with well-maintained roads. The mountains are known for producing gold and emeralds for the country of Axuum, but strangers are not permitted around the mines so outsiders have only a vague idea of where they might be.

UASHTA HILLS

The Uashta Hills lie between the Geb-el-Mardikh Mountains to the west and the shores of the Ruby Sea to the east, and mark the northern extent of the Kingdom of Axuum. To the south, the hills rise into the northern spur of the Tekle Mountains.

Receiving rainfall from winds blowing off the sea to its east, and well-watered by multiple streams running down from the Gel-el-Mardikhs, these rolling hills boast forests in the valleys and excellent farmland and pastures for grazing many sheep and cattle. Prior to its conquest of Imya, Axuum relied on these hills for much of its food. This still remains an important agricultural region for the kingdom.

Lone obelisks of stone are scattered throughout the Uashta Hills, and farmers occasionally find strange stone figurines or clay tablets when working new lands. Local legend tells that, long ago, these hills were home to a fey race which, upon the coming of humans, was driven either into the sea or beneath the nearby mountains. Whether there is any truth to this is unknown, but those who live here point out that each time any such relics turn up, priests from the temples of Mazaber arrive soon to seize them "for further study."

CHANNEL LAKES

Capital: San Caseo
Notable Settlements: Arenzana, Caduvar, Munigua, Ortís, Sallavinera, Syat
Ruler: Sebastos Eva-Gracía, Duquesa of Rebollar
Government: ruled by Empire of Alcaldar, represented by the Sebastos (Imperial Governor)
Population: 859,376 (857,815 Alcaldrich, 1,561 other human ethnicity)
Monstrous: tengus, dwarves (mountains), orcs (certain tribes occasionally attempt to raid canal system)
Languages: Alcaldrich
Religion: Muir and Thyr
Resources: trade, crops, fish, abalone and shells, beef, wool, parchment, leather goods, leather armor, saddles, horses, gold, copper, canal system
Currency: Alcaldrich
Technology Level: High Middle Ages (cities and fortresses), Dark Ages (small towns, rural areas)

A lock along the Upper Sangre River opens to permit passage of ships heading west to the town of Munigua on Lake Odraga.

The Central Lakes were a group of connected lakes and rivers about halfway down the west coast of southern Libynos that formed a girdle most of the way across the continent. They are now known as the Channel Lakes, a territory founded 275 years ago by the Empire of Alcaldar when it conquered the Kingdom of Ka'dufaar and other small groups of the area.

The empire's great undertaking was to use the lakes already present to build a water route right across the middle of south Libynos, thus freeing much shipping from having to travel all the way around the southern coast. This feat of engineering involved dredging the lower parts of the Sangre River to allow for the passage of large, oceangoing vessels, constructing locks on the Upper Sangre River where it flows down from the Zorinos Mountains, expanding the River of Gold between Cordona Lake and Lake Aur to also accommodate large ships, and finally building the River of Gold Locks to join Lake Aur with the Great Ocean Ûthaf.

Before the locks were begun near Lake Aur, some argued for cutting a path from Cordona Lake straight through the Seniaro Hills since that would be an even shorter route to the ocean. However, the simpler prospect of building through the less-severely sloped, open lands east of Lake Aur meant the southerly plan eventually prevailed. A land route exists through the Seniaro Hills, though, and was used before the river connection was completed.

Traveling through the Channel Lakes is not a trivial matter; it is a journey of about 1,700 miles, and it is made slower by traveling against the current of the rivers at some portion in every traverse. It also requires going through two series of locks, up to and down from Cordona Lake and Lake Aur. However, since the alternative is sailing more than 9,000 miles around the southern coast of Libynos, many merchants great and small are willing to pay the fees and go through the channel instead.

The Empire of Alcaldar put forth great amounts of effort and funds to complete the Channel Lakes. They make it clear to all who pass through that using the channel is a privilege granted by the empire to its allies and trading partners, and not available to all comers as are the open oceans. Unfortunately, the country of Castorhage abused that privilege eight years ago when Castorhagi ships attacked an Alcaldrich vessel in the neutral waters of the Boiling Sea. Since that time, the Channel Lakes have been closed to Castorhagi shipping, a consequence that they continue to dispute even after all these years.

Alcaldar itself uses the channel to move its merchant ships and military vessels more quickly to points in eastern Libynos, which allows them to be where they need to be faster than was possible in the past. In general, Alcaldrich traders proceed through the channel in their turn, just like all the others, but the empire's warships receive priority over any other shipping.

The entire territory of the Channel Lakes is under the rule of a sebastos, a title derived from an ancient Hyperborean term for an imperial governor. The sebastos has authority over the entire Channel Lakes region but is assisted by two exarchs who oversee sections of the channel itself. The sebastos herself is directly responsible for everything from the east end of Lake Istobal west to Caduvar and Ortís on the Sangre Sea.

San Caseo, City of (Capital)

Ruler: Sebastos Eva-Gracía, Duquesa of Rebollar
Government: sebastos (regional governor) appointed by queen of Alcaldar
Population: 18,075 (17,380 Alcaldrich, 695 other human ethnicity)

San Caseo was built by the Empire of Alcaldar to be the capital of its new region of Channel Lakes. For more than 200 years it served primarily as a support center for explorers, engineers, military units, and the hundreds of laborers who built the route through the center of Libynos. Now it has finally come into its own as an administrative center for the entire Channel Lakes and a trading city in its own right. It is governed by the sebastos, or imperial governor, who represents the queen in all administrative and legal matters, though of course nobles still vow their allegiance to the queen herself.

Although traffic on the Channel Lakes goes past San Caseo, that doesn't necessarily make the city a big trading center. It has good docks and serves as a port for some transshipment of goods, but most ships that go through the Channel Lakes are taking their cargoes to somewhere specific to trade at the end of the route. Some captains, especially those from large merchant groups or ones who expect to transit the channel frequently, prefer to have their customs inspections in San Caseo because that gives them a chance to call on authorities there and get their names known, perhaps even by the Sebastos. Many people of the Channel Lakes have adopted the custom of the grasslands people who habitually give courtesy gifts to people they meet; a small non-monetary gift for the harbor master or some imperial administrator (or a slightly larger gift for the sebastos) is considered polite and appropriate.

San Caseo receives goods and materials from the settled areas around the Channel Lakes, and trades with merchants from Alcaldar and other points in central and southern Libynos. It exports materials produced in the Channel Lakes area such as salted beef, wool cloth, parchment, and leather goods — especially good armor and saddles (including high-end saddles chased with silver) but many other leather items as well — and high-quality horses. Sometimes horses from the Grasslands of Wahm may go as far as Akados to collectors or breeders looking for something unusual.

ARENZANA, TOWN OF

Ruler: Archon Francisca Ybanes of Ortís
Government: archon (city governor) appointed by queen of Alcaldar
Population: 692 (almost all Alcaldrich)

For more than 200 years, Arenzana was the final link in the primarily land-borne trade route across Libynos at the Channel Lakes. The town rests at the bottom of a steep drop on the ocean side of the Seniaro Hills at the end of the Coast Road from Cordona Lake. With the completion of the River of Gold Locks almost 20 years ago, and the opening of the water route across the continent, the land trade has almost entirely disappeared. Arenzana now remains as the foothold of a small Alcaldrich colony on the coast of the Great Ocean Ûthaf. It has large docks that were built at the height of the land trade, but they are aged now and used almost solely by local fishing boats, a few traders, and the occasional small vessel of the Imperial Navy.

Besides fish for local consumption, the fishers of Arenzana harvest abalone. They sell the meat fresh when customers are available, but otherwise salt it or smoke it and sell it that way. Of most value are the shells, which are primarily sold to Alcaldrich traders and used for decorative purposes in the wealthy households of Alcaldar and its possessions.

CADUVAR, CITY OF

Ruler: Archon Lope-Ederono, Conde of Sorzano
Government: archon (city governor) appointed by queen of Alcaldar; bureaucracy
Population: 9,127 (almost all Alcaldrich)

Caduvar is usually considered the gateway to the Channel Lakes, a water route cutting through southern Libynos. Most of the city is less than 250 years old, having been rebuilt after Alcaldar's conquest of the Kingdom of Ka'dufaar. Formerly built almost entirely of wood, government, commercial, and religious buildings, as well as the homes of the wealthy (and the city wall), are now made of imported stone; this makes them less vulnerable to the fire that ravaged the old city during the siege.

A major port city, Caduvar is also home to a fleet of the Imperial Navy. The fleet has been deployed close to the city for the past year, providing protection against warships of the Castorhagi Navy that have been anchored off the coast for that entire time. (Happily, these warships have yet to try to interfere with ships entering the Channel Lakes system.) The port sees relatively little trade; it is primarily a first stop for ships coming from afar and heading through the channel, or a last stop before ships head out along the coast or (more likely) across the Sinnar Ocean to Akados. The port also provides protection from the wild storms that sometimes form in the southern part of the ocean.

Although San Caseo was founded as the capital of the Channel Lakes, it was in a relatively unpopulated area while Caduvar was in an area of established farms and small villages. Several exceptional soldiers were ennobled and granted the lands in the region of Caduvar, resulting in that now being an area full of haciendas; while some are the usual size, others are smaller than those of nobles with older titles. Nobles in this area include the duque of Texedor, the marquesa of Benifallim, the marqués of Tormos, and the conde of Millena. Abandoned, though, is the coastal hacienda of the duquesa of Berrocal that had half its population butchered by orcs more than a decade ago, and the other half stolen away as slaves. Even though the village and some farms were still habitable, any people who survived or managed to return had no desire to stay. Most of them moved to Alcaldar (or even farther) to be far away from the scene of the slaughter and the unlucky estate has been allowed to fall into ruin.

CHANNEL FORTRESSES

Ruler: See below
Government: military commander, usually a teniente or capitán, but as high as a comandante at key locations
Population: 30–100

The Channel Lakes are protected by a series of military fortresses along their length. Located at key transition points, these fortresses claim to provide protection for ships traveling the channel — against wild animals or wandering tribes, one would suppose, but there are very few of the latter and the animals are unlikely to be a danger to ships. In truth, the soldiers stationed along the route are more to protect the channel from sabotage by keeping the ships moving and knowing where all the vessels in transit are located and when they should arrive at the next fortress. They also keep anyone from getting too close of a look at the workings of the locks. After all, Alcaldrich engineers learned about river locks by careful study of the Canal of the Pharaohs in Khemit; the government does not want other nations who might desire canals to have the advantage of stealing the Alcaldrich developments.

Each fortress has a stone wall surrounding a keep of at least two stories, as well as barracks, stables, and support buildings. They are armed with a mix of ballistae or catapults and keep plenty of ammunition on hand in case they need to deal with a recalcitrant ship. The soldiers are also well armed to deal with smaller threats such as wild animals or sailors getting drunk while waiting for their ship's turn at a lock. The fortresses near the locks have larger contingents because they are responsible for providing the guard forces stationed at each lock. Every fortress has a handful of small, fast ships to carry messages and to do inspections of traversing ships if necessary. In addition, each location is well-supplied with horses, as those are easy to come by in this area. Independent farmers settled near some of the fortresses (especially those east of Lake Odraga), and the commanders do not discourage this, as it increases the resources available for the troops. The fortresses from west to east, as well as the names of their commanders, are found on the table on the following page.

Fortress Name	Commander	Location
Altzaga	Capt Arias Ximon of Alicantato	south bank of strait on Sangre River by Sangre Sea
Elduain	Cmdte Damian-Gonsalvo of Estancia Galdames	south bank of Lake Istobal next to Sangre River
Gabiria	Ten Gelmiro-Martín of Estancia Urrimi	north bank of Lake Odraga where Sangre River leaves it
Itsaso	Capt Ana-Enderquina of Hacienda Tormos	south bank of Upper Sangre River to the south of the highest lock
Lizarta	Capt Manuela-Ildaria of Estancia Vellone	west bank of Lake Cordona to the north of where Sangre River leaves it
Olaberria	Ten Margarida Natalez of San Caseo	southeast bank of Lake Cordona where River of Gold leaves it
Orexa	Ten Bianca Hordonez of Cadua	northeast bank of Lake Aur where River of Gold enters it
Ubidea	Capt Ansuro Telles of Arenzana	southeast bank of Lake Aur where River of Gold Locks leave it
Zerain	Cmdte Visturio Bernal of Ruente	northeast bank of River of Gold Locks where it enters the Great Ocean Ûthaf

A note on abbreviations: Ten—teniente (lieutenant); Capt—capitán (captain); Cmdte — comandante (commandant).

MUNIGUA, TOWN OF

Ruler: Exarch of Sangre-Odraga Alvar-Julian, Marqués of Vellone

Government: exarch (regional governor) appointed by queen of Alcaldar

Population: 1,574 (almost all Alcaldrich)

The town of Munigua is located on the eastern shore of Lake Odraga where the Upper Sangre River enters the lake; it is the seat of one of the two exarchs of the Channel Lakes system, the exarch of Sangre-Odraga. He is the administrator of the lakes, the lock system, and the associated population, from the east end of Lake Istobal to the west edge of Cordona Lake. The authorities of Munigua oversee Fortress Elduain in its ship inspections and fee collections from ships entering the channel from the west. They also protect the Upper Sangre Locks and oversee those keeping the locks in good working order. The foothills of the mountains are the one area where imperial troops really may be called out to defend the locks and shipping against wild animals and fell creatures.

The exarch at Munigua is the closest potential Alcaldrich ambassador to the dwarves of the Zorinos Mountains and their trade contacts at Syat. He is occasionally called upon to intervene with the dwarves on behalf of someone who falls afoul of their policies or to represent the Empire of Alcaldar to the dwarves on some matter.

ORTÍS, TOWN OF

Ruler: Archon Beatriz-Elvyra of Estancia Clariana

Government: archon appointed by queen of Alcaldar; bureaucracy

Population: 4,319 (almost all Alcaldrich)

The town of Ortís was built after the Alcaldrich conquest of the Channel Lakes to provide a secondary guard on the entrance to the lake system. Ortís has good docks and several ships of the Imperial Fleet are based here. In the past year, they have been busy providing security for the merchant shipping in the area as the naval vessels in Caduvar have been guarding that city against threatening Castorhagi warships.

Unlike the steep, rocky coast south of Caduvar, the seacoast in the area of Ortís has beautiful white sand beaches. Many of the wealthy people in the western Channel Lakes region have villas in the area to get away during the hot months to where they can enjoy ocean breezes and some sea bathing. An official seaside residence for the sebastos is maintained here year-round. Although the current officeholder rarely uses it herself, it often hosts visiting diplomats and is the site of occasional informal government meetings.

After the establishment of San Caseo and the growth of the Channel Lakes as a corridor for trade, many noble estates were granted in the area between Ortís and the capital city for the purpose of supplying agricultural products to the growing communities. A maintained road winds through the haciendas between the two cities, the only city-to-city land route in the region. Noble estates in the area include those of the marqués of Zapardiel, the condesa of Fresneda, the condesa of Lanzuela, the condesa of Saldón, and the conde of Yebra.

SALLAVINERA, CITY OF

Ruler: Exarch of Cordona-Aur Ynes-Urracia, Marquesa of Iruela

Government: exarch (regional governor) appointed by queen of Alcaldar

Population: 5,304 (almost all Alcaldrich)

The city of Sallavinera is located on the Great Ocean Ûthaf at the east end of the River of Gold Locks. It is the seat of one of the two exarchs of the Channel Lakes, the exarch of Cordona-Aur. She is the administrator of the lakes, the lock system, and the associated population, from the west end of Cordona Lake to the Ocean Ûthaf. The authorities of Sallavinera are in charge of ship inspections and fee collection from ships entering the channel from the east. They also protect the eastern end of the channel, with the assistance of Fortress Zerain on the north bank of the river.

Sallavinera is home port to the fleet of the Imperial Navy in Oceanus. The navy sometimes escorts Alcaldrich merchants on their voyages, but is primarily responsible for the security of Alcaldar's various colonies in Oceanus. The port has become an active trade center, as ships from up and down the coast of southern and central Libynos come here to interact with each other, as well as ships from Far Jaati, and traders of Akados looking to pick up some exotic cargo from Libynos before heading through the channel and then west. For the Libynosi traders, Sallavinera is effectively a neutral port, one that is patrolled enough to keep violence to a minimum. Since it is an Alcaldrich port, it is more organized and somewhat more under control than many in southern Libynos, but it gives merchants from Akados good exposure to the kind of colorful chaos they can expect elsewhere.

The city is less than 50 years old, so it looks a bit raw compared to most in Libynos and is still growing. It was built specifically to be a large port and administrative center, which means the streets are neatly arranged in a grid that fans out from the port. The primary buildings and the city wall are strong stone, but most of the buildings are made of wood from the forests to the south. To those at a distance — such as the nobility in Alcaldar — Sallavinera is an isolated village practically on the far side of the world. To those who call it home, though, it is a vibrant and fast-growing city that is the anchor of Alcaldar's power in eastern Libynos.

SYAT, TOWN OF

Ruler: Archon Sarracino Durán of Munigua
Government: archon appointed by queen of Alcaldar; bureaucracy
Population: 1,735 (almost all Alcaldrich)

The town of Syat lies in a valley in the Zorinos Mountains where the waterfall that is the origin of the Odraga River pours out of a high, rocky face. Its isolation has caused Syat some growing pains as it has received sporadic support from the empire. While work was done on the Upper Sangre River, Syat had good population growth and trade with the cities downriver. When work moved to the vicinity of Lake Aur, however, travel to Syat waned and the people there grew disenchanted with the empire. Alcaldar had to exert a very firm hand for about 25 years to convince the citizens of Syat that a little distance did not absolve them of any of their responsibilities to the empire.

When the army of Alcaldar first arrived in the valley, the people of Syat put forth the ridiculous claim that the cozy little stone town had been built by dwarves hundreds of years before for the purpose of trading with humans in the surrounding lands. Despite some supporting evidence, this was not given any credence until 11 years later when a large delegation of dwarves marched out from behind the waterfall. They were quite put out to discover the changes wrought in the town in less than a dozen years. After some quick diplomacy, a different residence was found for the local archon and the mansion of the head of the dwarven merchants' guild was reserved for dwarven use only. With dozens of months-long market days over the past two centuries, town leaders and dwarven merchants now usually maintain a cautious respect rather than hostility. This does not extend to humans doing any actual mining in the mountains, however.

Syat is home to some Alcaldrich traders who buy goods from the grassland tribes whether or not the dwarves are going to be trading soon. If no market day is coming up, the traders send the goods downriver to San Caseo. Some area residents mine the hills west of the Zorinos Mountains, being careful to stay far enough away from the mountains themselves to be within the letter of the dwarven restrictions. These prospectors have uncovered a little silver in the hills, but mostly they have found copper.

GEOGRAPHIC FEATURES AND POINTS OF INTEREST IN THE CHANNEL LAKES

CORDONA LAKE

This long lake is the highest point of elevation of the Channel Lakes, located on a plateau on the eastern edge of the Zorinos Mountains. Just to the west is a low pass through the Zorinos Mountains, along which the Upper Sangre River begins a descent to the hills and plains beyond. Alcaldar engineers dug a winding channel through the pass so the waters of Cordona Lake could empty to the west to join the Upper Sangre River. Here they built a water gate and the first of the locks providing passage for ships. To the west, more locks were constructed along the course of the Upper Sangre, which eventually empties into Lake Odraga.

Water also flows out of the lake to the south via the River of Gold into Lake Aur. Beyond that, another series of locks completes the connection to the Great Ocean Ûthaf. Part of the genius of the Alcaldrich engineering is ensuring that the waters of Cordona Lake are always sufficiently high to keep water flowing through both the Upper Sangre and the River of Gold. This is helped by the fact that the lake is fed by many streams flowing from the northern Zorinos Mountains. Several small villages along its shores fish as well as grow crops, but they do not produce a tradable surplus.

An overland trade route exists from Cordona Lake to the Great Ocean Ûthaf, which was built and used for 140 years before Alcaldar gained the engineering knowledge and experience necessary to build the river locks that make the Channel Lakes so valuable. The Coast Road takes the shortest route from a tiny port village at the east end of the lake to the cliffs leading down to the sea. A series of tight switchbacks takes the road down to sea level where the small port town of Arenzana still clings to the edge of the ocean.

KINGSBARROW GATE

This circle of tall standing stones is missing a single stone at its eastern point; nothing indicates that a stone ever stood there. Two pairs of stones each have another stone over the top like a lintel, one at the north point of the circle and one at the south. Each of the lintel stones is elaborately carved, although the two sets of carvings are very different; some of the symbols on each seem to represent animals while others are more abstract. Nearby to the east is a small hill or mound that rumor says was the burial place of the rulers of the Kingdom of Ka'dufaar, although it seems rather small to hold the bodies of nearly 800 years of kings. Supposedly, a king would be buried in the mound and then his spirit would go through the gate provided by the standing stones to reach the afterlife.

LAKE AUR

Lake Aur is the final lake in the chain that became the Channel Lakes. The River of Gold flows into it from the north, and from here the River of Gold Locks complete the link to the Great Ocean Ûthaf. It was named after the gold that was discovered in its northern end by engineers surveying prior to dredging the river from Lake Cordona. Apparently, tiny bits of gold had been carried by streams flowing from the Zorinos Mountains, probably for centuries, and much of it precipitated out of the water to the bottom of Lake Aur. This led to a big recovery effort before any more work was done on the channel system, which involved hundreds of people digging and washing to separate out the bits of gold. Now some prospectors pan for gold directly in the mountain streams, but it is not a large enterprise as much of the free gold seems to have been collected already.

A few small communities lie on the northeast edge of the lake between the two sections of the River of Gold, because the land is generally good and some fish are available. Lying as it does at the far end of the Channel Lakes, though, the population has expanded very slowly in the past 20 years, and no nobles have ever been granted land to establish haciendas in this area.

LAKE ISTOBAL

Named for King Istobal-Alcacé, who led Alcaldar in its first steps to empire, Lake Istobal is home to the capital city of San Caseo and the beginning of the channel. Here ships stop for inspection and to pay the necessary fees, and then begin their journeys up the Sangre River. They may stop either at the dock at San Caseo or at Fortress Elduain at the entrance to the river. Patrol boats carry inspectors who stop every ship entering the channel to be sure everything is in order and give them tokens that allow them passage through the locks. At night, a chain is raised across the river entrance (or exit, for ships traveling west) to be sure that no one passes through without the empire's knowledge and authorization.

LAKE ODRAGA

The second lake in the channel system, Lake Odraga was named for the Alcaldrich general who led the successful conquest of the Kingdom of Ka'dufaar, paving the way for the empire's eventual control of the entire Channel Lakes' region. Lake Odraga has the most fish of any of the Channel Lakes and sustains a small fishing industry. Much of the catch feeds people around the lake but some is shipped down to San Caseo for the larger population there. The lake has a current that flows west, but usually ships can catch enough wind in their sails to make an easterly trip without much difficulty. At the east end of the lake, customs boats out of Munigua take a passage token from each ship before allowing it to enter the Upper Sangre and the system of locks there.

Odraga River

The Odraga River begins at a waterfall in the Zorinos Mountains and flows quickly on its way down to Lake Odraga. The river flattens out as it makes a wide curve approaching the lake, making it possible to ford it at some places in the last 50 miles even though the current is still fairly strong. It has not been improved as the Sangre has, so it is only navigable by small boats. Northwest of the Odraga is mostly grassland with some small farming communities, while to the southeast, between it and the Upper Sangre, are miles of hilly country rising to the mountains. Those foothills were patrolled during the time the locks on the Upper Sangre were being constructed, but in the past 50 years the hills have once again become the home of many dangerous creatures.

River of Gold

The River of Gold flows from Cordona Lake into Lake Aur and descends slightly along its length. Streams flowing to it from the southern section of the Zorinos Mountains carried small amounts of gold into the river, which were discovered when the waterway was expanded as part of the channel system. Many people from the poorer quarters of Mhalta, Cadua, and San Caseo, and some inhabitants of the local area, spent months (if not years) sluicing for gold in the mud dredged out of the river, in return for a small percentage of anything they found. Travelers these days still keep an eye out for a glint of gold in the water, but since anything found technically belongs to the Empire of Alcaldar, people don't usually go to great effort to retrieve anything they may see.

River of Gold Locks

Before the construction of the locks, the river that ran from Lake Aur to the sea ran shallow and flat for nearly 40 miles before it wound a circuitous route down, dropping several hundred feet over its course through rocky rapids and steep-sided channels. Using techniques developed from studying the Hyperborean-built Canal of the Pharaohs in Khemit, the engineers of Alcaldar cut a new path for the river, straight to the sea, via a series of locks. They named this the River of Gold Locks.

Using this new route, ships can be raised from the level of the Great Ocean Ûthaf to the plateau of Lake Aur. From there they can sail (or be rowed or towed) against the current into Cordona Lake, and then downriver to the west where they enter the Sinnar Ocean. An adjoining set of locks serves the needs of ships traveling east, making it possible for traffic to flow in both directions at the same time. Small villages along the canal house people with the expertise to work the locks (and repair them if necessary) and small military forces to guard the locks (and the engineers), as well as a few people who cater to ships' crews by providing food and sundries while they wait through the slow process of traversing a lock. Entrance to the lock system is controlled by the authorities at Sallavinera, and they also have protective chains they raise each evening over the entrance to the locks so that no ships can pass through without authorization.

Sangre River

The name Sangre River now refers only to the portion of the river that flows west out of Lake Odraga, through Lake Istobal and then via a narrow strait into the Sangre Sea. (The river east of Lake Odraga is known as the Upper Sangre.) Its south bank has good land for farming, and many noble haciendas have been granted between Lake Istobal and Lake Odraga. These include the estates of the marqués of Hervias, the conde of Ollauri, the condesa of Zarratón, and the conde of Sorzano.

Sangre Sea

Named because its color at sunset is supposedly the color of blood, the Sangre Sea is a wide bay of the eastern Sinnar Ocean along the western coast of central Libynos. The Sangre River flows into it through a series of intervening lakes that have together been named the Channel Lakes. These Channel Lakes and their connecting rivers as a whole

provide a water route to the Great Ocean Ûthaf across a narrow width in the southern part of the continent of Libynos. This water route is entirely in the control of the Empire of Alcaldar.

Seniaro Hills

These rocky, rugged hills lie between Cardona Lake and the Great Ocean Ûthaf. On the eastern side, they drop precipitously toward the sea. Hunters and soldiers keep the wild animals down close to the Channel Lakes, but they are plentiful deeper in the hills.

A road (called the Coast Road) runs as straight as possible from the east end of Cordona Lake to the coast. Although the road is no longer well-maintained, it is still passable. The east end of the road is a steep descent to the town of Arenzana. The descending switchback road is well built and has been kept in much better condition than the road through the hills.

Upper Sangre River

The upper portion of the Sangre River twists and curves as it falls from the plateau of Cordona Lake to the flatter lands to the west. Three locks have been built where the river loses the most elevation, making it safe for ships heading west to sail downriver. Ships heading east, upriver, typically must be rowed or towed from the shore. Villages next to each of the locks house the engineers who keep the locks working and other families who offer amenities to the crews of ships waiting on the lock system, as well as soldiers to guard the locks and the ships in them.

The Upper Sangre River is subject to hazards not found on the lower Sangre or the River of Gold. For example, sometimes rock falls from the surrounding cliffs block part of the river and make it too narrow for two oceangoing vessels to pass each other. In such a situation, a small herald boat is sent to warn oncoming ships, and captains must take turns passing through the narrowed area until it can be cleared again. Rumor says that the river through the mountains was originally widened and smoothed by an incredibly powerful wizard who had an affinity for earth magic. He now lives in a tower somewhere in the mountains nearby where he can keep an eye on ships using his channel, and to this day he earns a certain amount of coin every time one does.

Zorinos Mountains

This range of mountains in the Channel Lakes region falls off into rough hills toward its southwest. It is split by the Upper Sangre River, a gap that was widened when the river was modified as part of Alcaldar's Channel Lakes system. The excavation done to widen and smooth the river's channel coincidentally uncovered silver in the rock. In addition, streams on the southeast side of the mountains deposited gold in Lake Aur. However, neither of these valuable minerals is being mined at the present time.

An unexpected feature of the mountains was their inhabitation by a large clan of dwarves. After a brief period when it appeared conflict might be inevitable, the Alcaldrich came to an accommodation with the dwarves that permitted the excavation necessary to create the Channel Lakes system, so long as the humans otherwise left the mountains alone. In particular, mining was prohibited anywhere in the mountains proper. (The hills to the west, at least, are not subject to the restrictions.)

So far, the empire has honored its agreement with the dwarves, despite its suspicions that large veins of gold and silver must be contained in the mountains. Panning for gold is permitted, but Alcaldrich authorities swiftly punish anyone they discover trying to prospect. That being said, frustration with these restrictions waxes and wanes over the decades, and at the moment it seems to be on the upswing again.

The wild foothills of the mountains between the Odraga River and the Upper Sangre are the habitat of many dangerous beasts but have also been found to have some of the valuable metals the prospectors covet. As long as the miners stay away from the mountains proper and don't let their mines wander in that direction, the dwarves have raised no objection — so far.

KUNG, KINGDOM OF

Capital: Town of Kung
Ruler: King Joran the Vanquisher
Government: autocracy
Population: 2,139 (Kungish)
Monstrous: orcs (central hills)
Languages: Kaduvahn; Bhanikhat
Religion: primarily none; a few worship gods of the Woodslands tribes
Resources: fishing
Currency: barter, Bhanakhiri
Technology Level: Iron Age

A hilly, rocky island off the west coast of the Yingozi Woodlands is home to the Kingdom of Kung. The capital (such as it is) is a town of a few hundred people near a small harbor on the eastern side of the island, built near the king's castle that is really just a fortified tower. The population does some farming and the climate would be good for it, but the soil is so poor that harvests are barely at subsistence level. Fishing is somewhat better but still doesn't produce much to export, so people have just enough food but are always short of coin.

The lives of the common people are made more difficult by the orcs that live in the central hill country. Although the island is large enough that the orcs and humans are not in constant conflict, it is not big enough for the humans to avoid the orcs indefinitely. King Joran comes from a long line of great warriors, and he and his soldiers beat back the orcs from time to time. However, the king can be bothered only with issues that affect his own comfort — such as threats to his food supply — so many of the unpleasant things in Kung go on unhampered.

One shady character the peasants call the Dread Warlock is rumored to be a necromancer or a vampire, or perhaps someone who can read minds and enjoys seeing people frightened. He has a tower on the western side of the island and seldom goes to the village; a few rough servants who stay with him get things from the village when needed. Every now and then peasants disappear, only to be found dead later with looks of horror or terror on their faces. However, no one has had the temerity to suggest that the Dread Warlock is at fault and the king should do something about him, because the king has not been inconvenienced by his actions.

YINGOZI WOODLANDS

Capital: none
Notable Settlements: Fortress Castrobal, Lanza Dorada, Fortress Leza, Varcial
Ruler: none
Government: tribal
Population: unknown (mostly tribespeople, 3,771 Alcaldrich)
Monstrous: orcs (in the west), chupacabras, raggoths
Languages: tribal languages, Bhanikhat; Alcaldrich
Religion: Father Sky and Mother Earth; nature spirits
Resources: exotic animals, pelts
Currency: primarily barter; Bhanakhiran, Alcaldrich
Technology Level: Stone Age (tribes), Dark Ages (Alcaldrich settlements)

South of the Channel Lakes, the land becomes open woodlands interspersed with clear areas as well as patches of actual forest. Rather than horses, the area is grazed by antelope, gazelles, and other grass eaters, as well as large animals such as giraffes and the great elephants. Their predators are here, too: lions, cheetahs, hyenas, wolves, and more.

The people of the woodlands are organized into tribal groups rather than nations. Villages are usually located in more thickly-wooded areas near streams, for the resources and any protection against the elements. Houses are generally made of logs or branches with grass roofs, but some tribes that move often use pole frames covered with hides. For transportation, some locals are able to acquire horses from the Channel Lakes haciendas, often by trading pelts. Others herd the antelope and might tame them for riding, though most aren't as sturdy as horses. Many youths enjoy the thrill of raising and training ostriches to ride, something that can also be a choice for slender adults. The tribes tend to be superstitious, and they venerate the spirits of their ancestors as well as worshipping nature deities or spirits. They see Father Sky and Mother Earth as the great creators, and believe each part of creation has its own spirit at some level. For example, a grove may have a guardian spirit, or a single tree, or an entire forest. They also fear the hungry fire that can sweep through the woodlands, burning everything in its path; to them the symbol of a burned tree represents evil.

The human tribes inhabit primarily the central and eastern parts of the woodlands, while the western portion has a larger number of humanoids, especially orcs. Pressure by the Alcaldrich gradually moving south from the Channel Lakes, and the humanoids spreading toward the east, is slowly pushing more human tribes south toward the Kanderi Desert and its very limited resources.

CASTROBAL, FORTRESS

Ruler: Commandante Alfonzo-Gudesteo of Hacienda Esterquel
Government: military commander
Population: 178 (Alcaldrich)

Fortress Castrobal was founded to give Alcaldar a foothold among the humanoid tribes of the western woodlands. That being the case, it is much stronger than the forts of the Channel Lakes, or even those of its colonies on the eastern coast. It has a stone wall, and the roofs of its buildings are slate to ward off attacks with fire. It also has a larger guard force, with more than 170 soldiers present. The fortress has an excellent well and deep cellars where the troops store enough supplies for a siege of months, though they could not withstand years. A rudimentary pier allows ships to dock and vessels of the Imperial Navy stop by on a regular basis, as Castrobal is considered important in Alcaldar's eventual program of expansion.

FORTRESS IULIANES, RUINS OF

Population: 0

Although the original builder of this old stone fortress is unknown, a succession of humanoid forces occupied it for decades. They used it as a base to gain power over each other and to launch quick attacks into the Channel Lakes area. After some particularly violent raids a dozen or more years ago, the fortress was completely cleaned out by a combined force of the Imperial Army and Alcaldrich marines and the surrounding area cleared as well. For some unrecorded reason, the two wizards with the group insisted it would be a bad idea to completely demolish the structure. Instead, the pair stretched their resources to establish wards and magical traps. So far, the precautions seem to have prevented another band of humanoids from settling in, but it is likely only a matter of time before that happens.

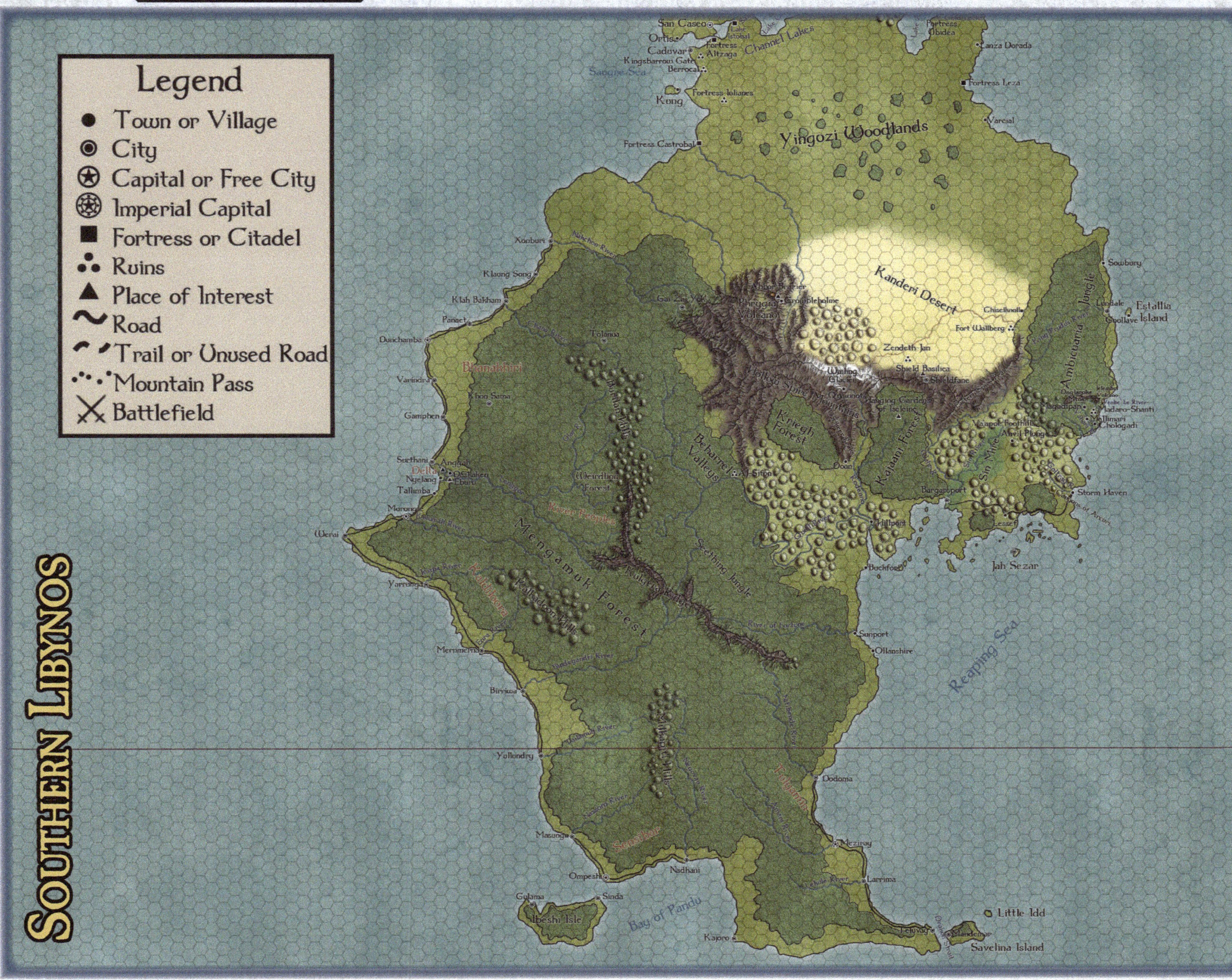

SOUTHERN LIBYNOS
Legend
• Town or Village
◎ City
✪ Capital or Free City
✪ Imperial Capital
■ Fortress or Citadel
∴ Ruins
▲ Place of Interest
~ Road
Trail or Unused Road
Mountain Pass
✗ Battlefield
Yingozi Woodlands
Kanderi Desert
Ambicuaria Jungle
Reaping Sea
Bay of Pandu
Saoune Sea
Channel Lakes
Mengamak Forest
Seething Jungle

Boats cluster at mid-day in the Floating Market of Anggah.

Lanza Dorada, Town of

Ruler: Archon Osoro-Antonio of Estancia Galdames
Government: archon appointed by queen of Alcaldar; bureaucracy
Population: 3,198 (almost all Alcaldrich)

Lanza Dorada was founded about 75 years ago by a paladin of Muir who was sent to the frontier to do penance for sins that were, in point of fact, just poor political choices. Lady Sancha Justenianes (and some companions who also were due for a few years away from court) built a handful of rough buildings, attracted residents, found resources to support the growth, and protected the hamlet, then village, then town, until it had the walls and guard force necessary to protect itself. Lady Sancha ultimately retired and passed away without ever returning to Alcaldar proper, and the town square features a noble statue in her memory.

The centerpiece of the town is the Frontier Temple of Our Lady of the Golden Lance, which is built of stone from the southern Zorinos Mountains although other civic buildings are local wood. The town is on a protected bay, so docks were built early on. Merchant ships as well as the Imperial Navy call here on their way up and down the coast. This is a prosperous town full of proud people, most of whom are also very devout. They are no longer quite on the edge of civilization, but they have a tradition of vigilance, and nearly everyone is trained to wield some type of weapon in defense of their community.

Leza, Fortress

Ruler: Capitán Menendo-Adulfo of Hacienda Ophelo
Government: military commander
Population: 122 (Alcaldrich)

Built about 50 years ago during the construction of the River of Gold Locks, a settlement has grown around the fortress but it is not actually a village. It has no community buildings nor have the residents shown an interest in taking over the organization of matters for themselves. Instead, they consider themselves as support for the fortress; they rely on the fortress commander for leadership and go to the sergeants when they need any assistance. The present capitán has been tasked with the specific duty of putting the settlement on the path to becoming a viable town. The protected harbor has docks for supply ships and the Imperial Navy uses the location as a stopover when convenient, but merchant ships very seldom call here. Developing resources for trade as well as local use is a high priority for the commander in his quest to forge this conglomeration of people into a town.

Varcial, Town of

Ruler: Commandante Felipa-Jimena of Estancia Sorueno
Government: military commander
Population: 273 (almost all Alcaldrich)

Varcial was founded a mere 18 years ago, its military force aboard only the eighth ship to pass through the newly completed canal system. The excitement for progress can still be felt here, as a small town quickly grew up around the initial fortress. Despite the increase in population, the dangers to this isolated community mandate that the military authorities retain control for some time yet. Although the town is walled, the fortress complex is large enough that the entire population can take shelter inside if absolutely necessary, thus reducing the space that must be defended. Varcial has an adequate port and is trying to develop new trade. Some of its people have found mineral deposits in nearby hills and are working to develop mines there that can bring income to the town.

REAPING COAST

Capital: none
Ruler: none
Government: varies
Population: uncertain
Monstrous: sea urchins, brine drakes (coast), froghemoths, hanunagas (jungle), bugbears, rocs, barbegazi (ice gnomes), mountain dwarves (hills/mountains), sand elves (desert)
Languages: Westerling, tribal languages, Zenzin, Alcaldrich
Religion: Hyperborean pantheon, Castorhagi pantheon, nature spirits
Resources: nutmeg, spices, tropical foods, antiquities, mining, lumber, handcrafts, trade, written material
Currency: Jah Sezain, Castorhagi, Axuumite, Alcaldrich
Technology Level: Renaissance (Jah Sezar), High Middle Ages (other cities), Iron Age (villages and rural areas), Stone Age (tribes of the forest or jungle)

The Reaping Coast makes up the southeastern region of the continent of Libynos where it meets the Reaping Sea. It runs from the Ambicuaria Jungle in the north, past the folds and features of the Hollow Spire Mountains in the center, to the genuine rainforest of the Seething Jungle far to the south. Records elsewhere suggest that much of this region was at one time colonized by the Hyperboreans, but little evidence is left to support that. Following the Great Crusades, settlers and traders from the lands of Foere and Castorhage developed outposts along the coast, many of which have become significant towns or even cities. Some are still definitely colonies, but others have long been independent of their distant founders.

ABHOR BRAZIER, TEMPLE OF

Population: unknown
Ruler: High Priestess Dealyn Rhó
Government: theocracy

This great temple sits on the side of the volcano Phrygia at about 14,000 feet above sea level in the northern Hollow Spire Mountains. The temple is built of black obsidian and appears to be a solid block 100 feet high with a single pair of brass doors. Four smokestacks rise 300 feet at each of the four corners of the structure. The temple is said to be dedicated to some evil deity of fire but was thought abandoned until recently, when great gouts of flame visible from miles away erupted from the temple's stacks. People claim flames burn there constantly these days, a sure sign that the temple is again occupied.

REFERENCE SOURCE: SPLINTERS OF FAITH 9: DUEL OF MAGIC

AL-SIFON, RUINS OF

Population: 0

This ancient ruined city lies at the eastern edge of the Seething Jungle, near the foothills of the southwestern spur of the Hollow Spire Mountains. Locals claim it is cursed, but the few adventurers who have been there speak of the extent of the ruins. A few main structures are discernable, including an 80-foot-tall cone-shaped structure and an equally tall step pyramid made of gray stone interspersed with rows of massive boulders

carved to resemble skulls. The majority of the city is overgrown with vines and towering trees, mostly lost to the expanse of jungle.

The death-priest Akruel Rathamon rose to power in Al-Sifon in –613 I.R. and marched the Cult of Aurikas from the ancient city against cities, towns, and homesteads throughout the coastal regions of the Reaping Sea. After decades of bloodshed, the Khemitian priest Shah Rasalt and his gathered forces fought Akruel's death cult to a standstill during the War of Divine Discord. After Shah Rasalt defeated Akruel in the little homestead of Lessef in –579 I.R., he marched his army to Al-Sifon and laid siege to the city of evil cultists. When Shah Rasalt finally left the Seething Jungle, very few structures of the ancient city were left standing. Unfortunately, evil never really seems to die, and some intrepid jungle explorers now claim the ancient city stands anew, rebuilt stone by stone, despite the encroaching jungle that surrounds it. Undead wander afresh through the paved streets and lurk in the haunted halls.

Several small settlements along the Quell River are located south of the ruins of Al-Sifon, and range from a few dozen huts to larger villages with names such as Ceza' Atan and Cata Luawn. Their inhabitants lead a simple, peaceful life unbothered by any supposed curse on the nearby ruins.

REFERENCE SOURCE: SPLINTERS OF FAITH 10: REMORSE OF LIFE

ANVIL PLUNGE, TEMPLE-HAMLET OF

Ruler: Patriarch Brovok Ashenchisel
Government: Church of Dargath
Population: 91 (dwarf)

Anvil Plunge is in the hill country near the northern end of the valley that holds the Sin Mire Swamp. The temple is an aboveground complex dedicated to Dargath, the craftsman god of the dwarves. The hamlet is surrounded by a tall, thick stone wall with guard towers at both the north and south gates. Visitors are admitted easily during the day, but the gates are closed at dusk and absolutely not opened again until dawn. Warehouses and stables line most of the inside of the wall; a general store is also located there. Barracks and houses sit in an inner circle of buildings. The shrines that make up the temple itself are in the center of the compound. Everyone in town is either a clerical follower of Dargath or at least a laborer in the service of the temple.

REFERENCE SOURCE: SPLINTERS OF FAITH 2: BURNING DESIRES

BARGARSPORT, CITY OF

Ruler: Mayor Berkoff Keleston
Government: mayor and city elders
Population: 10,484 (6,839 various human ethnicity, 840 dwarf, 730 half-orc, 630 half-elf, 525 orc, 420 gnome, 400 halfling, 100 high elf)

Bargarsport is a trade city located on the delta of the Wahr River along the Reaping Coast. Originally founded by settlers from Castorhage, an earlier version of the city drowned when a powerful tsunami rushed ashore and covered the people and structures in layers of silt and sludge. The trading company abandoned its investment at that point, deeming it pointless to throw good money after bad.

However, several years later the city was rebuilt, bit by bit, by residents determined to have their home back regardless of the opinion of a soulless company of Castorhage. The survivors built over the ruins of the earlier city that was now hidden in the soft mud of the delta, but they didn't completely forget that older city. Instead, they put the buried buildings to good use as the new city's sewers. Sunken buildings now carry the waste from the aboveground structures out to sea through an elaborate sewer network formed from homes, temples, and warehouses that stretches under much of the city.

Bargarsport is now once again bustling, though it is not as prosperous as it was previously. Instead, after its chaotic interlude, it has become a nearly lawless city where almost anything goes. No questions are asked, but much information is available — for a price. Many whisper that the powerful Alantyr family, which controls most of the importing and exporting, has its hand in the illegal trade as well. The official government is said to be on their payroll, and the only significant opposition is from the clergy of Ayianna, a minor goddess of luck who has been the city's patron deity. Her worship is literally underground, in a temple hidden somewhere in the inundated undercity where a host of worshippers gather to report on the goings-on in the city above.

REFERENCE SOURCE: SPLINTERS OF FAITH 3: CULVERT OPERATIONS

BUCKFORT

Ruler: Viobella Alivan, Factor
Government: Sun Coast Company agent
Population: 789 (630 Castorhagi, 135 other human ethnicity, 24 other)

Buckfort was founded by Castorhage's Sun Coast Trading Company to provide a port for large ships to dock and receive goods from the smaller ships needed to make port at the narrow, rocky harbor of Hillport. Both Sun Coast ships and others (for a fee paid to the company) use Buckfort for this purpose, making Buckfort a reasonably busy transshipping location. However, some ships still bypass Buckfort and anchor near Hillport, using that town's small ships to load and unload cargo at sea. This has reduced the profits the Company had hoped to make. They are currently looking for a way to take over the shipping business directly out of Hillport or perhaps even gain control over the town itself.

CHISELKNOLL

Ruler: Factor Malorette Berdmarstan
Government: administered by Royal East Libynos Trading Company
Population: 564 (488 Castorhagi, 65 other human ethnicity, 11 other)

This heavily fortified town sits near the top of the escarpment that separates the high Kanderi Desert from the Ambicuaria Jungle below. The height of the cliff here is about 500 feet, and steps and ledges carved into the stone wall — apparently using magic — facilitate climbing from the jungle below. For more than 300 years, Castorhagi expeditions have gone out from Chiselknoll to explore the ruins scattered across the desert. In some cases, these have comprised extensive archeological investigations that carefully uncovered and catalogued the remnants of people long gone. Under other supervisors, they have been little more than a quick toss for anything of current value. In all cases, most items of interest, of whatever size, have been removed to Castorhage, where they now decorate a public building or the home of some wealthy sponsor or purchaser. Expeditions from Chiselknoll never enter the desert without a large guard force and abundant supplies. When that is not possible (for financial or other reasons), explorers instead spend time studying and analyzing their findings or revisiting the area between Chiselknoll and Sowbury.

CHOLOGADI, TOWN OF

Ruler: Council Leader Mareatha Parkamlan
Government: council of five
Population: 1,871 (1,130 Foerdewaith, 553 other human ethnicity, 35 halfling, 20 dwarf, 18 gnome, 15 half-elf, 100 other)

Foerdewaith explorers established Chologadi centuries ago to serve as a frontier fort at the edge of the Ambicuaria Jungle. The town now primarily serves explorers, trappers, and traders. It has a decent port, and local traders are actively searching for a wider variety of goods to offer to counter the dangers experienced by ships sailing in the area. The council has arranged alliances with some local tribes, but the ties are tenuous. They are strengthened when, from time to time, several of the region's cannibalistic groups band together and try to eradicate any who refuse to join them; such circumstances remind both town and tribes of the value of combining resources.

REFERENCE SOURCES: ONS1 ONE NIGHT STANDS OR JUNGLE RUINS OF MADARO-SHANTI FROM QUESTS OF DOOM 2

CROMBLEHOLME, VILLAGE OF

Ruler: Governor Alcarascu
Government: typically a conclave of village elders, now ruled by the governor
Population: 90 (81 human, 5 half-elf, 4 elf [all female?])

Nestled just at the treeline in the Hollow Spire Mountains is the small village of Crombleholme, which is built upon small cliffs around cascading waterfalls about a half mile below the horrid structure of Abhor Brazier. A switchback road leads from the verdant valley to Abhor Brazier's brass gates. Dilapidated stone buildings lie mostly in ruin, and gardens of artichokes, fig trees, and grape vines surround the quiet village. The inhabitants tirelessly cultivate the crops and ferment the succulent grapes to produce a fine local wine.

Nearly forgotten by those outside the Hollow Spire Mountains, Crombleholme's out-of-the-way, idyllic setting turned into a nightmare when the fires of Abhor Brazier were re-lit. Now, the village is ruled by a merciless governor and cleric of Hecate that some claim is not human at all (although no one has seen her to confirm this tale). The villagers (all women now, as the men were put to death when the governor took over) tend to their assigned chores with little say in the matter. Some say they seem to be lost in a trance.

The village's one claim to fame is the abundance of hag stones — small rocks with holes bored naturally through them — that are found in the area. Many wear these small stones on leather straps around their necks to ward off evil hags.

DOAN, TOWN OF

Ruler: Mayor Greda Piltar
Government: mayor, by acclaim
Population: 832 (670 human, 125 half-elf, 25 halfling, 12 high elf)

This small town lies on the edge of an active caldera near the southern end of the Darikeer Peaks, a spur of the Hollow Spire Mountains. After the nearby supervolcano exploded — with the blast ripping upward out of the land since no one knew of the volcanic activity going on under their feet — the land dropped into the volcano's crater to form the current caldera.

Unfortunately, the edge of the dropoff ran through the middle of Doan, which resulted in half the town falling into the crater. The remaining town of Doan now leads a precarious existence as it balances on the edge of oblivion on the rim of the crater. Abandoned half-buildings still stand along the edge of the sinkhole in Doan, and a stair built of broken stones from the ruined portion of the town allow people to go up and down the side of the caldera. A wooden palisade guards the small town on the land side. The mayor, Greda Piltar, is a tough former adventurer who threatens to toss troublemakers into the sinkhole, and she looks more than capable of following through with this threat.

The city offers what aid it can to support the nearby temple to Ninevah, Goddess of Elements, that was re-founded among the geysers spewing upward throughout the dangerous caldera. A remarkable statue of shifting mercury stands in the middle of Doan and depicts Ninevah. The statue is composed of mercury that flows and changes shape throughout the day. The statue's most common form shows Ninevah standing atop a spur of rock surrounded by an ever-changing cloud of steam and spraying water.

REFERENCE SOURCE: SPLINTERS OF FAITH 8: PAINS OF SCALDED GLASS

ESTALLIA ISLAND

Capital: Goullave
Ruler: Exarch Madelena-Guntroda of Hacienda Texedor
Government: exarch (regional governor) appointed by queen of Alcaldar
Population: 28,250 (19,800 Littoric, 6,090 Alcaldrich, 2,060 other human ethnicity, 300 other)

An island in the Reaping Sea off the coast of the Ambicuaria Jungle, Estallia is a colony of the Empire of Alcaldar. After one of Castorhage's ships accidentally found its way to the small island during a storm and the company members aboard the vessel pressured the islanders to become a holding of the city-state, the people of Estallia Island instead responded positively to overtures from Alcaldar. It has been more than 90 years since the hereditary chieftain resigned and Estallia came under the empire's protection. Although there has been friction, the people of the island believe things certainly would have been worse if one of the trading companies of Castorhage had taken charge instead. Formerly known as Ixtal'a, the island's name was smoothed into something more harmonious to Alcaldrich ears after its annexation.

Nutmeg has long grown on Estallia, and since joining Alcaldar this has become the island's primary export. Connoisseurs claim Estallian nutmeg has a distinctive flavor, which has made it both popular and valuable. The island nation's secondary means of support is, of course, fishing.

The capital of Goullave is a town of more than 3,000 people at the southern end of the island, and Estallia has a few other towns and villages as well. The Alcaldrich started a small port town of their own at the northern end of the island. Granvilla, as they named it, has about 500 residents.

FORT WALLBERG, RUINS OF

Population: 0

The rubble of Fort Wallberg lies near the top of a 2,000-foot-tall dry waterfall, with switchback steps and ledges carved into the stone apparently by magic. The fort was used for many years as the base for profitable Castorhagi exploration of the ruined cities in the Kanderi Desert before it was overrun and taken by a coalition of desert bands. Eventually, the Castorhagi took it back with much loss of life, but just a few years later the desert-dwellers attacked again and this time utterly destroyed it. Without that base and given the strenuous opposition by the desert bands, the Castorhagi abandoned their exploration of the central desert and concentrated on approaching at Chiselknoll from the north instead.

HANGING GARDENS OF ISELEINE

Ruler: High Priest Jernigan Chimel
Government: Church of Iseleine, Matron of Peace
Population: 109 (various human ethnicity)

The Hanging Gardens of Iseleine are a center of worship consisting of vast gardens located in the north-central part of the dense Kajaani Forest. The primary temple, a sparkling edifice of glass and stone, sits among carefully cultivated gardens atop a granite pillar. The pillar itself rises from a steep chasm a quarter-mile deep and a quarter-mile wide in the forest, and the entire floor of the sinkhole is filled with verdant plant life. Even from the rim of the chasm, it is easy to see that the gardens below must be cultivated as well, because there are masses of single-colored flowers, and patterns appear in the interplay between the green and the blooming colors. A single stone bridge arches the 600 feet from the plateau to the western rim of the chasm. A long, carved stairway is also visible and winds around the granite pillar until it is lost in the mist rising from the lower garden.

REFERENCE SOURCE: SPLINTERS OF FAITH 4: FOR LOVE OF CHAOS

HILLPORT, TOWN OF

Ruler: Mistress Norallo Edameme, Head of the Traders' Council
Government: oligarchy of merchants, the Traders' Council
Population: 3,024 (2,875 various human ethnicity, 110 Castorhagi, 39 other)

Hillport sits at the confluence of the Rodenno and Quell rivers in the rough foothills that run from the Hollow Spire Mountains down to the sea. It lies on a small bay, protected by the rocky hills from the storms that pound the Reaping Sea. The town has a standing guard force and a strong volunteer guard, and is also surrounded by a strong wooden palisade. A regular sentence for any prisoners (for being drunk and disorderly, for example) is to spend a certain number of hours outside the palisade clearing brush from the town's perimeter.

Hillport was built primarily to allow traders access to products from the interior of the Kajaani Forest, the Hollow Spire Mountains, and the Seething Jungle. Unfortunately, the small bay near the rivers' mouth is almost as rocky as the surrounding foothills, which makes navigation to the port difficult. The town provides guide boats, but still only small ships are willing to come in to the port and they are never frequent enough for the amount of trade the town desires. The Traders' Council has a plan to encourage more ships to call at Hillport; they hired a bard (Grenhenbe Woribo) to travel to other area ports (such as Bargarsport, Jah Sezar, and Storm Haven to the east, and Buckport, Sunport, and Ollanshire to the south) and talk up the advantages of Hillport to the captains there.

JAH SEZAR, ISLAND CITY OF

Ruler: Governor Ghajden Shyd
Government: Church of Thasizier, with the high priestess, Ayire Jaysa, Master Scholar of the Mystic Erudite
Population: 43,118 (23,750 various human ethnicity, 12,950 high elf, 4,300 half-elf, 1,300 dwarf, 430 gnome, 358 halfling, 30 other)

The city of Jah Sezar covers the majority of an island in the Reaping Sea. Long piers extend off the island to allow a multitude of ships to dock during the sometimes-violent storms that sweep over the waters. The center of the island rises in a peak that reaches more than 2,500 feet above sea level. Buildings perch on the slopes of the massive peak amid a lush, tropical setting while cobblestone streets provide ample walkways up and down the hill. The people are very welcoming and kindhearted.

Sitting atop the central peak is the city's most famous landmark: the Theurgist Seminary of Thasizier. The temple's dome lights each night and can be seen for many miles out to sea; it casts a warm glow over the city and acts as a beacon to passing ships.

Crime in Jah Sezar is almost nonexistent thanks largely to the presence of the temple's priests working with the city's populace. During the day, apprentices and volunteers fan out through the city to assist the poor and to clean the neighborhoods that spread down the massive peak like sprawling ivy. Apprentices clean the seminary's walls using spells and offer their magical talent to keep other buildings sparkling as well. The city's residents appreciate the apprentices' efforts and feel a great deal of loyalty toward the clergy. In addition, the majority of the seminary's occupants are skilled spellcasters with years of adventuring under their belts, and they are very fond of the city of Jah Sezar. Most have little tolerance for evil deeds or discord within the beautiful city.

The island gets most of its supplies by ship, though careful householders are able grow a good deal of produce. Trade goods from Jah Sezar tend to be specialized or skilled items such as maps and charts, copies of rare books, or sheets of music. The population also includes many scholars and sages who can be hired (in person or by writing) to do research on particular topics in the seminary's extensive library. In fact, spellcasters of all races and types travel from hundreds of miles away to pay homage to the mage of divinity and to peruse the immeasurable underground library housed in halls and chambers that honeycomb the island's peak, and catering to their needs is an important industry on the island.

REFERENCE SOURCE: SPLINTERS OF FAITH 9: DUEL OF MAGIC

LESSEF, HAMLET OF

Ruler: none; guided by Almery Burgand, priest of Freya
Government: none
Population: 24 (mixed human ethnicity)

Lessef sits beside a dirt road connecting the cities of Storm Haven and Bargarsport, not far from the coast of the Reaping Sea. The hamlet lies at the base of a knoll, the only peak for 20 miles in any direction in the flat farmland, upon which sits a small, whitewashed church, Lessef's only true landmark. Called Poverty's Bethel, the shrine to Freya serves as a community center, temple, and shelter from the occasional dangers of the plains. A cemetery dating back hundreds of years surrounds the church with the broken monuments littering the hillside; the priest's house stands behind the shrine.

Several years ago, some of the elders hired an out-of-towner to help keep the town safe. Sheriff Dreng is more of a bully than anything, however, and makes up laws on a whim to keep residents in line. In the absence of a real government, most townsfolk turn to Almery Burgand for guidance.

A one-room tavern named the Pebble (but known locally as Scaby's Shack) is the only business left in town and survives by selling only the cheapest ale. A few farmers hide stills in abandoned houses, but Sheriff Dreng turns a blind eye to these if he's paid a fee to look the other way.

A massive — and decisive — battle during the War of Divine Discord was fought on the land that eventually became Lessef. Farmers still turn up truly ancient weapons or tools as they till their fields.

REFERENCE SOURCE: SPLINTERS OF FAITH 1: IT STARTED WITH A CHICKEN

LUNDALE

Ruler: Senior Factor Marvisa Toralino
Government: administered by Royal East Libynos Trading Company
Population: 10,088 (7,785 Castorhagi, 1,250 Littoric, 950 other human ethnicity, 103 other)

Located at the mouth of the King Prudus River, Lundale is the oldest Castorhagi city still active along the Reaping Coast. When Castorhage first began to build colonies in the area, many trading companies started settlements but not all were able to keep them up at such a distance. The most effective was the Royal East Libynos Trading Company, and even it had its setbacks. Lundale is now the largest city along the coast of the Ambicuaria Jungle and a major port of call for Castorhagi ships traveling up and down the east coast of Libynos.

MADARO-SHANTI, RUINS OF

Population: 0

Madaro-Shanti was once a powerful city-state that was highly advanced in magic and other arts. Jealous of its prosperity, a nearby tribe of sorcerers plotted its downfall. Within a few weeks, the city's inhabitants and its opponents killed each other off, most say with deadly magics. Any survivors fled the area, and the ruined city was left to the jungle. That was more than 100 years ago. Rumor is that many of the city's greater magic items were too difficult to carry off and so the survivors left them behind, but some explorers who have gone that way claim Madaro-Shanti is now cursed. In any case, no verified finds have yet shown up in the nearby port town of Chologadi.

REFERENCE SOURCES: ONS1 ONE NIGHT STANDS or JUNGLE RUINS OF MADARO-SHANTI FROM QUESTS OF DOOM 2

MAGADIPAN, TEMPLE-CITY OF

Ruler: High Hanu-priest Bezdionis
Government: Church of Pertikudeo
Population: 989 (521 Littoric, 310 half-orc, 135 hanu-naga, 23 awakened ape)

Until the fall of the nearby city of Madaro-Shanti a century or more past, the sect of the evil monkey-god Pertikudeo had remained hidden for fear of that city's wizards. The sect grew in the last hundred years — first quietly and then more openly — in the venerable temple-city of Magadipan, until now a town of almost 1,000 creatures spreads through the jungle around the edifice recently claimed by the monkey-god's worshippers. The population is mostly human or half-orc but also includes a significant group of hanu-naga and several awakened apes who act primarily as guards. One resource that supports the population is a deep well that taps into a seemingly endless underground spring.

The temple itself is ancient and towers above the low buildings of the town, but there is no doubt its carvers were friendly to monkeys as those animals can be seen peeking around columns and between leafy vines, and lines of carved monkeys march across the lintels of the doors and windows. The interior suggests that the temple may originally have been dedicated to a different power, as an ornate wall mosaic in the main room has been partially broken so all that remains is the lower part of a blue robe with a dark hand resting on a knee and several monkeys cavorting around a sandaled foot.

Recently the priests gathered several of the local tribes into the area by performing "miracles," supposedly by the power of their vile trickster deity. The rare traveler who manages to both find the town and also leave again can only speculate whether this gathering presages a substantial building program, upcoming mass sacrifices, or preparation for war.

MELLIMARI, TOWN OF

Ruler: Song-elder Arzanic Tojembe
Government: elder appointed by previous elder
Population: 895 (620 Littoric, 210 Foerdewaith, 65 other human ethnicity)

The small town of Mellimari sits on the Lesser Vahari River close to where the river divides into two branches on its way to the sea. The town is a mixture of indigenous inhabitants and descendants of Foerdewaith settlers who wanted to be out of their fortress and more part of the jungle. The townspeople cut timber and send huge logs downriver to the town of Chologadi, where it is processed for sale to traders from distant locations. They use some of the softer woods to produce elaborate carvings such as stylized jungle animals, exotic blossoms, and fantastic creatures from their ancestral stories.

Mellimari is led by an elder who sings the traditional stories while the others work, and gives judgments on conflicts based on nuggets of wisdom found in the stories. Arzanic Tojembe, the current elder, is 22 and has been in his position for only two years, so he is somewhat unsure of his leadership and may be intimidated by forceful strangers. His people consider him wise for his age and their legitimate leader, and encourage him to make good decisions for the town.

Although not a wealthy town, Mellimari is in an advantageous position for easy access to food and water so its people are generally well-fed and satisfied. This also makes it a good location for resupply on trips farther into the jungle.

OLLANSHIRE

Ruler: Adecolm Ollantyr, or Maret Sutley, his adjutant
Government: autocracy
Population: 278 (215 Castorhagi, 63 other human ethnicity)

Ollanshire is an attempt by Adecolm Ollantyr, an extremely wealthy investor in the Castorhagi Sun Coast Trading Company, to found his own town and develop it exactly as he wanted. The start was favorable, and he was able to convince many from Castorhage to move to this new location. Not everyone was happy with the arrival of the foreigners, however, including two nearby tribes of the Seething Jungle. In the past 10 years, Ollantyr has invested significantly more than he had planned in fortifications and guards for his town (which is barely bigger than a village), but at least the soldiers are happy to bring or start families, which increases the population. Ollantyr was hoping to see a profit by now, but despite his excellent port facilities, trying to ship the area's plentiful fresh fruit hasn't gone well. He now has his townspeople finding ways to preserve or use the fruit such that the products are still inexpensive to make but can easily be shipped back to Castorhage. (Exotic fruit liqueurs are his favorite result so far.) Ollantyr is also hoping to recruit some people to explore the interior of his colony, but so far word of the hostile tribes has kept people away.

QUAWNOT, VILLAGE OF

Ruler: King Waldron
Government: monarchy
Population: 135 (barbegazi)

This village of barbegazi (ice gnomes) used to live in pueblo-style homes built in caves inside the wall of the Wailing Glacier, high in the Hollow Spire Mountains. The small glacier's recent increased melting rate devastated the ice village when a large portion of the wall broke off. The gnomes now live in a makeshift community of stone and mud that is subject to the elements and vulnerable to attack by some of the large flying creatures that also live in the area. Scouts have been sent to search for a suitable new location in the mountains, but until they return, the villagers scour the muddy plain in front of the glacier for anything they can use and get under cover at the sight of any threat. If approached in a peaceable manner, the barbegazi willingly trade for food or weapons, or provide local information in return for any help.

REFERENCE SOURCE: SPLINTERS OF FAITH 6: MORNING OF TEARS

SHIELDFANE, CITY OF

Ruler: Mayor Kintus Hallete
Government: overseen by high priest of Shield Basilica of Muir, currently High Priest Lord Romel Sandusk
Population: 6,309 (3,915 various human ethnicity, 885 high elf, 505 dwarf, 380 half-elf, 255 gnome, 245 halfling, 124 half-orc)

The city of Shieldfane is built against the southern wall of the Shield Basilica of Muir. Those hoping to join the order of paladins, or those desiring the protection of a patrolled area in the middle of a wilderness, congregate here. It is primarily a trading post, with companies providing supplies for the Shield Basilica but also for adventurers, prospectors, and others eking out a living in the area. A small defense force protects the city from domestic troubles, with most members hoping to gain the positive attention of Muir's paladins through their actions.

The Shield Basilica of Muir was founded to protect the more-settled areas of the south from repeated invasions of humanoid armies from the Kanderi Desert. With the fortress physically blocking the way for armies (though small groups of travelers can still get through), the Shield Basilica has not had to go to war in many years. It is gradually transitioning to a training center for Muir's faithful.

REFERENCE SOURCE: SPLINTERS OF FAITH 7: THE HEIR OF SIN

SOWBURY

Ruler: Factor Warthan Harlix
Government: administered by Royal East Libynos Trading Company
Population: 4,563 (4,018 Castorhagi, 230 Littoric, 210 other human ethnicity, 105 other)

Founded after the destruction of Fort Wallberg to support Castorhagi expeditions into the northern part of the Kanderi Desert, Sowbury is more than 400 years old, but never grew beyond about 5,000 people, and even diminished in the last several decades. Its presence enabled the Royal East Libynos Trading Company to spread smaller settlements north along the coast. The city has a modest harbor and trades antiquities from the desert as well as products from the nearby settlements and the natives of the jungle, but Sowbury has never been the major port that Lundale is now.

STORM HAVEN, TOWN OF

Ruler: Mayor Anton Sidhall
Government: elected mayor
Population: 597 (525 various human ethnicity, 72 other)

The small town of Storm Haven is a port on a river delta fed by the Goltray River. Just two miles upriver, the river exits the Canyons of Arcuri through which it runs for more than 20 miles between 500-foot-tall stone cliffsides that surround the waterway.

While not a major trade stop, frequent storms along the coast force many ships into port here to seek shelter or repairs. Storm Haven is protected from the high waves of the ocean by an offshore coral reef, and is usually home for 15 to 30 ships that ply the dangerous waters of the Reaping Sea. Piers extend throughout Storm Haven, with the biggest along the seafront to anchor merchant vessels. Other piers along the delta entrances allow smaller vessels to moor safely inland. Overall, 60 ships can moor at the piers.

Throughout town, 20-foot-tall spikes rise from buildings and jut up from the streets. Townsfolk erected the spikes after a roc from the nearby canyons snatched a small boat and dropped it on the inn. The spikes and ballistae around town prevent the giant birds from snatching away sailors, cattle, and more small boats.

Storm Haven is a place where no one cares what you did previously in life; they only care about what you can do to help the town now. The community values fishing, net mending, and ship repair, and some of the best at these skills hang signs on pier-front businesses. Would-be laborers wander the docks when new ships arrive and offer to unload a current catch or seek work on the voyage out. A handful of arrivals seek riches, and legends of diamonds as big as a fist to be found in the canyons up the Goltray River are common. However, most treasure seekers who enter the narrow region between the imposing cliffs fail to return.

REFERENCE SOURCES: GLADES OF DEATH OR CANYONS OF ARCURI IN QUESTS OF DOOM 3

SUNPORT

Ruler: Mayor Malagar Kydrolin
Government: mayor and advisory council
Population: 1,012 (855 various human ethnicity, 130 Castorhagi, 27 other)

This port at the mouth of the River of Fortune in far southern Libynos is in the process of trying to grow from a fort and small settlement (tightly run by a trading company for more than 50 years) into an actual town, and the process is full of growing pains. The elected mayor finds his authority undermined by the local factor of the Sun Coast Trading Company, who is annoyed that independent trading ships calling at the recently improved port occasionally crowd out scheduled Sun Coast vessels. In the meantime, residents newly arrived from other parts of the Reaping Coast resent how much influence Sun Coast has over many aspects of life. Both the company and the long-term residents agree, though, that things will go more smoothly if the company doesn't have to look after all the town's issues anymore. Meanwhile, the years of development have settled into a steady stream of valuable products shipping out from the port.

Zendeth-Jan, Ruins of

Population: 0

Northeast of the Hollow Spire Mountains, in the southern part of the Kanderi Desert, Zendeth-Jan is typical of the ruins that lie scattered about the region. The remains of certain large buildings can still be seen, while other sections of the once-great city may either be revealed by the scouring winds, or buried deep beneath hard-packed dirt or shifting sand. One notable structure is the partial wall of a large building with a domed roof, possibly an arena or other type of public venue. Another is a six-sided ziggurat that looks as if it has been fought over several times. One low area collects water in the rainy season and supports enough plant-life to hold the moisture longer than other places; this watering hole attracts herd animals and the occasional predator. Otherwise, the ruins are inhabited by a variety of desert creatures, most of them dangerous, and sometimes roving bands of humans or humanoids.

Reference Source: Splinters of Faith 5: Eclipse of the Hearth

Geographic Features and Points of Interest in the Reaping Coast

Ambicuaria Jungle

Found at the eastern extent of southern Libynos, the Ambicuaria Jungle includes thickly forested hills and swamps along 600 miles of coastline from the shore of the Reaping Sea inland for more than 200 miles. It receives severe rains during the summer monsoon season and tends to be drier during the winter, but is hot at all times of the year. Its inhabitants are mostly scattered tribes of indigenous people in small towns and villages in the interior. The population becomes even more sparse in the western part of the jungle, where it nears the steep escarpment falling from the cursed Kanderi Desert. This escarpment reaches 3,000 feet at the southern extent, where it separates from the Eastern Spire Peaks, but decreases to a mere 100 feet at the other end, 400 miles north. Along the coast are towns and settlements that have been developed as colonies of other countries, including Castorhage and the westerners of the Crusader Coast. Having a long history of human habitation (apparently going back to some advanced civilizations thousands of years ago), ruins are plentiful and draw explorers.

Beharrel Valleys

North and east of the Quell River, the Seething Jungle intersects with the badlands that are the western foothills of the Hollow Spire Mountains. This area is littered with deep crevasses and plagued by volcanic activity, and the heat and humidity push the temperature to dangerous levels. This primordial section of the Seething Jungle teems with creatures and plants, some lingering from the untold past. It appears that some locations must be also tainted with evil, as stories are sometimes told of vile, twisted beasts that roam the jungle.

Reference Source: Splinters of Faith 10: Remorse of Life

Canyons of Arcuri

Over centuries, the Goltray River and its tributaries carved the Canyons of Acuri through rock as the river approached its mouth on the Reaping Sea. The waterway now runs for nearly 20 miles between 500-foot-high cliffs that are just 40 feet apart in some places. In wider areas of the canyon (where the walls are around 600 feet apart), the rushing river fills much of the canyon floor. The Goltray finally exits the canyon just two miles west of the town of Storm Haven where it empties into the Reaping Sea.

Within the canyon, paths along the sides of the river are hidden in the shadows of the high cliffs and thick jungle trees that rise to heights of 150 and 200 feet from the canyon floor. A secondary canopy of trees about 60 feet tall is below the higher treetops, and vines hang thickly from the stout branches. The double canopies and high cliffs leave the river and canyon floor in perpetual near-darkness. The thick foliage also traps moisture as it creates a dense hothouse of humid air along the surface of the Goltray River. Most of the canyon floor is in twilight during the day and complete darkness at night, and a person under the canopy may not even be able to see the canyon walls because of the thick trees.

Along the river (and in openings in the canopy where the sun reaches the ground), palm shrubs and bamboo palms grow thickly, as well as many other jungle plants that thrive on moisture. The dense growths along the river and in the canopy are also home to multitudes of wild creatures, some of which are rarely seen in other areas. The high walls of the canyons are said to be riddled with caves, and the rumor in Storm Haven is that an explorer found diamonds inside a certain cave, including one the size of his fist.

A small village called Arden's Grove is built among the branches of massive trees in a side branch of the canyon. The village is many centuries old, and its people stay to their high paths due to the dangers found on the canyon floor below. The folk of the town believe that it is named after a nearby tree spirit. Once the village had two parts spanned by a mighty tree bridge, but the other half was lost a few years ago to a clan of bugbears. These creatures continue to inhabit the portion they conquered and look for ways to force the humans out of the rest of the village. With so much of their attention taken up guarding against the bugbears, the people of Arden's Grove are reduced almost to subsistence living.

*Reference Source: Glades of Death
or Canyons of Arcuri from Quests of Doom 3*

Daglaroke Mountains

This small cluster of mountains sits off the Reaping Coast in the Ambicuaria Jungle north of the town of Chologadi. The steep slopes undergo frequent rock falls that make living in the area dangerous. It is the home mostly of goatherders and intrepid souls who climb the peaks looking for raptor eggs and other rare substances. Prospectors also traverse the mountains as they search for veins of valuable minerals or sources of gems. Rumor says that the mountains held a source of sapphires in the distant past, but that has been lost (or possibly mined out) for generations. The peaks are honeycombed with caves, some large enough for entire villages. Within these mountains is a high-altitude lake whose waters pour over a 300-hundred-foot high waterfall, the source of the fast-flowing Yenbe-le River.

Darikeer Peaks

The Darikeer Peaks are a spur of the Hollow Spire Mountains that lies between the Kriegh Forest to the west and the Kajaani Forest to the east. The peaks are distinguished by their shale and granite cliffs. The area was at one time known for its deep coal mines but they have been abandoned now for hundreds of years. The town of Doan, which sits on the edge of a volcanic caldera, can be found at the southern end of these peaks.

Eastern Spire Peaks

This range of mountains is an eastern spur of the Hollow Spire Mountains and forms the southeastern boundary of the Kanderi Desert. The southern slopes are home to various types of mountain goats and predatory birds, including eagles and hawks, and give rise to the headwaters of the Wahr River. The northern slopes, facing the desert, are largely barren and wind-scoured.

Fortune, River of

This river found in southern Libynos runs from the Kulgera Ridge through the southern part of the Seething Jungle and enters the Reaping Sea at the Castorhagi town of Sunport. Despite frustrating setbacks and even tragedies during implementation, well-protected supply depots for traders and prospectors are set about every 50 miles along the river, the better to enable profitable exploitation of the jungle interior.

GOLTRAY RIVER

The Goltray River flows from deep in the Va'apor Foothills into the Canyons of Arcuri on its way toward the Reaping Sea. Small tributaries run from narrow side canyons to join the main branch, which widens to 300 feet at its widest point. Leaving the canyons just two miles from the coast, the Goltray branches out into a multi-streamed delta at its mouth, where the town of Storm Haven sits on islands among the stream. The Goltray is sometimes called "The River of Veins" because of its numerous tiny tributaries, but also because the clay and silt in the water turn it a muddy red.

HOLLOW SPIRE MOUNTAINS

The Hollow Spire Mountains are in the heart of southern Libynos. To the east of the range lies the Ambicuaria Jungle. To the north is the Kanderi Desert, and in the south are the Kriegh Forest and the Kajaani Forest, each between arms of the mountain range. To the west and southwest is the Seething Jungle.

In general, these mountain peaks are high and cold, despite their southerly location, and the high elevations are inhabited by many cold-loving creatures. The strong storms that lash the jungle become snowstorms among the peaks and produce heavy snowfall that never really melts, making travel at high altitudes very difficult. The Hollow Spires get their name because the entire range is riddled with caves, chambers, and passageways. Rumors say these caverns are home not only to clans of dwarves, but also to rock-dwelling gnomes and many darker groups of creatures.

JELEMBUL VOLCANO

Jelembul is a peak in the Daglaroke Mountains. It lets off steam or smoke at irregular intervals, often enough that the locals pay attention but not so often that they seriously think the volcano is ready to erupt. People rarely go onto the flanks of the cone, as noxious (and sometimes dangerous) fumes vent from frequent cracks. Once in a while at night, lightning can be seen in the dark cloud over the peak; superstitious locals explain this as the fire demon in the volcano fighting off an attack by the sky god. Others claim some type of huge flame creature has a forge inside the volcano, and those are the sparks struck off its anvil.

KAJAANI FOREST

The Kajaani Forest is located between two arms of the Hollow Spire Mountains, its verges reaching up the slopes to the treeline. At higher elevations, conifers and other evergreens predominate, while the lower elevations consist of subtropical forest. The land between the mountain spurs slopes down in ridges toward the center, falling off even more quickly at it approaches the Reaping Sea at its southern end. On the west lies the Rodenno River, and on the east are the Wahr River and one of its tributaries. To the north, a long, dangerous pass through the mountains leads to the Kanderi Desert.

KANDERI DESERT

The Kanderi Desert was once a well-watered area, as evidenced by its numerous dry watercourses. One deep riverbed runs for hundreds of miles across the desert, all the way to its eastern edge where a deep escarpment drops to the jungle below. What happened thousands of years ago to cause this once-fertile plain to deteriorate to badlands and barren desert is unclear, but the ruins of abandoned cities and villages that dot the landscape suggest it was swift and severe. Some rain does fall in the desert in certain seasons, but any waterholes in low-lying places dry up quickly, and as a consequence the locations where water is available from underground (in a few small lakes, or some deep wells) are zealously guarded and vigorously fought over by the bands of people that do still call the Kanderi home. (Stories say the deep desert population includes an extremely reclusive tribe of sand elves, but most think that just a legend.) The Kanderi Desert is considered to be part of the Reaping Coast, though the hundreds of miles of the Ambicuaria Jungle to its east separate it from the ocean.

KING PRUDUS RIVER

This river is named after the Castorhagi king who supported the First Crusade for Tircople and received in thanks the right to colonize the eastern coast of Libynos. It runs from the eastern edge of the Eastern Spire Peaks northeast across the Ambicuaria Jungle to the coast of the northern Reaping Sea and the colony of Lundale. About 250 miles from the ocean, the King Prudus breaks into the deep bed of an ancient river, one that apparently once fell from the desert high above but is long dry, and follows that to the sea.

KRIEGH FOREST

This forest is in the western part of the Hollow Spire Mountains, between the spur called the Darikeer Peaks and the western branch of the mountains. It lies on a high, cool plateau and so consists mostly of varieties of pine trees. The forest is isolated enough that it is almost unknown to outsiders, and the northern part of it has many ancient trees and groves.

PHRYGIA VOLCANO

The massive volcano known as Phrygia stands in the northern Hollow Spire Mountains and serves as the location of Crombleholme (at its base) and the insidious temple of Abhor Brazier (14,000 feet above sea level on the side of its smoldering cone). Phrygia shakes and shudders occasionally (more frequently now, it seems, after the horrible fires of Abhor Brazier were re-lit) but few can remember the last time the volcano erupted. Visitors to Crombleholme claim that searing streams flow out of cracks at the base of the volcano, waterways that eventually cool and provide nutrient-rich water for the surrounding land. Many say the water tastes funny, however, although they can't remember why they feel that way.

QUELL RIVER

The Quell River rises deep in the Seething Jungle and wends its way through the foothills and badlands of the Hollow Spire Mountains on its way to the Reaping Sea at the town of Hillport.

The river boasts a variety of freshwater fish, but due to the numerous water snakes, the fish are not as plentiful as they are in some tropical rivers. Travel on the Quell offers an easy and comparatively fast route through the jungle (upstream as well as down), and many villages are located on its banks. The Quell is the route most used by explorers and adventurers trying to travel farther into the jungle, but the dangers overall mean that few get farther west than the fork where the river comes from the north and meets its main tributary, the Totono, coming from the south.

REAPING SEA

This sea curves around the east and southeast coasts of southern Libynos and is part of Mother Oceanus, the great southern ocean. The sea is prone to storms and frequently lashed by hurricane-strength winds; those who wish to trade along its coast must choose their seasons for travel carefully to avoid the worst of the weather. Its southern waters are calmer, with hurricanes being practically unknown along the Reaping Sea's equator-spanning west coast.

RODENNO RIVER

The Rodenno River arises from melt from the glaciers capping the central Hollow Spire Mountains and flows south along the eastern eaves of the Darikeer Peaks, where it is joined by numerous tributaries draining the main valley of the Kajaani Forest. The Rodenno tends to be thick with plants and full of fish. In general, the area along the river is lush and fruitful until it leaves the forest and passes through the rough foothills to the south on its way to its mouth, where it joins the Quell River at the town of Hillport on the Reaping Sea.

SEETHING JUNGLE

This jungle lies in southern Libynos, to the west of the Hollow Spire Mountains and along the southwest coast of the Reaping Sea. Most of the interior is unknown to any but local tribes, though rumors exist of vine-covered ruins deep in the jungle, suggesting the existence of an advanced civilization in ancient times.

The tree canopy is continuous, or nearly so, and allows little sunlight to reach the ground. The verdant canopy is full of animal life, including hundreds of types of birds, dozens of varieties of monkeys and other small climbers, and the ubiquitous tree snakes. Wild boar and deer are plentiful on the jungle floor, as are the jaguars that prey on them, but there, too, snakes are abundant. In fact, the disproportionate population of snakes is part of what gives the Seething Jungle its name, and also makes it so dangerous. Many types are not venomous, but with so many varieties not even the locals can be said to know all of them.

The indigenous people in the eastern part of the Seething Jungle live simple lives in small, rudimentary villages and are generally peaceful. The east-central area of the jungle has an ominous reputation, though, so in reality these gentle people have established themselves in an area where they are unlikely to be pressed by other tribes. Farther south and west, toward the Kulgera Ridge, the tribes are more aggressive, and likely to live in more-sophisticated villages or even towns. They have more contact with travelers from Kaldiloora or Tulyamin and actively participate in trading relationships with these countries. The farthest western portion of the jungle, in the upper part of the Totono River, is home to several groups of tabaxi. The cat-people's range extends across the Kulgera Ridge, where more tabaxi can be found living among the River Peoples.

SIN MIRE SWAMP

The Sin Mire sits in a low area surrounded by an arc of the Va'apor Foothills. In most of the swamp, the silty waters are about five feet deep, but deeper holes, small islands, and flatter fields of grass-covered wetlands are common. Tall trees draped with hanging moss fill the swamp. The Sin River runs out of the mire (and becomes a tributary of the Wahr). The Sin Mire grows a bit more every year, and many believe it is fed by some underground source of water. In actuality, the long-standing dwarven community of Anvil Plunge is the true culprit behind the growing Sin Mire, as a magical decanter used to cool their forges has been draining down the hill from the temple for centuries. Ironically, the dwarves completely fear the dangers of the deep swamp around them, even as they add to its expansion.

Over the years, the Sin Mire swallowed several villages or smaller settlements, and these ruins are scattered throughout the swamp. Rumor says that one of these drowned villages is inhabited by the dead, and that a dragon has taken up residence in another. Travel through the swamp is dangerous and slow and is really best done by boat.

VAHARI RIVER

The Vahari is a slow-running river that starts in the central part of the Ambicuaria Jungle and flows southeast to the Reaping Sea. At some point in the river's past, an earthquake thrust up a sharp promontory of hard rock in the middle of the river, like a ship's prow parting the waves. Rather than turning its channel to one side or the other, the river divides 50 miles from the coast and flows two different directions. The Lesser Vahari runs on the north side of the pinnacle and is joined by a few small tributaries before it reaches the sea near the town of Chologadi. The true Vahari runs south and curls among hills until the land flattens out 20 miles from the sea and its motion slows even further. The water flows into and eventually out of a long swamp on its way to the Reaping Sea through a small delta.

VA'APOR FOOTHILLS

These hills rise along the southeastern slopes of the Eastern Spire Peaks, and then cover more than 400 miles to the Reaping Coast. In the north, the hills merge into the Ambicuaria Jungle, while the range surrounds the Sin Mire to the south and southwest. These hills are the source of several rivers of the Reaping Coast, including the Wahr and the Goltray rivers.

WAHR RIVER

The Wahr River runs down from the southeastern side of the Eastern Spire Mountains, through a valley between the mountains and the Va'apor Foothills, and along the eastern boundary of the Kajaani Forest, to its mouth on the Reaping Sea at Bargarsport. The Sin River (from the Sin Mire) also feeds into the Wahr.

WAILING GLACIER

Local legend says that during an ancient time of evil and darkness, unnatural snow and ice fell high in the Hollow Spire Mountains and a river of ice came down from the peaks, moving faster than should be possible for such a thing. It covered the land all the way to the Reaping Sea and lasted for centuries even after the darkness passed. Eventually it melted, leaving behind strange land formations and boulders the size of huts in the Kajaani Forest. Whether the legend is true or not, the remains of a glacier are still to be found in the heights of the mountains. It is relatively small, and recently its decreased size has caused it to melt even faster, much to the consternation of creatures who make their homes on the ice. Intrepid travelers who have visited the glacier claim it moans when the wind blows, hence its name.

YENBE-LE RIVER

The Yenbe-le falls out of the steep Daglaroke Mountains and moves fast all the way to the Reaping Sea. Daredevil traders gather loads of the valuable products of the mountains and fill small, agile boats for the dangerous but exhilarating trip down the river to the sea. They sell their goods and their boats at the town of Chologadi, just a short journey south along the coast. The traders then purchase lowland supplies and donkeys to carry them, and make the long return trip along the river rather than on it.

SOUTHERN PARAMOUNTCIES

The so-called Southern Paramountcies hark back more than 2,000 years to the time when the exotic lands of extreme southern Libynos were the most distant of the far-flung provinces of the Hyperborean Empire. By the time their soldiers and sailors reached so far, the empire was stretched thin indeed. At that point, they were content to control strategic locations on the coastline and have their subject peoples bring them the riches of the interior. Being the latest settled, the area was also the first abandoned when the times of trouble began later.

Once five imperial provinces, two have been completely lost and the other three are changed beyond all recognition. All that is left of Hyperborea in the region are stone ruins and traditions whose origins have been long forgotten. Only a few people in the area even recall that it was once part of an empire, and none there think of it as "Southern Paramountcies" (that designation survives only in a few former Hyperborean areas outside of Libynos). Instead, the people of the region refer to the "ancient ones" who built their buildings and taught a little of their language, and then left before having a strong impact on the local cultures.

Bordered on the west by the Sinnar Ocean and Mother Oceanus, and on the east by the Reaping Sea, this region encompasses the vast majority of southern Libynos. The terrain varies from clement coastal areas to deep tropical jungle to the high, cold peaks of the Hollow Spire Mountains. One major feature of the west coast is called simply the Delta. The outlet of an extensive network of rivers, it is home to thousands of people who live on or around the water. Both Bhanakhiri and Kaldiloora tried to annex this region in the past but it had no major population center to conquer; when threatened, whole communities just float away. It has been useful enough as a neutral area between the two countries that it now survives unthreatened and at least semi-permanent settlements have developed. The entire Delta is effectively a free-trade area where someone of perseverance truly could buy or sell almost anything.

Castorhage has colonies on the Reaping Coast that were awarded for its assistance in the First Crusade against the Huun at the Sacred Table, and others from Akados also built settlements during the 250 years of the crusades. The degree of integration between colonizers and people indigenous to the area varies, with Castorhage in particular having seen unexpected setbacks in their interactions with some desert and deep jungle tribes.

BHANAKHIRI, OTTIARKY OF

Capital: Dunchamba
Notable Settlements: Gai Zai Yok, Gamphen, Khon Sama, Klah Bakham, Klaung Song, Panaet, Surthani, Tolanua, Varindra, Xonburi
Ruler: Council of Ottiarks: Sasithorn Wi Gom of Jewel, Intira Chana Sing of Silk, Ubon Phrae Savan of Sword, Klahan Tak Jiern of Iron, and Prasert Yok Khla of Gold.
Government: oligarchy
Population: 3,740,796 (3,724,941 Bhanakhiri, 15,627 other human ethnicity, 228 dwarf)
Monstrous: inphidians, tentamorts (jungles), quicklings
Languages: Bhanikhat; Gonidal in the Mengamuk Forest
Religion: Paramountcies pantheon
Resources: silk, cotton, shipbuilding, iron, weapons, precious metals, gems, jewelry
Currency: Bhanakhiran
Technology Level: Renaissance (Dunchamba, Panaet), Medieval (cities and towns), High Middle Ages (rural)

Bhanakhiri is in southern Libynos west of the Hollow Spire Mountains. Its primary cities are along the coast, but various towns and villages dot the interior. The country is run by a group of factions that compete to control various aspects of life and government. Bhanakhiri's currency, the bhan, is readily accepted in most of the surrounding areas.

Bhanakhiri's political and mercantile influence is divided among five factions: Gold, Jewel, Silk, Iron, and Sword. These factions might have begun as guild alliances, but they are much more than that now. The five leaders of the factions form the Council of Ottiarks, which governs the country. The individual ottiarks rule their specific areas of responsibility through their bureaucracies. As corpulence is considered a sign of prosperity and power in Bhanakhiri, most of the ottiarks (and many other rulers or wealthy merchants) are extremely plump. The exception is the unfortunate Prasert Yok Khla, who despite his wealth still practically has the body of a poor farmer. Another way people show their position is through their clothing. The ottiarks (and others who have assistants or servants to do their work for them) usually dress in expensive, colorful outfits with full sleeves, elaborate headpieces, and shoes with exceptionally long toes.

The factions are not concentrated in particular regions of the country; instead towns of various factions are interspersed to give the groups a degree of control in many areas. Cities or regions are governed by factional hexargs who answer to the faction's ottiark. Towns or villages too small to have their own hexargs are part of an area hexargate. (This is not to be confused with a regional hexargate, which is much larger and more prestigious.) Each faction has its own faction city, which holds the faction headquarters and arena and the estate of its ottiark. The city is ruled by the faction's chief hexarg as the ottiark is away most of the time at the council.

Individuals are born into a faction but can move into a different faction in adulthood. Members of factions may participate out of loyalty, or they may be hired to do a job. Those who are loyal to a faction are generally rewarded by trust from faction leaders and responsible (and profitable) positions within the faction. Those such as mercenaries or gladiators who joined a faction for money are not considered to be traitors when they change factions for a better offer, provided they are straightforward about their plans and do their job for a faction the entire time they are being paid. People expected to be loyal may get more privileges than mere hirelings, but if they violate trust — even trust they didn't want — they could be in great danger. One way a loyal member might show allegiance to a faction is to have a faction symbol tattooed on his or her body. Most-common locations are on the arm, chest, hand, or face, depending on how loudly a person wants to announce faction membership. Gladiators may get tattoos representing a faction or a sponsor; this can result in top gladiators having several tattoos as they change sponsors over the course of a career.

One of the popular pastimes in Bhanakhiri is attending the arena. Ancient stone arenas exist in Gamphen, Dunchamba, and Panaet, and others have been built in the past in other cities. In addition, each faction has its own arena in its faction city. The primary attraction is to watch duels between sponsored gladiators who fight for a rich purse on behalf of their sponsors. Those duels usually go only to first blood, so the best gladiators have learned to put on a good show while they protect themselves. The audience is encouraged to throw coins or other tokens after a good performance; some also throw other things after a poor performance, despite guards at the doors who are supposed to keep those things out.

Combat by single gladiators is not the only entertainment at the arenas. Faction mercenaries fight each other in various configurations, usually with blunt weapons but sometimes with live steel. In addition, there are various types of footraces and the wildly popular ostrich races. The swift birds are trained specifically to race, often by the very youths who ride them. They race faction against faction, and winning is one way young people can hope to come to the attention of a faction leader or a wealthy sponsor.

DUNCHAMBA, CITY OF (CAPITAL)

Ruler: Hexarga Wattana Buri Zai of Gold
Government: bureaucracy
Population: 203,149 (199,456 Bhanakhiri, 3,693 other human ethnicity)

Dunchamba is the capital city of Bhanakhiri and the location of Ottiarks' Hall, the meeting place of the Council of Ottiarks. It is a large city, full of bureaucrats and the people who serve and support them. Bureaucrats of all five factions run the various parts of the government, according to the currently negotiated division. Happily, it is not necessary to bribe officials to get something done. However, in important matters, a little gift as thanks in advance seldom goes amiss.

While the Council of Ottiarks is led by the senior member (currently Sasithorn Wi Gom of Jewel), the capital city is governed by a hexarg named every fifth year by the council's then-most-junior member to achieve a better balance of power. Each ottiark's city estate is of course served by faction personnel. The great hall, on the other hand, is staffed by hereditary servants who value the council as a whole more than they do any particular faction.

As the largest city, Dunchamba is well stocked with great temples, their carved, gilded spires glowing in the sun. The most popular of these is the temple of the god Sifkra, Who Loves Coins. Only a little less popular, though, is that of Anana, the Lady of Luck and Gold. Some city-dwellers also worship at the temple of Serena, the Peaceful Lady, while others attend the temple of Ahtizerr, The Magic One, or any of the numerous other locations.

One notable feature at each public building — hall, temple, inn, tavern, or shop (and even many private houses) — is the carved spirit house outside the entrance. Intended to attract the attention of wandering spirits who might otherwise enter the structure and cause trouble, spirit houses tend to resemble temples in their carved details and spires. One large inn that has stood in the same place for hundreds of years and seen many deaths inside its walls has a gilded spirit house nearly 10 feet tall to provide for all the spirits that might instead haunt its spaces.

The arena in Dunchamba is a marvel. Local people claim it is more than 2,000 years old, and it possesses an amazing system of chains and pulleys that can lift gladiators or pieces of setting right up into the middle of the floor. With all the factions represented in the city at all times, and many wealthy people living here much of the year, sponsored events take place in the arena several days a week. In addition to gladiatorial duels and battles between faction mercenaries, the area regularly hosts races. These include foot races of various lengths, dog races, and the ever-popular ostrich racing.

Ostrich carts are also popular in Dunchamba these days. With the right type of harness, a fully-grown ostrich can pull an adult in a lightly built cart, or even a sparse carriage with a driver and passenger. The Ottiarks consider themselves above such nonsense, but common gossip says that the wealthy faction leaders know they are too heavy for an ostrich, even with the lightest cart. The exception is the rail-thin Prasert Yok Khla of Gold, who seems quite pleased to drive himself around the city with a servant riding in the back.

A well-maintained road runs south from Dunchamba to Surthani, and also north to Xonburi. No government roads run into the interior; roads going east from the coast are built and maintained by various factions, and travelers must pay a fee to use them. There is no fee to use the rivers for transport, though there may be fees for the convenience of docking at a town or village along the way.

Just outside Dunchamba is a harbor built by the ancient ones, which was repaired and put back into use several centuries ago as the main base of Bhanakhiri's navy. The navy is commanded by Nayokoei (admiral) Arthit Lam Narathat. He has ships patrolling all along the coast, but the number of ships that can be stationed in Surthani is regulated by treaty with Kaldiloora. Negotiations are going on to increase that number temporarily, to deal with the pirate incursions in the area.

GAI ZAI YOK, CITY OF; CITY OF IRON

Ruler: Chief Hexarga Anong Bhan Surat
Government: bureaucracy
Population: 43,613 (43,464 Bhanakhiri, 111 dwarf, 38 other human ethnicity)

The Faction City of Iron is located near the faction's first mine, at the northwestern extent of the Hollow Spire Mountains. Although the faction has widespread interests now, it has never changed the location of its city, where its colors of red and black appear everywhere. Being near the source of the Nakchon River makes it fairly easy to ship raw materials and great forged items down to the coast and other cities.

Gai Zai Yok is as far away from the capital as it is possible to get and still be within Bhanakhiri, which means that the Iron bureaucrats have a great deal of freedom to be practical in their administration, not necessarily following every tiny regulation put out by the Council of Ottiarks. Because the area around the city is mostly unsettled and sometimes dangerous, Ottiark Klahan Tak Jiern has his house and gardens safely inside the city wall. If he wants a change of scenery while in town, he goes out to one of the mines for a few days.

The city has a gilded temple to Sifkra, Who Loves Coins, but the largest edifice in the city is dedicated to Newan, Lady of Fire and Water. Her worshippers are mostly found in Iron, though she has adherents among Sword and Gold as well. Most smiths have at least her symbol near their forge for a blessing.

Being so far from other large cities means the faction's arena is a major source of entertainment. With no other factions to provide regular competition, the Iron arena sometimes invites people from tribes in the region, and even dwarves from the mountains have been seen from time to time.

The distance from Gai Zai Yok back to Dunchamba sometimes makes the other ottiarks think they can agree on proposals without the participation of Klahan Tak Jiern because he is away at his faction city. However, he always manages to show up at crucial times, as did his predecessors before him. This ability is due to a secret that is closely guarded within the faction: a teleportation circle set up from Gai Zai Yok to the Iron faction estate inside Dunchamba. It has the ability to transport up to five people once per hour, as long as each time it is used by someone who knows the control words. Legend has it that Iron once saved the life of a great wizard named Muargaun in the Hollow Spire Mountains, and this magical circle represents his unending thanks.

GAMPHEN, CITY OF

Ruler: Hexarga Malai Daun Phet of Sword
Government: bureaucracy
Population: 34,489 (almost all Bhanakhiri)

Gamphen is one of the locations with an ancient arena; it uses the events staged there to draw people in to the city. They welcome traveling gladiators to events with purses provided by local sponsors and invite faction-sponsored gladiators to special bouts. Once in a while, the arena hosts local faction mercenaries competing against foreigners, but the outsiders sometimes don't understand the rules of the arena so those events occasionally end badly — which of course makes them wildly popular. The spirit house outside the arena is tall and highly carved to tempt away possible trouble from any resulting spirits.

Gamphen is also a center of cotton production, with most of the cloth woven here being sturdy fabric that goes to the army for uniforms. The city boasts an elaborate temple to Lohfa, Who Makes Things Grow, and one near the arena to Anana, the Lady of Luck and Gold.

KHON SAMA, CITY OF; CITY OF SILK

Ruler: Chief Hexarga Kanda Patham Et
Government: bureaucracy
Population: 55,932 (almost all Bhanakhiri)

The Faction City of Silk is a beautiful sight, draped as it is in the faction's signature fabric and with the colors of purple and white worked in throughout the city. Some of the public buildings are structures built by the ancient ones, and are of such quality that minor repairs have kept them usable after all this time. Located inside the jungle almost 200 miles from the coast, Silk is the one faction that does not have easy water transport from its faction city. On the other hand, the actual silk is not woven in Khon Sama; that is handled in fortified villages throughout the area and shipped to the coast by caravan or on local waterways. Instead Khon Sama is merely an administrative and merchant center, not just for the silk trade but for the faction's wide variety of interests. The city has popular temples to Sifkra, Who Loves Coins, and also to Lohfa, Who Makes Things Grow; more than any other faction, the main products of Silk are vulnerable to natural disruptions.

While Silk manufactures other types of cloth such as linen and cotton (and also builds ships, and participates in many other ventures), it has a monopoly on the production of silk in Bhanakhiri. It also tries to enforce its monopoly in the surrounding area, which in the past has led to raids on villages outside the country that had the temerity to offer even inferior wild silk.

The silk facilities are carefully guarded, and most people know only a few steps of the entire process. Those who grow up in one of the silk villages and learn the trade may find themselves nearly trapped by the strictures of the Silk Faction. Traveling to Khon Sama to see the city and attend the arena may be as far as most silk workers are ever allowed to go. It is unclear whether the other ottiarks know that Intira Chana Sing and generations of her predecessors have enforced such careful controls on her faction people. Even if they did, they would probably refuse to interfere in another faction's business as that could be a bad precedent for their own future interests.

KLAH BAKHAM, CITY OF

Ruler: Hexarg Thaksin Ban Kulok of Silk
Government: bureaucracy
Population: 67,619 (almost all Bhanakhiri)

One primary product of Klah Bakham is the army. The headquarters is nearby, the uniforms are made here, and most of the area's agricultural production goes toward its support. Another important product is ships. Silk has large shipbuilding facilities here, with logging and forestry interests upriver to support the construction. The Chana River also brings trade from the interior to the seaport for shipment elsewhere.

Although Silk controls the city, it by no means controls the military. The headquarters of the army is at Fortress Chengsang, a stronghold of the ancient ones built just outside the city, where Pholema (supreme commander) Kamon Trat Uthai of Gold and his general staff supervise the units around the country. The plains in front of the fortress are often filled with marching troops practicing their group maneuvers in case of war.

Because of the number of soldiers in the area, temples to Gonthor, Who Grumbles in the Sky, and Orgim, Who Loves War, are more popular in Klah Bakham than in most cities.

KLAUNG SONG, CITY OF; CITY OF SWORD

Ruler: Chief Hexarga Ratree Gam Lang of Sword
Government: bureaucracy
Population: 52,197 (almost all Bhanakhiri)

This is the Faction City of Sword, and the colors of black and orange are seen everywhere. In keeping with its name, weapons of all types are crafted here, and young people or foreigners who think they desire a career as mercenaries for any faction receive their basic training in Klaung Song. The faction arena is an important part of this training regimen, and the locals often find amusement in the fumbling efforts of would-be mercenaries. The largest temple here is to Gonthor, Who Grumbles in the Sky, as he is the god of strength and war as well as the storms.

Although Sword is a political and mercantile organization as much as any of the other factions, people tend to look to it for leadership in times of military need. This annoys the generals of the country's actual military and has resulted in some spectacularly bad decisions. However, Sword likes to encourage this to a degree, as it increases the faction's prestige, and they include a little bit of military perspective in their merchants' training. (They consider questions such as, "How would you defend a caravan traveling through this location?") Sword does seem to furnish an above-average number of soldiers to the army, though, and it is the largest military supplier overall.

The current ottiark of Sword, Ubon Phrae Savan, has a hobby of studying the history of battles so she is truly knowledgeable in the areas of strategy and tactics. She is also very interested in historical foreign battles and would be happy to hear accounts of those or to acquire new books to study.

PANAET, CITY OF; CITY OF JEWEL

Ruler: Chief Hexarga Pakpao Khun Nop of Jewel
Government: bureaucracy
Population: 48,894 (almost all Bhanakhiri)

Panaet is the Faction City of Jewel as well as having one of the ancient arenas, with carvings around the top only wizards and sages can read. Jewel took over Panaet about 50 years ago and has since used the ancient arena in place of the inferior facility in its previous faction city. Panaet is considered beautiful; the faction colors of blue and silver decorate the public buildings, including a few still standing from the time of the ancient ones. Mosaics of tiny chips of semi-precious stone adorn the temples here, especially those of Selena, the Peaceful Lady, and Sifkra, Who Loves Coins. Ottiark Sasithorn Wi Gom has an impressive mansion inside the city, but she also has a country estate a few miles to the northeast where she spends a great deal of her time.

The faction arena is a popular attraction that brings in plenty of coin for Jewel. In addition to sponsored gladiatorial duels, organizers bring in groups to do shows with trained animals, including elephants from deep in the forest. They also feature faction youth in ostrich races and sometimes invite teams from other factions to compete.

There has been some talk in the area of banning the ostrich racing. In the past few months, travelers on the road from here to Xonburi have been plagued by attacks from ostrich gangs. These are groups of armed youth on fast ostriches who swoop down on a caravan, take anything they can grab or cut away from a saddle, and then dash away. Certain people blame the racers. Others reasonably point out that the young people who do the ostrich racing are certainly not involved in the crimes as they are very serious about their birds and would never subject them to such hard usage, and that canceling the racing would do nothing to stop the bandits.

SURTHANI, CITY OF

Ruler: Hexarg Suchart Hin Saun of Iron
Government: bureaucracy
Population: 56,621 (almost all Bhanakhiri)

This city is the headquarters and launching place for merchants who want to trade with the great markets of the Delta. Each faction has warehouses and waystations here, but public inns are also available. It is also one of the nearest ports for those who come from a distance; the Delta itself is too shallow for oceangoing vessels, so the city's great docks do a brisk business. Surthani seems to have imbibed some of the free spirit of the Delta, because it is the most chaotic of the cities of Bhanakhiri, which are usually quite staid.

A unit of the army is stationed here, ostensibly to guard against attacks from Kaldiloora or from the River People. Since no such attacks have taken place in over 200 years, the posting has been considered a very soft duty. In the past two years, though, pirate raids have taken place on both Surthani and nearby Delta areas and the military has been called on to defend against those.

This is a city where Sifkra, Who Loves Coins, is worshipped but also important is Ghamia, the River Lady. Many of the less-lawful people in the area also worship Erka, Who Moves in Shadows; Surthani is the only city where a temple to her is publicly available.

TOLANUA, CITY OF

Ruler: Hexarg Sakchai Ubol Thani
Government: bureaucracy
Population: 21,179 (almost all Bhanakhiri)

Tolanua was the faction city of Jewel until about 50 years ago, when the faction took over the coastal city of Panaet, and the colors of blue and silver continue to be used here. The city still has many of the jewelers and gem specialists that originally gave the faction its name, so the city is protected by a strong wall and mercenary forces. The hills nearby once yielded several types of semi-precious gemstones. However, when the supply here grew scarce and easier sources were discovered elsewhere, the mines were eventually abandoned.

VARINDRA, CITY OF; CITY OF GOLD

Ruler: Chief Hexarga Lawan Pit Ji of Gold
Government: bureaucracy
Population: 48,256 (almost all Bhanakhiri)

Although nearly all towns and cities of Bhanakhiri are walled, the Faction City of Gold is exceptionally well-protected. Its wall is unusually thick and high, and many faction troops patrol inside and outside. It has been more than three centuries since one faction attacked another's faction city, but the historians of Gold are not going to let their leaders forget.

Inside, the city is as beautiful as mere money can make it and lavishly adorned with the faction colors of gold and green. The temples here are covered with even more gold than in other cities, if that is possible, and the temple of Sifkra, Who Loves Coins, is especially elaborate. The faction headquarters itself has gilded "gates of welcome" at its complex, and the arena is built of white marble. Varindra is generally rather clean, with the daily rains washing street trash into the well-built sewers and carrying it to the sea. The city and its wall are large enough that the estate of Ottiark Prasert Yok Khla is entirely enclosed.

Not only does Gold work precious metals, it mines them in the hills and distant mountains. The faction has a transportation network to support the mines, and others traveling to the interior can use the roads and waystations for a fee — one that gets higher the farther from the coast one travels.

Xonburi, City of

Ruler: Hexarg Somchai Map Hua of Jewel
Government: bureaucracy
Population: 45,313 (almost all Bhanakhiri)

Xonburi is the northernmost city in Bhanakhiri, with the Nakchon River representing the country's official border. Settlements have spilled over the river, however, and since there is not another single country that claims that area, they will probably continue to grow. Just east along the river is Fortress Munkulok, which houses a military unit to protect the border from invasion. However, the army is not responsible for the defense of the cross-border settlements. Instead, the settlers hired the usual mercenaries and also trained to take part in their own protection.

The merchants of Xonburi carry on a great deal of trade with the tribes that inhabit the forest and savannah areas north of Bhanakhiri. The good port also brings opportunities for trade, with ships calling from the Empire of Alcaldar to the north as well as ships from the far west. Furthermore, the Nakchon River allows factions (especially Iron) to ship raw materials and valuables to the coast for transport by sea to other parts of the country. Overall, Xonburi is a very active city where a purchaser can find goods of many types.

The primary temple in Xonburi is to Ghamia, the River Lady, but the city also has a prominent temple to Vreenon, Who Loves Birds. The temple to this nature-related goddess has proven to be a diplomatic boon when dealing with the less-sophisticated people of the wide region north of the river. Of course, Sifkra, Who Loves Coins, is also represented.

Geographic Features and Points of Interest in Bhanakhiri

Burilan Hills

The Burilan Hills run north and south through central Bhanakhiri, the northern section of a long ridge that continues through Kaldiloora. East of the Burilan Hills, water runs down into the system that flows toward the Quell River. To the west, most of the hills drain toward the Lenggor River or the Chana River in the extreme north. The hills have some mineral resources, but long-term mining in certain areas has depleted the supply in those spots.

Chana River

The Chana runs from the northern end of the Burilan Hills to the sea at Klah Bakham. It is a source of freshwater fish, but more importantly it is a convenient way to transport materials from the interior of Bhanakhiri to the seaport at Klah Bakham.

Nakchon River

The Nakchon River rises in the Hollow Spire Mountains and runs roughly northwest to the sea at Xonburi. It is useful for transportation from the mountains and is generally considered to be the northern border of Bhanakhiri.

Delta, The

Capital: none
Notable Settlements: Anggah, Daskaken, Eburu, Nyelang
Ruler: none
Government: local only, if any
Population: unknown; mostly River People, small numbers of Bhanakhiri, Kaldiloorans, and other human ethnicities
Monstrous: tabaxi, fae, inphidians, golden grippli, jungle treants
Languages: Delta Speech; Gonidal or River Speech inland
Religion: riverine spirits, ancestor worship, Paramountcies pantheon
Resources: fish, rare plants, exotic animals, skins, handcrafts
Currency: barter; Bhanakhiran, others
Technology Level: Iron Age (Delta); Stone Age (River Peoples)

Separating the countries of Bhanakhiri to the north and Kaldiloora to the south is the Delta. No one calls it anything else; it has never had another name. In the Delta are villages on stilts and villages made of hundreds of boats tied together. Marketplaces exist that are nothing but more boats. Some areas of dry land have existed long enough to have people build homes on them, but none last long. The Delta is always changing, and what is here today may be gone next month, or this afternoon.

The Delta developed from the flow of the Lenggor River. As it reaches the low, flat lands near the coast, the river broadens, slows, and separates into many long fingers that make their own ways to the sea through the surrounding forest. Some branches are met by the tide coming in and form a brackish mangrove swamp. Others flow out of the forest, wide and still deep enough to float rafts of boats.

The Delta is part of the land of the River Peoples. Between the Ular River to the north and the Lenggor River to the south, the tribes of the River People live isolated lives with their own strange language and their own traditions and superstitions. The inhabitants of the Delta are usually those who have left the seclusion of the deep jungle to deal with the outside world. They live in the Delta, perhaps returning upriver to obtain more goods to trade, or deliver new acquisitions. What these reclusive people might want with many of the things available from traders is anyone's guess, but things do make their way back into the secretive enclaves.

Another secluded group living among the River Peoples is the tabaxi, or cat-people. Having little use for fixed villages, families of tabaxi prowl the area between the Ular and Lenggor as well as over the Kulgera Ridge into the eastern part of the Seething Jungle. They sometimes interact with traders who can get them new and interesting weaponry, as weapons are nearly the only possessions of value to tabaxi.

The language of the Delta is a trade tongue (called Delta Speech) that uses a debased version of the speech of the River Peoples and is combined with many words learned from the ancient ones and handed down for generations, and some terms borrowed from its neighbors. A person who speaks Bhanikhat or Kaldilooran can probably understand a third of what is said, while someone who speaks the ancient language could likely comprehend more than half and communicate the rest through gestures. Most people now on the river speak some form of the Delta trade tongue; the only people who truly speak the language of the River Peoples are the tribes far upriver.

The deities of the River People are as strange as anything else. Most prominent among them are the Night Sisters — the powers represented by the moons. Noh-ro the Guardian, also called the Pale Sister, is worshipped by many, and is probably the favorite among the tribes. Less popular is Be-Le the Witch, the Dark Sister, but she is very important to some formidable people. The veneration of ancestors is also essential to the culture. The River People appear to have spirit houses similar in nature to those of Bhanakhiri, if less sophisticated in construction. The little buildings are specifically for the spirits of the ancestors, though, and people make daily sacrifices at these spirit houses, putting out food and drink to satisfy their ancestors and keep them from becoming angry with the descendants who are still alive.

Other beliefs are even more unusual. In a certain part of the deep forest, homage is given to some of the great powers among the fey. (See "Weirdling Forest" below for more information.) In addition, some among the River Peoples commune with powerful spirits called loa. Although some seem to be spirits of nature such as the sky, sea, and earth, they do not appear to be linked to the Kaldilooran creator-spirits. (People of both cultures emphatically deny any relation.) These loa choose to be caretakers of humanity and purveyors of justice, but rarely intervene unless properly invoked. The River People often entreat the loa in various daily matters, but that is in the nature of hoping perhaps something might go their way rather than expecting divine assistance.

ANGGAH, FLOATING MARKET OF

Population: varies
Ruler: none
Government: none

Several floating markets are scattered across the Delta, but the one called Anggah is without doubt the largest such collection. Scores or even hundreds of flat-bottomed boats fill the water of one quiet inlet off the main flow of the river. Although the sellers vary from day to day, the things sold are usually about the same. People sell directly off their boats and offer many kinds of fruit, fish, clothing, woven hats, flowers, household items, cloth, and handcrafted or rare items from the River Folk far upstream. Of course, food is always available; cooks grill or boil over tiny fires and serve noodles, rice, various kinds of seafood, sweets, hot drinks, and much more right from their boats. The boats of buyers are forced to interpenetrate through the mass of sellers, with lanes of clear water opening only occasionally to let the purchasers through. When a person wants to buy an item from a vendor a few boats away, the seller often uses a lightweight pan or basket tied to a long pole to reach across and collect the payment and then to deliver the goods.

DASKAKEN, STILT TOWN OF

Ruler: none; Takul speaks out for the people
Government: informal spokesperson
Population: 574 (almost all River People)

The town of Daskaken sits on one finger of the Delta where the trees spread out and the water is more open. Wooden houses with high-pitched roofs stand over the water on tall stilts, varying in height. Each has a walkway in front and a wooden ladder leading down to the water where one or more flat-bottomed boats are tied. Some houses are built near each other, close enough that a plank can be laid from one to another for people to cross. Most are at a distance, though, and seemingly randomly placed. Townspeople cross back and forth in their small boats, dodging the piles and each other and occasionally slipping right under a house that doesn't have fishing nets or rope lines dangling around the edges.

Some places sell cooked food, and boats go from one to another to collect up a meal; usually a child lets down the food in a bucket or basket and collects the payment the same way. Other places appear to be actual shops, or at least homes where people sell things. These places may have several boats tied up outside, and people emerge with bags or bundles that they stow in their own boat before casting loose and rowing away.

Daskaken has no official government. However, Takul is an older man who is generally considered wise and is usually to be found at his house, so any strangers with questions are directed to him. The stilt-town is typical of many semi-permanent towns or villages that have developed in the Delta, although some are slightly more organized than Daskaken. One was even built on a plan, with specific waterways between houses to help get boats in and out more easily. This level of detail was generally considered excessive, though, so it is unlikely to be repeated.

EBURU, ISLAND ORCHARD OF

Ruler: none
Government: none
Population: 32 (all River People)

While most food sold in the Delta is grown around the edges or upstream, this orchard stands on a plot of land high enough that the river actually went around it rather than simply wearing it down. It is large enough to hold stands of several types of fruit trees that are cultivated by many different growers. To protect the valuable fruit against thieves or vandals, most of the owners live in small huts on the island or in houseboats tied up alongside. Some competitors claim that the reason the island is so fertile is that in the past, criminals were executed and buried here since it is high ground, but this attempt at scaring customers away from the island's produce has been largely ineffective.

NYELANG, WATER TOWN OF

Population: uncertain
Ruler: none
Government: none

While everyone in the Delta uses small, flat-bottomed boats to get around, some denizens possess larger versions that they use as their actual homes. These houseboats are built with a covered wooden structure in the central section that is high enough that a person would merely need to stoop to enter. These usually have long, low windows that can be shuttered, or opened to let in air.

Hundreds of these houseboats gather at the place called Nyelang. In many cases, dozens or scores are lashed together, effectively making large platforms. People can step from boat to boat for hundreds of feet before needing to cross open water. The composition of boats is always changing as new people arrive and other owners decide to head for a new location. Those in the middle of a formation might consider selling their houseboat rather than trying to work it free, but those on an edge or untethered to a larger group can simply float away.

This changeability can offer a certain degree of anonymity to those who desire that. While boat dwellers might be interested in their neighbor's business when the person is nearby, in general they neither know nor care whence that neighbor came nor where the person might have gone next.

GEOGRAPHIC FEATURES AND POINTS OF INTEREST IN THE DELTA

LENGGOR RIVER

This river runs from the Kulgera Ridge northwest to the Sinnar coast. Many other rivers flow into the Lenggor from the north and east, increasing its volume. Its steep banks make it difficult to cross along much of its route through the rainforest, which isolates the peoples on one side from those on the other. In the low-lying lands toward the coast, the Lenggor broadens immensely and flows into a wide delta. Most of the delta area is forested, and part of it is mangrove swamp.

MEMATIKAN, DRY VILLAGE OF

In the mangrove forest, whole villages of little houses have been built supported by the roots of the trees. Residents come and go in their flat-bottomed boats, and traders can come right up to each house to buy and sell. When the Delta changed, however, one such village on the south edge of the Delta was left high and dry. Mematikan was once a thriving small community where residents made handicrafts and special foods that the traders would sell to outsiders farther down the Delta. When their channel started to dry up a few months ago, people packed their things and moved on. Many of the trees are now dying, watered only by the rains. Not everyone is aware of the change, of course, and some still come here looking for people from the former community but possibly finding trouble. A few of the houses have already deteriorated but many still stand, well enough at least for *other* things to move in.

MENGAMUK FOREST

This tropical rainforest extends for more than 1,800 miles along the western side of southern Libynos. The character of the forest changes somewhat over that distance, becoming more jungle-like south of the Lenggor River. East of the Kulgera Ridge, the jungle is even thicker and more tangled; that portion is known as the Seething Jungle and is usually considered by most observers to be a separate area even though the rainforest is actually contiguous from the Quell River and Hollow Spire Mountains in the east to about 100 miles from the western coast. The Mengamuk has some creatures almost unheard of elsewhere, such as the sturdy forest elephants and the little halfling elephants, which are no taller than a man's chest.

Sedili, Drowned Village of

Sedili was once a bustling village on stilts until a powerful windstorm and flood knocked down the houses. Residents piled their boats with what they could salvage and moved on. Few have returned to try to recover more possessions; the people of the Delta have little time for looking back. Others came behind, of course, to search for missed valuables. What they found was that the water dwellers had been even quicker. Alligators had moved in as well as other aggressive predators, which deterred most of the human scavengers.

A few former residents of Sedili have been heard to regret the loss of ancestral items in the tragedy — one a necklace, one a sword, and perhaps others — and they might pay good money for someone to deal with the dangerous interlopers and to conduct a good search for the missing items.

Ular River

Starting well north in the Kulgera Ridge (in the area the Bhanakhirin call the Burilan Hills), the Ular snakes its way south and then west. Joined by tributaries also coming from the Kulgera, it eventually meets the Lenggor and becomes part of that strong river. The wide Ular has long formed a natural barrier against expansion by the usually aggressive Bhanakhirin, leaving the River People to continue in their traditional lifestyle.

Weirdling Forest

East of the confluence of the Lenggor and the Ular, hard up against the Kulgera Ridge, is an area different from the rest of the Mengamuk. It is a center of power for the Green Lady, Who Loves Trees, and the Ancient Boy, Who Leads the Hunt. It has not always been so — the tales of the ancestors tell of a time when the River Peoples lived here in peace — but for many centuries now the fey have dominated this area.

The small fey may be annoyances, or even allies; usually they can be propitiated by gifts of bread, honey, or fermented fruit juices. Some are evil and must be warded off by protective hexes, so each house has woven signs above the door, and villages place them in rock around their fences. The great fey, though, are capricious, and dangerous in their uncaring. Those who wish to gain their favor must offer sumptuous gifts. The great spirits are not be impressed with a little food or drink; a banquet might be the least thing that could hope to win their approval. One reason the River Peoples need to trade with outsiders is to gain gifts lavish enough to draw the attention of the ancient fey."

Kaldiloora, Great House of

Capital: Morongle
Notable Settlements: Birriwa, Mernmerna, Tallimba, Werai, Yarrunga, Yullundry
Ruler: Prince Jarrah
Government: monarchy
Population: 1,236,759 (1,232,598 Kaldilooran, 4,161 other human ethnicity)
Monstrous: assassin vines, phookas, tigerrillas
Languages: Gonidal
Religion: Kaldilooran spirits
Resources: trade, spices, cabb'e and cocoa beans, linen, cotton, mining
Currency: Bhanakhiran
Technology Level: High Middle Ages (cities), Dark Ages (towns and villages), Iron Age (rural areas)

Kaldiloora is at the westernmost extent of south Libynos, on the coast of Mother Oceanus. It has a fertile, if narrow, coastal plain and dense rainforest in the interior. The country is named after the chieftain who united many related tribes into a single group, making them all part of his "house" and doing away with the clan warfare that was devastating the people. All people are considered to be part of the family of the prince, with chieftains being cousins who are in charge of smaller houses under the great house. As infants, people are given facial tattoos that designate

their house, so later in life it is possible to recognize where people were born if one knows a great deal about the tattoo patterns. However, the population of Kaldiloora is mobile enough that even knowing a person's birth town tells the observer very little. A person with no facial tattoos, though, is immediately revealed as an outsider. Towns and even cities are often named after famous local people, with those living there proud to claim to be part of that person's house. In fact, towns and villages have been known to change their names when a native person does something particularly notable; the smaller the village is, the less notable the action would have to be to cause a name change.

After uniting the nation, the first prince realized he needed something to keep his energetic people busy if he was to keep them away from their clan wars. He took an idea from the country to the north and instituted a series of gladiator games using the ancient stone arenas still standing in Morongle, Yarrunga, and Birriwa. Eventually, this developed into an ongoing set of elaborate competitions, with local winners going on to regional games and eventually nationwide championships. These competitions generated a great deal of excitement without the ill-will that led to previous conflicts and became extremely popular.

The people of Kaldiloora don't have deities as most people think of them. Instead, they pay homage to a variety of creator-spirits. These spirits were themselves created by the now-distant Sky Father, who gave them responsibility over various parts of creation. Rather than worshipping in temples, devotees of the creator-spirits acknowledge their influence in the many small ways of life, with shrines in the home or in common areas. For more serious occasions (such as weddings or coming-of-age ceremonies), people may travel to ritual locations. Many places in nature could honor one or more creator-spirits, so such locations are not hard to find.

Morongle, House of (Capital)

Ruler: Chieftain Alkawari
Government: chieftain appointed by prince
Population: 61,513 (60,485 Kaldilooran, 1,028 other human ethnicity)

The capital of Kaldiloora, Morongle is also the largest city, sitting near the mouth of the Kulumali River where the coastal road crosses the river over an arched bridge. The chieftain is a woman of about 40 years and several of the city officials are relatives of hers, as would be expected. This is no sinecure for them, as it might be in other countries; instead it shows the responsibility of the family as well as the chieftain to the house and its people. (Although chieftains are appointed by the prince, many locations have had the chieftainship in the same family for several generations.)

The city bustles with all sorts of craftspeople and merchants, as well as foreign visitors and diplomats here to see the prince. Morongle also has one of the ancient arenas and hosts local, regional, and sometimes national gladiator competitions at various times in the two-year cycle. For the larger events, the city is packed with people supporting the individuals and teams from various houses.

The prince's castle is east along the river a short distance outside the city. Another bridge crosses the Kulumali here, so the prince can send messengers or envoys to either side of the river without needing to go downriver to the capital first. The castle is built around a fortress of the ancient ones, carefully restored to provide extra protection for the castle's inhabitants in case of attack. Jarrah and his staff keep careful track of the events and needs of the country. However, he is not a formal person, and his meeting room, with its large table and open windows, gets much more use than his throne room.

South of the city is a newer fortress that is the headquarters of Kaldiloora's military, both army and navy. The army has small units stationed at small forts throughout the country, mostly to keep the peace and to assist villagers against dangerous animals and the strange creatures that are sometimes found in the Mengamuk Jungle. The navy, on the other hand, primarily patrols against pirates and any possible foreign attack on the coast. While peaceful traders and diplomats from other countries are welcomed, Kaldiloorans prefer to keep them only to occasional visits.

A tabaxi scout looks out upon a vale of the Kulgera Ridge.

BIRRIWA, HOUSE OF

Ruler: Chieftain Jarli
Government: chieftain appointed by prince
Population: 16,611 (15,970 Kaldilooran, 641 other human ethnicity)

Birriwa sits on the coastal road at the bridge across the long Bindegandri River that runs all the way from the Kulgera Ridge in the east. This makes the city a stepping-off place for merchants willing to take a risk for a profit, and for explorers who want to travel far into the jungle. Excellent woods, ivory, and sometimes diamonds from the Kulgera Ridge are among the trade products that come down the river to the coast. Sometimes strange items from the deep jungle or even the east side of the Kulgera make their way to Birriwa. Certain ship captains make a point of stopping here from time to time to acquire items for collectors far away who are willing to pay a premium for rare things.

Another feature of Birriwa is the ancient arena, which was repaired in the past and, with careful maintenance, is still sturdy enough to hold hundreds of on-lookers for the various gladiator games held here. Last year's team combat champions came from a small town near here. The team was not favored to win, so when the members became champions, the town renamed itself House of Gilbanung in their honor.

MERNMERNA, HOUSE OF

Ruler: Chieftain Yannathan
Government: chieftain appointed by prince
Population: 6,514 (almost all Kaldilooran)

Mernmerna is located on the southern bank of the Eora River where it reaches the sea. The city is responsible for maintaining the Eora bridge on the coast road. River access to the Kalkadoon Hills means merchants can travel back and forth easily, bringing products from villages as far east as the Lenggor River including ivory tusks from the forest elephants so prevalent in the central part of the jungle. The Kalkadoon Hills also have some precious metals and iron, though they have been mined enough that the remaining minerals are not so easy to get to as they once were.

One special thing about the Eora River is that its northern branch comes out of the hills in a fairly tall waterfall. This constant spray of water shows rainbows anytime the sun is out, and so it is a well-known ritual location for Rainbow Boa, creator-spirit of mountains and rain. Of course, a person may find a rainbow any day when there is sun following the afternoon rain, so people only make the journey all the way to the waterfall for especially important invocations.

TALLIMBA, HOUSE OF

Ruler: Chieftain Menindee
Government: chieftain appointed by prince
Population: 31,821 (30,756 Kaldilooran, 1,065 other human ethnicity)

Tallimba is primarily a trading port that serves as a base for merchants and travelers who trade with the Delta and also a place where goods can be shipped south or to other countries. However, the port is neither as large nor as well constructed as the port in Surthani to the north, so it does not get as much traffic from foreign ships. Menindee often acts as a diplomat to try to increase the reputation of the city; she invites the officers of any foreign ships to dinner with her and is sometimes able to convince merchants from the Delta to visit as well.

A road runs from Tallimba along the coast all the way south to Yullundry, a distance of more than 1,600 miles. Keeping the road in good condition and maintaining its safety is one of the primary duties agreed to by the cities, towns, and villages along the way when the road was first built. The distance helps explain why so much travel is done by ship; even small vessels that must hug the coast can move along faster than a single traveler or a caravan.

Tallimba has its own arena, a wood-and-stone structure that it built several generations ago and keeps in good shape. It is one of the few areas to regularly welcome outsiders to local matches. Recently, foreign sailors challenged some local athletes to a race up the rigging of their ship; now the arena's administrators are trying to figure out how to add a similar feature to its contests.

WERAI, HOUSE OF

Ruler: Chieftain Kuparr
Government: chieftain appointed by prince
Population: 23,429 (22,560 Kaldilooran, 869 other human ethnicity)

Werai is just north of the tip of land that is the westernmost point of Kaldiloora. To the north side of the city is the port, and beyond that beautiful beaches that the people use for recreation. South of the city, though, the beach is unspoiled as it is a spot sacred to Barramundi, creator-spirit of oceans and rivers. Here, supplicants may stand with their feet in the ocean and their backs to all the land there is, and call on Barramundi for their intention.

The people of Kaldiloora have always been curious and adventuresome, and Werai is the port most often used to go exploring to the west. Ships from Kaldiloora were happy to establish trade with the Aizanes Isles several hundred years ago and later traveled all the way to the Razor Coast. The latter distance is so far, though, that regular trade was never established. Kuparr has encouraged businesses in his city that support long distance travel, such as ship repair and refitting, outfitters that can provide supplies for long journeys, and the like. This is not only a benefit to Kaldilooran ships heading west; foreign ships circumnavigating southern Libynos, or those heading off to distant Akados, can stop at Werai and be sure they will be able to acquire necessary supplies.

YARRUNGA, HOUSE OF

Ruler: Chieftain Yarran
Government: chieftain appointed by prince
Population: 21,747 (21,120 Kaldilooran, 627 other human ethnicity)

Yarrunga sits on the coast at the mouth of the Imapa River, which runs west from the Kalkadoon Hills. In addition to the coastal road, a road passes through the jungle directly from Morongle to Yarrunga, cutting the distance between those two locations roughly in half. Yarrunga was built around a set of buildings of the ancient ones — a fortress, arena, public buildings, a bathing house, and others whose function can no longer be determined. Some of them were easily restored; others took a great deal of effort but were eventually finished. Now sages from all over southern and central Libynos come here to study the buildings and argue over the meanings of the interior mosaics and the words carved in the walls.

As a relatively central location, Yarrunga is where the national gladiator competitions are held. The games include a variety of athletic events as well as feats of agility, strength, and endurance, and individual and group combats. The mixed groups and women's team combats are particularly popular right now, and speculation is high about which contestants will actually make it through to the national competition.

A tall, open hill outside the city is a popular location for rituals invoking Great Eagle, the creator-spirit of wind and storm. About 10 miles from the city is an area people avoid: the ruins of a village

from the clan wars, burned and salted so that even now little grows there. No one would ever admit to it, but from time to time people use the village as a ritual location for Crook-beak, the creator-spirit who brought covetousness, jealousy, and taking into the world in his envy of the other Eagle spirit, who was created first while Crook-beak was created last.

YULLUNDRY, HOUSE OF

Ruler: Chieftain Parara
Government: chieftain appointed by prince
Population: 9,289 (almost all Kaldilooran)

Yullundry is at the southern end of the coast road on the northern bank of the Tailamuli River. The river flows out of the Milkapiti Hills, which have become well-known in the past decade for their ores and gems. Many miners work in the hills and ship their results down to Yullundry.

The area between Birriwa and Yullundry is some of the best cropland in the country, and many people make a living producing cabb'e beans and cocoa beans, which are the basis for popular drinks in Kaldiloora and other, more-distant, places. Some villages instead concentrate on spices, such as cloves and nutmeg, and trees are logged for their wood. Parara has encouraged more trading ships to stop in Yullundry, and her efforts to get the port in good condition, with officials and workers to see to the ships that come in, are having a good effect on the town's popularity and the income of its residents.

A grove of fruit trees in a valley a few miles from the town is used as a ritual location for Possum, creator-spirit of earth and plants. It is particularly popular for local weddings, but each group takes care to leave the grove no different than they found it so all can appreciate its sumptuous beauty. Another area nearby is full of flowering trees and many locals make the trek out to it to invoke Parrot, the trickster, who is the creator spirit of all strange and colorful things.

GEOGRAPHIC FEATURES AND POINTS OF INTEREST IN KALDILOORA

BINDEGANDRI RIVER

This river is about 700 miles long and runs from the Kulgera Ridge southwest to Birriwa. A bridge carries the coast road across the river there. Although not deep near its headwaters, all its feeder streams combine to make it fairly deep and fast by the time it reaches the flatter, open lands east of Birriwa. It has plenty of fish along its length, though the type varies depending on location.

From the headwaters of the Bindegandri, it is only about 50 miles across the Kulgera Ridge to the Seething Jungle, which is much wilder than the western tropical forest. Furthermore, explorers have found that the top of the Bindegandri is less than 100 miles from the beginning of an eastern river that flows all the way down to the Reaping Sea. Of course, those are some of the most difficult miles to traverse in the entire jungle, and the same destination could be reached by sea in just a few months. Nonetheless, there is occasional wild talk about developing an overland route from Kaldiloora to the Reaping Sea.

EORA RIVER

The Eora River is a fairly short river flowing from the Kalkadoon Hills down to the sea at Mernmerna, where the coast road crosses it at a bridge. It has two branches, both of which probably form just from the quantity of rainfall in the forest. However, the northern branch falls in a nice waterfall, while the southern branch just runs quietly out of the hills. After the two join, the river becomes rather fast, making it difficult to row a small boat upstream through that area. It also has different types of fish than other rivers in the country, with those that prefer faster water dominating.

IMAPA RIVER

The Imapa flows from the Kalkadoon Hills west to Yarrunga, where a bridge carries the coast road across it. Since it comes from underground, it is cool upstream. It warms up eventually and has plenty of fish farther downstream. Explorers following the river discovered it flows out of a series of caverns. The first is a squeeze to enter, but once inside the others are larger with incredible rock formations. Since that discovery, the caverns have been used as a ritual location for Bat, creator-spirit of the night and underground places. Of course, a person could invoke Bat on any night when the moon is gone and the sparkling footprints of the Sky Father can be seen across the sky, but caverns seem to have a special power for people that the night sky itself does not usually have.

KALKADOON HILLS

The Kalkadoon Hills are a set of hills about 300 miles east of the seacoast in Kaldiloora. They are not rough, but are high enough that waters to the west of them flow to the sea rather than joining the Lenggor River or flowing into the Bindegandri. The hills do have mineral resources but those that were easily accessible have been mined already, requiring more effort and possible danger to continue to develop the area.

KULGERA RIDGE

This long line of rather rough hills separates the Seething Jungle and the river basin of the Quell River to the east from the watersheds of the Lenggor River and the Bindegandri in the Mengamuk Jungle to the west. Although various valuable resources (including gold and diamonds) have been found from time to time under the Kulgera, the range is deadly enough that no sustained development has taken place. Instead, mines come and go, and villages are abandoned as being too dangerous. The gentler Burilan Hills are an extension of the Kulgera Ridge in Bhanakhiri.

KULUMALI RIVER

This short river flows from the northern end of the Kalkadoon Hills, northwest to the sea at Morongle. Two bridges cross the river there: one at the city itself and one slightly farther east near the prince's palace. The river is mostly collected rain, so the water is fairly warm and slow-moving. The river is full of fish, and many villages eat well from it.

MILKAPITI HILLS

Running approximately north-and-south about 400 miles east of the coast of Mother Oceanus, the Milkapiti Hills are part of the geographical separation between the country of Kaldiloora and Sensibar, its neighbor to the south. The hills have mineral resources that have been discovered relatively recently, so the two countries have not yet come into conflict regarding them.

TAILAMULI RIVER

This river is generally considered to be the southern border of Kaldiloora. It flows west-southwest out of the Milkapiti Hills to the sea at Yullundry. Its source is underground, so it is cold at its headwaters, making it unsuitable for tropical river fish until it warms up downstream.

SENSIBAR, KINGDOM OF

Capital: Ompeshi
Notable Settlements: Gulama, Kajoro, Masunga, Nadhani, Sinda
Ruler: Queen Lediana the Magnificent
Government: monarchy
Population: 1,177,186 (1,173,281 Equatorian, 576 Castorhagi, 3,329 other human ethnicity)
Monstrous: ettercaps, decapuses, tri-flower fronds, viper vines

Languages: Zenzin
Religion: Paramountcies pantheon
Resources: spices, exotic woods, wood carvings, ivory, trade
Currency: Bhanakhiran, Castorhagi
Technology Level: Medieval (cities), High Middle Ages (plantations), Iron Age (rural areas)

Sensibar is on the west coast of extreme southern Libynos. It is a wealthy country because of the easy cultivation of spices valuable to the rest of the world. Cloves, nutmeg, and cinnamon literally grow on trees here, and black pepper is also commonly grown. Cultivation is most often done on large plantations, though some smallholders produce their own crops. Wealthy plantation owners purchase foreign slaves and put them to work harvesting spices that are often worth more than the slaves. Traders from places such as Khemit or Castorhage sell slaves and high-quality weaponry and, in exchange, purchase spices and exotic woods.

Castorhagi merchants tried to convince the queen to grant them a monopoly in trade with Sensibar, but she has not yet agreed. Queen Lediana learned Castorhage has a monopoly on some of the same spices in certain parts of Far Jaati so she is reluctant to do the same. However, since they are one of Sensibar's largest trading partners, she doesn't want to push them away until she has an alternative. Presently, the queen has allowed Castorhage to establish a supply depot near the city of Sinda on Ibeshi Isle. The depot includes a series of warehouses near the port that the Castorhagi will build and own, where they can store supplies for their far-traveling ships.

The government appears to get plenty of money from taxing the trade on spices, but the queen also has another very quiet source of income. More than a century ago, a prospector found diamonds in the Milkapiti Hills near the source of the Negovan River. The king at the time hushed this up very thoroughly and then spent years having his own people search for and develop working diamond mines. Unofficial royal representatives sold the diamonds a few at a time through trusted intermediaries, and very soon the mines went from making a profit to bringing the royal family amazing sums of money. They have, perhaps, spent more than could be accounted for by the spice trade, but there is no one to call them to account, so the palace and the capital as a whole keep getting more ostentatious. The rest of the kingdom is not suffering, but neither are they living at the level of luxury found near the royal family.

OMPESHI, CITY OF (CAPITAL)

Ruler: Princess Kiumbwa the Dulcet, Cousin to Her Magnificence
Government: monarchy
Population: 64,676 (63,210 Equatorian, 125 Castorhagi, 1,341 other human ethnicity)

Sensibar's capital city of Ompeshi is almost luxurious, with gardens, beautiful fountains, and carriages pulled by exotic beasts to take people even short distances. Essentially, all unpleasant work is done by foreigners who are either paid and worked hard, or owned and worked harder. The poorest citizens work at trades such as dressmaking or innkeeping, and even then, they have hirelings to do any difficult work.

Life elsewhere in the kingdom is much better than most places but not as good as in the capital. To keep it from becoming overcrowded by people who think moving to Ompeshi would solve all their troubles, all Sensibrite visitors (including merchants) must register with the guard when they arrive and receive a pass that allows them to stay a certain number of days. If they do not return their pass on time, visitors are subject to magical search and arrest, followed by magically enforced exile from the capital. Foreign travelers are not subject to the same restriction, but they almost always stand out in the city so it is easy for the guard to keep track of them and be sure they are not overstaying their welcome.

Ompeshi has several lovely temples, as does each city of the kingdom, dedicated to the deities handed down by the ancient ones. Most important to this trading country is Sifkra, Who Loves Coins, but Lohfa, Who

Makes Things Grow, is just as important, and chapels or shrines to him can be found on nearly every plantation. Selena, the Peaceful Lady, is popular with many, as is Ahtizerr, Who Loves Magic. Ghamia, the River Lady, has a temple in Ompeshi but otherwise is mostly worshipped in cities and towns on the rivers. Vreenon, Who Loves Birds, and Anana, the Lady of Luck and Gold, have temples here because that it what the capital city should have, but not many actively worship there. The temple of Gonthor, Who Grumbles in the Sky, is mostly attended by soldiers and naval personnel visiting the city, and a larger temple to the god of strength and war can be found at the navy's base in Gulama.

The port at Ompeshi is up to date but not large, and it frequently becomes crowded with ships. The solution that has been instituted is to force ships to leave the dock after one day to make room for more ships to conduct their business. Some captains elect to just lie at anchor nearby in the bay, but any who plan to be in Sensibar more than a day or two are encouraged to dock instead at Sinda on Ibeshi Isle. No fishing boats are allowed to fill up the docking space at Ompeshi; fishing boats have their own separate harbor east of the city, which also happens to be downwind.

GULAMA, CITY OF

Ruler: Her Grace Lady Maua the Just, Second Cousin to Her Magnificence
Government: monarchy
Population: 21,198 (20,830 Equatorian, 45 Castorhagi, 323 other human ethnicity)

Gulama is located in a natural harbor near the western end of Ibeshi Isle. When more merchants and traveling ships began to call at Ompeshi and Sinda, the crown felt it best to move the naval facilities to a different location, which became Gulama. Shipbuilding yards are here, as well as the navy's training facilities and enough anchorage for most of the fleet. Active patrols keep foreign ships away from these waters. In the past several years, the queen has instituted, and Lady Maua has overseen, a significant increase in the size of the navy, including its force of marines. Under Lord Admiral Tarab the Long-sighted, Uncle to Her Magnificence, the navy has nearly doubled in size in 10 years and is almost to the place where it could hope to defend Sensibar against an actual attack by Castorhage — assuming most of that country's ships are busy elsewhere.

Given the wealth of the kingdom, the navy's facilities are more comfortable than those of almost any other country in the world, but participation is still more work than most other citizens ever do. The pay and benefits are excellent, though, and retiring from the navy is one of the few ways to guarantee owning a home in Ompeshi.

KAJORO, CITY OF

Ruler: Prince Ussi the Brave, Cousin to Her Magnificence
Government: monarchy
Population: 5,799 (5,695 Equatorian, 25 Castorhagi, 79 other human ethnicity)

Kajoro is built on the site of an ancient fortress and watchtower. The fortress has become the palace in the heart of the city, enhanced of course by gardens, covered walkways, and other changes over the years. The watchtower on the point overlooking the sea is topped by a lighthouse with a beacon that has supposedly been lit nightly for hundreds (some even say thousands) of years. Repairs to the outside of the watchtower have to be done — and then redone — as the new material weathers away, but the inside and the supports remain in good shape. Prince Ussi, who was a naval officer until an unfortunate injury ended his career, takes the city's responsibility to the watchtower very seriously and has been known to personally conduct surprise inspections of the facility.

The market of Kajoro gathers all the products of the east side of the Bay, and the city provides a large port for use by interested merchants. This resulted in the area being very prosperous. Only a little of the money is spent in luxury for the city or its lord; most is spent on improving the

lives of the common people and also to a degree the lives of the owners of the large plantations. Prince Ussi currently has people exploring the cost and difficulty of building a crown road inland from Kajoro about 50 miles and then north through some of the plantation areas. He is nearly ready to send out exploration teams to determine the best route, and then to start building out from the city.

MASUNGA, CITY OF

Ruler: His Grace Lord Feethan the Glorious, Second Cousin to Her Magnificence
Government: monarchy
Population: 5,396 (5,286 Equatorian, 15 Castorhagi, 95 other human ethnicity)

This city lies on the west coast of Sensibar at the mouth of the Nassoro River. It boasts an excellent port, and a good road also runs from here to Ompeshi. Plantations as far inland as the Milkapiti Hills ship their spices and other produce to Masunga to trade. In fact, many plantation owners have mansions in the city and directly oversee the sales of their goods. The crown puts certain limits on prices, however; spices cannot be sold below a certain minimum to avoid undercutting other Sensibrite producers.

Although Masunga is ostensibly at the limit of the kingdom, Lord Feethan turns a blind eye to people who wish to explore or even establish small settlements north of the river. He has so far been unwilling to send in the army unit he has under his command, so two groups have recently fared badly at the hands of tribes in the area.

One site of interest on the north side of the river is the ruins of an ancient fortress. It has long been a rite of passage for youth to sneak across the river at night and explore, but a group of historians who want to make a serious study of the place recently approached Lord Feethan. They promised to write up their findings for the royal library, and he offered them the protection of the military while they do their research.

NADHANI, CITY OF

Ruler: Princess Mwajume the Glimmering, Niece to Her Magnificence
Government: monarchy
Population: 17,921 (16,980 Equatorian, 67 Castorhagi, 874 other human ethnicity)

On a wide plain at the mouth of the Negovan River, surrounded by white beaches and clear blue sea, Nadhani is widely thought to have the most beautiful setting of any of the kingdom's cities. The city is built primarily of white stone so it, too, gleams in the sun. Unfortunately, Princess Mwajume has little interest in the upkeep of the city. She is more interested in using tax money to beautify or amuse herself and opens the public purse only for expenses (such as the upkeep of the port) that will bring in more trade and thus more tax money. After three years of official neglect, the city is finally starting to lose its luster.

Riches pour into the city in the form of sacks and barrels of spices, carvings and goods made of exotic woods as well as logs of the wood for use in ships or building, and even the occasional shipment of ivory from the forest elephants used as work animals far up the river. A crown-sponsored road connects Nadhani to Ompeshi in the west and all the towns and villages in between, and goods come from that direction as well. Trade is brisk; sellers don't dare undercut the official prices, but have no qualms about offering to throw in a little something extra or offer a special gift to persuade a buyer. With the princess looking the other way, an active slave auction system even developed, rather than slave purchases being handled privately as they are in the rest of the kingdom. Some people are starting to grumble about the departures from previous rulers, but others with long memories point out that things could be much worse. So far, no one is willing to journey 300 miles to Ompeshi to complain to her magnificence the queen, so the situation stays as it is.

SINDA, CITY OF

Ruler: Prince Salum the Erudite, Nephew to Her Magnificence
Government: monarchy
Population: 8,701 (8,346 Equatorian, 30 Castorhagi, 325 other human ethnicity)

Sinda is at the eastern end of Ibeshi Isle, approximately 50 miles southwest of Ompeshi. Originally founded as a naval base, it now focuses more on shipbuilding, although a few naval vessels are stationed there. Since the port facilities at Ompeshi are rather small, foreign ships are invited to dock at the island while they awaiting their turn in port, waiting to pick up cargo, or finishing any repairs or resupply. One of the royal family's improvements of the port at Ompeshi was to acquire magical communications devices, so the harbormaster at the capital can communicate with the harbormaster at Sinda rather than relying on message boats or some other type of signals.

One of Prince Salum's most important duties is acting as diplomat with pushy foreign merchants or officious envoys. That way, by the time they actually speak with Queen Lediana, they understand what is or is not proper for them to propose and she is not importuned by their unreasonable requests.

GEOGRAPHIC FEATURES AND POINTS OF INTEREST IN THE KINGDOM OF SENSIBAR

IBESHI ISLE

Off the southwestern tip of southern Libynos, Ibeshi Isle is mostly covered with plantations raising trees for the navy (a long-term proposition, to be sure) and food to supply the naval base at Gulama. A well-maintained road supported by royal funds runs from Sinda on the east coast to Gulama through the middle of the island. This makes it easy to get supplies to the navy and also for the noble plantation owners to travel to Sinda for a ship to Ompeshi.

NASSORO RIVER

The Nassoro flows from the south end of the Milkapiti Hills west and a little south to the coast of Mother Oceanus at Masunga. Its warm waters are full of freshwater fish. The Nassoro has historically been the northwestern border of Sensibar, but several noble plantation owners have been petitioning to expand their holdings on the north side of the river. Although that side is not claimed by another country, it is not empty and Queen Lediana expects some conflict if Sensibrites do move into the area.

NEGOVAN RIVER

The Negovan River and its tributaries run east of the Milkapiti Hills, primarily filled by all the runoff from the plentiful rains. It reaches the sea at Nadhani, where it empties into the Bay of Pandu.

PANDU, BAY OF

The Bay of Pandu is at the southwestern extreme of Libynos, surrounded on three sides by the Kingdom of Sensibar. Many people around the bay live off its fish. Along the east coast are many coves with exceptionally clear water where jewel-like fish, corals, and other sea treasures are at hand for the taking. Large pieces of coral for carving — worth little to Sensibrites but valuable in far-off countries — are often harvested in the bay.

TULYAMIN, PRINCIPALITY OF

Capital: Meziray
Notable Settlements: Dodoma, Larrima, Mandemar, Teluvay
Ruler: Prince Diodorus Momose
Government: monarchy
Population: 1,041,327 (1,039,656 Equatorian, 93 Castorhagi, 1,578 other human ethnicity)
Monstrous: leucrottas, nazalors, monstrous centipedes
Languages: Zenzin
Religion: Paramountcies pantheon
Resources: exotic foods, spices, cabb'e and cocoa beans, ivory
Currency: Bhanakhiran, Castorhagi
Technology Level: High Middle Ages (Meziray, Larrima, Teluvay), Dark Ages (cities and towns), Iron Age (rural areas)

Tulyamin is located on the Reaping Sea on the eastern coast of Libynos, at the very southern tip of the continent. The country is not large or populous, but it does produce several valuable spices such as cabb'e beans, cocoa beans, cinnamon, cloves, nutmeg, and pepper. The late Prince Vedastus encouraged his people to start planting the two types of beans when he saw how well they did in nearby countries, but at the time many thought the drinks made from them were just a passing fancy. Now those who cultivate either of the beans are doing quite well, and others are starting to grow them also.

Prince Diodorus has reigned for 17 years, and it has been a time of stability and peace. But the prince is nervous nonetheless. Castorhage has colonies only a few days' sail north along the Reaping Coast, and their merchant captains stop frequently in Tulyamin. Realizing the country could never defend itself against a determined attack by the city-state, Diodorus can only hope Tulyamin looks to be not worth the effort. He has heard that Queen Lediana of Sensibar is being pressured to grant Castorhage a trade monopoly and is afraid he would be unable to refuse if such a thing were demanded of him.

Tulyamin has a small army that is usually split between the northern and southern outposts of the country. The intention is that it could move quickly to wherever it might be needed, and the Prince's Road, a coastal road the length of the country, is kept in good repair to facilitate that necessity. The navy is somewhat larger and actively patrols up and down the coast out of its base at Larrima.

The population of Tulyamin is not highly religious, but temples are kept in each city to the most important of the ancestral deities. The first would be Lohfa, Who Makes Things Grow, followed by Ghamia, the River Lady. Vreenon, Who Loves Birds, and Selena, the Peaceful Lady, also have temples. One of the closest friends of Prince Diodorus is a wizard, Kabwe Mefume; his research discovered that the worship of Ahtizerr, Who Loves Magic, is really a very old-fashioned form of devotion to Thasizier, the god of goodness and magic, who is the patron deity of an important wizards' school on the island of Jah Sezar in the eastern Reaping Sea. That being the case, Thasizier's temples were updated just a few years ago, and the priests were sent to learn anything more they needed to know about the worship of their true deity.

MEZIRAY, CITY OF (CAPITAL)

Ruler: Lord Phares Momose
Government: monarchy
Population: 46,998 (46,628 Equatorian, 20 Castorhagi, 350 other human ethnicity)

The capital city of Tulyamin, Meziray is at the mouth of the Amani River where it empties into the Reaping Sea. The Prince's Road crosses the Amani just upriver from the city, on a bridge high enough that the flat river ships can sail under it. The city is on a small inlet that gives it a good location for a sheltered port, and the river and its feeder streams mean that a lot of producers can transport their trade goods to the coast fairly easily. The trade market is near the port, separate from the regular city market so the population doesn't have to fight its way through the trade goods just to buy bread. While merchant ships and their crews — even foreigners — are welcome in the city, everything is arranged to keep the regular people's lives as peaceful as possible.

The royal palace is on the west edge of the city, away from the bustle and odor of the port. It is no higher than two stories and is built

The lighthouse at Teluvay on the Drakon Strait is lit during a storm.
The lighthouse at Mandemar on Savelina Island is visible across the strait in the distance.

around a central courtyard that allows the rooms to be open and still be protected enough to please the royal guard. One long wing is given over to the quarters of the family and other nobles, while the opposite wing holds offices and public meeting rooms. Peace is important to Prince Diodorus, but some think the palace has become too quiet since the prince became a widower three years ago. He was left with only one child, a young girl. It has been many generations since Tulyamin had a reigning princess, and many people are uncomfortable with the idea. The prince's advisors frequently urge him to marry again, to give himself some companionship and to secure the succession with at least one more heir.

DODOMA, CITY OF

Ruler: Lady Batilda Negovan
Government: monarchy
Population: 7,461 (7,306 Equatorian, 10 Castorhagi, 145 other human ethnicity)

On the coast of the Reaping Sea at the mouth of the Nitibende River, Dodoma is the farthest north of Tulyamin's cities. It is not the northern border of the country, however; settlements run farther north along the coast and also inland along the river, which is entirely north of the city. The northern force of the royal army is stationed here in a refurbished fortress thought to have been built by the ancient ones millennia ago. Technically, Lady Batilda has the authority to order the army out, but she can't imagine ever needing it for anything unless some inland tribe decides to attack one of the northern villages. General Harith Sindato is not as optimistic as the lady, but is sure he can persuade her of her duty should the need arise.

As the northernmost port, Dodoma receives a lot of visits from merchant ships (both Tulyamin and foreign) before they make the several-days' journey on up the Reaping Coast, or as their first stop on the long southward trip. The city has a good port and a protective harbor, so it is a preferred refuge in the face of the many wild storms that brew up in the Reaping Sea. The fees are reasonable and the people friendly, so though the beer is different from what northern crews are used to drinking, Dodoma is a regular stop for many ships. In addition to the many foodstuffs available in the other cities, Dodoma sometimes also offers ivory from smallholders far up the river who use forest elephants to help their work and copper from a small mine in the Kulgera Ridge.

LARRIMA, CITY OF

Ruler: Lady Maida Kayanza
Government: monarchy
Population: 12,798 (12,690 Equatorian, 3 Castorhagi, 105 other human ethnicity)

The Lekule River comes down to the Reaping Sea at Larrima, and the Prince's Road bridges it where the road enters the city. The river is an important water route for people to ship their goods to a trade center. Despite its good port, Larrima doesn't get the foreign traffic that other cities do; ship captains find it faster to travel from Teluvay straight to Meziray, bypassing Larrima altogether. Local merchants make the trips back and forth from Larrima to the other two cities.

Residents of Tulyamin spread through about two-thirds of the peninsula, as the Sensibrites on the west coast have never extended more than about 100 miles inland. Other citizens live in towns and villages along the southern coast. Great storms destroyed some of those settlements at least three times in the past century, and those who live farther north can't understand why the inhabitants don't move somewhere less dangerous. The coasters, as they call themselves, say living in the area is worth the risk and just stubbornly rebuild.

MANDEMAR, CITY OF

Ruler: Lord Rostam Momose
Government: monarchy
Population: 6,510 (almost all Equatorian)

Mandemar sits on the northwest corner of Savelina Island, near an ancient lighthouse that was rebuilt about 400 years ago after a series of shipwrecks showed the renewed need for such a device. The town was originally founded to service the lighthouse but grew into an active port. It has long been popular to take sailing trips to catch some of the great ocean fish, and Mandemar, with its proximity to the open sea and the great Mother Oceanus, is the best place for adventurous people to hire ships for those activities. Naval vessels are also stationed here and patrol around the islands and the southern coast of Tulyamin.

As the ruler of Mandemar, Lord Rostam also oversees the welfare of the population of Savelina Island. Since the smallholders on the island are the main producers of the food for the people of the city, their success is of vital interest to the city dwellers and their lord.

TELUVAY, CITY OF

Ruler: Lord Idris Haruna
Government: monarchy
Population: 11,446 (11,020 Equatorian, 21 Castorhagi, 405 other human ethnicity)

Teluvay is at the southern end of the Tulyamin coast road. The southern unit of the army is stationed here, in a fortress much like the one built by the ancients in what is now the city of Dodoma. The troops under General Jumanne Athuman stay alert for any threats to the country or any threats to just the city that might come from (for example) a foreign ship in port. However, the most action the unit has seen in the past several years was rescuing people along the southern coast of Tulyamin after some especially bad storms.

Teluvay has an average port and is a stopping place for many merchant ships, but its real importance lies in the lighthouse that stands on a rocky spit east of the city. An ancient light tower was found in ruins centuries ago on Savelina Island and painstakingly rebuilt, and then the lighthouse at Teluvay was built to match. The lights guide approaching ships to the entrance of the Drakon Strait, but even more they warn southward-sailing ships of the land curved out in front of their path. Although it has been about 400 years, sailors still talk about the three shipwrecks that took place west of Teluvay in a single decade, when night or storm put ships off-course.

GEOGRAPHIC FEATURES AND POINTS OF INTEREST IN THE PRINCIPALITY OF TULYAMIN

AMANI RIVER

Flowing through central Tulyamin, the Amani River is filled primarily by the copious rainfall in the interior, which it carries to the coast of the Reaping Sea at Meziray. The river's dependence on runoff means that at some seasons it is much lower and at others it is high and fast, so villages that use it as an important means of transport must take those changes into consideration.

DRAKON STRAIT

Drakon Strait lies between the southeastern tip of the Tulyamin mainland and Savelina Island. It is about 30 miles wide and 60 miles long and lighthouses at Teluvay and Mandemar mark the northern corners. No one knows why it has the name it does; "drakon" is not even a word in the Tulyamin language. However, the oldest maps have the strait so marked, and later cartographers continued the tradition.

LEKULE RIVER

The Lekule is a short river flowing from the interior of Tulyamin's wide peninsula and is fed by rainfall. The ease of travel given by the river makes communication possible with the villages and smallholders in the center of the peninsula. The river empties into the Reaping Sea at Larrima.

LITTLE IDD

A slightly oblong island about 30 miles in the long direction, Little Idd lies 50 miles northeast of Savelina Island in the southern part of the Reaping Sea. The island is commonly supposed to be uninhabited, but people tell each other all kinds of stories about what is really on Little Idd. Parents tell their children that if they are not quiet at night, monsters from Little Idd will swim over and eat them. Old hands at sea try to frighten new sailors with tales of a murderer whose transport ship was lost in a storm. They say the killer washed ashore on Little Idd and lives there still, surviving on fish and seaweed, hiding in the caves, and killing anyone else who sets foot on the island.

It is true that there are caves under the rocky hills that cover Little Idd, and that someone could hide in them. Some stories claim that the island is a hideout for pirates. Others whisper that an army is hiding on Little Idd, on the far side where they can't be seen by ships at Savelina, and when they are ready, they will invade Tulyamin. This is one story that Prince Diodorus takes semi-seriously; the navy has standing orders to sail completely around Little Idd on a regular basis and to disembark for a closer investigation if they see anything out of order.

Really, though, Little Idd is uninhabited and everyone knows it, even though there is no way to actually prove it.

NITIBENDE RIVER

The Nitibende flows through the northern part of Tulyamin, through deep jungle to Dodoma on the coast. It begins in the southern part of the Kulgera Ridge and runs south to the Reaping Sea. The villages and other small settlements on or near the river and the streams that feed it give Tulyamin a claim to much of the interior jungle along the Reaping Sea, far past the country's most northerly city along the coast.

SAVELINA ISLAND

This island sits in the south part of the Reaping Sea, about 30 miles east of the tip of the Tulyamin mainland. Other than the city of Mandemar and the royal lighthouse, the island is only lightly inhabited, primarily by people who grow food or fish to supply some of the city's needs. The northern side is hilly, while the southern is low-lying, with mangrove swamps to the east that are often flooded during storms. Lord Rostam declared that each of the inland villages have a common building large enough for the coast dwellers to take shelter during storms if necessary.

One thing the island does have right now is a large population of wild pigs. Left behind when the owner dies, or escaped from a pen in a storm — one way or another, pigs got loose several years ago and are now breeding in the wild. Islanders take extra care to protect gardens or ground crops because the pigs certainly try to get into them. For those who can hunt the pigs, the wild creatures provide plenty of meat. Sometimes Lord Rostam gets together an expedition from Mandemar for the purpose of decreasing the wild pig population and also providing a great roast for the island's people.

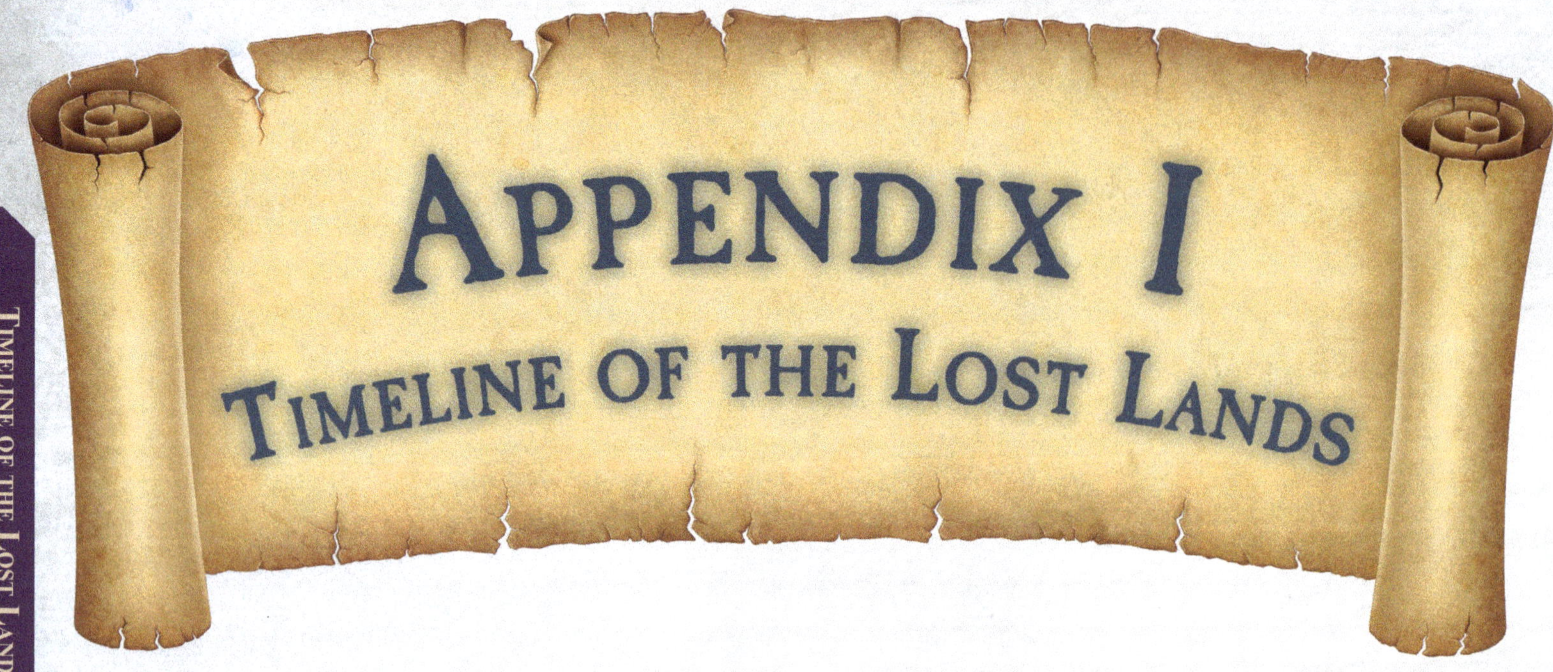

APPENDIX I
TIMELINE OF THE LOST LANDS

The following sets forth a timeline of major events in the Lost Lands, as currently recognized by leading scholars in Akados and Libynos. Needless to say, not all events of import have been listed, and some may reflect rumors or estimates based on such knowledge as is currently available.

For simplicity, all dates are given by reference to the Imperial Record of the Hyperborean Empire. Other calendars in common use can be converted based on their date of origination (the elven Erylle Cycle has its year 1 in –6484 I.R., the Khemitian Reckoning of Kings in –1518 I.R., the Xha'en Calendar in –1302 I.R., the Blessed Year of Mah-Barek in 480 I.R., the Regis Castorhagi in 1741 I.R., and the Huun Chronicle in 2496 I.R.).

Imperial Record (I.R.)	Event
	AGE OF GODS
c. 7 billion years ago	Creation of the world of Boros
c. 100 million years ago	Arrival of the Great Old Ones on the world of Boros
c. 30 million years ago	Beginning of the Primordial War among the Great Old Ones
c. 23 million years ago	End of the Primordial War; many Great Old Ones decline in influence, but survive in isolated locations
c. 20 million years ago	Fiery object from the skies called the Judgment of Xtu crashes into eastern Libynos creating Boiling Sea and devastates the populations of the Great Old Ones' nonhuman servitor races and the great beasts inhabiting the world
	AGE OF DRAGONS
c. 19 million years ago	Elemental and primal dragons arrive on Boros from Inner Planes and defeat unhuman races
c. 5 million years ago	Dragon Wars between the metallic and chromatic dragons
c. 1.2 million years ago	Giants arrive on Boros from Jotunheim and battle the dragons
	AGE OF MAN
c. 100,000 years ago	Neolithic human groups begin to spread over Boros
c. 25,000	Initial origins of communities that will become Khemit, Istaflumina, and Jaati on Libynos, and Xha'en in western Akados
	AGE OF STRIFE
c. 18,000 years ago	Oldest human cities founded, including Erethu, Gessh, and Ur on Libynos; the explorer Koshag of Ur sails Sinnar Ocean and establishes city-state of Xantollan on Pontos Island
c.17,000 years ago	Elven god Wayland the Smith unlocks the secret to passing between the elven homeland of Alfheim and the world of Boros; elves begin arriving on Boros
c. 15,700 years ago	Jaati colonists cross Mother Oceanus and establish city-state of Gtsang
c. 15,000 years ago	Beginning of Gods' War
c. 14,800 years ago	War between the dwarves of Niðavellir and the elves of Svartalfheim (drow); dwarves discover secret of gates of Wayland, and dwarves and drow arrive on Boros
c. 14,500 years ago	Thyr ends the Gods' War

Imperial Record (I.R.)	Event
	AGE OF KINGS
c. 12,000 years ago	Rise of Phoromyceaen civilization
–7031	Subterranean city of Barakus constructed by Phoromyceaen peoples under Duskmoon Hills
–6671	Arvonliet walks among mankind and elder races
–6650	Construction secretly begins on Arvonliet's Abyssal gate
–6627	City of Barakus falls
–6484	Thyr, Muir, and Kel overthrow Arvonliet, driving him from Boros and casting him into the Ginnungagap (where he becomes known as Orcus); Stoneheart Mountains raised over Keltine Barrier; elves migrate from Alfheim to Boros in First Exodus; last Phoromyceaen city, Lyemmos, disappears in a vast sinkhole

Imperial Record (I.R.)	Event in Akados	Event in Libynos
	AGE OF SILENCE	
–6470	Phoromyceaen Sorcerer-King of Tharistra, Gremag, obtains lichdom and inters himself in hidden caverns beneath Stoneheart Mountains	
–4891		Beginning of Pre-Dynastic Period in Khemit
–4483	Harul of Estresia founds shrine in Stoneheart Mountains above Keltine Barrier	
–4481	Harul of Estresia martyred, sainted by Thyr and Muir	
–4232	Beginning of War of King-Chieftain Aracor in Plains of Sull	
–4227	Arrival of *Obelisks of Chaos* in Sull; destruction of Broch Marfal; end of King-Chieftain's War	
c. –2000	Xha'en migration into the Plains of Xha begins	
–1520	First conflict between the Xha'en and the Senge tribesmen on Plains of Xha	
–1518		Narmer crowned pharaoh of Conjoined Double Kingdoms of Khemit; beginning of Ancient Dynastic Period
–1302	Last Senge tribes driven from Plains of Xha; founding of the city of Xha'ahan	
–1288		Menes crowned pharaoh of Khemit; beginning of 2nd Dynasty
–1138		Semerkhet crowned pharaoh of Khemit; beginning of 3rd Dynasty
–1025	Harul's Shrine discovered in vision by Beward of the Three Gods	
–1017		Djoser crowned pharaoh of Khemit; beginning of 4th Dynasty
–1013	Beward establishes St. Harul's Hold on site of shrine	
–943		Beginning of 5th Dynasty of Khemit
–833		Udimu crowned pharaoh of Khemit; beginning of 6th Dynasty
–722	Rise of First Yaltic Dynasty in Hawkmoon region	
–691		Teti crowned pharaoh of Khemit; beginning of 7th Dynasty
–629		Cult of Orcus in guise of "Aurikas" rises in southern Libynos
–613		Atrocities of Aurikas's priest Akruel Rathamon begin in lands along the Reaping Sea

Imperial Record (I.R.)	Event in Akados	Event in Libynos
–604		Arden rallies followers in Khemit under Shah Rasalt to bring war to the burgeoning empire of Akruel Rathamon; beginning of War of Divine Discord
–579		Shah Rasalt of Arden defeats the armies of Aurikas at Al-Sifon on Reaping Sea; Akruel Rathamon slain; end of War of Divine Discord
–573	St. Harul's Hold becomes High Altar of Thyr and Muir	
–518		Anendjib crowned pharaoh of Khemit; beginning of 8th Dynasty: university and library founded in Pharos
–488		Netrikare crowned pharaoh of Khemit; beginning of 9th Dynasty; First Intermediate Period
–450	First reports of incursions of Shadow from the Nam-i-Budhani (Lost Mountains) north of the Great Steppe	
–408		Menkare crowned pharaoh of Khemit; beginning of 10th Dynasty; Early Triple Kingdom
–360		Amunenhat I crowned pharaoh of Khemit; beginning of 11th Dynasty
–187	Construction of Lujhiran Dam on the Pantai River in the Plains of Xha completed	
–182	Tsathogga unleashes horde of demons in Irkaina; the god Arden sacrifices himself to entrap horde and stop the invasion; Tropic of Arden created	
–151		Beginning of 12th Dynasty of Khemit
THE HYPERBOREAN AGE		
–109	Polemarch Oerson leads Hyperborean Legion out of Boros and into Akados	
–107	Oerson discovers St. Harul's Hold and bestows gifts upon its patriarch	
–102	Wild elves drive Hyperboreans from forest; Legion advances along forest's edge passing through region that will become the Sundered Kingdoms	
–92	Elven high lords gather elven host; Oerson's Perilous March begins	
–91	Elves defeated by human and mountain dwarf alliance at Lake Crimmormere	
–90	Oerson founds city of Apothasalos	
–88	Oerson's advance checked at Helcynngae Peninsula; Legion withdraws into hills between March of Mountains and Forlorn Mountains; Stronghold Hjerrin erected in Lorremach Highhills	
–87	Remenos founded	
–83	Construction of Helwall begun, Legion breeds horses on plains east of Lorremach Highhills	
–73	Helwall completed, Heldring contained on peninsula; Exeter Province established, foundations laid for forts at Albor Broce and Sylvos	
–69	Town of Sessilbridge established	
–28	Death of Oerson	
–27	Rise of Valenthlis; outbreak of elven civil war	

Imperial Record (I.R.)	Event in Akados	Event in Libynos
−26	Wild elves withdraw to western Akados in Second Exodus	
−17	Monarchs of Boros send episcopi to Akados demanding increased tribute	
−11	Hyperborean Rebellion; construction begins on Tower of Oerson in Curgantium	
−8		Menkamin I crowned pharaoh of Khemit; beginning of 13th Dynasty; Second Intermediate Period
−3	Polemarchs Crassin and Odontius march south from Boros	
−2	Tower of Oerson completed	
1	Battle of Hummaemidon; birth of Imperial Record	
3	First citadel of Castorhage constructed on Insula Lymossus	
4		Hyperborean expedition to Libynos; Khemitites defeated at Battle of Phillistia; Khemit made vassal kingdom, effectively bringing northern Libynos into Hyperborean Empire
5	Porta Librum constructed at mouth of Talamerin River	Oeric receives vision of Sacred Table, begins construction of Tircople
7	Great Khan Jaganga arises among Hundaei and unites them into Invincible Horde	
8	Hyperboreans found city of Occibolos on the Binjerin River	
11	Vengeful mountain dwarves show Hundaei secret passes through Stoneheart Mountains; refugees from Hundaei expansion begin to arrive on Anaros Island and the Thousand Rocks	Tircople completed; Oeric abdicates claim on throne and appointed Pontifex; High Altar of Muir moved from St. Harul's Hold to Tircople
12	Oesson crowned as imperator of the Hyperborean Empire; first Hundaei cross the Stonehearts and appear in Hyperborean lands	
14	Hundaei besiege Apothasalos, which is relieved by Gnassus; beginning of Hundaei Wars	
52	Queen Talith Harwood of Solis Alunaris and King Reithon of Suomen Gron raise the Cinderhame Mountains to defend the Green Realm from Vilik Strad	
82		Beginning of 14th Dynasty of Khemit; Old Triple Kingdom Period
128	Hyperboreans colonize Insula Extremis, battle Heldring on Helcynngae Peninsula	
145	Jhohir and Rojhah in Plains of Xha join in a confederacy	
212	Hill dwarves of Irkaina teach ironworking to Hyperboreans	
288	Stratego Verin and his Legion destroyed by Heldring in Peninsular Campaign; militias raised from Helwall to Apothasalos fearing Heldring attack; coastal forts erected south of Matagost Range to guard against sea invasion, forts of Albor Broce and Sylvos expanded	
325		Rameses I crowned pharaoh of Khemit; beginning of 15th Dynasty
359		Hyperborean engineers complete the Canal of the Pharaohs in Khemit; opens travel from Sea of Baal to Ruby Sea

Imperial Record (I.R.)	Event in Akados	Event in Libynos
436		Merikare crowned pharaoh of Khemit; beginning of 16th Dynasty
c. 480		Religion of Mah-Barek founded in the Ashurian Desert
494	City of Occibolos burned and razed to the ground by the Hundaei	
515		Followers of Mah-Barek split into four churches
532	Invasion of Thousand Rocks/Anaros Island by Jhohir Confederacy is defeated by both weather and Anari warriors	
534		Karram, eldest grandson of Mah-Barek's First Disciple Fatimashan, founds Karramid Caliphate on Libynos
535	Jhohir Confederacy collapses	
562		Rameses II crowned pharaoh of Khemit; beginning of 17th Dynasty
678	Hyperborean Legions push into Great Steppes	
680	Hundaei settle near the Nam-i-Budhani (Lost Mountains) due to Hyperborean pressure	
681	Civil war erupts among Hundaei clans	
683	Hundaei cease to exist as a people; survivors flee to Sea of Grass or Libynos, remainder becoming the Shattered Folk of the Great Steppes	

Pax Hyperborea

Imperial Record (I.R.)	Event in Akados	Event in Libynos
687		Djedkare crowned pharaoh of Khemit; beginning of 18th Dynasty
689	City of Tsen founded	
712	Humanoids raid south from the Great Steppes; elven defense of Crynnomar Gap	
717	Remenos extends marchlands north; old forests of the elves cut for timber	
725	Wild elves withdraw further to the west of Akados in Third Exodus; Green Warder monoliths raised	
804		Beginning of 19th Dynasty of Khemit
872		Antiocham Solinius, First Tradelord to Hyperborean Imperator, begins policy of strengthening the city-states west of the Scythirian Mountains as counterbalance to the merchants of Khemit
908		Sekhemkare crowned pharaoh of Khemit; beginning of 20th Dynasty
928		Death of Antiocham Solinius; primary city west of Scythirian Mountains renamed Antioch in his honor; cities in the region become known as the Antioch City-States
968		Beginning of 21st Dynasty of Khemit
1020	Thyrian clerics open ferry across Stoneheart River and build chapel on central island	
1021	Nûk tribe of wild elves ends its wandering among forests along coast of North Sea and establishes Nûkland far from human influence	
1107		Inyotef I crowned pharaoh of Khemit; beginning of 22nd Dynasty; Third Intermediate Period; capital moved from Menefet

Imperial Record (I.R.)	Event in Akados	Event in Libynos
1228		Amyrtalos crowned pharaoh of Khemit; beginning of 23rd Dynasty; Middle Triple Kingdom Period
1233		Nepherities I crowned pharaoh of Khemit; beginning of 24th Dynasty
1300		Amenemhat crowned pharaoh of Khemit; beginning of 25th Dynasty; Fourth Intermediate Period
1328		Plye I (first Nubiar pharaoh) crowned pharaoh of Khemit; beginning of 26th Dynasty; Classic Triple Kingdom Period
1398	Founding of the Xha'en Hegemony by the first Ahra Emperor, Vaelos su Dis	
1444		Nedjemibre crowned pharaoh of Khemit; beginning of 27th Dynasty
1491	City of Tsen destroyed in a terrible cataclysm; the Great Darkness covers the waters of the Gulf of Akados region for three years; sea trade to the north ceases; Aka Bakar's tower appears on Feirgotha Plateau, who establishes the Kingdom of Arcady in the Stoneheart Mountains, and commences war against dwarves of Clan Craenog; Thyrian Stoneheart River ferry and chapel abandoned, construction begun on shrines to Thyr and Muir in upper Lyre Valley	Aka Bakar's tower disappears from city of Pharos in Khemit along with a third of the Pharos Legion
1494	Following the end of the Great Darkness, land route to the Irkainian Peninsula reopens; Apothasalos reestablished but never regains its former size and status; Occibolos reoccupied as little more than a town, now known as Oxibbul; Baen Halfhammer slain by Aka Bakar, Arcady gains control of Baen's Pass, establishes trade with gulf region	
c. 1500?		Huun arrive at Desert of Oreb in Libynos
1503	Wizards that escaped Tsen establish Gray Tower in Oxibbul as academy and guildhall	
1543	City of Rojhah falls to Ahra forces	
1544	City of Jhohir joins Xha'en Hegemony	
1546	Aban Rha and Thanalos join Xha'en Hegemony	
1548	Hobgoblin raids from Deepfells Mountains descend into northern fringes of Reme; survivors report a new hobgoblin kingdom arisen among the clans of Dragonbone Peak led by a seemingly unbeatable warlord; armies of the Northmarches fall back before the onslaught	
1554	Earthquake and tidal wave devastate Xha'en coast and the undersea kingdom of Caerulea; raids on Xha'en shipping by Caeruleans begin	
1557	Northmarches fall to hobgoblin armies; everything north of the High Downs becomes part of Hobgoblin Kingdom of the Deepfells; defensive line is created between the High Downs and the Green Mountains	
1558	Open war between Xha'en Hegemony and Caerulea	
1564	Adventurers infiltrate Dragonbone Peak and discover warlord to be hobgoblin demigod Kakobovia	

Imperial Record (I.R.)	Event in Akados	Event in Libynos
1571	Army of Deepfell hobgoblins and orcs invade Arcady	
1572	Aka Bakar defeated and Arcady falls, but Deepfell army is also destroyed in magical devastation	
1573	Kakobovia gathers remaining forces of Dragonbone and launches all-out attack on High Downs; at Battle of Ironhill, Grand Duke Borell I of Reme defeats hobgoblins of Dragonbone and personally banishes incarnation of Kakobovia from Material Plane; Reme begins to reclaim Northmarches	
1576	Peace treaty between Xha'en Hegemony and Caerulea signed	
1581	The Ophronya Dynasty of Djir seizes power and moves capital of Xha'en Hegemony	
1602		Nebirau crowned pharaoh of Khemit; beginning of 28th Dynasty; Fifth Intermediate Period
1610		House of Ammu gains control of Karramid Caliphate on Libynos; renamed the Ammuyad Caliphate
1636		Amasis VI crowned pharaoh of Khemit; beginning of 29th Dynasty; Late Triple Kingdom Period
1643	Gtsang agrees to join Xha'en Hegemony as a prefecture	
1740	Harmost Demos Castorhage declares himself King of Castorhage in defiance of Imperator Ivint III; Lymossus Legion burned alive inside Castorhage barracks	
1741	Castorhage founded	
1751	Recognized beginning of Eleventy Year War between Castorhage and the Hyperborean Empire	
1760	Boy Emperor Ziris su Dos Ophronya takes the Xha'en throne	
1781	Ziris su Dos Ophronya perishes in a "mysterious" fire and Sarilla sa Dan Huris takes the Xha'en throne as empress	
1861	Castorhage and the Hyperborean Empire sign the Eleventy Year War treaty	
1822	Humanoid raids from Black Forest begin on city of Oxibbul; Wizards of the Gray Tower turn them back	
1887		Antef crowned pharaoh of Khemit; beginning of 30th Dynasty
1915	Oxibbul abandoned in face of ever-greater number of humanoid incursions; remaining inhabitants retreat across the Fingers and establish towns of Elise and Glaivr; Oxibbul becomes a humanoid-occupied ruin	
1918	Wizards of the Gray Tower largely depart region, the few remaining establish the Library of Elise	
1921	Imperial capital of Xha'en moved back to Xha'ahan	
1922	Southern Xha'en nobles rebel against the Emperor Takar su Pan Huris	
1928	Battle of Taode River ends in a victory for Emperor Takar su Pan's forces; rebels flee into the Utterends	

Imperial Record (I.R.)	Event in Akados	Event in Libynos
1930	Port city of Penmorome established on Southvale coast	
1932	Evil treants from Fae Copse plague Penmorome and surrounding settlements	
1943	The Great Conflagration; citizens of Penmorome with soldiers of Parthos raze forests of Southvale with iron axes and fire; treants retreat into Black Wood and Fae Copse	
1944	Towns of Southreach, Guildford, Marwood, and Whitehaven founded; treants disappear from Fae Copse; refugees and outlaws begin settling in area of Hawkmoon, encounter kingdom of Seventh Yaltic Dynasty	
1948	Invasion from the sea as sahuagin strike the west coast of Anaros Island; Anari and Caerulean Kingdom join forces to defeat the attack	
1968		Menes XX crowned pharaoh of Khemit; beginning of 31st Dynasty
2112	Ghost Plague ravages Xha'en Hegemony, with spirits of all sorts roaming the streets and attacking innocents; monks, priests and other specialists are dispatched to face the threat	
2114	Ghost Plague in Xha'en Hegemony ends mysteriously	
2143	Earthquake strikes Insula Lymossus leaving much of Castorhage in ruins	
2193	Queen Coal of Castorhage comes to power; beginning of Years of Terror	
2214	Scouts report groups of humanoids crossing the Fingers and traveling at night to disappear into the Dragon Hills; River Watch established along Binjerin River	
2228		Djehuti crowned pharaoh of Khemit; beginning of 32nd Dynasty
2251	Queen Coal of Castorhage burned at the stake; Years of Terror end	
2279		Castorhagi explorer ship "Brave" makes landfall in western Libynos
2284	Castorhage colonizes Tandril Island, and establishes port of Trinidar	
2301	Forest Coast work camps established by Queen Malice of Castorhage as penal colonies	
2348	King Lertis Tevoy of Castorhage decrees construction of Great Road and supporting fortresses "to pierce the secrets of the Green Realm"	
2349	Hostilities between Forest Coast wild elves and Castorhagi work colonies begin	
2369	Battle of Tevoy sees complete destruction of Royal Army garrison by wild elf warband; Fort Tevoy abandoned, informally renamed "Fort Toofar"	
2371	Citadel of Tranith on Forest Coast destroyed by earthquake, wild elf raiders slaughter the survivors; outpost fortress of Fringe makes separate peace with wild elves and refuses entry to all Castorhagi soldiers and work parties	

Imperial Record (I.R.)	Event in Akados	Event in Libynos
2373	Forest Coast Great Road abandoned; Ilber Nole left as only fortification on Forest Coast	
2375	Xha'en Emperor Amaran su Bha Huris begins to experiment with necromancy, intending to cheat death and live forever	
2376	Beginning of Dragon Plagues in Utterends, lasting 5 years	
2390	Scouts report ruins of Oxibbul once again abandoned; Dragon Hills rumored to be teeming with humanoid tribes	
2395	Xha'en Emperor Amaran su Bha Huris is revealed to be a lich; calls up legions of undead to defend his palace and begins the Immortal Dynasty	
2411		Suserenre crowned pharaoh of Khemit; beginning of 33rd Dynasty
2471	Last clergy of Thyr and Muir depart St. Harul's; High Altar of Thyr moved to Tircople	
2475	Xha'en rebels besiege Amaran's palace and, with the aid of ancient Ahra artifacts, defeat Amaran and bring the Immortal Dynasty to an end	
2476	Tilgi Dynasty rises to prominence in Xha'en	
POLES OF BOROS SHIFT AND THE FALL OF THE EMPIRE		
2491	The poles of Boros shift; lines of impenetrable storms called the Tempest Meridians arise far out in the oceans east of Libynos and west of Akados, beyond which is something called the Goitre; an ice sheet begins forming over the continent of Boros; Fimbulwinter begins in Castorhage	Volcanic eruption buries Hyperborean city of Clandestine on Reaping Coast
2494	Ulnat tribe of the Shattered Folk arrives in the Far North and begins to settle beyond Wailing Mountains in abandoned cities of lost Boros	
2496	Hyperborea attempts to reverse the pole shift, but disaster ensues; Tower of Oerson destroyed; wildfires ravage Curgantium and spread across Akados burning Plains of Suilley and Matagost Forest; refugees flee across Dardanal Strait to Ramthion Island; last Yalts depart Hawkmoon and establish city of Coralis in Sinnar Ocean	Nation of Huun founded in the Desert of Oreb
2499	Hyperborean Imperial Court relocated to Tircople; western empire abandoned by Hyperboreans; chaos descends among survivors of Suilley Plain and Matagost Peninsula; Penmorome seals gates against all travelers; Endhome elects Senate to govern in absence of Imperial Court; Ramithi pirates give aid to refugees of Ramthion Island	Imperial Court relocated to Tircople; Khemitian capital moved back to Menefet
2506	Fimbulwinter in Castorhage ends	
2507	Qui Tai trading junk *Bountiful Harvest* makes landfall at Castorhage, opening a trade route with Xha'en Hegemony	
2509	Twelve Bloody Nights; Hyperborean imperator and pontifex roles combined; Trystecce the Ageless becomes imperatrix; High Altars of Thyr and Muir quietly moved to Lyre Valley	

Imperial Record (I.R.)	Event in Akados	Event in Libynos
	END OF HYPERBOREAN AGE IN THE WEST	
2516	Hyperboreans withdraw from Akados; Heldring cross the Helwall, forts of Sylvos and Albor Broce destroyed; Cult of Althunak rises to power among the Ulnat in the Far North	
2517	Heldring longships land on Ramthion Island and subjugate the populace; Heldring land in Southvale but cannot breach walls of Penmorome; Heldring advance checked at Stronghold Hjerrin in the south and withdraw to Exeter Province	
2521	Unnamed local chieftain brings Heldring mercenaries to Insula Extremis; Heldring conquer all of Southvale but Penmorome; found settlements of Wellesley, Weatherell, Freeport, North Bay, Penn, and Pike Point but eventually assimilate with local population	
2523	Heldring invasion of Insula Extremis begins; fortress of Farketh Knowe constructed for Heldring to rule Ramthion Island	
2524	Sea plague appears in Xha'en coastal provinces and begins to spread inland; plot by dissident nobles to trigger war with Caerulea is foiled and a cure for the plague is provided by the merfolk	
2527	Most Heldring in Exeter Province withdraw to Helcynngae Peninsula to take part in invasion of Insula Extremis	
2528	Cult of Althunak begins enslaving Ulnat settlements in the Far North; construction begun on City of the Lord of Winter	
2533		Binitis I crowned pharaoh of Khemit; beginning of 34th Dynasty
2553	The Cult of Althunak holds sway over the Far North from the City of the Lord of Winter	
2560	Daan forms his Cataphracts in service to Hyperborea	
2566	Daan acclaimed as Polemarch of Insula Extremis	
2576	Daan defeats Heldring at Battle of Agedium	
2580	Daan's Legion lands at Durwent and marches north to Tircople, following the coast of the Sinnar Ocean through Akados and Libynos	
2584	Cult of Althunak overthrown by Ulnat uprising in Far North; City of the Lord of Winter abandoned; Althunak imprisoned beneath Lake of Frozen Screams; Ulnat tribes scatter along Seal Coast	Siege of Tircople by Daan's Legion; Daan falls as he destroys the lich-queen Trystecce
2585	Daanites withdraw to Ynys Cyrmagh; Daanites name the rest of the world as *Lloegyr*—the Lost Lands	
2586	The Twin Regents King Alar and Queen Elspeth normalize Castorhage trade relations with Xha'en Hegemony	
2611		Ammuyad Caliphate asserts control over Antioch City-States
2619	Ammuyad Caliphate begins colonization of Isthmus of Irkaina, founding the Principality of Pelshtaria	Ammuyad Caliphate begins colonization of Isthmus of Irkaina

Imperial Record (I.R.)	Event in Akados	Event in Libynos
2623	Archmage Jhedophar builds tower in Green Mountains and creates school of advanced arcane arts	
2632		Last Hyperboreans quietly disappear from Tircople
2654	Birth of Macobert of House Foere	
2690	Knights of Macobert formed, mounted upon destriers bred in eastern Suilley	
	RISE OF THE FOERDEWAITH	
2698	King Macobert begins uniting Akados as Kingdom of Foere	
2720	Province of Aachen established extending to the Great Bridge	
2731	Swein Sigurdson discovers the Neimbrall Trail in Under Realms, leads his tribe of the Heldring through tunnel away from Helcynngae Peninsula to escape worship of Hel	
2734	Guided by vision from Wotan, Swein Sigurdson leads his people to emerge in Storstrøm Vale; colonization of Northlands begins; Swein Sigurdson named Køenig of Storstrøm Vale	
2738	Archmage Jhedophar's school of magic disappears and the location of his tower is lost	
2739		Resarmun V crowned pharaoh of Khemit; beginning of 35th Dynasty
2740	The half-troll Acregor Ironclaw founds the kingdom of Acregor in the Dragon Hills, reoccupying the ruined elven city of Aranost as his capital	
2744	Macobert marches his host across Irkaina to Tircople, reclaiming the city, and clearing the High Altar of Muir; he is crowned Macobert I, Overking of the Hyperborean Monarchy of the Foerdewaith	
2745	Foerdewaith provinces of Suilley and Matagost established; old Hyperborean forts at Salyos and Parthos rebuilt	
2746	King Prudus I of Castorhage gives fealty to Overking Macobert; Castorhage granted status of protectorate rather than vassal state	
2747	King Prudus I and three Foerdewaith inspectors-general found consumed in their beds by swarms of rats; Foere declines to send further inspectors-general to Castorhage	
2748	Construction begun on Lyre Bridge over Stoneheart River; Trademoot established at King's Bridge	
2751	Province of Burgundia established to maintain garrison forts at Salyos and Parthos; construction begins on city of Trevi	
2762	Overking Macobert and his Knights march on sealed city of Penmorome, Primus of Penmorome opens gates with welcoming celebration; city renamed Penmorgh, Primus Ostephion appointed Magnate of Penmorgh; Province of Southvale created	

Imperial Record (I.R.)	Event in Akados	Event in Libynos
2765	Death of Macobert; son Magnusson succeeds to the throne; issuance of Eastreach Decree; provinces of Eastreach and Pontus Tinigal established	
2768	Overking Magnusson completes imperial capital at Courghais	Plague strikes trade city of Bhutan in Ammuyad Caliphate
2769		Plague spreads to Hava, capital of the Ammuyad Caliphate
2772		Antioch City-States regain independence from Ammuyad Caliphate
2773		A new prince of Pelshtaria is chosen without the consent of the caliph, marking the end of the empire of the caliphate
2776	Death of Magnusson I; grandson Magnusson II succeeds to the Foerdewaith Throne	
2781	Red Plague strikes Kingdoms of Foere; one quarter of the population of the central lands dies including Magnusson II; son Osbert I succeeds to the Foerdewaith Throne	
2797	Red Plague returns and strikes central Kingdoms of Foere again; much of the kingdom's central territories are depopulated due to the high death toll; plague claims Overking Osbert I who is succeeded by his son Osbert II	
2801	Heldring armies cross Helwall again and roam along the March of Mountains, burning settlements and slaughtering their inhabitants; Overking Osbert II gathers a small army and marches south from Courghais to meet the Heldring in battle	
2802	Mitra appears to Overking Osbert II and predicts victory over the Heldring; Osbert builds a shrine to the Sun Father, and defeats Heldring at Oescreheit Downs; Helcynngae Peninsula pacified; Exeter Province split into Exeter and Cereduin provinces; Trebes constructed on ruins of Sylvos; war hero and nephew of Osbert II, Claud Oberhammer, given rulership of Troye and named Duke of the Rampart, Battle-Duke, and Sword of the Foerdewaith	
2803	Ramithi overthrow Heldring warlords on Ramthion Island; fortress of Farketh Knowe thrown down; construction begun on garrison town of Kingston; Keston Province established	
2805	Ramthion Island petitions for entry into Kingdom of Foere; Province of Ramthion created	
2822	County of Vourdon created	
2840	Foerdewaith settlers push through Crynnomar Gap into the Great Steppes	
2843	Twin royal heirs Kennet and Cale born to Overking Paulus	
2854	Trinidar and Forest Coast work colonies slip from Castorhagi control	
2856	County of Toullen established	
2858	Cale abdicates claim to throne and given port of Reme	

Imperial Record (I.R.)	Event in Akados	Event in Libynos
2859	Prince Cale of Reme blocks Castorhage's attempts to resume control of Trinidar and Forest Coast	
2861	Cale leads Colonization of Great Steppes	
2921		Yakbam of Nubara crowned pharaoh of Khemit; beginning of 36th Dynasty; capital of Khemit moved to Elephantine
2931	Caleen settlers reach shore of Lake Hali; humanoid attacks on the colonies begin	
2947	Shadow walkers lead humanoid hordes from Lost Mountains; Caleen colonies destroyed, Prince Cale is lost; Wizard's Wall raised at Crynnomar Gap	
2955	Alliance of the Elitan-i-pan Confederation founded in the Haunted Steppes	
2956	Long in decline, the Tilgi Dynasty of Xha'en is replaced by the aggressive and militaristic Rachar Dynasty	
2958		Huun invade Tircople; the Pontifex and First High Lord are slain
2960	First Great Crusade gathers at ports all along Sinnar Coast and Crescent Sea	Crusaders recapture Tircople and establish Crusader States; in return for aid in the crusade, Castorhage granted colonial rights in southeast Libynos
2970	Overking Yurid gathers crusader army at Pontus Tinigal and Tros Zoas and sails for Khemit on Second Great Crusade; in the absence of forces on crusade, the vampire lord known as the Singed Man rises in the Duchy of Kear and conquers it, ruling as its Infernal Tyrant; King Prudus II of Castorhage caught traveling in Kear at time of rising and slain; wife of Prudus, Constance, crowned queen of Castorhage	Huun besiege Tircople, overrun part of Crusader States; crusader army of Overking Yurid lands in Khemit and marches overland to Tircople; Khemit remains occupied by Foerdewaith forces for six years
2971	Second Great Crusade breaks siege of Tircople and drives Huun from Sacred Table	
2977	Battle-Duke Ormand of the Rampart charged with freeing Kear from the Singed Man; Foerdewaith army crushed by the Infernal Tyrant of Kear at Seilo Ford, Battle-Duke Ormand slain and rises as vampire spawn in the Singed Man's service	
2983	The vampire Ormand expands enslaved Realm of Kear from Eber to Tarry; Foere and Castorhage dispute political responsibility and neither raises further forces to try and dislodge the Infernal Tyrant	
3030	Founding of trade city of Bard's Gate at King's Bridge	
3035	Shengotha Plateau covered in unnatural glacier, decimating dwarven Clan Krazzadak; city of Bryn Tuk Thull entombed by ice; Year of the Hard Cold afflicts Stoneheart Valley, ruining the harvest, killing winter crops, and delaying spring planting	
3036	Famine strikes Stoneheart Valley and surrounding areas, starvation sets in across the region; Bard's Gate's expanding trade connections are able to import sufficient grain from the south to support the city's population; Bard's Gate council votes to provide their excess grain to the mountain dwarf clan of Silverhelm	

Imperial Record (I.R.)	Event in Akados	Event in Libynos
3037	Dwarven craftsman arrive in Bard's Gate from Halls of the Silverhelm and begin construction on retractable canal bridges	
3039	Silverhelm dwarves construct massive basilica temples to Thyr and Muir in Bard's Gate; High Altars moved from Valley of the Shrines into city	
3048	Turin the Pretender imprisons Overking Oestemor and declares himself Overking Turin I	
3050	Turin I defeats Battle-Duke Orferro at the First Battle of Aixe, cementing his hold on the Crown	
3058	Leothrand of Mitra rescues Overking Oestemor and hides him in Yolbiac Vale to rally his loyalists	
3060	Overking Oestemor brings Turin I to battle in Second Battle of Aixe; Oestemor prevails with the aid of Leothrand Cold-wielder	
3061	First Shabbisian Plague outbreak in Bard's Gate	
3073		Castorhagi settlement of Fort Wallberg on the margin of the Kanderi Desert overrun by desert bands
3081		Fort Wallberg retaken by East Libynos Trading Company
3095	Second outbreak of Shabbisian Plague in Bard's Gate	
3102	Infernal Realm of Kear reaches largest extent, stretching from Tarry to Tourne	
3106		Castorhagi settlement of Fort Wallberg destroyed by desert bands
3114		Nation of Yeera conquered by Kingdom of Imya
3120	Cult of Zaihhess constructs temple on Frontier of Reme	
3123	Third Shabbisian Plague outbreak in Bard's Gate; priests of Bast summon cats to destroy plague rats	
3124		Castorhagi settlement of Sowbury founded by Swyne explorers on Ambicuaria Jungle coast
3128	Sir Varral the Blessed destroys the Singed Man and Duke Ormand, freeing Realm of Kear; Duchy of Kear reconstituted under Foerdewaith Crown with nephew of overking given title in Eber; Castorhage annexes port of Tarry	
3129	Black-robed monks of the Brotherhood arise from ashes of Kear and beginning distributing alms and feeding the poor and displaced	
3133	High Church of Foere officially sanctions Black Brotherhood as a benevolent society, first Brotherhood temple constructed in Nains	
3140		Aaneterire crowned pharaoh of Khemit; beginning of 37th Dynasty
3149		Castorhagi settlement of Chiselknoll founded in margins of Kanderi Desert
3160	After years of declining population Hazad-Burgh falls to giant invaders	
3164	Duke of Northmarches leads army to throw down temple of Zaihhess on Frontier of Reme, Zaihhess imprisoned in Carceri	

Imperial Record (I.R.)	Event in Akados	Event in Libynos
3169		Crusader Coast overrun by Huun; Tircople sacked
3172	Fleet gathers in Reme to transport Third Great Crusade to Crusader Coast	
3173		Third Great Crusader fleet destroyed by storm as it attempted to land at Crusader Coast
3176	Black Brotherhood extends loans to Crown to offset financial hardships of loss of crusader fleet	
3181	Black Brotherhood becomes major banking organization throughout Foere with chapterhouse banks in every major city	
3190	Dwarf lord Durand Strong-Arm discovers gold and silver west of Blackflow River; establishes Durandel mines under Fae Copse in Southvale	
3199	Overking Oessum VIII calls for Fourth Great Crusade; armies and fleet gather at Endhome to sail for Crusader Coast; crown borrows extensively from Black Brotherhood bankers	
3207	Graeltor crowned overking after death of Oessum at Battle of the Sickles	Huun defeated by crusaders and their hill dwarven allies of Shamash Kush at Battle of the Sickles; Overking Oessum slain

The Age of Breaking

Imperial Record (I.R.)	Event in Akados	Event in Libynos
3208	Army of Light marches on temple-city of Tsar; Desolation of Tsar created	Surviving knights of Muir from Crusader Coast establish Holy Ecclessia at fortress of Perona on Iber Bay
3209	Last Justicar of Muir slain at Battle of Tsar	Tircople falls to Mguru tribes
3210	Army of Light defeats Tsar and pursues Disciples of Orcus into Forest of Hope where both disappear; Citadel of Orcus vanishes from Tsar; King Worrn II of Castorhage orders exploration for colonization of Bream Isles and Nether Sea (i.e., the Caerulean Ocean); Castorhagi galleon *Brave* sent on exploration mission	
3213	Foerdewaith Wars of Succession begin; Ramthion Island breaks from empire	
3214	Displaced wizards from throughout Foere gather in Bard's Gate and form Dominion Arcane, found Wizards' Guild	Holy Ecclessiast of Perona converts King Artoa of Alcaldar to faith of Muir
3215	Grand Admiral of Pontus Tinigal withdraws from Foere, declares himself Emperor of the Oceans Blue; Kingdom of Oceanus established on Pontos Island	
3216	Earl of Swordport mockingly declares himself Monarch of the Moonsilver Sea, assassinated by agents of Oceanus	King Artoa decrees Thyr and Muir as state religions of Alcaldar and establishes Holy Ecclessia Inquisitorial to protect the integrity of the faith; King Artoa assassinated, High Ecclessiast Roqemonte organizes Church Militans to seek out the assassins and deliver Muir's justice
3217	Imperial fleet gathers at Highreach to attack Kingdom of Oceanus; Foerdewaith fleet defeated at Battle of Kapichi Point; city-state of Endhome declares neutrality, Foerdewaith garrison expelled	
3218	Foerdewaith army marches on Endhome; army of Burgundia paid off by Oceanus and Endhome, surprises imperial army with flanking maneuver; imperial army withdraws to Troye without bloodshed; Oceander army occupies Endhome	

Imperial Record (I.R.)	Event in Akados	Event in Libynos
3219		The Day of Faith: 867 conspirators burned alive in Mhalta by Holy Ecclessia Inquisitorial; Istobal-Alcacé crowned King of Alcaldar by Holy Ecclessiast Roqemonte
3221	Foerdewaith garrisons withdraw from Salyos and Parthos; Kingdom of Burgundia declares its independence; armies of Matagost besiege Trevi; Burgundia sues for peace with Oceander; Oceander army withdraws from Endhome; Castorhagi colony of Farthest Point established on Lesser Bream; Castorhage begins trading with Gtsang Prefecture	
3222	Kingdom of Suilley declares independence; eastern region of Suilley erupts in civil war; Foere attacks western Suilley	
3223	Foerdewaith army defeated by Suilley at Battle of Bullocks Bale	
3224	Magnate of Penmorgh assassinated; Penmorgh appoints duke and allies with Burgundia; Southvale named a duchy of Burgundia; Duke Oden of Kear declares Kingdom of Vast as independent realm from Foere	
3225	Matagost attacks Southvale; Dwarves of Durandel aid army of Penmorgh and route Matagost army; Margrave of Bret Harth declares Kingdom of the North Heath across Meander River from Vast	
3226	Siege of Trevi lifted by human and dwarven army from Southvale; Matagost erupts into civil war; Suilley armies withdraw from Gundlock Hills drawing new eastern border at Trader's Way; Foerdewaith armies skirmish with Vast and North Heath along Meander River; last Marquis of Eauxe slain in battle	
3227	Burgundia garrisons coastal forts of Salyos and Parthos	
3228	Castorhage recognizes independence of Vast and North Heath and sends ambassadors to Eber and Bret Harth	
3233	Grand Duchy of Reme declares independence from Foere	
3238	Eamon Angus founds trading post in a valley of the western Stoneheart Mountains that will become the citadel of Dun Eamon	
3240	Reme recognizes independence of Vast and North Heath, sending ambassadors to Eber and Bret Harth; Short War between Reme and Castorhage; Castorhage capitulates after 7 months and agrees to permanently absolve all claims to Forest Coast	
3241	Tycho Free States founded on Forest Coast; the Camp first established on border of the Desolation of Tsar	Holy Ecclessiast Arman-Diego issues *Bulla Patent* that Alcaldar's divine destiny is to spread the Holy Ecclessia throughout Libynos and the world; King Istobal-Alcacé declares war on Caddesh and invades Caduvar on the Sangre Sea
3242		Alcaldrich invasion of Gulf of Caddesh begins while Alcaldar conquers Caduvar and establishes city of San Caseo on Lake Istobal as first vassal state of Empire of Alcaldar

Imperial Record (I.R.)	Event in Akados	Event in Libynos
3244		Northern Alcaldrich invasion stalls in Maighib Desert as Guurzan and Khartous aid Caddesh; Alcaldrich forces push upriver from San Caseo
3245	Armistice signed between Foere and Vast and North Heath kingdoms; former March of Eauxe depopulated and left abandoned as buffer zone; wandering companies of mercenaries and deserters increase in number as wars of the Sundered Kingdoms begin to wind down	Ships of Oceanus and Alcaldar skirmish in Sinnar Ocean
3262	Bream trader *Provision* makes landfall at the mouth of the Devil's Tail on coast of Haunted Steppes and discovers the Elitan-i-Pan Confederation	
3263		Alcaldar gains complete control of Sangre River system and entirety of Cordona Lake creating trade corridor across central Libynos
3269		Kingdom of Axuum conquers Imya; introduces Khemitian deities to Imya
3270	Attacks by sea creatures from the Sea-Throng disrupt Castorhagi trade from Bream Islands	
3272	Shadow Masks founded in Bard's Gate; Black Brotherhood begins construction of monastery on Hill of Mornay	
3274	Castorhagi colony of Neer established on Lesser Bream Island	
3282	Heldring expelled from the Domain of Hawkmoon, which becomes semi-autonomous under Bosworth the Great	
3306	Giants from Giantlands invade Southvale as far as Guildford; Duke Artimus Traverthal slain in battle; Burgundia refuses to give aid; men of the vale and dwarves of Durandel drive giants back; Duchy of Southvale secedes from Kingdom of Burgundia; Burgundia threatens war but does not invade; Mayor of Penmorgh becomes de facto ruler of Southvale	
3307		Battle of Olivár between Alcaldrich and Oceanic fleets in northern Razor Sea inconclusive but costly to both sides
3308		Alcaldar and Oceanus agree to *Doctrine of Apportionment*, under which warships of both empires will keep to their respective sides of the Sinnar Ocean and not interfere with the other's trade
3309	Border Keep constructed in Southvale to guard against further Giantlands incursions	
3311		Castorhage begins establishing colonies in Jaati
3312	Kingdom of Oceanus demands fealty from Burgundia, Southvale, and Ramthion Island; Oceanus invades Matagost Peninsula, quickly ending civil war and bringing its factions to heel; Southvale surrenders; Ramthion refuses; Burgundia agrees to pay tribute to Pontus Tinigal to avoid invasion, calls to Foere for aid with promise of fealty; Suilley attacks troops sent by Foere to assist Burgundia; Foere withdraws beyond the Rampart and names region east of Suilley the District of Sunderland; assassins sent by Black Brotherhood attempt to murder Overking Osment; Osment closes all Black Brotherhood banks and orders interrogation of all captured Brotherhood officials	

Imperial Record (I.R.)	Event in Akados	Event in Libynos
3313	Three more assassination attempts on Overking Osment; High Church inquisitors confirm Black Brotherhood's involvement with infernal powers	
3314	Overking Osment leads army of Foere to besiege Black Monastery on Hill of Mornay; the monastery disappears in a massive conflagration	
3317	Torwatch Keep constructed to keep watch over ruins on Hill of Mornay	
3329	Duke of Listonshire's bastard son allies with a cult and attempts to overthrow duchy; defeated and slain by uprising of peasants	
3330	Church of Mitra constructs Morninghaven Sanitorium in Hearthglen at Osbert's shrine	
3333	Burgundia and Oceanus reach peace agreement; Oceanus firmly controls Matagost, Southvale, and much of Sunderland	
3336	Keston Province and County of Toullen change their allegiance to Kingdom of Suilley	
3337	Oceander army marches from Matagost for Troye	
3338	Foerdewaith army defeats Oceanders soundly at Battle of the King's Road; Oceander forces withdraw back across Sunderland	
3339	Oceanus and Foere sign non-aggression treaty	
3350	Partisans of Southvale attempt to assassinate visiting King Phillipe of Burgundia in Penmorgh; plot is discovered and king escapes	
3351	Burgundia attacks Southvale; Oceander fleet lands at Parthos to aid Southvale; Oceanus also marches from Matagost; Trevi besieged by combined armies; King Phillipe slain in battle, succeeded by King Marteir	
3354	Trevi destroyed; King Marteir taken captive to Tros Zoas; Burgundia falls and Oceander armies lay waste to the lands, leave garrison at Parthos	
3377	Hetherington Quarrus Mabe of Castorhage first breaches Between	
3380	Knightly Order of Macobert largely destroyed in Courghais, the few survivors go into hiding	
3392	Tower of Bone appears in Fae Copse; dwarven city of Durandel falls	
3400	Rappan Athuk: The Dungeon of Graves discovered in Forest of Hope	
3402		Alcaldar begins construction on Upper Sangre River locks
3408		Anuphotet I crowned pharaoh of Khemit; beginning of 38th Dynasty
3412	Baron Atredi of Martyn's Nest raises fleet to destroy pirates of God's Tear Island	
3414	Lyre Valley grows wild and dangerous, High Altars of Thyr and Muir relocated back into city after too many parishioners and priests in the Valley of the Shrine go missing	

Imperial Record (I.R.)	Event in Akados	Event in Libynos
3419	Tecrad Avorill forms the Lyreguard as a free company of soldiers to serve as defenders of Bard's Gate, begins raising baby griffons and training recruits to be griffon riders; foundations of Citadel of Griffons laid	
3420	Baron Atredi of Martyn's Nest overthrown in Reme civil wars and replaced by council of ministers loyal to Grand Duke	
3422	Doom of Greenpool on Ramthion Island	
3423	Merchants of Endhome establish Grollek's Grove as trading post between four nation-states: Endhome, Sunderland, Suilley, and Duchy of the Rampart	
3425	Shandril of Freya founds village of Fairhill in Stoneheart Valley	
3436	Captain Aldrin Shaw of Eastwych deserts from the navy of Foere, relocates to Swordport; begins to gather small fleet of freebooters; Shaw's estate at Stormshield seized by governor of Eastwych	
3439	Conroi Expedition crosses Wizard's Wall to begin exploration of Haunted Steppe and makes contact with the Campachi; unseasonal torrential rains begin to fall on the eastern slopes of the March of Mountains, causing extensive flooding, washout of roads, and undermining of city walls and building foundations; Duchy of the Rampart, Kingdom of Suilley, County of Vourdon, Keston Province, and Count of Toullen are hardest hit	
3442	Captain Shaw's fleet driven from Swordport by earl's dragoons; flees to Razor Sea	
3443	The rains have continued for four years; casualties from flooding and mudslides have reached the tens of thousands, the destruction of property is on a massive scale, and trade on the South Road has virtually been brought to a halt causing economic recession in the lands east of the mountains; the noted scholar and philosopher Oscobar of Vermis declares the rains to be the work of the forces of Darkness and calls them the Fiend Rains, and predicts they will continue for another 13 years; the strange blind mystic Lun of the Mountain calls the rain Rynas' Tears, but she gives no explanation why; Lun says the rains will end in 6 more years	
3446	Captain Shaw destroys small Foerdewaith colony on Razor Coast and founds Port Shaw	
3449	After 10 years the Fiend Rains come to an end; the Borderland Provinces begin to dry out and dig themselves out of the mud; drainage to the lowlands of the Hearthglen have become a spreading marsh that is eventually known as the Creeping Mire	
3451	Last King of Castorhage, Worrn IV, dies in riding accident; Alice crowned queen; Oceanus opens trade relations with Port Shaw	
3452	Oceanus prohibits Castorhagi ships from trading on Razor Coast and attacks them on sight	

Imperial Record (I.R.)	Event in Akados	Event in Libynos
3455	The Creeping Mire continues to grow and attracts dangerous inhabitants, making the road to Morninghaven Sanatorium perilous; Mitran pilgrims begin to disappear from the Swamp Road en route to Morninghaven	
3461	Founding of Ghon Complex in Xha'en for the "humane" reeducation for family members of state enemies by the Rachar Dynasty; Castorhagi ship *The Lady Ruin* engages two Oceanic warships north of Razor Sea and sinks both	Alcaldar expands river between Lakes Aur and Cordona in eastern Libynos, begin construction on River of Gold Locks
3462	Castorhage and Oceanus open talks for Razor Coast trade	
3466	Unable to guarantee the safety of its pilgrims, the Church of Mitra sells Morninghaven Sanatorium to Baronet Wilbane Osterklieg who turns it into a prison for the criminally insane	
3467	Beginning of reign of Prince Kemal of Pelshtaria	
3471	Battle of Quandary Deep sees total victory for Castorhage over the sea-throng of the Sinking Place	
3478	Oceanus invades Ramthion and conquers lowlands; construction begins on the Damerhold	
3483	Ramithi resistance gathers in mountains at ruins of Farketh Knowe, elects *dux bellorum* to drive Oceanders into the sea	
3484	Ramithi resistance successfully repels Oceander army in Caterwaul Mountains; Oceanus turns responsibility to garrison Parthos over to Southvale; construction begins on Fort Kellstyn	
3485	Gathos the Cruel executes garrison of Parthos; renames city and declares himself first Tyrant of Lowport	
3486	Keston Province assumes control of Mourninghaven Sanatorium after arrest of Baronet Osterklieg	
3491	Six Castorhagi ships attack the Kraken's Teeth to force passage to the Sinking Place; *The Lady Ruin* and three others sunk, the remaining two retreat to Great Bream shipyards	
3496		Beginning of 39th Dynasty of Khemit; Modern Period
3497	Abysthor, High Priest of Thyr, disappears in the Valley of the Shrines; death of Prince Kemal of Pelshtaria, and ascension of his children Prince Adem and Princess Adelet	
3499	Bofred the Just raised as the High Priest of Thyr in Bard's Gate	Alcaldar opens Channel Lakes creating water route across central Libynos; Castorhage signs lease for long-term rights of passage
3500	Gnoll hordes attack Bard's Gate; Commander Avorill slain, Imril given command of Lyreguard; city's standing army instituted	
3506	Humanoid and barbaric human raiders descend from Wilderland Hills and burn village of Byrnum; beginning of Wilderlands Clan War; County of Toullen sends small contingent of troops to assist Keston	

Imperial Record (I.R.)	Event in Akados	Event in Libynos
3507	Kingdom of Suilley commits troops to assist beleaguered army of Keston Province against the Wilderlands clans; Exeter fortifies Albor Broce against incursions by the clans; shrines of Thyr and Muir lost to hordes of Orcus out of Stoneheart Mountain Dungeon; Clan Silverhelm seals its halls to outside world	
3509	County of Vourdon and Exeter Province send assistance to Keston and Suilley troops; General Cormien wins Battle of Broch Tarna breaking the strength of the hill clans and sending their margoyle masters fleeing back into the Forlorn Mountains	Castorhagi and Alcaldrich ships skirmish in Boiling Sea; Castorhagi ships barred from use of Libynosi Channel Lakes
3511	Rogue North Heath admiral launches a naval assault on the Tycho Free States, and is driven off with heavy losses	
3513	Calthraxus the Black attacks Bard's Gate mines and makes them his lair	
3514	Armies of Huun lay siege to Bard's Gate	
3515	King Ovar defeats Huun in Gulf of Akados and at Bard's Gate and pursues them into Irkainian Desert	
3516	Castorhagi ship *Devastator* anchors in Sangre Sea off Caduvar	
3517	Current year; rumors of Ovar's return from Irkaina	

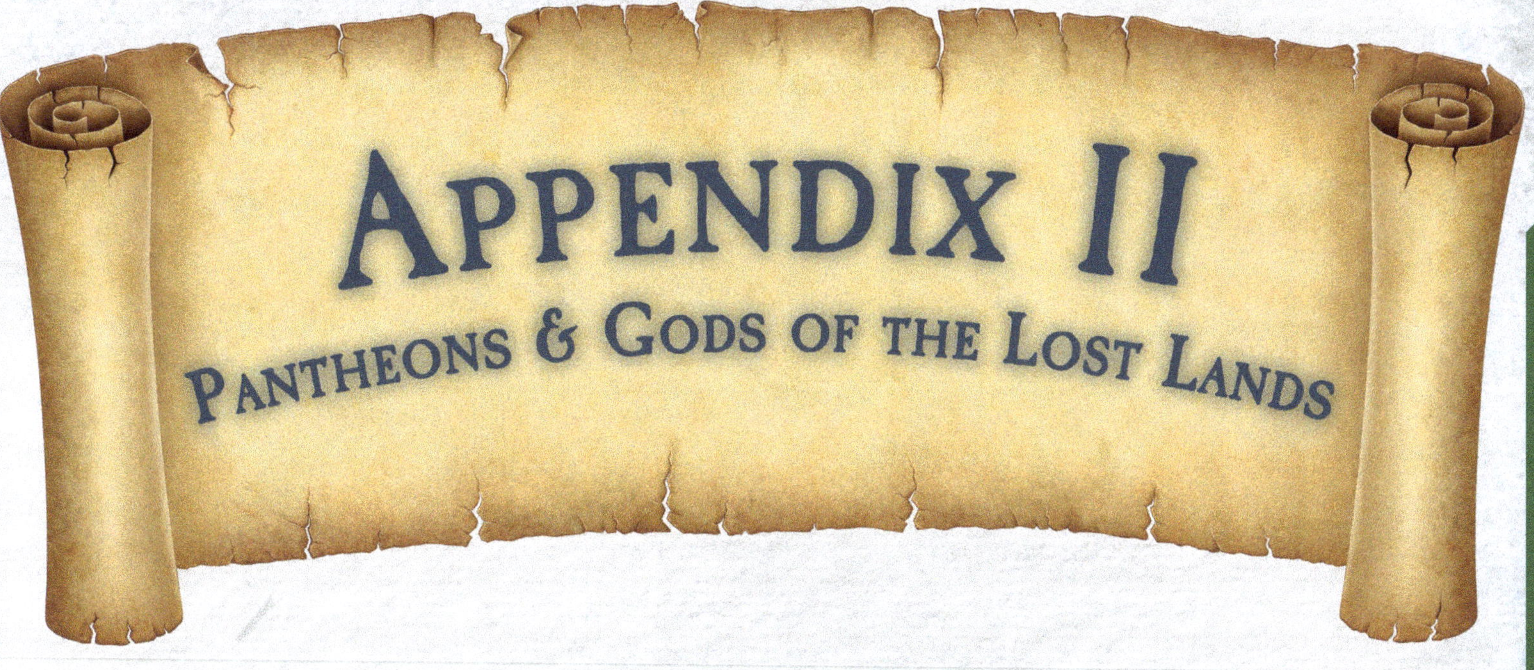

The following lists the major gods in the pantheons of wide adoption in the Lost Lands. It is not intended to be comprehensive as to all of the deities in any given pantheon, or of the many deities that are worshipped throughout the Lost Lands.

GODS OF AKADOS

FOERDEWAITH/HYPERBOREAN PANTHEONS

Name	Power	AL	Title	Spheres of Influence	Typical Worshippers	Notes
Ades	Greater	LE	Lord of the Underworld, The Gatekeeper, The Unseen One, The Host of Many	Death, Law, Repose	The grieving, the dying, death cultists	Created the Tower of Bone with Orcus and Demogorgon
Archeillus	Lesser	LG	God of Rightful Rule; Protector of the Nobility	Law, Nobility	Nobles, Foere traditionalists, magistrates and judges	
Arden	Greater	NG	God of the Sun	Air, Good, Sun, War	Not currently worshipped	Now dead
Arn	Lesser	NG	The Sunlord, Lesser God of Sun	Sun, Healing, Good	Good-aligned arcanists and celestials	
Bacchus-Dionysus	Greater	CN	God of Wine and Madness	Intoxicants, Revelry	Tavernkeepers, decadent nobles, those who produce or sell wine, ale or spirits, and those who simply want to have a good time	
Belon the Wise	Lesser	NG	God of Travel; Wanderer in White	Knowledge, Magic, Travel, Trickery	Rangers, bards, wandering wizards, those who make their living traveling	Originally, was a god of Libynos
Ceres	Greater	LG	The Revered Mother, Goddess of the Home and Midwives, Goddess of Healing, Mercy, and Patience, Goddess of the Millstone	Life, Community, Healing, Protection	Human matrons and mothers, midwives, bakers, millers, orphans, the poor, farmers, some civic leaders, halflings	

Name	Power	AL	Title	Spheres of Influence	Typical Worshippers	Notes
Da-Jin	Greater	NE	Lord of Death, Lord of the Burning Skull	Death, Repose	Necromancers, assassins, morticians, nihilists, murderers	
Dame Torren	Lesser	N	Goddess of the Four Winds	Animal, Air, Weather	Travelers, bards, people of Reme	Dame Torren is one of the three patron deities of Reme
Diana	Lesser	NG	Goddess of Fertility and the Hunt; Lady of the Wilds; Protectress of the Moons	Animal, Nature, Weather	Hunters, trappers and those who live or travel through the wilds	
Dre'uain the Lame	Greater	LN	God of Craft and Smiths, God of Industry and Hard Work	Artifice, Earth, Creation, Fire, Knowledge	Human, gnome, dwarven, and halfling craftsmen, inventors, laborers, union organizers, maimed workers, wounded veterans, beggars	Adopted from Gnomish pantheon
Freya	Lesser	NG	Goddess of Love and Fertility; Freyja	Earth, Fertility, Plant, War	Human females, farmers, midwives, hunters, druids	Adopted from Heldring/Northlands pantheon
Grox	Lesser	LE	God of Artifice and Darkness, The Deep Father	Artifice, Darkness, Evil, Knowledge, Law	Duergar, evil dwarves, lawyers, spies, scribes, alchemists	
Hecate	Greater	LE	Goddess of Evil Magic, The Arcane Mother	Evil, Knowledge, Law, Magic	Arcane spellcasters, women, hags, witches, crones, remnants of lost Arcady, some devils	
Jamboor	Greater	N	God of Knowledge, Magic, and Death; He Who Hears the Secrets of the Dead	Knowledge, Death	Arcane spellcasters, sages, seers, mediums, spies	
Kamien	Lesser	N	Goddess of Rivers, Streams, and Springs; The Sparkling Maiden; Old Widemouth; The Water Lady	Animal, Travel, Water	Women, nymphs, sprites, nereids, other water creatures and fey, prostitutes, boatmen, bargemen, fishermen, river giants	
Kel	Greater	LG	Goddess of Self-Sacrifice; Lady of Protection	Good, Healing, Law, Protection	Not currently worshipped	Now dead
Kudrak	Lesser	LG	Lesser God of Guardians	Community, Good, Protection, Strength	Farmers, guardsmen	
Mirkeer	Lesser	NE	Goddess of Shadows and the Night	Darkness, Evil, Magic, Shadow	Thieves, assassins, sorcerers, those seeking to hide for ill purposes	
Mithras	Greater	LN	Lord Storm; The Battle; The Soldier-God; Mithrae Invicto; God of War, Battles, and Soldiers	War, Law	Soldiers, generals, warriors, statesmen	

Name	Power	AL	Title	Spheres of Influence	Typical Worshippers	Notes
Moccavallo	Lesser	CN	God of Disguise and Treachery, Trickster God of Chaos and Disorder	Chaos, Trickery, Luck	Thieves, scoundrels, jesters, never-do-wells	
Muir	Greater	LG	Goddess of Virtue and Paladins	Law, Good, Protection, War	Humans paladins, Heldring soldiers, Alcaldrich knights, Justicars	Also known as Eostre by the Heldring
Note	Lesser	NG	God of the Harp	Travel, Luck, Music, Protection	Bards, musicians, travelers	Serves and travels with Oghma
Oghma	Greater	CG	God of Music	Art, Music, Travel	Bards, musicians, dancers and other performers	Patron god of Bard's Gate; adopted from pantheon of the Old Ways
Pan	Greater	N	God of the Wild, Lord of the Flocks and the Hunt	Animal, Fertility, Music	Bards, hunters, certain fey races	
Quell	Greater	CG	The Sea King; Lord of the Blue	Travel, Water, Weather	Explorers, sea traders, sailors, people that rely on the sea for their livelihood	
Sefagreth	Greater	N	God of Commerce, Trade, and Cities	Community, Commerce, Wealth	Merchants, traders, shopkeepers, bankers, caravan guards, travelers	
Solanus	Greater	NG	Goddess of the Sun and Healing	Sun, Light, Strength, Healing	Rangers, bards, healers, soldiers, undead slayers	
Stryme/Strym	Lesser	NG	Stryme the Mighty, God of Strength	Liberation, Protection, Strength, War	Soldiers, warriors, dwarves	Adopted from dwarven pantheon
Telophus	Lesser	LN	Lord of Crops and the Seasons	Nature, Plant, Sun, Weather	Farmers and halflings, some druids revering his natural cycle aspect	
Thursis	Greater	N	God of Battle	War, Death, Destruction, Evil, Magic, Strength	Warriors, mercenaries, and warlords	
Thyr	Greater	LG	God of Law and Justice; The Lawgiver; Tiwaz; Tyr	Law, Nobility	Human royalty, ruling and legislative bodies, some magistrates and judges	
Tykee	Greater	CG	Goddess of Luck and Good Fortune	Luck	Bards, gamblers, thieves, merchants, anyone seeking good luck	
Vanitthu	Greater	LN	God of the Steadfast Guard, The Gatekeeper	Protection, Law	Barristers, judges, guards, professional soldiers, military officers and nobles	
Yenomesh	Lesser	N	God of Glyphs and Writing	Knowledge, Magic, Protection, Runes	Wizards, scholars, sages, students, scribes, librarians	Adopted from Anunnaki pantheon of Libynos

Gods of the Anari (Thousand Rocks)

Name	Power	AL	Title	Spheres of Influence	Typical Worshippers
Ni Araha	Greater	NG	The Survivor, The Lady of Peace	Community, Good, Protection	Anari of the Thousand Rocks
Yisya Thun	Lesser	NG	The Watcher	Earth, Good, Water	Anari of the Thousand Rocks

Gods of Castorhage

Name	Power	AL	Title	Spheres of Influence	Typical Worshippers
Ash Queen, The	Greater	CN	Queen of Whores; The Hunger; Goddess of Lust, Nature, and Witchcraft	Animal, Beast, Chaos, Earth, Plant	Druids, mothers, fertility cults, satyrs, witches, hags, atavistic serpentfolk, nocturnals, intelligent plant creatures, rorkouns, gorynychs, bholes, dark young, living monoliths, some mongrelfolk
Baphomet	Greater	CE	The Rage Storm; Demon Lord of Anarchy, Beasts, and Anger	Animal, Chaos, Destruction, Evil, Fire, Water	Minotaurs, lycanthropes, therianthropes, chaaors, the Alcaldrich Order of Knights Templar in Exile
Brine	Greater	N	Ocean's Anger; Fish-Brother; God of Sea and Unsea	Animal, Chaos, Destruction, Water, Weather	Briny, brine mothers, fishermen, locathahs, some sahuagin
Father Canker	Lesser	N	Brother Choke; The Silent Assassin; God of Poison, Silence, and Smog	Air, Death, Trickery, Weather	Beggars, grieving mothers and fathers, belkers, some undead and psychotic thieves/murderers
Geryon	Arch-Devil	LE	The Liar; The Great Serpent; Lord of the Fifth; Patron of Betrayal and Deceit	Charm, Evil, Law, Scalykind, Strength	Politicians, con artists, barristers, justices, mongrelfolk, serpentfolk, lizardfolk, inphidians
Horseman, The	Greater	NE	End of Days; Lord of Disease; Supreme of Daemons; The Oinodaemon	Death, Destruction, Evil, Madness, War	Daemons, doomsayers, the insane, plague carriers, ghouls, some wererats
Jubilex	Demon Lord	CE	The Faceless Lord; Lord of Corruption and Decay; Demon Lord of Slimes and Oozes	Chaos, Evil, Water	Insane humans, lepers, intelligent oozes, ooze demons, spawn of Jubilex, slime nagas, some evil dragons
Lord Shingles	Lesser	LN	The Shadow on the Rooftop; Sovereign of the heights; God of Builders, Gables, Rooftops, and the Sky	Air, Artifice, Community, Knowledge	Architects, builders, gablemaesters, sprawlmasons, spider-hunters, daredevils, some burglars and vigilantes
Lucifer	Greater	LE	Prince of Darkness; Prince of Lies; The Adversary; The Prince of Light; Lord of Infernus; The Falling Tower; Satan	Charm, Evil, Law, Strength, War	Witches, corruptors, politicians, revolutionaries, the disaffected
Mammon	Arch-Devil	LE	Lord of Avarice; Lord of the Third	Artifice, Earth, Evil, Law, Trickery	Bankers, royalty, business owners, thieves, swyne, many Castorhagers (covertly)
Mithras	Greater	LN	Lord Storm; The Battle; The Soldier-God; Mithrae Invicto; God of War, Battles, and Soldiers	Animal, Glory, Law, Repose, Strength, War	Soldiers, generals, warriors, statesmen

Name	Power	AL	Title	Spheres of Influence	Typical Worshippers
Mother Grace	Greater	LN	The Holy Mother; Mother of All; Goddess of Family, Order, and Tradition	Community, Law, Nobility, Repose	Castorhagers
Papyri	Demigod	N	The Archivist; The Quiet One; The Lost Apprentice; The Thoughtful Silence; Goddess of the Written Word	Knowledge, Magic, Runes	Scholars, teachers, wizards, arcanists, alchemists, nagas, liches
Sister Shadows	Demigod	CN	The Unseen; Goddess of Alleys, Streets, Piers, and Pathways	Artifice, Darkness, Earth, Trickery	Beggars, thieves, dock laborers, street sweeps, commoners, ratfolk, mongrelfolk, skulks

ETHTUWATE PANTHEON (HAUNTED STEPPES)

Name	Power	AL	Title	Spheres of Influence	Typical Worshippers	Notes
Cajusta	Lesser	CN	The Mocking Jester, God of Comedy, Festivals and Mischief	Chaos, Fire, Travel, Trickery	Children, comedians, performers, satirists	
Drethra	Greater	CE	Mother of Mayhem, Goddess of the Moon, Darkness and Fire	Chaos, Darkness, Destruction, Evil, Fire	Conspirators, lycanthropes, murderers, pyromaniacs, spies, thieves	
Iluyugo	Lesser	NE	The Parasite, Goddess of Disease and Suffering	Air, Animal, Death, Evil, Plant	Diseased and disease-causing creatures, evil humanoids, torturers, sadomasochists	
Omay	Lesser	NG	The Great Mother Corn, Goddess of Fertility, Health and Marriage	Animal, Community, Healing, Plant	Animal breeders, parents, lovers, midwives	
Orlik	Lesser	LN	The Rotting Limb, God of Death	Death, Earth, Law, Repose	Assassins, embalmers, murders, soldiers	
Soncala	Lesser	LN	The Horse Lord, God of War	Animal, Law, Nobility, War	Diplomats, warlords, generals, riders, soldiers	
Srishwa	Lesser	NG	The Queen of Beasts, Goddess of the Hunt	Animal, Good, Nobility, Strength	Butchers, druids, good-aligned magical beasts, hunters, intelligent animals, rangers	
Tunkaku	Greater	N	The Great Giver, God of Creation	Air, Creation, Earth, Fire, Water	Chieftains, mystics, elemental spellcasters	Dead, voluntarily divided into the sun, sky, gods, the universe
Thaka	Greater	NG	The Golden Rider, God of the Sun, Harvest, and Life	Community, the Sun, Water	Chieftains, farmers, shepherds	
Ugutis	Lesser	CN	The Sin Master, God of Vices	Chaos, Charm, Darkness, Luck	Addicts, gamblers, hedonists, poisoners, sadists, seducers, sots, thieves	
Zuxaca	Demigod	CN	The Serpent Trickster, Demigod of Madness	Animal, Chaos, Madness, Trickery	Madmen, serpents, tricksters	

GODS OF HAWKMOON

Name	Power	AL	Title	Spheres of Influence	Typical Worshippers
Aletheia	Greater	LG	Goddess of Wisdom and Protection	Community, Law, Wisdom, War	Hunters, guardians
Bylkalla	Greater	N	God of Battle and Courage	War	Warriors and soldiers
Cavacendo/ Cavecendo	Greater	N	God of Fire and Horses	Animals, Fire, Liberation	Centaurs, dwarves
Elmarran	Greater	CN	God of Water and Change, God of the Depths	Chaos, Water	Mariners, fisherfolk
Gilyo	Lesser	CN	God of Travel and Caprice	Chaos, Travel, Trickery	Street dwarves
Hanijma	Lesser	N	God of Lightning and Beer, God of the Revel	Alcohol, Dancing, Luck, Revelry, Water	Brewers, revelers, sailors in storms
Igvys	Lesser	NE	God of South Wind and Decay	Death, Decay, Destruction	Those seeking to avoid a terrible fate
Inoska	Lesser	NG	Goddess of Secrets and Hope	Good, Liberation, Luck	Knowledge, Magic
Lusph	Lesser	N	God of the Sea and the North Wind	Storms, Water, Wind	Fishermen, mariners
Lyra	Lesser	LG	Goddess of Language and Creation	Creation, Healing, Knowledge	Craftsfolk, artists and bards
Majium	Lesser	LG	God of Magic and Mercy	Magic, Mercy	Magicians, sorcerers, residents of Coralis
Nekeler	Lesser	CE	God of Deserts and Lies, The Desert Walker, Subtle Deceiver	The Sun, Trickery	Bandits and petty criminals
Oon	Lesser	CN	God of Nature and Storms	Animals, Weather, Wind	Wild druids, wilderness scouts, nomads
Pelora	Lesser	NG	Goddess of Romance and Tragedy	Literature, Love, Poetry	Poets, bards, and wealthy folk
Quooembla	Lesser	LG	God of Wisdom	Wisdom	Scholars, teachers, students
Ulremara	Lesser	N	Goddess of Candles and Desire	Love	Courtesans
Zahm	Greater	LN	God of Money and Business	Commerce, Trade	Merchants

GODS OF THE HELDRING AND NORTHLANDS

Name	Power	AL	Title	Spheres of Influence	Typical Worshippers	Notes
Balder	Greater	NG	God of Bravery and Beauty	Glory, Strength, War	Male heroes and kings of good AL	Also known as Baldr
Bragi	Lesser	CG	God of Poetry and Song	Chaos, Glory, Travel	Skalds, chroniclers, travelers	Also known as Bragr
Frey	Lesser	NG	God of the Sun and the Hunt	Animal, Plant, the Sun	Hunters, frontiersmen, druids, some elves and fey	Also known as Freyr
Freya	Lesser	NG	Goddess of Love and Fertility	Animal, Darkness, Healing, Plant, War	Human females, midwives, spear maidens, hunters, druids	Also known as Freyja

Name	Power	AL	Title	Spheres of Influence	Typical Worshippers	Notes
Frigg	Greater	NG	Goddess of the Home and Hearth	Air, Community, Healing, Protection	Wives, mothers, stewards, spear maidens, spinners, hall builders	
Hel	Greater	NE	Goddess of Death; Lady of Pestilence	Air, Animal, Darkness, Death, Earth, Evil, Plant, Water	Diseased and disease-causing creatures, evil humanoids, evil druids, evil women, evil skalds	Member of Ginnvaettir (demons)
Loki	Greater	CE	God of Trickery, Fire, and Strife	Chaos, Evil, Fire, Luck, Madness, Trickery	Thieves, con men, gamblers, oathbreakers, arsonists, madmen	Also known as Loptr
Muir/Eostre	Greater	LG	Goddess of Virtue and Paladins; Queen of the Dísir, Goddess of Spring and the Dawn	Law, Good, Protection, War	Paladins, warriors, soldiers	Also in Foerdewaith pantheons; in decline; sister of Thyr and Kel
Njord	Lesser	N	God of Seafarers and Winds	Air, Luck, Travel, Water, Weather	Fishermen, seafarers, merchants, whalers	Also known as Njordr
Norns	Greater	N	Weavers of Fate: Uror, Verdandi, and Skuld	Artifice, Death, Fate, Glory, Knowledge, Luck	Seers	
Odin	Greater	NG	All-Father; Father of the Gods	Animal, Glory, Knowledge, Magic, Nobility, Protection, Runes, Travel, War	Jarls, warriors, arcane spellcasters, Bearsarkers, Ulfhanders, fathers, travelers	Also known as Wotan
Rán	Lesser	CN	Goddess of the Pitiless Waves	Animal, Chaos, Water, Weather	Druids, witches, sea creatures, some sailors, madmen	
Surter	Lesser	LE	God of the Fire Giants	Destruction, Evil, Fire, War	Fire giants, volcano giants, some fire creatures and other giants	Also known as Surtr
Thor	Greater	CG	God of Thunder	Air, Chaos, Glory, Strength, War, Weather	Heroes, warriors, ship masters, farmers	Also known as Donar
Thrym	Lesser	CE	God of the Frost Giants	Chaos, Evil, Ice, Trickery, Weather	Frost giants, Jötnar, jotund trolls, frost dwarves, ice trolls, some evil humans living in arctic areas	Also known as Thrymr
Thyr/Tyr	Greater	LG	God of Law and Justice; The Lawgiver	Community, Healing, Law, Knowledge, Nobility, Protection	Good-aligned jarls, members of the Thing, hirthmenn, orators, peacemakers	Also in Foerdewaith pantheon; in decline; brother of Muir and Kel; Thyr and Tyr and Tiwaz are the same god in different aspects

XHA'EN PANTHEON

Name	Power	AL	Title	Spheres of Influence	Typical Worshippers
Banra	Greater	LN	Goddess of the Underworld	Death, Law	Mourners, families with lost loved ones, funeral masters, morticians
Dakhan	Greater	LN	God of War and Justice	Law, War	Judges, soldiers, generals, nobles
Noradu	Lesser	LG	God of Nature	Animal, Nature, Plant	Druids, farmers, priests of nature
Jatan	Greater	LN	God of the Sun and Moon	Darkness, Light, Moon, Sun	Travelers, rogues, criminals, spies, merchants
Lainu	Lesser	LN	Goddess of Lakes and Rivers	Travel, Water, Weather	River-dwellers, fisherfolk, travelers, bargemen
Meita	Greater	LG	Goddess of the Harvest	Community, Earth, Good, Healing, Plant	Farmers, villagers, herders, grain and produce merchants
Quana	Greater	LG	Goddess of Love and Mercy	Good, Healing, Love, Protection	Lovers, poets, young married couples, parents, those in need of mercy and forgiveness
Gorni	Lesser	LN	God of the Mountains	Earth, Strength, Travel	Mountaineers, travelers, miners, mountain-dwelling folk
Estia	Greater	LN	Goddess of the Sky	Air, Nobility, Weather	Farmers, merchants, sailors, those dependent upon the weather
Oba	Greater	LN	God of the Oceans	Knowledge, Water, Weather	Villagers who dwell near the ocean, sailors, fisherfolk, merchant captains
Ara	Greater	LN	The Supreme God, Emperor of Heaven	Creation, Knowledge, Law, Nobility	Most Xha'en folk
Yainda	Lesser	LG	Goddess of Childbirth	Community, Family, Healing	Doctors, parents, children, midwives
Zakur	Greater	LG	God of Spring Planting	Earth, Plant	Farmers, villagers, merchants

OTHER GODS OF AKADOS

Name	Power	AL	Title	Spheres of Influence	Typical Worshippers	Notes
Bowbe	Greater	CN	God of War and Slaughter, Bowbe the Bloody, Bowbe the Baleful, Bowbe the Bearskin, Bowbe the Berserker	Chaos, Strength, Vengeance, War	Barbarians, raiders, reavers, and plunderers	
Cybele	Greater	NE	Magna Mater, Black Goat of the Woods, Goddess of Fertility and Witchcraft, The Dark Sister (the smaller moon - Sybil)	Creation, Evil, Knowledge, Magic	Witches, disenfranchised women, lycanthropes, degenerate cults, hags, harpies, some medusas	
Mocham	Greater	LG	The Earthpower, Stone of Battle	Good, Earth, Law, War	Formerly svirfneblin, deep dwarves, shaitan, earth elementals; Now unknown	Believed lost or dead
Oinodaemon	Greater	NE	End of Days; Lord of Disease; Supreme of Daemons	Death, Destruction, Evil, Madness, War	Daemons, doomsayers, the insane, plague carriers, ghouls, some wererats	Known as the Horseman in Castorhage
Orcus	Demon Prince	CE	Demon Prince of the Undead	Chaos, Death, Destruction, Evil, War	Orcs, orogs, monsters, undead, demons, evil humanoids	

Gods of Libynos

Anunnaki Pantheon (Istaflumina)

Name	Power	AL	Title	Spheres of Influence	Typical Worshippers	Notes
Anu	Greater	LG	The Father and King of the Gods	Air, Law, Magic, Protection	Kings, nobles, exorcists	
Apsu	Greater	CN	The Primeval Father	Chaos, Knowledge, Magic, Water	Magicians, sages, mystics	
Ea	Greater	N	The God of Wisdom and Magic	Earth, Healing, Knowledge, Magic	Exorcists, healers, craftsmen, wizards	
Erishkigal	Greater	LE	The Queen of the Underworld	Death, Earth, Evil, Law	Death priests, assassins, evil nobles, tomb robbers, necromancers	
Ishtar	Greater	CG	The Goddess of Love and War	Animals, Destruction, Protection, War	Prostitutes, concubines, eunuchs, warriors	
Kingu	Lesser	CE	The General of Chaos	Chaos, Destruction, Evil, Strength	Evil warriors, kings, raiders, slavers	
Marduk	Greater	LG	The General of Law	Air, Good, Law, Strength	Warriors, generals, charioteers	
Namtar	Lesser	LE	The Herald of Evil Destiny	Evil, Law, Luck, Trickery	Judges, evil viziers, oracles, sorcerers	
Nergal	Greater	NE	The God of Plague, Deathbringer	Air, Death, Destruction, Evil, War	Warlords, plague priests, evil cultists	
Sin	Lesser	N	The Moon	Air, Knowledge, Magic, Travel	Astrologers, scribes, pilgrims, travelers	
Tammuz	Greater	NG	The God of Fertility and Rebirth	Earth, Good, Healing, Plants	Farmers, peasants, landowners	
Tiamat	Greater	CE	The Primeval Mother	Animals, Chaos, Destruction, Evil	Evil warriors, sorcerers, nobles, evil dragons and draconic creatures	
Utu	Lesser	LN	The Sun	Fire, Law, the Sun, War	Holy warriors, judges, government officials	
Yenomesh	Lesser	N	The God of Glyphs and Writing	Knowledge, Magic, Protection, Runes	Loremasters, wizards, scribes, authors, historians	Adopted into Foerdewaith pantheon

Churches of Mah-Barek

Name	Power	AL	Title	Spheres of Influence	Typical Worshippers
Church of Fatimashan, The Blessed of Mah-Barek	Greater	NG	Church of charity, good, and the sun	Charity, Glory, Good, Repose, Sun	Charitable humans, some humanoids; only females are clerics
Sect of Zahrahan	Greater	CE	Sect of death, glory, and evil	Death, Evil, Glory, Nobility, Strength	Revolutionaries, violent zealots, would-be tyrants

Name	Power	AL	Title	Spheres of Influence	Typical Worshippers
Church of Hafaz, The Light of Mah-Barek	Greater	N	Church of esoteric knowledge, artifice and magic	Artifice, Esoteric, Knowledge, Magic, Rune	Scholars, philosophers, sages, elitists
Cult of Zargareth	Greater	CN	Sect of artifice, knowledge, magic, and entropy	Artifice, Entropy, Knowledge, Magic, Runes	Deranged inventors, anarchists, nihilists
Church of Koua, The Hand of Mah-Barek	Greater	NE	Church of intrigue, strength, and war	Intrigue, Nobility, Strength, Trickery, War	Bureaucrats, dictators, bandits, spies, thieves, assassins
Children of Abbashar	Greater	CE	Sect of chaos, destruction, and trickery	Chaos, Death, Destruction, Evil, Trickery	Madmen, murderers, deviant hedonists
Church of Marwan, The Mystic of Mah-Barek	Greater	CG	Church of performance, magic, liberation, and luck	Chaos, Magic, Liberation, Luck, Performance	Performers, bards, musicians, orators, artists
The Poppy's Chorus	Greater	CN	Sect of darkness, madness, and chaos	Chaos, Darkness, Liberation, Madness, Travel	Addicts

GOHTRA PANTHEON (JAATI)

THE TWELVE WHO SIT ON THE THIRTEEN THRONES

Name	Power	AL	Title	Spheres of Influence	Typical Worshippers
Hangrum the Wise	Greater	N	First Among the Twelve; God of Wisdom and Leadership	Knowledge, Weather	Rulers, judges, farmers
Eoya the Mother	Greater	NG	Destroyer of Evil; Fierce Protector of Family and Culture	Family, Good, Protection	Heads of household, paladins, artists in dangerous situations
Biale	Greater	NG	Creator of Worlds	Creation, Family, Knowledge, Law	Fathers, mothers, artists and artisans
Vihode	Greater	LG	Sustainer of Worlds	Law, Nobility	Most people to some degree, leaders, guardsmen
Sinenye	Greater	CG	Judge and Destroyer of Worlds	Death, Destruction, Law, Knowledge	Rulers, judges, most people to some degree
Chammu the Benevolent	Greater	CG	Rhino-headed Ruler of All Beings	Knowledge, Wealth	Nobles, scholars, business owners, hopeful people
Mitra	Greater	LG	God of Law, Justice, and the Sun; God of Oaths	Good, Healing, Law, Protection, War	Common folk, rulers, noble warriors, magistrates, judges, healers, the sick and disabled
Mithras	Greater	LN	God of War	Animal, Glory, Law, War, Repose	Warriors, especially those who revel in battle
Rhiaan	Greater	CN	Goddess of Air and Birds	Air, Animal, Chaos, Travel	Intelligent avians and flying creatures
Kal'Ay-Mah	Greater	LE	The Black One; The Black Mother	Death, Destruction, Law, Knowledge	Assassins, religious scholars

Name	Power	AL	Title	Spheres of Influence	Typical Worshippers
Gromm the Thunderer	Greater	CG/CE	God of the Storm	Air, Destruction, Strength, War, Water	Barbarians, bards, those who live in areas with harsh weather
Pandrume	Greater	CG	The Child God; Protector of Children; The Trickster; Purveyor of Magic	Air, Luck, Magic, Trickery	Children (more commonly told of in stories than genuinely worshiped), wizards and sorcerers

NOBLE DEITIES, WHO STAND IN THE COURT OF THE THRONES

Name	Power	AL	Title	Sphere of Influence	Typical Worshippers
Bablukar	Lesser	LG	Lord of the Golden Sword	Good, Healing, Law, Protection, Strength	Paladins, people who want to better the world
Gaijeikhan	Lesser	N	God of War and Victory; Commander-In-Chief of the Army of the Heavens	Glory, Strength, War	Military commanders; warriors, especially male; those who value masculine might
Hassith-Kaa	Greater	NE	The Great Serpent	Evil, Scalyfolk, Strength, Trickery	Nagas, serpentfolk, inphidians, intelligent serpents and reptiles, some assassins
Jengpata	Lesser	NG	Goddess of Speech; Mother of Wisdom	Art, Knowledge, Music	Artists, politicians, musicians, actors, leaders
Kremarra	Lesser	CE	Dragon Goddess of Death and Nihilism; The Monkey Eater	Darkness, Death, Evil	Cultists, dragonborn, half-dragons, lizardfolk, other reptilian races
Maitira	Lesser	N	Goddess of Beauty, Wealth, and Fortune	Light, Beauty, Luck, Wealth, Love	Women, poor folk, mothers, wives
Nagtel	Lesser	LE	God of the Heavenly Fountain; God of Rain, Justice and Night	Air, Darkness, Water, Weather	Sailors, farmers, lawmen
Orozim	Lesser	CN	Acceptor of Sacrifice, Messenger of the Gods	Communication, Destruction, Fire	Those seeking the gods' attention; people in extreme peril
Owomarari	Lesser	NE	Dark Earth Mother; Mistress of Monstrous Beasts	Animal, Darkness, Earth	Cultists, evil summoners
Rachiss	Lesser	NE	Mogul of Parasites, God of Pestilence	Animal, Evil, Plant	Evil druids
S'Surimiss	Lesser	NE	The Rat Queen, Goddess of Rats	Animal, Evil, Destruction	Wererats, some ratfolk
Thindawl	Demigod	NG	God of Truth and Virtue	Good, Honor	Most people other than criminals and those who live dishonestly
Zadastha	Lesser	NG	Goddess of Love	Charm, Communication, Good, Healing, Trickery	Poets, romantic authors, bards, lovelorn individuals

GUARDIAN DEITIES, WHO RESIDE IN THE GARDEN OF SOULS

Name	Power	AL	Title	Spheres of Influence	Typical Worshippers
Zaihhess	Demigod	CE	God of Death	Evil, Chaos, Destruction, Death	Necromancers, cultists
Zors	Demigod	CN	Fortune's Fool, Demigod of Luck	Chaos, Luck, Trickery	Gamblers, beggars, slaves, travelers, the poor, and prisoners awaiting execution

DEMONS

Name	Power	AL	Title	Spheres of Influence	Typical Worshippers
Shartang	Demon	CE	Demon King, Enemy of the Gods	Chaos, Darkness, Death, Destruction, Evil, Trickery, War	Demons, cultists, evil wizards

GRASSLANDS SPIRITS (CENTRAL LIBYNOS)

Name	Power	AL	Title	Spheres of Influence	Typical Worshippers	Notes
Father Sky	Greater	NG	He Who Sends the Wind and Makes the Grass Grow	Air, Darkness, Law, Void, Weather	Hunters, scouts, judges, leaders	Also known as Tiabene
Mother Earth	Greater	NG	The Birth-Giver	Community, Earth, Plant, Water	Common people and growers	Also known as Osi, Ulagooro
Brother/Sister Horse	Lesser	CG	The One Who Runs Across the Grass	Animal, Protection, Runes, Travel	Travelers, animal herders, horse breeders	
Little Pajero	Lesser	CN	The Red Cat	Chaos, Knowledge, Luck, Trickery	Explorers, the curious, those seeking knowledge	
Hungry Fire	Greater	NE	The All-Consuming, The Stealer of Grass	Death, Destruction, Evil, Fire	The angry, evil, and those who desire destruction	Also known as Komu

HUUN PANTHEON

Name	Power	AL	Title	Spheres of Influence	Typical Worshippers
Aku-te Selissa	Greater	NE	The Uncaring Mother; White Lady	Community, Family, Fertility	Mothers, children, young people; common people
Erishkigal	Lesser	NE	Amasser of Souls, Goddess of the Afterlife	Death, Earth, Evil, Law	Common people, relatives of those who have died or are close to death
Maas Tal-ek	Greater	NE	Destroyer of Worlds and the End of All Things; The Feathered God	Destruction, Rulership, War	Rulers, generals; those who want protection against enemies
Nergal	Greater	NE	The God of Plague, Deathbringer	Air, Death, Destruction, Evil, War	Common people staving off death; those who want revenge on enemies, military leaders

KALDILOORAN SPIRITS (SOUTHERN LIBYNOS)

Name	Power	AL	Title	Spheres of Influence	Typical Worshippers	Notes
Sky Father	Greater	LN	The Old Man in the Clouds; The One Who Moves the Sun, Moons and Stars	Air, Earth, Law, the Sun	Those who are coming of age, making agreements, or wish to show respect	
Barramundi	Lesser	N	Creator Spirit of Rivers and the Ocean	Repose, Travel, Water	Those who travel on water, fish, or explore the ocean	
Bat (fruit bat)	Lesser	N	Creator Spirit of Night and Underground Places; He Who Flies at Night	Darkness, Earth, Ruins, Void	Those who shelter in caves, or travel or hunt by night	Also known as Goloban

Name	Power	AL	Title	Spheres of Influence	Typical Worshippers	Notes
Crook-beak (eagle)	Lesser	NE	Creator Spirit of Jealousy, Covetousness, Taking, and Murder	Charm, Death, Destruction, Evil, Trickery	Those who resent others and wish to curse them, those who wish to take prosperity from others, and those who seek revenge for perceived wrongs	Also known as Wolokund
Great Eagle	Lesser	CN	Creator Spirit of Wind and Storm	Air, Fire, Weather	Those who want storms to pass, those who fear destruction and fire	Also known as Ewuti
Parrot	Lesser	CN	Creator Spirit of Colorful and Strange Things; The One Who Brings Color	Artifice, Chaos, Luck, Magic, Trickery	Those who make crafts, practice magic, trick others, and those who wish for color in their activities	Also known as Nuluganna
Possum	Lesser	NG	Creator Spirit and Caretaker of the Earth, Plants, and Animals	Animals, Good, Earth, Healing, Plants, Protection	Those who harvest plants and animals, those who wish for protection for their crops and livestock	Also known as Tua
Rainbow Boa	Lesser	N	Creator Spirit of Mountains and Other Earth Shapes; Sender of Rain	Earth, Scalykind, Weather	Those who travel through mountains or work under them, those desiring rain for crops or drought	Also known as Arutu

KEHNA PANTHEON (EASTERN LIBYNOS)

Name	Power	AL	Title	Spheres of Influence	Typical Worshippers	Notes
Athera	Greater	CN	Goddess of Fertility; Mother of the Seventy Gracious Gods	Community, Earth, Plant, Water	Everyone desiring fertility of the land	
Agamid	Greater	NE	God of Fire; Provider of Power through Sacrifice	Death, Evil, Fire, Strength	Those who crave power, rulers in times of desperation	
Baal	Greater	LE	God of Storms and Battle; Lord of the Earth	Air, Family, Strength, War, Weather	Common people, rulers in time of war	
Dagon	Greater	CN	God of the Sea and of Agriculture	Animal, Plant, Water, Weather	Sailors, fisherfolk, farmers, common people	Worshippers insist that this god is not the same as Dagon the Demon Lord
Ift	Lesser	CN	God of Deception; Last of the Seventy	Darkness, Liberation, Trickery	Ifthaaz: everyone; elsewhere: thieves, con artists	
Illion	Greater	LN	King of the Gods; Cornerstone of Law and Knowledge	Community, Earth, Law	Rulers, judges, sages, wizards	
Seventy Gracious Gods	Lesser/ Demigod	Varies	Minor deities of the many concerns of daily life	Varies	Common people	More popular in Ifthaaz

GODS OF THE PARAMOUNTCIES (SOUTHERN LIBYNOS)

Name	Power	AL	Title	Spheres of Influence	Typical Worshippers	Notes
Ahtizerr	Greater	LG	He Who Loves Magic	Good, Law, Magic, Protection	Good-aligned arcane spell casters	Equivalent to Libynosi Thasizer
Anana	Lesser	CN	The Lady of Luck and Gold	Chaos, Luck, Travel, Trickery, Wealth	Gamblers, rogues, bards, those who live by luck	Equivalent to Libynosi Ayianna
Erka	Lesser	NE	She Who Moves in Shadows	Darkness, Evil, Magic	Thieves, assassins, evil wizards and sorcerers, those who make their living in darkness	Equivalent to Hyperborean Mirkeer
Ghamia	Lesser	N	The River Lady	Water, Travel, Charm, Community	Women, boat or barge handlers, fisherfolk, swamp-dwellers, water creatures and fey	Equivalent to Hyperborean Kamien
Gonthor	Greater	CG/CE	He Who Grumbles in the Sky	Air, Destruction, Strength, War, Water	Barbarians, bards, mercenaries, adventurers, those who live in areas with harsh weather	Equivalent to Gohtra Gromm the Thunderer
Lohfa	Lesser	LN	He Who Makes Things Grow	Animal, Earth, Nature, Plant, Sun, Weather	Farmers, growers, druids revering the cycle of nature	Equivalent to Hyperborean Telophus
Newan	Lesser	CG/CN	Lady of Fire and Water	Air, Chaos, Earth, Fire, Water	Humans, druids, some artificers	Equivalent to Libynosi Ninevah
Orgim	Lesser	LE	He Who Loves War	War, Evil, Law, Magic	Evil monks, warriors, wizards, and nobles	Equivalent to Hyperborean Horgrim
Selena	Lesser	NG	The Peaceful Lady	Healing, Knowledge, Plant, Protection	Bards, monks, artists and artisans, gardeners, those who desire peace	Equivalent to Libynosi Iseleine
Sifkra	Greater	N	He Who Loves Coins	Commerce, Travel, Wealth	Merchants, seafarers, caravan masters, aristocrats, diplomats	Equivalent to Hyperborean Sefagreth
Vreenon	Lesser	CN	She Who Loves Birds	Air, Animal, Chaos, Travel	Intelligent avians and flying creatures, those who wish protection against birds	Equivalent to Gohtra Rhiann

PHARAONIC PANTHEON (KHEMIT)

Name	Power	AL	Title	Spheres of Influence	Typical Worshippers
Aapep	Lesser	CE	The Black Serpent; The Destroyer	Chaos, Death, Destruction, Evil, Serpent	Evil power-seeking humanoids, assassins, cults
Aker	Lesser	NG	God of the Earth and Death	Death, Earth, Protection	Embalmers, guardians, kings
Amemt	Lesser	CE	The Devourer; Eater of the Dead	Chaos, Death, Destruction, Evil, Magic	Evil humanoids
Amset	Lesser	LG	Guardian of the Dead	Animals, Death, Law, Protection	Embalmers, guardians

Name	Power	AL	Title	Spheres of Influence	Typical Worshippers
Amun	Greater	NG	God of the Sky and Sun, Air, Knowledge and Magic	Air, Knowledge, Magic, Strength, the Sun	Rulers, kings, scholars, nobles
Anhur	Greater	CG	God of War and the Hunt, Defender of Khemit	Animals, Chaos, Strength, War	Hunters, warriors, soldiers
Anqet	Lesser	CG	Goddess of Rivers and Water, Goddess of Pleasure	Chaos, Good, Magic, Water	Sailors, fishermen, pleasure seekers
Anubis	Greater	LG	Guardian of the Dead	Death [Good], Law, Luck, Protection, Strength	Embalmers, guardians
Apis	Greater	NG	God of the Sun and Life, Earth and Strength	Bounty, Earth, Good, Strength, Sun	Farmers, midwives, expectant mothers, pharaoh
Apuat	Lesser	CG	God of Messengers and Battle	Air, Strength, Travel, War	Messengers, warriors, barbarians
Aten	Lesser	N	The Sun; The Sun Disc	Air, Bounty, Fire, Strength, the Sun	Clerics, sages, wizards
Bast	Greater	CG	Goddess of Beauty and Cats, Good Luck and Trickery	Animals, Chaos, Good, Luck, Trickery	Nobles, women, those who desire luck
Bes	Lesser	N	God of Protection, Happiness, Music, and War	Luck, Protection, Strength, War	Fighters, rogues, bards
Buto	Lesser	LG	Goddess of Protection, Law, and Travel	Law, Protection, Serpent, Travel	Guardians, fighters, merchants
Chons	Lesser	CG	God of the Silver Moon, Time, Knowledge, Travel, and Trickery	Chaos, Good, Travel, Trickery	Musicians, bards, sages, merchants, travelers, pranksters
Duamutef	Lesser	LG	God of Death, Funeral Rites, and Protection	Death, Law, Protection, Strength	Guardians, embalmers, anyone after death of loved one
Geb	Greater	N	God of the Earth	Earth, Plants, Protection, Strength	Farmers, druids
Hamehit	Lesser	NG	Goddess of the Water, Fish, and the Seas	Animals, Bounty, Good, Luck, Water	Sailors, fishermen
Hapy	Greater	NG	God of Rivers, Oceans, and Streams; Lord of Fishes and Birds	Animals, Bounty, Good, Protection, Travel, Water	Sailors, fishermen, those who depend on the sea
Hathor	Lesser	NG	Goddess of Music and the Arts; Giver of Inspiration	Fire, Law, Sun, War	Musicians, artists, women
Herakhty	Lesser	NG	God of the Morning and Sunrise	Earth, Good, Protection, Sun	Farmers
Heru	Lesser	LG	The Watcher; God of Law, Order, Rulership	Law, Good, Knowledge, Strength, War	Rulers, nobles, lawyers, fighters, warriors
Horus	Greater	LN	The Avenger; God of War and Destruction	Destruction, Law, Sun, Vengeance, War	Soldiers, warriors, fighters, those seeking vengeance and retribution
Isis	Greater	NG	Goddess of Fertility and Magic	Bounty, Good, Healing, Magic	Women, mothers, wizards, clerics, sorcerers

Name	Power	AL	Title	Spheres of Influence	Typical Worshippers
Khebsenef	Greater	LN	Son of Horus; God of Death	Death, Law, Protection, Strength	Guardians, surgeons, physicians
Khnemu	Greater	NG	God of Creation and Invention	Artifice, Creation, Earth, Good, Healing, Luck	Craftsmen, artisans
Maat	Greater	LG	Goddess of Truth and Law	Good, Knowledge, Protection, Law, Strength	Judges, city officials, paladins, monks
Maftet	Lesser	CG	Goddess of Protection and Healing	Good, Healing, Serpent, Strength, Vermin	Healers, midwives, women, guardians
Mekhit	Lesser	CG	Goddess of War, The Eye of Ra	Glory, Protection, Strength, War	Soldiers, mercenaries, officers, generals
Menu	Greater	CN	God of War	Chaos, Destruction, Strength, War	Fighters, warriors
Meretseger	Lesser	LG	The Protector	Good, Law, Protection, Serpent	Guardians, warrior, keepers of secrets
Mert	Lesser	NG	Goddess of Song and Joy	Good, Healing, Knowledge, Trickery	Musicians, poets, artists, bards
Min	Lesser	CG	Protector of the Moon, God of Male Fertility	Chaos, Destruction, Good, Knowledge, Magic	Commoners
Mût	Greater	LG	Queen of the Gods, Mother Goddess, Provider of Life and National Prosperity	Fertility, Life, Wealth	Noblewoman, wives, mothers, growers, common people
Nefertem	Greater	NG	God of the Sun; Lord of the Sunrise; God of Healing	Good, Healing, Knowledge, Plant, Sun	Healers, surgeons, women, sorcerers, wizards
Neith	Greater	CG	Goddess of War and Wisdom; Guardian of the Dead	Death, Good, Knowledge, Law, War	Soldiers, hunters, fighters, paladins, loremasters, scholars, nobles
Nekhbet	Lesser	LG	Goddess of Protection and War, Childbirth and Fertility	Law, Protection, Strength, War	Warriors, women, farmers
Nephthys	Greater	CG	Goddess of the Dead	Chaos, Death [Good], Knowledge, Magic	Women
Nut	Lesser	NG	Goddess of the Night Sky	Air, Good, Knowledge, Protection, Trickery	Rogues, bards, guardians, paladins
Okdo-ad	Greater	N/CN	Primeval deities of water, air, darkness, and infinity	Chaos, Darkness, Water, Air	Nature worshipers, leaders in times of great danger
Osiris	Greater	LG	God of Fertility and the Dead	Death, Good, Law, Protection	Nobles, rulers, farmers, commoners

Name	Power	AL	Title	Spheres of Influence	Typical Worshippers
Pakhut	Lesser	CG	Goddess of Strength	Chaos, Destruction, Good, Strength	Fighters, barbarians
Ptah	Greater	LN	Creator of the Universe	Air, Bounty, Earth, Law, Magic, Sun	Craftsmen, artisans
Ra	Greater	NG	God of the Sun and Pharaoh of the Gods	Bounty, Good, Knowledge, Protection, Sun	Rulers, nobles, scholars
Renenet	Lesser	CG	Goddess of Protection and Fortune	Good, Knowledge, Luck, Protection, Serpent [Good]	Women, gamblers, guardians
Sebk	Lesser	CE	God of Evil, Betrayal, and Water	Chaos, Evil, Trickery, Water	Sailors, fishermen
Seker	Greater	NG	God of Death and Light	Death [Good], Good, Protection, Strength, the Sun	Commoners
Sekhmet	Greater	CN	Lady of Pestilence; Goddess of the Sun	Chaos, Destruction, Healing, War	Surgeons, doctors, healers, warriors
Serqet	Lesser	LG	Goddess of the Dead and Strength	Death [Good], Good, Law, Strength, Vermin	Fighters, guardians, necromancers
Seshat	Greater	NG	Goddess of Writing, History, Time, Knowledge and Architecture	Good, Knowledge, Luck, Magic	Record-keepers, scribes, sages, historians, story-tellers, architects
Set	Greater	LE	God of Evil and the Night	Death, Destruction, Evil, Knowledge, Law, Serpent	Evil power-seeking humanoids, evil monks, assassins
Shu	Lesser	LG	Lord of the Air	Air, Good, Law, Strength	Mystics, nobles, rulers, warriors
Tefnut	Lesser	LG	Goddess of Storms and Rivers	Good, Protection, Sun, Water	Farmers, fishermen, sailors
Thoth	Greater	N	God of Knowledge and Magic	Knowledge, Luck, Magic, Travel	Scholars, sages, travelers
Tuart	Greater	LG	Goddess of Fertility and Protection	Good, Knowledge, Magic, Plant, Protection	Women, expectant mothers, midwives, farmers

RIVERINE SPIRITS (SOUTHERN LIBYNOS)

Name	Power	AL	Title	Spheres of Influence	Typical Worshippers	Notes
Be-Le	Greater	NE	The Witch; The Dark Sister; Goddess of Knowledge, Magic, Evil, and Creation	Creation, Evil, Knowledge, Magic	Tribal shaman, witches, those desperate for a child, lycanthropes	Equivalent to Hyperborean Cybele
Noh-ro	Greater	N(G)	The Guardian; The Pale Sister; Goddess of Protection, Darkness, and Travel	Darkness, Protection, Travel	Tribal shaman, common people, druids, stargazers, those who wish to know the future, tabaxi, some fey, lycanthropes	Equivalent to Hyperborean Narrah
The Green Lady	Greater	N	She Who Loves Trees; Fey Goddess of the Forest, Animals, and Plants	Life, Light, Nature	Deep forest dwellers, tabaxi, fey creatures	Equivalent to Old Way Arialee
The Ancient Boy	Greater	CN	He Who Leads the Hunt; God of Animals, Plants, Chaos and Trickery	Animals, Chaos, Earth, Liberation, Plants, Trickery	Hunters, herders, druids, musicians, tabaxi, woodland fey, hybrid creatures	Equivalent to Hyperborean Pan
Loa Aizan	Lesser	N	Mistress of the Sea; Patroness of Commerce	Luck, Magic, Travel, Water	Fisherfolk, river travelers, traders, explorers, users of magic, those who desire luck	
Loa Damballa	Greater	N	Ruler of Air; Primordial Creator of All Life; Patroness of the Sky	Air, Chaos, Creation, Sun, Weather	Common people, tribal shaman, travelers, those desiring good weather	
Loa Legba	Lesser	N	Patron of Speech and Understanding	Animals, Knowledge, Law, Protection, Strength	Tribal leaders, storytellers, traders, travelers, any engaged in rituals	
Loa Oggun	Lesser	N	Lord of the Earth; The General; Patron of Smiths	Animals, Earth, Nobility, War	Tribal leaders, warriors, hunters, those who work in metal	
Loa Samedi	Greater	N	Baron Samedi; Patron of Death; Spirit of Fire	Darkness, Death, Fire, Law, Luck, Repose	Common people, tribal shaman	

OTHER GODS OF LIBYNOS

Name	Power	AL	Title	Spheres of Influence	Typical Worshippers
Anumon	Greater	LN (G)	God of Gates, Keeper of the Laws, Overseer of Creation	Creation, Law, Protection, Travel	Rulers, lawmakers, jurists, public officials
Ayianna	Lesser	CN	The Damsel of Fate, Goddess of Shadows, Luck, Greed, and Wealth	Chaos, Luck, Travel, Trickery	Travelers, gamblers, merchants, petty criminals
Iseleine	Lesser	NG	Maiden of Peace, Goddess of Art, Love, Beauty, and Passion	Healing, Knowledge, Plant, Protection	Physicians, healers, farmers, guardians
Ninevah	Lesser	CG/ CN	Lady of Miasma, Goddess of Elements	Air, Chaos, Earth, Fire, Water	Elemental spellcasters, builders, artisans

Name	Power	AL	Title	Spheres of Influence	Typical Worshippers
Thasizier	Greater	LG	Master of Magic, God of Good Magic	Good, Law, Magic, Protection	Good aligned spellcasters, scholars, teachers
Voard	Lesser	LN	God of Anguish, The End of Days	Destruction, Law, Strength, Travel	Warriors, soldiers, rulers

OTHER GODS

GODS OF THE OLD WAYS

Name	Power	AL	Title	Spheres of Influence	Typical Worshippers	Notes
Agrona	Lesser	CE	Goddess of Slaughter	Chaos, Death, Evil, Madness, War	Berserkers, warlords, warriors	
Annawn	Greater	LN	King of the Otherworld, Lord of Autumn	Darkness, Earth, Law, Repose	Families of the departed, preparers and guardians of the dead	
Aranrhud	Greater	CG	The Golden, Goddess of the Dawn, Weaver of Destinies	Community, Death, Earth, Family, Healing	Parents, midwives, healers, weavers	
Arialee	Lesser	N	The Morninglight, Fey Goddess of Nature	Air, Animals, Earth, Plants, Water, the Sun	Neutral and good fey, druids, intelligent animals, plant creatures, some elves	
Belenos	Greater	NG	God of the Sun, The Shining One	Good, Knowledge, Light, Protection, Sun	The Ancient Ones, most modern Daanites	Also known as Llywelyn, Maponus
Brigid	Greater	NG	Goddess of Spring, The Exalted One	Animal, Community, Family, Fire, Sun	Bards, poets, smiths, herders, farmers	Also known as Brigantia
Callyc	Demigod	N	Bel's Toad-Lord, Saint Toad, Callyc of the Held Gate, The Cromulent Keeper	Animal, Earth, Protection, Trickery, Water	Grippli, intelligent amphibians, some lizardfolk, some mist dragons	
Camulos	Lesser	CN	God of War	Death, Destruction, Glory, War	Fighters, soldiers, war leaders, martially-oriented rulers	
Chernobog	Greater	CE	God of Blood and Sacrifice, Old Bloody Head, The Black God, The Lord of Slaughter	Animal, Darkness, Death, Earth, Evil, Plant, War	Neolithic tribes (mostly extinct), some Daanite outlaws, occasional murderers and madmen	Also known as Crom Cruach, Crom Dubh
Danu	Greater	NG	The River Goddess, The Great Mother	Community, Earth, Healing, Knowledge, Plant, Water	The Ancient Ones, most modern Daanites	
Gofannon	Lesser	LN	God of the Smithy	Artifice, Fire, Knowledge, Rune	Armorers, blacksmiths, weaponsmiths, metalworkers	

Name	Power	AL	Title	Spheres of Influence	Typical Worshippers	Notes
The Green Father	Lesser	N	God of the Wilds, The Huntsman/Herne the Hunter (Foerdewaith), the Horned God (Erskaelosi)	Animal, Earth, Nature, Plant, Spring	Druids, rangers, hunters, guides, trackers, berserkers	Also known as Cernunnos (Tuathe De)
Lleullaw	Greater	LG	God of Law and Truth	Artifice, Good, Law, Nobility	Fighters, smiths, historians, lawmakers, rulers	Also known as Lámfada, Lugh
Manawydan fab Llŷr	Demigod	NG	Singer to the Gods	Music, Knowledge	Adventurers, bards, performers, craftsfolk	
Myrddin	Lesser	N	God of High Places, Lord of the Wild Air	Air, Knowledge, Luck, Sun	Druids, bards, poets, seers, prophets, aerial servants, creatures of the air, intelligent birds, some cloud dragons	
Narrah	Greater	N	The Lady of the Moon, the Pale Sister	Darkness, Nature, Magic	Druids, stargazers, lycanthropes, oracles, bards, some fey	
The Nameless One	Greater	N	The Cloaked Goddess, Lady of Secrets, Goddess of the Crossroads	Darkness, Magic, Travel, Void	Magic-users, fortune-tellers, travelers	
Nodens	Greater	N	God of the Sea and Healing; Nuada Silverhand; Llud Llaw Eraint	Water, Healing, Protection	Hunters, sailors, travelers, healers	
Oghma	Greater	CG	God of Song and Bards, The First Song	Creation, Good, Travel, Knowledge	Musicians, composers, dancers and poets, humans, elves, halflings.	
Sucellos	Lesser	NG	The Vintner, the Plowman	Earth, Intoxicants, Plant, Strength	Brewers, coopers, farmers, vintners, revelers	
Taranis	Lesser	CN	God of Thunder and Lightning	Air, Weather	Farmers, sailors, fisherfolk, those who depend upon good weather	

NEOLITHIC GODS

Name	Power	AL	Title	Spheres of Influence	Typical Worshippers	Notes
Agrona	Lesser	CE	Goddess of Slaughter	Chaos, Death, Evil, Madness, War	Berserkers, warlords, warriors	
Baal-Zag	Lesser	CE	The Howler in Darkness	Animal, Death, Strength	Evil rangers, cannibals, were-creatures	
Behemoth	Greater	LG	The Celestial Dragon	Air, Good, Knowledge, Law, Protection, Scalykind	Good-aligned dragons and related species, good and neutral lizardfolk, human and halfling paladins and dragon cultists	
Chernobog	Greater	CE	God of Blood and Sacrifice, Old Bloody Head, The Black God, The Lord of Slaughter	Animal, Darkness, Death, Earth, Evil, Plant, War	Neolithic tribes (mostly extinct), some Daanite outlaws, occasional murderers and madmen	Also known as Crom Cruach, Crom Dubh

Name	Power	AL	Title	Spheres of Influence	Typical Worshippers	Notes
Cybele	Greater	NE	Magna Mater, Black Goat of the Woods, Goddess of Fertility and Witchcraft, The Dark Sister (the smaller moon - Sybil)	Creation, Evil, Knowledge, Magic	Witches, disenfranchised women, lycanthropes, degenerate cults, hags, harpies, some medusas	
Dagon	Demon Lord	CE	Demon Prince of the Sea	Chaos, Destruction, Evil, Water	Aquatic humanoids and monstrous humanoids, evil human fishermen, water nagas, shrroths, hezrou, kraken, aboleths	Believed to be different from the god of the same name in the Kehna pantheon
Dajobas	Greater	CE	The Shark God, Devourer of Worlds	Chaos, Destruction, Evil, Water	Weresharks, sahuagin, intelligent sea predators, cannibalistic pirates	
Demogorgon	Demon Lord	CE	Primal God of the Earth, The Dark Creator, Demon Lord of Fate	Chaos, Creation, Darkness, Earth, Evil, Knowledge, Luck	Cultists, madmen, derros, crag men, dark folk, ropers, demons, bodaks, baregaras, demonic knights, the Fates, genies, aeons, black jinn	
Ellashah	Greater	LN	The Great Creator	Air, Creation, Earth, Fire, Water	Druids, elemental spellcasters; some isolated neolithic groups	Believed dead
The Father	Greater	CE	Father of the Sky, God of Violence and Warfare, The Demiurge	Chaos, Creation, Destruction, Fertility	Neolithic tribes (mostly extinct), Vanigoths of the Wilderland Hills, some Wildmen of the Mistwood, possibly others	Also known as Boros, Engur, Abzu, Buri, Dyaus Pitra, Nun, Lir, Wakea; imprisoned
The Goddess	Greater	CG/CN	Mother of Earth	Animal, Community, Earth, Fertility, Healing, Plant, Protection	Neolithic peoples, mothers	Also known as Erce, Gaia; sacrificed self to imprison Father
Keld	Lesser	CE	The Wicked, Lord of the Grimlocks	Chaos, Evil, War	Evil underground creatures, especially grimlocks, derro, morlocks	
Mocham	Greater	LG	The Earthpower, Stone of Battle	Good, Earth, Law, War	Formerly svirfneblin, deep dwarves, shaitan, earth elementals; Now unknown	Believed lost or dead
The Nameless One	Greater	N	The Cloaked Goddess, Lady of Secrets, Goddess of the Crossroads	Darkness, Magic, Travel, Void	Magic-users, fortune-tellers, travelers	
Ninevah	Lesser	CG/CN	Lady of Miasma, Goddess of Elements	Air, Chaos, Earth, Fire, Water	Elemental spellcasters, builders, artisans	
Pan	Greater	N	God of the Wild, Lord of the Flocks and the Hunt	Music, Wild Animals, Dancing, Fertility	Bards, hunters, certain fey races	

Name	Power	AL	Title	Spheres of Influence	Typical Worshippers	Notes
Shupnikkurat	Greater	CN	The Wild Mother of the Thousand Young, Goddess of Fertility, Birth, and Wild Beasts, The Mad Mother, The Black Goat, Magna Mater	Animal, Chaos, Earth, Fertility, Plant	Druids, mothers, fertility cults, satyrs, witches, hags, atatvistic serpentfolk, nocturnals, intelligent plant creatures, rorkouns, gorynychs, bholes, dark young, living monoliths	
Yaazotsh	Lesser	N	Eater of the Dead	Air, Death, Protection	Neolithic tribes, some modern healers and morticians	

GODS OF THE TULITO (AIZANES ISLANDS/RAZOR COAST)

Name	Power	AL	Title	Spheres of Influence	Typical Worshippers	Notes
Dajobas	Greater	CE	The Shark God, Devourer of Worlds	Chaos, Destruction, Evil, Water	Weresharks, sahuagin, intelligent sea predators, cannibalistic pirates	
Great Pele	Greater	CN	Mother of Fire, Eater of Land	Chaos, Destruction, Earth, Fire, Weather	Tulita, fire giants, menehune, creatures of elemental fire, fire cults	
Lakua Mao	Lesser	LE	The Red Misery	Destruction, Fire, Law, Scalykind, War	Underground creatures, usually evil, including goblins, derro, mites and grimlocks	Imprisoned
Paphu	Lesser	LG	Dolphin, The Herald	Charm, Liberation, Luck, Trickery	Tulita explorers, messengers, arcane spellcasters, fighters of oppression, lovers	
Tohoraha	Lesser	NG	The Whale, The Lore Keeper, The Watcher, The Great Traveler of the Waves	Animals, Knowledge, Travel, Water	Tulita whale riders, totemic tribes, fishermen	
Tumatenga	Lesser	LG	Grandfather Turtle, Old Angry Face	Glory, Law, Liberation, Protection, Nobility, War	Tulita leaders, warriors	

GODS OF NONHUMAN FOLK

DWARVEN GODS

Name	Power	AL	Title	Spheres of Influence	Typical Worshippers
Barator (Lost)	Greater	LG	The Crafter and Master of the Forge	Artifice, Earth, Law, Strength	Dwarven smiths, artisans, and craftsmen, dwarves of Clan Krazzadak
Bilis	Lesser	N	Dwarf God of the Otherworld, King of the Hollow Hills	Earth, Fire, Glory, Magic, Repose	Isolated dwarven communities, dwarven druids, recognized by Daanites and other human followers of the Tuatha De, some spriggans
Crugas	Lesser	N	God of Magical Crafts	Artifice, Knowledge, Magic, Runes	Dwarven smiths and armorers, craftsmen, and arcane spellcasters, Dvergar of the Northlands

Name	Power	AL	Title	Spheres of Influence	Typical Worshippers
Dargath	Demigod	LG	The Kingmaker, God of Craftsmanship and Creation	Artifice, Air, Earth, Fire, Law, Nobility, Strength, Travel, Water	Dwarves of Libynos, some elementals
Dwerfater/ Dwurfater	Greater	LG	Father of Dwarves	Earth, Good, Strength, Creation	All dwarves to some extent
Grox	Lesser	LE	God of Artifice and Darkness, The Deep Father	Artifice, Darkness, Evil, Knowledge, Law	Duergar, evil dwarves, lawyers, spies, scribes, alchemists
Pekko	Lesser	CG	God of Ale and Spirits, Lord of the Abundant Harvest	Chaos, Community, Good, Plants, Travel	Gnome, halfling, dwarven, and human brewers, tavern keepers, bakers, some farmers that raise hops and barley
Father Poga	Lesser	LG	God of Time, Lord of the Yule	Community, Darkness, Good, Time, Travel	Mountain dwarves, candy makers, Yuletide celebrants, chroniclers
Snorri Horrnison	Demigod	CN	The Swaggering Axe, Hero-God of the Targ	Destruction, Glory, Liberation, Luck	Mountain dwarves of Clan Targ, dwarven adventurers and gamblers
Stryme/Strym	Lesser	NG	Stryme the Mighty, God of Strength	Good, Liberation, Protection, Strength, War	Dwarves, soldiers, barbarians, fighters, laborers
Vergrimm Earthsblood	Lesser	LN	Keeper of the Mines, God of Miners	Artifice, Darkness, Earth, Law	Dwarven miners, architects, spelunkers, deep cave explorers
Yngret Yellow-hair	Greater	NG	Goddess of the Clanhold, Mother of Accord	Community, Fire, Healing, Law, Protection	Dwarven women, matchmakers, city guards, soldiers, and midwives

Elven Gods

Name	Power	AL	Title	Spheres of Influence	Typical Worshippers
Darach-Albith	Greater	CG	High God of Elves, Firstborn; Father of the Elves	Plants, Animals, Magic, War	Elven and half-elven warriors, wizards and rangers, a few drow
Queen of Spiders	Greater	CE	The Spider Goddess	Darkness, Death, Earth, Evil, Magic, Trickery	Drow, troglodytes, spider-obsessed humans
Rialae-Aibaru	Lesser	LG	Goddess of the Wandering Star, Lost Queen of the Elves, The Tear of Heaven	Law, Good, Travel, Magic	High and wood elves, warriors, wizards and rangers, some drow
Shae'loegn	Lesser	N	God of Forests, Prophets, and Seers; He That Walks Unseen	Animals, Darkness, Knowledge, Plants, Weather	Fortune tellers, diviners, prophets, mystics
Wayland the Smith	Greater	LN	God of Craft and Smiths	Artifice, Earth, Creation, Fire, Knowledge, Magic	Elven smiths, armorers, swordmakers, a few dwarven and human smiths

Gnomish Gods

Name	Power	AL	Title	Spheres of Influence	Typical Worshippers
The Dark Seer	Lesser	N	God of Delving and Deep Caverns, the Hooded Dark	Animal, Darkness, Earth, Knowledge, Scalykind	Svirfneblin, Under Realms fey (conshees, fyrs, killmoulises, mites, pesties, wechtleins), occasional troglodytes
Dre'uain the Lame	Greater	LN	God of Craft and Smiths, God of Industry and Hard Work	Artifice, Earth, Creation, Fire, Knowledge, Magic	Human, gnome, dwarven, and halfling craftsmen, inventors, laborers, union organizers, maimed workers, wounded veterans, beggars
Hammer Mittelschmerz	Greater	CG	God of Gnomes	Animals, Artifice, Chaos, Earth, Protection, Trickery	Gnomes, pranksters, those seeking vengeance
Iskardar	Lesser	N	Master of Invention, God of Gems and Wealth	Artifice, Earth, Knowledge, Runes	Gnome jewelers, finesmiths, scholars, academics, mathematicians, explorers, svirfneblin
Kittail Hillcaller	Lesser	CN (G)	The Wild One, The Wind in the Hills, Goddess of Freedom and Jest	Chaos, Charm, Liberation, Trickery	Gnome country folk, druids, hunters, trappers, frontiersmen, slywallies, some fey (mainly satyrs, korreds, and dryads)
Pekko	Lesser	CG	God of Ale and Spirits, Lord of the Abundant Harvest	Chaos, Community, Good, Plants, Travel	Gnome, halfling, dwarven, and human brewers, tavern keepers, bakers, some farmers that raise hops and barley

Halfling Gods

Name	Power	AL	Title	Spheres of Influence	Typical Worshippers
Hester	Lesser	NG	Goddess of the Hearthfire, Hester Full of Blessings, Mother Hubbard	Animals, Community, Earth, Fire, Healing, Protection	Halflings, married couples, human worshippers of Ceres
Mick O'Delving	Greater	CG	God of Halflings, The Little Miner	Artifice, Earth, Good, Luck, Protection, Trickery	Halflings, some burrowing creatures, drunks, Barefeet assassins
Pekko	Lesser	CG	God of Ale and Spirits, Lord of the Abundant Harvest	Chaos, Community, Good, Plants, Travel	Gnome, halfling, dwarven, and human brewers, tavern keepers, bakers, some farmers that raise hops and barley
Sotheryn (Dead)	Lesser	LG	Goddess of Fertility and Death; Lady Suzanne	Community, Good, Healing, Repose	Sotheryn is no longer worshipped, but is mourned and remembered by all traditional halfling families.

Goblinoid Gods

Name	Power	AL	Title	Spheres of Influence	Typical Worshippers
Snuurge	Greater	NE	Father of Goblins	Earth, Evil, Magic, Trickery, Vengeance	Goblins, hobgoblins, bugbears
Kakobovia	Demigod	LE	Hobgoblin Demigod of War	Death, Evil, Law, War	Hobgoblins, some goblins, some humans
The Destroyer	Lesser	CE	Warlord of Bugbears; God of Stealth, Violence, and Slaughter	Chaos, Destruction, Evil, Trickery, War	Bugbears, ogres, trolls, troblins, evil barbarians

Gods of the Gnolls

Name	Power	AL	Title	Spheres of Influence	Typical Worshippers
Crocutus	Lesser	CE	Eater of the Dead; Demon Lord of Gnolls	Animal, Chaos, Destruction, Trickery	Gnolls, flinds, and some ghouls, ghasts, and other intelligent eaters of carrion
Alquemedak	Lesser	CE	The Hyena God; Five Aspects: Master of Fortune, Taker of Slaves, Lord of Carrion, Giver of Plentitude in Exchange for Sacrifice, Smasher of Skulls	Evil, Trickery	Gnoll, plunderers, slavers, those seeking favor, those seeking to kill

Orcish Gods

Name	Power	AL	Title	Spheres of Influence	Typical Worshippers
Grotaag	Greater	CE	God of Orcs	Beast, Death, Destruction, Evil, War	Orcs, half-orcs, orogs, ogrillons, some goblins and ogres
Orcus	Greater	CE	Demon Prince of the Undead; King of the Dead/ Thanatos the Fallen; Deliverer of the Dead	Chaos, Death, Destruction, Evil, War	Orcs, orogs, monsters, undead, demons, evil humanoids

Avian Gods

Name	Power	AL	Title	Spheres of Influence	Typical Worshippers
Myrddin	Lesser	N	God of High Places, Lord of the Wild Air	Air, Knowledge, Luck, Sun	Druids, bards, poets, seers, prophets, aerial servants, creatures of the air, intelligent avians and flying creatures
Rhiaan	Greater	CN	Goddess of Air and Birds	Air, Animals, Chaos, Travel	Intelligent avians and flying creatures

Caerulean Gods

Name	Power	AL	Title	Spheres of Influence	Typical Worshippers
Awalea	Greater Demon	CE	The Terror that Lurks in the Depths, the Sea Witch	Darkness, Evil, Water	Evil sea-folk, the corrupt, those who desire to harm others
Cehenasla	Lesser	NG	Goddess of Mercy and Healing	Community, Healing, Protection	Most Caeruleans, healers, physicians
Eashae	Greater	LG	The Sea Mother	Community, Good, Water	Most Caeruleans, some surface fisherfolk and mariners
Taela	Lesser	NG	Goddess of Plenty	Animal, Plant, Water	Caeruleans of the upper depths, some surface fisherfolk
Tymannum	Lesser	LG	God of Battle	Glory, Law, War	Caerulean warriors, generals, leaders, a few surface mariners
Udamata	Lesser	NG	God of Art and Architecture	Artifice, Creation, Good	Caerulean artists, architects and builders

Draconic Gods

Name	Power	AL	Title	Spheres of Influence	Typical Worshippers	Notes
Behemoth	Greater	LG	The Celestial Dragon	Air, Good, Knowledge, Law, Protection, Scalykind	Good-aligned dragons and related species, good and neutral lizardfolk, human and halfling paladins and dragon cultists	

Name	Power	AL	Title	Spheres of Influence	Typical Worshippers	Notes
Kremarra	Lesser	CE	Dragon Goddess of Death and Nihilism; The Monkey Eater	Darkness, Death, Evil	Cultists, dragonborn, half-dragons, lizardfolk, other reptilian races	
Lakua Mao	Lesser	LE	The Red Misery	Destruction, Fire, Law, Scalykind, War	Underground creatures, usually evil, including goblins, derro, mites and grimlocks	Imprisoned
Moash-Sirrush	Lesser	NE	Bloodthirsty Dragon God	Destruction, Trickery	Evil-aligned dragons and related species	
Tiamat	Greater	CE	The Primeval Mother	Animals, Chaos, Destruction, Evil	Evil warriors, sorcerers, nobles, evil dragons and draconic creatures	
Utechner	Greater	LE	The Prime Wyrm, God of Rightful Ascendance of Dragonkind	Air, Earth, Fire, Magic, Scalykind, Water	The Hykadrion Order, dragon disciples, evil dragons, some half-dragons, kobolds	

Fey Deities

Name	Power	AL	Title	Spheres of Influence	Typical Worshippers
King Oberon	Greater	CN	King of the Fey, The Erl-King, Lord of the Wild	Chaos, Earth, Nature, Magic	Fey creatures, druids, nature worshippers
Queen Titania	Greater	CN	Queen of the Fey, The Fairest, The Queen of Air and Darkness	Air, Darkness, Nature, Magic, Love	Fey creatures, druids, nature worshippers

Gods of Rodents/Vermin

Name	Power	AL	Title	Spheres of Influence	Typical Worshippers
S'Surimiss	Lesser	NE	The Rat Queen, Goddess of Rats	Animals, Evil, Destruction, Vermin	Wererats, some ratfolk

Serpent/Reptilian Gods

Name	Power	AL	Title	Spheres of Influence	Typical Worshippers
Aapep	Lesser	CE	The Black Serpent; The Destroyer	Chaos, Death, Destruction, Evil, Serpent	Evil power-seeking humanoids, assassins, cults
Gallinda	Greater	NG	Lady of the Fountains, Snake-Mother	Healing, Scalykind, Travel, Water	Phoromyceaean healers, midwives, travelers, water nagas, lizardfolk, good water creatures, bronze dragons, mist dragons
Hassith-Kaa	Greater	NE	The Great Serpent	Evil, Scalyfolk, Strength, Trickery	Nagas, serpentfolk, inphidians, intelligent serpents and reptiles, some assassins
Set	Greater	LE	God of Evil and the Night	Death, Destruction, Evil, Knowledge, Law, Serpent	Evil power-seeking humanoids, evil monks, assassins

Dark Pantheons

Abyssal Horde

Name	Power	AL	Title	Spheres of Influence	Typical Worshippers	Notes
Akanax	Greater Demon	CE	The Lord of Terror, Beast of Slaughter	Darkness, Death, Evil	Murderers, berserkers, barbarians, evil spellcasters	
Alyheedra	Lesser Demon	CE	Demon Princess of Evil Water Creatures	Death, Nature, Water	Evil druids, sea hags, evil marids, elementals and sea creatures	
Althunak	Greater Demon	CE	Demon Lord of Ice and Cold, Master of Cannibals, The Winter King	Chaos, Earth, Evil, Ice, Water	Crazed cultists, lycanthropes, cannibals, ice daemons, snow brides	
Azazael	Greater Demon	CE	The Rebel, The First, He of the Mountain of Sacrifice	Destruction, Evil, Magic	Scholars, spellcasters, researchers, historians	
Baphomet	Demon Lord	CE	Prince of Beasts, Demon Lord of Minotaurs	Animal, Chaos, Evil, War	Minotaurs, lycanthropes, therianthropes, chaaors, the Alcaldrich Order of Knights Templar in Exile	
Beleth	Greater Demon	CE	King of the Abyss	Chaos, Evil, Fire	Cultists, fire-worshippers, arsonists	
Beliuri	Greater Demon	CE	The Temptress	Chaos, Charm, Evil, Trickery	Faithless lovers, spies, extortionists, power-hungry, evil sensualists	
Belphegor	Greater Demon	CE	Lord of the Gap	Artifice, Evil, Knowledge, Trickery	The slothful, those who desire wealth without effort	
Caizel	Greater Demon	CE	Deposed Queen of the Succubi	Chaos, Charm, Darkness, Lust	Pleasure-seekers, decadent wealthy, corrupt nobles	
Crocutus	Lesser Demon	CE	Eater of the Dead, Demon Lord of the Gnolls	Animal, Chaos, Destruction, Trickery	Gnolls, flinds, some ghouls, ghasts and other intelligent carrion-eaters	
Dagon	Demon Lord	CE	Demon Prince of the Sea	Chaos, Destruction, Evil, Water	Aquatic humanoids and monstrous humanoids, evil human fishermen, water nagas, shrroths, hezrou, kraken, aboleths	Believed to be different from the god of the same name in the Kehna pantheon
Demogorgon	Demon Lord	CE	Primal God of the Earth, The Dark Creator, Demon Lord of Fate	Chaos, Creation, Darkness, Earth, Evil, Knowledge, Luck	Cultists, madmen, derros, crag men, dark folk, ropers, demons, bodaks, baregaras, demonic knights, the Fates, genies, aeons, black jinn	
Fraz-Urb'luu	Demon Lord	CE	Demon Prince of Deception	Communication, Chaos, Evil, Knowledge, Trickery	Evil human and humanoid clerics, politicians, aristocrats, sorcerers, illusionists, adepts	
Jubilex	Demon Lord	CE	The Faceless Lord, Demon Lord of Slimes and Oozes	Chaos, Evil, Water	Insane humans, lepers, intelligent oozes	

Name	Power	AL	Title	Spheres of Influence	Typical Worshippers	Notes
Kostchtchie	Demon Lord	CE	The Deathless, Demon Prince of Wrath	Chaos, Destruction, Evil, Strength, War	Frost giants, aberrant giants, ogres, berserkers, deformed creatures	
Maphistal	Greater Demon	CE	Second of Orcus	Chaos, Evil, Protection	Worshippers of Orcus, evil fighters and spellcasters	
Mathribaunt	Lesser Demon	CE	The Mad, Demon Prince of Insanity, Evil Music and Orchestration	Art, Evil, Trickery	Nihilists, insane musicians, harpies, debased satyrs and korreds, redcaps, sirens, exiled Leng-men, shantaks, cambions, gallu-demons, nabasu, skitterdarks	
Marchosias	Greater Demon	CE	The Wolf, The Deceiver	Chaos, Communications, Evil	Greedy and power-hungry, corrupt nobles, evil spellcasters	
Orcus	Demon Lord	CE	Demon Prince of the Undead	Chaos, Death, Destruction, Evil, War	Orcs, orogs, monsters, undead, demons, evil humanoids	
Pazuzu	Greater Demon	CE	King of the Demons of the Wind, Demon Prince of the Middle Air	Air, Chaos, Evil, Protection, Weather	Nihilists, insane musicians, harpies, debased satyrs and korreds, redcaps, sirens, exiled Leng-men, shantaks, cambions, gallu-demons, nabasu, skitterdarks	
Semiazas	Greater Demon	CE	Father of Giants	Destruction, Evil, War	Giants, warriors, barbarians, berserkers	Also known as Samyaza, Sahjaza
Shibauroth	Greater Demon	CE	Demon Prince of Beasts and Blood	Animal, Chaos, Destruction, Evil, Madness	Savage barbarians, trolls, lycanthropes, barghests, minotaurs, beasts, evil druids	
Shur D'zhar	Lesser Demon	CE	Demon Lord of the Insane, Lord of Insanity and Murder	Chaos, Death, Evil, Madness	Serial killers, insane sadists, chaotic bandit chieftains, evil anarchists	
Sriasha	Lesser Demon	CE	Demon Queen of Lust and Hate, The Tempestuous Bitch	Chaos, Charm, Madness, Lust, Trickery	Serial killers, insane sadists, chaotic bandit chieftains, evil anarchists	
Stonechard	Demon Lord	CE	General of Orcus	Darkness, Destruction, Evil, War	Worshippers of Orcus, evil fighters, berserkers	
Tsathogga	Greater Demon	CE	Demon Frog God, The Devouring Maw, Demon Lord of Filth	Chaos, Destruction, Evil, Water	Human cultists, aberrations, tsathar, sentient frogs, greruor, hezrou, evil water creatures, the Violet Brotherhood	
Vepar	Demon Lord	CE	Duke of Dagon	Darkness, Evil, Water, Trickery	Worshippers of Dagon, evil mariners, aquamancers, aquatic demons, fiendish merfolk and tritons	

Name	Power	AL	Title	Spheres of Influence	Typical Worshippers	Notes
Yiv	Lesser Demon	CE	Demon Lord of Treachery	Chaos, Charm, Evil, Trickery	Evil chieftains or jarls, lawyers, merchants	
Zelton	Greater Demon	CE	Demon Sultan of Sloth	Chaos, Charm, Destruction, Liberation	Rulers, the rich, con artists	

Benthic/Oceanic Deities

Name	Power	AL	Title	Spheres of Influence	Typical Worshippers
Kunolo	Lesser	NE	The Hungering Tide, God of the Deeps	Death, Destruction, Evil, Fear, Oceans, Water	Pirates, evil sea creatures

Cthonic

Name	Power	AL	Title	Spheres of Influence	Typical Worshippers
Camazotz	Lesser	CE	The Bat God, Lord Underbelly, He Who Takes Blood in the Darkness	Animal, Chaos, Darkness, Death, Evil	sabosans, mobats, vampires, gugs, werebats, cloakers, greenskin orcs, chikes, evil lizardfolk, swamp trolls, vile drakes, some black dragons
Jubilex	Demon Lord	CE	The Faceless Lord, Demon Lord of Slimes and Oozes	Chaos, Evil, Water	Insane humans, lepers, intelligent oozes
Keld	Lesser	CE	The Wicked, Lord of the Grimlocks	Chaos, Evil, War	Evil underground creatures, especially grimlocks, derro, morlocks
Queen of Spiders	Greater	CE	The Spider Goddess	Darkness, Death, Earth, Evil, Magic, Trickery	Drow, troglodytes, spider-obsessed humans
The Crawler in Darkness	Lesser	CN	The Eater, The Shadow That Stalks	Darkness, Death, Void	Underground creatures, usually evil, including goblins, derro, mites and grimlocks

Infernal Court

Name	Power	AL	Title	Spheres of Influence	Typical Worshippers	Notes
Alastor	Greater Devil	LE	Hell's Executioner	Death, Destruction, Law	Worshippers of Asmodeus, executioners	
Amon	Greater Devil	LE	Duke of Hell, Vassal of Geryon	Darkness, Evil, War	Worshippers of Geryon, warriors	
Asmodeus	Archdevil	LE	Monarch of Hell, Lord of the First Circle	Darkness, Evil, Law, Strength	Cultists, the greedy and power-hungry, decadent nobles, corrupt or insecure rulers	
Astaroth	Archdevil	LE	Duke of Hell, Judge of the Damned	Evil, Law, Trickery	Judges, evil nobles	
Baalzebul	Archdevil	LE	Prince of Hell, Ruler of the Seventh Circle, Prince of Lies, Lord of the Flies	Darkness, Evil, Law, Treachery	Cultists, assassins, politicians, corrupt nobles, those who gain wealth through guile and treachery	Also known as Beelzebub
Baaphel	Greater Devil	LE	Duke of Infernus, General of Belial	Death, Evil, War	Worshippers of Belial and Lucifer	

Name	Power	AL	Title	Spheres of Influence	Typical Worshippers	Notes
Belphegor	Greater Devil	LE	Duke of Hell, Patron of Fire Giants, The Disputer, Lord of Sloth	Artifice, Destruction, Earth, Evil, Fire, Law	Fire giants, salamanders, devils (mostly barbed and belier), some smoke giants	
Belial	Archdevil	LE	Prince of Infernus, Agent of Darkness	Evil, Knowledge, Magic, Nobility	Evil magic-users, seekers after knowledge, cultists	
Caasimolar	Greater Devil	LE	Former President of Hell, Master of Infernus	Evil, Law, Strength	Worshippers of Lucifer, corrupt lawmakers and nobles	
Demoriel	Greater Devil	LE	The Twice-Exiled Seductress	Evil, Charm, Lust, Trickery	Worshippers of Lucifer, those who desire illicit love or undeserved wealth	
Dispater	Archdevil	LE	Lord of the Second Circle, Master of the Fortress	Charm, Evil, Law	Evil lovers, seducers, adulterers, decadent nobles, warriors, jailers, solicitors	
Geryon	Archdevil	LE	Lord of the Fifth Circle, The Great Serpent	Evil, Law, Strength	Serpentfolk, lizardfolk, human cultists and serpent-worshippers	
Gorson	Greater Devil	LE	The Blood Duke, Mammon's Lion	Destruction, Strength, War	Worshippers of Mammon, soldiers, warlords, mercenaries	
Hutijin	Greater Devil	LE	Duke of Hell, Marshal of Mephistopheles	Death, Glory, War	Worshippers of Mephistopheles, warriors and evil paladins	
Lilith	Greater Devil	LE	Queen of Infernus, Former Queen of Hell	Law, Evil, Lust	Worshippers of Lucifer, cultists	
Malphas	Archdevil	LE	Lord of the Fourth Circle, The Armorer, The Great Crow	Artifice, Evil, Fire, Madness, War	Armorers, blacksmiths, soldiers, evil fighters	
Mephistopheles	Archdevil	LE	Prince of Hell, Lord of the Eighth Circle, He Who Shuns the Light	Darkness, Evil, Law	Evil rulers, cultists, seekers of knowledge, spellcasters, liches	
Moloch	Archdevil	LE	Lord of the Sixth Circle, Master of the Hunt	Animal, Evil, Strength	Assassins, sorcerers, bounty hunters, schemers, spies, Knights of Moloch	
Titivilus	Greater Devil	LE	The Confuser, Duke of Hell, Chamberlain of Dispater	Communications, Evil, Law	Worshippers of Dispater	
Xaphan	Archdevil	LE	Duke of Infernus, The Burning Duke	Evil, Law, War	Worshippers of Lucifer